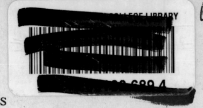
PENGUIN BOOKS

RETURN OF THE ARYANS

Bhagwan S. Gidwani was India's Additional Director General of Tourism and Director General of Civil Aviation till 1978. He served as India's Counsel at the International Court of Justice at the Hague, and as Representative of India on the Council of ICAO (UN) from 1978 to 1981. Thereafter, he joined ICAO as its Director till 1985.

His earlier novel—*The Sword of Tipu Sultan*—was a best-seller in India, with many translations and 44 reprints; it was followed by a major TV serial for which Gidwani also wrote the script and screen-play. The TV serial was telecast in India in fifty-two episodes in 1990 and 1991, and is being re-run. It has also been telecast in Europe, UK and USA.

Bhagwan S. Gidwani is based in Montreal and divides his time between international efforts to promote the safety and security of air transport and tourism and historical writing, research and teaching.

PENGUIN BOOKS

RETURN OF THE ARYANS

Bhagwan S. Gidwani was India's Additional Director General of Tourism and Director General of Civil Aviation till 1978. He served as India's Counsel at the International Court of Justice at the Hague, and as Representative of India on the Council of ICAO (UN) from 1978 to 1981. Thereafter, he joined ICAO as its Director till 1985.

His earlier novel—The Sword of Tipu Sultan—was a best-seller in India, with many translations and 44 reprints; it was followed by a major TV serial for which Gidwani also wrote the script and screen-play. The TV serial was telecast in India in fifty-two episodes in 1990 and 1991, and is being re-run. It has also been released in Europe, UK and USA.

Bhagwan S. Gidwani is based in Montreal and divides his time between international efforts to promote the safety and security of air transport and tourism and historical writing, research and teaching.

Return of the Aryans

Bhagwan S. Gidwani

PENGUIN BOOKS

Penguin Books India (P) Ltd., 11 Community Centre, Panchsheel Park,
New Delhi 110017, India
Penguin Books Ltd., 80 Strand, London WC2R 0RL, UK
Penguin Putnam Inc., 375 Hudson Street, New York, NY 10014, USA
Penguin Books Australia Ltd., 250 Camberwell Road, Camberwell,
Victoria 3124, Australia
Penguin Books Canada Ltd., 10 Alcorn Avenue, Suite 300, Toronto,
Ontario M4V 3B2, Canada
Penguin Books (NZ) Ltd., Cnr Rosedale and Airborne Roads, Albany, Auckland,
New Zealand

First published by Penguin Books India 1994

Copyright © Bhagwan S. Gidwani 1994

10 9 8 7

Typeset in Palatino by Rekha Printers Pvt. Ltd., New Delhi

Printed at Basu Mudran, Kolkata

To the land where the poet is no more, and the historian never was
To Liela, my wife
To Manu and Sachal, my sons
To Lori, my daughter-in-law
To Leah, my grand-daughter
and
To all those who will try to keep alive the memory of their roots for generations waiting to be born

Contents

Acknowledgements

I have had my share of anxiety, trouble and frustration in writing this novel. But I have had help and blessings too, from many, in abundance.

My thanks, first, to my wife Leila, who organized the translation of over 4,600 songs, and re-arranged the vast research material which once occupied five rooms fully, and was spilling over everywhere else in the house. I cannot reward her enough for her cheerful and extraordinary help.

My elder son Manu, his wife Lori, and my younger son Sachal, helped in a variety of ways. My brother Mangha, who is now no more, shared the same faith, and helped me tremendously with research. My debt to him is endless. My brothers, Narain and Durga helped too with advice and assistance.

Encouragement and assistance often came from my friend Kailash Nath. He also placed at my disposal a guest house where I could comfortably work on this project. His son Ravi Khanna and daughter-in-law Pratibha helped to compile some source material. My special thanks also to my friend Prakash Nath and his son Sandeep Khanna for their unstinting help.

In Montreal, Derek Menezes assisted with the collection of prehistory sources. Jehangir Guzdar, President, Daivam Transport Inc., placed at my disposal his organization to transport materials and records from many countries. Jehangir's questions also led me to a closer study of the pre- and post-Zoroastrian period of ancient Persia. Shirish Suchak, President, Chalais Holdings (Canada) was also always ready with help.

My thanks also to B.N. Jha, Joint Secretary in India's Ministry of Home Affairs for his encouragement and help.

In Chicago, Dial Gidwaney, President, Intra World Travel & Tours, helped in transporting mountains of documentation and archaeological records from all over the world. Dial also placed at my disposal many songs of the Vedic period collected by his father Dr Watanmal.

In Delhi, Papu Chablani and her husband Gulu helped. In Bombay, Kala Punwani, Kiki and Pritam gave me a place to work, and helped in many ways.

My salute to Marya Pushkarni, the gypsy girl I met in Prague, Czechoslovakia, sixteen years ago. She was thirty-six then, but small, slim and petite, with shining eyes and dark hair; and in the depths of her eyes was the same glint of a shy smile as in the waters of a deep well. No wonder, she was always called a 'girl'. From time to time, she sent me songs—over a hundred. She never put postage stamps on her letters, but somehow they always reached. I received her last two songs, a day after she died. Her songs did not help in writing this novel as they related to a later period—when the gypsies migrated. But her perseverance kept my spirits alive. I shall visit Prague to light a candle on her grave.

Leah Alesandro of Mexico too! She gave me a thousand clues to the Hindu influence on the art, architecture and sculpture of the Mayan civilization. I did not use the material in this novel, as so far I have not discovered direct evidence of the ancient Hindu explorers having travelled beyond to the west of Europe. Yet her patient and painstaking pursuit of the subject provides an inspiration to question the historians who have written to preserve not the *fire* but the ashes of the past. Leah is now no more; she died trying to protect forests from urban encroachment; but then she always believed that the dream survives even when the dreamer does not.

My thanks to Uma Khan for the excellence of her editing.

I am immensely grateful to archaeologists, librarians, directors of archives and museums, here and in a hundred countries, who unhesitatingly helped me obtain material for the novel. So many have also helped, over the last eighteen years, with translations of sources from foreign languages. Their list is endless, and if I do not individually mention them, I know they will understand, and forgive.

The responsibility for mistakes in this novel is entirely mine. Often, dates have left me confused, where I was not certain if poets, singers, and others had the lunar or the solar calendar in view. Hopefully, the reader will permit an allowance of thirty to ninety years, in the case of many of the dates used in this novel.

Introduction

This novel tells the story of the Aryans—of how and why they moved out of their homeland in Bharat Varsha (India) in 5000 BC, their trials and triumphs overseas, and finally their return to India.

I must present this as a work of fiction. But fiction is *not* falsehood. Nor a dream. Nor guesswork. Ideally it should be seen as a fictionalized alternative history that our mainstream historians have not attempted to write. In order to write the book I have had to rely on the oral history tradition—the songs of the ancients from prehistory which still remain in the traditional memory of the people of Angkor, Sind, Bali, Java, Burma, China, Bhutan, Nepal, Iran, Iraq, Turkey, Egypt, Norway, Sweden, Finland, Italy, Russia, Lithuania, Germany and India.

The language in these songs of prehistory is archaic, the idiom strange and the images unfamilar. Yet they carry the imperishable remembrance of the Aryan movement and migration from India; and the message in these songs is clear—that the Aryans originated from India and from nowhere else. It is the substance of these songs that dominates my story.

*

In order to tell the story of the Aryans, it is necessary to follow the drama of Hinduism back to its roots prior to 8000 BC.

My novel will therefore try to trace, among others:

- The origins of Hinduism, its roots in Sanathana Dharma and its pre-ancient root in Sanathana; and how the country came to be named Bharat Varsha;
- The origins of Om, Namaste, svastika, Gayatri Mantra, the sacred thread, marriage customs and soma wines;
- The establishment of the Hindu Parliament; guilds; the development of ships and harbours; legal systems; growth of cities; yoga; calendar; mathematics; astronomy; medicine; surgery; music, dance, drama, art and architecture; moral and spiritual beliefs; the written language; and material advancement;
- The Himalayan and trans-Himalayan expeditions by Hindu explorers to discover the source of the Ganga, Sindhu and Saraswati rivers;

- The founding of the Sindhu, Ganga, Dravidian and tribal civilizations; the rise and fall of Varnash (Benaras; Varanasi), Hari Hara Dwara (Haridwar) and other ancient cities.

While I wish to focus on the story of the Aryans, my hero in this novel is the pre-ancient Hindu. The Aryans of 5000 BC were born, grew up and died as Hindus. They were anchored in the timeless foundation of the Hindu tradition. While some readers may question such an assertion, it is strange to believe that the Aryans arrived on the world stage without precedents and ancestors; the fact is that there is no such thing as a spontaneous generation. History is rooted in continuity and advance and it is inappropriate to present the Aryans as 'strays' without their cultural precedents, traditional links and spiritual ancestry of the Hindu.

*

I cannot say that I found this subject. Rather, the subject found me; and gradually it came to obsess me. The impulse to study the history of the Hindu came to me, first, as I witnessed the anguish of my uncle, Dr Choithram P. Gidwani, and my father, Shamdas P. Gidwani, when the partition of India was announced in 1947. They both had different political faiths, though they lived as a part of the same family under the same roof in Karachi. Both spoke then of the cultural continuity of Bharat Varsha and its age-old political and spiritual frontiers. Both felt that by a succession of acts of surrender, the leaders of India had taken on the responsibility of dividing the country as they saw no other possibility of securing power in their own lifetime. Both felt that the Indian was being exiled from his own land. Both also feared the menace to partitioned India from outside, and a far greater menace from within. The spiritual tradition of the race, they felt, would not be able to protect India from the invader *outside* and the spoiler *within*.

I wish to make no judgement on their political views. My novels and I shall always remain apart from politics. However, the main purpose which their continuing conversation served was to invest me with the desire to study the history of the pre-ancient Hindu.

When Dr Choithram died, he willed everything to me. That 'everything' contained books, an old watch and eighty rupees. (In those days, politicians and their families did not acquire many assets and wealth and were judged by the 'magnitude of their non-possession'. It is only in the era after Mahatma Gandhi's assassination that politics became the most lucrative of all professions in India.) Dr Choithram also left me a package containing many hastily scribbled songs about the Aryans.

Ever since then, I felt a perpetual restlessness to study the subject. Initially, I contented myself with trying to collect material from various sources. It was some eighteen years ago, after I completed my research for my novel—*The Sword of Tipu Sultan*—that I started on the project of the Aryans in true earnest.

*

One version of history is that the Aryans originated *not* from India but from elsewhere. But the historians do not pinpoint any single region as the homeground of the Aryans. At the last count, they must have mentioned twenty-two regions in the west and the north from which the Aryans could possibly have sprung.

The difficulty in picking one single place from the twenty-two is understandable. None of the twenty-two regions showed even the slightest link with the high civilization and classical art and literature of India; and even as the historians came under the spell of the compelling fascination of the Vedas, the spiritual vision of the Upanishads, the philosophic content of the *Bhagvadgita* and the inspiration of the enduring epics of India, they must have wondered: how could it be that the Aryans came from this or that region, when that region itself showed no evidence of such philosophic development or artistic achievement or spiritual heritage? Especially as all these clearly flowered in India independently and unrelated to any other region, with no parallels or precedents elsewhere.

The main argument thus far, that the Aryans originated from outside, has been that Sanskrit had so much similarity to Greek and Latin and to all the languages now known as Indo-Iranian and Indo-European (including Italic, Germanic, Gothic, Armenian, Tocharian, Celtic, Albanian, Lithuanian and Balto-Slavic). But is it not possible that these western languages were enriched by the Aryans moving out of India to the other regions? And could it not have been Sanskrit that moved out to those countless lands instead of the reverse?

More will be said in my novel about how Sanskrit went out with the Aryans to enrich the language of many regions and was itself enriched by them. The novel will also explain how Tamil, the most ancient of all languages, remained largely unaffected.

The second hypothesis of the current historical view is weaker still. It relies on the divergence of skin colour and the physique of the races in India and, in particular, between the north and the south. My novel hopefully clarifies how the divergence arose.

The link of the pre-ancient Hindu with the Aryans should have been clear by now, given the plethora of clues that exist. In support of my argument I have read every word of the Vedas, Upanishads, epics and other Aryan literature. If the Aryans came from the far north or west, it would be amazing that they who wrote so much on so many subjects, simply forgot to mention their original homeland.

*

A date of 1500 BC has been ascribed to the *Rig Veda* but the grounds for this are somewhat flimsy. Certainly, the *Rig Veda* also includes a few songs of the ancient Hindu of the pre-Aryan period.

*

It is a perilous undertaking to criticize the mainstrean historical view but it cannot be denied that new discoveries and versions of our shared past deserve to exist. And I am not arguing here about a revisionist view of history. As I have made clear earlier I have no political axe to grind. Having said this, let me continue my argument. Initially, it was thought that the entire culture of India had to be refracted through the prism of Aryan life—and that only decadence and darkness existed in the land until the Aryans emerged.

But then, in one of history's more subtle ironies, came the excavations of Mohenjo daro, Harappa and others. These excavations clearly pointed to a flourishing civilization that existed thousands of years in the past, distinct from all others, independent and deeply rooted in the Indian soil and environment. After these discoveries, there was no longer an attempt to explain the origins of Hindu civilization in terms of immigration from outside.

Faced with this evidence, the histories of the civilization had to admit that the pre-Aryan Indus Valley civilization, with no known beginnings, was highly developed, thoroughly individual, and specifically Indian. But even so, it was maintained that the Aryans did not spring from the indigenous culture of India but were from a different culture and arrived, somehow, from somewhere else, at a later stage.

What led to this confusion was the evidence of the Aryan influence in many foreign lands. But, I submit that this was probably because the Aryans emerged from India and returned to their homeland, leaving behind, in various regions, the imprint of their language and cultural, social and spiritual affinities.

Hopefully, this novel will give a mosaic of a long-forgotten past to show that the Aryans did not belong to a different species, culture or race. Their cradle-grounds were the Sindhu, Ganga and Dravidian civilizations; and there is an unbroken continuity—spiritual, social and secular—between the pre-ancient civilization of Bharat Varsha and the Aryans of 5000 BC.

*

We now come to the assertion that the name 'Hindu' itself is of recent origin and that it came about as some foreigners had difficulty in pronouncing 'Sindhu'.

My novel explains how the people of Sanathana Dharma chose to call themselves 'Hindu'. It was a name that they adopted for themselves of their own accord, and not because some foreigner, somewhere, was unable to pronounce their name correctly.

Similarly, the novel will also explain the origins of the names of Shiva, Rudra, soma, Bharat Varsha, Burma, Bhutan, Sind, Afghanistan, Iran, Egypt, Tibet, Hindu Kush mountains, Himalaya, Saraswati, Danube and Volga rivers and scores of other names, here and in Europe, West Asia and the Far East, given by or under the inspiration of the pre-ancient Hindu and the Aryans of Bharat Varsha.

*

Even those who suspected that the Aryans might have originated in India, failed to follow up on their hunch. This lack was probably because

it was unthinkable that the Aryans should leave their homes, neither
to loot nor to plunder, nor for conquest, nor to persecute in the name
of dogma, nor to propagate their faith, nor to dethrone and destroy
the gods and idols of others.

But what I'm trying to say in this novel is that the Aryans who
left Bharat Varsha were not warriors or conquerors, not men of genius
or madness; they were not adventurers or soldiers/of fortune; and
certainly, they were not religious zealots, fanatics or crusaders. These
travellers simply had a dream that led them on towards the 'unreachable
goal of finding a land that was pure and free from evil—and it was a
road that led everywhere but finally nowhere' and at last they came to
realize that there was no land of pure, except what a man might make
of his own efforts.

*

There is some truth in the assumption that some Aryans came to India
from foreign lands. Many Aryans from India married there. They
brought their wives and children. But more so, many locals came with
them—and kept coming—inspired by the faith and values of the Aryans
of Bharat Varsha. These locals came with the returning Aryans in large
numbers from Iran, Assyria, Sumeria, Egypt, Finland, Sweden, Lithuania,
Estonia, Latvia, the Russian lands and Scythia, Turkey, Italy, Spain,
Greece, Germany and even from Bali, Java, Angkor, Malaysia and
Singapore.

Intellectually and emotionally, these men and women from foreign
lands came to bind themselves together with the Aryans of India in a
web of common ideas and reciprocal knowledge, with fellowship of
spirit, a communion of minds and a union of hearts. It did not take
too long for these visitors to be assimilated in India.

*

Not all the triumphs of the Aryans in foreign lands must be credited
to Indians alone. The help they received from the locals who joined
their cause and came to call themselves Aryans was tremendous. In
the deep recesses of the past, many who so helped, remain anonymous.
My novel gives an account of a few of them though I realize that
much more needs to be written about these heroic men and women.

*

If the reader is looking for a golden age of peace and plenty in the
past, this novel will disappoint him.

Our ancients were not all heroes or hermits; they did not walk
hand-in-hand with gods and angels. As we closely examine prehistory,
we find in it a cast of characters as varied as any around today. There
was cowardice and courage; there were hermits and harlots; loyalty

and treachery; yogis and tricksters; greatness and crafty stupidity—all existing side by side. Nor were the majority of people immersed in matters of the spirit. Some sang, others danced or told stories; some tried out new herbs and medicines, while still others sought to discover the physical laws of nature and find unity in diversity. Some occupied themselves with chiseling stone, drawing pictures, burnishing gold and weaving rich fabrics. Many dug wells or built reservoirs; some constructed granaries, dock-yards, huts, cottages; others made water-clocks, cloth-looms, boats, carts, chariots and toys; many more toiled in fields and farms, while a few made ships to cross the ocean.

But then, it has always been so—then and now—that those who live by the spirit alone are a mere handful, exalted above the life of their times, while the majority attend to mundane activities. And yet those few succeed in purifying and enlarging the heritage of mankind.

Even some of the rulers then were no less corrupt than those who are in power today; the only difference is that the means available to present-day rulers to manipulate the masses and spread evil are vast, if not unlimited.

The distortion of the caste system had not then entered Hindu society, but even then there was the system of slavery, howsoever benign. Fortunately, the system of slavery lasted only a few short centuries and was abolished both in law and fact in 5000 BC.

As a generalization, however, it can be said that the pre-ancient Hindu had more faith, less superstition, and therefore enjoyed greater laughter and joy in life. The affectionate bonds of the large family nourished him; he did not grow up inwardly torn, largely deprived of love, with his sights shattered and values confused. He did not allow many vague cults to exploit his credulity; nor did he idolize leaders who depended on disunity in the land for their existence.

There was also greater respect, even fear, of the doctrine of karma—the law of deed and consequence and greater preoccupation with achieving moksha (salvation). Judged by today's standards, the corrupt rulers themselves displayed less greed and greater self-restraint; but then as a wag uncharitably, and even crudely, put it, 'Mistake him not; his goodness arises not from his heart; he is simply afraid lest he go down the evolutionary ladder and be reborn as a cockroach or diseased and limbless.'

Even so, a reader seeking to discover a pure and golden age in the past may find melancholy fare in this novel. My effort has been to present our past as it was, with all its triumphs, trials, tragedies and terror, and not in a rosy light. In fact, the Aryans considered themselves exiled and moved out of their homeland only because they were disenchanted with the conditions there. That they found greater degradation, corruption, discord, superstition, anarchy, folly and frustration in every other country is quite a different matter.

Compared to other regions, there is no doubt that the Aryans sprang from a society of stability behind which lay ages of civilized existence and thought. No wonder then that the Aryans, soon after leaving their homeland, had the burning desire to return to the healing power of their roots, hometown and heritage. Yet it would be totally fictional to describe India, then, as a society of purity and perfection.

*

I have no special goals towards which I would like to lead the reader. I simply want to tell this story (or alternative history) as I believe that everyone must know where he comes from, where his ancestors resided and what his roots were. A civilization is kept alive only when its past values and traditions are recreated in men's minds, faithfully and thoroughly, without the element of fancy and distortion; and a generation that remains unaware of its roots is truly orphaned. The present silence, blankness, oblivion about our ancient past represents a theft from the future generations as well and the tragedy we face is that the soul of our culture could well wither away. Already, we are moving towards a cultural holocaust in which our children will have much intelligence, power and intellect but no wisdom, virtue, and the exaltation of spirit, and not even the faith to serve as the consolation of their dreams.

We have inherited an ancient culture. It has faced many waves of invasions, among others, from the Greek, Persian, Pathan, Mongol, French, Dutch and the English. Often with savagery they attempted to suppress our culture; yet the flame of hope burnt brightly against the dark background of foreign rule. Our culture endured, though our land has shrunk to less than half its size compared to the past. But then freedom in 1947 did not bring a fulfilment of our dreams. Day by day, the menace grows from within. In the final analysis, the greatest danger lies not *outside* our borders but *inside*, and in our soul and spirit.

What often saved us in the past was the awareness of our age-old culture and the need to hold fast to it, while weaving and refining it for the future. What might doom us in the future is the ignorance of our culture, with no roots to cling to. Culture is tradition and tradition is memory. The ancients knew that and that is why Bharat, who led the Sindhu clan, reintroduced Memory songs in 5095 BC, to keep alive the knowledge of the past, lest we run the risk of building our future without foundation or roots of growth.

In this era of vanishing worth and fading memory, historians have a role to play, to rekindle the dying embers of life and light in our society. But where history falters for lack of fact or interpretation, the field is open to the novelist. He who fails to guard his house—be it the scholar or the nation itself—must learn to tolerate an intruder.

Bhagwan S. Gidwani

Canada
July 1994

'....Much of our past is covered with the dust of time. Shall it always be thus?... No, there must be Memory songs to remember our knowledge. And thus our age shall be endless, a part of eternity, and not merely a fleeting moment.... Every culture needs to be preserved... even when we are no more, our culture must continue....'

—(From the declaration of Karkarta Bharat to the joint session of the Assembly of People and Council Chiefs, in the year 5095 BC)

...Much of our past is covered with the dust of time. Shall it always be thus?... No. There must be Memory songs to remember our knowledge. And thus our age shall be endless, a part of eternity, and not merely a fleeting moment... Every culture needs to be preserved... even when we are no more, our culture must continue...

—(From the dedication of Kartavya Bharat to the joint session of the Assembly of People and Council Chiefs, in the year 3059 BG).

Birth of Sindhu Putra

5068 BC

Bharatjogi heard the dogs barking. He paused in the midst of his meditation, opened his eyes and looked at the swollen river.

In the distance, he saw a small boat drifting aimlessly. Perhaps a boatman had not secured the boat properly and Sindhu river was claiming its prize, tossing it from side to side and playing with it as a child, with a new toy.

Glancing away from the boat which had moved closer, he went back to his prayer-mat to resume his meditation. His eyes were closed but his mind was not on his prayers. Two dogs and a bitch, who had adopted him after he had come to live on the island, disturbed his concentration with their barking.

Seated on his prayer-mat, Bharat shouted at the dogs to stop barking. He knew it was in vain. They had learned to obey all his commands except the command to stop barking. That, they were convinced, was their inalienable birthright, and no authority, human or divine, could deny them the freedom to bark. He smiled at his futile effort to silence them but understood why they were barking. Obviously, they had sensed the approach of the boat.

A boat would arrive every month bringing news, food, medicinal herbs and even some delicacies along with small casks of wine for Bharat. Three or four boatmen would disembark and stay for a day or two. Bharat, who longed for company, would quietly pray for high winds or a storm to delay their departure. Sometimes his prayers were answered. These simple boatmen had little to say but Bharat would ply them with questions. He did not care too much for their news or information; he was not even interested in the substance of their answers. He just wanted to hear them talking—to hear human voices.

This was Bharat's third year in isolation on the island. He was sixty-three years old, and had, on his sixtieth birthday, given up his worldly possessions to retire as a hermit as ordained by custom. It was open to him to join a colony of hermits and be within shouting distance of many who had also retired similarly, on their sixtieth birthdays. But he feared that sharing his misery with others would only multiply his own. Also, he loved his wine — in moderation of course—and this would be disapproved of since wine was to be used only as a libation to the gods. They would not be amused if he told them that the spirit of the gods was inside each person's body and soul and, therefore, wine must be consumed by man if it was to serve as a libation to the gods.

Also, he knew of the eternal air of grief in the hermit's colony — for Death is a cowardly assassin who largely strikes the old and feeble.

And so, he had decided to be by himself, on the island in the Sindhu River, alone, to contemplate eternity, study the stars and heavenly bodies, drink a little wine and, perhaps, compose some poems and songs—and if he did not pass most of his time in prayer and meditation which as a hermit he was expected to do there was no one to notice it.

Better, then, to avoid the doomed, crowded colony of older hermits, and live and die alone—in dignity and privacy.

Bharat knew that the small boat, adrift in the river, was not the boat that came monthly with his supplies. But the crazy dogs did not know that and kept barking. Possibly, they were hoping for the arrival of their regular boat and, with it, treats for them to eat, chew and play with.

Three years earlier, when the boat had arrived on its first trip, they had barked fiercely at the three boatmen, and were prepared to be violent, fearing that the intruders meant harm—and they were ready, at all times, to give their protection to their silent, contemplative, grave companion, Bharat; but soon, the dogs realized that the newcomers posed no danger, and had in fact proved to be great fun; and their distrust gave way to friendship.

The boat was now coming nearer. No, surely it was not their family boat. It was much too tiny and did not fly the family flag; nor did it have the bright colours and round railings which the boats they were familiar with possessed.

The dogs continued to bark, even more fiercely, now that the boat was getting nearer. This was not their practice when Bharat's usual boat approached. Then, the dogs would rush to the very edge of the water, stop barking and wag their tails instead; maybe they thought that the strength of their moving tails would supplement the rowing efforts of the boatmen, and bring the boat to the shore more quickly. But now they continued to bark and were even tugging at his feet and legs. Bharat rose from his sitting position to release himself from the dogs, and admonished them.

'You have no desire to pray with me and I have no desire to play with you. So let me alone and stop your yapping.'

The dogs heard him out in silence, gazing at him gravely, as if to absorb fully the wisdom of his words, for they knew that despite his limitations, he was often wise in his ways. But apparently on this occasion he had disappointed them. They resumed their barking and tugging, even more intensely.

He looked at the boat again which continued to move this way and that, at the will and pleasure of the windswept river. If it continued on its present course, it would not take too long to come directly opposite the spot where he was, though it would still be quite far out, in the centre of the wide river. He could of course swim towards it, for he was a strong swimmer despite his age and he loved to swim. But what for? He had already had his swim before dawn, and the boat, clearly, was empty. Let it find its own destiny. Instinctively, his eyes went up to the sky, as they always did, whenever he thought of destiny. Do all things begin from there and do all things end there? he wondered looking at the sky—and if they begin, why end; and if they have to end, why begin?

It was not a new question. He had asked it frequently, from the age of seven when his father had died, pierced by a poisoned arrow aimed by those who had come to loot their land. He had even asked his mother if his question was foolish.

'No, son, no,' she had replied, 'questions can never be foolish, only... only answers will sometimes be faulty.'

He had had questions all his life but rarely any answers. But he had no regrets on that score. Somehow, he felt that all his questions would be answered after his life ended. But even if they were not then answered, would it really matter? And when life ends, don't the questions end? Or is it that the questions remain and only the questioner passes?

On this occasion at least, the sky had a good excuse not to reply to his question. It was overcast. The sun had given up the effort to assert itself through the clouds, giving way to a gentle drizzle, followed by distant thunder and lightning. Then came the rain, pouring through the heavy velvet sky. He picked up the prayer-mat and went into his hut.

He called the dogs into the hut. They did not come. He called again but there was no response. This surprised him. The dogs always sought shelter when it rained. He too disliked the rain. His joints ached and he would have to resist the temptation to use the special ointment to ease the pain. He had not asked for it, but his wife had sent him the jar of balm made from diamond dust, mixed with the roots of the Naagadhoya plant, which flowers in the waterless desert, a day after the mating dance of snakes, on the night of the full moon.

Through the boatmen who brought the balm, she had sent a message saying that Vaid (medicine man) Raj had told her that air moist with the wetness of rain can sometimes cause the joints to ache, and he should use the balm if ever he suffered from such pain. The boatmen must have told his wife about the limp in his leg during the rainy season, even though he had asked them not to report it lest it worry her. He did not blame the boatmen for disobeying him for he liked these friendly spies. But he had never used the balm, preferring to suffer pain rather than depend on medicine. He feared that with advancing age the intensity and frequency of the pain would increase but he hoped that he would be able to suffer in silence and would not have to summon help from the village next to his island. He looked with distaste at the huge drum in the corner of his hut, which he would have to use to call for assistance in case of emergency.

His wife had commissioned the best artisans to make the drum, and they had boasted that its sound would cause horses to bolt, fish to leap out of water, and even wake up the dead within two yojna (ten miles) around.

Bharat had never used the drum and hoped he would never have to. Better to suffer in silence and privacy, away from strangers, since he could not be with his loved ones.

He was now thinking of his wife, and said a silent prayer for her well-being. He did that often, praying also for his sons and grandsons, and for the souls of his departed father and mother. The image of each of them passed through his mind's eye as he prayed for them.

He abandoned his questions and his mind dwelt again on his wife. She would have loved to visit him and he would have loved it too. But hermits could have neither family nor female visits. Perhaps there was merit in this rule; after all, how can you achieve total, or even partial, surrender to the gods if women and the family keep visiting you; obviously such visits can only dissipate any hope of attaining detachment.

He was glad though that women did not ever have to be hermits, whatever their age, and so his wife would not have to undergo the isolation imposed on him. He had wondered, once, about the discriminatory aspect of this practice which compelled men to retire as hermits, while a woman was free from such enforced isolation. But then he realized that a woman could never be asked to retire because her work never ceased. From being a wife, she moved smoothly and selflessly into the role of a mother and grandmother, giving all of herself, body and soul, in the service of the generations that followed, until her dying day. Man's tragedy, on the other hand, was that he lived alone, and for himself, from the moment he achieved manhood, until he reached his dying day; he had his ego centred around his own self, and if he loved his children and grandchildren, he loved them merely as extensions of himself and the older he grew, the more demanding he got, with his ideas fixed and mind closed. All that grew within him was a lust for power, while his advancing age continued to render him less and less capable of wielding it honourably. Happiness for man depended on what he could *get*; for a woman, it depended on what she could *give*. Retirement at the age of sixty years was, therefore, intended to save man from himself and also to protect society. Bharat often thought with a smile that he himself was an exception to the rule, and that his advancing years, in the midst of his people, would have added to his grace and dignity, and to the welfare of society; but then he also knew that everyone facing retirement thought this about himself.

Actually, Bharat could easily have saved himself from this enforced retirement as a hermit. He was the Karkarta (supreme chief) of the Hindu clan which lived in the villages and settlements along and around the river Sindhu, as far as the eye could see and man could travel. He, it was, who held the rod of authority and established the law of the land. He was the leader of his people, their guide, their mentor, their teacher and they were fond of him, and sometimes even treated him as their lord, for when things went well or badly, he decreed their rewards and punishments.

The institution of Karkarta had been established only nineteen generations ago when it was realized that the clan's dominions were expanding very rapidly and with it, its problems. And because the Council of Chiefs could never act promptly and was often divided, except in its common desire to make long speeches. Each of his eighteen illustrious predecessors as Karkartas were reputed to have died in harness before reaching the age of sixty. So there had never been an instance of a Karkarta who had to retire as a hermit, and it was assumed that he was free from such bondage; after all, a Karkarta who interpreted god's laws to man, was holy enough, and did not need to be a hermit.

Bharat had always suspected that at least some Karkartas had violated this law. True, a man's age could not easily be hidden, due to the unbroken immemorial custom of planting trees for each year of a man's life, right from the year of his birth until the age of his retirement, with the added injunction to plant new trees in place of those that died. But so what! Some people just wouldn't count what they didn't wish to count.

Yet, he did not wish to consider that option.

Therefore, he raised the question of his retirement when he was nearing sixty. The Council Chiefs smiled but took no action. Bharat insisted that the Council meet to establish a date for holding elections to choose his successor. After several days and many long speeches, the Council decided that the Karkarta had the right to remain in office until the end of his natural life. Bharat heard the long and carefully reasoned declaration of the Council in silence, nodding his head from time to time, signifying that he appreciated the wisdom and gravity of what was being said. At the end of the recital, Bharat thanked them for their careful and earnest consideration of the problem, but informed them of his conviction that the *higher* the office of the man, the *fewer* his rights and more numerous his obligations, and added:

'....You spoke of my rights, but I am convinced that as Karkarta and as the leader of our clan, I have no rights; only duties.... As for the rest, I am subject to the same law and subordinate to the same duty and have the same obligations to fulfil as all of us in this land....'

Then, sadly, he had passed the sentence of banishment on himself.

The irony of it all was that he had never believed that a man who was obliged to retire as a hermit forged stronger bonds between himself and his gods. In his younger days, after he had assumed the high office of Karkarta, he had thought of trying to repeal the practice of compulsorily retiring people as hermits at the age of sixty, but that idea went nowhere, for he soon realized that the system was so rooted in antiquity that any interference with it would be unpopular, leading to a widespread fear of inviting the wrath of gods, which might in turn be visited on their children.

To the Assembly of the People he said:

'...Each man has his own destiny, which he can change and alter by his own free will, effort and action, for good or evil. But it is evil for me, as Karkarta of this land and the leader of our people, to sacrifice a Rule of Law which I have sworn to uphold.... The unalterable, inevitable course of my destiny therefore leads me to retire and my anguish is no less than yours....'

Bharat honoured those who went to their retirement as hermits, by choice, well before sixty. Those were the ones, he thought, who would achieve a lasting personal relationship with the gods. Some even went in their early youth, seeking total isolation and immersion in their meditation; others went as disciples and devotees. But not all such hermits went into permanent seclusion. Many returned from time to time, back to their life amongst the people; some felt that the brief salute they had made to the gods was enough for the time being; others came back because their hope of reaching the gods had proved elusive; and there were those who, after a brief sojourn in solitude, came back believing that the way to reach the gods was through living and working with people and not under a tree in a forest or on a silent hill. But, then, a few of them went back again and again into seclusion to pray and meditate, thus alternating between isolation and activity. Bharat honoured all those who went of their own free will, prompted by devotion to the gods and guided by no ulterior motives.

There were, of course, those who merely pretended to be hermits and sought the safety of forests when the first war-cry was heard and raiders from the north or the east were about to attack and returned only after the raiders departed. These instant hermits would then claim that the enemy onslaught was weakened as a result of their prayers. And when others laughed at such claims these fair-weather hermits went about their business unabashed, consoled by the thought that men of God would always be taunted by the ignorant and the vulgar. Bharat himself smiled inwardly at these hermits but dealt with their requests with utmost seriousness when they urged that the time spent by them as hermits be taken into account so as to postpone their eventual retirement at sixty.

*

Bharat smiled as he recalled his arguments with those hermits. He realized that as Karkarta one was sometimes forced to be sincere without being too honest.

His smile deepened into satisfaction as he realized that those days of fear and flight were over. No longer would the people of his clan have to run to the safety of the forests. Those who had raided from the north and the east were enemies no more. The last major raid had occurred many years ago and the enemy had fallen—burned, blinded, with fractured faces and limbless bodies. Since then, repeatedly, Bharat had led his people to victories against hostile tribes and after his last decisive victory came an era of unbroken peace and harmony during which the tribes themselves had sought to become a part of the larger fabric of the Hindu clan. For more than two decades now there had not been a single armed attack on their borders from the north or the east.

Bharat often wondered why those who had been in the thick of a battle spoke less of it than those who had merely heard of it. He himself had led his people in countless battles against raiders but always with fear in his heart. His friend Suryata who knew of his fear, had said to him: 'Only the dead are without fear.'

Before each campaign, he prayed to the spirit of his father. His father had died while leading a charge against the enemy and he had often wept when a child because his father had been a fixture in his world, a part of the great universe and he had never imagined that he could die.

Bharat hated war. Anguish and death were its bitter fruits, he knew; and he thought not only of those lost on the battlefield but also of the widows and orphans left behind. Yet he also knew that there would always be wars, especially when there was unrest in the land.

Therefore, while he was tolerant towards those few who pretended to be hermits and fled to the sanctuary of the forest to avoid joining the battle against the enemy, it was another band of hermits that he feared. These were the hermits who returned from their temporary forest retreats from time to time, claiming that the gods had appeared before them with the command that they should go back amongst the people and spread the divine word and message. Each such hermit brought forth a different message from the gods, often at variance with, and even hostile to, that of the others. This did not at first confuse the people. The gods, they knew, were totally unique and incomparably splendid and could not be comprehended through a single, solitary image. Initially he too had listened to these false prophets with humility and respect. Later, he found them coarse, selfish, scheming and invariably greedy and intolerant, though some of them were simply stupid and victims of their own hallucinations. Each reviled and ridiculed the gods of others and prescribed his own method of worship; each declared that the eternal fires of hell would consume the unbelievers and those who prayed to false gods—and thus they moved around, whipping up a frenzy and demanding new forms of ritual and worship, but always with themselves in the forefront, as messengers or heralds or, sometimes even more arrogantly, as angels or prophets or sons of God. To do this, they often simulated false doctrines, created cruel hatreds and invented perilous lies and sometimes even performed conjuring tricks to give them the appearance of being miracle workers. Bharat disliked deeply these charlatans who with their fakery, fraud and falsehood were seeking to splinter men's belief into fragments all over the land. He knew that somewhere in the burning pit of these men's black hearts, a hideous voice was whispering, urging disunity, hatred and strife. Strange that these new and vile hatreds should lift their deadly heads when prosperity had began to smile on the lands of his clan—a prosperity that kept growing year by year, ever since the raiders from the north and east ceased their annual attacks. Is it that when danger does not threaten from the *outside*, people are compelled to create demons *inside* themselves, to rush towards their self-destruction? If that was so, a wise Karkarta would be well advised to keep fanning the flames of wars on his borders and shut out for ever every hope of prosperity for his people and their land. No, surely that was not so—and he believed what his people had believed for countless generations—that the gods sought to *unite* and not *divide* mankind with their mercy and compassion. He was convinced that if hell-fire really existed, it must have been created solely and exclusively for those false preachers who had no kindness and charity in their souls and who sought to divide and disunite their fellow-men with new resentments and new hatreds.

The rain and thunder increased in intensity; Bharat checked the ceiling and was relieved to see there was no seepage; the hut had weathered many storms in the past and would weather many more.

Long before he was to retire as a hermit, his wife had come to the island, with a group of men well versed in the art of building, and had personally inspected the construction of the hut. In fact, she had herself selected this island for his retirement—it was close to a village and yet so situated as to be almost invisible from it. She had planted fruit trees and flowering bushes, widened streams and erected fences to keep out wild animals. In his mind now, Bharat saw her, thought of her, talked to her; he was sure that she too was seeing him, thinking of him and talking to him. He realized that they could no longer meet and make love; but then they were more than mere lovers; they were companions in spirit.

The dogs were still out in the rain. They still appeared to be exercised about the boat drifting aimlessly in the river. Bharat was almost certain that by now someone from the village next to his island would have spotted the boat and towed it in—and if not, the next village would have done so. But what if none of the villages took the trouble to catch the boat?

Even as a child, Bharat had known that the river went far beyond the villages of his clan, into inaccessible terrain where no man had set foot. Some even said that Sindhu river went on and on to the end of the earth, gaining in speed and turbulence, until it finally reached the stairway to the sky, which served as the bridge to the abode of gods. He had never believed that. He was sure that the earth and the sky, and the space beyond it, were separate elements and could not possibly be joined by a staircase. He chose instead to believe a song he had heard, when he was only eight years old, sung by a wandering hermit about the haunting beauty and endless bounty of Sindhu river. The song had concluded on the following note:

'The Sindhu flows majestically; along the way, many rivers and streams come rushing from different directions to pay homage to her;
'She accepts them all lovingly, and thus overflowing, she goes on to meet her lover at a magical place where there is the River of all Rivers, with winds of crushing force and enormous waves;
'And Sindhu is so glad to meet her lover that she sheds tears of happiness, which turn her waters salty;
'And together, then, in the ecstasy of a tumultuous embrace, with pounding hearts and heaving chests and the cry of joy and pain that is heard when two lovers surrender to each other, they go on, to distant shores that no one has seen.'

Bharat had been fascinated by the hermit's description of the beauty and grandeur of waters that flow to distant shores, and had asked, 'But have you seen those unknown shores?'

'I have dreamt of them,' was the hermit's reply.

'Oh, a dream!' Bharat was clearly disappointed.

'Everything, my son, has at least two faces—its face in reality and its face in a dream.'

Bharat had blurted, 'But if it is merely a dream, what reality can it have?'

'My son, only that which cannot be dreamed of is devoid of reality. Everything that is great and blessed begins as a dream.'

Bharat had stared at the hermit. Perhaps, the old man was always dreaming, he had thought. The hermit had sensed that he had disappointed the child and had said, 'But there are those who have seen the great waters and their distant shores.'

'Where are they?'

The hermit had turned to face the river, his hand half-raised; and Bharat had not known if the hand was directed to the sky to indicate that the answer would come from above, or was simply a gesture to admit that he did not know the answer. Bharat had persisted. 'Tell me, is this your own song or did you hear it from someone else?'

'My grandfather used to sing this song and he had heard it from his father.'

Even when Bharat grew to manhood, the dream of tracing the source and destination of Sindhu remained with him; but it was only much later, long after he became Karkarta, that this dream was at last fulfilled.

Bharat was thinking now of the arduous journeys and perilous adventures that had faced him and his people, when they had set out to discover the path of the Sindhu river, from its source in the trans-Himalayas, to its destination, into the River of Rivers—the great sea. They had finally discovered it—but what came next? Bharat wondered. God gives us a glimpse into a small secret of the origin and source, but behind that glimpse lies the larger challenge of a greater secret. It was as though each discovery multiplied infinitely what yet remained to be discovered.

Bharat's mind dwelt again on the wandering hermit who had sung for him the 'Song of the Sindhu River' when he was eight years old. During this conversation with the hermit, Bharat had been holding the hand of Bindu, the girl he was expected to marry when they grew up. She was two years younger than him and their parents had already exchanged marriage vows on their behalf.

It was only when the hermit left and Bharat had released his hold on Bindu's hand that he realized how excited he had been during the conversation. He had gripped Bindu's hand so tightly that he could see the white marks of the pressure of his fingers clearly visible on the back of her hand. He had looked at her hand with concern and smiled a special smile to apologize. She had smiled sweetly back at him and pressed the back of her hand lightly to her lips. That was the last time they had exchanged smiles for she had died, along with her two brothers, during a sudden enemy raid the next day.

He had not shed tears at her funeral pyre. Nor had he shed tears a year earlier when his father died. Some said Bharat had achieved manhood before becoming a man, and others said that when the hurt is very deep the heart cries tears that do not reach the eyes.

After Bindu's funeral, he had gone quietly to the river. He had known what he had to do. He would call out to the sky and to the river to be witness to his terrible, eternal oath of vengeance against the tribes of the north and the east.

But the sky had looked impassively on as he called out to it and in the flowing waters of Sindhu he had seen visions that had melted his resolve. He saw the serene, stately face of his father, with his hand raised lovingly to calm him down; and then the waters brought to him another vision—of Bindu, with a smile in her liquid eyes, shining with the heart-sweetening, eye-kissing light; and she had waved to him—he had understood that she was not waving goodbye but was telling him that she would come back to him, always to be with him. Tears had welled up in his eyes; and when his tears fell in the river, he wondered if they would reach the River of Rivers and unknown shores that the hermit had described.

As the months went by, Bharat's mother started looking for eligible girls to exchange vows with Bharat, but he pleaded with her to stop as Bindu would reappear in her own house. She merely shook her head, knowing that one day her eight-year-old son would come to realize that those who depart never come back. Finally, she did tell him—'Those who have left us, have left us for ever. They will not come back and we must not wish that they should be back on this earth.'

'Why?' he had asked rebelliously.

How could she explain to the child the mysteries of life and death when she herself did not understand them all! But she had tried, 'Son, we are all part of God—one with God. God sends us out on this earth and expects us to do good deeds during our sojourn on earth. But there are those amongst us that do evil, commit sins and live with unholy desires. They do not go back to God when they die. No, they are reborn on this earth, in different forms, without knowing their former lives; and thus they are born and reborn, again and again, in lives of sorrow and misery, until they learn to live a moral life, with decency, honour and good deeds—and then, and then only, are their sins wiped out and they go back to God to be one with Him again.'

She had looked at him intently, wondering if he had understood her. He had and asked quickly, 'And what about those who do good on this earth and live sinless lives?'

She had been happy he had asked the question, for she had wanted to talk about Bindu. 'Those that do good, my son, attain moksha.' She had paused at the question in his eyes. She explained, 'Moksha is the liberation of the soul from the chain of birth and death.'

The question in his eyes had remained, so she continued, 'When a person on this earth lives an innocent life—a life of love, goodness, purity—like Bindu, she goes back into the loving arms of God—she and God are then one. That is moksha, total release from the cycle of birth and death. Then the person is a person no more but a part of the One Supreme, who is the God of us all.'

He had looked at her intently, as if trying to understand and had at last said, 'You mean, Bindu is a god!'

His mother had nodded, though it had not been her intention to confer godhood on anyone.

'Then she is a god!' he had said triumphantly.

His mother had not understood his jubilation, until he said, 'Then she can come back if she wants; gods can do anything.'

She had replied lamely, 'Gods have no desire for this earth.'

'But gods don't lie,' he had retorted. 'Bindu told me herself that she wants to come back to me and always be with me.'

To that she had had many answers, but none that she considered adequate. Time, she hoped, would heal the wound in her child's heart.

After some months, it became common knowledge that Bindu's mother was expecting a child. This surprised everyone, as she was long past the child-bearing age. Many feared that a miscarriage would result. When Bharat heard about her pregnancy, he quietly told his mother that he would marry her daughter. His mother smiled and asked, 'How do you know it will be a daughter? Bindu's mother goes to the river every morning to pray for a son. Her husband has also promised the gods that he will erect a temple in their honour if he has a son. Even their family astrologer predicts a son.'

'Are astrologers always right when they predict a son?'

She smiled, 'They are right half the time.'

He shared her smile but then asked seriously, 'Why do they want a son? Were they not happy with Bindu?'

'Of course they were; Bindu was the sweetest girl who ever lived; but see my son, with Bindu, her two elder brothers also passed away. Who can blame them for wanting a son?'

But Bharat, ignoring this, simply repeated, 'I shall marry her.'

Bharat's mother had averted her eyes to hide her tears, for she knew that he was grieving not only for his lost girlfriend but also for his departed father. And the memory of her husband, who was also her lover and her friend, came to her anew, reopening a wound in her heart that would never heal.

A child always knows, instinctively, when and why his mother's heart cries in pain, even if tears remain unshed and words unspoken. Bharat put his arm around his mother and she broke down, as he buried his face in her bosom.

A daughter was born to Bindu's mother. She too was named Bindu. Eventually, many years later, when he was nearing twenty-four, and she fifteen, they were married.

Bharat was now thinking of his wife, as he often did, in the loneliness of the island. He thought of their wedding night. He saw his wife decked in flowers and pearls, her face flushed with pride. He could hear the sighs and murmurs of admiration from the crowd, as she walked down, dressed in gold and brocade, to take the marriage vow and hold the hand of the man who was to be her husband. While the sacred fire was burning, Bindu's father formally offered his daughter to Bharat, on his making the ritual promise of always being true to her in all the five traditional aims —piety, permanence, pleasure, property and progeny. Then, with the recitation of sacred mantras by the purohit (priest), and offerings of grain, ghee and flowers to the sacred fire, their garments were knotted; and holding her hand, he led her seven times around the fire, while both repeated their vows.

For three nights, the newly married couple slept apart; the custom clearly insisted on continence for the first three days, during which many sacred ceremonies were performed. It was only on the fourth day that the marriage was consummated. This was of course to highlight the fact that the spiritual and emotional bonds of marriage were far greater than its sexual bond.

Actually, she was a bit younger than her fifteen years, but that was because the clan used a different calendar to determine a girl's age. The lunar calendar, in which each month began with the appearance of the new moon, determined a woman's age. For determining a man's age, however, it was the solar calendar that was used.

The cycles of the moon corresponded well with the menstrual cycles of women and it was regarded as natural that for them the moon should be relied on as the measure of age. That was not the only reason. The moon was considered auspicious and attractive, even mystical and romantic, and certainly cool and calm and it was therefore considered appropriate to link it with women.

But man—the farmer, the cattle breeder, the hunter, the builder, the trader, the traveller—was concerned more with the change of seasons; with the coming of heat, cold and rains, and of the rhythm of the Sindhu, with its rising and falling waters. The warmth of the sun and the heavenly gift of rains decided the fate of crops and determined the time to sow and reap.

The clan had clearly perceived that the sun was the surest guide to the change and return of seasons; and the moon, though a great charmer, did not have its phases designed to keep in step with the change of seasons.

Thus it was that the solar year, divided into three hundred and sixty-five and a quarter days—the proper measure of days between seasons—was regarded as appropriate for all official business, and for determining a man's age.

Even so, for all feasts and festivals, and for every auspicious and blessed event, it was always the moon and its cycles that guided the clan. But that was so because the clan had always retained a primeval fascination and special affection for the moon. An ancient, half-remembered song had spoken of the moon as a worshipper of Mother Goddess Sindhu and of Mother Earth whom the Goddess served, and the song had said—

'Even though we sometimes do not see it, the moon always revolves around Mother Earth, sometimes shining near our view but half the time away and hidden, shining over distant, unknown shores where Mother Sindhu goes on her enchanted journey to the passionate lap of the mighty River of Rivers.'

The song had then dwelt on the moonlit settings of lovers' meetings, and sung of 'woman's eternal capacity for love, that changed neither with rain nor shine, nor with the season of storms, clouds and lightning, to give gladness that never leaves those that love.' And the singer went on to ask: 'Why then do you wonder that the waters of Mother Sindhu rise in joy to meet and greet the new moon!' The same song spoke of the impatient energy of man and of his subservience to the changing and returning seasons that came with the cycles of the sun and it described surya (the sun) not as a worshipper of Mother Goddess Sindhu but as a god in his own right who worships other, mightier gods; and while the sun kept revolving round them, it was always mindful of those on earth, as its 'rays reach out to touch, bless, sustain and nourish the worshippers of Mother Goddess Sindhu.' The song had ended on the philosophical note—half sad, half amused—that we always tend to love those that worship us, rather than those to whom our worship is due, and thus it is that we venerate the sun and love the moon.

No one knew that ancient song in its entirety, nor even the identity of the composer with certainty, though it was clear that it was first sung by a woman, for the song had a passage that said: 'So, sisters, let men order their lives around the seasons of the sun, while we have the endless season of love with the moon.' Generally, though, the song was credited to Darmandevi, in the time of the fifth Karkarta, four centuries earlier. It was she who was also reputed to have composed a song that recited the seasons and cycles of the moon and the sun. But later, so many improvisations had taken place that no one could remember the original song, for the memory of man is short.

Many had worked on creating a synthesis of the lunar and solar calendars, but that was used chiefly for teaching arithmetic; often a teacher would mention a lunar date and ask students for the corresponding solar date. In an age when the art of writing was yet to be developed, such mental exercises were not too easy for Bharat, even as an adult.

Thus the custom of the clan, clearly, was to determine man's age according to the solar calendar, while a woman's age had to be determined by the calendar of the moon, with its lofty disdain for a change of seasons. Since the lunar year had less days (and it took a pregnant woman longer—nearly ten months—under that calendar to give birth), it sometimes happened that when a woman was only one year younger than the man on the eve of their marriage, it took around thirty-three years for the woman to become of the same age and then begin to overreach him. Normally, however, a difference of at least two years was maintained between the age of the boy and the girl when they married, though it had no practical significance, as after the age of thirty, a married woman who was also a mother, was always to be referred to with the prefix of Mataji (mother) and it was bad form, at any time, to refer to her actual age. She was supposed to remain thirty, except when she became a grandmother, and then she could proudly claim to be thirty-one, though that age remained with her even when she became a great-grandmother. The rationale for this was lost in antiquity, but Bharat thought that it had something to do with the concept of equality in their large and ever extending joint family system so that, for instance, the wife of the younger brother was not subservient to her much older sister-in-law because of her age; in any case the supreme command of the family remained solely with the mother or grandmother, as the situation demanded, and the rest were directly answerable to her.

Bharat never underestimated the traditional songs his clan sung. Such songs, he felt, must be preserved for the future. He knew that the stories and legends of the past, of the people who lived before his time, of rivers, mountain and valleys, of flowers, trees, birds and animals, of longings, yearnings and aspirations of the years gone by, were all woven into songs and poems—some of which had survived, while others were either only half-remembered or forgotten altogether. Even when his own father had died, many songs were sung, recounting his gallantry against the enemy. But now except for a few singers attached to his own family, hardly anyone remembered them; and whenever a new event took place, new songs were composed and sung, while the old ones were forgotten, and it seemed as though the event which those earlier songs celebrated had never occurred.

It was unfortunate that only a few, stray fragments of the knowledge of the past remained. How, then, could the people of the future discover how we lived, loved, worked, prayed and thought—and know of our hopes, fears and aspirations? By a dream? By a vision? No, there had to be an unbroken bridge of knowledge linking all of humanity as it evolved; otherwise all the past would be as nothing, and man would be groping to discover what the previous generation had already found and possibly even discarded.

He had come to the conclusion that there had to be songs—eternal songs, always remembered, never forgotten, handed down from father to son, to keep alive the knowledge of the past and the present — and these could be a gift to the future of man. Some things, he was convinced, had to remain permanent and every culture needed to be preserved.

Bharat smiled as he thought of the measures he had introduced after he became Karkarta at the age of twenty-five—measures to elevate the position, privileges and prominence of singers and song-composers. Many had laughed and some continued to laugh, even when he had explained to them, at length, their importance and why they were needed to transmit to the coming generations, through eternal songs and poems, the knowledge of today, so that each successive generation could draw upon that vast, collective pool of learning. 'Our Memory songs,' he had explained, 'shall be the treasury, the trustee and the guardian of the knowledge of our generation and through those songs messages of our times shall be passed on to all mankind for ever, through time and space.' And though many looked unimpressed, he had concluded by saying: 'Through the superb rhythm of our poets and singers we have the opportunity to reach out to future ages and to make our own generation endless, not a mere fleeting, unnoticed moment in the history of eternity....'

Bharat continued, 'Who amongst us will deny the legacy of wisdom to our children and to the children of our children?'

No one really had an objection to what their Karkarta had in view for they soon realized that while the Karkarta was peering into the cloudy mists of a distant future, he was also adding immensely to the storehouse of their entertainment; more singers, poets and song-composers would mean that people, at the end of their labours each day, would be regaled with new melodies and choice lyrics.

So people welcomed the idea of Memory songs, even when Bharat announced that singers, song-composers and poets who achieved eminence, should be exempted from retirement as hermits.

When Bharat had been considering extra privileges to encourage poets and singers, he had turned to his friend Daya for advice. They had tried to visualize the effect of their songs and poetry on future generations. The songs and poems would, they knew, have to be of at least three kinds; a few would deal with things as they existed in reality; but there would be many more of the second kind, which would concern themselves with only that which existed in the imagination— of the yearnings of the heart, or the longings of the soul, or the quest for beauty, or the exaltation of the spirit; and the third category would be that in which the singer combined reality with his imagination or flights of fancy, like the poets who sang of the bravery of their clan in every battle but never said a word about how cravenly many ran away.

How did one ensure that only that which was authentic was passed on? This question troubled Bharat and Daya only momentarily as they began to ponder a basic question: what is the meaning and essence of reality and imagination in poetry? Reality, they felt, meant the depiction of things as they were and of man as he was; but imagination in poetry and songs, they felt, reflected not only man as he was but what he aspired to be. Surely, then, imagination in poetry was as important as reality itself. In any case, would the coming generations not have the wisdom to separate fact from fantasy and make their own judgements? So, let there be songs to remember not only knowledge but also dreams; let poets weave into the recital of the times, the adornments of their fancy; and, only then, would their generation be endless.

Bharat's thoughts moved from Daya, back to the days of his childhood, as he thought of all those who had died before their time. He recalled how he had gone to the banks of the Sindhu after Bindu's death with a rage in his heart that cried out for revenge; he had glared, with anger welling in his soul, at the distant trackless passes in the faraway hills from which the raiders made their annual attacks to butcher his people and steal their cattle and goods; pillage houses and burn all that they could not carry. Yet he did not take the oath of vengeance and instead vowed to protect the people of his land from future attacks.

He had known that in the past the clan took shelter, deep in the forest, as soon as the enemy appeared. Later, a few courageous ones stayed behind to fight but failed due to their comparatively small numbers. His own father had gathered a large group to strike against the enemy but when he fell his men had tried to flee and most of them were killed.

His father's action to organize resistance had been against the advice of the presiding Karkarta who had feared that such an attempt, apart from being futile, might infuriate the enemy and make their vengeance swift and deadly; but Bharat never forgot his father's words. His father had spoken of shame and fear—*shame*, if people submitted passively to the enemy, and *fear*, that the attacks would continue so long as people failed to resist.

He was only seven years old when his father had died. Before the year was out, he had lost Bindu. It was after Bindu's death that Bharat had accosted the Karkarta's son, Suryata, who was his friend. 'When you become Karkarta, you must lead our people against them,' Bharat had said, his finger clearly pointing in the direction from which the enemies came.

Suryata, only a few months older than Bharat, understood the silent scream of anguish that lay beneath those words. 'I am the Karkarta's son and not entitled ever to become Karkarta,' Suryata had said quietly. Somehow, Bharat had not then known of the established convention which prohibited a family member from succeeding as Karkarta; he had assumed it to be a hereditary office, passing from father to son.

'But,' Suryata continued, 'God willing, when you yourself are Karkarta, I shall be by your side in battle against the enemy—and this I swear by the light of the sun that shines on us every morning.'

Bharat had wondered, momentarily, if Suryata was making fun of him. No, there was no hint of laughter in his earnest face and honest eyes; moreover, Suryata belonged to a family of sun-worshippers and would never swear by the light of the sun in vain. They had left together for a swim, both with the instinctive feeling of having drawn closer to each other.

Inwardly, the eight-year old Bharat had smiled at the possibility—held out by Suryata—that one day he could become Karkarta; but as he plunged into the Sindhu river, he had asked himself: 'Why not?'—and floating in the river, with his eyes closed, he had felt the warm glow of the sun and the presence of his departed father, of Bindu, and of the many others who had died in enemy raids. And then his mind had gone to the living—to the panorama of the land of his people along the life-giving waters of the Sindhu, to their valleys and plains, to the forests and broad fields, and to the faces and figures of men, women and children that lived, loved, laughed, worked and prayed

there. 'God! help me to bring peace to them,' he had prayed; 'God,
help me to give them hope, restore their dignity and renew their faith;
God, use me as You will, but help me to protect our people.' When he
had come out of the water, he had known what his heart had resolved
and it was to this resolve that he would devote his life. Later, after
reaching the age of fourteen, when he was allowed to bear arms, he
had often gone into battle against the enemy raiders. Still later, when
he became Karkarta, and the leader of his men, he knew that the gods
had granted him this opportunity so that he might bring safety and
peace to his people and his land.

Battles, Bharat had realized early in life, lasted only briefly and
victory did not necessarily go to those who fought with courage and
bravery, but to those who had the foresight to prepare for it. To his
friend Suryata he had posed the problem: 'We do poorly whenever
the enemy ventures into our land. So, either we must go and confront
them in their land or, somehow, prevent them from setting foot in
ours.'

'How?' Suryata had asked. 'How? By praying to the sun, as my
father does, to dissolve the enemy!' Suryata's tone had been loaded
with anger and irony, and Bharat had known that his friend's wrath
and bitterness had not been directed at him but at his own father.
Suryata's mother had been dragged away by the raiders and would be
going through unspeakable horrors if she were alive; his two brothers
and a sister whom he adored had been speared to death. Suryata's
father, who was then the Karkarta of the clan, had prayed every day
to the sun for the souls of his slain children and for the deliverance of
his wife from bondage; and many who had also lost their loved ones,
joined him in his prayers to praise their gods and glory in them, and
in every breath of theirs was resignation and acceptance of things as
they were and of hope beyond.

Suryata, whose father and grandfather were known as ardent sun-
worshippers, no longer worshipped the sun. But who could tell? Suryata
spent practically every waking hour watching the sun and making
constant drawings in the sand of its movements, size and direction. At
night, when the sun went into hiding, he kept looking at the sky,
watching the stars; and every one thought that he was waiting for the
sun to reappear.

The wise men of the clan, of course, knew that the sun splintered
into an endless number of stars at night so that men might sleep under
their cool shadow but at dawn it gathered them all together, in its
fiery fold, to make its majestic entrance in order to revive the universe.
There were other wise men who rejected that theory and held that the
rising and setting of the sun over the land around the Sindhu merely
proved that somewhere far away there were distant lands, and the
sun set over the Sindhu only to rise in those faraway lands. Yet, there
were also those who possessed extraordinarily playful minds and bold
imaginations; they looked at the flowing waters of the Sindhu river,

saw their constant movement, and wondered: is it the sun that moves out of our lives every day, or is it that we ourselves move out of its realm every evening to re-enter it at dawn? But then they were asked: how could it be that the earth beneath our feet moves, yet we neither see it nor feel it? The replies to this simple question were rarely forthcoming and, if at all they came, were in the form of questions which were designed to infuriate, rather than explain. For instance, the counter-questions were:

- How is it that you claim to see with your eyes and yet you cannot see your own eyes? What arrogance is this, that you must see and hear something before you will accept its existence.
- You grow old, moment by moment by moment, but do you see or feel the growth each moment?
- Is any heavenly body or element ever stationary or unmoving? So why be surprised if the earth moves!
- If you do not see the earth moving, so what? How can you see what the gods designed to remain invisible?
- In any case, how can you even imagine that the sun, a deity of the gods, loses its vigour and might and majesty at dusk, and sinks low in the west; instead, is it not conceivable that the earth itself moves us out of the brightness of the sun to bring us each night under the restful glow of the moon?

Many regarded the sun as 'our local star linked to the earth'; they believed that there were other 'countless worlds beyond our outer space and galaxy'; and that each star served as the sun for each of those worlds. Some proudly exclaimed, 'Our own star—the sun—is so much bigger than all the other stars!' Only to hear the retort, 'Yes, just as this sparrow in your garden appears larger than that eagle flying high up in the sky.'

Those who were regarded as the wisest in the clan, neither supported nor rejected any of these diverse theories. They welcomed every theory, in the hope that every new theory would be tested and mankind would thus advance, step by step, to an understanding of the mystery of the universe.

Bharat, at the age of eight, knew little of such philosophical speculation and learned theories. Even his friend Suryata, was unaware of them. But the fact was that Suryata had, on his own, lost all illusions about the might and majesty of the sun, and in fact had ceased to be a sun worshipper. He had watched the sun, initially to worship it—as his father did—but later abandoned this useless god who had been unable to protect his family. Why, Suryata had thought to himself, I have more freedom than the sun, for I can go where I please but the sun is undoubtedly lashed with an invisible rope and must strictly follow the path set for it. His feeling of superiority, however, did not last long; he had sadly told himself, 'The sun knows the path it has to take; it has its purpose in life and a promise to keep every day, but I float aimlessly, without any purpose or sense of direction' and had looked in anger at the sun and cried out in desperation, 'Go slave go; tell your master that I neither believe in you nor in your master, nor in anyone else.'

There was much that was personal in his anger against the sun. His father had led all the men of his village to a distant hill-top for prayers during an eclipse of the sun, and the raiders had attacked the unguarded village and slain his brothers and sister and dragged away his mother.

After his outburst, Suryata had shed silent tears. He felt he had sinned and deserved to be punished for his blasphemy. But the gods, who are often stern, can also be gracious. Suryata acquired a purpose in life. Like Bharat, he too was fired with the overpowering ambition to protect the people of his land from the hated enemies of the north and east.

While Suryata's father, the presiding Karkarta, intensified his prayers, Suryata and Bharat racked their brains to devise ways of foiling the enemy. First of all they had to discover the secret of the poisoned arrows of the enemy. The arrows of the clan were well-made with a much longer range but were far from deadly; the enemy, on the other hand, applied some material to the tips of their arrows which killed as soon as it pierced a victim's body. None could tell what that poisonous material was, though many of their friends, children like themselves, had put forward fanciful and even ridiculous theories.

It was many years later that Bharat along with his friends Yadodhra and Suryata had at last solved the mystery of the poisoned arrow-tips. Bharat recalled how he alone was given credit for this astounding discovery, though his effort had been negligible. Again, he recalled how Suryata, Yadodhra and particularly Yadodhra's father, Ekantra, had helped him. And how his friends and Yadodhra's father had contrived to elect, Bharat, regarded by many as the least worthy, as the Karkarta of his clan.

Bharat continued to reminisce about the past—how the impossible task of securing for him the high office of Karkarta had been accomplished, how dance, music and painting began to flourish in the clan, how new arts and crafts were developed and how finally the enemies of the clan were defeated and peace had returned to their land!

He was now thinking of how his people had evolved pictorial images of their knowledge; and how a language 'that can be seen' was developed so that people could write what they wished to say.

With an effort he put a stop to his nostalgia. Sadly, he realized that instead of being immersed in meditation, he had become prey to every stray thought that chose to enter his head. Is it that when one retires, one cannot concentrate at all?—he asked himself. A hermit is expected to gain wisdom in his solitude but I do not feel any wiser. Can one get wiser by withdrawing from the world?

Suddenly, the fury of wind and rain subsided. Bharat became conscious of light creeping into his hut as the clouds began to lift. He strained to hear the sound of the dogs barking. He could not hear them.

But immediately, Sheena, the bitch, entered the hut, wet and dripping, looking miserable and bedraggled, and started urgently tugging at his feet. Had one of the dogs drowned? he wondered. No, he reassured himself; dogs don't drown—not these dogs, anyway. Still, he followed Sheena out of the hut, and she escorted him to the river.

He quickened his pace when he saw a battered boat wedged lightly between the wooden poles which supported the pier. There was someone in the boat.

Bharat stepped into the boat, carefully, so that it would not sink under his weight.

A young woman lay in a crumpled heap at the bottom of the boat. She was naked, with an infant nestled against her right breast, and appeared to be dead. Bharat knelt by her side, felt her pulse and put his ear to her heart. There was no doubt. She was dead. Gently, he separated the infant from her breast. The infant, perhaps a few hours old, also appeared to be dead. It did not move or make a sound; and Bharat wondered sadly, while holding the limp infant in his arms, why it was given life if it had to be instantaneously snatched away.

Bharat had not seen Sheena entering the boat. Sheena began to lick the infant's face. Bharat did not stop her. In each life, there should be at least one moment of love and he was pleased that Sheena was giving her love to the infant who had perhaps died loveless; or was Sheena trying to lick the last remains of mother's milk which had dried on the infant's face? Mournfully, he looked at the infant while Sheena continued to lick its face, but as Sheena's tongue reached the infant's lips Bharat was startled to see a tiny, imperceptible movement in the baby's mouth; it was as if the infant had felt the nearness of his mother's breast. All of a sudden, a new hope sprang in Bharat's heart; perhaps the Angel of Death had paused to allow the child its last illusion of nourishment on earth, and maybe, if the child was taken out of the boat, the Angel would go away on errands elsewhere.

Bharat stood up, gathering the infant in his arms. He looked at the infant's mother, with her face set in calm repose, as if no sorrow had ever touched her life; and as he saw her thin and bony figure, he thought how frail her body was and how strong her spirit, that triumphantly, with her final breath, she had given perhaps her first and last breast-feed so that her offspring might survive.

Bharat left the boat, with the infant in his arms. I shall be back for you, he silently told the mother of the child; let me first take your son to the shelter of my hut.

He reached the hut at a speed he did not know he was capable of. Meanwhile, a strong wind began to blow and rain began to fall.

He set the child on the rug and gently rubbed its tiny body dry. He moistened his finger-tips with water and placed them on the child's lips and again on its tongue. There was no movement. The child was either in a coma or lifeless, but he kept hoping that it was alive.

After wrapping the child in a soft cotton shawl, Bharat looked gratefully at the huge drum in the corner of the hut. He picked up the drum-sticks, dragged the drum out of the hut, and began to beat the drum with all his strength, hoping that someone in the nearby village would hear, and come to assist him. After three or four beats, he tied a piece of cloth around his ears to muffle the awesome sound of the drum. Let it wake up the dead, he prayed, and renewed the drum-beats pausing, from time to time, to rest his tired hands.

Finally, he stopped and went into the hut to look at the infant. There was no movement. The infant appeared as lifeless as before. The three dogs were lying around the infant in a close circle, and he could hear the sound of their deep breathing in spite of the din of the wind howling outside.

Bharat hoped that the villagers had heard the drum-beats and would heed his summons. They would take their time, he feared, and meanwhile he must go to release the mother of the child from the boat. She was entitled to a last prayer for her departed soul and a funeral pyre so that her body might mingle with the earth. He would say the last prayer for her himself and leave it to the village to cremate her body. He hurried to the pier.

The boat was no longer there. Had it sunk? Bharat looked around and then dived into the river. No, there was no wreckage anywhere.

He came out of the river, dried the wetness from his eyes with the palm of his hand and scanned the river again, as far as he could see. Nothing. He walked up and down, to get a better view of the river from mounds and vantage points. The boat had vanished. Where? He did not know, but he suspected that the gust of wind which had assailed him when he was taking the infant to the hut must have pried the boat loose from the wooden poles of the pier and set it adrift once more.

He looked at the river, beyond to the horizon, seeing nothing, his eyes moist with tears, his heart heavy. He closed his eyes to pray for her soul but his prayers, as always, followed wayward paths and he ended with a plea for mercy and protection for the infant she had left behind.

He was about to return to the hut when he suddenly remembered that he had seen the petals of a wet, wilted, white flower—the kind that women wear in their hair—in the boat. Such fragrant flowers grew on his little island also. He went to the nearby plant, plucked the flowers and placed them in the river. As he saw them float gently in the river, he hoped that they would carry his prayer for the soul of the departed.

While returning to the hut, he heard the distant sound of hooves. His heart leapt with joy. Obviously, someone from the village was coming to help! He ran to the hut. He wanted to reach it as quickly as possible in order to prevent the dogs from going berserk with their barking. When he entered he saw with relief that the infant and the dogs were in the same position in which he had left them.

Outside, a horseman dismounted and entered the hut; Bharat recognized him immediately. He was Gatha, who had once belonged to Bharat's household as a slave. Bharat's wife had granted him his freedom in celebration when their second son was born. Even so, he had remained with Bharat's family, not as a slave but as a helper, entitled to wages and his share of the produce. A year before Bharat retired, Gatha had left to seek his fortune in new pastures.

Gatha bowed low and, with an air of concern, asked, 'Is everything all right, Master?'

Bharat, despite his greater concern, was astonished to see Gatha. 'You! Gatha!' he exclaimed.

'Yes, Master, I am the village headman.' Gatha replied simply.

Bharat smiled. He saw the invisible hand of his wife at work. She certainly would contrive to keep a family retainer in the village next to him. Gatha asked again, 'Are you well, Master?'

Gatha had not seen the infant who was hidden from view by the dogs. He had not even noticed the dogs. His eyes, full of anxiety, were fixed on Bharat alone. Bharat, overcome by the physical exertions of the day, could hardly speak. He pointed to the infant.

Gatha went nearer and the dogs, with surprising quietness, made way for him. What he saw startled him. Was it a child? Or, was it a doll? He touched it and stared at Bharat questioningly.

Bharat nodded his head as if that were answer enough to Gatha's unasked question, and softly said, 'I think this infant may be alive. Can anyone in your village nurse him to life?'

Gatha, picked up the infant gently.

Outside, other horsemen were dismounting. Gatha went out of the hut with the infant in his arms, followed by Bharat and the three dogs. The horsemen had come prepared with food, bandages, medicinal herbs, an antidote for snake-bite and a stretcher which might be needed if Bharat was ill or wounded. In fact, under Mataji's (Bharat's wife) instructions, most of these items were always kept in readiness by Gatha, to meet any sudden summons from Bharatjogi.

Gatha spoke to his men. They took charge of the infant and left. Gatha alone remained with Bharat. To reassure Bharatjogi, whom he loved and respected, that the infant would receive all possible care, Gatha said haltingly, 'There are women with newborn babes in the village, Master. They will nurse the infant and, if not, there are other villages. I have friends there and their headmen respect me.'

Bharat felt relieved and put his hand on Gatha's shoulder. Gatha, touched by this affectionate gesture, continued, 'Vaidji is on his way here. My men will catch him on the way and he will attend to the child. By the time I return, my men will have all the information on possible wet-nurses.'

Bharat thanked him and added, 'Please spare no expense. God, in his divine wisdom, has separated the infant from his mother and placed it in our charge. We must see to it that anyone who cares for the infant is amply rewarded. Take my word for it; when my boat arrives, I shall send a message to my family and they will definitely respond generously for the care of the infant.'

Gatha heard him with surprise. 'But, Master how can you worry about that? Surely you know that Mataji has placed large funds at my disposal for anything you might desire.'

No, Bharat did not know that; he had not even known that his wife had arranged for Gatha to be in the village next to him. He said nothing, but thought that his wife had broken yet another commandment by earmarking funds for the benefit of a hermit. Bharat knew that, to his wife, every commandment was sacred and had to be obeyed. But if such a custom stood in the way of the safety or happiness of her loved ones, she had no use for it. He had protested when he realized the arrangements she was making to ensure a comfortable retirement for him. 'This is not what a hermit must do!' he had protested. 'But this is what a wife must,' she had retorted. Later to his further protests, she had said: 'Let them come with their laws and rules and their customs and commands to bind me fast but I shall evade them forever—for I am bound to you and not to their sightless laws.' He had continued to protest but the fact was that he had learned to live with—and love and relish—the luxuries and comforts that she constantly arranged for him on this lonely island. Strange that throughout his tenure of thirty-five years as Karkarta, he had scrupulously adhered to every law, custom and commandment of the ancients—sometimes questioning, often grumbling, but never deviating. Now, however, in the sunset of his life, he had learnt to disregard all the austerities imposed on hermits. But then, he had always been kind to hermits when he was Karkarta. Why not be kind to himself now! Silently, he thanked his wife for keeping Gatha nearby to help.

Gatha's horsemen had disappeared from view behind the trees. Gatha remained to ask the question which had mystified him. 'Master, where did the infant come from?'

Bharat looked at the river, wearily, and pointed at it.

Gatha also looked in the direction of the river, and then intently at Bharatjogi. A tremor passed through him, as he recalled Bharatjogi's recent words—'God, in his divine wisdom, has separated the infant from his mother and placed it in our charge.' Overwhelmed by the thoughts rushing to his mind, he asked, 'The infant—he comes from the Sindhu river?'

Bharat merely nodded. Gatha remained astonished and did not know what more to ask. A hundred questions raced through his mind. Finally, one question emerged. 'That little infant... you mean Master, the little one is... is Sindhu Putra? Son of Sindhu river?'

Bharat's eyes met Gatha's and he wanted to explain but could not; he simply nodded; physical weakness had gripped Bharat; the exertions and tensions of the day had been too much for him; in any case, he was always a man of few words except when he was talking to himself. He saw that Gatha was still staring at him. He nodded again.

Gatha was not a man of immense curiosity. But he certainly was a man of great faith. Dimly, somewhere in his consciousness, he began to realize that he was a witness to the fulfilment of a prophecy of the past—that the son of Mother Goddess Sindhu would come to walk the earth. Still, he wanted to be sure, and in this instance he knew he would have to send a detailed message to Bharat's wife. She had to know everything. But then it was also disrespectful to ask the same question again. He thought for a moment and inspiration came to him. He asked, 'Master, by what name should the infant be known?'

'You gave him the name yourself Gatha,' was Bharat's response.

'What name?' Gatha wondered aloud—and then asked in a hushed tone, 'Sindhu Putra?'

Bharat nodded. Gatha had another question. 'Of what family shall I say the infant is?'

Bharat recognized the practical aspect of the question. It would be important for the nursing mother to know whose child she was suckling. But it would be far more important if the child died; it would then become necessary to know the family name for the last prayers to be said for its departed soul.

'Say that he is of my family,' Bharat responded.

'Rajavansi?' Gatha asked. Rajavansi was the name of Bharat's ancestral family.

Bharat thought for a while again. No, he no longer had the authority to confer the name of the family from which he had retired as a hermit on anyone. At last, he said, 'No, Gatha. Not Rajavansi. My family.'

'Your family!'

'Yes, my family. Bharatvansi.'

There was no such family, Gatha knew, for old slaves and servants know a great deal more than their lords and masters will ever know about such matters. Gatha also knew that if his old master hesitated to adopt the infant into the family of his ancestors, he also lacked the right, as a hermit, to start a family of his own. But Bharat was his master and he was not going to question him.

No, Gatha had no more questions though his mind was in a whirl. Respectfully, he looked at the pale, tired face of his old master and said, 'I shall do all I can, Master. You can rely on me.' Bharat was sure he could. He thanked him with his eyes and gratefully put his hand again on Gatha's shoulder. 'God will bless you for looking after this infant whom He gives to our care.'

Bharat watched Gatha mount his horse and waited until he disappeared from view. Wearily, he went into the hut.

*

Bharat was still at his rambling prayers the next morning when Gatha arrived. Gatha was beaming with pleasure and cried out, 'Sindhu Putra is crying! He is crying!!' Bharat nodded, happy to interrupt his prayers, and Gatha continued, lest he be misunderstood, 'and they say that an infant that cries so lustily will have a long life.'

Bharat was happy and asked, 'Crying all the time, is he?'

But Gatha said, 'No, no, most of the time he is glued to the breasts of Sonama. She lost her twins in childbirth and is grateful to have Sindhu Putra at her breasts.' Gatha saw his old master smiling with pleasure and continued, 'Sonama says he is hungry all the time, as a healthy infant should be; and she says he is greedy enough for two infants, which is as it should be, because she lost her twins.'

'Poor Sonama,' Bharat said. He did not know her, but he grieved over her sorrow at the loss of her twins in childbirth.

'Poor Sonama!' Gatha almost snorted; he could not permit anything to mar his old master's moment of happiness. 'Sonama is radiant with joy. She has found total solace in Sindhu Putra. She is the happiest mother today.'

Bharat believed him; he knew that only those who have endured real sorrow can truly experience happiness. He nodded.

But Gatha had not yet finished and continued, 'Vaidji is confident that Sindhu Putra shall live—and so is everyone else.'

Twice, during the next twenty-four hours, Gatha came to Bharat's hut. Bharat had assured him that he was a light sleeper, which was true. Sleep he regarded as the luxury of youth and snatched at every excuse to keep himself awake. The time to sleep would come soon enough.

Gatha came only to tell him that the infant was doing well. Yet how full was his heart when he made that simple announcement! He could see Bharatjogi's smile of happiness. There was much excitement among the villagers over the astounding news that Mother Sindhu had sent her child—Sindhu Putra—to be brought up in their village and Gatha, their own headman, had been given the high honour of serving as the guardian of Sindhu Putra!

Their cup of happiness was overflowing.

Gatha himself just wanted to believe what his villagers did. After all, how could an infant, barely an hour old, arrive at Bharatjogi's hut on his own! Surely, Goddess Sindhu must have brought him there.

Gatha's mind was untroubled, and his faith was strong, and if ever a doubt crossed his mind, he told himself that demons were always seeking to enter into the souls of the virtuous to implant evil suspicions. He had wrestled often with such demons in the past, and had always come away unruffled. And in any case, how could he be wrong if he believed what all the others in his village believed! He thoroughly enjoyed his new status amongst the people he served as the custodian of the infant, and if they heard in his voice a new tone of authority, or saw in his expression an air of grave concern, they considered it only fitting in a man whom the gods had chosen for such high responsibility.

Gatha kept Bharatjogi informed about the infant. His frequent visits to Bharat's hut did not trouble him although he knew that a hermit was not supposed to be approached nor his repose disturbed, except in cases of serious sickness or at times of momentous importance. But could there be a matter of greater importance than the emergence of Sindhu Putra?

*

A joint announcement was made by Vaidji and Mahantji (village astrologer) that if Sindhu Putra lived for twenty-four hours, it would mean that he had decided to live in their village; otherwise he would leave his body here and take birth elsewhere.

No one in the village slept. With bated breath, they waited for the twenty-fourth hour to begin and end.

At the end of the twenty-fourth hour a cheer went up which rent the sky. Sindhu Putra was brought out in the arms of Sonama with Gatha by her side, and Vaidji and Mahantji following closely behind. He was still crying lustily and Sonama put him to her breast in full view of everyone. They were all struck silent as if this was the most wondrous sight they had ever witnessed. Many applauded and then they all bowed in respect. They would not yet go to sleep for the celebrations would begin, now that Sindhu Putra had decided to make their village his home.

Thus did Sindhu Putra pass his first twenty-four hours on this earth.

'...He shall come, where you light up his path with worship and
    devotion;
and with reverence and love you shall wait;
where no false preacher's foot shall be set;
where no false temple shall you erect;
where no false idols shall you install,
forgetful of the true God of all;
for he shall come to the land of pure;
and nowhere else shall he endure;...
Yes, he shall come ...to the Land of Pure....

'...Listen then in your heart to the melody of the faraway
song floating from unknown shores to sing of the coming of him
who is to come....

'...Listen in your timeless watch for the approach of footsteps
of him who is to come....

'...And ...bind him to your heart, lest he should pass away
with silent, secret steps, eluding all watchers....'

—(from the prophecy of Sage Jyotisdas, in the village of Rohri,
5110 BC)

The Life of the Miracle

5068 BC

After a day of rejoicing, most of the villagers dropped off to sleep under the silvery moon, in deep, silent slumber, with an innermost sense of serenity in their souls. Even in the dreamland of their sleep, they felt as though their lives had been touched by something that was gentle, noble, beautiful and pure.

But not all of them slept. There were those who felt that this was not the time to sleep. They sat on the banks of the Sindhu and while the stars looked down on them, they prayed and sang hymns of praise to the river, which for countless years had given them nourishment for life, and now had even given its own son—Sindhu Putra—for the sustenance of their souls. They were convinced that there would soon be no evil on earth and would instead be kindness, tenderness, gentleness in all hearts.

Under Gatha's orders, when the infant was being brought from Bharat's hut, some horsemen had branched off to nearby villages to inquire about the availability of wet-nurses. Fortunately, they found Sonama in their own village; but, meanwhile, the news spread to many villages that Sindhu Putra had emerged; and many came from far and near to pay obeisance—and remained to pray.

Some, amongst these many visitors, wondered why Sindhu Putra had chosen this of all villages! Why had he not came to their villages which had so much more to offer—elegant housing, beautiful idols and many teachers and preachers of renown who taught the word of God. At first, it was a question they had idly asked; then a suspicion crept in slowly which took hold of their minds. Was it, they wondered, because this little village boasted of no temple and no preachers or prophets who professed to speak in the name of god? Many had even left this small village because Gatha, the headman, had been cold, if not hostile, to the presence of preachers.

Poor Gatha! His simple mind had hungered for priests and preachers. If they warned of thunderbolts from heavens, they also regaled the crowds with their stirring stories, tales, songs and hymns.

At times, Gatha's soul revolted against the indifference he was obliged to show towards preachers. But he served someone far more stern and inflexible—Mataji. She would not permit a single preacher in the village next to Bharat's island.

Bharat's wife had nothing personal against preachers; nor did she mind their fanaticism or the fire with which they spoke; it did not matter to her if they cursed the unbelievers and threatened those who followed different gods; let them ridicule the idols of others, if they wanted. But then she knew their ways and their real danger, according to her, was that they had never learnt to mind their own business and would be prying into the affairs of others. She wanted to protect Bharat from their insinuating ways and this meant that they had to be kept away from Bharat's island, for then they would pry and spew the venomous slander that Bharat, the hermit, was enjoying wine and luxuries, and that even the village-headman was maintaining a constant watch on the island to cater to the safety and comfort of the illustrious hermit.

The simple village folk did not know the compulsions under which Gatha worked. All they knew was that Gatha gave a cold welcome to any preacher who strayed into his village; and if the preacher chose to tarry, the headman became even colder. They did not know that Gatha himself went to other villages whenever the urge to hear a new preacher came over him; nor did he discourage his villagers from such visits. But preachers had learnt not to stay too long in his village.

The preachers, though always divided among themselves, would undoubtedly have combined to denounce him, but for the fact that he was extremely generous to them, and that each preacher was certain that one day Gatha would see the light, and come on bended knee to invite him, and him alone, to take permanent abode in his village.

In the silence of night, the visitors from other villages began to brood. Many were genuinely perplexed. Why had Sindhu Putra chosen this particular village? Was it because their own villages housed false preachers with vicious doctrines? And so they wondered whether they had been led astray. And thus was born the hope for a new future in Sindhu Putra. They began to feel that if they came to stay in the village of Sindhu Putra, their lives would be purer and nobler.

Mahantji was walking along the Sindhu river. He was not looking at the sky, as he always did, whenever anyone was nearby; for, above all, he wanted to be known as a serious and constant observer of stars which, according to him, held all the secrets of man's destiny. But now he was not even watching the reflection of the moon and stars in the river. He was just walking along, lost in thought.

He passed by a silent group of people sitting by the river without noticing them. They too were immersed in thought, for the miracle of Sindhu Putra had touched them deeply. But one youngster in the group had the temerity to address Mahantji, 'How come, Mahantji, that you who know all the secrets of the stars, could not foretell the birth of Sindhu Putra?'

Mahantji looked angrily at the youth, for he had dared to ask the very question which Mahantji was asking himself. That the young man was being chided by the others for his irreverent question did not console Mahantji, for he feared that the question would now remain in the minds of many and be asked repeatedly. He raised his hand to secure their silence. 'How could I reveal it! Was it my secret?' asked Mahantji in a tone of injured dignity combined with a sense of mystery. 'No; it was the secret of the Sentinel of the River and Sky.'

Many were shaken out of their reverie. Some even asked in chorus: 'Sentinel of the River and Sky! Who is he?'

Mahantji paused before composing his reply. He looked at them all in sorrow at their ignorance. Inwardly, he regarded it unfortunate that due to the dark, they could not see his expression of profound contempt. But his tone made up for it. 'Who is the Sentinel of the River and Sky, you ask! Who indeed! Have you lived here with eyes shut and minds closed? Have your eyes shown you nothing and your minds told you nothing? Have you been dead to all that is happening around you?'

The group was roused now, listening intently, though not many were impressed with Mahantji's verbiage. This time, it was a young woman who spoke, 'Speak clearly, Mahantji, and not in these riddles. You are talking to us now, and not conversing with the stars.'

Mahantji drew in his breath, and in a tone that would erase all doubts and stem all questions, began his oration: 'You ask, who is the Sentinel of the River and Sky! Who, I ask you, has for the last three years been mounting lookouts in tall trees at his own expense and waiting for someone to emerge from the union of the sky and the river? Who, I ask you, has been going around night and day along the boundaries of that island—waiting, watching and wondering? Who, I ask you, cleared the forest around the island—at his own expense and with his own labour—and dug up pits, and put up obstacles, so that neither a wild beast nor a drunken man should cross into this island? But think, think, you, you who never thought in all your lives; think, who came here nearly four years ago and had the stream widened and trees planted in the rocky island where neither man nor beast could find shade! Do you know that now there are more flowering plants and bushes in the island than all the men, women, children and animals in the seventy-seven surrounding villages? No, you do not know that, because you do not know how to count. But let me ask you, who do you think came here four years ago to plant them?'

Mahantji paused; the crowd around him was thicker now as others from nearby groups had also moved closer, attracted by the loud, long speech of the respected Mahantji, who rarely spoke; and when he did, he did so briefly. And he was not finished.

Mahantji continued, and now his tone was sharp and incisive, and he spoke as though from the depths of his agonized soul: 'And I ask you, was it not me, who four years ago suggested to you all that he be appointed the headman of your village?' Again, after a pause, Mahantji asked, 'You think, you presume to think, you dare to think, that I did not know that he had come to wait—and prepare for the coming of Him who has come!'

There was not a movement, not a sound; it was difficult to believe that so many people could be so still.

Long before Mahantji had finished, they had begun to realize whom he was talking about. Gatha! Their village headman! Their own simple Gatha, with his sleepy eyes, seedy smile and shifting glance! Gatha, who could not concentrate on a simple sentence or even utter half a sentence, without looking in the direction of the island! Gatha who could sing no songs, tell no stories, recite no hymns! True, he was fair in his dealings, considerate and even kind; whenever quarrels erupted, he was impartial; if someone was in trouble, he was there to help; if anyone needed seed, he had plentiful supplies to offer, and he was always ready with his gifts and knew who needed what.

But still. How could it be, they wondered. If there was beauty in his soul, somehow they had not seen it. And if there was beauty in his face and figure, somehow it had so far failed to excite passion or ecstasy in any woman's heart.

Mahantji had said what he had to say and he now concluded in a ringing tone, 'Yes, I was the one who knew that he who came as the Sentinel of the River and Sky was waiting for the advent of Sindhu Putra. Yet, you... oh the blind that shall not see, and the deaf that shall not hear and hearts that shut out the songs of the advent of Him who has come!'

And with these words uttered in his sonorous voice full of sorrow for mankind and contempt for his listeners, he marched on, away from them.

Respectfully, silently, they made way for him, but one of them asked in a tone bordering on worship, 'You knew then, Mahantji, you knew!' Mahantji stopped only to touch the bowed head of the man who asked the question, and then he passed on, leaving an unmistakable impression of mystery behind him.

They looked at Mahantji in awe, as he passed from among their midst with measured steps. But Mahantji was deeply wounded. Events had so conspired as to force him to confer on Gatha a title which he deeply wished for himself. Surely, he, with his intimacy with the stars and knowledge of the secrets of the heavens, deserved the title of the Sentinel of the River and Sky, rather than that simple-minded, half-witted Gatha.

But then as Mahantji continued his measured steps, he began to waver and wonder and almost came under the spell of the words he had spoken to the crowds. It was true that he himself had proposed to the village, four years earlier, that the newcomer Gatha should be appointed as the village headman. A stranger from far away had offered Mahantji several exquisite gifts to encourage him to nominate Gatha as the headman. Vaidji had also strongly supported Gatha's appointment. Somehow, Vaidji's stock of goats, cows, medicines and herbs had grown tremendously since then. And where, he wondered, does Gatha get all that he generously keeps supplying to the village! Gatha had even brought his own men from outside to serve as lookouts from tall trees, to keep a watch on the island, and generously paid for their food, lodging and other wants! Gatha, he knew, lived simply, had frugal habits, and did not at all look like a person with a hidden horde of wealth. The way he gave to others obviously indicated wealth—and if he has wealth, why is he not near the source of his wealth? In any case, why keep lookouts in a village which is in no danger from anyone?

Mahantji stopped, immobilized by the awesome question he had asked himself. Then was Gatha, really, the Sentinel of the River and Sky, as he had said?

He could go no further. He sat under a tree and, leaning his head against it, closed his eyes and prayed. For three days and nights he remained under the tree, speaking to no one, and barely touching the food that was brought to him. When passers-by wanted to talk to him, they were advised by onlookers not to disturb him, for he was a man who saw visions of things that lay hidden from the eyes of men.

The crowd bowed to Mahantji—for was he not the prophet with whom the stars had shared the secret of the mission of the newcomer Gatha, who came to wait for the coming of Sindhu Putra.

If Gatha was in seventy-seventh heaven, he did not know it. That was largely because he did not know how many heavens existed. The earlier preachers had spoken of one heaven. Later he had heard that there were seven heavens. But then the number increased each time he encountered another preacher. Each preacher reserved a place for himself, in the highest heaven, while the heavens just below were reserved for his believers—and the rest were for lesser gods, angels and some select mortals. The preachers did not often say so, but the implication that they retained the right to promote or demote various deities and entities to higher or lower heavens or even banish some altogether was clear.

But Gatha knew that if there was heaven on earth, he was in it— right at its centre.

He had performed the simple errand of bringing the infant to the village. In his life, he had performed far more demanding tasks but they counted for nothing. Now, however, they called him the Sentinel of the River and Sky. They hung on his every word, but since he had nothing to say, they gravely contemplated his silence and wondered what noble and profound thoughts must be passing through the vast recesses of his all-seeing mind.

They knew that their headman went out, at odd hours of the night, to see if the lookouts were awake and keeping their vigil. They knew that when the wind broke into a riot and storms followed, he would run to repair fences to prevent wild beasts from straying into the island where there was nothing to protect. Yet his own hut would remain tattered and untended for days, and he would let the rain pour in without complaint. Surely, then, he was waiting for the auspicious moment when someone, suddenly, silently, would arrive. And now He had come.

How did it matter if Gatha could not tell stories or sing a song. On those rare occasions when he joined the singing and chanting of others, it was like someone groaning in despair. They now knew that his heart was resonant with the melody of a faraway song, floating from unknown shores to sing of the coming of Sindhu Putra.

They now looked at their headman Gatha in awe, with pride and joy; and silently then bowed in his presence, for he was their own— their Sentinel of the River and Sky; and for ever, for as long as man lived, he would be known by that title.

Gatha went about, his head buzzing with questions which he could not formulate, and with thoughts he could not articulate. Much of what was being said in the minds and words of the men and women that crowded around him was not clear to him. But he knew he was happy. When he saw their new wave of respect for him bordering on worship, a surge of happiness flashed through him. He knew they had tolerated him in the past only because of his gifts to them and for his hard work—in fact, many had suspected that it was through bribes and the unseen influence of his unknown friends that he had come to acquire the position of headman, immediately on arrival in their village. They had continued to tolerate him even when he refused their request to accommodate preachers in the village, though some left the village in disgust to reside elsewhere, near their favourite preachers. Now the whole village recalled his prophetic words, when he had refused to admit preachers, for Gatha had then said, 'The time has not come.'

They had seen no hint of prophecy in those words when they were uttered. Some had charitably thought that Gatha feared that the villagers would slacken their activity if preachers came, for they always collected crowds and with their constant chanting, wailing and singing, took the minds of people away from their daily tasks. But some had warned Gatha that the village would suffer if too many left for other villages, in search of salvation of their souls. It was then that Gatha had said this.

As a matter of fact, the village had improved under his stewardship, for the simple reason that Gatha had a faraway benefactor in Mataji, who was prepared to carry all financial burdens of the village that bordered her husband's island.

Now all those who had ranted against Gatha's refusal to allow preachers into the village fell silent. And the villagers who had remained loyally in the village had nothing but laughter and scorn for those who had left.

Those who had left the village now wanted to be permitted to return. He gave in to their pleas with his characteristic brevity, simply saying, 'Come back.'

Shouts of joy greeted this. Happily, he told himself, that his two words were enough; he did not need to feel inadequate.

When others from different villages, who had never lived in Gatha's village, also asked to be allowed to come and live in his village, he listened with growing happiness and wonder and again, in his simple way, merely said: 'Come.'

The shouts of joy reverberated throughout the village square, frightening the birds away from nearby trees, though there were some who thought that the birds had been there simply to hear Gatha speak, and now flew off to inform others of what he had said.

The procession of preachers began. Each came to the village of Sindhu Putra in fervent hope. Each, unknown to the other, had often received gifts from headman Gatha. Each thought, therefore, that Gatha had a special corner for him in his heart.

What each preacher wanted was to be the exclusive steward of Sindhu Putra. Naturally, every preacher was convinced that the simpleton Gatha, the headman with the face and soul of a goatherd, was entirely unfit to bring up Sindhu Putra. Surely, Sindhu Putra's upbringing must be trusted solely to a person of worth and eminence, who has mastered the word and the way of gods—and who better than himself, thought each preacher. It pained each of them to see that other so-called men of god were also travelling the same route, to seek for themselves the guardianship of Sindhu Putra, but then each was warmed by the memory of their last conversation with Gatha, and of the gifts he had received from the headman. Surely, Gatha would have enough intelligence to recognize him—and him alone—as the true messenger of the gods and dismiss all the other spurious preachers.

To be fair to those preachers, it cannot be said that all of them truly believed that the emergence of Sindhu Putra was a genuine miracle. Many of them had thought, deeply and hard, and could think of many and diverse explanations for the phenomenon. But they guarded their thoughts and kept them locked up in their breasts. It was enough for them that people regarded it as a genuine miracle. A preacher would be foolish to stand against the floodtide of people's belief and run the risk of being swept away.

Miracles, the preachers knew, were opportunities which the gods provide for those who preach God's word to mankind. It was, however, a pity that the gods were often slow in performing miracles, and the preachers were forced, at times, to contrive miracles of their own.

But, here, at last, Oh Glory be! Here was a miracle ready-made, and people had already begun to speak of it in hushed tones.

What better opportunity then, than to wrest control of Sindhu Putra's upbringing, install him in their midst and speak in his name!

Thus, with hope surging in their hearts, and with every blissful anticipation of success in their mission, the procession of preachers proceeded to the village of Sindhu Putra. Some walked to their goal firmly with bold steps. Others, more prosperous, went on fleet horses; some chose the lowly donkey for their journey; there were many on bullocks, others on camels, and a few were carried by their followers in make-shift cots or more stately palanquins; and those who wanted to make a majestic entrance, were on elephants.

When the first preacher reached Gatha and demanded that Sindhu Putra be placed in his charge, Gatha pleaded that the infant needed breast-milk which only Sonama could provide. But the preacher, with his characteristic generosity, replied, 'Sonama shall also be with me, in my charge. She shall rank above all women in my congregation, and her breasts shall be more productive under my prayers and ministrations. My men shall build statues of her breasts to inspire all womankind.'

But Gatha knew that Sindhu Putra was not his to give; he remained silent, as he faced the long line of preachers who were arriving.

Preachers are never patient except with gods, and that too, on rare occasions. So it was not easy for them to tolerate Gatha's silence. They peremptorily demanded Gatha's answer, each claiming his own superiority, though some joined hands with others to form partnerships to advance joint claims for custody of Sindhu Putra.

Gatha simply said: 'I must ask.'

To questions of 'Who?' 'What?' Gatha replied, 'His father.'

'His father!' 'His father!!' was the surprised response of all those who heard him. Of course in Gatha's mind, Bharatjogi had acquired the attributes of the earthly father of Sindhu Putra. He was about to explain, but he bit his tongue. How can a hermit be given the attributes of a father! In any case, how could he explain his own relationship with the hermit, who was once his master, and whom he had vowed to serve all his life! He faced them in silence, not knowing what to say.

Whatever the thoughts that floated in the minds of preachers at this long, unending silence, the rest of the people understood, and their awe and wonder grew. 'Gatha can speak to the Father of Sindhu Putra!' they thought, and some of them even said so aloud.

'He speaks to Gods!'

'He converses with Gods!!'

'With Gods!!!'

Gatha left them in the midst of their wonder. His head was reeling from the onslaught of the preachers. At first, they had begun by praising him, cajoling him, coaxing him; then some spoke in loud tones; others even threatened, calling upon heavenly thunderbolts to strike him if Sindhu Putra was deprived of the devotional care which they alone could offer; and finally, the meetings became unruly, while more and more preachers came pouring in.

Gatha was no longer the timid headman he used to be. If one is called the Sentinel of the River and Sky, and constantly bathed in worshipful glances from everyone in the village, it is difficult to maintain a mien of timidity.

But then, again, when so many preachers began to show their fangs and claws and rent the air with their wrath and indignation, his old self returned and he was oppressed with doubts and fears.

Gatha knew that the decision could not be his; he must go to Bharatjogi and receive instructions. But he was tired. Ever since that fateful moment when the distant drum had sounded from Bharatjogi's island, a few days ago, he had not had any rest or quiet. He now wanted to go to his hut to sleep for a while before proceeding to Bharatjogi; but he saw the route to his hut lined with admiring crowds and threatening preachers, along with their quarrelsome followers and retainers. Above all, Gatha wanted to be alone. He turned back and went in the direction of the river. People followed him with their eyes, and then with their footsteps. He feared they would follow him into the river. He raised his hand. The effect was instantaneous. They all stopped.

Gatha went alone to the river. They all waited for him on the riverbank, hoping that he would soon come to them, after his swim. But Gatha made a detour, and from the bend of the river, went to the island of Bharatjogi.

The three dogs who, after careful and continuous consultation among themselves for the past few days, had come to regard Gatha as a loyal ally and trusted friend, escorted him to Bharat's hut.

Bharat looked at the tired man, who had already made so many visits to his island during the last few days.

Gatha would not, at first, drink the wine Bharat offered him, but out of politeness, he took one sip, and then because he liked the taste, he took another and yet another, while Bharat graciously kept pouring the wine for his weary visitor. Meanwhile, Gatha told Bharat of the demand by the preachers—and since a long recital always made undue demands on his mental faculties, he continued to sip the wine, absent-mindedly, to cover gaps of silence in his story.

Before he could complete his story, Gatha felt an urge to sleep. Wine and the weariness of the last few days were having their effect.

But Bharat had heard enough and understood it all. His mind went into a reverie. He thought of the infant and felt immeasurably sorry. Aloud he said, as though speaking to the infant: 'What will the world of men do to you, little one?'

Gatha took another sip of wine and nodded, hardly understanding what Bharatjogi said or meant. Bharat now spoke to Gatha. 'He is a child of this earth. Let him live like one. Chance brought him to me. Let him live his life as a human being, and not as a plaything of preachers or as anointed by gods.'

Gatha continued to nod; but he was half-asleep and did not know where his mind was.

Again, Bharatjogi's mind went into a reverie. Softly, then, he spoke and began to tell Gatha how the infant came in a boat, with his mother dead, and how the boat drifted away. Gatha's nods continued through his immense drowsiness but he hardly heard a word.

'Yes Gatha,' Bharat continued, 'keep him away from preachers. They are the enemies of the light. They will keep his soul chained away from the gods. Let him be burdened with the sins of ordinary men; let him share their sorrows and their joys; their laughter and their tears. But Gatha,' now Bharat raised his voice, 'Gatha, keep him away from preachers at all costs—away, away from preachers.'

Gatha woke up startled as Bharat raised his voice. He had dimly heard the last words and he almost repeated them: 'Yes, yes, Master, away, away from all preachers.'

Now Gatha desperately struggled against sleep and tried to look alert and awake. Bharat looked at Gatha's tired, sleepy eyes and said softly, 'Gatha, go to sleep.'

Gatha would have protested if he had heard those words. One does not sleep when the master is awake. Certainly not, when the master is speaking. But Gatha did not hear them. He was already asleep.

Bharat picked up a pillow, and stretching Gatha gently on to the floor rug, he placed it under his head.

The sun had set when Gatha woke up from his deep sleep. It was perhaps the first time in his life that he had slept during the day. He woke up in a happy frame of mind, as though from a pleasant dream; but he was immediately assailed by an oppressive feeling, bordering on despair. How had he dared to sleep in the presence of his old, revered master? he asked himself.

Bharat had not slept himself. He was outside the hut when Gatha woke up and was warming soup on a slow fire. He heard Gatha moving and brought in the steaming bowl of soup. Gatha started his abject apologies, but Bharat graciously cut him short and compelled him to drink the soup. Gatha at last confessed to him that he had never had such restful sleep, but then, he said, he had never had wine before. Bharat told him of the virtues of wine, if taken occasionally and in moderation, and insisted that Gatha carry a cask of wine from his large, accumulated stock. Bharat would not take 'no' for an answer, so Gatha gratefully accepted the gift.

Bharat's parting words to Gatha were: 'Gatha, keep the infant away from those men of god. Their hearts have no eyes, their souls have no ears, and their minds have no windows. They will place a thousand scars on the infant's soul. Keep him away from them.'

Gatha went into the river, intending to return by the same route he had taken in the morning. But he saw several small fires lit up on the bank. People were obviously awaiting his return. Many had misunderstood his raised hand before he had moved into the river in the morning. All he wanted was that they should not follow him into the river but they had thought that he was asking them to wait for his return. One does not treat lightly the wish of the Sentinel of the River and Sky, particularly when he is off on an auspicious visit to the father of Sindhu Putra.

Gatha realized it would not be in keeping with his new-found dignity to be seen travelling with a cask of wine. So he swam back to Bharatjogi's island; from there he took the land route, and crossing over the stream, he reached his hut. He was pleased that there was no one around. They were all keeping vigil on the banks of the river, waiting for him to emerge.

He ate a little and then as it was the usual hour for him to turn in, he tried to sleep. But it is not easy to sleep when you have already slept for seven hours. So he sat back. For a moment he cursed himself for his unforgivable conduct in sleeping in the presence of Bharatjogi. But the graciousness with which Bharat had treated him brought a warm glow to his heart. He looked gratefully at the cask of wine which his old master had pressed on him.

Gatha was happy. His heart overflowed with affection for his master Bharatji and Mataji. They have allowed me—a servant who once was a slave—to achieve so much in life ! Not only am I the headman, but Bharatji gives me charge of Sindhu Putra so that I come to be known as the Sentinel of the River and Sky!

He was dazed with the blissful memory of the worship and admiration showered upon him by the people of his village.

His cup of happiness was full. Thinking of the cup of his happiness, he turned to his empty cup. He was about to fill it with water but, on an impulse, poured wine into it from his newly acquired cask. He raised his cup and thinking of Bharatjogi, said: 'I drink to you, Master.'

But then he had to take a second cup to drink to Mataji.

A few hours later, when the cask was half empty, he remembered clearly what Bharatjogi had said: 'Not a shadow of a single preacher must cross Sindhu Putra. They must be scattered.'

He must go to do his duty.

It was late. But Gatha walked on. He was not aware that his steps were unsteady from the potent wine. Nor was he conscious of the wind. Nor of the darkness. When he reached the village square, he was astonished to see no one there. He wondered: do they not know that when the headman, who is also the Sentinel of the River and Sky, reaches the village square, they all must rush there forthwith. He had forgotten that many were at the river, and the rest would be sleeping at this hour. He sat down in the village square.

A villager returning from the river saw him. News spread. They all rushed to the village square, and even those who were sleeping, were roused.

Gatha was sitting in a trance. The wine was playing tricks on him. The crowd, after an initial burst of noise, was now quiet. Preachers, with hope in their hearts, stood in front of him. But Gatha's eyes were closed and his thoughts were nowhere.

At last, Gatha opened his eyes. He saw the crowds. He was pleased. His eyes were dazed and his mouth distorted with the effort to smile. Hope sprang anew in the hearts of the preachers.

Unsteadily, Gatha rose and then he grinned. The preachers were happy, for obviously he had brought good news after his supposed conversation with the Father of Sindhu Putra.

Gatha surveyed the preachers, one by one, grinning all the while. Then he began his announcement: 'Preachers, preachers all, come near.'

They moved forward with eagerness, ready to crush all others in their stampede. In utter silence, the preachers saw Gatha's broad grin. He was again struggling to speak.

'Preachers!' he said loudly and stopped. As he was groping for words, the smile left him. He was silent. The crowd also remained silent. Then he spoke calmly, in an even tone, as though he was telling them something quite inconsequential. He said: 'Get out.'

The preachers looked puzzled, as they realized the import of the softly spoken words. Then they glared in anger as if the thunderbolts with which they often threatened, were being directed at them. Many thought that the words so pleasantly uttered were intended for someone else, and some even began to ask questions, and raise their voices.

Gatha raised his hand. The grin reappeared on his face. His hand remained raised. Silence, all over. Now he made an even longer speech and said with a smile: 'Shut your mouth.'

They were speaking all at once. Gatha was not listening to them. He was desperately trying to remember the exact words of Bharatjogi. He could not. The hubbub in the village square was rising. Suddenly, with a burst of happiness in his heart, Gatha remembered. He raised his hand. Silence. Gatha cried out; now his voice was loud, clear, authoritative, 'Men, men, watch these preachers. Keep them away from Sindhu Putra. They will place a thousand scars on the infant's soul.'

This was the longest speech Gatha had made in his life and he felt fulfilled. He left with steps as unsteady as before.

The preachers would have strangled him, for these men of God were always ready to fight for a just cause when they were not outnumbered, but unfortunately for them, there were far more villagers than preachers in the crowd.

Villagers bowed to Gatha as he passed. They knew he never drank; yet he appeared intoxicated. Oh! the exaltation of spirit! The upliftment of the soul! The elevation of the mind! Yes! What else could it be!

These simple villagers knew that a yogi can levitate in the air, merely by meditating on the gods—and here they had Gatha who had just had a long, sustained and meaningful conversation alone, with the Father of Sindhu Putra! Would his spirit not be light, would his feet not be airy, and would his walk not sway with the rhythm of the spring breeze! And who knows, the gods may even have given him their soma amrit (the wine of everlasting pleasure)!

Thus the Sentinel of the River and Sky reached his hut, supported by his adoring entourage of villagers. But like a man who always thinks of his duty above all else, he did not immediately enter his hut. He turned back to ask, 'Did you hear what I said?'

'We did, we did,' they replied in unison.

'Will there be preachers in the village?'

'No, never, never!'

They escorted him into the hut and he said, 'I go to sleep now.'

'Good night, Sentinel of the River and Sky,' they said.

'Then I shall wake up,' said Gatha.

'Gods be praised' 'Sindhu Putra be praised'; 'Our Sentinel be praised,' were the sentiments voiced by many.

Once inside the hut, Gatha went to sleep. People who had accompanied him to the hut were now ready to return, each to his own home, but suddenly they stopped to ponder over what Gatha had said. It dawned on them that Gatha's words—both spoken and unspoken—always had profound meaning and significance. Gatha, after speaking about preachers, had said he would go to sleep but then he had also added that he would thereafter wake up. Why did he have to add that? Clearly, there was a wealth of wisdom in these words and an underlying message of sense and substance; yes, undoubtedly, Gatha wanted the preachers out before he woke up. They realized that they must attend to this task, without delay, and complete it, before Gatha woke up.

The preachers left—some quietly, others protesting. Some had to be forced out. The villagers vowed to stand guard so that the preachers never re-entered the village.

The entire valley resounded with the name of Sindhu Putra, as preachers returned through various villages, back to their own homes. Most preachers were tight-lipped and grim-faced and would answer no questions from villagers enroute, though some simply said that they were now returning after fully completing their mission of blessing Sindhu Putra.

There were one or two preachers who gathered enough courage to denounce Sindhu Putra. Their congregations reacted with shock and disbelief. Later, murmurs of protests were heard against them and many of their devotees left to go and live in Sindhu Putra's village.

Despite widespread rejoicing at the emergence of Sindhu Putra, there were a few individuals who worried about their future. They were the lookouts whom Gatha had recruited. Their task had been to keep watching the little island on which Bharatjogi lived. They did not know what precisely they were looking for, but they had to report everything to Gatha. Was the smoke of cooking fire visible? If so, this indicated to Gatha that all was well. Did any wild beast appear on the approaches to the island? If not, all was well. If a wild beast did appear, the lookouts had instructions to take immediate action and chase it away. Actually, fences to the island were so well placed that the possibility of a wild beast entering it was remote. But then, their employer, Gatha, liked to take all kinds of precautions. Precautions for what? They had not known earlier, but now they did. Obviously, he was waiting for Sindhu Putra to emerge.

Now that Sindhu Putra had emerged, would they not lose their comfortable jobs! The pay was good. They were lodged and fed well. Even the tree tops from which they had to watch, were fitted with a thatch on which they could recline restfully, with a canopy to protect them from the sun and rain. Ladders were placed against trees, so that they did not have to climb up and down like monkeys. A rope was hung from each tree, with a basket attached to it. Refreshments could be sent up and a youngster always waited below to serve them.

All they had to do was to report everything, however trivial, that was happening on the island. Gatha's questions were always endless. Did a boat stop at the island? For how long? What did it do? When did it leave? In which direction? What about the old hermit? Did he tend to his plants? Did he go for a swim? He did not appear at all today? But then, did you see smoke from the cooking fire? Did you see the dogs playing around? But above all, the question was: did you hear the sound of a drumbeat?

The lookouts did not know why they were watching the island. Actually, there was nothing to watch, for nothing was happening there.

In their curiosity, they had, initially, asked a question or two of Gatha. But Gatha, though he did not have a way with words, could glare meaningfully. Some said, when a wasp or a bee hovered round Gatha's face, he just glared at it and it quickly left him to sting someone else. So, the lookouts saw his glare and asked no more.

When the lookouts began their duty, there was no one on the island. Later, they saw a hermit. They reported this to Gatha, with excitement. Of course they feared that Gatha would chase him away, and they would be sorry if he did that, because his presence there would at least give them someone to watch, in the midst of their boredom of watching nothing on an empty island. Clearly they realized that Gatha could not permit the hermit to remain on the island. He had spent so much on the island, to widen the streams, put up fences and plant trees and bushes, and had paid a handsome amount to Karkarta's treasury to buy the island, exclusively for himself; surely he would not permit anyone to settle down there. So the lookouts expected that the hermit would soon be ejected.

However, Gatha had resolutely shaken his head when they asked if they should go to the hermit to ask him to leave. Thereafter, he often looked in the direction of the island.

This was because his old master, Bharatji, had arrived! At last! His real work—his mission—for which he had come had begun.

A man with a mission will always be misunderstood, at least initially. So it was with Gatha. The lookouts thought that Gatha's fear to eject the intruding hermit arose from a superstition, for it was well known that gods frown on those who disturb hermits. All that Gatha did was to ask them to watch every movement, every action and every inaction of the hermit.

They watched and, unknown to them, Gatha sent his fortnightly messages to Mataji. These messages had, throughout, an almost unvarying quality about them—'All is well, nothing to report; he was seen swimming, cooking, exercising.' These messages Gatha gave to a boatman whose boat crossed his village regularly on its way to the village of Mataji; the boatman was also in the pay of Mataji, and had a talent for memorizing messages correctly.

The only time there was something new to report was when the three dogs crossed over to the island. Gatha was livid. How had the fences been so ineffective! He was about to send out a patrol to chase away the dogs, but they were seen following the old hermit affectionately, wagging their tails and the hermit was even seen patting them.

Gatha did not remove the dogs. But he made the boatman memorize the message for Mataji. He waited for Mataji's decision and even feared criticism for allowing dogs onto the island. But Mataji was gracious. She realized that her husband, denied as he was human company, should at least have the affection of dogs around him—and she knew that a dog's capacity for love was far greater than most men's.

Despite the absence of anything spectacular, the lookouts kept a sharp eye on the island. Gatha had selected men of honesty. His own surprise visits were also far too frequent to permit any slackening.

But nobody should blame the lookouts for not being able to see the boat in which Sindhu Putra arrived. The sky was overcast and the waters of the Sindhu looked as if covered with a black blanket. Add to that furious rain, interrupted by threatening wind and thunder which shook, from limb to limb, the trees on which they sat! How could anyone blame them for their failure to see that boat!

But did that boat exist at all! Obviously not. Everyone seemed to know how Sindhu Putra had come. Certainly not by boat. Yes, everyone knew that Mother Goddess Sindhu herself had risen from its waters, holding her baby in her two outstretched arms; some said that she was wearing a crown of gold, studded with rubies and diamonds; others said, no, she was holding the crown over the head of the child with her third hand; but everyone agreed that the two outstretched arms reached out and began to extend themselves, more and more, until they touched the old hermit on the island. With trembling hands, the hermit took the child. The fourth hand of Mother Goddess, now extended itself and reached Gatha's head, blessing and anointing him as the Sentinel of the River and Sky. Simultaneously, from the heavens above, the joyous sound of drums was heard to proclaim the emergence of Sindhu Putra and that of Gatha as his sentinel.

Obviously, if Mother Goddess Sindhu brought the child in her outstretched arms, the question of failure of the lookouts to notice the boat could never be raised. How can you see that which does not exist! Even if one assumes that Sindhu Putra came in a boat, that boat must have been fashioned in the heavens. How do earthly eyes see a heavenly vehicle, unless of course the gods so will it! Natural eyes will see what is on this earth, but it is only given to elevated souls like Gatha to see the supernatural and recognize it.

Now of course, it was recognized that the lookouts too had a role to play in the unfolding drama of Sindhu Putra. They would now always be known as Watchers of Sky and River who waited for Him to come.

But they were now scared that their job was over and asked Gatha as much. He, in response, glared at them and instructed them to continue their vigil. From this it was inferred by all and sundry that Mother Goddess Sindhu would soon visit her son and that is why the vigil was maintained.

Thus the lookouts, with happiness in their hearts, and full of faith that they would always be employed in their comfortable, well-paid jobs, continued watching the island, keeping now a closer eye on the old hermit, for was he not the first on this earth to hold Sindhu Putra in his arms! Yes, he would be the first, no doubt, to greet Goddess Mother when she arrived to meet her son on earth.

Gatha's village was the smallest in the valley. How Mataji, unknown to her husband (Karkarta Bharat), managed to get that small area the status of a separate village, and the manner in which she manipulated her husband's functionaries and village elders, can be told in a separate, larger story. Enough here to record that this village was established and, eventually, Gatha was elected as its headman, after he was duly proposed and seconded by Mahantji and Vaidji.

The advent of Sindhu Putra in that small, nondescript village was a stirring event, enough to give rise to an ambition in the hearts of headmen of nearby larger villages. Should not Gatha's small village be merged with their own large village? Naturally, the headman of the larger village would automatically be the headman of the village so united, though Gatha could be given a seat on the village Council.

The headmen of the large villages nearby consulted their villagers, as obviously the action to merge would need their approval. Their villagers were delighted with the idea of the merger. All they asked was that Gatha, the Sentinel of the River and Sky, be asked to be their own headman too.

Somehow, the headmen of the larger villages lost their urge to seek a merger with the village of Sindhu Putra.

Sonama's husband, Muthana, was unaware of what was happening in his own village. He had taken no part in these momentous affairs.

He was lying dead drunk in a hut on the edge of the forest. The hut belonged to his elder brother who had migrated to another village. Since then, Muthana stocked wine in the vacant hut and whenever he wanted to drink either alone or with friends, the hut would be used. Sonama, with all her affection for her husband, was totally against his drinking and would not permit wine to be stocked at home, except for religious purposes—and that too, of the weakest variety and in limited quantity, as apparently she did not believe in the gods getting drunk, either.

Muthana had given up drinking ever since his wife became pregnant. He wanted to remain sober to greet his first-born.

Like all others in the Hindu clan, Muthana believed that the child within the womb of the mother has life right from the moment the seed of man meets the woman's seed, even though it would take around nine months for the infant to emerge. Again, like others, he also believed that somehow, every single thought and action of the parents during the period from the union of seeds (conception) to birth, would profoundly influence the child. So, he took a firm decision—not to touch a drink until the child was born.

Boundless was Muthana's joy when the Vaidini (medicine woman) announced that Sonama was in perfect condition and a healthy offspring should be expected. Later, in the advanced stage of pregnancy, when Vaidini announced the possibility of twins, Muthana burst out of his cottage, his hand raised high up in the air and his fist waving, as if he had been declared a champion of champions at the wrestling tournament. Then he kissed the earth, kissed the trees and finally came to kiss his wife's stomach, first out of love for her, and then out of love for those who were housed within her. He rested his face on his wife's round and comfortable stomach, and after kissing it all round, he quickly spoke to his unborn children.

After a moment, in a voice of mock-protest, he said, 'Sonama, how many times have I told you, never to interrupt me when I am speaking to persons of importance; here I was talking to my little ones and you disturb my chain of thought and flow of conversation.'

She laughed and wanted to know what had been said in that momentous conference between the father and his unborn children. But he replied with an air of importance, 'This should be a secret between a father and his son and daughter.'

'Oh, so you have decided the sex of each twin!'

'The gods always listen to me.'

'Really! When was it last that the gods listened to you?'

'When they gave me the best, the sweetest and the most delightful wife,' replied Muthana with feeling. And added, 'None can match my wife in the village or anywhere else even.'

With this statement, Sonama could never disagree. She looked at him with tenderness. He was not very successful at the farm; his bouts of drinking often kept him away from work, and his cattle remained untended sometimes. But all that did not matter any more. 'All right, but what did you tell my unborn children?' she asked.

'Your unborn children! I thought they were our unborn children.'

Graciously she agreed but returned to her earlier question. He shook his head and said, 'I was not talking to them. I merely listened to them. They were talking to me and they said they are very happy to have you as their mother and me as their father.'

But of course he was not telling the whole truth. Across the screen of her stomach, he had whispered to his unborn infants that he would be an ideal father, always willing to work hard to make their life easy and prosperous and would never drink again.

Sonama and Muthana lay side by side, sharing the same dreams.

Then, tragedy struck. The twins were born dead.

Sonama was crying in agony. She was inconsolable and he watched her quietly; and the more freely her tears flowed, the more terrible became his own silent despair.

Muthana left his cottage and looked at the sky. Then he spoke his first words since the tragedy. 'God, you rejected my offering.' He was thinking of his resolve to reform, to stop drinking, to be a conscientious worker, a model husband and a loving father. Quickly, with resolute steps, he went to the hut on the edge of the forest.

Wine did not ease his anguish, nor his loathing of life. He knew he had to drink more, and he did, until he fell, motionless.

Meanwhile, great events had taken place in the village, with the emergence of Sindhu Putra, who was now suckling at Sonama's breasts.

Muthana's younger brother suspected where Muthana was. While the village continued to be in the grip of rising commotion and excitement, he found him lying senseless in the hut. It was not easy to bring him to his senses. His brother did the best he could. Later, in a daze, with faltering steps, Muthana came to his cottage and dimly realized that in place of his lost twins, an infant had been found to suckle the breasts of his wife.

A confusion of emotions swept through him. How could anyone take the place of his lost twins? he asked himself. But he saw Sonama's happiness. His anger subsided. Then he kept looking at Sonama's naked breasts. Whether out of deeply-felt affection or from an unknown greedy desire of flesh, Muthana's hand moved to touch her breast. She stopped him. Why? She possibly did not know. Was it the breath of liquor on him, or was it because of the unsteadiness of his hand from over-drinking or was it really because she felt that her breasts were no longer to be touched by anyone since the holy of holies was suckling from them? Whatever her reason for the refusal, it had a devastating effect on Muthana. He felt rejected as never before.

He left, overcome by horrible despair, no longer aware of where he was going.

Beaten, tired and panting, he sat down on the ground, not knowing where he was. As he opened his eyes, he found himself opposite Kanta's cottage. Kanta was known as a woman of easy virtue, whose love and time could be hired by anyone who could afford it. He could afford it. He went in, knowing that here at least he would not be rejected.

Kanta, for the first time ever since she had set up her business in the village, was brusque with a customer who promised to pay well. She had to go to Sindhu Putra, she said.

Muthana felt as though the earth and the sky had collided to crush him in between.

They never saw Muthana in the village again. Some said that he had taken a boat to the River of all Rivers to discover unknown shores beyond; others said that he had gone to the lands in the north and east to prospect for gold, and yet others said that the gods had invited him to drink with them, and some even said that at times he wins against some lesser gods when these drinking contests take place.

'. . . I die for all people; and I shall go where I have to go for bearing false witness, but I go without tears, for what is false should have been true, so that the children of my ancestors remain unharmed, and the people of your land remain in peace ... and the battle cry is heard no more....'

—(Message for Karkarta Bharat from an ex-slave at the moment of his execution—5085 BC)

Hindu! Hindu!

5068 BC

Bharatjogi's mind went to images and pictures of the past.

'Hindu! Hindu!' The legendary cry reverberated clearly in his mind as his wandering thoughts recaptured the past.

His eyes were closed. He had sat down to pray, as a hermit should, but as usual his mind moved away from his prayers. He was now thinking of the last battle with the tribes of the north and east, when he, as Karkarta, had led his army deep into their territory.

'Hindu! Hindu!' He heard the cry again and saw himself at the head of his columns charging at the enemy.

'Hindu! Hindu!' The cry repeated itself and he felt tall, powerful and alive, certain that nothing could stop the onslaught of his people against the enemy.

'Hindu! Hindu!' he heard, as his spear pierced the enemy breast; and he felt the spirit of the gods with him.

'Hindu! Hindu!' was the cry as he charged. The field was littered with enemy dead, wounded and dying.

'Hindu! Hindu!' cried the enemy; and those who survived were fleeing to the high ground, in terror.

'Hindu! Hindu!' was the shrill, piercing scream of the enemy, as they called out to their compatriots to run and retreat.

'Hindu! Hindu!' Yes, it was a cry that struck terror in the hearts of tribesmen. Yet, there was a time when they had uttered those words with laughter and ridicule.

'Hindu! Hindu!' Bharat heard the low moan of the Chief of the enemy tribe who lay wounded on the battlefield. The Chief cried not for mercy, but for swift death. Bharat understood. The Chief was in pain from his terrible wounds; all the men by his side were dead or had fled; even his own son had run away. What he feared was the slow, lingering death, and, worse still if he survived, a life of slavery to the victorious Hindu. He wanted instantaneous death in dignity.

The Chief's teeth were clenched, his hands were powerless but his eyes kept darting to the spear, nearby.

Bharat looked at the Chief. Their eyes held each other in a silent, bewildering understanding. He glanced at the spear and shook his head to deny the Chief's appeal, and motioned to a soldier to remove him from the battlefield. The soldier misunderstood and swiftly with his sharp spear pierced the Chief's chest. Bharat saw a flicker of gratitude flash through the Chief's eyes, before they closed forever. He glared at the soldier but the deed was done. Quietly, he ordered, 'Remove the Chief's body. Give it to his people with respect.'

The soldier looked at Karkarta uncertainly. In the past, they always left the enemy dead and dying on the battlefield. But now Bharat was certain that this was a clear victory and the challenge of a fresh charge from the enemy had vanished. A conqueror can afford to be generous.

Yet that was not the only reason. That last glimpse into the eyes of the fallen Chief recalled to his mind what he had always known—that the soul of one man, when liberated from the body, is the soul of all men and that in the passage of time, we all become one soul, indivisible and merged with the One Supreme. Formerly, in the midst of battle, and amidst fears of its outcome, he had often forgotten that.

Bharat repeated the order: 'Yes, the body belongs to the people of the dead warrior. Give it to them.'

But a voice behind him quickly thundered, 'Yes, yes, give his body to his people, but not his head.'

It was Dhrupatta, his deputy commander. He dismounted from his horse and with one powerful stroke of his massive sword he separated the chief's neck from his body. He picked up the head by the hair, and holding it aloft like a trophy, he mounted his horse and galloped near the hill where the enemy had retreated.

From the hill, the enemy watched. Dhrupatta went nearer, well within the range of their arrows. The arrows did not come. Their eyes were focused on the head of their Chief, held high up in the air.

A mournful chant came from the enemy hill. The tribals knew that their Chief held the spirit of their god. He was to surrender it to his son before the moment of his death. But his son had fled when the Chief fell; and the Chief, obviously, could not surrender the spirit to him. The son, then, could never be anointed as the Chief; and oh the pity of it! The spirit of their god would fly away, always wandering, eternally unfulfilled.

The low chant rose and filled the air. Suddenly there was silence, for the tribals knew that the departing spirit of their god demanded a sacrifice. Quietly, the son of the Chief was brought forth and stood there, flanked by priests. He was the one to be sacrificed.

Bharat and his men watched from a distance. Dhrupatta was busy with his antics. He stood up on the horse, with the Chief's head impaled on his tall spear, and kept whirling it high in the air.

Bharat cried out in dismay, 'What are you doing?'

Dhrupatta understood the sense of what Karkarta said, though at that distance, he could not hear the words. He replied, whirling the trophy more vigorously, 'I think the fresh air will do him good.'

The tribesmen stood still. They knew that the spirit of their god would fly away from the body of their dead Chief as soon as the clouds gathered to conceal the sun, or latest at sunset. And the sacrifice must be completed quickly; already, the sky was threatened with clouds.

A tribal priest brought out his axe; others held the trembling youngster. The priests were chanting prayers for the sacrifice, but their eyes were on the whirling head of their chief. They waited for the whirling motion to pause before striking the boy with the axe.

Dhrupatta's arm was tiring; his horse too was restless with Dhrupatta standing over him for so long. Suddenly Dhrupatta, with one last furious whirl, flung the head towards his own troops.

The boy, who was to be sacrificed, saw his chance as the astonished priests watched their Chief's head flying through the air. He fled.

Dhrupatta smiled as he saw someone rushing towards him, with lightning speed. His sword was ready to strike, but then he saw that it was only an unarmed boy, obviously intent on surrender. He gently prodded the frightened boy with the back of his sword making him run even faster towards Karkarta's troops.

At Karkarta's feet, where the Chief's head had fallen, the son knelt, gasping for breath. Bharat picked up the head. Slowly he raised the boy. The sight of his sightless father's head brought tears to the eyes of the boy and he moaned. Bharat held the boy against his own body to comfort him.

The boy, Bharat knew, could not tell him much; he understood only a few of their words, if spoken slowly. But tribals never spoke slowly. A slave-interpreter—a tribal captured long ago by Karkarta's troops—tried to explain it all to him, though much had to be clarified by signs and gestures.

The slave-interpreter left no doubt that the boy was doomed to die, but worse still, the entire tribe was doomed as the Chief was unable to bequeath to him the power of the gods, as he had run away from the battlefield when his father fell. The tribe, consequently, would have to leave their land and move elsewhere.

'Move where?' Bharat asked.

'Anywhere, everywhere, but not remain in their present habitation, which is forever doomed.'

'Move elsewhere! Anywhere! Everywhere!' Danger signals flashed in Bharat's mind. Where would they move? Maybe they would infiltrate into the lands of his own clan along the Sindhu! Where else! Otherwise they came only to raid occasionally, but always went back. Now they would want to stay and die in the attempt rather than return to their accursed land!

'What happens if the boy does not go back?' Bharat asked.

'They will hunt for him all their lives. He is the one who must be sacrificed to the spirit of our departing god.'

So, our land will always be their target, Bharat feared. What will hold them back in their lands? he wondered. Nothing, he was told.

The tribal land was doomed, as the spirit of their god would be wandering without repose.

Bharat reached a decision. 'Go tell them their Chief gave me the spirit of their god. It reposes in my breast, happy and fulfilled.'

The interpreter had many objections. The Chief could bequeath the spirit of the god only to his eldest son, for the system of dynastic rule had to be maintained.

Could the Chief not adopt a son? Bharat asked. Yes, but only in special circumstances, for instance, when his natural son agreed to such adoption if he chose to become a priest or if the son fled from battle, deserting his father, as was the present case.

'Can you tribals adopt a son from our clan?' Bharat asked.

'Why not! Our tribals have adopted many children captured from your clan.'

'I thought you people killed or enslaved all those you captured!'

'Only a barbarian kills a child, away from the heat of battle. And only a barbarian would enslave a child or keep him captive,' was the contemptuous answer of the slave-interpreter.

Everything from Bharat's mind was erased, momentarily, except the thought of the captured children of his clan whom he had thought massacred or enslaved by tribals, and he asked, 'How is it, then, that we never hear about our captured children?'

'They are no longer children of your clan. They are children of our tribe.'

'And when they grow?' Bharat asked.

Clearly, the interpreter considered it a foolish question but explained patiently, 'When they grow, they are our people; some become hata (hunters), some itta (magistrates) and some even atta (priests) and all become ita (warriors). It is only in your clan that a slave is a slave for ever.'

The slave-interpreter spoke softly yet his contempt was unmistakable; and Bharat was thinking: the enemy is always a barbarian, but if you look with the eyes of the enemy, the barbarian is nowhere but within ourselves!

Quietly, Bharat spoke, 'Very well then, tell them that their Chief adopted me as his son, as his own son wishes to be a priest.'

But the interpreter explained that the breast of him who was to be adopted must be pierced to take in the blood from the breast of him who is to adopt.

At Bharat's order, Dhrupatta and the others stood in front of Bharat, to shield him from view of the far-away hill. Bharat asked Dhrupatta to draw blood from his breast with his dagger.

'With great pleasure,' said Dhrupatta with enthusiasm, as though he would love to plunge the dagger right through Karkarta's heart. But for all his flamboyance, Dhrupatta stopped as soon as the first hesitant drop of blood appeared. Bharat prodded him to dig deeper. As more blood flowed, Dhrupatta threw away the dagger and said, 'Enough, we killed their Chief today; we don't have to kill ours. I can wait.'

His words—'I can wait'—brought smiles all round, as he was expected to succeed as Karkarta, after Bharat.

'Go now,' Bharat told the slave-interpreter. 'Tell them, I am their Chief now, for their old Chief adopted me as his son and surrendered to me the spirit of their god.'

'Only a priest can make such an announcement.'

'Who can appoint a priest?' Bharat asked.

'Only the Chief of the tribe can.'

'Very well then, I am the Chief now. I appoint you as a priest.'

'No,' the interpreter objected. 'You cannot. I am unclean.'

'Unclean! How!' Bharat asked.

'My tribe knows that I have been a slave. A slave is not clean.'

Bharat understood the sadness of the slave. Bharat responded with the traditional words:

'I, Bharat, Karkarta of the land of the Mother Goddess Sindhu, here and now, set you free. As from this moment, you are no longer a slave; but a free man of the rya (people) of Sindhu.'

The slave shook his head. A slave, he explained, does not instantly become clean on gaining freedom. Purification ceremonies by priests, for one moon-month, must cleanse his spirit. 'My freedom cannot serve your purpose. You can take it back,' he said contemptuously.

Bharat also shook his head. The slave was a slave no more. The words granting him freedom had been spoken and he was already free. A free man of the rya of Sindhu cannot be enslaved except when convicted of a grievous offence.

Inwardly, Bharat smiled, happy somehow that he had freed the slave. Actually, he did not have the absolute right to free him. The slave belonged to a land-owner. However there was a convention that during hostilities the commander could dispose of private property in the clan's interest. In any case, Bharat had decided to pay the slave-owner from his own pocket.

But the problem of sending a priest remained. The freed slave came to his help and suggested that the old Chief's son could go as a priest. If Karkarta, as the new Chief, appointed him as the priest.

'But you said they will hunt him down and kill him!'

'Not if he is a priest. No one can dare kill a priest. In fact, your right to be adopted by our Chief is stronger if his natural son surrenders his succession to become a priest.'

It is not easy to understand everything readily through gestures and half-spoken words. But at last Bharat understood. The old Chief's son could be appointed as a priest; Bharat, being older, was to be regarded as the eldest son, in view of the assumed adoption, and also as he was supposed to have received surrender of god's spirit from the old Chief; clearly, therefore, Bharat was the new Chief of the tribe and had the right to appoint anyone who was clean (non-slave) as a priest. A priest cannot be held accountable for any faults—including fleeing the battle-field—committed prior to his priesthood. The interpreter further explained that the priest must wear the head-dress, in red, and be accompanied by a witness when he announces the transfer of god's power from one Chief to another.

The problem of finding a red head-dress for the new priest posed no problem. Quickly, Dhrupatta dipped a white cloth in the bodies of enemy soldiers who had bled to death on the battlefield.

The boy's head was draped with the red cloth; much of the blood dripped, forming lines on his face, but that did not matter, as tribal priests often painted their faces. Earlier, the boy had trembled in terror at the prospect of facing his people from whom he had fled. But the head-dress transformed him. He stood erect, unafraid and full of confidence in his priestly dignity.

How outward symbols change the spirit inside us! Bharat marvelled.

The interpreter also explained that anyone from his tribe could be a witness so long as he had not been a servant or a slave of the priest.

'Then you must go as the witness,' Bharat ordered. The order needed no response. Yet something in the ex-slave's eyes held Bharat's attention. Perhaps he has not understood, Bharat thought, and repeated the order. The ex-slave was still lost in thought. Finally, he nodded blankly and said, 'Of course, I must. You shall be obeyed, Karkarta.' Yet his anguish was clear. Maybe, thought Bharat, he was struggling to find the right words for his reply.

On the opposite hill, tribesmen were gathering. All eyes were raised to the sky, to see if clouds would move to conceal the sun. For then, the spirit of their god would leave the body of their dead Chief and wander away. Or else at sunset.

The ex-slave asked for a cask of wine. 'Is this the time to drink!' Bharat asked, astonished.

'No,' the ex-slave explained, 'the new Chief invariably sends a gift to the priests.'

'Would they be happy if I sent many casks of wine?' Bharat asked. 'The more the better,' the ex-slave said. 'The more you send, the more the priests shall believe; and hope for more in future; and they will ask themselves: what reason can he have to lie, who has so much to give, now and later!'

Bharat smiled. He saw enormous fallacy in this reasoning and asked, 'They do not suspect that he who comes bearing many gifts has his eyes on something in return?'

'Perhaps they do. But they think that what you give is theirs to keep, and what you seek you will grab from people.'

'The priests, and the people—are they not one?'

'Priests?—they are a class apart—the privileged class. How can they know how another class feels!'

Silently, Bharat asked himself: is it not true of my land as well? Why is it that those who are known as men of god are the least godly!

'What happens if the priests do not believe you?' asked Bharat.

'They shall believe,' the ex-slave said, 'because they shall want to believe. Or else they shall wander homeless without their priestly dignity and comfort. And when they believe, they shall bow to you as their Chief.'

Bharat ordered four mules to be loaded with wine casks brought for the campaign. 'These are my gifts to the priests,' he told the ex-slave. 'They can expect much more in the days to come.'

The ex-slave nodded gravely and astonished everyone by taking off all his clothes. No one in Bharat's clan or amongst enemy tribes ever appeared naked in public. But the ex-slave explained, 'A witness to the gods must appear as God made him—naked.'

The ex-slave spoke to the dead Chief's son, who went forward with measured steps. The ex-slave followed with mules loaded with wine-casks.

Bharat's troops watched seriously. Only Dhrupatta laughed, 'If our old slave goes naked, as God made him, would the tribals also think that God made him holding four mules loaded with wine casks?'

'Be silent, Dhrupatta,' Bharat urged.

But it was not easy to silence Dhrupatta and he said, 'Soon, the tribals will bow to you, if they believe our naked messenger and your frightened priest. But they will wonder why your own troops do not bow to you. I think our troops must kneel before you to increase the trust of those barbarians in you.'

Bharat smiled, 'A charming thought but please dismiss it. Free men kneel only before God.'

'Not even before their great Karkarta who leads them to victory and glory?' Dhrupatta asked, with mock-astonishment.

'No, but you can change the system when you are Karkarta.'

'That I shall. But even now I shall ask them to kneel to you.'

'Don't be ridiculous. You know that they will not kneel.'

'No?' asked Dhrupatta, as though surprised. Quickly, he called out to the troops. They came, lining up before him and Bharat. 'Now, kneel to God, for we have won a great victory,' Dhrupatta commanded.

They knew that this was no place to kneel to God, with the dead and wounded lying around. The place to do that was in the hallowed precincts of a temple. But Dhrupatta continued: 'Four casks of Karkarta's wine to those that kneel, all the way on the ground.'

They laughed. So this was some joke, not a prayer, for which they would get choice wine. They knelt.

From the faraway hill, enemy tribals now had their eyes focused on the two men and four mules moving towards them. The drum-beat which Dhrupatta organized drew their attention to the kneeling troops.

At the foot of the hill, the Chief's son stopped. The ex-slave tied the mules to a boulder. Slowly, he went up the hill.

Silence on the hill! Not a sound, not a movement! All stood rigidly, waiting for the naked messenger to reach them.

The ex-slave stood before the chief-priest. His face was raised to the sky and his hands were also raised, as if he was speaking to the gods. But apparently the priests could hear him. Alone, the chief-priest left the hill and kept circling the Chief's son. Certainly, they were speaking. However, it could not be seen if the chief-priest was looking at the mules bearing wine-casks. The chief-priest returned to the hill and he too raised his hands and remained gazing at the sky. This apparently was a signal for all the priests and tribals to do likewise. Even women with babes in their arms raised their infants, to achieve heavenly grace. Soon, the chief-priest lowered his hands, as they all did except the naked ex-slave.

The chief-priest wrapped a white cloth round the naked body of the ex-slave and knelt before him, followed by everyone on the hill.

Bharat and his men were watching and Dhrupatta said excitedly, 'They have believed him. They are kneeling to our ex-slave!'

'But why are they kneeling to him?' Bharat asked.

'Why not?' Dhrupatta rejoined. 'He announces the movement of the spirit of god from one Chief to another. Is he not then the messenger of the gods? Surely, they must kneel to him!'

The chief-priest was speaking to the ex-slave. Slowly, with his left hand, the ex-slave pointed to where Bharat and his men were standing, far away. The chief-priest, then, went down to the Chief's son. The boy pointed with both hands in Bharat's direction. Apparently, the ex-slave had schooled him well, while walking to the hill.

The chief-priest escorted the Chief's son to the hill. The boy again pointed in Bharat's direction, with his right hand. Immediately, on the hill, a chant began, led by the chief-priest.

'Hindu! Hindu!'

The chant rose, louder, as though they expected that the birds high up in the air would hear and fly to tell the sun. Louder and louder, the chant rose like a roar. It reached Bharat and his men. Clearly, they heard: 'Hindu! Hindu!'

It was a soulful cry! The tribals had not lost the spirit of the gods! It had not flown away into nothingness! The void they dreaded was no more! No, the spirit of their god was alive in the heart of the Chief of the Hindus. The Chief of the Hindus was their Chief now. They had their new Chief. They had the spirit of their god. They were not doomed. They were saved!

'Hindu! Hindu!' It was a joyous cry, of relief, gratitude, thanksgiving.

'What happens now?' Bharat wondered.

'They will come and kneel before you as their new Chief,' Dhrupatta said, 'But as our good ex-slave said, you will have to wait for sunset, for I see no clouds around, to hide the sun.'

However, for once, Dhrupatta was wrong. Possibly the birds, hearing the rising chant of the tribals, had carried the message to the clouds. The clouds clustered round and, well before sunset, hid the sun completely from view.

A mighty roar went up from the tribals. 'Hindu! Hindu!'

Tribals came, followed by priests, in an almost never-ending stream. The chief-priest paused only to inspect the dagger-cut on Bharat's breast, and then he knelt. They all knelt; and before their faces met the earth, they chanted, 'Hindu! Hindu!'

At a signal from the chief-priest, the tribals rose. A platform of boulders and wooden frames was quickly improvized. Bharat stood on it, raised his hand in benediction and the chant repeated itself.

'Hindu! Hindu!'

That evening, in his tent, Bharat asked for the ex-slave. I must thank him. Ours was only a military victory but the ex-slave has earned for us a victory that will last!

An interpreter carried the message to the chief-priest, who was glad that the new Chief was already taking his duties seriously.

Wrapped in a rug, the dead body of the ex-slave, cut up in several pieces, was brought to Bharat.

Bharat was horrified. 'Why!' he asked, at last.

The chief-priest misunderstood, for he did not know the language of his new chief and started pointing out that the body was cut into the correct number of pieces—one for the sun, one for the moon, seven for planets, one for mother earth, one for . . . .'

Later Bharat understood that a witness to the surrender of god's spirit from one Chief to the other must die.

'Why?' he asked. The answer was quite simple:

'So that he who is a false witness shall go straight to hell. So no one shall bear false witness.

'And he who is a true witness shall go straight to heaven. What more can a man want!

'But that no man shall come forth lightly to bear witness, except that he be inspired by a cause greater than his life. . . for his life shall be forfeit as soon he bears witness.'

Bharat wondered: where would I go? I, who encouraged him to bear false witness?

But why did he not tell me what would happen to him! Did he not know?

'Perhaps more than his life, he loved his people,' Dhrupatta said, seriously.

'His people!'

'Yes, his people; we; ourselves; for he was of the Sindhu, when you gave him his freedom. But he died also for the people amongst whom he was born; he realized that they too must be saved from the catastrophe that would inevitably result if the spirit of their god was lost and his people became homeless, rootless.'

'No, he perhaps did not know that he would have to die!' Bharat cried, as though to escape the moral guilt of sending the man to his death.

'He knew. He was a priest amongst his people before he was enslaved by us. I have checked.'

Bharat stared and Dhrupatta softly added, 'He also left a message with the old Chief's son, and he said: If all goes well, tell Karkarta that I die for the people; and I shall go where I have to, for bearing false witness, but I go without tears, for what is false should have been true so that the children of my ancestors remain unharmed, and the people of Karkarta's land remain in peace, and the battle cry is heard no more....'

Bharat listened in anguish. He did not believe in heaven or hell. It is on this earth that man receives punishment and rewards, whether in one life or in a series of lives; but the ex-slave, who died with such infinite love, for the people—his and ours—was not of this earth. For him, should be moksha, total liberation, and complete identity with the self of the One Supreme.

Dhrupatta broke in on his reverie. 'He left another message of a personal kind for another slave. He said all his clothes should be given to Dhanumati, a slave-girl, who was his only friend; and if he is entitled to a day's wages as a soldier—since he was a free man at least for one day—that too should be given to Dhanumati.'

'Dhanumati will receive his wages for all her life. Who is she? Where is she?' Bharat asked feverishly.

'They worked together. She is a slave in the fields of Sutukatta.'

'Send a courier now. Now, this instant. Order in my name that Dhanumati is no longer a slave.'

'I have already taken the liberty of doing that.'

'Thank you Dhrupatta, you always know what is in my heart.'

'But of course. How else can I become Karkarta?' Dhrupatta rejoined, hoping to bring a smile to the face of Bharat. But Bharat did not smile. He could not overcome his distress for sending the ex-slave to his death.

Dhrupatta understood his sorrow and said: 'What is done, is done. All we can do for our ex-slave is to pray for his soul.'

'Pray for his soul! No, Dhrupatta, no, we do not pray for such souls. We pray to such souls.'

'...Hinduism is the law of life, not a dogma; its aim is not to create a creed but a character and its goal is to achieve perfection through varied spiritual knowledge which rejects nothing and yet refines everything, through continuous testing.

'...Yet a Hindu must remain strong and united, for he must know that no external, outside force can crush him, except when he is divided and betrays his own....

'He who seeks to convert another to his own faith offends against his own soul and the will of God and the law of humanity....

'...What then is the goal of the Hindu? Through strength, unity, discipline... to reach the ultimate in being, ultimate in awareness and ultimate in bliss, not for himself alone, but for all....

'...This was the silent pledge that our ancients took when they called themselves the Hindu.... If I cannot abide by that pledge, how can I call myself a Hindu?'

—(From the 'Song of the Hindu'—5085 BC)

'Criticism! Opposition in the Parliament! We must learn to sit back and enjoy it. Even God loves opposition. Why else do you think He created the devil?'

—(Karkarta Bharat's advice to Dhrupatta—5080 BC)

The Parliament of Hindu and the 'Song of the Hindu'

(5068 BC with flashbacks to 5085 BC)

Bharatjogi sat down to pray, but as always a host of memories came crowding into his mind.

He was now thinking of Dhanumati, the wife of the ex-slave interpreter. He had learnt from her that she and the ex-slave interpreter had run away from their tribe. He, as a priest, could not take a wife or live with the same woman for more than six days in any moon-month. If he had, nothing would have happened to him, but Dhanumati would have been killed for corrupting a priest and her dead body would have been fed to the hyenas.

Unfortunately the two lovers found no sanctuary: they were caught by Bharat's clan, treated as enemy spies, and promptly enslaved.

Dhanumati cried often. Her lover tried to comfort her and his tears were only for her, never for himself, for he said, 'He who runs from the gods has to be caught by the devil. He has no other destiny!'

Indeed he was right to call us the devil, thought Bharat. Is it not devilish to hold two innocent lovers in slavery? Is it not devilish to hold anyone in slavery?

Bharat wondered if it was the sacrifice of the ex-slave and the story of Dhanumati that hardened his heart against slavery all the more intensely. But who knows how God reveals his heart to man!

And is it not always so! A sudden flash, an inward illumination— and all life then is seen afresh, anew.

Bells were ringing throughout the Hindu clan when they heard of Bharat's victory. Victories there had been before, against tribal outposts, or many villages. But now it was total victory, against all the combined armies of tribes, right in the heart of enemy land, with most tribal chieftains massacred; and even the hated tribal Chief of Chiefs slain, with his head severed from his body.

Some from Bharat's clan arrived even before the final victory itself, in anticipation, hoping to buy captured prisoners as slaves. From a distance they saw the ghastly spectacle of flight and pursuit, slaughter

and capture. Horses and men were thrown down; and many of the
wounded tribals were struggling to get up, but collapsed, without the
strength to escape. As far as the eye could see the enemy was defeated
everywhere, and the battlefield was strewn with their corpses, only
small patches of bloodstained earth showing between them. This was
total, final, indisputable victory, and all that remained was the mopping-
up operation, complete occupation of enemy land and speedy vengeance
for all their outrages of the past.

More and more people arrived at Bharat's tent, at the battle
headquarters. Some were slave-traders who brought ropes to carry
slaves back and they came hoping that the price of slaves would be
cheap because of abundant supply; others came to buy land in tribal
areas for farming and cattle; some needed mining rights for metals;
others, sites for precious stones; and some sought recruits for whore-
houses.

But there were also many who wanted nothing. 'You do not
conquer men by war but with love,' they said. 'Greed for gold and
lust for power are evil,' they urged, 'and avarice will destroy our honour
and virtue and tempt us to hold nothing too sacred to buy and sell.'

To the slave-traders, Bharat simply said that there would be no
slaves to sell, for none would be enslaved. They smiled, thinking that
Karkarta was merely trying to bargain for a higher price. Surely, the
clan, with its ever increasing territory needed slaves, and besides,
Karkarta's treasury was empty and desperately needed money.

But to their dismay, Karkarta was adamant. Some Council Chiefs
also came to plead. 'Why?' asked Nandan, their spokesman.

'Because they too are Hindus.' Bharat had replied. 'And a Hindu
shall not be a slave.'

'When did they become Hindus?' Nandan asked.

'When they called themselves Hindus, accepted our protection, our
way of life and our gods.'

'There are those who say that you have accepted their gods!'

'Of course,' replied Bharat.

'Then it is you who have ceased to be a Hindu.'

Bharat did not flinch at the accusation and asked, 'When was it
that a Hindu failed to accept the gods of others! When did we ever
reject a god in our endless, supreme quest! Did not our ancestors, who
first came to live by the side of Sindhu river, accept the gods of those
who were there before them? And did we not embrace the gods of
those who came in peace after them? Their gods, like ours, serve the
One Supreme, whose gracious purpose is to. . . .'

Nandan interrupted, 'Bharatji, we are speaking of slaves, not of
gods.'

'No, we are not speaking of slaves, we are speaking of God and
His love for His creation; we are speaking of man and his humanity;
and we are speaking of tribals and their right to freedom.'

'Yet you think nothing of the horrors those tribals perpetrated on
our people in the past!'

'Is it vengeance you seek? Or is it profit from the slave-trade?'

'Both. They tore children of our clan out of their parents' arms; our women were subjected to their lusts and they pillaged our temples and homes. They ravished. . . .'

'And they shall do so again, unless we ourselves have wisdom and restraint. Can you not see that vengeance sows vengeance, hate engenders hate, and blood breeds blood! What satisfaction can revenge bring? Does a single war end all wars? No. The enemy rises again. How can a victory today guarantee a victory in the future! No, the protection against war is not in enslaving an enemy but in ending the enmity.'

Nandan and Karkarta Bharat spoke for a long time but both remained inflexible. At last Nandan said, 'All right, they are Hindus, I concede that. But how does that protect them from slavery? The slaves that we already own in our lands also call themselves Hindus. They pray as we do and serve the same gods. See, how wrong your position is!'

'The wrong lies not in my position, but in the position of those who own slaves in our land.'

'And you yourself own slaves!' Nandan restored.

Bharat nodded sadly and Nandan asked, in a tone of triumph, 'How many slaves does your household have?'

'Many,' Bharat answered, as though admitting to a charge.

'And you will of course free them, instantly?' Nandan asked, with heavy irony.

Bharat looked at him, as if pondering over the question, and then nodded, 'Yes, half of them, instantly.'

'Half of them!' Nandan was astonished at the unexpected answer.

'Half I can liberate on my own.' Bharat said as though explaining his difficulties. 'Because my wife and I own our property in common; what right can I have to dispose of her portion, unless she agrees!"

Nandan stared at him, wondering if Bharat's mind was beginning to crack, and asked, 'How did this idea come to you?'

'You gave me this idea and I am grateful to you; yes, I must liberate my slaves.'

'No, I mean the idea that tribals must not be enslaved.'

'Who knows how God reveals his message to us! Maybe a slave spoke to me, or a priest or a witness or someone seeking refuge, or a lover, or his sweetheart. Who knows!'

But Bharat knew. He was thinking of one man who was at one time a priest, a lover, a refugee, a slave, and a witness, and who was now dead because he chose to die so that others may live.

'You are in error, Bharatji, those barbarians will never be good Hindus,' Nandan said.

'Are we good Hindus ourselves?' Bharat asked. 'It may take centuries for men to be fully men but we must prepare for that day.'

To those also who wanted to exploit tribals for their own profit, Bharat said—'Go, help them; peace is our primary requirement and poverty and riches cannot grow side by side. Only the rich fear death. The poor do not dread it, and are often sorry that it is so late in coming. For your own peace, for your own prosperity then, share with your neighbouring tribes the bounty of the gods; help them to help themselves, so that they too, like you, have a life of plenty. Their failure to grow is your failure more than theirs.'

Many ignored his words. There was no call to action, no duty to perform in that pious, elegant advice. It was simply the poet in their Karkarta's temperament taking charge.

But then he did free his own slaves. Not half but all, for even though his words were not heeded by many, apparently his influence over his own wife was considerable.

In an imposing ceremony, Bharat stood on the crest of the hill, while the tribals gathered in their thousands to hear him. Bharat said:

'Your gods are our gods. . . . Your people are our people.

'Know this then, that from this moment, all of you are free, never to be enslaved, except for those seven serious offences for which the law prescribes the punishment of slavery.'

The tribal chief-priest translated. He had been up all night trying to memorize everything to be said at the ceremony.

The ceremony continued. The Chief Purohit of Bharat's clan, recited:

> *Let us think of the splendour*
> *Of Her that is the One Supreme,*
> *She, that is one without second,*
> *That She may inspire our minds,*
> *Our words, thoughts and deeds.*
>
> *To Her, who is the unending time*
> *To Her, who is without beginning*
> *To Her, who is without end*
> *To Her, who began it all*
> *To Her, who is the seed of all*
> *To Her, who is the source of all*
> *And to Her, who alone is the self*
> *In the innermost heart of all,*
> *To Her, our prayer, our devotion, our love*
> *That She may inspire us, together, all, all.*[1]

---

[1]This ancient mantra refers to the One Supreme as 'Her' and 'She'. It was common also to refer to the One Supreme as 'Him' and 'He', as this was regarded as a matter only of linguistic convenience; the belief clearly was that He is the universal God who Himself is the universe, being both the creator and the creation, whose form the eye cannot see, though the heart can; and thus He is the woman, He is the man, He is the youth, He is the maiden, He is the infant, He is the old, for He includes within His own being the entire universe. . . .

The purohit sprinkled water and grain in the ceremonial fire and uncovered fruits and flowers. In the silence that followed, Bharat spoke: 'The holy water of Mother Sindhu is sprinkled in worship of the One Supreme. Sacrifice of grain is made to Goddess Agni (fire), that it may carry it to all deities on earth, in air, water, space, outerspace and beyond. These flowers and fruits are also our homage to the gods and we hope that they shall accept the subtle part of the fruits, leaving gross material as food for their worshippers.

'For know this: such are the only sacrifices that gods seek. For gods do not desire the sacrifice of blood and flesh—neither of humans, nor of animals, nor of birds; and those that permit or participate in such sacrifice shall be chastised by the spirit of the gods and punished by the law of man.'

The tribal priest translated rapidly. His heart was not in this announcement. He had remonstrated with Bharat, explaining that much of the tribal society's effort went towards placating the formidable gods whose benevolence was assured by constant human and animal sacrifices. He was convinced that continuity of life and prosperity of the tribe could be secured only by such bloodthirsty rites. Karkarta pointed to the famine and malnutrition in tribal lands and prosperity in his own clan, which had never indulged in human or animal sacrifice, and said, 'The surest way of inviting the wrath of the gods is to abominate their presence with the blood and flesh of an unwilling sacrificial victim.'

'Unwilling!' the priest protested. He explained that for the tribal it was the finest death to perish under a sacrificial knife. 'Such a fate to honour the gods is known as an honourable death.'

Karkarta shook his head. The priest wished to argue no more. How does one argue with a conqueror who spares the life and liberty of the conquered! Yet he spoke as if he was asking himself, 'Everything has life—human, animal and bird. The flowers, fruits and grains have life; the tree, the stone, the salt have life; and the drop of water that we sprinkle has life. All creation has life. The sacrifice of one or the other, is it not the same!'

Bharat was pleased. He knew that those who believed that all creation had life were on the right path; and the next step towards enlightenment could arise only from such knowledge and faith.

'Everything has life,' Bharat agreed. 'But then every life has a purpose and its own fulfilment and salvation to seek.'

They argued no more.

The tribals heard Bharatji with relief flooding their hearts, that none would be enslaved. His second statement, prohibiting sacrifices of flesh, was not readily understood in the fast translation. They had assumed that there would be sacrifices to gods. Virgins and warriors had already been selected as sacrificial victims. Now, instead of having their hearts carved out with the sacrificial knife, each was offered grain, nuts and fruits to keep before idols, and later to eat themselves, after the gods digested the spirit of their offerings.

This, the tribals were told, was all the sacrifice that their gods needed. No more! To many tribals it was strange that the clan which conquered them should have such tame, undeveloped and primitive ideas of sacrifice. How could the gods be satisfied with so little!

But the tribal chief-priest was true to his oath of loyalty. 'Be silent,' he said to them. 'Their Karkarta is now the Chief of our Chiefs and speaks to us with the spirit of Prajapati (the lord of all beings). Obey him in all things.'

Many obeyed. But obedience to the conqueror's command can be demeaning, even though he assumes the high position of the Chief. And some wondered: can even the Chief of Chiefs offend against the Way and the Will of gods, as revealed by our ancestors? No, that cannot be; and a few decided against the new wave, to escape to the mountains beyond and build a shrine to continue human and animal sacrifice.

It was to those rebels that the son of the former Chief, who was now a priest, spoke. 'Their Karkarta is now our Chief and he speaks the truth. The gods of Hindu are not hungry, nor thirsty, and that is why their clan is well-fed and prosperous.'

The rebel-leader heard him with contempt. 'So we desert our gods who are thirsty and hungry and run after gods of wealth and plenty!'

'No!' the youth pleaded. 'Their gods are our gods and our gods are theirs—and they all serve the same creator.'

The leader was in a rage and said, 'Foolish youth! Gods are not like these animal skins we wear, that we put them on whenever we want or discard them at will. Gods are with us, always, and forever!'

The youth made no response and the old man continued with rising contempt, 'You were the son of him who was the Chief of our Chiefs: after him you were to be our Chief; that glory is denied to you, as your own father disowned you; now you are no more than a junior priest. To what lower depths you will sink, in time, I know not. But be sure, a place in hell is always reserved for those who abandon their gods.'

They all looked at the youth, some in sympathy over the loss of his father, others in remembrance of days, not long gone, when they bowed reverently to his father, and to him, as heir-apparent. They saw his face, open and frank with innocence, and they felt sorry for him.

Briefly, the moon came out from behind the clouds in an overcast, starless sky. But the glow that they saw on the handsome face of the youth did not come only from the light of the moon. There was no longer distress on his face. All tension had left him. Somewhere, within himself, he felt the stirring of an emotion which thrilled him. He forgot the pain of his father's death; he forgot the gnawing guilt of deserting his father in battle; he even forgot his sin for the lie that led to his appointment as a priest. Suddenly, he became conscious of light and warmth; he felt his mind caressed. No longer was his spirit overwhelmed. Peace had returned to his anguished soul. Unafraid, he looked at the old man who had cursed him with a place in hell.

They watched, as he stood transformed, as though a vision rose before him. Then, he spoke in a faraway voice: 'The Creator bleeds when any of His creatures bleed. . . . Do not carry the sin of His blood!'

This is all they heard; perhaps he said no more, or perhaps he did, but they could not hear, for suddenly the rain came down with thunder and lightning. They saw him as lightning played hide and seek with his face, bringing out its glow and shadow. His lips were moving in prayer. They could not hear him. But they felt they heard the echo of his words in the thunder rampaging from the skies; and, distinctly, clearly, they heard that distant echo, repeat itself: 'The Creator bleeds. . .bleeds, when any of His creatures bleed. The Creator bleeds. . . .'

The rebels returned to their homes. They wondered and wavered. But not their leader. He left for the mountains, alone and undaunted. The voice of thunder meant nothing to him. He heard only his own voice.

Many myths rose about him. Some said, there on the mountain-top, he sacrificed himself to the gods.

Others said that he sacrificed himself, but the gods returned his blood and flesh back to him; and since then, at each sunset he kills himself but at each dawn the gods restore him to life; and from dawn to dusk he keeps beseeching the gods to accept his sacrifice.

Not so, some said. True, he sacrificed himself and the gods did return his flesh and blood, but that went on only for six evenings, and then the gods came down to the mountain-top and showed him the wounds inflicted on the gods themselves, through his sacrifice. Then he stopped. And now he sits meditating on the mountain-top, to understand the first step of the mystery of the universe, and shall come down to us briefly, every thousand years, as he crosses each step of that mystery.

Many of course rejected the myth that the gods came down to the old man to show him their wounds. How was it possible that the gods could be wounded!

But there were some who said that amongst all the gracious attributes of the gods, the noblest and highest was that of compassion. Surely the gods must have suffered wounds to know so much about compassion.

Many spoke about the old man who went to the mountains, alone, deserted by his followers. Not much of it went into Memory songs. But when Bharatji heard what the son of the old Chief of Chiefs had said he wanted his words to be woven in a Memory song—The Creator bleeds...bleeds when any of His Creatures bleed... Do not carry the sin of His blood!'

For the tribals who heaved a sigh of relief at being spared a life of slavery, it came as a surprise that Karkarta also meant that even their own slaves, the ones they held, were freed. It was a heavy price to pay but they had been prepared for worse.

The contrast, however, was glaring—that tribal lands should be free from slavery, with not a single slave, while Bharat's own clan still held its slaves as Karkarta could not interfere with the existing privileges and property of his own clan. In the tribal land, he had no such limitations as their Chief of Chiefs.

The tribals, who had to give up their slaves, felt that their new Chief had favoured the clan of his origin. Bharat's clan, on the other hand, was convinced that he had favoured the tribals.

Drupatta told Bharat, 'Since both sides have a silent grievance against you, surely you must have done something right.'

But the grievance was not that silent. Many in Bharat's clan complained loudly and harshly that he had interfered with their traditional right to enslave tribals when victory was won on the battlefield.

Bharat insisted that victory came not on the battlefield, but later, on the hill, when the tribals made peace and extended their hand of friendship.

'We could have annihilated them,' cried a Council member. 'And we should have. Their entire race should have been wiped out.'

Dhrupatta intervened, 'Then we would not have had a single slave; so why complain!'

There were those who laughed but Bharat did not. He faced his accuser directly and asked, 'For this evil of annihilating another race, that your words contemplate, who will bear the responsibility? He who leads our people or the entire Hindu clan? To whose karma (action) will it be accounted? Who shall suffer its consequences? I must know, if I am ever to lead our people in battle again. The entire clan must know if ever it has to go into battle again.'

Dhrupatta looked at Bharat in admiration. Trust him to change a political discussion into an argument on the role of gods and man's karma. But he nodded vigorously, as if moved by his words. Karkarta, however, had not finished and asked, 'But what exactly is your complaint? That I denied you the opportunity to grow fat and lazy by holding a few more slaves! That tribal lands are not open to your greed and exploitation! For that, you prefer that I should have rejected the hand of peace and friendship which the tribes offered!'

Now with contempt he continued, 'The pity is that not many of you know the value to place on peace. This discussion must therefore continue in an open assembly of the people of the clan.'

The threat was obvious. The Karkarta wanted a public debate. He would appeal to the people directly. The vast majority of the clan did not own slaves and had no intention of grabbing tribal lands. Many in the clan had often to enlist as soldiers in campaigns against tribals and go through the mud, filth, blood and horror of war. They had shouldered a heavy burden of bloodshed, fury and destruction from constant raids by tribals. They had sufficient common sense to realize that the idea of annihilating all tribals was no more than a figment of the imagination. Surely, in that rough terrain with impassable barriers and hidden caves, tribals could again amass large armies to lead future attacks. People wanted peace. And surely they would shout down the Council if it stood in the way of Karkarta's plan for lasting peace.

Nandan, who had led the critics, suddenly found himself in a conciliatory mood. He needed time to persuade and influence people to reject the idea of a union with the tribals. He felt he would succeed eventually, given time to mount a campaign against it; and he said, 'We are mature men; we represent people; we respect Bharatji. What he has done is no doubt with the best intentions for the good of us all. Time will tell what the future holds in store for us. We are in any case to meet tomorrow. The night will give us counsel. It would of course be unthinkable that a matter be referred to the people before the Council fully debates the issues.'

The discussion would have ended there for the day with an ominous threat looming the next day, except for the loud voice of Devdatta.

Devdatta belonged to no party and had no affiliations, for above all, he admired reason and logic. 'Our Karkarta Bharatji,' said Devdatta, 'leads our people by the power of his intelligence, his reason and his charisma. But the most intelligent men can sometimes be wrong. Is he not wrong when he says that he has not interfered with traditional rights? True, he has not interfered with the rights of our clan. But has he not interfered with the traditional rights of the tribal people by depriving them of their slaves?'

Karkarta's critics waited for his answer. Devdatta was nobody's friend and nobody's enemy, but his question held a glimmer of hope. If tribals could hold on to their slaves, surely the clan could contrive to purchase those very slaves from the tribals at nominal prices!

Quietly Bharatji replied, 'That action I took as the Chief of Chiefs of the tribal people and not as Karkarta of our clan, and it cannot be questioned in this Council.'

'Very true,' responded Devdatta, as if pleased with the answer. 'I take it, then, that our clan will not control tribals and their lands.'

Bharat saw the trap. Or was it an invitation? 'Our clan will control the tribes and their land only to the extent that the tribals will control the land and the people of our clan.' Bharat replied. He had not thought about it at all. There had been no time, but quickly he added, 'I foresee a unity of the two peoples, not domination by one or the other. I also visualize a joint Council and a joint Assembly, where both our clan and the tribes are represented with equal rights.'

'Good,' Devdatta responded graciously. 'As I said, even the most intelligent men can sometimes be wrong—and indeed I was wrong in this case.' He smiled, and Bharat weakly answered his smile, while Devdatta continued.

'I feared that there might be an intention to keep tribals as a subject race under our domination. But you, Karkarta, are honourable as always, and I salute you for combining the interests of the tribes and of our clan into one unified interest, from which all can benefit.'

Nandan seethed with anger. The empty compliment of Devdatta to Karkarta meant nothing to him, but it enraged him that Bharat should arrogate to himself the power to act as Chief of Chiefs of the tribals, without the clan's control, as though the tribal defeat was his own personal victory and not of the entire clan. And how could Karkarta even dream of bringing those barbarians into the clan Council and Assembly with equal rights!

All eyes turned to Nandan, as he shouted, 'Listen, Karkarta....'

But Devdatta raised his hand and interrupted Nandan, 'Nandanji, wait for your turn. I have not yet yielded the floor to you.'

Nandan glared but sat down, hoping that perhaps Devdatta had something sensible to say, and his earlier complimentary words to Karkarta were merely to soften him for the fierce, final blow; everyone knew that Devdatta was not a respector of persons, not even of Karkarta.

Devdatta's voice was now soft, even mournful, and he said, 'I should have said this at the very outset, but I did not know the direction in which the Council discussions were to proceed. However, I must say it now, that this meeting is clearly out of order.'

Devdatta was not in the habit of raising points of order. Everyone wondered. The meeting was being held on the fourth day of the moon-month, as usual. The quorum was there, with only two Council Chiefs out of the seventy-seven missing; even galleries for headmen and spectators were over-crowded. Not that headmen and spectators counted towards the quorum.

Bharat did not respond to the challenge. He waited for Devdatta to explain his point of order, though in his mind flashed the silent question as if to ask Devdatta: 'What are you up to now, old fox?'

Devdatta continued, 'It has always been the practice that when the Council discusses a question affecting some special interests of a particular group, that group is invited to participate in the discussions, even though it has no right to vote. For instance, when a question affects farmers, their guild is invited to participate. We do the same with hunters, fishermen, artisans, teachers, singers, painters, sculptors, builders and others. Regrettably, I do not see at this meeting, the representatives....'

Nandan was livid with rage. What was Devdatta saying? Obviously, that the tribals should have been called to the meeting! He must not be allowed to even utter that impossible, preposterous demand. No, he must be silenced before he infects others with that dangerous thought.

'What idiocy is this!' Nandan thundered. 'What sheer, utter nonsense are we indulging in! Have we lost all sense, all reason, all sense of proportion? Is this a Council of Chiefs or is it a meeting of jokers, buffoons and comics! If tribals can come and participate, why, tomorrow you will ask that slaves should also participate in the Council!' Nandan paused, choking over his words in fury.

Devdatta was looking at him in amazed silence and gently said, 'Nandanji, your habit of interrupting and speaking out of turn grows tiresome. Even if Karkarta does not call you to order out of the goodness of his heart, you must try to curb it.'

Devdatta continued, 'I did not speak of inviting slaves to participate, though I must say that if ever they came into the Council, much more sense would be spoken at our meetings.'

'But you spoke of the tribals,' Nandan shot back. 'Tribals in the Council of the clan!'

'Did I?' Devdatta asked innocently and looked directly at Karkarta, whose task it was as presiding officer to clarify any doubts about the proceedings. But Karkarta did not clarify; he was still wondering what was in Devdatta's mind.

'No,' Devdatta continued, 'I did not ask that tribals be invited to this meeting. Nandanji has the gift of looking into the future, and I shall certainly look forward to the participation of the tribals in future joint Councils and Assemblies. But for the moment my concerns are of a different kind, and I beg that I may be permitted to speak without interruption.'

Bharat nodded; Devdatta resumed, 'This meeting, I take it, was to discuss questions of war and peace with the tribals. Am I correct?'

Again Karkarta nodded. Devdatta looked as though he felt immensely encouraged by Karkarta's nod and continued, 'Whenever a special problem that affects a particular group is taken up in the Council, I know that you, Karkarta, yourself take pains to invite persons from that group to speak for them. I remember, last year, you postponed a discussion on the location of temples because the purohits had not been invited, in spite of our claim that the gods speak to us as clearly or unclearly as they speak to purohits and priests. It is with this in view that I confess that I am mystified that this meeting should be unrepresented by those who are primarily concerned. You understand my difficulty, Karkarta?'

Karkarta did not understand but did not wish to say so. Yet he had to respond, as Devdatta waited for an answer.

'This meeting,' Karkarta began with hesitation, 'is to consider questions related to the war concluded with the tribals and the issue of achieving a lasting peace with them. Tribals, of course, cannot be invited here until a joint Council of our clan and the tribes is established.

For the rest, the issue is general, of war and peace, and surely no special interests of any particular group are involved.'

'No!' Devdatta challenged. 'How many in this Council have lost their sons in successive wars with tribals? I ask because my impression is that when battles take place, not only are the Councillors faraway from the scene of battle but also their sons. Somehow, they are all engaged in important, clan-building activities, at the greatest possible distance from the fields where arrows fly and blood flows.'

Devdatta paused to catch his breath, 'I must ask, for I have carried on my shoulders the coffins of my three sons who died in battle, and I assure you that there is no load which is heavier than a father carrying the body of his son, towards the funeral pyre.

'And those who have lit fires at the funeral pyre of their sons know that that fire does not lighten your burden; nor does it illumine the darkness of despair in your heart; no, the fire mocks at you and even promises to return to consume more of your sons, perhaps in the hope that when all your sons are consumed, there will somehow be an end to the madness in your minds that seeks war, instead of peace.'

Devdatta's voice rose as he continued. 'Would you, Karkarta, take a roll call and ask how many Council members have lost their sons in the battlefield? If they have not, how are they qualified to speak of war and peace? Have you Karkarta, yourself, lost a son in the war?'

Quietly Bharat replied, 'No, I have not.' He did not add that his sons were too young for battle. Nor did he add that his own father died in battle when he himself was a child. But then Devdatta knew that. He was one of those who had carried his father's coffin on the last, mournful journey.

Devdatta continued, 'I spoke of my tears for my sons, but I speak also for those who lost their husbands and for the tears of those who lost their fathers when they were children.' His eyes caressed Bharat and now his voice rose, 'But I must deny that the Council alone can speak for the tears of the clan. Let us recognize that a special interest exists: of widows who lost their husbands to those dreadful wars, of children who lost their fathers, and of fathers who. . . lit the funeral pyres of their sons.

'Let that special interest be invited if the question of war is to be debated again. Let them tell you what is in their hearts; then see if what they say penetrates into the heads of those who never had to shed their tears for the loss of their loved ones.'

This was the first time that anyone had seen or heard Devdatta display emotion or speak with passion. He was usually cool and collected, speaking always to the point, in the fewest possible words, and with the calmness of reason and logic. When Devdatta finally sat down, weary, perspiring and drained, he himself wondered how he had strayed so far from his usual self-controlled and disciplined reasoning.

At a later stormy session the preachers demanded that the tribals not be considered Hindus. Devdatta then said, 'How can the horizons of our God be bounded by the limits of our clan! Do we or do we not worship a universal God? Or is it that we have rejected the God of the Universe in favour of a local god whose boundaries reach the limit of a stone's-throw?'

Bharat thanked Devdatta for interceding and was met with, 'Thank me by all means Bharatji! But in my heart there is anguish for the insult to our land.'

'What insult?' Bharat asked with concern.

'The tribal land today is known as the "Land of the Free", for you abolished slavery there. But here, in the land of your birth and mine, it flourishes. Is that not an insult? Tell me, you who always think of the future, what will the coming ages say of us?'

'They will say that in our midst lived a man of honour like Devdatta who sought to right a wrong and showed the true path.'

'Flatterer, flatterer! No wonder people love and admire you.'

'And I,' Bharat replied, 'love and admire you.'

'Then I shall die happy.'

'No, you shall live happily,' Bharat said. But both knew that Devdatta suffered from a terminal sickness from which there was no escape. His physician gave him eighteen months to two years.

'Perhaps,' said Devdatta, 'I shall do you one last favour after I die. You do need someone to intercede for you in the world beyond.'

'I need someone to intercede for me here.'

'You! You who are the Karkarta of our clan! You who are the Chief of Chiefs of the tribals! You need someone to intercede for you here?'

Bharat smiled, for he knew that Devdatta despite his heavy irony understood what was in his heart. Even so, he said, 'So much is being said by so many and so often against equal rights to tribals. Preachers, slave-owners, their hirelings, oh, so many—they are just out to mislead, misguide and inflame!'

'Surely our people will know what is right and wrong!'

'How will our people understand! Who is to silence the thousand voices that are raised throughout the land calling for vengeance! In their fury, those voices rise far above the soft and gentle murmurings of those few who urge mercy, compassion and brotherhood. How then will our people understand? Through a miracle? By a vision? From a dream? By inspiration?'

Devdatta did not reply. Bharat smiled ruefully and continued, 'No, my friend, I need people to intercede here. A Karkarta is powerless unless the power of his people is behind him.'

Their eyes held each other and Devdatta said quietly, 'I think I shall intercede for you on this earth itself.'

Bharat smiled politely but had no idea what Devdatta intended.

When they parted, somehow, Bharat had the impression that Devdatta walked away erect, with the light, precise steps of a soldier.

Devdatta died two months later, far from his home. All this time he had been on the road, night and day, through mud, slush and rain, speaking of the moral and spiritual need to unite with the tribals as Hindus, under the One Supreme; and to strengthen Karkarta's attempts to achieve union with tribal lands, based on peace, friendship and goodwill.

Sadly, Bharat reminisced over his last conversation with Devdatta when they had spoken of the need for peace and unity with the tribals. Devdatta had offered to help. Bharat's response had been polite. But how could he know the lengths to which Devdatta would go, at the cost of his fragile health!

Bharat questioned the Vaid. 'Why was Devdatta allowed such a journey?'

'He was a law unto himself,' the Vaid replied. 'I did not even know where he had gone and when and why. He squandered away his life in two months, when he could have lived for two years.'

No, Bharat said, Devdatta died like a soldier, on the battlefield, for a cause bigger than life. No, he did not squander away his life as the Vaid said. He lived it to the full. Yet Bharat's sadness remained.

Bharat was informed of Devdatta's dying wish—that his ashes be immersed in Sindhu river by the side of villages that he was not able to visit; and on immersion, someone should repeat his words calling for peace and unity with the tribal lands and add, 'I have not lived long enough to tell the truth to all, but let those who love the truth speak out, and if they shall not, let my dead ashes speak for me, not only to confound those that lie, but also to accuse those who, knowing better, fail to speak.'

Devdatta was right, Bharat thought. Mercy and goodness must speak out for themselves and only then can they silence the thousand evil tongues who for ever try to cloud and overwhelm the truth. It is not enough to have truth and honour on our side. One must fight for them. There is guilt in silence.

Devdatta is not dead, Bharat said to himself, for a hundred living tongues now speak with his voice and carry his message throughout the land. Devdatta's voice, even though he was no more, began to be heard in every nook and corner of the clan from those hundreds who carried his ashes; and people listened with respect.

'Ultimately,' Bharat said to Dhrupatta, 'the voice of truth will prevail. People will respond to Devdatta's appeal.'

'Maybe so,' Dhrupatta replied. 'Or maybe not. It may well be that people love to listen to the voices of the dead. Not many listened to Devdatta while he lived, but now that he is dead they possibly think that he spoke with the combined wisdom of all the sages and rishis of the past. I am sure that if I were to end my life now, people would consider me too amongst the wisest on this earth, which of course I am, even though not many are aware of it, at present.'

'I certainly know the extent of your wisdom,' Bharat responded cheerfully. 'But to test your theory of people's reaction, would it not be worthwhile for you to end your life now?'

'And deprive you of my constant advice! Never; I love you too much to do you that ill turn. Enough for me that you and I know of my wisdom.'

'Enough, if one of us knows of it.'

But Bharat was wrong to believe that people were willing to agree to a union with the tribals. His adversaries had mounted a widespread campaign throughout the clan against the tribals. It was so easy to excite people, play on their fears, rouse their hatred, and remind them of past tribal savagery. Preachers, always ready to be hired, went round. Stakes were high. Slave-owners, land-owners and the rich, mighty and influential had much to lose. Even ordinary people understood that equality for the tribals meant that the Hindu clan would have to spend a lot on their welfare. Why—asked preachers—why do we sacrifice our comforts and benefits for those that sought to violate our lands and people? Is it not the right time to compensate each family in the clan for the past depradation of raiders? Think not then of union with the tribals; instead let each family demand from Karkarta what they have lost from the havoc wreaked by the tribals. Think of your loved ones that died battling against them! Did your loved ones die in vain! The blood your loved ones shed matters no more to you! How can we be one with these savages and bring their corruption into our midst? No, they are a race apart, and we need neither them nor their gods, but only just and honourable reprisals for the havoc they caused us in years past.

Bharat knew that in the Council and Assembly he had sufficient strength to win acceptance for union with the tribals, even though the number of adversaries had grown. Yet he said, 'I shall not impose this decision on the people; they shall be the ones to decide.'

His adversaries laughed. They were certain that views among guilds and people had hardened against the tribals.

When Bharat spoke, he said little about the need to protect the tribals and treat them as equals. Instead, he was lost in a day-dream.

He was trying to recall the stories which Yadodhara's father, Ekantra, had told him in his childhood, of the birth of Hinduism and of the dreams and hopes of the ancient Hindus. He recalled Devdatta's words on his last journey. He remembered his conversations with Muni at the rocks. What Ekantra had said, what Devdatta had declared and what Muni had told him were no different from the ancient songs of Hindus, sung during the time that they called themselves people of the Sanathana Dharma, and even earlier, in the pre-ancient times of Sanathana.

For himself, Bharat had no more doubts. He was no longer overwhelmed by uncertainty. He realized he had understood the essence of the Hindu way of life.

As he spoke, there was no hesitation in his words, no effort, no groping. The words came out in a torrent; and later, a once-blind singer composed a song to commemorate Bharat's words on the occasion. It was called the 'Song of the Hindu'.

The 'Song of the Hindu' was heard in all the villages of the clan. To recite it fully, one needed time from sunset to midnight. But plainly and simply, it said what the ancients had always said:

'Our desires have grown immeasurable. But they should be desires to give, not merely to receive, to accept and not to reject; to honour and respect, not to deny or belittle. . . .
'God's gracious purpose includes all human beings and all creation. . . .
'For God is the Creator; and God is the Creation. . . .
'Each man has his own stepping stones to reach the One Supreme. . . .
'God's grace is withdrawn from no one; not even from those who have chosen to withdraw from God's grace. . . .
'How does it matter what idols they worship or what images they bow to, so long as their conduct remains pure . . . .
'It is conduct then—theirs and ours—that needs to be purified. . . .
'There can be no compulsion; each man must be free to worship his gods as he chooses . . . .
'Does every Hindu worship all the gods of all the Hindus? No, he has a free will; a free choice . . . .
'A Hindu may worship Agni and ignore other deities. Do we deny that he is a Hindu? . . .
'Another may worship God, through an idol of his choosing. Do we deny that he is a Hindu? . . .
'Yet another will find God everywhere and not in any image or idol. Is he not a Hindu? . . .
'He who was Karkarta before me was a sun-worshipper. Did the worshippers of Shiva ever say that he was not a good Hindu? . . .
'Do the worshippers of Vishnu feel that he who worships before the image of Brahma is not a Hindu?. . .
'How can a scheme of salvation be limited to a single view of God's nature and worship?. . .
'Is God then not an all-loving universal God?
'Clearly then, he who seeks to deny protection to another on the basis of his faith offends against the Hindu way of

life and denies an all-loving God....

'Those who love their own sects, idols and images more than the truth, will end up loving themselves more than their gods....

'In the Kingdom of God, there is no high and low. The passion for perfection burns equally in all, for there is only one class even as there is only one God....

'The Hindu way of life?....Always it has been and always it shall be...that God wills a rich harmony—not a colourless uniformity....

'A Hindu must enlarge the heritage of mankind ....

'For a Hindu is not a mere preserver of custom ....

'For a Hindu is not a mere protector of present knowledge ....

'Hinduism is a movement, not a position; a growing tradition and not a fixed revelation....

'A Hindu must grow and evolve with all that was good in the past, with all that is good in the present and with all goodness that future ages shall bring ....

'Yet he remains a Hindu ....

'Hinduism is a law of life, not a dogma; its aim is not to create a creed but character, and its goal is to achieve perfection through spiritual knowledge which rejects nothing and yet refines everything, through continuous testing and experience....

'Yet he must remain strong and united, for a Hindu must know that no external, outside force can ever crush him, except when he himself is divided and betrays his own....

'What then is the final goal of the Hindu? Through strength, unity, discipline, selfless work, to reach the ultimate in being, ultimate in awareness and ultimate in bliss, not for himself alone, but for all....

'This was the silent pledge that our ancient ancestors had taken, when they called themselves the Hindu....

'If I cannot abide by the pledge, how can I retain the right to call myself a Hindu?'

Bharat smiled at the last words in the song—he knew how the ancients had come to call themselves 'Hindu.'

There was hardly anything in the 'Song of the Hindu' about the need to protect tribals or to achieve a union with them. Bharat's adversaries saw nothing ominous in it. To them, it was simply an irrelevancy to restate the basic beliefs of the Hindu. Perhaps, Bharat had nothing else to say—they thought—so he chose to be irrelevant.

Yet, contrary to every expectation, overwhelmingly, people supported the union with the tribals when the time came to vote. Why?—asked Bharat's adversaries. Amongst the main reasons that most gave was the influence of the 'Song of the Hindu'. Though the song had little to do with the tribals it had challenged their inner faith.

A Union with the tribes was achieved with equal rights, equal protection and representation in the Council and Assembly. The expanded Council and Assembly came to be known simply as 'The Parliament of Hindu'.

Bharatjogi arrested his wandering thoughts and smiled as he saw Gatha approaching. 'I hope I did not interrupt your prayers, Master,' Gatha said.

'No, I am glad you have come.'

But Gatha's expression of gloom persisted and he said, 'They want to build a huge temple for Sindhu Putra in the village.'

'A huge temple for that little infant?'

Gatha nodded and Bharat said, 'Gatha, your people have to understand that the infant is not a god.'

Gatha nodded again. Of course he knew that the little one was not yet a god but was the son of Mother Goddess Sindhu brought by her to walk on this earth. Godhood would come later by the grace of his mother, when he was older.

Gatha broke the silence, saying, 'It is to be a large temple—the biggest in the land.'

Bharat smiled. Dreams cost nothing. Large temples were however expensive. He said so.

But Gatha assured him, 'Money is not the problem.'

'No!' Bharat asked. He had thought that everyone with the ambition to build a temple always needed money.

Gatha assured him, 'Money is there. Plenty. More than enough.'

'You have some hidden treasure in the village?'

'No, someone will pay for it all; a...a lady...a woman...a female.'

Bharat wondered over the confusion in Gatha's words but ignored it. 'Well,' Bharat said, 'even if you have the money, the question is: should not this money be put to better use? Why a large temple for a little infant!'

But the question troubling Gatha was different. 'About the lady...the woman, who is giving money for the temple, some have asked: is it not inauspicious to build a temple with her money?'

'Why? Who is she?'

Bharat was told at last that it was a prostitute who was donating fabulous amounts for the temple. His memory raced back. A long time ago, when he was the Karkarta, it was a headman who had complained that a whore had set up a field for the grazing of elderly cows. He had silenced the headman by saying that he must be complimented for creating an atmosphere in which even sinners felt compelled to perform saintly acts.

Just moments earlier Bharat had been determined to persuade Gatha to give up the idea of a temple. For he had seen no evidence of godhood in the infant. All he could think of was that somehow the mother of the infant had found herself in a boat. There, prematurely, the baby was born. Was she running away from someone? Or to someone? Why? Where?—he did not know. All he knew was that she had died and the baby lived; and a sudden gust of wind swept her boat away and the baby was left with him. How did that confer godhood on the infant? Gatha, he knew, had affection, even reverence, for him and treated his every wish as a command. But he ceased to listen when Bharat questioned Sindhu Putra's divinity. Even so, he had made up his mind to try to dissuade Gatha from having a temple to honour the babe.

However, now that Bharat heard the thoughtless objection against a prostitute donating for a temple his perspective changed. Why should the villagers object?

'What is the name of the woman?' Bharat asked, wondering if it was the same woman who had established the cow-field.

'Kanta.' Gatha informed him. The name meant nothing to Bharat. He was wondering: what is it that motivates a person of such a questionable trade to donate to God's work!

Gatha saw Bharat in deep thought. Perhaps his old master was against accepting a donation from a prostitute. Maybe he was even offended at the idea. Many others in the village had also objected. Still, he hazarded his question. 'We should refuse, Master?'

'Refuse what!' Bharat asked, startled.

'Her donation for the temple,' Gatha said, unhappily. 'Many have said we should refuse. Even Mahantji.'

'Tell your villagers that God would never refuse an offering made with love; tell them that they lack the right to dictate to God whose offering He shall accept, and whose offering He shall reject. Tell your Mahantji that if he aspires to be a man of God, he should develop a little more compassion and charity.'

Gatha looked sad, wondering how he was to say such terrible things to Mahantji. Bharat misunderstood his expression and asked, 'But tell me, are you also against Kanta?'

'Me? No. I like her. I am fond of her. I...I....' He blushed and said no more. He did not want to say that he used to pass a night of pleasure with Kanta, once a month.

'I am glad,' Bharat said. 'God's goodness and mercy shall reach her. Whatever her sins, there are no sins that God cannot forgive. And tell your villagers to object no more, for God's grace is denied to none. If they doubt your word, tell them plainly that it is the message from the father of Sindhu Putra.'

Gatha beamed. This was the first time that Bharatji had acknowledged Sindhu Putra as his earthly son. He had even shown enthusiasm over a temple intended for Sindhu Putra. Obviously then, Bharatji had no doubt about the godhood of Sindhu Putra, despite all his disclaimers.

'Do something for me?' Bharat asked. 'Say to Kanta that I honour her pious thought to build the temple. Say that in the presence of everyone. But privately tell her that I request that she give up her profession. And even if she has a compelling reason, she should try and somehow God will show her the way.'

'I will so order her.'

'No, let it be my request. It is for her to decide.'

'As you wish, Master.'

'No. As she wishes,' Bharat clarified, leaving no room for doubt.

'...Hear then how our river was called the Sindhu, and how our people came to call themselves Hindu....'

'...The past always clings to us. We may seek to renounce it but it does not renounce us. The body moves away from the past but the spirit is interwoven with it.... Yes, it is the past that comes to us in the garb of today, tomorrow, infinity and beyond....'

—(From Ekantra's Story—5131 BC)

'...And this oath binds not only us and our descendants, but all who may hereafter enter this land of the Sindhu through various pathways.
'...Let those who so enter this land in future swear also enternal loyalty to this land and its people or for ever remain out and away.
'...For he who enters here, and does not so swear, or he who having sworn violates his oath, let him and his seed be for ever accursed;
'...And for ourselves and for those that follow, we declare, that he who is disloyal to this land and its people, denies his own soul and betrays his own gods.
'...Mother Goddess Sindhu! Be then you the witness to this our oath, for ourselves and for those who enter this land after us. Chastise them and their seed for ever, if ever they fail to take this oath, or having taken it, deny or violate it.'

—(From an oath administered by Chief of 108 Hindu Tribes, to his people, after their entry into the land of Sindhu, 7000 BC)

'...This thread that binds 108 beads to represent our 108 Hindu tribes is washed in the waters of Sindhu. It is the sacred *thread of Sanathana Dharma ...to unite in a single bond all Hindu tribes with this land and its people. ...Remember among the highest virtues is the virtue of unity; and he who seeks to divide us or betray us denies his own soul.'*

—(Declaration by the old Chief of 108 Hindu Tribes—7000 BC)

The Name of My People

Gatha had just left. Bharatjogi was about to sit down on his prayer-mat, but he was in no mood to pray. Instead, he wanted to recapture the thread of the past memories he had been pursuing before Gatha arrived—how did his clan come to call itself 'Hindu'?

Amongst Bharat's friends, it was Suryata who first raised the question about the origin of the Hindu. The three friends—Suryata, Bharat and Yadodhra—were relaxing in a field, watching six elephants guzzling sugar-cane. Suryata was then nine years old, Bharat, a few months younger, and Yadodhra was eight. The field belonged to Yadodhra's father, Ekantra, now a hermit.

Ekantra lived in a large cave in a nearby forest. Often, he would be travelling around to meet other hermits, sadhus and munis. Everyone knew that the last part of life's road, as a hermit, had to be walked in single file, in prayer and meditation. But Yadodhra's father had different views; and he always travelled in style, carrying home-made food, fruits, candles, herbs and much more, which he freely distributed to other hermits. Wherever he went, he took his six elephants. When he returned to his cave, the elephants roamed free, except in the first week. During that first week the elephants would proceed to Ekantra's family home, tap gently with their trunks—enough to rouse everyone but not to break the door. The elephants would then move to the river to play in the water where Yadodhra's mother would also come to give them a brisk rub-down with a brush of pine needles and herbal soap. Thereafter, the elephants would proceed to the sugar-cane field for an extended meal. Finally, one of them would carry Yadodhra's mother to the forest-cave, while the others would be loaded with the provisions that had to be taken to the cave for Ekantra's needs and comfort. His wife would remain with her husband for two or three days, and sometimes she would take Yadodhra to the cave as well.

What kind of a hermit is he, some asked. Should a hermit so pamper himself with luxuries and even family visits! But Yadodhra's father was truly unique. There was no social obligation on him to be a hermit. He was less then forty years old and refused to believe that a hermit must necessarily lead an austere life.

The then Karkarta, Suryakarma, who was Suryata's father, was annoyed. He had fixed ideas about how a hermit should conduct himself and he spoke to Yadodhra's mother to protest against her husband's life-style. A hermit, Karkarta Suryakarma insisted, represented the soul of the entire people and its great ideals. It is essential, therefore, for a hermit to attain spiritual freedom and not be tempted by riches, attachments or family loyalties.

Yadodhra's mother listened to Karkarta Suryakarma with respect and agreed with every word he uttered. Why not! They both had a common aim—up to a point—to change Ekantra's lifestyle. Suryakarma wanted Ekantra to be a better hermit, while she wanted him to cease being a hermit so that he might return to her.

'Karkarta, you must speak to him,' she urged.

'I! I was hoping that you would speak to him.'

'You know well a wife's vow never to interfere with her hermit-husband.' Actually, she had never taken that vow. Ekantra had told her, 'Do what your heart pleases'—and it always pleased her to interfere with her hermit-husband in small ways.

Karkarta nodded in sympathy. But she had not finished. 'Yet the words you uttered are such as to tempt a wife to break her vow, for there is truth in your words, and truth must never be suppressed, though a vow also must never be broken. Clearly then, you must speak to him, lest a wife is encouraged by your words to break her vow.'

Suryakarma stared at her. Somewhere, in her words, he was sure there was a flaw, though he could not readily put his finger on it.

Ekantra's wife continued. 'You will visit my husband and tell him what it is your duty to tell him, will you not?'

Miserably, Karkarta nodded. How could he as Karkarta ignore the challenge of duty! She certainly was a woman of sense, because she had agreed with every word he said. Clearly also, she was a woman of piety, who would never break a vow of non-interference with her hermit-husband. He promised, 'In due season, I shall visit Ekantra.'

It may have been a private conversation, but how can there be privacy about a public figure! Yadodhra's mother saw to it that everyone knew of Karkarta's promise. Many volunteered to join Karkarta to see for themselves the opulence in which the hermit was reputed to live.

Yadodhra's mother had promised to take her son to her husband during Karkarta's visit—and when he asked if his friends, Suryata and Bharat could join him, she agreed. The more children her husband sees, the better to bring into his heart the nostalgia to return home. If Karkarta had an objection to his own son Suryata joining the party, she quickly silenced it, 'Your child and my child must know the voice of truth as you shall speak, and they who have their lives to live must be given the chance to be guided by your words of infinite wisdom.'

*

'And what did they say?' Yadodhra and Bharat asked Suryata while they watched elephants munching sugar-cane. Suryata was speaking about the question he had asked his father and uncles—where did the name 'Hindu' come from?

'But what did they say?' Yadodhra asked again.

Suryata ignored them and spoke instead to the elephants, 'Utu, Utu, Utu.' Quickly, at the familiar command, the friendly elephants interrupted their eating and raised their trunks.

'That was the response of my father and uncles,' replied Suryata, pointing to the raised trunks of the silent elephants. They laughed, knowing that elders generally point to the sky when faced with a question on the origin of 'Hindu'.

'Maybe,' Yadodhra said, 'my father will tell us all.'

'Would he know?' Suryata asked. Yadodhra gave him a withering look. His father, he was certain, knew everything.

Riding majestically on the elephants, the three children and Yadodhra's mother reached Ekantra's cave. Karkarta and his entourage were to travel more humbly by carts and horses, and the last few steps on foot, as is only fitting when one approaches a hermit.

Ekantra's wife told her husband to expect Karkarta in a day or two—not only Karkarta but a large entourage of fifty. He sighed and said, 'Yes, wolves always band together. They do not roam singly through forests.' In dismay, his wife indicated Karkarta's son Suryata with her eyes. But Suryata had not heard. He was curiously exploring the cave along with Bharat and Yadodhra.

It was a large cave, cut into rocks, which led to other smaller and larger caves, some of which went deeper underground. 'Did you make all these?' Suryata asked Ekantra, referring to the caves. Ekantra shook his head and explained that the entire cave-complex was an ancient miracle of nature and man working together. In the centuries gone by, many had apparently laboured long and hard to make the cave-structure habitable. At several points the ancients had cut into rocks to construct tunnels to lead from one cave to the other, along the platforms, canopies, projections, overhanging shelters and a network of ramps and stairs.

Ekantra claimed to having discovered no more than the cave-complex. Even credit for that discovery he would pass on to his little puppy dog, his elephants and an unknown squirrel. His dog was chasing the squirrel in the cluster of rocks. 'Crazy squirrel,' Ekantra had thought. 'Why can't he just climb a tree and call off the chase!' But soon, he heard his dog's agonized yapping. The dog had caught himself in a slit in the rock, behind which the squirrel disappeared. In his rush, the dog got his body halfway into the narrow opening, but was stuck, unable to go forward or get back. Ekantra tried to pull him out, but the dog got into a panic and its body seemed to expand with his quick, frightened breathing; in terror, it squeezed in and was entirely behind the opening. Ekantra put his hand through the crack; the dog licked his hand, but there was no way in which he could guide the dog out through the narrow opening; he would have to get men and tools to break into the rock to make the hole large enough for the dog to come out. He was about to mount his elephant to go for help, but the elephant ignored him and went to the rock to pry out a piece from it. He was unable but kept trying. 'Crazy squirrel, crazy dog, crazy elephant!' Ekantra cried. It was obvious to him that the elephant could achieve nothing, as the rock with the crach was not separate from the entire rock-complex itself and merely the work of nature. The elephant looked at Ekantra as though he wanted to reason with him, but then changed its mind—possibly realizing that humans didn't have that much understanding—and trumpeted his call to the five elephants who had remained below. Ekantra recognized it as a distress call and the five elephants quickly responded, their gait no longer majestic or stately but hurried and concerned. They paused, only mementarily, as though to consult amongst themselves, before taking up positions along the rock. How they arranged their huge forms so that the maximum pressure of each elephant should be directed at one spot, did not surprise Ekantra. What surprised him was that they should engage in such a futile exercise. He was worried that two of the elephants who had perched themselves higher on the slippery slope might fall and even collide with the elephants below. But he was wrong on all counts. The huge boulder—almost a rock in itself—was not a part of the original rock-complex. The elephants pried it loose and began balancing their pressure so that it should come down gradually and not fall headlong. Ekantra watched with surprise as it gently came down. The dog rushed out. He was quickly scooped up by the elephant who had organized the rescue. The elephant held him aloft in his trunk, ignoring its protests. The dog had forgotten the squirrel, but quite clearly blamed the elephant and Ekantra for not preventing his misadventure; in any case, the dog did not hold the grudge for long, and after briefly barking to complain, he went into Ekantra's lap. When the dust that rose from the fall of the boulder had settled, Ekantra scrutinized it. The elephants were not fooled; nor should he have been, he realized. Looking closely, he found it had the same texture and appearance, but there was a slight difference in its grass and weed-growth as compared to the rest of the rock cluster. Where did this huge boulder come from? Who brought it to block the cave-entrance? Why? When? And how many pairs of hands were needed to bring it there? These were questions which Ekantra could not answer. But what he could do was to bring almost an army of workmen to clean the caves of dust and debris, to repair the man-made works inside the caves, and to protect all pieces of art, statues, carvings and paintings there.

Yadodhra had visited the caves often. But this was the first time that Bharat and Suryata were there. The night before they had merely been in the first cave, which served as living quarters. Ekantra took them to another cave, down the slope, to reach a kind of a huge indoor bathing pool, with hot water seeping from the earth, mixing with cold water coming from the side wall of the cave, and all of it together being evacuated from an opening in the floor. They bathed and played in the water until Yadodhra's mother called them for their meal.

They all had questions about water seeping from hot springs, cold water dripping from the walls, statues of unknown gods, interconnections between caves, and a host of other marvels, both natural and man-made, found there. Patiently, Ekantra answered all their questions.

Suddenly Suryata remembered Yadodhra's claim that his father could explain how the clan came to be called Hindu. He asked Ekantra, 'Why are we called Hindu? Did the name "Hindu" come from the sky?'

Gravely, Ekantra nodded, 'Yes.'

'From the sky! From God?'

'From the sky, yes. From God, no.' Ekantra replied. The children looked puzzled. Ekantra warned them that it would be a long story. The children were delighted with the 'threat'.

'Come,' Ekantra said. He picked up a burning torch and led the way. They entered a side cave. The entrance was low and narrow but the hall inside was large. Somehow there was more light in this cave than what a lone burning torch could achieve. It was almost like daylight, though cool and mellow. On the ceiling the children saw some shining dots reflecting light. They did not know what they were. The walls were covered with paintings, some faded, and others fresh and bright as though painted recently.

Ekantra began, 'Many centuries ago there were people who lived along the Sindhu River, where we now live. Some strangers, then, came to live with them. They came from lands far away. How far, nobody knew. They may not have been too far, though it took them a long time to reach Sindhu. They had come across trackless passes, rocks and, some say, mountains—and often they did not know where they were going. All they knew was that they had to leave their own barren lands, overtaken by severe storms, and then by drought and famine, while they were under constant, murderous raids from neighbouring tribes; and they were desperate to find some other place, with water and food. On the way, they met other tribes, in similarly miserable conditions. They joined each other and the procession continued.'

Ekantra paused and brought the burning torch near a faded painting, to show men, women and children on the long march. Many were lying on the way—some, exhausted from their trek, others possibly even dead. A child was crying over its mother's dead body, and some were consoling him, while others encouraged him to join the march. The arresting feature of the painting was the haunting sense of misery in the eyes of everyone.

Ekantra continued the story.

'It is said that in all 108 tribes joined the trek. Many died on the way, but the rest dragged themselves along. But how long they marched, no one knows! Most of the time they were famished, finding little to eat. Often, they lost their way over trackless passes and reached the place vacated earlier. One evening, they had given up hope, for they could not even find water to drink. It was then that the oldest among them all called on them to pray. While they were praying, some youngsters spotted a few birds resting from their migratory journey. All they had to do was to aim well with their slingshots and the tasty meat could be theirs. But the old man remonstrated, "No, you cannot kill while you pray. Attend to the Lord."

'They wanted to throw stones at the old man in anger, but he was a powerful man, so they remained silent, in the hope that the prayers would end soon, and the birds would not fly away.'

Ekantra put the torch in front of another painting. It showed people in prayer. Their eyes no longer held the earlier helpless feeling. The expression of some youngsters was in direct contrast, with their eyes half shut in prayer but their gaze directed at the birds sitting far away. The painting showed only seven birds at the edge, but the impression was that there were more birds beyond, unpainted.

Ekantra continued: 'The prayers ended but the birds flew away. The youngsters silently cursed their leader.

'But somehow their luck changed thereafter. That night it rained. Tired and famished they still were, but no longer thirsty. They slept that night with hope. At dawn, they suddenly heard a sound, which they could not immediately identify. It was soft and musical, coming directly overhead, through the clouds; and it echoed continuously, "Hin Hin Hin, Du Du Du". Three times they would hear this sound, followed quickly by the hurried refrain "Hin Du, Hin Du, Hin Du".

'As the clouds shifted, they saw that it was a pair of high flying jatayu birds. The male would sing "Hin Hin Hin" and the female would quickly respond "Du Du Du" in a singsong. This would go on three times and then the male would say "Hin," and swiftly the female would add "Du," and this too would go on three times—and after a pause, they would restart the song again.

'Now children, as you know, the jatayu is a rare bird. It was rare even then. As you also possibly know, jatayu birds have a long life and a female jatayu gives birth to only one offspring in her life. Thus their number has been dwindling over the years. And perchance, if one jatayu bird dies, its mate dies too within a day or two....'

'Why?' Suryata interrupted.

'I don't know, son.' Ekantra replied.

Yadodhra was never happy when his father confessed ignorance. In the years to come when Yadodhra became celebrated as a sage, he would remain silent whenever he did not know the answer; and people always regarded his silence as a sure indication of his profound knowledge. But now he spoke, 'Maybe, the bird stops eating after its mate dies.'

Ekantra was silent. It was his wife who spoke, 'Or, possibly, it finds it impossible to live without its mate. Some hearts break more easily than others.'

Ekantra was reflecting: maybe my wife is right. He knew that a male jatayu collected food for the female jatayu and fed her; likewise the female jatayu would collect food to feed him; neither of them would eat what it collected, and without the one, the other died; but why die so quickly if the mate dies, when jatayu birds can live without food for days on end! The hurt in the heart, perhaps!

Ekantra waved away the speculation and continued: 'And so rare is the jatayu bird, that not many see them. And the opportunity to hear them sing is far more rare. Normally, the birds fly in silence, without their singsong duet, for it is well-known that they sing only when their offspring is due to be born, and that means that they sing only for forty-four days in their entire life span of 150 years, when their egg is about to be hatched and their song is only to tell other jatayu birds of the location of their egg, so that if a mishap occurs other jatayu birds will look after their young one.'

Suryata interrupted again, 'That means there must be other jatayu birds in the vicinity?'

'Not necessarily. Maybe the wind carries the voice across tremendous distances. Or maybe their song remains frozen where it is sung, and when other jatayu birds fly in that area, they hear it.'

'But if the jatayu song remains always the same—"Hin Hin Hin, Du Du Du"—how could the song speak of the location of the egg! Would not each jatayu pair have its egg at a different place!'

Yadodhra replied before his father could answer, 'The secret may be in the inflection of the song; or its tone, or even how many times it is sung, or intervals between the end of one singing sequence and the beginning of another. Maybe that is how one jatayu bird understands the message of the other.'

Ekantra merely nodded and resumed the story: 'The old man leading the tribes was convinced that the sight and sound of these rare jatayu birds was a sign from the gods that all 108 tribes must continue their quest together.

'Again, they saw the jatayus flying ahead, but suddenly the birds changed direction. When the tribes reached the point at which the jatayu had turned, the old man urged his people also to turn like-wise. But everyone saw that the new route would be rocky and treacherous.

'It was here that members of some tribes parted, for they insisted on following the earlier route, which at least had some rain-clouds. They lacked the faith their leader had that the song of the jatayu was a sign from heaven. "Why," they asked, "would the mighty gods choose to send a message through a pair of birds who are cursed with begetting only a single offspring throughout their life?"

'But many shared the faith of the leader, and gladly they moved to the impassable terrain. For days they trudged along. It was when their feet were weary and their spirits flagging, that the song of the jatayu was heard again, though they could not see the birds. Some say that the birds were not there at all and it was only the imagination of their leader which infected the others.

'Be that as it may, they followed the direction from which the sound of the birds came. However, as they went, they could see that everything around them was bleak and barren, with no sign of life. Then once again the song of the birds was heard, faintly, fleetingly, from far away—and they went on.

'One night when they were resting, a young man from one tribe and a young woman from another, strayed farther to look for privacy. But suddenly, what they saw made them shout to everyone. Below, in the valley, they saw the shining moon. It was like the moon shining up in the sky. "Have we reached the middle of two worlds with one moon above and another below?" But their leader saw through the mystery—it was water below, reflecting the moon. They forgot their weariness. Water, at that moment, was more welcome than the presence of two moons, and they rushed to the valley, hoping that this was the promised land.

'It was not. The water did not come from a stream. It was rain water, collected in a depression of land. But it served their immediate needs. There were a few roots, grass, even frogs, worms, insects—for wherever there is water, be it stagnant or flowing, there is life.

'But they knew that soon they would have to go on. In what direction? They did not know. Meanwhile, they rested by the side of the life-giving pool, which was fast depleting, as no fresh rain came.

'The leader sent 108 scouts on a futile search for signs of life elsewhere. Still, all the 108 tribes were represented in that motley multitude. The leader hardly slept, keeping awake for the song of the jatayu.

'Then one early dawn, the leader ordered the march, for he had heard the jatayu song, through no one else claimed to have heard it.

'The days and nights that followed were miserable, through blinding storms, and some, it is said, returned to the valley which they had left, only to find it without water and without life, and of them, only a few could double back, to make it to the main party.

'It was in the middle of a raging storm that the leader again claimed to hear the song of the jatayu but that, many said, was impossible because the noise of the wind was so loud and fearsome that nothing else could have been heard. But then the power of his suggestion was great and they followed him in the new direction.

'Well, children, to cut a long story short, this huge multitude of 108 tribes, after several adventures, at last came across pools of water on the way and small game and even birds, though the leader put a ban on hunting birds. This was his silent promise to the jatayu.

'Again then, before the break of dawn, it was not only the leader who saw and heard the jatayu. There they were, in the cloudless sky, in plain view for everyone to watch their graceful flight and hear the melody of their song—Hin Hin Hin, Du Du Du! It is said that never have the jatayu flown so low, and it was not only their musical duet that could be heard but even the flapping of their wings. Some ran in the direction of the flight of the jatayu, but they suddenly stopped in wonder, as they beheld, ahead of them, a vast expanse of the river.

'They had not known what they were looking for, but now they all realized that this was the magical place of their quest. They saw the immensity of water. They saw the rows of majestic trees that lined its shores. They could see birds flying back and forth. Yes, they could even see animals moving around.

'None spoke. Silently, they watched the magnificent spectacle. Some had tears of gratitude. It was the leader who broke their silence when he said, "We will pray to render our thanks to God," and many said, "Yes, and to the jatayu." And their silent prayer also was that there be no people in this magical land, for they feared that if there were people, they would resist new-comers, for such was always the way of all the tribes they had known.

'Prayers over, many picked up jagged, pointed stones, ready to hurl them if they met with opposition. But the leader realized that they hadn't the strength to fight and so he ordered them to throw away the stones and give every appearance that they had come in peace. Obviously, the local population here must be powerful. Why, they even had houses moving on the river! Those were large boats which they had never seen before. Apprehensively, they came down the hill.

'Two boys and an elder from River village saw the tribals at the foot of the hill. They looked at these obvious outsiders in surprise. Meanwhile, he who had led the march of the 108 tribes, stepped forward to announce his identity, for he knew that the custom of the tribes usually is that the visitor must immediately disclose the name of his tribe and his intentions—be they peaceful or warlike. But how was the leader to announce the names of the 108 tribes that he led! If he did, what would be the reaction? Obviously, a clear suspicion that if so many tribes have gathered, their intention could not be peaceful. He must, at all costs, avoid giving the impression that he led a vast number of tribes intent on mischief.

'An inspiration came to him. Are we really 108 tribes? Have we not marched together and suffered all along the way? Did we not think, act and behave as one single people? No, we are one tribe. But what is the name of our single tribe?

'It was then that a greater inspiration came to him as he thought of the refrain of the song of the jatayu—"Hin Du, Hin Du, Hin Du." With as much dignity and calmness as he could muster, the old leader faced the two boys and the elder, and proudly announced: "We are Hin Du tribe. We come in peace. We seek your friendship and your hospitality."

'The elder and the two boys understood nothing. But the elder saw the frightened faces in front of him—men bruised and wounded, women who could barely stand, and children who were emaciated. He realized there was suffering here—and hunger, thirst and fear. He spoke to the boys. They ran off.

'The leader saw the boys run. It was no different from the ritual of his own tribes. The information would no doubt be passed on to the Chief of the River village and he would decide their fate.

'They had not long to wait. The two boys had summoned many. Steadily, the procession started towards the hill where the tribals waited. Buckets of water, loads of fruits, sweets, honey, milk cakes, curds, wheat loaves, barley bread and cooked vegetables were brought in. Even cows were ushered in, to be milked on the spot, to serve, first the children, and then adults—and a tribal woman said to a child, pointing to a cow, "She is the Mother of us all and gives milk to our children. She is the Mother." The leader heard her and pledged, "She will always be a Mother to the tribe of the Hin Du."

'They feasted as never before. Vaids came to tend to the wounded. Herbs and special foods were given to undernourished children.

'The leader and many others were accommodated in various houses. For the rest, the villagers cleared an area by the riverbank, spread hay and soft pine leaves for them to rest on until proper housing could be found for all the members of the Hin Du tribe.'

Ekantra paused to run the torch quickly over many paintings. They had glimpses of tribals resting, eating; cows being milked to feed children; Vaids tending to the sick and wounded; long lines of villagers bringing food. The common feature among these was that many eyes were raised to the sky in thanksgiving, gazing at an abstract representation of two clouds. Bharat felt as though the clouds in the paintings had a sign of movement. Did the artist intend to show the flight of the jatayu?

'So children,' Ekantra concluded, 'they are right when they say that the name Hin Du came from the sky. It was inspired by a pair of jatayu birds who sang high up in the air. Yes, from the sky it came. But not from the gods. That was your question, was it not?'

No one replied. Yet the children were wide awake, looking at the paintings and lost in thought.

At last, Suryata asked, 'Are we descended from those 108 tribes, or are we from the people who originally inhabited the River village?'

'From both. The 108 tribes mingled and intermingled with the early River people and we are now one and the same race.'

Suryata saw a fallacy in the reasoning and asked, 'The 108 tribes—they called themselves Hindu; but were the River people also called Hindu?'

Ekantra nodded.

'How? Why?' Suryata pressed. Ekantra smiled, 'Must we finish all the stories tonight? Let us leave something for tomorrow.'

Bharat had a question, 'Who made these paintings?'

'They were made by different artists at different times.'

'When? When the tribes came?' asked Bharat.

'No, later; even so, they are centuries old.'

Quietly Bharat said, 'They were good people who made these paintings. They wanted us to know.'

They all stared at Bharat. He had spoken like an adult.

'Yes son,' Ekantra responded. 'He who does not know his past can never hope to recognize the future.'

They faced each other as equals and Bharat asked, 'This story you told us, surely others know it too.'

'Of course. It is known to many throughout the land. If you go to the ashrams of Sachal and Sindhri, you will see paintings even older than these, and they will sing songs for you of the trials of the tribes as they marched to the River village of our ancestors, and of their heartfelt gratitude to the jatayu bird, whose flight showed them the way, and whose song gave them their name. Go one day to those ashrams.'

'I shall.' Bharat said gravely, more as a promise to himself. 'I shall go to them all.'

Yadodhra led his friends out. Ekantra and his wife followed. 'The boy has a dream,' said Ekantra to his wife, referring to Bharat.

'We all have dreams when we are young.' Ekantra understood her sadness. He kissed her softly on the cheek. It was the kiss of a father for a daughter.

The next morning ushered in a beautiful sunrise but the story session with Ekantra was no more. He was in a foul mood. Karkarta Suryakarma had annoyed him. If Ekantra did not unleash the blazing intensity of his anger against him, it was out of delicacy, as he realized that Suryata, the son of Karkarta, was also there.

'How do idiot fathers come to have such bright sons?' he asked his wife.

'Is it any different with you and Yadodhra?'

He laughed, 'You are right to be proud of my son.'

'Your son! You are the one who renounced him!'

'I renounced nobody, nothing. I merely took the hermit's way to seek God and his goodness and to understand the ways of the universe.

If custom decrees that my property is yours and that my son is fully in your charge, so be it. It is a measure of my trust in you.'

'Search for God and goodness! Are you saying that a hermit's way is the only one that can lead to it?'

Ekantra shook his head and she quickly asked: 'Then why not renounce your renunciation and listen to Karkarta?'

'Listen to Karkarta! Anyone who wishes to know what he should do has merely to ask his advice and then do exactly the opposite and he can never go wrong.'

The meeting with Karkarta Suryakarma started at dawn, on a peaceful note. Karkarta began with the mantra which he repeated every day (later, a part of this mantra would be known as the sacred Gayatri Mantra, and included as a hymn in the *Rig Veda*), and he said:

'We meditate upon the adorable effulgence of the Resplendent Vivifier, Savitar; may he stimulate our intellects and inspire our minds.

'Behold then, the might and majesty of Surya and bow to him for he it is, Brahma in the morning, Vishnu at midday, and Shiva in the evening. Behold, behold! And bow.'

Whatever Ekantra's views on the might and majesty of the sun, it was incumbent on him, as the host, to praise the god of him who was his guest, and he gave a fitting response, 'I behold him Karkarta, I behold him, for the fair, shining dawn has come, bringing to us the sun of the sky, youthful, robed in white, driving forth the darkness of the night.

'Master of limitless treasure! Shine down upon us, this day, and all days to come.'

Karkarta was certain now that there was hope for this dissolute hermit. True, Ekantra did not repeat the ritual of bowing to the sun, but the words were elegant, even original, and his praise of the sun was pleasing.

Happily, Karkarta said, 'The Creator, Custodian and Restorer of order both in cosmological and human spheres has entrusted the sun to be guardian of rita (the sacred order of the universe).'

Ekantra was silent. Actually, he did not know that the sun had this monumental duty. He had heard that this belonged to Varuna— the deity of the air, atmosphere, space and outer space. He disbelieved that too, trusting in a more direct relationship between god and the universe. However if he had to choose between Surya and Varuna, as guardian of rita, he would choose Varuna, as that deity was present night and day, while the sun did a vanishing trick every night, to shine elsewhere perhaps. So how could the sun guard the rita, unless of course God intended that good order should prevail only during the day, while the night should be reserved for all evil deeds! But his inward smile did not appear on his lips.

Karkarta continued, 'And with deep regret, I have heard of the offence to the guardian of rita.'

'What offence?' Ekantra asked.

'The offence that as a hermit you do not lead a hermit's life.'

Dark clouds appeared on Ekantra's brow. 'If anyone has said this of me, he must be chastised. If the guardian of rita himself complained, he too must be chastised!'

'The guardian of rita be chastised!' Karkarta cried out outraged.

'No one, but no one, has the right to complain against a hermit, except he who is a hermit himself. Are you a hermit yourself?'

'I am Karkarta,' said Karkarta with injured dignity.

'So remain a Karkarta. But if you wish to assume the right to criticize a hermit, be a hermit yourself, to set an example to other hermits.'

'Perhaps my words were ill-chosen,' Karkarta said with humility. 'It was not my intention to criticize. I came with a different purpose—to beg you to renounce your renunciation.'

'How many sins will you place on your head in one single morning? Do you not know that it is sinful to stop anyone from being a hermit? Are you, as Karkarta, above God's law?'

'If you lived as a hermit should I would sooner cut out my tongue than say what I did. I know a hermit is above reproach. Yet I took the risk to serve a bigger, higher cause, and if there is a sin in that, I shall willingly bear its burden.'

Ekantra, touched by Karkarta's sincerity, said, 'I know you mean well and I honour you for it. But then I too have the right to hold my view. I believe that if the way of one devotee is different from the other, so be it. When God himself does not dictate, no one can command how each of us will achieve our salvation. There are many God-given rights to man and amongst them is his freedom to decide how, when, in what form, and if at all, he shall submit to God. That freedom is mine.'

'But then you will never know God nor even recognize him!'

'Enough if God knows and recognizes me.' Ekantra answered.

'They say you seek personal attachments and keep the company of merrymakers.'

'In darkness are those who worship the infinite alone.'

The debate continued but both remained inflexible.

'I shall pray for you,' Karkarta Suryakarma told Ekantra when they parted. He meant it. He felt no anger against Ekantra—only anguish that the man was so misguided.

Ekantra understood and relented. 'Thank you,' Ekantra said. 'What you said today was not in vain. I shall remember the words you uttered. Perhaps they alone will show the way to the future. What I said has no substance, for in my heart I hear many voices, and each of these voices seeks to pull me in different directions. Bear with me, then. I am still testing, experimenting, groping, in the hope that some day I shall know the way.'

The forest in which Ekantra's caves were located was large and was a favourite place for hermits and rishis. Karkarta Suryakarma went to visit them. Strangely enough, hermits who often found fault even with God, had no quarrel with Ekantra.

Viswamanna who practised severe austerities praised Ekantra. The Karkarta's entourage was not surprised, for everyone knew that Ekantra carried food, even soma (wine) for many hermits. He would mend their huts, repair fences, build fire pits and even hire workers when the task was beyond him.

Priyamannu, who was in samadhi for the first half of the lunar month, admitted that he opened his eyes, 'whenever God wills it or when Ekantra approaches.'

Suryamannu, the most celebrated hermit, and one whom Karkarta respected the most, because of the hermit's reverence for the sun, said, 'Ekantra is the true seeker of knowledge.'

And even Visera defended Ekantra's habit of riding—'How many can he reach with weary, blistered feet! Better to be on a horse or an elephant to reach as many as possible.'

When the Karkarta asked, 'Why must Ekantra go to meet so many to find truth? Is it not to be found with a guru or within one's own self?' Yogana answered: 'I had a guru once. I did not find truth. Nor have I found all of it within myself.' Karkarta was surprised for Yogana was known to have achieved perfection in yoga and meditation, and yet, Yogana continued, 'There is a vast surplus, uncovered so far by most human knowledge. Perhaps it shall always be so.'

When Karkarta mentioned to Rishi Satyayana that he feared that Ekantra's way of life would stand in the way of his moksha, the Rishi countered, 'What makes you think that Ekantra worries about his own moksha?' Karkarta was shocked and said, 'But everyone must worry about his moksha.' It was then that Satyayana enlightened him, 'Ekantra is more concerned that we attain our moksha.'

Suryakarma went home in a thoughtful frame of mind. He sent a cart full of provisions and herbs to Ekantra as a gift with a message, 'I was wrong to find fault with you. I learnt much in the last few weeks in the forest and I must thank you.'

Ekantra was touched. He told his wife, 'He is a great man. He admits a mistake.'

'But you of course are greater,' his wife smiled, 'for you never make a mistake.'

Ekantra's wife remained with her husband for weeks this time. Yadodhra, Bharat and Suryata left three days after the debate between

Ekantra and Karkarta. But during those three days, the children coaxed Ekantra into telling them the remainder of the story that he had promised.

'Well, children,' Ekantra began, 'the 108 tribes began to call themselves Hin Du—and your question was: "How did the original inhabitants of the River villages also come to call themselves Hindu?" The answer is simple.

'The leader of the 108 tribes was a linguist. He had to be. Each tribe had a different language and he had to learn all of them along the way to lead, encourage and inspire. He now made an effort to learn the language of the River villages. Soon, he was able to ask an elder of the River villages the name of their tribe. But their tribe had no name, the elder said. Each individual had a name. Why did they need a collective name? They simply called themselves rya. To this, the leader of the Hin Du tribe responded courteously, "Indeed, where is the need for a name! We once had various names for our 108 tribes and that only caused dissension. Now we are fortunate to have one name—the Hindu."

'The River people were no less curious. They asked how the newcomers acquired the name, Hin Du. But the leader did not yet know enough of their language to explain it all. He thought of the song of the jatayu in the sky. He looked up. The birds were not there, but, as always, the melody of their song echoed in his heart. Quickly, his hand went up to the sky. How else could he tell them of the song of the jatayu and where it came from!'

Ekantra placed the burning torch near a painting. It showed an old man facing a crowd of avid listeners; there was rapture on his face; his prayerful eyes were lifted upward and his hand pointed to the white clouds in the sky.

As Ekantra moved the torch away from the painting, Bharat felt that in that fleeting moment, he saw jatayu birds in those white clouds. He went near and Ekantra again brought the torch closer. No, the birds were not there. Perhaps, it was the effect of light and shade; or possibly, his imagination. But the impression repeated itself as the torch moved back. Ekantra understood. He too had experienced the same feeling every time the torch moved. He simply nodded and continued:

'The River people had no more questions. They saw the old man's hand pointing to the heavens worshipfully. Obviously, the old man regarded Hin Du as a God-given name. So ....'

Suryata interrupted, 'So the River people adopted the name Hin Du!'

Ekantra smiled. 'No, not so quickly. The River people merely wondered. Many were moved by the faith of the humble, sweet-natured old man. They knew that the faith of another is to be respected.

'Like early man, the River people too were/awed by voices that seemed to come from the heavens above and enticed by the unending parade of God's glory in the sky and on earth. Also, they believed that divine revelation was a source of truth but not the only source, for humans must also think, reason and ponder, and exercise their God-given free will. How could they, then, suddenly adopt a new name for their people! So it was later, much later, that the River people started calling themselves Hindu, though I cannot even guess at an approximate date. However, the process by which they came to call themselves Hindu began soon after our river was named Sindhu.'

Suryata was surprised. It had never occurred to him that the name of their sacred Sindhu river could be of human origin. He said so.

'God creates but we give names,' Ekantra replied. 'Even the names of the gods are of human origin. That is why we have thousands of names for God, and yet the search continues to find a perfect name. I doubt if God cares by what name we call Him. . . .'

Bharat interrupted softly, 'How was our river named Sindhu?'

Ekantra smiled. He got the feeling that he had just been called to order. He began the story of how Sindhu was named:

'The old leader understood that the River people had no name for their tribe. What he asked now was the name of their river. Here again, he drew a blank. They had no name for it, either. This surprised him; he knew how these people venerated the river and its life-giving waters, "No," explained the River people, "we have given no name to the river; it was here before our ancestors were. They gave no name to it, nor have we; though in our prayers we refer to it as *sarva shreshtha poojnay janani* (most respected mother of our people)."

'The old leader uttered the phrase "*Sarva shreshtha poojnay janani!*", repeatedly, so as to be able to pronounce it correctly. Kneeling to the river, he announced, "This sacred river is our Mother too and henceforth it shall be known to us as *sarva shreshtha poojnay Hindu nam janani* (most respected mother of all Hindus)."

'At his summons, his tribes collected. The old man spoke to them. The River people watched curiously and although they understood very little, they did hear him repeat "*Sarva shreshtha poojnay Hindu nam janani,*" whenever he pointed at the river. Often he forgot to pronounce the phrase correctly, for he spoke fast, in a mixture and mismatch of the diverse languages of various tribes. But it was even more difficult for the tribals to respond when he asked them to repeat the phrase so that they remember it. There were too many mispronunciations, mutilations and variations—some said "Sarva Shri Hindu," or "Sharva Hindu"; others, "Shreshtha Hindu," and yet others "Sarva Hindu Nam". The only consistency was that none uttered the entire phase correctly; and so it went on, until a group of children, with no desire to try the difficult phrase, which each one, in any case, pronounced differently, took the simple step of abbreviating it and cried out "Sa Hindu," "Sa Hindu"; and other children, imitative as all children are, took up the cry to repeat "Sahindu Sahindu", though even then there were variations, as some chanted "Shindu", others, "Shahindu", and yet others, "Shindu". But the loudest single, common chant was "Sindhu",

"Sindhu". Children would not stop chanting; it was, for them, a fun-filled rebellion against the old leader who tried to impose on them an impossibly long name. Even the elders cheerfully took up the chant, "Sindhu", "Sindhu", which was easy, as they had already got used to the word "Hindu", and the simple addition of the sound of "s" presented no tongue-twisting problems.

The old leader slowly nodded his approval. "Sindhu," he realized, was a good name for the river which the Hindus were to regard as *sarva shreshtha* (most respected), for appropriately it took the first sound of *sarva shreshtha* and combined it with Hindu. He lifted his hands and addressed the river in a voice of deep respect:

"O ye waters, You who art the source of joy and bounteous giver of wealth! You who art daughter of heaven! You who are *sarva shreshtha poojnay Hindu nam janani!*

Henceforth, so that your auspicious name we and our children may easily invoke and clearly remember, we seek your gracious permission to call you Sindhu, who is the Mother Goddess of us all."

'Many have said that when the old man finished speaking, a cool breeze blew across the river and rain drops fell. Clearly, this was considered a signal that the river graciously accepted its new name.

'From then on, although in ceremonial prayers the river is still called *sarva shreshtha poojnay Hindu nam janani*, in popular usage everyone called it by its abbreviated name—the Sindhu.'

Ekantra brought the torch near a painting which depicted the old man's invocation to the river, with thousands watching—their faces solemn and eyes worshipful.

But as the torch moved, the artist seemed to shift to a lighter touch, to focus on youngsters, with merry twinkles in their eyes; and behind them were goats, cows, chickens, parrots with their eyes wide open, in wonder, as if the animals and birds too had questions to ask.

Ekantra smiled and explained: 'There were a few youngsters who were amused at the old man's passion for names—name of their clan, name of his tribe, name of the river. A youngster even brought cows and goats for the old man to name each one of them individually. Another wanted him to bestow names on each of the thousand or more parrots which came to pluck fruit from trees around his house.

'The old man merely used to smile, knowing that they were trying to make fun of him. Often he joined in their fun and went through the mock-exercise of naming and renaming goats, cows, trees and birds, but even the most irreverent of youngsters never questioned the name of their holy river—and so it has remained all these centuries as the old man named it—the Sindhu.

'Perhaps the only lasting contribution that these youngsters made, apart from raising a lot of laughter—which is a wonderful thing in itself—was that they forced the old man to suggest a name for their

River villages also. At first he suggested names such as, "The Land of Sindhu" or "Land blessed by Sindhu", but the children objected to the length of the names and insisted that it be even shorter than "Sindhu" to show respect to the river; but the old man was without inspiration. He was delighted, however, when a youngster came out with the right name, linked to the river Sindhu, and yet, respectfully shorter.

'That is how, children, the region in which we now live, came to be called Sind.'

Ekantra had stopped, thinking that the story he had to tell had ended. But Bharat reminded him, 'You were to tell us something more, Uncle— how the River people also came to be known as Hindu?'

'It is a long story,' Ekantra again warned them.

'The longer, the better,' Bharat and Suryata replied.

Ekantra's wife intervened, 'Don't worry, children, he knows how to make short stories, long; but not how to make long stories, short.'

'My wife is always right. I never argue with her.' Ekantra smiled.

Ekantra began the story of how the River people became Hindus:

'Well, children, you know that all the tribes under the old man identified themselves as Hindus. However, they did not know how to refer to the River people, to distinguish them from their own Hindu tribes. Should they refer to them merely as the River people? No, the new Hindu tribe also inhabited the river villages now. Could it be assumed that they belonged to all the tribes since they had no name? In which case, asked a young man, could they marry the River village people as well.

'An elder took up this question with the old leader who stroked his beard' and admitted that others too had voiced the same concern over their children's marriages. He called a meeting of the Hindu tribes.

'But then he had not called the meeting solely to discuss the matrimonial alliances of young hopefuls. He had another, more important reason. He had a vision of the future. He wanted his people to take an eternal oath of friendship, unity and peace with the River people.

'The old leader belonged to what was once a ferocious tribe. Every tribe along the borders was its enemy. Battles for supremacy, looting and thieving were common among these tribes. Killing, pillaging and burning followed as a matter of course. Incessant warfare and natural calamities had made them, and all neighbouring tribes, destitute. Every winter, many died, not only from the depredations of nearby tribes but from drought and famine. Some men even lost the strength to hunt and women had hardly anything to cook in the family-pot. The old leader then decided that his tribe must leave to find a better place. As his tribe moved, they met other tribes in search of sanctuary. The tribes faced each other but no longer with hostility. Their common adversity curbed their desire to kill and maim each other, and none in any case had anything that the other could rob. The different tribes marched separately at first but then realizing that there was safety in numbers, joined forces. Most of them believed that this truce was temporary and that their traditional way of fighting each other would re-emerge when they found sanctuary.

'But the leader had a different dream. He did not want the tribes to revert to the old way of life. He wanted peace for his people. He was glad that the tribes did not fight during the march. But at times he saw to his dismay that small quarrels erupted, and the youngsters of one tribe glared at others, vowing vengeance for an assumed wrong. He had done all he could to bind the tribes together but ancient enmities die hard. Generally, he ignored minor disputes but once the youngsters started a quarrel which turned out to be ugly so he intervened harshly. Amongst the guilty was his own son. He let the others go unpunished but banished his son from the march. It was like a sentence of death, for it was impossible for a youngster to fend for himself in that inhospitable terrain.

'Request for mercy for his son came from the leaders of other tribes since they would lose face if they did not take similarly drastic action against their own kith and kin who had been involved in the incident. The old leader relented but his purpose was served. Everybody realized that he would hurt even his own son to keep the peace. Slowly but surely all the tribes came under his leadership without losing their individual identity. His discipline was strict but always fair and impartial. As they marched, the tribes became friendlier with each other. His hopes for the future revived. They soared when he thought that the jatayu birds had sent a message from the heavens. He and his people had been looking for a sanctuary where they could begin a fresh life and it had seemed as though the jatayu had led him to just such a place. But his heart sank when he realized that this richly fertile plain was already populated. For, this meant that they were now in danger of facing a tribe that might annihilate or enslave them. But it was too late to change course. The ordeal, he realized, had to be faced and if the gods willed it, they would die here and now.

'He found, however, that his fears were groundless. How different these River people were from all the tribes he had known! They welcomed the refugees, "Guests," they had said, "are sent by the gods."

'The old leader saw gratitude in the eyes of his own people. They had been tense, anxious, shaken, frightened, even desperate, before they entered the River village. They had come in with a cry for help and mercy, and the River people's response had been generous and spontaneous. The hearts of the tribals were touched.

'But he wondered how long the gratitude would last. Would greed, jealousy and petty rivalries, which had goaded tribes into warfare since time immemorial, not reassert themselves?

'At this meeting now, he reminded all his tribes—the tribes of the Hindu—of their eternal debt of gratitude towards these people:

"We were hungry and they fed us, we were thirsty and they quenched our thirst. We were naked and they clothed us. We were homeless and they gave us shelter in their hearts and homes. They nursed our wounds and healed our spirits and restored to us our honour, self-respect and dignity.

"How shall we respond to their mercy, their goodness and their humanity! Search your souls and you will find the answer. And I ask you to join me in an oath that shall bind you, your children and the children of their children for all generations to come." The old man, then bowed to the river and soulfully cried out:

"'Sindhu! Be you now our witness to the solemn oath of our people.

"For centuries, you were the source of life and being of the people who lived by your side.

"Willingly, these people gave us refuge and shelter by your shores so that your waters may also bestow upon us your bounty and your splendour and grant to us sustenance, health and strength.

"Hear then, our oath, Mother Goddess Sindhu!

"For ever we swear for ourselves and for our children, and the children of our children, until this universe shall last that we shall live with the people who dwelt here before us in peace, friendship and harmony and if ever the need arises, we shall protect them against ourselves and against all others;

"And we swear that this oath binds not us alone but all who may hereafter enter the land of the Sindhu through various pathways.

"Let those who so enter this land in future swear also eternal loyalty to this land and its people or for ever remain out.

"For he who enters here and does not so swear or he who having sworn, violates his oath, let him and his seed be for ever accursed;

"And for ourselves and for those that follow, we declare, that he who is disloyal to this land and its people denies his own soul and betrays his own gods.

"Mother Goddess Sindhu! Be then you the witness to this our oath for ourselves and for those who enter this land after us. Chastise them and their seed for ever, if every they fail to take this oath, or having taken it, deny or violate it."

The tribals readily repeated the oath. There were some however who wondered if the oath was necessary and one of them said: "I came to this land hungry, thirsty, barefooted, bruised, homeless. They made me one of their own. Will I ever forget the debt! Gladly have I taken the oath with my lips and my soul. But was it really necessary?"

'The old leader nodded. He did not tell the young man of his ancestral memory—how their own tribe had once permitted outsiders who had come as refugees and traders to enter; soon the outsiders grew numerous and powerful; suddenly, bonds of affection and gratitude were snapped; an era of mutual distrust and contempt commenced; and then came the day when the slaughter began; those of the original tribe that were not immediately killed were forced to flee.

'But the old man wanted to think of the future, not of the past and he simply told the youth, "The oath was for those who may forget. And for your children and theirs and those that follow them. Let each of us and each one that comes after us say to himself—I remember."'

Ekantra continued the story.

'The old leader had discussed with the elders of his tribes the matter of a name for the River people. The names, "older inhabitants", "early settlers", "River village people", were discarded for obvious reasons.

'The River village elders offered no help. They repeated that collectively they called themselves rya. Was that not enough?

'However, our old man was not one to give in so easily. He continued his friendly questions and they explained that their spiritual and philosophic tradition was known as Sanathana Dharma (eternal law of righteousness, without beginning, without end).

'But Sanathana Dharma or eternal law, the old man realized, was hardly a name. All it meant was that for the River people, this dharma or law had no known beginning and had never been introduced through a particular ceremony at a particular time, by any founder. Even so, the old man questioned: "Surely it did begin at some point?"

'The River village elders remained silent, though one of them, quietly, asked, "Must everything have a beginning?"

'Little by little, he came to know a bit about Sanathana Dharma. As he understood it, Sanathana Dharma had its roots in ancient, ageless ideas and ideals. It stressed that man must live by truth so as to be able to realize God; and the way to find God was mainly to serve His creation and be one with it. Thus it pointed to satya (truth), karma (right action) without attachment for reward, ahimsa (non-violence) and dana (liberality, charity). These were the steps leading to moksha (realization of God). These principles for individual perfection must always endure, without change. But additionally, Sanathana Dharma stressed man's obligation as a member of society and his conduct at various stages of his life and also according to his status. Obligations, for instance, of a student would differ from those of a householder; and far more was expected from a person of power and wealth. However, essentially, Sanathana Dharma demanded right conduct and its real message was: "You cannot find God apart from humanity and the rest of His creation."

'The old man had seen many immersed in bhakti (devotional prayers). "Is bhakti not a part of Sanathana Dharma," he asked. "Not so," he was told. "It is a matter of individual choice. If your heart overflows with love for God, you will engage in bhakti, but God does not dictate how much, or if at all, you must pray to him." Irreverently, an elder explained to him, "God, it is clear, has taken it upon Himself to love humanity. But humanity itself is bound by no such oath to love God." The same irreverent elder even explained that Sanathana Dharma did not concern itself with the origin of God. "It does not matter if God created Man, or Man created God, or if the First Mother created them both, or even the Last Mother. God exists. But even if you deny His existence, it matters not, so long as you follow satya, ahimsa, dana, dharma—and so long as your karma and conduct are pure. Then He Himself will be powerless to deny you moksha."

'The more he discussed Sanathana Dharma, the more charmed he was with it. Dana, for instance, was not directed only at offering material aid but also stressed respect and understanding for differing viewpoints. Non-violence extended far beyond the physical realm and was concerned also with respecting the feelings and sensitivities of god's creatures as also the duty to protect and refine environment; in certain cases, though, ahimsa could be discarded to fight for a righteous cause, but with self-discipline.'

Ekantra paused, thinking that his digression into Sanathana Dharma could not possibly have interested the children. But it had and so he resumed his story.

'"Well," the old man repeated to himself: "Yes, this is the tribe of God—truly, without a beginning." And he said, more as a prayer: "Surely this shall also be the tribe without an end." But a doubt troubled him. Sadly, he realized that God did not protect man against man, or tribe against tribe. Man was endowed with free will and God did not intervene. He left it to the tribes to protect themselves. Prayer, goodness, mercy, gentleness were no barrier against a powerful, ruthless, scheming enemy. Amongst his own tribes and in his own time, he had seen that unprotected men of God were the first to be slaughtered by the enemy; and tribes that merely worshipped God were squashed under the heel of conquering tribes. Yet this River tribe—this tribe of God—had been sheltered, away from the envy and fury of other tribes, possibly because none had found the way to their lush and prosperous land. But if they had found them, others would find them too. A beginning, he feared, was never by itself; one beginning always led to a thousand such beginnings.

'The old man tried to peer into the future of this land. He saw clouds floating in the sky—vague, shapeless and formless. Would they turn out to be treacherous and thunderous, shot with deadly lightning or would they merely pour gentle rain in due season?

'Suddenly, then, it was as if a lamp had been lit in a dark corner of the old man's mind and he was looking into ages and worlds beyond memory's shores, where the beginning and end of all things met—and he was hearing a whisper of longing of the ages without beginning and end.'

Ekantra continued: 'The old man reminded himself of the oath to defend the River people against all new-comers. "We shall be their arms; we shall be their protection; my own 108 tribes must remember what we owe these people. We were sharanarathis (refugees) and they were our sharna (refuge). We are linked with them in our hearts today and we must remain linked with them for ever, even in our name."

'To the River village elders the old man said, "We know what you are to us; you are our refuge; and henceforth to our tribes of Hindu, you shall be known as Hindu nam sharna (the refuge of the Hindus)".'

'Well, the River people continued to call themselves rya though the Hindu tribes began to call them Hindu nam sharna.

'The River people saw something appealing in this new name, yet something disagreeable. It was nice to know that you had given sharna to someone in need, but was it not really arrogant to style yourself as the "refuge"! Surely dana was an essential element of Sanathana Dharma. But what kind of dana was it if the giver prided himself on it? Shouldn't the giver of charity remain anonymous and humble? Is a guest not sent by the gods? How then are they the refugees and we "the refuge"! Who is the "refuge"? Is not God, the one and only, the first and last refuge?

'Besides, their argument was based on their dharma—that Mother Earth gives life and bounty but we are only a part of humanity; how could Mother Earth have willed that its bounty be reserved only for some? It never occurred to them that they were the exclusive owners of the land. How could they then refuse to share it!

'Meanwhile, the Hindu tribes worked vigorously and cheerfully, in the fields allotted to them, even though some of them had been lazy and unwilling to work hard in their old tribal villages.

'Their lands, lush and green, produced much. But their leader never regarded it all as their own. He gave away a good part as gifts to the River people and also to the hermits and rishis of whom there were many in the forests around.'

'The old man's liberality endeared him and his tribes to the River people. His own men, however, protested—"Even if we were their slaves we would not have to work so hard and give away so much." But the old man simply said: "It is because we are not their slaves that we must work harder and give away more." Whatever the merits of this answer the old man could also calculate coldly. He thought of the lands given to his tribes, the domestic animals donated, the housing provided, along with seed, tools and implements; and he realized that even in those material terms, his people gave away far too little. But if ever it was possible to calculate the price of affection with which these strangers greeted and treated his people, when their spirits were bent and broken, the debt, he knew, would be infinite. How do you calculate the price of the hospitality of heart!

'Yet it was not gratitude alone that made him resolve that his tribes should follow the path of Sanathana Dharma. Their very conception of moksha fascinated him—that the soul of man should be immortal to reach the level of the One Supreme and be one with Him; and until that was achieved through dharma, ahimsa, satya, dana and karma, man would live through a series of births and rebirths.

'Certainly, the old man wanted bonds of eternal friendship with the River people whom he called "Hindu nam sharna". In naming the River people Refuge of the Hindu, not only was he aiming to acknowledge the truth, but he hoped that the word "Hindu" included in their name would keep their bond alive, for ever, with his own tribes, and remind his own people of the eternal debt of gratitude they owed to them. Names could often divide, and that is why he had chosen a name which should unite and never divide.'

'How can names divide?' Suryata asked.

'Unfortunately, they sometimes do divide—not only men, but even gods of our mythology,' Ekantra replied. 'Take for instance god Rudra. This is the ancient name for god Shiva. As legend had it, beautiful Parvati named him Shiva, after their marriage. However, initially, even Shiva's favourite mount, the bull Nandi, would not move out of his pen if told that Shiva wanted him. He reacted only to a single name—Rudra.'

'Well, what does a bull know!' Suryata smiled.

'Maybe; but it affected many. Some continued to call themselves devotees of Rudra, while others styled themselves as devotees of Shiva.[1] And really, if you talked to an ill-informed devotee of Shiva, he would tell you that Rudra was not as adorable as Shiva.'

Suryata asked, 'Why did Parvati want god Rudra to be named Shiva?'

Yadodhra laughed, 'Who knows! Many myths abound; and one myth leads to a hundred legends and a thousand refinements. One story goes that Parvati was unhappy with Rudra's name because his full name and title was "Rudra Pasupati (Lord of beasts)", and he was known as a fierce protector of animals, birds and trees. Parvati wanted

---

[1]That this rivalry continued far beyond Ekantra's time is clear also from Vedic texts in which all other gods are asked to come to the place of sacrifice but Rudra alone is asked to go away. The aversion to Rudra, in Vedic texts, has given rise to the frivolous theory that Rudra was viewed with distaste because he was foreign to the Vedic Aryans, belonging to the pre-ancient Hindus of Sindhu civilization; thus this theory vainly tries to prove that the Aryans did not spring from the ancient, flourishing culture of the Hindu civilization but were foreigners who broke into the Indian subcontinent.

him to be known not as the Lord of beasts but as her own Lord. So she changed the name.'

Ekantra resumed: 'As I was saying, the old man did come across a stumbling block, as the River people, guided by humility, never came to call themselves "Hindu nam sharna". Was the old man disappointed? No. He knew that beginnings are slow, but eventually, they catch up. To his wife he boasted, "In fifty years, the entire River village tribe will call itself 'Hindu nam sharna". His wife found it impossible to contemplate an event fifty years away and asked, "And where will you be then?" The old man, thinking no doubt of the theory of rebirth of Sanathana Dharma, said, "In fifty years, why, I think I shall be reborn, and then you and I shall make love and marry again." His wife smiled, but said, "Did you not also speak of moksha whereby a person is not reborn but resides with God?" But her husband replied that moksha was not for an old sinner like him. This annoyed his wife, for she could not tolerate his being described—even by himself—as an old sinner, and she said quite clearly, "Dear husband, you are neither old nor a sinner". The old man, delighted to hear what she said, redefined moksha, to say that God undoubtedly suspended moksha for those who desired to return to earth out of love for someone.'

Ekantra saw a startled jerk from Bharat. Perhaps, his mind went to the vision of Bindu's promise to return to be with him. Ekantra asked no questions. Clearly it was something deep and personal that stirred Bharat.

Ekantra resumed: 'The old man was not relying only on the binding force of the new name "Hindu nam sharna", to bring the River people closer to his tribes. His was a fertile mind with many ideas. As it is, the custom in each of his 108 tribes was to marry within the tribe itself. No one sought a wife outside his tribe, except at dire peril to himself. But now that all 108 tribes had joined under a single banner, as the Hindu tribe, the old barriers were washed away and it became common, even popular, to choose a spouse from any of the erstwhile 108 tribes. The old man did everything to encourage it, so that the entire Hindu tribe should be bound by ties of love, blood and relationship. But what about their intermarriage with the River people?

'After grave thought, he took up the matter with the River people elders. There was ready acceptance. "What objection can we have, except that young hopefuls be suitably matched!" the elders had said. They explained their ancestral view—that offsprings would be healthier, stronger, brighter, if in choosing their life-partner, people moved away from near blood relationships. But of course it is impossible to avoid remote relationships, for, over time, everyone in the clan comes to be related to every one else. In any case, they viewed the old man's idea with favour, since such intermarriages would move them further away from blood-lines—with its resultant benefit to offsprings.

'This is precisely what was in the heart of the old man—to bring together in relationship his Hindu tribes and the tribe of Sanathana Dharma. He himself had married his own mother's sister's daughter and he never regretted it, even after hearing the theory of the River village elders; he was happy with his own offsprings who, though often wild in their ways, were the joy and delight of his heart.

'However, what bewildered him was the amazing variety of marriage customs in the River villages. But then children, you will not be interested in those, so let me leave them out, and....'

'Why, Uncle; please tell us,' Suryata interrupted.

'I would like to hear them too, Uncle,' Bharat said, gravely. Ekantra capitulated and resumed: 'Well, children, as I said, over these centuries, customs of marriage have come to us unchanged. The custom was for parents to exchange marriage vows when the boy and girl were small. This vow was tentative, to be confirmed one year before the date agreed for the marriage. The man had to be sixteen years of age (solar), and the girl, fourteen years (lunar). Six months before the marriage date, a meeting between the boy and the girl would be arranged, at which they were expected to garland each other. If they did, the parental marriage vows were confirmed; otherwise, they were regarded as non-existent. But I don't think an instance ever arose where garlands were not exchanged at the ceremony. If such a contingency was expected, naturally parents would mutually agree to rescind the vows: and the only restriction, then, was to keep secret if it was the boy or the girl who objected.'

'But then,' Suryata asked, 'why call it a vow, if parents—and even the girl and the boy—were not bound and could rescind it?'

'You are right, son,' Ekantra replied. 'At best, it was a tentative vow. But mind you, it did bind parents, if it was confirmed one year before the date agreed for marriage. Nevertheless, it did not bind the boy and girl who had to confirm it at the garlanding ceremony. But still I agree. The tentative promise of parents should not be called a vow. Perhaps when this custom began, the language of our ancestors was not as extensive as it is today. Now, if I make a promise, twenty words would spring to my mind to describe the extent, validity, duration, scope, ambit, confines, conditions, limitations, exclusions and reservations of that promise, and various events, stages, contingencies at which it can be altered, annulled, terminated or cancelled, in part or wholly. But in those early days, it may be that the words were few and the expression "vow" covered them all—and since the ancients used that expression, we continue it, though our understanding of it is no different than what it was in those times.'

Ekantra hoped that the children understood. Surprisingly, they did. Ekantra resumed: 'The garlanding ceremony was to reassure everyone that the boy and girl were exercising their free choice. The truth, however, is that, then and now, it is largely the choice of the parents that prevailed and prevails. What your children will do, in future, I do not know, but I married because my mother selected this very charming and virtuous lady for me.' Ekantra pointed to his wife.

She smiled, though it did not reach her eyes and said, 'Yes, but tell them also how the marriage vow is a bond for life unto death.'

Ekantra responded, 'Yes, no man can leave his wife, nor can a wife leave her husband, except when God claims them.' The children had no difficulty in understanding what he said—that a marriage bond is suspended if wife or husband becomes a hermit, otherwise it survives until their dying day.

Quickly Ekantra resumed: 'Marriage was then, as now, a spiritual, material and emotional bond. The boy and girl took the five-fold marriage vows of "piety, permanency, pleasure, property, and progeny". Then came the spiritual aspect with a ceremony of worship, including recitation of sacred mantras; knotting of garments; offerings of grain and flowers to the sacred fire and nine turns around the fire to honour the planets of God's creation and to make them witnesses to the marriage vows. The material bond was established as the husband's property became the joint property of both. The girl's parents were also to keep in trust the share of her property. Thus after deducting one-fourth for charity and one-fourth for father and mother, the rest of the property was divided between all the sons and daughters (including a child conceived, even though as yet unborn), and thus the girl's share was determined.'

'But how much does the girl get?' Suryata asked.

Yadodhra explained with a superior smile. 'If the parents have 100 units, twenty-five are for charity; twenty-five for themselves; fifty units remain; if they have five children including the girl who gets married, her share would be ten units.' Yadodhra looked at his father, who nodded with a smile.

'So little!' Suryata asked. 'Ten units out of 100!'

Yadhodhra smiled, 'But if the girl to be married was the only child, she would get fifty units.'

'I will marry a girl who has no brothers or sisters.'

'Ho! Ho! Ho!' Yadodhra teased. 'I know your marriage vows have been exchanged with a girl whose parents have twenty children.'

'Don't worry,' Suryata countered. 'I shall refuse to garland her at the ceremony. But no one has twenty children, unless he has many wives!'

Ekantra resumed: 'Well, children, that is what bothered the old man. In his tribes, a man could take more than one wife, and they did not regard marriage as something permanent. He for one would never give up his wife. But the custom amongst his people was that man and woman could part to remarry, while the system in the River villages was to treat a marriage bond as indissoluble, along with the rigid rule that a man must remain satisfied with one wife alone.

'The old man was charmed with the marriage customs of the River people. But he realized that if any of his people married into the River villages, and thereafter treated the marriage bond lightly it would only result in bad blood. His first action therefore was to warn his people of the marriage customs of the River people and their rigid rules. He thought his own people would be aghast. Not so.

To begin with, the women of his tribes were delighted. They were the ones who often suffered from the fickleness of their husbands. Besides, if the husband died, all the property went to the sons. The wife and daughters were merely entitled to meagre food and shelter. But property was not the main criterion for these women, who had in their lifetime seen nothing but want and penury which they shared with their husbands, and with the tribe as a whole. What counted with them was the attribute of equal respect that was accorded by the River people.

It was this aspect—of equal respect—that fascinated the women of the Hindu tribes. They saw that a woman of the River villages could be a teacher, an artist, or take on any job that a man could, except during the last five months of her pregnancy, and until her youngest child was nine years. She was in charge of family finances, children's education and all social and spiritual activities of the household. She had an equal vote and voice in the village administration.

Imagine the shock of the Hindu tribes when their women almost unanimously decided that their daughters should marry into the families of the River people.

The result? Well, you can imagine it. This certainly did not please the boys of the Hindu tribes. They could of course have retaliated and married girls from the River villages too, but then the wife would come under the protective umbrella of the five-fold oath.

In fact, the girls of the River villages were resentful as well, because they began to face competition from girls of the Hindu tribe and also because the boys of the Hindu tribes were reluctant to marry them since it would curb their freedom.

But Nature, children, is a great leveller. Both the girls from the River villages and the boys from Hindu tribes decided to teach the girls of the Hindu tribes a lesson.

Here again nothing was sudden, nothing hurried, nothing rushed; everything proceeded along patient, orderly lines, in which the old man had a decisive part to play.

'When the old man was approached by his people with the complaint that girls from their tribes were deserting to marry boys of the River people, he advised the boys to marry the girls of the River village. He reassured the young men by pointing to his own single marriage; was it unhappy? He asked them also to consider those from his tribe who had two or more wives, or those who were divorced, or those who had thrown out their wives. Were they happy? he asked them.

'The fact was that these young men were unmarried and had an idealistic view of marriage. At that stage of their lives they were certainly not thinking of divorce or multiple wives. After all, a man with no wife thinks only of having one wife. And with this initial idealistic approach, they were quite prepared to believe that men with multiple marriages and many divorces were never happy. Besides, the old man was clever in asking them to consider those who had remarried and divorced and somehow convincing them that they were not happy individuals. In constrast, here was the old man himself, full of smiles and cheer, and if there were lines and wrinkles on his face, they were eased, or perhaps even formed, by his constant laughter.

'Well, the old man so manoeuvred the discussion, as to convince them that all such happy cheerfulness springs from the fact of his remaining faithfully with one, single life-partner.

'I must tell you, children, that although I admire that old leader with all my heart, he also played on the baser instincts of those young men who were looking for wives. What had they got?—he asked them. Had they any property, except land and domestic animals donated by the River people? "What the River people have given, they can also take away," the old man warned them. "But think of what will happen if you marry a girl from their village? First, the girl gets property from her father. Will she eat it up herself? No, it will be for your children. And then think of what life can bring!" He expounded on his cyclic theory of life. Nothing is static, he said. Periods of comfort and safety can be followed by almost unending periods of penury and discomfort for those who do not plan ahead. A man can save himself from those eras of disaster by having a little property; a sure method to save oneself from an uncertain future was to have property and to be related to those with prosperity—and this was achievable only by selecting a bride from the River villages.

'But, children, I believe that the old man was only trying to convert those who were already converted. As it is, the young men of his tribes were already thinking of seeking brides from the River villages and he merely spurred them on, with all his eloquence, theatrics and drama.

'His last exhortation to the young men of his tribe contained two stern warnings.

'The first warning: if they married a girl from the River villages, and failed in their marriage vows, there would be the five-fold curse on them— first, of the One Supreme; second, of the gods of the Hindus, including the gods of all 108 former tribes; third, of the gods of Sanathana Dharma; fourth, of the gods of the new tribe, Hindu nam sharna; and fifth, which would be the swiftest, the most powerful and deadliest curse of all—his own curse. And he would enforce it without delay, without mercy, for "he who breaks his marriage vows with them will deal with me, and even before the first four curses can begin to take effect, so terrible will be my own action that the vow-breaker will wish that he had died long before he was born."'

Bharat intervened, 'Uncle, you spoke of the two warnings of the old man, but you told us of only one!'

'Yes, the second warning was there, but really it was no warning. The old man told them that if they married a River girl, he was not certain if children born from that union would be considered to belong to the Hindu tribe or to the tribe of the Hindu nam sharna of Sanathana Dharma. There was thus a clear danger of their children being lost to the Hindu tribe. The young men were polite enough not to laugh in the old man's face outright. The new Hindu tribe was far too recent for them to shed tears over losing its affiliation—and if indeed their children found their place in the prosperous tribe of Sanathana Dharma, what more could they ask for!

The boys were smiling too, no doubt in admiration of the old man's antics. Suryata spoke, 'This old man—he was very clever wasn't he?'

'Oh, indeed he was. And he was guided by the single-minded vision of uniting the Hindu tribe with the people of Sanathana Dharma.'

'He had the gift of laughter too,' Bharat said.

'No doubt about that,' Ekantra said. 'Often when we think of people from our ancient past, we seem to believe that they never laughed, never joked, never smiled, as though they were lifeless, inanimate objects. Entirely untrue. The ancients enjoyed life passionately, delighting both in things of the senses and things of the spirit! I am sure they smiled more readily, laughed more uproariously, and joked more often, than the present generation.'

'Why?' was the inevitable question from Suryata.

'Possibly life was simple then, and not so complex and demanding as today. Possibly because there were, then, not so many activities that we undertake nowadays; who knows!'

Quietly, Bharat said, 'Or possibly because they had greater faith.'

Ekantra looked at Bharat. He had himself wanted to say that it was faith which moved the ancients, that it was faith which dissolved their doubts, effaced their sorrows and misgivings, and that it was faith that brought laughter more readily into their lives. But he had not said so, fearing that the boys would not understand and he would be drawn into an explanation of something he could never explain—not to others, nor even to himself. How do you explain faith? Yet this boy, young in years, had no difficulty in understanding that it was faith that comforted the ancients, removed the burden of doubt from their hearts, yielding to easy, spontaneous laughter.

Impatiently, Suryata asked, 'What happened then?'

Ekantra smiled and continued, 'Then, my young friends, we at last come to the end of the story. The old man was wrong when he thought that the name "Hindu nam sharna" would be adopted by the River people. There was so much intermarriage between the Hindu tribes and River villages that all appearance of any division or difference between the two peoples was lost. None could distinguish who was a "Hindu" and who a "Hindu nam sharna". In any case, long names never have a chance, and therefore it is not at all surprising that both the "Hindu" and "Hindu nam sharna" came to be known simply as "Hindu". From then on, the River people and the Hindu tribes became so merged and assimilated with each other, through marriage, relationship, mutual acceptance of each other's gods and common bonds, that no one could tell them apart, and they all came to be known as Hindu. But it was not at all a one-way movement. The Hindu tribes became imbued—gradually, but inextricably—with the principles of Sanathana Dharma, while the River people came to adopt the name "Hindu". And from then on, till today, all of us, who are their descendants, are known with one single, common name—the Hindu.'

Yadodhra and Suryata clapped in appreciation of the story. But Bharat asked, 'Should not everyone in our land be told this story?'

Ekantra nodded as he looked at Bharat's grave expression and softly he said, 'Yes, some know it, but the rest should be told.'

Bharat said nothing. Something stirred in his mind. Perhaps a resolve that somehow, some day, someone, would begin to compose the ithihasa of his people into a Memory song for the future.

Bharat also had another question, 'Hindus, you said, adopted the principles of Sanathana Dharma. Hinduism then is older than Hindu—is it not?'

Ekantra simply nodded; but Bharat still had a doubt, 'Yet there are those who say that the Hindu is without a beginning!'

Ekantra nodded again and said, 'No doubt, they speak of pre-ancient Sanathana Dharma when they say the Hindu is without a beginning. After all, the two expressions—"Hindu" and "Sanathana Dharma"—are synonymous and interchangeable, and came to apply to all the people who then lived along the Sindhu, shortly after the 108 tribes led by the old man arrived there.'

Ekantra understood Bharat's unasked question and slowly said, 'I think you are trying to ask: when did the Hindu tradition or the Sanathana Dharma begin? I don't know, son. There are of course those who say that it is timeless, ageless, without beginning.'

Strangely, Yadodhra, who never said anything at variance with his father's views, intervened to say, 'Only God is without a beginning. All else started after His time.' He looked at his mother; clearly he was repeating something she had taught him.

'Yes, a thousand songs you must hear, a hundred paintings you must examine, before even the smallest clue of our ithihasa reveals itself. Be not misguided by the blinding, tearing hurry of someone who himself is misled, or repeats parrot-like, what he hears from others.'

'Sometimes, I fear, it is easier to know what the future holds than what is hidden behind the veil of the past.'

—(From Ekantra's story—5122 BC)

'Yes, a thousand songs you must hear, a hundred paintings you must examine, before even the smallest clue of our thithast reveals itself. Be not misguided by the blinding, tearing hurry of someone who himself is misled, or repeats parrot-like, what he hears from others

'Sometimes, I fear, it is easier to know what the future holds than what is hidden behind the cell of the past.

—(From Eloatin's story—5122 SC)

108 Gods and Their Message

5122 BC

Bharatjogi's mind continued to stray from his prayers and wander into the days of his childhood when he had heard Ekantra's stories on the origin of the Hindu. He had asked Ekantra the name of the old man who had led the 108 Hindu tribes. But Ekantra had said, 'For all I know, he may have had the same name as you do.'

'My name! Bharat?'

'Why not! Many famous Hindus have borne that illustrious name.'

Suryata intervened, 'And many infamous Hindus too!'

Ekantra smiled at the jest and told Suryata, 'True, son; but I think your friend Bharat will turn out to be a famous man.'

'Then you do know astrology!' Suryata asked.

'No son, I try to understand the path of stars but I do not believe in astrology. No one predetermines our destiny. Man has choices and free will and stars do not control the path we tread. . .' he paused, and spoke to Bharat, 'No son, I wish I knew the name of the old man who led the 108 Hindu tribes though I know that he followed the practice of Sanathana Dharma and passed the last days of his life as a hermit.'

'Where?'

'I believe at Gidudham. I inferred this from paintings at Manu's ashram, which depict the old man's funeral. Those paintings had a few details of the neighbourhood. Comparing them with other paintings, it seems that his last days were passed at Gidudham.'

Ekantra added, 'Yes son, a thousand songs you must hear, a hundred paintings you must examine, before even the smallest clue of our ithihasa reveals itself. Be not misguided by the blinding, tearing hurry of someone who himself is misled, or repeats, parrot-like, what he hears from another. Sometimes, I fear, it is easier to know what the future holds than what is hidden behind the veil of the past.'

Mounted on Ekantra's elephant, the nine-year-old Bharat had returned home from Ekantra's caves, certain that he would surprise his mother. She had always said that the Hindu was without a beginning. He told her about his discovery that Hinduism was older than the Hindu! His words bubbled. 'Hinduism is older than the Hindu! Yet Hindu and the ancient Sanathana Dharma was the same! It is that which makes the Hindu tradition ageless, timeless!'

But his mother simply nodded. Clearly, he was not telling her anything new. He smiled, 'Of course you knew. That is why you are regarded as the wisest woman in the clan.'

'Wait till you get married,' she said. 'Then you won't regard me as the wisest woman, even in this household.'

Later, they spoke more about it. Bharat asked his mother, 'All right, Hinduism is ancient and its root of Sanathana Dharma is even more ancient. But tell me exactly how ancient is it?'

'I don't know, son; maybe, as ancient as God's first creation.'

'And how ancient is God's first creation?'

Her eyes met his as she sang from an old song:

'Then nothingness was not, nor existence then,
Nor air nor depths nor heavens beyond their ken,
What covered it? Where was it? In whose keeping?
In unfathomed folds, was it cosmic water seeping?

'Then there was no life, no birth, no death,
Neither night nor day nor wind nor breath,
At last One sighed—a self-sustained Mother,
There was that One then—and none, none other.

'Then there was darkness wrapped in darkness;
Was this unlit water, unseen, dry, wetless?
That One which came to be, enclosed in naught,
Arose, who knows, how, from the power of what!

'But after all, who knows and who can say
Who, how, why, whence began creation's day?
Gods came after creation; did they not?
So who knows truly, whence it was wrought!...

'Does that First Mother herself know, now?
Did She create, or was She created somehow;
She, who surveys from heavens, above us all,
She knows—or maybe She knows not at all.

'Did She Herself create the One God!
And gladly gave Him the Creator's Rod!
But so re-fashioned Time and Space,
That He was more, and She was less?
Did She then turn future into past?
So He came first and She was last!

But surely, She told Him all, all!
Then how could He not know at all?

'Or perhaps He knows it not, and cannot tell
Oh! He knows, He knows, but will not tell. . .'.

This pre-ancient song also appears in the *Rig Veda* —'Hymn of Creation'—X:129.

There are however notable differences between this song and the *Rig Veda* hymn. In particular, the *Rig Veda* does *not* refer to:

- Creation of the First Mother
- First Mother as the Creator of the One God
- Future turning into the past
- Time and space being re-fashioned by First Mother, so that She becomes *less* and *last*, while God becomes *more* and *first*.

It has not been possible to discover how certain elements of this pre-ancient song which was sung at least up to 5122 BC came to be omitted in the *RigVeda*, composed around 4600 BC.

Bharat's mother smiled as she concluded the song, 'At least, this is the oldest song I know, even though I don't know exactly how ancient Hinduism is.'

'How old is the song?' Somehow ancient songs always moved him.

'I don't know. Some say this song was sung long before our clan moved to Sindhu river, when we lived in caves.'

'Did our people live in caves? What kind of caves?'

She laughed. 'You have returned from the caves today itself; and you said, its bath-house was as big as our whole house; but I am sure there were small caves too.' She continued, 'Of course, things do not always grow bigger with time and age; sometimes, our memory also shrinks. Even the song which I recited now was once a very long song.'

'How long was the original song?' Bharat asked.

'How many questions you ask! It was very long. Some say it took seven days and nights to recite it. But much of it is forgotten now.'

Someone should really try to have all those forgotten songs remembered, Bharat had thought to himself.

Bharat asked endless questions about the nature of the One Supreme. His mother, in order to stem the flow, recited an ancient poem explaining the impossibility of describing the Absolute:

There the eye goes not,
Nor mind, nor thought;
We know not, understand not,
Nor whence, why and what!

> How could I teach
> By thought or speech
> What I know not!
>
> Yet who knows!
> In absolute silence,
> With silent footsteps
> The Absolute may arrive
> To dwell for ever
> Where He always dwelt—
> In your self.
> Where else!
>
> Then you must know
> Yes, you shall know. . . .[1]

Bharat had not, then, fully understood the poem. Even so, he saw in it a glimmer of promise. His mother could explain no further, and merely repeated what the ancients always said: 'The Absolute is attainable only in silence—the silence of within.'

The Absolute is attainable only in the silence of within! Not very illuminating for a nine-year-old. Later, he understood. The heart has an inner ear that hears all that the soul silently whispers.

And much later, as Karkarta, he saw to it that both the poem and its explanation were woven into a Memory song.

Since then, Bharat had visited Ekantra's caves often, with Suryata and Yadodhra. He saw the entire collection of Ekantra's paintings. Bharat's wonder was endless and his questions, many.

Ekantra did not mind. Only children know how to ask important, difficult questions. The rest were afraid to unburden their hearts and so their questions remained unanswered and their doubts remained unresolved.

A set of three paintings sparked off interest in Bharat. The first showed the old man, who led 108 Hindu tribes, offering a rosary of beads to a River village elder; the second showed a puzzled look on the elder's face, as the old man separated beads to show the string passing through them; the third depicted the elder kissing the rosary.

Ekantra told the story, pointing to the first painting:

'Here is your friend, the old man who led 108 tribes. This is his last day on earth. He offers his rosary to the River village elder. This

---

[1]The thought in the first two paragraphs of this pre-ancient poem appears also in the later *Kena Upanishad*-II:3. However, the Upanishad does not include the hope expressed in the last two paragraphs of this poem.

was his only possession as a hermit. He explains to the elder that the rosary has 108 beads, each representing his 108 Hindu tribes.'

Ekantra now pointed to the second painting:

'Here, the elder protests to say, "But old man, you belong not only to the 108 tribes but also to our rya. Should there not be 109 beads to include our people also? Or is it that we do not count, neither on this rosary nor in your heart?" But the old man smiles; he separates the beads to show the thread on which they are strung, and says, "This thread that binds them represents you and your people. It is the sacred thread washed in the waters of the Sindhu and blessed by your gods who are our gods too. It is the thread of Sanathana Dharma, to unite, in one single bond, for ever, all Hindu tribes with your land and people. I leave this rosary in your keeping to remind people that unity is the highest virtue; and he who seeks to divide or betray us, denies his own soul."

'The third painting,' Ekantra said, 'is clear. Here, the elder soulfully accepts the rosary from the old man, kissing it reverently as an everlasting pledge.' Ekantra added, 'That is why you see every household in our land with a rosary of 108 beads.'

'But that is a mala (rosary) of the gods!' Suryata said.

It was Bharat who answered 'Of course it is; but did you not hear the old man's words "that among the highest virtues that God honours is the virtue of unity?" '

Ekantra nodded, 'Yes, it is a mala of the gods to remind the Hindu of his pledge of unity.'

Looking at the paintings, Bharat had said, 'How clear they are!'

'No, they are faded,' Suryata rejoined.

'Their language is clear,' Bharat said. 'I can see their language.'

Suryata smiled, 'Language is heard, not seen.'

Ekantra intervened, 'Yet there are those who are working on a language that can be seen.'

'How!' they asked; Ekantra explained, 'twenty-one yojna (105 miles) from here, lives Muni Manu. He has taken a vow of silence, except on full-moon day, though many say that he speaks a lot in his sleep. He is developing a language that can be seen.'

They had many questions. He explained, 'Basically, his theory is simple. Assume, Bharat, that he wants to put your name in a language to be seen. He sketches a bow and arrow and designates that sketch as the sound "b". Then if any word begins with the sound of "b", like Bharat, baba or budhiman, you will first have to draw a similar figure of bow and arrow. But differences begin with the second sketch. In your case, the second sound of "h" will be indicated by drawing a heart; the third sound of "r" may be represented by a rose.....'

'Or a rat,' Suryata interrupted.

'Why not!' Ekantra agreed. 'Only remember, Suryata, that the rat's figure will decorate your name too, as you also have "r" in your name.'

'Oh! The rose is all right then, Uncle; let Bharat have it too.'

Ekantra continued, 'Similarly, the last sound of "t" in your name, Bharat, could be depicted by a triangle. Such a triangle will also be used for Suryata, for the last sound in his name.'

'But then how can anyone know that my name is distinctive and ends with "ta" and does not collapse like Bharat's?' Suryata asked.

'Fear not,' Ekantra replied. 'Muni Manu's idea is that symbols must show the direction in which sounds proceed. For instance, we spoke of a triangle to represent the sound "t". If the word is complete with that sound, as in Bharat's case, the triangle stands by itself; but if the sound goes on as in Suryata's name, one side of the triangle is extended. There are other directions too, for the sound to proceed—"i" "aa", "ia", "ie", "ee", "u", "o", "oo", "ou", "ow" For these, Muni Manu is devising various symbols; so your name, Suryata, will be pronounced correctly.'

'Which symbols?' Bharat asked.

'I don't know, son; maybe circles, semi-circles, squares, dots, stars and many figures that you see in our mandalas (geometrical patterns). All I know is that Muni Manu will do a great job. Don't forget, he is the one who invented the concept of zero and its symbol when he was young, no more than twenty-five years old.'

'Twenty-five years old! Isn't that very old!' Suryata asked. Ekantra smiled at the perspective of a nine-year-old, while Bharat's mind was on the wonder of a language that may come to be seen and not merely heard.

Suryata asked, 'If then only a hundred words are there, each say, with four sounds, it means 400 drawings with perhaps 800 symbols, just for 100 words. Who will take that trouble?'

'You! Everyone!' Bharat said, angry that someone should question the value of a written language.

Gently, Ekantra explained, 'Suryata's doubts are not without significance. But Muni Manu's method is simple. I gave an example of bow and arrow the sound of "b", but perhaps only the tip of an arrow may be selected for the "b" sound. The important point is that once an arrow-tip is chosen for a sound, it will be used to denote only that sound—and none other. Now if, out of bow and arrow, only arrow-tip is chosen for the "b" sound, maybe the string which ties the two ends of a bow can be selected for the sound of "s" as in Suryata.'

'A string, left loose, looks like a snake,' Yadodhra said.

Ekantra wondered if his son was having a dig at Suryata, but he said, 'Exactly. Therefore if a string is used as a symbol, a snake will not be used at all. Muni Manu will avoid symbols that look alike.'

Suryata intervened, 'This symbol of string or snake to denote the sound of "s" as in Suryata is not a good choice.'

'It was only an example I gave,' Ekantra replied.

'Even so, the sound "s" should have the symbol of surya, the sun. My father would be pleased.'

Ekantra smiled. Certainly, Karkarta, the sun-worshipper, who was Suryata's father, would be delighted with symbols of the sun all over. Suryata continued, 'I will be pleased too.'

'You! In that case, I shall discuss it with Muni Manu.'

'But you said he does not speak!'

'He hears; and if I say that the request comes from you, he may even speak; he knows that only children make honourable requests.'

Surprisingly, Yadodhra said, 'I know what Muni Manu will say. He will say that a circle is the symbol of the sun, as of all heavenly bodies and the earth; it is also the symbol of zero—of nothingness—from which the universe began and from which we begin our counting in our arithmetic, and yet we continue with it throughout.'

Ekantra was wondering. Surely, I did not plant that thought in his mind! Two years earlier, he had taken Yadodhra into the forest and left him alone with Muni Manu for a few hours while he delivered medicines to an ailing hermit nearby. Later, Muni Manu said to Ekantra, 'Bring the boy again, he clarifies my doubts.' Yet, Yadodhra told him that Muni Manu had not spoken to him and both of them just drew figures and sketches on the ground. Ekantra wondered: Is there really something like transference of thoughts and ideas without the need to speak words!

There and then it came to Ekantra that his son possibly had the gift to see the unseen and to hear the unspoken. I must, he decided, devote more time to my son even if I have to give up my life as a hermit. But then it may be that prayers of the sun-worshipping Karkarta, and his own wife, rather than this chance remark of his son had suddenly changed his mind.

Suryata interrupted his silent thoughts, 'I thought a muni like all other sadhus and rishis would be concerned only with prayers and worship. How is it that this muni was interested first in arithmetic and now in a language to be seen? Are these not worldly pursuits?'

'All worldly progress too comes from these unworldly people. True, the material fruits of their discovery are enjoyed by worldly people, while the unwordly discoverers go on to reveal God's glory hidden in all things. A silent rishi is a man of God, not merely because he prays; he wants to make this earth a better place than he found it.'

'. . .Sindhu river was always there, long before the mountains came, and then slowly, imperceptibly, the mountains rose, but each day no more than one-millionth measure of one angula (finger's breadth, 2cm), and thus the mountains were uplifted gradually, completing in each cycle of million days, a rise of one angula. . . . If the mountains had come in all their might and height in one single sweep, perhaps the river would have been blocked and the mountains themselves would have lost the sure foundation that they now have—and who would wish to obstruct the flow of Mother Goddess Sindhu or provide mountains with a floating foundation, rendering them unsure of their place on earth?. . . Nature works with patience, and neither will mighty mountains bang into waters and earth, nor will rivers explode, suddenly to rise to the heights of mountains and the sky. . . . Everything evolves gently, slowly, smooth as a continuous drama in time, with the same "tranquil calmness of the One who fashioned it all."'

—(From 'A verdict on the antiquity of the Himalayas, surrounding mountains and Mother Goddess Sindhu,' pronounced by Yadodhra, around 5078 BC)

. . . .These four returning survivors told the story of their painful wanderings of nine years—and how ultimately their expedition had reached the source of Sindhu river—this greatest of the trans-Himalayan rivers rising at an enormous altitude, near Mount Kailas in southwestern Tibet. They did not then know that it was one of the longest rivers in the world and longer than any that crossed the Indian subcontinent; nor did they know of its annual flow of 450,000 square miles, which is twice that of the Nile in Egypt and three times that of the Tigris and Euphrates combined. No, they did not know all that—for the age of statistics, and even of the written word had not yet arrived. They did not even know of the existence of the Nile, Tigris or Euphrates. . . .Indeed, many of these details would remain unknown to the four survivors who returned.

Yet, these men who were not the children of the mountains and were brought up in the warm sunshine of the plains, were the first to discover the source of this great river, hidden in the midst of the highest and most formidable mountains of the world.

—(From later songs—date unknown but possibly of AD period—celebrating the discovery of the source of the Sindhu river in 5080 BC)

Onward to the Himalayas and Tibet

5068 BC

Bharatjogi's mind was still dwelling on images of the past. What else have I here on this lonely island, except memories?—he told himself. He thought now of the expeditions he had organized to discover the source and destination of Sindhu river. It had always been a matter of the deepest interest to him—where the gracious river came from and where it finally rested!

Many people had volunteered to join the expeditions and finally 220 men were selected—including Nandan's two younger brothers.

The Sindhu expedition was split in two parts—with one group proceeding to the north and the other to the south. No one knew which would be the longer, more arduous route.

Bharat, accompanied by Yadodhra, was to lead a group of eighty men on the route to the south of Sindhu river. Nandan's younger brothers joined the group of 140 to the north.

Bharat's wife was concerned and asked him, 'Why are you taking only eighty men while the other group has 140?' But Bharat countered, 'Did you not always say that I was equal to at least sixty men?' And his wife's angry retort was, 'No, I have always said you are equal to a thousand men, so why don't you go alone?'

Bharat explained to his wife that he was taking Yadodhra who had studied currents and much more; and he was hopeful that the southward journey would be swift and easy. In any case, as Karkarta he could not be away for too long, and if the expedition took too much time, he would return and if necessary send in more men to reinforce the teams.

The northern route? Only four survivors returned from the group of 140 that went to discover the source of Sindhu river. For nine years they were all unheard of and given up for lost.

Then at last, after nine agonizing years, four survivors returned, exhausted, dazed and crazed, unable for days to tell a coherent story of their incredible journey, covering 320 yojnas (1,600 miles) each way. In terms of time and distance they had covered less than a mile per day, but except initially, each was a day of danger—and sometimes of disaster. Only twenty-four had survived to reach the source of the Sindhu as it rose at an altitude of 16,000 feet (southwestern Tibet annexed by China). Nandan's two brothers were among those twenty-four, though they were not among the four who finally returned.

Initially, the progress of the 140 men on the northern route along Sindhu river was brisk. They had mules, horses and great enthusiasm. It did not take them long to reach the confluence of Sindhu river, at an elevation of 2,000 feet, with the river from Kubha (so named by Sadhu Gandhara, now known as Kabul river—and mentioned also in the *Rig Veda* as a tributary of Sindhu river—map reference: 33.55w; 72.14e).

From Kubha (Kabul) river, the expedition moved to a spot beyond which lay what was then known as Taraka desa (the land of demon Taraka). At this spot, a Rishi who was a devotee of god Skanda—and assumed the name of Skanda Dasa—had established an ashram.

Later Vedic literature somehow pictures Skanda as a war-god, born from the marriage of Shiva and Parvati, who destroyed the terrible demon Taraka, whom all the gods including Shiva could not destroy. Vedic legends also hold that the marriage of Shiva and Parvati was contrived by the gods to give birth to this demon-killer god Skanda. However, in pre-ancient, pre-Vedic times, god Skanda was regarded as a fertility-god, gentle and kind, and concerned with improving the earth's bounty; his killer-instincts were related only to destroying weeds or jungle growth which obstructed crops, plants or fruit trees. Thus in the pre-Vedic era, god Skanda gave no evidence of wishing to kill demon Taraka; all that god Skanda was reputed to have done was to keep a watch on demon Taraka who was under a curse that if ever he came to fertile lands, his demonic powers would be taken away. But meanwhile—so long as he remained away from fertile lands—he could roam free in the region of turbulent storms: the region named as Taraka desa. Demon Taraka was thus trapped in the region of Taraka desa as he had no wish to give up his demonic powers.

It was this terrible land of Taraka desa that the expedition had to cross in order to reach Skanda desa where god Skanda himself was reputed to be on watch to see that demon Taraka remained trapped in his region.

Rishi Skanda Dasa, with fifteen disciples, joined the expedition. The Rishi was convinced that when Taraka desa ended, they would reach the auspicious spot from which god Skanda himself was supposed to be watching—and the hope was that the source of Sindhu would be found there. Yet it was the Rishi who warned them that the route through Taraka desa would be long, hard and treacherous. From his brief excursions up and down, he knew something of the sudden dangers that might lie ahead in that mountainous region.

The 140 members of the expedition knew little about mountains. They were simply going forward, in faith, to discover the source of Mother Goddess Sindhu, and if mountains came in the way—well, they would somehow cross them with God's help. But the Rishi cautioned them that gods may not be able to see them all the time through the blinding snow and fog that they had to battle through. Certain that this man of God knew the ways of the gods better, they heeded his advice and now equipped themselves with loads of goods which the Rishi himself obtained for them—dry foodstuff, skins to wear, stitched skins to serve as sleeping bags, tents, thick ropes, rope ladders, poles with sharp edges on one end, and hundreds of other items including balms and herbal medicines. All this was in addition to their own equipment, which also included axes, spears and hammers. They looked in dismay at these vast loads collected by the Rishi and asked, 'How can we carry them all the way?'

The Rishi's ominous response was, 'Maybe you won't have to carry them all the way. The mountains may demand their due.'

They loaded their mules and along with the Rishi and his disciples, moved into Taraka desa. Their horses were left behind at the Rishi's ashram as it was feared that they would be useless in this rocky terrain.

Initially it seems that the demon Taraka was in a playful mood and though the journey was slow and painful, they could still manage it.

But soon the lofty mountains began to close in towards the Sindhu river. Like a torrent in fury—deep, relentless, dark and grey—the river hurled itself through ravines of naked rocks.

Their mules, terrified by this forbidding terrain, became a source of danger to them. They had to let them go. The mules retraced their steps faster than they had come and the Rishi feared that they even failed to hear his blessing.

Perilously, the expedition continued, through terrible storms; they heaved a sigh of relief, thinking that their journey was nearing its end when they saw the valley widening itself and a clear, jade green river foaming down to meet Sindhu river. It was the river that came from the mountain range which Sadhu Gandhara had named Hindu Kush to mark the birth of his son, Kush, at the foot of those mountains.

Compared to the torrential, forbidding grey waters of the Sindhu, this tributary river appeared so inviting with its clear, transparent waters that despite the icy-cold, they went in for a dip. Here they had their first casualty. An avalanche of boulders hurtled down suddenly from the mountainside. The expedition-leader was killed. His head was smashed. The waters changed colour from jade green to grey, as boulders and mud kept pouring in. They called this river Girgit (which meant a chameleon). Later this river would come to be known as Gilgit river (map reference: 35.47n; 74.35e).

There would be more casualities thereafter. Sindhu was narrowly confined within mountain walls with no outlet and forced to turn south-west. Another river joined the Sindhu from the east. Reinforced, Sindhu twisted and swirled down the trough between Hindu Kush to the west and the huge ramparts of Nanga Parbat to the east.

This meeting of rivers—though a confluence is regarded as holy—actually frightened them. They were in the midst of appalling storms and landslides and fearsome noises, as though the demon Taraka was challenging them to a demonic duel.

They named this tributary river Asura.[1]

Inch by painful inch they went on, sometimes protected by clefts, crevices and caves from blizzards, landslides and falling rocks. The entire area was filled with chasms and gorges which seemed to be made by some superhuman, malignant will. They heard earth and sky shake and rumble. They did not know then that they were passing through an unstable region subject to severe storms and earthquakes which had left their mark on the terrain. They lost three more men where Asura river met the Sindhu. Often they gave up skirting along the Sindhu river to take other passes to shelter themselves from falling rocks, though they always kept a distant watch on the river so as to retrace their steps to follow its course.

They finally reached another confluence of rivers, after having battled through snow and fog and taken a route both treacherous and circuitous. Every confluence, holy though it may have been, held immense terror for them. Rishi Skanda Dasa saw a few plants and shrubs ahead, and assured them that the land of god Skanda (Skanda desa) must be near. No one, it seemed, was in the mood to believe him, but the Rishi pointed far into the tributary river. It was a glacier, or rather the remnant of a glacier afloat on the ice-bed of the river.

'Sikhara! Sikhara!' Rishi shouted with joy (sikhara meant a temple-tower, normally with rounded top and curvilinear outline, though at times it could also be a rectangular truncated pyramid. The broad base of a sikhara was intended to give an atmosphere of solid strength and steadfastness and the top itself of single-mindedness and refinement). Whether the glacier looked like a sikhara or not cannot be checked but it seems that they were all impressed and even bathed at the confluence. They named it the Sikhara river. (It is now known as Shigara or Shigar river.)

From the confluence of the river Sikhara (Shigar), the Rishi rushed. They all followed him and reached a spot which the Rishi immediately declared was Skanda desa (the land of god Skanda). He had good reason for saying so, for legend had it that the demon Taraka could not hold sway where the land became fertile, due to the benign hand of the gentle fertility-god Skanda. The Rishi was certain that from this great height, god Skanda was watching Taraka trapped in the region which they had just left, where not a blade of grass grew.

---

[1]River Asura is presently known as Astor; the meaning of Asura has changed with time. Asura, then, meant a god who had fallen from grace, banished from godhood and assumed demonic qualities. He continues, however, to have the potential to regain godhood after penance and good deeds.

The expedition rested in this land of god Skanda (the land of Skanda is presently known as Skandu or Skardu—now in Pakistan and its first town on upper Sindhu, 7,500 feet above sea level—map reference: 35.18n; 75.37e).

The Rishi's search was over. He had reached the end of his quest—the land of god Skanda. With his fifteen disciples, he remained there, while the expedition prepared to move on.

One of god Skanda's functions, as the legend then had it in pre-ancient times, was to keep an eye on demon Taraka—trapped between Taraka desa (Tarbela) and Skanda desa (Skardu). But more than that, god Skanda himself was said to be doing penance for demon Taraka's troubled spirit. The only way of doing penance, according to this gentle god was not so much by prayer but through toil.

For himself too, the Rishi wanted a life of toil, to establish an ashram, to tend the earth and make it fertile. But that had to wait. He collected herbal remedies for days together so that he could treat the sick among the expedition-members. Thereafter, he devoted his energy to repairing and making tools and equipment for their journey since so much had been lost on the way. To their food-store, the Rishi added nuts and berries collected on the mountainside.

It was only after the expedition members set off that the Rishi set about establishing his ashram at Skanda desa along with his disciples. He started planting walnuts, apples, melons, nectarines, apricots and several crops of cereals.

Later, faraway, in small pockets and caves, the Rishi came across the locals. He encouraged them to cluster around his ashram and in the course of time they too became devotees of the fertility-god, Skanda.

The Rishi, being a devotee of the fertility-god himself, did not believe in Brahmacharya (sexual abstinence) but in the institution of marriage. He felt that the right time for Brahmacharya was below the age of seventeen and above seventy. Most of his disciples, at his original ashram at the entrance of Taraka desa were married couples.[2] It was not uncommon for bachelors, unmarried girls, widows and widowers to join his ashram, but somehow soon they all felt encouraged to marry.

The Rishi's sorrow at the new ashram at Skanda desa was that of the fifteen disciples who came with him, only five were bachelors—the rest had left their wives behind. The bachelors were already preparing to lose their identity as bachelors, with the influx of local girls into the new ashram, but waited until the idea—that a woman has to be married to only one man and that marriage is an indissoluble link for life—could be understood by these girls.

[2]The Rishi's ashram at the entrance of Taraka desa is presently known as Tarbela—now a town in Pakistan after the partition of India—map reference: 34.08n; 72.49e.

The Rishi too had left his wife behind. He made many excursions, near and far, into the fringes of Taraka desa to study the right season and proper route to travel to his old ashram, to bring his wife and the wives of ten others. There are those who say that he prayed not only to god Skanda but also to demon Taraka, and even a poem is attributed to him, questioning the gods for their harsh treatment of demon Taraka.

> *I ask not what his sin was;*
> *Nor how he broke your laws;*
> *But to banish him for all time!*
> *Does the punishment fit the crime?*
> *He deserves no mercy, you say!*
> *Gods! You too may need it, one day!*

Either the gods or demon Taraka or possibly both smiled on the Rishi, and he was able to understand, somehow, the vagaries and moods of seasons on the route to his old ashram. With his five bachelor disciples and thirty-eight locals, he reached his old ashram without a single casualty.

After a brief rest there, he left the old ashram again with his wife, the wives of ten disciples and 176 others—men, women and children—this time taking care not to separate men from their wives or parents from their children. He appointed his worthiest disciple as the head of the old ashram who would later be called Rishi Skandatara, though many called him Taraskanda to give precedence to demon Taraka's name.

Guided by the Rishi, the entire group, carrying assorted loads, and children in protective baskets, reached Skanda desa without mishap. All along the way, demon Taraka, the poets say, was playful but never vicious. His demonic laughter howled after them right through the journey. He also hurled boulders but only just after the group left a particular spot or just before they reached it so nobody was ever hurt.

The Rishi even performed two marriages on the way and it is said that the laughter of demon Taraka followed the rhythm of the marriage-mantra recited at the ceremony.

Again a poem has been attributed to the Rishi, interceding with the gods on behalf of the demon Taraka who had listened to his prayers for a safe journey:

> *Banished he is, banished in pain*
> *Yet, he heard and heard again;*
> *Count! for all the mistakes he made,*
> *Has he not fully, finally paid!*

The Rishi's pleas seeking forgiveness for demon Taraka were, however, not too excessive. Like the others of his era, he realized that the demon Taraka was only a myth which presented an aspect of the innermost self. All gods, all demons, all heavens, all hells, all worlds and all voids were within us—and the myth was intended simply as a story, in the setting of a dream, to manifest the symbol of images within us. Thus, a myth was not to be confused with actual events but had to go to the very heart and essence of reality to take us on a voyage of the spiritual discovery of our deeply felt longings and dreams. The adventures and exploits of gods and demons were simply markers to the way of the spirit. Even his own god Skanda and all the idols were no more than symbols to lead man to the One Supreme and to focus man's faith on Him and Him alone.

The Rishi was not one to take a myth literally and dissect it as a reflection or replica of day-to-day events; but then nor was he the one to take a myth lightly. All he saw was that demon Taraka, like other troubled spirits, had a human face. And he prayed for all. But here poets take us further afield to say that god Skanda heard this revelation from the Rishi's prayers (it was common for Rishis to enlighten gods) and on hearing this, god Skanda smiled for the first time in his life, and felt relieved from the strain of constantly watching demon Taraka— for the demon was a demon no more and had aquired humane and divine qualities. In sheer joy, then, god Skanda rushed to Mount Meru (a legendary mountain where his father Shiva and his mother Parvati resided), and cried out:

'A miracle! miracle wrought by Time
A sinner has reached the Sublime!'

And the poets tell us that when god Skanda told his parents the tale of demon Taraka having achieved higher reaches of goodness, they were pleased; and they allowed the son to roam free on the earth to make it fertile. Thus he had permission to leave Merugun (Skanda Dasa's residence was called Merugun or Murugana by Shiva and Parvati). It was here that Shiva and Parvati came down from Mount Meru to give birth to their child Skanda, so that he might keep a watch on demon Taraka. The area was mountainous with some minor features of Mount Meru and therefore they named it Merugun which literally indicated a terrain with some features of Mount Meru. It would have been arrogant for Shiva and Parvati—and gods were never arrogant lest they be replaced—to name the region Skanda desa to honour their son, though it was proper for people to call it so, out of respect for the gods. Thus it is that Skanda desa and even the child Skanda himself were also known by the name Merugun and Kumar—which means, son.

Thereafter god Skanda—released from the odious task of watching Taraka—moved around actively as god of fertility, responding graciously whenever anyone from the earth cried out for his help. If a woman wanted a child, she had only to pray to him. If a man lacked vigour or potency to make his wife pregnant, again, he had only to invoke god Skanda's blessings. It is said that his blessings were so all-pervasive, that at times when the wife of an ascetic or a sanyasi (one who renounces the world) would pray to god Skanda, the sanyasi would somehow interrupt his renunciation to return to the wife—briefly—to give her a child. It seems god Skanda's father Shiva, who was after all the patron god of hermits and ascetics, was not too happy with his son's interference in deflecting them from the path of sexual abstinence, because of his wife's prayers. But mother Parvati defended her son. Her view was that it was the sanyasi himself who wanted to interrupt his abstinence and so smoothly, through his meditation, he planted the cry of desire in the wife's heart—and after having enjoyed himself he came forward to complain against their benevolent son. The song—'Counter-complaint Against Sanyasi'—ascribes the following to Parvati:

> Was his renunciation real and true?
> Then how, where, and from whom
> Came the desire and why?
> Was it his wife's or his own cry?
> Were gods ever so high
> That a sanyasi, they dare defy!

As she developed her argument, she even said:

> For all vices, everywhere everyone
> Blames wife, god or the demon;
> Then, let the Lord of Karma resign
> And join the drinkers of spurious Soma wine!

Finally her view was that a sanyasi who renounces the earth but leaves alive the flame of desire in his wife's breast is not a true sanyasi.

None know what Shiva's reaction to Parvati's views was.

Legend however has it that god Skanda listened to every prayer. Birds chirped for plants. He gave them plants and the earth smiled. Animals asked for forests. Again, he obliged and the earth smiled. The earth itself asked for nothing—but then the earth is the mother, and even if you hurt or ignore her, she will smile—and if you love or caress her, she will still ask for nothing. And god Skanda who knew the secret of a mother's heart and could hear the unspoken longing, went round kissing the earth and it became green and fertile; its sighs turned into a smile.

Thus god Skanda was now known to be always young, fragrant, beautiful and smiling, and if he came across a heart burdened with grief, he would move in to remove that sorrow, unasked, because he did not subscribe to the views of the other gods that prayers must he said before the gods could respond with favours.[3]

Before going on to roam the earth, it seems that god Skanda first blessed the land where the Rishi established his new ashram, and it is said that poplars, walnuts, lemons, melons, nectarines and apples grew to enormous sizes. Those who did not believe in such myths of course saw that the land grew green and fertile from the endless toil of the Rishi and the ever growing number of disciples around his ashram.

Meanwhile, the expedition plodded on to discover the source of Sindhu river. They had thought their troubles were over at Skanda desa, but greater ordeals awaited them.

Tragedy struck at the confluence of the river which they named the River of Sorrow (Shok river). Fed by mighty glaciers on slopes of the Nanga Parbat Massif, Karakoram and Kohistan ranges, river Shok did not, at first, present a terrifying appearance. Through storms and fog, they did not see a mighty glacier sliding down the river, nor did they see when the ice dam broke with its implacable waters rising cliff-high. They lost six more men in a single catastrophic sweep of the river. Two were wounded, unable to move. They were to be carried back to Skanda desa when the sun reappeared.

They died during the night.

Clearly, they were now in a region far more severe and merciless than Taraka desa. He who led them asked for volunteers to return to Skanda desa, while he would lead just twelve men to risk their lives. He cajoled; he begged; and he ordered—and they all refused to return.

The fearsome journey continued, slowly, painfully. For days on end they had to find shelter under mountain clefts, unable to advance even a few yards. Yet they reached another confluence, where Sindhu joined one more river. There, blocks of solid ice were falling around them. The invisible sky rumbled and it felt as though the earth below their feet was shaking and rattling. They named that river Ghar ghar— an imitative sound to describe fearsome conditions of thunder and rumbling. (Presently, river Ghar ghar is known as Zanskar—in the Ladakh region; map reference: 35.00n; 78.00e)

The distance between Shok (Shyok) and Ghar ghar (Zanskar) rivers, as they met the Sindhu, was possibly 150 miles, and yet it took months to cross—and often shelter had to be sought in ice-covered caves.

What kept them going was not faith alone. In some of those caves, they found evidence that men had been there, long before them. There were no footprints, no skeletons, and yet there were unmistakable traces of someone having passed through, or even lived there. They saw that

[3]It is therefore not clear how or why god Skanda is demoted as the killer of demon Taraka and is dismissed with little fame in the post-Vedic period. But then myths do change from time to time.

evidence in a cave in which they were trapped by ice. While trying to break out with their axes, they misjudged and hit wrong spots. Suddenly, they came upon a strange find—a few beads with holes on either side. Surely the holes were man-made; and the beads were exactly like those found near Sindhu river in Larkan region (presently known as Larkana, in Sind, which is now part of Pakistan—near the Mohenjo Daro ruins—map reference: 27.19n; 68.07e).

Later, in another cave, they found a stone idol, merely the face, crudely chiseled, but unmistakably that of god Rudra. Subsequently, they found a stone axe and also a round plate. They did not know what the plate was for, as engraved on the plate were three triangles. Again, they found a rattle—the kind that a child plays with.

We will go on, they resolved. If a Hindu has been here before and crossed over, how can we fail!

Between rivers Shok and Ghar ghar, they lost three men. If one life can be considered more valuable than another, then indeed they lost three most valuable men. He who was leading them was dead. The physician was dead. The third, an artist, with the task of charting the route, was also dead.

It is the artist's death which later caused controversy, after a poet sang that 'he died but should not have died when he did.' Many then told the story in greater detail:

The barks and leaves, on which the artist drew, had lost their shape and form. The pigments and colours had dried up. All he had was a long pointed needle, but he was forbidden to use it for etching on skins, which were being used for clothing, tents and sleeping bags. But then, he had sharp eyes and a memory for detail. He was hopeful that on his return, in the warm sunshine of his home, with a cup of soma wine in one hand, and a paintbrush in the other, he would draw and paint a thousands pictures of every little twist and turn in the route. Thus he went on, trying to remember all and giving names to rivers, mountains, gorges on the way—so that an accurate route-chart be drawn for future Hindu explorers—and Karkarta Bharat had said, 'You will not be the last to go on that route; your charts must speak to those that follow you, so they neither falter nor fail.'

But he hoped he would be able to recall many route-features. To many features, he gave names to help him recall the scenes—and lest he forgot, he would tap everyone's head playfully with his long needle and make them repeat the name. The last name he had given to a place was Tribhanga where over high cliffs rose pinnacles of ice in various forms and figures, standing high above the cliff-tops; and when the sun came out, even slightly, the ice pinnacles changed their colours, though blue was often predominant. One such pinnacle, slim and taller than the rest, stood out distinct from the rest, and they all had to agree with the artist that it was the figure of a lovely woman, decked in all her jewellery and colourful dress, striking a playful dancing pose, with one leg bent and the body slightly turned at the hips. But he did not tap everybody's head repeatedly with the needle to make them remember Tribhanga, for he knew that ice formations can be temperamental, changing from time to time; and what appeared to be the figure of a dancing girl today would later possibly look like a ferocious lion or a clowning monkey. But others charged him with trying to keep to himself the memory of the voluptuous dancer— Tribhanga.[4] When they were approaching the confluence, he made imitative sounds to describe thunder and rumble, and kept saying 'Ghar ghar, Ghar ghar'. It was just then that the boulders fell and the earth seemed to give way—and the team leader and the Vaid were killed and the artist was buried under a mass of stones.

They dug him out. He was unconscious. When they saw his legs, they knew he would never walk again. They put him on a stretcher. Long after, he opened his eyes and through pain and delirium, he saw his friends roped to his stretcher, carrying him perilously, over treacherous, pathless terrain. Weakly, he begged them to leave him behind. He pleaded. They ignored his pleas. Later, he asked for his sketching needle. That was not surprising for he would often be waving it in the air to make imaginary etchings, so that they remained embedded in his memory. They gave him the needle, though for some time his hand was too shaky to hold it.

At the confluence of the river when they set the stretcher down, they found that they had been carrying a dead man. With that needle, he had slashed his wrist to bleed to death. The blood had congealed.

They knew he had died by his own hand—to save them from the peril of carrying him. But to take one's own life! Was it not a denial of God! No, in their hearts, they knew that in this case, it was a renewal of faith—a sacrifice to a cause that was bigger than one's own life. Yet, none would admit to the other that the artist killed himself and it was as though by common—but unspoken—consent that the fiction arose that he too died along with the Vaid and team leader.

The expedition moved along in the domain of falling rocks of ice, where blizzards ran wild and the cold was congealing. The artist was no longer with them to cheer them up or speak of the vastness and grandeur of the mountains. They had eyes to see but had lost the heart to admire.

Many died around them. Something even died within them. Each step was like a mile. In the thin cold air, they had difficulty in breathing. Their minds and bodies fought desperately to conquer fatigue and they

---

[4]Tribhanga, under the inspiration of the Rishi, was acknowledged as the goddess of dance. Dancers paying homage to her would keep changing their dress during the performance, but the final act would always be in a red dress—from the blood donated by the artist as his last act in life or the first in after-life.

feared that they would not be able to go on. They did not then know what later Hindu explorers of the Himalayas would discover—that the higher one goes, the severer is the environment, and lungs are unable to push, in that rarefied atmosphere, the required amount of oxygen for the bloodstream.

But these men—untrained and inexperienced—what did they know of the mountains! They came from the lowlands of Sind and knew little of the conditions they were to face. In fact they would not even have had an idea of how to clothe and equip themselves for the journey but for the Rishi's assistance. They understood nothing of the constant headaches, breathlessness, inability to drag their bodies and sometimes, even loss of control over their muscles. Often they could not find an even patch on the terrain to rest. Caves were not easy to come by. They often had no strength to make an ice-shelter (igloos).

Yes, something had died within them and they felt it deeply. But their new leader cried out, 'We shall not die of this cold, nor of the mountains; no, we shall die of having lived!' His words, by themselves, perhaps made no sense, but the others understood.

From Ghar ghar river in Ladakh with painful steps they skirted Sindhu river, as it crossed the south-eastern boundary of Jammu and Kashmir (elevation of 15,000 feet—4,600 metres), while the mighty Himalayas closed in on them. Almost each yojna (5 miles) took its toll of life. They were dazed most of the time and sometimes moved as though in a trance; but often they were not moving even an inch. Then there would be times when their bodies seemed to them like terrible dead loads—standing apart from their mind and spirit. Many lost their equipment. But others lost their lives, and somehow, the equipment matched with the living. They could no longer build fires to cremate bodies. They had no idea that cold ice could protect dead bodies and that future explorers might find them for cremation. Prayerfully, they consigned the nude bodies of the dead into the river—praying for the departed and for themselves.

They had crossed possibly about 40 yojnas (200 miles) from river Ghar ghar when they heard a continuous noise above the wind. They paused to listen. It was the sound of a lion's roar, but a constant, unending roar. For some reason—or perhaps for no reason—the twenty-four who had survived felt that they had reached. Indeed they had.

They had found, at long last, the source of the river Sindhu—this great trans-Himalayan river rising at an altitude of 16,000 feet.

Silently, the twenty-four survivors stood at the source of the river and heard its lion-like roar with mixed feelings—each thinking perhaps his own thoughts—their minds dwelling possibly on those that fell on the way, and wondering how many would fall on the return journey. The feeling was inevitable—how far we travelled, how hard the way, how high our hopes, and . . .!

Yet there was a quiet glow in their hearts. In silent awe, they faced the Sindhu. They were unable to speak. It was their leader who realized the inappropriateness of silence on so auspicious an occasion. Surely a prayer was called for. Maybe the men were even waiting for him to begin the prayer.

He was their 12th leader. Eleven before him had died on the way. It was for him to speak. He was a simple man, who knew how to pray, privately, silently, but not how to lead the prayers. He began,

'Tat Tvam Bhagwant' (Thou art from God); 'Tat Tvam Bhagwant'.

He kept repeating the phrase, not knowing what to add. They joined his chant, repeating after him. 'Tat Tvam Bhagwant.'

He kept repeating the chant and the others followed. Louder and louder they chanted, so that the Sindhu may hear them above its lion-like roar.

As they repeated the chant, it had the effect of a mantra on them. Peace entered their hearts. The questions whirling in their minds, ceased. They felt blessed. At last, the leader spoke, loudly, clearly.

'Daughter of God, who art our Mother Goddess! With the roar of the lioness you leap and, at your command, mountains part to give way, to tear for you a route to our land, so that you may nourish us, sustain us, give us your grace and bind us with your everlasting love. . . .'

He did not finish, but stood along with the others, eyes closed in silent meditation. Later they felt he had made a long speech. He had not. Like all of them, he had felt that words were no longer necessary. And like all of them, he was simply reaffirming in his heart their love for Mother Goddess Sindhu. After a long while, he opened his eyes, and repeated the chant again:

'Tat Tvam Bhagwant.'

There are those who say that this oft-repeated chant—Tat Tvam Bhagwant—along with the few simple words of the expedition leader— came to be regarded as a mantra, though much was added to it later. The mantra itself was called by the shortened, simplified name Tibata Mantra (an abbreviation of Tat Tvam Bhagwant) and that is how possibly the entire region of Sindhu's source got the name of Tibet. That may be so. But on inspiration of those Sindhu pioneers, the river would come to be known even to Tibetans of later ages as Seng-ge-Kha-bab (out of the lion's mouth).

Doubts were expressed about how many reached Sindhu's source. Some poets had said that twenty-four survivors were present at the source of Sindhu whereas others said that twenty-two saw the spectacle. Both figures are correct, as another poet explains:

Twenty-four reached that awesome height
Twenty-two saw that glorious sight
For two it was as dark as night,
Robbed as they were by the Giver of light;

> *Shining he was, yes, softly, up, high, above*
> *Shooting from the ice below, cruel arrows somehow.*

The poet could have made an effort to be a little clearer—but then, that is how poets are. What he meant was that it was the reflection of the sun's rays as they fell on the ice and snow that blinded the two men. It was then unclear how men can lose their eyesight simply by the sun's reflection leaping back from the ice. Later, as more Hindu explorers went into the Himalayas, the realization came that the sun's rays, even those of a softly shining sun, reflected through ice and snow, can be deadly to the eyesight.

The twenty-four survivors remained in Tibet for months. They needed time to heal their wounds and prepare for the journey home.

Throughout, they could see that birds reigned supreme in the sky. Every kind of bird was there—pheasant, cuckoo, nightingale, robin, mynah, lark, owl, hawk, eagle, jungle-fowl and even ducks, cranes and gulls. Streams abounded with fish. They saw many animals but no men. It was a region of wild flowers, edible roots and fruit trees. They built fires and for the first time after such long deprivation, they ate cooked food, and it seemed to them that its aroma was so great that it would reach their homes in lower Sindhu.

Forests surrounded them—large willow trees, oaks, birches, teak, bamboo, spruces, fir, pines, spreading yews, poplars, thorn trees, babul and several others. They experimented. From these trees, bushes and vines, mixed with the rushes found in streams, they made ropes stronger than they had before. They sharpened their spears and axes and made many more—though wooden, for they did not come across metal there. From willow trees, they found that they could make better baskets than from bamboo. From the durable Khrespa tree, they made not only bowls and food containers, but also a sort of helmet for their heads, which though it would not save them on their return from falling blocks of ice or boulders, was a protection against small rock splinters and ice stones. Every basket and container was wound with thick ropes, so that most of these could be dragged, instead of being carried—and ropes, which had often saved their lives, would in any case be necessary, even if baskets had to be discarded. Skins to wear, skins as sleeping bags and even for tents, they had enough, for many had died and their gear was carried by the living. Even so, the skins were tattered. Pine needles and thread from river rushes helped to repair them.

This silk-like thread also proved useful as a lining within two folds of skins, to provide better protection against the biting cold. Patiently, they made ropes from thread, which were then flattened with rock hammers and tied at appropriate spots to hold as lining between two layers of skins. The Guild of Tailors, back home, would not have thought much of their handiwork but it served its purpose.

Their first task was to build a hut. They saw many animals nearby—mostly small—but they also heard the sounds of bigger animals. Once they had heard the growl of a lone tiger. From a distance, they had seen bears, a wild boar and a leopard. These wild animals were not likely to attack them with so many smaller animals around. Even so, they built their hut well above the ground, with strong support from the poles and planks they had cut from trees. Even the stairs, which they made to lead to the hut entrance, were light and portable, and when they were out the stairs were kept away from the hut. They were trying to make a quick job of building the hut, but the leader wanted excellence, which would stand the wind and the vagaries of various seasons.

'Are we going to be here for ever?' one of them asked.

'Some of us are,' the leader had replied.

They knew he had decided that the two blind men in the group had to stay back. One more whose arm had lost all its feeling and strength had also to be left behind. Who else! they wondered.

Somewhere, they knew there would be human habitation in this region. But they were not too keen to discover people as yet. People, they knew, could be temperamental—and the group of twenty-four felt they were far too few and much too weak to take the risk.

Later, the men who were left behind and also subsequent Hindu explorers would discover how simple, kind and gentle the people of the region were, though often they lived poorly and in unfortunate circumstances.

To domesticate cattle, the twenty-four survivors erected two large pens outside the hut, one on ground level, and another interconnected with it by a movable ramp, on a higher level. It took several trips to the forest and a long time to coax and cajole cattle into the pens and be responsive. The first cup of milk that their cattle yielded was like nectar to them—better than any soma wine that they had ever tasted. Later the cattle became so mild that the blind could milk them.

They prepared to return. The two blind men and the one with the disabled arm had to remain. Three bachelors were selected to be with them. It was their fault. The leader organized endurance contests amongst bachelors for running, climbing and obstacle clearance. They assumed that those who did the worst would be left behind. Each strained to excel—and those that did, were chosen to remain. The leader justified it by saying, 'We know what dangers we will face, and we have faced them before, but what of the unknown dangers these men may encounter!'

The return journey was as terrifying as before. They did not suffer as much from the overpowering headaches, fatigue, depression and

breathlessness which had earlier tortured them; their acclimatization
to higher altitudes of rarefied atmosphere had by now been achieved.
But danger from falling rocks, cascading ice and sudden landslides
lurked everywhere. A chaos of ice and snow, trembling mountainsides
and rumbling rocks, blizzards and avalanches were with them all the
time. Yet they were fortunate. It seems their leader had developed a
sixth sense which warned them of the hazards ahead. At every change
in the wind, at every faraway rumble, he seemed to guess the right
direction of his group, the right time to rest, and the right spot to
choose for shelter.

Not for too long though. They could see their leader, ahead of
them, as always, scouting the route. Suddenly, he was lost from view.
The snow and ice under him had given way. Two others, though much
behind, but tied to him with the same rope, were being pulled forward.
Others held them. With every ounce of their strength, they pulled at
the rope, hoping that somehow their leader would come back to them
at the end of it. Impossible!

Then came blizzards—terrifying, unending and deadly. Whatever
was not tied to their bodies was blown away—and they too were in
the same danger, throughout. Much of their equipment was lost. In
the thick fog, they could not see each other, at a distance even of
inches. All seemed to be lost. One of them at last reached Skanda
desa. The Rishi himself, accompanied by many others, led the search
for more survivors. Two more were found the next day, half-dead, but
they revived at Skanda desa. Later on, another was found faraway,
trapped in a cave surrounded by ice and boulders. He was not in a
terrible state. He alone had his sleeping bag, tent, and enough food to
sustain him for a few days. But it would have taken him months to
break out from the cave. The Rishi's party took four days to break
through, after they had been warned by a continuous bark from a
'half-wolf' belonging to a local devotee of Skanda Dasa. Meanwhile
five bodies were located. No more, even though the search went on
for months.

The four returning survivors continued their journey from Skanda
desa after a rest there. The journey to the Rishi's old ashram at the
entrance of Taraka desa posed no real danger. The Rishi himself
accompanied them with a large group. It was a route which by now
had become familiar to the Rishi and his disciples and more so to his
mules. Already, the Rishi had established sixteen shelters on the way,
and hoped to have ninety-two more built. Some of his local devotees
were even housed at five of those shelters to plant trees and bushes
there. 'Why?' many asked. The question was natural; there was so
much land around Skanda desa itself, with springs, streams and
tributaries of Sindhu; why go into the inhospitable, rough terrain of
Taraka desa? The Rishi's reply was simple: 'This is also God's earth.
Who knows another Hindu like you may wish to cross over to pay his
homage to the high mountains beyond. Why should any demons bar
his way?'

Even before the four survivors reached the old ashram at Taraka desa, some of the Rishi's men had rushed to the lowlands to convey the glad tidings of their safe return, along with the news of the six who had remained behind in the Tibet region.

There was joy—wild and tumultuous. All 140 had been feared lost. That ten of them survived unleashed a wave of happiness. Yet it also renewed pain—of those whose loved ones would never return. True, in the years gone by, they had given up hope of their ever coming back, but with the return of these four, grief for others, allayed for so long, came back to wrench their hearts more cruelly than before. Even so, every house was brilliantly illuminated with myriads of twinkling earthen lamps—put up also by those who had lost their loved ones.

Bharat, Dhruputta, Yadodhra, Nandan and others had sped forward to the Rishi's ashram to welcome them on behalf of the clan and to escort them back home. The four survivors embraced Nandan first for he was the one who had lost both his younger brothers on their return journey from the source of the Sindhu river.

Even as the four survivors embraced Nandan, each of them was perhaps thinking of the question which Nandan's youngest brother had posed, on their return journey from the source of Sindhu. He had asked: 'What came first? The mountains or the Sindhu river which flows through these mountains?' How, they wondered, could their Mother Goddess Sindhu be of later creation! Yet they paused as they looked at the vast, formidable mountain range, which they had named the Himalayas (the perpetual abode of snow—hima means snow; alaya means abode).

Nandan's youngest brother fell on the way, while his question remained unanswered.

For nine years, Yadodhra considered the question, and finally gave his view. Sindhu river, he said, was there long before the mountains came, and then slowly, imperceptibly, mountains rose, but each day no more than one-millionth measure of one angula (finger's breath, 2 cm), and thus the mountains were uplifted gradually, completing in each cycle of a million days, a rise of one angula.[5]

Yadodhra also explained how the slow rise of mountains enables the river to cut into unfathomable transverse gorges, steep-sided jagged peaks, glaciers of stupendous size and deep valleys.

Thus his pronouncement was simple—that mountains rise slowly, so that the Sindhu and other waters continue to flow without obstruction; and with the slow rise in their height, the waters rise with

---

[5]By this reckoning, for a mountain to rise one metre, it had to take 140,000 years, and for each thousand metre rise, 140 million years had to pass. On the basis of this calculation, it would appear that the highest mountain peak in the Himalayas should have taken about 1,238 million years to form.

them, gathering speed and momentum, always to ensure that the river flows broad and strong to the land. Yadodhra, therefore, had no doubt about the auspicious purpose of those mountains.

He justified his statement on the basis of calculations but also explained his belief that nature worked with patience.

This aspect, along with some mathematical data, was included in a Memory song on Yadodhra's 'A Verdict on the Antiquity of the Himalayas.'

Amongst the six left behind in Tibet, only the man with the disabled arm was married. As it is, mostly bachelors had been selected for the expedition. Years later, Rishi Skanda Dasa travelled to this region, with a team that included unmarried girls. But for this purpose he was a little late, for by then the five bachelors were already married to local girls from communities they located in the Tibet region.

The Rishi, however, was able to revive strength in the disabled arm of the one who was left behind. Yet, somehow, nothing is known about him—whether he crossed the mountain to return or just remained there.

The clan heard, from the four survivors, of the trials and triumphs of the 140 men who went out on the northern route to trace the course of Sindhu river, 130 of whom lost their lives while four returned and the other six remained behind.

These four men told the story of each one of the 140 men and how ultimately twenty-four of them reached the source of Mother Goddess Sindhu river—this greatest of the trans-Himalayan rivers rising at an enormous altitude (16,000 feet), near Mount Kailas in southwestern Tibet. They did not know then that it was one of the longest rivers in the world, though certainly they knew that it was longer than any that crossed their land; nor did they know of its annual flow of 450,000 square miles, of which about one-third would be in the Himalayan mountains and foothills, while much of the rest would find its way in their own land. Nor did they then know that its annual flow was twice that of the Nile in Egypt and three times that of the Tigris and Euphrates combined. No, they did not know all that—for the age of statistics, and even of the written word had not yet arrived. Nor did they know of the existence of the Nile, Tigris or Euphrates. If they had been called upon to estimate the distance they had covered, they would possibly have considered it to be colossal, beyond reckoning; but actually, they had covered only about 1,600 miles each way. (Sindhu river is 1,800 miles long, from its source in Tibet to the Sindhu Sea—Arabian Ocean.)

Indeed, many of these details would remain unknown to the four survivors who returned and to the others.

Yet, these men who were not the children of the mountains and were brought up in the warm sunshine of the plains of Sind, were among the first to witness the source of this great river, hidden in the midst of the highest and most formidable mountains of the world.

'These people—truly they are the people of Sanathana Dharma!'

'No, they are more ancient than that. They are the people of the Sanathana. It is from them that our Sanathana Dharma arose.'

'Yes, but then they are Hindus! Are they not?'

'Yes, they are Hindus. They are the very root of the Hindu.'

—(Conversation between Yadodhra and Bharat as they speak of the people living by the side of the Sindhu river, as it meets the Sindhu [Arabian] sea)

'These people—truly they are the people of Sanathana Dharma!'
'No, they are more ancient than that. They are the people of the Sanatana. It is from them that our Sanathana Dharma arose.'
'Yes, but then they are Hindus! Are they not?'
'Yes, they are Hindus. They are the very root of the Hindu.'

—(Conversation between Yadodhta and Bharat as they speak of the people living by the side of the Sindhu river, as it meets the Sindhu [Arabian] sea.)

From the Himalayas to the Arabian Sea

5068 BC

It had not taken too long for Bharat and his men to return, safely, in triumph, after witnessing where Mother Goddess Sindhu river ended her journey. How different that expedition was from the deadly trans-Himalayan route to the north to trace the source of the river!

They had started the journey by briskly skirting the southern route of the Sindhu. Initially, at times they even swam in the river when the land route became too difficult and rocky. Soon, however, the river turned fast and fearsome so that neither a boat nor the strongest swimmer could have survived its fury. How gentle Sindhu was when it passed through their land and how fearful it had now become! Was the river displaying its anger at being followed, to discover the secret of its destination! Yadodhra assured them that the river was simply trying to goad them into following it with equal zeal.

They went on and on. Certainly, it was not a journey of danger or distress. Nothing of the trials and tribulations that assailed their compatriots on the northern route came in their way. All they needed was the patience to cut through jungle growth and difficult passes along the banks of the river, which increased in fury each step of their way.

No one knows who saw it first. Perhaps they all saw it together. Now they all knew where their beloved Mother Goddess Sindhu went.

It was the River of Rivers or the Sindhu samundar (Sindhu sea) or the Hindu samundar (Hindu sea), as they variously called it from then on. They saw what was beyond their imagination, beyond their dreams, and spellbound they watched the foaming bodies of water, with waves of enormous magnitude and frightening power.

Silently, they watched the magnificent spectacle, unable to utter a word. There were tears in their eyes, not from the spray of sea water but from the joy of discovery and thankfulness.

Cautiously, reverently, they moved to taste the water. It was salty.[1]

Bharat clearly recalled the words of the wandering hermit about Sindhu's tumultuous journey to distant shores that no one had ever seen. Perhaps Bharat's companions were also thinking of Sindhu's distant destination beyond this sea. He simply said, 'With each discovery, the mystery deepens.' Silently, they nodded. And one of them began to hum an old song:

> He reveals much to conceal more
> Behind each gate, a closed door.
> Play Your games, God, it matters not
> I know what is in my lot
> And if in searching You, I fail
> You will find me—is it not?

They walked backwards, facing the sea, as though fearing that somehow this vast miracle would vanish if they turned their eyes away.

A little distance away, they unpacked their gear and set up their tents. Further on high ground, where there was some grass, they tethered their animals. They undressed and proceeding along the shore, took a dip in the waters where the sea was not turbulent. Each prayed in his own way. Each knew that the other was praying. Bharat wondered what different gods they were invoking in their prayers. But they were all invoking the One Supreme, for the miracle they had witnessed was far too great for the gods of their choosing.

They should have been tired after their long journey but the excitement kept them going. In their hearts was the joy of those who are the first to witness such magnificence. This was no time to rest! Still undressed, save for a cloth band around their waists to serve as underwear, but carrying their spears, bows and arrows from the tents, they drifted along, in wonder, far along the shore of the sea. Along the way, Bharat's party had met no one. Here too, as they looked around in various directions, they could see no one. Suddenly, however, they heard the sound of running feet behind a clump of trees.

Danger? No—simply a group of children frolicking and playing hide and seek. Beyond the trees, they saw the village. The children, seeing these obvious strangers, had questions which Bharat could not answer, as he did not understand their language. The children laughed and asked many more questions, quickly sensing their inability to understand. They laughed even more when Bharat spoke, as children can respect silence, but not sounds that make no sense. Bharat joined their laughter, and a bond was struck in the universal language of laughter.

---

[1] Till the later Vedic period, both names—Sindhu sea and Hindu sea—survived, but as more seas came to be discovered, it was the name Sindhu sea that became prominent. It is only in recent times that the Sindhu sea has come to be called the Arabian sea.

An elderly man was coming from the village, with a child who had run to inform him of strangers in their midst. He wore a necklace of white beads which could not be seen from the distance against the background of his white robe. Bharat felt sorry that he and his men were halfdressed, but in the warm air, after a prayerful, refreshing dip in the sea, with none around, they had not felt the need to dress, while walking along the soft, cool earth of the shoreline.

The old man smiled and touched his necklace, possibly to indicate his rank, or to introduce himself. Bharat had the impression that he understood a word or two, though most of what the old man said was beyond Bharat's comprehension. However, clearly the old man was gracious and his tone, friendly. He pointed to the sea and then in the opposite direction, and Bharat pointed to the opposite direction to indicate where they came from. Politely, the old man waved to the village, inviting them to come in.

They reached the village square, ringed by huts. Many had collected to meet the visitors. A number of questions were asked but each group had to answer its own, as there was communication only by gestures. Again Bharat had the feeling that he could understand some words. Everyone was addressing the old man as Shreshtha. He was obviously the chief of the village. 'Shreshtha' in Bharat's language meant 'respected' or 'honoured'. For instance Sarva Shreshtha (most respected) was the title given to Sindhu river. Bharat asked, pointing to the old chief, 'Sarva Shreshtha'? The old man readily understood it as a question to ask if he had the title of 'most respected'. Vigorously, the old man shook his head to deny it, but then smiled and pointed to the sea, the sky, the river, the trees, and even a far away rock and repeated 'Sarva Shreshtha' for each of them. And finally, the old man lifted both his arms high up to the sky and said soulfully, 'Sarva Shreshtha!' Bharat understood. The old man was referring to the whole universe— God's cosmos—as 'Sarva Shreshtha'. Again, the old man pointed his hands at himself to exclaim, 'Sarva Shreshtha!'—and he laughed as though the question of his being thus considered was far too ridiculous. Suddenly however, a doubt entered his mind and he quickly suppressed his laughter. Pointing his finger at Bharat's chest he asked 'Sarva Shreshtha?' Clearly, he was asking if Bharat's men considered Bharat 'most respected'. It was now Bharat's turn to deny it, and he did so with the same vigour and dramatic gestures which the old man had employed; Bharat pointed not only to the sky, river, sea, trees and rocks, but stepped up to a hut where a fire was lit, to point to it as 'Sarva Shreshtha' (most respected) and waved his hands to indicate that the wind itself was also to be so regarded. At each new example that Bharat gave, the old man nodded emphatically in agreement, delighted that his own gods were the gods of the visitors from far away.

The old man introduced them all to his wife and family. He pointed to his wife, putting his arms affectionately around the old woman, his two grown-up sons, their wives, his daughter and her husband, and his grandchildren, indicating, in each case, the child's parents.

Yadodhra pointed to the old man, and then to the land beyond, and asked 'Shreshtha?' Actually, he was asking if there were other villages also in the land, with other Shreshthas (chiefs). The old man misunderstood and thought he was being asked if any other person in his village was also a Shreshtha, along with him. He smiled, put his hand on his heart, closed his eyes and then pointing to the sky, made a broad, sweeping gesture to all who were present, and raised a single finger as though to indicate that they would all have to choose a new Shreshtha after he went into the sky. That led Yadodhra to ask 'Shreshtha, will you go to the sky when you die?' The old man understood the question from the gesture, despite the unfamiliar words. He shrugged his shoulders, as though to say, 'Who knows where ultimately we go!' Slowly he pointed to a bird flying overhead, then to a butterfly hovering over a nearby plant, and finally to two pregnant women standing in the group of his people, and softly he said something, but his meaning was quite clear, as though to say, 'And who knows in what form, in what guise, and how, we return! Maybe as a bird, a butterfly or a new born babe! Who knows!' Sadly, he looked at Bharat and Yadodhra, certain that they had not understood him and apologetic that he could not explain more clearly. But they had understood—clearly, vividly—and yet wondered. The gestures are the same, the thoughts are the same—only the words differ. Even the questions are the same—is it that the quest of one man is the quest of all men!

The old man saw his guests in thought. He felt he had failed them. He was a man of courtesy and he believed that when a person asks a question so deep, he has a right to know the answer fully. But he realized that he could explain no more. If they were men of his own tribe and understood his language, he would have had merely to say one word and they would have understood. He said that word to himself audibly. 'Karma,' he said.

Bharat heard him. Yadodhra heard him. They stared at the old man, in bewildered silence, as they heard the familiar word—karma. They repeated, 'Karma!' The old man simply nodded, glad that they could correctly pronounce the new word he had taught them. But they kept looking at him as though they had seen him for the first time. At last Yadodhra asked softly, 'Old man, when did we meet before?'

But he realized his impoliteness and corrected himself quickly and asked, 'Shreshtha, when did your people and mine meet before and when did we part?' To this, the old man had no reply. Even if he had understood the question, he would have been unable to answer it, for he knew not if and when his people and theirs had met—and parted. He saw their astonishment though and feared that he was to blame for mentioning to his visitors an obviously unfamiliar word—karma—

without explaining what it meant. But how could he explain! He did not have the words to tell them that sin is the erosion of spirit and that all evil deeds come to haunt you through a series of rebirths. How could he explain that conduct in present life would exalt or abase a person's status in the next life, and yet the person would have every opportunity towards redemption! Indeed, how could he make them understand the concept that those who lead sinless lives of sacrifice and charity and good conduct will live in bliss, as one with God, having escaped the endless series of births, deaths and rebirths! Did he have the words to explain that the gods themselves must pass away to be replaced by other gods, and that gods, humans, animals, insects, plants, indeed everything on earth, the planets, and in the entire universe, lived under the same law! How was he to explain that good conduct nourished the soul.

The villagers and Bharat's men sat at places indicated by the Shreshtha. It was apparently their custom to eat the communal meal together.

A woman with a bucket of water first came to the Shreshtha, but he pointed to Bharat, to give precedence to his guests. It was a wooden bucket and she also had a large wooden cup with a stick inserted into a slot (like a ladle). Bharat cupped his hands to hold and sip the water, but the woman smiled, gesturing that it was for washing hands. The water had flower petals floating on top. After he washed his hands he was given what looked like a leaf, cut into a square. He waited for the Shreshtha and saw him wipe his hands dry with it. He followed suit. Soon, others came to place before each of them round earthenware plates covered with leaves. The food service then began. They were first served thinly rolled, fresh, hot bread and three kinds of fish and two kinds of vegetable—one yellowish like cauliflower and the other, green spinach. Shreshtha rose and chanted a prayer but apparently ended with a speech to welcome the visitors, as all the villagers smiled in greeting. Shreshtha then pointed to the food in front of Bharat and said 'Sarva Shreshtha' to indicate that food also had a divine aspect. Bharat nodded and the Shreshtha was pleased at being able to communicate so effectively.

It was a delicious meal, worthy of being washed down with soma wine, except that instead of soma, a whitish drink was served. It was pleasant, aromatic and fruity, tasting predominantly of coconuts, but somehow Shreshtha was keen that the children should drink it quickly, for he kept pointing to them and repeating 'Tawdy, Tawdy,' which Bharat thought meant that the children should drink it quickly. As it is, the children did drink it quickly. Most women had declined it and the few that accepted it also drank it fast. Shreshtha himself and most men kept it aside, to drink later. Bharat followed their example. Shreshtha tried to explain—and Bharat understood—that it was a drink that ferments with time and has the kick of a liquor or wine. Shreshtha pointed to the head of a child and then whirling his own finger around, and rolling his eyes, he tried to indicate that a small boy could get drunk with it, if he allowed it to ferment.

It surprised Bharat that everyone was talking, laughing, gesturing during the meal—and some were even making loud remarks to others some distance away. At times, when Shreshtha spoke, there was silence but then he spoke very little, and almost all the time he was smiling at others' observations, and sometimes even laughing when a joke appealed to him. How different it was from Bharat's own clan, where the custom was rarely to speak during meals, and often it was said that only a fool spoke with his mouth full.

Once the meal was over, water came again, to wash hands, this time with the fragrance of lemons. Everything was taken away, except the cup with the drink. Those who did not have their cup before them were being served something else. Yadodhra, whose ambition seemed to be to taste everything, handed over his cup and was rewarded with the new offering in exchange. It was sweet, rubbery and took time to chew. Shreshtha's wife, sitting next to Yadodhra, told him that it was called 'halwa' and Yadodhra explained to Bharat what it was. Bharat was pleased that he had not exchanged the cup for the sweet. Yadodhra seemed to be pleased with the exchange.

The children left as it was time for them to sleep and only the adults remained. There was talk, more noise, more laughter around the square, though suddenly everyone became silent as the singers came to perform. Was it an everyday affair, or was it being done in their honour?—Bharat wondered. It was an everyday affair, he later learnt.

The first song appeared to be well-known and popular—apparently a favourite—for practically everyone from the village joined in and clapped along with it. It was the second song which was new and aroused curiosity and attention. Bharat liked the tune and the rhythm, though he did not understand the words. But clearly, it was sometimes sad and sometimes merry, judging from the listeners' reactions.

After the song, Bharat and his party were ready to leave. Shreshtha offered the hospitality of the village for their stay, but Bharat did not want to impose and tried to explain that they would like to be by the side of the sea to witness and watch it again and in any case they had also pitched their tents there. Shreshtha understood and, along with his two sons, went with Bharat and his men to escort them back.

Everyone in Bharat's party was silent on the way back. Their eyes, hearts and minds were on the sea. The joy of discovery was still with them. Somehow, the route back along the seashore seemed different, but then evening shadows could mislead and they paid no attention. Later, they did. Their tents and gear had been washed away with the tide. Fortunately, the animals were tethered on high ground and were unharmed.

Shreshtha laughed—for laughter came to him easily—but was quickly apologetic. He escorted them back to the village. Taking them to the far end of the village, he pointed to two large huts. 'Shreshtha huts' he called them, and Bharat thought that these were Shreshtha's own huts but he later understood that they were intended for visiting Shreshthas from other villages and their groups. Are there many Shreshthas like him? Bharat asked and the old man had no difficulty in understanding the gestured question; he nodded, pointing in various directions, to indicate that there were many of them, all over.

Meanwhile, hectic activity was on with some vacating their huts to double up with others so as to make way for the eighty visitors. Bharat begged that so much not be done, and that they could all squeeze into the two huts available but to no avail.

When everything was arranged to the Shreshtha's satisfaction, he bade them goodnight and, pointing to himself, gestured to the sea. Clearly, he would be going to the sea while they slept. Excitedly, they asked whether they could accompany him. He promised to wake them up in time.

Long before sunrise, Bharat and his men went to the sea and, in fishing boats, participated in the catch. They were no longer half-dressed. Each one had been given a set of clothes. Shreshtha had waved away their thanks, as though it meant no trouble, but many of his people had obviously been up all night stitching the clothes for them. No wonder then that Shreshtha's wife and some other women were sleeping when they returned.

Hundreds of boats were in the sea and most of them belonged to other villages. Bharat and Yadodhra were in Shreshtha's boat; a few others from their party were also in boats belonging to the host village, though many found a place in other boats. Everyone, it seemed, was keen to invite the visitors to their boats. Bharat was introduced to other Shreshthas and each of them was ready with an invitation and offered to escort him and his group to his village.

Their boats, Bharat saw, were faster, more manoeuverable and rugged. Smoothly, effortlessly, they glided over rising waves, as though the waves themselves were assisting the boats' rise, slope and descent. Bharat was not a boat-builder and knew little of carpentry, but he was intrigued with the design. Many from his party also examined the boats minutely, so much so that another Shreshtha asked them if they had no boats. They explained with gestures that they had boats but not this vast ocean. This totally confused the other Shreshtha because he assumed that they were saying that they had boats but no water. Did their boats then operate on land? The question was flung from boat to boat, and ultimately Yadodhra explained that they had the river Sindhu, but not the big ocean that the people here had. Yadodhra, while explaining, indicated that the ocean belonged to Shreshtha and his people. He was set right immediately—it was they who belonged to the ocean and all of nature, not the other way round.

For six days Bharat and his party remained with the sea-people.

Bharat was not too concerned over the loss of their tents and gear. The return trip, he was sure, would not by itself be troublesome, now that the route was known. And, in the meantime, his hosts had seen to all their wants. He regretted the loss of his soma which he would have liked to share with his hosts. Clothing? All of them had by now been given two sets of clothes, washed each day by someone from the village. What troubled him was how to gather food for the journey back—both for men and animals. Actually, he had brought spare animals, expecting the journey to be longer; he did not need all, now that there would be so little to carry. He decided to leave many animals with Shreshtha and ask for food and supplies. He did gesture to the Shreshtha that he would leave some animals behind, but did not have the heart to ask for food for the journey; instead he asked for an axe, a fishing net and a few items like rubbing stones to light a fire. Shreshtha nodded as though he had already decided on all that.

All neighbouring Shreshthas had been invited on their last night in the village. It was a festive occasion with more music, dancing, better wines, though the meal itself was about the same as before.

With Bharat's permission, two bachelors from his team had decided to stay back. They were being formally accepted by the village. All the unmarried girls came forward as though to inspect them and each cried out to the other, pointing out their flaws, and making fun of them. But then it was merely a mock-ritual of the kind that was invariably carried out whenever a young man from another village came to settle in their village. As they were continuing their banter and 'ridiculing' the two hapless strangers, the voice of a lone singing girl came floating over the distance, as she came nearer:

'With every rose, he gives a thorn
With every dark night, a fresh morn
Why this cry then? remember, he once,
Gave us the handsomest amongst men born'

The singing girl then pointed directly at the Shreshtha and asked with a challenge in her ringing voice: 'Who is the handsomest of all?' Almost everyone shouted back, 'Our Shreshtha! Our Shreshtha!' Actually, this was a variation in the usual mock-ritual. Normally, at such rituals when young men came from other villages to join them, the Shreshthas of these villages were not present. And who can blame the villagers for boasting pleasantly about their own Shreshtha on their home-ground. Other Shreshthas joined the fun, raised their wine-cups to toast the local Shreshtha as indeed, 'the handsomest amongst men born.'

Then the Shreshtha was asked to speak. The old man rose. He was not too tall. No one could have seriously called him the handsomest of men. Yet there was dignity in his bearing. His face was weather-beaten and wrinkled, and there was something in it that suggested a capacity for tenderness. He looked around with shining eyes, as though he felt a glow of pleasure at being surrounded by so much laughter and began to speak, 'Truly I am the handsomest of all, for my wife has told me that herself, and she also tells me that she always speaks the truth.'

Then he went on to speak of his pleasure at having other Shreshthas around him, of his joy at having Bharat and his team visiting them, of his happiness at having two of Bharat's men joining their village. Finally, glaring at the girls who had criticized these two men, he said, 'Fear not, these two young men will have nothing to do with you, for their Shreshtha—who is called Karkarta in his land—has promised to send two beautiful girls for them, from his own village.' At this, the girls started their mock-cries and crowded round Bharat saying, 'No, no, send us men, more men, yes, more men, if they are all as handsome as these two wonderful specimens'. Immediately it seemed that in their eyes, the two earlier 'rejects' were transformed into the finest specimens of mankind. Shreshtha sat down, while Bharat, who understood only after some explanation, laughed and agreed to encourage more men from his land to come to their village.

In those six days Bharat and his men saw and learnt much about the sea-people. He thought with a rush of warmth, how carefree and happy they were with their simple pleasures! Everyone seemed to delight in poetry, song and music. They loved conversation, not only because each thought that he had much to learn from the other, but for the sheer pleasure of it. Their huts were smaller than those of Bharat's people though their boats were superior; their tools were advanced, they loved their wines, though their best wine was not as superior as soma; these sea-people were forever friendly, laughing, joking and making merry and loved life; they painted beautifully but there was no evidence of great architecture; they had no notion of money and relied on barter; the forest was fenced off with huge boulders, possibly uprooted by human labour from the sea, some hundreds of years earlier—no one knew when—rendering it impossible for wild animals to cross over, even if they wanted to; it was prohibited to hunt in the forest or kill birds anywhere; they raised poultry and cattle in pens; meat was eaten on special occasions. They generally ate seafood, poultry, eggs and vegetables; they fished three days in a week, saying that fish needed time to multiply and they needed time to play, rest, be with children, plant flowers and vegetables; trees could be cut down only in the park on the fringe of the forest, with the requirement to replant; each village was an independent community with a Shreshtha as its head; and the Shreshtha's own hut was no different from the huts of others, and he was not given any extra privileges but the respect he enjoyed was immense; each Shreshtha had however two extra guest-huts in his charge, which were bigger and better, and were for visiting Shreshthas; a Shreshtha was in charge of all village functions, and inter-village contacts such as barter, though generally he delegated many duties to others; there was equal respect for men and women, and both went in for fishing, farming, weaving and other activities, though generally it was the man's task to cook the food, while the women served communal meals; intermarriages among the villages were common and welcomed; generally the boy moved to the girl's village on marrying, but the boy's parents could not move to the girl's village, even temporarily, until a child was born; a boy could not marry before the age of sixteen, and the girl, not before the age of fourteen, but parents could waive that by a year or so; there was no age limit for persons to retire as hermits; a hermit was free to go into the forest if he wanted to lose all contact with the outside, but regular visits to him were frowned upon, as the forest had to remain undisturbed as far as possible; many hermits found refuge in tiny islands on the sea.

Bharat saw no temples, as the earth, sky and sea were themselves regarded as temples, and a person could pray anywhere; most of them however kept idols—made with great art and intricacy—in their huts, though the two guest-huts were kept free of idols, for each visitor had his own favourite gods and some of them believed in none, so the argument was—'Why impose one god, when they believe in another!' or even, 'Why impose a god at all, if they believe only in the One Supreme!'

There were no whores; there were no priests; there were no slaves.

Bharat and Yadodhra wondered. So much was common between the two peoples and yet so much different! Even the conception of gods and the names were different. And how generous they were! They had piled baskets of foodstuffs, salted fish and other supplies, including casks of wine, for the visitors to carry. Shrestha had declined to accept thanks for himself, explaining that many of these gifts came from others, including those who had not met them.

Bharat and Yadodhra were having their last look at the sea. Soon they would go to the Shreshtha to say goodbye. 'I have never seen them at prayer,' Yadodhra said.

'Their whole life seems to be one long prayer,' Bharat replied, and both thought of what the old man had said about the earth and sea being God's heritage for all mankind.

'He spoke of karma too.' Yadodhra said. 'The word is the same. Their concept is also the same as ours.'

Bharat nodded and Yadodhra added looking at the waves, 'I think we were here in some long-forgotten landscape which was once familiar to our people. Their people and ours were together, here.'

Bharat smiled. 'Maybe; but I know of no song, ancient or modern, which celebrates our people ever having seen the sea.'

'Yet you told me of the hermit's song about the River of Rivers.'

'True, but the song spoke of something unseen, something far away, something unreached and unreachable, except in a dream.'

'Perhaps their ancient songs may sing of our land and people. Surely we were together once,' Yadodhra said and slowly added, 'if we were not here before, then surely they were amongst us, once.'

They went into the Shreshtha's hut. His wife served them with freshly-made sweets and a cup of milk. Yadodhra again, like the detective he thought he was, began his cross-examination though, as always, in the friendliest of spirits. He had already, more than once, used words like Hindu and Sindhu, just to see if they were at all familiar. They were not. He had also used several common terms of the Sindhu people to see if the Shreshtha's people had the same words. He found no meeting ground. He had repeated words such as acharya, arati, bhakti, brahmacharya, buddhi, daya, dana, dharma, guru, sanyasa, yogi, satya, samskara... they didn't recognize these or ten thousand other words he used. They practiced yoga but called it by a different name. They performed bhakti, but named it differently. The only common words he discovered were: karma, moksha, Brahma, tulsi and god Rudra.

Shreshtha himself rarely asked a question. Yet he never seemed to mind if Yadodhra kept questioning him, though at times he indicated with a gesture and a smile that Yadodhra's head might burst with so much knowledge. This time, Yadodhra was making his last attempt.

He pointed at Shreshtha's grandson, then Shreshtha's son, thereafter at Shreshtha himself and finally kept waving his hand upwards. Obviously, he was asking about Shreshtha's ancestors. Shreshtha replied with a smile and gesture that they were all dead. Yadodhra shook his head. That is not what he was asking. Again he pointed to himself, then to Bharat, and to his men standing outside, calling each a Hindu. Now he was pointing to Shreshtha's grandchildren, sons, and Shreshtha himself, and waving his hand upwards to include his ancestors as though to ask if there was a common dharma or spiritual bond or link. Shreshtha shook his head. His sons had a polite smile; only the grandchildren seemed to be curious. Again Shreshtha shook his head, to indicate that he could find no satisfactory answer.

Shreshtha's wife, busy warming thin, wafer-like biscuits on the fire, looked up at Yadodhra, and asked, 'Sanathana?'

Yadodhra heard her, unable to believe his ears. Shreshtha nodded and repeated 'Sanathana!' He wondered if that was what Yadodhra was asking.

Yadodhra's clay cup of hot milk had dropped into his lap. It did not break but the milk spilled, soiling his clothes. He did not notice it. In a hushed whisper, he asked, 'Sanathana Dharma?'

Both Shreshtha and his wife noticed his excitement but shook their heads. Quietly, Shreshtha corrected him and repeated, 'Sanathana.'

It was as though Yadodhra had not heard him. But he had heard—clearly, distinctly. His face beamed with joy, as if he was, by some mysterious enchantment, hearing a melody of an enticing song from generations past. When he trusted himself to speak, he said with his voice still quivering with excitement, 'Sanathana Dharma, Shreshtha, Sanathana Dharma! You are from that ageless, ancient dharma of righteousness! You and I are links from the same past. You and I are links of the same future!' Yadodhra rose, while Bharat removed the fallen cup from his lap, but Yadodhra was still speaking:

'Let me embrace you, Shreshtha, for the past, for the present, for the future.' He almost stretched out his arms to embrace the old man.

But Bharat intervened to cut in, 'Do not, please, embrace Shreshtha with your wet clothes!'

Shreshtha's wife took Yadodhra to the next room and gave him a thin cotton cloth which she had intended for a bedsheet. He wrapped it around him and came to embrace Shreshtha.

Shreshtha smiled at the gaudy cloth with red and white stripes that his guest wore but was happy that, mysteriously, a deep well of curiosity in Yadodhra's heart had been satisfied. Gladly they embraced.

Yadodhra, who always had questions, asked no more. But Bharat did. He wanted to know if the Sanathana Dharma of his people meant the same thing as the Sanathana of Shreshtha's people. He was certain it was so, yet he had to ask. In his own land, he knew that Sanathana Dharma was a bonding of those who believed in Sanathana. But was Shreshtha's own understanding of Sanathana the same as his?

Such questions are never easy. Without the same, common language, they are impossible. Yet Shreshtha and his wife and even their sons tried to explain. She put a pinch of salt in water; it melted, and she shook her head to show that Sanathana could not melt. She took a piece of cloth, burnt it over the fire, and again shook her head to indicate it could not burn; she brought Yadodhra's wet trouser, shaking her head, to indicate it could not be drenched; she broke a biscuit in two, and again shook her head to show it could not be broken. Shreshtha's wife stood firm on the ground, while Shreshtha pretended that he was trying to move her, and thus they explained that it was immovable. They closed their eyes and shook their heads to demonstrate that it was always awake and alert. They pointed to the sky and the sun and the sea to show that it was all-pervading, ageless, abiding and eternal.

Yadodhra was sitting in a reverie, certain that he had understood all that there was to understand. Bharat was learning from the examples of Shreshtha and his wife, of their conception of Sanathana, which was no different from his. He understood from their explanations that it was unbreakable, insoluble, everlasting, eternal, imperishable, infinite, awake, alert, all-pervading, unchangeable, that it could neither be drenched, nor dried, nor burned, nor cleaved. Yet all the time, as they gave each example, they pointed to their hearts, as though to emphasize their belief that God and the human soul were the same. Truly, it was Sanathana Dharma that was at the heart of their description.

Bharat looked at Yadodhra, but Yadodhra sat with the deep satisfaction of one who had solved a great mystery. Indeed it seemed that all was revealed to him. Leisurely, affectionately, he was patting the cloth with red and white stripes which he wore round his waist in place of his discarded wet trousers.

Shreshtha had come to see them off. They looked at the Sindhu samundar for the last time and embraced Shreshtha affectionately. Bharat was silent but Yadodhra spoke pointing to Shreshtha's heart and his own—to show that they were the same people, from the same race. Shrestha had no difficulty in understanding him. He, in any case, had always thought that all men were brothers.

On the way back Yadodhra was lost in thought. More than finding the source of the Sindhu river, more than the sight of the vast, unending ocean, what satisfied him the most was the discovery of these people with a pre-ancient link with the Sanathana Dharma, of which his father Ekantra had spoken with such feeling and emotion. He did not, then, know that later, people from the Sindhu region would meet the people from the greater Ganga civilization in the east and discover a common ancestory, culture and link binding all of them as one people, from one single race. There, they would see, how their own holy river, Saraswati, meets with the Ganga and Yamuna rivers, leaving some of its waters to merge with these two rivers and yet charting a majestic path of its own to even carry some of the waters of the Ganga and Yamuna to their own Sindhu river, as both the Saraswati and Sindhu flowed to the Sindhu sea. Nor did Yadodhra, then, know that the explorers from his region would one day meet the people of the magnificent Dravidian civilization in the south and discover the long-forgotten link that once bound them together, in their ways of living, thought, attitude, ideals and culture—though the language they spoke was different.

But Yadodhra's mind was not on the unseen future. He was thinking of the past—he was convinced that somehow hidden in the mists of centuries gone by, there had been a close and continuous living contact between his people and the people who lived by the side of the confluence of the Sindhu river and the Sindhu sea. At last he spoke to Bharat.

'Shreshtha's people—truly, they are the people of the Sanathana Dharma!'

But Bharat replied, 'No, they are more ancient than that. They are the people of the Sanathana. It is from them that our Sanathana Dharma came.'

'Yes, but then they are Hindu! Are they not!' Yadodhra asked.

'Yes, they are Hindus. They are the very root of the Hindu.'

'. . .There are those who believe that suddenly, out of nothing, without preparation, without foundation, without forethought and even without warning, God creates a miracle and, lo and behold, all mankind is immediately touched with reverence and awe by that miracle, and all life is rearranged, remoulded and reshaped around it!

'But the truth is, that while God can indeed perform any miracle of His choosing, the way He works is neither sudden, nor capricious, nor arbitrary. He had all the choices while constructing the universe. It was His will to choose the set of laws that the universe obeyed. But having done that, He allows the universe to evolve according to those laws, and never does He intervene to break them. Clearly, then, He Himself has chosen to follow the very same physical and natural laws which He has set for mankind; thus God (or, call it nature, if you will) stands in His majesty, dreaming, breathing, planning and creating, but never deviating from the physical and natural laws of the universe of His creation.

'Everything, then, is the result of His endless patience, and nothing is ever sudden, and all is orderly, thought-out and carefully crafted and moulded, and yet it must obey the physical and natural laws of the universe. But when there is hope and hunger for a miracle in the landscape of the human soul, and when people begin to hear in their dreams, the sound of the footsteps of Him who is to come, then surely they will see what seems to be His miracle. . . .Yet, ask yourself, who made this miracle—God? Man? Who?. . .'

—(From Rishi Ekantra's lectures to his students, around 5121 BC, recalled in the Memory songs of 5080 BC)

He Comes, He Comes,
Ever He Comes . . . .

5088 to 5068 BC

Much had happened, long before Sindhu Putra emerged at the Island of Silence, and even before Bharat retired as Karkarta; and many had their roles to play.

Villagers who were polite, called her 'The Lady of Easy Virtue.' There were other epithets too, by which Kanta was known but epithets never tell all the truth or even half the truth.

As to the accusation of being a cheap prostitute, the fact is that her fees were moderately high. She set a high value on what she offered.

The charge of being dirty also fails, considering how filthy her customers often were, while she usually smelt like a rose.

Nor was it correct to call her a heartless bitch. Her love was not always for sale. Sometimes, she gave herself free and freely, out of the sheer joy of love. Was she heartless? What about that occasion when she gifted away her jewellery to a girl whose mother complained that her husband had squandered his all in her whorehouse and could not afford to get his daughter married! And would she ever permit boys, not of the right age, to enter her house? No, never, even if they came rolling in with costly gifts, stolen from parents.

It was unfair, too, to call her an easy, money-grabbing harlot; she worked hard to earn what she did and suffered unspeakable horrors.

But the fact also remains that Kanta was a prostitute, a whore and a harlot; and she was attracted to this profession of selling her body by the same consideration which attract many of her kind to it—lust, greed and selfishness, though not necessarily their own.

Kanta was married to Satrash, a farmer who later become a preacher when he heard the word of God. She followed his lead. But then, he had chosen to follow God's word chiefly so that he could seduce Devadassi, the young girl who danced in the temple. Devadassi had taken a vow to remain a virgin in the service of the gods until the end of her days.

Although her heart was innocent and she had submitted to Satrash on his pretext of purifying her body, Devadassi knew that she had committed a revolting outrage against god, as the oath of a brahmacharini (a virgin's oath of life-long chastity in God's service) cannot be lightly taken or broken.

For three days Devadassi lived in agony and finally she threw herself into the black waters of the Sindhu on a moonless night.

Meanwhile Satrash, not knowing what Devadassi contemplated, was terrified. He had not expected Devadassi to react so terribly to what he considered a simple act of love. The day after he deprived her of her virginity, she had not appeared in the temple. When some went to ask the reason, she refused to answer. The head pujari decided that he himself would speak to her.

Satrash feared that Devadassi would tell all. He knew the penalty for molesting a virgin and he rushed to tell Kanta that they must leave immediately. He gave no reason. Kanta was expecting a child, due any day. She pleaded but he was adamant. Finally, she refused because the life of a child to be born, she said, was more important than any vision he might have had to serve the gods elsewhere.

He told her then that it was not a vision from God but the fear of man and his life was in danger—and was that not more important than the life of a child yet to be born? There and then she decided to leave, clear in her mind that she would walk to the ends of the earth, sacrifice everything and everybody, to protect her husband.

Kanta began to pack. All that she begged was to go to her father's house to say farewell.

'No, no, you cannot! Devadassi will be there.'

'But of course Devadassi will be there and if not, I will go to the temple to meet her.'

Devadassi was Kanta's sister.

It was only then that Satrash told her of his heinous sin. He sounded penitent. 'The devil made me do it. The devil made me do it.' Satrash wailed, 'God give me death!'

Kanta was staring blankly into space. Thought and emotion left her. Then she knelt on the floor and sobbed, hitting her head against the floor, hoping that the hurt to her head would, somehow, ease the throbbing pain in her heart. She stopped banging her head only when she heard a movement inside her body, as though her unborn child was pleading with her to stop.

She remembered the old curse: 'Their seed shall never die but shall burn eternally in hell-fire, and the spirits of their ancestors will be summoned, from wherever they reside, to burn with them for ever— for that shall be the punishment for him who commits the sin of plucking the chaste flower of God in the brahmacharini.'

He Comes, He Comes, Ever He Comes.... / 173

This, she knew, was one of the eighty-eight curses in an ancient hymn: 'Crime and Punishment'. It sang not of the compassion of the gods but only of their wrath. While many hymns composed in Karkarta Bharat's time (some new and others inspired by songs of centuries past), sang of the love, mercy and tenderness of the gods, the old pre-ancient curses were not easy to forget.

Kanta shivered. She knew the gods were watching. They would see the seed of her husband in her belly—and that seed would, for ever, be cursed. For ever! She must run, hide, away from the searching gaze of the ever-watchful gods who stood guard over their village. But gods were everywhere; where could she run to! Where could she hide! She shuddered—'My seed is cursed, how does it matter where I go!'

Quickly, he sought to reassure her. 'No, nothing happens to our child. I was the one who was tempted. I was the one who was seduced.'

She stared at him, speechless with repulsion. She would never believe that of Devadassi, her little, innocent sister—half woman, half child—whose heart was filled with pure devotion to the gods.

But Satrash was a marksman with many arrows. If one fell short, he had another. 'Yes the devil tempted me; he seduced me. But we must go away from here; otherwise, our unborn seed is in jeopardy.'

Kanta was sobbing; Satrash continued, 'I know of a place where we can lose our identity, where neither god nor man can reach us.'

He had thought of running away by himself, leaving Kanta behind. But she was his protection. Her father, then, would have him hunted and killed. It would be impossible for the old man to bear the burden of one daughter seduced and another abandoned. Yes, she must serve as his hostage. 'You must save our child.' He spoke in a tone of complete humbleness of spirit.

But if she heard him, she did not respond. Tears welled up in her eyes and her heart was moaning in pain. She was telling herself, 'All my life I wanted to hear God's voice; now at last I hear it, and all it tells me is that the seed within me shall burn in hell.'

She was shivering, while Satrash repeated softly, 'You must save our child.' Again, he kept chanting these words in the form of a mantra, though he changed them slightly to say, 'I must save my child.'

He repeated this softly uttered chant until it reached the emptiness in her heart; and suddenly, with dazzling clarity, she was telling herself that she must move to save her unborn child—away from this village—away from the curse of god and man.

Avoiding the river, Satrash and Kanta went towards the forest. He walked; she was on her horse; he even exchanged greetings with passers-by and pointing to her pregnant condition, said, 'She now has wild tastes, so I go to collect wild flowers for her.'

Hidden from villages, they went along the inside edge of the forest. When dusk fell, they rested on the outskirts of a large village.

Satrash watched village fires subside and, alone, he moved to the river. He knew where the boats were tied and also knew how inattentive the night-guards were. But he was afraid of their dogs. He went into the river, at a distance from the boats. With silent strokes, he swam towards them. There was one small boat which looked trim and fast. Remaining in the water, he pulled it slowly downstream, so that its movement did not attract notice. When he reached the desired spot, he tied the boat to a boulder and fetched Kanta. He left the horse behind, and helping Kanta into the boat, waved farewell to the village: 'Take my horse. My horse for your boat!'

Kanta fainted on entering the boat. She remained in delirium while the boat travelled downstream, for days. At last Satrash heaved a sigh of relief when he saw, in the far distance, his destination—a row of three barren rocks jutting out of the middle of Sindhu river.

These rocks were known as the Accursed Rocks of the Mad Muni.

Those who knew this stretch of Sindhu river would advise others never to set foot on these rocks. The only inhabitant, they said, was a demented recluse, who spoke to no one but cursed everyone who ventured near his rocks—and then he cursed not only people but their gods, one by one, name by name.

Once, these rocks were a place of worship. A man of god had come there with his wife and eight-year-old child and built a temple.

Then, one stormy night, lightning struck. Fire erupted in their cottage. The man and his wife perished. The child survived.

Headmen of surrounding villages decided that the child, when he grew up, would run the temple. Meanwhile, they chose a trustee to look after the temple and the child.

A child's hunger to regain the love of his lost parents would probably match all the yearnings of the universe; and initially, the trustee spoke with such gentleness that he felt a glow of warmth in his heart and a hope that the deep wound within him would heal.

The ritual for custodial care required sixty-six promises from the trustee to the child. The trustee recited them all. From the child, only a few words were required. Obviously. The ancients who devised the ritual believed that the less a child speaks, the better it was for everyone.

The child repeated the words of the ritual: 'I shall obey all I hear from your lips, as long as the gods keep us together.'

He recited feelingly. Somewhere in his innocent ecstasy was the hope that he would recapture the rapturous love of his lost parents.

The child's parents had believed that a temple was merely a place of worship. The trustee knew better. To him, a temple was business, like any other. With a foresight borne out of that vision, he planned improvements. Piers were constructed to facilitate the handling of boats. Steps were built for easier climbing. Boatmen were offered food to divert passenger-boats to halt at temple-rocks. Instead of a single place for offerings, he had several new idols made, each with an in-built bowl or niche, for multiple offerings. Raised walkways were provided for the satisfaction of being seen while making large donations. He established shops for selling food, cereals, flowers. Devotees would buy these as offerings to the idols and back they would go for resale. It made sense as prices at the temple-shops were cheaper, with the competitive advantage of resale.

The number of devotees rose. So did their donations. The trustee felt a glow of satisfaction. He had struck a gold-mine.

But the child! It was he who occupied the trustee's mind. He was foisted on him, as part of the deal, to take over the temple. But what had he taken over! A decrepit temple building with nothing to encourage the worshippers to loosen their purse-strings! But he, by his foresight, turned it into an imposing building, with attractive approaches, ornamental plants, and with every incentive to visitors to be generous.

The trustee felt entitled to a just wrath against the child. But then how do you appeal to god against man's law, which, in its stupidity, was concerned more with protecting children than their custodians!

Apparently, the trustee concluded that the proper course was to make the boy unworthy of running the temple. Hopefully, the boy could be coerced into giving the temple to him, after eight years—as a person must be at least sixteen years old to make a gift of property. Meanwhile, he wanted to break his spirit, dominate his every thought, and teach him to obey every command, with no will of his own.

The child was given menial tasks to perform. He was obliged to sleep in the open, never to enter the temple. Never before had he heard a harsh word. Never had he been hit. Now it was common.

He was only a child and had no words for his suffering. Through tears, he would recall the vision of his parents. But it seemed to him that his parents whose memory he loved more than himself had become remote, uncaring, like faraway stars. In his heart was the bleak, endless expanse of a silent wasteland.

Only once did he disobey the trustee's order and enter the temple in the silence of dusk. He carried a mala of beads. It was the only possession he had. He was seen. Retribution was swift. The trustee came; the boy was praying, eyes closed; the trustee hit him. The rosary dropped. The trustee was about to kick the fallen boy, but seeing the rosary, stopped.

'Did you steal it from the temple?'

'It was my mother's,' the boy mumbled. The trustee saw the cheap rosary; he was even more angry with the boy's parents, who left behind nothing of value. 'Your mother was a whore,' he shouted, and relishing the shock on the boy's face, added, 'And your father was a pimp.'

The boy faced the trustee in silence. No voice penetrated his mind, no movement and the trustee had to repeat the order, 'Get out.'

All his emotions, feelings, senses, were stilled. All he kept hearing and re-hearing was the echo of the trustee's order—'Get out.'

He was ready to obey. He left the rocks and went into the river to reach the forests beyond. His vow to the trustee echoed within him— 'I shall obey all that I hear from your lips, as long as the gods keep us together.' He now vowed that the gods should never keep them together and he threw a clenched fist in defiance against the gods, if ever they dared to bring them together.

He left the rocks at the age of twelve and became a silent wanderer, often in the depths of forests. Many questions raged in his mind, to which he could find no answers. He returned to his rocks, after twenty years, on the day the trustee died.

He did not know that the trustee was to die that very day! It was simply a coincidence.

Many stories were told about this muni while he wandered in the forests after leaving the rocks at the age of twelve, without saying farewell. Rarely did he reply to questions. Some said that he spoke to the trees and birds and that they understood him.

There was a story that when he was eighteen years of age, a little girl, five years old, brought him a long staff (walking stick), for his walks through the forests; she told him that it belonged to her father but he also had another walking staff; he asked her to bring the other staff as well. She refused, protesting that her father was blind and needed it. When the girl reached home, she tearfully told her poor blind father of the impossible demand of the impossible muni. But her father said that it was improper to refuse a muni, and he handed over the staff to his daughter; she went reluctantly and gave it to the muni, but in anger she asked him, 'How can you take this staff? Do you not know my father is blind?'

The muni gently said, 'I knew little one that your father was blind.'

The girl stamped her foot in disgust and ran to her hut. Her father was asleep. In a surge of sympathy, she placed her hand on her father's forehead, and said, 'I shall be your staff, Father, and we shall walk together, always, hand-in-hand.'

Her tears flowed and some of those tears fell into her father's eyes. The father opened his eyes. And then... the miracle occurred! He could see! He was blind no more!

Trembling with joy, he went to thank the muni, but the muni replied, 'I had nothing to do with you, old man; maybe your daughter's tears washed away your blindness.'

And when the old man said that he would go to the temple to render thanks, the muni said, 'Men go to temples to lose sight not to gain it.'

The muni became angry when the old man wanted to touch his feet, but calmed down when the little girl went quickly to sit in his lap.

The whole village heard of the miracle and flocked to see the muni, but he had left for the deep recesses of the forest.

From the villages, near and far, many came to pay homage to the muni when he re-entered the temple after the trustee died.

They were disappointed. The headmen even more so. The trustee always welcomed them respectfully. This muni ignored them, as if they did not exist! When a headman asked him to begin singing, all he got was a glare, though later the muni said he knew no songs but the headman was free to sing, if he wished. When the muni was told to begin the sermon, he asked people to close their eyes and listen to the sound of their hearts. Sound of their hearts! Why come to the temple then? The muni agreed that it was foolish to visit a temple to listen to the sound of one's heart.

This mad muni did not even acknowledge the generous offerings of visitors. Instead, his eyes went to those who bowed low before idols, but made no offerings; they were boatmen, largely slaves, who had brought devotees and they had only their devotion to offer; they bowed and remained far behind. The muni brought them forward; and he said, 'They are the ones who heard. They are the ones whose eyes were closed. They are the ones who were listening to the sound of their hearts.'

But what is surprising about it—wondered some; they are slaves, with no minds of their own. They were asked to close their eyes, so they closed them; they were asked to listen to the voices within, so they were trying to do that. Why should that intrigue the muni! But to bring slaves forward, ahead of the headmen, was galling.

As the muni refused song and sermon, the headmen asked for at least a question-answer session. Many moons had passed since the last temple service. The trustee, ailing for a long time, was telling visitors that the gods were dissatisfied as he had not collected enough to expand the temple and therefore the gods were thinking of calling him back. While that tearful plea made visitors generous and increased the trustee's wealth, the temple service with question-answer sessions remained in abeyance. After the trustee's death the people hoped for its revival by the muni.

The muni however would not oblige. 'Who am I to answer? Who am I to teach? Listen to your heart. Listen to its sound. Listen to its silence.'

When a headman protested that if persons listened to their own hearts, each would have a different story, the muni seemed happy and said, 'Then all those different stories will be the many stories of god.'

But another headman was angry. His slaves were sitting ahead of him. Loudly, he said, 'It is an insult to the gods to leave this man in charge of the temple.' Others tried to pacify the infuriated headman. No, let us give him a chance; this is only his first service.

Many began to leave, some in anger, others in sorrow. Only the slaves, somehow, sensed the anguish that filled the soul of this muni.

The muni halted a slave-woman. 'Take all this,' he said, pointing to the gifts brought by devotees, 'and give equally to all the slaves here.'

'No, Muniji, no; our masters gave these for the gods.'

'Are the gods so poor and worthless as to need these?' the muni asked. He commanded, 'It is in god's name that I ask you to take them. Take!'

The angry headman shouted again, 'Mad muni, you have no right to be with these idols of gods.' The muni nodded, as if he fully agreed.

The headman rushed to lead the people who would heed his call to leave. Blocking his way, unwittingly, was the slave-woman to whom the muni had spoken. In his anger—for he wanted to be seen as a man of wrath in a righteous cause—the headman pushed the woman roughly. She fell against a stone idol. The wound to her head was not deep but there was blood.

The muni saw her blood on the idol. Looking at the headman, in a hoarse whisper that could be heard by many, he commanded, 'Go!'

With horror, they saw the muni removing the idol with the slave-woman's blood. He kept it outside. They protested, but he asked 'Why! Are your gods so weak that they must remain indoors!' It was a beautiful idol, which the trustee had got specially made, with its hand raised in blessing, while its smiling eyes rested on the bowl held in its left hand, to receive the offerings of devotees. The headman shouted at the sacrilege. The muni dragged the idol and threw it in the river.

He was mad. They were certain.

Yes, he was mad, mad beyond redemption! They left in anger.

The headman, who had chastized the muni, tarried. With help from some others, he recovered the idol from the river. Unfortunately, his boat capsized and he alone was drowned while the others were saved. Some said the boat was overloaded, but many feared that the mad muni had a powerful curse.

From that day on, crowds to the rocks thinned, then became a trickle and finally none came, each telling the other to avoid the doomed rocks which came to be known as the Accursed Rocks of the Mad Muni.

Even so, some came not to worship but to inspect, fired with hope from the headmen that the mad muni would be banished and a trustee would be appointed. Naturally, the temple's spiritual and material rewards would go to the trustee. They disturbed the muni; some asked when he would leave, others threatened action against him if he damaged any more idols.

Suddenly, a huge fire was seen burning on the rocks. Unfairly, it was said that the mad muni had set fire to the temple. The headmen halted their consultations to appoint a new trustee; in fact they had already sent a deputation to Karkarta to have the mad muni banished; but now, there was no need for a new trustee, as only the barren rocks remained, with no temple. Soon the madman would leave and then they would build a temple there, to honour the gods whom the mad muni had dishonoured.

It was to these barren rocks that Satrash guided his boat. Rumour had intensified the demonic qualities and violence of the mad muni.

Satrash hoped to hide in these rocks which none approached. He would beg, plead or bribe the muni—but if nothing works, well, the mad muni can be dashed against the rocks to share the fate of his idol; and surely, people would regard it as just retribution... And then... I can resurface to build a temple here. What more can a man ask for, than to be the master of a temple!—That had always been his highest ambition.

Satrash need not have been worried. The mad muni had mellowed.

After the raging fire, when the last embers cooled, a semblance of calm came to the muni's turbulent mind. He went into a trance, deep within his subconscious depths and somehow it seemed that someone, from somewhere unseen, was flooding his mind with new awareness.

Suddenly though, that tranquil feeling deserted him, as he saw a young woman standing before him.

She was Roopa, that little five-year-old girl of the blind singer, who innocently sat in his lap, thirteen years earlier; since then, she had grown into a vivacious, charming girl, and he had seen her from time to time; she would bring him food but never disturb his meditation. When he left to reclaim his rock-temple, many had gathered to greet him and she threw flowers in his path.

Now, as he saw Roopa, his mood became dark and angry; somehow he feared that the brief moment of peace that he had found in his inner consciousness would be lost. 'Why have you come?' he asked.

She was smiling. He was cold and stern. He repeated his question.

The smile did not leave her, though she was quaking within, aware of his searching eyes on her. 'Why did you come?' he asked again.

'To sit by your side,' Roopa said. She saw the anger in his eyes and blurted out, 'Only for a moment, if that is all you shall grant.'

He was silent. Something in her fear softened him. She forgot what was to be her first greeting to him though she had rehearsed it well. But then it is sometimes wise to be foolish. She kept before him fruits and nuts. 'I picked them here,' she said. Obviously, she had been here for quite some time. It was the hour of sunset.

'How long have you been here?' he asked.

'I came here at dawn. You were meditating, so I went to collect fruits. But this is all I could collect. I am clumsy, you know.'

He saw her hands, bruised from rock-climbing. Gently he spoke, 'I must eat what is gathered by these bruised hands. You must eat too.'

'I ate before. Later. You eat. I am not hungry. You eat.' Even in her babbling, she wondered—Why am I unable to speak to him without my heart pounding! He commanded, 'Eat now.' Both began to eat. She felt his eyes on her. She felt shy. She had come with many desires whispering in her breast, and now she was afraid to face him, fearing that somehow he would see her dreams.

Sadly, he looked at her and asked, 'Where is your father?'

'He is in Karkarta Bharatji's village, as a singer of the clan.'

'That is high honour,' the muni said.

'It comes from you, Muni, from you!'

'From me! How?' he asked.

'My father sang many songs for Bharatji. But the very first song was about you, Muni.' He was surprised, 'Song about me!'

'Yes, the song my father composed, of how you speak to birds, trees; how birds are silent when you meditate and how animals, tame and wild, follow you into the forest, none attacking the other and how. . . .'

'I never heard such a foolish song in all my life,' he said, but she wanted to defend the song she loved. Quickly, she said, 'But Bharatji liked it. He said it should be remembered as a Memory song.'

'Memory song!' This was a new expression for the muni.

'Yes, a Memory song. Bharatji feels that certain songs should be sung and resung, so that the coming generations will hear them too and know what the people of our times thought, felt and said.'

'Really!'

'Yes really,' she said, undisturbed by his irony. 'Bharatji says that everything will be lost unless there are such songs. He believes that everyone must know what their roots are and before people venture into the future, they must know the past, lest they run the risk of building without foundation.'

The muni snapped in icy tones, 'So this Karkarta would impose every absurdity that every demented singer can imagine on future ages!'

'No Muni, no! Only songs that speak of truth—of goodness and beauty—of our feelings and longings, our prayers and hopes, even our fears and torments. Bharatji says people must not be trapped by the times in which they live and the future must be told of what is in the landscape of our hearts and souls today. . . .' She saw his amused glance and paused, 'You are laughing at me, Muni, are you not?'

'No, I was just thinking, you should have been here at the temple to give a sermon to the people who were clamouring for it. They left me in anger and they will always be angry with me.'

'Yes, I know; they were asking for your banishment.'

'What!' He was surprised. 'How do you know?'

'That is why my father rushed to Karkarta. We heard that headmen around here sent eighteen persons to Bharatji, seeking to banish you from the temple. We reached when Bharatji was speaking to them and....'

He interrupted, 'So you and your father spoke and I was saved!'

'No, Muni, no; my father was dying to speak; he even interrupted to say that they were talking nonsense. But Karkarta said, "Let the accusers be the first to speak." So we sat with silent contempt.'

'And your expression of silent contempt saved me!'

She smiled, 'No, Bharatji decided that you could not be banished.'

'Why?' he asked.

'Oh! He silenced them all; many, many reasons he gave.'

'Tell me,' he insisted. But she hesitated, 'They said foolish things, not worth repeating. Karkarta spoke with the voice of reason.'

'And why should I not hear that voice of reason?' he insisted.

She began the story of Karkarta's meeting:

'...On the charge of you insulting the gods, Bharatji's reply was:

"It is then a question between the gods and Muni. Do our gods need our protection from Muni? A quarrel between man and his gods is a private affair. How can I accept the view that a man cannot ask the gods the questions that torment his spirit! If the gods do not answer, or his understanding is not illuminated, why can he not question the gods further?... But even if a crime has been committed against the gods, it is for them—not man—to avenge it...."

'Then, on the charge of your belief in the devil, Bharatji replied:

"...Does it matter what gods or devils he believes in? Your own preachers say their gods are true but the gods of others are devils. Tell me then, who are the true gods and who is the devil?..."

'Karkarta then gave them a long lecture on the identity and nature of God and the devil and finally said:

"...So long as Muni believes in a creature of God, it seems he may come to believe in God.... Is the devil a creature of God, or is he created independent of God? If he is created independently, then you admit that there are two creators—God and the devil.... In any case, by what right do we interfere with a person's belief, or the path he chooses, to reach the truth?..."

'Bharatji confounded them further, on their main demand and said:

"...You ask that he be banished. Where? To your village! Do you want a scoffer of gods and a blasphemer, as you call him, to be in your midst to corrupt your minds! Or is it your suggestion that he be sent to other villages, far from you! Then you would admit to the principle that undesirables from other villages can be banished to your villages. In any case, he is at his own rocks within his own temple. You are the ones who go to disturb his peace; he does not come to you. So he has banished himself. Yet you go to him and then come crying that the company of this godless man of sin degrades you! Did it not occur to you to let him be in his isolation and keep yourself away from the temptation of his company so that you might achieve your self-appointed goal of remaining chaste and pure—if indeed, that is your goal! But if you have come seeking his banishment outside our clan and outside our land, then you are guilty of harbouring evil in your hearts, for remember this, he, like all of us, is a rya and no one, and I repeat, no one has the right to exile a rya, and make him arya. As Karkarta, I do not have that right; the Council of Chiefs has no such right. Why, even if all the people of our rya are unanimous, they cannot deprive a single man of his basic right as a rya."

'Courteously then, Bharatji dismissed their plea. It was then that my father wanted to speak but Bharatji stopped him again and said:

"Those who complained against Muni have already said so much in his favour that I fear when you begin to speak for him you might say much that is against him. But the case is decided and judgement has been given. Do you want to reopen it?"

'But my father said that all he wanted was to sing a song. Bharatji was delighted and my father sang so soulfully that there were tears in many eyes; and when he sang of how you restored his eyesight....'

At this the muni interrupted her, 'Foolish girl, how often must I tell you that I did not restore his eyesight! Your tears did that.'

She looked at him boldly; nobody could rob her of the knowledge of that miracle; she said, 'I know what I know; my father knows what he knows; and God knows what we all know. That is enough for me.'

He retorted in fury, 'Do you know what I know? I know you are mad, your father is mad and your Karkarta is mad!'

She smiled to soften his anger. He misunderstood and said, 'No wonder you smile. You must wonder how I who am called the mad muni can call you, your father and Karkarta mad.'

Her heart froze; pain washed over her in waves and she cried out, clutching at his hand, 'No, no, Muni, no; sometimes I don't know why I smile; sometimes I smile because my heart says one thing and I am thinking something different. Sometimes my heart loses its limits in joy and I smile because of the gladness of your presence.'

She was trembling. To calm her, he placed his hand on hers. For a few heartbeats, they faced each other. Her love rose up like a wave, crushing her, filling her, fulfilling her, and she was smiling, embracing him with her eyes; she was at peace now, happy that in her silence she had told him what she could not utter in words. She had always feared that she would carry her unspoken love in her sleeping and waking dreams, but now the voice within her had shouted the message of her heart to his.

The muni spoke. She scarcely heard. He repeated, 'You must go back.'

'Where?' she asked, as though surprised.

'Back to your village,' he replied.

'I have no one there,' she said.

He Comes, He Comes, Ever He Comes.... / 183

'Then go to your father,' he urged.

'But he is in the village of Karkarta,' she replied.

'Then go there.'

'But I have just come from there,' she smiled. 'And Karkarta Bharatji said that I must give you his salutations and regards.'

The muni refused to be diverted and asked, 'Where is the boat?'

'What boat?' she asked innocently.

'The boat in which you came to these rocks.'

'I don't know. The boatman left me here and went away.'

'Did you not ask him to come back for you?'

'Why would I do such a thing?' she asked.

'But you said you came to sit by my side only for a moment.'

'Oh, that! No, Muni, I shall always be by your side.'

The roles were now reversed. He was the one who was pleading. Sadly, he looked at her and said, 'I can offer you nothing.'

'That is more than I expect. I came expecting less than nothing.'

'This is no place for you. You have to go back, child.'

'Child! Child!' she challenged. 'Do I look like a child to you!'

His eyes brushed her young, inviting breasts and he said, 'It is because you are no longer a child that you must go away.'

'No, Muni, no!' Her playfulness disappeared. 'I have nowhere to go. Even as a child I promised myself that I would be yours. God heard that vow from me every day for thirteen years. He knows!'

The muni glared but she continued, 'If you will not have me, let me at least live here. I shall keep still. I shall fill my heart with your silence and ask for nothing—neither word nor smile.'

'Is that all you want?' he asked sternly.

'No. My desires are many, but you will not even hear the whisper of my wishing; only let me be on these rocks, near your footsteps.'

He looked at her, his eyes full of profound, silent sorrow. Slowly, he walked away and sat at the bank of the river. But the river kept flowing on, heedless of him and his grief.

At the core of his heart was emptiness. How could this girl, bubbling with life and laughter, have come to share his loneliness! Possibly she floated on the bosom of a blissful dream of long ago; but these rocks—they would shatter her dream to bits. In humbleness, he prayed: 'Oh! Limitless One, let her youth blossom in pure joy; protect her so that she does not, alone and unguarded, commit a wrong to herself. Hear me, God....'

Suddenly, the muni's wandering prayer stopped; and he went into meditation. An inner quiet descended on him. When he finally rose, he saw fruit and water near him and nodded his thanks silently.

For days, they hardly spoke; sometimes he helped her to clear the heavy rubble from the remains of the charred temple; and if his hand then touched hers, her heart would silently leap in joy.

At last, he called her to his side. The sun was about to set, but its last flickering glow still remained. He spoke with tenderness of disorderly games that the mind plays in idealizing past dreams and images; possibly, in her childish fancy she had believed that he restored her father's eyesight, and then, in a flash, the thought of surrendering herself to him eternally came to her; and this was the shadowy foundation of her dream: to pass her life with him in these forbidding rocks. 'But you must not hear the whisperings of a dream based on fantasy. You must not permit yourself to be bewildered by what you told yourself when you were five years old, nor must you wound yourself with your own hand. Your desires are the desires of youth and flow like a fountain, but how can they seek to drink from my cup which is broken and will always remain empty.'

He continued, pointing to the setting sun, 'No, like the sun, this evening, that is deepening into orange and ruby, I want you to feel joy—deep tranquil joy—to let it sink into your very soul, in anticipation of the life that awaits you, away from these accursed rocks.'

He spoke now in calm despair, 'I alone know the loud and unceasing storms that rage in my heart. They are right who call me mad. I am not a man of God. I am unworthy even to call out God's name. I insulted God's creation and taunted those who came to pray.'

'But Muni, they angered you with incessant questions, interrupted your meditation; even wounded a slave-girl! I heard it all when Karkarta remorselessly questioned the eighteen jackals who accused you!'

'Yes, I broke their idols! And, in breaking their idols, I robbed them of the cherished fragments of God's grace. God forgives all blasphemy against Himself, but not a crime against His creation. And you wish to live with a man steeped in sin, drowned in sorrow! A man who can offer nothing because he has nothing to offer even to himself!'

He looked at her. But her eyes were closed in silent prayer—'God, you know there is no sin in my Muni. But there is some unseen, hidden wound in his heart—deep, unhealed. God, lift the burden of his prolonged and measureless torment. He simply wants to know you. Give him that knowledge, that understanding—limitless, everlasting.'

She concluded her prayer; yet she did not open her eyes; her trance continued and she heard herself, locked in debate, defending her Muni against accusation from the gods and finding the gods at fault.

The muni watched her, fascinated. He knew that before a worshipper, through yoga, becomes one with the spirit, certain visions, of mist, nebulous smoke, lightning, are experienced within, with an inner glow, and then the yogi's face appears transformed and a radiance shines through it when passing into the stage of samadhi. He now saw the same glow and radiance on the face of the young woman before him.

A golden mist of sunset descended on the rocks. Roopa remained in her state of oblivion. Himself, a seeker of silence, the muni did not intrude on her silence. But he wondered: what is the flame that burns deep within her and showers its light on her face? Or is it the evening sky, and its light and shadow, playing on my imagination?

He saw the moon rise, in its perpetual mystery, over the rocks. He had often wondered in the past: does the moon come to us or do our nights go to catch a glimpse of it? But now he was not concerned with the pale sky-wanderer of the night. He was wondering over the mystery of the woman in her trance of fathomless silence.

He watched as at last she rose. Slowly she walked towards him. It was dream-walking; her eyes were closed and her mind was in silent stillness. She stood before him for a moment, opened her eyes; her glance embraced him and then they slept side by side.

The song of the morning birds awakened her with the memory of his hand on her breast. They moved into each other's arms, warm and half-asleep and in the last clear moment, before they sank into the promise of each other's bodies, they knew, with a triumphant surge, that they would be together, for ever.

Exhausted and exhilarated, they lay in brief, dreamless slumber; for love does not know its own depth until the moment of its fulfilment.

The sun was rising and the birds tried to pierce the morning's warm silence with their songs but Roopa and Muni heard only each other's heartbeats. No other voice penetrated their consciousness, while they lay merged, finding their fullest flowering in each other.

Later, the muni told Roopa, 'God is truth, power, glory, compassion, purity, grace, order and purpose. But God is also love. Of all things, love is the greatest, and most powerful. It is the generating seed of all existence and fulfilment. This, I had forgotten.'

'That is not all you forgot,' she said. 'You also forgot to bring flowers for the morning prayers.' That only proved his point, he said, that so potent was the power of love, that one forgot all else.

With a sigh of relief, Satrash brought the boat to Muni's Rocks. He picked up his inert wife and began the climb.

Roopa saw them. Satrash, his face lined with worry and weariness, placed Kanta at her feet. As soon as Roopa saw Kanta's conditon, she ran into the hut and brought water. It had the perfume of flowers.

She massaged Kanta. Soon, Muni's voice boomed, 'I thought you wanted me, so I left my prayers and told the gods to wait a while, for a longer session.' They carried Kanta in. Muni brought herbs. Some he burnt, applying ash to Kanta's body; others she sipped with water.

Kanta recovered after three days, during which Muni and Roopa hardly slept; Roopa knew how much Muni missed his meditation. His reply was: 'God is nourished when His creation is served. He meditates for those who cannot meditate in their attention to His creation.'

With joy, Roopa sensed the immeasurable peace in Muni's heart.

Even Satrash was puzzled. Mad this muni certainly was, but his madness did not have the violent quality for which he was well known.

Everyday, Satrash ate nuts and fruits. To Roopa he said: 'Muniji hardly eats anything. The village will have more to offer and if you permit....' But she said that the muni ate only what grew on the rocks.

He nodded, 'But I could catch fish for him, around these hills.'

'Muni does not believe in himsa. Nor will he permit fishing from these rocks. So, if you need fish for yourself, you must go to the village and eat it there too.'

'Oh no, I believe in ahimsa too. But I thought I must do for Muni what I would never do for myself or for anyone else.'

How strange, thought Roopa, that this man of ahimsa would commit himsa to feed Muni! What is the point of adopting the God-given principle of ahimsa, only to abandon it to feed the loved one! Even so, she was touched by Satrash's gesture of devotion to Muni.

Kanta gave birth to a son. After two days, the baby died.

Kanta remained tight-lipped, holding her dead baby against her breast. She had no tears, no words; her unspoken grief cast a pall over them all. When Satrash came near, she recoiled as if his shadow on her dead child would doom it for all eternity. To Muni she cried piteously: 'Muniji, out of your mercy, save my child'

'Your child is already saved,' Muni replied.

She met his eyes. They were soft, tender. She laid kisses like a necklace on her baby's face. Silently she placed the baby at his feet. He picked up the baby and cried out to the river:

'Goddess of Sindhu! Princess of limitless treasures! I behold your beautiful vision, robed in white and blue, and I bow to you.

'For nine months this infant lay in the womb of his mother, in innocence. For two days he lived in innocence.

'For the innocence in which he lived and died, let him go to the realm of the liberated.

'Count also that I pray for him with my heart.'

Calmly, Kanta heard. But as he was lighting the cremation fire, she cried, 'No, no, do not burn him. Spare him, for he will always burn in hell.' Her inauspicious utterance upset Muni; he shouted, 'How can you speak of this little one burning in hell—he who was helpless, innocent. He suffered, yes, but he caused no suffering!'

Kanta was in the grip of a nameless terror. Hoarsely, she whispered, 'He is of the accursed seed, eternally to burn.'

'Who told you this?' Muni asked in anger.

'It is the curse of the gods for the sins of his father.'

Muni was aghast; in a towering rage he said, 'Any god that curses an innocent child is himself deserving of a curse. How can ancestral sins be on our heads! Are our own sins not enough!'

Kanta believed him. The torment within her ceased as she heard Muni chanting to the deities of Sindhu, sun, fire, atmosphere, outer space:

'Protect his soul. Keep winds and waters sweet for him; let his nights and days, dawns and sunsets be sweet; may all the regions he passes through be sweet; may his resting places be sweet.'

Kanta's mind was at peace. It was when she was sprinkling ashes in the river that the ache in her heart returned. Muni realized that there was a heavy burden in her soul; he began his invocation again:

'Goddess of Sindhu! This mother has placed in your loving fold, ashes of her son, who is henceforth your son. Be then yourself the loving mother of this child.'

Kanta saw a ripple in the waters and Muni said, 'Sindhu accepts. Grieve no more. Your child is now the putra (son) of Sindhu.'

'Sindhu Putra?' she asked, in a voice hushed with wonder.

Muni nodded; then to reassure her, he said, 'Goddess Sindhu accepts your child. If there is the hidden burden of anyone's guilt in your heart, be sure it cannot hurt your child's soul. The love of Goddess Sindhu for your child will be no less than yours.'

Kanta heard him with relief flooding her heart. But then, there never is an end to human wishing and she said wistfully: 'Only, I shall never see my child again!'

'Who knows! Goddess Sindhu may bring him back for a sojourn here!'

'He can come back! To me, as my son!'

Muni realized that it was a question every grieving mother would ask. Yet how was he to explain to her that the atman (soul) seeks liberation only to be reunited with the One Supreme, free from the cycle of rebirth and death!

Earlier, when he had invoked the deities, he had felt confident, powerful. But now he found it difficult to answer a simple question from a simple woman. Easier to speak to the gods than humans, thought Muni, for the gods neither heard nor replied. At his irreverent thought, he smiled.

Kanta saw that smile. She needed no more assurance.

But Muni's mind was still on what she had asked. He was thinking of the goal to attain moksha—liberation from the cycle of birth and death, in the final, eternal ecstasy of reunion with the One Supreme.

Attainment of liberation? Muni knew it was not an attainment as such because moksha is actually the birthright of an individual. Man himself frees himself to reach that highest level of emancipation; man's life is simply the soul's pilgrimage, back to man's original right of mystical and spiritual union with the Supreme. Even if liberation is not realized in one, two or more lives, an individual is sustained in all the stages of transmigration by the message that none is denied his birthright—to be one with the One Supreme.

How is it possible then, Muni wondered, that the child would not attain moksha! Muni thought of karma—the law of action and retribution, which governs mankind and operates in the moral realm as inexorably as in the physical realm. Every action produces a result. Every deed, good or evil, has an inevitable consequence leading either to a final release from the birth-death cycle into moksha or to further immersion in the painful cycle of rebirth and death. Each creature is fashioned by his past deeds, and not by blind chance, fate, destiny or the configuration of the stars. It is simply the law of sowing and reaping and a person reaps only that which he sows. Yet this child lived in innocence and God could not possibly will that he be given another life to pay for the sins of earlier lives. The Supreme is just not capricious and if He wanted the child to expiate for the sins of his past lives, his life could not have ended in two days. The child of two days committed no sin—neither denied his soul nor betrayed his Self— and if he did not acquire true knowledge, it is God who needed forgiveness—not the child—for the child was denied time and opportunity to acquire it.

Muni was now certain that he had the answer. To Kanta he said, 'Your child is no longer a creature of God. He is one with God. His self is united with the creator. He is free, pure, limitless, without beginning, without end. If he chooses, he shall visit you.'

Kanta looked at Muni, fascinated. To her, he was an oracle of God. He added, lest she harbour hopes of seeing her child again, 'Yes, your child and the creator are united; all you can do is to have a temple in your heart for him and the creator, who together are one.'

'A temple in my heart.'

'The heart is where temples of love are. Temples of brick and straw do not last! My parents built such a temple here. It burnt. They died in a fire. Again, it burnt, after I came here.'

Soulfully, Kanta said, 'I shall always have a temple in my heart. But I shall also build a temple, a great temple, for my Sindhu Putra.'

Muni did not hear her. Briskly, he moved; someone was coming up. Possibly, another visitor with designs of turning me away from these rocks, he thought. Well, I will dismiss him quickly.

But Roopa heard Kanta. 'Yes, you do that,' she said, hoping to channel the grieving mother's mind in new directions.

'Yes, a temple with gardens, flowers, fountains,' Kanta said.

The visitor, a young man, bowed respectfully. 'Muniji, I bring greetings from Karkarta Bharatji.' Muni nodded sternly, ready to shout him away. The youth continued, 'Karkarta will shortly visit villages in the vicinity. He seeks the honour of visiting you.'

Muni suspected irony, 'Did you say "Honour of visiting me?"'

'The words are Karkarta's. But I believe they are well chosen.'

Muni groped for words of politeness, 'Karkarta is welcome.'

'Karkarta wanted to know if any special time would suit you, so as not to disturb your prayers or meditation.'

Dark clouds of suspicion again gathered on the muni's brow at such excessive respect. 'Tell me young man, is this a game to soften me for a blow? Is your Karkarta coming here to charge me with burning the temple? Tell him, I did not burn it. Or does he want to get me out of these rocks? Tell him, I shall not leave. If need be, I shall lift these rocks with my bare hands from their very foundations and hurl them to the centre of Karkarta's village. Do you hear me?'

The youth's voice was gentle, 'Karkarta has no such designs. He will come in respect for you. Utmost respect.'

Muni felt contrite. 'I am sorry. I spoke harshly. Forgive me.'

'You had every right; I believe, many disturb you foolishly.'

'No. The foolishness has been mine, to disturb their faith in their idols.' Impressed with the youth's bearing, he added, 'I wish I had your elegance of speech, but I suppose some people are born lucky.'

Muni saw a fleeting shadow of sadness in the youth's eyes and realized that somehow he had, again, said the wrong thing. Possibly, to show friendliness, he asked: 'What is your name, son?'

'Asudra' the young man replied. The peculiar name surprised Muni and he wondered at it.

Sudra literally meant a slave. Asudra would mean a non-slave. Later, with the total abolition of slavery, the expression 'sudra' went into disuse. In those pre-ancient times, the caste system did not exist. However, centuries later, long after the Aryans returned to India, slowly, the caste system was introduced. Sudra, then, came to mean a person of low caste and the expression 'asudra' had no meaning though it was sometimes applied to those, who by their personal attainments, had elevated themselves to a higher caste, since in those early Vedic times the caste system was flexible, and it was clearly recognized that one could attain the highest state by one's deeds, not by one's family or birth—for instance, Vasistha, a celebrated sage of the Vedic era, was born of a prostitute; Vyasa, another celebrated sage, was the son of a fisherwoman; and similarly, Sage Parasara's mother was a chandala girl, belonging to a family that dealt with the disposal of corpses. It was later, after the incursion into India of the Turks and other foreign armies, that the caste system came to acquire a stranglehold, making it virtually impossible for anyone to move to a higher caste. The term 'asudra', thereafter, lost all meaning.

Thus in the larger historical context, the caste system of the Hindu is recent, so much so that even the Sanskrit language—both ancient and modern—has no word which directly or indirectly means 'caste'.

Also, it was usual to give a first name, along with a family name. Maybe, thought Muni, he belonged to a well-known family but did not wish to show off.

'Asudra! What family?' Muni asked with a friendly smile.

'I am of no family. My mother was a slave. She could not tell who my father was. I hope I have not dishonoured you with my presence.'

'Dishonoured me! No, son, no, I dishonour myself for allowing such a thought to enter your mind.'

Muni looked at Roopa. She left and soon reappeared bringing fruits and nuts. 'Let us all eat together,' Muni said.

When the frugal meal ended, Muni and Asudra conversed. Asudra told his story:

In order to keep up the population of slaves, and to ensure that the offspring were healthy, the strongest of male slaves were sent out by slave-owners, often in relays, to impregnate the female slaves. Asudra was the product of one such loveless union. No one knew who his father was.

Asudra's mother was a slave. His mother died when he was three. He was not strong. He inherited the physical weakness of his mother. His master was keen to part with him.

Mataji purchased him. She called him Asudra (non-slave) and instantly gave him free status. Later, it was suggested to him that Asudra was not a proper name, but since he was proud of that name given to him by Mataji at the moment of his freedom, he decided to keep it. It was, for him, the only sure link between his unknown past and uncertain future.

Bharatji later appointed Asudra to serve as his liaison officer with the headmen.

Earlier, Bharatji had wanted to adopt him, but the law permitted adoption only when the natural father of the child agreed to it or when the natural father was dead. As nothing was known about his natural father, these conditions could not be met. However, Karkarta had already set up a body of learned men to consider a revision of the law since he felt that a father who abandoned his child or who could not be found for three years could be presumed to have agreed to such adoption.

Meanwhile, Bharatji had given Asudra the right to use his family name—Rajavansi. He used that name for his official duties and was called Asudra Rajavansi. But he had felt it improper to use the family name when Muni had earlier questioned him; he had felt that he could not appear before Muni in the garb that really was not his. . . .

The life of every man is always a deep, dark forest, Muni was thinking. His eyes were moist as he said, 'Asudraji, what you say of Bharatji inspires respect. But he is wrong in believing that adoption requires the permission of the natural father, even if none can locate him. The law cannot be so inflexible.'

'How, Muniji! This law, inspired by the ancient sage, Yakantra, is repeated and reinforced by many. Nobody questions it, believe me.'

'I believe you but I also believe that there is much that is wrong in treating unrelated songs or stories as sources of true law.'

Muni went into a long explanation and concluded, 'True, songs on adoption owe their inspiration to a poem by Yakantra—who lived some six centuries ago. But he was also a poet and story-teller, who drew more from his imagination than from reality.'

Muni continued, 'This Yakantra loved children. He wanted children not to be in awe of the gods, but to love the gods. Children, he felt, must not regard the gods as infallible. He believed that once children love the gods as one of their own, there would be time enough, later, for them to understand the ways of God. His song on adoption was simply a story to amuse children. Let me tell you Yakantra's story in his own words, and let you be the judge.'

Muni began Yakantra's story as narrated to the children.

I, Yakantra, when I was five years old, was playing with my wooden marbles. I played alone. Soon I saw Yama (God of Death) charging on a buffalo. Now this Yama is a cheerful fellow, even though he comes only when someone has to die. And you know, it is necessary that some have to die so that they may go and visit other worlds too. The world is only one of the many that God had created and is still creating. So Yama comes to help and greet those who are fortunate enough to travel to other worlds.

That day, of course, no one was to die on that street, otherwise my parents would have told me so. Parents know everything, though sometimes they don't tell all. But if you give them a lot of love and listen to them, they will tell you everything. Sometimes, without your asking, they will tell you all, if you are good and loving.

So I wondered why Yama was charging on his buffalo! But my question was unasked. You know why? His buffalo had displaced my marble just before it went into the winning hole. I became angry. Of course if Yama was going on some real duty, I would have realized that he was in a hurry. But did I tell you that my parents had not told me that anyone was to die that day?

So, I threw the marble at Yama. No, no, children don't laugh. What I did was wrong. Never act in anger and never throw marbles at Yama. You lose them that way, because when marbles hit Yama, they break, so you have to go to your father to buy more marbles, when he is saving money to buy a horse for you when you grow up.

Well, when my marble hit Yama, it broke too. Yama also became angry. I became afraid and ran. Now children, one should always have the courage to face the adversary, otherwise everyone picks on you. So you must exercise your body to make your muscles strong. But don't forget to exercise your legs too; if the adversary is strong and powerful, use your legs and run. So, you know now why I ran.

Now, while running, I rushed to the forest with Yama chasing me. A lion cub was in my way and I collided against it. Now, children, do not make the mistake, ever, of running into a lion cub or a little animal. The lion's mother, father, aunts and uncles, were all hidden there, and they thought I was attacking their boy, so they all rushed toward me. So be careful; even when you go to play with an animal-child, its parents may fear that you intend harm, and, in ignorance, may attack you. But also children, never go to a forest alone. Take your parents there. They enjoy your company, though they are sometimes busy.

Well. Yama stopped being angry and wanted to protect me from the ferocious lion attack. So he quickly picked me up from the path of the lions. But that was his mistake. Because Yama cannot touch anyone who is alive. So I died and went to heaven.

Oh! It was great fun to be in heaven! I loved it.

But my father called out to the gods and asked them to explain Yama's conduct. All the gods met. I saw them because I was in heaven. They were worried because it was not my time to die—and yet, I was in heaven. So how could they answer my father's charge!

So you know what the gods did? They adopted me as their own son. They told my father that I was no longer his son but theirs.

But not so, said my father. 'What right do you gods have to adopt my son, when I, his father, am living and have not given consent?'

Now children, the gods could have set Yama on my father also. Then he would have died too, and no longer been able to question them. But the gods are fair and just. They said, 'Two wrongs cannot make a right.'

You know children, even if the gods had wanted my father to die, I could have prevented that. Because being adopted by the gods, I was a god myself. But children, as you all know, gods are good, fair, just and kind. Their hearts are full of love. So they met again. They had to agree to send me back to earth, to my parents.

But as the gods had already adopted me (and, children, an adoption cannot be broken), I go to heaven whenever I like. I take my dog there too, and god Indra gets annoyed when my dog chews his rug.

And children, as I have already died, I cannot die again, so I shall always be here, and when your children and grandchildren are born, tell them to visit me, for I shall always be here to tell them stories.

Ah children, you are laughing. You don't believe my story! Well, I don't believe it myself either.

Asudra stared. 'Surely, this could not be the basis for the belief that a father must be proved dead or found to consent to adoption!'

'I know of no other source. Words from his song-story were taken out of context and woven by later poets into their songs—in particular, the words "What right did you have to adopt my son, when I, his father, am living, and have not given consent?" Even children laughed at Yakantra's story, believing not a word of it, though they enjoyed it immensely. Yakantra himself laughed at it. Yet our people, wise with age and old with white hair, choose to believe it.'

'Why?' Asudra asked. 'But why?'

'There are those among us who believe that whatever is rooted in antiquity is authentic, worthy, pious. For them, it is as if the ancients never laughed, and all they were concerned with was to leave their ponderous utterances to guide us.'

Muni paused to smile, 'There are of course others who credit the ancients with nothing but primitiveness, ignorance and indolence—devoid of reason, rationality and intelligence. But the truth. . . .'

'And the truth?' Asudra was quick to ask.

'The truth?' Muni echoed. 'Our ancients had their half-truths and we have our half-truths. I wish I could say that the truth lies somewhere inbetween. But man's quest for truth continues and the ultimate truth is still beyond us. Meanwhile, a person must simply follow the path of ananda (bliss or happiness), so long as it is with ahimsa to others and oneself.'

'Ahimsa to oneself?' Asudra had wondered aloud.

Muni nodded. 'Of course. Your body is the temple of your soul. Must it not be kept away from impurity? If ahimsa imposes a duty to avoid hurt or harm to another, how can you conceive of hurting your own body! Is it not then necessary to avoid over-drinking, over-eating, indiscriminate sex, and even associating with people of violence!' Muni added smilingly, 'Yes, people of violence, like me.'

He continued, 'Yes, you can hurt your body, willingly, in a higher cause, or to protect your soul—and when such rare demands are made, one must respond to their call, even to sacrifice one's life.'

Asudra nodded and Muni added, 'But above all, it is your own soul that you must protect with ahimsa. The soul of man is a part of the supreme. When liberated, it attains the world of the Lord of Creation and becomes one with the Lord. Your soul is not a creature of God, but God himself. God is pure. Yourself—the soul within you—must remain undefiled, untouched by sin. For remember, the soul has to be in union with the ultimate for eternal bliss. Therefore practice ahimsa also with your self and soul.'

Asudra nodded. 'I had thought ahimsa meant avoiding physical injury to other people.'

'To people? No son, no. Ahimsa is not restricted to humanity alone. There may be forgiveness for transgressions against humanity, for humans can provoke and retaliate. But what forgiveness is there for a man who will wantonly offend against a cow, an elephant, a lamb or a deer! Or for a man who aims an arrow at a parrot or an owl, or destroys trees and offends against nature! What use can the soul of God have for the soul of a man who permits himself to do dark, evil, ugly things to other creatures of God! Do you believe that man was created, simply, to destroy beauty and the treasures of the earth in which God Himself breathed life with infinite love and endless patience! Do you believe it is man's destiny to become a destroyer of things that live with nature and be surrounded by creatures hostile to him, fearful of him, fleeing in terror at the scent of his flesh and the sound of his footsteps!'

Asudra felt Muni's rising vehemence as he continued, 'You also spoke of physical injury. But the hurt to the heart can be deeper. It is that which I often forget. Yet neither knowledge, nor wisdom, nor prayer is above the principle of ahimsa.'

Muni now spoke gently. 'Perhaps I am too old to learn God's ways. But you, who are young, should never be without the hope of moksha, to join in union with the very soul of God, as your mother has done.'

'My mother! moksha!' Asudra, always calm, was shaken to the core. 'My mother has moksha!'

'What else! She was a slave, you said—chained to man's will, with no pleasures of her own, unable to speak her heart out, living in filth, misery, subject to man's cruelties. You think God does not reserve a special place in the heart of His soul for the victims of man!'

Asudra was in a daze.

'My mother! Moksha!' Asudra whispered to himself. But Muni heard.

'Yes, your mother,' Muni said slowly, measuring each word. 'Because the soul of God has the heart of God.'

A flash of ecstasy passed over Asudra's face, as Muni continued,, 'Yes, we are discussing that one must follow one's own ananda and if it can be achieved with honour, go fearlessly where you want to go. So, if Bharatji still wishes to adopt you, go for it.'

'My adoption! Bharatji considered it when I was a child. Only children younger than twelve years can be adopted.'

Muni laughed. 'Let me then tell you another story by Yakantra:

'....Children of this valley came to God, sad that their parents came home, weary from work, with no time to tell them stories. So they asked God either to abolish work or give them a story-teller.

'....God stroked his long, white beard, and thought long and hard; then he decided that work could not be abolished, but the children's request for a story-teller was just.

'....Now God had a young angel, who was only ninety years old, and he was His best story-teller. But God said, "I cannot send him, for everyone on earth must have a father, so I must ask someone worthy, someone good and honourable on earth to adopt this angel."

'....But then a three-year-old child cried out, "I will adopt him." Again, God thought long and hard, and said "What can be more worthy and more honourable than a three-year old child!"

'....So, children, that is how I, Yakantra, an angel who was ninety years old, came to be adopted by a child of three years....'

Concluding the story, Muni smiled, 'So if Yakantra is the authority on adoption, you are eligible for it until ninety years of age.'

Asudra laughed. 'I love, respect and honour Bharatji, but now I would not wish to be adopted. I shall remain the son of my departed mother and my nameless father. If I had a hatred in my heart, it was for my father who brought me, loveless, to this world. But now I know that he too was helpless—a victim—as much as my mother was.'

'Of course,' Muni said softly, 'a victim of his own past life, for which he paid in this life, to go to his final goal of moksha.'

Asudra nodded. 'I shall go to Yakantra ashram and hear his songs to try and separate fact from fantasy.'

'Not an easy task. There is, sometimes, more truth in fantasy than in fact. But let us not misjudge Yakantra. His moments of laughter were few but when he was with the children his heart was full of cheer and he could laugh easily. For the rest, his was an eternal, unceasing search, but again with faith, for he said, if I cannot reach God, then God shall have to come to me. You should hear all his songs.'

Asudra nodded. 'Yes I must.'

'Go to Lurkan. They will guide you to the ashram of the yogi of a thousand years. That is how Yakantra is known by some. Each successor of Yakantra takes the same name. Thus he keeps his promise to children to remain a thousand years on earth and a thousand years in heaven.'

Muni also had a question. 'Bharatji was concerned over the phantom of an adoption law, torn from Yakantra's words of laughter?—and yet, is there not a law that persons from slave-stock cannot be taken into public service? Then how did he give you this position?'

'The law preventing former slaves in public service was adopted only a century ago, in fear that the then Karkarta would give a place of honour to a son born from his affair with a slave-woman. It was not a law based on custom and Bharatji could abolish it.'

'And no one objected to his admitting ex-slaves in public service?'

'Many grumbled, but they were consoled by the belief that ex-slaves would never reach the level of intelligence needed for public service.'

'Is that the reason that Karkarta Bharatji gave?'

'No, Bharatji said: freedom is freedom; and when a slave is freed, he must have all the attributes and opportunities of a free man.'

'Did not people realize that Bharatji was changing the law in order to appoint you?'

'No, Muniji. Bharatji abolished that odious law, long before considering me. He had no individual in mind—only the principle.'

'And were you as good as the others when Bharatji selected you?'

'I had to be, because Bharatji said that my past entitled me to receive twice the training, but for the sake of my future, I had to be three times better than the others.'

'But if Bharatji is so enlightened, how is it that he does not abolish slavery altogether, if indeed he wants the gods to be on his side?'

'He also wants people on his side,' Asudra replied. 'When he first suggested the abolition of slavery, they made such a noise that if he had persisted, they would have removed him from office.'

'And is it good to hold office amongst such people?'

'Should not a man lead his people in the hope that one day he might change them? This Karkarta is a man of God but he is also a man of the people. He will bring the two nearer each other.'

Muni sensed Asudra's love for Bharatji and ceased his questions. 'Tell Bharatji he is welcome, and if he brings you, I shall be doubly pleased.'

That night, Kanta slept, lost in her dream of building a temple for her son, whom Muni had called Sindhu Putra.

Satrash was thinking: if I remain at this miserable rock, eating nuts and fruits, I shall soon grow the tail of a monkey.

Satrash had noticed that Muni cast many ferocious looks in his direction. But he was always very gentle with Kanta. Why such ferocious glances at me and melting glances at my wife! Maybe Muni is like me. He likes women around. He smiled as he addressed Muni silently. 'You live horribly; you eat poorly; your head is in the clouds; your spirit wanders nowhere, but at least, like me, you know what it is to be sought by the hunger of desire.'

He tried to wake up Kanta. She was in a deep sleep. She saw her son with thousands cheering him; Oh! they called him the healer, teacher, path-finder; and he bowed to her—he... to whom all bowed! He kissed her cheek; and in ecstasy she heard him, but only his first three words, 'Now, mother mine....' The remaining words were lost, for then, Satrash finally shook her out of sleep.

She heard Satrash in a daze, desperately trying to recapture her lost dream and wondering what it was that her son had left unsaid. Plaintively, she asked, 'Where is my son?' Grimly, Satrash replied, hoping to shock her into reality, 'He is in Sindhu river.'

But sweetly she nodded, as though glad that he knew; 'Yes of course. He came to me. I must build a temple for him.'

'Of course,' Satrash said, 'That is why we must leave in the morning. We have to hurry. The temple must be built.'

She was awake now. She stared at him. The memory of what he did to her little sister would never leave her. The wound would remain.

But, he knew the right words, 'The temple...shall be my atonement...or else the burden of my sins will be heavy...for us...for our son.'

And as she heard these words, and looked at his downcast face, she recalled Roopa's words, 'There is no sin for which there is no atonement, for God in his limitless mercy....' Kanta was ready to leave.

Muni went into meditation after saying farewell to Kanta. Even so, Kanta stopped again, steps away from Muni, and silently prayed, 'Protect my son, tell Sindhu to give me back my son; my son is not Sindhu Putra; he is my son, mine.... Protect him....'

She did not hear herself speak; she thought the prayer was in her heart, not on her lips; but maybe her heart gave voice to her silence. Muni opened his eyes, as if awakening from a dream. His voice was calm as he spoke, 'The body of your son died. The God in him did not die—cannot die. Unborn, undead, he shall love, for he is the creation of God and he is the creator of God, for God and he are one.'

Kanta asked the question that tore her heart. 'But will he return to me?' It was more a cry than a question.

Muni smiled. She pines for him whose soul is liberated and is with the One Supreme! But why not! His brow cleared and in the gladness of a song he said: 'He comes, He comes, He ever comes, He....'

His voice rose above the tumult of the wind that blew across the rocks. His eyes were closed and his face glowed as if the vision he saw clasped him to its bosom. He was now singing the song in his heart. And yet Kanta felt she could hear him clearly, distinctly.

Roopa watched her Muni, enthralled. She saw the rapture on his face—a new glow, a new radiance—luminous, shining! She knew that at last he had abandoned the vale of tears and all phantoms of the unseen had left him; that he had made his joyful discovery and was blessed; his endless quest was over and the peace and love of God were within him.

Roopa felt she could hear in her heart the song that her Muni began—'He comes, He comes, He ever comes, He...' She knew that one day she would sing that song in its fullness so that everyone could hear it.

Love, she realized, was the liberating force—love, mercy and compassion for God's creation.

Satrash rowed to the nearest village for food. He threw Roopa's food into the river. Fish did not pop out their heads; he smiled, 'Even those dumb fish have more sense than Muni and his woman and will not touch this trash.' He rowed away from the shore and stopped at a large village. It was easy to lose oneself in bigger places, he knew.

Satrash's ambition to set up a temple, with himself as its master, remained. He met Jhadrov, the town's richest man.

Jhadrov was charmed by Satrash. Joint crimes and shared secrets form bonds more powerful than love and friendship.

Satrash spoke of a new wave in the heart of humanity. Temples, there were many to the spirit of the gods—but none to the spirit of man!

God, Satrash explained, created man in his image. Only in man could God find his fullest flowering. Think of the body of man and woman! Its beauty, grace and desire for fulfilment! How could it be that the supreme ordained it thus, for nothing! How could the body be chastized, denied, or subjected to austerities to remain unused! In all God's creation, it is this human body which is the height of His achievement. Should, then, the Almighty's greatest work remain purposeless! No, man's body is the real deity and should be bathed in worship, touched with love and offered homage. In the ecstasy and orgasm of the body of man lay the perfect symbol of the union of God and humanity.

The need, Satrash felt, was for a temple dedicated to the spirit of man—to worship God through man-supreme.

Who could that man-supreme be! Obviously, a man of wealth and intellect.

'Our tragedy,' Satrash explained, 'is that there is no single, central belief. But mankind desperately needs a man-supreme. And think of how many gods we have! Thousands!'

He paused. 'And that fool Karkarta Bharatji—when he is told of someone's claim that a clay replica of a lizard is an idol of the gods— he cheerfully says: "No harm done. Gods come in many shapes and forms." And when he is told that there are already too many gods, he laughs: "There is room for more!" And do you know how he explained that stupid remark? He said that with so many gods around, at least one or two gods would be nearby to hear him and grant his prayers; but otherwise, who knows, with only a few gods to attend to so many, his own prayers may go unheeded. "So give me more gods. The more the merrier," he said! Such is the calibre of the men elected to guide the destiny of our land!'

Jhadrov's concerns extended to everything that could be bought and sold. Certain activities—whorehouses, slave-trading, gambling— he left to others whom he controlled. His visible interests were respectable and included mining of metals, jewellery, farming, inns, land clearance and construction.

He had no scruples where business was concerned, for obviously business existed for the sole purpose of making money, and for that, he would lie and cheat, so long as he kept within the law. But certainly, he knew the distinction between right and wrong. He wondered, however, if the man before him who spoke with such artful eloquence, knew of such distinctions. I must probe his depths, he thought. Meanwhile, he said, 'Such a temple could easily fail!'

Satrash smiled, 'In this land of ours, with a million gods, has even one god failed? Every god is honoured.'

'And how will your temple ever over-reach other temples?'

'The temples we have are helpless because their pujaris are powerless. Would they dare to speak against Karkarta? No; they have no real following and do not speak with the voice of a single god; so, Karkarta in his arrogance, even makes laws against temples.'

'What laws?'

'For instance, laws against pujaris if they fail to report a crime or laws to deny sanctuary to criminals hiding in temples.'

'But these are good laws,' Jhadrov observed.

'It is immaterial whether a law is good or bad. A temple is God's abode, outside the pale of man's law.'

'And a temple, you think, should control Karkarta!'

'That is the natural order. God rules man and not the other way round. Therefore, all power must emanate from the temple.'

'You spoke also of Sindhu Putra. So many prophecies speak of his coming. Is he the god of your dreams?'

Satrash clarified, 'Sindhu Putra could qualify. But who knows, others may come to adopt him. So our temple may come to honour him, depending on how Sindhu Putra's story unfolds. For the goal, I repeat, is not the God but man-supreme, to whom I shall be pledged.'

Jhadrov understood that Satrash was giving him his pledge. But he was not yet ready to accept it.

Conversations between Jhadrov and Satrash continued. Both were intoxicated by what they were finding in the depths of their souls.

Jhadrov liked the idea of the temple. It would, he realized, earn a new image for him. Maybe, it would also serve as a cover for some unsavoury aspects of his business. But initially, it must be a spiritual centre...later it could change, if circumstances permitted....

Satrash wholeheartedly, agreed. Jhadrov had hundreds of questions. Satrash answered them all. Yet, Jhadrov thought—I must have the full measure of this man before I give him the slightest measure of my trust. Jhadrov would never employ anyone, unless he was for sale, body and soul, exclusively, to himself.

Satrash bared his soul. He told Jhadrov all about his past, even of his molestation of Devadassi. He knew that with agents everywhere, Jhadrov could easily discover it all.

Jhadrov continued his questions—less about the temple and more about Satrash. Only one question from Jhadrov about his wife's health caused Satrash uneasiness. But he quickly reassured Jhadrov that this would not upset his work, 'She is strong. She will get well soon.'

'Good; I am sure she will help you fully to lead the temple activities,' said Jhadrov and he saw a wave of happiness on Satrash's face, at this first indication that he would finance the temple. But he continued pleasantly, 'I am glad you told me she is a great dancer.

better even than her sister who danced exquisitely in a temple.' Satrash nodded unsurely; but Jhadrov enlightened him, 'So you will present yourself as a motivated devotee and master of the temple, to inspire faith, by your own example, and by the example of those who are nearest and dearest to you. Husband and wife must therefore be a team bound by a common cause. You agree?'

'Of course. My wife has no existence apart from me.'

'Naturally,' Jhadrov responded. 'I accept your cost-estimates for the temple. I also accept your word that you will serve me in all things, body and soul, with no reservations; but your wife must serve me too, body and soul, without reservations, for you both work with me as a team and not individually. You better consult her.'

Jhadrov saw a shadow of hesitation on Satrash's face; he was pleased. Every corruption has its natural limits, he knew. There is no such thing as a totally corrupt man. Always, a small, half-forgotten seed of sentiment will remain at the core—that last, almost invisible, nearly vanished layer of decency. It will be a challenge to crush that final barrier of conscience in this depraved man, thought Jhadrov; only then can the man be said to be wholly sold to me.

Meanwhile, Satrash wondered. Surely, he has no amorous designs on my wife. He has not even seen her. Is he testing my loyalty? He thought of the rich smell of victory and the joy of achievement once the temple was set up. 'My wife and I shall always be at your command.'

'Better consult her. Later, let her not plead wifely virtue when I claim her.' Jhadrov was bitingly clear but Satrash replied, 'I speak for myself and her.'

Jhadrov and Satrash discussed suitable temple-sites. No land was available in the town itself. The huge forest next to the town would be even more ideal but Karkarta did not permit construction in forests. Why not eliminate the forest to make way for a magnificent temple?— asked Satrash. How? Small fires keep erupting in forests; they often go out quickly; but who can control nature when it decides to be malignant with a huge fire that destroys the forest altogether? All that is necessary, here, is for man and nature to act hand in hand. But what if Karkarta insists that the area remain free for the forest to regrow? Not likely. Villages will have immense problems with displaced wild animals and will never permit the forest to grow again.

It was the hour of sunset. But the radiance of the setting sun could hardly compare with the glow from the fires that raged in the forest.

In the charred ruins of the forest, the headman discovered the first miracle—a pattern of ashes from burnt leaves, with clear lines and curves, along with figures of idols, animals and birds. The headman discussed this miracle with Satrash and explained to his flock, 'A clear sign. We must have a temple here.'

They walked deeper to find charred pieces of trees, some in the shape of a woman, an infant to her breast; others resembling men and women embracing an idol; and a few patterned like a temple.

News of these miracles spread. Visitors from other villages, whose trips were also organized by Satrash, were even more enthralled. They found many similar charred figures. The judgement was clear: 'A temple,' they said. Satrash added, 'Yes, a temple that the gods want here.'

Villagers, pujaris, headmen—everyone—begged Satrash to construct a temple. Mysteriously, he had come to be known as a man of vast resources. With a show of utmost reluctance, he finally agreed.

Foundations of the temple were now being laid, in forestland, cleared and cleansed by fire.

Urgent and pressing pleas went to Karkarta to sell forestland for temple construction. At a meeting in the village square, when Asudra announced Karkarta's decision to give the land, only one lone voice was raised in protest. A sadhu rose to ask, 'By what right does Karkarta give away forestland to construct a temple?'

Politely, Asudra replied, 'Sadhuji, the forest is no more. It was the prayer of all the villages around that, in its place, a temple should be built.'

'A new temple to destroy a million ancient temples of God!'

Asudra was lost, 'What ancient temples!'

'What do you think the trees that stood there are?'

'But they are dead!' Asudra said. 'They are gone! Burnt out!'

The sadhu realized that it was sheer ignorance, not mischief, that prompted Asudra's reply; gently, he said, 'Forests grow! They regrow! God's temples renew themselves. But man must not rob them of the part of the earth that is theirs.' He then started pleading: 'Millions of trees have perished; homes of birds have been destroyed; animals of the woods are scattered, slaughtered. But that beautiful landscape is not gone forever. It shall regrow unless man is too stupid, too greedy and too thoughtless.' He continued: 'Your Karkarta is endowed with reason. He cannot create a beautiful, plentiful forest, but he has the power to preserve what he is powerless to create. They say he encourages Memory songs that people will hear ten thousand years from now. Should he not help the earth to remain richer, more abundant and bountiful, ten thousand years from now? But if you prevent forests from reappearing, what will you leave?—an earth that is scarred, poor, ugly and desolate. Is that the future he wants? To create such sores and wounds on the face of the earth? But remember then, many will curse him for it, not only today, but even ten thousand years hence, if the earth so scarred, lasts that long!'

Asudra still tried to reason, 'But please understand, Sadhuji, the forest is already dead. While fires raged, Karkarta prayed that they stop. But they did not stop. It was God's will.'

'Then let God's will prevail. Let your men do nothing; build nothing. Rains will come. All nature will then sigh and wake up refreshed. In time the forest will regrow. Its bounty will return. Animals will come back to it. Birds will sing their songs. And I shall tell them all to sing a song to bless your Karkarta and his memory, not for ten thousand years but for ever and beyond.'

A headman, next to Asudra, felt it opportune to step in. 'Sadhuji, ours will not be an ordinary temple. It will honour Sindhu Putra.'

The sadhu glared. 'Then build that temple elsewhere.'

'Where, Sadhuji, where?' the headman asked in a superior tone.

'Anywhere, but not in the forest of God's temples.'

The headman smiled, hoping to impress the villagers with his finesse, 'And please tell me Sadhuji, who will build such a temple?'

The sadhu's ire was aroused now, 'You go and build it. Let a whore or a pimp or a prostitute build it. I don't care; but not on forestland!'

Now clearly, the sadhu alienated many. None can say that a whore should build a temple and get away with it. There were gasps of disgust.

Another headman, wishing to share the limelight, said, 'Sadhuji, we allowed you the hospitality of our village. We never complained against your sleeping anywhere, nor your nakedness. But when you insult our temple, and speak of prostitutes and pimps, I must ask: are you fit to be amongst us? Really, I protest. . . .'

The sadhu interrupted, 'Protest all you want, till you are blue in the face and till the river starts flowing backwards! But you shall see me in your villages, and in all your land, no more. I am not your rya any more, and I shall never be your rya. I am no longer of the Sindhu. I am arya. I hereby renounce you all and your entire land. This land is not mine and I am not of this land.'

There was a murmur in the crowd, though the voice of the murmur had many tongues. Many did not care; some were sad and a few felt they were silent witnesses to a tragedy of their own making, and their silence itself was blameworthy.

Asudra sensed the sadhu's agony and said, 'Sadhuji do not go angry. Renounce your last words. I beg of you.'

The sadhu looked at him with sadness but his words were terrible. 'I curse the temple that you build in my forest. I curse those that build it. God's grace shall belong to those that build the temple elsewhere.'

Asudra pleaded, 'Sadhuji, do not leave in anger!'

'I do not curse, you, nor your Karkarta, for you know not what you do,' the sadhu said. 'But tell Karkarta that the thunderbolt of God shall fall on him and on his land if he listens ever again to those who rob ancient temples of gods in forests to build false temples of man.'

From her cottage, in the forest clearing, Kanta could hear the bustle and din of temple construction. Peace was returning to her heart. The wound over the loss of her child was replaced by her hope for the temple. The pain at the molestation of her sister remained, but the desparate anger against her husband subsided. Had not Roopa said, 'God shall forgive if repentance is real. . . .' And obviously, his repentance was genuine. Who else would take on the gigantic project for such a temple! Yes, he had atoned for that horrible moment of unthinking lust.

Satrash had brought many statues of Sindhu Putra for Kanta—each different from the other, for who could know what Sindhu Putra would look like when he walked the earth. She kept them by her side so that they would guard her spirit during her sleeping and waking hours.

Slowly, Kanta started feeling less devastated and her faith in the future grew.

Satrash surveyed the scene with satisfaction. He knew that every idea is realized gradually, but happily, here everything was being done all at once. The fire had swallowed the forest. Temple construction had begun. Jhadrov's purse was at his disposal. Idols and carvings for the temple were being made, far away, under Jhadrov's orders.

The only thing that marred his happiness was his suspicions about Jhadrov's intentions as far as Kanta was concerned. Jhadrov's conversations always ended with inquiries about Kanta. Satrash could no longer plead that she was unwell. The bloom in her cheeks had returned. She was spontaneous in her greetings to Jhadrov; she knew that her husband relied on him for the temple. That Jhadrov wanted no credit for it himself only increased her respect for a man so selfless.

But why did Jhadrov want her! Kanta was pretty but not a stunning beauty like her sister, Devadassi. Jhadrov could have the most beautiful girls as his mistresses. Why then! He remembered his first conversation with Jhadrov about Kanta. He had then assured Jhadrov that his wife had no existence apart from him and her body and soul would belong to Jhadrov. He had even boasted of her talent for dancing. Surely, Jhadrov, with so many concerns, would promptly forget all that. But no; Jhadrov kept alluding to it.

'Your wife is looking well and I am so glad,' said Jhadrov. 'I am sure she is ready to honour your pledge.'

'She will, in time,' Satrash replied, miserably.

'In time!' Jhadrov rejoined. 'We must be orderly in our tasks. Everything must go by a definite pattern, as we agreed.'

'I just want time... to be a little reasonable to her. . . .'

'And when did a reasonable man ever achieve anything?'

'My wife . . .she has led such a sheltered life. . . .'

'We all lead sheltered lives to begin with. But there comes a time when we must discard our shelters, if our goals are to be fulfilled. Greatness must function that way or else it ceases to function.'

204 / Return of the Aryans

The words were without menace; rather, Jhadrov spoke like an unwilling prophet who was simply expounding the law of nature.

'I shall consult Hiranbai. She will know the right way to persuade my wife,' Satrash said; and Jhadrov nodded indifferently.

Hiranbai was in charge of training the girls who were to dance at the temple.

Satrash went to Hiranbai for help. She was surprised. 'Why?' She would have understood it if a man wanted to take his wife out of the clutches of another; but that a husband should seek to put his wife into another's trap was hardly natural.

Lamely, Satrash said, 'There are reasons that my heart alone knows.' He kept before her a heavy purse and said, 'Serve me in this and count me your friend in all things, for ever.'

Gladly Hiranbai undertook the task. She was not daunted by Satrash's claim that his wife was firmly stuck to the path of piety and virtue. Surely, they had been married long enough for his own corruption to have rubbed off on her.

Kanta was delighted to see Hiranbai. Although her cottage was almost next door, Kanta had never met her, face to face. All she knew was that this fine lady had been appointed by Jhadrov to train devotional singers and dancers for the temple. Satrash had told her never to approach her or talk to the girls who were in her charge, as they had all taken a vow of silence with strangers, until the temple was constructed. He had told her, 'One day, your neighbour will come to you herself, and then be ready to follow her footsteps, fearlessly.'

It was a new experience for Hiranbai to be treated with heartfelt reverence and be addressed as 'Respected Sister.' How else was Kanta to treat a lady who devoted her life to the temple!

Hiranbai encouraged Kanta to talk. She had to understand her fully so as to trap her totally.

Kanta spoke of her joy at the temple being constructed; she spoke of her son, not with sorrow, but faith that he was coming back as Sindhu Putra. She told Hiranbai of Muni and Roopa and how Roopa would plant for her son the flowering trees whose reflection would be seen in river Sindhu. Clearly Kanta was entirely devoted to the One Supreme and absolutely convinced of the coming of Sindhu Putra.

Hiranbai heard her transfixed. Throughout her life, she had never met a truly virtuous woman. My God! she thought, is this the girl I am to corrupt! She, a child, whose every word, every whisper, every wish, every sigh, is centred on God and the coming of Sindhu Putra!

She looked at Kanta's shining eyes and thought—am I so God-forsaken, so wretched in soul, that I, of all persons, be chosen to degrade this innocent girl! No, that shall not be!

When Hiranbai was leaving, Kanta bowed to her, 'Respected Sister, bless me.' Hiranbai nodded and averted her eyes to hide her face.

She, who had never shed tears, ever since that terrible night when she was twelve years old, now could not stop crying.

Hiranbai was born in a brothel. Her mother, Sundarima, managed the whorehouse. The whorehouse was known to belong to Hanauti, though Jhadrov was the real owner.

It was Sundarima's ambition to keep her daughter away from prostitution. She had saved a fortune to retire to a village where none knew her. There, she would live like a virtuous widow and bring up her daughter respectably, so that she would be able to marry into a good family.

Sundarima made up a story about her family to improve her daughter's marriage prospects. She could recite the names of nine ancestors, who of course never existed. Her husband was supposed to be named Vassi—a respectable farmer who died in his youth.

To achieve a virtuous background, Sundarima had purchased, six years earlier, a field outside the village where she was to retire. The field was exclusively for elderly cows to graze in. She had it fenced and connected to a nearby stream for water supply.

The cow-field was reputed to honour her husband Vassi's memory. None knew Vassi when the cow-field was set up, for he was simply an imaginary husband that Sundarima adopted. But slowly, Vassi's name was getting known in the village, associated as it was with this pious act. Every year, the field was improved to feed more cows and Vassi acquired the reputation of a virtuous man—some even claimed that they had known Vassi and he was a man of honour.

Barely a month remained before Sundarima was to retire. The management of the whorehouse was to go to her twin sister, Madhuri.

For the last few days she worked overtime to earn all she could, to add to her wealth in her new village. Although her main job was to manage the whorehouse, Sundarima had her own customers too. Many mature men found her desirable; and they came for their last, farewell fling with her. Her purse was getting full.

Sundarima had kept her daughter away from all whorehouse activities. She had hired teachers to train her to sing—but not the songs of earthly love, flesh and sex. By the time she was twelve years old, young Hiranbai could sing more devotional songs than most temple singers. Her songs overflowed with the love of gods and deities; their majesty and mercy; their goodness and godliness. When other whores heard her devotional songs, some laughed and said: 'Well, her mother teaches us to corrupt men, but she trains her daughter to corrupt the gods!'

One day, late at night, after Sundarima was in bed, someone knocked. She was tired and disliked the man at her doorstep even though he was an old customer. He had absolutely no refinement or sensitivity.

She was about to refuse but recalled that he was always generous and did not take up much time either.

Suddenly, as he entered, Sundarima realized that her daughter was also sleeping with her on the same bed, and not in the next room, allotted to her. She woke up the child to send her away to her room.

The man looked at the girl, his eyes glued to the outline of her small, tender breasts and said with a grin of lust, 'I want that girl.'

'No!' Sundarima said firmly. She pushed her daughter into the other room. With a forced smile, she said, 'Come; she is only a child.'

'I want her,' the man said grimly.

She shouted, 'No, you will not have her. No! No! She is not ....'

Silently, he pushed her away from the door which led to the next room. He went in and bolted it from behind. The little girl screamed.

Outside, Sundarima was screaming. Whores collected. An axe was brought to break the door. Sundarima rushed in. Others stood by, afraid.

The man was on top of the girl, even though she had fainted. Sundarima pulled at him but he would not move until she tried to put her thumbs in his eyes. He then got up, grabbed Sundarima and flung her out of the window. She fell in the street, one floor below.

Sundarima was dead.

Murder was uncommon. If anyone took the life of another, he knew that he would be damned forever after. Even a murderer's life was not taken. The murderer would lose civil liberty and be sold as a slave. The only restriction was that the victim's family could not hold him as a slave lest personal vengeance intervene. Such a slave could never be freed. Half his property went to the victim's family and the other half was confiscated by Karkarta, unless the murderer left behind needy children. The victim's family, if he was an earning member, was entitled to the full benefit from Karkarta's treasury, of all it was deprived of, if confiscation of the murderer's estate did not meet their needs.

The simple principle was that not only the murderer but society itself was responsible to the victim's family.

Rape was also uncommon. It carried the same punishment as murder. But if the offence was against a child below fourteen, there was the additional punishment that the criminal would be castrated so that even as a slave he would not be able to gratify himself with women-slaves.

Many considered castration barbaric but the crime itself was regarded as even more horrendous. Therefore, they sought not to eliminate this punishment but to discover a better, less crude and more humane method of castrating the criminal.

Of course, the status of the victim was never a factor. It did not matter if the victim was a whore or a slave. They too had the right to life and protection against molestation.

However, the offender's status was important. A person of high social status would be punished more rigorously; but as murder or rape carried mandatory punishment, the rich and poor were treated alike. For other crimes, yes, the accused must prove that he had low social standing. Otherwise, he was in danger of receiving severe punishment.

The principle of equality before law had support. But Karkarta Bharat was impressed with the argument that law must follow life's pattern which offers unequal advantages; and a person placed by life in a position of advantage should be less tempted to commit a crime. Thus it was fitting that punishment to the rich and powerful be more severe.

The man who raped Hiranbai and killed her mother would surely have received the mandatory punishment of enslavement, confiscation of wealth and castration. But Karkarta's court was not invoked.

Hanauti, owner of the whorehouse, pleaded that the matter be hushed up for the good name of the whorehouse. The whores refused. Hanauti had to agree that the culprit be caught and punished.

Quickly the man was caught. Hanauti, with six men, brought him, tied and gagged to the whorehouse. The whores wanted to kill him, there and then but Hanauti intervened. He ordered the six men to take the prisoner away, deprive him of his manhood, and sell him as a slave.

Meanwhile, he brought a large purse, saying that it was surrendered by the culprit's family for Sundarima's daughter. Also, he vowed to seize the criminal's farm and house for the daughter's benefit.

Hanauti was persuasive: 'Let justice be done; let the criminal suffer as he would at the hands of the authorities; but let all his wealth come to Sundarima's daughter. Why give half to the authorities!'

How can anyone sell a free man as a slave without the knowledge of the authorities? But the leader of the six men said, 'No problem! My slave died yesterday. Will this criminal agree to be sold as the same slave?' The culprit nodded his head in agreement. But the leader added sombrely, 'Yes, he will be sold, if castration does not kill him; the fearful fact is that some do die with shock and injury.'

His sorrow was not shared. Jubilantly, an old whore said, 'Whether he lives or dies bring me a little piece of his lost manhood. I shall spit on it.' Other whores joined the chorus, 'Yes, Yes.'

In the morning, upon reflection the whores realized that they had been a party to serious crimes. They moaned—that madness came upon them, that in the terror of the night and frenzy for revenge, they agreed to have the criminal mutilated and enslaved!

The worst was that the criminal died while he was being castrated. The whores received a jar with pieces of flesh, covered with blood, as proof of his lost manhood. The man, they were told, lived only a few moments, in horror and pain, after being castrated.

Oh, horror of horrors! Why had they taken the law into their own hands! Terrible would be the punishment when the authorities found out.

And the questions—would they not all be answerable? By what right had they presumed to judge a man guilty? Was it not his right to be considered innocent until Karkarta's court decided otherwise? Did he confess? With his mouth gagged! By what right, this private vengeance? And how could anyone assume the right to deprive him of his manhood? Did it not matter if he lived or died? What was it, then, if not murder?

How do you keep a secret from the authorities if it is shared by so many! It was then that Hanauti showed himself to be a man of resource. The whorehouse would be closed for renovations, he said. All the whores would go to different whorehouses with handsome bonuses. They swore never to divulge the gruesome story.

Through this turmoil, little Hiranbai was unconscious. When her eyes opened, fever gripped her, and she lived through delirium and pain. Every night, in the agony of a nightmare, she saw the horrible face of the man who had molested her; she would then wake up and sob.

Sundarima's sister, Madhuri, moved to a new location to manage a large whorehouse. Hiranbai went with her. They loved each other.

As Hiranbai grew up, she helped Madhuri to train new whores. But herself? She would never sleep with a man or allow him to fondle her. She began to be known as the 'virgin whore'.

Some suspected that Hiranbai was impotent but others argued that a female could never be impotent, though most men were.

Hiranbai demonstrated her talent only in order to teach the other prostitutes.

Those who felt that she wanted not a man but a woman were also wrong. Man or woman, front or back, she just would not indulge in the act. She watched it as a phenomenon, untouched by the waves of passion that seemed to precede it.

With each passing day, Hiranbai learnt more; she knew the erotic zones and fancies of each customer and which whore to pair him with to double his pleasure. Her fame as a talented tutor of prostitutes spread.

For herself, Hiranbai had no ambitions. Only in remembrance of her mother, she asked Madhuri that the cow-field set up by her should remain. Willingly, Madhuri agreed. Each year, their old retainer would go to the cow-field, leaving a purse with the headman, for its upkeep. The headman was convinced that it came from the saintly family of Vassi.

Once, Hiranbai went to visit the cow-field. Her mother's memory came to her anew, with tenderness. But she felt restful. An older cow looked at her with gentle eyes.

The headman had seen Hiranbai's cart as it passed. He recognized the old retainer; maybe the lady was of Vassi's family. Quickly, with his companions, he followed, to meet the family-member of pious Vassi.

The retainer met them first and confirmed that the young lady was indeed the daughter of the person who had set up the cow-field.

He introduced the headman, pujari and others to Hiranbai. The headman was charmed to see the young, fresh looking woman. To impress her and others, he said, 'Ah, Vassi, in whose honour this cow-field was established, was a great soul, of noble deed! A man without sin.'

Cheerfully, Hiranbai said, 'Yes, he never committed a single sin.' After all, she felt, how could a man who had never lived, ever commit a sin!

Respectfully, the headman asked where she resided, and was dumbfounded when she said she belonged to a whorehouse in a distant village.

She had seen no reason to lie. She was not ashamed of what she did. The headman cried out in outrage: 'You are a whore! A whore!'

'No,' she corrected, truthfully. 'I assist my aunt who manages the whorehouse. Sometimes, I tutor whores in their business.'

The headman opened his mouth to say something. The mouth remained open but he said nothing. The pujari saw the headman's anger and said to Hiranbai, 'God bless you, child, for your good work for all these God's creatures.' His hand swept to the cows resting in the field.

She was touched by the pujari's graciousness. She took out some gold pieces and said, 'Would you accept these for your temple, pujariji?'

'Would it not be nicer, child, if you came to the temple to offer this yourself? Our temple is small in size but large in the love of God.'

The headman intervened angrily, 'You will accept money from a whore?'

'Why not!' The pujari extended his hand to take the gold pieces and said, 'Thank you, my child. But do visit the temple, if you can.'

'Not this time, pujariji,' she said gratefully.

'Well,' the irrepressible pujari smiled, 'if you don't visit the home of God, maybe God will have to visit your home.'

The headman was livid, 'God will visit a whorehouse!'

The pujari smiled and said, 'The God I know keeps all kinds of company. Your house, my house, her house, it is all the same to him.'

'How dare you speak of God visiting a whorehouse?'

'Why! Will you stop God from doing that?' asked the pujari.

'No, but I will tell the whole village that you are a mad man.'

'Why tell them what they already know! Everyone has been calling me mad since I was ten years old.'

The headman turned on his heel and left. The others followed. Only the pujari remained.

She saw the pujari's sorrow, 'I wish I had not given my identity.'

'No, child. The truth is always best.'

'But on my account the headman is angry with you too!'

'Don't worry, child. He is young. Young blood boils quickly. May God forgive me, but I too cursed ladies of your profession once.'

Hiranbai smiled. 'I am sure you never cursed anyone in your life.'

'I did when I was ten years old. My father ran away with a whore, leaving me and my mother destitute. My mother died quickly. I cursed that whore repeatedly. But then I understood. Who am I to judge! I asked God's forgiveness and it came flooding in.'

She misunderstood and asked, 'Your father came back?'

'No, child. God's forgiveness came to me. It had nothing to do with events as they unfolded.'

She wanted to hear more; the pujari continued: 'My father never came back. He died seven years later. When I heard he was dying, I went to be near him, as a son should. He died moments after I reached.'

'And she?' asked Hiranbai.

'She was stricken by the same deadly disease. She had got it from my father. Devotedly, she looked after my father in his last years. I looked after her for over a year and she died in my arms. She blessed me when she died and called me her son.'

Tears came to her eyes. She did not know why. Were they there because a ten-year-old child lost his mother after his father ran away with a whore? Or were they there because of the emptiness in her own life? Or was she weeping for this simple man because he felt elated that a whore who destroyed his life blessed him on her death-bed and called him her son?

Impulsively, she knelt and said, 'Pujari, pray for me.'

The pujari smiled, 'I have prayed for you; but God must be bored with me for I keep praying often and sometimes I think I even disturb His sleep. But I know He loves to hear new voices. So let Him hear yours. He has sharp ears and He hears every prayer.'

The headman complained to Karkarta's representative that it was disgraceful that the village had a cow-field owned by a whore.

At last, Karkarta's response came. But instead of answering the headman's weighty question, Karkarta Bharatji contented himself with asking a set of questions which his representative recited with relish:

● If the whore pays for the field, am I to assume that it has affected the morality of the cows?

● Do we have the authority to take over private land maintained for public purpose?

● Suppose we take over the land, will the village pay for its maintenance? Surely the intention is not to deprive the cows!

● If a saint performs a saintly act, it is in the nature of the saint to do so. But if a sinner conquers her own nature to perform a saintly act, like maintaining a field for the benefit of the cow Mata (mother), is her act not more saintly than the act of a saint?

● Should we not be enormously proud of the headman who creates such an atmosphere that even whores are tempted to perform saintly deeds?

Much of this annoyed the headman. But the last question gave him solace. Indeed, his was a village of purity, where even sinners acted with goodness and piety. And naturally the credit was his.

Hiranbai was now thirty years old. Her aunt Madhuri had died five years earlier, leaving her a fortune. Hanauti begged her to stay on as manager. She agreed. She had no other place she could call her home.

She continued to help whores to perfect love-making techniques, and devised new, erotic, provocative dances for them.

Hiranbai went to various whore-houses to train and teach. Revenues went up so high that the unseen owner of the whore-houses decided to give her a generous percentage of the profits—for he wanted to make sure that such excellent workers would never want to leave.

Suddenly, Hanauti offered her a fabulous bonus if she took a new assignment to train thirty young singers and dancers for a temple. A temple? She was thunderstruck. Hanauti knew nothing. She refused.

But she was tempted when the real owner, Jhadrov, sent for her. Why should I not accept this offer and, thereafter, really retire?

She had no desire or illusion of happiness. The one person she loved—her mother—was snatched away when she was twelve. Madhuri too was gone. No, she had no one to love but only a terrible blind hatred—for the man who ravaged her body and killed her mother. But that man was dead and she could not even seek vengeance!

In Hiranbai's heart was an open, festering wound and its memory would remain. Maybe, its memory would remain even after death, if the tale of an old whore was to be believed. That whore had said, 'No one burns in hell. People just remember in hell. They remember clearly, vividly, sharply, whatever happened on earth. It is the land of memory. They just cannot forget anything. Never. Neither sleeping nor waking. Not for one moment.' And heaven? 'Heaven is heaven because it is the realm of forgetfulness. What more can a person want than to forget all—everything!' the old whore had replied.

For herself too, all that Hiranbai wished was forgetfulness—to erase that horrible night of eighteen years ago. She was not in search of happiness. She did not know if happiness ever existed for anyone. Was happiness not simply a pretense? And now even a brief conversation with Jhadrov convinced her that this man of immense wealth also had unsatisfied ambitions. He too hungered.

Was anyone happy then? Only children. But they grew up and lost the illusion; for happiness, she was certain, was simply an illusion.

No, happiness was not what Hiranbai sought. But then why not accept Jhadrov's offer and thereafter retire! And she thought—maybe if I am away, that haunting, horrid memory will cease; maybe even my mother's spirit will be happy if I leave. Well, why not! Life in retirement would be empty. But how could it be emptier than it already is!

She accepted Jhadrov's offer.

And now. . .now, as she left Kanta, Hiranbai was thinking: evil grows. It never subsides. I even took on the task of corrupting a girl whose heart sings out in innocence and ecstasy. And she asked herself: is my soul really so crippled, so grotesque, so hideous, that it must seek to strangle the soul of another! And for what! To feed my body! For a few pieces of gold! For a moment of triumph!

Outside Kanta's cottage, Hiranbai looked up through her tears, 'Am I that godless? Have I fallen so far from grace that I should have been given this shameless task! Why then was I chosen to smother a soul that is innocent and fill it with corruption? Why?'

It was hot. She did not want to go to her cottage. There was too much evil there. She walked in the opposite direction.

She walked without seeing anything, her mind in a whirl; she faltered but went on, as if to escape from the cry in her soul.

In the distance, the faint noise of construction could be heard from the temple-site. It grew louder as she went on. But she did not hear it.

Suddenly, then, she saw, staring at her, the face that had haunted her, day and night, ever since the horrible night when she was twelve. It was the face of the man who raped her and killed her mother.

She stood rooted. There was sickness in the pit of her stomach. Her senses told her it was an apparition, a ghost, a spectre!

No, the face was there, really there, staring at her with a smileless grin, and it was even speaking. It was Thani.

Thani was not killed that night, eighteen years ago. It was a drama by Hanauti at the order of his master, Jhadrov, to reassure the whores.

Thani was only a distant cousin of Jhadrov's wife. Still, family is family, and Jhadrov could use Thani's services. Jhadrov would employ only those whose loyalty to him would be total. And who could be more loyal than a murderer and a rapist, sheltered at his orders!

Why, even a small-time leader of dacoits would not recruit anyone unless the man had a past worthy of the gang. Jhadrov was not a leader of a gang of dacoits, but he saw merit in this method of employment.

Hiranbai was frozen to the spot as she stood facing Thani, unable to think, move or speak, for the storm raging in her.

Thani had been supervising temple-construction. Suddenly, he saw a woman from afar. He came forward, ordering the workmen not to move. He could not recognize her. But it was enough that she was a woman!

Thani grinned. He and his workmen had orders never to go near Hiranbai's cottage or the singing girls' hostel; for who knows what excesses they would commit! But, here came the woman herself, from forbidden territory! Obviously, she was looking for a man. And was he not a man! Was he not the biggest and the strongest of them all?

Thani approached her. She stared. What could it be, he thought, but frustration. He could see that she was not young, nor too pretty. But he liked mature women; in fact, he liked women of all ages.

'Welcome lady; welcome to my land,' Thani repeated as the woman looked as if she had not heard him. Was she pretending to be coy?

Then suddenly, as she heard him, all feeling left her; it was as though all emotion, all sensation disappeared from her mind and even her own personality departed; and in its place, someone else came into being. Yes, it was the same man, with the same scar on his forehead! Yes! The little finger was missing from his left hand—the hand with which he had muffled her screams, eighteen years ago.

Is she trying to undress me with her eyes! Thani wondered to himself as her eyes travelled from his face to his hand.

She struggled to speak. At last she asked, 'What is your name?'

Thani grinned. She doesn't want my name; she wants me, my body. He simply said, 'Thani.'

She nodded. Now she was in command of herself and said, 'Meet me in my cottage, seven days from today, after sunset.'

Whatever Thani wanted, he wanted it there and then, and not after seven days. He moved to touch her. She recoiled. Thani played his winning card and said, 'It is forbidden to approach where you live. . . .'

'How close can you come?' she asked coldly.

'The boulder, there.' He pointed to a distant boulder.

'Meet me there, then, seven days from today, at sunset.'

'No, now!' he said.

'No!' she said with a firmness that surprised him. Her eyes were cold, hard, commanding; and he wilted, 'I shall wait for seven days.'

Hiranbai reached her cottage. She gave Satrash's purse to her old retainer with instructions to return it.

'We receive; we do not return,' the retainer said.

'Sometimes, we return, little one.' He was called 'little one' ever since her grandmother first employed him and christened him thus. The name stuck over the years. Hardly anyone knew what his real name was.

'I must ask you for something,' Hiranbai said.

'Anything but my life,' he said smiling.

'Why not your life?' she asked, getting into a playful mood.

'I must live to look after you.'

She smiled but said seriously, 'I want a horse cart; two fleet riding horses, for you and me. Also, a fast boat waiting at the pier. And provisions for a long journey—seven days from today, at sunset.'

'Are we running away?'

She nodded and he asked, 'Why?'

'Don't ask.' But he did, 'Where shall we go?'

'I don't know. I shall think about it,' she replied.

'Why not back to our whorehouse in Baddin?'

'No, that will not be safe.'

'You mean there is danger!'

She nodded; the retainer said, 'Don't worry I shall be with you.'

'No, you will escort me to the boat and return; you will tell the dancing girls that I have left. I shall leave funds with you for them, if they too wish to leave.'

'Then I shall follow you. Where?'

'No. You won't know where I am. Let my sin not fall on your head. I shall leave funds for you. Go where you want. Live in peace.'

'What are you saying, daughter Hiru!' He lapsed into his childhood name for her.

'I have said what I have said,' was her firm answer.

He spoke quietly, 'I know why you will not tell me. You fear that I shall not keep my mouth shut. But I know where you go; so you better take me to keep an eye on me lest I blurt out your secret to the others.'

She smiled, 'And where will I be going, my little know-all?'

'You will be at my own cow-field.'

He always called it his own cow-field. His real name was Vassi. Hiranbai's mother, though a woman of ingenuity, could think of no other name, and had quietly 'borrowed' the name of her retainer for the imaginary gentleman in whose memory the cow-field was established.

It was true. Hiranbai had planned to go to the cow-field. She could think of no one she could trust, except the pujari there.

'How did you know I was going to the cow-field?' she asked.

'Where else? That is where your mother wanted you to go.'

She nodded sadly, 'All right, follow me there if it is safe.'

'I shall follow you to the ends of this earth, be it safe or unsafe. But what is the mischief in your heart? Why this hide and seek?'

'Do not ask.'

Jhadrov was pleased with the progress of work, but then came the inevitable question. Satrash told him miserably of Hiranbai's failure.

Coldly, Jhadrov said, 'I had confidence in you, why did you lie?'

'No, no, I did not lie to you . . . I had hoped. . . .'

'Hoped!' Jhadrov exploded. 'And I am to sink my name, my wealth, my reputation, on the basis of your hopes!'

Satrash pleaded, 'My wife is not important. She....'

'Who speaks of your wife? We speak of trust—of violating your pledge; you lied that you could even control minds, if all else failed.'

Satrash had spoken of opium and bhang to control others' minds, never of his wife. How could Jhadrov misunderstand! Pitifully, he said, 'My wife will never take such substances, even if I tell her to. She smells everything she eats.'

'Very discerning, but perhaps she is cautious only when you offer her something,' said Jhadrov with irony. 'You want me to try?'

'By all means,' Satrash said without understanding.

'And you must not intervene!' It was an order, not a question.

Satrash said nothing. Jhadrov responded to his silence, 'Good; if I fail, I shall blame you no more. Expect me at your cottage soon.'

Kanta greeted Jhadrov. He told her, 'I have a gift for you.'

A sparkle came to her eyes. 'What is it?' she asked.

'Muni and Roopa remembered you and gave me prasad (offering to the gods).'

'For me!' she was delighted.

'No,' he replied playfully. 'For me and for your husband too.'

She laughed. 'Give it to me please.'

He took out a little box and Kanta extended her hand.

'Not so fast, young lady,' Jhadrov said. 'First, your husband.' To Satrash he said, 'Open your mouth.' Satrash gulped whatever Jhadrov placed on his tongue. Jhadrov smiled at Kanta, 'Now who? You or me?'

Kanta smiled back. 'You first, you are the elder.' He ate and playfully closed the box while Kanta cried, 'But what about me?'

'Oh I forgot! Old age!' He brought a piece to her lips; reverently she opened her mouth and swallowed it. 'Thank you,' she said.

Kanta was about to leave them for their discussion. Her head reeled. She stumbled. Satrash rose to help her. Jhadrov hissed, 'No interference, you said! Remain where you are!'

She pitched forward. Jhadrov helped her to her room and returned.

The heart of the little man that Satrash was, manifested itself. He sat without stirring. He was beginning to believe that Jhadrov was sexually attracted to Kanta. Little did he know that to Jhadrov, sex was a way to express power and domination; a means to an end; no more.

Satrash was in the throes of self-pity. He loved to seduce the wives and daughters of others. But it hurt that his own wife should be seduced.

Once, long ago, he had loved Kanta. When the first hot flood of his desire cooled, there was nothing left—no love, no affection, no comradeship—not even the pleasure of intelligent conversation. He had then sedulously courted other women. His final exploit was to seduce her sister.

But his luring of women he regarded as the natural order of things. That someone should seduce his own wife was, for him, a reversal of the natural order. He felt sick, though not from the potion which Jhadrov had given him. That was a fake. Only Kanta was given the real thing. But he felt helpless, as if he too had been drugged.

Sadly, meditatively, he began to realize that all achievements, each fulfilment, every accomplishment, made demands on man's conscience. But must he stifle his conscience and allow his wife to be seduced!

Possibly, Jhadrov had an inkling of what he was thinking. He commanded, 'Go out. The fresh air will do you good.'

Like a dog trained to obey, Satrash went out.

Kanta opened her eyes. She was sure she was in a deep dream. She was naked and in someone's embrace. She could sense his warm breath on her cheeks and feel the soft touch of his limbs on her body. There was the fragrance of perfume in the air. Someone was making love to her, unhurriedly, gently. She smiled happily, receiving and returning the joy and ecstasy!

She lifted her arms to put them around her dream-prince, raised her bosom to meet his beating heart, locked her lips with his and then opened her eyes to behold him who was giving her such limitless pleasure.

But as she opened her eyes, the dream was shattered. In her revulsion she saw that it was no dream-prince. Was it Jhadrov? It looked like him. But no, it was a fiend with bloodshot eyes and the smoking lips of Satan. Fearfully, she rose and Jhadrov almost fell from the bed. Her hand clutched the statue of Sindhu Putra. She picked it up as if it were as light as a feather.

Jhadrov cried out as the heavy metal statue connected with his head. It was like the cry of a mortally wounded wolf.

Satrash heard the cry. He rushed to the doorway. 'What have you done?' he asked as he saw Jhadrov, his head battered and bleeding. Kanta did not hear him. She was in a daze. She did not even recognize Satrash. All she saw was someone who had seduced her sister and was now an accomplice to her own seduction by a fiend from hell. With a strength that came of the powerful drug she had taken, she flung the heavy statue of Sindhu Putra at Satrash. He saw it coming, turned to run, but it hit him on the back of his head, and one of its pointed corners remained embedded in his head. Bleeding, whimpering, Satrash reeled outside the house and fell down.

Hiranbai was returning from her meeting with Thani.

She had undressed Thani, teasingly and lain on top of him. He was grinning. If that is how she wants it, he would let her have it her way, he thought. When his own desire to undress her reached its peak, the blade of her dagger found his unprotected throat. There it remained, before going deeper though the blood had begun to flow. She told him who she was. Thani struggled and even managed to pick up a large stone. Thrice he hit savage blows at her ribs. She did not flinch. She pushed the dagger deeper and twisted it. Blood gushed all over. Thani sank with a gurgle. He was dead.

The joy she expected over his death eluded her. She walked back with painful steps. The blood on her clothers was not just Thani's. His blows with the heavy, pointed stone had cut through her flesh and ribs.

Moaning with pain, she reached Kanta's cottage, after what seemed an eternity. There she stopped to rest, before proceeding to her own cottage. She nearly fainted when the death cry of Jhadrov awakened her. A moment later, she saw Satrash reeling out of the door. She went forward and bent over him. He was dead. She saw fragments of his broken skull with the metal statue sticking out of his head. Kanta, all naked, stood at the door. 'I killed him,' said Kanta laughing triumphantly. Hiranbai nodded as though nothing more needed to be said. But Kanta continued, 'I killed his master too!' Hiranbai went in, slowly. She saw that Jhadrov was also dead.

Kanta was hysterical and kept repeating, 'I killed them all, all.' Hiranbai wanted to stop her but could not. Then she pointed to the statue of Sindhu Putra still stuck in Satrash's battered head.

'Sindhu Putra killed them,' Hiranbai said quietly.

Kanta stopped in wonder and then said, 'Sindhu Putra!.... my son. . .he is very powerful. . .is he not?'

Hiranbai nodded and despite her terrible pain gathered Kanta in her arms. She knew that the hurt in Kanta's heart was deeper.

Kanta and Hiranbai left with Vassi for the cow-field.

The next morning, the bodies of Thani, Satrash and Jhadrov were discovered.

Wonder and awe spread. Inquiries began.

Vassi had arranged everything for a swift journey. He had not expected Hiranbai to be in pain, nor for Kanta to join them. But he managed.

All Hiranbai's jewellery, gold and silver was packed. Vassi ransacked Satrash's cottage and removed a large horde entrusted to him by Jhardov for massive expenditure on temple construction. Vassi also took from Hiranbai's basement all that Jhadrov had left with her for payments to the dancing girls. Then there were the vast quantities of expensive jewellery 'lent' by Jadhrov which these girls, ostensibly from good familes, were supposed to wear while singing and dancing at the temple.

Vassi thought of taking Jhadrov's horse which was waiting for its master. But superstition held him back. He untied the horse to let it roam free and merely removed its saddle-bag of gold pieces.

Jhadrov's empire passed to his younger brother, Ranadher. Temple construction was abandoned. Ranadher never accepted his brother's idea that the temple would provide the road to power. To him, money alone was the source of power, and the rest, meaningless. His motto was: 'Build nothing, buy everything and if you cannot buy it, destroy it.'

The hunt was on for the two missing women, Hiranbai and Kanta, and the old retainer, Vassi. Ranadher was determined that they be caught.

At the dead of night, Vassi knocked at the pujari's door, near the cow-field. The pujari gave them disquieting news. Several men were already watching the cow-field. Although Hiranbai had thought that her mother's cow-field was a secret, some inmates of her old whorehouse knew about it and had innocently blurted it out to Ranadher's men.

Hiranbai decided that they must go on to a distant relative of her mother's. But she was too weak to travel. They remained hidden in the pujari's hut for twenty-eight hours. Vassi and the pujari dug deep holes in the mud-floor of the hut to hide the valuables. They knew from Hiranbai that where they were going such wealth would attract terrible danger.

Ghulat, the distant relative of Hiranbai, welcomed them. He was always happy to welcome relatives, to relieve them of their wealth.

Hiranbai pleaded that she had left everything behind. He took all she had—and it was not too little either. For a moment, he toyed with the idea of surrendering them to Ranadher. He knew of the rich reward offered for their capture. But his hatred for Jhadrov's family was far too intense and even exceeded his love of wealth. Jhadrov's father was responsible for the merciless death of Ghulat's father.

No, the refugees must earn their keep, Ghulat decided. He ran a whorehouse and a gambling joint in the frontier town. Vassi was too old to be a good pimp and could be given menial jobs. Hiranbai was too ill to serve as a whore. Kanta...well, she was pretty enough to serve as a decoy at the gambling joint and to sleep with customers.

Kanta was horrified, unable to speak. The alternative was that all three be sent to Ranadher.

Vassi's suggestion that he should go to the pujari, retrieve some gold to give to Ghulat, was discarded, for then Ghulat would demand more and more, knowing that they had secreted it somewhere. It was then that Hiranbai said, 'No, Vassi, no, that money belongs to Kanta.'

'To me!' Kanta asked, surprised. 'Why?'

'Did you not say you were destined to build a temple for Sindhu Putra? That money shall be for that temple. Only for the temple.'

Kanta was silent. Hiranbai continued, 'Too much evil I have done.

Too many I have corrupted. Even you, I sought to corrupt. Maybe the temple will atone for a part of my sins.' She was in tears as she begged, 'Promise me, Kanta, that you shall build that temple.'

Kanta's eyes met hers and, she thought, those are Roopa's eyes. She said simply, 'I promise.'

Hiranbai trained Kanta from her sickbed. She became the most celebrated prostitute at Ghulat's whorehouse.

Hiranbai never recovered despite the attention from Kanta, Vassi and an incompetent Vaid. She was on her death-bed; and her last words were, 'Remember Kanta, remember the temple of Sindhu Putra!'

'I remember,' Kanta said through her tears.

Hiranbai heard her and died with a smile on her lips, in Kanta's arms.

Ghulat was killed in a brawl with drunken customers. Some say they were Ranadher's men masquerading as customers. Vassi tried to save him and received severe cuts on his face.

Just before Ghulat died, bleeding from deadly wounds, he whispered to Kanta to go to Thatta—a distant village—and dig under the cow's statue in the valley between two twin hills and bring back whatever she found. She was amazed. Such a journey would take days and surely he was dying. She said nothing but Ghulat understood, and raising his voice in defiance, shouted, 'No, I shall live... live...live.' His voice trailed off, blood spurted from his wound and he died.

Ghulat's camp came under the control of another—far more vicious than Ghulat. Quietly, Kanta and Vassi left. They had to find a better Vaid to attend to the injuries to Vassi's face.

After many towns, they found a competent Vaid. He cured Vassi but his face was so disfigured that Ranadher's men would never be able to recognize him. Hiranbai was no more—and Kanta, somehow, was unafraid.

They ran short of money. Still, they never thought of touching the valuables left with the pujari, for those were kept in trust for the temple. Kanta knew how to sell her body and the Vaid was her first customer.

Kanta and Vassi moved from place to place and finally reached Gatha's village, next to the island where Bharatji retired as a hermit. For Kanta, it was an ideal place to settle down and set up the only business that she knew.

Later, Kanta and Vassi went to the pujari's village to bring all the gold, silver and jewellery concealed there.

Kanta thought also of the dying request of Ghulat to go to Thatta. She knew that Ghulat wanted it while he lived but that could not be.

Still, it was a dying wish and maybe it would ease the pain to his roving soul, if she fulfilled it. She went to Thatta with Vassi. There, digging under the solitary statue of the cow, in the isolated valley, they found the hidden horde of Ghulat's vast wealth secreted by him, his father and grandfathers over five generations of crime.

'We are immeasurably rich,' Vassi said, surveying the treasure.

'The temple shall be immeasurably rich,' Kanta said. Vassi agreed.

On returning from Thatta, Kanta dragged Vassi out to look for land for the temple. They wanted the temple to be unique, incomparably splendid—reaching the clouds with shimmering walls, impressive arches and its cool reflection in the clear waters of Sindhu.

That night Kanta slept with the unending dream of the temple until Vassi woke her up with the astounding news, which like wildfire had spread all over the village, of the birth of Sindhu Putra.

From the garden outside her house, she could not hear the chattering of birds. Instead she heard in her heart the echo of the song 'He comes, He comes, ever He comes'—the song that Muni had sung when she had parted from him and Roopa.

Hurriedly she dressed. But a customer called. It was Muthana, seeking solace in Kanta's arms after his rejection by his wife, Sonama. Kanta refused and went to the village square, followed by Vassi.

Crowds had gathered to watch Sindhu Putra, being suckled by Sonama. They were infuriated to see Kanta and Vassi. A prostitute and her pimp! At this auspicious occasion!! They would have thrown out the two, but Gatha put up his hand to restrain them.

Gatha himself was a patron of Kanta. In his younger days, when he was thirteen, an older woman divested him of his virginity, though he was reluctant to play with her. But the woman had warned him that semen goes to the brain if a man does not lie with a woman regularly. Ever since then, he had tried to follow her advice. He had ample chances in Karkarta's village, with so many slave-women around. It was only when he came to this village as its headman that opportunities for sharing a bed with a woman were not easy to come by. Gatha had therefore welcomed Kanta with open arms, literally and figuratively, when she desired to set up her home in his village. He visited her home every seventh night after full moon, for he was a man of precise and punctual habits. Now as Gatha saw some females hissing at Kanta, he looked stern and waved Kanta in. His new-found authority was sufficient to secure obedience.

Kanta went forward with uncontrollable tears, certain that it was her own son. Surprisingly, the infant gave up the breast of Sonama and started looking in Kanta's direction. Kanta thought—truly, he is my son but he is also a god and she touched the infant's tiny foot. Everyone seemed to see the infant move as though wishing to be taken in Kanta's arms. Sonama moved the infant to her breast. The infant rejected the breast and cried, again turning towards Kanta. Sonama and Kanta looked at Gatha. Gatha nodded. Kanta took the babe in her arms. The infant who had had enough from Sonama's breasts, nestled against Kanta's bosom and promptly fell asleep.

Kanta felt whole, complete. With her son in her arms, and with an air of authority, she said, 'There shall be a temple for my Sindhu Putra. The biggest and the best temple.'

Gatha, used to such demands, gave his stock answer, 'It costs money.'

'Yes! The money is all there.' She looked at Vassi. He had brought only one of the heavy boxes; he spread out the gold and jewellery.

The crowd gasped. The village had never seen so much wealth.

'What? How?' Many were asking. 'So much!' 'From where?'

'It belongs to Sindhu Putra,' Kanta said. 'For His temple.'

The questions from the crowd continued. 'But from where?'

'It always belonged to Sindhu Putra,' Kanta replied.

The village was familiar with many minor miracles. But always, somehow, each miracle made demands on their money. After each miracle, the organizer would invariably end up demanding donations. But this was the rarest of all miracles—the first in which the gods not only sent out Sindhu Putra but also gave untold wealth for his temple.

'There is more,' Kanta said. 'Ten times as much, more, more, for it must be the best, the greatest temple for. . . .'

She did not have to complete the sentence; the infant woke up from the nap in her arms to face the crowd. Clearly, Sindhu Putra was nodding his approval.

The crowd bowed. Truly, the miracles were multiplying! Mother Goddess Sindhu sending her son into their midst! A prostitute, in a poor village, with such untold wealth!! The infant Sindhu Putra nodding at her words with approval!!! Most of them were watching Sindhu Putra, though there were many who could not take their eyes off the vast display of wealth.

One or two even wondered why the gods had to use a prostitute to serve as a treasurer and banker for Sindhu Putra's temple. Surely, the gods didn't frequent prostitutes. Or did they?

Did they!

'. . .What was he (Sadhu Gandhara) then? A sadhu! An explorer! A man of God! A ruler! A chief! A reformer! What!'

'He was a human being.'

'Surely, he lives with God as part of God's Eternal Self'

'No, he lives with us, as part of us all on this earth. He is a Hindu.'

—(Conversation between Dhrupatta and Sadhu Gandhara's wife, 5069 BC)

To Discover the Edge of the Earth?

5071 BC

Dhrupatta was elected as Karkarta of the Hindu clan after Bharat's retirement as a hermit.

Many expected Nandan to oppose Dhrupatta for the office of Karkarta.

Not so. Nandan spearheaded the campaign to stop Bharat from retiring and earned great popularity in consequence. Again, Nandan surprised everyone by supporting Dhrupatta. Dhrupatta was elected unopposed.

At Assembly meetings also, Nandan's support for Karkarta Dhrupatta was total. Dhrupatta had the soldier's temperament of being a man of few words, honesty and humour. It was not in him to veil his intentions under silky phrases. Nandan smoothed Dhrupatta's path in early stormy meetings. Gratefully, Dhrupatta appointed him as the head of Council.

Nandan sponsored no agenda of his own. He fully supported Dhrupatta who was keen to continue Bharat's policies. If some wondered, Nandan's answer was simple: 'A new Karkarta must be given time,' though in his heart he added, 'to make mistakes.'

To his friends, Nandan confided that he would wait for a better opportunity, but did not discourage them from opposing Dhrupatta vigorously. To supporters of Bharat, and now of Dhrupatta, he frankly admitted, 'Yes I opposed Bharatji, but only to bring out the best in him.' And then he asked his two famous questions: 'What do you learn from a friend who simply agrees with you?' 'Is a Hindu who questions even his gods to remain silent when his friend the Karkarta speaks?' And he confused many by adding that, 'Dissent is often a surer test of loyalty than hostility.'

Also, Nandan gave massive evidence of his regard for Bharat. After Bharat's retirement, the first measure which Nandan introduced was that 'Bharat's Ashram' be set up in scenic surroundings for singers and poets to keep alive Bharat's idea of Memory songs.

Madhava—an avid supporter of Bharat—had once almost sworn that he would always oppose anything and everything that Nandan proposed. He ate his words and voted for Nandan's proposal for 'Bharat's Ashram'.

Was Nandan inconsistent? No; he was always considerate to the dead and the dying and the retired and retiring; his view was: why kick those who are already kicked out! As for his support to Dhrupatta, he realized that a new Karkarta rode on a wave of popularity and it would be unwise to oppose him, initially. Also, he did not contest the election as he felt he had no chance. True, he could have made it difficult for Dhrupatta to win. But the result would have been that both of them would have been eliminated, leaving the field open for a compromise candidate. Nandan was younger. He could afford to wait.

Shortly after Dhrupatta's election as Karkarta, a long-lost sadhu arrived. He was Dhrupatta's father, Gandhara, who had left his home at the age of thirty-four, to become a wandering sadhu. Now at last he had returned, with a young lad, twelve years old, who could not speak their language but had a captivating smile.

From all over Sind, people came to listen to Sadhu Gandhara's tales of the faraway land of Avagana (Afganistan).

Actually, Gandhara was not a sadhu in the traditional mould. His ambition was to travel to the end of the earth. Somehow, he wanted to reach the earth's edge, if there was one, and discover what else lay beyond. He wondered: does one fall off the edge of the earth into an unending abyss? Or does one jump over or walk straight from there to the other side? If there is the other side, is it visible, or are we all covered within a huge dome, in which the earth, sky and heavenly bodies are enclosed, with no possibility of reaching out? Or is it an open dome, where we simply move in circles, with no beginning and no end? Many such questions haunted his mind. But his years of travelling had shown him that the earth was unending, in so far as his feeble body could carry him, and if the edge of the earth existed, it was beyond his reach.

Later, the sadhu gave up his wanderings to settle in Avagana. He spoke of its cool climate, luscious fruits and friendly people. They loved him there and called him a teacher. But it was not of the gods of the Hindus that he taught. Basically, he trained them to domesticate animals, instead of merely hunting them. From him, many learnt that wild cows produce milk only for their own offspring, undomesticated hens cannot produce surplus eggs and that it was better to have wool from domestic sheep than kill animals for their skin. Patiently, he showed them how to obtain milk, eggs and wool by the domestic breeding of animals. He taught them how to build huts with wood, stone and clay, instead of having to live in caves or tents propped up with animal skin. He also taught them how to make sauces and wines from fruit.

Sadhu Gandhara described plains and meadows in that land, fertile with fruit trees. He felt that the land was ideal for the farming of grain too. But he did not know how to go about producing wheat or rice. Nor did he know how to grow cotton, make textiles or weave baskets.

Now the 'teacher' returned to his land, bringing a boy who would learn these arts and take back his knowledge, seeds and implements.

For himself, the Sadhu had no wish to return. His wanderlust was exhausted. No one was surprised; surely, a father would retrace his steps to be with his own son, at the last moment.

Dhrupatta was lost in the wonder of having his father back. He had questions only about his father's well-being and asked little about Avagana. It was Nandan who had questions about metals, marble and precious stones in that distant land. With enthusiasm, the sadhu described the terrain, rock formations, its ups and downs.

But as Nandan's probing questions continued, the sadhu became evasive. He saw the hunger in Nandan's eyes. Was it the expression of a well-fed predator stalking a site for a future kill?

Later, Nandan visited the sadhu often, with many friends. But the sadhu exercised the privilege of his old age by promptly going to sleep. Their questions, he feared, arose from greed.

The sadhu's wish that the land of Avagana and the land of his birth should come closer together, evaporated.

Sandhu Gandhara was dying. He sought a promise from Dhrupatta about the boy, Kush, who had come with him. 'Send Kush back when I am gone. He will know how to return.'

Dhrupatta objected. 'But Father, did you not say earlier that he must learn the arts here? He can be with us. I shall look after him personally, I promise you.'

'No. He will learn the arts here but he will learn the ways of your people too. Your people are greedy. There, we have no slaves.'

'Greedy! No slaves!' Dhrupatta repeated, surprised.

The sadhu's words were now proud, triumphant. 'There are no slaves—not within forty yojnas (200 miles) of my home. I bought them all.'

'You bought them!' Dhrupatta was losing the drift of the conversation.

'Yes, I bought slaves in exchange for the huts I built and animals I domesticated. I set slaves free and they worked with me to build more huts and domesticate more animals so as to gain freedom for more slaves. They built better huts than I could but they didn't know that. Like a lord, I only supervised.' There was a merry twinkle in the sadhu's eyes, but now his tone was serious. 'Let your brother go back. He knows the way. Your mother will be lonely without him.'

'My mother! My brother!'

'Kush is your brother, acknowledge him or not. He is born from my wife whom I married, a long time ago.'

Dhrupatta put his arm around the boy and took his father's emaciated hand, 'I acknowledge him as my brother and his mother as my own.'

'Then I shall die happy, for I leave no one lonely,' the sadhu said.

The boy bent his ear to the sadhu's lips, who said much to him. When it was over, the boy tearfully addressed Dhrupatta. The words were foreign but Dhrupatta understood. The boy was acknowledging him as his brother, but as the boy's hand gestured to the door, he thought the boy wanted the family to be brought in to meet his father. Actually, Kush was simply acknowledging Dhrupatta's family as his own.

Dhrupatta opened the door to let the family in. The sadhu smiled and said, 'I thought I would leave you all today—but no, not today when you are all welcoming a new member of the family. God has agreed to give me till tomorrow to bid farewell to all of you.'

Sadhu Gandhara died the next day.

Dhrupatta was twelve years old when his father, Gandhara, became a wanderer. Gandhara was a builder of huts, houses, granaries and temples. His wife had gone to visit her father's family. On her return, an accident in the river drowned her along with her brothers and sisters. Her parents, left childless, begged that their grandson Dhrupatta remain with them. Gandhara agreed. They adopted Dhrupatta.

Gandhara built a tree house for his son and left for regions unknown. There was no reason to call him a sadhu. But they did.

Now that he had returned to pass his last days in their midst, and died at a ripe old age, where was the need for sorrowing! The custom was that when a person died at an advanced age, food would be distributed, donations made to temples, and a dinner given on the third and twelfth day of death for family and friends; and speaking of the dead was not forbidden so long as there was something good to say or even to laugh at. It was not to be a festive occasion but tears did not flow and anguish remained unexpressed.

But they saw the grief of the twelve-year-old son who came with the sadhu. He did not know their customs and saw no need to suppress his tears.

Already, Kush felt that he did not belong there. When Gandhara's body was cremated and his ashes sprinkled in the Sindhu, the boy jumped into the water and scooped up some ashes into his hands. The priest shouted at him to return the ashes to the river. The boy was about to strike the priest who made the mistake of reaching for his hand to recover the ashes. Further ill omen!—when the priest leaned back, away from the infuriated boy, the grain, flowers and fruits for prayers fell down. Dhrupatta intervened and allowed Kush to keep the ashes. The priest's cry was silenced by the gift of a cow from Dhrupatta's wife. Infact, from then on, the priest ceased to regard the event as an ill omen. She was certain that with two cows, the priest would even have seen some real, spiritual merit in those events. But then, she was not feeling too generous.

Dhrupatta heard the complaint, with a 'sympathetic' remark from the pujari that none could blame Dhrupatta's wife for her small gift, as she hardly knew her father-in-law. Dhrupatta was surprised, since his wife was normally generous. He however did not intervene, as such matters were entirely within his wife's domain.

Dhrupatta remembered his promise that his twelve-year-old brother would go back. But how can I send him alone! Whom should I send with him? He recalled his father's distrust—'Your people are greedy for land, for slaves.' Dhrupatta regarded his father's judgement as unduly harsh. Even so, he decided to go himself, with his brother. Surely his father trusted him, whatever his reservations about others!

Also, Dhrupatta decided to take a team of farmers, potters, weavers and artisans who would teach their crafts to those in Avagana.

Nandan favoured the expedition but insisted that Karkarta must not lead it. Nor should the expedition be privately funded. The clan should sponsor it. Besides, it must include fighting men who could lay claim to the land and anything valuable found around Avagana.

Dhrupatta shivered. His father's warning of his people's greed came to him anew. Nandan accepted Dhrupatta's rejection calmly, 'Well, have it as you like. There will be opportunities in future.'

A chill wind blew through Dhrupatta. What future opportunities! To enslave Avagana? To take their land? Was that his father's fear?

For days, Dhrupatta isolated himself in his house—natural for a son who had but recently lost his father. But quietly, he saw many.

At the joint session of the Council and Assembly, Dhrupatta proposed a policy resolution. Those, not in the picture expected merely a simple announcement of his intention to lead an expedition to Avagana. Instead, came a long resolution, and its substance was:

'From my late father, Sadhu Gandhara, I have learnt the route to Avagana and beyond. From him I have also learnt of routes available to other unknown lands and destinations in many directions. While I myself shall proceed to Avagana, I plan to send other expeditions along other routes. Exploration of one route might itself lead to the discovery of other regions and I thus foresee an era of exciting and fascinating exploration and discovery. Think of the secrets to be revealed! Think of the expansion to the frontiers of our knowledge!

'True, new lands have, often, come under the sway of our clan, but this was achieved by aimless wanderings and also because of those who attacked us from their lands, forcing us to march into their lands. Fortunately, the wise policies of Karkarta Bharatji brought us not only more land, prosperity and plenty, but also peace and harmony on our borders, with none to threaten us and none threatened by us.

'In peace, therefore, we must begin this journey and in peace only, should such steps continue.

'Let us now declare, for all time to come, that in all our explorations, we shall be guided strictly by the policy of peace and certain definite principles—and amongst them will be:

- No land or goods or property belonging to another shall be taken over by us, by force, fraud, trickery or even purchase, if the price is not fair or the seller is unwilling to sell;
- Except for the seven deadly crimes, no person shall be enslaved in these new lands; his custody too shall be with people of those lands and in no way shall we profit from his slavery;
- No person from our clan shall buy or acquire a slave in discovered lands except for the purpose of setting him free, forthwith;
- Violation of these conditions shall attract serious penalties; all land and gains obtained by such expedition, or its members, shall be regarded as illegal. Such lands and gains may thereupon be delivered to the local population or the charities of the clan and amongst them will be a new fund administered by Karkarta for purchase of slaves in order to set them free.'

Dhrupatta received a standing ovation from many. Some suspected that it was pre-planned and reluctantly rose to join the others.

Indeed, everyone's heart was set on discovering new lands, but there were those like Nandan who did not appreciate the need for such conditions. What was the sense in the effort, expense and danger of an expedition, if you could take neither slaves nor property!

But already, speaker after speaker was supporting Karkarta's resolution. Even those who never usually spoke were now making long speeches of support. Nandan was fuming but did not wish to break with Dhrupatta. He realized that Dhrupatta would carry the day, unless he encouraged those who wished to oppose.

Nandan spoke. His manner was friendly, even silky. He complimented Dhrupatta on his forward-looking policies. He added that he would not object to the specific conditions proposed by Karkarta as he had not, within the time available, considered them fully, but his doubt was of a different kind. What he feared was that establishing conditions for the future would limit Karkarta's own freedom to deal with situations as they arose.

Nandan's remarks inspired a few questions: 'Is it not unwise, even illegal, to legislate for the unknown future?'

Dhrupatta's retort was simple. He said, 'Surely we legislate only for the future and not for the past.'

But some rose to denounce the measure which would tie the future into knots and thundered that a future Assembly would undoubtedly reverse the measure, which was thoughtless, hasty and ill-conceived.

There were some with no strong views. Still others who were upset that Dhrupatta had consulted some privately but ignored them. They seemed ready to abstain, while Nandan's friends thundered out their objections.

To the surprise of many, a youth rose. It was not his turn to speak, for Dhrupatta had an order of speakers in mind. But there was applause from the spectator's gallery when the youngster rose. He was the son of a head of the Council who had recently died. In his place, Dhrupatta had appointed Nandan as Council head. The Assembly seat vacated by him went to the son who was elected unopposed, which was, in a way, ironic because his own father had once proposed that the rule that prevents Karkarta's family members from succeeding as Karkarta, should be equally applied to all Assembly elections as well. He did not want public offices to be degraded to a father-to-son succession. His proposal was defeated and his own son eventually profited from its defeat. The other amusing aspect was that the youngster looked so boyish that some wondered if he had reached the legal age for standing for elections, although he was actually older.

Now as the youngster rose, everyone applauded in memory of his father and also as this would be his maiden speech. They just wanted to encourage him, knowing that speakers often suffered from nervousness when making their first speech.

Dhrupatta had not waved to him to speak. The youth simply rose. Dhrupatta who heard the applause and remembered that the youth had just lost his father, did not have the heart to lecture him on the procedure followed when intervening in debates. He simply allowed him to speak. In his heart though Dhrupatta wondered where this loose, unguided arrow would go.

There was no nervousness in the youth.

'Most respected Karkartaji! Let your Resolution say what is unsaid there but what was obviously in your heart. I propose therefore, honoured Karkartaji, that to your Resolution, let another thought be added, as an overriding condition, in the following words:

'We go on this quest of exploration and discovery of Avagana and elsewhere, not for economic benefits of profit to the clan, but because we recognize the moral and spiritual bond with the earth.

'This moral and spiritual bond can never permit us to dispossess the land of another or to hold anyone in captivity or to take undue advantage of the lands that we explore and discover.

'To those who may fail to understand our impulses and emotions in embarking on these quests, we declare that we regard that Mother Earth is the real presence and that we are only a small part of its children. We go therefore in the spirit of humanity's humble relationship with its entire environment and the greater universe.

'Thus we go with clean hands and the cry of peace in our hearts.

'Therefore any person who joins expeditions for exploration, takes an oath, permanently binding upon himself and those that come after him, to abide by the policy of Karkarta's Resolution and the four conditions which are recited therein.'

Dhrupatta shouted 'I agree'; even though it was undignified for Karkarta to display such haste in accepting amendments. Spectators broke into applause. Those from the Sahiti region, from which the youth had been elected, would not stop applauding. Even some Assembly members joined in the applause.

The applause took a long time to subside. Dhrupatta looked at the youth fondly and asked if he had more to say.

'Yes, respected Karkartaji, I was waiting to thank you for your kindness in permitting me to speak.' For no reason whatsoever, this wholly innocent remark led to renewed applause.

Dhrupatta could not have asked for a better ally to ram his Resolution through. The youth's good looks, his demeanonr, and his ignorance of procedure, were themselves an asset. Maybe, he would have been ignored if it had not been his maiden speech. Maybe, he would have been ignored if his father had not died recently. Maybe . . .but the fact is, he spoke elegantly and carried the crowds with him.

The youth's debut which delighted Dhrupatta, caused agony to those who were of Nandan's opinion. Nandan did not want to oppose Dhrupatta openly. Nor would he dignify the youth by debating with him. He was, after all, the Council head. He whispered to his neighbour Sahaji.

Three speakers had the floor before Sahaji. Each complimented the youth for his historic contribution which they strongly supported.

It was then Sahaji's turn. Dhrupatta expected fireworks. Slowly, Sahaji surveyed the Assembly, and his gaze rested on the youth from Sahiti. Then he spoke: 'I heard with wonder, Karkarta's Resolution. With even greater wonder, I heard the amendments of the member from. . .from. . .' he paused as though to leave the insulting impression that the member was unknown. But as he paused, the crowd itself roared 'Sahiti, Sahiti' making it clear that they knew the member, even if he did not. Dhrupatta took no steps, as the presiding officer should, to restore silence while the crowd kept up the chant.

Nandan groaned in spirit. He knew that the insult which flies off its course, returns to haunt its source.

Sahaji reddened. Some Assembly members who forgot, for the moment, what the decorum of the august body should be, were even laughing.

Sahaji resumed his speech but without his usual flourish. Lamely, he asked: 'Can the member from Sahiti explain how he expects oaths and acts of the members of an expedition to bind future Karkartas and Assemblies!'

Dhrupatta, as presiding officer, was prepared to answer. He did not want the youth to be grilled and, in any case, no member could demand an answer from another member. Karkarta and Council Chiefs were obliged to answer questions but not ordinary members. But the irrepressible youth from Sahiti rose, in the belief that the responsibility to answer lay with him. With a sigh, Dhrupatta addressed him, 'You do not have to respond to questions unless you specially wish to.'

The youth declared: 'Respected Sahaji, how can I even accept the view that future generations would be so misguided as to remove the moral basis of our exploration! Has it not been said in the Memory song—the 'Song of the Hindu'—inspired by the illustrious Bharatji, that 'a Hindu must grow and evolve, with all that is good in the past, with all that is good in the present, and with all goodness that future ages shall bring. . . .'

Spectators went into riotous applause—some as they remembered Bharat; others because the 'Song of the Hindu' was close to their hearts; and those from Sahiti were prepared to applaud their own, all the way. Again Dhrupatta failed to silence the spectators. The youth resumed:

'But honoured Karkarta, I appreciate Sahaji's fear. Things happen. Events evolve. People change. Memories fade. I submit, therefore, let your Resolution, with all that has been said here, be remembered in the Memory song. . . .'

Again the crowds misbehaved and cheered wildly. They loved the idea of the Memory song.

But Sahaji shouted, 'How. . .how. . . how can you have a Memory song?'

The youth apparently misunderstood and innocently asked Dhrupatta, 'Respected Karkartaji, are there limits to what this Assembly can recommend? Is it beyond our competence to suggest a Memory song?'

Sahaji felt his blood pressure rise, while patiently, Dhrupatta explained that no limits existed to the Assembly's powers to evolve any recommendations, unless it was, 'physically impossible or morally untenable', and he wondered, at length, how a Memory song could be treated as having those defects! The crowd went berserk with applause.

It was Devaji who rose to clarify that Sahaji was questioning not the Assembly's competence but the need for a Memory song.

'The need for such a Memory song!' The youth shot up again, like a loose arrow. 'But there was wisdom in Sahaji's words. How else do we keep the future with us? Did not Karkarta Bharatji say: "A Memory song penetrates to the depths of our feelings. Let it also penetrate to the depths of ithihasa?. . ." '

There was no need to say more. The applause was unending. At last, Dhrupatta simply announced, 'There shall be a Memory song on today's proceedings, unless anyone cares to oppose it; and in that case we shall put the matter to vote. Any opposition?'

There was none. Who wants a Memory song to eternally indicate his name as the one who opposed it!

Nandan allowed his thoughts to wander. Enough damage was done by Sahaji and Devaji and he had been the one to encourage them. He was sure that but for that young fool's intervention, there would have been a sufficient minority to oppose the measure and thus lead to a demand for a direct vote by the people. Such a demand required one-fifth of the Assembly members. But who would dare now, after all the theatrics of that young upstart from Sahiti, along with the threat of a Memory song! Dhrupatta had been smart to put the suggestion for a Memory song to the Assembly but that, Nandan realized, was the correct procedure, as all suggestions on the main Resolution had to be voted upon first.

But then it is not always necessary to win in order not to lose. Gracefully, Nandan rose, 'It gives me pleasure to support Karkarta's Resolution.' Dhrupatta was grateful, but a trace of suspicion still lingered, as the opposition had come mostly from those known as Nandan's supporters. 'I thank you,' Dhrupatta said, 'but the Resolution stands along with amendments proposed by the member from Sahiti, which I accepted.'

'It is because of those amendments, Karkarta,' replied Nandan, 'that my support for your Resolution is all the stronger.'

The Resolution, so reinforced, was adopted unanimously.

It is not easy to compose an inspiring Memory song about dry, drab Assembly debates. But the imagination of the composers soared to lofty heights when they sang of the moral and spiritual bond with the earth, as a basis for its exploration by man.

Someone gave out the story that Dhrupatta's father Gandhara was more than a sadhu and was the Chief of Chiefs of Avagana.

Many found it difficult to picture the sadhu as Chief. But then others questioned his credentials as a sadhu. He admitted that he ate meat, though for years he had given it up. His occupation was to build huts, grow fruit trees, and indulge in earthy, material pursuits. Infact, till his dying day, his heart was set on teaching the arts of farming and cloth-making to the people of Avagana.

Apparently, he had not even tried to find out whether the people of Avagana believed in the gods of the Hindus!

Dhrupatta refused to confirm or deny any of this. 'All I know is that he was my father. If he was a sadhu, it is between him and the people. If he was a Chief, that too is a matter between him and the people of Avagana.'

Gossip was not uncommon. It was rumoured that Dhrupatta was going to Avagana, more for collecting his inheritance, than escorting his brother. Dhrupatta laughed. His wife was hurt at such gossip. Dhrupatta laughed again but his wife could not be brushed aside lightly. And so he went to the extent of renouncing publicly in favour of his little brother, Kush, any shadowy claim that he might have had in Avagana.

Earlier Dhrupatta had thought only of Avagana. Now that the Parliament had adopted the Resolution, he felt encouraged to organize expeditions to explore distant lands in seven different directions.

Dhrupatta's caravan left for Avagana. Kush was jubilant, though full of tears when parted from his many new-found relatives. But how would he carry all their gifts? No problem; his sister-in-law, Dhrupatta's wife, had brought two mules which, she said, were gifts from two other mules—she was referring to her two grandsons.

The caravan had long lines of pack-animals with a vast variety of goods. Instead of the team of twelve, as originally planned, the expedition now had eighty-eight—mostly farmers, artisans, pottery, textile and basket makers. There was also a Vaid and an artist to draw route-charts.

The journey, arduous though it was, continued uneventfully. At times the expedition was watched and even surrounded by force. But hostility melted as soon as the strangers saw Kush. Apparently, he was well-known, even though his own home was still far way. The locals treated Dhrupatta with utmost courtesy—not for his being Karkarta of the Hindu clan, but as the elder son of Sadhu Gandhara.

Many in Dhrupatta's party began to believe that, indeed, stories of the sadhu being a chief were true! How else was little Kush treated with such courtesy! But it also seemed that there was no common chief. Friendly villagers would escort the party to the edge of their village but would never dare cross into another village.

There were, however, seven locals who joined them and went from village to village, fearlessly. They wore thongs around their necks like a garland. Dhrupatta asked Kush, who knew only a few words of his language. The boy, pointing to the thongs, simply said 'Hindu.'

Hindu! Dhrupatta wondered. All he understood was that these thong-wearers were his father's disciples and known as Hindus and somehow these thongs made them safe and inviolable in each village.

The artist sadly remarked on the fact that they had not seen a single woman on the way and was made great fun of for this very pertinent observation.

The expedition, however, did see a woman in the next village.

She was horribly mutilated. Her tongue was torn out. Her nose, lips, ears and breasts, cut off. She was helplessly writhing in pain.

Dhrupatta's impulse was to rush to help her. But the men in his party, who wore thongs, blocked his way. Dhrupatta shouted, 'Why?'

The villagers wondered why this distinguished visitor was so excited; and one came to ask as much. He spoke to Kush and then to his people. One of them picked up a huge rock to smash it in the face of the writhing woman. Dhrupatta saw fragments of her skull scatter on the ground.

Later, Dhrupatta understood that their sense of hospitality made the locals comply with his plea to end the woman's suffering, though they thought the request was odd, and even unfair, in view of her offence.

What was her offence? Pregnancy, he was told. Simple. She was the wife of an impotent husband, so obviously it was a case of adultery. Why did an impotent man have a wife? Why not! He bought her, as he had bought three other wives; and now that one of his wives was killed, he would buy one more. Was it not terrible to kill someone carrying a child? Certainly it was; but she was not carrying the child; she was killed after giving birth; the child was innocent; he did not share the mother's crime. What about her paramour who committed adultery? Oh, he belongs to our village and will pay for twelve years towards the upkeep of the child. What happens if he cannot pay? Then his family—his father, brothers, sons—must pay; after all, the family is responsible for its members; if the family cannot, the entire village must pay, but surely, the aggrieved husband and the innocent child cannot suffer!

They realized, now, why women were not visible. Women were guarded, never permitted outside their caves. With some men holding more than four, five or more wives, many had none. No wonder, outsiders entering their village were presumed to be after their women. What else was there to steal? Intruders were therefore dealt with severely. The only exceptions were Gandhara 'Hindus' with thongs round their necks. But then they were under oath never to covet another man's woman—nor to have more than one wife.

As Dhrupatta's men trudged along the difficult terrain, they saw the horrifying spectacle of what the villagers did to intruders.

Two men had been caught. One had his limbs cut off and was awaiting death to release him from his agony. They would start on the second only after the first died but even so, his eyelids were cut, so that his eyes remained open to witness all that happened to the first victim.

The first victim died in agony. Dhrupatta wished they would spare the second man, not from death but from torture. The man deserved to die, for such was the law of their land. It was hardly relevant that in his own land of Hindu the death penalty did not exist. But why inflict such brutality and gruesome torture!

Quietly, Dhrupatta went forward to present his sword to the man in charge of butchery. The man admired the shining sword. He touched its sharp edge. Dhrupatta cautioned him by a gesture. The man smiled unconcerned. His finger bled. Sadly, the man viewed his own stone axe and wooden dagger and smiled as though to compliment Dhrupatta on his sword. But Dhrupatta had not finished showing off. He touched the thick neck of the victim and gestured that with one stroke it would fly off. The Master of Ceremonies seemed to doubt it. The crowd challenged him to try. Dhrupatta again gestured to show how the stroke should be executed. As he stepped back, he saw gratitude in the victim's eyes.

With one broad, powerful sweep, the Master of Ceremonies wielded the sword. The neck flew up and then curved down, falling in the midst of the crowd. The unseeing eyes of the dead man were open; his lifeless face appeared as before, except that the lips were twisted. Dhrupatta was certain that the man grinned at the end, happy at his swift death. He wondered if the man smiled before his neck was severed or after, but he dared not ask the Vaid who would regard the question as frivolous. Indeed, the Vaid would have explained that the last lip movement of the dead man was his final prayer to God for forgiveness.

The Master of Ceremonies was triumphant and the crowd, impressed with the sword. But the ceremony continued. The dead man's limbs were cut off. The custom was inflexible. For those who came to steal their women, such dismemberment must take place, even after death.

After this gruesome deed, the man came to return the sword. Dhrupatta declined and with a sweeping gesture gifted it to the village.

The crowd was pleased and the Master of Ceremonies delighted. He began swinging the sword, happy with its swishing sound and motion. But Dhrupatta pointed to the dead man, to clarify that it must be used only for enemies who stole their women. The crowd roared its approval.

Many gestures were then involved, for Dhrupatta to explain that dismemberment of limbs must take place after the neck is cut off, as this special sword was designed to smite a criminal in full possession of his limbs and senses, so that he felt the full fear of death.

The debate that followed was intense. What however tipped the balance in his favour was Dhrupatta's appeal to their sporting instincts. His gestures clarified that the neck would fly higher, faster and farther, if the criminal was not already wounded.

The decision, therefore, was clear. In future, limbs must be cut off only after the neck is severed with this mighty sword.

It was the Vaid who later criticized Dhrupatta. 'You should have advised them not to take the man's life.'

'We did not come here to interfere with their laws.'

'No!' the Vaid was sarcastic. 'But you did interfere and change their ritual! And to bribe them, you gave them a sword, to kill instantly!'

'Only to teach them to take life humanely, if it must be taken.'

'Then be so kind as to not distribute swords elsewhere. Or soon, lives will be taken that need not be. What would prevent villages holding such swords to band together to steal other's women?'

'But Vaidji, the whole village was there! Everyone in that entire crowd understood the condition with which the sword was given!'

'The entire crowd, yes; and crowds are always more dangerous, more fickle, more insane than the combined will of all its individuals.'

Dhrupatta thought of those simple, sincere people. Poor and primitive they were, yet with so deep a sense of hospitality! They had no guile or greed. Surely, these men of honour would keep their word.

It was Kush who spoke. He was trying to frame his sentence in words foreign to him and said, 'One man, one woman.' Dhrupatta appreciated his brother's effort to say that none should have more than one wife but the Vaid tried to spoil his pleasure by saying, 'Now there you have a boy with vision. He will be a leader of men.' This was the Vaid's way of saying that Dhrupatta himself was deficient. But Dhrupatta was delighted with the compliment to Kush. He remembered what Bharat used to say of this Vaid who was no respector of persons —'He is kind only to those who are in pain. The rest he ignores or chastises. Respect for status, he has none. He sees too many men of status, naked and with all kinds of ailments and sores in their bodies and brains.'

They saw extreme poverty in the region. Rocky areas and deserts predominated. Vegetation was scanty. Patches of trees, here and there, were a bounty of nature, and there was no one trying to plant trees or tend the soil. Meat was their main diet, but with their primitive hunting implements, it was not easy to get a regular food supply; and people relied largely on mongoose, hedgehogs, bats, moles, rats and wild dogs.

The scene changed dramatically as they neared the town of Sadhu Gandhara's ashram. Here, the beauty and bounty of nature were in abundance and people had laboured hard to assist nature. Avenues were lined with trees. From gardens along the way, they heard the sounds of birds. Some they even identified as pheasants, partridges, cranes, pelicans and parrots. There was hardly a man who did not wear a thong.

The entire town lined up to greet the visitors, whose greatest thrill was that they could at last see live, smiling women, showering them with flower-petals and blowing kisses at Kush.

This was the region that the locals called Gandhara, in honour of the sadhu. Locals pronounced it also as they pronounced his name— with a sound that moved between G and K, like Kandhara or Qandhara.[1]

---

[1] Even now, it is associated with the sadhu's name and called Qandhara or Kandhara, in Afghanistan—map reference: 31.35n; 65.45e.

Dhrupatta's party stopped before a hut in the centre of a beautiful garden. The fragrance of roses, jasmine and lilies filled the air. Dhrupatta and Kush dismounted.

Sadhu Gandhara's wife stood in the doorway as her two sons entered the garden. Dhrupatta had not expected her to be so young. She looked at them affectionately and stretched out her hand. Silently, Kush brought out a cloth-purse which held his father's ashes scooped up from the river. His mother placed it against her heart. She embraced Kush and extended her hand to Dhrupatta. 'Your father spoke to me about you so often that I feel this meeting is not the first between us. Yet he spoke of you as a young boy, like my Kush.'

She spoke faultlessly in his language, though with an accent. Apparently, the sadhu had taught her well. 'My father,' Dhrupatta replied, 'had the image of a youngster in mind when he thought of me. He left us when I was no more than a boy.'

Perhaps she detected sorrow in his voice and said, 'Fate brought him to me, and to this land, to do a great deal of good, just as fate brings you, his son, to continue his good work.'

He responded with courtesy, 'In the presence of my father, I acknowledged you as my mother. Feel free to command me in any way.'

She kissed him lightly on the forehead and said, 'In the presence of your father, and within the hearing of God, I too acknowledged you as my son. But a mother makes no demands on her son. I shall only speak to you of your father's wishes... and mine, for this land.'

She added, 'But come, first, we shall bury your father's ashes.'

They went to the back garden. The fragrance of flowers mingled with the breeze as they walked in the garden carpeted with roses, tulips and jasmine. A pit had been freshly dug. Men from Dhrupatta's party and large numbers of locals were there. Gandhara's wife sprinkled a little of the ashes in the pit and gave some to Dhrupatta and Kush so that they could follow suit. Thereafter, she scooped the earth to cover the ashes. The two sons helped. Dhrupatta was thinking of the custom in his own land—where people were cremated and their ashes sprinkled in the river, as indeed was done for his father.

Maybe she understood what he was thinking and said, 'All life comes from the depths of the earth. There the spirit of your father shall hear the whispering of flowers and the singing of trees.'

Dhrupatta did not speak of his conviction that his father's spirit was one with the Eternal Self, hearing the exhilarating music of the universe. He simply nodded though he wondered why only a bit of the ashes were sprinkled, and the cloth-purse was still almost full.

Dhrupatta introduced her to the members of his party. She touched the Vaid's feet as he had looked after her husband in his last days to ease his pain. She spoke to him so sweetly that even he asked if there was anything he could do for her. Quickly, at her summons, ten youngsters came forward, and she told the Vaid, 'They are yours. Teach them your art to look after our people.' They touched the Vaid's feet and called him 'Guru'. The Vaid was one of those who was to return with Dhrupatta but there and then he decided to stay back.

Dhrupatta marvelled at her captivating ways. Of his party, forty were to remain behind to teach arts and crafts, and the rest were to return. Now she was sweetly encouraging many more to stay back. He was glad that he had selected bachelors and widowers to form his team.

The sadhu's wife had made impeccable arrangements for their stay, acting upon the information supplied by the thong-wearing locals, of Dhrupatta's imminent arrival. Huts were erected. Trainees to learn new crafts were chosen. Areas for farming, tree-planting and mining were selected.

Only once did she deviate from Dhrupatta's views. When Dhrupatta advised his men on what should be given away free, she cautioned him saying that the locals were a proud people and would dislike charity, 'Help them to help themselves'—was her advice—and he agreed.

The first objective, she said, was to get slaves in exchange to set them free. Slaves were of no use to their masters, here; the main occupation was hunting and game was not easy to come by with the result that the masters had to hunt for themselves and for their slaves.

'Why do people have slaves here, then?' Dhrupatta asked.

'Why do people have more than one wife? Some foolish ideas of ego, prestige, vanity. Maybe like me, even. Why do I have a hut with four rooms, when Kush and I need only one!'

She continued, 'But henceforth, it will be different. These people, as my husband said, can no longer survive on hunting alone. Now that they will learn farming with your help, slaves will be extremely useful to their masters. And that is why we must buy slaves, before their masters learn how useful they can be in farming land.'

'Yes, we can buy them cheap now,' Dhrupatta said.

'Only to set them free, forthwith,' she said, leaving no doubt.

'Of course. There shall be no slaves in this land if I can help it. My men and I promise you that.'

It seemed she was waiting to hear only that. She went out and spoke to the people outside. There was applause. Dhrupatta understood nothing but she explained when she returned. 'It means that you are the successor of Sadhu Gandhara—and sadhu of this land and its people.'

Dhrupatta was puzzled. But she continued, 'It means that land between here and Kubha, around and beyond, is to be administered by you. You are the sadhu now.'

Dhrupatta understood. Clearly, his father was more than a sadhu, and held a commanding position. She repeated, 'Yes, you are the sadhu.'

'No, I am not!' Dhrupatta said. 'I have no rights or claims on this land. Even if I had any, I renounced them in favour of Kush.'

'Kush is too young. How can he administer this vast region?'

'Then you administer for him, until he is of age.'

'I wish that were possible. In Gandhara, yes, they have learnt to tolerate a woman in charge, thanks to your father's teaching. But below this region, and beyond Kubha, and around, a woman is considered chattel, with less liberty than a slave.'

'But I have to go back to my land.'

'I know. But you can appoint someone here to act as your headman.'

'How can I do that! I do not have the right.'

'Right! No one is conferring a right on you. What is being imposed on you is a duty.'

Their eyes met and she continued, 'Yes, you did renounce your right in favour of Kush. But you did not speak of renouncing a duty. Perhaps I misunderstood, because ever since I heard of your coming, my heart was filled with hope.'

She dropped her eyes and said, 'But the decision must be yours, and whatever it be, you must know that you are a part of me, for you are my husband's son—.'

Dhrupatta wiped out all objections from his mind and simply said, 'It shall be as you wish.'

'No, as you wish.'

Dhrupatta smiled inwardly: yes, the decision is mine. Is there anything stronger than the chain of love? But quietly, he said, 'Yes, that is what I wish. Who do you think should be headman here?'

'Someone who is not a woman like me, nor a child like Kush.'

'When can Kush take over?'

'Not before there is hair on his upper lip and on his chin. But why not appoint our respected Vaid?'

The Vaid was startled, 'But I don't even know the language here!'

'My husband did not know the language initially. Perhaps you will permit me to interpret your words to my people.'

'It will be an honour, Madam, an honour,' the Vaid replied instantly.

But Dhrupatta wanted to be clear beyond a shadow of doubt. He did not want her to be a mere interpreter of the Vaid's words. For the first time in his life he spoke sternly to the Vaid.

'Let me understand, Vaidji. You agree to be the headman. . . .'

The Vaid interrupted, but with unusual politeness, 'If that is your wish Karkarta, and if that is the desire of the lady of Sadhu Gandhara.'

'But,' said Dhrupatta, 'let us understand this fully. Is it clear that in all matters you will act exactly according to the wishes of this lady,

242 / Return of the Aryans

whom I acknowledge as my mother? Further, is it clear that she holds
my authority to dismiss you and appoint anyone in your place?'

Everyone expected the Vaid to flare up. He was not known to be a
man with a cool temper. But he replied formally, 'Karkarta, be assured
that it is exactly on those conditions that I accept the appointment.
You have my oath. My only stipulation is that should I ever consider
her wishes as opposed to the laws of God or Nature, I shall resign.'
To her, he said humbly, 'Dear lady, I know that will not happen, but
we speak of the future, and as I bind myself with an oath to serve you
for life, I must provide for unknown dangers that may lie far beyond
the horizon of today.'

For no reason, her eyes were moist. She said, 'My husband also
said what you have in mind. He said that some who begin by serving
people sometimes turn vicious when they take up the rod of authority
and then are unable to understand the superior and eternal law of
Sanathana Dharma. But Vaidji, I shall not disappoint you.'

'And I, dear lady, shall not fail you,' the Vaid gallantly replied.

Later, Dhrupatta learnt why she had retained most of the ashes. They
were to go for immersion to distant lands, she explained.

'What are those lands where the ashes are to be immersed?' he
asked.

She did not reply immediately. Her mind lingered on the precious
memories of days gone by. Those lands! She tried to recall and count
them one by one. 'First, the mountains of Hindu Kush and Kubha;
second, Hari River; third, the village of Hari rath; fourth, the village of
Sindhan; fifth, Kama River (river of love); sixth, Kara Kumari desert
(desert of the blue-black girl); seventh, Indra ka River (River of god
Indra).

Dhrupatta heard her astonished. They sounded like Hindu names—
so familiar, yet strange. 'Where?' he asked. 'Are they Hindu lands?'

'No,' she smiled, 'but these names were given by a Hindu—your
father.' She pointed to a line on a route-chart etched on the wall and
continued: 'Your father first came to this place—the one we all call
Gandhara and set up his ashram. Soon he moved to the north, to a
place he called Kubha (present-day Kabul), to honour the memory of
his disciple buried there. That disciple died while protecting your father
who was at prayer. Then, your father's wanderlust led him 20 yojnas
(100 miles) to the north where he came face to face with the mountains.'

'You also went with my father?' Dhrupatta asked.

'Oh no. I had not met him then. Well, he went along the mountain
range and, at last, with terrible difficulty, crossed over. Every day he
met adventure and, every night, danger. Yet, he went on, always in
the hope of finding the edge of the earth. Somewhere, he felt, the earth
would end. Later he felt that the earth was endless. Even so, he went

on and on, crossing rivers, mountains, swamps, villages, and finally, reached a river which he named Indra ka river.[2] There we met.'

She described the terrain. They both pored over the route-chart. Dhrupatta was amazed. How did his father cover thousands of yojnas on this breathtaking, dangerous journey, alone, unaided!

She continued: 'My own father was dying from wounds. He had been mauled by a bear. Your father came into our cave to shelter from a blinding storm but stayed back to look after my father. We did not understand his language; but it was his care that eased my father's pain. He had herbs and medicines and often went out to find more.

'Your father tried to catch fish to feed us. When the river was frozen, he would break the topmost layers of ice to get at fish through the hole in the ice. He tried and tried but caught no fish. However, one day, he went into a trance to pray to god Indra, and thereafter the fish came in large numbers as though wishing to be caught. He therefore named it the Indra ka river.'

She continued, 'The time came for my father to die. Your father treated me like a child. I was so much younger. He promised my father that he would look after me as his own daughter. Your father understood the word 'daughter' well, as that is how I was introduced to him.

'But my father had bigger ambitions. He wanted your father to marry me. Maybe he understood the look in my eyes and heard the voice in my heart. Or maybe, he felt that marriage would protect me. I could never go back to our village. We were banished, as my brother had hit the Chief's son for trying to molest my mother. My mother and my brother were beheaded—she, for causing temptation to the Chief's son, and he, for hurting him; and my father and I were banished, subject to death if we reappeared. My village was then our whole world.

'I think my father died a thousand deaths before your father agreed to marry me. My father joined our hands in marriage.

'There were a few unfortunates like us living in caves nearby. Your father always helped them with fishing. They all came for the wedding party and one of them even brought an empty cask which had once held wine. We filled it with water and pretended that it was wine and we danced all night. My father said, "Never, never have I been so happy. I die happy. Promise, all of you, to drink to me when I die."

---

[2]Indra ka river is presently known as Indigirka river, which drains into the Arctic Ocean. Location: former Soviet Union; map reference: 70.48n; 148.54e. Subsequently, controversy arose over it. It was alleged that Sadhu Gandhara could not have travelled so far into that inhospitable terrain and that later Hindu explorers and settlers who reached another river, mistakenly assumed it to be the Indra ka river of the sadhu's discovery, and so named it. There is not much substance in the controversy.

'I kissed my father. Your father kissed him. All the guests kissed him. My father was smiling. But he was dead. We remembered his words to drink to him. We drank water again from the wine cask.'

She paused, her eyes moist, suddenly realizing that she had strayed into a story about her father. 'I am sorry,' she said. 'I digressed....'

'No,' Dhrupatta said, 'Tell me all about my father—and you.'

'All! It will take months to tell you all about his fantastic journey of endless years. But let me try. Your father wanted to return to Kubha (Kabul), but not by the route he had come. He knew I would be unable to cross the mountains. So we went on, in the west, hoping to proceed on to the south to avoid mountains and finally, to reach Kubha.

'Throughout, your father was kind and considerate to me. But I was his wife only in my imagination. He treated me like a daughter. The journey was rough and full of perils. The wind was cruel and pitiless. Often, we were in each other's arms, protecting ourselves from the biting cold. But to him, I was still his daughter. We rested near a river.'

It was at this river that I decided that he must know that I was more than a daughter to him. I did what a wife should do, to bring her husband to herself.' She smiled. It was Dhrupatta who felt shy, though he smiled back. He wondered at how uncomplicatedly she, Kush, and people of this region expressed their emotions.

She continued: 'By the side of that river we became united as husband and wife, not merely in name but truly—and that is how he called it Kama river (river of love).[3] Your father told everyone there that indeed the river was blessed by Kama (God of Love), and they all began to believe that a swim in the river would bless their love life.'

She continued: 'News of Kama river's love-power spread; and even couples from far away came to seek its blessings. They all regarded your father as the Priest of love. And you know what happens when people have faith in their hearts! Somehow their hopes are realized and their dreams, fulfilled. Gratefully, many gave animal skins and furs to your father. With these, he improved his mobile home.'

'Mobile home?' Dhrupatta asked.

'Oh yes, your father travelled with a kind of home, everywhere. It was mainly skins, dried grass and river vegetation, mounted on poles. It could be set up anywhere to protect us from bad weather, any time. It was small when your father came to Indra ka river, but when he left with me, it was larger and accommodated both of us, in a tight fit.

'Now, with many gifts, our mobile home was grand, with layers of furs and skins, and even slits to see through and flaps to close them. But your father was greedy. He suggested to everyone that

---

[3]Even now, it is called Kama river; located west of the Ural mountains; former U.S.S.R.; map reference: 55.45n; 52.00e.

Kama's blessing would increase with more gifts. All he received, he gave to the many unfortunates who lived nearby. That spread his name and the river's fame, as he gave those skins as gifts from Kama river and not from himself.

'He could not speak much of their language but he was a great actor. He spoke with signs and gestures more clearly than you and I speak with words. He was also lucky. No, I should say God favoured him. And why not? God had no better servant. He was greater; yes greater than all the 108 gods that serve God.'

Pride for her husband shone in her face as she continued, 'Yes, Kama river gained fame. Even the Chief of the region came with his wife, on hearing of it as the river of fertility. He was young and in love with his wife but four years of marriage had brought no offspring.

'The Chief bathed with his wife and gave only a small skin to your father, and that too because the Chief's wife insisted. This did not surprise your father as he always said that the rich are never generous.

'But it is not always so; the Chief returned. At last, his wife was pregnant. He wanted renewed blessings. The Chief had loads of skins. And as your father chanted his prayers, one by one, the Chief handed over the skins. It was clear that your father would have to keep chanting till sunset to relieve the Chief of all his skins. Your father met the challenge and in the end the Chief parted with them all.

'However, it troubled your father that the Chief could not go near his wife during the pregnancy and two years of breast-feeding; the custom was that the Chief must have another wife to serve him during the period. "Why?" asked your father. But once a custom is established, who can oppose it? Your father did. He went into a fit of trembling, as though lightning would strike and the sky would fall if the Chief parted from his wife. I moved away lest I laugh at his acting.

'The Chief left perturbed, but returned with his mother, five step-mothers, his wife's father and mother, his wife's three step-mothers. Your father frightened them, first by silence, then with rapid chants, and finally with every gesture that spelt the ruin of the entire family if the Chief took a second wife. Bystanders were frightened for your father's life, for with the Chief was the dreaded Chief of an adjacent region who, it was said, tolerated no opposition and even killed without reason. But they need not have feared. That dreaded Chief had four wives and was planning to marry the fifth, but he was happy if other Chiefs married no more. A Chief with many wives acquires large family backing and influence—and it pleased him if the other Chiefs remained content with one wife. He had the ambition, one day, of removing all the minor Chiefs to become the sole Chief of Chiefs.

'By then, your father's dramatic performance convinced them of the tragedy waiting to overtake them all if the local Chief remarried.'

She smiled. 'Yes, they must have asked themselves: What is the gain to this man if the Chief does or does not marry; surely he speaks not from self-interest; he is not greedy—did he not refuse the gifts they brought and give them to the poor bystanders! They knew also, he was a visitor who would leave soon—so he was not building a base there as a priest. So why not believe him?'

Again she smiled, 'And your father, in one surprising gesture, took hold of the dreaded Chief's whip. With his dagger, he cut pieces from it, and went to the Chief whose second marriage was being considered, and put it round his neck, chanting "One man, one wife". Soon, they understood that the thong was a pledge to have only one wife. The Chief touched the thong and gave the pledge after the dreaded Chief encouraged him to do so.'

'Did he keep the pledge?' Dhrupatta asked.

'I am sure he did, as soon after, we received from the Chief's father-in-law, a gift of two horses and six mules and donkeys. He had six wives but he obviously wanted his son-in-law married to a single wife—his own daughter—and was delighted with your father's effort.'

'Meanwhile, many came to your father to take the pledge "One man, one wife." He had no thongs for their necks but some wore leather strips or anything round their necks to mark their pledge.'

Dhrupatta asked, 'What made him crusade for "One man, one wife"?'

'He blamed me,' she smiled. 'When the Chief and his wife visited us at first, the wife was sad as the Chief gave him a poor skin. Quietly, she gave me a pearl without her husband seeing it. Your father said her kindness to me was reason enough to save her from another wife for her husband. But then that is not so. There was always something deep in your father's heart that moved him. He did not care about the pearl; I gave it to him for safekeeping. The next day, a couple came to the Kama river to get married. They were poor and for days they had waited to catch a rabbit, as a gift for your father. Your father gave them the pearl as a wedding gift. Later, he told me, "You wanted the pearl to be kept safe. These two will really keep it safe." I am sure he was right. Poor though that couple was, they loved each other too much to part with a wedding gift."

Her smile deepened, 'But your father was fair to me. Instead of the pearl, he gave me the rabbit and the condition he imposed was that I should release the rabbit, in wild vegetation, away from human habitation, which I was happy to do.'

Dhrupatta shared her smile and she continued, 'Yes, both Indra ka and Kama are a part of our life and your father's ashes must go there too.'

Sadhu Gandhara's wife continued her story: 'We left Kama river in style. Many saw us off. We had horses, mules and donkeys for travelling.'

Dhrupatta was puzzled, 'Then how did you travel before? On foot?'

'No,' she said, 'we had animals.' She paused, reluctant to say more, but then spoke slowly, 'Before leaving Indira ka river for Kama, we had gone to the Chief's village. The old Chief was dead. The son, whose head my brother had struck with a stone, was the new Chief.

'It was a dark night. The Chief's animal were unguarded. . . .' Again she paused, reluctant to offend her husband's memory by admitting that he stole the animals.

'So my father took them!' Dhrupatta prompted. She nodded, sadly. Dhrupatta laughed to put her at ease. 'My father was human. But every god in the firmament must have applauded his action in stealing the animals of the Chief who caused you so much suffering.'

'My husband was human, yes. He did what he thought was right—always. He did not care for applause—neither from humans, nor from the gods and his heart never led him astray. My reluctance to speak of this was so that it may not serve as an example to those who will know of it in isolation, without the surrounding circumstances.'

'Yes,' she continued. 'From Kama, it began as a beautiful journey. But later, it was terrible. Both our horses and three donkeys died. There were blinding storms and we often lost our way. To make matters worse, I became pregnant in the middle of nowhere.'

'Kush?' Dhrupatta asked.

'No, Kush came later.' She continued, 'It was at the fringe of a desert that I could proceed no further. Some cave-dwellers there gave us what little help they could. I gave birth to a baby girl. Your father called her Kara Kumari (black girl) as she was almost blue-black in colour from her premature birth. She lived for six days.

'Your father wanted to cremate her but it would have offended the cave-dwellers. The fire-God is not summoned to consume the dead. Your father buried our daughter, who was to be your sister, in the desert.'

Dhrupatta's mind went to his unseen little sister buried somewhere in an unknown, nameless desert. But she clarified that the desert had a name. 'Cave-dwellers had no name for the desert. Your father gave it a name. He called it Kara Kumari desert (desert of the blue-black girl).'[4]

'Yes,' Dhrupatta said impulsively, 'the ashes must go to Kara Kumari.'

She resumed: 'By an effort of will, my health improved. The weather was changing and he too was keen to ensure that I reached the safety of his ashram in Kubha (Kabul).

---

[4]Kara Kumari desert is now known as Kara-Kum desert; location: Turkmen Soviet Socialist Republic; Map Reference: 39.00n; 60.00e.

'I was such a burden to him! Yet he never complained. On and on we went, with nothing but the desert ahead and almost certain that we were lost. A moment came when I nearly collapsed with thirst. He laid me on the ground, sheltered me with his body and I could hear him praying "Harihara, Harihara" (Hari: god Vishnu; and Hara: god Shiva).

'Suddenly in the midst of his cry to Harihara, when he uttered "Hari...", he stopped as if he had seen a miracle. In the distance he saw what appeared to be a stream. "Hari, Hari, Hari river," he shouted, and raced towards it, dismissing the fear that it was a mirage. Indeed, it was a river!

'Only after I had quenched my thirst did he drink water. The river gave us fish and strength. After a rest, we followed its course. We met people trying to eke out a living from the river. They became friendly when your father showed them better methods to catch fish, build fires and cook food. Like us, they too began to call it Hari river.'[5]

She continued: 'Many joined us along the Hari river, accepting your father's view that the river would be more productive as we moved. It was indeed so. Our last donkey had died. Your father made a basket of driftwood, grass, bark and river weed. I would sit in the basket and he would pull it with a rope. In rough terrain, it would come apart, and he would carry me in his arms until he repaired it.

'Your father called this basket a rath (chariot). Once my ride in it was so smooth that I went to sleep; when I woke up, it was to see water foaming among the boulders and a rainbow woven across the river. It was lush countryside. I asked what the place was and your father, never at a loss, said it was a place where the rath from Hari river had brought us, so obviously its name should be Hari rath (chariot of Hari river).'

Her story continued: 'At Hari rath (Herat),[6] we rested. The local cave-dwellers were frightened of us at first. Strangely, most of them were old men or children. Soon they realized that we meant no harm and they began to point to the south, to warn us of the terrible danger from there. It was clear that a raiding party often came to take away their women and young men. Resistance meant instant death and indeed there were empty caves with nothing but skeletons of the dead.

---

[5]The river is still known as Hari river (Haridud). It originates in the western slopes of Kuh-e-Baba range and forms a border between Afghanistan, Iran and erstwhile U.S.S.R., before crossing into Soviet Central Asia, to disappear finally in the Kara-Kum (Kara Kumari desert). Map reference of Hari River: 35.35n; 61.12e.

[6]The place continued to be called Hari rath. However, different pronunciations came into play. Presently, Hari rath is known by the name Herat. Location: Afghanistan; map reference: 34.20n; 62.12e.

'They believed that one day the gods would send strong bodies from heaven to embody those skeletons and they could then take revenge from the southern raiders but until then, it was their lot to suffer.

'What did the raiders do to the young men and women captured by them? The women were sold to men who wanted wives. The men were sold as slaves, though some were trained to join raiding parties. Their own young men, snatched from these very caves, had come with raiding parties to attack them.

'Why did the cave-dwellers not resist? How could they! The raiders came on horses, with spears, whips; they were strong and cruel; they came yelling, shrieking, killing everyone close at hand; then they trussed up young women and men and speared whoever was nearby, just to strike more terror; "Oh they are ungodly, ungodly!" cried the cave-dwellers.

'But then you know your father. He was a true Hindu and he believed that it was more ungodly not to resist evil aggression.

'But only the children listened to your father. Even those who came with us wanted to return, unwilling to risk death and abduction. All they needed was rest, to heal their sores and bruises. Besides, they were catching fish and your father had taught them how to salt and preserve it for the future. They wanted to go back quickly, with abundant food, and were even making raths (travel baskets) with your father's help.

'Your father too was not keen on staying long; his heart was on proceeding to Kubha as soon as I recovered. But he cautioned everyone. What if the raiders came charging in while we were still there?

'It was decided that every night two men would watch from a south hill. It would be easy to spot the raiders as they invariably came at night with burning torches. Jagged stones were collected and kept ready in huge mounds. Children practised stone-throw and adults were taught to make spears from trees with sharp, pointed tips. Your father taught them to extract oil from fish and plants. The oil was stored in a cave overlooking the route. A fire was always kept burning in that cave, so that at a signal from the hill, wooden sticks dipped in oil and fire could serve as burning torches to be thrown at the raiders.

'Apart from the children, most of them treated these exercises as futile. The locals thought there was no protection from the raiders; other expected no attack in the short period they were to be there.'

'But the unexpected happened. The attack came. The lookouts on the hill were possibly dozing. By the time they saw the burning torches of the raiders, the enemy had even crossed beyond the hill. The fire had almost died out and the lookouts took time to light their signal-torches. At last, they signalled. Luckily, a boy and a girl, hiding behind a stone-mound to have a private moment to themselves, saw fire-signals from the hill and began yelling; the boy threw stones at our cave. Fortunately also, we were not asleep.'

She smiled, as though reliving that night, 'We rushed to the cave where torches dipped in oil were kept. The old watchman there was asleep. But luckily the small fire was burning. By the time we were ready to throw our burning torches, almost half the raiders had passed below the cave. The three of us—the old man was up by now—threw burning torches. It was the old man's torch which caught a raider first. But then our torches also began to hit them, as the raiders rode very close to each other. The tail-end of the raiders stopped, while their front-line had already begun their furious ride, unaware of what was happening at the back. The old watchman, in a frenzy at his success, rushed out of the cave, holding two burning torches. As the raiders stopped to spear him to death, they became easy targets for us to fling our own fire-torches at them. Their horses bolted; the raiders scattered to move away from the range of our throw. For them, this resistance was totally unexpected. Two of them dashed to our cave. One was easily caught by a burning torch aimed by your father, but the second raider came close, to hurl his own fire-torch at us. It missed us but landed in the cave. Your father speared him, but we had to rush out, as a huge fire developed in the cave. The stored oil had caught fire from the burning torch thrown by the raider. The raiders gave not the slightest attention to us. They were all watching the huge blaze in the cave.

'By now, everyone was aware of the attack. The vanguard of raiders went with frightened yells to the caves to empty them of their occupants.

'Some children, however, reached the stone-mounds and started hurling stones. In the caves, too, there was some resistance, as the Hari river residents, at least, had kept their spears ready. Your father reached the stone-mounds to direct the stone missiles.

'I am ashamed to say, I was terrified. The courage with which I had hurled burning torches earlier, left me. I found refuge in the cave of skeletons. Your father remained to lead the children in stone-throwing.

'The raiders were distracted. Some fought in the caves against the feeble resistance offered with wooden spears. But many raiders hurt by stones rushed to the stone-mounds. Your father now directed the youngsters to move in a large semicircle to the skeleton-cave where I was hiding. Many came, carrying stones to hurl at raiders. Some youngsters were hurt but your father himself cut down three raiders with his own long sword, which was sharper than anything that the raiders had. He himself stood guard at the skeleton-cave, from which the children now threw stones. The children had a fresh target as the raiders who had remained behind, dazzled by the burning cave, also reached the scene of this confusion.

'The raiders, certainly, were confused as at all their previous raids the victims hadn't even attempted to fight back. Some of them even threw away their torches, to avoid being easy targets for our stones.

'Stones were now in short supply. We were in the dark. And then I made my most terrible mistake.' She paused to smile.

'In that pitch dark, I picked up what I thought were stones, and hurled them. They were skulls of the dead stored there. Suddenly, the raiders saw those skulls with their torches. Previously, they were confused. Now they were frightened. The superstition, that skeletons of the dead would one day come to embody brave warriors, was already in their minds. How else could they account for this strange resistance from people who had never resisted before! The raiders had seen their men stoned, unhorsed, burned, killed, and in flight! What else could this be except that their skeletons were coming to life! They were shouting at each other. Apparently, they were leaderless. Some mounted their horses. Others were unable to find their horses, scattered by stones.

'Your father was in his element. He again led the youngsters to the stone-mounds. Stoning began in right earnest. Even adults joined in after hurling their spears. The raiders lost their nerve and began to flee. The lookouts on the south hill atoned for their earlier folly by hurling boulders from the hilltop on the retreating, frightened raiders.

'The price was heavy. Twenty-three of our people, including five children, were killed. Only nine raiders died. Yet we rounded up twelve horses. Apparently, some raiders doubled up on their horses while fleeing.

'Yes, the price was heavy, with twenty-three dead. But earlier attacks had been deadlier—and at least no one was abducted! The raiders fled leaving their dead behind!

'We mourned our dead. Everyone was grateful to your father. But initially, they were puzzled. Why did I throw skulls, so reverently stored? But I was saved the embarrassment of explaining that in the pitch dark I had mistaken the skulls for stones.' She smiled, 'Sometimes, language-barriers help; they concluded what I never had in mind and looked at me with new respect, as they realized that it was my throwing of skulls which had led to the dreadful fright that caused them to flee forthwith. Everyone was now convinced that your father was a great fighter and organizer, which of course he was, but that I too was a great strategist for having thought of creating for the raiders the frightening illusion of dead skulls having come to life.

'For the next few days at Hari rath, your father gave lessons in horse-riding, as we were the proud possessors of twelve horses left behind by the raiders. Opinion was divided on what should be done if the raiders returned to seek revenge. Some from Hari river favoured returning forthwith. Your father hoped that the demoralized raiders would not return but he insisted on defensive steps.

'He organized defence with boulders, pits and ditches, as obstacles in the enemy path, with continuous vigil from the hills, a signalling system by day and night, and even an inspection team to keep every lookout awake and alert. He promised to return to set up an ashram there.'

She continued, 'We left Hari rath with the four horses. We wanted two but the villagers insisted that we took four. We took the eastern route to reach the mountain range below which Kubha lay. We had had many breathtaking adventures and narrow escapes but it was always me who caused the greatest trouble to your father.

'At the foot of the mountains above Kubha, about 20 yojnas (100 miles) away, we rested. We had to. I gave birth to my son. Your father named him Kush which was the short form of my father's name.

'Your father also named the mountain range Hindu Kush in honour of the beautiful, bouncing son I had.' Dhrupatta's arm went around his brother Kush, who smiled, realizing that they spoke of his birth.

She continued: 'We rested at Hindu Kush valley for quite a while before resuming our journey. At last we reached your father's ashram at Kubha. He had left Kubha alone but returned with me as his wife and a little son Kush after an absence of many years.

It was a rousing welcome; many joined his ashram to call themselves 'Hindu' and took a pledge against slavery, abduction and exploitation.'

Dhrupatta asked and she told him the story of the thongs. He already knew how, on the spur of the moment, his father had put a thong round the Chief's neck at Kama river, to bind him to the pledge of 'one man, one wife.' Later, he realized that such outward symbols were needed for a growing number of his 'Hindu' disciples, to remind them of their pledged word; besides he wanted his disciples to be identified in the villages as persons who came to help and meant no harm.

Some suggest that the modern practice of wearing neck-wear possibly grew from wearing thongs round the neck. This is doubtful; no Memory song supports this theory. Also later, in Avagana itself, thongs were replaced with the 108-bead necklace. None wore thongs in the land of Sindhu. The Sindhu people kept 108-bead rosaries for prayers, but they were not worn as necklaces; however, it was common in the lands of Sindhu to wear a sacred thread (*Yajnopavita*). This sacred thread was a cord of three cotton threads, each of nine twisted strands. The three threads represented the gods Brahma, Vishnu and Shiva and the nine strands represented the planets. The sacred thread, hung over the left shoulder and under the right arm, was generally worn at the age of seven and thereafter continuously. However, tribals adopting the Hindu fold could begin wearing it at any age. The Gayatri Mantra was recited when the sacred thread was worn.

Incidentally, it is said by some that wearing the sacred thread started around 5125 BC, in the time of the eighteenth Karkarta, Suryakarma, after his wife Gayatri was abducted by the tribal raiders and that Suryata, his son, was the first to wear it, as a measure to invoke the protection of the gods. However, judging from early songs, it seems that the system of the sacred thread is far more ancient. Possibly, this mistaken attribution to Karkarta Suryakama arose because his wife was called Gayatri and he himself was a sun-worshipper. And what is more, the Gayatri hymn in the *Rig Veda* is addressed to the old solar god Savitar (the Sun god). On the other hand, the Gayatri Mantra recited even in Suryakarma's time, at the time of wearing the sacred thread, referred not to the Sun god alone, but also to Brahma, Vishnu and Shiva and was intended to glorify the various manifestations of God rather than seek protection.

'Did my father go to Hari rath again?' Dhrupatta asked.

'Oh yes. He went but without Kush and me, and with many followers, horses, draft animals, provisions and weapons to protect the people of Hari rath and surrounding areas. There he came face to face with awesome tragedy. Raiding enemies had come in vast numbers, ably led, to wreak havoc. Only seventeen survived to tell the gruesome tale.

'Your father visited many nearby colonies of cave-dwellers attacked by raiders. Their situation was worse. None knew the location of the raiders—only that they came from the south.

'With his many followers, and some from Hari rath, he took the southern route. It was not too difficult to find the raiders' camp. Everyone was frightened of them but the raiders were afraid of none. They had not taken the trouble to guard against a surprise attack. Your father attacked. The raiders were taken unawares and were soon at your father's mercy.

'Your father's victory led to the release of eighty-four women whom the raiders held prisoner. Slave-traders were also caught, leading to the release of 216 more. Unfortunately, among them were only two women from Hari rath. The rest had been sold by the raiders and could not be located.

'Your father established an ashram at Hari rath and another ashram on site of the raiders' camp which he called Sindhan, after his beloved Sindhu. The Sindhan Ashram was fully armed, always charged to go into action against raider activity anywhere in the region, while the ashram at Hari rath concerned itself with civic problems.'

She paused, her eyes moist, her hand on the purse that held her husband's ashes. 'Yes, the ashes must go to Hari rath and to Sindhan too.'[7]

She continued, 'But then even after Sindhan, your father led expeditions, mostly peaceful, but there were engagements in which blood was shed to liberate the abducted women and enslaved men, and to free the regions from those that terrorized them. There too his ashes will go. Your father carried marks of eight wounds from those expeditions.'

Dhrupatta nodded. He had seen the scars of those wounds on his father's body at the cremation.

She was silent. Her eyes went to the small fire burning in the kitchen. Perhaps she saw in it the image of the flames that must have consumed her husband at the cremation.

It was Dhrupatta who spoke, lost in wonder over his father's travels and exploits. 'What was my father! A sadhu! An explorer! A man of God! A man of the people! A ruler! A chief! A reformer! What!'

She looked at him. Quietly she said, 'He was a human being.'

Dhrupatta thought that she had possibly misunderstood his remark and felt that he was trying to diminish her husband by placing him in a particular category. He wanted to correct the impression and said, 'He lives with God; he is far above us; he is a part of God's Eternal Self.'

'No,' she said. 'He lives with us as a part of all of us. He is a Hindu.'

[7]Presently Sindhan is known as Shindhan. After Sadhu Gandhara's time, it became unclear if the name was Sindhan, based on Sindhu, or Hindan. Later, as a combination of both, it came to be known as Shindhan. Now its name is established as Shindhan. Location: Afghanistan, south of Herat. Map reference: 33.18n; 62.08e.

'...He who was one of us went ahead through dark, stormy nights and ordeals of patient, arduous journey to discover those lands in the immensity of this earth and the infinity of the universe. Why? To enlarge the heritage of humanity. He knew what every Hindu of Sanathana Dharma knows—that the children of this earth are all bound as members of one single family....'

'...Do we not then dishonour our family affiliation if we fail to support humanity in all the lands discovered in the bosom of this great earth?...'

—(From woman-councillor, Hansuya's address to Hindu Parliament—5069 BC)

The Family of Man

5069 BC

Dhrupatta returned from Avagana to the land of Sindhu.

Little has been said, over the centuries, of the Pledge of Hindavana that bound the Hindu nation with the people of Avagana. Perhaps there was little to tell, except that it was a pledge of unity and eternal friendship. The Memory song that survives has 156 words, and the possibility is that even originally, it was not longer. The song spoke of the approval by the Hindu Parliament of the pledge made by Karkarta Dhrupatta to support Avagana in the spirit of unity and oneness, without seeking reward, return or remuneration. And, supplying all the goods, services, implements for farming, cattle, seeds, teachers of crafts, artisans, builders and others that the people of Avagana might need to lead a self sufficient, fuller and more abundant life and further, that every Hindu who entered Avagana would be bound by the principles of Sadhu Gandhara which totally excluded slavery, exploitation and greed.

Dhrupatta returned from Avagana with twenty-two of the eighty-eight men he had taken there. The sixty-six left behind would go to various parts of Avagana under the orders of the Vaid who was now the headman. Their task was to train the people of Avagana in farming, tree-planting, well-digging, housing, arts, crafts and, where necessary, to defend their villages from attacks by raiders. The small number of sixty-six was certainly insufficient for the vast area to be covered—and Dhrupatta decided that he would send more of his people. Meanwhile, he brought with him a contigent of ninety-four men and seven women from Avagana. They would be settled in the land of Sindhu for a year to learn new arts and crafts and to return to their homes thereafter as teachers and instructors.

Dhrupatta submitted his Pledge of Hindavana to the Assembly for approval. There were those who could not resist the insinuation that such generosity to Avagana was the result of the family affiliation of Karkarta himself. Would he, asked some, have been so liberal but for the involvement of his own father, Sadhu Gandhara? Would he have placed this enormous load on his own land to support Avagana if his father did not have his second wife and son there? Did he not acknowledge them openly as his own mother and brother? Was Sindhu's wealth to be frittered away to meet the family obligations of its Karkarta?

But these questions were quickly quashed by the staggering response of the people. Volunteers came by the hundreds, demanding to be sent to Avagana, at their own cost. Some, of course, were looking for adventure—even an escape from boredom—but many had searched their hearts and understood what the obligations of the Hindu should be towards what Sadhu Gandhara had begun.

When Sahaji rose in the Parliament, ostensibly to support the Pledge of Hindavana, he ended with the snide observation that among the many good reasons in its favour were also the family affiliations of Karkarta Dhrupatta. Immediately, however, the woman Councillor, Hansuya rose, charging Sahaji with 'trivializing, debasing and degrading the debate with his insidious, ignominious and unscrupulous reference to the family affiliations of Karkarta, in order to divert attention from the cardinal Hindu principle of supporting humanity in all the lands that may be discovered in the bosom of this great earth.' She glared at Sahaji.

There was perhaps much more she had to say, but the applause from the spectators interrupted her and she sat down, happy and flushed.

The youth from Sahiti was the next speaker. He now knew the correct procedure in the Parliament and should therefore have addressed Karkarta. Instead, he chose to look directly at the spectators and said, 'Like you, I too wish to applaud our sister Hansuya, but I wait to hear your voice, for you have not yet said whether you all consider yourself bound by the family affiliations of Sadhu Gandhara!'

Pandemonium! Dhrupatta took time to restore order. Later, he mildly admonished the member from Sahiti for his undisciplined conduct, who apologized in turn but with a smile that showed quite clearly that he was not altogether overcome by repentance.

None who spoke, thereafter, attributed the slightest personal or family motivation to Dhrupatta.

The Pledge of Hindavana was approved unanimously.

With the ratification Pledge of Hindavana, caravans of volunteers left for Gandhara to place themselves under the Vaid to serve Avagana, in fulfilment of the pledge. With them went large loads of goods, implements and domestic animals needed in Avagana.

So many had volunteered for the task along with generous donations that Dhrupatta sought the assistance of the guilds to screen and select the men and materials to be sent. About goods and implements to be sent to Avagana, there was little doubt. As for the individuals, it was only those who thought clearly, felt nobly and acted rightly that were chosen.

'...From where do the earth and universe arise?... Where and how far do they go?... Is not God playfully challenging us to find what he momentarily hides from us? ...Yes, He knows of our compelling thirst to open the secret of the earth... and of our restless minds that for ever will seek to unveil the mystery of the universe....'

'...But then go on and on with the realization that God is in your heart as you are in His... and be in harmony with nature and all on the way—neither to destroy nor to dispossess... but to enrich all and everything....'

—(From the Song 'Aim High and Look Far, Traveller, Go On and On', sung for the expedition to trace the source of Sindhu river— 5084 BC)

Death of Karkarta

5069 BC

Karkarta Dhrupatta died—suddenly, violently, needlessly—and he was killed by those whom he sought to save.

Ancient singers as they gazed back, across the centuries, at the tragic incident, found their admiration for Dhrupatta overcast by sorrow. Some criticized his carelessness in choosing the wrong man to lead an expedition to the east of Sindhu. It was this mistake, they said, that led to Dhrupatta's death. Others blamed it on his impulsiveness.

The fact is that after Dhrupatta's return from Avagana, seven expeditions left in various directions. Routes for those expeditions and their leadership were recommended by committees. But as Karkarta, he was the one to give final approval—and to that extent, he can be criticized for choosing the wrong man as leader for one of those expeditions.

Sakhara was chosen as the leader for the expedition to an eastern route. A close look into Sakhara's background might have revealed that he was a man of arrogance and violent temper, unfit to lead.

No one knew how his name was recommended by the guild-committee. Was it because his father was the head of a guild? Or was it the memory of his philanthropist grandfather, Sakha, who was known as everyone's friend, and had done so much good that a large village in Sind was named after him (Sakhar or Sukkur)? Or was it because Sakhara agreed to recruit men and buy equipment for the expedition at his expense?

These questions remain unanswered. What is clear is that Karkarta accepted the recommendations and Sakhara's name was approved, along with those who were to lead the six other expeditions.

There was no doubt as to the conduct expected on these expeditions. All such expeditions were to be guided by the song 'Aim High and Look Far, Traveller, Go On and On'. This was the song established first in Bharat's time, when an expedition left to trace the source of the Sindhu River; and it was updated by the spirit of resolutions adopted by the Hindu Parliament before Dhrupatta began his expedition to Avagana. All the expeditions were to follow its guidelines. The song left little to the imagination. It clearly stated that by the words 'aim high,' it was calling on travellers to follow the 'ethical tradition and heroic living'—with adherence to peace, the pledged word, compassion and honour. In particular, the song called on explorers 'to be in harmony with nature and people on the way—neither to destroy nor dispossess.

Thus the song suggested abandonment of a particular route if there was opposition or hostility from those whose lands were to be crossed. Besides, to leave no doubt as to what was intended by 'aim high,' the verses closed with the phrase 'hrdi-ayam', suggesting that each member must travel with the realization that God was in his heart.

The rationale of the words 'look far', was explained as the 'compelling thirst to open the secret of the earth' and of 'restless minds overwhelmed with the spirit of adventure and exploration to seek out the universe and unveil its mystery.'

Sakhara, who was selected as leader of the expedition to an eastern route, knew by heart, the entire song. The pity is that he remembered nothing of it when a village on the eastern route sought to bar his entry.

Sakhara had with him eighty-six men. All, with the exception of five, were selected and recruited by him at his expense. He would have willingly recruited even those five, but the committee itself had to nominate a Vaid, route-plotter, priest and two others to study the deposits and potential of the terrain. These five served under the expedition-leader but were to give their own reports on their return. For instance, the artist would liaise with artists from other teams to arrive at a larger picture of the route-pattern; physicians would exchange information about herbs (and their medicinal value) found in distant lands; priests would observe the rituals, customs, dance and music of tribals to understand their common and diverse strands.

To begin with, Sakhara was only mildly angry when a tribal village barred his entry. He had otherwise been in the best of moods.

Karkarta Dhrupatta himself had seen off his expedition. It was a coincidence, as Dhrupatta was in the vicinity as Nandan's guest, on his tour of the eastern tip. Yet Sakhara saw it as a special honour.

Besides, Sakhara was cheered through all the tiny tribal villages they passed. He felt like a conqueror. Now, suddenly, this cheerless village-Chief, whose language he did not understand, sought to bar his entry! The Chief had ten men who, though unarmed, were equally cheerless.

The expedition-priest came forward to explain to the Chief that they would not even stay in the village but go beyond. He had in his hand a gift for the Chief. But the Chief refused. His reply seemed to indicate a possibility of death. Actually, he was not threatening them. He was simply saying that someone in his village had died; and the spirit of the dead always remains nearby for three days, to bid farewell to familiar places and people; and that nothing must be done to distract the spirit by the presence of strangers, as the danger was that if the spirit wandered into a stranger's body, it may lose its way and therefore be unable to leave it; and the result may be that its promised destiny to reach Vaikuntha (the spiritual world) would be disrupted.

The priest understood nothing but the refusal was so strong that he advised Sakhara to leave.

It was then that something seemed to explode in Sakhara. Perhaps, the violence in Sakhara's nature arose from some deep mysterious psychological well. He was annoyed with the Chief but what really angered him was that the priest was presuming to tell him what he should do. His dislike of the committee's five nominees whom he regarded as the 'eyes and ears of others' turned into contempt. Ignoring the priest, he ordered his men to go forward and cut down the villagers if they resisted. The order shocked even his own men. They hesitated. The Vaid saw the look of hatred on Sakhara's face as he repeated his command. Both Vaid and priest tried to physically block Sakhara and his men. For a moment it seemed that all reason had left Sakhara and he was capable of any madness. The physician, unafraid, gripped Sakhara so tightly that he unhorsed him. Some sense of rationality came to Sakhara as he fell off his horse. He did not feel as strong and powerful any more. Sullenly, silently, he got back on his horse, wheeled it to the left, away from the village. They all followed.

Soon, Sakhara halted and indicated they should camp there. It was an unsuitable spot, with a limited view, hidden by hills and dunes. None, however, wanted to argue with the leader, obviously livid with rage.

It was the artist from Sakhara's expedition who reached Dhrupatta in Nandan's village. Tumbling from his weary horse, the artist gave him the savage news. Sakhara had destroyed the tribal village. The physician and twelve others who had refused to obey Sakhara's orders were held as prisoners by Sakhara; none knew where the priest was; he himself had escaped to bring the news and it was fortunate that Dhrupatta was still in the eastern part.

Dhrupatta leaped to his swift, sudden decision, waiting only to give Nandan some quiet instructions. He mounted his horse. Nala, the headman and the artist joined him. The three galloped away furiously.

Before Dhrupatta and his two companions reached the outskirts of the village, they were ambushed, surrounded, stoned and killed by those whom Sakhara had dispossessed.

Little is said in the ancient songs about Dhrupatta's death. Some question his wisdom in rushing, unarmed, into danger. True, he went to discipline and dismiss Sakhara. But could he not have waited for a day? Why did he not wait to take soldiers. Instead, as Nandan said with tears, he instructed Nandan to follow the next day with soldiers, spare horses and provisions.

Even so, Nandan left that evening itself.

Nandan's party returned with the dead bodies of Dhrupatta and two others. Nandan reproached himself publicly and said he should have physically stopped Dhrupatta from rushing to his doom. It was difficult to visualize how Nandan, though younger, could physically stop the bigger, stronger Dhrupatta. Those who had seen him leaping on to his horse, spoke of the intense fury on his face. None could have stopped him, they said.

Yet, Nandan blamed himself and said, 'How can I forgive myself! This most gracious of men was a guest in my house when fate dragged him to his untimely end. . . .' Nandan attended Dhrupatta's funeral in tears. Quietly, then, he left for home and went on an indefinite fast, refusing to touch food until he felt forgiven. He broke his fast six days later when Dhrupatta's son himself brought food with the assurance that the family respected him and that they did not feel that he had failed them.

Practically every ancient song exonerates Nandan. Poets speak of his honour and restraint in that tragic episode. Possibly, only one verse survives, which casts a doubt. That verse speaks of the moment when Dhrupatta parted from Nandan for his last, fateful journey.

> Four were with Nandan, when they parted;
> First, Dhrupatta—but alas! he is dead;
> Second, Nala, the headman—but he too died;
> Third, artist Hema—no more with us to guide;
> Fourth, Nandan's conscience—but was it not always dead?
> Who knows then, what was said or unsaid!

The song, judging from this verse, was not elegant. Certainly, it was not composed by a mature poet. Possibly the innuendo itself had no substance. No wonder then that the song influenced no one.

Nandan stayed away from the campaign to elect the new Karkarta. He devoted himself, instead, to sending large caravans of aid to Avagana. As Council Chief, until the election could be held, he was in charge; and he ensured that every policy of Bharat and Dhrupatta was carried out. The only change he made was to stop the expedition leaders from recruiting members of the expeditions themselves.

Nandan was prepared to hear the cry of vengeance against the village which killed Dhrupatta and his two companions. But Dhrupatta's family opposed it. Provocation, they said, came from the Hindu clan itself. They were the ones to shed blood first. And what would vengeance achieve? Would it bring the dead back to life! Tearfully, the artist's widow agreed. Nala's son, Devadhara, was in Avagana, but there was mercy, not vengeance, in his heart when he heard the sad news.

With Nandan's help, Dhrupatta's son led an expedition to the tribal villages to repair the damage, to rebuild their huts and replant their fields. Nandan assisted him in having wells dug for them. Nandan also established a memorial park on the spot where Dhrupatta fell.

All along, Nandan was self-effacing, drawing attention to the greatness of his predecessors and pleading his unfitness to replace them. Yet the clamour rose that he, and he alone, must be their next Karkarta.

Nandan was elected as the twenty-first Karkarta of the clan.

'No one is above the Law;
Not even Him that made the Law;
Verily God cannot destroy him who conquered himself;
For he who conquers self is the very self of God;
And God and he are one;
Where is the duality then, when they are one!
Yes, one—one-without-the-second;
And how can God destroy him without destroying Himself?
He can but He cannot!

'...Then God looked in wonder and awe at the spirit of the man who had conquered his self and Rudra asked God:
"Is he then a God like You?"
And God said, "No, he is not a God like Me. He is Me."'

—(From Kunita's Dance-Drama—5300 BC)

The Path of Glory

5068 BC

It was a momentous year. It was the year in which he who was named Sindhu Putra was born and emerged at Bharat's Island of Silence.

It was the year in which began the construction of the largest and the most magnificent temple in the land—to honour Sindhu Putra.

It was the year in which Gatha the headman came to be known as the Sentinel of the River and Sky.

It was the year in which Nandan was elected as the twenty-first Karkarta.

It was the year in which messages came from six expeditions of resounding successes in discovering new lands, streams, rivers and mountains.

It was the year in which a suicide took place. Sakhara was, at last, tracked down, far from the village he had destroyed. He was alone, ailing. No other member of his expedition was found and the search continued. When Sakhara was brought to face the inquiry, he recovered sufficiently to hang himself. People shuddered and recalled the hymns of the Law of the Ancients, that the soul of him who takes his life shall be condemned for one kalpa (at least 12,000 years), during which it shall not take a body; and thereafter to start life all over again from the lowest level of the evolutionary ladder and wait for 1,000 kalpas (12,000,000 years) to take on a human form again, to go into the cycle of birth, death and rebirth—a cycle to be broken only by moksha through good karma.[1]

The concept of a man going back to the lowest evolutionary level was explained in a single cryptic line—'For he it was who threw the ladder on which he rose and stood.'

---

[1]Kalpa was a measure of time but with a qualitative aspect. In the case of suicide by a person who led a pure life, the kalpa was 12,000 years, during which the individual remained in a bodyless condition. However, if suicide was committed by one who led an impure life, kalpa was multiplied 360 times and such a soul would suffer isolation for 4,320,000 years. Thus kalpa ranged from 12,000 to 4,320,000 years, depending on the kind of life the person led. No method of calculation was given to count and balance good and evil deeds to determine kalpa for each suicide.

However, the hymn spoke of sinless suicide caused by the 'law of paramount necessity, to avoid greater danger, with burden unbearable to heart and soul', but no examples were given as clarification, except the addition, 'for them, none shall withdraw grace.'

As to why a person who led a pure and noble life would commit suicide the hymn clarified: 'Let none be tempted to reach the Eternal Self before his time or else who knows how long he shall have to wait!' Even in the case of austerities by a yogi, the hymn required that such austerities should be within physical limitations and not be used as a 'vehicle to accelerate a journey that is not of His choosing.'

Incidentally, later, kalpa came to mean a cycle of 12,000 divine years or 4,320,000 human years.

During that year, the news that all the members of Sakhara's expedition were safe also came. His entire contigent had simply abandoned him, leaving provisions and two horses for him. They were afraid to remain with him, convinced that he would continue to give insane orders. They did not go back for fear of retaliation by the villages they had vandalized at his orders. They deviated from the precribed route, fearful that Sakhara would follow the same route. Joy and relief flooded the hearts of those whose loved ones were involved. But some demanded an inquiry. Nandan put his foot down (improving his reputation) by refusing an inquiry which would have revived the pain of the clan over Dhrupatta's death.

But Nandan also agreed to limit the guild-committees' role. Henceforth, Karkarta alone would be responsible for the selection and conduct of expeditions. Everyone agreed. Implicit in that agreement was also the acceptance that Karkarta had absolute authority for all future expeditions. How else could he have full responsibility!

It was the year in which Kush returned briefly to collect a handful of ashes from the cremation of his brother Dhrupatta.

Nandan had reason to be pleased with that eventful year. The clan was growing. Its lands were expanding. His predecessors may have started the process but results were emerging in his time as Karkarta. Luck surely was with him and he was glad, for he had many grand designs for the future. But first, he thought, I must win over those who do not agree with my policies; I must watch my enemies to silence them; I must keep an eye on friends so that their loyalty to me remains undivided; and to the rest, I must appear as a leader guided by the gods towards lofty ideals of virtue, honour and integrity.

Nandan courted preachers and pujaris—not the silent ascetics in the forests, but only those whose voices were heard everywhere.

He went to Gatha's village. When so many believed in Sindhu Putra, he did not want to lag behind in showing his devotion.

Nandan did not believe in miracles—certainly not in the miracle of Sindhu Putra. He could not work out who was behind the fraud. All that he learnt was that everyone in the village was a devotee of Sindhu Putra, while Kanta and Sonama were his earthly mothers, and the hermit in the nearby island, his earthly father.

Nandan was among the few who knew the identity of the hermit on the island. The two mothers—who were they? One, a prostitute, and the other a woman whose husband deserted her as soon as Sindhu Putra was born! There was also the mystery of the prostitute's wealth which she intended to use in building a fabulous temple. Nandan wondered: how much does a village prostitute earn? But whatever the rates of prostitutes, he was certain that no prostitute could make that kind of money in a thousand lifetimes.

What did it all amount to? Nandan wondered. Obviously, Bharat, while ostensibly a hermit, was enjoying himself with two women, one of whom gave birth to the child from this illicit relationship; and now they were going to use the ill-gotten wealth, no doubt acquired by Bharat as Karkarta, to build a temple. Yes, that was the explanation!— the only way that all the pieces fitted together.

Nandan did not intend to share his suspicions with anyone. If people learned to ridicule a past Karkarta, the institution itself would suffer.

Nandan was convinced of Bharat's involvement in this mystery. He even learnt that Gatha, the headman, was a servant—earlier a slave—from Bharat's household. Also, there was a lot that was odd about his election as headman and even about forming the village itself as a separate unit. Undoubtedly, there was a conspiracy. Nandan disliked mysteries unless they were of his own making. This one made no sense. But, with his fear of the unknown, he must break whatever links he could in this chain of conspiracy. For, he had begun to wonder whether Bharat had some secret political ambitions for the child. Or, perhaps, he intended to oust Nandan from his present position of power by using the child's name and influence with the people to do so. First, he thought, I must remove Gatha as headman. Karkarta, of course, could not remove a headman. It was an elected office. But he could amalgamate villages and call for the election of a new, common headman.

In a way, Nandan felt grateful to Gatha. Thinking about Gatha gave birth to Nandan's idea, that the many posts of headmen could easily be abolished. As it is, the duties of the headman had decreased radically.

Nandan's mind went to the past—to the time when headmen had heavy responsibilities. The headman, then, was in charge of barter and trade, with a huge granary to store grains for farmers, until buyers came to exchange them for cattle, domestic fowl, clothing and other goods. He also controlled large tracts of land where cattle would graze, until barter deals were finalized. Similarly, he maintained warehouses for textiles and other goods until buyers were found. Apart from being a shrewd bargainer, the headman had to be a master mathematician, expert accountant and gifted with a phenomenal memory, for often he had to give away cattle in advance, in return for a promise to receive goods later, or to obtain grain, seed and supplies for his village with the promise of payment at a later date.

But no more. Around 5300 BC, pressures on the headmen decreased when the ninth Karkarta, Devi Leilama, inspired the formation of guilds which eventually took over many functions, formerly entrusted to headmen.

Nandan's mind went to Devi Leilama's times.

Nandan was proud of the ninth Karkarta—Devi Leilama—who was elected as Karkarta in 5333 BC, at the age of forty-nine. She was Nandan's ancestress; her daughter had married Nandan's great-great-grandfather.

Devi Leilama was a widow. Her husband had died when she was twenty. He met his death in a collision in a boat race. She did not remarry and devoted her time to forming a guild of boatmen who were largely transporters and fishermen.

Her initial interest in forming the guild was to ensure safety—that safer boats be built, that none under age should ply a commercial boat, and that none should imbibe any liquor before or during a boat ride—neither boatmen nor passengers. Floating, mobile boat-shops in the river were persuaded to stop selling liquor. River-front shops were also warned not to sell liquor to boat-traffic. Hawkers, who appeared from nowhere at boat-races, could no longer sell liquor.

The guild grew. Boatmen staggered their schedules so that their boats did not travel half-empty. Fishermen established zones for fishing. Bulk buying by the guild began. Improvements in boat-design were initiated.

Devi Leilama guided the guild through many stages. Her only daughter Kunita kept pressing her to establish another guild, for singers, dancers and dramatists. Kunita was an accomplished singer and it was she who organized the first spectacle of song, dance and drama on the river. During this spectacle, twenty-five boats were lined up on the river, in an extended semicircle, to serve as a stage. Hidden behind each boat were canoes with fire torches, to give the effect of light and shade to the stage. The main drama started from the central, large boat, but the scene often shifted to the twenty-four side-boats and, at times, the action continued simultaneously in all the twenty-five boats. Additionally, there were many other boats plying in reserved river-lanes, with musicians, singers and sound-effect men. These boats came within sight and hearing of the audience on the waterfront. The task of these musicians and singers was simply to synchronize their songs, music and sounds, with the dramatic action going on in the twenty-five boats. Without this 'play-back', the audience would not have known what was being said or sung on the faraway stage.

The public appreciation of Kunita's spectacle of dance, music and drama was tremendous. Financially, however, it was a disaster, due to the costs of costumes, props, make-up and stage extravaganza.

Devi Leilama realized that artists were incapable or unwilling to calculate costs before, or even after, a performance. She decided to listen to her daughter Kunita's plea to establish a new guild for singers, dancers and dramatists.

Her idea was simple—that Karkarta, the headmen and others—the rich and famous—must pay if they wanted performances in their areas and in return they would get quality but not the right to interfere with the content.

The eighth Karkarta saw the profound effect of dance-dramas on the people. He suggested that the songs and dances be improved. He agreed to be the patron for the next five plays and pay for them fully. He wanted not only artistic excellence but strict control over expenditure. Karkarta's son was an expert in financial affairs and Kunita and Devi Leilama promised to consult him on costs.

The five plays, for which the eighth Karkarta was the patron, were a roaring success. Karkarta's reputation as a patron of the arts grew. But there is no evidence that his son helped to tone down the costs of these plays. What came to pass is that the Karkarta's son married Kunita. It was he who was Nandan's great-great-grandfather.

Kunita organized another play just before she got married. But it was not a great public success. The Guild of Singers, however, profited greatly from it as a wealthy merchant agreed to pay generously. He was Suryadana, ancestor of Suryakarma, the eighteenth Karkarta whom Bharat succeeded. All that Suryadana, the sun-worshipper, wanted was that the play should show the greatness and grandeur of the Sun god.

For this play, a structure was set up with two platforms, one above the other, to serve as two stages. Unseen men, hidden in false ceilings over each stage, dangled a huge, gold-coloured object to depict the sun.

The main theme of the play was that the sun never sets. Commentary by the narrators leaves no doubt about it. The play wanted to show that when it was thought that the sun was setting, it was actually moving to the other side of the earth where also 'there dwell God's creation under the sun.'

Not many were charmed by the play. Artistically, there were faults with stage-management; the passage of the 'sun' over the earth was not smooth or majestic; at times the 'sun' stopped, ran and even shook drunkenly. Also its movement diverted attention from the action and songs on stage. The two-stage idea was inconvenient to viewers, forcing them to crane their necks to watch the top-stage.

And there was no entertainment! There was no hero fighting decisive battles, vanquishing dark and evil forces, dispensing enlightenment and dispersing foes! Nor was there a heroine who, with her grace and suppleness, would charm the hero; and where were the adventures, the suspense, the ultimate triumph of good over evil, and a happy life ever after for the hero and heroine? True, everyone venerated the Sun god but worship was a private affair and, when it came to entertainment, people wanted to have stories of humans who rose to great heights in battle, love, passion, sacrifice and achievement. As Kunita herself later admitted, 'God is a super hero but the hero of the play must always be a human.'

The play did, however, spark some quiet interest among those whose hobby it was to watch heavenly bodies like the sun, moon, stars and planets to try and understand the physical laws of the universe. They would silently be drawing mandalas (geometrical figures) to represent the movement of heavenly bodies and wondering how the cosmos worked, how the sun and moon were seen to alternate, with night following day. These silent ones would later be known as astronomers but even amongst them were those who were concerned not only with identifying what physical laws the universe obeyed, but also with the very basic question of understanding the mind of God in order to explain why the universe began and why we exist. The question of *what* the laws were was important. But it was the *why* that mattered most in their minds.

Even so, the sun worshippers were delighted with the play. What Suryadana, who paid for it, wanted was a presentation of the sun's glory and greatness. Kunita had excelled herself. The sun was shown as a god who never sets, was always in motion and eternally present. In gratitude for this, Suryadana built a huge theatre.

Kunita went on to produce seven children in the next seven years and the burden of running the Guild of Singers fell on Devi Leilama. Suryadana's generous donation spurred the Guild on to further achievements. Her son-in-law, the eighth Karkarta's son, was always there to help with the finer financial details; as for the rest, she had a genius for delegating responsibility to competent poets and dramatists.

It was then that the eighth Karkarta suggested to Devi Leilama to assist in organizing a few more guilds. Suryadana also encouraged her.

For Suryadana, with his extensive business dealings, it made sense to have a guild for merchants. Guilds bought and sold in bulk and were welcomed by traders with large stocks. Also, guilds could assure quality and prompt payments. It was never satisfactory to deal with the headmen to buy or sell in bulk. Headmen were elected officials and however honest and God-fearing they may have been, had no head for business. In fact, it was because they were honest and God-fearing that they could never develop a head for business; they were timid, never able to negotiate, much less take a risk.

Devi Leilama organized a Guild of Merchants and, thereafter, three more guilds—one for artisans; a second for those engaged in spinning and weaving textiles; and a third for the makers of perfumes, herbs, medicines, essences and oils from flowers and plants.

However, before the eighth Karkarta died, he suggested that Devi Leilama be elected as Karkarta after him. The clan saw nothing extraordinary in electing a woman. She had already been on the Council for years.

On her forty-ninth birthday, Devi Leilama was elected as the ninth Karkarta. She went on to establish more guilds and also encouraged greater cooperation among them. The guild of Vaids functioned closely with the Guild of Perfumers in the search for herbs and medicines from plants and flowers. The Greengrocers' Guild worked with the Guild of Boatmen so that their produce reached all the centres without any damage. The Artisans' Guild worked with the Artists' Guild to design better carts and chariots.

Following the discovery of gold dust along the Sindhu river, Devi Leilama established a new service for the mining of metals and precious stones. The service was not formed on the lines of a guild; its entire cost came from the clan and all finds of gold, other metals and precious stones belonged to the clan.

From then on, gradually, barter began to be replaced by direct sales which were paid for in gold and other metals. The price of all metals was quoted in terms of gold. A minute division of the weight of gold (raktikas) was established as the gold unit which represented the pre-announced weight of grain or the area of new land sold by Karkarta on behalf of the clan. In point of fact, raktikas (gold units) as such, did not phyically exist, as the clan had not then found the method of achieving an exact, uniform weight for small particles of gold. It represented a ten thousandth part of Prastha (equivalent to 565 gms or about 20 oz.). Thus 100 raktikas would be equal to 5.65 gms or 1 raktika would equal 0.00199 oz.

With the establishment of the gold unit and the growing strength of the Merchants' Guild, a new class of traders emerged, with strong partnerships. The headmen's responsibility for barter and trade virtually disappeared. They still maintained granaries and warehouses but only for emergency supplies in drought or crop-failure—but then, in such cases, the question of prices did not arise as Karkarta established prices in those situations, based on the severity of conditions and the buyer's capacity to pay—and often, the distribution was free.

Nandan came back to the present with a start and decided that since headmen no longer served a useful purpose, he would tempt Parliament into doing away with the election of headmen altogether.

Parliament members, he knew, loved principles but they loved their privileges far more—and he would appeal to their principles and privileges to convince them that they were more capable of recommending to him the right people to be appointed as headmen. Once the system of appointing headmen was established, he could ignore their recommendations and make his own appointment. It would not be easy, he knew. But was anything worthwhile ever easy?

Also, Nandan felt, why not listen to those who have been complaining that headmen were ignorant of the problems affecting guilds!

He decided to reserve posts and fix quotas. It was necessary to divide people in order to unite them under the single banner of the head of the clan.

Nandan's mind raced from the headmen to the Assembly itself. He knew that it would be impossible to do away with elections to the Assembly: the public outcry would be far too intense. The alternative was to make the Assembly powerless. He would follow Bharat's policy to include in the Assembly representatives of the new lands that joined the clan. The only difference would be that the representatives from the new territories would be 'elected' only by those whom he sent out to be in charge there.

Yes, people must remain divided, to be united to his higher cause! Again, he thanked Gatha silently for provoking this chain of thought.

The ancient singers have said a great deal about Nandan's actions but very few have tried to probe into his mind to discover the impulses that moved him.

Deep down, Nandan had a burning passion. He loved his clan. He was convinced that the inscrutable wisdom of Providence and the inexorable process of destiny had so ordained that his clan would always be in a preeminent position. If he needed any proof of that, all he had to do was to look around at the barbarism of other tribes.

As a young lad, he had joined Bharat's expeditions against the tribal raiders. In those arduous journeys, he saw the terrible condition of various tribes. His companions would be moved to pity but his own dominant thought was one of thankfulness for the culture of his own clan. He disapproved of Bharat's friendly treatment of the tribals. He gave up soldiering. He wanted to dictate policy rather than be a puppet of policy.

With this family wealth and prestige, he was soon elected as an Assembly member, after his success in several civic fields.

Nandan loved his clan as he saw it: free, proud, clothed in honour, steeped in culture, industrious, frugal, just and benevolent. Like Sadhu

Gandhara, he too did not know how far the earth extended. But he was convinced that his own land and clan were the greatest.

To him, it was regrettable that Bharat and Dhrupatta were obsessed with ideas of uniting with the tribes. He was sure that their initial motives were not foolish or evil; they honestly felt that their clan's rich culture could assimilate new tribes, so why have enemies on the borders. But when the clan expanded to the furthest frontiers of the land, it was time to call a halt. It was extremely expensive to assimilate them. They had to be provided with food, clothing and shelter. And besides there was the danger of their culture being contaminated by that of the tribals.

Nandan had developed something in the nature of a religious faith in the paramount importance of his own clan and its culture. He would tolerate no challenge to it. To the new territories, he would be benevolent, even helpful, but he would see to it that his clan would remain cold, aloof and distant from their culture and way of life. Nothing must stand in the way of the greater glory of the Hindu clan.

Yes, that indeed was the prayer and passion of Nandan in his early days as Karkarta—'God! Let me be the one to lead the Hindu on to the path of glory.'

'. . .I believe God had a choice when He created this universe and He had freedom to choose the laws that the universe obeys. . . . That is the real, everlasting miracle which arose from the mind of God. But if I am called upon to believe in an unending string of miracles, which are talked of from day to day, I must also believe that the initial conditions which God chose were so imperfect as to need the aid of constant miracles to support His universe—and this I shall never believe, that God's mind conceived something imperfect. . . .

—(Attributed to Bharatjogi in a Memory song—5065 BC)

Should the Gods be Educated?

5068 to 5065 BC

Bharatjogi waved away his dreams and memories of the past as he saw his dogs wagging their tails. He looked up. Gatha was approaching.

From a distance, Gatha cried out in ecstasy, 'Sindhu Putra speaks! He speaks!'

'He speaks, does he! And what does he say?' Bharat asked with a smile.

With delight, Gatha spoke the infant's first words—'Da da da.'

'He is a true Hindu, then!' Bharat rejoined.

Gatha was surprised; he asked seriously, 'How so, Master?'

But Bharat had no intention of being serious. 'Did you not say that the infant's words were "Da da da"? What else could they mean, other than daya, dana and dharma!'

Gatha started. He had not seen the deep significance in those first sounds of the infant, barely five months old. Nor did it occur to him now to doubt his old master's words. Surely, all infants begin with 'ma ma'! He almost gasped, 'I never thought of that, Master!'

Immediately, Bharat regretted his thoughtless jest and said, 'No, Gatha, I was joking—a foolish jest. Forget it.'

But Gatha was not about to forget it. The earthly father of the infant was at pains to deny the divinity of the infant. Even now, his first thought had been to invest the infant's initial words with divine significance; but he had then quickly denied it. Soulfully, he looked at his ex-master, as though to thank him for giving him that meaningful clue to the infant's first utterrance.

'Thank you, Master,' Gatha said, brimming with gratitude. His words did not surprise Bharat as he had just extended a cup of wine to Gatha. If Bharat heard in Gatha's voice an uplifted tone, he attributed it to a desire for wine. 'Yes,' said Bharat, 'let us have a drink to celebrate the first words of the infant.'

In the past, Gatha had declined wine, ever since that night when he went to sleep in Bharat's hut. But how could he refuse it now! The new significance of the infant's first utterance had to be celebrated!

Gatha drank in silence, content to give himself up to the enjoyment of wine. He spoke only as he was leaving with a wine-cask which

Bharat pressed on him and said, in a voice from the depths of his soul, 'If today Sindhu Putra speaks of daya, dana, dharma, just imagine what he will say and do when he walks on this earth with firm footsteps!'

Soon after Gatha reached his hut, Mahantji visited him. Instead of the usual greeting, Gatha asked, 'Did you hear Sindhu Putra's words?'

'Of course,' Mahantji replied, 'da da da.'

'And do you know what they mean?' But before the startled Mahantji could reply, he enlightened him, 'They mean daya, dana and dharma!'

Mahantji did not bat an eyelid. 'But of course. This is what I came to tell you. But you are great, Gathaji! You know all!'

Gatha nodded. Here was confirmation, if indeed it was needed, of what Bharatji had said. He looked at Mahantji with affection and asked, 'Have you told the others of the significance of Sindhu Putra's words?'

'No,' Mahantji replied. 'I came to suggest that you should.'

That was another aspect of Mahantji which Gatha admired. So self-effacing he was—always wanting Gatha to be in the forefront.

'Call the people here, then.' Gatha ordered.

'Here! But such announcements are made in the village-square.'

'No, call them here.' Gatha was peremptory. He knew that the wine had rendered him incapable of walking to the village square.

Mahantji left to call the people. Let them laugh at Gatha, he thought. For himself, he wanted to remain away from the fantasy of giving to the babble of the infant such profound significance.

People gathered outside Gatha's hut. He took his cot out to stand on it, so that they could all see him.

'Da. . .da. . .da. .,' Gatha said loudly, as though to scare away the noisy crow in a nearby tree; and then swaying, he added, 'Today was Sindhu Putra's first discourse. He said: daya, dana, dharma. . . daya, daya. . .dan. . .' He fell down on his cot, overpowered by wine. They all followed his obviously prayerful posture and knelt, all the way, on the ground.

Mahantji followed their example to avoid inviting public wrath. But the pain in his joints from which he often suffered forced him to get up. He dragged the cot with the sleeping Gatha inside the hut.

They all realized that Gatha, their Sentinel of the River and Sky, was in a deep trance.

Quietly, Mahantji faced the crowd. What do I tell these village dolts?—Mahantji asked himself in self-pity—that their headman is drunk and was babbling! Who will believe me? Have I not already suffered a jolt for opposing a temple to be built from tainted money!

Mahantji spoke. Slowly at first, but gathering speed, he told them of the first discourse of Sindhu Putra, on daya, dana and dharma. This only confirmed to the people what their Sentinel had said before going into a trance. But Mahantji was captivated by his own oratory. The speech took hold of him, rather than he of the speech, and the discourse went on until it began to rain. Then he sent the people away. Everyone left with their souls uplifted.

Now the story that went round spoke not of the simple babble of Sindhu Putra, but of his entire discourse on daya and dana as two of the essential pillars of dharma. When the story reached other villages, it achieved even greater dimensions, to include songs sung and stories told by an infant who could not as yet utter a single, coherent word! Devotees came from all over and remained to pray.

Bharat remembered Gatha's joyful words—'just imagine what Sindhu Putra will say and do when he walks on the earth!' He recalled them not with joy but with dread. The little one is not a god, he thought. What will he be when he grows up? A god that failed?

Bharat did not see the beautiful landscape of that glorious morning; in his mind's eye, all he saw was the lone figure of a child passing silently through a desolate graveyard of shattered dreams, lost illusions and crushed hopes.

Sindhu Putra was three years old. His every wish was a command. He went through mountains of toys made by loving devotees and it took him only a moment to break them and demand new ones.

'He is not of this earth,' Gatha said. The child threw tantrums. They all echoed Gatha, 'He is not of this earth!'

Bharat understood. A child without curbs or controls, without training or instruction, is a child unfit for this earth or for any realm of God. A child whose every cough and cry puts the entire village into dread is doomed, as no one dares teach him better ways. Blind love and unquestioning obedience to a child of three!

Bharat felt responsible. It was I who picked up the child from his dead mother's arms. Did I not then and there make a covenant with her and the gods that I would look after her orphaned babe? But I failed even to squash the image of his assumed divinity! Why, in utter foolishness, I even blessed the temple-project for the infant, just to oppose the village prejudice against Kanta's donation! Why was I so blind? The gods imposed a duty on me and I failed. A mother left her babe in my arms and I failed!

He spoke to Gatha. But Gatha could not understand the need to discipline a god. Bharat could not decide what to do. He thought of sending the child to his wife but abandoned the plan because then thousands would collect around her and nothing would be achieved.

He prayed for a solution. It came quickly. He thought of Muni and Roopa, the daughter of the once-blind singer. He had often visited the rocks before he retired. But are they still there?—he wondered.

Maybe, Gatha could go to the rocks and find out. But no; Gatha would then put two and two together and learn where Sindhu Putra was being sent—and Gatha could not be trusted to keep Sindhu Putra's whereabouts a secret.

One inspiration follows another. He requested Gatha to go to the singer and beg him to come to his island, adding that 'sometimes, I get an urge to hear the old songs again'.

Gatha reached the singer's cottage late at night. To Gatha's suggestion to leave the next day, the singer said, 'Why tomorrow? I am ready now.' Before an hour had passed, they were on their way.

There was fear in the singer's heart. Gatha had said that Bharatjogi wanted to hear the old songs. Why? he wondered—Is he dying? He recalled his last words with Karkarta Bharat, 'Allow me to come to you in your retirement, to sing for you.' But Bharat had said, 'No, your songs are for the people here, not for a hermit.' Now he was summoned. Why?

Actually, Bharat had not reached the point of desperation; he realized that children knew when and where to misbehave. How sweet-tempered the child was during his weekly visits to him! If he threw a tantrum, an inquiring smile calmed him. Maybe the environment had something to do with it. In the village, if a speck of dirt sullied the child, it was quickly wiped away. Here on the island, the child played on the soft earth with the dogs, to his heart's content. During all his visits, the child was playful, smiling and cried only when Gatha tried to wipe the dirt off him. But from all accounts, he was a terror in the village. Yes, the time was ripe for his education. Later, it may be too late.

Suddenly, Bharat saw his favourite singer. Gatha was tying the boat, while the singer rushed on. He embraced Bharat and asked in a shaking whisper, 'Are you well, Bharatji?'

Bharat reassured him, 'Would I trouble you if it was merely a question of my health! Is an old man like me afraid to face the gods?'

The singer was delighted. Then he really was called for his songs!

'That too,' Bharat said, 'but much more.' What could be more important than Bharat's health and his own songs, the singer wondered.

Gatha reached them but waited only to extract a promise from the singer to sing for the villagers later.

Bharat opened his heart to the singer. The singer had heard a great deal about Sindhu Putra. Who had not?

Bharat then told the singer how destiny had guided a boat to his shores, about how he had first found the child and how the myth about the child being invested with divinity had grown despite his efforts to prove the contrary.

'What makes you certain that this is not God's own miracle?' asked the singer.

'I do not deny God's ability to perform any miracle of His choosing. But in my sixty-six years I have not yet come across any miracle, unless of course one holds the view that every chance occurrence, every passing cloud and every gust of wind is a miracle of God.'

'And apart from these?' The singer questioned. 'Have you witnessed no miracle which touched your heart?'

'The only other miracles I have seen are those which are contrived by humans to mislead and misguide. I believe God had a choice when He created this universe and He had the freedom to choose the laws that the universe obeys. That is the real, everlasting miracle which arose from the mind of God. But if I am called upon to believe in an unending string of miracles, which are talked of from day to day, I must also believe that the initial conditions which God chose were so imperfect, as to need the aid of constant miracles to support His universe—and this I cannot believe—that God's mind conceived something imperfect!'

The singer smiled, 'Would you really say that everything in this God's universe is clear to you? Everything?'

'No, not even the fraction of a fraction. But that is the failure of our knowledge. As our knowledge grows, so will our understanding—and the realization then is inevitable that what we see as a miracle was only in accordance with God's laws when He began his universe.'

The singer did not wish to argue and contented himself with the observation, 'Every time I look at the earth and the sky, I know He, that created us all, is there, and with each day that dawns, He creates a new miracle. . . .'

'Yes, that is His miracle,' Bharat interrupted, 'but must I accept the notion that He sends the Son of Mother Goddess to us to take on our sins, or lead us into paths of purity, or cure us with a wave of his hand!'

'My eyesight with which I see you, Bharatji, is a miracle in itself.'

Bharat knew the story. He recalled his own belief in the reincarnation of Bindu. But those were miracles of man's faith and followed God's laws.

Their conversation continued. 'Even if Sindhu Putra is destined to be a god,' Bharat said finally, 'do you not see that he must learn the ways of the earth if he is to live on it. How can a god be without proper education!'

The singer confirmed that Muni and Roopa were still at the rocks. Muni, he said, had mellowed; he no longer had a running tussle with God. He was even rebuilding the temple that had been destroyed by fire. What had delayed the temple was the fact that Roopa, during the last six years, had three children—two daughters and a son.

The next day, the singer and Bharat left for Muni's rocks. Gatha asked no questions when told that the mission was related to Sindhu Putra.

Bharat returned, happy with all the assurances from Muni and Roopa.

Soon he announced that Sindhu Putra would have to leave for an unknown destination, for his education.

It almost led to a riot in the village. How could he, who was destined to dispense enlightenment, go elsewhere to receive enlightenment? No, they could not let Sindhu Putra go!

Even the singer found no favour with the villagers when he sang historical and mythological songs to show that those who came to be honoured as gods or goddesses had received the most rigorous education in childhood. But Mahantji clarified that those were not gods initially and it was simply the case of humans achieving godhood; here, however, it was the case of a god being downgraded to human level. Where was the parallel, then? Unfortunately, the singer had no songs to prove that a god who sprung from a river was ever educated on earth. Mahantji's argument was, thus, unassailable. But could it stand against the resolve of the earthly father of Sindhu Putra!

Kanta was devastated. Hers was an important, vital voice. She employed hundreds for her magnificent temple. Everyone respected her smallest wish. She put her foot down. Sindhu Putra shall not go. She was on the warpath.

Bharatjogi and Kanta met. She cried, 'Where and why do you wish to send my Sindhu Putra away from me? Do you not know how long I waited for my son to come back to me!' With tears, she began her incoherent story. He hardly understood her but discerned a deep wound in her heart as she kept asking, 'Where would you send him—why?'

His heart went out to her. He begged, 'Tell no one, please but I must send him to the rocks of Muni and Roopa.'

Bharat was astonished to see Kanta's transformation as soon as he uttered those words. It was as though a flash of light split the darkness in every corner of her mind and her entire soul was illuminated. Her tears stopped. She smiled.

'But of course, of course,' she cried out. 'What a fool I am! Of course, yes, of course.' She fell at Bharatjogi's feet and shed another stream of tears. Bharat lifted her face from his feet, not knowing what to make of her. She kept smiling through her tears, 'Thank you, thank you; yes, that is where my son has to go. He ended his last journey there. That is where he must start his next journey. Where else! Send him! Send him there!'

Kanta left, promising that no one would hear from her of Sindhu Putra's destination. Bharatjogi insisted on that, certain of Muni's wrath if crowds gathered at his rocks to catch a glimpse of Sindhu Putra.

When Kanta returned, they saw her face, serene and happy. Obviously, the battle with the hermit was won. But Kanta cried out, 'No, my son must go where the hermit-father takes him.'

Who could oppose Kanta! She was, they knew, the first miracle which Sindhu Putra wrought on earth. Did not treasures of untold wealth drop from the sky into her house when Sindhu Putra emerged? Was she not building a magnificent temple for him? And what was it, if not a miracle, that a lowly prostitute, overnight, gives up her sinful ways to devote herself totally to Sindhu Putra? Truly, she was dwija (twice-born or born-again). If some doubted divine inspiration in her, they were quiet. Nobody questions a person of such immense wealth who gives gainful employment to so many.

Later, with a smile, Bharat told the singer that he himself should begin to believe in miracles because the woman, convinced that she was Sindhu Putra's mother, came storming in to quarrel with him, but ended by kissing his feet!

Who could oppose Kamla! She was, they knew, the first miracle which Sindhu Putra wrought on earth. Did not treasures of untold wealth drop from the sky into her house when Sindhu Putra emerged? Was she not building a magnificent temple for him? And what was it, if not a miracle that a lowly prostitute, overnight, gives up her sinful ways to devote herself totally to Sindhu Putra? Truly, she was dwija (twice-born or born-again). If some doubted divine inspiration in her, they were quiet. Nobody questions a person of such immense wealth who gives gainful employment to so many.

Later, with a smile, Bharat told the singer that he himself should begin to believe in miracles because the woman, convinced that she was Sindhu Putra's mother, came storming in to quarrel with him, but ended by kissing his feet.

'. . .Those carvings in the caves of pre-history. . . beginning with the lotus flower and ending with fish, birds, beasts, and finally with the human figure. . . were they there to show what came first and what came last? But then, why arrange them all in a circle! Is the artist asking you to believe in a cycle of creation, evolution, re-creation and destruction? Maybe he wants the circle to indicate the earth itself. But is the earth circular? Why not? The moon, sun and stars are circular. Is anything in nature a square or rectangle? Our own human body, our face, hips, buttocks, a woman's breasts—are they not all in curves and circles?. . . The question also remains—why is so much space left blank after the human figure? Is it to indicate that the process of creation is not yet complete and the space is left for a later artist to carve a superhuman or post-human figure, still to be created?. . . Maybe, the large space between the human figure and other creatures was intended to warn all creatures to maintain their distance from man, lest he destroy them. . . .'

—(Conversation between Ekantra and Bharat — 5122 BC)

Who Will Unite My People?

5065 BC

The night Bharat and the singer escorted Sindhu Putra to the boat to leave for Muni's rocks was calm and beautiful.

Sadly, Bharat heard the mournful wail from his dogs that had been left behind.

The moonlight was well blended with the night and Bharat had no difficulty in rowing the boat. The singer sat back with Sindhu Putra who went to sleep. Bharat was silent too. He was thinking of what lay ahead of the child, in the years to come. He had sought no assurances but Muni and Roopa had given them, generously. Muni had said, 'Don't worry. He will receive a better education than this father.'

'His father!'

'You, of course,' Muni explained. 'He has none other. God brought him to your shore and you accepted him as your own.'

Yes, the child, he felt, was a part of him, like his own son.

The breeze helped the boat along, as Bharatjogi's mind went back to his own school days.

Bharat remembered his early school days. He had no guru. Like most children of his age, he attended school with a large number of students. School discipline, though firm, was never as demanding as under a guru. Nor did the school concentrate on God-realization, as a guru would. Teaching at school was devoted to rules of good conduct, polite speech, health, yoga, arithmetic, painting, music, sculpture and activities like farming, cattle-breeding and mining. Compulsory classes were few, and a student could skip many, except those related to good conduct, health, yoga, arithmetic and sports.

Bharat excelled in sports. He was a good swimmer and could handle a small boat. Among the games that he played well, was kabaddi, which involved catching the opponent while reciting various poems as evidence of holding one's breath, until the opponent was caught or unable to hold his own breath. Bharat still remembered some of the rhymes he had to recite while playing kabaddi, six decades earlier.

Would Muni and Roopa teach such games and rhymes to the child? Bharat wondered. He had pleasant memories of his school, with its two yearly sessions, each of ninety days with a holiday of 185 days between sessions. Most learning, in any case, was imparted at home by the parents. Given a choice, he would have sent Sindhu Putra to a large school. A guru would not accept so young a child, as a student goes to the guru out of his own free will and not because his parents' have chosen to send him—and to exercise such personal choice, a student had to be much older. In fact, search for a guru began after the student completed school sessions.

But do I have a choice? Bharat asked himself. Muni's rocks would not have the advantages of a large school or a guru. But then, I am not seeking to send him to a seat of learning. All I want is an escape for him into anonymity, to grow up as a normal child should, away from the worship of those who treat him as a god. Besides, he would have the company of Roopa's three children. That would be enjoyment enough!

Then why do I worry? he asked himself. Does one really learn that much at school or from a guru? After all, I learnt much more, later, from Ekantra, who was neither my schoolteacher nor my guru.

A host of memories surged into Bharat's mind, while the boat moved on. He was ten years old when Ekantra left his caves to live with his wife and son, Yadodhra. Even so, Ekantra often went to supervise the workmen who were protecting the caves, section by section, from the ravages of time, wind and weather. He knew that, if unprotected, nature would take over and these treasures would be lost to mankind.

Ekantra sometimes took Yadodhra and Bharat to the caves. He even entrusted to Bharat some minor tasks to preserve statues and paintings.

It never pleased Ekantra to cover a painting but that is what had to be done if it had to be protected. Ekantra would look at it lovingly— happy to answer every question, if only to delay covering the painting— and Bharat was always there to ask the questions.

Ekantra could explain most of the paintings and carvings but there were some he could not. There was a huge carving which covered an entire wall from ceiling to floor; and one had to stand on ladders to be able to see the whole thing. Figures in the carving were arranged in a circle. There was only one human figure. The rest were: a lotus flower in water; a plant with leaves; a plant with a flower; a tree; insects; a butterfly; a bird in flight; fish in water; a tortoise emerging from water onto land; a peacock on the ground; a snake entering the water; a boar in a forest; a monkey in a tree.

Surprisingly, these figures were followed by mammoth, monster-like figures of animals with crocodile faces; birds with wolf faces; and fish with large canine fangs and sweeping tongues with tusks. If these incredible figures followed a scale, each was a hundred times larger than the largest figure. However, a distinctive feature about these fantastic, monstrous figures was that a line was drawn across them, as though the artists were dissatisfied with this fantasy of unrealistic figures and wished to cancel them out.

Thereafter, figures that followed on that carving were small. Amongst them were a large number showing human faces with bodies of beasts, like the man-lion, man-monkey, man-gorilla, man-wolf; and finally the human face emerged with the human body, upright.

The entire circle was not complete in the sense that while all the figures were at an equal distance from each other, a large space was left after the human figure, before the lotus figure began.

Ekantra had many theories but few certainties. Even ignoring the fantastic, monstrous figures which seemed cancelled out—possibly as figments of the imagination, or of species long extinct—it was not clear what the carving intended to show. Maybe, it was there to show a few of God's creations; or was it there to show what came first and what came last? But then, why arrange all the figures in a circle! Was the artist illustrating his belief in a cycle of creation, evolution, destruction and re-creation?

Possibly, the circle indicated the earth itself. But was the earth circular? The moon, sun and stars were circular. Was anything in nature in the form of a square or rectangle? The human body, face, hips, buttocks, women's breasts—were they not all in curves and circles?

The question also remained—why was so much space blank after the human figure? Was it to indicate that the process of creation was not yet complete; and was the space left for a later artist to carve a superhuman or post-human figure, still to be created? Where did the circle begin? If it ended with the human figure, it obviously began with the lotus—and was it intended to show that the process began with a flower and developed to the creation of man? Maybe the large space between the human figure and other creatures was intended to warn all creatures to maintain their distance from man, lest he destroy them!

No, there were no certainties as to what was in the minds of the artists who had laboured over these carvings.

The statue which Bharat admired most of all in Ekantra's caves was of the old leader who had led the 108 Hindu tribes. The eyes were half-closed and deep-set, as though he was looking outside and inward. The expression was dignified; features, regular; eye-brows bushy, both apparently growing together, though the bridge between them was lighter; the ears were somewhat large. The shawl he wore over his left shoulder and under his right arm was decorated with a trefoil pattern. Round his head was a fillet with a circular buckle in the centre, with a similar buckle on his right arm. He had a short beard, whiskers and closely trimmed moustache.

Bharat also saw many nude figures in the caves. Amongst them was the statue of a dancing girl—slim, beautiful and naked, except for a necklace and bangles covering one arm, her hair arranged in an elegant coiffure. She had a mischievous smile, a provocative posture, with one arm on her hip and one leg half-bent, with an impression of movement, vivacity and invitation. After he overcame his initial shyness and surprise over the nudity, Bharat realized that artists were always fascinated with the beauty and rhythm of the human body. Even at that tender age, Bharat admired the exquisiteness with which the artists had modelled lips, breasts, torso, and hips. In later years, he shared the artist's feeling for line and form, even though he was unable to paint well.

A number of paintings were of the First Mother, credited in many tales to be the First Creator, who abdicated in favour of God. But then everyone knew that to be a charming myth, for the creator was neither man nor woman, neither 'this' nor 'that', but the imperishable Self within each and all of us. So even Bharat knew in his childhood days that the statue of the First Mother was to be treated with respect as a symbol, but could not be confused with reality. What delighted Bharat was that every artist had shown the First Mother differently. Depending on the painting he was looking at—she was tall, she was short, she was angry, she was calm, she was flying on an elephant, on the crest of a wave, on a tiger, on the wings of a swan, holding a baby in her arms, making toys, combing a child's hair, looking at children in a comic pose, or sometimes just standing by herself, with a serene look. One painting showed her looking comically frustrated as she tried to teach her son—God—the laws of creation, with him listening with only one ear!

Obviously, as Ekantra explained, these symbols—be they of First Mother or the gods—were devised as aids to see the deeper divine reality of the Infinite and the Absolute, the in-dwelling Spirit which is the source and origin of all creation. The ten-year old Bharat understood that but said, 'These symbols are good too, to enjoy God, and to laugh with Him.' Ekantra agreed. Why not! Maybe even the earliest man drew such comic figures when his children wanted to know their spiritual roots—and how else could he do it except by drawing comically in the sand to teach and entertain them at the same time! Surely, he wanted his children to love and laugh with God!

Many carvings had lessons for Bharat. Men and women in yogic postures were obviously intended to teach yoga. Paintings of bulls and cows, the pipal tree and the tulsi plant showed the respect they enjoyed. Carvings of horses and elephants proved their role in people's lives. He could not understand the paintings of animals with only a single horn, nor of some monstrous over-sized beasts. Ekantra did not know whether these animals were now extinct. They both feared that the

Jatayu would become extinct—and their feeling was that if a species of creation was no more, something precious was lost to the universe.

Bharat had grown up ready to take up arms against tribal raiders. He had distinguished himself in many skirmishes. Yet all along, he and his friends wondered about the secret of the poisoned arrows of the enemy.

Yadodhra dumbfounded them by saying, 'My father knows the secret but will not tell.' They did not believe him. They knew that Yadodhra thought his father knew everything. Ekantra knew a lot and always shared his knowledge. If he had known, he would have said so.

Ekantra was silent when Bharat asked him if he knew the secret. Later, when Bharat and Suryata persisted, Ekantra said that poisoned arrows were not essential since the clan was stronger than the tribals. The clan had built walls to halt and harass the enemy. True, the tribals had the advantage of poisoned arrows, but the clan's arrows were superior, had better aim and a longer range. Also, the clan's swords and spears were longer and sharper. Its horses were better trained and faster. Surely, the clan could do without poisoned arrows. In any case, Ekantra urged, the secret was not his to give away and he was under oath to divulge it only in an emergency which, he hoped, would never arise.

It was after several murderous tribal raids that Ekantra, at last, succumbed and agreed to share the secret of the death-arrow.

He took Bharat, Suryata and Yadodhra—who were no longer boys but young men—on a trip beyond the village, through many forests, to a rocky region. Climbing over the rocks and descending on the other side, they found patches of uneven ground with tall weeds. Ekantra led them to a small cluster of rocks which concealed a broken down hut. Someone, long ago, had apparently lived there. Beyond the hut was what they were looking for—a clump of small trees.

These were not joy-giving, life-sustaining trees. They were trees of death which yielded the poison for the arrows. Yet even at this distance, they had a persistent, inviting aroma.

They could not immediately reach the trees, for there was a deep, man-made pit, running all round with sharp, thorny bushes. Someone, sometime had seen to it that no animal or man, attracted by their pleasant fragrance, strayed towards those trees of death. In the hut they found logs which served as a bridge across the pit. They were afraid to touch the trees, but Ekantra said that the trees, by themselves, were not poisonous. The poison was in the sticky sap which oozed when a cut was made in the tree; the sap was to be dried in the sun till its perfume disappeared and then it would become a deadly poison, for which there was no antidote once it got into the bloodstream.

How many oaths Ekantra forced on them before divulging the secret of the poisoned arrows! Even after these many decades, Bharat remembered them:

- They would not be the first to strike with such arrows, but would use them only if the tribals used poisoned arrows;
- A tribal-prisoner should be sent back with a poisoned arrow to warn his tribes that such arrows would be used against them, if ever they used their poisoned arrows;
- Only those with proven skill for marksmanship must use these arrows; they should be aimed so as to avoid the danger of them falling into the river, lest creatures that dwell in it are poisoned;
- Also, they must be aimed clearly at the enemy and not at the innocent animal he is riding. After a battle, search parties would retrieve such arrows lying around or stuck in trees, lest any living thing, bird or animal, licks or treads over them.

Ekantra insisted that the route to the Tree of Death should be known only to Bharat, Suryata and Yadodhra—and that they should not breathe a word of it to anyone else. Further, he insisted, 'Let it be known that only one of you knows the secret of the arrow of death.' He selected Bharat, 'not only because he is already proving to be a natural leader but because he is the least talkative among you all.'

Thus, credit for the discovery of the poisoned arrow was given to Bharat alone, and he began to be known both as a fighter and a discoverer.

It was Karkarta Suryakarma who most regretted Ekantra's decision to leave his caves and resume living with his family. Who was now going to perform all those services for the rishis and munis in the forest? Gladly, he permitted his son, Suryata, to join Yadodhra and Bharat to take supplies for the rishis from Ekantra's home. He also appointed Ekantra's wife as Council member for the welfare of the hermits. Speaking of Suryakarma, Ekantra asked his wife, 'How did I ever come to exchange harsh words with such a good man!' He added, 'Henceforth, I shall not quarrel with any man.' Deliberately misunderstanding him, she said, 'Good. Let all your quarrels be only with a woman—me.'

Bharat's trips to the caves ceased, since Ekantra was now living in his family home. But that meant more opportunities for Bharat to meet him. Once he asked, 'However did the tribals discover the secret of the poisoned arrow before we did?' Ekantra replied that the secret was known to some in the Hindu clan centuries before the tribals had it, and concluded with, 'would you blame them if they chose to show wisdom and restraint?'

But Bharat asked, 'A deadly weapon with the enemy!—does it not impose a duty on us to acquire and use it, if he strikes first?'

'Yes a Hindu must remain strong. But he must also remain wise, for without wisdom what is strength? The strength of a fool and a bully.'

Thoughtfully, Ekantra added, 'That is why I think you, Bharat, should one day be Karkarta of this land.'

Bharat laughed and Ekantra said, 'You laugh because this is the first time you have heard of such a possibility.' Bharat confessed that it was Suryata who once spoke of his becoming Karkarta, but that was when he was eight years old and had lost his father and his childhood sweetheart, Bindu. Bharat told Ekantra how then, during his swim, he saw a vision of the panorama of the land of Sindhu and its people, and of his resolve to serve his people. Ekantra nodded at Bharat and said, 'He who leads people must be guided by a vision. And he who holds a weapon of destruction must be guided by responsibility.'

Bharat thought no more of Ekantra's reference to his becoming Karkarta but apparently he had misjudged Ekantra's persistence.

Suryakarama, the then Karkarta, was ailing. He decided not to stand for re-election on expiry of his seven-year term. A Karkarta was, of course, elected by the people, but the outgoing Karkarta and Council members always had enormous influence with the people.

It was to Suryakarma that Ekantra went to prepare the ground. Suryakarma was surprised. What were Bharat's credentials? True, he had discovered arrow-poison and was a fine soldier. But were these the virtues to seek in a Karkarta! Suryakarma, like many pious persons, had a sneaking contempt for soldiers, whom he regarded, at best, as a necessary evil. For him, it was unthinkable to contemplate Bharat for this high office. After all, so vast was the power of Karkarta, that he could veto Council and Assembly decisions, though the Assembly could, in some cases, demand a direct reference to the people. Again, if a Karkarta misused his power, the Assembly could initiate steps to dismiss him, but this too involved a direct appeal to the people and a tedious procedure.

Suryakarma thought to himself that if he drew up a list of 500 eligible persons as Karkarta, Bharat's name would not appear even then.

But Ekantra was not the only one canvassing for Bharat.

Yadodhra had organized a large group of friends to seek support for Bharat's candidature, even though the election was two years away.

Many spoke of Bharat's amazing discovery of the poisoned arrow, with stories of his ceaseless search and arduous journeys, in the face of grave danger, to discover this vital secret to protect his land.

Every soldier knew of Bharat's bravery on the battlefield. Old soldiers remembered how gallantly Bharat's father had died fighting tribal raiders.

Then came Bharat's marriage and that also helped, as many recalled, how he had come to exchange marriage-vows with the girl, even before she was born. The story was not exactly true, but it appealed to romantic sentiment.

His youth was against him, but people often forgot this when they saw his handsome figure.

Even so, all this might not have mattered if the Council Chiefs had not been impressed as well. True, every adult in the clan had a vote and was obliged to vote, except in the case of illness or emergency, as failure to vote attracted the penalty of a fine and disqualification from holding public office. The adults exercised votes for themselves and for their minor children, as it was recognized that a person must vote not only for the present but also for the future of his children. (Yadodhra was delighted that Suryata, who was already married, had twins and this meant four votes for Bharat.)

Initially, the only Council Member committed to Bharat's cause was Ekantra's wife. She was in charge of the welfare of hermits. Most hermits were unconcerned but some listened. Why would they not believe this kind and gentle lady, whose only mission in life seemed to be to look after them! A few hermits did spread the word round in Bharat's favour, to anyone who came to listen to them.

Pressure came on Karkarta Suryakarma, like an avalanche, from a number of rishis who inhabitated the forest in which Ekantra's caves were located. Yadodhra had taken over Ekantra's task of distributing supplies to them. Respectfully, Yadodhra discussed with them his father's view in Bharat's favour, and while many remained silent, there were those who endorsed it. Yadodhra saw to it that those who endorsed Bharat or even politely wished him well, sent messengers to Suryakarma and the Council Chiefs, requesting support for Bharat. The messages were so many that Suryakarma began to entertain doubts. He sent his own son, Suryata, to check. Suryata returned, not only to confirm the messages already received, but many more. It seemed that all those men of God, who had never taken the slightest interest in elections before, had suddenly become deeply enamoured of Bharat's success. It did not occur to Suryakarma to inquire of Suryata how he was able to consult so many within so short a time.

Suryakarma began to waver—did I misjudge this young Bharat!

It was Suryata again who provided the clinching argument. Almost casually, he spoke of Bharat's worship and veneration for Surya. This surprised Karkarta and Suryata responded with, 'Bharat's reverence for the sun deity is as great as mine—if not more.' Suryakarma could not believe it and Suryata had almost to swear. But Suryata spoke the truth, for he himself no longer had any special reverence for the sun, even though he came from a family that had worshipped the sun for generations. So how could Bharat have less respect than him for the sun deity!

This decided the issue. Suryakarma had no personal ambitions yet his heart overflowed with joy that a sun-worshipper should be a Karkarta after him. It did puzzle him for a moment—how was it that he had known nothing of Bharats's devotion? But then he knew very little about him anyway.

Suryakarma ignored his misgivings. The next Karkarta would also be a sun-worshipper! He felt a warm glow in his heart. Bharat was now his favourite candidate.

The election was still some time away but Suryakarma's health worsened. He sent for the Council Chiefs and begged them to use their influence to elect Bharat. They too had received messages from every quarter to favour this 25-year-old youngster. Some Council Chiefs saw merit in having an inexperienced, immature young man as Karkarta. He would undoubtedly listen to their advice with respect.

For the rest, Bharat's youthful looks, his soldierly bearing, his exploits against raiders, his discovery of arrow-poison, the courage with which his father had fought and died, and even his romantic marriage, were enough to endear him to young and old.

Yadodhra insisted that, as a candidate, Bharat must address people with a flourish. He must be eloquent about his achievements. But people saw in Bharat's silence a sense of humility and modesty that they liked. Yadodhra, however, continued to complain and Suryata suggested that the least Bharat could do was to close his eyes and tell people—'Let us all pray together'—and that warm glow of joint prayer would heighten people's belief in Bharat's godly ways. Bharat said that would be dishonest. Yadodhra retorted that honest men never stood for election to public-office and never won elections, but looking at Suryata's glare, who thought that this was a veiled dig at his father, he quickly added, except in the past.

Later, somehow, Bharat found the words, as he recalled the vision he had seen of the land and people of Sindhu. His words then flowed easily as he spoke of Sanathana Dharma and the hopes of the first Hindus who settled by the side of the life-giving waters of Sindhu—and he often ended with the prayer—'God bring peace to my people; give them hope, restore their dignity and renew their faith.'

One by one, other candidates left the field and, on election day, Bharat was unopposed. Even so, the election had to be held, for the candidate had to secure three-fourths of the vote even if he was the only one. The last Karkarta, Suryakarma, was a compromise candidate, elected after three other unopposed candidates successively failed to get the qualifying vote of 75 per cent. There was no such upset in Bharat's election.

How many votes did Bharat get? No one knows. The practice was to stop counting votes as soon as the candidate obtained the stipulated number. The intention, obviously, was to choose a Karkarta and not to engage in a popularity contest to compare with the votes of previous or future Karkartas.

The boat moved on. Bharat interrupted his day-dreams and wondered—why are all these visions of the past rising before me, in an unending parade!—they are pleasant visions in themselves but why then do I have this sense of loneliness and despair!

He looked at the child sleeping peacefully as the boat moved. Where is the need for sorrowing, he asked himself. I learnt so little at my large school. I had no guru. God guided my path to Ekantra. He was the one who orchestrated my rise to the position of Karkarta at the age of twenty-five. After that campaign for the first election, there never was need for another. People gave me their love in abundance. I left my land strong, united, prosperous. Ekantra was the one who taught me, helped me, inspired me, to keep my pledge to the gods and to my clan of the Hindu. Why then this strange, desolate feeling! Ekantra is no more. But this child will have Muni to guide him. How then can I ask for more!

Now he knew, his sorrow was not for the child but for himself. In his loneliness on the Island of Silence, his one ray of happiness had been the weekly visit of this child. He would have little to look forward to in the years ahead. Only memories!

Bharat had the feeling of being robbed of those too. The singer told him of all that was happening. Yes, the clan was more prosperous; diversion of Sindhu into new channels, completed in his time, had begun to pay rich dividends; new lands were under cultivation; new villages and towns were springing up; expeditions to faraway lands had met with astonishing success; the clan's territory had expanded. People had more wealth, more amenities, more leisure.

Even so, when the singer told him all this, he felt dejected. Clearly, new winds were blowing. New threats of disunity were forming. The rule of law was being eroded. Favouritism, influence, partiality and wealth were coming in its way. The clan was expanding, with new lands coming under its sway, but new kinds of divisions and hatreds were creeping in. To safeguard his own position, Karkarta Nandan had pitted guilds against each other and even enlisted preachers to support the causes he championed.

'Why does he wish to create divisions? To what end?' Bharat asked; and the singer said, 'So that he may keep the people and the guilds divided, and each may learn to quarrel with the other, and each may look to him alone for protection, and to none other.'

Bharat was shocked when he heard of the proposal that headmen no longer be elected but appointed by Karkarta. 'Nandan can do a lot of damage in these fifteen years as Karkarta,' said Bharat.

'Fifteen years! Why only fifteen years?' asked the singer.

'He is, I think, forty-five years old now. Did I not establish a principle that a Karkarta, like every one else, must retire at sixty!'

'Did you really!' the singer asked. 'Council and Assembly ruled that a Karkarta can, if elected, serve till the end of his natural life. You simply chose to walk away and did not offer yourself for re-election. When Nandan came as Karkarta, his first official act was to approve a number of Council and Assembly decisions and amongst them was also the decision that Karkarta does not have to retire.'

'And the precedent I set has no value then?' Bharat asked.

'To a man of honour, yes. But to Nandan, no.'

'But what about the people? Surely Nandan faces them for re-election, after his seven-year term!'

'Exactly. That is why he has to create even more divisions among them, so that he alone remains the single, solid symbol of unity.'

The singer also told Bharat of the complacency in the clan, as more wealth poured in, with less effort. With new territories came more comforts and luxuries. New expeditions were being sent out to bring more land under the clan, with the promise of a free hand to those who undertook such enterprises, to deal as they chose, with tribals there.

True, the singer added, some had begun to worry over the divisions and blocks forming in the land that Bharat had left united. But those voices—few and scattered—were lost in the wilderness. 'And you know the faith our people generally have in those that lead them!'

Bharat wondered—where will this sickness—this deadly disease of disunity in the hearts of our people—lead them?

Gently, the boat moved on. The singer saw Bharat looking wistfully at the sleeping child—obviously worried about him. With a reassuring smile, the singer said, 'When he returns from Muni's rocks, he shall walk as a god should.'

'Let him walk as a son should,' was Bharat's reply, as he resumed rowing the boat, and his silent prayer was: let him finish what I left unfinished, to unite our people once again.

He repeated the words to himself, 'Let him walk as my son should.' The words seized hold of his mind and took complete possession of him. He prayed, 'Yes, God, give him the vision to walk as my son should. . . and give him the strength to unite the people of my land. . . .'

...Then the Lord God discovered that, at times, the gods serving under Him were wanting in some elements of grace, learning and wisdom. So He decided: let each god be given a consort, so that he may learn from his goddess. But when humans have free will, can goddesses have less? So goddesses chosen as consorts declined to attend their own weddings with the gods and only when such gods, through meditation, yoga and a sacrifice of ego, reached a level of acceptability, did the goddess chosen for them come forward to consummate their marriage. . . . Oh! Have you not heard of Brahma's sorrow, solitude, penance and renunciation, until at last he began to perfect himself, and only then, did Saraswati come forward to accept him as her consort!. . .'

'. . .In each swan's life is a promise that at least once, goddess Saraswati shall ride on her, and in each poet's heart is the yearning for her vision. Thus it is that this goddess of learning, art and music—always beautiful, shining, fair and young—is constantly on the move on earth, except when she holds classes in heavens to spread learning among the gods; and it is said that her husband, god Brahma, had called upon all gods so that they may 'learn more and brag less'; and even Brahma himself attends those classes—to see that various gods do attend and not for his own learning, for surely all is revealed to Brahma. Is it not?'

—(Both quotations from Poetess Damayani—5400 BC—whose poetry often claimed that goddesses were superior to gods, just as women are superior to men. Damayani was reputed to be happily married, and it has been said that her husband helped her with her poetry. She stopped composing poems after his death and became a hermit.)

Saraswati River

5065 BC

Nandan's idea to remove Gatha as headman come to naught. He had suggested that the village be merged with bigger villages and everyone agreed but vowed that Gatha should be the headman of the amalgamated villages. Everyone was certain that the suggestion for the merger arose in Nandan's mind from his deeply-felt respect for Sindhu Putra. But Nandan realized that no one other than Gatha would be tolerated as headman and he would not be opposed by any of the headmen from the other villages.

When Nandan realized that no one would dare to remove Gatha, he floated the rumour that Gatha was being considered for Council Membership, certain that Gatha would run to him, like a petitioner, to beg for this most coveted office; and then it would not be difficult to make him divulge the secret of Sindhu Putra!

The villagers heard this. Certainly, no honour was too great for their Sentinel!

But Gatha refused to even consider the honour of Council Membership. He wanted to remain rooted in the village and wait for Sindhu Putra's visits. Besides, he had a mission—to remain next to Bharat's island.

Sindhu Putra's name thus rang again in the land! For his sake, they said, a simple headman was offered this honour! For his sake, a simple headman refused this honour! For his sake, Karkarta Nandan even considered an ex-slave for an office of such prestige! The fact however is that Nandan never intended to make the offer.

The temple was a constant reminder to the village of the child who had lived in their midst for three exhilarating years, even though now he could visit them only once a year. Everyone was fascinated by the temple. For architects, artists, sculptors and painters, Sindhu Putra's temple held a growing fascination not only because it was the largest, but also as its design followed a unique pattern. All earlier temples were circular in shape, since the circle was regarded as an image of perfection and wholeness, with no sharp or artificial lines, representing a symbol of nature from which man emerged and to which man longs to return. But this temple was based not on the circle but on the square; yet as it grew in height, it rose in curved planes, each merging with the other in natural rhythm; and each decorated with sculptures and figures of different sizes; and the impression from the ground was that they were of the same size.

When Vassi initially saw the temple's square structure, he cried out sorrowfully, 'Are they building a temple or a structure to house their cows and camels!' But the artist explained that a temple must begin with a square as the fundamental form and only thereafter must curves and circles be depicted, to show humanity's movement, action, adventure, and finally, its goal of highest spiritual wisdom. 'Man must refine the world he lives in—and a temple depicts stages in that progress, leading finally to a realization of the Absolute.'

The village grew into a town. Large—two and even three-storey—houses replaced the huts. Every house had windows and balconies facing the temple. Roofs, though fancifully turreted, had platforms to enable householders to sleep there at night, in warm weather, or to view the temple-dome, with its sweeping curvilinear lines of fluid grace. Outer house-walls were decorated with paintings with endless scenes —Sindhu Putra feeding from Sonama's breasts, smiling, blessing and sometimes in a serene pose. Some covered their walls with awnings to protect the paintings; others were delighted to redo their paintings when the rain washed them away. Many simply covered their walls with sculpture, impervious to the rain.

Large baths were constructed for the devotees to wash in, before entering the temple. The village-square was enlarged to provide nine fountains for drinking water for visitors. Surrounding villages also constructed inns to cope with the overflow. Another large square provided huge water-troughs for animals—mules, donkeys, horses, elephants, camels—as pilgrims' caravans were arriving and departing each day. But less were departing than arriving, as many—some in faith and others with wounds to heal—chose to stay back.

Thus hour by hour, year by year, the legend of Sindhu Putra grew.

Nandan's mind was on the land of his people. How far could it be extended?

Centuries earlier, his people had branched out from the Sind to settle in Panchanad (Punjab), where the Sindhu flowed along with its five main tributaries—Sutudri (Sutlej), Vipas (Beas), Parusni (Ravi), Vitasta (Jhelum) and Asikni (Chandrabhaga or Chenab).

Thereafter, the people from Sind moved again, along another river— Saraswati—which joined the Sindhu, as they both flowed to the sea.

This then was the homeground of Nandan's people—the region of seven rivers (Sindhu, its five tributaries and Saraswati). The region, in its entirety, came to be known as Sapta Sindhu or the land of seven rivers; the *Rig Veda* uses the expression Sapta-sindhavah to point to this region.

While 'Sapta-sindhavah', in the *Rig Veda*, undoubtedly refers to the region covered by these seven rivers—Sindhu, its five feeders and Saraswati—it is worthwhile to clarify certain other matters:

The *Rig Veda*, composed after 5000 BC, hardly mentions the Ganga and the Yamuna rivers. The Ganga is mentioned only in one late hymn and, from this, many infer that the *Rig Vedic* people knew of the Ganga and Yamuna only vaguely; and that for them the rivers par excellence were the Sindhu and Saraswati, which is why these two rivers are mentioned repeatedly, respectfully and glowingly in the *Rig Veda*; besides, the *Rig Veda* even mentions the feeders of Sindhu (including the five in Punjab, as also the rivers which join the Sindhu in Afghanistan and Surat).

However, though Sindhu and Saraswati are prominent in the *Rig Veda*, and the Ganga is hardly mentioned, the inference that the *Rig Vedic* people ignored the Ganga or were mostly unaware of it, is not justified. The fact is that the people of the Sind had themselves visited the Ganga well before 5000 BC, along with the great civilization that flourished around the Ganga. Why the *Rig Veda* virtually ignores the Ganga is attributable to the fact that this most ancient literature in the world arose not in one single mighty sweep in the mind of a single author, but also included a compilation of some pre-ancient Memory songs, sung for thousands of years. The earliest Memory songs of the Hindus were naturally about their homeground, which began with the region of Sind, thence to Punjab, and thereafter to the region between the Sindhu and Saraswati rivers, which they regarded as the holiest of holy grounds—Brahmadesa.

It was after witnessing the source of the Sindhu river rising in Tibet, and after Sadhu Gandhara established his ashrams in Avagana that the people of Sindhu came face to face with the great Ganga civilization, which in itself was a part of the great tradition and root of Sanathana Dharma. Thus the inference that Ganga, known and respected by the people of Sindhu before 5000 BC, was unknown to *Rig Vedic* people, is hardly warranted. The *Rig Veda* simply included some of the songs of the early Hindus, sung well before the people of Sindhu and Ganga came together to recognize their common ancestry and roots, and to move forward as one people.

Nandan knew that with population growth, improved farming techniques and larger cattle herds, the need for more land had grown; and this had served as a lure for many from Sind to extend their settlements to Punjab and northwards. To the east, however, along the Saraswati river, people moved not for land, but as pilgrims.

Nandan proudly recalled that the Saraswati river was discovered by his own ancestor, Brahmadasa, some nine hundred years earlier

(6010 BC). Brahmadasa was the direct ancestor of the eighth Karkarta, whose son married Kunita, daughter of Devi Leilama, who herself became the ninth Karkarta in 5333 BC.

Nandan allowed his mind to dwell on his ancestor Brahmadasa.

Brahmadasa, at the age of eighteen, became a disciple of Rishi Vaswana. He had no ambitions except to seek spiritual enlightenment and to remain a lifelong brahmachari (student; with celibacy and chastity).

Suddenly, after eight years, he felt his spiritual strength deserting him. The rishi's daughter, who came to the ashram every year for a fortnight in spring, became the centre of his day-dreams.

Rishi Vaswana's daughter was ten years old when Brahmadasa saw her for the first time at the ashram. She knew neither shyness nor fear then, and would chatter incessantly. Her father would sometimes speak to her sternly, but she could melt him with a smile. Every time she came, she brought home-cooked food and sweets for her father and his disciples. She became quieter as she grew older but she always had a merry smile for Brahmadasa, possibly in remembrance of their first meeting.

Brahmadasa had been at the ashram for only a month when she startled him by jumping down from the tree under which he was praying. Before he could ask who she was, she demanded to know why he was sitting under her tree. In a daze, he tried to leave but she asked him sternly how he could leave without completing his prayers. She then ran off but soon returned with sweets. Quietly, he ate at the command of this wild girl who had tumbled down from the trees and at last asked who she was. She feigned surprise and said, 'Surely you know, your father and mine are one!' She was right in a way; she was the natural daughter of the rishi, who was also his spiritual father. And, it was common to so regard the guru. But he understood nothing.

Later Brahmadasa laughed as heartily as the other disciples in the ashram. Older disciples cautioned him against sitting under the tree as the rishi's little daughter had claimed rights over it because when she was a child her father had jokingly told her that she was born from that tree. Also, it was nearer the duck-pond and she would sit under it to feed the ducks flocking around her. True enough, when he had sat under the tree the ducks had waddled out of the pond but soon trooped back, apparently disappointed to see him. Poets tell us that a bond developed between Brahmadasa and the little girl as he took on the task of feeding the ducks.

As Brahmadasa meditated on love's ecstasy, a feeling of inconsolable woe soon overtook him. He knew that he would be unable to pronounce to her the words in his heart. In his soul was the cry of despair that men feel when they are startled by their inner weakness.

He had come to the ashram for enlightenment, to be away from turmoil, lust and attachment—as a brahmachari for life. Even if he lived to be a hundred, he wanted to see nothing of the earth beyond the tall, dark trees that enclosed the ashram. Why was he then being drawn by some strange, irresistible force? Why was he the prisoner of a destiny unknown?

All night, Brahmadasa would toss and turn restlessly. When at last he slept, he saw her in his dreams and the naked body of his dreams merged with himself, as together they went on an enchanted journey. But he would immediately wake up, tormented with the question— What can I offer her? Nothing but pain and anguish.

Brahmadasa went about his duties listlessly. When he sat for his usual meditation, he could not concentrate and feared that God was not in his heart. God's place had been taken by another.

He saw the rishi's daughter coming in his direction. She did not speak to him. Her usual greeting was missing. Her perpetual smile was not there. She simply gazed at him mysteriously, as if she too were guarding a secret. He had the intense desire to confess his love to her, to hold her in his arms, but he controlled himself.

Brahmadasa feared that he had fallen from grace. He counted his sins. He had violated his vow of brahmacharya for he discerned no purity as he contemplated her nearness to him. Also, had he not contemplated violating her vow as well? Everyone knew that the running battle between the girl and her mother was finally over and she was at last permitted to join her father's ashram, as a devotee, from her eighteenth birthday, instead of merely visiting it each year. Worst of all, he had allowed the shadow of his unholy desires to fall on a girl whom he and every disciple addressed as 'sister', for she was the daughter of his rishi—their spiritual father. Was it not moral incest that he contemplated!

Brahmadasa felt he had committed a revolting outrage against his conscience and against the rishi's ashram. He, by his evil desires, had violated its nobler code and soiled its purity.

At the dead of night, Brahmadasa left the ashram. No one can explain why he took the route to the vast eastern desert. Maybe, because every other route led to human habitation and he wanted to be alone with his sorrow in the barren, endless desert. Poets simply speak of his going on and on, plodding wearily, day after day, month after month and no one explains what he lived on in a desert that was known to have no edible plants, only thorny bushes and poisonous snakes.

In fact, little is known of his journey except that poets at times speak of sandstorms that propelled him forward, or even blocked his path, whirling around him with violent ferocity and accumulated force. But then, the storms raging in his heart were far more terrible.

Brahmadasa did not know where he was going but he continued.

Suddenly, the storms around him subsided, the wind was calm and yet he heard thundering noises ahead, as if two hurricanes were battering at each other. He gazed ahead. He could not see the setting sun. Its view was blocked and it seemed to him that the howling winds had formed themselves into a solid mass of white sheets rising in the sky. He ran forward, his body feverish but his mind glowing in hope. Surely, this was to be release at last—the end of his journey on earth—the end of his life itself. What else could it be in the midst of those battling storms with winds that rose like pure white metal, shimmering in the flame-coloured light of the setting sun!

As he ran, drops of water fell on his head. He looked at the immeasurable sky above. It was clear, cloudless, with no hope of rain. He felt blessed. He knew of the custom of sprinkling Sindhu water in the last moments of a person's life. Now it seemed that someone was looking down from the heavens above and sprinkling drops of auspicious water on him.

The cry in his heart was stilled. He felt forgiven. The vision of the girl he had left behind rose before him. He could see her smiling. They embraced each other—for the past and the future.

He raced forward to meet what he thought were battling storms, to end his life Here, the poet criticizes Brahmadasa to say:

> *'Whatever your innermost strife*
> *By what right can you end a life?*
> *How can you decide its time*
> *Except for a cause—exalted, sublime!'*

Tirelessly, the poet explains that escape or penance is not a 'cause—exalted, sublime' and does not justify ending a life. But then he breaks out in joy to say that heavenly grace saved Brahmadasa.

Brahmadasa felt dazed as he strode above the sand dune to watch the dazzling sight below.

It was a magical place where two rivers met. Brahmadasa had never seen a confluence of rivers before. He watched it fascinated.

Later he would learn that one of these two rivers was the same Sindhu which flowed through his own land. The second river came from elsewhere and would later be known as Saraswati.

The continuous roar he had heard was not of storms locked in battle. It came from the waters of the two rivers—Sindhu and Saraswati—as they rushed headlong to greet each other; and as they met, sprays of water rose high in the air—and then the waters of the two rivers joined together and in their immensity flowed as one single river.

No one knows how long Brahmadasa stood there, transfixed, gazing in awe at this confluence. He saw birds of various plumage swooping down but could not discern whether they were out to catch the small fish leaping out as the result of the two rivers rushing towards each other. Nor did he see, in the distance beyond, the tall, majestic trees, plants and flowers that the two rivers nourished.

Slowly, he moved, as though in a trance, towards the confluence. I shall, he thought, drift into eternity as the waters cover me softly, gently, invisibly. Drowsiness flooded his ravaged body as the waters leapt over him. He felt a moment of complete peace as never before.

Then as he lay, contentedly, to die, it seemed as though another voice came to him, louder than the call of self-surrender, and he rose, refreshed from the cold waters, with the desire to live and love.

On the bank, he meditated. The gods, it seemed, agreed that there was no sin in his love for the girl he had left behind.

Brahmadasa opened his eyes. Instead of the assembly of gods that he expected to see, all that faced him was a lone swan in the river. He smiled, wondering how long ago it was that he had last smiled!

There and then Brahmadasa decided to renounce the brahmacharya oath and ask the rishi for his daughter's hand. But he was too weak to travel.

That night, he slept under the stars with the sweet anticipation of happiness. He woke up refreshed and saw the waters glistening in the first rays of the sun. The swan was there. He greeted her cheerfully, 'Good morning, fair lady, are you also as lonely and lost as I was?' The swan nodded in agreement.

The poet here also explains that it is possible to see a swan without goddess Saraswati riding on her, but impossible ever to see the goddess without the swan, who serves as her chariot. He describes Saraswati as the goddess of learning, art and music, always beautiful, fair and young, with a musical instrument in her hand, worshipped by students, artists and musicians and loved ardently by her consort, god Brahma. The goddess has no swan as her favourite, as in each swan's life was a promise that, at least once, the goddess would ride on it. Constantly therefore, Saraswati is on the move except when she holds classes in heaven to spread learning among the gods; and it is said that god Brahma called upon all the gods to attend those classes so that they may 'learn more and brag less,' and Brahma himself attended those classes, though cautiously the poet adds, 'but that must be to see that various gods do attend, and not so much to learn, for surely all was revealed to Brahma—was it not?'

Thus goddess Saraswati then had a role of high importance. Later Vedic literature, even after the *Rig Veda*, maintains her cult but does not assign to her the importance that she enjoyed around 6000 BC.

Brahmadasa's cheerful mood did not last. Clouds came. The swan flew away. The sky looked gloomy and threatened rain. The grief which was allayed for a while returned to wrench his heart as he remembered that the rishi's daughter was herself to take the vow of brahmacharya on her eighteenth birthday—and that day he knew had past while he had been in the wilderness of the desert. How could he now claim her hand!

With despair, he realized he had nowhere to go. He remained there for days, weeks. . . . The nearby plants and trees with their fruits gave sustenance to his body. His spirit, however, was beyond healing. The birds flew overhead, heedless of him and his grief. His sole, silent companion was the swan who came to sit in the water opposite him. Even when he moved along the river and chose a different spot to sit, the swan would fly to take her position in front of him. She knows my sorrow, he thought, or perhaps I should know hers—and he wondered, has she too lost her loved one? Has she been passed over by goddess Saraswati? Often he forgot his sorrow and prayed for the swan and, in his day-dreams, he saw goddess Saraswati riding on her, but the face and figure that the goddess assumed was of the rishi's daughter. He spoke to the swan, talked to himself, and knew that he was raving, going mad, out in the open, under the hot sun and chill winds of the desert nights. But even in the blaze of the sun, he would not go far so as to remain close to the swan; and in the evening when the swan flew away, he remained there, for he did not know how to build a fire to protect himself from the cold.

Then came a miserable, desolate morning when the swan did not appear. He scanned the skies but she was nowhere to be seen. She did not appear for the next few days, while he sat staring into empty space in despair.

Brahmadasa kept peering into the sunlit sky, vainly trying to catch a glimpse of the swan. He had a fever, racked by mental anguish and pain.

He fainted.

It was there, at the confluence of the Sindhu and Saraswati rivers, that Rishi Vaswana and his daughter found Brahmadasa.

Nobody knows how Rishi Vaswana came to search for him in the desert. It may be that a disciple or even the rishi himself saw Brahmadasa take the desert route. It was not uncommon for the rishi and his disciples to continue their meditation through the night.

The fact however is that Brahmadasa's sudden disappearance had surprised the ashram. The rishi himself was philosophic—'Who knows when and where the spirit moves you and to what blissful consequence!' He was certain that Brahmadasa had left to follow his own bliss.

Even later, when the rishi's daughter said that she would not embrace brahmacharya, her father only mildly wondered how his daughter had suddenly become so obedient to her mother's wishes and agreed to lead a normal householder's life. The rishi too was not keen on his daughter following brahmacharya but had no wish to stand in the way of her quest for bliss.

Rishi Vaswana had married when he was eighteen years old. The call of the forest came to him when he was twenty-two. He was childless. He promised his wife that he would not lead the hermit's life exclusively, until he gave her a child. It is said that while most women prayed for children, his wife's prayer was to remain childless. Meanwhile, the rishi alternated as a householder and a hermit. Years passed and at last a daughter was born to her.

Vaswana retired to the forest as a hermit after the birth of his daughter. Later, he set up an ashram and came to be renowned as a rishi. He regarded brahmacharya as only one of the many paths leading to grace and he realized that this path too was littered with pitfalls. So he was quite unconcerned—even glad—that his daughter had at last decided to follow her mother's advice to forget about brahmacharya.

But what did attract the rishi's notice was the look of anxiety and torment in her eyes. At night when the rishi heard her sobbing into her pillow, he went to comfort her. The secret was out. She told him all.

The next day, the rishi left the ashram with his daughter. He did not go immediately to the desert but to a village to meet the explorer Kripala. The explorer was unable to join the expedition but he placed at the rishi's disposal, men, materials, equipment and animals for the journey.

The wind howled in the desert and all visible space was filled with grey sand, but they went on, now to the right, now to the left, and the rishi often thought of abandoning his search, but when he saw his daughter's despairing look, he continued. They finally reached the spot where the sound and spray of the confluence of the rivers could be heard and seen. Undeterred, the rishi and his daughter went on, though the rest of the party halted. They reached the spot where Brahmadasa had fallen.

Brahmadasa opened his eyes to find himself on a bed of dry grass with a fire glowing nearby, a tent above his head, and the rishi's daughter by his side. He was sure he was in some heavenly realm.

When Brahmadasa regained his senses and saw the rishi ministering to him, fear entered his heart. But the rishi reassured him: nothing should hinder you from loving each other; there was no reason to be ashamed of your feelings. Why should a man live without love when the gods themselves cannot! Has anyone heard of a god without his consort?

There and then the rishi decided that the two should exchange marriage vows though the formal ceremony could only take place when the rishi's wife was present.

Brahmadasa begged that the marriage vows be exchanged by the side of the river. The swan, he feared, would not be there; even so, she had been his sole companion in his misery and isolation and he wanted to be near her favourite spot to exchange the vows. But now the poet's voice rings out in joy as he sings, 'But the swan was there! She was there!' Another poet is even more ecstatic and claims,

'Though we beheld not her face;
Her goddess was there too, yes;
Oh she, Saraswati of ineffable grace;
Herself, yes, herself, came to bless.'

Other poets doubt goddess Saraswati's presence, though there are those who ask, 'Why else would Rishi Vaswana kneel except that he saw the goddess on the swan's back?' But there was every reason for the rishi to kneel. To him, the river was holy and auspicious.

With reverence and homage, then, the river, associated as it was with the swan and its goddess, inevitably came to be known as Saraswati; and to the people of Sindhu, it was as sacred as Sindhu itself.

'...And hear my secret before I die,
For none knows it—not even I.

'I saw God, up and high,
And Devil, down, with triumphant cry,
And a child suckling a mother's breast,
A wolf stealing a bird's nest,
A priest robbing the temple chest,
A youth rushing nowhere in haste;
I saw a widow weep, a maiden sigh,
And a singer, who knows not how to lie.

'But then as I wondered who, how and why,
The truth came to me, by and by,
That each one I saw, on earth and sky,
Was none other—Yes—it was I.'

——(From the poem recited by Sura, the dramatist, at his farewell performance, 6000 BC)

Saraswati & Soma

5065 BC

Nandan smiled as he recalled the songs about the discovery of Saraswati river by his ancestor Brahmadasa who married the rishi's daughter. Soon thereafter, the region between the Sindhu and Saraswati rivers began to be populated and Nandan knew that much of the credit for this belonged to the explorer Kripala.

Sixteen years before the discovery of Saraswati river (6010 BC), the Sindhu Council of Chiefs had commissioned explorer Kripala to lead an expedition to the desert to discover all that it had to offer. Karkarta's institution was not then established and the matter fell within the Council's jurisdiction which placed large amounts at Kripala's disposal to recruit men, buy materials, acquire camels and draft animals. Kripala, without going into the desert, saw with his trained eye, from a distance, all that the desert had to offer; so after two years, he reappeared, to report that he found nothing there but flying snakes, lizards, reptiles and inedible, thorny bushes.

Later when everyone became aware of the amazing discovery of the Saraswati river, the explorer Kripala came in for a lot of criticism. But he brazenly claimed that the river was not there when he had visited the site and must have appeared after his inspection, sixteen years earlier. As also the Sindhu, which, too, he declared had changed its course, which is why he had not come across it.

Few believed him and it was clear that Kripala had never ventured deep into the desert but remained in his forest-hut.

Some said that he had intended to explore the desert but a woman he had pursued with lifelong devotion finally agreed to marry him.

Still others maintained that the Sindhu Council had foolishly sanctioned a niggardly amount for exploring the vast desert and the cost must have been ten times more. Therefore, to prepare for the expedition, Kripala wanted to increase the amount available to him; and he tried his hand at a game of dice with the honest intention of using his winnings for exploring the desert. Unfortunately, he lost. 'Then blame the throw of the dice—why blame him!' concludes the poet.

During the two years that Kripala was hiding in his hut, when he was supposed to be out in the desert, not all his time was spent in marital bliss with his newly wedded wife. His wife, who quickly became pregnant, acquired an inordinate desire for mushrooms. He, on his part, by careful grafting, pruning, planting and replanting, finally developed what he called the soma plant, in honour of his wife Soma Devi. From this plant, he extracted and brewed a wine called soma amrit.

Before soma wine came on the scene, wines and liquors were made from grain, cereal and fruit; all of these required extensive fermentation. Some of these were bitter while others sweet; but none of them was comparable to the superb and exquisite wine that Kripala developed from his carefully nurtured mushroom plants. It was bitter-sweet, slightly hallucinogenic and it was said that it transported men to the realm of gods. There were quite a few rishis, sadhus and visionaries who favoured the wine in their quest to commune with gods and sacred powers—and they called soma the drink of the gods. Also, there were poets who could not be inspired to compose a single hymn without a few sips of soma. However, it must be said that the vast majority of rishis, poets and visionaries firmly believed that its exhilarating effects were illusory and misleading.

Few found themselves neutral when discussing the virtues of soma; some considered it a 'divine drink, that inspires awe and wonder'; to others, it was an 'inebriating drink, leading to bragging and false perceptions of reality.'

However, irrespective of whether or not soma heightened poetic qualities, the fact is that for private or social drinking and revelry, it was incomparable and much in demand. Its popularity brought wealth and renown to Kripala. Zealously he guarded the secret of its preparation. As his customers grew day by day, he hired more workers to increase production. But he was careful to assign to many workers certain duties that only confused and confounded the spies seeking to learn his secret. Some workers were given the task of collecting honey, provided the bees were not driven out by smoke; honey-barrels were then buried ten feet deep; after eighteen days, they were dug out and the top, thin layer of honey was scooped out for retention, while the remaining honey was sent for resale. Actually, honey was never used for making soma and the whole idea was to mislead spies sent by rivals. Similarly, sugar was openly purchased as if to be used for fermentation, though it was never used. Kripala also used workers to collect certain flowers at sunrise to make a paste which was dried in the sun for sixty-four days and kept in the shade at night, to be finally burnt over a slow fire, with the ashes sent to Kripala's cottage. This too had nothing to do with soma but was only a drama enacted to fool rival wine-makers. Besides, in these hundreds of acres, various varieties of mushrooms were planted but only six varieties were useful for soma. Workers brought, at random, 1,000 mushrooms to Kripala's cottage, and he and his wife Soma Devi alone would select the right varieties for treatment, crushing the rest into pulp so that everyone thought that all the mushrooms had been used. Kripala's strategies for disinformation were many and, in fact, for each worker needed for useful work, he had at least two for tasks to misguide his rivals. But then he could afford to employ so many, for he was doing extremely well, especially since everyone who saw the frantic activity in his fields thought that the expenses of making soma must be considerable.

Kripala even appointed singers to recite mantras to his plants, claiming that these recitations kept the plants happy and smiling and invested them with potency and flavour.

Kripala's competitors went to the trouble and expense of honey gathering, sugar-buying, flower-crushing, paste-making and indeed many rituals and experiments—all to duplicate soma. They failed.

True, this extensive effort by his rivals resulted in many kinds of liquors being produced, but none as superior as soma. These liquors came to be known as sura and it was said that they transported a person not to the realm of the gods but often to a terrible headache the next morning.

There was an element of gross unfairness in choosing the general name of 'sura' for these poor imitations of soma. Sura was actually the name of an excellent actor and a great performer of those times. He gave solo shows in which he took on all the parts—for instance, to depict the conversation of a god with a woman and a child, he would rapidly change masks, to switch from god to woman to child in quick succession. What made Sura a great actor was that he could change the pitch, tone and inflection of his voice so rapidly and dramatically that he often made the audience forget that it was only one performer playing all the parts. His gift for tragedy was awesome and his gift for comedy, irresistible, and yet his goals were larger than mere entertainment. He was concerned more with the celebration of life in all its forms and phases, so that man may overtake the gods in goodness. Sometimes, he presented a fast-moving play in which gods, birds, animals, men, women, children—in all thirty-one—were depicted with cloth and wood cut-outs, and he would go behind each to sing appropriate lines. And it was said that he never faltered and sang in thirty-two different voices—his own as narrator and the rest for the thirty-one illusory participants. He could imitate everyone's voice, tone and mannerisms. He could laugh with the bitter scorn of a doomed god or ask a puzzling question with the innocence of a child.

Then, when imitations of soma came into the market, people unthinkingly called them sura, to emphasize that they were imitations. But what they should have realized was that these liquors were poor imitations of soma whereas Sura, the actor, was superb—and often superior—when he sought to imitate. Incidentally, Sura, the actor, never drank sura, the liquor. He always drank soma—except on the day of his performance when he drank only water, lest he forget his lines, though many assured him that soma aided the memory.

Clearly, Kripala left his lasting imprint on future ages. He realized the importance of image and publicity and surrounded himself with song-composers and poets, whose task was to sing of the heavenly qualities of soma. These singers went around—in market-places, at piers, assemblies—and their rousing hymns in praise of soma were heard everywhere. Kripala also began organizing special functions for soma poetry with public contests and magnificent prizes. Quickly, it became a fashion of the times to sing songs extolling the virtues and splendour of soma and to invest it with qualities of the divine.

Kripala fanned the flames of soma's roaring success as though his soul's salvation depended on it. All his life he had craved recognition. It had eluded him. He had failed in his profession as an explorer. Now, at last fame came to him as the creator of soma and he wanted more of it. He kept on demanding from his poets the ultimate in praise of soma. They obliged.

Kripala must be honoured as the first of those pioneers who understood the value of publicity and public relations in promoting a product. But did he really intend to leave such a lasting impression on ithihasa? Whatever his intention, his hiring and inspiring so many poets and singers to sing of soma has led to possibly the greatest and most delightful hoax of all times. The snowball effect and continuing inspiration of soma songs became so intense that centuries later, Hindus of the later-Vedic or Aryan period came to believe that the pre-ancient Hindus of Sanathana Dharma venerated soma as a deity. Thus it is that in the Vedic era—centuries after Kripala—soma acquired a far more elevated position and was personified as a god. The *Rig Veda*, itself, has several hymns to honour 'god' Soma who came to be regarded as a special god of the Brahmins and is referred to as their 'king' or patron deity. However, in the pre-Vedic period of Kripala, when kings were unknown and Brahmins did not exist as a caste—as there were no castes then—soma, with all the publicity and poetry around it, had no claims to such a high position, despite all the efforts of Kripala and the singers. On the other hand, the *Rig Veda* of ten Mandalas (books) has one whole Mandala—the ninth book—exclusively devoted to hymns in praise of god Soma. For instance:

'... *O sacred Soma, conqueror of high renown, flowing on thy way, make us better... Bring forth to us your sacred light, the light divine, and all pure felicities... Strengthen our skills and mental powers, drive away all our foes, O Soma, O Purifier, give us our share in the sun through your wisdom and grace... O almighty Soma...*

Not only have the compilers of the *Rig Veda* exclusively devoted its entire ninth book to the worship of god Soma, but in its other books as well there are similar songs of adoration. Soma is referred to as a 'supporter of heavens', 'lord of strength', 'giver of happiness', 'the lord of speech'. But then, composers of the *Rig Veda* were scholars, philosophers and sages. They sat in the isolation of their forests to hear and repeat some songs as they were sung and resung hundreds of years before their time. It is doubtful if they themselves imbibed soma or saw in it the divine virtue which some ancient poets attributed to it under Kripala's inspiration. But certainly they were charmed with the songs on soma—their lilt, imagery and fine phrases. But then, not every historian who narrates ancient tales of war or love is necessarily a great warrior or lover.

The fact is that Kripala and his descendants left foundations which were not easy to uproot. Kripala's own sons, Som Kavi and Som Bhakt, born and brought up in the midst of Soma poetry, themselves became renowned poets and fathered a generation of singers, lyricists and composers who sang of soma for hundreds of years.

And in fairness to the *Rig Veda* period, and even to pre-ancient times, it must be said that soma poetry is largely allegorical; and soma achieved that high status and recognition only in song and literature and not so much in the hearts and habits of people. In day-to-day life, certainly, it was not so highly esteemed; women in any case hardly fancied it. Even amongst men, except for festive occasions, it did not reach a fraction of the importance that the *Rig Veda* poets assigned to it. However, in the Vedic period it did achieve a high level of acceptance with the priests who were unhappy with mere offerings of fruit and flowers to the gods—for fruit and flowers did not command as high a price. The priests found it profitable to recommend soma as an offering to the gods. For even if the priest did not drink soma himself, he could always resell it to the next devotee and encourage him to make that his offering.

After the discovery of the Saraswati river by Brahmadasa, many criticized Kripala for his earlier failure to survey the desert. However, it was widely rumoured that it was Kripala's soma which brought Brahmadasa back to life and so his stock was high with some. Brahmadasa's condition when the rishi and his daughter found him was said to be critical and yet a few sips of soma revived him.

Even so, Kripala's own feelings of guilt over his failure to survey the desert were immense. To redeem himself, he built rest-houses and ashrams, all the way to the confluence, for rishis and poets.

Rishi Vaswana's daughter and Brahmadasa would not part from the river. Here again, a poet says that at their marriage ceremony there, he saw a vision of goddess Saraswati sitting on the swan's back. A later poet disputes this and asks, 'How could goddess Saraswati be

present at the wedding of another, when she was not present even at
her own wedding!' This remark about goddess Saraswati's absence at
her own wedding was simply a myth voiced by Poetess Damayani
that at times the gods were found wanting in some elements of grace,
learning and wisdom, so much so that the goddesses declined to attend
their own weddings and it was only when such gods, through
meditation, yoga and a sacrifice of the ego, reached a level of
acceptability, that the goddess chosen for them came forward to
consummate the marriage. Poetess Damayani named goddess Saraswati
as one of those who absented herself from her wedding with Brahma
and her poem describes Brahma's sorrow and solitude, until at last he
perfected himself, and only then did goddess Saraswati accept him as
her consort. But then Damayani's poems were all like that—and she
always wanted to prove that a goddess was superior to her consort,
and a woman to a man.

    Some hold that Damayani did an ill-turn to goddess Saraswati by
depicting her as superior in her early years of marriage to Brahma and
that is why the later *Rig Veda* poets, enticed by Brahma's greatness,
ignored goddess Saraswati, though they treated river Saraswati as
auspicious.

Kripala went ahead, building more ashrams for rishis and poets on the
route to the confluence of Sindhu and Saraswati. Also, he had a
passageway dug for streams to flow from rivers, creeping deep into
the desert, to form man-made lakes to serve the ashrams he built there.
Small, scattered oases sprang up in the desert and greenery lined itself
along the waterways.

    Was it simply due to his feelings of guilt, or even devotion to
Saraswati river that Kripala went to such lengths? Some say Kripala
made another astounding discovery. His soma mushroom fields began
from the border of the desert; and as he extended his fields deeper,
away from the desert, he found to his dismay that something, somehow
was missing in the aroma of his soma. It was then that he realized
that it was the desert air blowing over his plants that lent the final,
lasting touch of grace and charm to his soma. Kripala then chose to
extend his soma fields into the desert, by careful plantation, soil-
treatment and man-made lakes and streams, along ashrams that he
provided for the rishis!

Kripala hoped that the region between Sindhu and Saraswati which he
nourished and nurtured would be known as Kripaladesa (land of
Kripala) or Somadesa (land of soma—to celebrate his wine and the
name of his wife, Soma Devi). But people are fickle and the region
began to be called 'Brahmadasa desa' (land of Brahmadasa); and since
this was a tongue-twister, they simply called it 'Brahmadesa'.

Saraswati river is now no more—having lost itself in the desert of Rajasthan. In Kripala's times, it flowed broad and strong, joining the Sindhu river well below the confluence of the Sutlej. Many have sought to criticize Kripala for being the first to dig out several streams and man-made lakes to flow from that river. Similarly, in later centuries, Karkarta Nandan has also been criticized for developing a congregation of twisted streams from the Saraswati river in order to irrigate the desert. Criticism against Kripala and Nandan is based on the belief that they, amongst others, were responsible for drying up the Saraswati. But the criticism is unjust, for Saraswati river flowed thousands of years after that and has been celebrated in the *Rig Veda* as one of the most sacred rivers, along with the Sindhu, even though the Yamuna and Ganga are hardly mentioned.

Karkarta Nandan came out of his reverie with a smile. Even Kripala was prominent in his family tree. Kripala's daughter Somavati had left the soma fold to marry the son of a well-known maker of sura wines. Three generations later, the great granddaughter of Somavati would marry Brahmadasa's grandson.

Nandan believed in blood-lines. It gave him a feeling of pride to be descended from Brahmadasa, discoverer of Saraswati river; from Kripala, the creator of soma; from the eighth Karkarta, one of the greatest patrons of art, music, dance and drama; and from Devi Leilama who became the ninth Karkarta—the first woman to hold that high office and the first to establish guilds.

Nandan thought of his predecessors—Dhrupatta and Bharat. Could they boast of such illustrious lineage? No wonder they were failures. And failures they were, according to Nandan, for depriving the clan of untold wealth in slaves and territory.

People themselves, Nandan was convinced, had been far more sensible than those leaders. Again he recalled how lured by the thrill of discovery and prospect of more land, his ancestors had moved from Sind to occupy the land around the five rivers (tributaries of Sindhu river—Jhelum, Chenab, Ravi, Beas and Sutlej). The new lands were barren and unoccupied. Huge boulders washed down by floods of countless centuries dotted the landscape. At most places, the boulders were embedded deep in the earth like a rock formation growing underground. The trees if they had ever grown there, must have been washed away periodically by the mighty sweep of waters in torrents of flood. Only thorny bushes grew there, like weeds, with roots so far under the earth as to require an extraordinary effort to remove them. By some mystery of nature, craters and ditches appeared everywhere. Yet, people of Sindhu filled the earth, planted their crops and built their homes. They erected barriers and bulwarks against flooding rivers, channelled the waters into reservoirs on low land and diked them in, for use when the floods stayed away. Thus slowly, they made the land responsive. More and more people from the Sind region began to move to the now inviting soil! Multitudes of majestic trees were soon clinging to the shores of rivers, tamed by human hand and the fields were full of barley, wheat and fruit—and the sound of music, song and laughter.

Again, the people of Sindhu moved into the forbidding desert region of Brahmadesa (between Sindhu and Saraswati rivers). Ashrams were established in the region. Each devotee who went to visit those ashrams was fired with the ambition of planting at least five trees there. The desert was a desert no more. There was an oasis as far as the eye could see.

Yes, Nandan was convinced, those were the achievements of his people—to go forward, occupy the land, make it green with vegetation and forests, for the prosperity of the clan.

Yet what did Bharat do?—Nandan asked himself. He spared the tribals who repeatedly and shamelessly attacked our clan. All their land should have been ours and all their people should have been our slaves. Instead, Bharat made them a part of us and even gave them equal representation in the Council, Assembly and guilds.

Nandan had once asked Bharat, 'I suppose you will be delighted if one of those tribals becomes Karkarta of our land?' And Bharat had replied, 'Certainly not', but had said, after a pause, smilingly, 'certainly not while I am Karkarta, but after I retire, why not!' That was Bharat's way—flippant, faulty and foolish—and Nandan decided never to ask such questions again.

'One land and One people of Sanathana, Sanathana Dharma and the Hindu.'

—(From the Act of Union for the Merger of Lower and Upper Sindhu—5078 BC)

'How can there be different levels of humanity!'

—(Question from Shreshtha of lower Sindhu, 5087 BC)

'...Fidelity to one's land and culture is consistent with compassion for others....All men are children of the Immortal... and it is treason to the majesty of the One who is Real to act otherwise....'

—(Attributed to Sage Yadodhra, 5070 BC)

'One land and One people of Sanathana, Sanathana Dharma and the Hindu.'

—(From the Act of Union for the Merger of Lower and Upper Sindhu—5078 BC)

'How can there be different levels of humanity?'

—(Question from Shreshtha of lower Sindhu, 5087 BC)

...Fidelity to one's land and culture is consistent with compassion for others ...All men are children of the Immortal... and it is treason to the majesty of the One who is Real to act otherwise....

—(Attributed to Sage Yadullah 5070 BC)

Together Again!

5088 to 5065 BC

Many years had passed since Karkarta Bharat first established contact with the people of lower Sindhu. Since then, the process of assimilation proceeded at a fast pace, with intermarriage, intermingling of people, travel, trade and the acceptance of many common customs and beliefs. If the sea-people were children of Sanathana, were not the upper Sindhu people also from that same common root? Did not both believe in karma, which insisted on the primacy of the ethical and identified God with justice and the rule of law? Did they not also both believe in the spiritual realization of moksha though they had different words to express the concept? Above all, did not both believe in the reality of the supreme universal spirit, even though they found it impossible to describe the nature of that spirit fully, but enough to accept the principle that God and the human soul are the eternal, inseparable rhythms of that same spirit? This community of ideas and sharing of the same faith even led to the entire region being called Sind.

Even so, while this process of assimilation between two peoples continued, some differences in their respective customs remained. Bharat, like other Hindu thinkers of his age, never believed in colourless uniformity and readily conceded that different points of view or customs of others were equally worthy of respect. God, he was certain, had not yet finished the revelation of His wisdom; and tradition was forever in the process of being evolved anew by progressive enrichment from fresh ideas and mingling with other peoples.

Many customs of the lower Sindhu impressed Bharat but the one that was nearest to his heart was the total absence of slavery. The old Shreshtha of lower Sindhu could not, at first, even understand the concept of slavery, 'How can there be different levels of humanity!'

Even before they began to understand each other's language fully, Bharat had initiated steps to achieve a union of the upper and lower Sindhu. An Assembly of sixty-six Shreshthas of lower Sindhu approved unanimously, the resolution on 'One land and One people of Sanathanah, Sanathana Dharma and Hindu.' The Parliament of the Hindus was reformed to include representatives of lower Sindhu. Clearly, in all resolutions of merger and unity there was a reference to the respect for different customs and traditions. The sea-people of lower Sindhu had not even asked for this safeguard and assumed it to be implicit in the union but Bharat was pursuing an agenda which was after his own heart and he moved a resolution in the Parliament which in its first part provided that:

> Neither the sea-people of lower Sindhu, nor anyone descended from them, wherever they may be, can ever be enslaved except on committing a deadly offence to be prescribed by the Assembly of sixty-six Shreshthas of lower Sindhu.

The last part of the Resolution went further to provide that: 'Except for such a slave so convicted, any other slave entering into lower Sindhu shall be deemed to be free, forthwith.'

Nandan—then a Council Member—saw the trap. The last part of the resolution made him see red. He asked, 'Does it mean that all that a slave has to do is to run away to lower Sindhu and he will gain instant freedom? Is this what the sea-people demand as the price of their union with us?'

Bharat did not reply. Yadodhra—attending as special invitee—intervened, 'You know very well, Nandanji, that the sea-people abhor the notion of two levels of humanity. To them, it is a negation of the divine law.'

Negation of divine law or not, Nandan found it intolerable that every slave could find sanctuary and freedom simply by crossing over to lower Sindhu. He could tolerate the first part of the resolution which guaranteed safeguards against slavery to the sea-people. After all they were Hindu. Of that he had no doubt. They were not of the barbarian tribes, out to raid and loot. He felt as one with them, linked by the pre-ancient tradition of Sanathana which he respected and honoured. Yes, that guarantee was due to them to achieve a union. But how could he accept the notion that a slave unconnected with the sea-people gained freedom merely by running away to their land!

Nandan unleashed his objections. Yet there was fear in his heart. He passionately wanted this union with the sea-people. His clan desired it. The spiritual and emotional link was undeniable. Besides, there was evidence of wealth in the land. How would the clan react if Nandan was held responsible for obstructing a union with the land where Mother Goddess Sindhu rested in the lap of the Sindhu sea!

In the past, Nandan had opposed every union—but those unions were with the tribals; and he had always advocated that the tribals be enslaved and their lands be occupied, to push farther the frontiers of the Hindu clan. But now, it was different. He recognized the emotional bond with the sea-people—they were his own long-lost people from a bygone age.

Bharat listened to Nandan with amusement and relief. He had simply put in the last part of the resolution to draw attack away from the first part. He was keen only on the first part—to give permanent guarantee against slavery to the sea-people. He was quite willing to throw out the second part which he regarded, all along, as a non-starter. But he saw the hesitation in Nandan's invective and understood its source. He kept the comedy alive and asked, 'I must ask you, Nandanji, what are we to do with this last part of the Resolution?'

Nandan, so appealed to, softly said, 'It should be amended.'

Thus Nandan left the door open and Bharat said haltingly, as if in distress, 'Then help me with it, Nandanji, please, though remember that it has also to be approved by the sixty-six Shreshthas of the sea-people. . . .'

Nandan's replacement of the second part of the Resolution ran thus:

'No slave shall enter the land of the sea-people. If any slave, however, enters their land with the permission or connivance of his owner, that slave shall thereupon be deemed to be free forthwith.'

Bharat accepted the suggestion, though he looked perturbed, as if his mind was weighed down by the fear that the sea-people might reject it.

At the Assembly of sixty-six Shreshthas, which Bharat attended, as honoured invitee, there was no discussion when the Act of Union and Resolutions was adopted, other than many joyful statements welcoming the merger.

It was much later—when Nandan got closer to the Shreshthas—that he learnt that the issue had never been raised by them, though they considered it gracious that Bharat voluntarily responded to their sentiments. Quickly, as if the question were not important, Nandan asked the Shreshthas who were dining with him, 'Was that Resolution about slaves so important to you in considering the proposal of the union?'

The question surprised them. A Shreshtha said, 'Surely the union was a foregone conclusion with or without the Resolution?'

Nandan asked, 'But if the Resolution did not exist, and we wanted to bring our slaves here to work for us, would you have objected?'

'We of course cannot contemplate owning a slave. Nor can we permit any of our people to be enslaved. That is our custom and you naturally honour it. By the same token, we were bound to honour your custom.'

'So?' Nandan asked, feeling that his question was unanswered.

'So, if you had brought your own slaves here to work exclusively for your people, maybe our people would have learnt to live with that situation, to respect your customs. But you, Nandanji, were wise. Karkarta Bharatji clearly mentioned that you worked day and night to so phrase the Resolution that our land would remain totally free from slavery and not a single slave would set foot here. Obviously you thought that if slaves enter here, and even if they work exclusively for you, somehow it would influence us to view slavery with favour. You wanted to save us from that temptation. Am I correct?'

Nandan nodded with a smile that lit neither his face nor his heart.

Clearly then it was Bharat who, on his own, imposed this burden on his people. Why? Obviously to keep lower Sindhu away from slavery. How could Bharat be so unpatriotic as to impose this burden on his own people, when none even asked for it!

Later when Nandan became Karkarta, he asked Yadodhra, 'Was Bharat not being unpatriotic in imposing this burden on his own people?'

'He may have thought,' Yadodhra replied, 'that fidelity to one's culture and land is consistent with consideration for others. Obviously, Bharat wanted to protect them from the influence of slavery.'

'Yet to impose the condition on his people unasked!' Nandan fumed. 'I have talked to the Shreshthas. None of them had asked for it.'

'Shreshthas may not have asked: no one may have,' Yadodhra said, 'but Bharat always heard voices of his own. Maybe he heard a voice that said all men are children of the Immortal, that it is treason to the majesty of the One who is Real to permit or promote slavery. How can we prevent a yogi from hearing the voice of his conscience?'

'Yogi!' Nandan exclaimed, surprised. 'Yadodhraji, Bharat became a yogi recently. I speak of the time when he was Karkarta and when the union with the sea-people was established.'

'I know Bharat became a yogi recently. But in my view, he was always a yogi.'

Nandan laughed at this play of words. 'I suppose next you will compare Bharat not to a yogi but to a god!'

'Is there really a difference between a yogi and a god!' Yadodhra meant it not as a question, but an answer.

Nandan gave up. Obviously, Yadodhra's mind was wilting from the ravages of old age which is why he was being absurd enough to compare Bharat with a yogi and a god!

Silently, Nandan recalled a story of how some barbarian tribes confer godhood on their chiefs. If the chief led an unblemished life, with honesty and honour, he did not need godhood. But if the chief was brutal, harsh and sinful, he compelled his tribe to go through the ritual of conferring godhood on him. The chief did this because he was certain that the gods were not accountable for their earthly sins, and could not, like humans, be consigned to hell; certainly, for the gods, there was no place other than heaven. Thus it was, concluded Nandan, that Yadodhra's feeble mind was trying to conceive Bharat as a god to free him from hell for all his lies and sins.

Nandan's hatred for Bharat grew as did his hatred for Sindhu Putra, whom he regarded as Bharat's illegitimate son, from an affair with Kanta.

'Honour the hermit by all means . . . but remember that interests of humanity cannot lie simply in deep passions of spiritualism. For a civilization to grow, it must first learn to harness the forces of bounteous nature; and with effort, labour and persistence, it must nurture them to grow to eliminate hunger and want and to achieve for its people material joys and rewards. . . . Then only can it be possible for humanity to think of a higher life, to be serene with the love of wisdom, to lead a life of meaningful self-denial, and to dream strange dreams and burst forth in joyous songs.'

—(From Karkarta Nandan's address to the Parliament of the Hindu—5063 BC)

'...The first condition, then, for thinking minds to blossom, is a settled society which provides material needs, wealth, security and absence of external and internal enemies. . . . Leisure shall then follow and only then is renunciation well earned. . . .'

—(From Karkarta Nandan's address to the Parliament of the Hindu—5065 BC)

My Land, My People!

5053 BC

Nandan, the twenty-first Karkarta of the land of Sindhu, sat idly under a great tree in the garden of his house. It was still early in spring and the young, fresh foliage, swaying with the wind, allowed the sunshine to dance on his sparsely covered body. There was a peaceful expression on his broad face as he gazed across the lovely park which dropped down in the far distance towards the Sindhu river.

This was Nandan's sixtieth birthday and also the first holiday he had permitted himself during his last fifteen years as Karkarta.

As he contemplated the Sindhu river and the silvery vista of the city on either side, he felt that he could look deep into the entire north and south. His mind went far beyond his field of vision to the foaming sea and distant mountains with their immense range and elevation; to mighty rivers with their abundant bounty; to lush forests and broad fields; to well-built cities with their wide avenues; and to the valleys and plains, teeming with life and activity.

The election of Karkarta was now a mere formality; and undoubtedly Nandan was Karkarta of his people for life. After which, he wanted to see his younger son, Sharat, elected to the office for he could think of no more worthy successor.

That Nandan's son, Sharat, was a man of outstanding ability was acknowledged by everyone. In Bharat's time, he was given charge of improving the drainage system of a village which was fast growing into a town. Not only did he do that job efficiently, but advocated that all future villages and towns must be planned, keeping in view the problem of drainage. He is credited to have said: 'An animal, an insect, a fish creates no waste and no hazard, but each human being creates a waste of 1,100 times his bodily weight and twice the hazard.'[1]

---

[1]The narrator who cites this statement does not clarify if the waste of 1,100 times an individual's body-weight relates to a period of a month, year or even lifetime. He simply goes on to explain how animals, insects and fish 'create no waste and no hazard, but only nutrients to feed and fertilize another life.'

Karkarta Bharat had been impressed with Sharat's ideas as the young man kept in view not only an efficient drainage system but the need for granaries, gardens, bath-houses and fountains—with a pleasing view, from every spot, of scenes of nature. Along the river, he planned no housing, for there he thought only of flowering plants and trees and walk-ways and promenades, where people may come to listen to the rush of the wind and torrents of the river, the music of birds and the rustling of trees, to remain whole of heart and fresh in spirit.

Sharat was promoted to Town Planner by Bharat, shortly before his retirement. In Dhrupatta's time, he became a leading member of the Architects' Guild. In Nandan's time, he rose to be its president, but, on his own merit, and not because of his father's help. Sharat had also taken on the more onerous duty of tending to Sindhu river.

The Sindhu was at times a challenging river. It rose and fell in response to the accumulation and melting of snows in the high mountains whence it came. Now and then, overfed by sudden storms, rainwater and streams, it would burst turbulently over its banks, imperiling villages on its shores. People had to wrestle with it often, diking it in times of flood and tapping its precious waters in times of drought to divert them for irrigation. Shortly after his decisive victory against the tribals, Bharat established a civic authority, under a Council Chief, for the planning and control of the river-system, whose task it was to have dams built and canals constructed to control the floods and also so that swamps were drained and distant fields irrigated.

On his own merit, Sharat virtually came to head this authority, though a Council Chief was nominally in charge. Nandan continued to resist appointing his son as Council Chief and liked to hear what some said of him—'To another man's son, Nandan would give what is due even well ahead of time, but to his own sons. . . .'

Let Sharat be one of the Council Chiefs now, resolved Nandan, and in a few years he will be senior enough to become the head of the Council; then I can retire and he can succeed as Karkarta.

The only obstacle that had to be overcome was the age-old prohibition that a Karkarta's children could not succeed to the office. 'Well one more hurdle to encounter—and overcome,' Nandan told himself.

Nandan looked up as a messenger approached and placed before him a bulky package. 'From Naudhyaksa (superintendent of ships) who sends his regards on this auspicious day,' the messenger said.

'From Naudhyaksa!' Nandan asked. 'From my elder son Vasistha, you mean! Now he is called Naudhyaksa, is he?'

'It was a title conferred on him by the combined decision of the sixty-five Shreshthas of the sea-people of lower Sindhu.'

'Sixty-five Shreshthas! I thought lower Sindhu had sixty-six Shreshthas.'

'We still have sixty-six Shreshthas,' the messenger responded with a smile, as if enjoying Nandan's joke. The sixty-sixth Shreshtha was, of course, as they both knew, the wife of Nandan's elder son Vasistha.

Vasistha himself had gone to lower Sindhu, several years earlier, as a junior member of a large group sent by Bharat under an experienced boat-builder, Naupati, to study the boat-building techniques of the sea-people. Most members of the group returned after a while, but Vasistha, along with his two seniors—Naupati and Pilava—remained. He and his two seniors were making phenomenal progress in building bigger, faster and more dependable boats, which could be used for longer voyages in rough weather.

Under Naupati's guidance, they had at last built a huge sea-craft with upraised bow and stern to overtake the fastest boats and yet withstand the turbulence of waves. Naupati was killed on an experimental voyage of this ship when an anchor-stone, tied loosely, struck him.[2]

After Naupati's death, Vasistha worked under Pilava, with 210 sea-people, to build sturdy sea-going vessels. Under Karkarta Bharat's orders, every assistance was sent to them. The land was scoured for suitable woods, leather, baskets, ropes. Special cutting, trimming and sanding implements were made for them.

The team-leader Pilava also died tragically. During a sudden storm, he went into the sea alone, at night, to study the behaviour of waves—their flow, force and depth in a storm-tossed sea. He never returned. It was the night the town was celebrating Vasistha's wedding.

After Pilava's death, Vasistha led ship-building activity and put his heart and soul into it. Nandan was unable to persuade Vasistha to return home, along with his wife, since all Vasistha was interested in was ship-building. He was entirely unmoved by his father's suggestions that one day he might become Council Chief or even Karkarta.

It was then that Nandan began to think of grooming his younger son Sharat for the office of Karkarta.

Vasistha, on the other hand, tried to interest his younger brother in ship-building. It was left to Nandan to interrupt the collaboration between the two brothers by reminding Sharat that his work back home remained unfinished. Nandan, however, promised to send every assistance to Vasistha.

Nandan kept his promise, and soon men and materials poured in to help Vasistha and the progress they achieved as a result of this was remarkable.

---

[2]It was in Naupati's honour that all ships from then on were called Nau. His name Naupati, literally, meant 'husband of Nau' (pati—husband). As a poet explains, his original name was Thukra, son of Bhoja, but he changed his name to Naupati on the death of his wife Nau, because she had, with her dying breath, called him that.

Vasistha had also discovered a suitable location for a dockyard, southeast of the mouth of Sindhu river, near the Sindhu sea (Arabian sea). It was a sheltered harbour into which two rivers flowed (Bhogava and Savarmati) though these rivers have since changed their course. In this ideal setting, both for sea and river navigation, he began construction of a massive dockyard of burnt brick reinforced by mortar, bitumen and other building materials. When it was finally completed, it measured 170 dhanus by 35 dhanus (approximately 1,000 feet by 200 feet). Through a gap in the eastern embankment, ships were intended to be sluiced into the dockyard at high tide through an inlet 40 feet wide. Where the inlet cut into the side of the dockyard, a low wall retained sufficient water within the docks at low tide to permit the ships to be moved. A loading platform about 1,100 feet long ran along the western embankment of the dockyard.

Nandan was impressed with the achievement but could not resist adding that had slaves been permitted, it would have finished even sooner. Vasistha's reply was simple: 'But there would have been no pride in our achievement then.'

Nandan silently regretted that his son had assimilated the philosophy of the sea-people so completely. Yet he loved his son; and he loved the sea-people too, for he realized that 'the links that bound them were far stronger, more ancient and abiding than those that divided them.'

Nandan broke free of his thoughts as his wife and grandchildren came out to see Vasistha's gift. His wife opened the large package, covered with layers of bark. The youngest child shouted with excitement, 'It is a toy!—For me!'

It was not a toy. It was a model, in miniature, of a sea-going vessel. Apparently Vasistha's team had nearly completed the vessel. Nandan examined the model wordlessly. He began counting the many tiny oars depicted on the model but soon gave up.

'It will have a hundred oars?' he asked the messenger.

'108,' the messenger responded.

'What is this on the sides?' Nandan asked, pointing to two minor projections on either side of the model.

'They are devices that will serve as the ship's stabilizer,' replied the messenger. 'They will help the ship withstand the battering of a storm-tossed sea.' He referred to them as 'Nau-manda' (possibly rudders, though the poet gives no clear explanation). He further explained that their present ships largely hugged the coast, afraid to go into the deep, except in fine weather, but the new vessels would be quite different.

'Naudhyaksa, your son,' the messenger added, 'also has a request.'

'Consider it granted,' Nandan promptly responded.

'He seeks your permission to name his ship after you and fly your flag.'

Nandan felt thrilled that his son should wish to honour him so. But said, 'Thank my son—your Naudhyaksa—and tell him that my time for such an honour, if it is ever to come, has not yet arrived. But if he wants my suggestion, let the ship be named after Pilava, his senior, who first dreamt of such a ship and who died in the effort to discover what angry waves can do to our ships.' And so, the ship when it was ready bore the name of Pilava.

The child looked sadly at the projections on the ship model which he had thought were wings. 'Why did Uncle put in Nau-manda?'

'Did you not hear? To stabilize the ship.' Nandan replied.

'He should have put wings instead. The ship could fly then.'

'Ships don't fly.'

'They do! Ma tells me stories of flying ships in which gods and goddesses travel. I saw a vimana (flying chariot) in a drama.'

'Yes, ships and chariots fly in stories and dramas but in real life, the flying ships are yet to arrive.'

'When?'

'When little ones like you grow up, when they dare a dream, when they work to realize it; then ships and chariots shall fly.'

'They will?'

'Certainly they will,' replied Nandan. 'With persistence of effort and labour, I know of no dream that can remain unfulfilled.'

His grandson still had questions—'Will flying ships fly to the moon?'

'In time, why not!' Nandan smiled. 'Maybe beyond to the planets, stars, and galaxies unseen and unknown.'

'Are there people living on the stars and planets?'

'Maybe,' Nandan replied wondering, like all grandparents, why children always asked unanswerable questions.

But it seemed that the child knew the answer and was merely testing the limits of his grandfather's knowledge. Jubilantly, he said, 'Ma says that Sage Yadodhra said that people live in planets.'

'If your mother told you that why must you ask me?' Nandan asked.

'She said you would know better.'

Nandan smiled. Indeed he did know better—not if there was life on the planets, but what Yadodhra had said. The sage had said:

'The possibility of life on the planets remains. How can we have the arrogance to believe that life exists nowhere except on the land and waters we inhabit! But if there is no life on some planets now, the chances are that there was life there in the past, which is now extinct because of misuse of the planet and violation of God's laws; and God waits with His immeasurable patience to renew and refresh life there, perhaps in a form and shape altogether different. Here too on this earth—were we to abuse God's laws—it is not as if the earth would vanish; no; only we would disappear. . . .

'. . .And then there are planets and stars still in the making, as the miracle of evolution continues, endlessly; what is building is forever building, unstopped and unstoppable; and surely there shall be life in those planets and stars in the future. . . .'

Interpretations of the sage's pronouncement were many. The idea of life on the planets was charming. But Nandan was interested in this world, in this life; and the question of life on the planets did not worry him at all. There was one certainty he had. It was that life existed all over, on earth itself—beyond the snow-peaks of the Himalayas, beyond the gigantic rivers and beyond the vast sea surging in lower Sindhu.

Affectionately, he looked at the model of the ship of 108 sails sent by his son. The sea he realized was vast but, he thought, it must end somewhere—and then their ships would lead them to discover the lands beyond.

Silently, he resolved to halt all the other public works that could wait, in order to send unlimited materials and men to assist the ship-building projects of the sea-people in lower Sindhu.

Let those ships be a reality in my lifetime, Nandan prayed, and let me be the one to guide my people to lands beyond—and to glory.

Two years after Nandan had seen the ship-model, the first major ship was ready to sail in Sindhu sea. It met with disaster on its maiden voyage. Vasistha and the rest of the crew went down with it.

Although Nandan was devastated by this, he redoubled his efforts to help with the ship-building project.

Six years later, Nandan's assistance was slowly being rewarded. Ships from Sindhu sea reached the deserted coastlines of Persia and the Gulf.

But these six years were eventful not only in sea-exploration and building better ships. Nandan sent out teams in all directions to discover and occupy distant lands. He even encouraged his people to go and settle in those new territories. He was convinced, like Rishi Skanda Dasa—though their aims and ends were different—that lands left unoccupied would attract demons.

What Nandan really longed for was to blaze new trails, to extend and expand Hindu Varsha (the land of Hindu).

It was not only in the exploration and discovery of new lands that the clan advanced. There were other impressive gains.

The efforts of Muni Manu, who was working on evolving a full-fledged written language, had succeeded even before Bharat retired as Karkarta. Although Muni Manu had taken on this task some 50 years earlier, he diverted to a number of other fields, notably astronomy and mathematics, including equations for minute divisions of time, starting with heartbeats, and later extended to bodies falling to the ground with a co-relationship of weight, speed and distance. Not all this was entirely theoretical and apart from other applications, even came to be used to compare competitive performance in sports and races—of men, animals, carts and chariots. Later, Yadodhra joined Muni Manu and both of them worked on the age of ancient trees, earth, mountains, rivers and on the concepts of time and space.

Finally Muni Manu had completed the alphabet and the signs and symbols to go with it, in order to clarify sound, intonation, emphasis, sex, number and other distinctions. Bharat, Nandan and the others were very impressed when they first saw a presentation of the written language. Nandan remarked, 'It has the precision of mathematics and the expanse of a story-teller.' Along with 'words to be seen' also came advice about materials on which, and tools with which, they could be written, sculpted, etched or painted—and how the bark and leaf be treated, depending on whether the written word was intended 'for the time being,' or was a record for 'generations waiting to be born.'

Everyone had watched the first presentation of the written language with fascination but with a touch of sadness, for it was conducted by Muni Manu's granddaughter. Muni Manu had turned blind when he completed the last sign and symbol.

A poet explains that Muni was working on 'borrowed sight', and his story is that Muni began losing his eyesight in the midst of his work and would have turned totally blind, leaving it unfinished, but for the 'prayers of his granddaughter Kriti who asked the gods to take away her sight and give it to Muni Manu so that his life-work be completed', and the poet adds that Kriti, thereupon, lost her eyesight, and when Muni Manu completed his work, her eyesight was restored, while Muni Manu lost his. Another poet disagrees. He says that Muni Manu's granddaughter never lost her eyesight but simply had pain in her eyes; and it was sheer coincidence that the pain disappeared when her grandfather lost his own eyesight. This poet gives credit for the cure of her temporary eye infection not to a miracle, but to treatment by Sage Dhanawantar and his wife Dhanawantari, and simply attributes the loss of Muni's sight to nature, over-exertion and his advanced age.

The written language did not become popular overnight. It spread slowly. It took great effort on Bharat's part to overcome the opposition of the Teacher's Guild and include it as a compulsory subject in schools. Slowly, however, it began to gain ground as more and more people saw its advantage. Poets had the assurance that their songs would remain as they recited them, without being mutilated by the failing memory of their listeners; lovers could send messages and not have them shouted by irreverent messengers, to their sweethearts; and for everyday trade, buying and selling on credit, moneylending and banking, everyone recognized the superiority of the written word.

Nandan had taken pains to learn the written language. As Council Member under Bharat, and as Council-head under Dhrupatta, he supported every move to encourage the language. He agreed that 'the written word is far above any human invention and shall represent the very essence of our sanskriti (culture and civilization) to unite people.'

Was it not really so? As it is, spoken languages of various peoples in the Sapta Sindhu region differed in many ways. Yet with the written language, a synthesis began to emerge, where the words used by others came to be accepted and adopted as synonyms and alternative words to express the same thought, rather than rejected. The written words were thus influencing the spoken language and the emerging common language became richer, more expressive and highly versatile.

And certainly, the synthesis brought people nearer to each other, emotionally and culturally.

There were, of course, some who complained that when alien words were accepted and absorbed into a language, its purity was lost. But a poet retorted, 'Only the unborn and the dead are pure; so is it with humans and so is it with the language.'

Nandan supported the written language from public funds in schools and outside. He kept insisting that the written word would bind culture and civilization of the land of Hindu.[3]

Nandan also gave every assitance to Sage Dhanawantar who, along with his wife Dhanawantari, had developed a comprehensive system of medicine. Certainly, here, Nandan was taking a risk with his popularity, as the sage was intensely disliked by many purohits and priests.

The sage had been forced into a running battle with the purohits. He had been seeking dead bodies for dissection to study and teach anatomy, and even to discover the cause of death, so as to prevent the same disease from striking others. But the taboo on interference with dead bodies was widespread and the purohits carried out a furious tirade against Dhanawantar and his disciples. The body, the purohits argued, served as the temple of the soul and had to be respected even after death. Everyone was entitled to prayers and cremation; and dissection of the dead, the purohits held, was an abomination. A live slave could be bought but not a dead one, for even a slave was entitled to respect at death.

No one knew for certain if Sage Dhanawantar had actually dissected a human body. Some asked him but his reply was, 'If a physician never betrays a patient's secret, is he not to guard his own secret!' A case which caused some furore arose when hermit Dhrona declared that his body be given, after death, to the sage for dissection.

---

[3]A minor controversy later arose over the origin of the words sanskrit and sanskriti. Some said that these two words were derived from the names of Muni Manu's two granddaughters—Sansi and Kriti. Others feel that possibly the word sanskriti itself may have formed the basis for naming the two granddaughters.

Dhrona became a hermit at the age of twenty-eight. He was healthy and strong and expected to outlive Sage Dhanawantar. No one therefore took his declaration seriously. But he died after a brief illness at the age of forty-four. Purohits approached Karkarta Nandan to declare that such a 'will' was unlawful. 'Ashes to ashes, let it be, and neither desecrate nor abominate what was once a dwelling of the gods'—the purohits argued. Fortunately for Nandan, the question of disposing Dhrona's body ceased to be a live issue; Dhrona's family quickly came forward to cremate the body, with the assistance of a number of purohits, who despite their deep concern that custom be preserved, were not abashed enough to demand a large fee for carrying out the custom.

However, many were convinced, from the drawings and descriptions of Sage Dhanawantar, that such intimate knowledge of the functioning of the body is impossible without dissection. How else could he have drawn such precise illustrations of internal organs!

Sage Dhanawantar described the six 'winds' which cause bodily functions—udana, from the throat, causing speech; prana, in the heart, for breathing; somana, fanning a fire in the stomach to separate digestible food; vyana, causing blood-movement to and from the heart; ojas, a diffused wind throughout the body producing energy for bodily functions; and apana, semen for sex and procreation.

The sage explained how food is digested and how blood, bone, marrow and semen are formed. He listed functions of the spinal cord; and located eighteen centres in the brain which, he thought, were the seats of learning, memory, the nervous system, psychic energy and other impulses.

Many of Sage Dhanawantar's views on the interrelation of the brain and heart were, later, criticized. For instance, the sage speculated that there could be another diffused 'wind'—circling near the heart. It was the wind of the 'inner voice' of the heart, which sought to measure, weigh and assess all that the brain wanted to do—and sometimes it encouraged or even opposed what the brain contemplated, though it was always the brain who was the commander and could reject or accept what that 'wind' of the silent voice whispered.

Many had difficulty in accepting the sage's views on the adverse effect to the health of an individual as the result of the brain rejecting the advice of the 'inner voice' of the heart.

Even the sage's wife Dhanawantari was criticized for her theories.

She conceived three main stages of the functioning of the human brain. In its first stage, the brain receives and interprets outside signals (such as by eyesight, sounds, the sensation of touch or smell). In the second stage, processing takes place to analyse those signals and to evolve a plan of action; and the third stage is the brain-output, to issue commands to the body for movement, speech, or any other action or inaction.

No one questioned these three stages. But the sage's wife went further afield to speculate on two other organisms of the brain which influenced these three stages. The first organism, she described, as 'the stream of the conscious', which holds 'the power to reason, along with a memory of past experience, words heard and taught, a sensation of comfort or pain... or remembrance of the sound of music of long ago.... or a place of scenic beauty that once enchanted us....' The second organism was 'the stream of the unconscious', serving as the source of 'inspiration, insight and originality, which comes spontaneously in a flash to blend with conscious thought....'

She further speculated that 'the stream of the unconscious' had another 'current' too, which arose before we were born and remained alive after we died and that much of its content came from our past series of lives and would go forward to our next series of lives, 'enriched or seasoned by the experience of our sojourn in the present life.' This hidden, undying 'current', according to her, could be tapped by the wise for its knowledge of the 'infinite unknown' and 'the memory of what happened before we were born and a preconception of what may happen after we die.'

The complaint of critics was that the sage and his wife often forgot the boundary-line between scientific study and philosophy. But the sage always held that one leads to the other.

The fact however is that even in their errors, the sage and his wife advanced medical knowledge.

Much has also been said about the code established by Sage Dhanawantar for his disciples. To summarize, his instructions were:

'The health of your patients and their recovery is of paramount importance, even at the cost of your own health.... You do not choose your patients. Their pain and agony calls to you. Do not pass it by...be they master or slave, rich or poor, man or animal' (possibly, veterinary medicine as a separate field had not yet taken root).

'By all means, pray for and with your patients, if you wish.... And surely, if your prayers have no effect on your patients, they are at least good for your mental health and to guard your soul.'

Little needs to be said about the material progress made by the people of Sindhu in that period. The *Rig Veda* and particularly the findings of the Indus Valley clearly demonstrate that Sindhu artisans and merchants enjoyed an extensive trade of goods ranging from cosmetics and jewellery to gambler's dice, wine-cups and children's rattles. The artisans worked in clay, bronze, copper, gold, silver, precious and semi-precious stones. Clearly, they had attained real artistry and designed much that was not only for utility but also for beauty.

The Indus Valley finds and also the poetry that survives cast a revealing glow on the people who made and used them. Their world and their lives had apparently a lighter side—happy, laughing children playing with toy horses, elephants and rams, with mountings for wheels and holes for drawstrings, and adults taking pleasure in statues and objects imbued with kindly grace.

Even more significant are the excavations of beautifully planned cities, brick-walled public-baths, granaries, assembly-halls, schools, wide streets, shopping areas and harbour-works, built long centuries before the Aryans.

playing with toy horses, elephants and rams, with mountings for wheels and holes for drawstrings, and adults taking pleasure in statues and objects imbued with kindly grace.

Even more significant are the excavations of beautifully planned cities, brick-walled public-baths, granaries, assembly-halls, schools, wide streets, shopping areas and harbour-works, built long centuries before the Aryans...

'Fear them the most, who treat their conquered with gentleness, and fear them even more when they offer gifts.'

—(Chief Jalta, 5050 BC)

'But then as a Hindu, how could he believe in hell except on this earth itself! Hell! Does it not presuppose a place where God is not, or that there is a being, uncreated by merciful God, and so absolutely evil as to deserve total, everlasting punishment?'

—(From a song dismissing the rumour of suicide by a team leader, 5050 BC).

To Far Frontiers

5051 BC

Nandan's instructions to his contingents, which he sent out to discover new lands, were to avoid quarrels and not to occupy lands clearly occupied by the tribals. Initially, at least, he preferred peaceful occupation. But disputes often did arise over demand for passage. Sometimes, tribals themselves began hostilities as they wanted no outsiders nearby. Many tribal groups also moved seasonally from place to place, over a vast terrain, which they regarded entirely as their own. Several 'mistakes' therefore arose—some by accident, though many by design. But Nandan was not too worried about injustices to little men. He was more concerned about his vision of the future.

It was always the tribals who suffered whenever hostilities resulted. Nandan's teams were well-armed and ably led. The spoils of victory often included a new harvest of slaves. The Tribal Chief, however, was never displaced; his authority over his people was left intact; he was expected to keep peace and serve as a source to supply future slaves. The tribals had their own slaves, gained from their continuous warfare; they found these new-comers reasonable in demanding not too many slaves, and never their goods and women.

The tribal Chiefs were given gifts and honoured with invitations to visit the Sapta Sindhu region. The visiting Chiefs were dazzled by the region's wealth and brilliance. What also amazed them was the condition of the slaves. They saw comfortable living quarters for the slaves, with good though simple food, along with leisure time for amusements, and even a cup of wine on festive occasions. A Chief remarked, 'Your slaves live better than all our free people do!'

A visiting Chief told a Chief named Jalta about how mildly the slaves were treated in Sapta-Sindhu. Jalta was unimpressed and said, 'Fear them the most, who treat their conquered with gentleness. . . .'

Actually, Jalta was Chief only in name and prestige. He had distributed his lands among his three sons and passed his time in sport and hunting, along with a number of friends.

Later, one of Nandan's expeditions reached the hunting grounds which Chief Jalta regarded as his own. Beyond lay the lands of the three Chiefs who were his sons. He refused to let the expedition pass. With his eighty men and women, he stood to oppose the larger contigent. He was soon unhorsed and overpowered. They demanded three slaves from him, for his foolishness in denying them passage and opposing them with arms which involved minor injuries to two of them.

'We have no slaves,' Jalta responded.

'Then let three of your free men be our slaves.'

'Take me. I am equal to three of them,' said Jalta.

'No, you are the Chief. You cannot be touched.'

Jalta argued. No, he was told. Give us three slaves on your own; or we imprison all and occupy the land. He argued no more.

Jalta went to his group and spoke to them. Three of his men came forward. He led them to be enslaved. Courteously, the team leader thanked him and tried to give him the usual gifts. That was the practice and Nandan had insisted on it—to give lavish gifts, invest in goodwill, leave no enemies behind and keep the myth alive that slaves were offered freely in exchange for gifts.

Jalta asked, 'Am I free?'

'Yes, of course,' he was told; and Jalta said, 'Then I am free to accept or reject your gifts.' He turned away, leaving the gifts behind.

The team leader camped there for the night. Sentries were cautioned to watch lest 'this hot-headed Jalta resorts to some other foolishness.'

The sentries watched Jalta's people chanting. Only Jalta was in a ceremonial robe. He was collecting firewood in three piles. Slowly, Jalta lit three fires. Flames erupted. The chanting became louder. The sentries woke up the camp. They watched. The team-leader wondered. What were the fires for. Maybe some strange tribal ceremony!

Suddenly, the chanting stopped. Was it a prelude to a sudden attack? It was not.

In the glow of the fire, they saw Jalta walk to the first fire, his hands raised high. He did not stop. He went into the fire. If he cried out in agony, none heard him. With his robe and hair visibly burning, he leapt from the first fire into the second; and thence with almost his entire body in flames, he leapt to the third fire. There he collapsed. Slowly, the fire consumed him.

'Why?' The team leader asked aghast. The tribal priest later enlightened him, 'For his three sins in leading his three men to slavery. He chose to burn in three fires here, rather than in hell everlasting.'

'But the sin was not his! We took the slaves.' The team leader argued.

'Then you too will burn, everlasting, in the three fires of hell,' the tribal priest replied firmly.

The team leader released the three slaves. He also decided to avoid the hunting grounds of the dead Chief and took a different route.

Nobody knows whether it was compassion, remorse or superstition that led him to this. What is known, however, is that shortly thereafter, he resigned and died in his home-town, when his cottage caught fire, in the dead of night. Someone said that he had set fire himself. But a poet calls this 'pure speculation' and adds, 'the mere fact that he had given away all his worldly goods and had left the stable door open and horses untied, enabling them to bolt away with the onset of fire, was no proof that the man intended to take his own life.'

Nandan's heart swelled with pride at the new discoveries. The wealth and land of the clan grew. But, suddenly, deep in the eastern territories, resistance broke out and his advancing expeditions were halted and harassed with casualties. But Nandan was less worried about those external enemies. It was the internal enemies that concerned him and, among them, he regarded none more formidable than Sindhu Putra.

'Will the fish then walk on land?
Will men eat water and sand?
Will the sky then fall on ground?
Will rivers flow faster than sound?
Will the earth ascend high upwards?
Will time fly its arrow backwards,
To end before it all began?
That promise of God and man!

—(From the song 'Will Discoverers be Colonizers?'—5049 BC)

'Surely, we went to seek God's earth, not to battle with its inhabitants!'

—(From the 'Song of Complaint' of an explorer in the eastern region—5049 BC)

'Will the fish then walk on land?
Will men eat water and sand?
Will the sky then fall on ground?
Will rivers flow faster than sound?
Will the earth ascend high upwards?
Will time fly its arrow backwards,
To end before it all began?
That promise of God and man!

—(From the song 'Will Discoverers be Colonizers?'—5049 BC)

'Surely, we went to seek God's earth, not to battle with its inhabitants'.

—(From the 'Song of Complaint' of an explorer in the eastern region—5049 BC)

The Tribes Strike Back

5049 BC

Onslaughts began against Nandan's contigents in the eastern territory. The tribals struck at night, springing from trees, bushes, boulders and rocks. If at all they came into view during the day, it was to hit and run, after an ambush. As time went by, they grew bolder.

It was all so senseless, thought Nandan. He had no wish to occupy by force any territory that belonged to another. His strategy simply was to occupy as much vacant and uncontested land as possible, in the first round; and leave, for the present at least, isolated pockets which were in tribal occupation. No wonder his contingents had penetrated so far, deep into the eastern region.

Suddenly, without warning, these surprise attacks were followed by the appearance of an army of a strange eastern tribe. It came far from its own territory, to harass and molest Nandan's teams. They stole nothing, looted nothing—and if they caught any of Nandan's men, they killed there and then, swiftly, without cruelty, but also without mercy. They spared animals and left them there, unharmed.

Why were these ferocious men and women of this eastern tribe willing to kill and be killed, needlessly, far from their own territory which none threatened? A poet remarks, 'What else, but the warning in their ancestral tribal memory against a fast-approaching alien!'

Many tribals were caught by Nandan's men. Strangely, they spoke no language. They could not formulate a single word. Sometimes, they would yell when they attacked, or cry triumphantly when they retreated after inflicting losses. But mostly, they came silently, killed silently and left silently. When they were captured and wounded, tears came to their eyes freely and a cry from their throat, but never a word would they utter from their lips.

Even Sage Dhanawantar could not explain how, in the evolutionary process, the vocal chords of everyone in this tribe had been suppressed. However the sage, like the others, never regarded evolution as a spent force but one that was still working, with many more changes in store.

Undoubtedly, among themselves, they understood each other perfectly with sign-language and signals. How else could they organize such well-coordinated attacks, manoeuvres, ambushes and withdrawals!

It was in captivity that their behaviour was the strangest. They would not move and had to be dragged or tied. They would not eat or drink while their hands were tied and even chose to starve. But it was never feasible to take off all their chains, for then they felt that it was their duty to flee, though they could plainly see spears trained on them. Yet the attempt to flee was often made, resulting sometimes in serious injury or even the loss of life of the captive.

Captors were not unduly harsh with them but even then, many died on the way, for it seems that the will to live left them during captivity. Those that survived proved to be unwilling and unsatisfactory slaves, impossible to train, even for the simplest tasks.

They were mute but had sharp ears and eyesight. Yet they would react neither to gestures nor shouts. When provoked, they would assault their master but never his wife, child or slave. They could not be tamed or moulded. Among the least of their offences was tearing off their clothes and walking naked, as they wanted to wear only their animal skins, and not the woven cloth, which somehow they regarded as a badge of slavery.

As slaves, they were an embarrassment; their resistance evoked sympathy in many quarters, and certainly, they were a terrible example to other, docile slaves. Nandan ordered that no slaves should ever be brought to Sindhu from that detestable eastern tribe.

A vast number of the tribals died in skirmishes with Nandan's forces. They wore no armour and were an easy target if ever found in the open. They had long wooden poles with pointed ends, wooden spears and short-range arrows, but no shields. They mostly attacked on foot. No wonder many of them perished. But even so, they kept coming. It was easier to kill than to capture them, for they never surrendered and had to be overpowered by force. Even when swords and arrows flew thick and fast against them and they were cornered on all sides with nowhere to run, they fought on, ready to face death rather than capture.

Nandan had no wish to involve his contingents in long, drawn-out engagements. He ordered his forces to halt and regroup. The eastern tribes became even bolder. Their onslaught increased.

Many other tribes witnessed the discomfiture of Nandan's contingents. Somehow, even faraway tribes became aware of it.

The three Chiefs who were Chief Jalta's sons came with their warriors. Their land was by-passed by Nandan's men when Chief Jalta was consumed by fire. There was no danger to them. Yet they marched through treacherous routes to reach within striking distance. There they waited till the eastern tribes attacked Nandan's forces; and then they rushed, yelling like a rabble, without an attempt to maintain formation, hoping to make short work of the enemy. But Nandan's troops struck back, after losing many in initial surprise; and the tribesmen who were not instantly killed or wounded, withdrew in disorder. Among those captured by Nandan's men was the youngest Chief—the fifteen-year-old son of Chief Jalta, known as Jalta the Fourth. His two elder brothers who escaped unhurt were known as Jalta the Second and Jalta the Third.

Again, rumours spread far and near, of this battle. But then, a rumour has many voices; and the story depends on who tells it and who hears it. Some spoke of tribal heroism and of total death in Nandan's camp. Others told a truer tale. But the fact that emerged was that Nandan's troops were not invulnerable. Their losses were heavy.

Withdrawal, Nandan knew, meant loss of face and renewed attacks, now that the aura of invulnerability had vanished. Further advance was also fraught with danger, with sustained campaigns. It was not always easy for Nandan to control all flow of information and already reports were reaching Sindhu from returning, wounded veterans, of casualties in the eastern region. 'Surely, we went to discover God's earth and not to battle with its inhabitants!'—complained some.

Nandan decided that his troops should neither march forward nor return. Instead, a ring of forts should be established throughout the eastern region, where, safe from attack, his contingents would control the area around. Construction of forts began in earnest.

A number of people reminded Nandan of the Hindu Parliament's decision, not long ago, that exploration and discovery of lands was for a 'moral and spiritual bond with the earth, never to dispossess the land of another or to hold anyone in captivity'; and that no slave could be acquired in 'discovered lands, except for the purpose of setting him free.' But theirs was a voice in the wilderness.

There was hardly anyone in the Parliament to question Nandan. He had seen to it that it was filled with those who supported his policies; his control over expeditions sent out to explore new lands was tight; and few had access to much of the information. Many of those who knew chose to remain silent and looked away to brood on different matters—their own future, their privileges and their own well-being. Their covetousness waxed greater. Their minds and conscience darkened.

'Let me recount all the strands
Let truth worry where it stands.'

'...Will dreams of the Divine ever hover in the breasts of girls ...? Can gods be tempted by the lust and flesh of humans! But why not!....Gods are invented by humans—Can they not then have human imperfections!'

—(From 'Songs of Sindhu Putra', by a later poet—around 4900 BC)

A God on the Move!

5054 BC

The years passed pleasantly for Sindhu Putra at Muni's Rocks. There was laughter, mirth and games with Muni and Roopa's children.

As teachers, Muni and Roopa were not demanding. Their training came not like an avalanche but gently, through stories and tales, verse and song. They sought to implant in children the ideas of right and wrong, truth and virtue and belief in the One Supreme; but more so, they wished to invest in children a thirst for knowledge, a philosophical outlook, a compassionate heart and a mind that inquires and questions. The serene environment of the Rocks encouraged peace and quiet contemplation as Muni guided them through yoga and meditation.

Sindhu Putra was to remain at Muni's Rocks till his eleventh birthday. But he was not keen to leave. Nor did Muni and Roopa wish to part with him. Bharatjogi said with a sigh, 'If it is his wish and yours, so be it, for another year.' This went on till his fifteenth birthday.

'This time, Sindhu Putra should leave,' Muni told Roopa.

'He loves to be with us. I am sure Bharatjogi would agree.'

'Perhaps. But now, he must leave,' was Muni's response.

'Why?' Roopa asked, puzzled at Muni's firmness.

'Because I have seen hunger in his eyes,' Muni replied.

'Hunger! Hunger for what?' Roopa asked, surprised.

'For your daughters,' Muni responded.

Roopa smiled. Happily, she asked, 'Which one?'

'Both,' Muni replied evenly.

'Both!' she said, in surprise. Muni nodded. Roopa's smile deepened, 'He is young. They are young. One day, he can marry one of them.'

'Meanwhile, he should go,' Muni countered. But Roopa objected, 'He belongs to us. If he leaves, he may not come back.'

'If he belongs to us, he will be back. Those that do not come back, be sure, they never belonged to us in the first instance.'

'God will guide his footsteps,' Roopa said as Sindhu Putra left but Muni rejoined, 'God guides no man's footsteps. That will and choice belong to man.'

A feeling of loneliness grew upon Sindhu Putra as he left to live in Gatha's village. He had a cottage in the temple compound. He was surrounded by adoring crowds. Why then this feeling of isolation and fear that he had to face the world as a stranger! At times, a vision of the two beautiful girls at the Rocks rose before him, but when it disappeared, his spirit was again overwhelmed with sadness.

The crowds around him sought his blessing. Wordlessly, he would give it, merely by raising his hand. Often, he did not know how to reply to a question but simply smiled with tenderness, as if that were response enough. It was. But if the questions persisted, he asked them to look into their hearts to find the answer and take the path of *Sat Chit Ananda* (follow your bliss). Clearly, he felt, Muni was right when he said—each man answers his own question. . . . Each man must come to his own decision. . . . Decisive issues lie in the heart where battles between right and wrong are fought hourly and daily until man is fully aware of his purpose in life and the direction he has to take.

Did this thought lie in Sindhu Putra's innermost consciousness?— Or was he simply repeating parrotlike what he had heard from Muni? When the questions grew, he went into a prolonged silence. Was it because he could not answer or was it that he was seeking answers from within?

The crowds around him grew. They came swarming from far and near and, in his presence, they seemed to find a solace and calmness of spirit. Many came with a cry of pain from some nameless torment. Somehow, their panic disappeared, replaced by calm strength. 'They heal themselves,' Sindhu Putra simply replied, when many chose to praise him for his healing presence. 'How? By what miracle?'—they asked. 'By the miracle of their own faith'—was his reply.

He preached no sermon, chanted no prayers, spread no gospel, established no idols, invented no new faith and everyone—even professional preachers—felt comforted, for if he supported none, he also opposed none. If some preachers muttered that 'Sindhu Putra says nothing because he has nothing to say,' they were met with sufficient contempt from people to silence them. Sindhu Putra heard of their remarks. 'They are right,' he said. The crowd bowed in reverence. 'What humility!' they said.

It never occurred to Sindhu Putra that he had in him a spark of divinity—except that spark which is in every human being. He was no god, he knew, though he also knew that the more he said so, the more it was attributed to his humility. 'How modest he is!' many had said in wonder. A preacher wanted to retort, 'Oh, he has much to be modest about!'—but kept silent lest people turn against him.

Yet in the core of Sindhu Putra's heart, there was a depression that could find no relief. Many saw the sadness reflected in his eyes. But it surprised no one and they said—'Those gentle eyes reflect the sorrow of us all!'

A later singer, trying to explain Sindhu Putra's dilemma says:

> *'... Godhood was thrust on him. ... Yet he sought only human affection...*
>
> *... He sought to live by the divine principle, but not be divine himself. ...*
>
> *.... His words!—were they from his heart—from deep within?...*
>
> *.... His words! But they were strange to him! Who planted them?...*
>
> *.... Whose part am I playing? he asked—Why do I say what I say!..*
>
> *.... And he longed to be true to himself...and chose silence*
>
> *.... But silence leads to a bigger lie...*
>
> *.... For they invested his silence with the message of the divine....*
>
> *.... And he asked—why am I unable to utter the words in my heart?*
>
> *.... Why do I not advance beyond the bonds of this spurious image?...*

*

Sindhu Putra moved from Gatha's village to Bharatjogi's Island of Silence, next door. As it is, Bharatjogi was regarded as his father, though not in the biological sense. Sindhu Putra himself wanted to believe that Bharatjogi was his father. He longed to belong. Also, he had an abiding affection for the old man.

The Island of Silence had ceased to be silent. The secret was a secret no more, that the hermit there was none other than the great Karkarta who had retired before his time. Many came to visit him, out of affection and curiosity. It was left to Gatha to restore order and lay down the law—who shall visit, and when, and even to erect barriers beyond which none could proceed and disturb the hermit. But even so, there were many visitors. Bharat's wife, Mataji, when she heard the reports, said: 'The hermit is a hermit no more. The lifeless custom of not visiting a hermit is deader than before.'

The singer who was once blind escorted Mataji to visit Bharatjogi. Thereafter she visited the island, often.

Now that Sindhu Putra stayed at the island, Gatha became even more stern with visitors. He was able to enforce his restrictions only because Sindhu Putra agreed to visit the village temple every day.

Sindhu Putra loved Bharatjogi. But rarely understood him. But in the poet's words, 'Who says to love is to understand! For if that were so, no father would love his son and no son, his father—and when did one generation ever understand another?'

Bharatjogi spoke out against slavery. How could Sindhu Putra understand—he who had never seen a slave! He knew though that Gatha had been a slave, once. 'Were you treated badly?' Sindhu Putra asked.

'Oh no! Never!' Gatha replied, aghast that anyone should think that he could have been treated shabbily in Karkarta Bharat's household and added, 'It is given to few, the love that I received.'

Also, how could he grasp Bharatjogi's concept of unity! His world moved—from Gatha's village to the Island of Silence and thence to Muni's Rocks. Were they not all united in that tiny world of his?

Bharat spoke to him of the land of the Hindu—of the majestic mountains of Himalaya and of the images and idols of the gods Rudra and Brahma that the Hindu explorers found there. He spoke of the source of Sindhu river at Tibata and of the mighty Sindhu sea which he himself discovered. He told him of the land of Sanathana; of rivers, forests and habitations beyond. 'We were all together, once before,' he said.

Even Bharat realized, as he spoke on, that such a vast panaroma was far beyond the comprehension of the fifteen-year-old boy before him. Yet his urge to speak of it to this youngster was boundless; and he wondered: Why am I pouring my heart out to this child?—to what end!—to what consequence!—what will he understand?

But Bharat was wrong in assuming that he had failed to excite the youth's imagination. It was however not the concept of unity, as such, that led the youth's mind to distant lands. Instead there was a simpler question in his heart: where did my mother come from? He longed to know the answer.

He stood with Bharat at the spot where his mother's boat was found—and lost. Bharat showed him where he had scattered white flowers for his mother. But his question—where did she come from, where was she going, and why—remained unanswered. Perhaps someday, he thought, I shall travel far and my feet shall touch the land she walked on. He knew he could hope for no more.

The concept of unity apart, the boy did not even comprehend the shape, size and dimensions of Bharatjogi's perception of the land of Hindu. He understood that on one side stood lofty mountains and on the other, a deep ocean, while in between the land went on and on, in all directions. He had never seen mountains nor the sea and the rough lines which Bharat drew to indicate the land mass were hardly illuminating. With his well-ordered mind, matured from Muni's training, Sindhu Putra wondered, 'Surely, someone should attempt to make a chart!'

'Someone has!' Bharat triumphantly said. He spoke at length about Ekantra, who was his mentor and the father of his dearest friend Yadodhra. Bharat added smilingly, 'They call him Sage Yadodhra now. Why not!' Seriously, he continued, 'I do not know how Ekantra unearthed so many charts. Most of them were disfigured with age and the drawings had almost disappeared. He had to study them all to prepare his own consolidated charts. Those were Ekantra's proudest possessions and he parted with them only moments before he closed his eyes for ever.'

He continued, 'It was with the aid of these charts that Yadodhra inspired the trans-Himalayan expedition to Sindhu's source in Tibata. Those charts also led us to Sindhu sea. Yadodhra went with me and our journey was sure and swift—and how rewarding it was!'

Bharat paused; his mind went to the sea-people of lower Sindhu, with their pre-ancient link with Sanathana—the ageless root of the Sanathana Dharma and of the Hindu.

Sindhu Putra acquired yet another mother.

He saw Bharat's wife, Mataji, arriving at the Island of Silence. He had never met her, but he knew she was expected that day. Respectfully, he bowed to her. She recognized him. Many portraits of him were displayed throughout the land. She teased: 'You are Sindhu Putra, the one who is honoured as the son of Mother Goddess Sindhu!'

She heard the note of distress in his voice as he replied, 'My mother was a nameless woman who died in the lap of the river. My honour lies in having Bharatjogi as my adopted father.'

She felt sorry that she had spoken thoughtlessly. She hugged the boy and said contritely, 'How can a son of my husband not be my own son! Will you not accept me as your mother?'

Wordlessly, the youth nodded and she hugged him tightly.

Later, Mataji said of Sindhu Putra, 'Every woman would like to have him as a son or a sweetheart depending on her age.'

To Bharat, she spoke with mock-sternness. 'You reside in the shadow of a god who calls you his father. Every day, Kanta and other women come to minister to your wants. What kind of hermit are you!'

'One of a kind,' he replied. 'But why don't you come to live here?'

'Who will look after our children, then?'

'Our children are grown up, well settled and so are their wives.'

'And our grandchildren?'

'Their parents will look after them,' Bharat responded.

'Parents cannot look after their children. Only grandparents can.'

'I thought we did a good job of raising our children.'

'Times change. Parents no longer have our wisdom.'

However, the fact is that Mataji had decided to pass six months each year at the island. Since this decision synchronized with Sindhu Putra's stay at the island, some have said that it was his presence that attracted her to stay there for so long. But apparently, they did not know the extent of her love for her husband. She often said that he was all her world. But her children and grandchildren also, she had said, were all her world.

Sindhu Putra did not stay too long at the Island of Silence. Mataji had asked Bharat, 'Why do you keep him cooped up in the island?'
'Because villagers surround him, convinced that he is a god.'
'Then why don't you send him away? To see, learn and grow!'
'He will be recognized everywhere,' Bharat said. 'Everywhere they will surround him and hound him.'
'Why not to Yadodhra? You keep chattering of Ekantra's charts with Yadodhra! How can the boy understand, unless he sees them?'
'Yes, he must see the charts. He must understand. But Yadodhra will be furious. Hundreds will invade his ashram to greet Sindhu Putra.'
'Yadodhra! He can silence a thousand shrieking devils with a single shout. None can dare approach his ashram if he forbids it.'
'Really! He still shouts as he used to? He is my age, you know!'
'Yes, I know. He is young—like you, though not as handsome.'
'Only the eyes of love will view an old man of eighty as handsome!'

Bharat and Mataji discussed plans for Sindhu Putra's travel. 'The singer,' she suggested, 'can take him to our house by boat. Let him meet the family. They will give him all he needs and escort him to Yadodhra's ashram. He can have one of our best horses.'
'A horse! Why?' Bharat asked.
'Because I have never seen a god riding a donkey,' Mataji said.
Bharat smiled, 'Have you seen a god riding a horse?'
'Yes, when you came riding a white horse to marry me.'
Bharat laughed, 'I doubt if he learnt horse-riding at the Rocks.'
'Then my grandchildren will teach what Muni neglected to teach.'

'Will Sage Yadodhra show me those charts?' Sindhu Putra asked.
'Yadodhra will do anything you ask in my name,' Bharat smiled. 'But if he does not, tell him you know the story of the voice in the jar.'
The story of the voice in the jar! It was a simple story--of Yadodhra's very first experiment—though Bharat related it with relish, reliving an event of his childhood, seven decades earlier:
'Yadodhra was barely seven years old. His father had once explained that sound is carried by air waves. So if air did not exist, sound could not reach others. Thus sound transmission, his father explained, came from a sound-producing source only on motions of air.
'Yadodhra, certain that he understood it all, had a brainwave; he concluded that if he spoke into a jar and closed it immediately, covering it on all sides, his voice would not travel, due to absence of air, and the jar would retain his voice; and later when the jar was opened, the same imprisoned voice would be heard as it would then be free to travel on the motions of the air around it.

'Secretly, Yadodhra collected a number of jars. In each, he spoke his name and even described his greatness. Then he covered them tightly with cloth to prevent the air from escaping with his voice.

'Already, he had announced that he would, on a certain day, perform the greatest magic feat of all times. That day came.

'Crowds of children collected. Jars were opened. But alas! No sound.

'Yadodhra was heart-broken. The anguish in his eyes moved me to pity. Quickly, I assumed blame and said that I had carelessly dropped Yadodhra's magic powder, which was eaten away promptly by pigeons and squirrels and hence Yadodhra's magnificent magic-feat was ruined.

'Everyone blamed me. For Yadodhra, they had praise as he gave them all many rides on his father's elephants. But quietly, Yadodhra put his arms around me and promised that whenever I asked for anything, possible or impossible, he would do it for me.

'So,' concluded Bharat, 'remind Yadodhra of that promise, if he is reluctant to show you the charts.' Sindhu Putra smiled, 'Your debt is for you to collect. I cannot hold that experiment against him.'

'Indeed,' Bharat said, 'one can only honour him. For, even at the age of seven, he tried to uncover a secret of nature's process. Since then, all his life, he has been striving to discover the unknown. For him, no question is useless; no theory, impertinent; no experiment, a failure; and no myth, sacrosanct—everything must be tested, checked, proved and disproved. Only...' Bharat smiled, 'he makes no rash pre-announcements as he did when a seven-year-old. He waits, with unending patience, to unveil a truth of nature.'

'And he succeeds, does he not?' Sindhu Putra prompted.

'That he does; but he knows also that mysteries multiply with each discovery and if a few tantalizing clues are found, they will be surrounded by fresh problems and paradoxes. Perhaps, it will always be so and the eternal mystery will remain incomprehensible for ever.'

'Only a trickster or a lunatic would like to be known as a god, while he lives. For a sane or an honest man, on earth, the burden of godhood would be impossible to bear in his lifetime.'

—(From Sage Yadodhra's address to his students, 5054 BC)

Messages from the Past

5054 BC

'Thieves and gods will always hide themselves,' sang an irreverent poet to commemorate Sindhu Putra's departure from the Island of Silence for Yadodhra's ashram. The village was uninformed of his departure. He was seen off only by Bharat and Mataji and the seven dogs who barked sorrowfully to inquire why he must leave.

Yadodhra welcomed Sindhu Putra with open arms. He had a hundred questions about Bharat. He was delighted that Mataji was with him and said, 'He is no more a hermit then! I too shall visit him.'

'He will be delighted to see you,' Sindhu Putra responded.

'Delighted! He will jump with joy; he will dance with glee; his heart will sing,' said Yadodhra but added, 'Oh but not for my sake!'

'What else!' Sindhu Putra asked.

'No, for the treasures of knowledge my students have unearthed and to see the charts which, at last, we have corrected and updated. You also want to see those charts, is it not? He sent you to see them; yes?'

'I hope to see them, if you permit.'

'Do you know what those charts are about?' Yadodhra asked.

'I believe they indicate the lands of the people of Sanathana, Sanathana Dharma and of the ancient Hindu,' Sindhu Putra replied.

'And who were the Sanathana people? Men from another planet?' asked Yadodhra stridently, the school-master in him coming to the forefront.

'No, they are from our world. Sanathana were our own ancestors. From them emerged Sanathana Dharma, which itself led to us—the Hindu.'

'Bharatjogi schools his son well,' Yadodhra responded. The words were complimentary but tinged with irony. 'But I suppose,' Yadodhra continued, 'you should know all that is there in the charts.'

'I do not,' Sindhu Putra replied with simplicity.

'No! But I heard a claim that you are a god.'

Yadodhra saw distress in the youth's eyes; and quickly added, 'I know you do not claim it. And, it is, after all, only at the end of a life that one can say if someone was a god or not. A person's karma alone will determine that. Gods are not born, they are made—self-made—through their own effort, passion and commitment.'

Sindhu Putra told him his story. 'I am an orphan that Bharatjogi found in a storm-tossed, battered boat, and certainly, I am no god.'

In a swift change of mood, Yadodhra put his arm around him, 'You are my dearest friend's son and surely that places you above any god.'

Yadodhra's ashram was a beehive of activity. Every student was busy in some activity or the other—some in faraway fields to plant crops and flowers in different kinds of soils, others to treat iron and various metals and yet others to study the effect of still water, rushing water and dripping water on diverse materials, and even on rocks and stones. Some were making and mixing various dyes and paints. Their activities were endless but to what end? 'Until the mystery is no more,' Yadodhra said.

Sindhu Putra pored over a map, depicted not on bark and leaf but on a huge, wall-like structure. It was square in shape and four times his height. By its side were other, smaller wall-sections, with several charts. Yadodhra explained, 'My father tried to preserve the original charts. They kept deteriorating. He made copies on larger barks, preserved them with wax, to protect them from the elements. Even so, copies deteriorated faster than the ancient originals. That danger is no more. Charts are now reproduced on this massive stone wall which will soon have a protective canopy on top.'

Yadodhra stood below, while Sindhu Putra went up and down the ladder, to study the map. Yadodhra kept shouting explanations. The youth hardly comprehended anything. Many lines were in various colours; others were inlaid with beads and some overlaid with small broken stones. From Yadodhra's observations, it was clear that the huge map portrayed all the information from various ancient charts to depict lands where the ancient Hindu lived successively from the age of Sanathana to the present. The map also included lands where the Hindu once lived but then abandoned for a number of reasons—such as drought, lure of abundance elsewhere and even to seek safety from tribal attacks.

Yadodhra added: 'My father's difficulty was that he had not seen the Himalayas or the Sindhu sea. It was our good fortune to reach beyond the Himalaya and to touch the Sindhu sea. Even so, my father saw route-charts with rough drawings in caves. Their very repetitiveness convinced him that the Himalayas existed and the Sindhu sea was waiting to be discovered.'

Sindhu Putra had doubts, 'What kind of a chart or drawing can show a mountain as great as the Himalaya is known to be! Could it not be a depiction just of any rock-terrain or a small mountain!'

'True,' Yadodhra answered, 'but look at the evidence. First, there are inartistic sketches of a mountain. Second, on the righthand side of such sketches is a column with crude drawings of men. Each man stands on the shoulders of the one below him, and as the righthand column rises, the figures of men become progressively smaller and ultimately men come to be represented by tiny dots. It was difficult to count the dots, for they often overlapped, but clearly there were some thousands of them. No it was not art—but a message in the form of a scale—to show that the mountain peak was higher than the combined height of five thousand men. Third—and this was even more peculiar —that in all such repetitive, inartistic drawings found in many caves, was a box in the lefthand corner in which there was a tiny sketch of a pyramid. Apparently, ancient route-plotters and explorers had agreed on a common code: that all drawings of the Himalayas shall have this symbol of a pyramid to distinguish them from others.' Yadodhra paused to ask, 'You see the advantage of this now?'

Sindhu Putra saw nothing. 'What advantage?' he asked.

'The advantage of providing a link between a number of drawings on the same subject. My father found so many charts and drawings in different caves. Some were repetitive, while others differed in certain aspects. But he quickly realized that all drawings with the "pyramid" symbol related to that mountain that he had not seen, and yet it existed, somewhere, not too far.'

Yadodhra saw the puzzled look on Sindhu Putra's face, and added, 'Perhaps I go too fast. The fact is that there were many drawings of the mountain with different perspectives. Some showed terrain of certain sections, with mighty cliffs and high waterfalls; others showed only foothills; a few had a close-up of vegetation, trees and forests; and many depicted streams flowing through the mountain, some coming together to form rivers to flow over land and finally rivers reaching out to meet one large body of water.'

'The Sindhu sea?' Sindhu Putra asked.

Yadodhra nodded. 'Yes, even drawings of Sindhu sea had their own distinctive symbol—a fish with the face and breasts of a woman. This one single common symbol was given on all the sketches of the Sindhu sea so as to make it clear that they pertained to that body of water, and not to any river or stream, which also had their own separate symbols. Similarly, drawings of the Himalayas also could not be confused with sketches of other mountains which too had their separate symbols.

'But even with distinctive symbols, it was not easy to get the message of the ancient route-plotter or chart-maker.' Yadodhra led him to a distant wall, 'Now, see this copy of an earlier chart.'

It was the sketch of a mountain, with men standing at its foot, birds flying above the foothills, but far below the rising mountain were mountain goats, apparently unable to climb higher, with some of them tumbling down, while the mountain rose majestically, covered with a sheet of ice, though innumerable ice boulders had detached themselves, as though they were hurtling below.

Yadodhra continued, 'See that corner box with the sketch of a pyramid? There is no doubt that this chart depicts the high and mighty Himalayas. But see also the circular lines by the mountainside. I took them to be clouds. But later, I understood; they were meant to indicate severe, swirling storms. It was simply a chart of difficulties and climatic conditions that climbers will encounter.'

They went to another wall-section. 'See this,' Yadodhra said. 'This is a copy of a chart of Sindhu river. We know now that Sindhu is a trans-Himalayan river. But what did ancient route-plotters do! They drew river lines above and beyond the Himalayas. Foolishly, some of us thought that the ancient plotters suggested that Sindhu stood in mid-air or sprang from the sky. No, they were wiser than many of us.'

Sindhu Putra spoke. 'But there are two symbols on this chart!'

'Yes; the pyramid for the Himalayas and Mother Goddess for Sindhu. Whenever a chart had more features, symbols for all the features were given. Thus, to show the confluence of Sindhu river with Sindhu sea, the chart would have symbols for both. But I feel that the Mother Goddess symbol should have been avoided. Why? Because each plotter drew Mother Goddess differently—some simply as a symbol, others with reverence to elaborate it—and at times it became difficult for us to relate one with the other.'

Yadodhra continued, 'But, even so, my father who had seen neither the Himalayas nor the Sindhu sea, saw the connection and realized that they did actually exist, not merely in the imagination but in reality. It was as though, with these charts, he could look into the hearts and the eyes of the Hindu who had seen them in the past.

'These charts also inspired Bharatji to send an expedition to seek Sindhu's source in Tibata and later to the Himalayas. He and I went to the mouth of the Sindhu to look at the Sindhu sea. Without these charts to inspire us, how many more generations it would have taken!'

Later, Yadodhra explained many charts and the consolidated map. Sindhu Putra asked, 'How many rivers are shown in these charts?'

'Far more than we have discovered,' was Yadodhra's reply.

'Is it not possible to conceive that the ancient Hindu merely saw the Himalayas from a distance?' Sindhu Putra asked. 'Where is the proof that he actually went in, climbing high and deep into the mountain?'

'How else did we find idols of our gods in the mountain! Our explorers there saw images of Rudra, Brahma, Vishnu and other deities.'

'Yes; Bharatjogi told me of that,' Sindhu Putra said. 'He also told me about the exquisite paintings in your father Ekantraji's cave.'

'Yes, there are beautiful paintings in the caves which my father discovered. They were on the walls and ceilings of the caves. Your father and I admired them together, with wonder and awe. But the charts, with symbols of which we now speak, were not displayed. They were wrapped in layer after layer of protected covering, to preserve them. Obviously, they were not intended to fascinate but left by ancients as clues to guide us in our search or call it research.

Sindhu Putra asked, 'Were there no similar paintings—for instance, of the mountains—on the cave-walls?'

'Paintings of mountains, yes, but by no means similar. Paintings on cave-walls were imaginative, captivating. There was one painting of the mythical 420,000-mile high mountain, Mount Meru, which is known in all our children's stories as the dwelling-place of the gods. You would love to see that painting for its artistry, with its flowing streams and beautiful golden houses inhabited by spiritual beings, the devas, attended by heavenly singers, the gandharvas, and divine dancers, the apsaras, while the mountain itself, rising from the centre of the universe to the heavens, is surrounded by several concentric rings, around which are the moon, the sun and planets, with the earth between the seventh and eighth outer ring. The feeling that the artist evoked was that the top was studded with real blue sapphires and from this radiated the blue colour all across the heaven; the other realms were seemingly covered with glittering rubies, yellow and white gems, with a dazzling interplay of splashing colours. No one who saw this painting could take his eyes off it. Yet its beauty apart, everyone regards it as a painting which simply captures a charming myth and not a real mountain waiting to be discovered.'[1]

Yadodhra continued, 'But route-charts or sketches that simply identified physical or other features of the terrain were not on display; they were made by prosaic explorers with no art or aesthetic sense— but only with the detail that was essential to identify the place. And they were carefully concealed—to excite us, to lead us on to a voyage of discovery, on to the paths that the ancients had treaded before.

Sindhu Putra asked, 'But what was the compulsion the ancients had of communicating with the coming generations!'

'Why did your father encourage the Memory songs? We all wish to belong—to the future and the past.'

Yadodhra continued, 'But ours is the opportunity to do much more. The ancients had no leaf or bark large enough and their charts had to be in several sections. Often, they were glued together but the glue came off and in many, even symbols were obliterated. Also, distances

---

[1]Even now, Mount Meru continues to dominate the landscape of the Hindu imagination and is celebrated in Hindu and Buddhist art.

kept ancient chart-makers apart and perhaps the effort to consolidate information on a single map was never possible.

'But,' Yadodhra said jubilantly, 'we, my friend, have no such problem. We have massive walls here to copy every chart. If needed, I shall build many more, as my students keep discovering more charts in various caves. The future must never be robbed of its past.'

News went round among Yadodhra's students of Sindhu Putra's visit. His name was well-known as one who was regarded as the son of Mother Goddess Sindhu. Not that students truly believed it—for Yadodhra had trained them to be sceptics—but curious they certainly were.

Yadodhra noticed the curiosity. At evening prayers when all the students were gathered together, he rose to introduce Sindhu Putra and made it clear that 'he is no god, nor son of Mother Sindhu, but the son of my dearest friend, Bharatjogi, the most illustrious Karkarta that this land has had.' Then, Yadodhra joked: 'But, boys and girls! If ever you are in frantic search of a living god and if you are at my ashram, I alone must be regarded as that living god.'

'...So why blame the young, shy slave-girl, with a faded white flower in her hair, and a blush in her cheeks, who was the first to proclaim that the land she was in was Bharat Varsha (the Land of Bharat).'

—(From a song-story by an unknown poet, around 5054 BC)

'...Thus this bride of Sindhu Putra, who was a slave no more, became a slave of slaves, and her heart lost its limits in joy, for he who was the lord of her dreams and master of her thoughts was elusive no more and now came to remain in the very depth of her being and in the body of her body, even though she saw him not face to face....'

—(From the song—'Brides of Sindhu Putra', around 5054 BC)

'...There was a time perhaps when the divine, universal Father created the earth and established His law. But man banished God and created his own law. Your Father exists no more and this is not his land.'

—(Foreman's cry to Sindhu Putra, song-story, around 5054 BC)

Bharat Varsha

5054 BC

For days, even at night with fire-torches, Sindhu Putra pored over huge charts and maps. His wonder grew. His wanderlust made him restless.

'Why not!' Yadodhra said, when the youth expressed the desire to travel. 'Who knows, maybe one day you will discover new lands and fill in the many gaps that still remain on our map!'

Sindhu Putra knew of those gaps. He even asked, 'How is it that the charts go on and on but the actual discoveries are so few?'

'Once the search begins—and it has begun—can anything remain hidden!'

Sindhu Putra knew also that Yadodhra's students were trying to discover more charts in the caves all over. Without them, Yadodhra's map would be incomplete, though meanwhile, Yadodhra had drawn bold imaginative strokes to fill in the gaps. Even so, the sage was careful, and when relying on his imagination, used a purple colour. 'The purple is the colour of my question mark,' Yadodhra said. But why not leave the gaps blank? Why fill them at all? Yadodhra explained —'Only to challenge myself and to dare others to prove me wrong. First, in the absence of facts, I establish a possible theory—an illusion of knowledge. I shall shed no tears if my theory is extinguished when the fact emerges.' He argued that empty blanks might even misguide 'and if the initial path of a stream is known, then our reasoned imagination must guide us to draw its probable further course and final destination, even though they are yet to be discovered. Foolish, would it not be, to show a stream that stops midstream?'

Sindhu Putra discussed with Yadodhra plans for travel and routes to follow, initially, to reach the cave-complex discovered by Yadodhra's father Ekantra, and the twenty-one caves discovered by Yadodhra and his students, with their treasures of art, paintings and charts.

'Wear the garb of a muni or sanyasi,' Yadodhra advised. 'None will bother you then.' To dispel Sindhu Putra's doubts, he said, 'Your youth is no obstacle to the saffron robe. The four distinct stages of life—child, student, householder and hermit—are simply guidelines. Our land is full of hermits and ascetics who skip the student and householder stages to pass their life in meditation, with all earthly ties broken. Your own Muni of the Rocks was an ascetic at the age of twelve.'

'I lack the knowledge of a muni,' Sindhu Putra replied.

'You have the gift of silence. That is more mature than knowledge.'

'Yet to go out in a garb that does not belong to me!'

'Would you rather travel like the god you are supposed to be? Be sure that out of every hundred wanderers in a saffron garb, at least ten wear it either to cheat or to protect themselves from robbers.'

'Robbers respect the saffron robe then?' Sindhu Putra asked.

'Respect, no; superstition, yes. Besides what will it profit them to molest a lonely wanderer in a saffron robe? A man of substance would travel in style—maybe in a chariot and be escorted.'

To Sindhu Putra's reservations about travelling on horseback, Yadodhra asked, 'How far will you reach on your weary feet?'

'But does an ascetic travel on a horse?'

'My father travelled on an elephant,' was Yadodhra's reply. 'You are not that elevated. A horse will do for you.'

Sindhu Putra rode on. He lost his way. It was his fault. With Yadodhra, he had fully discussed the routes to reach the caves. However, he felt tempted to deviate from the route—to pass through towns and villages, to see for himself how people lived and worked. This was the first time he was alone and unescorted; he wished to see everything himself, unaided by another. None, he was certain, would recognize him—with his head shaved, ash smeared on his forehead, a saffron garb to cover him, with the hood concealing his head and ears. Even so, obviously he was an ascetic passing through—and entitled to consideration. Everyone made way for him; some offered him food, others asked for blessings as he silently passed by, sometimes acknowledging greetings, sometimes declining food.

Now, after days and weeks of aimless wandering, he was hopelessly lost and thought that by turning eastwards, he would be able to cut across to the appointed route. At last, far away from a town, almost in the midst of the wilderness, he reached a large plantation. It was the hour of dusk, when work normally stops in fields and farms. Also, it was a full-moon day, when hardly anyone works. Yet from a distance he saw many at work. He smiled as he recalled Sage Yadodhra's words to his students, 'God may not respond to prayers but certainly His bounty and blessings flow to those that work harder—and when a man, weary from work, falls asleep without praying, it is God who guards him through the night, and prays for him.' When a student irreverently asked the sage, 'But what about hermits that pass their time, not in work, but solely in prayer?' Yadodhra had replied, 'Maybe they are doing penance for never having worked at all in their life. Maybe, now that they are too old to work, theirs is a lifelong regret of having been as indolent and lazy as my students.'

His smile deepened, as he also recalled that there was no holiday on full-moon at Yadodhra's ashram, and students stopped their work, not at sunset, but at midnight or beyond. Well, people here too seemed to be working hard.

Sindhu Putra's smile disappeared as he approached the spot where people were at work in the plantation. He could see that they were slaves, acting under sharp, curt orders from the foreman.

No one paid attention to Sindhu Putra. Apparently, ascetics and sanyasis often sought food and lodging there. The foreman simply pointed to a hut which the owner had provided just for that purpose.

Sindhu Putra, however, did not pass on. He alighted from his horse and asked, 'Why are slaves working at this hour, on a full-moon evening, when no one can be made to work?' It was the first time he had spoken in many days and his words came out loudly.

'Because there is work that remains to be done,' the foreman replied, contemptuously. He was in no awe of ascetics. They came and went, always seeking something, never giving anything in return.

Sindhu Putra glanced at the slaves. Among them was a young woman, perhaps no older than him. She was busy at work, with her back to him. He saw her hair, adorned with a white flower. Was it the same kind of flower that his mother wore? He moved forward to see.

The foreman grinned. Maybe, this sanyasi is not after food or lodging, but has different appetites. He had met some ascetics like that, who loved the 'human touch'. Well, he would send him on his way forthwith.

Meanwhile, Sindhu Putra went near the woman. Yes, it was the same kind of flower. Lightly he touched it. The woman turned back, startled. She saw it was a sanyasi! Where did he come from!

She always prayed silently whenever asectics passed by, hoping that somehow they would hear the prayer in her heart and carry it to Him who grants all prayers. She was about to touch his feet but he moved back. 'God bless you, Mother,' he said.

The foreman halted his words and the young woman smiled at being called 'Mother', but Sindhu Putra was in a different realm—his mind on the woman with a white flower in a boat who gave him birth and then left for nowhere. In a daze he wondered: 'Was my mother also a slave, like this girl with the white flower!'

The spell broke, as roughly the foreman shouted at the girl to attend to work. Sindhu Putra faced the foreman, 'When did they begin to work?'

'At dawn, last night, last year—how does it matter to you?'

'Is there not a law that says that no slave shall work on full-moon day and their work stops at dusk?' Bharatjogi had told him of those laws he had introduced, as Karkarta, to reduce severity on slaves. But then, during Nandan's time, nobody even remembered those laws.

Derisively, the foreman asked, 'Whose law is that?'

'My father's law!' Sindhu Putra thoughtlessly thundered. Clearly a slip! He had replied on an impulse, stung by the foreman's tone. What he had been trying to say was that his father Bharatjogi had made that law as Karkarta. But even as he said it, he realized his blunder. He was to travel incognito and not reveal his identity.

The foreman totally misunderstood Sindhu Putra's reference to his father's law. He was sure that like many sanyasis, the youth was simply referring to God, as the divine, universal Father.

'Your Father's law is honoured only in your Father's land. Not in this land of sin and sorrow,' the foreman said. Sindhu Putra stared, as the foreman continued, perhaps from a deep and powerful remembrance of a long-past wound which had suddenly re-opened, 'There was a time when your Father—the divine, universal Father—created earth and established His law. But man moved away and created his own law to banish God. Your Father exists no more and this is not His land.'

At last Sindhu Putra understood that the man was denying God! In his tiny world no one had ever questioned the existence and paramountcy of God. But here this odious, godless man....

In Sindhu Putra's heart there was always the silent loneliness that an orphan feels. Solace came from those around him who loved him and whom he loved in return. Yet he always felt the presence of Another whom he loved all the more. Now this evil slave-driver was trying to shatter his faith!

The foreman's words had pierced him and he stood frozen, trying to forget. Sindhu Putra's voice rose to an angry pitch, 'This is my Father's land. . .!' he stopped. For him, anger was a new experience. He had never raised his voice to shout.

The foreman heard the shout and stepped back. Clearly, this was one of those lunatic sanyasis who turned violent, if crossed. Certainly, he could hold the sanyasi back with a single blow. Still, the plantation owner would not appreciate his hitting a sanyasi.

The effect on the slaves was, however, magical. They heard his shout and even in the dim light of dusk, they saw the sanyasi shaking. It was from a frenzy of anger, but it appeared no different to the trance of a holy man, deep in the midst of a powerful vision. The girl, with the flower in her hair, came closer and asked, 'Who are you sanyasiji?'

All thought of hiding his identity left Sindhu Putra. No, he would not tell an untruth to a girl with a flower of the kind that his mother wore on her last, fateful journey. Nor to these simple slaves.

'I am Sindhu Putra,' he replied simply. Sindhu Putra! Sindhu Putra! The slaves stared in astonishment. They knew the name of him who was known throughout the land as a god destined to walk on earth. 'The son of Mother Goddess Sindhu!' came the chant from many slaves —they knew the lore. And they moved forward to touch his feet.

Sindhu Putra raised his hand, determined that he must avoid this aura of divinity. Quietly, he announced, 'I am the son of Bharatjogi. That is my highest honour. No more—but no less. I neither possess nor seek a higher honour.'

He silenced them but did not halt their move to kneel before him. He stopped them, raised his hand again and commanded, 'Let us all stand and silently pray.'

*

Here the poet, whose songs tell this part of the story, is largely silent. He does not speak of the effect of the prayer on the slaves; nor if the foreman joined the prayers or suspended work. The poet simply says that when the prayer ended, Sindhu Putra caressed the flower in the hair of the girl, making a movement with his lips, as if planting a distant kiss—and then he mounted the horse and rode out in a tearing hurry.

Yet the poet does add that thereafter, every wandering minstrel, and every passing visitor to the plantation, was told the story of Sindhu Putra's brief visit and his soulful cry that all this land around was his father's—and clearly, unmistakably, he had identified Bharat—formerly a Karkarta and now a hermit—as his father. Many, then came specially to listen to the songs and stories of the slaves and 'to have the joy of spreading them to others, and even the foreman's severity was no more, as visitors listened to slaves—and their stories and songs made it clear that Sindhu Putra himself had proclaimed that the entire land be known as the land of his father, Bharat.' And that is how the land came to be known as Bharat Varsha.

The song of despair that fills the night
Is heard the next day by birds in flight.
Trees and flowers hear it, as they wake
But why sing it—for whose sake?
He hears it not, perhaps, neither now nor then
Maybe, the gods hear it; before or after? Who knows,
                                              when?

—(From 'Songs of Sindhu Putra', around 5054 BC)

'The earth is sacred. Do not smear it with blood'

—(Sindhu Putra's cry at the fort, 5054 BC)

The song or despair that fills the night
Is heard the next day by birds in flight
Trees and flowers hear it, as they wake
But why sing it—for whose sake?
He hears it not, perhaps, neither now nor then
Maybe the gods hear it, before or after. Who knows,
when?

—From *Songs of Simha Putra*, around 5654 BC?

'The matrix is sacred. Do not smear it with blood.'

—(smaller Runes are at the fork 5054 BC?)

The Mask of a God?

5054 BC

Thunder and lightning rent the air as Sindhu Putra rode out of the plantation. For the slaves he left behind, this was an omen from the heavens, to mark the visit of the god who came briefly in their midst.

But Sindhu Putra himself was in a bewildered daze as his horse went dashing forward, unmindful of the thunderstorm.

He had gone into the plantation to find a well or a stream, and hopefully to rest for the night. When he saw the slaves working late into the dusk, he remembered Bharatjogi's words on the plight of slaves. Then came the strange conversation with the foreman. To what end? To what useless inconsequence?—Sindhu Putra wondered. He could not recall it with clarity—neither the words, nor their sequence, though it had taken place only moments earlier. All he remembered was his searing, blinding rage at the foreman's words.

How foolish I was to get into that rage!—he thought. Why did it matter that the foreman disbelieved in the One Supreme? Did not Muni of the Rocks say, 'Conduct, morals and action are the basis of karma and not the irrelevancy of faith, belief and creed....' And did not Roopa's song say, 'the Real is in each of us, whether we know it or not.' He remembered also what Yadodhra said, 'If the reality of the One Supreme depended simply on people's acceptance, it might as well cease to exist. God is not like a headman seeking an election. God *is*.' Even Bharatjogi had said, 'The tree that gives shade to the believer does not withdraw it from the non-believer and so is it with the light of the sun.'

Sindhu Putra realized that he had been even more foolish in revealing his identity. He should have foreseen that, despite disclaimers, it would end up by his being treated as a god—as in Gatha's village.

The only sensible action he took was to ride out, fast, before they knelt and prayed to him. But he then asked himself: Yet why did I flee like a thief in the night?

The horse galloped on. The night was dark and the moon was content to remain in hiding, with clouds disputing its passage. Sindhu Putra did not pay the slightest attention to where he was going, his mind tossing from his recollection of his conversation with the foreman, to the condition of the slaves, and on to the white. flower of his lost mother. A feeling of guilt was slowly creeping in—as he feared he had left the slaves in a condition worse than he found them—as the foreman would certainly vent his wrath on them for his interference.

Suddenly, the thunder stopped. Gentle rain followed. The horse slowed down. The rider and horse were thirsty and welcomed the rain. Both rested for the night under the ledge of a rock.

When he woke up, Sindhu Putra became conscious of the light and warmth of the sun. He felt his mind caressed. He was no longer distraught. The questions of the night before had ceased and, instead, he now felt within him the stirrings of a new emotion.

He recalled Bharatjogi's words on the plight of slaves and his condemnation of slavery. Sindhu Putra had listened to him with respect, as always. But to him, slavery was impersonal, distant. Now he felt these words of Bharatjogi re-echoing in his heart and he began to understand them in the innermost consciousness of his being.

His water-flasks were full from the rain of last night. Nuts, dry fruit and the salt in his saddle-bags were enough for a few frugal meals. The horse too was content with the bounty of the land and rain-water puddles. The only difficulty was that he was in the middle of nowhere, with no idea of the route he must take.

He mounted the horse with the hope that what he had once heard was true—that a horse somehow finds the way, if nowhere else, at least back home. But the horse waited patiently for the rider to make up his mind. Sindhu Putra rode east.

Little was known in Gatha's village of Sindhu Putra's movements during these months. There were speculations, though. Some said he was at the Sindhu sea; others heard he was at a Himalayan peak. But that was impossible, considering the vast distances involved and the short time he had been away, though many argued that time and distance posed no barriers to the gods. The most persistent rumour however was that he had declared his will and wish that the land be known as Bharat Varsha. Why, some asked. Is it to honour his father who was once the Karkarta and now a hermit?

Meanwhile, Sindhu Putra rode on—not always in a straight line, for the horse often intervened and even refused to move in the intended direction. But the rider and the horse had reached an understanding. The horse had an instinct for locating distant water-holes, grasslands, and even trees and plants with edible berries and roots. Suddenly, the horse would slow down, prick up its ears, sniff the air noisily—and then, a long unspoken conversation would begin between the horse and rider, with the horse suggesting a deviation in the route. But there were other times when the horse was not so polite and would stop suddenly, rooted to the ground, refusing to move forward. It was not an impulsive act, as Sindhu Putra discovered. It happened when there was danger ahead. Once, there was the risk of straying into a swamp. At another time, the rocky track would have led to a disastrous fall. Ever since then, the horse had the power of veto over the direction they were to take.

Day after day Sindhu Putra went on, meeting none to guide him. Suddenly, the horse stopped. From then on, the land went downhill, to disappear in a forest of tall evergreens, which climbed up the hills in the far distance and merged with the blue of the sky. Yet, one large hill stood incongruously apart, holding the promise of a settlement nearby. It was bare at the top, as if human hands had been at work to shave off its greenery. Sindhu Putra dismounted and led the horse cautiously downhill.

Sindhu Putra reached the distant hill after a long, arduous journey of four days and nights. The vast forest of evergreens he had to cross had neither food nor water. The horse was tormented by hunger and thirst and his head drooped sadly.

The paths had become more overgrown, thornier, narrower, steeper and darker, as Sindhu Putra approached the hill. But now, in the open, he could sense a flurry of activity going on, at the hilltop.

Sindhu Putra did not know it, but at the top of the hill, a fort was being constructed. It was to be one of the forts which Karkarta Nandan had decided to establish at strategic points in the eastern territory to control the area around. On the other side of the hill, hidden from view, was a large township.

The sentry on the hill had been watching Sindhu Putra's approach. He had seen many in the past approaching the hill but never anyone from the treacherous route which Sindhu Putra had taken.

'Who goes there?' barked the sentry, ready to throw his spear.

'A traveller in need of water, food and rest for his horse,' Sindhu Putra replied.

The sentry's doubts vanished. A tribal would have yelled, fled or attacked. The stranger spoke his language and sounded educated.

'Welcome, sir, approach,' the sentry said, intrigued that the stranger spoke of the needs of his horse rather than his own. The sentry took his pitcher of water and also the bucket of water kept near his mule, tethered nearby and went down. Gratefully, the horse and Sindhu Putra had their fill of water. Sentry saw that apart from their need to eat, they both needed attention. Sindhu Putra's robe was tattered; even so it was clear that it was the garb of a sanyasi; his face and body were bruised from overgrown, thorny bushes in the forest.

Next to the sentry's hut, under a canopy, was a drum. The sentry's drum-beats, which he struck in a curious pattern—indicative of a coded message—summoned men from the top.

Sindhu Putra was escorted along the half-concealed, narrow, winding path that led in a gradual rise and fall, not to the hilltop where the fort was being constructed, but to the township, behind the hill.

The headman of the township welcomed Sindhu Putra. Curious onlookers also gathered. A visit from a sanyasi was rare. During the four years that he was in charge, the headman had received only three sanyasis. Two of them were persuaded not to go into the eastern territory and returned after a brief, pleasant stay. Only one, who was apparently a raving lunatic—and he gave every evidence of it by his shouts and loud, unceasing laughter—refused to listen to reason. He went deep into the tribal lands. He was never heard from and many thought that he must have been killed by the tribals.

The headman escorted Sindhu Putra to his cottage. The headman's wife gave him herbal water with which to wash his bruises. He declined wine but gratefully accepted fruit juice and wheat-rolls. He was given a white garment to wear, while his saffron robe was repaired. 'It will be as good as new,' the headman assured him. 'My wife is an expert in needlework.' The wife smiled, as the headman added expansively, 'Actually, she is better than everybody at everything she does.' But she was hardly paying attention to her husband. She was wondering, 'How young this sanyasi is! Why he is no older than what my son would have been, had he lived!' She shook her head to wave away the memory of her miscarriage, fifteen years ago.

Soberly, the headman's wife said, 'I shall repair your robe but it may not last long. Let me also make another robe for you. I will ask Sehwani to make a saffron dye. She is good at making and mixing colours.' She did not need to ask if he had another robe; it would be a rare sanyasi who had more than one robe. If often sanyasis were seen, standing for hours, waist-deep, in cold waters of the river, it was not for bath or prayers alone, but mostly because they had washed their robe in the river and were waiting for it to dry on the riverbank—and their eyes would remain wide open, in the midst of their prayers, lest some mischievous urchin should hide the robe for a prank.

Actually, Yadodhra had given Sindhu Putra two more robes. He had draped both on the horse to protect it from the stinging thorns in the overgrown forest. Somewhere in that forest, the robes were lost.

After a relaxing bath, Sindhu Putra needed sleep. It was mid-afternoon, but he had not slept for four nights, warding off persistent gnats and flies in the forest; yet he politely answered the headman's questions. He was looking for Sage Yadodhra's caves, he said, but had lost his way. The headman did not know where the caves were but he had certainly heard of Sage Yadodhra. Who had not! His respect for the youth rose. Surely, if he comes from the sage's ashram, he must be a sanyasi of quality. The headman promised to have him escorted to wherever he had to go and meanwhile offered the hospitality of the town.

The headman escorted him down the road towards a cottage, intended for honoured guests. On the way, the headman pointed to the neat rows of huts which housed soldiers, workers, transporters, and even fortune-seekers in the eastern terrotory. New housing, the headman said, was being built near the fort; the fort itself would dominate the area around and, he added proudly, 'Our contingents and colonies shall then be invulnerable from sneak attacks and our forces shall be able to move out at will to strike terror amongst those who seek to terrorize us.'

The headman was proud of the town and pointed to gardens carpeted with flowers and trees. Sindhu Putra was not surprised that the headman ignored a large, shabby part of the township—ugly, barren and miserable—with broken-down huts, crumbling walls and shattered ceilings. After all, the township was in a state of transition, waiting for the fort to be built.

The moon was riding high in the cloudless sky at midnight, when Sindhu Putra awoke from his sleep. In the silence of night, he heard the distant noise of construction from the fort-site. He walked to the open courtyard. The guest-house sentry came to offer food. Sindhu Putra declined and watched the glow of fire-torches far away at the fort-site.

'How long do they work?' he asked the sentry.

'From sunrise to midnight. But already the fort has taken too long to build. That is why they are working past midnight, now.'

An hour later, the noise from the fort-site subsided. Sindhu Putra completed his bath and prayers and the sentry brought a light meal. The sound of countless footsteps was audible from the street and the sentry enlightened him, 'They are back from the fort, but in less than five hours they will march back to work.'

Sindhu Putra wished to sleep again, to resume the normal rhythm of night and day. But the silence of the night and fragrance of the flowers mingling with the breeze, led him to the garden outside. He lay down on the cool, soft grass, listening to the breathing of sleeping nature and watching the magic and beauty of the sky, sparkling with bright, shining stars and the golden moon. It was in this dream-like state that he heard the melancholy strains of a song floating out of the wide, open spaces. He walked beyond, to hear the song more clearly, but there was a deep, wide ditch separating the lowly section of the town, littered with dilapidated huts, from which the song came. He closed his eyes and tried to listen.

He heard no words—only a sad, haunting melody—as if he was hearing a voice from the bosom of the night that sang of the silent shrieking of the soul and the unspoken despair of the heart.

The sentry's footsteps distracted him. He was leaning too near the ditch and the sentry had feared that the sanyasi might sleepwalk into danger.

'Who is singing that song?' Sindhu Putra asked the sentry.

'Maybe someone who cannot sleep; but I hear no song!'

Sindhu Putra heard the haunting melody no more. He went back to the garden, his mind still on the melody. After a long while, he dozed off and, in his dream, the melody came to him again. Somehow, it seemed to him to have a pleading, summoning note about it—as though someone was seeking to call him somewhere.

Sindhu Putra woke up at sunrise, as he heard a noise from the street. Obviously, columns of workers were marching to the fort-site. He went in for a wash, hoping to go out quickly to see them, and even visit the fort. But as he was stepping out, a girl came.

She was Mithali, thirteen-year old daughter of Sehwani, the maidservant at the headman's household. She brought the robe which the headman's wife had repaired. She apologized for coming when he was about to leave. He waved it off saying he had nothing important to do and had simply thought of going to the fort-site; since he did not know the way, he had thought of following the workers. She seemed puzzled, 'But workers go later—three hours past sunrise, after their morning meals.'

'The sentry told me that they go at sunrise and return after midnight.'

'Oh they!' She seemed troubled and changed the subject. 'The fort is easy to find. Besides, the headman can always take you there.'

'The headman, I am sure, is busy,' Sindhu Putra said.

'The headman is never busy. He keeps others busy,' she said. He laughed.

It was actually Mithali who took Sindhu Putra to the fort. The headman came to call on him, in a fluster. He had just received a message that Karkarta Nandan would be arriving. The visit was twenty days away but the headman felt that he had to complete ten thousand things before that. Even so, the fort-commander, to whom he had spoken a day earlier, wished to welcome the distinguished sanyasi to the fort.

Mithali brought a mule for him to ride on. He refused to ride while she walked. She also declined to ride and said in jest that the mule was a snob and did not like servant-girls to ride on it; after all it was the headman's own mule. They both walked.

They went up the hilly path and came upon the fort. The headman had said that the commander himself would receive him at the fort-entrance. But the commander had rushed out to inspect distant outposts, as soon as he heard of Karkarta Nandan's impending visit.

Many came forward to greet the sanyasi. But his eyes went to a section with a large number of half-clad, sullen and miserable persons tied to posts with long ropes around their waists, slaving under the watchful eyes of sentries. A slave—hit on the chest by a stone-block—had fallen. Many slaves tried to crowd around him; and his prone body hindered the work of others nearby.

With a loud oath, a man walked authoritatively to the fallen slave and cursed the sentries for not removing him; he cut the rope that tied this slave to the others and pulled the body roughly, unmindful of the jagged stones and boulders over which it was dragged. The victim's face bled. With another oath, the man barked the order that the slaves must continue work. This was Dasapati—the man in charge of fort construction.

There are those who say that Dasapati was not always that cruel—and it was the news of Nandan's visit that spurred him on to a merciless hurry to get everything finished in time. Others say that he had always had a cruel streak but he kept it in check when the commander or headman were nearby. Dasapati and the headman had their own functions though, nominally, both came under the commander's control.

The sanyasi strode forward to where the fallen slave lay, ignoring Dasapati's smile of greeting and sat by the side of the wounded man. He lifted the man's head to keep it in his lap. Blood fell on the sanyasi's robe. He tore a portion of his robe to tie the wound, but first, he wanted to clean it free of dirt and sweat. Piteously, he cried out, as though she was the only one who could hear him, 'Mithali! Mithali! water, please, water!' Many others heard him but no one helped. Everyone expected an explosion of anger from Dasapati.

Mithali ran to the ledge where the waterpots were kept. They were too high. She could not reach them. She looked around for someone to help but none did. Mithali jumped high twice, thrice to reach a waterpot. Perilously, she clutched it, but it broke into bits against the wall, and some of its pieces crashed against her head. Her clothes were drenched but she had no water to carry to the sanyasi. Her eyes full of tears, she reached the sanyasi, and sat by his side. He lifted the wounded man's head from his lap and placed it on hers. With her wet shirt, he cleaned the wound.

Dasapati glared at the sanyasi in mounting fury. Clearly, he was in the way of work. The slaves around him had to stop as they had no place to manoeuvre. Others ceased work to watch the spectacle.

But even his own diseased mind was telling Dasapati that it was improper to tangle with a sanyasi. Not that he cared one bit for the saffron robe, but this sanyasi was the headman's guest, and even the commander wanted to receive him with honour on hearing that he came from Sage Yadodhra's ashram.

Dasapati feared nothing from slaves who could be forced to work, but he feared tantrums from the many skilled workers from town—

and now that Karkarta was to visit, he must not antogonize them, if work was to go on at full speed. Bull-headed he certainly was, but he was not without natural cunning. Clearly, he realized—what everyone knew—that a sanyasi is 'untouchable' (achhut).

Strangely, a sanyasi, in those times, was referred to as achhut (untouchable), in the sense that none could lay a hand on him in anger, or molest or harass him. Even a thief, without faith, would have enough fear of the supernatural not to rob him.

Besides, even in affection or respect, everyone would bow to him from a distance but none would touch him, except when the sanyasi himself invited or permitted a touch. This was due to the fear that even a respectful or affectionate touch might distract the sanyasi, if he was deep in prayer at that time. As a poet explains, it is not necessary that a sanyasi's eyes must remain closed when he prays:

> 'You ask why he prays wide-eyed!
> How else will your image abide
> In his heart, and thence reach Above
> To grant you forgiveness, wisdom, love?'

The poet may not be correct in presuming that some instant image-transmission took place, straight from the sanyasi's heart to the high heavens above, but everyone had to assume that a sanyasi could be at prayer, with or without his eyes closed; and none should touch him for fear of disturbing his prayers. Another poet also sings:

> Halt not his sparks that fly
> To reach right to the sky;
> Keep your distance, and let him be
> Untouched—as he prays for you and me.

Thus it is, that a sanyasi would—affectionately and reverentially—be referred to as achhut or 'untouchable'. More strangely, it was in the modern era, after foreign conquerors entered India, that the term 'untouchable' came to be applied to persons of the Sudra caste of Hindus, though no longer with affection and reverence. However in pre-ancient times, even in Sindhu Putra's days, the caste system did not exist.

Dasapati was still glaring at the sanyasi, uncertain about what he should do next to remove him. Now he smiled to himself. He found a new target. That little chit of a girl—Mithali, daughter of a servant-woman—had dared to sit by the sanyasi's side and even had the injured slave in her lap! She would pay for her impudence and that would be a lesson for the sanyasi who had encouraged her.

With a grim smile, Dasapati strode forward. Mithali did not see him. He caught her by her long hair and was about to drag her. He could not. The sanyasi had risen. He held Dasapati's offending hand in a tight grip and twisted it. Dasapati's left hand shot forward, instinctively, to strike, but the sanyasi held that too. It was as if all the strength in Dasapati's arms had drained away.

Dasapati was a big, powerful, thickset man. His reputation was fearsome and he was known for his ruthlessness and violence. How could this sanyasi, slim and slender, hold this man rooted to the spot, despite his every effort to break free!

Against the irresistible force, Dasapati's face turned purple with anger? His neck swelled and some even claim that its veins were visible for all to see. At last with a purposeful jerk, the sanyasi released his grip on Dasapati's imprisoned wrists.

Dasapati glared at the sanyasi, malevolently, with madness in his eyes. He gripped the dagger in his belt and spoke, as if to pronounce a sentence of death. 'You have abused the hospitality of the village.'

'And you have abused the hospitality of God's earth,' the sanyasi replied.

Dasapati's mind exploded. He again gripped Mithali's hair and shaking his fist, dagger held high, right in the face of the sanyasi, asked, 'You low-down lunatic! Who do you think you are?'

A crushing uneasiness took possession of the large, silent crowd. No one knew who was menaced—the sanyasi or Mithali?

Quietly, the sanyasi spoke, 'Who am I, you ask! I am Sindhu Putra.'

Sindhu Putra! None of them had seen Sindhu Putra before but was there anyone in the land who had not heard of him! Sindhu Putra! Many moved forward, daring at last to prevent Dasapati from committing a grievous, heinous sin. But it was not necessary. Dasapati himself stood immobilized. His grip on Mithali's hair relaxed and although his fist with the dagger was still high in the air, he was in a state of shock—far too bewildered to speak or move a muscle.

Sindhu Putra! The whisper went all around. It rose to a cry, a roar, a chant. Only the slaves were quiet. They comprehended nothing of the excitement around them. Most of them had their eyes riveted on their wounded comrade in Mithali's lap. Their fear had been that it was he who was menaced by Dasapati's dagger.

Mithali wanted to touch Sindhu Putra's feet. She could not rise for fear of dropping the injured slave's head. Tenderly, Sindhu Putra looked at her and her tears no longer held the terror of the last few agonizing moments. Sindhu Putra touched her head and her tears flowed now, 'easily, freely, joyfully, and though she could see him not, through the mist in her eyes, her body trembled in ecstasy.'

The injured slave opened his eyes. Possibly, Mithali's tears fell on his face and revived him. Standing above him, he saw a youth from the race he had learnt to detest. Sindhu Putra saw raw hatred in those eyes. Mithali saw the look and shivered.

Sindhu Putra picked up the injured slave. A mournful groan came from the slaves. They, comprehending nothing, feared that their comrade was being separated, to be slaughtered or thrown down the hill. Sindhu Putra heard the groan. He went into the midst of the slaves. Gently, he lowered the injured slave. He tore off his own robe to bandage his wounds and kept the rest under the slave's head as a pillow.

The half-clad Sindhu Putra looked at the slaves. They were mostly men—he saw only four slave-women. And how young most of them were!

The injured slave was as old as Sindhu Putra. He was the fifteen-year-old son of Chief Jalta and was named Jalta the Fourth, and had been captured by Karkarta Nandan's troops in the eastern region.

A young slave-girl gently massaged the injured slave, hoping to revive him. She was chanting a soft, mournful tune. It was the same melody Sindhu Putra had heard the night before, in the garden. He turned to her and asked, 'Did you sing that song last night?' She looked up, understood nothing, lowered her eyes and continued her song.

The poet identifies the slave-girl as wife of Jalta the Fourth. She had rushed headlong into the field of battle when her husband was surrounded; she too was imprisoned as a slave. They were married when she was twelve months old, and he, sixteen months, by the desire of their parents, according to tribal custom. Their marriage was not consummated, for the appointed time for such consummation arrived when both were in captivity—and the poet quotes Jalta the Fourth— 'Captives do not make love; nor do they breed.' This was not universally true, for captives elsewhere made love and produced offspring. But he was speaking for himself and his tribe.

Sindhu Putra left the slaves and faced the crowd. Some sought his blessing; others knelt to touch his feet. He pointed to the injured slave and said, 'Go, touch the feet of him, against whom you sinned.'

Suddenly, his voice rose and he said, 'Go, free all the slaves.'

There was no movement and his voice rose still higher, as he cried out, 'This I ask you, in the name of my father.'

The poet says that Sindhu Putra's repeated references to the Father, again and again, were often understood as references to his earthly father (Bharatjogi), and this forcefully reinforced in the minds of many, 'at the plantation earlier, and now elsewhere, the name and concept of Bharat Varsha—the land of Bharat.'

Sindhu Putra and Mithali were leaving the fort-site. Everyone wanted to follow them but Sindhu Putra raised his hand to halt them. 'Do not follow me until you have followed my will,' he said and then pointing to the slaves, added, 'Let them go free.'

But he did not leave immediately. In the corner, he saw a woman with a white flower in her hair. With people crowding and jostling, the flower fell. He went closer, picked up the flower, and caressed its petals. Carefully, he put the flower back in her hair and made a movement with his lips, though nothing was heard. He touched the ground where the flower had fallen. 'This earth is sacred,' he said. And, pointing to the slaves added, 'Do not smear it with their blood.' Then he left.

They watched him leave and went to Dasapati. He was sitting alone, on a high boulder—his mind in a whirl. He knew something terrible had happened to him in his encounter with the lad who called himself Sindhu Putra. But what was it? Why did my heart freeze with nameless terror? Why was my arm numb, unable to strike?

Even now, he felt a helpless sensation coursing through his arm!

He thought he had at last found the answer. His mind went to the stories of the yogis and rishis who, by prolonged meditation and austerities, had acquired the power to dominate others' wills. Such a sanyasi would look with deep concentration into the eyes of others and by a profound and deeply-willed desire learn not only their secrets but could even coerce them to act by his will. Dasapati had heard of miraculous cures by such ascetics; and Sage Dhanawantar had also said that healing by 'transference of thought and will' was possible in some cases. The sage particularly praised this art for emergency surgery, when herbs to dull the patient's pain were not available.

Yes, thought Dasapati, I was subjected to some such 'will-domination' by a manipulating charlatan who had learnt the secret of this mysterious art. Yet the one who did this to me was a mere boy! But then it was well-known that this boy was isolated and immersed for years in the Rocks of Mad Muni—and maybe he learnt the art there.

Even so, was it not said that a yogi who practises such an art needlessly, for his amusement or to promote evil, loses his power over that art?—and certainly, Dasapati regarded an action to control or dominate his will as the highest evil. But that line of thinking, he realized, led nowhere—why would a person lose his art, if he misuses it in his own way!—a soldier may, in a good cause, aim an arrow to kill an enemy in battle, whereas a robber aims an arrow in an evil cause for self-gain; but does the robber lose his power as a marksman? No, concluded Dasapati, the simple fact is that I was duped by the boy who played the masterful trick of his black art against me. This did not console him. He still felt bitterly mortified and humiliated but at least he understood how he had been tricked.

The crowd faced Dasapati. He heard their demand—that slaves be freed. Some self-satisfaction came to him and he thought—these simpletons have been duped far more than I was; I at least have

396 / Return of the Aryans

reasoned myself out of that deception but they continue under the spell. 'Go back to work,' he barked. 'Let the slaves resume their work.'

The crowd remained unmoved. Dasapati felt the need to explain, in order to regain his lost self-esteem. 'I did not hurt the lunatic sanyasi out of respect for our headman whose guest he was. Besides, it is not in me to show disrespect to a saffron robe, however unworthy this man was to wear it—and no wonder he himself felt the need to tear it, and walked out, half-naked, like a slave. Even then I forgave him, for he is known as the adopted son of former Karkarta Bharatji, and our own esteemed Karkarta Nandan would not have appreciated my harming him. But do not misunderstand my forbearance.'

He felt relieved after his long speech. It was an excellent explanation he thought, and no one, he was certain, would ridicule him ever, for his attitude of weakness towards the sanyasi.

But the crowd did not move. Dasapati glared. Someone from the crowd said, 'Free the slaves. That was his will.'

'That I shall not.' Dasapati retorted, 'Before I do that, I shall kill them. Yes, I shall, upon my soul and yours, if we have a soul.'

The blasphemy of his possible denial of the soul had no effect. Many knew that Dasapati had never believed in God or the soul, though he had a vague, formless idea of the supernatural, with a meaningless play of chance forces. But then they had nothing against Dasapati on that score; for, after all, an atheist is simply exercising his God-given right to investigate and understand for himself the eternal rhythm of the spirit, and there was hope that someday, the precious echoes of God's voice would reach his soul. Normally though, such a remark would have led to a friendly discussion. But now, everyone was silent.

Dasapati smiled weakly and said, 'Let us resume work.'

An old man took a step forward to say, 'You do not have the right.'

Dasapati was startled. 'What right?' he asked.

'The right to kill slaves. You said you would. Karkarta Nandan does not have that right. No one, but no one, has that right.'

'I have no intention of killing them,' Dasapati replied. 'We need them for work. You too, my friend. Go back to work.'

The old man stood his ground, and said, 'The slaves must be freed.'

'Go, old man,' Dasapati said. 'Go and join that stupid sanyasi. I don't need you. I need younger men to work here. Go!'

'I cannot,' the old man mournfully replied.

'Why not?' Dasapati asked, 'You need your wages so badly!'

'Sindhu Putra asked that we not follow him until we have followed his will to free the slaves.'

'Who will free the slaves! You?' Dasapati asked with irony.

'I am hoping you will,' the old man said.

Dasapati looked as if there was insanity stamped on the old man's face. The man continued, 'He is the son of Mother Goddess Sindhu.'

'If he is a god, why did he not free the slaves himself?' Dasapati shouted back. 'Why did he leave to run off with a servant girl?'

'He knows what he does. He knows what we do.'

Dasapati glared. Plainly, he saw that the same madness had affected the entire crowd. He changed his tactics and said, 'You know that Karkarta Nandan is to visit shortly. Maybe he will free the slaves, if our work has already progressed at a fast pace.'

He scanned their unresponsive faces and added, 'Karkarta has also authorized an increase in wages. There will be a bonus too when Karkarta arrives. So let us not miss the opportunity.'

'It is good of you to increase our wages,' the old man said.

'So,' Dasapati cut in, 'get back to work then. Right now!'

The old man looked back at the people behind him, sadly, as though he realized that as a spokeman he had failed them. Another spoke, 'Dasapatiji, it is not a question of our wages. The slaves must go.'

Dasapati thought: surely in this devil-ridden multitude, there must be someone with a grain of sense who has withstood the spell of that artful sanyasi! His eyes fell on a woman. He could rely on her.

It was she who wore the white flower in her hair. Her son was killed outright in a tribal raid. Her husband was captured and was presumed dead. For her work at the fort-site, she was not tempted by wages. She had enough savings. She was even entitled to a pension—which she did not claim—as Karkarta Nandan, in order to lure families to settle in the region, had offered pensions to those who, by mischance, lost their earning members. She simply wanted to do her bit to make her people strong against the tribals, as an offering to her son and her husband, lost to her. Others sometimes complained against maltreatment of slaves. She never did.

At it is, slaves at the fort-site were treated differently from all other slaves in the land. There were laws, made in Karkarta Bharat's time, to ensure humane treatment of slaves and those laws regulated hours of work, housing conditions, sanitation, food, rest periods, worship, holidays and other matters. What one Karkarta does, another Karkarta can undo, but Bharat had taken precautions. He gave the appearance of not laying down a new law but of restating the ancient law, and for this purpose, he had old songs recalled and resung. The result was that both the ancient tradition and the legal system, as enunciated by Bharat, seemed to be in line with each other in laying down decent conditions for slaves. There were even instances in Bharat's time, of slave-owners being deprived of their slaves because of persistent violations. Undoubtedly, the same laws continued in Karkarta Nandan's time too but enforcement was entirely lacking. Even so, it would not have been possible to subject slaves, publicly, to any glaringly harsh treatment, without raising a clamour. But this was the eastern region—remote, far from the inland, subject to tribal attacks and full of stories of tribal cruelty, real or fancied. Visitors were few and hardly any outsiders even saw the fort-site. Besides, these were no ordinary slaves.

At first they had been carted inland. They created hell for their new masters with their threats, unruly conduct and even assaults. A decision was made to move them back to the eastern region. Thus they were brought to work on the fort-site. Initially, even Dasapati had to go slow with the severity against slaves, for there were many skilled artisans working for wages at the fort-site and he could not offend their feelings by an open demonstration of cruelty against slaves. Slowly however, his brutality asserted itself. True, Dasapati's masters never told him to chain the slaves or subject them to severity but they gave him a deadline for completion of the fort, and surely they knew that it could not be met without crushing the slaves and distorting their lives. Some workers complained initially. A few left in disgust. But many no longer saw the suffering of the slaves as their own. Dasapati concluded that sudden and isolated acts of cruelty against slaves lead to protests from others, but if such severity is continuous and systematic, protests are stilled and even the cry of agony from the slave is viewed as a nuisance. Even so, Dasapati tried to recruit only those workers who had suffered personally from tribal raids and were unlikely to be squeamish over the plight of the slaves.

The woman, who now faced Dasapati, was recruited by him personally. She never averted her eyes if a slave cried out in anguish. The cry of the slave had, for her, the sweet sound of vengeance for the last, agonized cry she had heard from her son when he died under the tribal raider's axe. She was the one who had supported the view that slaves be made to work till midnight. Daspati could always rely on her sensible and supportive attitude. Even now he saw in her face a calm expression that distinguished her from the others, who were speaking all at once, making their impossible demand that the slaves be freed.

'Speak, Sarama, speak,' Dasapati invited her. He could not hear her response. He raised his hand to ask for silence, 'Let Sarama speak. Or is it that you wish to hear your cackle, over and over again.'

They were all silently looking at Sarama. There was accusation in their eyes, as though they already knew what she was going to say, as she had never questioned Dasapati's conduct. One of them even thought of a retort—'Vengeance does not dissolve pain. It only multiplies it.'

But as the poet tells us, 'they did not know that she had seen a vision, as even Sindhu Putra had—he, of his lost mother, as he picked up the fallen flower to put in her hair, and she, of her lost son.' The poet explains her vision fully, but to summarize:

'When Sindhu Putra had come to pick up the fallen flower, she had heard his silent footfalls and saw his soft smile; she had heard his silent voice when unmistakably, he called her "Mother!" Through the mist in her eyes, she had seen not the youthful sanyasi, nor Sindhu Putra, but her own little son. She felt the touch of his golden hand as he put the flower in her hair and a feeling of tremulous joy passed through her heart. She knew she stood before her child, face to face, and there was something he was asking. As she saw him leaving, he picked up a handful of earth—maybe to collect a pebble—and he looked at her again and at no one else and there were tears in his eyes—and she saw that others were ready to do his bidding, to free the slaves, but she—alone—had stood speechless. When he took his leave from the crowd, others called him, shouted, begged and even implored him to stay, but she stood silent, lost in the midst of the clamour of her heart! Why did she not stretch her eager arms to hold him in the depths of her being. . . .'

Thus the poet goes on to speak of her exaltation at seeing the vision of her own child, and of her anguish that she did not clasp him to her bosom, and finally, the poet speaks of her tears that 'cleansed all bitterness, eternally to remain pure and beautiful.'

Tears still welled in her eyes, and she saw the accusation in the eyes of others around her, as Dasapati questioned her. Vainly, she struggled for a voice.

But, at last, she found her voice. Now she faced Dasapati. With trembling lips she said, 'Deny him not! Let the slaves go free.'

Everyone heard her, amazed. Her calm, gentle look of sweetness disturbed Dasapati even more. He spoke, 'There are penalities for stopping work. This fort is to make us strong, invulnerable against tribal attacks. What you are all contemplating is treachery—no less.'

He realized he had made no impression on them and pleaded, 'You know I do not have the right to release slaves. Even the commander lacks that right. Karkarta Nandan alone can authorize that. We have to wait for him.' He looked at the old man who had acted as the spokesman, 'Do you understand that I do not have the right?'

It was a fair question. Certainly, Dasapati had no authority to grant outright freedom to slaves. They were not his personal slaves. But surely, he could stop them from working forthwith while making a request to Karkarta Nandan to release them altogether.

Respectfully 'Kakaji' (the old man) explained this alternative.

'I have no authority to stop their work,' Dasapati rejoined. 'Slaves are placed at my disposal to work, not to be released from work.'

Kakaji nodded, 'You must do what you must. And we, what we must.'

Lines were now rigidly drawn. Workers refused to resume work unless the slaves were released. Dasapati thundered:

'I shall put the slaves to work. You go where you have to go.'

But they said they had nowhere to go, for they could not follow Sindhu Putra until they had done his bidding and they must remain at the fort-site until that was done. 'For how long?' Dasapati asked, and they replied, 'For as long as it takes—maybe days, months—who knows!' Dasapati asked the practical question, 'Who will give you food here?' But they seemed not to worry—'He will provide.'

This was perhaps the first threat in the land of a sit-in strike, combined possibly with hunger-strike, but what can one do to free people except to threaten their wages, housing and future prosperity!

Dasapati was about to lose his temper beyond recall. He ordered his assistant, Tahila, to put the slaves back to work instantly, sparing 'neither the rod, nor the whip nor the lash.' But the mild-mannered Kakaji intervened firmly to say, 'Give up then, for ever, the prospect of our working for you, even for a moment, as long as you and we are alive. This I swear. And Tahilaji, that goes for you too.'

Tahila whispered to Dasapati—and for the first time in his life, Dasapati listened to Tahila's advice—'Nothing good can come out of all this so why not let the commander take the responsibility and blame! He is to return in three days but why not recall him earlier!'

The sun was still shining. Tahila raised long poles with highly polished, shining shields at the top—a signaling device that would be repeated by guards posted on various hills at a short distance from each other. Later, after sunset, there would be fire-signals but those might be unnecessary, if the message reached the commander earlier.

The headman was summoned too and reached immediately. The commander arrived after sunset. It took him time to understand the situation and he went methodically over each little event that led to it, questioning everyone. Even so, he wondered—how did things go so far!

The commander disliked Dasapati, but rarely interfered, except when Dasapati became excessive in his ill-treatement of the slaves. Dasapati himself was careful not to be too stern with the slaves on those rare occasions when the commander was present. Certainly, the commander wanted the fort to be ready in time, but he was convinced that Dasapati's cruelty arose from basic insecurity and did not lead to quicker results. Even so, he was puzzled, as the protest came not from the slaves but from the free men and women; and the protest was not that there should be less cruelty against slaves but that they should be freed.

The commander dismissed Dasapati's charge of the sanyasi's black arts dominating others' wills. Also, he brushed aside the headman's view that it was the god in Sindhu Putra that spoke to these people. His own reason and intelligence would not permit him to believe that a living god could walk on earth. Yet he could appreciate Sindhu Putra's feelings on seeing a slave wounded by Dasapati's callousness, and no doubt that was what had led to his demand that all slaves be freed.

'Where is Sindhu Putra, now? In the guest-house?' the commander asked.

The headman knew. Sadly he reported, 'He is not in the guest-house. Mithali said that from here he went straight to the slave-quarter.'

'Alone?' the commander asked. The headman nodded. The commander kept to himself his fear for Sindhu Putra's safety. Slaves may not be able to distinguish between a friend and a foe from an alien race. All slaves were at the fort-site, except those who were too sick. But even the sick could hurt. How would they know that he had tried to help the slaves at the fort-site!

The commander went step by step. The solution was not too difficult. A little more than one-third of the workers at the fort-site were slaves and less than two-thirds were wage-earners. The slaves worked till midnight and the wage-earners till sunset. If the slaves were let off from work, it simply meant that the wage-earners would have to do all the work allotted to the slaves. Wage-earners agreed—both for long hours without payment and to do the unskilled, back-breaking jobs assigned only to slaves. Kakaji—the commander decided—would see to it that they all held their honour in forfeit if they failed to do what was expected of them. The commander made no threats but challenged that there would be a strict accounting by Kakaji, and on Kakaji, everyday.

Surely, Kakaji is not in charge!—Dasapati objected. No, I am in charge, the commander said—and this annoyed Dasapati even more.

The commander saw the intense light of new faith burning in the eyes of all the men and women and he was certain that it would not burn out too quickly. But to be doubly sure, he spoke of Dasapati's statement reported to him—the promise of increased wages. Dasapati protested that he had offered that in different circumstances. But the commander asked, 'Yet you said to them that Karkarta has so ordered!' Dasapati explained that he had Karkarta's authority to increase the hourly wage by 22 per cent during daylight and 44 per cent at night, if circumstances so warranted. 'Good,' the commander responded, 'I am glad you have exercised that authority with effect from this morning.'

Now that an agreement had been reached with the workers, the commander ordered that the slaves be marched to their quarters. To Kakaji the commander said, 'You all may also leave, but after midnight.' They remained.

There were two distinct groups of slaves. The minority were from Jalta's tribe; the rest were from the silent eastern tribe who could not articulate a single word. There was a bond of sympathy and friendship between the two groups in the face of their common adversity.

None of the slaves understood what was going on. They had seen frenzied excitement ever since the man in the saffron robe had come and gone; and now they were released early from work! Somehow, the slaves were fearful, expecting only evil from these detestable aliens. Meanwhile Jalta the Fourth revived and that brought a sigh of relief to them.

Sentry Hardas, during the march back, told the slaves what had transpired during the day at the fort-site. Hardas could speak the language of Jalta's tribe. A poet tells the story of his earlier contact with the tribals and how he had learnt their language:

Some four years earlier, the contingent to which Hardas belonged, was moving forward to battle against tribes in the eastern region. The tribals had initially taken shelter behind a row of their huts. These were quickly set on fire with the contingent's fire-arrows. The tribals retreated to the trees beyond. Hardas heard a scream from a hut in which fire was raging. He rushed into the hut and, in the din, could not hear his commander ordering him to return. He came out of the hut, with searing burns all over his face and body, bearing in his arms a tribal child. Fire and smoke had apparently overpowered his senses, and instead of returning to his own troops, he went blindly in the opposite direction towards the tribals, faltering, falling, slipping, but all the while protecting the child. Both sides stopped shooting their arrows, lest he be hit. At last he reached the tribals and there he fainted.

Hardas returned to his own people after six months, when his wounds healed under the constant care of the tribals. Some tribals wanted Hardas to remain with them for ever, as a member of their own tribe. The tribal chief however rebuked them and the poet repeats his words: 'As you would not wish to foresake your own tribe to join another and yet be considered honourable, how do you ask another to do the same, except that you consider him without honour—and of what benefit is a man of dishonour to you! To himself! To the gods!' The poet adds that the chief's view was challenged by the mother of the rescued child, who wanted Hardas to stay back and it would seem that the chief was not much of an autocrat except in the field of battle. The mother began with a series of questions—for instance: does our god belong to our tribe alone and to none other?

But if her questions had no effect, her threat had. She said that she would marry Hardas and surely the husband of a woman of the tribe could not leave. The fact is that she was already married, but then she had obtained the permission of her husband—the father of the rescued child—to this second marriage. In such a case, the only restriction was that both husbands (or if there were more than two, all of them) would so exercise their conjugal privileges that there should be no doubt as to whose seed was carried by her next child. This, the poet tells us, called for a rigid scheduling with large intervals, and the result was that a woman with more than one husband had to be content with less sex than a woman who had only a single husband.

However, Hardas pleaded that he was already married and as a Hindu he was not entitled to more than one wife. Strange though this custom seemed to the tribals, they realized that it was possible that the gods laid down different customs for different people; and naturally Hardas was honour-bound to follow the custom of his people. All that the mother could do then was put, in accordance with the custom of her people, a 'raksha' (bracelet) round the wrist of Hardas, in a token adoption of him as her brother.

The tribals parted from Hardas with love and gifts. The chief was moved to tell him: 'God guided your footsteps once to us; should your steps be guided to us again, you shall be an honoured member of our tribe. I am only a minor chief, but Jalta the Second, to whom I sent the message, agrees, in consultation with tribal-priests and tribal elders who are custodians and guardians of our law and custom.'

Hardas was not received effusively by his own contingent. Firstly, his intervention to rescue the child had halted the battle for a while, depriving his contingent of a victory, as the tribals were able to regroup. Secondly, Hardas, on return, refused to carry arms against the tribals, claiming that amongst them was his adopted sister who had tied a raksha round his wrist. His commander simply relegated Hardas to the lowly position of sentry at the fort-site.

Hardas was useful to Dasapati in interpreting orders to slaves. Dasapati did not initially object to his speaking with the slaves often, thinking that Hardas was trying to improve his language skills. But later he flared up as Hardas began to plead for the slaves. Dasapati could not dismiss him. He could appoint and dismiss civilian workers but not someone from the army. What Dasapati did was to move Hardas away from the slaves and post him in a far corner; his new task was to serve water to the workers. Sometimes, Dasapati would call him to interpret his orders to the slaves, but he would then go back to his duties as water-carrier. It gave Dasapati a sense of power to assign a soldier to such a lowly task and it pleased the workers to have someone at their beck and call to serve them water; even Hardas was pleased to do something useful—to quench others' thirst rather than witness the misery of the slaves.

Now as Hardas marched back with the slaves, he had a single thought—to speak to the slaves about Sindhu Putra. These slaves, he knew, were hardened by cruelty and abuse; they expected only evil from the aliens who held them in bondage. Some were impressed with what the man in the saffron robe did when Jalta the Fourth was injured, but others suspected it was an attempt to revive him, simply so that he could be put to work again for those odious people.

Hardas had seen the look of apprehension in the commander's eyes when he heard that Sindhu Putra had gone to the slave-quarter.

Hardas had already failed Sindhu Putra once. That was when piteously, Sindhu Putra had cried for water to wash the bleeding wounds of Jalta the Fourth. Hardas was the water-carrier with a pitcher of water in his hand—and was it not for him to heed the call? But he had stood there, immobilized, afraid of Dasapati's anger. Helplessly then he had watched Mithali reaching for the water pot, which broke into bits over her head. Still, he had stood rooted to the spot and simply watched the spectacle as it unfolded.

Now, Hardas was in terror over what the slaves might do to Sindhu Putra, unguarded, in the slave-quarter.

Actually, it was not a part of his duty to escort the slaves back. There were other sentries for that purpose. But it was a day of strange events and an extra sentry raised no eyebrows.

Hardas spoke eloquently of Sindhu Putra to the slaves. It was left to Jalta the Fourth who had recovered sufficiently to ask, 'How can a god of such goodness be born among people of such great evil!'

But the answer came from the slave-girl. 'It is only amongst people of great evil that gods manifest themselves.' And she asked, 'Where else are gods needed more, except among the damned and the doomed and where the devil rides high?' Again she asked, 'And did you not see how their god went back, in defeat and disgrace, with his tears flowing, but not a single follower, except the girl he came with?'

Hardas listened to her with sadness, but perhaps she had said the right words. In their own abject misery and pain, the slaves still had room in their heart for sympathy for a god, tearful and disgraced and rejected by the very people who terrorized them. The slaves would not bow to that god; for he was after all a god of those wicked and wanton people and must be tainted by their corruption; but their bond of sympathy with that god was enough to wish him no hurt or harm.

Sindhu Putra sat in the slave-quarter. He was trying to concentrate on his prayers. He could not. He felt dispirited, bewildered. What folly tempted me—he asked himself—to reveal my identity as Sindhu Putra! But what is wrong with that—he tried to rationalize—surely that is my name! Did I lie?

He knew however that his lie was all the greater. He saw the adoration in the eyes of everyone as soon as he announced his name; they bowed to him as to a god. And what did I do? I started posturing like a god and demanded that they must do my bidding!

Why did I do it? he asked himself. He knew that somehow he was overcome by a nameless terror when he confronted Dasapati. Yet when the hated man was subdued and powerless, he felt a strange surge of triumph; and to a question that could be ignored without an answer, he announced himself as Sindhu Putra. And what was in my heart at that moment—he asked himself—yes, to stand out flamboyantly as a god, so that all may come to worship me. Yes, I stood there, preening myself and masquerading like a god, that I am not—and never was.

He knew that as an infant—nameless, motherless and undoubtedly abandoned by his father—he was found in a broken boat in the river. Unwilled by the hermit who adopted him, a legend grew that he was the son of Mother Sindhu. Falsely now, by his words and actions, he had acted the part, as if he truly were a living god. Again he racked his brains to find an excuse and asked—'But did I really lie?'

He had seen an act of violence against a slave. He felt as if he himself were a victim, and the blood of the slave was his own blood, and the wound of the slave was his own wound—and in his fright he ran to help. Then, he saw the girl, Mithali, threatened; again he was frightened. Impulsively, unthinkingly, he blurted out his name, lest Dasapati renewed the violence. That he could forgive himself—but not what came thereafter. He had glowed inwardly at the effect of his name on everyone and when Dasapati had stood paralyzed and others had gazed in fascination, he had felt an exhilarating sense of triumph. He knew that he had only to lift his finger and they would all do what he wanted.

The lie, then, was not in his words for they were innocent, but in the way he moved amongst them—feeling, acting, behaving, gesturing and even strutting like a god!

Even at Muni's Rocks, he had been taught that to lie, it is not necessary to speak an untruth—one can do it even more effectively through silence or by conduct and behaviour. Yes, that is what he had done with heartless ingenuity, as though he truly was the spirit of god hovering over the waters of Sindhu at the creation of earth, and had now come to walk on earth in response to mankind's prayer.

Even when he left the fort-site with Mithali, that sense of exhilaration was still with him. He had felt like an all-conquering god, with a heavenly song in his heart and his spirit raised to the realm of light as though he could see what no one else could divine.

But now in the slave-quarter, he began to realize how superficial and heartless he had been. Like footprints washed by waves, his exhilaration disappeared. He became lost in sorrow and reverie.

Even in Gatha's village, where they viewed him with reverence, he made no call to action, demanded nothing and asked none to change their ways! What has happened to me since then? At the plantation, I failed but there at least I had the grace to run away. Now here. . . .

He began to dread that at the hidden core of his heart, unknown to him, was the terrible temptation to proclaim himself a god—and he trembled. 'God, watch over every step I take and every word I utter'— he prayed, but his heart was not in the prayer, for Muni's words came echoing back at him—'Man makes his own destiny.' Indeed that is what Sindhu Putra himself had come to believe, as a part of the doctrine of karma—that man has liberty in the realm of thought and action; he is not a pawn of fate nor a slave of necessity; he is an active agent, a doer, a creator; and the spirit in him can triumph to rise above and beyond his heritage; clearly thus, he believed that the human being is the source and essence of freedom and there is no unfolding of a pre-arranged or pre-determined plan.

'Yes,' he accused himself. 'It was not an outside will from an unknown source that led me into this falsehood. I myself willed those words and actions to relish the thrill of being regarded as a god.'

406 / Return of the Aryans

This self-analysis only increased Sindhu Putra's anguish. He thought of the days ahead, amidst people in the township, bathed in their worship and he shivered. He must run and hide—but where? Mithali had spoken of the dreadful slave-quarter which the townspeople never entered. He decided to go there. Mithali wept; she wanted to be with him; but he insisted that she went back to the headman's house.

The slave-quarter was plunged in the dusk of the evening when the slaves marched in. They watched him curiously—and even Jalta the Fourth had no hatred in his eyes; his wife told him what the man in the saffron robe did for him. Even so, the slaves found it impossible to believe that this half-clad youth was a god. He had neither the venerable age nor the splendid adornments of their imagination.

'Is he really a god?' the slaves asked Hardas who alone entered the quarter with them, while the other sentries remained outside the perimetre, as usual. 'Why does a god have to pray?' 'To whom does he pray?' 'How did he become a god?' Sindhu Putra heard the questions but did not understand, for Hardas had not translated.

His mind was on his own questions that were tormenting him. But as he opened his eyes and saw the slaves around him, a new fear assailed him—has my posturing at the fort-site deluded these simple slaves into believing in my godhood! I must speak and erase any such thought from their minds—and from my own—and he said, 'I am no god. I never was a god... never shall be. Yet, all my life, I wish to devote myself to search for the eternal rhythm of God's spirit, to hear the precious echoes of God's voice and to understand the mystery of divine reality. . . . Those that call me a god are in error. I pray. . .but I do not even know the pathway which a seeker must choose. . . . For the rest, my brothers and sisters, I am like you, and I pray to the God that lives in all of you. . . .'

Hardas translated, carefully, as though the words were etched in his heart. To the slaves, the mystery was not in Sindhu Putra's words. They wondered—how did he understand and address their questions! To Hardas, it was no mystery—how can a god fail to understand!

Jalta silenced Hardas to ask: 'When your own god says he is no god, do you believe him to be a liar? Do your gods always lie?'

Yet they wondered—how did he understand? But then, he had answered, not their questions, but his own, that tormented his heart.

Their wonder was even greater that he denied his godhood! Tales of their priests were different—and in those tales, gods came forth in a shining blaze of glory, roaring and thundering, with the claim that they were the first and the last, the origin and the dissolution, and that all must take refuge in them or else they would be punished with destruction everlasting and for ever be denied the glory of His power; and only those that believed in them would be saved and the rest would perish in eternal hell-fire. If a trace of modesty ever crept into their exhortation, it was only that those gods chose not to call themselves the all-mighty God who created the universe, but simply His Viceroy on Earth, or His Son, or His Prophet, or Messenger, or First Chosen Deputy to speak to His chosen people.

But this God! He denied all such claims for himself!

Sindhu Putra closed his eyes to resume prayer. The slaves saved a portion from their scanty food-rations and kept it by his side.

A silver half-moon was shining. Sindhu Putra was at his elusive prayers. Hardas alone kept vigil for him. A woman in the slave-quarter sang. It was the same voice which Sindhu Putra had heard the night before, but it no longer had the sad, plaintive, summoning cry.

'What does the song say?' Sindhu Putra asked. Hardas translated:

'In the desolate desert of lost hopes, untold
Where the wind cries and the moon shines, unseeing and cold,
Where stars twinkle, only to sneer and mock,
At the unmoving god we made of clay, sand and rock
Where Death stalks with ghostly steps by day....
And the Devil laughs, all night, all the way....
Amidst the caravan of the defeated and the damned
Where all pathways are closed and doors are slammed....
A stranger comes by an unseen way....
With silent steps... a golden day....
He comes, He comes, Ever He comes....'

Sindhu Putra repeated the last words—'He comes, He comes, Ever He comes...'—and said, 'We too have a song that begins and ends with these words.' Actually, it was a song which Muni sang at the Rocks when Kanta parted from him after the death of her child. The song celebrated God's love and compassion—a god whose footsteps are near, who hears every soulful cry...and He comes... ever He comes.

'Many of their songs,' Hardas said, 'are almost like ours. Words differ but the sense is the same.' Sindhu Putra was thinking—Bharatjogi is right; everyone, everywhere has one soul, one aim, one goal. The bond may be invisible, yet it exists.

'Slaves were freed early, tonight! How?' Sindhu Putra asked.

'Such was your will, Master,' Hardas replied.

'You think it is possible that they would free the slaves?'

'Everything is possible for a god,' Hardas replied with emotion.

Sindhu Putra tried to pray but his mind, unbidden, went on a journey of its own. He thought of Bharatjogi's dream to free the slaves and unite the land. He recalled also what the once-blind singer told him of Bharatjogi's prayer when as a child he was going to Muni's

Rocks— 'God, give Sindhu Putra the vision to walk as my son should. . .to unite our people!'

His mind then leapt to a recent conversation when the singer told Bharatjogi, 'We have gone too far downhill. For unity and freedom, we need more than a new Karkarta. We need a god.'

And Bharatjogi had laughed, 'Do we not already have enough gods? The strong in spirit find God everywhere in their deeper self, without searching elsewhere; and the rest of us find our gods in water and fire; and in images and idols of wood and stone. And yet you seek a new god!'

But the singer simply said, 'I seek no new god. But I wait that a god may reveal himself—even to himself!'

Yes—said Sindhu Putra to himself now—the once-blind singer is right. It needs a god to stop the ugliness of slavery and the degradation of the slave. It needs a god to recapture Bharatjogi's vision of freedom and unity. Yes, let me be that god! Let me be, as I was today at the fort-site, and if they would honour my word as the word of a god—so be it. Again he heard in his mind the song 'He comes, He comes, Ever he comes.' Yes, let it be their solace—that I have come.

But another wave of thought and feeling came flooding into his mind. I will be living a lie. By what right do I degrade godhood to pass myself off as a god? Are the foundations of freedom, justice, unity to be based on a fraudulent lie? There is a god above and inside of us all—and will He not see to it that the dream of freedom and unity shall one day be fulfilled? But he remembered what Muni said, 'Evil grows—to rise like a flood. It may not subside. Even so, God does not choose to interfere with the world of man. Man moves his world, by his own actions, by his own will and by his own karma.'

Karma?—what kind of a karma would it be to pass myself off as a god! Did not Yadodhra say that 'only a trickster or a lunatic would like to be known as a god while he lives.' Do I then live the life of a trickster or a lunatic and be forever damned, condemned and scorned for this grievous sin, in my own mind, and before God, who sees all! Is this to be my karma—when all I wanted was an opportunity to devote my life to truth and piety—hopefully on the way to moksha. Why then am I drawn by this strange, irresistible idea? And what is it telling me! To live the life of a lie! And what of my moksha then? What use will the soul of God have for a dishonourable trickster who falsely wears the garb of a god on earth?

My moksha! But is it really important? Does it matter if my own moksha is unattainable, if I can take on the sorrow of those who suffer? How can I think of my own salvation, when others suffer!

He tried to gather all the diverse images flashing in his mind and to combine them into a single whole. He failed. His mind went again to Muni who said that God does not have to interfere with man's joy or suffering. Obviously then, it is by the hand of man that the suffering of man can rise or cease. Is it not man's duty, then, to intervene! Did not Yadodhra also say that it was not enough that a devotee should surrender himself to the divine in prayer, piety and meditation. The doctrine of grace and salvation meant much more—that anyone who gave up his duty to pass his time merely in prayer or to proclaim the Lord's name, but devoted not his energies to protect righteousness, was a sinner. How can anyone lose himself in inner piety alone when hearts heavy-laden cry for help or when there is even a single person who is maltreated or humiliated! Thus prepared though he was to exalt the life of contemplation, he was convinced that man could not make himself a perfect instrument for his use or attain the highest spiritual wisdom unless he sought out the action and adventure to fit God's transcendent pattern, purpose and will.

What then is the purpose of life—Sindhu Putra wondered. Is it to achieve spiritual destiny? And is this destiny to be achieved by ceremonial worship, chanting of prayers, a code of personal ethics, an inner piety or by total devotion to the Lord? Does devotion to the divine involve a surrender of man's duty on earth? Are they not sinners who merely proclaim the name of the Lord and in their assumed devotion surrender their duty on this earth? Can man seeking a surrender to the Divine obtain a release from the problems of the earth or be indifferent to them? Surely man's purpose is to live on the earth and save it. Life is, therefore, a mandate for action and none can be anchored in the Eternal Spirit by mere renunciation.

Thus Sindhu Putra kept unburdening his heart to himself. Perhaps that alone served to cast away his doubts. His mind began to resolve itself. His decision was made—yes I will take on the burden of giving shape to Bharatjogi's dream of freedom and unity; I shall not proclaim myself as a god—he decided—but nor shall I deny it. If suppression of truth is worse than an outright lie—so be it.

The procession of those who might disapprove of the course he had determined, passed before his mind's eye—and amongst them he saw those he loved and admired—Muni, Roopa, Yadodhra, the once-blind singer, and even Bharatjogi—who, he feared, would hold that such questionable means could not achieve an honourable result.

As to his own moksha, with a hopeless wave of his hand, he surrendered all claims, all hopes, all aspirations to it. He was, he realized, about to set out on a course that was based on falsehood, howsoever noble its aim. He was about to hold himself out as a god— if not by his own words, at least by his silence and conduct. Moksha shall not be mine—he told himself ruefully. But the renunciation of his own moksha no longer seemed to matter to him. He thought more of the simple, frightened men and women he had seen at the fort-site in bondage. Surely, in this God's good earth with its endless series of lives, they too counted for something—and if my moksha is the price, so be it.

'...But those were not the tales of Hindus. They were the tales of the tribal priests—and in those tales, gods came forth in a shining blaze of glory, roaring and thundering, with the claim that they were the first and the last, the origin and dissolution, and that all must take refuge in them, or else they would be punished with everlasting destruction, and for ever be denied the glory of His power; and only those that believed in them would be saved, and the rest perish in hell-fire. If a trace of modesty ever did creep into their exhortations, it was only that those gods chose not to call themselves the All-mighty God who created the universe, but simply His Viceroy on earth, or His Son, or His Prophet, or His Messenger, or His First Chosen Deputy to speak to His chosen people....'

—(From 'Songs of Tribes', date unknown, but around 5500 BC)

'...Tyranny itself serves to inspire the cry for freedom. No wonder, the cry for freedom is mute when captives are treated with mildness.'

—(Attributed by a poet to the Commander of the Eastern Region, 5054 BC)

Go, Take Your People & Go!

5054 BC

Nandan glared at Dasapati, the headman and the commander. He had summoned them to his headquarters. The commander's report, conveyed by a messenger, had mystified him. The only thing that was clear to him was that there was a revolt of townspeople. But revolt for what! Not for wages, nor for less work or privileges, but to work endlessly, in place of the slaves who must be freed! And the instigator! Sindhu Putra!

Nandan wondered—how had that scoundrel found his way to that God-forsaken land which even his father Bharat had never seen! And what had made him incite a revolt, amidst strangers, so far away from his own temple, his land, his people! Was it some deep-seated conspiracy by Bharat that his ill-begotten son win laurels in a faraway land, so that he return like a conquering hero to begin his nefarious activities here? What else! Nandan knew that every success, achieved elsewhere, was magnified, but what people saw as happening in their own midst was often treated as ordinary. So! He wanted a string of successes in a distant land and would then burst forth here to begin such revolts!

Nandan had postponed his visit to the eastern region and was now questioning the three men responsible for the township and fort-site. Dasapati's account he heard with contempt. How could he accept that the boy dominated the will of all by a spell of black art! Even Sage Dhanawantar had said that a person's mind could be put to sleep only if he willingly subjected himself to that will. This thick-skulled bully, Dasapati, who caused such terror among the slaves, must really be a weakling at heart! Nandan's assessment of the headman was no different. The headman had said that Sindhu Putra spoke with the voice and heart of a god—and Nandan wondered why he had not realized earlier how soft in the head the headman was! Only the commander was objective. The commander could not say if Sindhu Putra was simply a rabble-rouser or was guided by a higher motive, but if the townspeople felt moved to support his demand to free the slaves, the reason must partly be found in the cruelty which Dasapati's nature compelled him to adopt, and to the natural flow of sympathy from decent, honest, free people.

'What is the progress of work on the fort?' Nandan asked.

'We were behind schedule when all this started. Now without slaves, we are ahead. Each day, our people complete twice the work.'

'Then slaves are no longer necessary at the fort-site?' asked Nandan.

'That question does not arise, Karkarta,' the commander replied. 'If the slaves are made to work, the wage-earners would stop their work.'

'They would give up their wages, privileges, land grants and...?'

'Dasapati threatened them with that loss. It did not work.'

'They may not take Dasapati seriously. Maybe you could tell them.'

'I shall tell them so in your name, Karkarta,' the commander replied softly, but the implication was clear. He would speak in Karkarta's name and Karkarta would lose face. Nandan changed tack.

'You think I should send the slaves elsewhere under Dasapati?'

'No, I think Dasapati has served his purpose,' the commander replied.

'What purpose has he served?' Nandan flared up. 'Except to create this fiasco! We never had such madness anywhere else before!'

The commander did not reply. But he thought that tyranny itself serves its purpose when it inspires the cry for freedom. Elsewhere, slaves were treated mildly and no wonder then that the cry for their freedom was muted.

'Surely,' Nandan began, 'we can send slaves elsewhere, if not under Dasapati, under someone else, who will know how to handle them!'

'That will serve no purpose,' the commander replied. 'The demand is that they be freed, to go back to their own land.'

'Are we so dependent on them? Why not dismiss them?'

'We can,' the commander agreed. 'And replace them with new workers. There are many seeking high wages and land grants that we offer there. But it leads to a new situation. The present workers are determined not to leave the fort-site until their demand is met. What will be the result when the new workers arrive? Possibly a confrontation between the two groups, or maybe the new group will also be influenced into making the same demand.'

'Are we not,' asked Nandan, 'overrating the influence of this rebellious group on the new workers that we select to replace them?'

'Possibly,' the commander replied. 'But if we go by the example before us, the result may turn out to be the same. This new, sudden wave has not overtaken the wage-earners alone. All the townspeople have joined in the same demand. Bhavnan, the merchant, in whom none ever discovered previous evidence of generosity, has joined hands with Lekhan, the horse-trainer, to donate huge sums to set up a food-kitchen for the slaves.'

'Why!' Nandan was surprised. 'Have we denied food to the slaves?'

'No. But Sindhu Putra refused the food sent for him. He would eat only what the slaves ate. The townspeople now send good food for all.'

The commander saw the headman's pleading look. He did not tell Nandan that the headman's wife herself was in charge of running the food-kitchen.

The commander continued, 'Not only the townspeople; even my sentries are affected. Sentry Hardas now lives in the slave-quarter with Sindhu Putra.'

Hardas! Somehow the name was familiar. Nandan asked, 'Is he the one who was held captive by the tribals for several months?'

'No, not captive. He was their honoured guest. He rescued their child. They tended his wounds and cared for him as one of their own.'

Nandan muttered under his breath—'Now he is one of their own.'

The commander continued, 'Certainly, we can eject our workmen from there, forcefully, and bring a fresh group of workers. But where does that leave us? Our authority will be questioned; we will lose face.'

Dasapati, wilting under their contempt and neglect, now spoke firmly, 'All that is required is to arrest that rascal Sindhu Putra.'

The headman's face turned pale. The commander looked at Dasapati with pity. Nandan simply shook his head. True, Nandan had earlier toyed with the same thought. But he had dismissed it. Arrest Sindhu Putra! The reverberations would thunder throughout the land. And would they ever stop! No, that unfortunately was not feasible. He looked at the commander and asked, 'Your advice then is that the slaves be freed!'

The commander nodded. But Dasapati said, 'Karkarta, be sure, the day these slaves are freed, the workmen will also stop their work forthwith.'

Nandan looked at the commander, waiting for him to respond. The commander said: 'Dasapati may be right. But he is wrong, if he is right....'

'What!' Dasapati interrupted. The commander continued, 'I would welcome it, if our workers went back to their earlier laziness, once the slaves were freed. Because then they will know that their victory was hollow—based on empty promises which they could not keep. Their conscience will trouble them for that falsehood; their enthusiasm, in future, to follow new, unknown paths on the inspiration of any newcomers will wither; they will return to their earlier mould of obeying lawful authority and cease to interfere with affairs that are not their own.'

Nandan looked at the commander with respect. He dismissed them and promised to give his decision to the commander in the afternoon.

Karkarta Nandan may have had a few character flaws—but a foolish consistency was not one of them. He watched the weather vane and knew which way the wind was blowing; and he had no intention of being caught in a whirlwind of cross-currents. He realized that the situation in the eastern township had to be contained before more damage was done. The commander was right—he concluded—there was no sense in converting a small, insignificant issue into a major disaster; no gain in giving the misguided township the feeling of a hard-won victory; and no point in trying to confer martyrdom on anyone. And there was every danger that if the matter was left unattended for too long, the news would spread and ill-wind from the township might turn into a chilling whirlwind influencing and infecting everyone in the land.

Later, Nandan gave his instructions to the commander. 'Let slaves at the fort-site be freed to return forthwith to their lands, with a warning that they shall be re-enslaved, and never freed, if they step into our land again. Sindhu Putra shall lead them to their lands.'

'I shall send soldiers to escort them out,' the commander said.

'No, I don't want my soldiers at risk. I want no new clashes. The slaves are under Sindhu Putra's protection. Let them so remain.'

Their eyes met. Nandan was calm, unwavering, decisive. The commander had a question. The slaves to be freed belonged to two tribes but the route beyond the fort was infested by many tribes, hostile to each other. It was impossible to hope that these slaves would reach their homes unmolested; and what would happen to Sindhu Putra, alone, amidst these slaves! Would they not turn their ferocity against him, in their first flush of freedom from the hated captors of his race?

Nandan shook his head, 'Our soldiers shall not escort them.'

The commander understood but said, 'They face the danger of deadly attacks from other tribes. I shall give them limited weapons for self-defence.'

'No. They go with nothing. If such weapons are used by them against Sindhu Putra, we shall be accused of arming them to harm him.'

'Would it not be said that we led them, along with Sindhu Putra, into attack and ambush, unprotected and unarmed?'

Nandan smiled, 'Such an accusation would be unjust. Does a god need protection! How can I act from want of faith! I leave the task of escorting slaves to Sindhu Putra because I am led to believe that he is more than a mortal man who controls the weaponry of the gods.'

'Hardas must be punished,' Dasapati said.

Responding to the commander's question, Dasapati specified charges—'desertion, remaining in the slave-quarter without permission and making us all look ridiculous!'

The headman intervened, 'Why not learn from Karkarta's compassion! Graciously, he tells us to free slaves. Why go after Hardas?'

'Because he is a deserter,' Dasapati thundered.

'He is a captive of conscience,' the headman pleaded.

But the commander told the headman, 'If Dasapati charges Hardas as unsuitable for service, and demands immediate action, without need for further enquiry, I cannot ignore him.'

'I do so charge and I do so demand.' Dasapati said quickly.

'Very well.' The commander assumed a stern, judicial expression, 'Please remember then, that in view of Dasapati's clear, categorical charge of unsuitability for future service, and the demand for immediate termination of service, I do, hereby, in my capacity as the commander, in the presence of the headman, Dasapati, Tahila, and my Deputy Vashi, terminate, as from this moment, the services of Hardas, with benefits.'

'With benefits!' Dasapati almost choked.

'How can I deny benefits of past service?' asked the commander. 'Unless the charge is grave and the demand is for dismissal with disgrace!'

'But of course the charge is grave, more than grave,' Dasapati urged. 'And the demand certainly is for dismissal with disgrace.'

'You should have clarified that beforehand,' the commander said.

'I clarify it, now,' Dasapati replied hotly.

'Dasapati, surely you know the procedure. If the charges were so grave as to demand dismissal with disgrace, the case should have been heard fully to enable Hardas to reply to the charges. But you wanted an immediate decision. You tie my hands and then ask for what is beyond my power.'

'Let the full-scale enquiry be held then,' Dasapati demanded.

'Please, Dasapati, do not make me appear ridiculous in my own eyes. How can you suggest that after rendering a decision, I should submit the matter to an enquiry. What would everyone think! That you and I have some personal, deep-seated animosity against Hardas to subject him to two enquiries for one offence. Please, let us not lose the appearance of objectivity, if we are to retain the respect of others.'

'Do what you wish,' Dasapati replied with impotent rage.

'I am glad you take such an understanding view of the situation,' the commander said.

'I am a slave not when the rope ties me but only when I think I am a slave.'

—(Attributed to Jalta IV, in the Song 'Sons of Jalta I'—5054 BC)

'If she is the mother, she will constantly pray for him, bless him, guard him, protect him. Why should a son be denied the presence of his mother!'

—(Attributed to Sindhu Putra—5054 BC)

'Tat Tvam Asi (Thou art That)—But this is simply the Hindu belief of the pre-history period of Sanathana Dharma and Sanathana that man and God are akin—that all creation is a manifestation of God—that we are all fellow-workers of God— that all humanity stems from a single root and in all humanity is Brahma, the infinite spirit, and none can say where man ends and the divine begins—that we all belong to the real and the real is reflected in us all with no barriers between the self and universal spirit—that there is only one single, indestructible, abiding, imperishable reality, and truly He is I, as I am you, and you are Him. Tat tvam asi (Thou art that)—that the human soul is coexistent with God Himself, not as an emanation from Him, not as a part or effect, but as an eternal verity, birthless, ageless, and undecaying—Ayam Atma Brahma—This self-soul is Brahma....'

—(Explanations by Jalta's Virgin-Wife & Hardas—5054-5050 BC)

'Thus I do homage to the God in each and all of you.'

—(Sindhu Putra explains 'Namaste'—5054 BC)

Namaste!

5054 BC

The commander did not intervene even when Hardas joined the slaves to move out with Sindh Putra. Dasapati raised an accusing finger and said, 'He must be prevented from leaving with the slaves.' The commander refused. 'You are the one who made me remove him from service. He is no longer under my authority and can go wherever he chooses.'

The commander, however, felt a twinge of conscience when Devita, wife of Hardas, joined the party. In his heart of hearts, the commander wanted Hardas to accompany Sindhu Putra so that he should have at least one companion if a distressing situation arose. But he did not wish that Hardas' wife should brave the danger. He decided to stop her.

Hardas too was pleading with her to remain behind. But she said, 'My place is by your side.' And she smiled and added, 'Once before, the tribals tempted you with a wife. You think I will take that risk twice!'

Jalta the Fourth heard Hardas and the commander arguing with Devita. He then saw her imploring the commander. The words were unfamiliar but he had a clear idea about their argument—they were afraid of her safety amongst the tribals. Hardas, meanwhile, was begging Sindhu Putra to dissuade her from joining them.

Jalta strode forward; he felt outraged at the thought that she was being prevented from joining them because of a fear of tribals.

He forgot that he had been a slave, he forgot the degradation heaped on him in captivity; he remembered only that he was the chief of his people and that the honour of his tribe was being defiled. His words were now loud, commanding, passionate. But neither the commander nor Sindhu Putra understood a word of what he said.

At the commander's request, Hardas translated. 'He said that none shall harm a single hair on my wife's head; that the entire tribe shall protect her; that he holds his life and honour in forfeit; that he proclaims her as his mother; and declares lifelong retribution of all his father's tribes against those who seek to offend his mother.'

Sindhu Putra looked up as if from a reverie. A vague, melancholy association of words and ideas flocked in his mind and he said, 'If she is the mother, she will constantly pray for him, bless him, guard him, protect him.' Then in the hushed silence he added, 'Why should a son be denied the presence of his mother!'

The commander brooded unhappily over these irrelevant and unconnected words and wondered—where will this thoughtless youth lead them? With a resigned air he said to Devita, 'Go with God'.[1]

Again, the commander abstractedly heard Dasapati's shrill complaint that Karkarta had ordered that slaves be sent out with nothing. 'That is exactly what is being done,' the commander replied.

'Then why all these loaded mules and horses?' asked Dasapati.

'They belong to Sindhu Putra, Hardas and Devita,' the commander said. 'Or do you suggest that I should deprive them of what belongs to them?'

'That was the spirit of Karkarta's order,' Dasapati insisted.

'Then that order would be lawless and Karkarta would never give it and you and I would never obey it.'

The entire population of the town turned out to bid Sindhu Putra farewell. Sindhu Putra singled out Mithali. He placed his hand on her head. Mithali quivered in ecstasy. It was then that Sindhu Putra did what brought a gasp to everyone's lips.

Looking at the headman's wife, he joined his palms. With palms pressed together, he raised his hands to his forehead. It was no different from an exaggerated version of the respectful Namaste of later times, which causes no surprise nowadays. But in Sindhu Putra's times, it was the gesture of a slave. No free man, unless he was an actor taking on the role of a slave in a theatrical performance, would ever demean himself by adopting such a gesture.

The origin of this gesture of raising hands, with palms pressed together, was not shrouded in mystery. Captors of newly captured slaves always took the precaution that the slaves march with their hands tied together, and raised, to remain visible in order to guard against concealing a weapon or an attempt to untie the hands of another slave. Later, this gesture was enforced as a compulsory greeting by all slaves, even though they may be docile, and the only difference was that the hands were not tied but were expected to be raised voluntarily by the slave, with palms pressed together, to greet a free man. It was like a badge of dishonour and was imposed at the insistence of wage-earning workers who did not wish to be mistaken for slaves.

---

[1]Here a poet intervenes, loudly, to claim this as evidence of the commander's conviction that Sindhu Putra was a god, for how else would the commander ask Devita to 'go with god.' But others view it simply as a traditional statement of farewell, commonly uttered all over the land to bless those who are about to depart.

It was this astonishing gesture of the slave that Sindhu Putra made—with his palms pressed together and raised to his forehead—as he faced the headman's wife. Involuntarily, her hands moved, though not to greet him in the same fashion but simply to touch his hands.

Sindhu Putra passed on to greet others with the same unvarying gesture of the slave, his lips moving, but none heard what he said.

Everyone seemed nonplussed. Many bowed. Some kissed his robe; the nearest that some came to repeating the slave-gesture, was when they raised their hands to hold Sindhu Putra's hands in their own.

Many saw Sindhu Putra's lips moving. The words were inaudible.

From a distance, Jalta the Fourth watched with contempt. Earlier, he had told his virgin-wife that he would ensure that Sindhu Putra was accepted as a member of his father's tribes. And she had replied, 'Yes, a god and his tribe belong together.' He had smiled, not ready yet to accept him as a god, but with a growing bond of affection.

Now, however, Jalta felt uncontrollable fury against Sindhu Putra, as he saw him moving from person to person among those hated people, repeating the demeaning gesture of a slave. Why is he degrading himself? No, he does not belong to us—never shall—he said to himself.

Meanwhile, as Sindhu Putra moved on, greeting each with the same gesture, he came to face to face with a child barely two years old, in the arms of an eight-year-old girl. Unnoticed, the child, as children often do, was trying to imitate Sindhu Putra's gesture of the slave. Sindhu Putra smiled; perhaps the eight-year-old girl felt that as his lips moved into a broad smile, he had omitted to utter the silent chant of blessing with which he had favoured all; and as he was moving on, she felt sad and complained: 'Baba, will you not bless my little brother and say for him what you said for all the others!'

Sindhu Putra arrested his footsteps, looked at the eight-year-old girl and the two-year-old child. To each he said, 'Tat tvam asi.'

The silent words were silent no more. To each as he now passed them, the words were clear, distinct, audible—'Tat tvam asi' (Thou art that). What did these words mean? Many knew and understood, though each perhaps may have explained it differently.

Many no longer felt bewildered by his strange slave-gesture—and realized, he was simply holding himself out as a slave to the God within us all—as his submission to the ultimate. The urge for the same humility came over some... then over many. They too raised their hands, palms pressed, in the same gesture, to reciprocate Sindhu Putra's greeting; and they chanted Tat tvam asi even more soulfully than Sindhu Putra—for whatever their doubts about the supremacy of ther own self, they were convinced that facing them was a youth who had found fulfilment in the heart of the Eternal.

Others, whom Sindhu Putra had passed earlier, rushed forward with their belated slave-gesture. The chant of Tat tvam asi filled the air.

While the townspeople were in ecstacy, Jalta watched, bewildered. Why were the townspeople making slave-gestures to Sindhu Putra! Inappropriately, he laughed. He was convinced that there was madness in the air. Many slaves, by his side, joined in his laughter. His virgin-bride and the Chief of the silent tribe remained quiet.

Sindhu Putra, at last, walked towards the slaves. Here too, his hands were raised to the forehead, palms pressed against each other. It was Jalta's virgin-wife who raised her hands to make the same gesture. Chief of the silent tribe—and then his men—followed her example.

Jalta's fists were clenched. Anger reentered his heart—why must I suffer the ignominy of raising my hands in the gesture of the slave! Even during his captivity at the fort-site, he had told himself, 'I am a slave not when the rope ties me but only when I think I am a slave.' He glared at Sindhu Putra. Maybe, truly he is a god—but then he is a god of that hated race—not ours! And what is his purpose? To make us slaves for ever! Not in body alone, but also in spirit! That willingly, we submit as slaves! Slaves of that hated race! Never!

In defiance, Jalta raised his fist at the silent townspeople across the distance. The slaves standing next to him also raised their fists, with a mighty roar, in a show of solidarity. Many townspeople saw the raised fists and heard the shout. They misunderstood. They saw it, not as defiance, nor a challenge, but an invitation for a rallying cry—and their cry went up, loud and clear—'Tat tvam asi'!

It was Jalta's turn to ask Hardas, 'What are they saying?'

Hardas explained, 'They say there is God in you and to Him and to you, they salute.'

Jalta misunderstood. He pointed at Sindhu Putra to accuse him, 'Yes, there is god among us. But he is their god, your god, not mine, not ours!' His accusing finger was still pointing at Sindhu Putra.

Silently, his virgin-wife kissed his outstretched finger, as Hardas began to explain the meaning of Tat tvam asi—'The God in you—He that resides in you—He whose divine flame ever burns in You—You whose soul is the same as that of God's own....' Even as he spoke, Hardas wondered how, and from what source, these words were tumbling from his lips! Were they the result of his discussion in the slave-quarter with Sindhu Putra who spoke of the words of Muni of the Rocks!

Jalta wondered—first, they make us slaves, then they make us gods; first they are treacherous and callous, then they are stupid and dazed. But he wavered, as he noticed, possibly for the first time, the lips of his virgin-wife resting on his hand. Perhaps it was the plea of that love which overcame his resistance or maybe it was because Sindhu Putra came to stand before him just then, but as the poet tells us, 'his hands rose in silent, spontaneous salutation as fervent as Sindhu Putra's, though with what thoughts—who can say!'

The hands of all the slaves rose in unison, in the same silent salutation—but, again, the poet tells us, 'It was no longer the gesture of the slave; it was the affirmation of their freedom; and they saw with the eye of their own inmost heart, the unique splendour of "oneness", of "at-one-ment", breaking through the darkness of their mind—and thus it became the salute of the liberated and the free!'[2]

As for the mantra 'Tat tvam asi' itself—it was certainly not invented by Sindhu Putra. This mantra appears in many ancient Memory songs, sung well before his time; maybe, he had learnt it from Muni, Roopa or the once-blind singer. The fact however is that the mantra itself remains current in the later Vedic, post-Vedic and the modern era. It was quoted in *Chandogya Upandishad—VI-8-7*. Besides, its many variations, current in Hindu thought in the centuries before Sindhu Putra's time, have also found a pride of place in other Vedic literature—for instance, in the *Brihadaryanaka Upanishad*, we have: *Aham Brahmasmi*—I am Brahma, the infinite. *Isa Upanishad* also recaptures the mantra which was current in the age of Sanathana Dharma, when it says: *Yas tvam asmi so ham asmi*—you are indeed that I am. Again, *Isa Upanishad* expresses itself in the thought and words of the pre-ancients when it repeats 'Soham—I am He, that am I.' The *Mundaka Upanishad* also reflects the words of the ancients of Sanathana to say *Idam sarvam asi*—thou art all this. Again in the *Mundaka Upanishad* is the reappearance of the words of the elder of the River-village of the Sanathana Dharma, who greeted the old man who was the first to call himself a Hindu—and he had said, *Brahma eva idam visvam*—this whole world is Brahma.

These and similar quotations appear and reappear throughout Vedic literature to recapture the Hindu belief of the pre-history period of Sanathana Dharma and Sanathana, that man and God are akin—that the human soul is coexistent with God Himself, not as an emanation from Him, not as a part or effect, but as an eternal verity, birthless, ageless, and undecaying—*Ayam Atma Brahma*—this self-soul is Brahma....

---

[2] Slowly at first, but swiftly then, the slave-gesture became a common form of greeting, to salute and celebrate the flame of divinity that each acknowledges in the other—'Tat tvam asi'. It is passed on to the modern age as 'Namaste', even though the pressed palms are raised not always to the level of the forehead, but often stay below the chin or even at the breast.

'God! to save a god, how many must die!
Are you God, deaf to the innocent's cry!
Keep your gods then to yourself, God,
Or else, one day they'll steal your rod!'

—(*A poet's cry against Sindhu Putra for bloodshed in thirteen tribes—5054 BC*)

'*A fire was lit in the heart of the non-believer to consume him quite. And a believer emerged to go forth—onward into the light.*'

—(*From the Song, 'Commander! Whose Silent Call Commanded Thee?'—5054 BC*)

The Long March

5054 BC

The slaves were slaves no more. As they marched out to freedom, they wondered about Sindhu Putra—this god of the alien people marching with them, is he also our god! But how is that possible?

They heard Jalta's virgin-wife, as she haltingly explained 'Tat tvam asi'—and the words were hers, simplified, in their own idiom, what Hardas had explained. She spoke of the majesty of all mankind and of the conception of God as the ultimate cause from whom we are all born, through whom we live, and unto whom we return and merge. And they wondered, recalling their own ancient myths:

- But then what about hell everlasting and hell-fires unending!
- What about that mistake of God's First Servant, steeped in original sin, whose hands trembled as he fashioned us all!
- What about our exile, then, from deathless heaven to this desolate earth for our failure to be fitted into the God image by that mistake!
- Is this youth the promised Redeemer! Is he the one prophesied to slay the banished First Servant, whose legions of thousand devils and ten thousand serpents guard the routes to the gate of heaven!

Each marched with diverse thoughts—but many wondered why their hearts were cleansed of hatred against the people who had held them captive.

Jalta troubled himself with no such wandering thoughts. He was concerned about sudden attacks from the hostile tribes on the route. In the exhilaration of freedom, he had forgotten that terrible danger.

They carried no weapons and had no protection and there were too many tribes on the way to allow them to pass unmolested.

At his bidding, everyone halted to collect jagged stones. It would be a poor defence, but then, better to die fighting than be slaughtered or enslaved without inflicting a penalty. If some wondered why it was necessary to take precautions with a god in their midst, Sindhu Putra disappointed them. He took out his long knife from his saddle-bag and advised them to use it to make wooden, sharp-ended javelins and spears from trees.

Hardas took out the weaponry he had brought, concealed on two mules. It included an axe, six swords, a few daggers, short spears and knives. He began making new spears from trees and encouraged others to do so, lending them his knives and axe for this purpose.

It had to be a long halt to make a number of spears and sticks.

Everyone saw Jalta's sadness. He was torn between the desire to reach his lands without delay and to prepare for defence. It was not simply the nostalgia for his home. He and his virgin-wife had decided not to consummate their marriage during captivity though its time had arrived. Now they were free. But the two priests from their own tribe, enslaved with him, had died in captivity. They now had no priest for the ceremony to sanction consummation. I am the upholder of law in my tribe, he argued with himself. How can I break the law!

Sindhu Putra understood Jalta's sorrow. Hardas had told him. He held the hands of Jalta and his virgin-wife. Hardas translated, 'The time has come, says Sindhu Putra, for you two to be joined as man and wife.'

Jalta shook his head while Hardas translated. It cannot be done, unless there is a priest to witness and sanction it.

Sindhu Putra's hand moved to his breast, then heavenwards and finally it pointed to everyone present there. All he meant was that he was a witness, the gods above were witness, and everyone there was a witness. But the effect was different. It was as if he had said—I am the one sent from the heavens to lay down the law for all.

Can you disbelieve a god who seeks to fulfil your own heart's desire! If Jalta had any lingering doubts, they were laid to rest by encouragement from the Chief of silent tribe, in his clear sign language. Why stop the rhythm of your heartbeat and the urge in your body to wait for the senseless chant of an old priest! Perhaps if they had older men among them, they could have warned them of the power of priests who alone could command, and even drown, the voice of God.

Jalta and his virgin-wife needed no more encouragement. Blessed by Sindhu Putra, they went far behind a grove of trees and lay down in the soft, cool grass. There was little they said to each other, their thoughts wandering to reenact the dreams of their past, and re-discovering them in the beating of their hearts and warmth of their bodies. Gently and unhurriedly they moved and together they stitched an unbroken tapestry of love and fulfilment. No, they would never forget their first mingled cry of joy, pain and ecstasy!

The Chief of silent tribe raised his hand to stop work while the couple lay together, unseen, behind a clump of trees. He wanted no noise of hacking trees to disturb the couple. It was then that Sindhu Putra went to him, with his slave-gesture (Namaste), to plead that work go on. Cheerfully, the Chief gestured to countermand his order. The couple was blissfully unaware of noise. They heard only their own heartbeats.

The Chief wondered: is Sindhu Putra then expecting an imminent attack? Even Hardas asked. Sindhu Putra replied, 'Who can attack if you are ready!' To Hardas, the answer was clear—'Be prepared, and the enemy would not dare.' But Hardas doubted if the Chief would understand. The Chief did and his sign language was clear and expressive—'Peace belongs to the vigilant—to him who is prepared.'

Later, when the march recommenced, Jalta wondered how he would meet the criticism for abandoning the time-honoured custom that required a priest to sanction consummation. But he would argue— what could I do against the advice of him who was known as a god! Surely—they would argue back—he is not a god of our tribe. So what! Did not this god secure our freedom and save our lives? But Jalta feared they would sneer. Is your freedom, or even life, so important, so blessed, so auspicious, that it confers godhood on another! Don't you understand that it was his own tribe that held you captive and then released you; so all that is necessary is to imprison you, degrade you, and then release you and you reward your captors with godhood! And your life! Why not confer godhood on a sperm of your father's semen, or the womb of the mother, or the goat or the cow that gives milk!

Do I have an answer for the priests?—Jalta wondered. He thought of the long, treacherous journey ahead to their homeland; he feared fierce enemy attacks on the march. Many would die. Perhaps he himself would fall. But his silent prayer was that his wife survive and out of their union, a child be born to be the chief of his tribe.

To his wife, Jalta said, 'None must doubt the sanctity of our union, nor question the right of our offspring to be the chief.' She had no idea of the thoughts whirling in his head and simply smiled.

He gazed at Sindhu Putra and continued, 'I shall declare him a god. None can then question the validity of our marriage or the legitimacy of our child. I shall call on all the tribes to accept him as a god from now on.' Again, she smiled, intrigued over his last phrase and simply said, 'But that he always was and is.'

He decided to make the declaration there and then. He walked to the Chief of silent tribe. In their joint captivity, he had learnt enough sign language to 'converse'. Chief asked no questions nor reasons, but agreed readily, willingly, touching his own heart and even Jalta's head— no doubt to bless Jalta for the pious thought.

The march was halted for Jalta's announcement. He declared Sindhu Putra as god of all tribes 'from end to end, for all time, from the first arrow of time, to time unending.' Appropriately, the Chief of silent tribe repeated the declaration in sign language.

But others deal with the account unemotionally. Sindhu Putra, they assert, understood from Hardas that Jalta's announcement was made, possibly, to raise the morale, in case of attack, and to assure the tribesmen not to lose heart, as they had a god in their midst. Nandan's poet-great-grandson again asks, 'Why did he not deny his godhood?' But a poet replies, 'How can a god deny what is true?' And later, the cry of the poet-great-grandson of Nandan would be heard across the centuries that this false, conniving god, Sindhu Putra, stood silently by, jubilant at accepting the homage from all.

Later, Nandan's great-grandson would correctly assert that the tribal custom in no way permitted Jalta to anoint a god; it was left to the twenty-two tribal priests to make such a recommendation, and when the last of those twenty-two died, another group of forty-four priests was to consider that recommendation; and thus there were no 'instant' living gods, appointed in a hurry, to walk their tribal earth. A poet argues that 'what is true of lesser gods, cannot be applied to Sindhu Putra,' which led to the frustrated retort from Nandan's great-grandson, 'How can gods be less or more! Or do we speak of lifeless pebbles on the seashore!'

But other poets argue: Why blame Sindhu Putra! It was Jalta's declaration, not his. Jalta had wrestled with his mind and concluded: If I live, I shall fight to justify my declaration; but if I die on the march, I will be sheltered by it, with none to question the sanctity of my marriage and my child. The dead, he knew, were treated with respect and much was forgiven them. His brothers too, he was confident, would fight to protect his honour and memory. And the poet adds, 'Thus through error Jalta reached the truth!'

Soberly, Jalta watched his motley army carrying all kinds of sticks and blunt spears freshly hewn from trees. They would frighten no one, much less hurt or harm any hostile tribe. He dared not hope for the miracle that they would not be attacked.

Slowly, they marched, day after day, with their pitiful weapons, taking care not to make any noise. Alert and thoughtful, they scanned passes ahead for movement, wondering if the owl-hoot or birdsong they heard were signals of enemy lookouts calling out to their tribes to attack. When they were in valleys and gorges, they looked up fearfully, wondering if boulders would be hurled at them, to begin a furious assault. As they passed more and more dangerous passes, traditionally controlled by hostile tribes, the enemy inactivity surprised them and covertly, Jalta and many others kept looking at Sindhu Putra, wondering if it really was a god guarding them. The Chief of silent tribe simply nodded with a smile as if he understood the question in Jalta's mind and was answering it in the affirmative. But even he looked concerned when they reached a pass well within enemy land.

But nothing happened. They passed unmolested. Their relief was immense. Jalta said, 'My mother must have prayed for us, last night.' He almost bit his tongue as Hardas translated. From his priests' tales, he knew of the wrath of the gods who tolerate no challenge to their absolute authority—and here he had praised his mother's blessings and not of the god in their midst. But Sindhu Putra's expression creased into a soft smile. His eyes lit up and putting his hand on Jalta's shoulder he said, 'There is, then, nothing, my brother—nothing—to fear, any more—when the mother prays for you and me.'

But they knew—even if Sindhu Putra did not—that one treacherous pass still remained. This pass was dominated by a murderous and vigilant enemy tribe which certainly would not let them pass unmolested. The lay-out of the terrain was also such that they would be in a frightfully vulnerable position even against a small number and that fearful tribe always had a large attacking force. It was unthinkable that their lookouts would not be watching.

The land of this enemy tribe was rough and barren. It had not always been so. There was a time when it had been lush and green. But over the centuries, the tribe had violated the ageless oath of mankind to wildlife, and started the slaughter of animals and birds even for sport. Either as cause or effect or from the just wrath of the gods, their forests were now dwarfed. Now they relied on warfare and catching slaves and sold able-bodied slaves to tribes far away. The wounded and the weak amongst their prisoners would often serve to feed the tribe itself.

Jalta was convinced, as was the Chief of silent tribe, that whatever their good fortune all the way across this vast distance, there was little hope that this terrible tribe would not attack. As though their worst fears were about to be realized, they could now hear the noise of a distant drum. It rose as they went along.

What else could these drum-beats signify, except to call the tribe to arms! They looked at Sindhu Putra but he seemed calm.

Jalta ordered his men to re-form in single file, in a zig-zag pattern, so that the onrush of the enemy horde did not wipe them out in a single sweep; and some may have a chance to hit back or escape.

The Chief took time to reorganize his men, despite Jalta's plea for haste. The Chief gazed at Sindhu Putra as if he wanted to unburden his heart, but could not form the words. Sindhu Putra held his hand.

Full of faith, the Chief of silent tribe began his task of forming his men in lines, except that he asked twenty men to form a circle around Jalta's wife. 'Why?' Jalta asked—grateful and surprised—but the Chief gave a hurried, gestured explanation which could mean that either the Chief adopted Jalta's wife as his own daughter, or as daughter of the tribe, or that the child in her womb needed protection—and in any case she had to be safeguarded. The Chief looked at Hardas' wife, but thought that she needed no protection, as she was immediately behind Sindhu Putra.

Jalta and the Chief were side by side, ahead of their troops.

The drum-beat was now louder. Its echoes reverberated menacingly. Clearly, the blow was about to fall.

They went on and on, fearing that each step would take them to an ambush—terrible, treacherous and deadly. The drum-beats resounded and the enemy was obviously on its way, ready to slaughter them.

But no; the blow did not fall; none blocked their way. Even so, they did not slacken their speed. 'Let us help the miracle'—was the thought in their minds as they kept running. They crossed the danger-point, their hearts pounding, but did not slow down, nor did they speak; each was thinking his own thoughts, but as a poet tells us, there was only a single thought they all shared, and it was the same as before—and as they gazed at Sindhu Putra, they all felt that it was a god who was guarding them all.

They heaved a sigh of relief as they neared the outskirts of the village of Jalta the Third. Here, as nowhere else, lookouts were watching with keen alertness. It did not take long for the group of Jalta the Fourth to establish their identity. The reunion was joyous and the drum-beats to announce the safe return of Jalta the Fourth, his wife and his men, were louder than any that had been heard in the village before.

How did this miracle of miracles occur? Were the thirteen hostile tribes, on that perilous route, in a total state of daze and stupor, or had they grown suddenly supine or benign! Why this inactivity on their part! Was it some black art or magic—as Dasapati might have said? What then! Was it really the miracle of Sindhu Putra?

Many poets have chosen silence, as if to lead to the inference that it was indeed Sindhu Putra's miracle. But not all the poets. There are some who say:

As soon as Sindhu Putra marched out with the slaves from the fort-site, the commander felt impelled to move with the full contingent of his troops into the eastern region to close all the routes of the thirteen hostile tribes which could possibly harass the slaves marching with Sindhu Putra.

The commander had fully adhered to Karkarta Nandan's instructions that the slaves must leave without anything—particularly without arms and weapons—defencelessly. There were no other instructions from Nandan and therefore none else that the commander felt obliged to follow.

Certainly, Nandan knew of the peril that the slaves would face on the way from the thirteen deadly tribes—and it may be that the thought crossed his mind that it would not cause him ceaseless anguish if all the slaves were slaughtered, along with Sindhu Putra himself, on the route. Maybe, he even expressed that private thought to himself. But then how could it constitute a direction to the commander!

It was, in any case, the commander's duty, on his own initiative, to make a show of strength and even carry out selective sorties against hostile tribes, to keep them in check. Somehow, the commander decided that this was the right moment to do so, in full force; and he chose, as his target, the thirteen tribes that could pose a danger to the slaves marching with Sindhu Putra. In his campaign, he made no frontal attacks, but went with speed to simply block the routes, preventing the movement of the hostile tribes towards the passes through which the slaves were to march.

Hostilities did break out—intense and furious. The last battle was fought in the area from which loud and repeated drum-beats were heard by Sindhu Putra's party. It was bloody and fierce. The tribals were beaten back but the commander himself lost his life.

Some say, the commander died instantaneously as the tribal arrow pierced his heart, and they all claim that his features were composed, his eyes peaceful, as if he was in a relaxed, untroubled, dreamless sleep. But some poets add that the commander's hands were clasped together, in what was once the slave-gesture. Others argue that it could be that the commander's hands moved in an instinctive, reflex action, simply to clutch at the arrow in his heart, to pluck it out but somehow the hands got together, never to reach the arrow—and he was dead in the meantime, with hands clasped.

His sudden movement across the routes of thirteen tribes was, initially, so carried out as to give an impression to his own troops that he was keen simply to make a show of strength, without of course shirking from hostilities if he was challenged; and challenged, he certainly was, time and again.

The miracle of miracles, then, was not that none of the hostile tribes chose to molest Sindhu Putra's march. How could they, with the solid wall of the commander's troops blocking them! The miracle, as a poet said, arose in the heart of the commander—'A fire was lit in the heart of the non-believer that consumed him quite; And the believer emerged to go forth with all his might.'

The freed slaves, who marched with Sindhu Putra, knew nothing of the commander's decisive push into the eastern region. To them, the failure of the thirteen vicious tribes to attack them was simply the miracle of Sindhu Putra. There was wonder in their hearts, but no doubts and no questions in their minds.

It took a little time but the entire Jalta tribe gathered—men, women and children—to greet the new arrivals. The two elder brothers of Jalta the Fourth were also there, along with his mother.

When the tale was told to all who gathered there, none doubted how this miracle had occurred. They knew nothing of the commander's campaign against the thirteen tribes. Their scouts and lookouts had heard incessant battle-drums from the distance, but that was not surprising in this war-torn territory, where each tribe was at the throats of the other. All that the jubilant Jalta tribe knew was that their sons and daughters had walked through the valley of death, defied the devil, and come out, unharmed and safe, because of the god that escorted them.

When Jalta the Fourth guided his blind mother to Sindhu Putra, she half-embraced him shyly, though wondering if her greeting was too familiar. Sindhu Putra hugged her tightly. From the once-blind singer, he knew how the blind 'see', and he guided her hand to his face so that she may touch his features. He did not know that the blind shed tears. She did. Yet she was in an ecstasy of joy and said, 'If you were not a god, you would be my son.'

Jalta the Second, her eldest son, intervened with a jest, 'Mother, be careful, you have three sons already as chiefs, and there isn't enough land to go round for yet another son who would be a chief.'

She stared at them with her sightless eyes, and said, 'Chief! You will call him a Chief! He is Chief of all Chiefs! Nobler, mightier, greater....' She was about to say, 'greater than your father,' but the memory of her husband was far too precious—and painful, for always in her sightless eyes was that last terrible image of her husband consumed in three fires. In a hushed tone, she concluded, 'Yes, he is nobler, mightier, greater than all. Honour him then, all of you.' She herself turned back to grope for Sindhu Putra's feet, to touch them as a mark of reverence, but he held her hands tightly and clasped his own hands over hers with palms pressed, in the familiar gesture of 'Namaste,' and said, 'Thus I pay homage to the mother in you, Mother, and to the God in you, Mother.'

'He who leads his people does not have to be a total scoundrel. But nor can he afford to be godly. Certainly, he must serve the devil more than he can serve god. Sometimes, a Chief may sacrifice an individual to serve the larger greed of the community; or he may declare a war that a god considers unholy. From a Chief, his people expect courage, but a god may demand honour. How then is it possible for a person to be a leader and yet serve god! And when that inevitable conflict arises, whom does he abandon—his people or his god? But then it is often easy to abandon god. Not so easy to give up power!'

—(Chief of silent tribe announcing his abdication—5053 BC)

The First Word of God!

5053 BC

The Chief of silent tribe and his men were honoured guests in Jalta land. A messenger sped to their homeland to spread the glad tidings of their safety. The messenger, however, was told not to announce the names of those who had died in captivity. Such sad announcements would have to wait until the Chief visited the families of those who had lost their loved ones.

The Chief's younger brother, who acted for him in his absence, rushed to Jalta lands to escort him back with honour. The Chief declined, and indicated that he would always be by Sindhu Putra's side. He wanted to surrender the Chief's office in his brother's favour.

The brother objected. Apparently, a Chief had no authority to resign without his people's consent, until he reached the age of fifty. To get that consent, he had to appear before his people, and not send messages by proxy from a distance. Nor could he appoint a successor without the consent of his people. For that too, he had to appear before his people. Both his resignation and the appointment of a successor would be considered illegitimate, if these were decided on foreign soil, away and apart from his people.

The priests who accompanied the brother were sad that the Chief wished to resign. But they agreed with his forceful arguments, that it was not possible to be a Chief and yet serve a god; sometimes, a Chief might sacrifice an individual to serve the larger greed of the community; or he might declare a war that a god would consider unholy; he might even enslave a person for whom a god would demand freedom. From a Chief, his people expected courage, but a god demanded honour. How then was it possible for a person to retain his position of guiding the destinies of his men and yet serve a god! And when that inevitable conflict arose, whom did he abandon—his people or his god?

Even so, the priests pointed out, forcefully, that he was on foreign soil, among alien people—howsoever friendly they were; and all that he had said was wise and just, but it had to be said in the presence of his own people, on his own soil. That was the law and how could the Chief, who was the upholder of the law, flout it?

The Chief's brother was mystified over the Chief's reluctance to go to his homeland, even briefly, to resign. If indeed the Chief's decision to abdicate was firm and final, the brother wanted his own succession to the chiefship to be regularized in the proper way so that no one questioned its legitimacy now or in the future.

The younger brother went straight to Sindhu Putra, with the gesture of Namaste—for that greeting was now beginning to be familiar to everyone. His hand-movements and signs, even without help from Hardas, made it clear that it was his heart-felt desire that Sindhu Putra accompany them to their land. He pointed to all his people to convey that it was their fervent prayer too. Sindhu Putra readily accepted the invitation and even started drawing lines on the floor, in an effort to understand the route to that land. The brother kept drawing lines, as Sindhu Putra went on encouraging him, not only to indicate the route to his own land, but the routes around and beyond, with the physical features of mountains, forests, rivers and deserts. Sindhu Putra was thinking that Sage Yadodhara's charts though not totally accurate, were not far wrong either.

After which, the brother went to interrupt the heated though silent exchanges still going on between the Chief and the priests. With a dramatic flourish, he announced that Sindhu Putra wished to travel to their land and expected the priests and the Chief to join him in that journey. The argument was at an end. The priests smiled. The Chief nodded sombrely.

True, the Chief of the silent tribe wanted to remain by Sindhu Putra's side, but he did not want to take him to his land. His tribe had slaves and his new god, he feared, would demand their freedom.

Mournfully, the Chief stood alone, unable to shake off his gloom, while his brother, Rohan, and the priests moved to Sindhu Putra. They found him poring over the lines which Rohan had sketched to indicate lands far away. Already, Sindhu Putra was thinking of Yadodhra's charts and had begun to draw lines. The priests watched him politely, but suddenly, an old priest, Khashan, held Sindhu Putra's hand, to stop him from drawing further. With a smile, the old man began to change a few lines with delicate movements of his stick, and went on to draw new lines and add more features, twists and turns. His sketches were not too clear, but his gestures were certainly attempting to indicate hills, mountains, streams, forests and populations of birds, animals and humans. At last, he completed his silent presentation of showing a number of streams joining together to tear through the mountains and form a single huge river the shore of which was densely populated and had temples and tall huts.

The sudden onset of despair which overtook the silent Chief did not pass in a flash; he realized he would now have to face his people along with Sindhu Putra; how was he to be true to his new god! How would he pit himself against his people to remove slavery? How? How would the faith that moved him enter their hearts? They would say that the other tribes had slaves too since time immemorial.

Actually the Jalta tribe was the only exception which tolerated no slavery. But then the Jalta tribe was not ancient. It was no more than 800 lunar years old. Unlike the other tribes, it did not claim its descent from the sun or moon or other heavenly bodies. It was formed by a priest in disgrace, in love with a pregnant slave-girl. They had escaped and found sanctuary in the forest. Later, some runaway slaves who had escaped from other tribes, joined them. But they were all men. The priest did not restrain them from raiding outposts of various tribes to capture women, lest his own wife become the centre of their amorous attention. It was, however, his wife who laid down the law when the first batch of captured women was brought. She declared that none be held as slaves and women who wished to leave, be escorted back, with honour and safety. 'No masters, no slaves', she thundered, would be tolerated in their midst. If the priest himself was visibly trembling, no one realized that it was in fear for his safety from these violent men. They all thought that this man of God had been overtaken by some higher emotion, somewhere from high above. Their confidence in the priest and his wife became all the more unshakeable as the captured women refused to return to their earlier miserable existence. It was then that the priest's wife called upon her husband to bless them all, but for some strange reason—maybe in terror—he forgot the chants, with which he was familiar as a priest. Instead, his wife's words rang in his ears, and he went from person to person, repeating, 'No master, no slave', and his wife demanded that they all repeat this vow. They did. The ritual had its cleansing effect. They felt their own taint of slavery erased.

The priest's wife was still not done. She demanded that each man build a hut and wait for a woman to claim him; and the priest then pronounce them man and wife, 'for that is how free men and women must wed to have children who are forever free.' Somehow, they curbed their passion to have those women there and then, convinced as they were of the wisdom and piety of her words—that she simply did not want even a shadow of slavery, ever, to mar their offspring.

Since then, she became the acknowledged leader of these runaway slaves and captured women, though the exact line of command was uncertain. It was assumed that the priest heard God's voice, from time to time, and conveyed it to her; accordingly she performed the day to day tasks of governing the group. The husband certainly had no time for such affairs, as he had to devote his undivided attention to listening to God's voice—and the gods, as everyone knew, speak at all odd hours, suddenly, and are eternally angry if no one is around to listen to them. The fact however is that the priest was lazy.

From those small beginnings, the Jalta tribe began. Thus it was not actually a tribe initially. The runaway slaves who joined it came from different tribes and so also the captured women. There was nothing homogeneous, no oneness; but there was something which bound them together. It was their knowledge that they were hated and hunted by all the tribes. Perhaps that alone made them stronger and more cohesive. At times when hostilities with other tribes erupted, their losses were considerable, especially when they forgot to follow the drill for withdrawal, retreats and ambush laid down by the priest's wife. They knew what would happen to them if they were caught by raiding tribes, for a recaptured slave dies a slow lingering death after agonized torture. Surrender was therefore out of the question and they were prepared to sell their life dearly; they chose to court death rather than be captured. Consequently, their feats of heroism were many and though they were despised by outsiders as emerging from slave-stock, led by a discredited priest, they began to be feared. That too gave them a feeling of nearness to each other, a sense of belonging as a single tribe.

Other tribes could easily have wiped them out, if only they joined together to crush the upstarts. But the tribes hated each other equally and could never unite to form a joint front. It was this realization which inspired the priest's wife to a vision of the future. She called off all attacks against tribes which were nearest to them. If her people wanted to capture women or booty, they had to go to the distant tribes and not their neighbouring tribes.

An ancient song tries to explain her motives for this 'long-distance strategy', though it embraces too many theories. 'Maybe,' says the singer, 'she wanted to curb their instinct to attack frequently, knowing that they would pause if the nearest targets were denied, or maybe she wanted to teach them the value of the element of surprise when the distant enemy feared no attack'; or 'maybe', continues the singer, 'she wanted them to learn the art of forward-planning when targets were far away, and the march endless and, on return, even burdensome for survivors.' Finally, the singer says, 'Maybe she wanted peace on her borders and looked far into the future and saw that this was the only way to achieve it.' As to her 'look far into the future', the singer obliges us with a glimpse—'The distant tribes, chagrined at the sudden attacks of the slave-tribe, would march speedily, ready for instant vengeance, and in their thrust would take the shortest route to reach the slave-forest, with no regard for frontiers of other tribes enroute, with whom they had no quarrel, except that they were in the way and must therefore be crushed too and thus, borders were violated; and they all became embroiled in new battles which raged far away from the borders of the slave-forest. . . . Is it surprising then that the neighbouring tribes became weaker, even decimated, by these repeated onslaughts; and the distant tribes, over-burdened with captured booty, had no wish but to march back to their homes, while the slave-tribe remained untouched and unmolested. Thus, while bordering tribes became powerless, there was an era of continuing peace in the slave-forest which made the slave-tribe all the more strong under the skilful command of the priest's wife who at times even sent out her men to defend the neighbouring tribes against hostile attacks, earning if not the lifelong support of her neighbours, at least their truce for the time being, enough to discourage them from an attempt to attack; and thereby she achieved lasting peace on her borders and nourished the continuing strength of her people, who were now united in many ways—above all in their single-minded devotion to her. And they would never fail in their vow to honour their pledge of "no master no slave", and would even demand it from their descendants for all time to come.'

The priest's wife had insisted that the tribe must be known not by her name but by the name of her husband—Jalta.

She bore eleven children—the first two were sons, the rest, daughters.

Even after her two sons were born, she declared that succession as the chief would belong to the eldest daughter 'except when there are only male issues, and in that case, the eldest son shall succeed, but from him too, it shall pass to his eldest daughter on his death.'

For nearly 800 years since its formation, the Jalta tribe continued its tradition of having the eldest daughter as its Chief and the only exceptions that intervened were when the eldest daughter died without any female issue. This was the case with Jalta who was consumed in the three fires of his own making. He had no sisters and thus he became the Chief of his tribe. He too had three sons and no daughters.

Jalta territory had grown enormously along with its prosperity. Many of their neighbouring tribes withered away. The problems of the Jalta tribe were beginning to be vast. There was also danger looming large from Karkarta Nandan's advancing contingents. To meet these challenges, Jalta had decided that the tribe's territory should be divided among his three sons, with independent command as Chiefs, with again the proviso that the office of the Chief would, after them, belong to their eldest daughters.

Whatever changes time had wrought to the Jalta tribes, the principle of 'no master, no slave', remained unbroken and sacrosanct. To contemplate its breach was regarded as the highest sin and betrayal of her who founded the tribe.

The silent Chief had thought of the Jalta tribe, as it was the only one which disallowed slavery. But was it not an impossible dream? How would a comparison with the new tribe of Jalta, no more than eight centuries old, influence people of his ancient tribe who prided themselves on customs rooted in antiquity? Why was he trying to clutch at straws?

He feared that he would simply be a target of ridicule if he suggested to his tribe to free the slaves. Surely, they would ask who this new god of his was. And what had he done? He had secured his freedom but then they too released their slaves sometimes when they served them well. Did that make them gods? Why, priest Jarasanda freed his woman-slave Arundhati because she bore him a child! Did that make him a god? And what about Prasta Pitamana who released his three woman-slaves whom his grandsons were trying to seduce? Was he a god too! Then maybe his grandsons were because they were the cause of their freedom!

Would they not also laugh if he made too much of their safe journey, unmolested by the thirteen vicious tribes? Maybe, they would point to the old priest, Khashan, to ask: do you know how many journeys the old man has made for the last thirty-three years to lands near and far? And was he ever attacked?

No, they would simply mock, the Chief told himself. The task of freeing the slaves was beyond him. With a heavy heart, he went out into the open to be alone with his melancholy thoughts.

Suddenly his gloom vanished, as he saw someone familiar in the distance. It was his cousin Narada, his dearest friend, riding out towards him on his mule.

Narada and the Chief were devotedly attached to each other. The Chief had hoped that Narada would be among the first to come down to the Jalta lands to greet him. He was disappointed at his absence. His brother had no explanation—except that Narada must be immersed in his constant study of the stars.

The Chief ran briskly, his arms outstretched, to greet his friend. He almost collided headlong with the mule before Narada could dismount.

They embraced and Narada asked in his sign language, 'Why were you trying to kiss my mule instead?'

'Why not?' the Chief replied. 'He is the one who brought you to me.'

Outwardly, there was nothing impressive about Narada except that he was older than the Chief and looked at least ten years younger. 'I am too young to be old and too old to be young and nobody wants my company,' Narada used to say; but actually, he was welcome everywhere. He was respected as a dreamer and a visionary. He himself had little time for others, as day and night he was busy studying stars and planets. He could have asked for anything. His father was the Chief of the tribe. After him, Narada was nominated as the Chief. He declined. The tribe protested but he insisted that he had a vision from above that the office must go to his first cousin and dearest friend who was next in line. The tribe knew that he studied stars though they were unaware that he also received visions from above. Since then, many came to him and he sometimes obliged them with what could never be checked for a hundred years, or with something that was never at hand, like the solar eclipse.

Narada had also refused to serve as the Chief-priest. He insisted he must remain free to lead a life that was totally empty. Empty? He was never idle. All his time was spent in studying the heavenly bodies. He had only two close friends—the Chief and Khashan, the old priest.

Narada gazed at the Chief. He touched the Chief's hair and then his heart—as if to say, 'Your hair is whiter, your eyes in sorrow, your heart heavy with grief.' The Chief nodded sadly and Narada smiled— 'Then I was right in refusing to be a Chief?'

But silently the Chief retorted, 'Is my sorrow not yours too?'

Narada embraced him again to sympathize with the Chief's suffering during captivity. The Chief shook his head to express a greater anguish.

The Chief poured out his heart. It was a long tale—and it ended with the Chief's anguish that he was about to betray his new god. 'How can I face my people and demand that they free their slaves!'

Narada was pitiless. 'There is no question of your going to betray your god. You have already betrayed him!'

Narada insisted that the betrayal started when the Chief decided to resign from a distance. 'You wanted to remain away so as not to face your people and carry out your god's will. And now, the fear in your heart is that your god will discover your betrayal when you fail to call on the people to free their slaves.'

The Chief nodded. Narada was right. True, the seed of his guilt lay in trying to shirk his responsibility. But this realization only increased his gloom.

Narada laughed and thumped his own breast. 'Here I stand before you, my dearest friend! I, the greatest shirker in the tribe! I, who escape all responsibility and accept no duty—neither from man nor from the gods! Why this grief then? What is there to fear?'

The Chief's gloom only deepened. 'You made me the Chief—to escape responsibility, so that I remain rooted to it. How does that help me?'

Narada was smiling, his finger raised high as if to remind his friend of the common belief that the sky sends visions to him. In spite of his gloom, the Chief smiled, too, knowing that Narada saw no such visions. Narada's smile grew broader.

They sat for hours. Narada's curiosity was immense. He wanted to know everything—each detail of the Chief's captivity, of those who died, of how they were freed, of their long march to Jalta lands.

Why these questions?—to what end?—the Chief often interrupted. But Narada continued his relentless inquiry, until there was nothing left to add or clarify.

Narada still had one more surprise. Instead of going with the Chief into Jalta village, he mounted his mule to return and warned, 'None must know that I was here or that we met.'

The Chief protested, 'But everyone must know that you left your place to come here. Then how could we not meet!'

'You think that if they knew that I was coming, they would allow me to travel alone! No, they still think I am holed up deep in my study.'

They embraced and Narada's final advice was—'Enter your land on full-moon day and your first words must be to demand a sacrifice to the gods.'

The Chief shook his head. 'Why must a horse die?' Every major sacrifice, apparently, meant that a horse had to be killed. The Chief knew that like him, Narada also hated that anything living should be sacrificed. They were both powerless to stop this age-old custom.

'No horse shall die,' Narada assured him. 'The lie shall lead to the truth, as truth often leads to a lie. . .' and then he faltered—'Maybe your god—be he a true god or false—maybe he would be pleased. But the true God of all, who knows!'

A week before full moon, Narada emerged, suddenly, from his retreat, dishevelled and distraught, to run down the path leading to the Chief's house, drawing maximum attention to himself. Many were there, hoping to welcome the Chief. It was left to Narada to announce that the Chief could not arrive before full-moon day and then would demand a sacrifice. No one asked how he knew. Was anything ever hidden from the man who conversed with the stars! Nor did they ask what the sacrifice would be. Obviously, a horse—for that was the most auspicious of all sacrifices.

The crowd grew. Narada, his eyes half-closed, saw the six men and two women he was searching for. They came to him at his signal. Then he addressed the crowd in 'sign language', with tears streaming from his eyes. First, he announced the names of those who had died in captivity at the fort-site and earlier. There were tears now in all eyes, for none knew till then, who had died and who survived. Narada then dwelt on the survivors—their sorrows and suffering in captivity. He made it clear that all of them would have died but for their heroic Chief, who not only looked after his people constantly but even summoned the spirits of tribal ancestors, by his will-power, austerities and meditation. Yet the tyrants who held their people captive were powerful. Even so, the Chief never gave up hope. He dissociated himself from the powerless gods of his own, and asked the God of All, for a new god. What made the Chief frantic was that from spirits of the dead, he learnt a frightful secret that the danger was not only for the captives but for the entire tribe. An ancient curse was to take effect and the fate was to be more terrible than death.

Now Narada received undivided attention, as he added, 'The Chief himself died a thousand deaths as he foresaw the tribe's awesome fate. He continued his austerities. But enough of this. . . .' Narada pointed to the men and women he had selected. He promised that they would later announce the successful outcome of the Chief's efforts.

Narada, then, simply made short points in sign language to indicate that the God of All could not resist the Chief's devotion and demand; He sent a new God; the Chief offered his tribe's allegiance to the new

God; also, the Chief promised a personal sacrifice and another by the tribe; the new God thereupon secured freedom for the Chief and his companions; boldly, the new God escorted them through the lands of the thirteen hostile tribes, but raised a screen of unseen smoke so that none could see or attack them, as they passed through the valleys of death; at times though, the smoke disappeared, as some of the Chief's companions had passing doubts about the powers of this new God—and the gods cannot exist without faith; but this God was too powerful. His deadly arrows flew invisibly and the enemy was paralyzed.

The rest, Narada said, would be narrated by the six men and two women; and he added, 'Now the new God will come on full-moon day; and the Chief shall demand a sacrifice to save the tribe. Are you ready?'

Ready? Of course we are, said all. Why one horse only? Two, three, ten! Narada shook his head. No, not the horse sacrifice.

What then? Surely not a goat or a sheep! The occasion was too great for such a lowly sacrifice!

Narada explained: the Chief's personal sacrifice was to resign and leave the office to his brother. It was a personal matter between him and his God.

They felt sad. Now that Narada had revealed all, their love for the Chief overflowed. Still, who could stand in the way of his promise to a God!

As for the tribe's sacrifice, Narada spoke haltingly. Building up the effect artfully, he shocked them. Not the horse. It had to be a human sacrifice.

Human sacrifice! They were aghast. Surely gods were not bloodthirsty. They knew of the human sacrifice in other tribes. But never in their own tribe. They sadly wondered who would have to die among them.

Narada softened the blow. None from the tribe would die.

'Who then? Do we go to war with other tribes to capture victims?'

'No wars, no captures, no blood. Only our slaves.'

'Our slaves! But why does the God want them killed?'

Again Narada softened the blow, 'No, slaves will not to be killed.'

'What then?'

'Simply to free them. The slaves shall be slaves no longer.'

'Why', 'What for?', 'But why?' 'But....'

'Why!' Narada looked up, high in the clouds. 'Because the new God reached a covenant with the God of All—if the Chief and our people are freed from the fort-site, he shall have all the slaves of our tribe freed.'

'How many slaves have to be freed?' they asked.

'All.'

Narada was in no mood now to soften the blow any more, and he firmly said, 'Yes, all. And never must we hold a slave again.'

Their questions ceased. Their doubts remained. Narada addressed those doubts. 'The tribe must honour the Chief's promise if it is to be saved. But maybe some among us will refuse to part with slaves. So I must recall how this God unleashed his deadly arrows against the thirteen tribes. And I ask: is it wise to incur the wrath of such a powerful God? If we do, maybe this God will wipe out only those who deny him; but who knows!—maybe, he will destroy the entire tribe. Do not, I beg of you, invite his wrath by retaining your slaves. Save the tribe, save yourself, your loved ones, your children.'

All heads were bowed. Only one man challenged, 'What about your own slaves?'

'They are free as of now.' He had inherited slaves. They were more his friends. Their boast was, 'Narada belongs to us.'

A few raised their hands to gesture that their own slaves were also free forthwith. Many hands were, however, unraised. They were afraid to affirm and yet terrified to refuse. Hopefully, Narada's vision may turn out to be untrue. They scanned faraway paths, hoping that the Chief arrive before full-moon day, to disprove Narada's fearful vision.

Narada left with the eight persons he had summoned. It was not a random selection. They were the 'Keepers and Guardians of Tribal Knowledge.' Like the Memory singers of the Hindus, their task was to keep alive knowledge for future generations.

This group of eight remained in Narada's retreat for four days and nights.

Meanwhile, doubters there were, as always. Away from Narada's piercing eyes, they consulted each other. Unfortunately, the priests were absent as they had left to escort the Chief back. At last one priest returned, two days before the full moon. It was old Khashan, who had sat with Sindhu Putra, to sketch the route-patterns of the lands beyond.

News of Khashan's arrival spread. They stopped their questions when they saw his stony expression. Khashan went straight to his hut. There his expression softened. His two daughters and all his slaves gathered round him. To the slaves, he intimated that they were free forthwith. The slaves protested, 'We belong to you.' Khashan shook his head, 'We all belong to the God of All and He belongs to us all.'

Jabli, a woman in tears, approached Khashan. Her husband was one of the captives freed along with the Chief. Narada had included his name in the list of survivors. Even so, she wanted to be sure. 'Is my husband alive?' The old man nodded to confirm it. A new rush of tears started to the woman's eyes, of joy and relief, to replace her tears of anxiety. Others too had questions about those that had died in captivity. Khashan gave the information, which was no different from what Narada had said. Finally, Jabli asked: 'When is the Chief bringing my husband here?' The old man did not know.

The crowd was rooted to the spot—the old priest comes direct from the Chief but does not know when the Chief plans to arrive! Yet Narada knows it all! For the rest, he confirms that Jabli's husband is alive and all his information matches exactly with what Narada said. Clearly, he did not meet Narada ever since he left with the priests for Jalta land; where was the opportunity for them to meet? Yet his every word confirms Narada's vision. His first act itself was to free his own slaves!

Khashan's every gesture and action were the conclusive proof they needed to believe in Narada's vision. Many went, with heavy hearts, to free their slaves. Having done so, they became fanatic—with a mission to convert those who still vacillated. The danger, they urged, was not only for those that resisted, but for the entire tribe.

The last straw was still to come. Drum-beats—slow, solemn and measured—announced that a parade would begin thirty-six hours before full moon. At that appointed hour, the six men and two women emerged to lead the Ithihasa Parade.

Many later poets have found it difficult to understand how the Ithihasa Parade of the silent tribe operated. The task of the parade was to elaborate the vision which Narada had narrated in summary form. The parade presented the tale of the superb heroics of the Chief and his men; of how they fought valiantly when the tribe was threatened; of how the Chief protected the tribe, though captured he was in the end, with many men; of their trials and tribulations in captivity; and of the death of so many. But above all, the tale presented the amazing spirit of the Chief who in the midst of his captivity lost neither his dignity, nor his love, nor his faith in the values he cherished—his meditation and austerities that compelled the God of All to send a new God to assist him; the Chief's promise of a sacrifice—both personal and tribal; his freedom and the freedom of his people; and the dramatic march through the lands of the thirteen bloodthirsty tribes; and how the new God protected them; how perilously close they came to disaster when some doubted the new God; yet how this God set into motion such a whirlpool of destruction sweeping into the thirteen tribes that their bloodchilling screams rent the earth and sky; and finally, unharmed and in a blaze of glory, the Chief is to arrive on full-moon day, accompanied by the new God. 'Render unto this God, then, what is promised unto Him. Deny Him not,' was the repeated refrain of the parade.

It was a compelling tale, that moved suspensefully and powerfully. If it paused at times, it was only to challenge and question—'Is there then any amongst us who will violate the Chief's pledge to this new God?'

The difficulty of the later poets arose not because the Ithihasa Parade told its tale in sign language. Certainly, sign language is as expressive as the spoken word. But there was more to this Parade. Many joined the Parade, with musical instruments, to keep in tune with the tale as it was unfolded. Almost everyone in the vast crowd there was either swaying his body or clapping his hands and even dancing, as people would normally do, when a song is sung. From time to time, the Parade would halt and sixteen masked dancers would perform to the accompaniment of sign language. It was not different from a musical song dance drama, except that no voice was heard.

But how is it possible that a song can be sung in sign language, voicelessly, and yet be accompanied by music and set to a tune that makes people sway and dance to its rhythm! A song in sign language!

No wonder most later poets, convinced that a song is the function and the result of a voice, ignored the song of the Parade in sign language, as something fictional and mythical. Later, Devita, wife of Hardas, when she became well-versed with sign language, would sing the song, giving voice and words to it. But many regarded it as a figment of Devita's imagination.

In his song, Nandan's great-grandson is clear that the Parade took place, that the silent song-dance-drama was enacted, that people were spellbound and swayed and danced to the lilting, uplifting rhythm of the 'song' rendered in sign language. Having said that, he accuses Narada and Khashan for this falsehood and fraud, though the chief villain, according to him, was Sindhu Putra who on the advice of his father Bharatjogi, conceived this grand design to set himself up as the god of all tribes.

Most poets however disagree with Nandan's great-grandson. They insist that it was faith that moved Narada and Khashan. Even poets who find it difficult to accept that Sindhu Putra was a god are ready to acknowledge that he was fired by a god-like vision to free the slaves and achieve unity—and one of them sang—

'More he did than what a god would
No less than what a god should
So blame the gods that failed
Why curse the lad to godhood nailed!'

The Ancients had no problem in accepting that a song could be sung voicelessly and yet carry a tune, rhyme, rhythm, melody and lilt. Among the ancients, many held that a song was not simply a function and the result of a voice, but could be independent of it. To Sage Dhanawantar, a song was basically a function of the brain and a feeling in the heart; and when the voice was not available, there were other methods, such as sign language, to 'sing' a song. Sage Yadodhra also spoke of songless birds and silent insects who conveyed their 'songs' and 'words' voicelessly to their compatriots across vast distances. Yadodhra even gave examples of the speechless fish and water-animals who communicated their 'thoughts' to each other, hundreds of miles away in the boundless river and ocean.

It was on full-moon day that Sindhu Putra entered the land of the silent tribe. The Chief and his men were with him along with a large contingent led by Jalta the Fourth and his wife. It was Jalta's mother who had told her son, 'The Chief escorted you to your land, now you be courteous yourself.' She also said, 'Let everyone, far and near, be our friend.'

Coldly, her eldest son, Jalta the Second, asked, 'I suppose you want us to be friends even with those that caused our father to burn!' Jalta the Third also spoke, 'And with those who kept our brother, his bride and our people as slaves!'

'Yes,' she answered, 'for are they not also from the tribe of Sindhu Putra?' She added, 'But then, there is evil in us all and goodness in us all—in the universe, among tribes, in individuals. There is virtue and there is vice; there is wisdom and there is folly—and they alternate.'

'But you are all wisdom, Mother,' Jalta the Fourth said.

'Yes, but I have foolish sons,' the mother replied.

The entire tribe was there to greet the Chief, his party, and above all, Sindhu Putra, whom they had already accepted as their own god, 'sight unseen'. The Ithihasa Parade song had schooled them on how they should greet their god. Respectfully, their hands were raised in Namaste and then the tribe's silent song of welcome began. It had alternating moods, with overtones of past sorrow, and the joy of the present. Everyone watched the fast hand-movement of so many, participating in the song, though only those who understood the sign language could 'listen' to the song. Later, a poet even asserted that 'clearly, with his inner ear, Sindhu Putra could "hear" the song of the silent people, in all the richness and beauty of its melody.'

Sindhu Putra went through the crowd. From Devita, he had learnt how to express *Tat tvam asi* in sign language. He greeted each with Namaste and *Tat tvam asi*.

Many poets say that the people of the silent tribe did not grasp the significance of *Tat tvam asi*. Even so, somehow, faith had overtaken the frontiers of their knowledge and consciousness, and it seemed that all their questions were answered, unasked; and they had the feeling that their life had become purer and beautiful. Their hearts no longer ached for the unattainable. They felt that a god had come to fill the void between the earth and sky and that he had blessed them all.

Yet, poets love to contradict themselves and they also speak of the longing in the hearts of many, as Sindhu Putra went through the crowd. Perhaps, some even remembered the ancient prophecy of the tribe, handed down to them from one generation to another:

452 / Return of the Aryans

'Then the lord God shall send forth this command and you shall hearken and obey, that He might reveal unto you His First Word that you yourself shall utter, and having uttered it, it shall be yours as it is God's and you shall then know that the First Word was always there within your reach and grasp, waiting for all eternity to be uttered, except that it was the covenant that you shall not come upon this inheritance unless the Lord God Himself sends down the Witness and the Source. . . .'

Was Sindhu Putra then the god foretold in the prophecy! Was he the Witness and the Source! Dare they ask?

An old woman, however, was not daunted. Leaning on her son for support, she was much too frail even to raise her hand for sign language, and kept nudging her son to ask the question. The son refused. Three times he declined by vigorously shaking his head. Sindhu Putra did not notice it, but a priest was furious to see the youth shaking his head. Quickly, with enormous pride in his own importance, the priest faced the young man with a rapid protest: 'Are you denying Sindhu Putra?' The youth waved his arms to refute the charge, while everyone stared at him. Finding his own explanation inadequate, the youth knelt at Sindhu Putra's feet. It was now Devita's turn to explain the gestures of the son and the mother, who herself began to find strength for a few limited signs.

'She is the mother of this young man,' Devita explained, 'and she waits to hear from you the First Word of God that she might utter it herself.' Devita was not clear what it all meant or what the First Word was, for she knew nothing of their ancient prophecy. Sindhu Putra, however, was lost in thought.

Sindhu Putra simply raised his hand to the sky and then placed it on his heart, in humility. As a poet explains, all he meant was that the 'First Word of God resides in every heart.' But the effect of his gesture was magical. It was as if his simple gesture promised that he would be the one to receive from above the First Word of God and he should be the one to communicate it to them.

The old woman was in tears. He nodded to reassure her. He did not know that hers were tears of joy. Those nearby shared the old woman's ecstasy that the ancient prophecy was soon to be redeemed. They were quick to transmit it to the others through their hurried sign language; and with each telling and repeating, the hope grew into certainty; and there was now in everyone's heart, the exalting, exulting assurance that the First Word of God would be revealed and even uttered by them.

Later that day, Devita learnt much about the pre-ancient prophecy; and Sindhu Putra understood the enormity of the hopes he had raised.

It is easy to claim knowledge of the First Word of God. Many in the past—some guided by faith, others for motives of their own—had come forward to communicate the First Word to mankind. But how to get it uttered by those who had never articulated a single word!

Sindhu Putra did not know how it was that the people of this tribe found it impossible to articulate words. It was not as though they lacked a voice altogether. They could yell and even laugh. Their voices could be used for elementary exclamations to indicate joy and anger. But they just could not form words either to speak or sing.

It is not known if Sindhu Putra was aware of the discourse of Dhanawantri, Sage Dhanawantar's wife, to her students. According to her, voice and speech were two different aspects of human sound. Human speech, she said, was activated first by the will to speak, formed in the brain, and thereafter received its driving energy from a sound generated at the back of the lower throat. As it travelled higher in the throat, the sound was moulded and a voice pattern shaped; and finally then, speech sounds emerged, refined by the articulatory organs of the mouth, such as lips and tongue. Her view was that as humans evolved enough to walk upright, they no longer had to use their mouths like other animals for food-gathering; instead, they developed dexterity in their hands to gather food; they thence had the opportunity to devote their lips and tongues to more verbal articulation. She even speculated that in the future course of evolution, verbal articulation may become unnecessary and humans may come to acquire the ability to directly transfer thought signals without speech; and in such cases, the mouth along with tongue and lips may become even more specialized—for the sensation of feel, touch and taste. Yet, she could not clearly explain how it was that the evolutionary process of word-articulation had missed this silent tribe—maybe some hereditary defect, aggravated by inbreeding, arising from marriages among very close relations.

Throughout the day, Devita had to repeat to Sindhu Putra words of the ancient prophecy of the silent tribe. Perhaps he hoped its frequent repetition would somehow reveal the secret of its fulfilment.

Sindhu Putra knew what these simple people expected from him. He was thinking: here is the largest tribe in the eastern region, ready and willing to surrender their slaves, for their faith in me! Yet is it right that I steal their faith for myself?

But then, how else do they give up their slaves? No, they have already decided to surrender them, have they not? So what? Surely, they can change their minds and return to their ways, to cling to their slaves? Must I continue to betray myself and pose as a god, simply for slaves?

But this was a mock-battle in his mind. His decision was already made. He was committed to the cause of freeing the slaves. The

incoherent, chaotic thought that he was putting his own conscience to
hazard, by allowing people to believe in his godhood, came to trouble
him. But again he waved it off. There was no turning back from his
commitment to liberate the slaves. Perhaps God would understand!
Perhaps God would forgive! But if not, so be it. Let the punishment
for the falsehood be his, so that others may go free.

He sat, bent forward, his cheek supported on his hand, his brow
knitted in deep thought. He was no longer questioning his own karma,
or his sin for his masquerade as a god. Instead, his mind was on his
futile search for the secret that lay hidden behind the ancient prophecy.
What is the First Word of God? What is the First Word which the
tribe must utter for the first time? And yet that Word was always
within their reach and grasp! But they could not utter it unless a god
manifested himself as the Witness and the Source! What then was that
First Word?

His thoughts led him nowhere. He feared that the First Word of
God would never come within his grasp. What would be the
consequence of his failure? Already he had sensed a vague suspicion
and envy among the tribal priests. Maybe, the priests could kindle in
the hearts of these simple people, resentments against a false god who
promises but cannot perform, and yet seeks to deprive them of their
cherished slaves. Sindhu Putra almost smiled at the thought. He would
then be free—released from the burden and bond of godhood. But the
smile was short-lived. His mission to free the slaves would then fail!

The silence around Sindhu Putra was unbroken. Everyone waited
for him to speak. But he seemed in deep meditation; quietly they left
to remain outside the hut.

Actually, he was not meditating. His mind was filled with a maze
of confused thoughts. At times, he went deep into the past, to search
for a clue to what could be God's First Word. Again he was bewildered
by his own arrogance that he should aspire to discover the Word that
none had discovered before. What was his claim to such knowledge
and illumination? And even if he were inspired to divine the First
Word, how was he to find a way for the mute tribe to utter it?

A feeling of helplessness came over him and he heaved a deep
sigh. It was more a groan than a sigh. He was not even sure if he
heard the sound of his groan. But swiftly, his soul was on fire. A
thought hit him so hard that it made him leap right up. It was as
though he had heard an echo from a long forgotten age.

His eyes were now wide open. In his heart was tumultuous
excitement. His turmoil was no more. Instead there was the radiant
joy of blissful fulfilment though all he could have heard was his own
whispered groan and a sigh. Yet his feeling was that his mind had
reached deep into a limitless past and stretched far into the infinite
future and the gates of perception were opened wide for him and he
could see all—all.

He stood up, swaying unsteadily, as though intoxicated. He uttered a sound to match and imitate his own groan. He tried it again. He felt an overwhelming emotion and was filled with it to bursting. Tears came to him but they were tears of thanksgiving and he knelt to pray.

Well before dawn, the Chief and many others peeped into Sindhu Putra's room. They found him kneeling in prayer. Those that went nearer him had the feeling that there were tears flowing from his eyes.

They tiptoed out. Outside, a sea of people had collected. Many asked what their new god was doing. The Chief's hand-signals said, 'He prays.' But others added, 'He weeps.'

He weeps! For whom does a god weep? they asked. For us; who else! For no reason at all, tears came to the eyes of many.

The sun had risen. Silently, the crowd waited. Only the twittering of birds and the murmur of the breeze could be heard. Hours passed.

Evening shadows were about to fall, though the sun was still gleaming in a far corner, when Sindhu Putra emerged. He walked through the crowds. His steps were sure and firm, as if he knew where he must go, in this unfamiliar village. They all followed. He turned to the valley ringed by hills. Suddenly, he stopped and sat down on a stone. It was not a comfortable seat. But he looked calm, serene, rested.

Silently they watched him. He had closed his eyes. Was he listening for a voice from within? A vision! An illumination? Many in the crowd were afraid even to blink lest something escape them, unseen!

Then suddenly it began. With his lips parted, Sindhu Putra emitted a sound, emanating from the base of his throat, though everyone was certain that it came from his heart. It was a long inarticulate sound and some would swear that it had the intonation of 'O', while others were certain that it sounded like 'AU', by the impulse rolling forward in the mouth; then gently Sindhu Putra closed his lips, while continuing the sound. Clearly, without effort on his part, the sound changed itself, and came out as 'M'. Thus the entire phenomenon of this sound-utterance came to be heard as 'AUM', or more clearly, 'OM'.

There was silence as Sindhu Putra uttered this OM mantra. But the hills were not silent and they reverberated to return the echo of the sound. They all listened, in awe and wonder, as Sindhu Putra repeated the sound. Again the hills responded with the echo.

No one knows at what stage the crowd joined in the chant. Maybe, they all were moved to join in, all together.

OM! It was an intonational, inarticulate, universal sound that required no effort from the mute and speechless; whosoever could utter a sound, could easily chant OM; and the silent tribe chanted it easily, effortlessly and worshipfully.

OM! OM! OM! The chant went on. And the hills resounded—OM! OM! OM!

OM! Was it the symbol, the name, the essence of the Infinite and the Imperishable? Was OM everything? Was everything from OM? Did Om identify God in all his fullness—in His transcendence and immanence?

Those questions would come to them later. For the moment, there was only one realization in their minds, as they came under the enticing spell of this mantra which they recited again and again—yes, indeed OM was the very First Word that God of All had uttered.

OM! they chanted, and they felt in the depth of their beings a cosmic vibration, mystical and radiant! It was like the flowering of a spiritual consciousness, carrying with it exalted experience, and an overall vision of reality combined with humility, that transcendent truth is yet to be discovered and the eternal search must continue.

A golden mist descended from the sun, setting on the green hills around them. The chant continued. OM!—and their hearts were lofty and soaring, in the ecstasy of love and beauty within. With each chant, they came more under the magical spell of, what was to them, a truly sacred utterance of utmost power and mystery.

And they wondered—did the universe itself arise from this word—OM?

Later, for centuries, even up to the modern era, scholars would emerge to analyse, examine and interpret the sacred symbol of OM. The silent tribe itself needed no explanation. It was after all a sound that a mute or even a baby could produce, without effort or preparation. All it involved was to begin from the base of the throat, with lips open, the sound of A and U, and connect them together to coalesce into the sound of O and finally close the lips while continuing the sound, with the inevitable result that the entire utterance emanated as OM. It was purely intonational and needed no articulatory function from tongue and lips, except that the lips would be open when the sound began, and they would remain closed while the sound continued to its end.

The silent tribe readily recognized OM as a natural symbol, nature's word, a pure genuine impulse of the heart, as distinct from a word of knowledge arising from the head. Surely then it was nature's own mantra, their very own mantra, a part of their being. No wonder it produced harmony, peace and bliss in their hearts. With it, came also the realization that this sacred utterance was always within their 'reach and grasp', as foretold in the prophecy, but they had patiently waited for a god to manifest himself as 'Witness and Source.'

For all these 7,000 years, philosophers, theologians, spiritualists, poets and scholars would weave their learning, love and fancy around the magical mantra of OM. Some would say that OM covered the full range and entire phenomenon of sound, travelling from one extremity to the other—from throat to lips—beyond which no sound existed. Others held that OM was the symbol of supreme Brahma, the ultimate and infinite reality. Yet others characterized OM as an 'idol' representing the divine ideal, arguing that an idol does not need the shape and form of a statue but can be subtle, like sound itself (to them sound was the subtlest of all idols, even more subtle than fire, because only one of the five senses viz, the ear, detects it). Some even claimed that OM was the real name of the Almighty and that it was also the key that unlocked the kingdom of God. Some thousands of years later, the Vedic Upanishads would also extol concentration with the aid of OM. For instance *Mundaka Upanishad* would say 'OM is the bow, the soul is the arrow, and Brahma is the target; one must pierce it with a concentrated mind, and become like an arrow, one with it' (Mu. U, II 2. 3-4). The *Bhagvadgita* recognizes OM as a mantra which existed from creation's beginning—*Om Tat Sat*, to express absolute supremacy, universality and reality of the inexpressible Absolute. The *Bhagvadgita* also reserves the highest goal for those that utter the single symbol OM while they remember the Almighty (VIII 13). Again in the *Bhagvadgita*, Lord Krishna would declare the existence of the syllable OM in all the Vedas—'Oh son of Kunti, I am the taste in waters; I am the Moon and Sun, I am the syllable OM in all the Vedas; I am the sound in ether and manhood in men' (VI 8). To the vast majority in the Hindu fold and beyond, OM came to stand for the pure consciousness that pervades the three stages of walking, dreaming and dream-sleep, and it came to be known as pranave, to mean that it pervades life and runs through prana or breath.

Modern scholars also say that OM is a Hindu mantra. That may be so in the sense that it was a Hindu—Sindhu Putra—who first uttered it. But it was uttered for the sake of the silent tribes. They inspired it and they were not Hindus when the mantra was first uttered. It is true that eventually the tribe became a part of the Hindu fold, but that was later. The fact however remains that for a long time the sacred utterance OM was regarded as the mantra of this silent tribe as it had been foretold in their own prophecy. Certainly, they rejoiced when other tribes adopted their OM mantra, as for instance, Jalta tribes embraced it from the very inception. The slaves freed by the silent tribe would also go back to their lands to spread it all over. Almost instantaneously, it found acceptance throughout the vast territory of the lands of the Hindu. The Hindu took it up worshipfully, lovingly, longingly, in their hearts, and later in their sacred literature. But that does not make it an exclusively Hindu mantra!

Another misconception about the OM mantra maybe that it comes from the Sanskrit language. The fact is that the mantra was uttered before Sanskrit matured. Besides, the word OM in Sanskrit is not subject to the conjugation, reflection and grammatical manipulations applied to all the other Sanskrit words. This is simply in recognition of the fact that it is a natural word—that exists in silence, in the heart, in meditation, independent and apart from any language. Hindus and Sanskrit made good use of it, but it can belong to all and every language—and does. The words omnipotence, omniscience, omnipresence, refer to the infinite power, knowledge and presence of all-seeing God, in many languages. Every prayer, everywhere, when it reaches its point of silence, will utter OM in its various formulations, like Amen and Amin.

People from the silent tribe, who soulfully chanted OM with Sindhu Putra, would remain unaware of the rich and colourful analysis which succeeding generations would extend to this mantra. But they needed no such analysis. The feeling in their heart was of radiant joy and pride over the revelation to them of the First Word of God. That they could ever utter that word was, for them, the height of bliss. Their hearts were full to overflowing. Nothing that later scholars have said to extol and exalt the magical utterance of OM could ever match their own indescribable feeling of bliss and fulfilment.

OM! The silent tribe chanted with Sindhu Putra in the valley ringed by hills—their minds released from all wayward thought. In its place was the feeling that their ears had opened to the song of the universe and their eyes, to the radiance of the mind of God.

'Humanity is more ancient than slavery, class and colour. . . . Do these differences make you or me less or more Hindu or human? . . . Is a Hindu to carry out the will of the Transcendent Supreme by freedom and unity solely within his class?'

—(Attributed to Bharatjogi—5052 BC)

Messengers from a God

5052 BC

The slaves of the silent tribe were free. Many wanted to go back to their own diverse tribes. But some wished to go nowhere, 'We have lost links with our ancient tribes. This is our home now.' And Sindhu Putra said to the silent tribe, 'They are of your tribe now and your tribe is theirs.'

Who could deny him! Yet, the silent tribe—large and numerous—was never open to anyone that did not belong to it from descent through time immemorial. Readily now, the slaves were accepted by the tribe as their own. Some departing slaves even demanded a pledge that if their own root-tribes rejected them, they could return. They received assurances, which in modern parlance would amount to 'dual citizenship', enabling them to return any time, as free citizens of the silent tribe.

Jalta the Fourth embraced the Chief and said, 'My mother says our tribe and yours are brothers and must unite. Such is also the wish of my brother and mine, that we unite, as one tribe.' Hardas and Devita translated for Sindhu Putra, who spoke before the Chief could reply, 'Unity! Yes, such is the wish of my father too.'

Everyone was stirred. They misunderstood, as many in the past had done. Sindhu Putra's mind was not on the Divine Father but on Bharatjogi, who sought unity—unity of the Hindu with tribals and unity of the tribals among themselves.

Soulfully, the Chief and his brother said, while the priests applauded, 'Our tribes and Jalta tribes are one—truly as brothers.'

The wife of Jalta the Fourth spoke to the silent Chief's brother, Rohan, 'You speak of brothers only. May I speak of my sisters?' She clarified that she would like Rohan to marry her sister. The priests almost jumped in to ask: 'How can our new Chief marry outside the tribe?' But immediately remembered their new bond of unity. The Chief's brother responded, 'With pleasure, if my elder agrees.'

Elder? He pointed not to his elder brother but to Sindhu Putra, who was much younger. Both the Chief and Sindhu Putra nodded assent.

'It is good,' said Devita 'that the new Chief will marry a Jalta girl. I hope boys from the Jalta tribe will also find wives from silent tribe.'

'Why not!' Hardas joked, 'to marry a silent girl who shall not speak—that is my idea of heaven on earth!'

However, intermarriages became fashionable. It almost became their proverb—'God comes to you, but to seek a wife, go far out.'

OM—the first Word of God had been revealed to the silent tribe.

OM—the First Word of God had been uttered by the silent tribe.

But much more was to come to them from one generation to the next. Infusion of freed slaves into their own tribe and their inter-marriage with them, coupled also with even more frequent marriages with the Jalta people, almost put a stop to their intense inbreeding.

The result was miraculous. Their children and grandchildren could speak.

The tribe knew nothing about Sage Dhanawantar's discourse on 'evolutionary processes and heriditability of physical and mental defects'. Instead the tribe gave credit to the OM mantra for their miraculous transformation from a silent to a speaking tribe. True, it took years, but some said, 'If only all of us had uttered the OM mantra, more often, and with total faith, it would have occurred much sooner.'

*

Not only was the silent tribe the largest in the eastern region, it had also the largest number of slaves—larger than its free population. As many slaves were leaving, they sought Sindhu Putra's blessings. To them, he said: 'Go in freedom, remain in freedom. Never be a slave, never a master. Let none be a slave, never permit it, and be not a witness to it.'

Did Sindhu Putra realize the consequences of this exhortation? Was he charging them with a mission—'Let none be a slave; never permit it, and be not a witness to it!' At least, the slaves thought so.

Slaves, afraid to venture out in small groups lest they be recaptured en route, and remembering their new, heroic mission, began to band together to travel to their diverse homelands. When they left, it was an army on the march. They struck at various tribes, sometimes without provocation, if only to free slaves, in order to fulfil their mission or swell their numbers. There was a tragic randomness about it. Brutality and slaughter resulted. And the question would be heard across the centuries: did Sindhu Putra, the prince of peace, sanction all this! This violence! This bloodshed!

Yet Bharatjogi's dream of abolishing slavery was being fulfilled, at least in tribal lands, away from Sindhu—but not so much by change of heart as by the murderous violence of militant slaves on the march; and the innocent died along with the guilty.

The slaves on the march would overcome many tribes. They would establish a new order in those lands. New order? Initially, it led to chaos. More blood flowed. Lines of command were blurred; men, women, children fled, while slave-armies tore across the land freeing many, wreaking vengeance on those that opposed them.

Several tribes retaliated. The slaves fled. The tribes often ignored the elusive slaves and attacked the silent tribes knowing that the source of trouble came from the slaves unleashed by that tribe. But the silent tribe was much too strong. Its unity with the Jalta tribe made it invulnerable. Enemy tribes were routed. Badly shaken, they fled, leaving their dead behind and during their disorderly retreats, slave-armies would pounce on them and their lands.

A scream of anguish rose. But through all this turmoil, more and more slaves were being freed.

Chief of the silent tribe resigned. Rohan, his brother, was nominated as the Chief. Soon, unfortunately, Rohan was killed while leading his forces against a fierce attack by the enemy tribes.

Rohan's wife was in her seventh month of pregnancy when he died. She was promptly appointed as Acting Chief of the tribe for sixteen lunar years and three months, until the child to be born to her crossed the age of sixteen, 'thereupon to assume the office of the Chief— be it male or female.'

Never before had a female been appointed as their Chief. Yet, in this case, Sindhu Putra 'had blessed the glorious seed that lay in her body. What greater qualification could one seek from a Chief!'

As it was, tradition was preserved, as she gave birth to a male infant. Yet their minds became attuned to the idea of a female Chief; and in the generations that followed, women did achieve that position.

Among the freed slaves were forty-four from Hindu contingents, captured by the silent tribe after Nandan's forces had begun their infiltration to the eastern region. To them, Sindhu Putra spoke directly. They knew what was expected of them. It was to spread Sindhu Putra's message of freedom and unity on their return to the land of Hindu. There was no call to arms or violence. In any case, the land of Hindu was much too large and far-flung; its armies, too powerful and vigilant; its abhorrence for avoidable war, far too pronounced; and its system much too constitutional. If a change was desired, it had to be achieved through the hearts of the people and not by violence.

Protected by an armed escort, this group of forty-four left for their land; and the message of Sindhu Putra was heard all over the land of Sindhu.

*

There were two among the freed slaves, father and son, who came from far-off Daksina (deep in the south). They called the land, Dravidham, and themselves, Dravidas. They were simply explorers. For seventeen years, they had been travelling until they were caught in the land of the silent tribe, where no outsiders were ever allowed.

They were promptly enslaved. The treatment meted out to them was benevolent since they were placed with a benevolent master—Khashan.

The two slave-explorers would not eat meat, nor kill a living thing. Many wondered how it was possible for them to travel for all these years, through forests, deserts and barren lands, and yet remain vegetarian. Maybe only grass grew in their homeland, with no animals around. Not so, said the Dravidas. They spoke of the contract between God and man, whereby birds and animals would remain protected. However, they said there was no contract between masters and slaves and it was a slave's duty to escape. Khashan agreed. They were planning an escape-route when Sindhu Putra arrived to usher in mass freedom for all.

Initially, the silent tribe thought that these Dravidas came from a different world since they were darker in complexion. Then the Dravidas explained that the sun shone more brightly in their land, that they worshipped the sun and constantly bathed in the sun; and their temple-tops were so designed that each change of the sun's position illuminated their fine texture in new ways, as though flecks of gold and multi-coloured jewels were dancing on them, in the vivid motion of light.

No wonder, many thought that these two strangers were story-tellers, with their tall tales of magnificent temples, towers, art and sculpture in the land of the deep south. They spoke of gracious rivers and mighty seas, myths and legends, songs and poetry—oral and written—and of the respect of man for man, of man for God, and of man for all creation and its creatures.

There was another batch of twenty-six among the freed slaves from the Ganga civilization—a civilization as yet unknown to the people of Sindhu.

The day was not far off when people from Sindhu and Ganga would meet face to face. The people of Sindhu would then marvel at the vitality and grandeur of the people of Ganga—the clarity of their language, the richness of their minds and the vigour of their thought. They would meet the thinkers of Ganga—some with an intense sense of individuality, and others, immersed in the heritage of the past. From them, they would learn much of the cultural continuity of the land and the depth of their philosophical thought. Above all, the Ganga would offer something new, something fresh, something vital, something vivid to those among the Sindhu people who sought an answer to the eternal question in their hearts.

But that meeting of the people of the Sindhu and Ganga was yet to take place. Meanwhile, Sindhu Putra was lost in wonder as he spoke to the twenty-six freed slaves. Some of their words he understood. Even some thoughts they expressed—slowly, haltingly—were close to his heart. They called themselves Sanathani. He wondered: was it the same as Sanathana Dharma? Or Sanathana? They nodded when he spoke of karma; they bowed when Brahma and Shiva were mentioned, though they did not react to the other name of Shiva—Rudra. And they spoke of worshipping Shiva in various forms, even in the form of linga (a short cylindrical pillar with a round top, as a phallic symbol to denote fertility and creativity, but not sensuous or lustful pleasure). Was it at all different from the worship of lingum to which the Dravidas referred in the land of Daksina though they spoke also of yoni (the female counterpart of lingum to represent the symbol of regeneration). Was it any different from the Rudra Linga in the land of Sindhu?

With a thrill, Sindhu Putra asked, 'Have we been there before?'

Some wondered why Sindhu Putra spent so much time with the freed slaves from Daksina and Ganga. Why was he drawing lines and charts to understand the routes to their lands? Surely a god knew all!

But the questions that arose within Sindhu Putra were insatiable. He realized that Yadodhra's dream of lands faraway was real, even though his charts were incomplete. I must complete his charts for him—and if men from Daksina and Ganga found their way here, surely those lands are not beyond reach. Maybe, one day I too shall be there, and see myself if they too were once the lands of Sanathana Dharma and Sanathana, at the dawn of civilization!

*

The men from Daksina declined to go back to their land. They told Sindhu Putra 'We are explorers and will follow you to the ends of the earth.'

'But what happens when I wish to go to your land?' he asked.

'Then our land will be refreshed anew, more glorious than ever before; and we shall follow your footsteps there.' They remained.

Of the twenty-six from Ganga, ten remained with Sindhu Putra.

Forty-four freed slaves from the Sindhu contingents returned to their land. Their mission: to spread the message of freedom and unity. Two of them reached Bharat. The time was ill-chosen as Bharat was ailing. But as he listened to the tale of what Sindhu Putra had done, everyone heard his cry. It took them time to realize the joyful significance of his cry and even tears. Suddenly, he felt recovered, refreshed.

From Bharatjogi, the two visitors went to Kanta. Temple bells were rung to call in the faithful. The two emissaries spoke from the temple podium. The heat with which they spoke was not Sindhu Putra's. But to these simple men, a god's wish was a command that must be obeyed forthwith. Their wrathful words hung over the temple like a brazen curse etched on red-hot metal, burning in the consciousness of all—'Release your slaves lest you offend God and be yourself mortally wounded.'

466 / Return of the Aryans

Kanta announced that the temple would remain closed to those who still 'deny and defy Sindhu Putra by clinging to their slaves.'

But Bharatjogi put his foot down, 'How can temple-doors be barred to any one! A sinner, a doubter, an unbeliever, even a blasphemer has the right and surely, his need is greater.'

Kanta reversed her words. But the objective was achieved, for others challenged, 'Let slave-owners enter the temple and be cursed by the gods directly, face to face.' When the slave-owners began to visit distant temples, a shrill cry came from many, 'God's arrows reach everywhere and the farther they travel the faster they become—and more potent.'

Bharatjogi urged, 'Persuade with love,' but in moments of passion and frenzy, who listens to the voice of reason, even from the most exalted!

Those who freed their slaves were honoured with garlands. The few slaves that remained in the village were quietly purchased by Kanta and freed forthwith. How could she deny her son's wish! The price she paid was not cheap, as unknown to her, Mataji was buying slaves to set them free; and with the two of them bidding, the price went up.

Gatha's village was now entirely asudra (non-slave).[1] But it was not just Gatha's village! The movement began everywhere. Thousands joined the forty-four emissaries of Sindhu Putra to demand obedience to his message.

A preacher went through twenty-seven villages, one after another, 'freeing' his slave in each village. He earned respect, donations, and commanded a passionate frenzy against slavery. Unfortunately for him, he was caught in the twenty-eighth village, where it was learnt that his 'slave' was actually a hired hand, falsely 'released' twenty-seven times. The angry villagers confiscated his two horses and money-bags to buy twenty-seven slaves, each in the name of the village he had cheated. Thus this preacher too served to strengthen the new wave. But there were hundreds who were honest and they went from village to village to cajole, coerce, beg and plead compliance with Sindhu Putra's wish. Some even imagined that all slavery was about to be over. But how could that be! More than half the slaves, engaged in public works, were clan-property and only Karkarta could free them. Karkarta Nandan had no such intention.

Nandan felt as if he was under siege. Even those who owed their rise to him began to find arguments to respect Sindhu Putra's wishes.

Nandan's mind was crystal clear. He would not release his slaves; nor would he integrate with the eastern tribes. He shunned all such advice.

---

[1]Addition of 'a' before a word often denoted the opposite; for example, himsa meant violence and ahimsa would mean non-violence; similarly, dharma-adharma; rya-arya.

But when a team came, he dared not refuse to meet them, for it was led by Bharatjogi, a respected hermit, who was once the Karkarta.

Nandan's eyes were cold and glittering; his smile, mocking, as Bharat asked that the slaves be freed and the land, united.

'How is a hermit interested in the affairs of men?' Nandan asked.

'Affairs of men? Are they divorced from God's affairs?' Bharat asked.

Nandan mocked, 'You were Karkarta yourself. You were ahead of your times, always in a hurry. Some even joked that you moved so fast, that you might overtake yourself. Yet you did not abolish slavery!'

'Times change; one moves with the everchanging stream of life. In my time, thanks to you, there was intense opposition to freeing slaves. Today's demand is to abolish slavery; and the time for action is now.'

'That is not an enlightened judgement; maybe it is the judgement of your son, Sindhu Putra. He is your son, is he not?'

'Yes, not through blood but love.'

'But whose bloodlines has he then?' Nandan asked, his voice silky.

Bharat understood. Nandan wanted to trap him into an admission or a lie. 'I know as much as you do, or they,' Bharat pointed to his team. Nandan saw everyone's eyes on him as they wondered how it was possible for this Karkarta to be unaware that Sindhu Putra was the son of Mother Goddess Sindhu!

Nandan changed tack. 'You also know that it is not open to Karkarta to abolish slavery on his own. It would call for action by the Council and Assembly. And then a vote of the people.'

'Of the people's vote, I am assured. And if I have your permission, I can address the Council and Assembly.'

'That right is not yours, Bharatji!'

'I know; that is why I ask you to do it.'

'I was elected as Karkarta to honour age-old customs. You, who are no longer Karkarta, find it easy to play upon people's heartstrings. But even you should know that all the traditions of life would be in jeopardy if we disowned the customs that are time-honoured and ancient.'

'Humanity is more ancient than slavery.'

'Maybe. But I also believe in progress, enrichment, in going forward, not back to poverty and decadence. I am not against freedom or unity. I believe in freedom for the Hindu and unity among the Hindu.'

'God conceived man as man; not as a Hindu, distinct from tribals.'

'And you perceive no difference between a Hindu and a tribal!'

'As I see the difference between you and me—your short stature, your handsome features, your wealth, your commanding personality— all so different from mine. Do these differences make you or me, less or more Hindu or human? Is a Hindu to carry out the will of the Transcendent Supreme by freedom only for himself and unity solely within his clan?'

'Yet that unity in our clan is what you seek to break! To set up slaves as our equals! To bring to us the corrupting influence of union with the tribals! To tear apart the oneness of our fabric! And your seditious son! By what right does he consort with the enemy tribes? By what right does he seduce forty-four of our soldiers to send them out to spread his treason? By what right, I ask?'

Bharat watched Nandan's rising anger in silence. He waited for Nandan's temper to cool. But his own team was furious. They mistook Bharatjogi's silence for weakness. One of them rose—the once-blind singer—and shouted, 'And by what right do you dare to shout down a god's voice? The entire clan has heard Sindhu Putra's message and demands freedom for the unfortunates and unity with the tribals. Will you dare shout him down when he comes to confront you?'

Nandan was livid. With Bharat, he could have continued to trade blows. Bharat was an equal, an ex-Karkarta. But it was the temerity of the singer that infuriated him. In fury, he said, 'He shall not confront me!' His voice rose as he continued, 'He went to enemy lands, violating the law. He remains there to violate the law. He assaulted Dasapati. He caused the death of our valiant commander and our men. He contrived the escape of our slaves, repeatedly. He spreads sedition against the clan. No! He shall not enter this land. Never!'

The brutally affronting words sped out of Nandan, beyond recall. Everyone froze—even the Council-members. Bharat watched Nandan in pity. What is it, he wondered! Frustration! Ravages of age! What happens to a man when he grows old! Yes, there is sense in sending people out as hermits at sixty, before their minds become warped.

'Karkarta Nandan,' Bharat said softly, 'that right is not yours.'

'Why? Because he is your son who pretends to be a god?' Nandan asked in fury.

'Because he is of the rya. None should demand that a rya be made an arya. It is not dharma even to contemplate such an action.'

'Allow me to be the judge of my own adharma or dharma.'

Bharat rose and said, 'Then there is little to discuss; and I must leave you to discover what dharma is and what dharma is not.' Bharat and his team left before Nandan declared the audience at an end.

'...Gods come to earth in order to save mankind, but not themselves. They protect others but who can protect them against man's onslaughts?'

—(Attributed to Jalta's mother in 'Song of Jalta Ma', 5052 BC)

Did the God Fly Away?

5052 BC

Nandan's emissary, Chautala, reached the eastern township to meet the new commander of the eastern region. Karkarta's orders were simple, crisp and clear—Sindhu Putra is not to enter the land of the Hindu.

'Why?' asked Vashita, the new commander.

'Orders are orders,' said Chautala, but he smiled. Vashita was a dear friend. He was to have married Chautala's sister but she had died before they could. Vashita remained a bachelor, with a lifelong devotion to her. To Chautala, he was like a brother. Vashita, unknown to him, owed his promotion as commander to Chautala's influence, which was considerable, both as Council-member and Nandan's trusted advisor.

Chautala explained, 'Sindhu Putra heads the enemy armies and seeks to create mischief here.'

'What mischief?'

'Even your own reports speak of his possible mischief. Did you not report that he united the mute tribes with the Jalta people and the two together unleashed onslaughts against all the other tribes?'

'Yes, but after those deadly battles and bloodshed there is finally peace; no more hostilities; slavery is virtually over and all the sixty tribes in the eastern region are united under Sindhu Putra's banner. But where is the mischief against us?'

'You amaze me! Sixty tribes united under the single banner of Sindhu Putra! Slaves are slaves no more! And yet you see no danger!'

'Then my reports are at fault. When I spoke of tribes uniting under his banner, it was purely in the spiritual sense—not to command armies, nor to pose a threat—but to seek freedom for slaves and unity amongst the tribes through moral force.'

'And that poses no threat! Instead of sixty weak, divided tribes, warring with each other, we now face one huge tribe—formidable, united, single-minded—on our borders. No threat to us, did you say!'

'The threat begins from us. They will not face us until we move into their land. Even now, with all their united strength, they are no match for us.'

'So we sit back till they get stronger and more united!'

'Even from our own forty-four men who came back, the message is clear—the plea is for friendship and unity.'

'Unity! To get submerged into the sea of sub-humanity! And I suppose you would like to give up your slaves!'

'That would be an inconvenience,' said Vashita with a smile.

'So, my friend, keep away from that inconvenience and prevent Sindhu Putra and his people from entering our land.'

'But suppose he enters alone, without the tribal army?'

'Then it will be all the easier to stop him, without fear and fuss.'

'On what grounds?'

'His crimes against our land are many.'

'Then why not let him enter and try him for those crimes?'

'You must really be a great soldier and a great commander!'

'How so?'

'Because so much in you is so impractical. How can we try Sindhu Putra in our land when thousands upon thousands regard him as a god!'

'And you think they would applaud our stopping him from entering his own land, even when he comes alone, without an alie army!'

'Hearts do not grieve over what eyes do not see and what ears do not hear. Here you are remote, faraway, unseen. Who will know if he came alone or with an army? Who would be aware that he was turned away? If complaints mount, there are always explanations and even promotions to a higher command. But why argue in circles? What is it that I said earlier?—Yes, I said—orders are orders—so let it rest on Karkarta's conscience, not on yours.'

'Did not a former Karkarta say: question the order that is immoral or unlawful.'

'We are not in Bharatji's times.'

'Yet the wrongful act shall be mine. How am I exonerated by pleading that I followed the unlawful order of my superior?'

'No one shall call upon you to explain. . . .'

'Yet I must call upon myself to explain myself,' Vashita interrupted.

Their discussion continued. Chautala pleaded. Vashita was unmoved. Chautala spoke of his efforts to get Vashita the command of the region.

'I did not know that,' Vashita said. 'You give me yet another reason to resign my command, for I cannot pay the price you seek.'

Chautala felt stung. 'Price! It was not to seek a price but out of love for you. . .and for my little sister. . . .'

Vashita was touched, 'That love shall always remain, whatever your path and mine. But I must request you to relieve me of my command.'

'That I shall not. But I accept your request for long sick-leave.'

'I made no such request. I am not sick.'

'Don't make a liar of me,' Chautala laughed. 'And as to being sick, we are brought up to believe that he who questions Karkarta Nandan's orders must be sick—in mind, if not in body.'

The tension eased. It was a way out, thought Vashita. He smiled, 'So be it. I request sick-leave.'

'I grant it.' Chautala said. Both left the township together, after Rochila was installed as commander. Somehow, Chautala had feared that Vashita would be inflexible and had brought Rochila along.

Rochila, the new commander, did not suffer from Vashita's scruples. He knew the purpose for which he was brought there.

Yet it was Nandan himself who queered the pitch for Rochila. In a moment of unthinking rage, he had made his premature announcement that Sindhu Putra not be allowed to enter his own land.

From Gatha's village, hundreds began their march to the eastern township, to stand in the way of those who would dare obstruct Sindhu Putra. But not only from Gatha's village. All over the land, people marched. With anguish, Kanta remained behind. How could she desert the temple? Or leave Bharatjogi, now seriously ill after his meeting with Nandan? Yet she was active. With unlimited funds, her retainer Vassi went about supplying carts, horses and provisions to those who wished to march to the eastern township. Soon, Kanta saw that Gatha, together with other headmen, was doing that too, though his funds were limited, supported as he was by Mataji's slender resources. Yet Gatha and his colleagues were better organized and were not fooled by spurious claimants. Kanta's funds were now freely available to Gatha.

Did all these thousands march merely for the love of Sindhu Putra? Many, yes; but some there were who went for the sheer enjoyment of it. A free horse, a cart-ride, provisions, a fun-filled vacation—why not! They were the ones who shouted the loudest for Sindhu Putra. Of them, quite a few became fascinated by their own oratory and later began to cling to Sindhu Putra's cause, in faith and silence.

But then there were also a few—perhaps no more than fifty—who were unconcerned with Sindhu Putra personally. To them, it was a principle that was being violated. How can rya be refused entry into their own land and be made into arya? No, they did not believe in Sindhu Putra's godhood. They marched because he was not a god. Their argument: if he is a god, how could his entry be prevented by man—even by Karkarta? It is because he is *not* a god that we must move to protect his right as a man—a rya in his own land.

Rochila, the new commander, was furious when the vanguard of protesters arrived. His instructions to them to go back were of no avail. His words were harsh and he asked, 'What will you do if I prevent Sindhu Putra's entry? Will you kill me?'

'No, we would rather kill ourselves than allow you to kill your own soul,' they said; and their eyes held neither fear nor defiance.

This was the first time that the remote eastern township learnt what was being contemplated. To obstruct Sindhu Putra! They stared accusingly at their headman. But he had known nothing. Immediately, he took on the task of looking after the needs of the protesters, as they kept arriving. First, he spent his own funds; later, official funds earmarked for visitors to the township. Protestors or not, they were certainly visitors!

Rochila summarily dismissed the headman. But that raised the headman's prestige sky-high. No one ignored him anymore, or laughed at him. At his request, many townsmen vacated their huts to double up with others, to accommodate the new arrivals. His wife gave up evening meals on alternate days and that became the rule for all adults so as to conserve food for the visitors. Some even followed stricter self-rationing. They all felt relieved, though, when Vassi arrived with cartloads of provisions.

Rochila saw and heard all this with growing anger. He faced Vassi, who remained undaunted, and asked, 'When has it been declared a crime to bring food?' The shouting match went on and Vassi said, 'I have faced Jhadrov, Ranadher and Ghulat and lived in whorehouses all my life; what makes you think I am afraid of you?' Looking at his disfigured face and hearing these infamous names, Rochila wondered— My god! this Sindhu Putra has both gangsters and saints on his side! He ordered a search of all new-comers for weapons. They had none.

What bothered Rochila was that his own soldiers were whispering, muttering, complaining. Some asked for release from the army; others sought sick-leave; a few disappeared. He moved most of his contingents two yojnas forward, to avoid further contagion from the township and new-comers. Also, Sindhu Putra had to be faced away from their gaze.

Rochila knew that if the tribes sent out any army under Sindhu Putra, to get into his land, there was only one possible route for them to cross over. He occupied a commanding position on that route. His spies went out to discover if the tribal army was on the march. The battle, he was certain, would be quick and intense and the tribal forces would be crushed instantly. But what of Sindhu Putra, he wondered. Rochila decided that weapons would not be aimed at Sindhu Putra directly; but who knows how the battle would begin and how end!

Rochila's only doubt was what would happen if Sindhu Putra slunk in, quietly and alone, under cover of night, without an army. Then he could easily avoid the main route and use narrow, side-tracks to enter undetected. But then, what reason would Sindhu Putra have to crawl into this land, like a thief in the night, when he commanded the armies of sixty tribes, including the dreaded mute and the Jalta people! Even so, Rochila decided to send out spies to find out.

Mithali, the servant girl in the headman's household, who had accompanied Sindhu Putra to the fort-site, followed Rochila's contingent on her mule. She undertook the task of serving water to the troops. Rochila was pleased; at least someone—albeit a child—from the township had a sense of duty. He patted her and she gave him a winning smile.

He did not notice her absence after they reached their commanding pass. Her mule remained behind. His own fleet horse was missing.

Far away from Rochila's command post, at a tribal village, Mithali was caught and brought to the village commander, who was once a slave. He was sure she was a spy. Already, they had caught a spy from the township and Mithali saw his head stuck on a pole. The village commander held her by the hair and she kept sobbing piteously, 'Sindhu Putra! Sindhu Putra!' The commander heard the venerated name and relaxed his hold on her. 'Sindhu Putra?' he asked. She nodded through her tears. Still, she could be a spy—he thought. He took her to a tent occupied by the administrator sent by the mute tribe. The administrator was annoyed at being woken up that early but when he saw Mithali, he embraced her. He was one of the slaves at the fort, and he had seen Mithali with Sindhu Putra when the water jars had broken. But he could not understand her language, except that she kept shouting 'Sindhu Putra'. Her gestures and tears however convinced him that it was necessary to reach Sindhu Putra who was in danger. The administrator commandeered two horses for himself and Mithali, as her stolen horse was weary; and grabbed food that both he and Mithali could eat on horseback. They thundered forth. When Mithali was overcome with sleep, he would snatch her from her horse and they would both travel on the same horse. For himself, he needed no sleep if Sindhu Putra was in danger. They stopped only briefly at the tribal villages to secure food and horses.

It took days, but at last they reached the Jalta lands. Sindhu Putra was there. Warning of their arrival had reached them by drum-beat. But to her lasting shame, Mithali was asleep, overcome by weariness, when they arrived. 'Let her sleep,' Sindhu Putra said. But soon she woke up with tears of shame streaming from her eyes.

Sindhu Putra learnt of the danger that faced him in his own land, with Rochila's army waiting to block him—to wipe him out if he came with a tribal army... and even if he went alone.

Sindhu Putra, in any case, had no intention of marching with an army. At best, Hardas and Devita, the father and son from the Dravidham civilization, and the two from Ganga civilization were to join him, though hundreds were determined to escort him until the last frontier village.

He decided he would go openly. He saw their anxious faces and said, 'I am a Hindu, entering my own land of Sindhu. Who can stop me!'

Everyone's fear vanished and they felt, 'Indeed, who can stop a god for going anywhere at his will! Who indeed!'

Jalta's mother, however, was silent. Her ancestral memory told her that gods came to earth in order to save mankind, not themselves.

They could protect others, but were they protected against man's onslaughts? Yet, how could she say this and incur everyone's wrath for want of faith in this new and mighty god! Quietly she spoke, 'A sin it would be for them that seek to prevent you. And in their misguided attempt, how many innocents may lose their lives! Yet, there is a way to avoid that temptation to them and save them from committing that heinous sin. So easy it is to cross into your land from various passes! And since you cross with no army, who can detect your entry with only a few companions? But if you go openly and someone dares to stop you, imagine the friction between your tribe and our sixty tribes!—and yet what you really seek is unity and not division.'

Many were annoyed—she dares lecture a god! Quickly she added, 'Forgive me if my love tempts me to speak like a mother to her son.'

This was perhaps the best thing she could have said. Sindhu Putra responded, 'Mother, I shall do exactly as you say.'

Sindhu Putra left with a few companions. Rochila's spies would have discovered him. But their attention was diverted elsewhere.

Jalta's mother had made preparations of a different kind. Under her instructions, a huge army of sixty tribes moved towards Rochila's camp, along with Jalta the Fourth and the former Chief of the silent tribe. Slowly, noisily, the army lumbered along, resting and frolicking on the way. They seemed to have no care in the world except to ensure that no outsider came near enough to see their leader. Viewed from a distance, but hidden by tall companions and shielded by banners of escorts, it was clearly Sindhu Putra himself who led the army.

Jalta's mother herself had selected this look-alike of Sindhu Putra. In build, height and general appearance, he looked exactly like Sindhu Putra. His hair was dyed and cut to match and even some colouring was applied to his face. 'How can a mere man look like a god?' Jalta the Fourth had protested, but his mother asked, 'How does a god look like a man?'

She became theatrical too, and the look-alike also wore a light crown of gold, though Sindhu Putra never had such adornments. For the rest, a decorative umbrella, with long tassles, held for him throughout the march, also prevented a clear view. At each stop, the tribals would bow to him for all to see; and his tent was the first to be set up.

Jalta's mother had one regret. She found the look-alike not among her own people, but from the silent tribe. But she consoled herself with the thought that a mute could not speak and would therefore not talk nonsense.

This elaborate hoax was carried out because Jalta's mother was certain that the enemy had spies. They would 'see' Sindhu Putra at the head of the huge army. They would look nowhere else for him. She was right. The spies 'saw' not only Sindhu Putra but also Mithali riding with the tribal army.

Rochila was delighted at the report, not only of Sindhu Putra and his army, but also about the 'horse-thief', as he called Mithali. Soon they would be in his trap. Pity, they were moving so slowly, but what can one expect from undisciplined barbarians led by a mere boy!

Sometimes, the best-laid plans will go awry. Jalta's mother's instructions were: 'Return instantly when you receive the message that Sindhu Putra has crossed into his land.' The two tribesmen who guided Sindhu Putra through devious paths reached the tribal army to report that indeed Sindhu Putra had finally crossed over into his own land, undetected. The silent ex-Chief and Jalta the Fourth however decided that the masquerade must continue. If Sindhu Putra's own people could contemplate obstructing his entry, they were capable also of any evil and would maybe harass him if they found him in his land, until he reached his own village. The words of Jalta's mother rang in their ears—'Gods, when they take human form suffer from human weakness. They can bleed. . . .' Yes, the masquerade must continue, more vigorously, so that no one even dreamt of searching for Sindhu Putra in his own land.

Now the tribal army rushed ahead with speed and Rochila was delighted as he heard of it from his spies.

Far away, on the west of a hill, the tribal army stood facing Rochila's contingents. The terrain dividing them was rocky; even so it would take just half a day to rush at each other's throats. But Rochila was in no hurry. They were the ones who marched hither. They were bound to make the first move. Let those lunatics rush to their doom. Why should he sacrifice a single life to move to their guarded position!

Everyday, in the bright sunshine, Rochila would go a little forward alone, to enjoy the spectacle of the tribals bowing to Sindhu Putra. 'Soon, you will bow to me—that is, if you survive,' said Rochila, as if speaking to the tribals, 'and he, to whom you bow, will kiss the dust.'

But Rochila was losing patience over the totally unexpected inaction of the tribals. Were they waiting for more reinforcements?

Meanwhile, the tribal army was getting ready to depart. But not Sindhu Putra's look-alike. He astounded his silent Chief to say, 'Let our entire army return. Alone, I shall go, unattended, towards the enemy. Let them block my entry. I shall then return to catch up with you. Perhaps they will kill me. So be it. Their hunt for our real God shall cease. Our God can then reappear, mysteriously. He is the Master. He alone shall will what He must will.'

The look-alike would hear no more arguments that warned him of certain death and asked, 'Would you not die to protect a single hair on His head? Then why is the privilege of dying for Him to be denied to me?'

Formerly, they had bowed to the look-alike to keep the enemy spies off the scent. Now they bowed to him with respect. He had been a good-for-nothing lad, dismissed from his last job of mixing wines, for drinking more than he mixed. He was also known as a coward who in the past had often run away to the hills, when the enemy tribes raided his village.

The next morning ushered in a beautiful sunrise. Rochila saw the lone horseman—Sindhu Putra—on the crest of the hill. Everyone in the tribal army was bowing to him and then mounting their horses. Surely the attack was about to begin. But each tribal went in the opposite direction. Rochila smiled—obviously a petty trick. The tribals were no doubt hiding behind the hill to tempt him to rush towards the lone Sindhu Putra. Now even the men holding banners and the decorative umbrella over his head disappeared and Sindhu Putra stood alone, unattended. Sindhu Putra waved back, as though in farewell to the retreating tribal army. Rochila smiled again at this obvious pretense.

An hour passed and now the lone horseman began his descent towards Rochila's contingents. Two of Rochila's men climbed up the long poles. Indeed, the tribal army was retreating, fast and furious.

Slowly, the look-alike's horse was inching towards Rochila's contingent. The day wore on. Rochila waited, certain that the tribal army would double back. He waited.

The look-alike increased his speed, possibly certain now that the retreating tribal army was beyond pursuit.

Rochila was ready with his javelin. But he had no intention of throwing it at Sindhu Putra. That task was given to his men. Not that he had moral scruples. But he was too high up and he maybe blamed for it and through him, Karkarta Nandan. Let the deed be anonymous, so that no one knew whom to blame for losing his head in the heat of the moment.

As the look-alike got nearer, Rochila saw that he was on the horse which Mithali had stolen. Another reason for him to die.

A line was drawn where Sindhu Putra was to be stopped. The look-alike looked back. Was it to say farewell to his land for ever?

Rochila's voice boomed, 'Sindhu Putra! Set not your foot on the line. This land is not for you to enter—ever. Go back!'

The look-alike wanted to reply, 'Are you trying to prevent Sindhu Putra—a Hindu—from entering his own land of Sindhu?'—as this is what Sindhu Putra himself had wondered. But how could the look-alike say all this—he, who was a mute! But I can utter the First Word of God—he thought, and he folded his hands in the gesture of namaste, and loudly, he intoned 'OM'. Forward went his horse, crossing over the forbidden line.

No one knows for certain to this day what it was that moved Rochila's men. Was it the Namaste, the familiar gesture of Sindhu Putra?

Was it the look-alike's smile of self-assurance, as though he feared no evil? Or was it this new mantra—OM—which they had not heard before? OM! What did it mean? OM—why did it stir something in them? Had they not heard it before? Why then was it familiar?

Earlier, the look-like had thought that he would cross the alien land with a sinking, fearful feeling. But now, he went with no fear. All he prayed was: let the First Word of God—OM—be my last word when I die. He saw weapons aimed at him. Softly, not as a rallying cry, but from his heart, he intoned a long-drawn OM, certain that it was to be his last breath. In hushed silence, everyone, perhaps unknown to each other, dropped their weapons and moved nearer to him. Why? To arrest him? No, poets say, it was to form a guard of honour.

Rochila glared, furious at the cowardice of his men. He aimed his own javelin directly at the look-alike. Did the horse see the javelin before the look-alike did? Without warning, the horse pricked his ears and raised his forelegs high in the air. The look-alike fell but it was the horse that caught the javelin aimed at the look-alike. The man and the horse lay side by side. The writhing agony of the horse stopped. The horse died.

There and then Rochila died too, with a javelin through his breast. No one ever admitted to hurling it, but poets later ran wild with their fantasies—it was a thunderbolt from the gods, some said. No, others said, the horse took out the javelin from its body to hurl it back at Rochila. The realists among them questioned: How is it then that the horse still had the javelin stuck in its breast?

Again, none would ever know if Rochila's men had already decided to rebel against their commander, or whether it was a sudden impulse inspired by the utterance of the First Word of God—OM?

Whatever be the truth, the fact remains that both the horse and his old master breathed their last at the same moment—and the poets have mourned the death of only one of them.

Escorted by Rochila's contingent, and even by Rochila himself—for his dead body was carried on the stretcher—the look-alike reached the township. A cry of agony rent the air from the thousands there. Was it Sindhu Putra on the stretcher? The look-alike stood up on a horse to see the crowds. My God! Everyone cried. Blood on Sindhu Putra! It was the blood from the horse that had died to save him.

Many came to the look-alike with questions. But how does a mute answer! They respected his silence. They wanted to take him to the guest-house. He shook his head. With frantic gestures, he moved the crowds back and drew a circle on the ground, with a radius of three hundred feet, making it clear that he would remain alone there. Then with his head bent, eyes closed, face shielded by Namaste, he seemed in meditation. No doubt, he wanted none to see him closely, lest he be recognized. The headman pleaded to enter. The look-alike raised a forbidding hand. Clearly, he was in communion with the divine father and none dared disturb him.

But Mithali, who had hidden behind a rock when the tribal army retreated, emerged at last. Stealthily, at a distance, she had followed the look-alike and was a silent witness to much of the drama.

Mithali reached the outer fringes of the crowd. The headman knew she was the one who had run off to be with Sindhu Putra. He placed her on his tall shoulders and she cried out, 'My friend! My friend!' Foolish girl!—everyone thought; what a way to address a god! But the look-alike looked up and with a gesture invited her to come into the circle. The headman rushed in with her on his shoulders, but again, a gesture halted him. Alone, Mithali ran to the look-alike. They embraced.

No one will know what they concocted with unmoving lips and elaborate gestures. Soon Mithali came to the crowds outside the circle and said to the headman, 'He wants silence, with everyone back in their homes. If he walks, he wants no one to follow him, neither with footsteps nor with their eyes. He is in communion with his father and shall obey his father's command.' To the headman, her shrill words were, 'Obey him yourself and see that all do likewise in all he asks!'

Many wondered. A servant girl to speak thus to her master! But she touched the headman's feet, 'These are not my words, Master!' They were touched. And the headman asked. 'Should I not send food for him!'

Mithali agreed, 'Yes, please. And mattresses and twelve horses.'

'Twelve horses?' the headman asked, astonished.

'Yes, with feed for them and poles to tether them. He wants to speak to the horses of the death of the horse that brought him here.'

'Yes, of course,' the headman said, without surprise.

Many say that all this was Mithali's invention. The look-alike wanted only one horse to escape, now that he saw that there was no danger to the real Sindhu Putra, judging from this affectionate reception. The sooner he escaped, the better, lest his identity be discovered.

Twelve horses, food, pillows, bedsheets and mattresses arrived.

On one of the horses, Mithali went round commanding everyone to retire. The silhouette of Sindhu Putra could be seen, even on that moonless night, and if some saw a glow on his face, it was simply a reflection of the glow in their own hearts. Even when everyone had retired, Mithali kept circling round on her horse, as if to disperse those who still remained.

On one of her trips, to and fro, the look-alike jumped on her horse, while the eleven horses blocked the view. The look-alike's silhouette could still be seen, made up of mattreses and pillows. Everyone had been hearing Mithali's horsehoofs, no doubt busy with her task to keep the people away. But now, she and the look-alike, mounted on a single horse, were headed elsewhere. They crossed the township into no-man's land.

Suddenly, the look-alike pulled up the horse, as he heard an owl-hoot, shrill and rising from a short tree. It was no tree, really, but a tribesmen covered with bark and branches, on a waiting-watch for the look-alike. He took Mithali and the look-alike to the horses tethered nearby. The tribesman and the look-alike left. Mithali rode back to the circle in the township but not directly; she kept going in all directions, as though still on her task of keeping everyone away.

As the first light of morning broke, they saw Mithali alone, sleeping there peacefully. 'Where is Sindhu Putra?' And Mithali said, 'He flew away to meet his father.' Yes, what else could it be! All twelve horses were tethered there. Surely, he could not have walked out!

It was a memorable day for the township.

*

But equally memorable was that very day for the village of Gatha. It was on that day that the real Sindhu Putra reached Bharatjogi.

Later all were astounded that Sindhu Putra was present at the same moment at two different places, removed by a journey of many days!

But did not Mithali say that Sindhu Putra flew away! Surely gods can do what no man can!

'...Why do gods intervene in the business of politics? Do they not know of the dirt in that business—and do gods know enough of dirt and business? No; only man can excel in it. And the darker the man's conscience, the more he will glow in that business.'

—(A later poet's rage over Sindhu Putra's meeting with Nandan, 5052 BC)

Farewell Bharat!

5051 BC

Bharatjogi was on his sick bed, weak, frail, emaciated. Sindhu Putra touched his feet and kissed his forehead. Bharat opened his eyes for the first time in several days. His eyes moved to the far end of the room as though to speak to someone else, 'My son has come! Yes, I am ready now!' To Sindhu Putra, he said, 'I knew you would come, son. Who could prevent your coming!' He attempted to laugh but it ended in a cough which would not stop. Everyone was worried. Only Mataji dared tell Sindhu Putra not to excite Bharat, nor to encourage him to speak. Sindhu Putra placed his head on Bharat's heart. The cough ceased. Bharat smiled. He could now feel himself bathed in a ray of light. The agonizing pain in his body melted away, leaving a sense of well-being. He asked in a firm voice, 'Tell me all, son.'

But Sindhu Putra's eyes were moist with tears. Bharat smiled, 'No, son, no. There is no need for tears, nor for delay. The Visitor waits.' His glance moved to the doorway. No one was there, but Bharat continued, 'He kept vigil by my bedside to wait for your homecoming. Let us tax his politeness no more. Thank him for the few extra moments he gives us.' Prayerfully Sindhu Putra gazed at the empty doorway, with the gesture of Namaste, his lips moving to utter 'OM'. But his tears were still there as he spoke.

Sindhu Putra told Bharat of his journey; of the release of the slaves at the fort; of Namaste; of the abolition of slavery in the silent tribe; of OM; of unity among Jalta and the silent peoples; and finally of unity among all the sixty tribes with the total abolition of slavery.

Deeply moved, Bharat half rose to embrace Sindhu Putra and looked at the doorway to say, 'My son! My son! He shall liberate the slaves—all the slaves everywhere! He shall unite our land!'

But a troubling thought came to Bharat through his joy. 'How will I remember all the names you tell me of the sixty tribes which you united?'

'Those names exist no more. They are all together now, known by a single name—Bharat Varsha.'

Bharat lay back on his bed with a wave of happiness flooding him. But again he asked, 'Why Bharat Varsha? Why not your name?'

'It was not my decision, Father. They took the decision.'

'How? When? Why?' Bharat asked.

'I simply said that it was my father's wish that this land be free of slaves and united,' Sindhu Putra replied.

None understood. But Bharat did; and he laughed, speaking to the empty doorway, 'Forgive me, Father, if my name got mixed up with yours. And forgive me for being happy about it.' Again he laughed.

Bharat asked, 'How did you enter? Were they empty threats then?'

Sindhu Putra wished to say nothing. Too many were present there. His look-alike, along with the tribal army, may still be on the way. They may all be in danger if the secret was out, prematurely. Sindhu Putra bent forward to whisper for a long time in Bharat's ear. It could not be a secret of the gods, for Bharat was laughing. It was the hearty laugh of a young man bursting with energy and vitality—and the laughter would not stop. At last Bharat spoke, 'Life is beautiful.' He looked again at the empty doorway, 'And greater beauty is yet to come.'

Quietly, with tenderness, Bharat asked for Mataji's hand, and thereafter, everyone present came forward to clasp his hand. Everyone, then, except Mataji and Sindhu Putra, left to wait outside where the crowds kept vigil. Mataji washed Bharatji with water from the confluence of Sindhu river with Sindhu sea. After the wash she put a new robe on him. Bharat asked Mataji with a smile, 'Am I presentable to go where I am going?'

She smiled through her tears, sprinkled water towards the sky, and said, 'Wait awhile. Give them time to be presentable to receive you.'

They held hands. Their eyes were closed. Silently, they were speaking to each other. When both opened their eyes, he spoke to Sindhu Putra, 'Tell me the last word again.' Actually he meant the first word of God. Sindhu Putra intoned 'OM'. Then holding Sindhu Putra and Mataji's hand, he looked at the doorway, and quietly said, 'Thank you for waiting. I am ready now.' Mataji and Sindhu Putra saw his smile and heard a long-drawn 'OM' from his lips.

Bharatjogi died.

'As for me, the battle is over and lost,' Nandan said. There was much he did not understand. One reliable eyewitness report said that Sindhu Putra, with his army, was facing Rochila's contingent and soon the tribal army would be wiped out. Another eyewitness report, equally reliable, was that Sindhu Putra was actually at Bharatjogi's deathbed. The first report was sent four days earlier and the second report only the day before. Nothing made sense. It was absolutely impossible for Sindhu Putra to reach Bharatjogi in that short time, even if Rochila himself was mad enough to escort Sindhu Putra on the fleetest horse.

Actually, Nandan had not yet received the report of Rochila's mysterious death, the disappearance of the tribal army and Sindhu

Putra's triumphant entry into the eastern township. Even so, he felt unhinged even as the tip of this vast mystery unfolded.

Only one thing was clear to Nandan—that he was destroyed. Why did this sudden madness descend on me to announce that I shall prevent Sindhu Putra from entering the land! Now he is with his dead father and I shall be laughed at for ever! Nandan realized that a man who leads his people can recover from any disaster except ridicule. And the next election—will they vote for me or laugh at me?

All his plans, with this single false step, had gone awry. He worried not so much about himself, but about the future of his clan, and the future of his son Sharat. He had done away with the odious law that the son cannot succeed his father as Karkarta. Ably, his friends had argued—why should we place such a limitation on people's choice? Does it not offend against an individual right of a rya to stand for election, and against the collective right of the ryas to elect anyone they choose? No, we have no individual in view; it is the principle behind such prohibition that is offensive.

Yes, that law was no more. But who will wish to elect my son to succeed me! He now carries, not my legacy of greatness, but my taint of ridicule. And who will stop the floodtide of freedom for slaves, when this Sindhu Putra is thrice blessed—with the image of a god, with breaking barriers to block his entry into the land, and now with the tears of all, over his father's death. 'My sun has set,' Nandan said.

'There never was a sunset that was not followed by sunrise,' Sharat said. 'Your sun will rise; even your son will rise.'

*

Sharat rushed to Gatha's village, leaving word for the others to follow.

Bharatjogi's body lay in state. Normally, the body was cremated by sunset of the following day; but this time a promise was given to villages far and near, that they would be given time to arrive.

Lovingly, men skilled in the art had prepared Bharat's body for its last journey. Its countenance retained the vigour and dignity which marked the great man during his lifetime. Mataji closed his eyelids and kissed his lips which still held a faint trace of his last smile.

Sharat bowed to Mataji and Sindhu Putra and said, 'My father prays that Bharatjogi be cremated in Karkarta's town.'

The once-blind singer intervened to ask 'Why?' Sharat bowed to him and said humbly, 'It is the clan's main town and Bharatji was our most illustrious Karkarta. The clan reveres him, mourns him.'

'Everyone mourns him in this village too,' the singer retorted.

'Of course. He belongs to this whole land which is beginning to be known as Bharat Varsha. My father wishes that he be escorted in an open, decorated carriage, for all the villages to see him and pay their respects.'

Mataji and even Sindhu Putra wondered why the singer obstructed the honour to their beloved Bharatjogi. Mataji simply said, 'Yes and I agree and thank you for the thought.' Sindhu Putra nodded.

'The honour is for the clan,' Sharat soulfully replied.

Sharat had many men. Yet he himself slaved to make a single cart by joining many together, decorating it with flowers and gold-threaded cloth. A hundred and eight horsemen were to precede the cortège: five hundred to follow.

Muni reached with Roopa. Muni bent to kiss Bharat's cold brow. He commented on the lavish arrangements. 'So much for a hermit.' But later Sharat said, 'He was more than a hermit,' and everyone agreed.

Sharat asked Sindhu Putra, 'Will you join Bharatjogi's journey?'

'Yes of course. He is my father. He guided me through life.'

'He is the father of the entire clan,' Sharat said. 'My father, though too ill to come here, will honour your father in a special way.'

'How?' Sindhu Putra asked. He began to like Sharat, but suspicion lingered; was it not Nandan who had tried to block his entry into his own land?

'He will release slaves and abolish slavery,' Sharat said simply.

'What!' Sindhu Putra exclaimed, unable to believe his ears. 'But how! When? I thought your father opposed it!'

'Your father Bharatjogi's inspiration convinced my father.'

'Yet everyone says that your father decisively refused my father.'

Sharat smiled sadly, 'What was my father expected to do! If in the presence of all he had announced the abolition of slavery, can you imagine the storm of protest from those who favour slavery and oppose unity! Your father had the same difficulty when he was Karkarta, even though he was more popular than any Karkarta can ever hope to be.'

'But your father even said that I could not enter our land.'

'Of course he said that, but only to protect you. Not from the tribes, but from those, here, who insist that slavery must be maintained. Once they knew that my father was going to block your entry, they had nothing to fear. Otherwise who knows to what lengths they would have gone to stop you!'

Sindhu Putra remembered what Bharat had once said—to lead people, a leader must sometimes appear to be sincere without being too honest. He felt sad at misjudging Karkarta Nandan and quickly said, 'It will be an honour to meet your father.'

Sharat responded, 'Thank you. But none must know of his intention to abolish slavery. Otherwise, the entire campaign might be defeated.'

'I understand,' Sindhu Putra said. 'But tell me, do you think he will also agree to unity with the sixty tribes of the eastern region?'

Sharat laughed, 'Strange! You ask what is in my father's heart. He wants to request you to arrange a unity meeting with the eastern tribes.'

A happy smile lit up Sindhu Putra's face and his heart. And he thought: how wrong I was about Karkarta Nandan! He remembered Muni's words—the life of every man is a deep, dark forest.

Later poets would say, surely Sindhu Putra was no god; how easily he was fooled by Sharat and Nandan! But others argued—man can easily understand man's villainy, lies and duplicity; but not a god. God trusts.

*

Nandan was one of those who carried Bharatjogi's body to the cremation pyre. Everyone knew he was unwell and everyone admired him for the effort. Later at the Memorial service, Nandan spoke, 'Whatever we do to honour Bharatji is less than what he deserves. Yet what is it that we can do? To confer on him a title, "Foremost amongst us all?" or "The shining light of the Sindhu?" or the "Most precious jewel of the Hindu?"...'

Everyone appalauded but Nandan contradicted himself. 'No, Bharatji coveted no empty titles. He had a mission, a dream. We must translate that dream into reality and that will be a lasting memorial to him. For this, my son Sharat and I shall consult Bharatji's son, Sindhu Putra, and I hope you will all agree with our joint decision.'

But, of course, everyone said. A joint decision between a Karkarta and a god! Who can oppose such a combination! Who indeed!

*

At Sindhu Putra's meeting with Nandan and Sharat, Nandan said, 'What I have to say is for your ears only.'

Sindhu Putra nodded; Nandan continued, 'Keeping before me the views of your illustrious father, it is my wish to take the following steps; first, to release all slaves under my charge on behalf of the clan; this right I have in consultation with the Council; second, to request—as I cannot demand—that all private individuals should free their slaves; third, to appeal to the Parliament of Hindu to approve legislation to abolish slavery for the future; fourth, to appeal to the people to approve the Parliament's legislation, as it will require the direct vote by all the people of the clan; fifth, by virtue of that approved legislation, to ensure that all who still hold slaves are obliged to let them go; sixth, to grant compensation to some needy or handicapped persons who are particularly hurt by releasing their slaves; seventh, to consult with you on how best to achieve unity with the eastern region which I believe now consists of a single tribe instead of sixty tribes.' Nandan paused, and then continued, 'I would wish that this seven-point programme, when implemented, be known as the Bharat Programme. But I must ask you, if you agree or whether you have any reservations about any of it?'

'I? Karkarta, yes, of course I agree, fully. With all my heart. My father could have asked for no more!'

'Thank you. As to scheduling, we will go ahead with the first six points, and tackle later the question of unity with the eastern tribes.'

Sharat intervened, 'Why Father? I thought you were keen on unity.'

'So I am. But remember, there are those who oppose the abolition of slavery and others who oppose unity. I do not want the two groups to join together to defeat us on both points. And suppose we are defeated on the question of slavery. Of what use is unity then? To subject the eastern region to slavery again? What do you think?' He looked at Sindhu Putra, who responded, 'You are right, Karkarta. But the sooner the question of unity is taken up, the better it would be.'

'Of course. That is why I want you, Sindhu Putra, to create an atmosphere of unity in the eastern region. And you, Sharat, must continue to take the pulse of the Council and Assembly to see who will support what. Don't forget I have no more than six months as Karkarta.'

'How?' Sindhu Putra was disturbed. He wondered how the seven-point programme could be implemented in so short a time.

Nandan explained, 'The re-election of Karkarta takes place in six months. Surely, I cannot stand for re-election.'

'Why not?' Sindhu Putra asked.

'If I stand for re-election, those who oppose me personally would also oppose the measures I propose. Even otherwise, to ensure the success of these measures, it would be better if I am away from the fray, to take a principled stand rather than make them a part of my election platform. You see my difficulty?'

Sindhu Putra did not and asked, 'But what if matters drag on beyond six months and the next Karkarta favours slavery and opposes unity.'

'That is a risk, of course.'

'Who is likely to be the next Karkarta?' Sindhu Putra asked.

'Who knows! I hope not Kulwant nor Prakash nor Bharadawan. They hate tribals and favour slavery. Even Jethan and Kalyani—I doubt if they are inspired by Bharatji's dream.'

'But surely there must be some who support us,' Sindhu Putra asked.

'Oh yes, take the Council. Apart from Sharat here, who is seniormost in the Council, and of course deeply committed, there are Madhu Janak, Gulara, Ajit—not well-known but . . . .'

'But why not Sharatji?' Sindhu Putra interrupted.

'Me!' Sharatji interjected and broke into a laugh.

Nandan's expression was thoughtful as if he were pondering deeply over this suggestion. At last he said, 'But yes, Sharat, my son; why not!'

Sharat laughed again. Nandan silenced him, 'I begged Sindhu Putra's presence here, so that he may advise us, guide us. He makes a suggestion and you laugh, without even considering it. Surely we owe him that courtesy. What is your objection?'

'I am your son,' Sharat weakly responded.

'Do I need to be reminded about it?' Nandan asked, frostily.

'I am not fit for the job.'

'I know that. No one is fit to be Karkarta. But when a person achieves that position, he grows to be worthy of it. God guides him.'

'I don't like the job,' Sharat argued.

'So take it and resign after Bharatji's Programme is fulfilled.'

'What makes you think I shall be elected?' Sharat argued.'

'There is much in your favour,' Nandan argued. 'You are my son. That entitles you to some respect. You are seniormost in the Council. You are committed to Bharatji's seven-point programme. There is an overriding reason too—that Bharatji's son, Sindhu Putra, is asking you to do it.' Nandan looked directly at Sindhu Putra.

Sindhu Putra spoke, 'Yes, Sharatji, yes, I request that you accept.'

Sombrely, Sharat looked at Sindhu Putra and saw the renewed appeal in his eyes. 'Yes, I must. I shall not deny you; Never. I accept.' He looked as if a hammer blow had struck him on the head but in his heart surged a wave of happiness.

'It is not enough that you accept,' Nandan said, 'people must accept you. You must consult Sindhu Putra on how to proceed. He suggests your name; you are his nominee for the election, not mine.'

'No, Father, I feel doubly blessed. I am certainly Sindhu Putra's nominee, but also yours, I hope.'

'Yes. But let Sindhu Putra be the first to press for your election.'

Sindhu Putra nodded, though not certain what he had to do.

Nandan's next observation enlightened him. 'Next week, I shall announce my programme to abolish slavery; also, my decision not to offer myself for re-election. Then, you, Sharat, can announce your intention of standing for election. Or maybe. . .' he paused, 'no, let it not be you. Let Sindhu Putra announce you as his nominee. Then we are closer to the truth, as after all he was the first to suggest it today.'

The meeting ended but not before Sindhu Putra told them of what he had heard of the great and glorious civilization—of Ganga in the east and Dravidham in the south.

'You must guide us to the wealth and riches there,' Sharat said, but clarified, 'the wealth of the mind and the riches of the spirit.'

'God, it seems to me, grants our wish and prayer only to defeat us.'

—(Attributed to Karkarta Nandan, 5052 BC)

'Only a fool would run after a principle that offers no profit.'

—(Attributed to Karkarta Sharat, 5052 BC)

Free, Free at Last!

5052 BC

At a special session of the Hindu Parliament—and none knew why it was suddenly convened—Karkarta Nandan announced his commitment to abolish slavery. He spoke of the 'Bharat Programme' and even hinted at the seventh point—to achieve unity with the sixty tribes of the eastern region and other tribes, 'whenever found, in regions yet to be explored and discovered.'

There was a stunned silence, but not for long. From the spectators' gallery, men leapt to their feet with roars of applause. Later, some said that these men were brought from Gatha's village to create the illusion of massive support for the 'Bharat Programme'. But that is doubtful, for on that very day, Sindhu Putra was to appear in his temple; and who would leave the village to witness a mere Parliament Session!

Not everyone was delighted by Nandan's announcement. Many felt bewildered, resentful. Their questions were many but could hardly be heard in the uproar. Nandan heard the rumble of thunder in those questions, but stood meditatively, with tightly sealed lips.

When the applause subsided, Nandan announced his retirement.

Those who applauded before, were now silent; some were dismayed; for others, it was amazement that smothered their anger. Nandan chose to ignore all questions, except the one that enquired his choice for the next Karkarta. He said, 'I have no favourites; but no, I speak incorrectly; I have favourites and each one of you, here, is my favourite. For the rest, your wisdom will guide you to choose our Karkarta.'

But this was no answer. A retiring Karkarta always recommended a candidate, though the final choice remained with the people's vote.

And questions came, one after another, but Nandan had already closed the Session, smiling on them with ineffable contempt.

Why did Nandan retire? Many explanations have been offered. Perhaps Poetess Papupatni (possibly 5010 BC) is nearest the mark. She quotes from a Memory song of her father in which she says that a situation arose where Nandan had to promise Sindhu Putra that he would abolish slavery and even unite with the tribes; he also had to repeat that pledge in Parliament. But equally, he was determined never to implement that pledge. And so he asked himself: do I wish to be remembered as a Karkarta who violated his pledge? Why not, then, leave the field to another Karkarta! My own flesh and blood—my son. But is not a son bound by his father's pledge? Yes, a son is, but surely a Karkarta is not bound by the promise of another Karkarta—and my son shall face our people, not as my son, but as Karkarta in his own right, uncommitted by any pledge that I make.

In Gatha's village, the temple was overflowing when Sindhu Putra appeared. Normally, he simply blessed all with Namaste. But now, he spoke to express the hope that if Karkarta Nandan retired, the office would pass to his son, Sharat.

Some wondered why he spoke of so distant an event; where was the indication from Karkarta Nandan of his wish to retire? But soon, reports arrived that on that very day Nandan had announced his retirement.

While many grappled with this miraculous coincidence, some grieved. The gods, they felt, should be concerned with the salvation of man's soul, not with the worldly ambition of man's prominence, position and power.

There was resentment in some quarters that Sharat wanted to be elected as Karkarta. When the law was changed to remove the bar against blood relations of a Karkarta from aspiring to that office, there was an implied promise that it was intended for the remote future and not to benefit Nandan's family. Some felt betrayed at his embracing the 'Bharat Programme'.

But then how could Nandan confide his compulsions, even to his inner circle of friends? Apart from the fact that a secret divulged to one reaches many, how could this proud man admit that the only way he could salvage his reputation and secure the future for his son was by joining with Sindhu Putra and even introducing the 'Bharat Programme.'

If some opposed Sharat, it did not worry Nandan. He had misunderstood the situation earlier, but understood it perfectly now—that none could defeat Sharat with Sindhu Putra by his side. It is all to the good, he thought, if some opposition to Sharat develops, for undoubtedly he shall win, but that opposition will be the excuse later, for Sharat to distance himself from the 'Bharat Programme', and even from Sindhu Putra. When Nandan's friends complained bitterly against the 'Bharat Programme', but said they would be silent, out of regard for him, he said, 'It would be a disservice to conscience. Speak as you should.' And they spoke. But theirs was a cry in the wilderness, against the avalanche unleashed by Sindhu Putra.

Nandan's planning was faultless. He encouraged Sharat to have many private meetings with Sindhu Putra, but not publicly, lest he were goaded into making a public commitment to the 'Bharat Programme'—'Let your words not return to haunt you as a broken pledge!' Nandan said.

'Yet, Sindhu Putra may object if I make no public statement.'

'No,' Nandan said, 'he understands that you do not wish to antagonize anyone. So long as he believes in your commitment to the programme, he will not worry.' Nandan smiled. 'Gods always trust—yes, gods and simpletons.'

But some, who were neither gods nor simpletons, distrusted. The once-blind singer went to Sage Yadodhra who laughed at his grief over Sindhu Putra's involvement. The sage said, 'His father Bharat was Karkarta. Why should Sindhu Putra not aspire to a higher goal—to become a Karkarta-maker?'

'But he will be betrayed!', the once-blind singer complained.

'Then he will be wiser next time; or do you think gods need no wisdom?'

Sadly, the singer said, 'And after elections, Sharat will discard the 'Bharat Programme' like a heap of garbage!'

'Commit him, then, fully! Or let him deny it and be exposed!'

Overnight, the once-blind singer became Sharat's strongest supporter. His group of sixty-six singers went to all the villages—to sing to all of Sharatji's deep commitment to the 'Bharat Programme'. The singer himself remained nearby, to regale everyone, in the temple and elsewhere, with his songs, and though his words varied, his theme was always the same—'that Sharatji's mind, heart and soul, and all his hopes and aspirations were centred on the success of the Bharat Programme.' Soon, new song-slogans were heard from the sixty-six singers: that if the Programme was not implemented quickly, Sharatji would retire a hermit.

Who can blame Sindhu Putra if he thought that the once-blind singer had learnt it all from Sharat himself! And who can blame Sharat if he thought that the singer was simply the mouthpiece of Sindhu Putra, to commit him deeper! My father is wrong—thought Sharat—when he says that Sindhu Putra is a simpleton. Yet dare I deny my commitment to the Programme?

Soon, they all heard Sage Yadodhra's words—'The call to be a hermit springs from the heart, unconditioned; so why Sharatji's vow to retire, if the Bharat Programme is not fulfilled in half a year! Yet a dreamer or a visionary must sacrifice, supremely, for the sake of his dream and vision. Truly, therefore, I honour the commitment of Sharatji that has led to his irrevocable vow. . . .'

Who could ignore the sage's words! Everyone knew that the Programme was Sharat's brainchild. And Sindhu Putra always gave him credit for inspiring it.

Sharat was elected the twenty-second Karkarta of the Hindu clan.

Opposition to Sharat had withered away. Unhappiness there was in some hearts over his victory. But no one was as unhappy as Nandan. God, it seemed to him, granted our wishes and prayers only to defeat us!

Nandan realized that he had rejoiced too soon over his son's victory. His every hope was centred on his son taking up the burden he had set down for him. Instead, day by day, his son became a stranger to him. Was it, Nandan wondered, a temporary aberration, in the first flush of pride at being elected Karkarta of the land! No, he feared that Sharat was finding himself committed to the 'Bharat Programme'.

Was Sharat totally out-manoeuvred by the once-blind singer and Sage Yadodhra? Not so. He was moved more, as he sat with Sindhu Putra, Yadodhra, and a few slaves freed by the silent tribe. Some of these freed slaves were from the Ganga civilization and the other two were explorers from Daksina. Yadodhra's interest lay in his supplementing his own charts, with the help of these freed slaves, to discover if their faraway lands had links with the ancient Sanathana. But as Sharat heard and reheard their glowing recital of the green, fertile lands—rich, abundant and advanced—in material, spiritual and artistic attainments, many of his old ideas began to drift away. He started realizing that there was a vast world outside. All of a sudden, he saw a clear vision of the future. But was that future attainable without Sindhu Putra's help? Who held the key to the lands of the sixty tribes? Who would lead him to the lands beyond?

Sharat was thinking—even if I can break free from the shame and ignominy of abandoning my assumed vow, will I ever be permitted to move into tribal territory, without battling each inch of the way? How and when do I then reach the lands beyond! And who will protect my flank? Is slavery really such a dire necessity for my land? And unity with the tribals? Surely, the vacuum from the abolition of slavery can be filled by the cheap labour of tribals; and their lands will then be open to create wealth for my own clan. More; they would serve as gateways to lands far away.

My father is right, Sharat thought, when a person achieves Karkarta's position, he begins to see everything afresh, anew, without the blinding mists of the past. Yes, my father is right in that, but wrong in all else! Sharat saw the 'Bharat Programme' in a different light—not for the principle behind it, but for the benefit it could bring—and he was convinced that only a fool would run after a principle unless there was profit in it.

Sharat put his heart into the success of the 'Bharat Programme'. Slavery, he said, was a crime against humanity and a sin against God; he urged that the unity and brotherhood of man, under the fatherhood of God, must remain among the clan's higher ideals, as it had been under ancient Sanathana Dharma and Sanathana which had never entertained different levels of humanity.

The once-blind singer felt ashamed for doubting Sharat as the new Karkarta rushed through all the hurdles against the 'Bharat Programme.'

Nandan begged, threatened and cajoled his son to remain away from this dangerous course. But Sharat said, 'Times change and we have to move with the everchanging stream of life.'

Sharat could not have used more brutal words, for these were the very words that Bharat had uttered at his last meeting with Nandan. Nandan argued no more. Sharat was pleased. All his life, he had been controlled by his father. Now, he was his own man.

As for Nandan, he did what a retired man would do when he feels he matters no more and is unheard, unloved, unwanted. He died.

But Nandan was wrong to feel unloved. Sharat was desolate. Sindhu Putra shed tears, for it was Nandan who had first inspired the 'Bharat Programme' when least expected to. The entire clan mourned.

At Nandan's funeral, Sindhu Putra put his arm around Sharat and addressed the entire gathering. He said, 'For his father's sake who is one with my father, hear him in your heart.' They heard. It is not easy to ignore the voice of the dead. Slave-owners halted their campaign against 'Bharat Programme', which was due to go for People's Vote in seven days. And later, many would say that even in death, Nandan served his clan.

The 'Bharat Programme' was approved with overwhelming support. Slavery was abolished in the Hindu Clan, in law and in fact.

'It is the union of the Hindu with the Hindu. . . .And how can Hindus not unite?. . .'

—(Jalta Ma's declaration at the Sindhu Council—5050 BC)

'Truth, as ultimate reality, has to be eternal, imperishable, and unchanging; but how can such infinite truth be captured by our finite minds, conditioned and limited as we are by time and space!. . .And arrogant it would be for anyone to hold that he or his sect holds the sole possession of truth. . . . Did not the Song of Hindu say that a Hindu must learn to refine everything by continuous testing and experiencing. . .to reach towards ultimate awareness. . .!'

—(Sharat quoting from the 'Song of the Hindu' at the Sindhu Council—5050 BC)

Mahakarta

5050 BC

Jaltama (Jalta's mother) was nominated by the sixty eastern tribes as their plenipotentiary to negotiate terms of union with the Hindu clan.

Strange, thought everyone, that they chose an old, blind woman to speak for them! What will she know! What will she say!

Sharat's men received Jaltama with honour at the border, to escort her to Karkarta's town. But she asked, 'Will Sindhu Putra be there?' No, he would be in Gatha's village. She insisted on going there first. She was told that she was already late and the Council meeting to approve the union was to take place very soon.

So she suggested, 'Why don't you hold the meeting in Sindhu Putra's village? I shall wait there, until you come.'

As their objections rose, her native distrust of outsiders came to the forefront. Why were they avoiding a meeting in Sindhu Putra's presence? Actually, she was being unjust. They were simply thinking of the custom of holding Council meetings in Karkarta's town. But now that her suspicions were aroused, she insisted that the meeting take place in Sindhu Putra's presence, or not at all.

She went to Gatha's village, with her entourage of sixty, escorted by Sharat's men.

Both she and Sindhu Putra moved to touch each other's feet, for she was the mother and he a god; immediately after which they embraced.

Sharat had said—So what! Let the meeting be held in Gatha's village. At least one thing was certain, she would readily agree to everything in Sindhu Putra's presence and create no problems.

Many—not just the Council members—gathered in Gatha's village. For this was a historic occasion—the first Council meeting outside Karkarta's town and in Sindhu Putra's presence!

Gatha made impeccable arrangements. Who can blame him, if he gave the seat of honour to Sindhu Putra!

Gatha stationed 'repeaters' at strategic points, to repeat what was being said at the dais, so that through the relays from one 'repeater' to the next, spectators, even in the back row, were informed of proceedings at the dais.

Sindhu Putra blessed the meeting with 'OM', and blessed all who sought unity and union. Karkarta Sharatji then welcomed Jaltama and her sixty companions, explaining that the purpose of the meeting was to achieve union between the clan of the Hindus with the people of the sixty tribes of the eastern region. . . .

Jaltama should have waited for Sharat to conclude, but she rose to object, 'We are not sixty tribes but a single tribe.'

Interpreters had no difficulty, but others had. Did Jaltama represent only the Jalta tribe! It was left to Sindhu Putra to explain that all sixty tribes were now united as one single tribe, and a reference to sixty tribes was a matter of ithihasa and did not reflect present reality.

Graciously, Sharat thanked Jaltama and resumed his address to say that the purpose, then, was to achieve union between the clan of the Hindu and the people of the eastern tribe. But again Jaltama rose to correct him and said, 'It is the Union of Hindu with Hindu.' Here the interpreters failed. Doubts arose. Was she claiming that all this would benefit only the Hindu clan? She clarified, 'You spoke of a union between Hindus and our people; but then our people are Hindu too!'

Sharat turned to Sindhu Putra and asked, 'Are they Hindus?' Sindhu Putra simply nodded and Sharat echoed the question in everyone's mind when he asked, 'Since when?' Sindhu Putra's glance rested on Jaltama. Quietly, he said, 'Always.'

Always! No one asked Sindhu Putra to clarify. The fact is that these tribals began to call themselves Hindu after Sindhu Putra came into their midst. But, as a poet explains, Sindhu Putra's mind went to the ancient past of which Bharatji had spoken to him—of the days of Sanathana Dharma and Sanathana and he was convinced that the people of the eastern region belonged to the same common root; and what is wrong, asks this poet, if Sindhu Putra said that they were 'always' Hindu?

Sharat gave up his idea of a long address and simply said, 'All we have to do here, then, is to formalize the steps that will make our ties stronger, and bring us all closer in our relationships, movement, travel, trade, land-use, for we are already united in our hearts.'

Jaltama heard him attentively, thereafter, merely nodding her head vigorously to agree with each item that Sharat proposed—and these items were many, such as, the free movement of people in and out of each other's regions and beyond; free trade and movement of goods; freedom to purchase land when buyer and seller freely agree; respect for each other's customs, attack on one region to be treated as an attack on both; joint action against raiders; arrest of criminals who run away to other regions; assistance in exploration of new lands; guild membership; representation to all in the council and assembly; voting rights.

The list went on with assenting nods from Jaltama.

Finally, Jaltama spoke, as Sharat concluded and said, 'All you said is what is near to our heart and we agree. Yet you did not speak of what is also near to our heart—no master, no slave!'

Sharat quickly replied, 'But we have abolished slavery!'

'Yes,' she said. 'For in the Kingdom of God, there is no higher or lower. . .and there is only one class, even as there is only one God. . . .' Everyone applauded, for obviously she quoted from the 'Song of the Hindu.'

Sharat nodded as if it was not necessary to say anything. But it was; and softly she challenged, 'Yet you spoke of the past and the present. But should we ignore the future? The future may then ignore us too. That is why our people have sworn for future also, that slavery shall not come into our land, ever. Is that your pledge too, to bind all who come after you?'

Sharat nodded only slightly, but it did not matter, for she gave words to his nod and said, 'I am glad that it is your sworn pledge too. Then we are agreed on this, and on all else, with no reservations.'

The poets tell us, here, that many were puzzled, as they heard Jaltama. They marvelled at the intelligence of this tribal matron and they wondered—how did we ever come to be fed on the absurd belief that tribals were primitive. How did the stupid thought that every person with different beliefs, language and customs, was a barbarian find its way into our minds. Who is a barbarian then? Them or us?

Sharat now came to his final question, 'Who will be the Chief or Karkarta of your land?' In his heart, he hoped they would not nominate the woman before him, for somehow she disconcerted him. She may have a big heart but she has a bigger mouth, thought Sharat.

But her unexpected answer delighted him, 'Of course Karkarta, you shall be our Karkarta too. How can there be two Karkartas, if we all are a single Hindu clan?'

Sharat felt thrilled, but he was not alone. The Council, headman, crowds, everyone shared the thrill. But Jaltama had more to say, 'Yes, you must be our Karkarta; and for us, and I am sure, for you too, Sindhu Putra shall be Mahakarta.'

Mahakarta? The word was new, but the meaning was clear. Jaltama used Sharat's language to invent a new title—Mahakarta! It simply meant, the Great Leader (maha—great).

Sharat tried to smile though his heart froze. How was he to react to this absurd woman's impossible suggestion that someone be superior to him! Even for the future, how could he discredit the very institution of Karkarta and submit to the higher authority of an unelected Mahakarta!

Her subsequent words, however, gave him, if not comfort, at least an escape route, for she said, 'He shall guide us all in spirit, and when troubles come or problems arise, he shall be the one to resolve our doubts and bind us together.'

'Of course,' Sharat shouted, but he intended only to stop the flow of further words from her, lest like a loose arrow she zigzag into some other explanations to bind him even more. But his sudden enthusiasm was regarded as his wholehearted acceptance of Mahakarta. Already many were chanting Mahakarta, delighted with the new title for Sindhu

Putra. The meeting after all was held in the heart of his homeground—in his temple compound—and his devotees in the crowd outnumbered all.

Sharat continued without a pause, 'I thank you and now that there is a meeting of minds on all main issues, our people shall meet again to fill in the details; and all that remains is for us to seek Sindhu Putra's blessings to end this meeting.'

Jaltama nodded and it was amidst the crowd's repeated chanting 'Mahakarta', 'Mahakarta', that Sindhu Putra rose to bless all.

Later, Sharat consoled himself with the thought that titles meant nothing. All pretenders to godhood were invested with all kinds of titles—merciful, divine, all-powerful, all-wise—but they were empty and meaningless in terms of earthly power. Let them chant Mahakarta. How could it lower Karkarta!

Much later, when the Resolution of the Union with the eastern region was moved in the Hindu Parliament, there were some who raised the question that the Resolution did not mention Mahakarta anywhere. Sharat was ready and he said, 'Mahakarta, as we call Sindhu Putra, guides our spirit, our aims, our goals, our quest. But ask me not to include him in this Resolution. Never shall I lay Mahakarta open to any such indignity. No he remains out, above and beyond any questions and criticism of imperfections in our resolutions.' This puzzled many, but Sharat willingly answered, 'In the past, in our countless resolutions, we never suffered from the temptation to say that they were inspired by the One Supreme or any divine authority. The reason is simple; our thoughts, ideas, words, actions will remain imperfect, and it would be arrogance to claim that we have encompassed the Perfect Himself, within the ambit of our Resolution. We have a long way to go,' and now he quoted Hindu thinkers who held that truth, as ultimate reality, had to be eternal, imperishable and unchanging, but that such infinite truth could not be captured by our finite minds, conditioned and limited as we were by time and space, and above all by ignorance. And then he quoted from the 'Song of the Hindu', as Jaltama had done, to say, 'A Hindu must learn to refine everything through continuous testing and experiencing. ... to reach the ultimate awareness. . . .'

Even from the special gallery, reserved for special invitees, Jaltama and Jalta the Second nodded. They were guests now. Later their people would take their place in the expanded Parliament of the Hindu.

The Resolution of Union with the tribes of the eastern region was adopted.

'. . .Then heavenly maidens showered flowers and each flower had a thorn facing outward for outsiders and flower petals inward for the people of the land. . . . And for ever, the vow to protect their borders against hostile intruders came to be repeated by every mother to her new-born babe, before he fed on her breast-milk. . . .'

—(Myth inspired by poets on the death of the Vaid, headman of Avagana—5049 BC)

People on the Move

5050 BC

Later poets, viewing the people's migration and movement in Karkarta Sharat's time, concluded that there was, then, intense curiosity and passion for discovery of the world beyond. It was not so.

Most thinkers of that age were looking inwards—plunged in their spiritual, philosophical and metaphysical speculations; and ordinary citizens were involved, simply, in day to day affairs, with the same inertia that afflicts each generation. After all, it was sheer necessity, not curiosity, that drove people out of their caves in the early dawn of time, to locate and live by the side of plains and broad fields near mighty rivers, great forests and the coastline of Sindhu sea. Only a few—mostly munis and hermits—moved, far from home, goaded by some inner compulsion. Theirs was a wanderlust that prompted them to plod along the lands beyond, their eyes turned towards deeper knowledge, with a question in their minds—have others found the answers that elude us?

Others like Sadhu Gandhara, Sage Yadodhra, Karkarta Bharat and Dhrupatta, who were neither pleasure-seekers nor ascetics, also went far afield, and even led expeditions. Theirs was the abundant vitality and deep curiosity to discover the fullness and beauty and infinite variety that might be found elsewhere—everywhere. Then there was Karkarta Nandan who was neither plunged in deep thought nor entangled in speculation. He sought no answers to the hidden mysteries of life but was guided by a compelling urge to make his clan rich and strong with what could be found in the lands beyond.

But by and large, people hated change and had no desire to seek new neighbourhoods or discover the lands beyond. Yet inevitably, compulsions came for mass migration and movement. Thousands upon thousands of slaves were freed not only in the Sapta Sindhu region but also in vast eastern lands. They moved, some to reunite with their roots, others to flee from the land that enslaved them, and yet others who feared that this new wave was temporary and soon they may be enslaved again.

But not only slaves. Others too were on the run. While the transition in Sapta Sindhu was peaceful, it was in the eastern region that blood flowed. Jalta and silent tribes remained peaceful, but many of the sixty tribes were in turmoil. Through bloody attacks and bloodier retreats, men were fleeing everywhere, anywhere, before calm was restored.

From the Sapta Sindhu region, itself, messages went out to outlaw slavery, reaching even the Himalayan pockets and Tibetan lands where Hindus had settled after discovering the source of Sindhu river. As it is, Karkarta Bharat had banned the acquisition of new slaves in those lands. But many had taken their own earlier slaves there. Not only slaves then, but those who found life difficult without slaves, were on the move. And everywhere, in Hindu settlements, word reached that slaves were to be freed.

Messages also reached Avagana. The Vaid had retired as headman and was now a hermit in the Hindu Kush mountains. But he was not alone. While he was headman, he had been sending mountain-grown medicinal plants and herbs to Sage Dhanawantar, with reports of his cures. After the sage's death, his wife Dhanawantri went to Avagana. She remained with hermit-Vaid. Some said they were married, though he was seventy years (solar) and she, sixty-four (lunar), so maybe it was more a spiritual marriage.

Kush was grown up and in charge of the Avagana region. The pledge of Hindavana prohibited slavery there and no one who entered there, could retain his slaves. But then not all of Avagana was under Kush. There were many pockets under the stranglehold of warlords. Kush's mother and Vaid were against forcefully freeing slaves, hoping instead for a change of heart among the people.

But Kush heard a different voice within, as he learnt that Sapta Sindhu had totally outlawed slavery, in all lands under Hindu influence. He prepared for battle to free all of Avagana from slavery. His mother restrained him. He contented himself by sending out messengers to territories which were not under his control, in order to influence locals against slavery. Many of his messengers were butchered, but rebellions followed; slaves were freed; yet a vacuum developed when nobody was in charge; robber-barons and slave-lords across the borders saw their opportunity. They moved in from all over, particularly from Mashhad (map reference: 36.18n; 59.36e) and Zabol (map reference: 31.02n; 61.30e) in modern Iran and from Khorog and other points in the erstwhile Soviet Union.

Massacres followed. Kush moved at the head of his army. Vaid left his ashram to head another army. Dhanawantri went with him. Kush defeated the combined armies of intruders and the poet speaks of the rivers of blood that flowed at Kushka and Kushk-e-Kohneh, so named to celebrate Kush's victory. (Kushka river on the Afghan-Iran-Soviet border; and Kushk-e-kohneh near the border. Map reference: 34.52n; 62.31e.)

Vaid's victories were equally spectacular (on the borders of the erstwhile Soviet Union), but he felt degraded as in a moment of red-hot anger he had ordered the hanging of four men at Charshanga (near the Afghan-Soviet border). Three of them were warlords but the fourth was innocent; he was simply the brother of a warlord.

A local poet justifies the hanging to ask, 'What else was he to do to those three that violated women, burnt children alive and ordered terrible massacres and brutal tortures for the sadistic pleasure of degrading and breaking the human spirit! And why should the brother of the merciless warlord not suffer for the crimes of his family members? Why then this vow of silence?' This was the poet's reference to Vaid's resolve never to speak again, after he had uttered his terrible words. To himself, Vaid could justify killing in the heat of battle, but not after the battle was won and calm restored.

Many in Avagana would have found it impossible to understand Vaid's anguish. The tribal custom there was simply to behead or hang the murderous enemy and his family and only a 'weakling, soft in head, would hesitate'. Dhanawantri had no intention that her Vaid should ever be considered a weakling or soft in the head; and when questions arose over his silence, she said that Vaid had taken a vow never to speak, unless everyone in Avagana solemnly swore that they would never permit intruders to occupy their land but would rather die fighting than surrender.

Many in Avagana took the oath and then many more—and some even claim that everyone in Avagana took it. Meanwhile, Vaid remained silent until his death, years later, and a poet says, 'As Vaid's spirit moved to heaven, even the heavenly maidens who came to receive him, called out—'Vaida! Vaida! Your vow shall be honoured for ever in Avagana—and then Vaid spoke to bless the defenders of the land for ever, and showered flowers which maidens had brought for him, and they fell all around Avagana, but each flower also had a thorn facing outward for outsiders, and flower petals inward for the people of Avagana.' Another poet takes this flight of fancy even further to say, '. . .and for ever, this "Vaida Vow" came to be repeated by every Avagana mother to her new-born babe, before he fed on her breast-milk. . .' There are those who have said that in the myth which Dhanawantri let loose, were the seeds of the nationalism of Avagana, and their fighting spirit against foreign intruders. On the other hand, some Indian writers, inspired by Europeon commentators, say that nationalism is a product of the eighteenth, nineteenth and twentieth centuries. They are right, but only about European history.

To Dhanawantri also belongs the distinction of developing in Avagana a system of empirical surgery. The taboo on the dissection of dead bodies in the Sapta Sindhu region had not penetrated into Avagana; and battlefields gave her the opportunity to improve the surgical training of her students, who became experts in plastic surgery, far beyond anything known at that time; they could repair fingers, noses, ears and lips injured or lost in battle or under torture.

Thus the mass movement of people began from all over to all over—
from Avagana, from the Himalayan high lowlands, from the Tibetan
region, from the eastern territories, and even from the Sapta Sindhu
region—and the slaves, the guilty, the innocent and the uprooted were
on the move, fired with the hope that there was a better, safer land
elsewhere.

'Yes; links do not snap. The past does not die. It relives; and a generation that does not know its roots is orphaned.'

—(From 'Songs of Ganga'—a poet's response to Kashi— 5455 BC)

'Man has never learned to simplify, only to complicate. Often he does not say what he feels but what he thinks—and sometimes he thinks too much and, in the process, gains much knowledge but also larger confusion and greater grief.'

—(From 'Songs of Ganga'; Hermit Nashtha to Kashi— 5455 BC)

'. . .Raiders yelled and shrieked to terrify all. Brahmadatta too wanted his men to yell "Ganga Mai", "Ganga Mai", as they rushed at the enemy. It was to be a frightening, ear-splitting, soul-searing cry. But then Gargi said, how can anyone yell "Ganga Mai!" . . .it is an utterance of homage from the heart. . .a prayer of the soul. . .reverence inspires it. . .and piety. . .and love. . . . Do you then wish our men to go forward to kill the enemy, or offer him comfort and solace?. . ."

—(From 'Songs of Ganga', commemorating 'Battle of Haridwar'—5455 BC)

'Those who forget the language of their people are like dogs that change their bark,' said the Chief. But she said that dogs never change their bark, though people can change their speech; and the Chief growled, 'Then learn from our dogs, who are superior to the people you surround yourself with.'

—(From 'Songs of Ganga'—'Cry of the First Chief'—5455 BC)

Ganga Mai

5050 BC

Many who did not join the caravans of those seeking sanctuary elsewhere, chose to cluster around Sindhu Putra. But Sindhu Putra himself was on the move. Some say it was Yadodhra who inspired Sindhu Putra's quest. Others claim that he moved at the request of those who had arrived from the Ganga civilization, crossing through the once hostile eastern region where now Sindhu Putra's name was enough to guarantee safe passage, and even an escort, towards Gatha's village.

Of the twenty-six slaves from the Ganga civilization freed by the silent tribe, ten remained with Sindhu Putra; the rest returned to their homeland. The sixteen long-lost sons were received in a delirium of enthusiasm by their people. Even Gangapati XIII, the Supreme leader of the Ganga clan, left his town near the confluence of the three rivers to welcome them.

The Supreme leader of Ganga was popularly known as Gangapati, though his full title was Ganga Sarva Pati. The etymology of this title—Ganga Sarva Pati—is not clear. By itself, the title means the chief protector of the Ganga region; but a poet claims that the actual title was 'Ganga Saras Pati', or the protector of both the Ganga and Saraswati river-regions. Another poet doubts this and asks: 'How is it, then, that the title mentions Ganga and Saraswati but forgets the third river—Yamuna. But then another poet explains Yamuna's omission saying, 'Yamuna was, after all, Ganga's tributary, and when the two rivers met, they were one, and flowed as one, in each other's embrace, mingled and inseparable, to the sea. So why speak of Yamuna as separate! But Saraswati, impetuous as always, rushed headlong through the confluence, as though to meet and part in the same single moment; and it greeted and was gone in one breathless heartbeat, leaving a little of its waters behind, but taking no less from the Ganga to flow through Brahmadesa, and thence flow on, in Sindhu's embrace, far away to its own sea.'

However, whatever the etymology of the Gangapati's title, the fact is that in his time all the three rivers—Ganga, Yamuna and Saraswati—flowed broad and strong to meet in a confluence in his home town

Trivenisangam Prayagraja (map reference: 25.27n; 81.50e; presently known as Prayag, Allahabad in Uttar Pradesh, India).

Gangapati's joy in greeting the sixteen men released by silent tribe was genuine. Everyone had thought that they were irrevocably lost. And these sixteen had news also of the ten who remained behind with Sindhu Putra!

'Why did these ten remain behind?' was everyone's question.

'To assist Sindhu Putra in freeing the slaves in his land,' they said.

'Then surely Sindhu Putra is no god, if he needs our men to assist him,' said many and they looked to Gangapati for confirmation.

But Gangapati said, 'How can I say if he is a god or not! But God, I think, needs man. Why else did He create us?'

They remained silent out of respect—but also from surprise. No one ever walked through their land calling himself a god. Hermits, sages, rishis, munis they had; also philosophers, artists, and poets, just as they had drunkards, lunatics, whores and crooks; and inbetween a vast layer of those who worked hard to till the land and produce goods for everyday necessity, beauty and joy. But they knew of no god that actually walked on earth, whom people could see, touch and even converse with. And if there was to be such a god, surely he would be born by the side of their auspicious Ganga and no-where else. How was it that their Gangapati failed to see what was so obvious!

Not many knew how the institution of Gangapati first began and it is not surprising that some regarded it as eternal. But actually, it was not that ancient. The story of how it all began has been told by a few poets and can easily be summarized:

The First Gangapati, before he assumed that title, went by the name of Brahmadatta and his wife was named Kashi. They were wandering in the Himalayas. No one knows what catastrophe or curiosity drove them there. But they are known to be the first to witness the glacial ice-cave at an altitude of 12,770 feet in the Himalayas, which later would come to be known as Gai-mukh (the mouth of the cow). From the belly of that ice-cave flowed two torrential streams, crashing against each other and throwing up their foam, white as milk, and thence parting, each rushing in a different direction. Brahmadatta and his wife chose to follow the path of one of the two streams. They did not know then that it was the Ganga river itself, for initially it appeared like any other mountain stream, no more than 20 angulas (40 cm or 15 inches).

They simply called it Kshira-subhra (white as milk), as that seemed to be the colour of this rushing icy stream. The other stream, which they did not follow, turned out to be Saraswati.

A later poet says that both the Ganga and Saraswati rivers flowed from the nipples of the same divine cow in the glacial ice-cave in the central Himalayas and thereafter each followed a different course to sustain life along its route, but Saraswati later went underground, and somehow that occurred at the same time as the tribals began sacrificing bulls and eating their flesh.

Slowly and painfully, through trackless passes, formidable peaks and deep gorges, Brahmadatta and his wife followed the course of the river and at last they reached the plains where the Ganga finally breaks through the last outriders of the Himalayas to enter the plains at Hari Hara Dwara—(home of the gods Vishnu and Shiva) now known as Haridwar (map reference: 29.52n; 78.10e). According to Brahmadatta's reckoning, they travelled only 60 yojnas or 300 miles from Gai-mukh to Haridwar (including detours where the terrain was impossible)— but the journey took them nearly a year. All along the way, they met no one; but at Haridwar, suddenly, they saw a number of people along the riverbank.

People viewed Brahmadatta with caution as he limped slowly towards them, carrying his wife on his shoulders. Obviously, he was an outsider with his garb of animal-skins, a wild look in his eyes and his strange way of speaking; but some of his words were familiar though he spoke with an atrocious accent and pronunciation. However, obviously, he meant no harm and needed rest for himself and his wife. The husband and wife were fed, their wounds washed and a hut given to them to rest in. Later, neither his strange speech, nor his wild appearance nor anything else mattered, once the people of Ganga learnt that he had witnessed the source of their holy river. He drew for them sketches of the glacier and the icy cave and described vividly the two milky-white streams, one of which was their Ganga. In those sketches, people clearly saw figures of the divine cow from whose nipples flowed the two milky rivers—Ganga and Saraswati.

Soon, the time came for the Hari Hara Dwara people to flee—to go into hiding for a while, far away—as tribal raiders were expected. Punctually, each year, without fail these raiders came, largely to hunt animals, but if any men or women were around, they would drag them away, dead or alive. The only persons that the tribals left unmolested were children and hermits immersed in their meditation by the river-side. For the hermits, they would even leave an offering or two.

Brahmadatta was terrified too, though his fear was of a different kind. He wanted people not to flee, but remain around him. His wife's legs were frozen from frost-bite on the mountain. Even otherwise, she was in pain, unable to move. And she was expecting a baby.

Brahmadatta, who had perhaps never known fear before, was simply terrified. He felt totally incapable of looking after his wife in her delicate condition through childbirth. Also, he feared that to move her would be the death of her and the life inside her. The prospect of a tribal raid appeared to him distant and unreal and he shouted, 'No one shall attack until my child is born. No one!' Few believed him. Many left. For, after all, Brahmadatta spoke 'not from inner conviction but from a wishful hope'. Only two women decided to remain behind— with their husbands, though they sent their children with the others.

Strangely, Brahmadatta proved to be right. The tribal attack, punctual and invariable for so many years, did not materialize. A poet ascribes this to the 'will of Brahmadatta' and asks, 'He who witnesses the auspicious source of the holy river—can he not will all?' But another poet claims that the tribals failed to attack because they were busy defending themselves against onslaughts from neighbouring tribes.

The fact, however, is that a bouncing baby boy was born and the tribal attackers were nowhere to be seen.

To the returning people who admired his little son, Brahmadatta proudly said, 'He is me, me!'—and some thought this to mean that the child's name should also be Brahmadatta.

From then on, whatever their other doubts, it was clear to many that this man who had witnessed the source of their holy river could alter events. No wonder, with his emergence, the raiders, so punctual otherwise, just evaporated. The idea floated back and forth and even a few of those who had abandoned the place due to annual attacks were tempted to return and reside there again, under his protection.

It was now Brahmadatta's turn to worry. He saw their faith. He had no such confidence in his own will-power. He was certain that some lucky chance had held back the raiders. And he feared they would come again. If in his earlier preoccupation with his wife's condition and her impending delivery he had been blind to the possibility of attack, his fears for the safety of his wife and child now redoubled. Should he not move on? In any case, he was a wanderer and had never wanted to be rooted to a single spot! So why not leave and follow the course of the Ganga to see where it flowed and where it rested.

But it was his wife who intervened. She could not then understand the language of Hari Hara Dwara but had a 'larger understanding' of what people around her were hoping or saying. A poet is categorical that she told her husband that he had a greater promise to keep—to protect these people from attack.

He reminded his wife that he had made no promises to these people and truly, he never had. But she retorted, 'Why do they then come swarming back here in growing numbers? Why do they feel a strange force in you that is replenished every time they see you? Why are they no longer fear-stricken? Why are their hearts touched and their panic replaced by solace and a calmness of spirit? How is it then that you say that you made no promise!'

Brahmadatta went to the oldest hermit, certain that this man of non-violence would have the wisdom to offset his wife's rash advice. The hermit agreed, 'Only God gives life and takes life; nothing that man does shall alter that.' So far they were in agreement and

Brahmadatta was delighted but the hermit added, 'Yet it is given to man to teach men what God did not need to teach—that is, to live and die in dignity.'

Thus it was that Brahmadatta, a simple mountaineer, took on a new role—to protect Hari Hara Dwara. When he gave serious thought to it, he realized that the task should not be too difficult. The raiders, as he learnt, always came at the same time, along the same route, arrogantly expecting no resistance. Because of their memory of earlier massacres, villages invariably went far back into hiding, when the raiders were due to arrive. The raiders stayed no more than fifteen days and left after corralling cattle and finally driving it away. Sometimes if their catch was not sufficient, they burnt huts and crops in anger. No wonder, many who once belonged to Hari Hara Dwara chose to remain away permanently.

At Brahmadatta's summons, some came back, at least to listen, hoping to hear that with his will-power he would keep the raiders away permanently. But he said, no, they would all have to fight to protect the land. Each year, they knew, they had to run and remain farther back. As cattle grew scarce, the area of the raider's operations widened. He asked, 'How far back will you run? And where will you hide when the entire region is at the mercy of raiders?' Not many were impressed. That prospect was far too distant. But his final appeal had more success—'And meanwhile, there is no one to protect the offspring of the divine cow—what then?' The poets here explain nothing, but obviously he meant that the divine cow at the source of the Ganga would be displeased. As it is, everyone knew that amongst the animals that the raiders captured and dragged away, were the cows that roamed around Hari Hara Dwara—and sometimes during their stay, the raiders would even roast a few cows to feast on them; when the raiders departed and the villagers returned, they would reverently wash the bones of the cows and bury them with a prayer.

Brahmadatta's message was thus clear. 'Face the raiders or face the displeasure of Ganga Mai (mother Ganga).' Many chose the displeasure of Ganga Mai, certain somehow that she was benign, while the raiders were certainly malignant and merciless. But a few remained behind to fight. And even those that decided to return to their fields and farms, far away from the danger zone, promised solemnly to help with labour and implements and any other sacrifice they could make to help defend their land. Only their own lives were beyond the pale of sacrifice.

Brahmadatta was not too dismayed as he viewed the groups of men ready to fight against the enemy. They had no fields or farms, but as a poet remarked, it is always the man of wealth who fears to die in the fear that somone will enjoy his wealth after he is dead.

Brahmadatta made no promises and when someone asked how many were likely to survive enemy attacks, he replied, 'I hope enough to cremate all of us who die.'

However Brahmadatta's first battle was not against the tribals but against the farmers who returned to their fields far away. He made them responsible for food for his warriors and to work on the foothills of the mountains to collect large boulders. He also requisitioned their draft animals and took away their wood to build carts to transport stones and building materials. He was deaf to their complaints that their crops stood neglected in the fields; and when protests arose, he threatened them with savagery worse than the tribals. With his little army behind him, they took him seriously. His men may have been afraid of tribals, but against their own, their courage was never in doubt.

Many poets exaggerate Brahmadatta's exploits. He was more an organizer than a fighter. The advantages he had were that the time and route of attack were known; and though his own army was small, he knew that it outnumbered the pitiful enemy force that normally came to attack. Actually, he was not trying to meet a single attack and feared that once the tribals were repulsed, they would return to attack in greater force to avenge their defeat.

Brahmadatta's first command was an assault on the Ganga itself. He ordered a canal to be dug, in order to divert water to flood the valley which the raiders habitually crossed.

Brahmadatta's other command was to build a series of dome-pits. These were simply man-size ditches in the earth in which a man or a woman may hide, but the top was covered with a dome of stone-work joined by bitumen and mortar, removable only by the combined strength of two or three men. Through slits in the dome, a person hidden in the pit could shoot his arrows and even jab with his spear if the enemy came too close to the dome. Nor could the defender abandon his post, until his own men came to release him. All this took time, but Brahmadatta hoped that he had a year to prepare, though many feared that since the raiders had not come this time, they might rush in any day. Hundreds of dome-pits could have been readied with wood, grass and clay, if he had not insisted on stone domes, but as he explained, 'Dome-pits are for hurting the enemy and not for our cremation.'

Brahmadatta is also credited with having a fort constructed, but that came years later. For the present, what he constructed was only a wall, rather than a fort. Deep and wide trenches were dug around the wall, to be filled with mud and water, to make them slippery like quicksand, ready to yield to pressure and pull a man down. The wall was connected with dry earth by a plank to be removed by the defenders when they reached the other side to scale the wall. Rope ladders connected the bottom of the wall to the top and those were to be pulled up when the defenders reached the top. But the defenders were to stand not only at the top of the wall but all along the wall where, from halfway up, were many projections for them to stand and throw stones or shoot arrows.

But Brahmadatta was not concerned just with defence. Everyone had to practice with bow and arrow, spear attack and stone-throws. Wrestling, jumping, fencing, running, dodging, kicking and even yogic exercises were the order of the day. Along the valley, which the new canal was to flood, open pits were dug for the best warriors, to pounce on the enemy who, hopefully, would be struggling through the rising waters. They were even taught to yell frightfully while attacking.

Brahmadatta himself had never seen a battle before, but from what they told him, it was clear that the shrieks and yells of onrushing raiders came well before their arrows began to fall—and the effect was terrifying. Brahmadatta did not know if raiders yelled to gain courage for themselves or to terrify others, but he saw some sense in it.

Yelling exercises began, though they were initially a failure. Brahmadatta had asked everyone to yell 'Ganga Mai, Ganga Mai' loudly as they rushed at the enemy. But none shouted or shrieked to his satisfaction—and a poet quotes Brahmadatta, '. . .and then Gargi said to me: how can anyone yell Ganga Mai . . .it is an utterance of homage from the heart. . .a prayer of the soul. . .reverence inspires it. . .and piety. . . . Do you then wish our men to go forward to kill the enemy or offer him comfort and solace?. . .Gargi was right and therefore. . . .'

No longer then, did they cry Ganga Mai, though poets do not say what the cry was. But no doubt it was frightening, ear-splitting and soul-searing. Brahmadatta was satisfied. Whether the cry frightened the enemy or not, he was certain that it built up the courage of his men.

Every child took up the cry. Many shrieked better than the adults. And when they started banging drums and shrieking simultaneously, the effect was doubtly frightening. But Brahmadatta never intended to use children in battle. The raiders always spared children and it would be senseless to invite the wrath of the enemy on children by using them. But the use of drums was a good idea, he thought. Raiders themselves beat drums on their departure, to call their men, still hunting for animals. So why not a drum-beat—to inspire them to leave, before they arrived!

Brahmadatta and Gargi apart, everyone had an assigned duty, though a poet observes, 'Gargi it was, whose task was to see that none forgot his duty.' In the morning when everyone assembled, after prayers, each had to repeat what his primary, contingent and subsidiary duties were—who was to be in the dome-pits; which group was to move stone-covers on pits; who was to take positions along the flooded valley; which marksman was to stand where; who was to scale the wall; who would remove the bridge-plank from the moat, and the rope-ladder from the wall; who kept—and how many—arrows and stones on wall-projections; who took whose position, when some fell.

Really, it was an anti-climax when the raiders did come. Almost everything went wrong with the preparations at Hari Hara Dwara. The canal did not discharge enough water in the valley to flood it. Many ran here and there, forgetful of their assigned duties. Confusion reigned everywhere. There was no reason for men, hidden in open pits along the valley, to remain paralyzed. But they were, even though the contingency of water failing to reach the valley had been anticipated. Raiders were coming on, leisurely, unchallenged. Soon, their yells would begin. Alone, Brahmadatta ran towards the valley to ensure that his men, hidden there, would begin the attack. Gargi followed him, but he ordered her back to see that the men in the dome-pits and the 'fort' wall were ready.

The planning had been faultless and arrangements impeccable; every contingency had been thought of. But actually something unplanned came to the rescue of Hari Hara Dwara. Three boys and two girls had hidden themselves behind a clump of bushes along the valley, contrary to orders. They knew their men were to begin attacking as soon as the raiders crossed a marked spot in the valley and then their yells and shrieks would start. The raiders crossed that mark but nothing happened. Suddenly, then, they saw the raiders stop. Obviously their men had begun the attack. The children were much too excited to pause and verify. They began their drum-beat and shrieks. And now, as though by a miracle, the chosen warriors of Hari Hara Dwara hidden in the pits along the valley, shook off the fear or lethargy or whatever it was that had assailed them, and came out of their pits, yelling and shouting.

Why had the raiders suddenly stopped? It was surprise, more than anything else, at seeing a lone man—Brahmadatta—running towards them. Normally, people ran away from them. But they heard the yelling and soon men were emerging from pits in their flank—yelling and shrieking. Ahead, it was not a lone man any more. Gargi had disobeyed orders. She was frantic that Brahmadatta must be protected. Any and everyone she could find was asked to abandon his post, to rush to the rescue of Brahmadatta. Everyone was yelling. Confusion. Pandemonium. Only the raiders seemed certain that it was a masterly ambush in which they were being caught. What else could they think with men rushing in front, men behind, and men alongside! They were not warriors; simply looters who had never faced opposition before. Many raiders ran back. No one stopped them. The first of the raiders remained immobilized. Their leader alone rushed forward and many say he wanted to surrender, while a number of raiders at the back kept running away.

Brahmadatta collided against the leader of the raiders in his rush and forgot that he carried a dagger in his belt and a bow and arrow in his backstrap. He simply picked up the leader and threw him in the midst of raiders at the back. Many raiders sat down to surrender with their hands on their heads. But even as they started to surrender, many at the back were still running away.

Many have, later, given a heroic account of this first historic battle of Hari Hara Dwara, crediting Brahmadatta with the masterly strategy of surrounding the raiders from three sides and crushing them. None has given an account of casualties. Fortunately, the comic-poet has left his version in his song entitled 'Oh terrible was the toll; none remained the same and whole.' He tells us that the 'first casualty was the raider-chief whose head was bruised when Brahmadatta threw him in the midst of his comrades, but so thick was his head, that not a drop of blood fell. The second casualty was our own Motara, who fell from the top of the "fort" wall into the moat below filled with mud and water and he ate enough mud to feed three hungry men; and truly the mud-bath made him look handsome while the mud remained on his face. The third casualty was that Gargi lost her voice and could shout no more, because of all the shouting she did when sending people into battle after Brahmadatta, but she regained her voice after two days and I know not which is a greater tragedy—her losing the voice or her regaining it, for now she keeps shouting at me, louder than before. The fourth casualty was the five children who disobeyed orders and went to hide along the line of attack. They were scolded sternly for disobedience, and then praised lavishly for their heroic conduct—and thus balance was achieved. The fifth casualty was that everyone's head at Hari Hara Dwara is swollen with pride, but then the raiders' heads are shrunk with shame, for such is the purpose of life—always seeking balance amongst unbalanced men, and. . . .'

The problem that Brahmadatta faced was: what should be done with the tribal prisoners? There were actually only forty-eight prisoners. Many had run away even at night while in custody.

To Brahmadatta's question—what was to be done with the prisoners—a hothead suggested, 'Kill them.' Brahmadatta stared at him in outrage. He did not know that this hothead had run away even before the raiders were sighted. 'No,' Brahmadatta said, 'that I cannot do.'

'You don't have to do that. We shall,' the hothead urged.

'No, he who commands or permits a sin commits it himself,' Brahmadatta replied—and the poet mentions this exchange to prove the point that Brahmadatta already considered himself their leader both in battle and peace-time.

Another advised, 'Let these tribals be held as prisoners.'

'And we shall have to feed and clothe them?'

'No. They can remain prisoners at farms, back there. The farm-owners shall put them to work and feed them if they work properly.'

It was perhaps a new concept—slavery. They had no word for it in their language. Nor did they understand it fully.

'Why do you think that the farm-owners would agree?' Brahmadatta asked.

'The farm-owners are already rushing here to celebrate our victory. They are interested in paying well if we sell these men to them.'

'How can a man buy or sell another?'

'Cattle is bought and sold. What is the difference?'

'Which farm will have so many workers?'

'They will be distributed in different farms, one by one.'

'For how long will they work for the owners?'

'For ever.'

'No,' Brahmadatta said. Gargi and many others shook their heads too, to reject the idea, though it is not clear if the objection was moral or practical.

In dismay Brahmadatta asked the raiders, lined up before him, 'What shall we do with you?' But it was a pointless question. He knew that they did not understand him, even though he tried the two or three languages he had picked up on his travels. As it is, the raiders spoke to no one. They did not even speak among themselves. They had not asked for water or food, even by signs, though later it was served to them at Gargi's orders. They were young. Only their leader was old. Silently they stood, unmoving, with no expression, 'neither of guilt, nor of shame, nor of fear, but perhaps in philosophic resignation, ready to accept whatever was to follow'.

It was Kashi, Brahmadatta's wife, who stood up. She was sitting at the back. Limping she came forward. Frost-bite in the mountains had left its permanent mark on her. People heard her speak rarely and never in public. But now she spoke, directly, to the prisoner-chief of the raiders. He did not respond to her first sentence, nor to her second. Obviously, she was shifting languages. It was her third sentence that elicited a response.

Kashi's first question was, 'Our Chief asked you—what are we to do with you for this attack against us? What do you say to that?'

'Only your Chief can decide that, lady,' the prisoner-chief replied courteously.

'If we let you go free, will you swear never to come here again?'

'This is for our Chief to decide, lady.'

'But you are their chief, are you not?' Kashi insisted.

'No lady, I look after the goats of our Chief.'

'Then why did you come here to attack us?' Kashi asked.

'When our Chief sends us to war, we go. He is the Chief, lady.'

'And these warriors of yours, are they goatherds too?'

'Not all; some tend to other animals. Most of the warriors ran away.'

'What will your Chief do, if we set you free? Will he attack again or will he appreciate our gesture and leave us in peace?' Kashi asked.

The prisoner had a troubled expression. Finally he said, 'How can I answer for the Chief, lady? He will do what he decides to do.'

'But you can persuade him, can you not?' Kashi asked.

'I, lady! I do not speak to the Chief! He does not speak to me! I receive orders from the headman, who receives it from the priest, and they too receive orders from those that cannot speak to the Chief.'

'Then persuade the headman, persuade the priest. Maybe your Chief has nothing to do with these raids!'

Mournfully, he replied, 'Nothing happens unless the Chief desires it and none speak for him unless he commands it so and those that disobey cannot live.' It sounded as if he quoted from a ritual.

'If we let you go, will you at least promise for yourself and your men that you all shall not join in any future attack on us?'

'Of what use are such promises to you lady, if we are commanded to march again against you? We die, if we disobey.'

'Oh! so you would prefer to die here, instead of there? Surely our people have a right to kill you here, if you give no promise!'

'That right is theirs, lady,' he said sadly. 'But here we die alone. Disobedience there, brings death to our family too.'

Silently, Kashi was saying, 'Why can't you lie, old man?'

Everyone was watching Kashi with surprise. None—not even Brahmadatta understood a word of this strange conversation. Some wondered—is she herself from the tribe of these prisoners! Impatiently, Brahmadatta asked, 'What is their chief saying?'

Kashi faced Brahmadatta and spoke in the language of Hari Hara Dwara which she had learnt recently. Each word came slowly, but distinctly, 'He is a victim himself. They are all victims. Let them go!'

The silence was broken by Kauru, the man who had suggested the sale of prisoners as slaves and he shouted, 'He is lying to you, woman!'

Woman! It was a term of endearment if a husband so addressed his wife. A parent, midwife, teacher could say that to scold in good humour. But from strangers, it was an insult. A poet says, 'even Gargi, who had not regained her voice, shot deadly arrows at Kauru with bloodshot eyes, and her hand threw a spear which was not there.'

Brahmadatta wanted to hear more from his wife. But Kauru appealed to them, 'The farmers will pay well. Forget the lies of this miserable prisoner!'

Kashi's voice rose, 'This old man is as incapable of telling a lie as you are of telling the truth!'

Insult! Counter insult! Brahmadatta came to a swift decision, 'It shall be as my wife says. They shall go free.' Some say that Kauru's disdainful attitude to his wife prompted his sudden decision. Others declare that he was divinely inspired and could look into the future.

Two days later, the prisoners left. But meanwhile Kashi spoke to their chief to translate for Brahmadatta and Gargi. 'Tell him,' Gargi prompted, 'to use his influence and never to attack our land again.'

'Your land!' the prisoner-chief exclaimed. 'My people were here before your ancestors ever set foot here. We were the ones driven out.'

But he could not tell when they were driven out. Ten generations ago? He did not know. It was simply ancestral memory, passed to them in age-old songs, with no dates, no time-frame, yet clear, vivid, as though it were a day old.

Questions then were many. Were they all driven out? Were any of them left behind? No, they all had to leave or die, though two hermits —a man and woman—stayed back. Later, an orphaned child ran back and the intruders permitted him to stay with the woman-hermit.

The prisoner-chief added that his people would never hurt a hermit, as all hermits were reincarnations of the two they left behind. Nor would they hurt children, for such was their Chief's command.

'Your Chief is then merciful!' Gargi asked and Kashi translated.

'Merciful! He is the Law. He upholds the Law.'

Kashi herself wanted to know what his people did after they were thrown out of Hari Hara Dwara. The old man knew little of the distant past, except that his people wandered in barren, desert lands, weary and hungry with the fruits of the earth denied to them. There were no plants with edible roots, nor fruit-laden trees, nor soil suitable to grow cereals. Their first Chief, from whom their present Chief was descended, taught his uprooted people something new—to catch animals and eat them. Many followed his lead but some declined and argued—how do you kill God's creatures to satisfy your hunger? The first Chief spoke of the law of necessity. He said also that it violated God's law to act differently from other creatures which ate smaller creatures and some who even ate their young. But the arguments never ceased and some asked, 'Was not man evolved to seek a higher destiny?' All arguments should have stopped when the first Chief finally declared that he was commanded by God to do so. Many obeyed the divinely-inspired order of the first Chief. But those who remained steadfast in their refusal to eat meat had to be treated the same way as the animals themselves. Thus it was that the first Chief saw to it that they all became hunters.

Brahmadatta was surprised. His own ancestral knowledge was that man was a hunter first, before he began to cling to the earth to garner its fruits and harvest its crops. He asked, 'But surely, old man, all the tribes began by eating meat and then turned to the earth to feed them!'

'Not in my tribe; maybe in yours, Master,' the old man replied.

Maybe the old man is right thought Brahmadatta. Even Kashi had mentioned that none in her ancestry ever ate meat. He had met Kashi on a mountain exploration. She had been nine then. He had been starving. Her mother and father had given him food. Kashi herself had run to her goat to bring him milk. Four years later, Brahmadatta had come back to the same spot, with gifts for those friendly strangers, but Kashi's parents were dead, along with all their neighbours. A huge, cruel mountain-slide had wiped out their entire settlement. Kashi alone survived, as she had been away gathering flowers under a mountain cleft. Brahmadatta and Kashi did not understand each other's language, but somehow he had persuaded her to leave with him. Later, they became man and wife.

The prisoner-chief spoke also of the ancient songs that told of many fleeing at night in different directions, to escape the first Chief's wrath for not joining the hunt for animals or to eat meat. And again, Brahmadatta wondered: does Kashi come from the stock of those who ran away?—how else does she speak the language of this old man? Suddenly, he asked, 'Those who fled from the first Chief—where did they go?' Slowly, the old man replied, 'Who knows! Everywhere perhaps. But as the first Chief marched in all directions, many of them were found dead. And the first Chief said that it was disobedience to him that killed them and not starvation.'

'Did any flee to the mountains?' Brahmadatta asked and described the mountainside where Kashi lived. But the old man did not know.

He then spoke of how the tribe wandered around hunting for animals and how the first Chief's domains grew larger. But that was inevitable, as it needed only a little patch of earth to sustain life with what could be grown there. But to hunt, one had to cover an ever-widening area. Animals, rarely suspicious before, began suddenly to fear man and wandered far away and the first Chief's people had to cover vast areas. The first Chief taught his men always to win, not only against wild beasts but also against all the new people whose settlements they came across. He set up a new system of joint endeavour in which many together stalked the prey—be it a wild beast or a colony of people. He made his men fearless and laid down two axioms: animals feel, while humans think, and therefore pain belongs to animals and rewards to man and a man can always trap and kill an animal whatever his size, strength or reach; we think and plan; they doubt and waver—and it meant that those who listened to his voice alone, would be stronger than those that listened to the many voices of doubt and discord.

The old man continued, 'Land occupied by the first Chief grew in size and prosperity and his prophecy was that his son would have greater vigour and wisdom and the son of his son even greater, and so on, for all time. And thus it is, that our present Chief is the strongest and greatest, though his son will be even stronger and greater.'

'And those who fled from the first Chief? Did your tribe ever come across their descendants?' asked Brahmadatta, his eyes on Kashi.

'The first Chief announced that they all died.' The old man's eyes were on Kashi's face and he added quietly, 'If some survived, or had descendants, our first Chief would have known—for he knew all. Not that he was obliged to tell all, for he spoke to God directly and would tell only that which had to be told. Great was our first Chief!' The other prisoners nodded. Apparently his last words were a ritual utterance, to which they all had to agree. 'Yes,' he added, 'only the first Chief could know who lived and who died and he did say that they were all dead.'

Yet his eyes still rested on Kashi, as if he saw a new link from an old past. Kashi whispered, 'Maybe we were together once.'

The old man whispered back, even softer, 'Yes, perhaps, a thousand years ago your mother and mine were the same.' His eyes darted to his companions. They had not heard him; even so, he changed the subject, as if he was continuing his whispered words. 'Yes, but how was your leg hurt, daughter?' This was the first time he had called her 'daughter,' instead of 'lady.'

She told him of the fall in the mountains during her pregnancy.

The old man spoke, 'I live amongst cattle, daughter. But sometimes I tend to village-people when they are hurt. And you should rub your leg with the oil of the zalzari tree, soaked in sunhera herbs.'

She knew nothing of the zalzari tree or sunhera herbs. He too realized that the tree grew neither near the mountains nor near the rivers, but in dry, desert air. Cheerfully, he pointed to a tall tree visible at a distance, in the direction from which they had come, and said, 'Who knows, maybe even that tree may yield that oil after some time!' That seemed a foolish remark to the other prisoners, as the tree pointed to by him was tall, not stunted and thorny like the zalzari; and there was no sunhera plant, with scarlet flowers, blooming nearby. (The zalzari tree and sunhera plant, together, were called the 'odd couple' and had to be within four hundred yards of each other; if the plant was cut off, the tree died within days; similarly, if the tree was destroyed, the plant did not survive.) But the prisoners thought no more about it, certain that he was rambling on to keep in the good graces of the captors and obtain their early release.

Brahmadatta's main question still was: 'Will your Chief attack again?' To this the old man did not even try to hazard a guess. He simply said, as if quoting from a ritual, 'Our Chief is mighty and merciful and he is mighty and merciless; he decides as he wills; except when God calls on him, and then, together, they determine what must be done.'

'Have you seen God call on him?' Brahmadatta asked with irony.

'God walks unseen and speaks unspoken,' the old man said softly.

'And yet you say that God and your Chief discuss and decide on the course of action! You don't even say that God commands your Chief!'

The old man was bewildered, 'When did God ever command man? Did God not leave man free to do what he wills?' He paused. 'God is with us twice—when we are born and when we die—and yes, the third time, after death, to those who have lived decently—and with them, He always is.'

Everyone looked at him intently. Was it different from their own belief in salvation after a life filled with noble deeds!

Gargi said, 'You seem to believe what we ourselves believe!'

'This land that you call yours was ours too, lady. It is the land that nurtures the mind. How then can you and I think differently?'

'And your Chief,' Brahmadatta pressed, 'he believes that too?'

The old man was aghast. 'Our Chief! He is above and beyond us! He walks with God in his mysterious footsteps. He knows what God knows. He knows what He believes. Who am I to say?' The other prisoners nodded.

Was it respect or fear?—Brahmadatta wondered and asked, 'Do your headman, priest or Chief order many to be killed?'

'Not the headman, nor the priest. Only the Chief can order that a man be killed for an offence. And he is just and fair, always, when he punishes or does not punish.' His companions nodded assent as he added, 'The headman can order a man's foot to be cut off. The priest can order that both the feet of a man be cut off. But no more; sometimes this is to the criminal's advantage, as a priest cannot order the second foot to be cut, if the man has already lost one of his feet at the orders of the headman. And certainly, our Chief does not order a man to be beheaded unless he comes to his punishment, full and whole, with both feet, intact and uncut.'

To Brahmadatta's main question—would their Chief attack again?— the old man had no answer. But he gave them some insight into their Chief's mind. Sometimes, he said, their small columns—like his own— were repulsed by the other tribes. Often, the Chief ignored the repulse when he wished to forgive, but at other times he would unleash mighty armies to wipe out the tribe. Their Chief invariably sent out small columns, regularly, at the same time, so that other tribes may know in advance and escape inland to save themselves. After all, he wanted no bloodshed. He simply wanted their animals and produce, though sometimes he would move to occupy their territory; and those who obeyed his law would be spared; and others killed or enslaved. But an attack against himself, he never forgave. Last year, he sent out no columns, as seven tribes banded together to attack the Chief's land. He not only repulsed them but now all the lands of those tribes were under his control and all their men were killed. Only the children and women had been spared.

'He respects women, then?' Gargi asked.

'Who does not!' the old man asked. 'Who else will look after the children?'

Brahmadatta asked, 'If a column like yours is repulsed, and if your Chief decides to attack, does he attack at the same time next year?'

'You ask, Master, what I cannot answer. Our Chief may, in his divine wisdom, consider our repulse a challenge; or in his divine

humour, he may forgive it, like the lighthearted acts of children. All I
know is that tiny, miserable columns like mine are sent on time, but
the mighty armies of our Chief move like the roaring of the wind, at
the moment of his divine inspiration, uncontrolled by all but the Chief
Himself. Great is our Chief!' Again, all the prisoners assented.

'You mean, the attack from your armies can come at any time?'

'Not any time; only when our Chief so desires.' This was no answer.
Yet the old man could give no promise—not even to save his life.

And similarly to many more questions, the old man's answers were
non-answers, though he was sincere and not evasive and said, 'I am a
goatherd, I speak mostly to cattle, and they speak to me not. I know
little about your questions, Master.' He did not even know if originally
his ancestral tribe emanated only from Hari Hara Dwara, or came from
further inland. His answer was, 'Our Chief would know—or the
hermits,' and he pointed to the hermits sitting along the riverbank.

'Our hermits!' Gargi asked surprised.

'Our hermits! Your hermits! What is the difference?' he rejoined,
irritated for the first time. He was convinced that these hermits were
reincarnations of the two hermits left behind, centuries ago.

'You have hermits in your lands? Are they respected?' Gargi asked.

'Of course! They are God's people. The Chief honours them.'

'Even if hermits say what displeases the Chief?' Gargi asked.

'Nothing that the hermits say or unsay displeases the Chief. The
hermits seek answers. The Chief knows all the answers. Nothing is
hidden from him. Where is the scope for displeasure?' His companions
assented. Clearly, the old man believed in God's majesty; but believed
no less in the majesty of his Chief!

Kauru meanwhile returned, with gifts from the farmers who hoped
that the prisoners would be sold to them. Proudly, he announced, 'I
have talked to the farmers. They have agreed to pay more than they
had earlier offered.'

Kashi dashed his hopes. She demanded that the gifts be returned.

'No,' Gargi thundered. 'They sent these for the sake of the prisoners.
Let them be given to the prisoners.' Kashi gratefully hugged her.

The old man had a parting request, 'Much your people gave us,
daughter; we always leave offerings for the hermits. Is it permitted?'

The prisoners bowed to the hermits, gave their gifts and went their
way.

'God be with you,' Kashi said to the old man when they parted.

'God be with you! Daughter of thousand years! Daughter of
Sanathani!'

Daughter of Sanathani!. Kashi wondered. How did he know that
every mother in her mountain-settlement was called Sanathani? To
Brahmadatta, the explanation was simple—the Hari Hara Dwara people
themselves were known as Sanathani. So what was so surprising if the

old man thought that she belonged to Hari Hara Dwara and called her 'daughter of Sanathani'? Her surprise now was greater: how did Sanathani move so far upwards from Hari Hara Dwara to her mountain?

'People move. Wanderlust, necessity, love, who knows! Maybe centuries ago your people moved from Hari Hara Dwara to that mountain.'

'Then why did I not speak the Hari Hara Dwara language? Why did my people speak the tongue of the old man whose ancestors fled from here?'

'But you do speak in more than one tongue!' Brahmadatta countered.

'Yes, that is because my father came from another mountain.'

'See! Love brings everyone together!'

But even Brahmadatta wondered. Did Kashi belong to the people of the First Chief driven out from Hari Hara Dwara? Perhaps, she did, as she spoke their language. But then those people were not known as Sanathanis! They were known as the 'First Tribe'. Only the people in Hari Hara Dwara were known as Sanathanis. Yet Kashi's people never spoke the language of Hari Hara Dwara. Strange that Kashi should speak like the 'First Tribe' but bear the name of Sanathani!

Brahmadatta gave up this idle speculation which took him nowhere and finally said to Kashi, 'Enough that we belong to each other.'

But it did matter to Kashi. Later, it was a hermit who took them a step further. He was not the oldest hermit and certainly not the most revered. Nor was he always meditating. Often, the comic-poet sat by his side and both spent their time laughing. Many suspected that the two together were laughing at them. But the comic-poet denied it, saying, 'We laugh only at God who created you.' And when someone said, 'You forget that God created you too,' his reply was 'When did I say that everything that God did was a mistake!'

Kashi and Brahmadatta were fond of the comic-poet, not for his poetry, but because he and his wife were amongst the four who had remained behind to help Kashi with her delivery. Even when Kashi hardly understood the language of Ganga, he would recite his poems to her; and his own wife's smiling request was: 'No one who understands his words appreciates his poetry; so Sister Kashi, please listen to his poetry—but, please, only when I am outside the range of hearing.' Actually, Kashi listened to him, carefully and gratefully, and if she learnt the language quickly, it was thanks to the comic-poet.

It was to the comic-poet then, that Kashi first posed the question about her roots. But to avoid a comic answer, she placed her little son in his arms, and said, 'Not me alone but my son must also know.'

Soberly, he asked, 'Why must this little one know of links that snapped perhaps two thousand years ago?' But he answered his own question, 'Yes. Links do not snap. The past does not die. It relives; and a generation that does not know its roots is orphaned.'

'So?' Kashi asked for all this hardly answered her question.

'So, go to Nashtha.' Nashtha! It was the name of the young hermit.

Later, Kashi understood why hermit Nashtha would know. Nashtha was descended from the orphaned child who had run back to the land that was his—while his own people were driven out to wander in barren lands under the first Chief.

Nashtha ignored Kashi. He simply stuck his tongue out to tease her little son, who responded by showing his own tongue. He took the child in his lap. The child put out his hand to push Nashtha's tongue back in. 'There is much that your child already knows,' said Nashtha.

'There is more he must know,' Kashi said.

'He will ask, when he must!' Nashtha replied gruffly.

There, the first conversation ended, for Nashtha had closed his eyes to pray. Kashi bowed to Nashtha and left after whispering, 'To your star-dust, I bow.' These were the traditional words of farewell of her own people—and these were the very words she heard from prisoners when they were parting from the hermits. And she said these words in her language of the past—and not in the tongue of Hari Hara Dwara!

She did not know that Nashtha heard her and opened his eyes.

The next day Kashi left with Brahmadatta who had to meet farmers inland. The comic-poet spoke to Kashi on her return, 'Nashtha is asking after you.' She went to Nashtha. 'Why should the hermit Nashtha ask for her?' some asked. 'Why not? Maybe he is very fond of Kashi,' the comic-poet replied. Perhaps, here, he said too little or too much. For everyone saw that everyday she was near hermit Nashtha singing songs for him.

Nashtha told her little, but asked if she knew the songs of her ancient people. She sang for him the songs that her mother had sung. People, passing nearby, recognized neither the tune nor the words.

'These are not songs of my ancients,' Nashtha said. 'They are sad, tearful songs. My people sang to laugh, to dance, to make love.'

'Maybe these songs were sung in tears, after my people lost their home here.' But suddenly she brightened up and hummed a tune with half-remembered words. It was a soft, restful, contented tune—a lullaby with which her mother put her to sleep in her childhood days.

She saw his tears. She stopped. 'Keep singing,' he ordered, but she replied, 'I don't know all the words.' Again, he commanded, 'Sing! I know the words.' He opened his eyes after the lullaby had ended. Quietly, he pointed to her sleeping son and said, 'The song ends and the child of our people sleeps.'

Nashtha's story was simple. Nine hundred yeas ago, his people were driven out of the land of Ganga. From Hari Hara Dwara? No, that was the last point of exodus. His people came from further inland, beginning from a city called Varnash, after its destruction by intruders.

Where was that city? Not far, but the way was barred as many new tribes had settled there, 'displacing those who uprooted our ancient people.'

Nashtha's ancestor, the orphaned child himself, came from Varnash and fled with the first Chief. But he soon ran back. He was cared for by a woman-hermit—one of the two hermits who remained in Hari Hara Dwara. Later, this woman-hermit's daughter was sent back to her by the first Chief.

'Why did the first Chief send her back to Ganga?' Kashi asked.

'Because she would not eat meat,' Nashtha replied.

'But the first Chief even killed those that refused to eat meat!'

'No one sheds his own blood!' Nashtha said.

'His own blood!' Kashi asked, surprised. Nashtha explained—the little girl was the first Chief's own niece and the woman-hermit was his sister; it was this sister who had brought up the first Chief since his own mother had died when he was an infant. When the sister became a hermit, he became the loving guardian of his niece. But when the first Chief fled the land of Ganga, the niece wanted to go back to her mother and even refused to eat; so he sent her back to his sister, though many say that he himself came, disguised, to bring her. Later, this girl married the orphaned boy who had run back to Ganga. And it was from this union that Nashtha traced his descent.

'Was Sanathani the name of the Ganga tribe which fled?' asked Kashi.

'Yes.' But then Nashtha explained how the name Sanathani itself came to be adopted by the intruders who occupied the land of Ganga, 'Simply by the process of assimilation; the culture of the conquerors was overtaken by the gentler, civilizing culture of the conquered.'

'But how! Did not the conquered all flee with the first Chief?'

'No,' Nashtha replied. 'How could all of them flee! Many remained. It was simply the first Chief who said that all the people had fled Ganga to join under his banner. He wanted his people to so believe, lest anyone was tempted into returning to Ganga. He was keen that the numbers of his followers should swell, not shrink.'

'How many joined the exodus and how many remained with Ganga?'

'Who knows? Maybe intruders killed one out of every ten and maybe one out of every thirty remained behind, and all the rest fled, to follow the first Chief, and even other chiefs who fled in different directions. But then maybe one out of every fifty fled from the first Chief too—perhaps like your people—to find sanctuary elsewhere.'

Kashi asked, 'If one out of every thirty did not flee to follow the first Chief and remained behind, how is it that their ancient language does not survive in the land of Ganga?'

'Yes, the language did not survive in the land of Ganga, even though you and I, here, are now conversing in that tongue. The language survived only with those that fled, even though so many remained behind. The intruders were far more numerous; and those of our people that remained behind were afraid to give out their identity or to emphasize their separateness. The result was that they adopted the language of the intruders and, over time, forgot their own words and songs.'

'But you said that the intruders were overtaken by the culture of the ancient people of Ganga from whom we spring?'

'Yes, I did. Intruders imposed their language or maybe they did not impose it and our people adopted it from fear or because the intruders were in a vast majority. Yet the culture of our people did not perish under the onslaught of intruders, even though our people adopted some of their external influences. The culture that came with the intruders—the culture that survived by brute force—died, absorbed by the more humane, the more intelligent and spiritual civilization of the Sanathanis of the Ganga that the intruders came to conquer.'

'Surely the conquerors brought their own culture too?'

'Yes, the conquerors did bring their culture but in the end it is always the gentler, more humane culture that survives. The conquerors have the power to win by force; but is power the same as wisdom, enlightenment or culture? And thus it is that much of their culture withered away and the rest of it mingled with the culture of the conquered Sanathanis.'

'But how could the culture of so few that remained behind in Ganga come to overtake the culture of so many that came from outside?'

'Numbers? Do they matter? The smallest minority, even a single individual, can influence culture. Don't ask me how. Maybe it is the land we live in or the soul-sustaining waters of the Ganga. All I know is that if a culture retains its God-given values of truth and righteousness, it lives.'

'But what part of our culture was adopted by intruders, if our language went out with the first Chief, to disappear from this land?'

'The beginnings of assimilation were slow. But in time, the intruders even gave up eating meat. They rejected the doctrine that denied to any God's creation its rightful place in God's universe. They began to believe in equality, certain that God treats every aspirant with favour. And so they too chose the path of piety, prayer and meditation. It obviously did not blind them to the need to protect righteousness.

'The woman was accorded equal status with man. But even greater was their belief in compassion, justice and fairplay and, above all, in sinless conduct and positive good deeds to achieve the final goal of salvation (mukta). They were guided no longer by the fear of the supernatural but by the love of God whose presence they felt all the time, all the way.'

Kashi came to her main question, 'Yet for me there is a missing link, somewhere. When the ancient people left Ganga with the first Chief, they carried their language. Their own people who remained behind, retained their culture but lost their language and spoke the language of the newcomers. So much is clear. But then what about my people at our mountain settlement? We spoke the First Tribe's language—the language that the people of Ganga abandoned—and yet we called ourselves Sanathanis, as the people of Ganga do. Do I then belong to the First Tribe or Hari Hara Dwara?'

Nashtha smiled, 'To both—you belong to the Sanathanis of Ganga and to the First Tribe. The prisoner-chief was right to call you the daughter of Sanathani, for that is what you are. And he was right too when he called you their own daughter of 1,000 years.' He paused to explain, 'What puzzles you is that your people at the mountain-settlement did not speak the present language of Ganga, and yet called themselves Sanathanis like the people of Ganga. But the answer is simple. Your people and the people who fled Ganga under the first Chief were both Sanathani. That name remained with the people of first Chief for at least eighty years—and then, by the order of the grandson of the first Chief who ruled in his place, the name Sanathani was discarded and even outlawed.

'Why?' Kashi asked. Nashtha explained that when the first Chief fled, he convinced his people that not a single Sanathani was left behind, and that they had all fled from the hated intruders. As it is, the name Sanathani did disappear from Ganga itself for some time, as even those Sanathanis who had remained behind kept a low profile initially, for fear of persecution from intruders. But soon, not only the name but even the dharma (law) of Sanathani began to re-emerge, stronger than ever before, as intruding tribes came under the sway of its culture. Everyone in the Ganga—ancients and newcomers—began to call themselves Sanathanis. It was then that the grandson of the first Chief decided that his own people must not be called Sanathani. He had the same dream as the first Chief had—of reconquering Ganga. He feared that if his people continued under the same name as the people of Ganga, they would identify with each other as the same tribe—and over time their enmity would subside, yielding to friendship. He had to keep alive the separateness and past enmity. So he renamed his people the 'First Tribe' to distance them from the Sanathanis.

Nashtha then voiced his conjecture about Kashi's ancient people, 'Your people also, I think, fled the Ganga along with the first Chief; like him, your people too were Sanathani and unfamiliar with the language of the intruders. Somewhere along the line, your people and the first Chief parted. Is it surprising then that your people spoke the language of the first Chief but remained unaffected by his grandson's order to outlaw the name "Sanathani"?'

Nashtha could not say how her people parted from the first Chief. 'Maybe, the first Chief permitted your people to go free as he allowed his niece to, who was my ancestress.'

'He may have been kind to his niece. Why to the others?'

'Who knows! All I know is that the first Chief had a terrible reputation—but it was an image he himself had created. Everyone spoke of his killing those who disobeyed him. But that was not true. In the dead of night, he would arrange the escape of those who refused his orders, for instance, to eat meat or join the hunt for animals. He spoke of killing people at the slightest excuse, but no one ever saw him doing that except in extreme cases. Even those who died of natural causes, or in fighting or hunting, were said to be killed by him—and he never denied it. Yes, the sins he committed were many, but he was not as evil as he painted himself, in order to inspire fear and obedience.'

'But why did he have to pretend to be more cruel that he was?'

'He had a single dream. He saw his people flee the Ganga, starved in mind and body; they appeared beyond repair. He did what he had to do, to change them into a strong, cohesive force—to listen to him, single-mindedly—and his dream was to return to Ganga and live there for ever, but not under the rule of intruders.'

'And he died with his dream unfulfilled!' said Kashi.

'In a way, yes. He wanted to charge at the head of his people to reconquer the land but that proved impossible. He came alone.'

'He came!'

'Yes, at the age of seventy, he nominated his son the Chief, and left himself—and no one knew where he went, though his people said that he had gone to meet the gods. But the ache in his heart had returned and slowly his footsteps turned to Hari Hara Dwara.'

'And no one stopped him?'

'Who would trouble an old man of seventy, who comes looking like a hermit? He came to his niece, my ancestress, and her husband, the once-orphaned child. They escorted him to Varnash. There he died and his last hope was that someday his soul would return to embody his ashes in the Ganga, so that he could lead his people to reconquer the land of Ganga.'

'He had lost his faith in mukta then?' Kashi asked.

'No, he was convinced that for the evil he had done, mukta was lost to him. And he sought neither mercy from God, nor offered repentance, and died with defiance on his lips saying—"God, you deserted my people but I shall not desert them. And what I did, I shall do again, in each life that is mine." The fact is, he had one life-long love—for the Sanathanis who fled with him. He lived and died too, with one tribal hatred—against the intruders and for that he was prepared to sacrifice his soul and every hope of mukta. Nothing else mattered to him. But I think he was a better man than he thought he was.'

Nashtha smiled, 'Tell me now, yourself, where do you belong? To the Sanathanis of Ganga or the "First Tribe"?'

'To both,' Kashi replied.

How did Nashtha know of events that happened hundreds of years earlier? Later he told Kashi. Both his ancestors—the orphaned child and the first Chief's niece—had matured as well-known poets and singers of songs. They had almost forgotten their language of the past and sang in the new language of Ganga. It was the first Chief who shouted at his niece when he stealthily entered the land of Ganga— and the seventy-year-old Chief could still shout with passion at his niece who was now fifty years of age—and said, 'Those who forget the language of their people are like dogs that change their bark.' But the niece told him with a weak smile that dogs never changed their bark, though people could change their speech; and the first Chief growled, 'Then learn from our dogs who are superior to the people you surround yourself with.'

Nashtha continued—'Some ten years after the first Chief's ashes were immersed in the Ganga, his neice lost her husband; and she wanted to compose a song in his memory. Her mind went back to the events of the past—how her husband as a child had run back from the contingent of the first Chief and was sheltered by her mother, who was a hermit, by the side of the Ganga. The first Chief—who was her mother's brother—had sent her back to her mother but himself came in disguise, years later, to witness her wedding; again, the first Chief had come in disguise, when his sister—her mother—had died. She thought also of the last time that the first Chief had come to her briefly, only to die in her husband's arms.

'But,' added Nashtha, 'the words in her song did not flow as she thought of the first Chief—and of the empty, sinking feeling he had in his last moments when he feared that his people would forget their roots, if they forgot their language. She began her song in the language she used to speak in the days of her childhood—and then the words and the feelings came to her easily, effortlessly. It was to be a song in celebration of her husband's life, but it went on to sing of her land and the people—and of the people who left with the first Chief whose new land she had not seen. She could only speak of their longings to return to the land of their roots. Few could understand her song and even her children did not understand the language in which it was composed. But then sometimes a poet does not compose a song for others. Yet a song dies if it is not recited to another. And she began to recite it to her youngest granddaughter, barely two years old. But the child grew and she kept hearing the song and even learnt the unfamiliar language that her grandmother taught her. Since then—whether it was as a promise to the grandmother or otherwise—someone in the family would be taught that old, archaic language, along with the song. Even so, the song that I inherited as part of my family tradition came with many words and verses missing. Strangely, it began as a lullaby and ended with it too but otherwise had no connection with the rest of the song and I am not certain if it was intended as part of the song or was simply a lullaby that her ancestress had sung to her granddaughter.'

After this Kashi and Nashtha were together often. Once Kashi asked, 'How did the old prisoner-chief express the belief that god is with us only twice—when we are born and when we die and perhaps the third time, eternally, if we have lived our life with honour?'

'Is that not what you believe, Kashi?'

'The last part—yes. But I also believe what the people of Ganga and my own people believe—that God is with us, always.'

'Only words differ. The beliefs are the same. When the old man said, God comes to an individual at birth, he did not mean that God comes empty-handed. God leaves a gift behind—the gift of conscience. It is for the individual then to use or abuse it. And, God, he said, comes again when the individual dies—but that is only to see how His gift of conscience was used or misused—and if it was used well, there is then the third meeting that the old man spoke of—when differences vanish between the soul of man and the soul of God—for then they are One for all eternity. Is there really a difference between what you believe and what the old man said?'

'But why different words? Why change a simple, beautiful thought—God is always with us—into a complicated formula of three visits?'

'Man has never learned to simplify, only to complicate. Often he does not say what he feels but what he thinks—and sometimes he thinks too much and, in the process, he gains much knowledge but also larger confusion and greater grief.' He paused. 'Actually, it was the first Chief who changed the words in that concept to create a belief in God's three visits. But in no way did he try to alter the doctrine of mukta, whereby salvation and identification with the soul of God are achievable through righteousness, pure conduct and noble deeds. Indeed, mukta remains a common word—like many others—in the language of the people on both sides.'

*

Brahmadatta kept travelling inland to collect men and materials so as to be ready for Hari Hara Dwara's defence in case the 'First Tribe' attacked. Kashi would often be by Nashtha's side. This led Kauru to recall the innocent words of the comic-poet who had said that Nashtha may be fond of Kashi. Kauru distorted the words and spread the malicious canard that Kashi was unfaithful to her husband. No one perhaps believed him but gossip travels, creates laughter and reaches the husband only after others hear it. The comic-poet dismissed it by simply saying, 'His pious father, who was a dhobi, washed dirt out of people's clothes, but he likes to put dirt on people.'

Brahmadatta heard of it accidentally when the comic-poet's wife was hurling abuse at Kauru, who ran off. Brahmadatta went after Kauru, lifted him by the scruff of his neck to throw him headlong into the river. Many collected and the comic-poet, fearing that Kauru would die, cried out, 'No! No! Do not pollute the river!' But what stopped Brahmadatta was that the oldest and most revered hermit, Parikshahari, woke up suddenly at this commotion and demanded silence. In his rush, Brahmadatta had reached the very spot at which Parikshahari meditated.

'What do you want?' Parikshahari asked, angry at being disturbed.

'I want to kill him.' Brahmadatta said, still clutching Kauru. 'But that is no reason to disturb my meditation,' the hermit said.

Brahmadatta apologized, mumbling, 'He accused my wife. . . .'

'Did you hear the accusation?'

'No. . .I. . . . .'

'Then go wash your tongue and clean your ears,' the hermit ordered.

But many came forward to accuse Kauru, their anger all the greater over Kauru's charge against a hermit—Nashtha.

Parikshahari stared at them as if to discover what lay behind their eyes. Meanwhile, the crowd grew larger. Finally, he said, 'No sin is attached to hermit Nashtha. There is no stain there for God to wash.' Sadly, he then looked at Kashi's tearful face and spoke, 'But a woman charged with unfaithfulness to her husband must prove her innocence. She must walk ten steps through fire. If she comes out unscathed, she is blameless.'

Brahmadatta now had the urge to pick up the frail Parikshahari and snuff the life out of him. But the hermit raised his hand to silence the crowd and said, 'But that must wait. For a charge so serious, the accuser himself must first go through fire for thirty steps, and if he comes out unharmed, the woman must then go through her test of fire.' He turned to Kauru, 'Please feel free to repeat your accusation, while they build the fire.' But Kauru mumbled his retraction, apology, plea for forgiveness—everything.

The chill went out of the atmosphere and the crowd smiled, but not so the hermit. Sternly, he told Kauru, 'Your retraction achieves nothing. All it proves is your fear of fire. And punished you shall be, unless you are forgiven by the chaste lady you slandered.'

Then Kashi simply said, 'Let him go.' The crowd was disappointed. The hermit alone was cheerful and said, 'That is how God punishes— through forgiveness—and that is how a mother punishes. Henceforth, Kauru, always address her as "Mother Kashi".'

*

Kauru was once more to play a role in Kashi's life. Lookouts had been placed by Brahmadatta in selected spots to watch for large-scale tribal movements towards them. Kauru was one of those lookouts.

Kauru espied a lone boy approaching a distant tree and hiding himself in its thick foliage. What aroused his suspicion was that the boy seemed to be coming from the opposite direction, stealthily, on all fours. Kauru ran to the tree. The frightened boy, meanwhile, clambered to the top of the tree on hearing Kauru's shouts. The boy would not come down and mumbled his response as Kauru shouted all the more. From his response, it was obvious that he was a tribal. Kauru picked up stones and hurled them at the boy who fell from the tall tree, bleeding and unconscious. Kauru picked up the boy and carried him like a trophy, slung on his shoulder, shouting, happy and proud, that he had caught a spy. Many followed him, some pleading that he put the boy down. He reached Brahmadatta's hut. There he flung him at Brahmadatta's feet.

The boy was no more than nine years old. Kashi cried out. She washed and bandaged his bleeding head. Brahmadatta rushed to the Vaid but he had gone inland to tend to a sick cow. With Kashi following slowly, he ran to a hermit, for help.

'He is already with God,' hermit Nashtha pronounced.

'But why did he come here?' Brahmadatta asked.

'I don't know,' Nashtha said. 'Maybe to run away from his people; maybe to meet someone; or take something or bring something. Who knows!'

Something flashed in Kashi's mind. She wanted to run; her limp held her back. She pleaded, 'Take me where the boy was found.'

Brahmadatta carried her. Under the tree were the broken pieces of a jar, along with an oily substance on the ground. As they pieced together the broken bits, they saw a hand painting of the zalzari tree and sunhera plant which the prisoner-chief had described. And there was more—a woman's face and figure, which looked like Kashi's, with her hand on her outstretched leg.

Many questions remained! Why did the prisoner-chief not come with the gift himself? Maybe he was afraid, as his people would have noticed his absence. But why send a child and put him in such danger? What danger! The prisoner-chief's single experience of Ganga was that its people were kind. If they sent back their attackers with gifts, would they harm a child! Tribals never hurt a child. Why would the people of Ganga!

Kashi wept. She scooped up the earth below the tree into which the oil from the broken jar had seeped and said, 'A little boy died in his effort to bring this gift to me and I must accept it.' She rubbed the earth on her leg. Soon, a tingling sensation began in her leg; later the sensation became intense, as if wasps were stinging her leg from within. All night she was awake with the pain. Even so, every day, she rubbed her leg with that earth, until it lost its oiliness and was dry as dust. The limp remained. She could not run, but she walked easier, better.

It was a coincidence, but on the day he noticed an improvement in his wife's leg, Brahmadatta went with Gargi to the inland farmers. They demanded that in future, the tribal prisoners be surrendered to them. This was to be the price for increasing their aid. Earlier, Brahmadatta's response had not been too negative. But now he flatly refused. 'No prisoners, no slaves,' he said gruffly.

It was left to Gargi to explain Brahmadatta's gruffness to the farmers. 'If we hold them as slaves, their onslaughts will then move inland, against you.' And finally, she threatened, 'But before the tribals attack you, Brahmadatta's forces will march against you to take what we need.'

'Surely our people will not attack their own people!' they said.

'When our people refuse to help us, are they our people?'

'Brahmadatta is an outsider. Why is he in charge?' they asked.

'He was the one ready to shed his blood for you. His child is born in our midst; and you call him an outsider!' Gargi grew angrier. 'Tell me who among you would help and who would not, so we may distinguish a friend from a foe.'

'We speak with one voice,' the leader of the farmers said.

'Then, each of you must wait to be dispossessed by Brahmadatta's army.'

Army! The comic-poet swears that he became sick trying to restrain his laughter. But the farmers were too stricken with fright and one of them said, 'Go not angry, sister Gargi! Let us reason with patience.' The leader felt deserted as the others also began to offer help.

The impulse to defend Hari Hara Dwara spread deeper in the land to people faraway, who were in no immediate danger. Gargi went everywhere. She was stung by the reference to Brahmadatta as an 'outsider', and she now spoke of him as a man who came from the mountains to defend them, to create a mighty force to face the enemy, unmindful of danger to himself, his wife and infant son. She intended no more, but the legend of Brahmadatta grew. Did he come from the mountains? Yes from high mountains where the gods resided! Yes, he was the one before whose unsheathed sword the invaders fled! Yes he it was who with an uncaring shrug released prisoners with the fearless message to their Chief, 'Come again, do your worst and die.'

Volunteers poured in. Feverish preparations went on. The wall was made into a fort. The canal-trench from the Ganga, to flood the ravine, was rebuilt, so as never to fail. Innumerable pits were dug and traps installed. But that was the second line of defence. At the first line, even beyond the huge tree in which the little tribal boy died, hundreds of new dome-pits were built for sharp-shooters with iron-tipped arrows. And far ahead of them were relays of runners, sentries and lookouts on high vantage points, to give advance notice by lowering banners during the day and by fire-torches at night. Huts were built where there were none before and tents rose like weeds, as everyone had to live near his duty-station. Deeper inland, swarms of workers toiled, none harder than those engaged in the task of smelting iron into weapons. It was far more difficult than smelting bronze or fashioning wood but the trouble was well worth it. Everyone had a task suited to his abilities.

A year passed, the usual enemy column did not materialize. Some heaved a sigh of relief. Others remembered the prisoner-chief's words —'Mighty armies of our Chief move like the roaring of the wind, at the moment of his divine inspiration. . .' and they feared a terrible attack without warning. Brahmadatta and Gargi redoubled their efforts. Volunteers poured in, inspired by the legend of Brahmadatta's heroism, but equally so by the extensive defensive arrangements they saw.

The attack came. Indeed, it was like the 'mighty roaring of the wind'. But it blew away like a whimper. The raiders could not even get beyond the first line of defence. Nothing is known of the casualties.

Three more attacks came in the next fourteen months. The last one was more deadly than the rest. It was watched by a youth whom the raiders brought in a palanquin. The tribals lost 114 and many more were wounded. The rest tried to run away except the forty-two guards around the palanquin and the eight who carried it. They were apparently ready to lay down their lives. In fact eight of the sixteen casualties of the Ganga forces arose as they tried to storm the defenders of the palanquin. Brahmadatta called back his men to form a distant circle around the palanquin, far from arrow-range and spear-throw. Alone, Brahmadatta went forward, visibly unarmed, warning his men, 'I shall wring your necks if you move or make a noise.' The tribals around the youth aimed their arrows at Brahmadatta, who simply raised both his hands as though to leave his chest unguarded. The youth spoke to his men. They lowered their bows. Brahmadatta bowed courteously as he reached the palanquin. The youth stepped out. Respectfully, Brahmadatta escorted him. The tribals followed.

Kashi asked her usual first question, 'What are we to do with you?'

'You will of course have me killed,' the youth answered. Kashi shook her head and anxiety now marred the youth's face as he asked, 'You will put me to slavery?'

'No,' Kashi replied firmly, 'we shall never do that.'

'Then be it for your Chief to decide the ransom for my release.'

'We seek no ransom. You are free to leave whenever you wish.'

'What do you seek in return?'

'Nothing—only a promise, never to attack us again.'

'That promise is not mine to give! I am merely the Chief's younger son. He alone decides.'

'Then our only request is that you so advise your Chief.'

'That I cannot presume. I can only convey your request to him.'

'Then we are satisfied,' Kashi said. 'And we leave it to your goodness to keep us informed of the Chief's decision.'

'I shall keep you informed but only if the Chief permits. I give no promise.'

'We seek none,' Kashi said. The youth left after a day's rest.

Two months later a priest from the First Tribe came to Hari Hara Dwara. To Brahmadatta he said, 'My message is from the Chief's younger son. There shall be no attack in his father's lifetime.'

Lifetime! Why not for all time?

But the priest said, 'How can his father promise for the future beyond his time, when his first son shall be greater and wiser than him?'

How old is the Chief?—was the question; they must know how long they could be certain of peace. The priest was unwilling to answer but finally confided, 'The Chief is just past 343,599 days.'

Impossible! That was over 940 years (based on 365 1/4 days per year)! But the priest patiently explained that it was not permitted to count a Chief's individual life-term. Counting began from the first day of the first Chief. When a Chief died, there were prayers for the dead but no ceremony or celebration to mark the emergence of the new Chief. It was as though a man died but the Chief lived on eternally.

But this merely gave a clue to when the first Chief began to reign. Kauru brought wine which made the priest more informative. Clearly, the present Chief was not too old but strong 'in mind and muscle' and his wife was expecting a child.

Indeed, an era of peace was ahead. They fortified Hari Hara Dwara, but no longer in panic—simply to safeguard the distant future.

Brahmadatta led an expedition down the Ganga from Hari Hara Dwara. It was not an uneventful journey as they crossed exciting rapids and waterfalls in the lovely though lonely country. Sudden attacks came from tribesmen hidden behind dense groves of reeds and grass. Fortunately, the attacks were ill-organized and Brahmadatta's contingent suffered no mishaps other than minor injuries. The attackers belonged to new tribes, which had moved in to displace the earlier inhabitants and seemed unconnected with the original inhabitants of Hari Hara Dwara or the First Tribe. Many attackers were caught and even Kashi did not understand their language. They were sullen, under-nourished, wretchedly emaciated, but initially refused gifts from Brahmadatta.

Cautiously, Brahmadatta's contingent moved, day after day, fighting through sixteen skirmishes on the way—none of them serious except for those who attacked them.

Suddenly, they stopped and looked about in wonder, as if seeing the earth for the first time. There was not just one river. There were three! Here was the milky white Ganga river they had been following! Here was another river, blue, glistening with flakes of silver in the brilliant light of the sun! And here was yet another, shimmering like gold! Where did they come from? Did they rise up, unseen, from the earth!

They walked slowly, as though in a trance. But the spell was broken when they heard a roar. Another attack? They readied themselves to meet the enemy. But there was no threat. It was the 'sangam' (confluence) of the three rivers—Ganga, Yamuna and Saraswati. And they saw the Yamuna, a river of blue water, becoming one with the Ganga, as they both flowed together, united and strong; while Saraswati, the river with ripples of gold, rushed through to chart a separate course, as though it came simply to embrace the two rivers and also say farewell at the same moment.

They watched fascinated the picturesque dance of colours as the three rivers met to rise in a foam of pure white.

They gazed at the Sangam[1] in silence. There was no need for words. It was as though the waters spoke in the language of the sky.

Slowly, they moved to bathe in the waters of the Sangam.

But then suddenly, viciously, came an attack from the riverbank. Brahmadatta's shout rose to call his men to arms. Lifting Kashi, he rushed to the bank, followed by his people, while arrows flew around. But the attackers did not remain to fight. They ran.

Casualties? Gargi's arm was bruised from an arrow; eighteen men of Hari Hara Dwara were injured, but only slightly. Kauru alone, with three arrows in his chest, died in the waters of the Sangam itself. He smiled. He pleaded that they not move him away from the Sangam, but only help him to remain afloat. They held him and saw around him a colour that was not in the Sangam earlier—the red colour of his blood. He was looking at the immeasurable, impassive sky. Above him, a dark cloud moved. He smiled. Then there was a stillness and peace. He was dead.

And many wondered over Kashi's words about Kauru—'He died sinless—always sinless.' Imagine calling a man like Kauru 'sinless'! But, the poets said Kashi was right—and they began to convince themselves that he who dies at this auspicious Sangam, 'sinless he is and sinless he always was,' because 'Sangam is the source of redemption,' 'be it a million of his births and billion of his sins, Sangam washes them all,' 'there is pardon for all faults, and attainment of mukta if one breathes his last at Sangam,' 'if sinless you are at the moment of death, does it not stand to reason that sinless you always were!'

Thus Kashi's characterization of Kauru as 'always sinless', when he died at the Sangam, encouraged many, in later generations, to believe that all their sins would be washed away if they died at the Sangam. But perhaps all she meant was that he was in God's realm and it is not for us on earth to count his sins, for judgement belongs to another. Or it may be, she thought, that he died with the clan and for the clan; that if he had not been there, the arrows aimed for him would have found another, worthier target and therefore all his past was forgiven to him for this final sacrifice.

Sangam or Sangayam—where Saraswati, Ganga and Yamuna meet—came also to be known as Prayaga or the place of sacrifice—as Kauru lost his life there and nineteen people were wounded; pra signifies extensiveness or excellence; yaga means sacrifice. A later poet

---

[1]Some poets assert that while sangam is a popular word for a confluence of rivers, this particular confluence was called Sangayam, to represent the meeting of Saraswati (sa), Ganga (ga) and Yamuna (Yam).

ridicules the idea that so small a sacrifice should be considered 'extensive' or 'excellent'. But then, life was not so cheap in Brahmadatta's times and battles did not involve so many injuries and deaths. Incidentally, later, with the emergence of foreign tribes, Prayaga was often polluted with the sacrifices of animals, including magnificent horses. But people of Brahmadatta's time, totally unfamiliar with such 'blood sacrifices', would have regarded them as inauspicious, inhuman and ungodly. Presently Prayaga is known as Allahabad (place of Allah or God) in Uttar Pradesh, India—map reference: 25.27n; 81.50e.

Brahmadatta, moved by Kauru's death and the injuries of the others, swore that he would make the route from Hari Hara Dwara to the Sangam so safe that even 'our dogs shall walk unmolested from tribal arrows and assaults. Enough have we sacrificed already!'

Brahmadatta's return journey to Hari Hari Dwara was less perilous with only seven skirmishes and no casualties.

Everyone in Hari Hara Dwara had heard of the enchanted, magical Sangam, and everyone sought to rush towards it. But they held back, as they also heard stories of the perils and bloodshed en route, magnified a thousandfold by those who had returned. How then did it cost only a single life and minor injuries? Many wondered, but a legend was already growing around Brahmadatta and people told stories of him as they tell stories of legendary heroes—how he deflects enemy arrows to render them harmless—how unerringly he took his people to Sangam—how his followers could come to no harm! But there were questions. How could he not protect Kauru? Kauru! Do you not recall Kauru's insult to his wife Kashi! But Kashi had forgiven the insult. So what—why would her husband forgive? Yet did he not show consideration to Kauru by making him sinless? No, Kashi did that. Nonsense! Does Kashi speak with a voice different from her husband's?

But the questions ceased and so the answers were unnecessary, as they all heard Brahmadatta's grim resolve to clear the route to Prayaga (Sangam).

Truly, they realized, he was inspired. Many volunteered to assist Brahmadatta. None, he ordered, should leave for Prayaga until the route was cleared. This was for their protection but maybe what he wanted was their single-minded attention in clearing the route, not only of hostile tribes but also of rocks and boulders; to level the terrain, make tracks for men, mules and horses to pass; to build rope-bridges and even to plant trees.

Only one man defied his order and moved to Sangam on his own. It was Tirathada. He glared at Brahmadatta who let him pass with the traditional blessing—'Go with God'. Later, Tirathada was not found at Sangam. For two decades no one knew where he was. Many were convinced that he died for his defiance of Brahmadatta's order. But then, he was seen at last near Ganga Sagar, in the Bay of Bengal where the Ganga divides herself into several streams—some said 108 though now there are fewer—to complete her incredible 1,560 mile journey. But then it was also said that Tirathada left not in defiance of Brahmadatta but with his blessing to chart the path that the people of Ganga were to follow.

Thousands worked for Brahmadatta to clear the path to the auspicious spot where the waters of Ganga, Yamuna and Saraswati mingled, 'with more colours than seen in the rainbow, as though diamonds and sapphires, rubies and emeralds and threads of gold and silver dance to meet the sunlight as it breaks into myriad hues and tints, passing through each drop of water.'

The route from Hari Hara Dwara to the Sangam was safe, secure and free from hostile attacks. Poets do not speak of the cruelty of Brahmadatta's men, as such, though they speak of how Kashi moved 'with a compassion that knew no bounds, to wipe a tear from every eye, for she said that these too were the children of Ganga and the hostile were hostile no more, bubbling with friendship and fellow feeling, except when Brahmadatta was around; and to him they bowed, in remembrance of their fear of him, and they called him, Gangapati (Protector of Ganga).'

Gangapati! It was a title by which even the fearful and hostile referred to Brahmadatta. In Hari Hara Dwara, Gargi used this title to impress farmers and to demand aid in his name. She saw the magical effect of the title and insisted that everyone refer to him as Gangapati.

Gangapati Brahmadatta led a larger contingent to Varnash—the town which was supposed to have been viciously destroyed some 900 years earlier, when intruders came to uproot the Sanathanis.

The journey was arduous, slow and painful. Throughout, they saw wretched hamlets, with people sheltered in rock-caves—some ready to fight with sticks, stones and primitive arrows, while others demanded a tribute to let them cross. Brahmadatta had come ready with gifts. Even so, attacks came from tribal pockets. He lost three men.

At last, from a distance, they saw a large town. Perhaps, it is not Varnash, they thought, and hermit Nashtha's calculations were incorrect. How could it be Varnash!—the destroyed city ! This place seemed to be teeming with people, horses, animals and structures that looked like temples, larger than any seen in Hari Hara Dwara.

The name Varnash was given to the city by the first Chief when his people were uprooted from the land of Ganga to go into the wilderness. And the first Chief described this once-thriving city to say, 'Not a blade of grass grows there any more; no more, a bird flies over it; nor are men, women and children there; and the river has the colour of red as the usurper bled our people; and all temples are below river-level, as usurpers lit fires with their unclean hands; and even the usurpers fled after laying waste our land, everywhere.' Thus spoke the first Chief as he called on his people to leave the land of Ganga, to rally under his banner and flee from Varnash and Hari Hara Dwara, to the lands beyond.

These words remained in the minds of the people and had been exaggerated by myth and distorted by time. Few knew the ithihasa of Varnash. The image, though, in everyone's mind was simply of a desolate, destroyed city with past glory and grace; but the legend left behind by the first Chief spoke also of dire peril to those that approached it.

Brahmadatta halted. The legend held no terror for him. But he realized that the tribe that had occupied the city would be invincible. If they erected such tall structures, if they had so many people, so many horses, what could his small contingent achieve! And such tribes, he feared, would not permit him to enter. He overruled Kashi who pleaded that she should go alone to scout the area. 'Who will harm a lone, lame woman!—and maybe I speak their language too,' she urged, with her heart set on entering the land of her ancestors. Brahmadatta silenced her. He was actually thinking of going back at the urging of many around him. But then, to them, Gargi spoke stridently in the voice of hero-worship, 'Gangapati never goes back—always forward!'

Gangapati wavered, 'Let us rest before our next move,' he said. 'Look also for a spot from which we can observe unseen.'

Gargi deployed men to go round. Kashi followed her. Later, from the top of the mound, Gargi saw a village group, far away, moving leisurely in the direction of the mound. She ran back to warn Brahmadatta. They all regrouped far behind, in a bamboo grove.

'But where is Kashi?' Brahmadatta asked, after they had settled in the grove. Whispers turned into shouts but Kashi was nowhere to be seen. Brahmadatta and Gargi ran to the mound where she had last been seen. They saw Kashi, far away, almost abreast of the men from the village. Brahmadatta stood on the top of the mound, his sword unsheathed, ready to rush to his wife's rescue. But he saw that the group passed Kashi by, without noticing her. Oh! But she approached them! The group halted. They were speaking to her! They pointed to the back while she pointed to where her men were hiding! Kashi walked with this group of strangers; they halted near another mound on the way! No, it was not a mound, but a large statue. And they were lighting little, flickering fires around it. Were they candles? And the entire group knelt—Kashi too.

The group waited there as Kashi returned to Brahmadatta's mound with two others—a man and a woman. And her call could plainly be heard, 'I am with my brother and sister. There is naught to fear.'

'Welcome strangers who art strangers no more!' cried out the man accompanying Kashi. Brahmadatta returned the greeting and called out to his people. Cautiously, some peered from the cover of the grove to ask, 'Have we surrendered to them?' And a poet says that Kashi replied, 'Yes, we surrendered to their love.'

Poets tell us further that 'Kashi was right in her faith but wrong in her language.' Maybe, because the people of Varnash spoke not the language of the first Chief but of Hari Hara Dwara.

Brahmadatta's question surprised the townspeople when he asked, 'Is this Varnash, the destroyed city?' 'Certainly not,' they said. 'How could God's city be destroyed!' But he pressed on, 'What is its name?' He was told—'It is the city of God, with as many names as God has.' 'A thousand?' he asked. 'No,' he was told, 'more than a thousand, for the names of the Nameless are limitless.' Brahmadatta persisted, 'But every city, everywhere, is of God.' Thoughtfully, they said, 'Of course,' as if that were answer enough.

Actually, they had no specific name for their Varnash. To them, it was the city of God. They never travelled out, so where was the need to name it! This is where they were born; and this is where they would live and die!

But the desire to travel now arose in their hearts, as Brahmadatta spoke to them of the magical Sangam where three rivers meet. 'I shall take you there,' Brahmadatta promised.

The people of Varnash heard, enchanted, the tales of these visitors from far away. To everyone, Gargi referred to Brahmadatta as Gangapati (Ganga's protector). She was simply seeking respect for her leader and truly it had a profound effect on her listeners.

A town-elder met Brahmadatta and said, 'I was wrong perhaps to agree that every village everywhere is of god, for there are villages with godless people.' He explained how their city suffered from tribes to the east. 'We bought peace by paying annual tributes to those tribes. But their demands rise each year and often they take whatever they wish, even after getting the tribute. They say we entice their animals here, but that happens because the tribals cut their own trees, never replant them and have scant vegetation. Each year, the danger from them rises and whenever they get time from their own warfare, they rush here to demand more. Last year, they destroyed the city's outskirts and we fear more damage next time.'

'No one,' said Gargi, while Brahmadatta was plunged in thought, 'no one shall attack this city. Gangapati shall not permit that.'

Gangapati's silence was treated as total commitment to protect the city. Surely a man of great resolve has to be a man of few words! And if there was anguish in Brahmadatta's heart, no one noticed it.

Actually, when he thought about it, his misgivings were no more. If he could protect Hari Hara Dwara where the inland farmers were lukewarm in their support, surely here with so many people—and all ready and willing—he could work miracles!

He asked for volunteers. Everyone was ready to volunteer. He and Gargi selected many for different tasks. But then came the hurdle. The volunteers would not learn to aim arrows or wield a sword or hurl a spear. They would not learn to kill. It was not for man to take a life that God sanctifies—they said. Brahmadatta tried to reassure them, 'Our arrows do not kill. They draw a little blood to frighten the enemy. Even our swords—they wound but rarely kill.'

And Gargi thundered, 'Fools! They come to destroy God's city, God's temples and you hesitate!'

They also heard Kashi's softer voice and that seemed to prevail, for she said, 'God has need of us. Why else did He create us! We have to have a purpose.'

'But to kill for it! Is that the purpose?' they asked.

'No', Kashi said, 'killing can never be a purpose. Protection of God's earth is. Protecting our temples and our children is. But only if you have the courage to do it without hating your enemy, without hurting him after he is caught. And only if you win him back to the ways of God with love.'

'But you are asking us to shed blood, to do violence . . .!'

Kashi interrupted, 'Do you love these tribals or do you hate them?'

'Of course we hate them. They attack and destroy. . . .'

'Then it is foolish to ask you to show courage, for truly you are men of violence without the courage to fight or love.'

Some said that this woman Kashi who was lame in her foot was also lame in her head. Others were not so certain that the faith of another was to be so ridiculed. But a few were quiet. They too believed that God had a purpose in creating humanity, but was she right in saying that man must fight to protect God's realm? Surely the all-powerful, all-seeing God could protect His realm. Why did He need man? But the fact was—and this brought a doubt to their minds—that God did not protect His realm and man could play havoc with it unless stopped by other men.

Brahmadatta and Gargi reached a decision—they would get their violent, battle-hardened veterans from Hari Hara Dwara to protect this city of God. The decision delighted the people of Varnash.

But again came Kashi's softly voiced question: 'You will allow others to do violence on your behalf, to shed blood that you fear to shed! Violence was in your hearts, I knew, when I heard that you hated the tribals. But I knew not that the spirit of your violence was so limitless.'

Perhaps Kashi would not have spoken thus if she had known the hurt she would cause. She was challenging their cherished belief in ahimsa and even ridiculing it. Surely, they did not need this diminutive woman to preach the principles of ahimsa to them. Many would have liked to have insulted her outright but who can speak roughly to the wife of Ganga's protector!

Yet arguments there were over what Kashi had said.

At the town sabha the city-elders wanted to silence such arguments. They wanted friendship with Gangapati and an elder said, 'Forget about her; you know what wives are! They speak from their hearts.'

Sadhu Mithra, the eldest said, 'The heart is the source of all goodness.'

'Also of evil,' another elder joked.

'Maybe evil is in my heart and yours; but not in the heart of her whom you seek to ridicule,' said the eldest.

No one really wanted an argument with the eldest. He was constantly in the temple-courtyard, often at prayers, though he was also a singer of songs and teller of tales. In his younger days, he was a builder of temples and a sculptor of idols. He never really participated in meetings of the city-elders though he was the chairman for years. He never voted even when there was a tie-vote, never called anyone to order, except by glaring at them. He never went to the town-hall for meetings, and they all had to come and sit uncomfortably under trees in the temple courtyard to hold the sabha meetings. His views were listened to with respect only because he spoke so rarely. Sometimes, he was outrageously unreasonable too—demanding that another temple be built, another school, another park, another idol, when the city was reeling from the tributes that had to be paid to the tribals. The townspeople loved Sadhu Mithra. If he wanted it, they would have voted all the city-elders out of office, to bring in new blood. But he never interfered with the elections. He himself was not elected by the people as the city-elders had to elect their own chairman. But they would have been booted out of office by the townspeople if they had failed to elect him—and they knew that. No one knew the secret of his power. He did not, himself. All he knew was that he loved the city and its people and they loved him in turn.

The elders were silent, keenly aware of the need to avoid an argument with their temperamental chairman at this important meeting.

Gangapati was to appear before the sabha to discuss plans for defence. The elders were assured that the warriors would come from Hari Hara Dwara, while earth-works, defensive forts, pits and the like, would be local responsibility, under Gangapati's guidance.

An elder escorted Gangapati and Gargi in. On behalf of the Sadhu chairman, the elder spoke welcoming Gangapati warmly and thanking him for his promise to bring his warriors to defend the city. He went on to speak of the city's gratitude and commitment to pay for everything. . . .

Sadhu Mithra cut him short, to ask Gangapati, 'Where is your wife?'

This wholly innappropriate question surprised Gangapati. Was the Sadhu trying to stop the elder from his commitment to pay all the expenses! But he mumbled, 'She is at the camp. . .or a temple.'

'If you permit it, I would like to meet her,' Sadhu Mithra said.

'That will be an honour. I shall bring her to you.'

'No, I shall go to her.' Sadhu said.

Brahmadatta had heard much from the city-elders about this eccentric Sadhu who tolerated no nonsense, except his own. Why must he go to Kashi! Brahmadatta himself was amused at Kashi's elaboration of ahimsa to the townspeople. His own understanding of ahimsa was different—you cannot love your enemy and seek to kill him at the same time—the killer instinct dies in you, if thoughts of love intervene —nor can you switch over from hate to love, once the enemy is defeated —how can human emotions move from hot to cold in a single instant! He had seen the hurt of the townspeople at Kashi's words. Now it seemed to him that this Sadhu was intending to chide his wife for her views. That, Brahmadatta was determined never to permit.

He looked straight at Sadhu and said firmly, 'My wife speaks her mind as she sees fit. That is her right. But it has nothing to do with our resolve to protect the life of this city.'

'Yes—you will save the city's life. But she will save the city's soul.'

Sadhu and Kashi met. Poets agree that each had questions for the other, but not many answers. It did not worry Sadhu. The important thing, he felt, was to ask questions and the answers would follow. Both were however certain that man's journey was not purposeless and God too needed man.

Sadhu and Kashi even discussed whose side God was on. Those that attacked or those like them who sought nothing except to defend themselves? But why did they attack? To seek shelter, warmth and food, of which someone, sometime deprived them? And did the land belong to those that occupied it? Did not these very people of Varnash dispossess those who had occupied it some 900 years earlier when the first Chief was driven out with his people! And the first Chief himself —did he not go out to dispossess others! This circle of greed needed to be broken with dana and daya.

Brahmadatta sometimes half-listened to these discussions between Kashi and Sadhu Mithra. He waved them away. He was a man of action. For him, the reality was to hate the attacking enemy, meet their threat and root them out. But he wondered too—ahimsa itself calls for action and courage, far more demanding!

Some say Sadhu Mitra asked Brahmadatta to teach him to wield a sword. Ridiculous!—say others. Would an old man of seventy do that!

But what did happen was that hundreds from Varnash volunteered for armed training under the Sadhu's encouragement. And as he heard the whoops of joy and blood-curdling cries of the trainees, Sadhu Mithra remarked to Brahmadatta, 'How easy it is to raise the beast in man! But how does the beast within him die?'

*

But Kashi and Sadhu spoke on other matters too—on the ithihasa of

Varnash. Sadhu said, 'I have no doubt that he who called himself the first Chief fled with many from here, for our songs speak of an exodus 900 years earlier when other tribes came here with their new language and new laws but then settled to follow our laws. There is however no song that speaks of the destruction of our temples which have been here for thousands of years. Even in the songs of the exodus, they sing of the glory of gardens and temples and the sacred waters that they were leaving behind.' And the Sadhu told her further, 'The exodus was not to the west alone, but the east and south too. Your ancient language is still remembered in many parts of the tribal lands that are threatening us till today.'

Now, she was certain that this city of God was never destroyed. It was a canard by the first Chief to swell the numbers of his followers.

Later, Sadhu took Kashi to his own temple which was flourishing long before the exodus began and was celebrated in the songs of the exodus. She listened to those songs too and knew it was not just the first Chief who had led his tribe away, but many others, to the east and the west, north and south.

The battle-training went on under Gargi's strict supervision. A more arduous task was also undertaken. On the outskirts of the city, which had been razed to the ground by tribals only the previous year, the citizens of Varnash began building a fort. A fort? Actually, seven idols were placed at the site. Who would regard it as a fort under construction! To tribals who saw it from a distance—and some came to inspect it at close quarters—it clearly looked as if it were a temple. Meanwhile, the entire city worked and those who were not making arrows, sling-shots, swords and other arms, were busy hauling rocks to the site. But why a stone-structure? Even brick-work with clay would suffice against the ineffectual arms of the tribals. No, a temple had always to be built with stone from the Ganga; bricks were for houses and sheds. Only a stone structure would give the impression that it was to be a temple, and hopefully, tribals would not see it as a challenge and begin their attack, while it was still being built.

A tribal child once came near the idols and left a clay figure. Sadhu said it was an idol of the tribal god. Brahmadatta demanded a large boulder, cut, chiseled and polished to have the same height as the seven idols. On that stone, he placed the small tribal idol. From a distance, it appeared that there was nothing on that stone-base, so tiny was the idol. But the tribesmen came to peer closer. They bowed and left.

Some from Varnash were delighted that the tribals bowed to the idols of their gods. No, said others—they bowed only to their own god. But then Sadhu Mithra said: 'He who bows to his God surely bows to your God!'

Sadhu went often to peer closely at the small statuette, his head resting on the head of the stone-base. From a distance, tribals watched;

some came closer. They saw him prostrating himself before the idol of their god. And from their distance, the tribals bowed too. But the old man was not kneeling in prayer. With the instinct of the sculptor he had once been, he was peering at every fine detail of the tiny statue. It was the statue of an archer-god with ten faces and heads; and all round its body were figures—sun, moon, stars, lions, horses, goats, snakes, trees, mountains, water. Sadhu called many to feel and describe for him the intricate details on the figure, for there was a limit to what his weak eyes could discern. And now the distant tribals saw many bowed heads before their god.

With loving care, Sadhu went on to sculpt a large statue of the idol and some said that it was probably a hair shorter than the seven statues of their gods, while others said it was actually even taller.

Gargi removed the statue from the temple when Sadhu was not there and placed it along with the other idols on the site. 'Only for two or three days,' she said. Sadhu was philosophic about it, and a poet said, 'Perhaps even the artist from the sky controls not what He creates!'

Some were happy that the false idol was removed from the temple. But Sadhu held that idols were neither false nor true but all of them— be they with familiar or strange countenances—be they loving or frightening—were simply there to focus attention on the One Divine Reality.

The effect of the new statue on the distant tribals was remarkable. A few of their youngsters who had previously come to hurl stones, held back—and some came, slowly, not to throw stones but flowers. And Gargi asked Sadhu with a straight face, 'Should I send the statue back to the temple?' Sadhu shook his head, 'No. They will think their god has been dethroned!'

Meanwhile Kashi plunged herself into the service of the city. Her cottage became an ashram to assist the needy. Many flocked to her. And her questions were many. If it is God's city, why do we not keep it as pure and clean as God would wish it? Should anyone go hungry, naked, maltreated or humiliated? Her voice was soft, her eyes gentle as she asked, unlike the others who went out on her behalf to ask difficult, strident questions: too much wood is burnt at temples for sacred fires—how could fires be sacred if they were caused by tearing the limbs of trees? Why did they think the trees shed leaves and branches, if not for the sacred fire? Why throw so much food in the river after it was served to the idols? Should the fish not eat? Fish knew where to find their food, they said, but some children didn't— and their food destroyed natural river-food for the fish. And why pollute the holy river with the dead, unburnt bodies of children? Why was it that some children didn't go to school? Not enough schools? Then why not open more? Many gave much to temples. But Kashi was the one to demand offerings from temples to help the needy. The needy? She had food-kitchens opened near the tribal quarters too with

Sadhu Mithra's help.

Yet poets speak less of this aspect of Kashi's work than of her effort to revive old songs about the exodus. Actually, she had merely to express a wish and singers and poets—always hungry for appreciation—came to her to recite and re-recite the half-remembered songs that their ancestors had once sung. Was she the only listener? No. Gratefully the singers found that the entire city listened; for the past always holds us spellbound; and the tales of our roots stir not only an emotion but also a memory, deep in our subconscious, from a different time centuries ago, as though we were there ourselves to participate in that event.

The city re-heard from those songs the cry of the exodus and the lament of those that fled nine centuries earlier. But the songs were not only of the first Chief who led his people to the west but of many— like Bhangal Baba, Burman, Bharhut, Madhyarani, Nagakani, Horiya, Bahari, Dukhadan, Vindhyara, Hawoorash, Mandala, Meghkanya, Mynakhel and Nipavali—each of whom led their groups, not to the west alone, but in all directions—north, south and east. Only the first Chief's songs spoke of the devastation left behind but the songs of the others who fled at the same time sang of the beauty and grandeur of the temples, flora and fauna that they left and of their hope eternal, that someday, somehow, they would return to their land of Sanathani. Maybe the first Chief spoke of the devastation in his heart or maybe he just wanted his people to follow him and not think of running back to the land of past glory which the invaders had occupied!

And then Kashi knew that she belonged not only to Varnash but to the land and people all around.

*

Meanwhile, the tribal chief of the eastern tribe fumed. He viewed the 'temple-site' with growing anger. Brick by brick he had razed the outskirts of their city. Now they were building a temple there! He wanted nothing but a barren, no-man's land in his west. Already he was under pressure from the attacks of tribes in the east, where he had made the mistake of extending himself right up to their borders. To him, what now made sense was a large belt of bleak desert area all round his land to which no animal was tempted to flee and from which no one hostile may approach unseen. Temple or no temple, he would rush and crush them. But he waited—let them clear the area, even more; yes, let them also pile up huge boulders. Maybe those would later serve as defensive spots for his archers and then he would go on to raze their land around. So what if they had never attacked a temple before! Every new necessity created a new rule of law—and with the growing attacks on him from the east, surely a new set of rules must evolve to replace the old order. He was no longer bothered by the idols staring at him from the fort-site. Even when the statue of his god was put up, he said, 'So what!' All that his warriors had to do was to be careful that all the idols remain unharmed, to retain the love of their own god and to restrain the wrath of the gods of others. Later though it did lead to a new idea, prompted by many of his trusted advisers. Why not wait and let them complete the temple! Why not, then, take over the temple. There was some discussion over this, however. Some suggested that the seven false idols be done away with; while others were of the opinion that they should be given a minor place in the pantheon.

Perhaps the tribal Chief would not have listened to this new wave of thought but for a peculiar chain of events. The first link in that chain was that a celebrated tribal artist was at work, sculpting an idol which would be taller than the combined height of all the seven idols that stood on the temple-site of Varnash. (A poet asserts that this sculptor was the father of the little boy who had earlier left the little statue at the temple-site.) The tribal sculptor was not working alone, as many artists, all over the tribal land, had collected to help him; and the work went on within 'shouting distance' of the temple-site. The sculptor's ambition was that his statue should face the temple of Varnash, be even taller than the temple itself and dominate the entire area around.

The second link in this strange chain, as a poet tells us, was that, 'someone then showed the tribal Chief the sketches of the ten faces of the idol that were to be sculpted by the tribal artist; and one of those faces was his—and then the desire for immortality entered his soul, as he thought of the idol with his own face amidst the clouds, while his piercing eyes surveyed his entire land for all generations to come, long after he was no more.'

Let the attack wait, he decided. 'Let the temple be built. I shall have the idol, with my face, moved on to the top of that high temple and the clouds shall dip low to pay their respects.'

Across the distance, Sadhu Mithra saw the feverish activity of the tribal artists as they built a framework for their idol. Maybe, Sadhu thought he saw a mistake in their rough structure; or maybe an artist cannot see another artist at work, without feeling the urge to be with him. The fact is that Sadhu felt impelled to walk across towards the tribal land. Some said he should have known better; it was always dangerous to cross into tribal lands. As it is, the tribals glared at him, at first, and yet as he began gesturing towards their structure, they smiled.

Sadhu did not return that night and the only harm that came to him was that he had to fast as the food they generously offered him was meat and even the soup was laced with meat gravy. But then he was used to fasting.

From then on, every day, Sadhu would walk across to work on the statue, 'climbing up and down their ladders and stools, like an eighteen- year-old'. Once, he even had a cartload of tools brought in for the tribal artists. Later, when the tribal chief visited and saw him there, he asked, 'Who permitted him to come here?' It was the chief artist who came forward boldly to claim responsibility. 'I did,' he said and the other artists joined in to say, 'We did.' But Sadhu simply pointed to the idol in the making and said, 'He called me and I came.'

The Chief could do no more than glare; and here, the poet jubilantly burst out to cry, 'But then does not an artist, a sculptor, a poet, a singer, have a licence far above that which maybe granted to a hunter or a peasant!' This poet's assumption of greater dignity for his own class apart, obviously, the tribal chief restrained himself from ordering Sadhu out, as he too wanted the idol to be completed as soon as possible.

Thus the work on the idol continued peacefully with 'loving care'; and on the fort-structure with 'rushed frenzy.'

*

Poets speak of the seven battles for the city of Varnash. Others speak of seventeen battles and yet others of twenty-seven. But how many battles can one fight in a space of 228 days! Maybe there were only seven battles or even less.

The fort stood, high, majestic, commanding the landscape. And the innumerable boulders at the site were not for the 'temple' interior, but for the defensive walls.

The realization that the 'temple' was not for prayers but to block his path finally dawned on the tribal chief. Boldly he strode forward to strike. He was certain that those who never fought before would vacate the fort and flee on his approach. But they did not.

The Chief was the first to aim his arrow. His people then shot theirs. There was no retaliation. Fearlessly he charged. And then havoc spread within his ranks, as arrows rained on them from a hundred points in the fort.

The Chief retreated, hurt not in his body but in his very soul. He and his father and grandfather before him had embraced the policy of leaving Varnash intact, except for occasional attacks and a levy of tribute. The city was like a treasure-house, to which they could turn to replenish their wealth from time to time, while his people squandered it for pleasure, for hunting and to battle with other tribes. It was in the east and south that he wished to expand, to occupy land and capture slaves. But it was never his plan to destroy Varnash or to occupy it. 'Yes', his great grandfather had said, 'untold wealth shall be ours at one stroke, if we enter their city, occupy its land and subject them to slavery. But think of the genius of our people to exhaust the inexhaustible! How long will it take us to squander the wealth! And who do we then turn to, when all that is finished? No, let them be in comparative peace, to pray and to labour hard—for whether they know it or not, they pray and labour more for us than for themselves.'

This then was the ancestral policy by which the Chief had guided himself earlier. Even now, his ambition was limited—not to have the entire city within his grip but merely to grab its outskirts and raise the tribute.

Now, the ghosts of the past rose to haunt the Chief. The 'temple' was a temple no more! Not prayers but sling-shots, stones and spears spewed forth from it! Behind its outer wall were not plants and shrubs but hidden, unseen marksmen with deadly arrows! And his own people said, 'The dogs hiding there have developed the fangs of a wolf.'

But the Chief was afraid of neither dogs nor wolves, nor lions, nor tigers. He hunted them all. There were stories of his killing a lion single-handedly. He regrouped, attacked again but returned, defeated.

The Chief was like a tiger at bay. Tribes to his east and south heard of his discomfiture against a city celebrated for peace. They laughed. Then they marched. Desperately, the Chief charged against the fort, breaking through its outer walls, but again he retreated, leaving many of his men wounded, dying and dead.

Fierce battles which were raging on the Chief's eastern and southern borders came closer home and were now being fought near the centre of his land. He made one last desperate attempt. Skirting the fort in an arc, from a distance, he broke through, unmindful of how many of his men fell, to enter the city of Varnash. He was certain that the city would lie defenceless, at his mercy, and he would create such havoc there that defenders from the fort would run out to seek his mercy.

But it was of no avail. He simply ran into the second line of defence, strong and alert, which Gargi was herself commanding. For the Chief, there was no going back. Perhaps there was no way forward either. Still he rushed. He found himself beyond that line of defence, but now he had only thirty-six men around him. All his other companions had fallen. Through the city of Varnash he went, his thoughts now centred not on victory, but escape. No one barred his way. The city itself lay in panic. Had the tribals broken through! Was it their vanguard tearing its way through!

The Chief rode on, his naked sword held in his teeth, as he aimed his arrows at whoever he saw in the distance, while his horse tore across the land. And suddenly the Chief found himself alone. Were his companions felled by the men of Varnash! He rode on, beyond Varnash, to the mound from which Brahmadatta had once viewed the distant city. He glanced backward only once, and saw little, for his eyes were moist with tears; the only thankful thought in his mind was that he had already anointed his son as his successor; and his only prayer was that the elders of his tribe would not disown his son.

Where the tribal Chief went, no one knows. Some say that he ultimately reached the land of the First Tribe, where he was honoured, but left that too, to become a hermit. Others speak of his death at the Sangam of Ganga, Yamuna and Saraswati. But there was evidence only of his horse having died there, while he went on.

What happened to the Chief's thirty-six companions? The Chief had outridden them. They saw not the fear they roused in the city but the stark terror in their own hearts. This was no way to go—rushing deeper into enemy land! But where could they go. They halted, perhaps without words, overcome by the one common desire to seek shelter before the city-people gathered to hack them to pieces. They went into the courtyard of the temple. Sadhu Mithra was there, alone. They brandished their swords as if to cut him down. Calmly, the Sadhu said, 'Let us pray together.' They sat down to pray.

*

Kashi was dead. An arrow struck her in the chest, as the few tribals tore briefly through the city. Brahmadatta himself had rushed from the fort when he heard the report of the tribal Chief breaking through Gargi's barriers. He did not know that the Chief was simply on the run, with a pitifully small number of people with him.

Kashi rested in Brahmadatta's arms. Silently, he gazed into her shining liquid eyes, as she spoke to him of her son, of her land and people. The perpetual sparkle of her eyes was, then, no more.

There was no victory celebration. Everyone thought of Brahmadatta's unshed tears. Some said that the thirty-six captives in Sadhu's temple should be killed to pay for this terrible deed. But Sadhu said, 'Then Kashi will have lived and died in vain.'

Silently, Brahmadatta agreed. And Gargi too nodded through her tears, as she recalled Kashi's words of mercy and love.

Gargi readied the people of Hari Hara Dwara to leave instantly. Kashi, she said, must be cremated at the Sangam and her body must be prepared by those well-versed in the art, to remain fresh for the journey. 'No,' Brahmadatta said, when at last he spoke, 'Kashi must be cremated here, in Varnash—in the land where her ancestors lived and died before they fled with the first Chief. That was her last wish.'

Kashi was cremated in Varnash. Her ashes were immersed in the Ganga.

The city of Varnash was renamed Varuna Kashi (to mean: 'God of favourable wind that brought Kashi to us'). It came to be called Kashi. Later, it assumed the name of Benaras and Varanasi—abbreviations of Varuna Kashi. Some however say that the name Varanasi was given because the city, built on the left bank of the Ganga, was situated between two of its tributary rivers named Varuna and Asi or Ashi.

But the fact is that these two names—Varuna and Asi or Ashi for the two rivers—came long after the city was named Varuna Kashi.

Whatever be the change of names that the city of Varnash went through, one name remained constant, unchanging—Kashi—in memory of the little woman who died there. As Sadhu Mithra said when her ashes were immersed:

'...This is the place of Kashi, and eternally it shall be known by her name; briefly she came to live amongst us, where her ancestors once lived. They however left in hate. She lived in love and blessed the city with love, and her dying words to her husband were not to lift his arms against those at whose hands she had died, but to heal their wounds with love. And here, as we sprinkle her ashes, is she amongst us? Yes, in our hearts as she is lifted to heaven...'

To every devout Hindu, since then, the place is known as Kashi (map reference: 25.20n; 83.00e).

Sometimes, people will hear only words—and perhaps only those that they want to hear. They heard Sadhu Mithra's eulogy, as the flames from Kashi's cremation rose. And he said, 'From here, this auspicious soul goes heavenwards to be one with God.' And this led to the belief, across the centuries, that the journey to heaven must begin from the city of Varnash (or Kashi, as it was now called), and there were those, then and now, who in the last days of their life would make the final effort to reach Kashi and realize the dream of their existence—to die at Kashi and be lifted to God's realm.

It is not as if the Sangam at Prayaga had lost its fascination. It would always be revered as a luminous centre charged with shakti (cosmic energy). The mingling of waters at the Sangam of Ganga and Yamuna, rising fifty feet above the sand banks to flow triumphantly together and Saraswati's gushing embrace with colours of gold and silver, diamonds and sapphires, presented a dazzling and unforgettable spectacle.

Varnash had no such comparable spectacle to offer—only the simplicity of reverence. But then, it was said, that at the Sangam one dies sinless but at Kashi one is transported to God's realm. Is there a difference?

*

A scream of anguish rose in the tribal lands, as the tribes from the east and south marched. There was a cry of despair, a heartbroken lament for mercy.

Tribal elders were pitted against each other—some behind the Chief's son, others with their own claims; many sought alliances with the enemy tribes in an effort to grab power. Fighting erupted all over. Famine stalked the countryside.

Just beyond the fort lay the idol on which the tribal artist had been working. The idol had fallen and the artist was dead.

No one knows who killed the artist or how the idol fell. Later, Sadhu Mithra would repair the idol. He had meanwhile found the artist's little son who had left the statuette at the 'temple site' near the seven idols. A tribal had seen the boy wandering around in a daze. He had taken charge of the boy and kept him as a dasa—slave or servant. Sadhu Mithra 'purchased' the boy from the tribal.

Sadhu adopted the boy—Dasa—as his son. Many years later, long after Sadhu Mithra was dead, the boy would grow up to be acknowledged as a celebrated artist of Kashi. He also became the chairman of the sabha. He was younger than many sabha elders but instead of the title of the Eldest, he chose for himself the title of Dasa—servant of the sabha. He, it was, who constructed a pier at the spot at which Brahmadatta's wife Kashi was cremated and her ashes immersed. It was also the spot at which the first Chief was reputed to have been cremated (nine hundred years earlier). The site came to be known as Dasawamedha ghat. Later, he also converted the fort into a temple and installed there the tribal idol on which his father had worked and which Sadhu Mithra had repaired.

*

Months went by. Tribes from the east and south moved on, to pillage and burn. The Chief's son rushed to Varnash to seek refuge.

Brahmadatta stirred himself. With the Chief's son, he moved into tribal land. Some said he did not want aggressive new tribes to be at the doorstep of Varnash, sanctified as it now was with his wife's name —Kashi. Others said he went with the inspiration of Kashi's last words —'heal their wounds!' Hundreds from Varnash followed him—apart from the 'veterans' who fought alongside him. Why did so many follow him?

Some said it was the 'guilt' of camouflaging a fort as a temple that made the entire city go out to assist the tribals. As it is, many had, earlier, spoken of the immorality of such a deception, though Gargi's shout silenced them—'War is not a game and there are no rules to follow—except to win.'

But it seems that it was Kashi's inspiration that moved many to follow Gangapati in order to assist the tribals. The others that followed him were certain that Gangapati was always on the path of honour and victory.

Thus, many who followed Gangapati to assist tribals were not fighters. They came on a mission of mercy with food, clothing, tents and medicines. They had heard harrowing tales of what was happening in their neighbouring tribal land—of men whose eyes had been put out, others whose limbs were cut off, and yet others whose tongues had been torn off, while starvation faced the rest.

Even Brahmadatta cried as he saw the devastation in the tribal lands and asked, 'Is there no God to forbid such revolting cruelties?'

And Sadhu Mithra's reply was heard and re-heard, 'There is a God, surely. For He it is who sent you to us and to them—to set it right!'

Who, then, would not follow Gangapati! He who was sent by God!

Only one poet speaks of the fear in Gangapati's heart. All the battles he had fought in Hari Hara Dwara, Sangam and Varnash, were defensive. For he had never marched out to meet the enemy.

Gangapati installed the Chief's son as the Chief. Why? Perhaps because he was the legitimate successor. Perhaps someone was needed, around whom others may rally to restore a semblance of order to a battle-torn land. Perhaps others vying for that position were corrupt, cruel, selfish, greedy and inefficient. Perhaps a grateful Chief who was indebted to Varnash would be less of a threat. Perhaps the Chief and his ancestors were benign, compared to all the others. Maybe it was a combination of all these factors.

Thereafter, Gangapati himself had to do very little fighting. The new Chief felt invulnerable. Fearlessly he faced tribes to the east and south, as Gangapati blessed him and the troops with the water of the Ganga that he said would make them bhiti-hrt (fearless) and if they died in the attempt they would be avyaya (imperishable).[2]

Who could stop the onslaught of the valiant Chief! And who would not surrender before a Chief who offered mercy and compassion to the defeated—for Brahmadatta had schooled him well. Attacking tribes fled to their lands though some found refuge in Kashi. The Chief returned flushed with victory. The last part of his journey he performed on foot, as was only fitting, when he came to bow to Gangapati.

The new Chief reigned in peace. There was peace in Varnash too, for the Chief remembered the blessing of Gargi, for strength and valour against his enemies, which ended with the warning, 'But he who seeks to harm Kashi, let his arms wither, let his eyes lose their sight, and let him and all those that follow him, now and hereafter, themselves and their descendants, be cursed!'

Gangapati had simply nodded, wordlessly.

There was an eerie silence in Brahmadatta's heart. He quietly went about his self-assumed task of rendering the route from Varnash to Sangam and Hari Hara Dwara safe and even comfortable for travellers and pilgrims. Tribals often blocked the path. Fearlessly, he would rush ahead of his men to face the tribals, unmindful of the arrows that flew around him. Death, it seemed, held no terror for him.

Gargi understood the well of loneliness in his heart. She increased the force composed of veterans and volunteers around him—and soon

---

[2]In the later Vedic age, both these names—Bhiti-hrt and Avyaya—would be amongst Gangastotra-Satanamavali and the Ganga-Sahasranam stotra which enumerate 108 and 1,000 of Ganga's names, respectively, to be chanted devotionally.

these men would be known as Gangapati's Guard. She brought his son from Hari Hara Dwara. Always, thereafter, the son would accompany the father on his perilous journeys, first in a litter and then on horseback.

No longer was Gangapati's spirit overwhelmed with sorrow. His love for his son overflowed; along with it, his fear for his safety. His mind dwelt on the future of his son—and of those of his son's generation and beyond. When he looked into his son's eyes—they were like Kashi's, with the same glint of a smile and he thought of the vision of oneness and unity that Kashi had inspired. He recalled the songs that Kashi had unearthed—of the cultural continuity of the Sanathanis that once were together but broke apart in new diversities of sect and language.

And Brahmadatta realized that it was not enough to win a few skirmishes or battles or keep the tribals at bay. He had to win their hearts. They were together once. Why should they now be apart! He became conscious of the conception of a common link of Sanathanis, with its culture of deep humanity and spiritual strength.

He had no idea of the geographical frontiers of that common culture—where it began and ended. But certainly, it was there in the settlement from which his wife emerged, in the mountains from which he himself had come, in the lands around Hari Hara Dwara, Prayaga, Varnash, and in the lands of the First Tribe, and in the lands to the east, north and south of the tribes whose Chief he had recently installed beyond Kashi. Where else? Somehow, a feeling came upon him that it was there, all along the course of the Ganga—wherever the river flowed.

Thereafter, the blood and fury almost disappeared from his battles and the end of each round of hostilities was followed by his gentleness. Whenever the tribals blocked his path, he would try to avoid battle and, instead, enter upon a long, patient siege.

It took time, effort and even some unavoidable bloody skirmishes, but at last the tribal attacks ceased. Instead, small settlements grew alongside the tribal villages. The initial, uneasy truce gave way to tolerance, and later, even to harmony, friendship and assimilation.

The impassable tracks on the route between Hari Hara Dwara and Varnash gave way to pathways lined with plants and trees. Rope-bridges stood where rivers, ravines and deep ditches made the crossing difficult. Each tribal village on the route felt honour-bound to protect and assist the traveller and the pilgrim. Now the bulk of Gangapati's Guard was formed by tribals. Many Sanathanis from Hari Hara Dwara and Varnash wondered initially at the enrolment of so many tribals for Gangapati's Guard, but Gargi's taunt silenced them—'These tribals pray only before a battle and after they die when God can hear them; while you. ....' But then Gargi was often unfair and the fact is that the tribals were not the only ones who were ready to lay down their lives. There were deeds of valour and heroism by Sanathanis as well, and certainly they had a greater understanding of the need to show mercy and charity to the defeated after a battle was won.

Brahmadatta's son grew up speaking many tribal languages and watching his father's battles from a distance. Gargi's instructions to him were clear—'Just watch the battle from afar; keep your distance and do not go anywhere near the place where arrows are flying and swords flashing.' There were hand-picked men from among Gangapati's Guard whose task was to watch over the son.

The only thing the son was allowed to do was clear the route. He did the job admirably. At the age of fourteen, he was not only amongst the most competent workers, but an excellent supervisor as well. He grumbled at his father's refusal to allow him into battle; and he also criticized the caution with which his father approached a battle. His father would patiently explain that the intention was not to die, nor to kill, nor to wound, but to heal and rebuild a long-forgotten sense of unity and oneness. But the son would complain of the delay and disruption a long siege caused and, 'why take months, when a single thrust would wipe them out in a day!'

At last, the work on the route would be complete. The moment would come when Brahmadatta and his son could look forward to an era of tranquillity and rest. A little away from Sangam at Prayaga, Brahmadatta built a cottage for himself. It was mostly his son who worked on it and on the ornamental gardens around it. Well-wishers came from all over to assist and admire. Gargi was back at Hari Hara Dwara. Gangapati's Guard however remained with him—no longer to fight battles, but only as friends, to be nearby. And the son assisted them too, to build their cottages. Prayaga became a town teeming with activity. Visitors and pilgrims came to witness the magical Sangam and pay their respects to Gangapati, around whom legends kept growing.

Brahmadatta was happy to tend his corner of the herbal garden. His passion was to discover more of the medicinal properties of herbs. He had gathered hints of such new uses from healers at Varnash and many more from the tribals. Gardening absorbed him. Yet he remembered his old promise to Gargi to take her to Ganga's source. He and his son reached Hari Hara Dwara just as a bloody battle erupted.

*

The old Chief of First Tribe was dead. He was the one who had promised that during his lifetime there would be no attacks on Hari Hara Dwara. With his death ended the promise not to attack.

A formidable army came to attack. Everyone was needed to fight this threat. The old restriction of keeping Gangapati's son away from the battle no longer applied.

The son distinguished himself in battle, combining the lessons of caution he had learnt from watching his father, with an aggressive thrust to reach the enemy flank and mow them down. The enemy retreated in disorder. But for him, the battle was not over. He led the assualt on the retreating forces and the cries of the wounded and dying rent the air as their bodies were crushed into the mud. The son was cheered at the end of the battle. In a flush of pride, he later even complained at his father's earlier refusal to allow him into battle. But Gargi brought him down to earth with a shout, 'Your father wants you to learn the arts of peace, the art of healing, not the art of slaughter!'

But arts of peace had to wait. Three more bloody battles for Hari Hara Dwara had to be fought. The new Chief of the First Tribe was slow in learning his lesson or perhaps he did not care for the anguish of his people. In each of these battles, Gangapati's son distinguished himself, never waiting for the enemy to reach defensive lines, but charging like a whirlwind to strike and kill. But at times, the enemy did reach the defensive lines, if only because he charged at them from the flank and then they had nowhere to run.

Contingents came from Prayaga and Kashi to help Hari Hara Dwara. They arrived after four massive battles were already won. Everywhere, the name of Gangapati's son rang as the victor. Brahmadatta himself would magnify his son's valour and victories, and slur over his own.

In the contingent from Varnash was also Dasaswamedha, the son of the tribal artist adopted by Sadhu. He and Brahmadatta's son became friends. Dasaswamedha had come not so much to fight as to seek Gangapati's permission to convert the fort at Varnash into a temple. But he realized that it was not opportune to discuss this subject just then, as the mood in the aftermath of battles for Hari Hara Dwara was to strengthen the forts all over, not dismantle them.

Brahmadatta's health was failing. He insisted on escorting Gargi to the Ganga's source. She declined, 'Wait till you get better.' But he argued, 'What if I get worse?' And she replied, 'Then Gangapati's son shall take me there.' No longer did she ever refer to his son by name, not even when she spoke to Brahmadatta. She always called him 'Gangapati's son'.

A mission was unfolding itself in Gargi's mind—that the son must take over the father's role of protecting the land and people of Ganga. To her Gangapati was not simply a title of respect and affection, but a title of authority and duty, to pass from father to son.

Gargi feigned deafness whenever anyone referred to the son by his name. 'Who?' she would ask, as though the name made no sense, and finally, 'Oh! you mean Gangapati's son! Then why don't you say so?' To the son, she spoke of his mother's dream and his father's struggle to realize that dream, to render the land safe from depredation and violence.

Brahmadatta died. The news spread like wildfire. Tribal lands east of Varnash were in turmoil. From north, south and east, the tribes marched, certain that the tribal Chief whom Gangapati had installed no longer had anyone to protect him. The Chief himself felt compelled to join the invaders threatening Varnash.

And Gargi's cry was heard—'Gangapati lives!'—for the title was accorded to Brahmadatta's son, not by Gargi alone, but by all.

Brahmadatta's son—now known as Gangapati II—marched to the relief of Varnash. At Prayaga itself, the tribals created disorder on hearing of Brahmadatta's death, but many veterans of Gangapati's Guard were settled there and the rebellion died as soon as it started. Gangapati II and Gargi reached Varnash by forced marches, but the picture was not so grim. Dasaswamedha and many others were sheltered in the fort and tribal attacks were only just gaining in strength.

Young Gangapati II repulsed all the attacks. Peace was restored in Varnash. Gargi shuddered at the carnage. Gangapati II was neither as cautious nor as merciful as his father. But she consoled herself—where was the time to plan the defence? Where was the scope for mercy against ruthless raiders? And he was so young! Again, she spoke to him of his mother's dream of unity and the oneness for which his father struggled. She protected many from his wrath—even the tribal Chief who was caught. 'Your father protected him once. Let him be under your protection,' she said. The Chief was allowed to go back unharmed to resume ruling over his tribe. But he tarried, until he received permission to enter the fort and touch the feet of the idol whom he and all the tribals regarded as the idol of their god. There, at the feet of the idol, he took an oath never to threaten Varnash again, whatever be the compulsions against him; also, to the surprise of all, he declared Gangapati II the overlord of his land.

Overlord! Gangapati II laughed. But not Gargi. Nor would she allow anyone else to laugh. 'You are the overlord,' she emphatically told him, 'not only of the lands to the east of Kashi, but of all lands around Hari Hara Dwara, Prayaga, Kashi and elsewhere.' She then spoke to him about what 'overlordship' meant—not to seek imperial power or lustful ambition but to protect and serve people, never to be a server of wrong but to be just in all ways, ardent in piety and eager for justice, and to lead people to be courageous in adversity, prudent in decision, fearless, temperate and honourable, and to remember 'that while no man may lord over you, God does, and His law must be obeyed.'

'But my father was never called an overlord!' he protested.

'Everyone knew in their hearts that he was the overlord!'

Thoughtfully, he changed the subject. 'I am glad the Chief swore never to suffer from the ambition to control Varnash.'

'His ambitions are far greater,' Gargi said, with a knowing smile. 'What! Treachery! Again?' Gangapati asked.

Gargi smiled again, 'No, he wants you to marry his daughter.'

He shook his head as if to say no. She nodded as if to say yes. 'Surely, Gargi ma,' he said, 'the final decision to marry is mine.' 'To speak, yes. To determine no,' Gargi replied.

'Funny kind of overlord I am, that I cannot even choose my own wife! My father chose his own!'

'Your father was alone, an orphan. Are you an orphan?'

No, he always said, Gargi was to him both father and mother. She hugged him to her bosom and told him not to worry; she had not yet seen the girl, nor discovered all that needed to be discovered.

Later, the Chief visited Varnash with his daughter. Gargi was charmed by her but more so, Gangapati II. 'Patience!' Gargi urged. And a decision to exchange marriage vows later in the year was reached.

Gargi's one wish remained—to witness Ganga's source before she died. Gangapati II joked, 'No, if you have to die, I won't take you there. Who else will guide the overlord!' She smiled, 'I promise you, I shall not die at Ganga's source.'

The trip had however to wait, until they were both satisfied with the arrangements for the defence of Hari Hara Dwara, Kashi and Prayaga, if any contingency arose. At last, he escorted her to the source of the Ganga. Hundreds joined them in their pilgrimage.

Gargi kept her promise. She did not die at Ganga's source as it leapt from the face of the glacier high in the Himalayas. 'This is a moment to live eternally,' she said.

But she died, after their return journey, about 2, 250 feet below the source of the Ganga.

Many names were given to the spot where Gargi breathed her last. Some called it Gargitri, others called it Gangoisthri (the lady of Ganga —as Gargi came to be known) or Gargi Gangoisthri (Gargi, the lady of Ganga), but later it came to be known simply as Gangotri.

Gargi's last words to Gangapati were—'Be you a rememberer of Kashi and protector of Ganga from mouth to mouth!' What she simply meant was to 'protect the land of Ganga from its source to destination'. The source of Ganga is in the glacial ice cave known as Gaimukh or Gomukh and the destination, of course, would be the other mouth, where Ganga finally rests, on her journey through Varnash and beyond, even though Gargi herself did not know where that other mouth (or destination) would be, or if it would ever be found.

From the spot where Gargi was cremated, Gangapati II went— some say, alone—back to Gaimukh to sprinkle Gargi's ashes there. But not all; the rest he intended to sprinkle at the other mouth, if ever he found it in his lifetime. Those ashes he left in the safekeeping of Dasaswamedha and his instructions were clear—

'Sprinkle them, when my day is done;
Hers and mine, at Kashi, as one. . .'

On his journey back, his mind was on Gargi. Truly, she had been both father and mother to him, as he had been fond of saying. His own mother, Kashi, he recalled lovingly but remotely, though her words of love were always repeated to him. His father! How little was the time they spent together! For his father had always been surrounded by people or in the throes of a siege or rushing from place to place. Rarely were they together and he had always kept him away from battle. When he was finally caught in the furious battles of Hari Hara Dwara, he overheard with a shudder his father's question to Gargi— 'Does my son love to shed blood?' And he also overheard Gargi's defence —'No, he does what must be done—and he has the courage to do it. He is his mother's son and yours—to keep your dream alive.'

And he remembered how in an overflow of affection, he had once asked, 'Gargi ma, how is it that you never married my father when my mother was no more?' She was about to strike him but her hand rested on her heart, as a wistful, faraway look came into her eyes. Softly, she said 'Time! Who knows what steps it keeps!' He did not understand her and she added, 'But we were always joined in spirit— perhaps as you and I are!' He had seen the hurt in her eyes and heard the sigh in her words.

He also remembered Gargi's explanation of an overlord—it was not to lord over people but to be their first social servant—to protect them, to serve them, to fulfill their needs, to bring them together and to ensure that Chiefs and Council Elders governed righteously. He even recalled her growing dissatisfaction with the word 'overlord', though initially she had adopted it eagerly, on the basis of the declaration of the Chief of the eastern tribe. Instead of overlord, she had coined an entirely new title for him—Mahasammatta Raja—'the great Chosen One Who pleases God and Man'.[3]

Gangapati laughed whenever Gargi said that he be named Mahasammatta Raja. But the last laugh belonged to Gargi—only she was not around.

Gargi's plans had been well-laid. As soon as she and Gangapati left for their pilgrimage to the Ganga's source, the Council Elders of Kashi promptly called a meeting of all the townspeople. The decision was clear and unanimous. Gangapati was to be their Mahasammatta Raja (the great chosen raja or king). Kashi sabha had invited leading

---

[3]In its origin, raja may have meant one who pleases God and man—possibly derived from the verb 'ranjayati' which means 'he pleases'. A poet however says that Gargi was not thinking of the verb 'ranjayati'. Gargi had been brought up by her grandmother Raji. Out of love for her, Gargi had named her only son Raja. Unhappily, both her son and her husband died in the same incident and it was with the memory of her undying love for her son that she thought of the new title—Mahasammatta Raja. This dispute on title-etymology apart, what Gargi clearly had in view was that the raja would be chosen by the people and it would be the people's pleasure to bring in the raja and their pleasure to part with him.

citizens from Prayaga and Hari Hara Dwara and they too, on their return, organized their own meetings. The decision there was the same.

But this was not all. At Hari Hara Dwara, they not only elected Gangapati as raja but also set up for the first time, sabha.

A messenger was sent to the Chief of the eastern tribe, informing him of the honour that had been conferred on the Gangapati who was to marry his daughter. The Chief's response was that 'every man, woman and child here too accepts and honours Gangapati as raja of all our lands and beyond.'

Gangapati returned from Gaimukh. He was about to reject their submission to him but their last words silenced him—'It was as Gargi wished it. . .her last wish. . . .'

But even his reluctant 'acceptance' speech would lead to a later question. A poet quotes him to say -

'Your battles, you yourself must fight:
For my own hands shall remain tied tight.'

What did he mean? Some said he expected greater valour from the people when fighting their battles, and not just when he reached the battle-field. Others held that he wanted no bloodshed, but would follow his father's tactic of patient siege or winning his opponents with love. Maybe, only one poetess—Vidyapatni—singing some 2,000 years later (3560 BC) was close to the mark when she said, 'Conjecture it may be—for who am I to speak with certainty of what lies in another's heart—but I do believe that Gangapati II, the first to be called a raja, was always haunted by his father's fearful observation—"Does my son like to see the colour of another's blood?"—and Raja recalled how violent were the battles he had fought, and how freely the blood flowed in those—and he asked himself, "Am I then seduced by violence? And does violence excite me to greater violence?"—and he realized that violence was not his mother's legacy, nor his father's, nor of mother Gargi.'

Poetess Vidyapatni of Kashi also sheds light on another aspect to say, 'But then across these twenty centuries other rulers heard of Gangapati's observation that people must fight their battles, themselves. And the rulers saw the wisdom of those words. No longer then would the rulers charge to the forefront but would direct battles from behind, afraid not so much of the violence they may do unto others, but fearful of the violence that might be done to their person, if forward they personally advanced. And thus it was that the brave words of Gangapati made cowards of them all, for they heard simply the shell of the words, and saw not the spirit that inspired that utterance.'

Poetess Vidyapatni goes on to give more information about other rulers who followed the practice of remaining behind their troops and adds, 'And yet to continue the myth that their spirits were always in the forefront, the ruler's personal horse would move, riderless, far ahead of its troops, and the horse was free to roam or rest as he chose, and the troops expected merely to follow; for how else could they sustain the myth of the horse holding the spirit of the ruler! Should the horse, then, enter the land of another and its people not block its path, they were assumed to have surrendered to the ruler himself, to accept his overlordship. But if they moved to detain or capture the horse, it would be regarded as a challenge to fight. Naturally, the rulers were wise and would take no chances with the wayward whims of an unthinking horse who might stray into a land far more powerful. It fell therefore to the lot of many to render one route barren and bleak with boulders blocking the way, while the other route would have food and water troughs and, miraculously, even a mare ahead to entice the stallion. If the stallion refused to be enticed away, the priest accompanying the heroic fighters would confer and decide that the horse had surrendered the spirit of the ruler to another stallion; and after due ritual and ceremony, it would be the task of another stallion to continue, though it had to be ensured that in appearance, size and colour, the two horses be indistinguishable from each other.'

Gangapati II married the daughter of the Chief of the eastern tribe. The Chief invited, for the festivities, every chief from all over. He was simply being cautious, aware as he was of the time-honoured custom that none who is invited will attack during the half-year of festivities of the wedding of the first daughter's first wedding. Many chiefs came. Even the Chief of the First Tribe sent his younger brother—the one who had been captured and released by Brahmadatta at Hari Hara Dwara. 'When can we have lasting peace?' Gangapati II asked him, and he spoke of his own roots, and of his mother Kashi who had belonged to the people of the First Chief. 'Please convince your brother that I am one of your people, of your own blood. All we seek is a word from him that there shall be no more attacks against us.'

The Chief's brother was silent. Gangapati added, 'Your father assured us peace in his lifetime. He kept his word.' The Chief's brother replied, 'My father was a man of honour.' Their eyes met and he said no more. The message to Gangapati was clear. He had no influence over his brother and the attacks on Hari Hara Dwara would probably not cease.

> 'Let none be idle; hear ye the call!
> Marital bliss for Raja, martial arts for all!'

That was how someone snickered at Gangapati II's order. On returning from his wedding, Gangapati decided that Hari Hara Dwara should be turned into an armed camp—strong, invulnerable, inviolable. He was convinced that the First Tribe had aggressive designs.

Promptly then he went to Prayaga where he had left his bride.

The burden to fortify did not fall just on the people of Hari Hara Dwara. Gangapati II had brought contingents from his father-in-law's land, from Kashi and Prayaga, to assist them. There was even a complaint from the veterans of Hari Hara Dwara—'We protected our city often before; why do we need outsiders?' 'No,' said Gangapati, 'there are no outsiders here. The land of Ganga is one, indivisible.'

But he himself left for Prayaga! Why? Some said it was customary for newly-weds to seek privacy. But many held that he simply wanted his people to be self-reliant; others argued: why have a raja if you have to be self-reliant? Some hoped that the raja would appear if a crisis developed, but many asked—'Is he a god or a Garuda bird that he will fly the distance from Prayaga?'

But whatever the reason for Gangapati's absence, the fact remains that defensive preparations went far beyond the plan he had left with the commander.

When Gangapati II visited and pronounced the arrangements 'perfect', the commander said, 'Yes, until they can be improved.' Gangapati embraced him.

The First Tribe attacked. Gangapati II arrived three days later. But the attack was long over. It had lasted no more than a day and the raiders had been routed. How many of our people died—was Gangapati's first question; and the commander, who had lost only twenty-four men, said, 'We lost twenty-four more than we should have.' For, after all, in the words of the commander, 'a heroic battle is that in which the heroes do not die.'

It was the commander himself who died in the next battle. Gangapati II, watching from a distance, raced to take over command, at the fall of the commander. But the raiders were already fleeing. Somehow, the Ganga forces had come to adopt the commander's slogan 'In us, we trust.'

*

The commander was given a hero's funeral, though his own cry had been, 'God! Give us no heroes; simply bless us with those who will do their job well, or even half-well.'

At the commander's cremation, Gangapati II reached several conclusions—that it is not wise to protect only defensively; that one must enter and even remain in the land of those that feel tempted to attack; that it is not enough to rely only on volunteers to defend or attack; that fortifications must be kept constantly in repair and readiness.

Months later, he was ready to move against the First Tribe. He marched, though on that day his wife gave birth to a son. 'Better to start a journey on this auspicious day, when the stars are in the right configuration,' he said. It was a carefree remark made in a happy mood over the great event of the birth of his son. Later, he even clarified that whenever something good and great happened, the stars found themselves in an excellent configuration—and not the other way round.

Finally, he said that the stars were never improperly placed and a person must do whatever he must do, whenever he must do it. However, the fact is that many continue to hold Gangapati II responsible for the widespread belief in the configuration of stars before starting a journey or a campaign.

Gangapati II intended no more than a short probe into the land of the First Tribe—not to strike or to wound decisively, but merely to serve notice that he was ready to attack with serious intent unless their Chief stopped his mischief. But nobody obstructed his advance. Villages, as he passed through, did not come out to welcome him but there was no show of hostility, no anger, once they were assured that they would not be molested.

As Gangapati's forces moved forward, they carried four prisoners. But all the four were his own men, who had, without provocation, tried to harass the villagers of the First Tribe. A priest accompanying his forces protested over their continued imprisonment. Gangapati agreed to release them and allow them to return to Hari Hara Dwara. 'How will they go back, on their own, through this alien land?' asked the priest. But Gangapati replied, 'You can accompany them if you wish.' The priest no longer interested himself in the subject. And none dared ignore Gangapati's message, 'These tribals here are our people. Harm them and you will be harmed more.'

Gangapati had come as far as he wanted in search of an elusive enemy outpost in the territory of the First Tribe. He wished to go no further—for he had to have Hari Hara Dwara within easy reach in case he was forced to retreat. He had planned on a campaign of four months, though only two months had passed.

Should he go back? What would he show for all this effort of bringing a huge force with cartloads of provisions and arms! He had no intention of burning tribal villages, nor looting them—even if they had something worth looting, which they did not.

But then the decision was made for him. At first, it was just a feeling that covertly from a distance, hidden in the underbrush, enemy eyes were watching. Later, quite openly, a few horsemen emerged from behind the hills, only to ride furiously away, as soon as his army came into view. He was certain that he was within striking distance of an enemy outpost. Confidently, he rode beyond the hills. But there he saw a sight that startled him. Spread out in the valley below was a vast, unending mass of tribal troops. 'My God,' he said to himself, 'it is like an ocean.' He rode back to his camp and sent out scouts. They saw tribal lookouts on the return route. This, then, he realized was not the time to go forward or retreat. He decided to dig into a defensive position and wait for a better opportunity.

Nearly a fortnight was to pass before the tribal attack materialized. Meanwhile, the tribesman were gathering openly and Gangapati's men were sweating day and night to dig trenches, erect earthworks and put up barriers.

Two palanquins arrived among the tribals amidst much pomp and ceremony. On that very day, the tribal attacks began in waves, one after another. They were repulsed. Gangapati's casualities were few, for his men were well and securely dug in. The tribal losses were many and their disfigured corpses lay along the route of attack. But it could not be a matter of grave concern for the tribals when their army was swelling day by day with new arrivals!

From the tribal prisoners who had been captured he learnt that the two palanquins had brought the Chief of the First Tribe, his son, their wives, even his granddaughter.

'But why bring women and children to the battle site?' he asked. The chilling answer the prisoners gave was that the Chief regarded this not as a battle but a sporting event—'he is simply teasing you, tickling you, playing with you, by sending out a few sorties, before his entire army moves in for the final kill.'

Gangapati had only himself to blame. He had miscalculated enormously. He had come merely to strike an armed outpost of tribals —to serve as a warning to them for the future. He had had no idea of the massive numbers he would have to face; nor had he expected that the Chief of the First Tribe himself would gather his entire army to halt him. All the stories he had heard of the First Chief spoke of his never leaving his own palace, much less his own town; but then he realized that those were stories about the last Chief.

Gangapati's second miscalculation was even more serious. He should have retreated before the two palanquins arrived. No one would have halted him, then. Obviously the First Chief had wanted to be present at the kill.

To Gangapati, it was clear that even if every arrow that his men released achieved a fatal aim, and if every sword and spear killed a hundred tribals, the enemy would still have enough to trample over them. True, tribal sorties, so far, had been disorganized, wavering, faltering and uncertain, as if their hearts were not in the attack; but how much organization does such a massive unending force need!

The tribal attacks suddenly ceased. The long lull brought no comfort to Gangapati; he realized that until then the tribals sorties had been sent out only to probe and play; but now they were getting ready for the final blow.

Rain was pouring down in sheets. Tents were put up in the enemy camp for the Chief's party and even large canopies were erected to protect the fires on which were being roasted goats and other animals for the Chief's food. 'Meanwhile, we live like rats,' Gangapati thought. But he had no intention of dying like a rat.

At night, with two hundred men and many spare horses, he left the camp, leaving the rest behind, with a brief farewell, 'Live to fight for us,' he said.

'We will live to die for you,' they said. And the poet tells us that 'none of them knew who would die first—they that remained or those that left, but each prayed for the other.'

Cautiously, stealthily, holding their horses by the bridle, Gangapati and his men struck a pathless route to the far left through the tall grass. This was not the route for retreat nor for going forward and no tribal lookouts were on the watch. Even so, the only noise that Gangapati's men made was to slash through the tall, thorny growth which blocked their way. But the noise of the rain was far louder.

Keeping to the west of their camp, they went as far as they could. The next morning was cloudless. Now they had to creep, for even the grass was tall only in patches and offered little cover for the men and much less for the horses. Suddenly, their hearts were in their mouths and their spears were at the ready for they heard a rustle in the grass and a shout. But it was only a tribal youth with his girl, seeking a private moment of love. They had to take them along as prisoners, lest they gave out their movement to the others. All Gangapati promised them was, 'If we live, you will live; and we will try to leave you in safety with a horse and much more, well before we face danger.'

The initial fright of the boy and girl was soon over and instead they were simply curious. They had escaped from their village in search of a better place. They did not know that they were so near the zone of battle where their own Chief was camped. Even more strangely, they did not seem to care whether their Chief won or lost. 'One Chief or another! What difference!' was their attitude.

The two youngsters advised Gangapati about the villages that lay en route. Their own village lay ahead. To avoid that, he decided to go north, but not too far, lest he was discovered by enemy eyes. He went a little distance, then turned east, to avoid a direct line to the villages, and finally he turned north; there too he made several detours, to avoid other villages, on the advice of the youngsters.

At last, Gangapati and his men reached a spot from which the Chief's camp was visible.

All the while, Gangapati prayed for rain so that their movements would remain hidden, but the clouds remained tantalizingly dry. He knew that on horseback they could cover the distance to the tribal camp in a few hours. But discovery, then, was certain, and death, inevitable.

They plodded on at night on foot, resting and fretting during the day. After what seemed an eternity, they reached within striking distance of the hour's ride.

Nobody was looking out for them. But clearly they were too late.

It was an hour before dawn and they saw tribal horsemen in massive waves, followed by unending lines of foot soldiers, tearing down towards their camp in the south. The entire tribal army was on the move.

The gamble had failed. All that Gangapati had hoped for was to attack the tribal camp suddenly, create a diversion, ride, run, slash, hack, strike and sell their lives dearly, so that his men left behind in the camp below, could retreat quickly and quietly, while tribal attention was totally focused on this sudden, senseless diversion. 'Let them sit back to celebrate their victory with our deaths,' Gangapati had said, 'and let them believe that they have annihilated the entire Ganga army, so that our retreating men go unpursued and unharmed.'

Long before he had left his camp, many had felt that it would be a foolish gamble and he had said, 'All gambles are foolish but, who knows, a fool may be lucky sometimes!'

Where was the alternative! Either they all sat back and died together in the camp as they must or they took this insane gamble so that some of them might survive. It would be a slender chance—a wind-blown straw in the midst of a raging river—but that is all they could cling to.

There were claps of thunder and the rain pelted down as Gangapati saw masses of tribal horse and foot soldiers almost half-way to his camp which he had left, days ago, to create a diversion. But the diversion had no hope now. I must rush to the camp, he thought—let us all die together in the camp. No longer was he afraid of being seen. No longer did he want to take a devious route back to the camp. Straight—in a direct line—he wanted to rush, with the fury of madness, to die along with his comrades at the camp. At least he would have the chance of riding at the flank of attacking tribals. He barked his command. His men mounted. He halted only a moment to give a horse to the girl and boy they had brought along, with all the things he had in the saddle, 'If ever you are in the land of Ganga, tell them that I died with love for them all.'

Furiously, he and his men began their ride towards the camp. The fog was getting thicker. He hoped to reach the tribal flank, unseen. But suddenly he reined in his horse. The horse pulled up with a jolt; many horsemen behind lost their balance. The fog from his mind lifted and he now realized what he must do. His camp, he realized, was beyond help. To die with them would be of no avail.

Gangapati shouted his order. His men could hardly see through the enveloping fog. In a blinding, tearing hurry, they changed direction, to rush not to their own camp, but towards the tents and canopies of the First Chief, even though they could not see them. But they were no longer two hundred, as twelve of them, unaware of his new order, were already speeding in a mad rush to the tribal flank on its way to their camp.

The 188 men with Gangapati now saw the bare outline of the Chief's tent. They did nothing to hide themselves and as Gangapati would later say, 'God was at work,' though actually it was the fog at work and the rain, that drowned the noise of their horse-hooves. They saw no one—neither the Chief nor his courtiers—and their javelins and spears flew and their swords were at the ready.

The Chief of the First Tribe was dead. His son was wounded. The women and children with them were unhurt. The Chief's fifteen courtiers died instantly.

Later, everyone would credit Gangapati with the foreknowledge that tribal troops always had to maintain their distance, to remain away from their Chief and his entourage, and never even lift their eyes to see the Chief's women. They would even credit Gangapati with a vision that pierced through the thickest fog to enable him to unerringly reach the Chief's tent, avoiding the heavy tribal guard that stood three hundred feet ahead and behind the Chief.

Much of what happened in that swift, sudden assualt on the Chief's tent would remain a blur. Gangapati denied being the first to throw his spear. No one heard his order to head for the tent. Instead, in excitement or panic, many simply started throwing their spears at the tent, long before they saw the outline of any person in that fog. Gangapati denied that it was his spear that had killed the Chief. Actually, his spear—distinctive from the rest—had hit the goat that was about to be slaughtered by the cook for the Chief's mid-morning meal.

Nobody knew how eight men of the Gangapati contingent had died in that one-sided mêlée, when not a single tribal had lifted arms. Obviously, it was the tragedy of mistaken identity and they were killed, unwittingly, by their own men.

Did the fog lift then, so that the tribal guard saw their dead Chief and heard the command of the Chief's wounded son to surrender! Or did Gangapati take the son, with a sword-point at his throat, to the tribal guard to call on them to throw away their arms! The versions vary. The facts are however clear. The tribal guard surrendered on the orders of the Chief's son, who himself was, henceforth, the Chief. The commander of the tribal guard was dispatched, along with a whole lot of others, to halt the attack on Gangapati's camp below. They reached too late. Everyone in the camp was dead, their bodies hacked to pieces.

Later, many said that each man of Ganga in the camp killed a hundred tribals but the tribals were a thousand to one. The twelve men of Ganga who had failed to hear Gangapati's order and had raced headlong towards the camp, were also killed on the way.

One incontrovertible fact, however, was that Gangapati and his one hundred and eighty men were the sole survivors of the huge army that had marched from Ganga. Their victory was total. The entire army of the First Tribe had surrendered.

But a poet exaggerates when he speaks of the surge of supreme self-confidence that Gangapati II felt at this moment of victory. In actual fact he was wondering how long he would be able to survive with his one hundred and eighty men in this hostile land! Would he have to carry the Chief's son at dagger-point to Hari Hara Dwara! The son was bound to die on the way. Already, he was showing signs of weakness from his wound, though three tribal Vaids were in attendance on him. But how can one recover from a serious wound, when confusion, shame, terror, and rage alternate at being commanded by an outsider!

His father's death was not too difficult for the Chief to cope with. That made him the Chief. But what kind of Chief! To be the mouthpiece of an alien barbarian!

Gangapati was certain that this new Chief's promise of safe-conduct to him was a sham. He was sure of a murderous assault, the moment he left the Chief. Yet he wanted the Chief to live, for he alone could order the tribals. Who would otherwise listen to Gangapati, except his own one hundred and eighty men! Gangapati demanded the presence of the dead Chief's brother whom he had met at his marriage festivities.

'He was in disgrace with my father,' the new Chief replied.

'Then remove the disgrace! You are the Chief,' Gangapati ordered.

'It will take time. He is far away.'

'I have time,' Gangapati said ominously. 'But do you?'

The Chief commanded his guard. The dead Chief's brother arrived the next day. He came as a prisoner, with his hands tied. Gangapati had failed to explain his intent clearly. He apologized.

'A conqueror has rights,' the Chief's brother said. But later, he relented when Gangapati explained the circumstances.

'I want you to be the Chief of the First Tribe,' Gangapati told him.

'That right is not mine,' the brother replied.

'I shall see to it that the new Chief abdicates in your favour.'

'That right is not his,' said the brother.

'Why?' Gangapati asked.

'He has no right to abdicate. . . .'

'But if he dies?'

'Even if he dies, or if you kill him, the right is not mine. It belongs to his son.'

'But he has no son! Only a daughter!' Gangapati countered.

'Hopefully, he will have a son,' the brother said. Gangapati understood, at last, that the new Chief's wife was expecting a child.

He asked, 'Assume it is a son. Can an infant be Chief?'

'Yes. All his father has to do is appoint a regent to administer for him until he reaches the age of fifteen.' The brother added, 'Even if it is a daughter, the eldest daughter becomes the Chief-in-waiting, to be married at the age of thirteen, and her first son becomes the Chief, while the Regent administers on behalf of the daughter, and later for her son, until the age of fifteen.'

Gangapati's head was reeling. Still he said, 'So be it. You be the Regent, then, if the Chief dies.'

'It is for the Chief to appoint a Regent. Why will he appoint me?'

'He will,' Gangapati said grimly.

Their eyes met; the brother said, 'If you get me appointed as Regent by threatening the Chief, or by spilling his blood, I cannot accept.'

'I have no intention of spilling his blood. He is near death's door, as it is. But I must insist that he appoints you as Regent.'

'Then I do not accept.'

'I am in command here,' Gangapati barked. 'I can have you killed.'

'Your mother and father could have had me killed years ago, when I was captured at Hari Hara Dwara. Perhaps, it is only fair and fitting that I die by your hands.'

'You do not understand me,' said Gangapati. 'Sadly, my choice is limited. I may have to threaten the Chief—but only with words—to appoint you as Regent, in case of his death, which I fear is imminent. If you do not accept the appointment, what is my alternative? To kill the Chief before he dies on his own, to kill his living daughter, to kill his wife who is bearing his child, and maybe even his mother and everyone else who is in the line of succession to the Chief! You alone shall live, to carry the guilt of their death, to your dying day!'

It was now the brother who pleaded, 'Do not carry the blood of innocents on your head! What will it avail you, if you leave our tribe in chaos, trauma and travail, leaderless, unguided, so they turn on each other in a bath of blood. How can you contemplate such savagery!'

'Because,' said Gangapati, pitilessly, 'you leave me no choice.'

The brother reached a decision. He agreed to be Regent, if the Chief so decided, provided the Chief died on his own, while receiving every care and attention to get well. Nothing more was said to prevent Gangapati from making a simple threat to the Chief.

The Chief declared solemnly, in the presence of his wife, the Chief Priest, courtiers, commanders and others that in the case of his death, his uncle, the late Chief's brother, would be Regent. The brother took an oath, on his life and honour, to perform the duties of the Regent, and knelt before the Chief in a token of submission. They all knelt, each wishing the Chief a long life.

A long life, however, the Chief did not have. He lasted nine more days, despite every care for his health and comfort.

Gangapati II left for Hari Hara Dwara with a hundred and eighty men. Was it a triumphant return? They had lost more men in this campaign than in all the battles that he and his father had fought. But then, everyone said that only great risks and losses can lead to great victories and achievements. Had he not secured permanent peace with the First Tribe? Was he not now the overlord and raja of the dreaded First Tribe! But those that said this were not accurate. Peace he had secured, though not as their overlord nor as their raja. The unborn Chief's uncle, who was now the Regent, had said to him plainly, 'Our tribe has never been reduced to subjection. Nor has it ever violated its pledged word. All I can promise you is friendship, respect and peace from my tribe, in return for yours.' Gangapati sought no more.

Later the bond between the First Tribe and the people of Ganga grew. There was peace in the valley of Ganga—and prosperity.

The late Chief's wife gave birth to a son.

Fourteen years later, the peaceful reign of the Regent was over and the son took over, in law and fact, as Chief of the First Tribe, amidst pomp and ceremony. Peace continued.

The new Chief of the First Tribe made one, single, imperative demand from the people of Ganga—that Gangapati's daughter marry him. But then this was also the demand of Gangapati's daughter and many said that the boy and the girl had even exchanged marriage vows on their own, in their quiet meetings during Gangapati's visits to the First Tribe and the Regent's visits to Ganga, when the children had accompanied them. So who could object! But Gangapati's wife did and clearly said, 'Their own marriage vows do not make a marriage!' She relented only after her demand was met and the Chief took an oath to outlaw multiple marriage not only for himself but also for his successors.

*

Ever since his return from his triumph over the First Tribe, Gangapati II was sure of one thing—that of all the foolish enterprises of man, the enterprise of war was the most foolish. And the only way he knew to avoid war was to build up strength so that no one was tempted to attack his people. He realized that only a brain-dead imbecile would have faith in the word of neighbouring tribes—and to be weak was to tempt an attack and invite disaster, particularly when so many of their tribesmen, with uncertain loyalties, were living in their midst.

He demanded forts and defensive works to be built all over. He insisted on improvements in weapons—and to pile them number upon number, weight upon weight. He organized drills and displays of speed and strength—in archery, horse-riding, chariot-races, spear-throw, yoga —and to these spectacles, he invited chiefs from far and near. To entertain? Yes, but the might was there for all to see and the warning was there—unspoken.

Spared from attacks, the land of Ganga became green, lush, fertile. Some said that but for the futile expense on forts and battle-exercises, it would have been far more prosperous.

Gangapati II's first son, who was born on the day he left to invade the First Tribe, was already being called Gangapati III. His daughter, who later married the Chief of the First Tribe, was born a year later. Always, Gangapati II said, 'I want peace for my children.' But no one misunderstood; he wanted peace for his people—and all people everywhere.

There were some who said that Dasaswamedha 'stole' defensive walls and forts built at Kashi under Gangapati II's order. However all that Dasa did was to set up temples within and behind those walls.

'Give people not only empty walls but something more to protect,' said Dasa to the local commander who protested about this misuse. But these temples were no temples either. Everyone who entered there was certainly free to pray—and many did, though initally they were confused by the different idols and varying forms of worship and rituals. This bewildering variety arose as Dasa encouraged into these temples, not only locals but many from the First Tribe, his own tribe and the tribes beyond—not so much to pray as to paint, sculpt, chisel, and carve. While the artists worked, the temple-dancers danced and the worshippers sang. And many came in then to entertain and be entertained—and often everyone participated in sheer joy and there was no entertainer but only entertainment.

Again, the local commander protested—is it a fort, a temple, an art-gallery, a theatre—what? But Gangapati II approved so long as the fort-structure remained unharmed. Also, Gangapati enticed the best singers and dancers from these fort-temples for his spectacles, organized annually to entertain chiefs from far and near.

These spectacles then, took on the character of festivals at which songs, dances and costumes drew their inspiration not from Kashi alone but from a treasure-house of the myths and legends of countless tribes. And, the poet tells us, with joy, that ever since then, the art of Ganga was 'never the same,' and he calls it 'a mosaic—rich and colourful—in which the creative genius of the people of the Ganga assimilated and refined a multitude of the artistic impulses and rhythms of a hundred tribal lands.'

Thus a common tradition of song, art and dance evolved in Ganga and all the tribal lands around; and a poet described it as a 'brilliant blend in which much was absorbed but little set aside—and yet never uniform for departures were many and innovations many more.'

A poet clarifies that it was always Gangapati II's hope that one day he would be able to go along the course of the Ganga river, to discover where the Ganga rested.

Many said that the treaties of friendship and peace that Gangapati II entered into with various tribal chiefs were intended to make his passage safe along the course of the Ganga. Others said—nonsense, he wanted peace simply for the sake of peace.

His friendship with the tribal chiefs did help to make Gangapati's passage safe and smooth, at least initially. He was known as the overlord of the First Tribe though that was not strictly true. He was simply a friend and ally and also the father-in-law of the Chief of the First Tribe. Besides, the Chief of the eastern tribe was his own father-in-law; and many tribes beyond were tied to him with treaties of friendship.

It was a journey that was to have three hundred people embarking on it—a hundred each from three regions—Hari Hara Dwara, Prayaga and Varnash. But it began with more than two thousand. They could not be held back. Meanwhile, large contingents arrived from the First Tribe to join them. Many joined them not only from the eastern tribe, but beyond.

Some left, when the rigours of the journey proved too harsh, but others joined in their place. The result is that nobody knows exactly how many there were. All that is known is that over 1,800 reached the mouth of the Ganga with Gangapati II.

Poets do describe the journey but only sketchily. They speak of the enthusiasm with which the pilgrims went. Pilgrims? It was like an army on the march. The entire surrounding plain appeared to be in motion with men, horses, baggage carts, pack-animals, and even bullocks and elephants—with vast quantities of provisions and foodstuff for this journey into the unknown. Tribals added even herds of cattle, 'but only for milk—for Gangapati's command was clear that none should eat flesh of animal or fowl while on this auspicious pilgrimage. . . .'

If there were soldiers in this huge group, the poets do not say so, for they speak of it as a pilgrimage. Yet at times, they do refer to the 'four hundred guardians.' Maybe, these were the four hundred battle-hardened veterans that Gangapati II took; for the poets speak not only of the friendship but also the 'awe' that these 'guardians' inspired. In any case, the vast number of pilgrims was protection enough, though its very bulk and mass was unwieldy, rendering it difficult to move fast.

Poets speak of vast deserts, swamps, mountains and forests on the way. They speak of many rivers that came to meet Ganga in 'loving and reverent confluence' (particularly those that came to be known as Gandak, Bari Gandak, Kosi, Son and Mahananda).

Later poets speak of their bewilderment at the Ganga branching off in two directions, 'but Gangapati led us on.' Nobody clarifies how Gangapati was able to lead them in two different, diverse directions. Could it be that he led in one direction and doubled back to lead in the other? Or is it that he headed in one direction, leaving someone else to lead in the other, though the poet is clear that 'Gangapati was with us all, each angula of the way.'

The poets also speak of mighty Brahmaputra's homage (as tributary) to the Ganga. But of this they speak fleetingly, and all their awe and wonder is reserved for the innumerable channels and streams into which the Ganga flows—but many clarify that too, to say that those streams were not innumerable—they were 'exactly one hundred and eight—the one hundred and eight mouths of Ganga,' that led to Gangasagarsangam (confluence of Ganga with the sea).

Little is said by the poets, thereafter, about the journey itself, as though nothing else mattered, or would ever matter; and all the efforts and energies of the poets were concentrated on the myriad mouths of the Ganga and the magical meeting of the river and the sea.

However, they do mention that Gangapati II and all those who accompanied him bowed to Tiratha Da, the Sadhu who in Brahmadatta's time (Gangapati I) left Hari Hara Dwara to wander the land. Tiratha Da had built a temple on the tiny island near Gangasagarsangam. There were four locals who were devotees at the temple. But Tiratha Da and these devotees quickly left to 'visit one hundred places during the one hundred years we have'—and it is not clear if sixty-six-year-old Tiratha Da expected to live for another one hundred years or if he was counting the total number of years that all four of them, put together, had.

Nobody knows why Gangapati took six years to return.

The poets even speak of the 'sweet forest (Sunderbans?) where the wildest of animals looked at us with tenderness, as though to bless us while we went our way, on to our luminous path.' While it is not easy to separate fact from fancy, it may well be that they met with no tragic loss of life on the way. Initially, their journey was through the lands of friendly tribes whose chiefs were known to Gangapati; later, they passed through many regions—some without, and others with people; but even in these areas where there were large congregations of people, 'there were no chiefs but only individuals with whom we shared our food, while they sought to gift theirs to us,' which seems to indicate that the locals were not miserable or destitute in the remoter regions which were without chiefs.

Gangapati returned to Varnash from his journey after 2,200 days. Some of his men stayed back near Gangasagarsangam. Even so, he entered Kashi with nearly 3,800 men (numbers are confusing, but apparently many joined him on the way, on his return).

Since his return, many, if not all, began to call Gangapati II the overlord and raja of all the land from Gangasagarsangam. He silenced them, 'I went as a pilgrim and as a pilgrim I returned.'

'Knowledge of ithihasa without feeling is an empty shell. It will not preserve the fire of the past but only its ashes.'

'I would sing of heroes but heroes are no more;
I would sing of men but men are men no more.'

'Civilizations are kept alive only if their knowledge and vision are recreated in people's minds.'

—(Quotations from 'Songs of Munidasi, Dasaswamedha's daughter'—5385 BC)

'One cannot simply wish away the past and adorn it with ornaments of one's choice—and he who forget his ithihasa assumes the peril of robbing his children of their heritage and their future growth.'

—(Attributed to Gangapati XIII—5050 BC)

Knowledge of History without feeling is an empty shell. It
will not preserve the fire of the past but only its ashes.'

I would sing of heroes but heroes are no more;
I would sing of men but men are men no more.'

Civilizations are kept alive only if their knowledge and vision
are recreated in people's minds.

—(Quotations from Songs of Murithael, Dessuamedha's
daughter—5385 BC)

One cannot simply brush away the past and adorn it with
ornaments of one's choice—but he who forgets his lifespan assumes
the peril of robbing his children of their heritage and their future
growth.'

—(Attributed to Gangnath XIII—6050 BC)

Tears and Triumphs at Ganga

5050 BC

Gangapati XIII's mind was on the ithihasa of his ancestors, as he received the sixteen men who were once enslaved by the tribes. Gangapati XIII asked himself: would the tribe ever have dared to hold our people as slaves in the time of Gangapati I or Gangapati II? Never! He remembered how Gangapati II marched 30 yojnas to free a boy snatched by the tribals. Gangapati II lost six men on that sortie and found that the boy had already been killed. But the lesson that Gangapati II left behind for the tribals was so harsh that it remained 'memorable for all those that lived.' No one dared hold a man, woman or child of Ganga as a slave. How then did they reach this sorry pass?

It was Dasaswamedha's daughter who, together with many, had started with the story of Gangapati I and his wife Kashi, though she was born long after their time. She had said that civilizations were kept alive only if their knowledge was recreated in people's minds.

She continued with the story of Gangapati II and went on to recite the lines about the early times of Gangapati III. But suddenly she stopped and her final verse said,

> 'I would sing of heroes but heroes are no more;
> I would sing of men but men are men no more.'

Her associates were critical of her. They felt that it was not their task to judge but merely to relate the story of their times. What would ithihasa be, they asked, if it was coloured by our feelings! And they argued that they must simply pass their knowledge on to others—not their feelings. She said nothing and blessed their efforts to continue, but in her heart she felt that knowledge without feeling was an empty shell. Since then, the group of historians grew from generation to generation, and continued with the story of Gangapati III, and of each Gangapati that followed. It was then an oral tradition, but in the time of Gangapati XI, when the written word began, the ithihasa groups were among the first to use the written language.

Gangapati XIII did not have the heart to continue his reflections on ithihasa. Yet he knew that one could not simply wish away the past and adorn it with the ornaments of one's choice—and he who forgets his ithihasa assumes also the peril of robbing his children of their heritage and their future growth.

Regretfully, he realized that with the end of Gangapati II, the golden age of Ganga ended. A poet said with a smile, how wrong that assessment was! Actually, gold came into the land of Ganga only in and after Gangapati III's time. Gangapati III was reaping the glory of his father but unlike him, he took the title of the Overlord and Raja seriously.

Yet Gangapati III's intentions were pious and honourable. He wanted safety and friendship in all the lands from 'mouth to mouth'— from Gangasagarsangam to Gaimukh. He searched for peace, order and discipline in all the lands around too—not for conquest but for harmony —so that visitors and pilgrims travelled unmolested and their bonds grew through art, trade, common culture and even intermarriage. From songs inspired by his grandmother Kashi, he knew of the single common root of all these tribes which had broken away from each other, not too long ago. Why are we not together then, he asked and felt that the task to bind them together should be his. He was, after all, the undisputed ruler of the land of Ganga around Hari Hara Dwara, Sangam at Prayaga and Kashi. But then he also regarded the land of the eastern tribe as his own. Surely, he thought, my title as Raja of that land comes to me by right of inheritance from my father; besides my own mother was the eldest daughter of the Chief of that tribe. And the First Tribe? He had no doubt that he was its Raja and Overlord too. Did not my father—Gangapati II—conquer it? Is not my baby sister married to the Chief of the First Tribe? Even so, rarely did he utter a word to proclaim himself as its overlord. Sometimes, though, his actions spoke louder than words.

He sent his contingents all the way to Gangasagarsangam. They were welcomed everywhere, for they came with aid and assistance for the locals. Also, they brought gifts that fascinated the locals. His men built huts for the locals as well, to entice them away from their caves. They planted trees and crops with implements that the locals viewed with wonder and awe. All the way to Gangasagarsangam, the countryside was dotted with men from Gangapati III's command. Their task: to build tracks, roads, bridges, huts, rest-houses and even temples to house the idols of the tribals. Local volunteers also began to assist them. At each place, the most helpful tribal was appointed as chief to coordinate all local activity. He was given gifts with the promise of many more to come. The best hut was his. Trees and crops were under his charge so that he distributed fruits and produce among his people fairly. Above all, he was given a horse—a noble animal, rarely seen in those parts. With chiefs in charge, Gangapati III's men passed on, with only an occasional visit to inspect. And they had every reason to be delighted with the progress.

The locals—given a chief when they had never had a chief before—had unmatched enthusiasm and affection for Gangapati III. They had huts, clothes, crops, tools, implements, temples and even a promise of protection against raids from their neighbours. It was as if all their cherished dreams had come true!

But total order and total chaos are seldom apart. And thus it was that many chiefs, invested with control over temples and distribution of necessities, became idle and corrupt, while some degenerated into brutishness and insolence. Gangapati III's men intervened. A system of rewards and punishments for chiefs came into play. Chiefs were made and unmade. Often, this power was exercised by Gangapati III's men at a level well below what he would have wished. But Gangapati III's commanders were much too busy to go into each and every tribal area.

Gangapati III's commanders also learnt something new—that the lower the level of inspectors, the quicker were the results. These low-level men could be as brutish as the worst chiefs themselves; and they dismissed a chief or appointed another with ease, without waiting to see or hear who suffered or what anguish lay behind the scenes. The results were swift and sure and the work went on faster than before and no time was wasted in trying to examine what was fair or just. In fact, so successful were these low-level shakers and movers that soon they were the only ones sent to expedite results.

Gangapati III himself was given only the good and great news of the progress achieved in those remote areas. With great pleasure he would send in more aid to reward local chiefs, who redoubled their efforts to achieve greater progress. And local volunteers, then, were volunteers no more. It was forced labour—just a step away from slavery. Chiefs raged to drive their men to extract the impossible and when that failed, there was the lash and the whip—or much worse. Men, women, boys, girls were caught anywhere, everywhere and brought to work. A cry of terror rang out but the inspectors from Gangapati III's command did not hear it. Among the inspectors were also those who were more concerned with personal pleasure and plunder.

Some reported the rumblings of anguish to Gangapati III. But he was convinced of the moral soundness of his policy. The sufferings of a few, he felt, were temporary but the rewards to fulfil 'the dream everlasting, of unity and oneness, as it was in reality once before, were permanent.' He was quoting from Kashi's song but was disturbed when someone reminded him that Kashi's song was pervaded with love, mercy, tenderness and compassion, based on an age-old Sanathani law. Lamely, he said, 'Each step forward costs an effort and demands a sacrifice; and this I promise, that those that suffer today will be rewarded one day.'

After this, no one spoke of the despair of the tribals far away, but only of the progress achieved, and of the fact that more aid was needed in order to achieve the desired goals.

Gangapati III gave all he could. He requested Chiefs of the eastern tribe and First Tribe for help. Willingly they gave all he asked. His requests multiplied, and later, they ceased to be requests. They were demands—and then, commands—of tributes to a sovereign.

Did Gangapati III have a clear idea of the pitiless suffering he caused? Maybe. But then he had a mission to fulfil and a dream to realize—and his commanders had targets to meet.

Yes, Gangapati III had a gracious mind, tender heart, compassion, deep humility, and honourable intentions. But of what avail all that, when he had wrapped himself in a strange innocence that tolerated the misdemeanours of his commanders and others serving him in the tribal lands!

Yet none really opposed Gangapati III—this pitiless, pious man who lived frugally, spoke elegantly, extended help to all in need—and whose every thought, word and deed was inspired by Kashi's songs. And those songs revived the dream to recapture the unity of the past. All he forgot was that this would not have been Kashi's way of doing things. Can a deed of honour be achieved through means that are without honour?

Even in the time of his successors—Gangapati IV and then on— there was little criticism. In fact, the policy became entrenched—that targets must be met and armies remain ready, always, to march.

It was in Gangapati XI's reign, that finally, it could be said that the entire land from Gangasagarsangam to Gaimukh, including the land of the eastern tribe and First Tribe became one and indivisible, under the direct command of Gangapati. And a poet sang:

'...There is peace everywhere—silent, sullen, desolate. There is prosperity everywhere—but joy nowhere.
....Much is gained that I can touch, feel and see—but something is missing, something lost, something gone, and I know not what, whither and whence!....'

And this poet sang this song at Gangapati XI's court, when they were celebrating the merger of all the lands under one single Ganga banner. How unwise!—said many. But the poet had something to say too—

'...And the seed of wisdom sprouts into a giant tree to darken this view of our sky, and the star that shone brightly before, is no more;
....Did the star fall, to splinter into pieces, or did it go too far above and beyond our vision?
...But why shed tears over an unseen star, when we have no more tears to shed for ourselves and our wisdom!...'

Pity, said some, that this great-grandson of the comic poet of the time of Gangapati I should sing with such irrelevance and irreverence!

Slavery had come to be accepted officially in Gangapati VI's time. But only in the tribal lands. Slaves were not brought to Kashi, Prayaga or Hari Hara Dwara. Only once, a group of thirty-two slaves was brought to Kashi, under Gangapati VI's orders, and more were to follow. Dasaswamedha's great-granddaughter demanded their release. She was refused. She went on a hunger strike. 'What will it achieve?' asked some. 'My death,' she said, calmly.

But on the fifth day of her fast, she was not so calm and said, 'With my death shall die the soul of you all and the soul of this city!' It was a curse and there were few who took it lightly, coming as it did from the keeper of Dasa's temple.

Gangapati VI agreed to send the slaves back to their tribal lands, but she demanded that they be freed forthwith. In a towering rage, Gangapati VI finally agreed to free them and she broke her fast on the eleventh day. Most of these slaves became inmates of Dasa's temple.

But she again went on a fast of thirty-two days—this time against herself—for she said that she had sinned in obtaining the release of slaves by means of a curse that was 'unjust and unjustified, and it arose from my hunger and frustration and not from the voice of the gods.'

She was weak but cheerful after her fast. She ate frugally. But that night, peacefully in her sleep, she died. Strangely—and no one explains why—the curse which she disowned as 'unjust and unjustified' now came to be accepted with full force; and it seemed that everyone agreed that the soul of the city would die, along with their own, if slaves were ever brought in to work there.

But away from Kashi, Prayaga and Hari Hara Dwara, everywhere in the tribal lands under Gangapati VI, right from Gangasagarsangam, slavery was on the rise. And the system continued under each Gangapati thereafter. Hardly anyone knew of the suffering of the slaves, not even Gangapati, for on his rare visits, the slaves were paraded as willing, docile, well-fed though unruly in their conduct and strange in their habits. They even sang songs and danced to entertain not only the Gangapati but all visiting dignitaries. But those were simply 'puppet performances'.

Gangapati XIII could not wave away his recollections of the ithihasa of his ancestors. How firm was their authority and how unchallenged their command! Chiefs from far and near came to bow to a Gangapati and to them his word was law. He made them, he unmade them. And he was always fair, just and even generous. He gave more than he received, for he wanted the tribals to advance 'to higher levels and be one of us, as they were once before.'

Then how did all this change?

Gangapati XIII knew when it began to change, but he did not know why. It was in his grandfather, Gangapati XI's time, that the eastern tribe revolted. The revolt was put down quickly but it erupted again in Gangapati XII's time. The revolts were against their own chiefs. Nor were they popular uprisings but arose from conspiracies of lesser chiefs; yet they challenged the Gangapati's authority as overlord.

The First Tribe also rose in revolt, though no one knew against whom and what. The Chief of the First Tribe was beheaded by his own nephew and since then no one knew who was in charge. Minor new chiefs sprang up like weeds, each to command his own little village.

Gangapati XII's army moved in to bring order to the chaos. An eerie silence followed, but again, more revolts erupted. Revolts over what? Not for freedom, only for power. And more innocents were slaughtered, looted and enslaved than ever before.

But far more disquieting were the disorders all along the route to Gangasagarsangam. People from Kashi, Prayaga, Hari Hara Dwara had moved, from Gangapati III's time, to populate the riverbank of Ganga, right up to the one hundred and eight mouths of Ganga and even to the islands in the sea. They went not on pilgrimage but to settle down, alongside the tribals. For hundreds of years now, they had lived in harmony, married, intermarried, with common customs, language and rituals. Some had even forgotten their contact with Kashi—but not quite—for in their declining years, their footsteps would revert to that city to die and be cremated there, in order to be transported heavenwards!

These people, originally from Kashi and around, were traders, farmers, artisans, artists, teachers, builders, wine-distillers, horse-breeders and tool-makers. Trade caravans moved regularly to and from Kashi and elsewhere to buy and sell their goods. It was their pioneering effort that made the tribal lands fertile. Not only new art forms but many articles of daily necessity and beauty sold in Kashi came from these faraway lands. And there was peace and harmony.

But then, why these sudden riots and revolts? Why these night-raids? Why kill a chief, when there was none coming forward to claim his place! Why this senselessness? To what useless inconsequence? Regular caravans stopped. The flow of trade ceased. Instead, the armies moved in.

But what could the armies achieve? Silence, obedience, order—and after the army moved away, violence, murder, mayhem. How many could the army punish! And were the offenders not always able to hide themselves? Only the fools and innocents suffered, as always.

The riots and revolts multiplied. Gangapati XIII moved in his armies. But he knew how futile it all was. It was a game of hide and seek. Order would be restored at ten places and disorder would erupt in a hundred more.

Nobody remembered that this process of disintegration began long before Gangapati XIII's time. Even in his grandfather, Gangapati XI's time, tribal disorders had become widespread, gathering speed and fury, day by day. In this father's time, they had presented a frightening spectacle.

Yet everyone blamed Gangapati XIII, as if it were all his fault.

But then that was not the only tragedy for which he was held responsible. It was his elder brother who was to be Gangapati. Everyone remembered the charming, smiling, handsome youngster, who jumped over a waterfall and died needlessly, crashing against a rock, in response to his younger brother's shout (in jest) that he was drowning.

The younger brother grew up withdrawn, inward looking, always guilty over his elder brother's death. Nobody ever saw him laugh or smile after the tragic incident. He declined to be trained for his role as Gangapati. His mother died. Some said it was grief over her elder son's death that killed her; others said it was her disappointment over her younger son. His father looked at him with loveless eyes; he found it impossible to forget the image of his favourite son, lost to him. But he had no more sons; and the right to succeed as Gangapati belonged to this ugly boy who stared at the floor all the time and mumbled his replies, keen to leave, not to go to his friends—for he had none—but to be with his blind dog. Even the dog, some said, went blind after it was given to him.

The boy wanted to talk to no one, see no one. If he did not kill himself, maybe it was because he did not wish to leave his dog loveless. Sometimes, he would sit by the side of hermits and munis in the forest. They rarely spoke, and he, never.

His one resolve—never to be Gangapati but to retire as a hermit—faltered, as the years passed. He saw the silent plea in his old father's eyes, shaken as he was by the riots and revolts in tribal lands. This was no time to leave his father without solace and his people, leaderless. A sense of understanding arose between father and son— enough to heal some of the wounds in the son's heart. Perhaps the father too remembered his wife's dying words to be gracious to his last loving son who had an 'entire universe of love buried in his heart.'

His father, Gangapati XII, wished it and so the son got married. His father waited for a grandchild. It was not to be. Some said his wife was barren; others said the husband was incompetent. His father died six years after the son's marriage. The son took over as Gangapati.

Everyone knew of the disasters in the lands far away. They blamed the new Gangapati in their hearts. He accepted all the blame. Never did he shift blame to his father, grandfather or even to his own people in distant lands who, for short-term gains, were conspiring with the rebel factions.

Many knew that the troubles had started long before his time. But so what! Obviously, the stars went into inauspicious configurations the moment it appeared that he was to emerge, eventually, as Gangapati.

They could forgive him for the poverty imposed on them due to mounting army expediture in distant lands. They could forgive him for disasters faraway, as fortunately there was not any visible danger to their original homeland. But what was unforgiveable was that he failed to provide them with a future Gangapati.

Priests around Gangapati XIII made it clear that while a Sanathani could not have a second living wife, that custom did not apply to a Gangapati. A Gangapati, they said, lived not for himself alone, but for his people and his duty to provide a successor overrode all prohibitions.

'Why can I not adopt?' he asked. A poor alternative that would be, they said; the bloodlines of Gangapati I and II and all his illustrious ancestors would then be lost.

'What makes you think my wife is barren? Maybe I am,' he argued.

'Never,' they said. 'Unthinkable that anyone from Gangapati I's line could be barren!' But privately, some feared that indeed he was sterile. And the priests prescribed not only a second wife, but a third, if the second failed.

The priests went out, scouring the land for a suitable second wife for Gangapati XIII. They were looking for a bride of beauty, chastity, from an ancient family but also a girl from a fertile line whose mother and grandmothers should have borne a number of children. Yes, fertility was the need of the hour. But above all, each priest looked for a rich family who would be truly grateful and generous to him.

But Gangapati XIII had no intention of remarrying. The priests had assumed that his silence meant acquiescence. But how could he remarry? His elder brother, whom he loved more than his life, was no more. His father was no more. The only person whom he loved and who loved him, dearly and tenderly in return, was his wife. And they wanted him to marry another!

In his mind, Gangapati XIII had also rejected the priests' assertion that much would be lost if the bloodlines of his ancestors were lost by his adopting a child. He never believed that greatness flowed through bloodlines. He knew of too many men of evil with honourable ancestries.

But from the priests, the news went round that Gangapati was to remarry. Many courted priests, lest their daughters went unnoticed. Stars were studied; horoscopes were cast; and priests were loaded with gifts.

Even before the priests spoke, Gangapati XIII's wife urged him to remarry. He silenced her, 'Never again speak of my remarriage. It displeases me and the subject is closed. I forbid it now and forever.'

And since a Sanathani wife was always taught to obey her husband's commands, if they fully met with her wishes, she never raised the subject again.

With fury, he now heard the proposals from priests. Curtly, he dismissed them. The priests consoled themselves with the thought that perhaps he would remarry, if his wife was no more. As it is, she was pale and appeared sickly. A priest callously said this. And then this silent Gangapati, who had never had a way with words, muttered something that would always be quoted to heap ridicule on him. He said, 'My brother died, my mother died, my father too! They are not replaced. The dog I loved is dead. He too is irreplaceable.'

Can madness reach higher! To compare his wife to a dog! The priests left angry and speechless. Many, with daughters, sisters and other females to be married, were angry with the priests and Gangapati. But the rumour that went around was that Gangapati was sterile and remarriage pointless.

But that was not the end. The army commanders fumed too. His orders were clear. 'Hands off,' he said. They were not to join any new tribals factions—never to attack new chiefs who took over the lands of other chiefs—never to loot their land, but simply to evacuate their people from the threatened areas to safe spots.

He even designated those areas around riverbanks to which the people must be evacuated for protection. Displacement of one chief by another meant little to him. 'But the chiefs overthrown are chiefs appointed or supported by us,' his commanders protested.

'Can you assure me that the chiefs you appointed proved to be more honourable than those that replaced them?' Gangapati XIII asked.

'No, they were crooks too. But they were our crooks,' the commanders said. 'We lose face if they lose.'

'Better to lose face than lose blood and lives!' he said. The only exception he permitted was that if the new chief terrorized his people, they could move in but, again, not to loot; only to evacuate those who wished to move out and leave it to the remainder to choose a new chief. 'But remain there, if conditions permit, to see that the people choose their new chief freely.'

His scheme may have worked. Perhaps, fear of intervention and the hope of being left alone would have had a restraining influence on the new chiefs. But his own commanders never gave the new policy much of a chance. 'He will lose all the land by his folly,' they said. 'Do we not know what the problem is in the field?' And they said much that they would not have dared to in the times of earlier Gangapatis.

Gangapati XIII sent civilians to oversee the movements of his armies. That made him even more unpopular. The commanders easily fooled and frightened the civilians—and they returned full of praise for the army, though not for the man who sent them on such foolish missions.

Gangapati XIII himself moved at the head of the army reserves, as revolts and bloodshed in the First Tribe seemed to have gone out of control. Many feared the worst; some even hoped for the worst. But Gangapati redeemed himself. Wherever he moved, he succeeded, far beyond his own and anyone's expectations.

The fact is that he had more than his little army—he was Gangapati. And the legend had taken root that a Gangapati is invulnerable, invincible, inviolable. The disorganized forces of rebels—unified by no principle or loyalty other than their greed and desire to loot—would flee at his advance, leaving their leaders to be caught.

The legend of Gangapati grew, as his army never terrorized those that fled or surrendered, never took any slaves, never looted and often distributed food. At places, rebel commanders were tied and trussed up by their own men and left in the way of Gangapati XIII's advance, while men waited to surrender.

Far away, fighting broke out amongst rebel factions, to loot the earlier looters. Some even brought that loot to keep at Gangapati XIII's feet, as proof of their loyalty, so that they may be among the new local chiefs to be appointed.

Gangapati XIII left the First Tribe in peace and order, though he alone knew that he had failed. What he had wanted was to leave a chief there, who would be the people's choice. But there was no way he could discover what the people wanted unless he stayed back for months, if not years, to discover that. But he had promises to keep elsewhere. All he did was to leave behind two of his men—Jethmalan and Pratav—and gathered around them all the tribals who aspired to be chiefs, so that they could decide on the future governance of the First Tribe. Pratav even sent for his wife Mayadevi, son and daughter, to give an appearance to the tribals that everything was calm and peaceful in the land.

Gangapati XIII returned in triumph. Fickle as people are, they now saw him in a different light. He gave all the credit to the army of reserves that followed him and took personal blame for the twelve lives lost in the campaign. But that only made each of his soldiers praise him sky-high. There had been no feats of heroism—only the bother of rounding up the surrendering rebels and keeping back the rush when food was being distributed to destitutes. But that is just the kind of situation in which the returning soldiers' imagination can soar high. Only a hard-won victory brings silence and even humility.

Gangapati did not tarry long to bask in the admiration of his people.

He left for the eastern tribe. There, too, there was a 'repeat' of what had occurred with the First Tribe. His greater difficulty, actually, was to restrain his own men from rushing forward before the tribals had a chance to surrender or flee. Fed on their imagination of earlier 'victories,' they were fearless. No wonder he lost twenty-six men even though the tribals kept themselves at a far greater distance than in the First Tribe.

Again, Gangapati III returned in triumph—a triumph he did not feel inside of him—'I have returned with twenty-six less men than I should have. But how many more shall we lose in the future?'

Peace, he realized, was illusory and, at best, temporary. Countless rebels from the eastern tribes had fled to other lands, making the task of his own distant commanders even more difficult. 'What then of the vast routes and lands that lie beyond—right up to Gangasagarsangam—who can protect them?' he asked himself.

The First Tribe and eastern tribe, he knew, were tied with his own people intimately over the centuries, with growing bonds of kinship, intermarriage, blood and language. By now, they were all Sanathanis. Gangapati II's bride had come from the eastern tribe. His daughter had married the Chief of the First Tribe. But the other Gangapatis and their children had also intermarried, though Gangapati VI had moved far afield to marry a tribal girl from Gangasagarsangam.

For the people too, it had become a common practice to choose brides and grooms from lands far away. And as the ties grew, people all along the lands up to Gangasagarsangam came to regard themselves as Sanathanis.

But there was a difference. The First Tribe and eastern tribe were next door and their bonds were closer; they were brought up on fear and respect for Gangapatis, over the centuries, ever since Gangapati II's resounding victories there. They had adjoining lands. But how far did that fear and respect travel? And again, he asked himself, 'Who will protect those vast territories up to Gangasagarsangam when my commanders and I speak not with one voice!'

But happily, Gangapati XIII found that his commanders now listened to him. Even the new batch of civilians sent by him spoke with newfound authority and the commanders heard them with respect. As the poet said—

'The voice of the victor is not easy to ignore;
And wisdom was seen, where none was perceived before!'

Gangapati XIII saw the sudden burst of affection among his own people. He was touched. Yet his anguish was even greater. He understood what was in their hearts and why there was this change of feeling.

Before he had marched with his little army to the First Tribe, events had reached the stage where his people felt threatened—at Kashi by the eastern tribe and at Hari Hara Dwara by the First Tribe.

Is our last day nearing?—was the fearful question being asked by his people. Will this Gangapati XIII drive us all to slavery, death and destruction! A scream of anguish rose also in faraway territories and everywhere there was the cry for help.

It was then that Gangapati XIII moved. To many it looked like a foolish step. They thought he should remain to protect Hari Hara Dwara and Kashi against attacks. But he simply left behind the main army, while he moved with untrained, untried reservists. Nobody expected him to be victorious. But he surprised everybody with victories that were total and outright. And nobody argues with success.

He continued, however, to argue with himself. How long will this success last, even in these contiguous lands! He dared not march too far forward on the route to Gangasagarsangam for then it would be difficult to double back if Kashi or Hari Hara Dwara were threatened! His commanders would certainly fight and defend them more valiantly than he could; but then he also knew that there was something in the hearts of his people that made them ascribe paramount importance to a Gangapati, so much so that if he were not around, everything might collapse.

What should I do to change that perception, he wondered. He was also worried about the tribal lands far away. How could he expect his commanders to get chiefs elected in various tribal lands, when he himself could not achieve that in lands much less hostile! But, above all, how could he tell his people that peace was short-lived! That lands far away were in unceasing turmoil! That savagery and bloodshed were on the rise! That this chain of violence would rear its ugly head again!

He was always reserved and reticent and rarely uttered what was in his heart. Gangapati XIII now simply had to raise his finger to command complete obedience. But at the centre of his heart was quiet desperation. He did not know what he really wished to command. He went through the motions of making Hari Hara Dwara, Sangam and Kashi invulnerable—a task that remained almost neglected since the time of Gangapati III.

Gangapati XIII saw the people's love and joy in him. He saw it reflected in their hearts, in their actions, in their words. But there was something that they wanted passionately, ardently, even urgently. They wanted their Gangapati to give them a future Gangapati.

There never was a question of his remarriage. He would have to adopt a child—and his wife encouraged it. But somehow, it seemed to him that she still hoped against hope that she would be able to bear a child. He decided to wait and adopt a child only when she was past child-bearing age.

'God has a purpose and, meanwhile everything moves, everything changes, everything passes—and perhaps man too shall pass.'

—(Atributed to Sindhu Putra—5046 BC)

Visitors to Ganga

5046 BC

Sindhu Putra reached the land of Ganga. He was not alone. Thousands had marched with him. Often, he travelled by horse, mule, camel or elephant, and occasionally in a litter. There were times when he could move fast, like the wind itself, without stopping, but sometimes came across terrain that remained impassable for hours.

Poets speak lovingly of the journey—of shining streams and beautiful forests everywhere; of murmuring brooks and the scent of wild flowers; and the splendour of the snowy mountain-tops far away. But also of barren lands, treacherous passes, and tracks that led nowhere; of detours that took days, only to reach a spot fifty feet away. The poets also speak of works of art, of clay and stone, in the midst of lonely landscapes; and of paintings, carvings in caves along myriad lakes, though clearly there had been no one around for hundreds of years.

At many places, crowds waited to greet Sindhu Putra. With the vast movement and migration of people, his name was known everywhere. And if there were isolated spots where he was unknown, the entire population would hear from those who reached ahead, of a god who was to arrive in their midst.

Sindhu Putra himself said little to those that came to greet him. He simply blessed them all. Many from various villages joined the march. Sometimes, entire villages would move—men, women, children and babes-in-arms. Contingents came even from distant villages and the vast, unending procession continued. It rarely occurred to them to ask themselves to what purpose this long journeying. They were simply following a god.

Only once did Sindhu Putra intervene when the entire village gathered to join his march. From a distance, two emaciated boys and a girl watched wistfully and Sindhu Putra asked, 'Whose children are these?'

They were village-orphans, he was told. The villagers fed them but the children did not belong to anyone, nor would they starve for food, as there were cattle and fruit-trees all around. And the poet adds, 'He looked into the eyes of the orphans and saw what lay behind them. He said, "Come, be with me," and their eyes were sad no more; but he waited to ask if there were any more children unattended. And they told him of an unwed mother who lay dying, with her infant just born, and an orphan girl who waited on her; and like a hurricane he ran to her hut, though none knows how he knew where her hut was. Or maybe he guessed it from their gesture. . . .

'But then even gods do not always run faster than time and the mother was dead when Sindhu Putra reached, or maybe it was willed that she live only till he arrived; and even through his tears, Sindhu Putra saw all and heard the infant's cry; and he saw a vision of his own birth, merged into a living reality, as though the infant and he were two lives that moved together, inseperably tied up with one another and yet apart.

'And he prayed for the dead woman and called her "Mother," and kissed her hair which held no white flower and wondered why and where she lost it. . . .'

The poet goes on, but with little more to tell, except that Sindhu Putra picked up the infant and led the weeping orphan girl out. The crowd was waiting patiently, ready to march with Sindhu Putra, while the sun was still shining. But delay was added to delay, as Sindhu Putra waited to gather firewood to cremate the 'woman he called "Mother," and her ashes he kept, to immerse in the holy river called Ganga, still far away.'

Sindhu Putra walked the last part of the journey to the land of Ganga. Couriers from Gangapati XIII had already reached him, with fresh horses and cushioned carts to escort him. He rode briefly to show his gratitude for the courtesy but then walked. For him, it was a pilgrimage to Ganga mai (Mother Ganga).

Gangapati received Sindhu Putra. Behind both waited huge crowds. There was disappointment in Gangapati's heart, as he viewed this pale, fragile youth before him who looked even younger than he actually was. Certainly, he did not look like a god, nor even an ascetic or a dreamer. The youth's words had no flourish, no fluency, even taking into account the language barrier.

Quite a few words of Ganga and Sindhu were common. Many new words Sindhu Putra had learnt on the way from the men of Ganga who accompanied him. Even so, in response to Gangapati's eloquent words of welcome, the youth merely mumbled a word or two (*Tat tvam asi*) and clasped his palms together (in Namaste) like a mendicant.

And Gangapati wondered—yet this boy is known as a god in the land from which he comes! And Gangapati knew, better than anyone else, of the turmoil that this lad had caused not only by freeing slaves, but by sending them out everywhere, with the mission to free others. For the ways of these freed, missionary-slaves were not always peaceful or godly. They moved in armed bands to strike in murderous raids and even took the risk of being enslaved themselves. Already, they had created havoc in the First Tribe and elsewhere. Some said that

Sindhu Putra never sanctioned such himsa. But so what? What kind of god was he if he was unable to control his men!

As it is, Gangapati had never believed that Sindhu Putra was a god. Would a god waste his time with the single, insignificant issue of slavery! Gangapati himself regarded slavery as a necessary evil of a temporary character and not something that would last eternally.

He viewed the evil in slavery in the same way as 'enslaving' animals —such as horses, asses, camels and elephants—to use them in the fields, for personal transport or as beasts of burden; and his question was, 'Is it that there is a divine spark in humans and none in dumb animals?' He foresaw an era in which a vehicle would be found to ply on land, in much the same way as a boat sailing on a river without the aid of animals. Meanwhile, the 'slavery' of the animal was as necessary as was that of humans—'though it too shall pass away in time.'

Gangapati was convinced that if ever a god walked the earth, he would definitely concern himself with the greater problems of humanity —of life, after-life and mukta. Why would a god need to unleash an army of slaves to create disorders and divisions? How then was he different from a chief seeking a power-base for himself? Is that what he was after? Yet, when Gangapati looked at the lad, he did not appear as someone aspiring to be a chief either—simply a bewildered youth.

In any case, Gangapati XIII had no serious worry on the question of slavery. Ever since Gangapati IV's time, when Dasaswamedha's great-granddaughter went on a fast to prevent the entry of slaves into the land of Ganga, it had become an established practice never to permit slaves to enter. What Gangapati IV had done was to have huge areas ceded to him in the lands of the First Tribe and eastern tribe. The slaves were kept there to work under the supervision of Gangapati IV's men; and their produce was exclusively for the benefit of the Gangapati's lands. Initially, it was a secret, later an open secret, and finally no secret at all. Subsequent Gangapatis perfected the system, expanding the slave-areas and increasing vastly the number of slaves. The slaves were far too well-guarded to suffer from encroachments or rebellion.

Gangapati XIII shrugged his shoulders and put away his passing thoughts. He was about to introduce Sindhu Putra to his wife and to the entourage of sixty men and women standing well behind him.

And now poets speak long and lovingly of a strange event—and many describe it as a miracle, while others go a step further to say that it arose from a heart full of faith that moved the heart of God! But there were some who simply called it a coincidence, even though, at times, they marvelled at it too.

Poetic fancies and descriptions apart, there is no dispute over the basic facts of this event. What simply happened was that before Gangapati XIII introduced his wife to Sindhu Putra, he was already

staring at her, fascinated by the white flower she wore in her hair. His
eyes—as a poet tells us—'seemed vacant, wondering, wrapped in the
emotion that always came flooding over him whenever he saw a
woman's hair decked with a white flower.' Gangapati himself thought
it a rude, impertinent stare. But not his wife. There had been doubt
and faith alternating in her mind and heart—would this god be the
one to answer her constant prayer for a son? And the poet tells us—
'Now as he stared at her, straight and direct, her will gathered itself
into a silent cry of faith. It was as if a door was opening to receive her
prayer, and a soft voice was asking her, "Come in, dear child!" But
that is not what Sindhu Putra had said, when she reached him. He
simply said, "You have the same flower that my mother wore." All
she heard or understood was the word "Mother," and she said, "That
is what I long to be—mother." Maybe, the waves of her passionate
yearning reached him, or maybe, someone translated her words more
clearly; Sindhu Putra understood that she was childless. With another
show of rudeness, he went into the throng of his own people behind,
and brought out the motherless infant he had picked up from the
village. He startled everyone by placing the child in the waiting arms
of Gangapati's wife and said, "Be you then the mother of this babe".'

This was not what she had hoped for. She was praying for a son
to be born from her own womb—not to adopt an unknown child
brought from some faraway land. 'But as she held the soft, warm
body—so light and so lovable—she felt she was holding the future, the
earth and the sky, the sun and the moon.'

Gangapati was seething with anger. If a son had to be adopted, he
had already formed a clear idea of whom he would adopt. He did not
want his wife to be enchanted with a strange, stray, nameless infant
from nowhere. He steeled himself to not even look at the infant in his
wife's lap. But she brought it near his face. A vague suspicion struck
him. He moved the sheet around the infant's waist. It was a girl!

A girl! Gangapati was too furious to speak. He wanted a son, to
be a future Gangapati, and this clueless clot had foisted a baby girl on
them!

Even Gangapati's wife cried out, 'But I wanted a son!'

Her vehemence troubled Sindhu Putra; quietly he said, 'God will
give a son too.' (And the poet here points out, repeatedly, that it was
a blessing—not a prediction).

'When?' Gangapati shouted fiercely—it was the pent-up frustration
of years in his heart rather than anger solely at the youth.

Now, Sindhu Putra was truly bewildered. Helplessly, he flung out
his hands, and said, 'As soon as God wills it. What can I say? Who
am I to speak "when" that shall be! It is in God's hands.'

But then perhaps every gesture of a god is noteworthy—not only
his words. In utter helplessness, as Sindhu Putra spoke, he had half-
raised his hands, his palms showing and his fingers parted. The young
daughter of the chief of the eastern tribe, who was in Gangapati's

entourage, had her eyes riveted on Sindhu Putra's fingers. She was an accomplished dancer and, to her, hand-movements meant more than words. In excitement, she shouted, 'Look! Look! Ten fingers! He means ten months! Did he not say, it is in God's hands!'

Nonsense—thought Gangapati. But pitifully his wife asked Sindhu Putra, 'God, do you mean ten months?' Sorrow entered Sindhu Putra's eyes. Silently he lifted up his finger. That should have convinced everyone that he was leaving it all to God above. But is that what people thought?

Even when Sindhu Putra was escorted to the guest house, and for days and weeks thereafter, rumour, wishful hope and faith combined; and many shared the belief that a prediction had been made by the new god that Gangapati's wife would have a son in ten months.

'Utter and absolute nonsense!' said Gangapati, firmly and furiously —keen also to avoid cruel disappointment to his wife, from any false hope of pregnancy. But he did not disallow his wife from retaining the girl-infant. He had seen the glow on her face as she held the child. No harm done, he thought, even if she wants to adopt her. He would later adopt a son fit to be Gangapati after him. He now thanked his lucky stars that this crazy new god had not palmed off a boy on his wife. That would have complicated his adopting a son later to succeed as Gangapati.

During the next four months, two maids of Gangapatni became pregnant. But Gangapatni herself was untouched. Yet she was happy, fulfilled, as never before, with the girl-infant.

Many looked on Sindhu Putra as a god that failed.

But at the end of the fourth month, Gangapatni felt something was happening. It gave her a ray of hope. The next month, she was certain.

Her son was born twelve months and twelve days after she first met Sindhu Putra. Almost everyone regarded it as the miracle of Sindhu Putra. A few saw it as a coincidence—yet even for them, it was much too marvellous.

Only one poet tells the story, simply and plainly. He calls it a coincidence, pure and simple. He argues that Gangapati's son was not born by the miracle of Sindhu Putra—neither by his blessing nor through his prediction. But by the mere fact that when Gangapatni became mother to the infant-girl, the birth-juices in her body flowed. This the poet pointed out had happened in innumerable cases, where a childless woman adopts a baby and 'something happens within her deep,' to stir her and give birth soon after.

'Nonsense!' said many, to the poet who sought to give this simple and prosaic explanation. But even so, some argued, 'Whose miracle was it then to give an infant-girl to Gangapatni?' Here, the poet agreed that indeed it was a great coincidence, as without the infant-girl constantly in her loving lap, nothing could have stirred the movement in Gangapatni's womb. Another said, 'Yes indeed! The miracle-maker presents a miracle and yet forgets not the physical law.'

But one question was raised, 'Did not Sindhu Putra promise birth in ten months? And yet it took twelve!' The answer was simple. 'Oh yes, but did he not twice raise his figure heavenwards, too?'

Sindhu Putra was hardly aware of the ups and downs in his esteem during the first year that he was in the land of Ganga. He did not even know that Gangapati initially regarded him as a fake and that many others had laughed at him. If he heard or saw them laughing, he was certain they were laughing with him, not at him.

Some around him suspected that their god was being laughed at, but they only huddled around him protectively all the more. A few wondered how a god could be so untouched by disrespect from some. Others saw it simply as a godly virtue.

If Sindhu Putra was touched by something, it was by the magnificence of the land. Nature had been abundant but it was the miracle of man's toil that impressed him. When he looked at the distant fort in the moonlight, it looked like a golden mountain squared off in straight lines. At first he thought it must be Gangapati's palace. But Gangapati had a humble home, less conspicuous than the homes of rich merchants.

In fields and farms, he saw oranges and lemons, grains and cereals, trees and plants which provided wells of oils, grapes for wines, oceans of onions, tomatoes, cauliflowers and eggplants. Everywhere, he saw jars and clay-pits in which to stock grain for lean periods and innumerable basket-lined silos for grain storage.

Their fabrics were as fine and attractive as those woven in Sindhu, though they were more conservative, not as gaudy. Many were at work, smelting and casting weapons and ornaments of high quality and making distinctive tablets and seals. He admired their filigreed silver, glazed pottery, shining metalware and intricately carved statues.

Their houses were designed for comfort and their public baths, temples and meeting places were erected with every convenience in view.

He saw the marvels of their irrigation and engineering skill, their broad streets, well-built houses, elegant temples, granaries, chariots, gardens and fountains; and he felt that there was much they could teach, as also learn from, the people of Sindhu.

More than the magnificence of the art and architecture there, for Sindhu Putra it was the Ganga river itself that held the greatest fascination. In the murmur of her waters, he could hear the voices of ages long gone by, as though he had been there, once before, centuries ago. He found peace and solace there—for whirling in his mind were questions that many asked, to which he had inadequate answers. And those questions came, one after another.

Gangapati XIII had no questions. In the first four months, Gangapati had been cold, though always polite to Sindhu Putra. But there were others who crowded round him, some to learn, but many more who simply wanted to find flaws in order to feel superior themselves.

His mistake lay, perhaps, in trying to answer their questions. He should have realized that the sages and rishis of Ganga—the great thinkers and philosophers—who sat in silence in the forests and along the riverbank had no questions to ask.

Sometimes the questions he was asked were foolish and absurd. But in his humbleness of spirit, he would reply. Yet anyone could find flaws in his replies.

How did he know of the existence of God? he was asked. His reply simply was: I feel it in my soul. When I see the multitude of trees clinging to Ganga and the stars in the sky, how can I doubt that God exists! Then there were many questions:

What is man's duty? Conduct that is pure and includes a striving for unity, justice, harmony and freedom. He who seeks salvation shall not permit another to be held a slave.

Will a man who acts towards these goals achieve bliss? Maybe not; but his purpose is not to seek bliss—only to assume the sorrows of others to free them from grief.

But what about those that only pray and meditate? Truly, they honour God and God honours them. But maybe they do not do God's work. They are born in life but they do not participate in it.

What about those who do not believe in God? God is always with us, even if we are not always with him. He will judge the believers and unbelievers alike—by their intent and conduct. Non-belief in God may itself be the starting point of a relentless search for truth.

Then you see no difference between believers and non-believers? Believers and non-believers—they all spring from a fragment of god's splendour; and it is possible for a man to be deeply spiritual without believing in God, just as it is possible for a believer to commit ungodly acts.

Can you describe God? Only in my heart, in silence, where there is no utterance and the definition is unknown.

Why do people die? Because they are born. Death is their birthright. For some, it is the end of a journey into the bliss of moksha. For others, it is the start of another. Each generation must die so that the next generation is born.

Like us you speak of karma that leads to rebirth or mukta (moksha; salvation). But what about a totally evil man who through all his successive births commits only evil and never obtains salvation? That would be God's failure—and God does not fail.

Why will someone who is totally evil journey towards salvation ever? Because his soul is pure. Like the journey of the Ganga, finally, to the sea, the soul knows of its ultimate pilgrimage to salvation.

Yet, the Ganga waters go to fields, they quench the thirst of animals and people, and some even evaporate in the sun. So how do you say all of it reaches the sea? Water turns into water; that which evaporates becomes vapour and comes back as rain; that which is consumed in the fields or by people and animals returns as water to find its way into rivers and the sea.

God created the universe? Yes, but before Him was She—the Mother.

Many felt that the answers he gave had no depth. And to many more questions, his answer simply was, 'I don't know.' In Gatha's village, people simply sought his blessings. Here, they were trying to test, even to trap him.

There was no poetry in his words, no fine phrases, no eloquence, no flourishes. His replies were slow, halting, diffident, as though he himself were searching for the answers. Often, he would quote Yadodhra to prove the point that water returns constantly as water wherever it goes, never losing a drop anywhere. Sometimes, he would quote Muni, Roopa, Bharatjogi. Are they gods? they asked. No, they were his teachers. Teachers! Then he was not divinely inspired!

The fact also is that he never gave one, single conclusive answer. Sometimes he groped and often contradicted himself. Yes Ganga is a place of pilgrimage. But so is Sindhu; so is every river, sea and all God's good earth; every place of work; even a cow-pen. A temple? It does not have to be erected; no, you don't need a sacred fire; your prayers shall rise as flames.

Again, where he fell short was in expressing the ultimate reality of God. It had to be infinite, eternal, imperishable and unchanging. But then—he pleaded—how could something infinite, eternal, imperishable and unchanging be understood or comprehended by their finite and limited minds which were restricted by time and space? A finite man could not understand how the mind of a finite fish worked; how would he be able to grasp the mind of the Infinite? What a foolish example! thought many. Again, was God unchanging? If He was the first seed, was it not possible that like a seed it transformed itself into a tree? If the progress of humanity was continuously in motion, why should it not be assumed that God too progressed in the same fashion! Was humanity not in His image? Did our duties not change—there was no slavery a thousand years ago! If a man must move to meet a new challenge, why must it be assumed that God remained unchanging?

These questions from so many troubled him sometimes; his mind went further afield. He even thought of the giant birds and animals that he was taught had vanished from the face of the earth—of the 250 foot long makara (predecessor of the crocodile) whose fossils were found by the people of Sindhu; of the garuda bird, who reached the combined height of twenty tall men, whose fossils he himself had seen; of the jatayu bird, larger than a cloud, whose flight caused a shadow to fall from one end of the village to the other, and who was known to lay an egg each spring, but was now shrivelled in size and laid a single egg throughout its life-span of 150 years; of the doli fish which carried camels, elephants and other animals from one shore to another in flood and drought or simply for pleasure; of the Hinmana ape-bird, which flew from one mountain top to another, to throw down herbs and plants for sick animals and fish; and of the biggest of them all, the mighty dandarah (maybe, a dinosaur), who would with one flick of his abrasive tongue gather in his mouth weeds, thorns, and underbrush for a tenth of a yojna (half a mile) uprooting everything but leaving trees untouched, and spitting out insects and birds, unharmed.

Maybe, he thought, what these mammoth creatures were supposed to do was all a myth. But there was no doubt in his mind that they really and truly had existed. He had seen their fossils and bones. Painstakingly, they had been searched, re-searched, assembled and reassembled by the people of Sindhu and Ganga long ago and even in his own time. Bharatjogi had spoken about them; and Yadodhra had even shown him some of the fossils, carefully preserved. Their size, dimensions and possibly even approximate weight were no longer simply guesswork. Many had wondered though, why it was that their ancients, so busy with their paintings and carvings in the caves, left not a single drawing, nor a single clue, of what those creatures looked like or what exactly they did. But to that, Sindhu Putra knew the answer—man, howsoever ancient, came long after these giant birds and animals were gone.

But why did they disappear? To make place for man? But if they went, would not man also abide his hour or two in this vast scheme of eternity and disappear? Even the earth itself, which began long after the beginning of the universe, would it not also disappear? And the universe! But why? Surely God must have a purpose. Or—a chilling thought came to him—is God simply experimenting? Does He not know who will fulfil His purpose on earth? Or, is it that God simply created the first seed of life and it was the will of creation itself that created, destroyed and re-created further creation?

And he wondered aloud, 'Is God then a symbol, like other idols, to help conceive the ultimate truth?' But he had no answers to his own questions. All he believed—but it was faith that guided him here —was that God had a purpose and meanwhile everything moved, everything changed and everything passed—and perhaps man and earth too would pass.

In his confusion at the various questions flung at him, Sindhu Putra even reached a stage when he could neither affirm nor deny—and much less try to prove—the existence of God or soul. He even said that it was unnecessary to ponder over the existence of God and in what 'formless form' He is, was, or should be. He spoke of only one certainty in his mind—that it was man's duty to live sinlessly and to achieve unity, harmony, love and freedom.

Some sneeringly asked, 'Why do you not begin a new faith away from us Sanathanis and away from your Hindu ancestors to spread these new ideas?' But his reply was: 'I know not who my ancestors were. But I pass the same ancient path that my teachers followed. Whatever I know, I learnt on this path. And the path renews itself with fresh flowers of new knowledge and higher thought. What will I achieve elsewhere?' He added, 'A good Sanathani is a good Hindu, and a sinless tribal is both a good Sanathani and a good Hindu. Is there a difference?'

Sometimes priests, learned men and even Gangapati's courtiers who questioned Sindhu Putra carried an echo of his insufficient answers and self-doubts to the rishis and sages in the forests. They heard it all silently; their own faith did not wither; yet some said, 'A god he may or may not be; but perhaps, he may come to achieve the goodness of a god.'

But not many took these rishis and sages seriously. These forest-hermits, they knew, were always generous, even to the mosquitoes that drank their blood or the wasps that stung them.

But then man is fickle. News of Gangapatni's pregnancy spread and those that scoffed before, clustered round Sindhu Putra to worship.

Sindhu Putra himself remained untouched, for he did not seem to know that many of them had ridiculed him earlier—and again a poet cries out, 'How little gods know! And how much more is known to man!'

'I know not who my ancestors were. But I pass the same ancient path that my teachers followed. Whatever I know, I learnt on this path. And the path renews itself with fresh flowers of new knowledge and higher thought. What will I achieve elsewhere?'

—*(Sindhu Putra in response to the suggestion to establish a new faith,—5046 BC)*

'A sinless tribal is a good Hindu, whatever gods he worships, or whatever gods he worships not.'

—*(Sindhu Putra's answer to the question, 'Are they Hindus?'—5046 BC)*

I know not who my ancestors were, but I pass the same ancient path that my teachers followed. Whatever I know, I learnt on this path. And the path renews itself with fresh flowers of new knowledge and higher thought. What will I achieve elsewhere?

—(Shudra Putra in response to the suggestion to establish a new faith.—504? BC)

A sinless tribal is a good Hindu, whatever gods he worships, or whatever gods he worships not.

—(Shudra Putra's answer to the question, 'Are they Hindus?'—504? BC)

Mahapati

5045 BC

When Gangapati XIII became aware of his wife's pregnancy, he vowed to himself, 'I shall release all my slaves if a son is born.'

Later, as the pregnancy progressed, he said, 'At least, half the slaves.' Again he said, 'Many.' In her eighth month, he said, 'Some.' As his wife went into labour, he said, 'All, yes all.'

When his bouncing son was born, how could he remember, among so many vows, what he had promised! But, in gratitude, he went to Sindhu Putra. Thousands followed him. Many more joined him on the way.

Everywhere, Gangapati XIII heard the same cry, extolling Sindhu Putra as Mahapati (Great Protector). It was a new title, but why should they not create a distinct title of their own, when the people of Sindhu call him, 'Mahakarta'! Was he not the one who protected the land of Ganga by providing a continuity of succession. Was he not their very own then!

Gangapati XIII bowed to Sindhu Putra. He even called him 'Mahakarta Mahapati', combining both titles of Sindhu and Ganga. Sindhu Putra asked for nothing and Gangapati felt relieved.

When Gangapati returned home all he wanted was to look at the magic and wonder of his infant son, but his wife asked him, 'Did you deny him?' 'No,' he said, 'I called him "Mahapati," and all shall so address him, always.'

Again, she asked, 'But did you deny him?' 'No,' he replied, 'he asked for nothing.' And she said, 'Then you did deny him!' and her eyes went to her infant.

Miserably, Gangapati XIII said, 'I shall release some slaves.' He went out to order the release of nine hundred slaves, held in an eastern land.

He returned to find his wife still plunged in melancholy. But then, childbirth at that age could be tiring—he thought.

It was some forty days later that fear set into Gangapati's heart. Even in his sleep, the infant used to smile and it charmed and captivated the parents. Suddenly, Gangapatni saw that smile turn into a grimace and then a twitch. The next day, the infant was unable to breastfeed and had fever. Vaids came. It was not serious, they said. But the fever continued. The infant's tiny body shivered.

In Gangapatni's eyes, there was an icy dread as she gazed at her infant; a beseeching look, as she spoke to the Vaids; but clear accusation when she glanced at her husband.

Suddenly, Gangapati XIII said, 'I shall go to Sindhu Putra. I shall promise that I will release all the slaves if he cures my son.'

She turned coldly on him, 'Do not bargain with a god! Release your slaves! Then go near him!'

She was really asking for the impossible. Dozens of messengers had to be sent to release all the slaves held faraway from the land of Ganga, in so many scattered areas of the eastern tribe and First Tribe. Besides, so many arrangements had to be made. But he swore on the life of his infant that he would release them all.

He rushed to Sindhu Putra who had gone far into the forest—a half-day's journey. He found him. 'Pray for my son,' he begged and Sindhu Putra said, 'We shall pray together.' Gangapati returned home in the early hours of the morning.

Coincidence, chance, fate, destiny—call it what you will. Some said there never was any danger and it was just something that all infants went through. Others said, the change of medicine prescribed by Vaid Raj had worked wonders. The child was sleeping, no longer fitfully, and the fever was gone.

Gangapatni and Gangapati thanked Vaid Raj profusely. But in their hearts they knew it was the miracle of god, not of man or medicine.

All the slaves of Ganga, held everywhere, were freed. With hundreds to help him, they were placed in charge of Sindhu Putra. So much he asked for—to feed, clothe and transport them, to repair their broken bodies and spirits and even to send some to their homelands! Nothing was denied him.

The freed slaves wanted to distance themselves from the people who had enslaved them. They began calling themselves, 'Sindhu Putra's slaves.' For the first time, Sindhu Putra shouted, 'Slaves you are not and never shall be!'

They called themselves 'Hindus' and they learnt that a Hindu could never be a slave.

Leisurely, then, Yadodhra arrived, travelling by slow stages. He spoke with the magnificence of a sage. He told them of the era of Sanathana and Sanathana Dharma. He declared that every Hindu in the land of Sindhu was a Sanathani Hindu. He spoke of the glorious heritage of 'togetherness' of the Sindhu and Ganga, with 'pride in my heart and yours.' Some poets called Yadodhra a 'modern', in the sense that where his knowledge of ithihasa deserted him, the bold stroke of his imagination replaced it.

With a dramatic gesture, Yadodhra escorted Sindhu Putra to bless Gangapati XIV as the 'first Sanathani Hindu who was always a Sanathani Hindu for all generations.'

It did not take too long—perhaps a few years, or maybe a decade or two—for everyone in the land of Ganga to be called a Sanathani Hindu, and later, simply a Hindu. Even Sindhu Putra had said, 'Call yourself a Hindu by all means, if it please you; there are no compulsions. The eternal guarantee of God's love is with you, whatever you call yourself. And remember, God's gracious purpose includes all and in his kingdom there is no higher or lower; and the passion for perfection burns equally in all, for there is only one class as there is only one God, who is all-loving and universal.'

Meanwhile Sindhu Putra pleaded with the Chiefs of the eastern tribes and First Tribe to release their slaves. Each offered to free five hundred slaves. He felt disappointed. What he possibly failed to realize was that the Chiefs had no centralized command like Gangapati, who could with one stroke release all his slaves. These Chiefs had many smaller chiefs, warlords, priests and prominent and leading figures who held their own slaves. Why would the Chief invite a rebellion by making such an impossible demand!

But what a god cannot do, his lieutenants certainly can. Slaves freed by the Ganga were like huge armies, in the charge of men from Jalta and Silent tribe who had followed Sindhu Putra. They moved leaving turmoil, murder and massacre in their wake. The slaves were freed but a blood bath resulted.

Did Sindhu Putra worry? Some said, no; he had already left for lands far away. But others said that he had cried, 'I am beyond redemption.' Some asked 'How could a god be beyond redemption when redemption is denied to no man?' But a few clarified that what he had said was that he was beyond redemption for 184,000 lives.

A hundred and eighty-four thousand lives! Why such an absurd figure asked many; but others replied, 'Gods are never absurd.' A man of learning clarified that for some it was necessary to go down the ladder of evolution and be reborn as a human, after successively passing 184,000 lives of various creatures. 'But surely, gods are not subject to that!' argued some. But the reply was: 'Be it man or god—the rita (moral law of the universe) is the same; gods live and die and are replaced; like stars—some are being built anew, while others splinter into fragments.' The argument went on until the learned man concluded that it was better to share one's knowledge with trees in the forest than with ignorant men who refused to believe him.

Meanwhile, Sindhu Putra was already on the move—to the Daksina. He had with him the explorer-father and son who had been freed by the silent tribe. But the wonder of wonders was that among the multitudes freed around the land of Ganga, there were seventy-eight whose roots were in Daksina. They could hardly speak their original language, for they were born in the land of Ganga. They were third-generation slaves whose grandparents had been enslaved. They too joined Sindhu Putra. But then there were thousands who followed, not because of the lure of Daksina but to be with Sindhu Putra—many out of love and devotion, but many more also because they were too old or too afraid to join the slave armies which moved to the eastern tribes on their way to Gangasagarsangam.

Gangapati XIII himself moved to the land of Sindhu, escorted by Sage Yadodhra. He called it a pilgrimage, but some say it was not without the hope that one day his son would be ruler over the united land of Ganga and Sindhu. Yadodhra could have told him that rulers were temporary, 'that the glorious on earth return to ashes and silence, passing like the shadow of a bird, but the earth and its waters are the lasting reality, and they remain in their beauty and gentle murmur.'

But none moved as fast as the slave-armies. From the First Tribe, they moved back to the eastern tribe—and then, along wayward paths, to Gangasagarsangam and in all directions to the east and north—and poets claim, 'it was all then the land of Hindu, with not a single slave in sight.'

They do, however, admit that it did not all happen in a single sweep; and some even speak of a hundred different directions in which the different slave-armies marched, always swelling with new recruits. Little is said of the battles they fought or the commanders who led them—though there is frequent mention of the former Chief of silent tribe and the Chief of Jalta—though it is not said which one: second, third or fourth.

The time-frame is not certain, neither is their reach. Some poets said that for each angula that the slave-armies occupied, there was a yojna beyond their control. But then surely an army does not have to occupy each inch of the territory to exercise control or to have the slaves released. However, what is certain is that within a relatively short time, the slave-armies were in control of the route along Ganga to Gangasagarsangam, though battles to secure commanding positions in the lands above and beyond continued to rage.

In modern terms, it would mean that initially, they controlled large parts of Uttar Pradesh, Bihar, West Bengal (in India) and Bangladesh.

Later, some slave-armies branched off to strike out in different directions.

Thus the slave-armies extended themselves and went as far as—(in modern terms) Bhutan's border with Tibet and in the east to Burma's border with China and Thailand, not only to free slaves but also to settle them in new lands.

At what stage, and under whose command the armies moved to modern Orissa and Madhya Pradesh is not known, though the poets speak of a 'criss-cross of seven armies from seven directions.'

However, the poet who hazarded a guess that the slave-armies were proceeding to Nepal is wrong. It was Rishi Newar of Kurukshetra forest[1] who went to Nepal with twelve disciples.

The songs of Rishi Newar are quite clear: 'There are no slaves here; and there never were; all men, women, beasts and birds and all living beings and all living things are gods here; only we thirteen are no gods, but guardians of the gate; and we shall see that all who approach come to honour and worship and be honoured and worshipped in turn, or for ever they remain out and away.'

And poets are all agreed that no armies, even if Sindhu Putra commanded them, would ever invite the wrath of Rishi Newar of whom it was said, 'If ever he cursed, mountains would fall and rivers rise, and the seed of him who is cursed by him shall wither into waste.'

---

[1]Kurukshetra forest in those times began at the town of Panipat—map reference: 29.25n; 76.59e—about 50 miles from Delhi and covered towns presently known as Thaneshwar, Kurukshetra, Patiala, up to Chandigarh—map reference: 30.44n; 76.47e.

'... Not even at the foot of the gods, for god I am not;
Nor among noble worshippers, for that I am not;
The road I travel, is the one I sought;
Another life, to atone, has to be my lot....'

—(Sindhu Putra's request that none keep his statue in a temple—5039 BC)

'Music is humanity's earliest heritage. It was there before language, before thought. Perhaps it was evolved before man finally emerged, in his uniqueness, to walk on two legs, distinguished from the rest of his ancestry. Maybe, it arose when there was only a sensation and impulse in the mind of our earliest ancestress when she sang a lullaby to her first-born human. That is why even today, an infant, before it can hear or utter a sound, is receptive to music or a tune or lullaby to soothe it to sleep. For the infant, it is a familiar sound heard for countless generations long before he was born.'

—(Dravidham explanation on the 'Origin of Song'—5044 BC)

Not only is every individual equal in the eyes of God, but he must remain equal in the eyes of humanity...and the question of a class...or different levels of humanity, is unthinkable.

—(Age-old Dravidham belief explained in 5044 BC)

'Whichever god you accept, He is that god and Dharma is His will.'

—(Ancient Dravidham belief explained in 5044 BC)

To the Land of Tamala

5044 BC

Sindhu Putra moved to the south with thousands of others. If some poets call it an army, they are quick to clarify that it was an army of pilgrims, who carried no weapons. Who, they ask, would attack 'such a huge multitude, led by a god himself!' But there are poets who also add that ahead of this multitude moved large bands of scouts, trained and armed, 'perhaps unknown to Sindhu Putra but ready to lay down their lives, though they said that god himself needs no protection, but there were also those who followed him.'

South? Sindhu Putra thought that the land of Dravidham would be reached as soon as they got below the Sapta Sindhu region, beyond the confluence of the Saraswati and Sindhu rivers. But Dravidham, to which the father- and son-explorers were leading him, was far, far away.

Meanwhile, the father-explorer kept them all regaled with tales of the beauty and poetry in his land. But the main task he undertook was to teach them all his own language. 'Why?' asked some; and he replied, 'So that you may not only see the exquisite beauty of my land, but also learn to sing its great songs.'

'Is your land, then, more beautiful and your songs more enticing?'

But his reply was, 'I cannot tell a lie and yet the truth may hurt your pride in your land and your poetry! So silent I remain.'

But silent he rarely was. Sindhu Putra had advised everyone to try to learn the new language; and the old explorer would be shouting numbers, words, odd sentences, in order to teach them; though often he would recite poetry and songs. Those in front would try to repeat what he said, but by the time it reached the back, with constant repetitions, it was vastly different and even he could not follow what they repeated.

The old explorer spoke about the origin of his people. When they pointed to his physical difference, and asked 'Are all your people as dark as you are?' His reply was, 'Not all my people are as handsome as I am, but yes most of us are dark.'

'Did you then come from some other planet from a dark sky or from the sea on a moonless night?'

'No,' the explorer replied. 'The songs of our ithihasa say that we were always here and came not from a planet nor from the sea. Our legend tells us that we originally came from a tamala tree of dark leaves and bark which holds within itself the promise that the darkness in man's mind shall one day be dispelled by reverence to the Lord and devotion to truth.'

'How can man spring from a tree?'

'It is a myth, my friend. Only to demonstrate that at the beginning there was a tree, and then came in slow stages the life that evolved from that tree. But don't be surprised if my earliest ancestor was born, if not from a tree, at least under a tamala tree, for in those days the sun was stronger on our barren landscape and women often gave birth under a tree.'

'But then why don't you call yourself the people of tamala?'

'How can we!' the explorer explained, 'our legend also has it that while the first man came from tamala, our first woman came from the silk-cotton tree (Bombax Malabaricum), whose flowers of deep scarlet bloom at the onset of spring. Besides, our first priest sprang from the sami tree, as it is said to hold within itself the radiant fire of the Lord. And then our first yogi came from a pipal tree; and the hermit sprang from a banyan tree, which lives and renews itself through centuries, offering shelter to birds and their nests and even solace to hearts burdened with sorrow and minds seeking wisdom.'

'When did it all happen?'

'My friend, I told you, it is a legend, a myth. It arose in the mind of man before man came on the scene like a dreamsong, a rhythm, a feeling for poetry.'

'How could the mind of man exist before man came into being?'

The old man's hand simply gestured to the sky as he said, 'Nothing and all things come from that which is not; and nothing and all things go into what is not! Man's mind? It is not all matter. The largest part is spiritual—invisible, undecaying, undying, unmeasurable. Then there is also the will that evolved man into being.'

'Where did that will come from?'

'From the heart of all spirit, will, desire, atoms, cells, elements, non-beings and beings from which man successively evolved.'

'How much of man's mind is then physical matter?'

'I shall take you to the ocean. There you will see, at times, a huge wave, foaming white, riding on the crest in a vortex of ceaseless activity. That much of our minds is matter. The rest of the vast ocean is comparable to the unseen, unperceived spiritual portion of the mind.'

Someone laughed, 'Then we who live are really bigger than we are!'

'You are bigger than you are, dead or alive,' the explorer replied. 'Only the physical matter of your mind dies with death but the larger— the spiritual part—is indestructible and changeless.'

'Good!' they laughed, 'then we never really die!'

They teased him, 'Then everyone in your land is immersed in matters of the spirit?'

'No,' he said. 'Some sing, others dance or tell stories; some try out new herbs and medicines, while others seek to discover the physical laws of nature, to find unity in diversity; but many dig wells or build reservoirs; some erect granaries, huts, cottages; others make water-clocks, cloth-looms, boats, toys. Many more work in fields and farms.'

'So many earthly, material activities, then?' someone quipped.

The explorer laughed, 'All these are essential fragments of the human pursuit to eat, drink, live, dress and travel. Can man plunge into a spiritual ocean before his basic needs to live are met?'

He paused, 'But one day—maybe a thousand years from today—when all physical knowledge will be available to discover unity and balance among physical laws. . . .'

A thousand years! Some laughed at this distant time frame. But he thought they ridiculed his hope for such quick results. He said, 'Maybe it will take two thousand years or five, but then the physical laws of the universe are, as I said, like a tiny wave in a vast expanse of ocean. We will still have to see where God's finger points, to hear His voice and know His Mind—why He brought the cosmos to us—and us to the cosmos, why there is a universe and why we are here!'

Again, they went into the question of human origins in the north and south, to ask why the physical characteristics of his people were different. 'I don't know,' he said. 'As we from the south came from beautiful trees, I think, maybe, excepting your god Sindhu Putra who undoubtedly sprang from a lotus, all of you originated from a tree in which a dark-brown monkey lived with a pink mate.'

But he added seriously, 'I shall take you to our rishis who study man's evolution. They will explain how ancestry, mountain air, climatic change, proximity to the sea, and inter-marriage affect man's appearance and complexion. It may even depend on when your first ancestors evolved into man and through what creatures and how long they have been on earth under the bright sun.'

He even explained that those said to originate from the earliest tamala tree were darker than those that came later from the banyan tree. What was the time frame, he was asked. He did not know.

All he could give them was his ancestral knowledge that plants came to earth some 555,000,000 years ago, and the tamala tree evolved about 333,000,000 years ago, while the banyan tree came 222,000,000 years back. Other creatures evolved around trees, on earth and water, and from them evolved man, at different stages, though each man did not evolve at the same time or through the same creatures.'

'How could different creatures bring out the same result?'

'It was the energy of spirit and will that caused man; and not the creature through which man passed and evolved. Perpetual movement there maybe, for nothing stands still—be they atoms or stars—but perpetual repetition there is not.'

They asked, 'What was there before trees, before plants?'

'All I know is that you and I were not here. Or maybe we were, since the spirit is birthless. But in physical terms, maybe there was nothing; only the spirit pervaded; then came space, and atoms, and the will of the spirit and atoms to form, combine and evolve. That is how physical creation is constantly created and recreated; and that is how you and I are fated to meet and talk today, till we meet to merge with each other and be One.'

'Does the tamala tree of your ancestors still exist?'

'It does and it does not; like a river—with its waters changing every moment. We have thousands of tamala trees in place of that mythical tamala.'

Every question he answered raised a thousand. He promised that the thinkers and sages of his land would answer them. But he startled them by saying that his land had a banyan tree (*Ficus benghalensis*) which was 5,000 years old. The glorious canopy of this tree had a circumference of eight acres which could shelter 100,000 people; it had thousands of prop roots, developing into secondary trunks to support the widespreading and constantly extending branches.

The explorer tells tall tales—they thought. But later, they found that the tree was actually larger than he had described it.

Back they came to the question of why his land and people were called Dravidham. 'No,' he said, 'we do not call it Dravidham. You do!'

He explained, 'In our land of the Tamala tree, we call our people as you do. In your land you call them rya; we do the same and we too call them "our people" That is all.'

'How did you then become a Dravidham?'

He had a long story to tell. The day he and his son were caught and enslaved by the silent tribe, other slaves noted their different physical appearance and kept asking where they came from. He did not know their language and so could not explain. In frustration, he pointed up at the sky; and others started ridiculing him, as coming from the land of Devaloka (celestial beings) or brought here by daivam (divine fate). Once when his son was beaten up, they said, 'devas got the danda' (celestial beings got the stick—were severely punished). Later when he became friendly with the other slaves, he told them of many concepts, and they were all translated as daya, dana and dharma. So again, in fun, they were being called Devarishis (sages of heaven). Out of these dozens of words—all beginning with 'd', da, dan, dev, daiv, and so on, 'they started playing a game of coining more such words to apply to us and thus it came to pass that they called us people of Drav, Dhru, Druv and finally of Dravidham.'

'But then what really is your land? Where are you from?'

The old explorer laughed in a childlike fashion and took dancing steps round and round and sang:

'I am from Dravidham, Dravidham
But Brahma idam visvam.'
(This whole earth is Brahma)

They laughed and his son joined him too to sing:

'Soham, Soham, Soham
(I am He; that I am)
From Dravidham, Dravidham!'

Many joined in the laughter, song and dance; and their songs were many; and some of them became their marching songs; for instance:

'We go to Dravidham, Dravidham
With satyam sivam advaitam.'
(with tranquil bliss, undivided)

Sometimes Sindhu Putra too joined in their frolic and rollicking songs as they marched.

Was it all a charmed journey? All along the way, many more joined them. Some poets speak of Sindhu Putra's scouts that went ahead and of the cry that was heard when the slaves were being freed. But was Sindhu Putra aware of such a cry!—the poets are silent.

It was long after they reached the fragmented Deccan interior that they felt that they were really in the land of Dravidham. There were no slaves there.

The old explorer explained that there was no precedence of one group or class over the others. Priests? They were appointed by the head of the family. Family? It meant all the people—a thousand or more in the village. Head of the family? Often, the eldest female—mother or grandmother—with a group of ten female and two male advisers.

The two male advisers were the priest and village doctor. They were perhaps the most 'responsible' males in the village, as they were held responsible for much that went wrong. The priest was blamed if anyone in the village misbehaved. The Vaid was blamed if anyone was sick. His job was to prevent sickness, not merely to cure it.

There were no orphans below the age of fifteen. If a child lost both parents, the family-head decided which couple adopted it. Neither man nor woman could have more than one living spouse. Widows and widowers were specially encouraged to marry if they were below thirty-six years of age. Ten or fifteen villages would join together to form a common unit, called a nagara (a city with built houses). The family-head of each village would be represented on the nagara Council.

Each nagara would have a park in front and a park where it ended. Another park would adorn the central village of the nagara with beautiful trees and flowers—among them would always be the most beloved of their flowers, the lotus in its various varieties. There was another flower—the rose—which Sindhu Putra had never seen before— neither in Sapta Sindhu nor in Ganga.

Each sub-family—wife, husband, their unmarried sons, daughters, sons-in-law, grandchildren—had a large house, with a veranda, behind which were living quarters and bathrooms. Married sons, often, moved in with their wives' families.

Each house had its temple, apart from the large village-temple— 'Where else can all the people and gods meet?'

Every nagara prided itself on its landscape of gardens, architecture, its temple, artificial fountains, public squares, bathing pools, drainage system, its statues, idols, frescoes painted in caves and figures cut into rocks.

There were no theatres and the everyday song and dance performance would be either in the open-air public square or in the temple itself. For dances in the temple, there was a dress code and all performances there were devotional. Performances at the public-square were full of fun or for folk-art and never too classical.

Peasants, farmers, craftsmen, traders, dancers, singers, poets, athletes, entertainers, sculptors—all came under the benevolent authority of the family-head who decided also on inter-village activities and exchanges, within and outside the nagara. As a member of the nagara Council she could influence and was influenced by the Council itself.

Sindhu Putra felt at peace among the people of Tamala. Their charm and variety began to grow on him. He found them gentle and thoughtful, even as they sat enjoying their wine or listening to music or watching their dance performances. Their songs were many—some spoke of passionate love, others were songs of the sea, which was natural, as the Tamala people had taken to the sea very early. Many of their songs showed a deep feeling for nature; some sang of unity and balance in nature, with a sense of wholeness; others attributed divinity to each element of nature; yet nature was not treated as subservient in relation to man but described for its own sake.

There were some who sang of the elusiveness of God, though the singers and even listeners remained unburdened with despair, as if this inexhaustible mystery added to their enchantment of life. There seemed to be no bafflement and brooding in their songs. Instead, there was a faith that was both intense and joyous.

But not all the songs were concerned with subjects that were full of meaning and significance. Some poets gave themselves wholly to the love of the language itself, with the magnificent use of alliteration, imagery, romantic phrases and lyric elements. Others sang simple folk songs, some of which were about heavenly lovers and earthly mistresses.

Many songs were full of fun and laughter and sang of idle and nagging husbands and autocratic wives. Then there were duets and choruses where the men complained that they were loved only for their bodies and not respected for their minds and the women quickly retorted that they could not respect what did not exist! And then a newly-married daughter would enter to complain that she ate very little because her husband ate too much and the other women would clamour to advise:

> 'Oh feed him well, for a body is all he has got:
> How else do you think, you have a mind, and he has not!'

Although these songs were merely light-hearted, the fact remained that in their matriarchal society it was common to treat the man as a sex-object. There were songs about henpecked wives, as also songs poking fun at the head of the family and even at the head of the nagara Council, all of whom were women; for instance, someone would ridicule the Council's advice that to avoid the perils of inbreeding, boys for marriage should be found from 'five villages away or preferably from another nagara' and the singer would sing:

> 'She looked in her village and around,
> And this is what she found,
> All rotten to the core within sight and sound.
> So she brought from far, a groom tied and bound;
> But alas! the new-comer did not improve our breed,
> We only had an incompetent stranger to feed.'

And thereafter the song would stray into the 'incompetence' of grooms from other villages in the art of love-making, comparing them with the 'competence' of the local boys, with subtle suggestions and overtones of eroticism. But then, occasionally, there would be a retort from the 'strangers' who had been brought within the fold—and their songs would tell of how 'barren and infertile' the 'land and its mistress' was before they came and how the local boys—

> 'Either left the bed in haste;
> And their wives remained as if unwed and chaste;
> Oh, love's offering, how it withered in waste!
> But then came we—the best, the very best!'

There were many 'Tamala' songs which were terse, without poetic beauty or elegance—simply pointing to a moral. For instance, there was one about a poor farmer who earned only ten pieces in a month and piously gave one-fifth to charity. Even when he began to earn more and more, it did not hurt him to give one-fifth away; but when, over the years, the gods smiled on him, and he began to earn the colossal amount of 500 pieces, it hurt him to give as much as 100 of those in charity; he went to a priest, who blessed him profusely, saying that there should be no compulsion where charity was concerned and it was enough if he continued to give just two pieces as in the beginning. The farmer silenced his own misgivings at breaking his vow but followed the priest's advice—to give two pieces in charity. And indeed, so miraculous was the priest's blessing that from then on, the farmer began to earn only ten pieces per month; and thus he kept his vow of giving one-fifth in charity and no longer grieved at having to part with only two pieces.

Sindhu Putra enjoyed the music, songs and dance of the people of Tamala, or Dravidham as his people called them. Most of all, he loved their 'mood music,' with its different beat, tempo and rhythm, for each occasion. From the courtyard of the temple would float the strains of devotional music, so that the minds of those who approached would be emptied of stray thoughts and concentrate on the divine. In fields and farms, the music would have a fast beat, to encourage the tempo of work; on the riverbank, before a class started its yoga or meditation, there would be a soft, quiet beat to usher in the mood of peace; but far away, where people sat around the village parks and fountains, there would be music with an entertaining lilt, working up to a climax of rapid ornamentation; and beyond the fringe of the forest, or on the riverfront where men went to walk and think, the music would be in a rhythmic texture to aid reflective thinking. For sportsmen and athletes who ran and jogged, again the music would take on the beat of their running steps.

The musical instruments of the Tamala people were many, though they largely used a bow-harp with 12 strings, a pear-shaped lute played with the fingers, conch, shell, drums small and large, cymbals, gongs, tinkling bells, flutes—single and double and reed instruments of various kinds.

'Do these people do anything without music?'—asked some who had come with Sindhu Putra.

But the old explorer had much to say, 'Music is humanity's earliest heritage. It was there before language, before thought. Perhaps it was evolved before man finally emerged, in his uniqueness, to walk on two legs, distinguished from the rest of his ancestry. Maybe, it arose when there was only a sensation and impulse in the mind of our earliest ancestress when she sang a lullaby to her first-born. That is why, even today, an infant, before it can hear or utter a sound, is receptive to music or a tune or lullaby, to soothe it to sleep. For the infant, it is a familiar sound heard for countless generations long before he was born.'

Many laughed at his impossible explanation and teased the explorer, 'How do you know so much, old man?'

'It is because I am old that I know so much,' he replied. 'But go, listen to our "songs of remembrance," and you too will know.'

'And these songs of remembrance? Do they tell the ithihasa of music?'

'Not of music alone but much more.'

More than the wide range of musical instruments, what impressed the new-comers was that the singing voice itself was treated as a musical instrument. The singer would sing softly, performing long, complex variations on a simple, wordless melody, often as an accompaniment to a dance or at a wedding or funeral or an invocation to the gods; the voice would then be neither loud nor throaty, but as though it floated from a remote distance, passively, never intruding, never drawing attention to itself, but only to the event that it accompanied. A song, normally, would arouse an emotion but this kind of song, that stood by itself without any musical instruments, was more for 'creating an atmosphere of its own, that is calm and tranquil, like the gentle, unperceived, unnoticed air around us, while every eye and ear, and every feeling and emotion is turned and tuned to the event that it accompanies.' Another poet maintained that an accomplished Tamala singer could achieve even more than merely creating an impersonal atmosphere, for his singing could 'uplift the feeling to an ineffable, aesthetic sensation, when the grief of the sorrowing parents at the funeral pyre of their child is obliterated and, in its place, comes the moment of certainty that the child lives always in their hearts, as a part of the universe, and in the lap of the divine—and then grief is felt no more as grief, but transforms itself into love and faith—and sometimes that single brief moment would have the dhvani (reverberation) that the stream of life must go on with that love and faith for ever.'

The new-comers were equally fascinated by the dance of Dravidham, with its forty-four postures of the eye and eyebrow, eighty-four of the hand, eight of the neck, nine of the feet, six of the breast, four of the torso, and 108 of the fingers, with every movement fully controlléd and significant depicting an emotion, feeling or object.

There was grace and artistry in their body movements and facial expressions as they danced to present an image of various emotions like love, surrender, mirth, terror, devotion, surprise, wonder, awe and pity; those emotions were easily recognizable, though it was difficult to grasp the beautiful but complex code of hand-gestures which identified gods, animals, flowers, sweethearts, lovers and demons.

To begin with, the visitors mostly enjoyed the grace, poise and charm of the movements and it was only later that the entire story became comprehensible to them. There were other classical dances—some masked—which were far more developed and demanded a greater understanding of mudra (hand-gestures).

The new-comers could only enjoy watching these fascinating spectacles as spectators, but what they could freely participate in were folk-dances which were many and largely required the vigorous use of arms, legs and body without subtle gesture or complicated poses.

There are some who say that Sindhu Putra felt at peace in Dravidham because he came under the spell of the beauty of the land and the love of its people for simplicity, justice and equality. But at least one poet put it differently and said that Sindhu Putra's enchantment arose from his 'triumph of freedom'. He explained that in the land of Sindhu everyone bowed to him as a god, sought his blessing and expected a series of miracles from him and called him, Mahakarta. In the land of Ganga too, first he was honoured as a god of the Sindhus and later as their own, and the miracles attributed to him were many and they called him Mahapati there. But here in Dravidham, they respected him, honoured him yet they sought no miracles from him. Gods, they felt, came to purify the earth, not to perform conjuring tricks. They honoured him all the more when they listened to his mantra 'OM,' and they recognized its power and mystery. They had hundreds of mantras of their own—some to bring peace of mind, others to eject evil thoughts and a few even to cure mental illnesses.

'Do your mantras work?'—someone asked the old explorer.

'Each one of them works—until it doesn't,' the explorer said.

Sindhu Putra's 'Namaste' gesture was adopted as a part of the repertoire of Tamala classical dancers, in a series of hand-gestures; and it depicted either acceptance or devotion or surrender, or even resignation, depending on the accompanying body-pose and the elevation of the gesture. It did not take too long for Dravidham to accept this familiar gesture as a form of greeting, as well.

Did Dravidham treat Sindhu Putra as their own god? The old explorer had difficulty in understanding the question. Where is the question of your god, my god, their god, and our god, he asked. Is not a god of one, the god of all; and is not the god of all, the god of one? How do you own a god? Or limit and confine him? Besides, in Dravidham's conception, a god was not required to show magic potency, 'to lift mountains into the air and crumble them into dust.' Nor did divinities descend to earth to salute him graciously. In fact what they believed was that a god who walked on earth conformed to the pattern of the earth. How could they believe otherwise, when they treated a tulsi plant, a tree and a cow as gods! Also, in the Dravidham conception, nothing was believed to be permanent, not even gods, though abstractions which inspire gods and men—like truth, love, service, virtue, ahimsa—were undying and determined man's everlasting destiny. Not gods, but God alone, was the imperishable reality and integrity and moved the universe by the abiding supreme principle of moral law. None but God was the 'real integrity before, between, behind and beyond the shifting panaroma of nature and universe.' For the rest, different gods were simply symbols and path-finders and even temples and statues of gods were merely inspirations in the 'approach towards salvation.'

Nor did Dravidham believe that the efforts of various gods could lead them to salvation. For that, the individual had to strain himself and build up his self with thoughts and deeds in which knowledge, love and action had to mingle to raise 'self by self.' All that was expected from a god was that he should rise to great heights mentally and spiritually, to reach a realm of truth to find his ultimate salvation—the final triumph of the soul; and such a god, by his example, would point out the path to others 'tempting many but forcing none to follow it.'

There are some who say that the philosophical conceptions of Dravidham were beyond Sindhu Putra's comprehension. Others disagree—'How could the "knower" not know all!' But everyone agrees that somehow he felt completely and utterly free. Maybe because none sought miracles from him, nor troubled him with questions which he could not answer. Maybe, he was no longer racked with guilt for having to posture as a god in order to free slaves and unite the land.

Sometimes, the people of Dravidham spoke to Sindhu Putra with a familiarity that shocked his companions. A family-head even chided him for remaining unmarried and said, 'I never heard of a god without a consort!' And again she said, 'A god or a man—what can he bring to his marriage, except his youth?'

There was so much that Sindhu Putra found different in the mentality and atmosphere of Dravidham. People were far more introspective and yet more mystical. Certainly, their minds were speculative and prone to niceties of philosophical and metaphysical discussion, and yet there was such a passionate, devotional abandon in their worship—pujey or puja, as it was called (pu means 'flower,' jey means 'to do').[1]

Their puja was simply an expression of their supreme longing and intense love for the Lord, 'without seeking a result, but merely to adore the divine, to contemplate his ineffable power, in the spirit of self-surrender.' There was nothing reflective, speculative or contemplative in puja. It arose simply from 'meekness in utter humility of self to the abiding grace and will of God'. And when a wise one among the new-comers remarked, 'Surely with so much puja, these men seek something!' the old explorer disabused him. 'How nice it would be, if God were a shopkeeper with a weighing-scale to grant so many boons, for so much puja! But the trouble is that He waits neither to give nor to receive!'

What also surprised the new-comers was that thinkers, philosophers, and even hermits and sages from forests would often flock to join in the puja. In the land of Sindhu and Ganga, such 'elites' often kept aloof from worship for it was believed that for those who had become accomplished, having drunk 'the nectar of wisdom, nothing more

---

[1]Centuries later, the Dravidham concept of puja would be expressed far more elegantly in the *Bhagavada Gita*, IX.26—'Whoever with devotion offers Me a leaf, a flower, a fruit, or water, that offering of love of the pure of heart, I accept'.

remained.' But again, the old explorer had a rejoinder, 'The greater the thinker, the greater his devotion!'

And the gifts placed before the idols during puja! How insignificant they were! Often a flower, sometimes a banana, and at times a little water from the holy river Kaveri. In Sindhu and Ganga, it would be mountains of fruit, thousands of garlands, Soma wine, ghee and even jewellery. In some primitive tribal lands—not yet under the influence of Sindhu and Ganga—it would even be pasukarma (animal sacrifice). But the old explorer said, 'In puja, we surrender ourselves to the Lord. What else can we give to the Giver!'

Sindhu Putra's mind went to the demands of priestcraft elsewhere, and of the diffidence of the poor in approaching the temple when they did not have enough to offer for worship.

Close to Sindhu Putra's heart was also the fundamental belief of Dravidham, that not only is every individual equal in the eyes of God, but that he remains equal in the eyes of humanity—and the question of a class or caste is unthinkable. To the people of Dravidham this concept was known as 'human sisterhood,' which brought a smile to the lips of the new-comers because the correct expression, they felt, was 'human brotherhood.'

But then the Tamala people even placed the name of a god's consort ahead of the god's name.[2]

For Sindhu Putra, the Tamala conception of oneness and social equality had its own fascinating and even practical appeal. Of the thousands who followed him, many were freed slaves, who neither joined the armies moving to Gangasagarsangam nor went back to their ancient homelands. Yet a freed slave did not instantly earn respect— and met with contempt from many, even though they were slaves no more. Solace came to them when they clustered round Sindhu Putra, but they never had the 'feeling of belonging anywhere,' until they reached Dravidham. Now, the memory of their previous crushing fear and hopelessness was gone and they walked erect, unafraid to look anyone in the face as equals among all equals, in the land whose people regarded equality amongst the essentials of the supreme moral law.

The old explorer even carved for himself a new, though unpaid profession—as a match-maker to find brides and grooms for these new-comers, slave and non-slave alike.

In a long and laborious poem, a poet explains that much that Sindhu Putra admired in the land of Tamala was clearly perceivable to the naked eye but 'the higher reaches of their greatness he saw only through the eyes of Sage Yadodhra.'

The sage arrived in Dravidham long after Sindhu Putra had reached. Accompanying him were the former Chief of the silent tribe

---

[2]Some thousands of years later, this practice would gain ground elsewhere too, and the name of the god's consort would often be placed first—like Radhey Shyam, Sita Ram.

and many of his men. But there were hundreds of others who followed Sage Yadodhra, once they knew that he was to join Sindhu Putra. Many in Sindhu and Ganga respected him as a great sage but many more had reverence for him as Sindhu Putra's 'father's friend'; and often the line between the earthly father—Bharatjogi—and the Divine Father would be blurred.

Sindhu Putra was delighted to see Sage Yadodhra and the former Chief of silent tribe.

There were also three children who were known as the sons of Manu of Tungeri. Actually, it was to meet Manu of Tungeri that Yadodhra had deviated from the route.

Manu of Tungeri was a celebrated sage who lived alone in an isolated part of the forest, separated by a mountainous terrain, near the Tungeri (Tungabhadhra) river. So rocky and rough was the way, that many waited on the main route while Yadodhra went on this side excursion, with a few of the hardiest among them, to meet Manu of Tungeri.

But Manu of Tungeri had died at dawn on the day that Yadodhra reached. Manu's last words of solace to the three children around him had been, 'God shall come to claim you as his sons.'

When the children saw the venerable Yadodhra descending from his litter, they were certain that a god had come, but he told them, 'I shall take you to Sindhu Putra, who is a god greater than me.'

Were these children, no more than five years old, the sons of Manu of Tungeri? Impossible. Manu of Tungeri was reputed to be nearly eighty years old. There was no evidence of a woman living around him. And as they saw him lying in repose, his skin so fair, it was impossible to believe that these dark-skinned children had come from his loins.

'They are God's children,' Sage Yadodhra said, as they joined him in the litter, after the cremation. And thus did he present them to Sindhu Putra when they finally met, 'and Sindhu Putra gently raised the children to kiss them on their foreheads and their eyes which were moist with tears, and he accepted their homage as a father.'

However, the fact is that though many started calling them the children of Sindhu Putra, he demanded that they be known as sons of Manu of Tungeri. It would be disrespectful, he said, to forget that Manu of Tungeri was their father. When someone said that they could not be Manu of Tungeri's sons because of the disparity in age and their dark complexion, he asked, 'Will you then deny me my father Bharatjogi, if I am the son of an unknown?'

Of Sindhu Putra it is said that, 'It was the heart of Dravidham that touched him,' but of Yadodhra it is said that 'it was the mind of Tamala that fascinated him.' Certainly the yoga of Dravidham was far more advanced than that of Sapta Sindhu or Ganga. The Tamala people laughed more easily and yet worked harder. And the language of Tamala was rich and abundant, with a wonderful structure, and yet exquisitely refined! And it was so poetic in its content and so rich in its philosophy, that Yadodhra often found it difficult to translate its words and phrases into his own language.

Many thought that Yadodhra was comparing the languages of Sindhu and Ganga with that of the Tamala. But this was not so. He speaks of the language of Sindhu and Ganga too, as full of beauty, imagination and deep thinking. His reverent approach to the language of Tamala was all the greater because it followed a different discipline and he was actually astonished to come across a language of such strength and dignity which, apart from its vitality, had such a romantic, devotional approach.

Their script was equally advanced. It was different and distinctive from the language of Sindhu and Ganga, with a sound system that was rich in consonants and it had varied vowels to give it a crisp character.

The writing materials were no different from those used in Sindhu and Ganga and often consisted of dried and smoothed palm-leaf and sometimes thinned strips of wood and bamboo and even cotton and silk for decorative writing. In Sindhu and Ganga, there was greater use of the inner bark of a tree than of palm-leaf. For the rest it was almost the same—the use of reed pens to apply charcoal and colour dyes; sometimes their pens would be different—of wood and even metal, with sharp pointed ends to scratch writing material; the scratches would then be filled with powdered charcoal dust or paint dyes—and this facilitated stylized, angular and calligraphic writing.

But rarely was there an attempt to reduce day-to-day matters to writing. Changes in the configuration of stars, the shifting direction of waves, appearance of comets, eclipses, storms, the effects of certain herbs on humans and animals would be noted. Even calculations relating to astronomy, cosmology, physical laws, mathematics, weights, measures, calendar and eras would be recorded. Poets would also note their long and continuing epics, lest they forgot 'how they commenced and how they were to end, as what the father began the son may continue and leave to his tenth great grandson to finish—if ever it was to finish.' Yet their myths, their ithihasa and their songs of remembrance, by and large, relied on memory.

The rule of thumb, largely, seemed to be that what began before the age of writing was rarely written. It was actually Yadodhra who pleaded that all those pre-ancient songs be committed to paper. 'Why?' they asked, 'when everyone remembers them!' But his argument was persuasive. 'What about those who are far from Dravidham! How will your knowledge be transmitted to them?' He even sat and discussed with them the art of permanency in writing—how to wax, lacquer and seal so that the writing was not disfigured by the ravages of time, and how written leaves and strips could be bound and covered with waxed wood.

What impressed Yadodhra most about Dravidham was how far advanced their system of Mathematics was. From them he learnt the decimal system of numerals. Later, the decimal notation and mathematical lore of Dravidham would be learnt by the Sindhu and Ganga people; and somehow Yadodhra, long after he was no more, would be credited with having developed the system. But then as it is, credits for discoveries and inventions are often mistakenly given. For instance, the Arabs learnt Mathematics some 5,000 years later, around the eighth century AD, and although they clearly called it Hindusat or Hindisat (the Indian art), the western civilization which learnt it from the Arabs credited the Arabs with the invention. Again paper as such may have been invented in China in the modern era—second century AD—but the wafer-thin wooden strips used as writing materials were known in Dravidham around 5100 BC. These wooden strips, cut and shaped into squares, were held together by a cord passed through holes, to make it resemble a book.

It was Lilavati—a woman—who, around 6000 BC, developed mathematical lore in Dravidham. The name of the mathematician who devised the decimal system, some hundred years later, remains unknown. Even Lilavati's name would have been lost, but for the fact that this mathematician dedicated his work to Lilavati. His invocation said—

'Oh Lilavati, from whose fountain of knowledge I drank; my salutation to you!...

'...And then I thought of a drop of water, a stone or other matter, and wondered if I could break it in ten parts and again each part in another ten and so on and on—a thousand, million, billion times—would it finally disappear into nothingness. Perhaps to the naked eye, yes, but something—a tiny fraction—will always remain!

'...So to my pupils I said, let us begin with a tiny dot; and let it move one place for each division of ten parts—and soon convinced they were, as was I, that howsoever far we went in our calculation, nothingness was not reached.

'...Oh Lilavati! Here then is the illustration of our calculation...

'...Oh Lilavati! Let this simple, small dot (decimal notation) with its place-value and the use of zero be my offering to the vast river of your knowledge....'

Since then, for thousands of years, even in the modern era, mathematical lore by many in Bharat Varsha would begin with the dedication or invocation 'Oh Lilavati!' It was as though the author of the work sought to draw strength from Lilavati's pioneering work. Even in the post-Vedic age, it was common for a group or a class-room of mathematicians to begin their work with the invocation 'Oh Lilavati!'

'Was she a goddess then?' some asked. 'No,' said the sages of Dravidham, 'she was simply a far-seeing person, very wise, very hardworking, who sought to understand the inifinity of God's creation and remained convinced that the inifinity, howsoever divided and subtracted, would remain infinite, though she could not prove it in mathematical terms and left it to others to so prove.'

Yadodhra's fascination with the mental adventure of the Tamala people apart, what he was keen to find were the diverse strands which united them with the people of Sindhu and Ganga. The basic values of Dravidham—of truth, beauty and freedom—were they really different, asked Yadodhra. Their love of nature, their tolerance of the ways of others, their splendid achievements in art and culture—did they really set them apart? Were the ideals of the Dravidhams not theirs as well though they were sometimes disregarded. Yet it was not as if they did not appreciate the inner beauty and significance of the Tamala ideals.

And as Yadodhra's mind went over the panorama of his own land, and the dreams of its people through the ages, he realized that there was no limit to the links that bound his people with the land of Tamala.

Both believed that the infinity of the soul outlasted the drama of life. Both also believed in karma to affirm the presence of the past in the present. Yet how inflexible was this order of deed and consequence in the mind of Tamala! To them, desire itself was tantamount to a deed and they held that 'one became virtuous by virtuous desire, and vicious by vicious desire—and desire itself was a karma unless there was a conscious annulment of that desire.' To the Sindhu and Ganga mind, 'there could be no merit or demerit in desire unless it manifested itself in conduct or action.'

And how difficult was it in the Tamala conception to escape from one's karma? Mere repentance, penance, austerities and even puja were not enough to offset the evil karma. For penance to succeed, it had to be atonement of a high order, to admit the evil, to undo the evil, to restore conditions that existed before and then undertake a fast to perform austerities and penance. Bhakti by itself did not cancel the previous karma; it merely led to jnana which in turn led to the purity of desire so that an individual could contemplate only virtuous karma. Thus, bhakti arose from sraddha and as its devotion glowed it purified the heart to prepare the mind for wisdom and higher consciousnesss.

'Does God demand bhakti?' 'No, it is a one-way offering of self-surrender; a God who makes demands would have needs, and God has none.'

Here Yadodhra smiled as he again recalled the remark of the old explorer, 'A temple is not a marketplace; bhakti is not a commodity for sale; and God is not a super shopkeeper to sell so many boons for so much bhakti!'

Even the concept of moksha had its differences. The virtuous deed must be done for its own sake and not for the sake of moksha; only the voluntary act done devotedly and wholeheartedly, without attachment to the result or reward, would make for perfection.

Besides, in the Tamala conception, it was possible for an individual to achieve moksha during his or her lifetime (jivan-mukti).

But then Yadodhra asked how, if moksha meant re-identification with the soul of God, was it that a person, who achieved moksha in his lifetime, was not treated as a god? But the initial Tamala reply was simple, 'He that enters into Him, he alone knows.' But that was not the only answer as Yadodhra learnt later; and some said, 'Who can judge until the end of an individual's life! And then is it for us to judge?' The old explorer tried to explain in his own way—'A liberated individual is a citizen of heaven, but exists on earth; is he not then subject to the temptations of the earth?' However the explorer found it difficult to explain why a liberated person, who had attained the ultimate wisdom, would be drawn to earthly temptations. All he could do was to repeat the stories of the gods themselves being banished for arrogance or misbehaviour from the Kingdom of God. But then he laughed, for he knew that those were simply charming myths.

Yadodhra himself did into believe in moksha during ones' own lifetime, but it pleased him, all the more, that in Dravidham there were so many different answers, however speculative. There was no emphasis on a particular, single point of view, and it seemed that each Tamala thinker encouraged a supreme personal adventure. As it is, some would exalt the life of contemplation, anchored in the timeless foundation of spiritual existence. Others would take joy in action and regarded work or service itself as a form of prayer 'which is most pleasing to the One supreme, for He Himself is a ceaseless worker and His creation is not a single act or a series of acts, but continues as an eternal, ongoing process.'

Each profession had the equality of merit with an equal claim to respect, 'for who can say who is superior—a peasant or a poet; a philosopher or a cattle-herder; a bhakt or a dancer; a brick-layer or a sculptor; a tree-planter or a singer; a cleaner or an artist; a priest or a washerman!'

Yadodhra found the people of Tamala friendly and open to new ideas. And they said, 'Whatever god you accept, He is that God and dharma is His will.' They built no rigid walls around their minds; and even a sage or a hermit, though entitled to respect, was not regarded as the mouthpiece of divinity.

Yes, Yadodhra saw the many differences that distinguished the Tamala conception of karma, bhakti, moksha and the many varying philosophic convictions and ethical aspirations. These, he was certain, could be inspired only in a society of stability, behind which lay ages of civilized existence and thought.

And yet, despite these differences, Yadodhra saw a sense of togetherness of ideas, a communion of minds and a union of hearts.

With him, it was an article of faith that the people of Sindhu and Ganga were once together with the Tamala people, though he could not say how, when, or why they were parted for these long centuries.

Some add that Yadodhra's belief in Tamala's togetherness with Sindhu and Ganga was reinforced by the pre-ancient charts discovered by his father Ekantra. Others point out that he saw 'a common heritage, a single family of beliefs and cultural affiliations,' and if he did not see total uniformity, 'it delighted him, for he believed that unity lies not in a duplicating sameness but in harmony.' And how could differences not emerge, thought Yadodhra. Distances apart, the cultures of Sindhu and Ganga absorbed to blend tribal people of various ideals and temperaments. Besides, did Tamala culture not admit of so many variations within its fold and did it not even delight in them!

Yes, they have no rigid uniformity—thought Yadodhra. Some, here, believe in action, others in renunciation; some in acceptance of life, others in abstention from life; some are drawn by the aim of self-salvation, others feel the need to hold that all activity and duty must drop away from him who has achieved spiritual freedom; yet others believe that the duty of the liberated is all the greater.

But in Yadodhra's mind, these were not differences that divided. They were simply aspects that made a unified whole into a gracious harmony. As in Sindhu and Ganga, here too, there was no tyranny of dogma to fill people's heart with intolerance or a doctrinal orthodoxy through which no fresh winds could blow.

Mankind, Yadodhra believed, was still in the making; and creativity operating in human life commited man to knowledge and progress, so that man could surpass himself to achieve the goal of material and spiritual ascent. If humanity was continuity and advance, how could a single, rigid, stagnant, dogmatic view help in the perpetual, unfolding drama between the visible and invisible!

Thus Yadodhra went from one Tamala sage to another, always learning something new and even listening to their pre-ancient songs, none of which, however, gave a definite clue to the 'once togetherness' of the people of Dravidham with Sindhu and Ganga.

The only real, visible link he found was in their practice of yoga. But even here, there was a difference. The Tamala yogi was convinced that in the stage of deep meditation he could rediscover his life and personality as it existed in his previous life and then the sinful acts and omissions of his life that led to his rebirth would become clear to him. For ever then, the ascetic who made such a voyage of discovery into his previous life would cover his body with ashes to remind himself of past temptations. Many Tamala yogis however kept aloof from such curiosity to discover their 'pre-birth past' as they regarded it as an egoistic act which detracted from samadhi (deep meditation to dissolve personality in total concentration of the whole mind).

Tamala songs too, even on the creation of the universe, evolution of the earth and birth of the first humans were different. In one of their songs, God was shown only as the creator of the first soul-atom and from this evolved everything as a part of the natural and spiritual life in which heaven mingled with the earth, right from the start. The song then went on to say how each evolutionary stage was aimed at its perfection—be it a leaf, a flowering tree, a swift-running hare, a fluttering butterfly, a deep-water fish or a four-legged ape—and so it was with man; thus, it is not as if a human being came from the darkness of a vacuum, differing from all who had gone before, though it may well be that in the perpetual drama between the visible and invisible many links were lost or remained undiscovered.

Clearly, this Tamala song recognized that man was not simply a plant or an animal but a thinking, spiritual being and he sprang not from nothingness but remained a part and product of the organic wholeness of nature.

The Tamala even had a disturbing song-myth, not so much about the emergence of humans but of the time when humans co-existed with their immediate predecessors. The song-myth, summarized to its bare essentials, said:

...Then after the blink of an eye, came the earth, with frozen waters all around. (The poem clarifies that the 'divine blink of an eye' represents five billion years.)

...And as the waters melted, in a half-blink came the grasses and the trees, the birds, bees and the beasts, the vertebrates and mammals.

...In yonder island, where the frozen waters had not yet fully melted, there emerged a unique being called apasu-apurusha (neither animal nor man), who would later be known as vraon for that was the sound he made as he walked, panting.

...Why were vraon's steps painful? Because he was born of those who only a few generations ago, by trial and error, learnt the art of walking on two hind legs, leaving the forelegs and forefeet free to gather food, fruit and fashion tools.

...The art of speech also came to the vraon as his mouth was released from food-gathering, and the erect posture helped in the control of his breathing... except as he walked on his two hind legs....

...At about the same time, and 'only a tenth of the blink of an eye separates that day from today', emerged man, on this strip of land by the side of melted waters.

...This new being—man—was unique; distinct from all, even from the vraon who was his nearest relative... But then it was the 'vraon who lived on land, had dolphins and whales as his ancestral cousins and also the creatures that lived in the trees, and around'... so believe not that man arose from a vacuum of 'nothingness and nowhere...'

...The very first contact between vraon and human led to a misunderstanding and a tragedy. From a distance, swimming in the waters, vraon had admired the furrow or plough used by men while working in the fields. Vraon wanted to 'borrow' it to fashion a similar agricultural tool for himself. He knew that after dusk, men did not need it since they invariably left it in the field. He crossed over to pick it up.

...He did not know the concept of private property. To him, all things left on God's earth belonged to all. But as he was picking up the furrow, he saw a woman there.

...This vraon had only ever seen men and never their women, and whenever he had tried to come nearer, the men had frightened him away with their shouts, lest he trample on their newly-planted fields.

...Now that he saw this delicate, beautiful woman, decked in a garland of flowers, full of grace and charm, he was almost certain that she was a god or goddess....

...He asked her as much but she, understanding not his speech, graciously smiled as she perceived his posture of respect and the admiration in his eyes... for as it is, many creatures, large and small, frequently passed her by, never contemplating harm to her, or from her.

...But when vraon saw her smile he shook with happiness, as a feeling of indescribable joy possessed him, and he reverently came nearer to touch her, but at his touch, the fear of the unknown sprang in her heart and she fainted in his arms... and this sudden posture of submission, he thought, signalled that she had accepted his prayer to go with him to his land... Vraon raced and then swam to his land, carrying her limp body, his heart a whirl of happy excitement for 'the God of whom he had only thought and dreamt before, he had now seen and touched, and the God was even in his arms.'

...The vraons, all over his land, shared his wonder and awe, and they doubted him not, for he was amongst them the most learned and beloved, the strongest and the ablest, the kindest and gentlest, not only to them 'but also to the four-legged, and those without legs and feet, and those that crawled on earth, and those that flew over trees.'

...When this woman, whom they regarded as their goddess, recovered from her fainting spell, she found herself in a strange forest, with vraons all around. She cried and when they saw a goddess weeping for them they cried and wept as well. She ran here and there and they followed her... and as she at last faced the huge body of melting water, she knew she was far from her land and could not swim an ocean so deep and vast....

...She sang sorrowfully, hoping that the waves lapping in the midst of melting waters would carry her voice across to her people. The vraons heard her fascinated, 'for a song was in the sensation of their thought, but never had they heard it before with their ears nor articulated it with their voice.... And now they tried to sing after her, but 'it frightened her more, and soothed her not.'

...Wherever she went, they followed her. They brought her the choicest fruits and flowers, and every night made a fresh bed of soft leaves and twigs for her...

...She had nowhere to run and hide and knew she must rest, for she was in the third month of pregnancy.

...Meanwhile, the man whose wife was thus taken away by the vraon was heart-broken. He recalled how every night, as she returned from her walk in the dusk of evening, 'she used to fetch and carry for him, rubbing his body and feet, even when he was not weary. She would rise before him and eat and sleep after him and it was as though she lived only for his pleasure and well-being.'

...He and his nine brothers searched for her everywhere, but to no avail.... But then months later, the secret was out from the 'four-legged ones who had learnt the art of inadequate speech but never raised themselves to be vraons, and I know not what passion consumed them—was it jealousy of the vraons who always protected them, or was it their fellow-feeling for a man who lost his mate?'

...And as the story of the four-legged was told, the man who lost his wife and his companions, flew into a rage and prepared for battle, 'while the four legged showed them the way.'

...The woman, meanwhile, had twins—both sons. The vraons regarded them as God's own offspring...

...She pined for her people, but her initial fright was gone. The vraons waited on her and her children, hand and foot. Her happiness in her two infants apart, she realized that these simple, strange creatures were simply offering her their worship and devotion, and sought nothing from her, except her presence to bless them.

...Herself, she began to devote her efforts to their welfare, to show them how to light a fire, to cook meals, to make toys and tools.

...But like a sudden thunderbolt, the avenging men arrived, crossing over the 'streams of the sea,...' and in their own fright, 'they struck at every vraon they saw; and the earth became crimson with the blood of the fallen...'

...And at last, they reached the vraon who had taken the woman away; and the husband and his nine brothers struck a powerful blow on his head... and each spoke later of how at his blow, the head of the vraon fell as though he had ten heads, but he had only one; and as that head flew to earth, it muttered its last prayer to the 'goddess' he had brought from the land of man...

...And 'thus died the noblest and the best vraon.'

...But the slaughter did not cease, for there is 'no mercy in man's vengeance and rage....'

...And the woman-goddess, who was in the forest playing with her two infants and the vraon children, heard the shrieks of the 'slayers and the slain,'... and she came running... and the vraon children with her would also have all been slain if she hadn't obstructed the killing, ready to be slain herself.... and so the killing ceased.

...Thus only a few vraon children were saved and the adult vraons who were not slain went into the water to 'share their future destiny with the dolphins and whales of the sea.'

...But, there was an adult vraon who still lived. He was a hunchback, short of height, his speech unclear, his physical growth retarded, his face disfigured, possibly because of his mother's fall from a tree, just before his birth.

...The hunchback had crouched among the vraon children and had therefore been left unmolested. Later, as the men scoured the island to see if any adult vraon remained, they saw the hunchback, but were so full of laughter at his grotesque face and comical figure, that they took him to their land as entertainment...

...The woman also—a goddess no more—was taken to her husband's domain. The husband viewed her with open distaste, convinced as he was by some that the children she bore were not his but of the savage vraon.... Thus it was that her two children were left behind, along with the vraon children, to fend for themselves....

...Although she cried for all the children left behind in the island of vraon, none heeded her, for many had turned against her—and she no longer was anyone's woman but simply a worker needed in the field.

...She spoke no more and none understood her grief, except the hunchback who did not speak either but kept busy making little toys out of wood, straw, sand, clay and pebbles, as once she had taught him on the island of vraon... 'for all else was clumsy about this little hunchback, except his undersized, nimble fingers that could turn lifeless clay and straw into lively works of art, and though she was his first teacher, her mind was filled with wonder and a strange stirring at the rhythm, grace and movement of the figures he created.'

...The children of man clustered round the hunchback for they, unlike the adults, had never noticed his deformity, nor did they ever laugh at him and now that he produced toys for them, they loved him.

...Even the adults stopped laughing and wondered how this deformed hunchback could create such beautiful figures, filled with a mystery of loneliness and grandeur that awakened such emotions and reverberations in their hearts. He, however, merely pointed to the sky when they asked what those figures represented.

...But what they could not understand was why the figures were without eyes. How could the gods and goddesses be unseeing and blind?...

...The hunchback pointed to the woman who was his goddess in reply. Some took this to mean that he implied that the gods refused to open their eyes as long as this accursed woman was in their midst. As it is, her presence was a constant reminder to her husband of his shame... and he felt that even if the vraons had not ravished her, many were continuing to laugh at him... Instantly, he commanded his brothers

to transport her to vraon island and she begged the hunchback to join
her...

...But the hunchback declined and they all said that so accursed
was she that even the 'last of the vraons wishes to keep his distance
from her.' They were certain that the children of vraon who were left
on the island 'uncared and amidst the hostility of the four-legged, could
not have survived.'

...But when the woman, transported by her husband's brother,
reached the vraon island, she found that the vraon children and her
own had survived under the tender care of the four-legged 'whose
mischief led to the malice of man for which they now atoned.'

...The woman found solace with her two children and lost herself
in the welfare of the orphaned children of vraon... and she also looked
after the four-legged...

...Meanwhile, from man's domain, suddenly, the hunchback was
found missing. Children grieved; men searched everywhere. They were
certain he could not have gone into the water to reach his old island...
for when they had first brought him, they used to throw him, cruelly,
out of fun, into the water, and they knew he could not swim.

...None knew where he was hiding and even the four-legged ones
could offer no clue as to where the hunchback was...

...Eight hundred days later, the children climbed a tall tree to pluck
its fruit... and they saw the hunchback far away, outside a cave near
the waters and cried out in delight. The adults left their work in the
fields to run after him.

...Maybe terror seized the hunchback's heart, for he had seen these
men kill before; or maybe another impulse moved him... Or maybe his
work was done.... He dived headlong into the water, clutching at a
large piece of driftwood. The swift current moved him far away. There
was no way to save him, they thought.

...They went into the cave, which apparently was the hunchback's
hide-out. There they stood silently, lost in surprise, at the myriad figures
he had created. There was no mystery and romance in these figures
not even joy or enthusiasm. It was as if the hunchback had a definite
story to tell... and, fearless and unashamed, he had created these figures
so that they could understand his story.

...The figures simply represented the anatomical parts of man and
woman... and separately, of the vraon and his mate, which would give
birth to an offspring... There was neither undue delicacy nor coarseness
and he had obviously aimed at exact accuracy while modeling,
perfecting each detail... except that he had enlarged the reproductive
organs to five times their actual size, so that the distinction between
the vraon and human organ was clear even to the most careless
observer. The man's linga was in the form of a cylindrical pillar with a
round top, and the vraon linga was very different in size, shape and
curves. The woman's yoni was also shown along with the vraon yoni,
and the differences were many.... There was also a second set of smaller

figures, where a man's body was intertwined with a woman's, a vraon body with its vraon mate, and the bodies of the four-legged with the four-legged. By the side of the human figures were the figures of the human linga and yoni, but these were made almost to a scale, unenlarged. Similarly, by the side of the vraon and four-legged figures were the reproduction of their lingas and yonis, so that the distinctions and differences were obvious. And so as to make sure that there was no doubt at all, there were the miniature figures of the human, vraon and four-legged infant, behind each set of figures.

...Perhaps even with this wealth of detail, much might have remained obscure to the ignorant, but then a man spoke, 'who rarely, if ever spoke for he was of those whose ancestors were said to spring from a banyan tree, and he passed time in forests, some-times witnessing, though participating not, in the events and affairs of men....'

...And this hermit said that there was no mystery in the message here but simply that neither man nor woman could mate with the vraon or four-legged, 'and only a mind that is barren and a head that is blind' can conceive of such a union or believe that 'such a union can ever conceive.'

...The hermit had sharp eyes and noticed that there was an etching on the cave-wall. They brought fire-torches to see it clearly. The etching showed a series of circles, crudely drawn, with sharp stone edges. The bottom circle showed an area with fallen trees and boulders—and amidst them a human figure, around which a number of vraon figures had fallen—some limbless, others headless; the next higher circle simply depicted heavenly bodies—like the sun, moon and stars; the third higher circle showed nothing but empty space; and the top circle showed a lone face, but so sketchily drawn that it could be of god, man, woman, vraon or even the four-legged....

...Again, the hermit explained the artist's conception...'The first circle represents the space of earth where things fall; the second circle has heavenly bodies from which not things, but nourishment falls on earth; the third is outer space; and the fourth is the space beyond outer space where God, in his lonely splendour, rested to plan and work, after his tireless sojourn of the three circles below.'

...Yet it was the face of God in the top circle to which their attention was riveted. The throat was blue-black, actually more blue than black, and it was a colour that was not difficult to achieve by mixing charcoal with the paste of crushed nila (blue) flowers.

...But where did vraon find red colour to smear on God's face, when men themselves have been 'searching in vain to reproduce the colour of red flowers, which neither their juice nor paste yielded!'

...The mystery was no mystery. The pattern of dried drops of blood on the cave-floor was there for all to see, and the hermit explained that it was vraon blood which had more 'red than white in it.'

...And they wondered why the hunchback shed his blood to decorate the face of God... and the hermit replied, 'God demands no one's blood, but the vraon gave it...'

...And as they went out to follow the trail of dried blood, it led them to a plant, with whose thorns the hunchback had obviously cut himself to draw blood and paint the face of God.

...The hermit sat back to pray and said, 'The God of vraon and the God of man is the same,' but what he said was nothing new for everyone knows that the God of all creation is one, 'even if man has no memory of his spirit, while all other creatures have.'

...All other men then again went to the edge of the water and saw the storms over the sea and determined that as soon as the storms subsided, they would go over the waters to bring back the 'woman wronged.'

...Regretfully though, they realized that the hunchback vraon, weakened by loss of blood, and unable to swim, could not have survived even a moment in the storm-tossed water.

...But they were wrong, 'for who knows why the storms came and how swiftly the currents moved!... and how the driftwood to which the hunchback clung, raced to the island of vraon, through clear streams of melted water in the frozen sea!'

...And in the clear morning sky, when the sun shone more piercingly than it did at midday, the vraon children saw the hunchback in the water....

...And they shouted with frantic joy and even the four-legged took up the cry... and the hunchback heard them, as he opened his eyes from his dizzy spell and saw the woman-goddess waving him on... and the hunchback too lifted his hands in silent salutation....

...But as he lifted his hands, the driftwood left him and he had no more support to save him from drowning, and it seemed as though he had come there not to live, but to die—but only 'after his one last, final salutation to his goddess and to the isle of vraon.'

...The woman-goddess jumped into the water to save him, but then all the vraon children jumped in after her as they saw, in the distance, boats loaded with men coming towards them... and it revived in their minds the memory of the last massacre and bloodshed by man....

...The two children of the woman-goddess waited for a moment, for they were, after all, the children of man and therefore 'blessed with reason and cursed by fear,'... and then they too jumped, clinging to the driftwood that had parted from the hunchback.

...And thus died the hunchback who was 'the last of the vraons; but also the first of the vraons'.

...But perhaps he did not die. Nor perhaps the woman-goddess herself, for it is said that 'she is still swimming in the waters holding the hunchback in her arms and sometimes when you hear the cry from the sea, it is not for herself she cries, nor for the vraon in her arms, but for all, on earth, water, air and the sky.'

...Her two sons? Who knows where the driftwood carried them! Maybe they went to rule over lands where the sun rises, while it sets here... for such is the story that my ancestors told me, but then they also said that maybe they were wrong... and possibly the two sons ruled over lands nearby, where the moon rises at the same time as here... but one certainty my ancestors had was that the two sons were in the land where man, vraon and the four-legged lived side by side, with none shedding the blood of another—for that was the last wish of the last vraon who disappeared into the waters after his last salutation... and it was also the cry of the woman-goddess who was their mother.

*

Yadodhra heard this song-myth in its entirety, over many days, for it took 188 hours of recitation. How different it was from the myths in his land of Sindhu and even Ganga! There, the myths were always heroic—of divine compassion and human virtue; and when they touched on earthly matters, they sang of women of grace and charm, of men who were valiant and true, and of the sweet pining of lovers and the joy of their reunion—and there was always a happy ending, with villains vanquished, heroes triumphant and songs of eternal love ringing through the ages.

This song-myth, on the other hand! How terribly it began and how terribly it ended, with none certain if the blameless, pure and innocent died, drowning in the pitiless, half-frozen sea!

Yet Yadodhra appreciated that a myth is simply a dream-drama, with little factual relevance to living elements; and if the myth spoke of early man's horrific cruelty and bloodshed against the vraon, its silent moral obviously was that the essence of humanity lay in movement—in a continuous progress towards refinement and not in an arrested moment, frozen in time. God did not begin everything on one glorious morning and create man into a god-like being.

Even so, Yadodhra saw similarities in this song-myth and the myths of Sindhu and Ganga, which spoke of the physical universe forming some five billion years ago and the earth that came two billion years later, while man emerged only around 500,000 years ago, towards the end of the Ice Age as a unique and distinct being, to coexist with the ape-man. Compared to the four-legged, the ape-man may have been a thinking, forward-looking, planning, imagining being, who, apart from walking erect, could speak, laugh, sing, shed tears, and even draw, paint, sculpt and use basic tools and implements.

Yet as the Sapta Sindhu myths also made clear, the ape-man and man were not in direct ancestral or evolutionary line, and both, despite some obvious similarities, followed different and divergent streams of evolution. Again, like the Dravidham myth, the Sindhu and Ganga myths also touched on the part played by the trees and animals of land and water (and even of air), in the final evolution of man, 'and yet this arose not as an accident but as a cosmic process whose ground and driving force began with the first and ultimate cause.'

Thus the Dravidham myth of man's evolutionary relationship with the dolphins and whales of the sea did not sound strange to Yadodhra's ears. The Sindhu and Ganga myths even hinted at the vastly different anatomical structure of the sex-mechanism of man and ape-man; and the implication that the two could not mate with each other or beget an offspring was clear. The only difference was that the Dravidham myth was explicit, leaving nothing to inference or implication.

To Yadodhra, it seemed that somehow in the dim past, this very Tamala myth-drama must have been enacted in Sindhu and Ganga, in one form or another—maybe with different players, different costumes and even different music, but essentially the same!

Even the phallic symbol. In Dravidham, it was the hunchback vraon artist—an ape-man—who created it, while in Ganga, it was said to be handed down to man by the ten-headed god. No; some said it was a god who wore ten crowns—one for each of the nine planets and the tenth for the earth. But then was not the vraon worshipper of the woman-goddess credited with ten heads? That was simply an illusion, as ten brothers struck a simultaneous blow at the vraon's head. Again, didn't some tribal communities—now in the Hindu fold—have gods with ten heads and ten pairs of eyes to watch all that happened on, above and below the earth! But then did not other tribal communities— also in the Hindu fold—regard those ten-headed gods of rivals as demons?

Yadodhra gave up his analysis of the similarity between myths. Myth is, after all, a story of the inner spirit of human hopes and longings. Its message is universal. So how is it surprising if similar myths spring up in different cultures or places unrelated to each other!

Yadodhra could even concede that the similarity of the Dravidham god—Shiva—with the Shiva of Sindhu and Ganga, was simply a coincidence. In one of his 108 forms, Shiva was represented in Sindhu and Ganga as 'Daksinamurti' (south-facing) and in that aspect he had a red face and blue neck (was it somehow the inspiration of the vraon myth that travelled northwards?). In Dravidham, on the other hand, Shiva was shown as wrapped in meditation, as a god of divine power, mythical stillness and ineffable grace, who was also the Lord of Dance (Nataraja), having inspired 108 celestial dancers, each of whom inspired 108 different dances.

Shiva, depicted as a mystic divinity in Sindhu and Ganga, was known as 'nila-lohita' or the 'blue and red one' and these were the colours with which the vraon hunchback had painted his god. Besides, in Sindhu and Ganga, the word 'Shiva' itself meant 'the Auspicious One,' and this meaning is retained in modern-day Sanskrit as well. At the same time, 'Shiva' or 'Sivapu' in the Dravidham language, then and now, would also mean 'the red one' and some say that this 'sameness in redness' of both Shivas was inspired by the vraon song-myth (first recited well before 7000 BC) in which the hunchback artist had painted the figure of god with his blood.

Again, in Sindhu and Ganga, the equivalent of the Dravidham 'Sivan' would be Rudra (from Rudhira or Rudhita which means 'red' or 'blood') and the red-faced Rudra, in Sindhu and Ganga, was simply another form of Shiva. In that form Rudra, always depicted in the blood-red colour, was known as Pasupati and was highly honoured.

That was the position in Yadodhra's times. But many centuries later, in the Vedic period, Rudra came to be regarded by priests as an inferior—and unwanted—manifestation of Shiva. As Pasupati—or protector of animals—he was grim and angry: 'if the sacred fire was fed with too much firewood, he would demand why so many trees were cut and that this would deprive the pasu (animals) of their domain and heritage.' Nor would he ever approve of a sacrifice of blood and flesh for the gratification of the gods or man. He was expected to 'curse the priest who officiates at the sacrifice, and also him for whom the sacrifice was offered; and he would thwart the purpose of the sacrifice and bless only him who was sacrificed.'

A running battle, often on comic lines, went on between the priests and god Rudra who was regarded as the protector of the dumb and the helpless; and some priests even helped foster the depiction of Rudra as someone who was out of place in a temple but lurked in cremation grounds, with unlit fires, wearing a garland of skulls and surrounded by evil spirits and demons. This mock-battle culminated in a cry in the Vedic rituals asking Rudra to remain away, while all the other gods were respectfully invited to the place of sacrifice. In *Aitreya Brahmana* (III. 3.9-10) was the insinuation that Rudra cared only for pasu and bhuta (ghosts and naked spirits who died violently without sraddha or prayers being said for them by their descendants). Again, this to some, seemed a reference to the vraon-myth in which the vraons died 'violently with none left to pray for them.'

Thus, with the Vedic priests at least, the high pre-ancient glory of Rudra was no more and a priest even asked, 'Is he then our god or is he the god of the demons who went to war with the first man who sought to furrow the land to plant his crop?' So great, was the priestly anger, that the name of Rudra appearing in the *Rig Veda* (II.3.1) was deliberately mispronounced as 'Rudriya' in *Aitreya Brahmana* (III.3.9-10); but worse still, even the mantra *'Abi nah'* (towards us) was modified, so that Rudra remained away from the place of sacrifice.

A new twist was given to the vraon myth in 1800 BC by Priestess Uma. (It is not clear why she was called a priestess; was she the wife of a priest? Or was she a priestess herself in her own right?) She said that Rudra was actually the vraon-god—the first to obey the Sacred Law—who sacrificed 'himself to himself,' and with that sacrifice all vraons went to reside in heaven with the gods, so that man may rule the earth, inspired by the Sacred Law that vraon left to guide man. She is said to have quoted a verse from the *Rig Veda* itself (Hymn of Primeval Man)—

> 'With Sacrifice, this god sacrificed to sacrifice
> Himself, the first to obey sacred laws
> And thus his mighty beings (vraons) did rise
> To reside where the imperishable spirit was.'

Some who try to discover the factual content in the myth consider Priestess Uma's contribution rather far-fetched! As it is, this quotation does not seem to conform fully with the *Rig-Vedic* verse, which is itself obscure. Some have suggested that this verse itself was not originally a part of the *Rig-Vedic* hymn but was added under Priestess Uma's inspiration.

Incidentally, Priestess Uma is also credited to have said that the red dot (tikka) which women wear on their foreheads is a 'symbol of the blood testimony' that the woman-goddess taken by the vraons was pure and chaste in thought and deed.

Yet Yadodhra's conviction that the people of Dravidham were once united with Ganga and Sindhu did not arise from a similarity of gods or myths for he always said, 'A myth may ultimately lead you to the truth but rarely to a fact.' What Yadodhra had was the evidence of Ekantra's charts; but more than that, as he discussed the Sacred Law of Dravidham, with Tamala sages and thinkers, he was convinced that with its concept of dharma, ahimsa, karma and moksha, it was simply a purer and more pristine reflection of the Sanathana Dharma of the upper Sindhu, the Sanathana of the lower Sindhu and Sanathani of the Ganga. In all its essentials, he could see no basic difference between the Tamala Sacred Law and Hindu Dharma. The names of gods and deities often differed and so did their magical power and potency. But then as a Tamala song said, 'Gods may change, sacred rites may differ, but dharma is changeless, with its virtues of ahimsa, compassion to all creatures, auspicious thought, purity, earnest endeavour, generosity, hospitality, contentedness and freedom from avarice and envy.'

Was it Yadodhra's wishful thought that led to the conclusion that sowewhere, sometime, his people were together with the Tamalas? The fact is that he was not the first to voice that view. It was a spontaneous reaction of the Tamala thinkers as he spoke to them of the precepts of the Hindu. True, the Tamala concepts of their Sacred Law were more refined and sometimes more demanding. But then even in Sindhu and Ganga there were differences in conception and approach, influenced by local colouring and social adaptations. Yet was that not inevitable in a liberal faith that tolerated, and even respected, all views without the regimentation of a single monotheistic, inquisitorial belief which would produce a nice, tidy system of one's own possession of the truth, the whole truth and nothing but the truth and even attack the faith of another!

The social customs of Dravidham, as Yadodhra discovered, were also different. It was the woman who played a leading role as the head of the family. She led the family worship, controlled family property and, in civic life, she—more than the man—was intimately concerned with the administration of the nagara. In intellectual life, many women were poets and philosophers; and in everyday worship, goddesses occupied equal, if not higher positions, than the gods.

Yet Yadodhra learnt that it had not always been so. The vraon song-myth had affected the texture of the Dravidham tradition and influenced even their social and legal systems. A woman came to be regarded not only as more compassionate but also as more rational, for the myth had said, 'Seven women pleaded against war with the vraons, but 777 men thundered that it must be as they had willed....'

The myth also quoted a girl trying to defend the woman who was taken to the Isle of vraons—'Wronged she is not by the vraon, but by the hundred tongues of our men!' Another woman went even further, 'Wronged she was by the vraon, you say! So be it, but was she wronged with or against her will?' And the myth went on to accuse those who persecuted on the basis of rumour, gossip, malice and prejudice, 'and even if a thousand tongues of men speak with one voice, there are a thousand reasons to believe that truth resides in none of them, but in the heart of that woman, wronged.'

Despite these differences in social customs, which Yadodhra viewed with utmost respect, he and most of the Dravidham sages saw a clear and indissoluble pre-ancient link between the Tamala and Hindu philosophy—'We began together, maybe we shall recommence our journey together.'

As they travelled from one nagara to the next, Yadodhra occupied himself with the Tamala thinkers and philosophers. Sindhu Putra however happily passed time with ordinary folks. Unlike Yadodhra, he had no immense curiosity in the intellectual and spiritual. Yet he saw that the lives of the Tamala people were never empty. They had deep affection, a sense of great value for love, friendship, family attachments and human relationship. There was a spark of poetry in their make-up and abiding faith in the unseen reality and respect for others which gave them a sense of exaltation in companionship, even with strangers. Yadodhra spoke of the triumphs of the Tamala intellect, their sense of social justice, freedom and, above all, unity—and Sindhu Putra agreed.

But the former Chief of the silent tribe gestured that the land of the Tamalas lacked unity; he explained by pointing to the vast distance that separated each of their nagaras from the next, with a terrain so difficult to cross that it was impassable in certain seasons; in fact, it was considered great if as many as four nagaras could join together for the spring festival and dance. Even the Tamala proverbs lamented over lovers staying five nagaras apart,

'Who will ask in vain
Where or when
Shall we meet again!'

Yadodhra laughed at the Chief as this was not the kind of unity to which his powerful intellect was directed. But Sindhu Putra was impressed. More so, as he had already been wondering how he should occupy the time and energies of the vast multitudes of people who had followed him from Sindhu, Ganga and all over.

Word went forth from Sindhu Putra to his followers—'You shall be the path-finders, bridge-builders, river-crossers, terrain-levellers' and the former Chief of silent tribe assumed leadership of the project.

Some say that Sindhu Putra had not realized that such activity would bring lustre to the material well-being of Dravidham. Others asked, 'How could anything be hidden from a god?' The fact remains that this toil to build paths and tracks, to connect all the nagaras, began to show its results. The bountiful produce of one nagara, never, thereafter, withered away, but reached the other nagaras where it was needed, well in time. Everyone saw the fascinating possibilities of this new beginning, though earlier it was thought that it was intended only for people to 'move, meet, and mingle,' and not so much for economic prosperity —'but in abundance it came, all the same.'

This 'route building' went on 'blessed by Sindhu Putra, extolled by Yadodhra and supervised by the former Chief of the silent tribe, at whose summons, thousands more poured in, from the silent tribe to assist and for their silence and devotion to work, they were compared to the silent ascetics of Dravidham, who combined work with worship and were known as Aravalu. Thereafter, it came to pass that people from the silent tribe, pouring into Dravidham, to work there under the command of him who was once their Chief, were also respectfully called Aravalu; and many said that Dravidham is one and indivisible from end to end, because Aravalu and Tamala are indivisible.'

Aravalu means 'the speechless people.' The prefix 'a' means 'not' and rava means 'voice or sound'—and this is retained in modern Sanskrit as well. Those of the silent tribe who worked at Sindhu Putra's request on these projects came to be called Aravalu (and it came to mean 'silent devotee'—and later, many also referred to the Tamala people, as Aravalu, when they performed a service with devotion, without seeking a reward or return). But as it is, the speechlessness of the silent tribes vanished altogether in a few generations of their intermarriage with the people of Ganga, Sindhu and particularly Dravidham. Yet the root-name of Aravalu lingered for generations.

Yadodhra's health was failing. Sindhu Putra wanted to escort him back
to his land of Sindhu. He was his last link with his father Bharatjogi.
But Yadodhra declined, and said: 'Sindhu, Saraswati, Ganga, Yamuna,
Kaveri. . . . He is manifest in all waters.'

Yadodhra was cremated by the side of Kaveri river. Sages,
philosphers, thinkers, mystics, ascetics from all over Dravidham
travelled to pay their respects to him. The foremost among them—
Tirukavi—spoke thus of Yadodhra—'. . .Thus him we salute, the
illustrious Hindu who was from the ancient root of Sanathana, Sanathani
and Sanathana Dharma, but also from the ancient root of the sacred
law of our people of Tamala—Yes, we Hindus all. . .'

Few understood Tirukavi, for she spoke with a rush of emotion,
through tears. Yet it was the first declaration in Dravidham that the
Tamala people regarded themselves as 'Hindus all.' Not that it was
such a dramatic or revolutionary declaration!

From the Dravidham point of view, the name of one's faith, even
the name of God, and the form of its expression, were relatively
unimportant and as Tirukavi always said,

> 'Every name is of One Name;
> All names speak of One that is the same.'

To the Dravidian mind, it was always clear that 'Shiva is Vishnu
and Vishnu is Rudra who surely is Brahma; And verily they all manifest
that One Atma' (soul). Actually this was no different from the Sindhu
belief in *tad akam* or that one—'She that is universe but more; she that
is heaven but more; she is the mother, father, son, all gods, the whole
world but more; she is the creation and birth, but more. . . . Verily,
She is the atma—soul.'

Even so, Tirukavi's soulful declaration of 'Hindus all' had a stirring
impact on all those who had come from Sindhu and Ganga and more
so on the vast numbers of ex-slaves who followed Sindhu Putra. Their
sense of 'belonging' and 'acceptance' grew, for this was what they had
dreamt of in captivity—a land without a master or a slave. And it was
as though they were now reunited with their past dream in a land
that was theirs and with people who were their own—Hindus all!

They were determined to work harder, longer, to overtake the work-
plan of building paths and tracks to connect the nagaras of these people
whom they regarded as their own. As it is, day by day, the plan was
getting to be more ambitious than simply levelling and clearing routes.
Little townships were set up to provide homes for new-comers in barren
lands so cleared. Of necessity, this involved planting trees and crops,
diversion of streams; and digging more wells and reservoirs of
enormous sizes. The townships grew, each with a small temple—and
the deities there were modelled on the available idols of Dravidham.

But far more furiously, work went on to 'cut rocks, fill ditches,
bridge ravines. . . .' so that 'by Sindhu Putra's will, the 8,400 nagaras
of Dravidham were one, from beginning to end.'

The prosperity of Dravidham grew. Their feeling of oneness with the people of Sindhu Putra grew. Tirukavi's declaration of 'Hindus all' seeped fully into the mind of Tamala, all the more, when they saw temples that the new-comers had built to honour the gods of Dravidham. Far greater was their admiration for Sindhu Putra—this god of the new-comers who had no aim other than to serve them and sought nothing in return! To them, he came to embody the highest ideal of Tamala goodness.

Yet when the foremost amongst the Tamala artists wanted to sculpt a statue of Sindhu Putra, to be kept in a temple, Sindhu Putra demanded that none should keep his statue in a temple; and a poet paraphrases his words—

'. . .Not even at the foot of gods, for god I am not;
Nor among noble worshippers, for that I am not;
The road I travel, is the one that I sought;
Another life, to atone, has to be my lot. . .'

This denial of his godhood actually endeared him to many; some wondered though, how he felt that he was not amongst 'noble worshippers.' And they wondered too, how with a life so auspicious, he could think of being denied moksha and being subjected to rebirth and another life! Yet he was firm and no statues rose, nor were images made.

For the six years that he was there, Sindhu Putra threw himself, body and soul, into the concerns of Dravidham—for its health, happiness and prosperity—and the results, as everyone could see, were spectacular.

They called him Periyar (the great one).

The widely scattered nagaras of Dravidham and several dispersed areas came closer to each other, 'bridged by townships, and separated no longer by impassable ravines, while gardens sprang from wastelands.'

Commerce began but not just between the nagaras of Dravidham. A caravan left for Sindhu, to the village of Gatha, carrying sandlewood, oil, cosmetics, painted pottery, garments, toys and ornaments of gold and silver, with a request from Sindhu Putra to Gatha to interest guilds and the merchants of Sindhu to come and buy and sell for 'they would find in Dravidham, the same abundance and yet so different and charming.'

The Periyar! He was also, then, their bridge to lands unknown. But many, enthused by the faith of Sindhu and Ganga, regarded him as greater. Yet he disappointed them when they asked him for the mystery of the universe and he replied, 'He who could answer your question shall not be reborn.' Obviously, it was a reference to Sage Yadodhra, but at least one poet says that he meant 'Him that first and for ever sprang from Mother Goddess.'

The growing prosperity and movement of people increased the disputes in Dravidham. Sometimes he was called upon to settle those; but largely, he resolved them more with love and an appeal to their reason, though he did step in, for instance, to have another well dug or to divert a stream, when the dispute was related to the sharing of waters. Yet when the disputes were serious, as those between the Councils of two or more nagaras, he suggested that they resign unless they could themselves resolve the dispute by a certain date; somehow that sufficed, and they felt that their 'Periyar was wiser in his indecision than they who made the decision.'

At a joint assembly of all nagara councils (though not all of them participated and many sent 'messages of accord') a decision was taken that Periyar should be the guiding spirit of every Nagara Council.

Their Periyar! He criticized none and nothing—neither an individual, nor a custom, nor a ritual, nor a doctrine. He had no message of enlightenment to offer and prescribed no rule of conduct or way of life; but many chose to see much, not in the words he uttered, but the life he led, and the attention he gave, unasked, to their welfare. The one emotion they recognized in him, clearly, was his love for them all, that arose from a gracious mind and a tender heart. And that impressed them more and made up for the absence of embroidery in his words and his refusal to engage in discussions on the nature of infinity. 'That discussion,' he would say, 'may take all eternity, but meanwhile much work remains to be done.' And clearly, they saw that his heart was set on spending every moment in the service of Dravidham and its people. In return, the people of Dravidham gave him 'their love in abundance and found comfort in his presence and were thrilled to claim him as their very own Periyar and themselves as his people—Hindus, all.'

'A man sees little and grieves much; surely God who sees all will grieve all the more.'

—(Attributed to the Chief of silent tribe in 'Songs of Silence'— 5036 BC)

'Gods are mighty, Gods are great;
But mightier are the guardians of the gate.'

—(Complaint against the Silent Chief for barring access to Sindhu Putra, 5036 BC)

Hindus All

5058 BC

Thousands wanted to join Sindhū Putra as he left Dravidham. He held them back. 'Your work is not finished here,' he said. That was obvious. The work-plan, as it had ambitiously evolved, would take not a few years but more than a generation—to build paths and bridges; dig wells and reservoirs; plant gardens; and divert waters.

Even so, he left with a huge group which included the former Chief of silent tribe, the three sons of Manu of Tungeri, and many Tamala men and women, none of whom had been outside Dravidham, with the exception of the old explorer and his son. Joining the son was also his wife and his four-year-old child.

Sindhu Putra left his vast workforce in Dravidham, with Dharmadassa, the speechless Aravalu, a remote cousin of the Chief of silent tribe in charge. As Dharmadassa was the first Aravalu to marry a Tamala girl, he was often known as Tamala Aravalu (silent Tamala); and later, he was called 'the first, very first,' by the silent tribe and even by the others, as his son born from the Tamala wife could speak effortlessly. He called his son Dharmalila.

This reference to Dharmadassa as 'first, very first,' and his son's name as Tamala Dharmalila, caused confusion among the modern historians, inspired by Herodotus and other western sources; and he came to be regarded by some as the founder of the ancient Dravidian civilization and his name was variously mentioned as Dharmila, Damila, Dharmaza, Dharmozi, Dirumalai, Tirumalai, Termilai, Dhamir, Damrike, Trimmli and so forth.

The fact is, however, that while Dharmadassa—this silent Tamala Aravalu—did do a lot of work in Dravidham, the Dravidian civilization itself flourished thousands of years before his and Sindhu Putra's time. In fact, Sindhu Putra would cry out everywhere, 'Learn. Learn, from the age-old culture of Dravidham!. . .'

No one knows whether, in Dravidham or even on his journey back, Sindhu Putra did hear the roar and rumble of battles raging in the far

north and west, fought by commanders acting in his name, to free the
land and slaves from warlords. And poets simply ask, 'How can you
meet savagery except by savagery that is equally remorseless?'

Yet many add that Sindhu Putra knew nothing of the bloodshed,
as none burdened him with undue information and each time, he
'simply blessed messengers who reported freedom and thrice-blessed
him who achieved it.'

Thus, as he travelled, he received joyous news, from time to time,
of lands freed but not of tears, agony and bloodshed.

At Ganga, he heard the sad news that Gangapati XIII was dead.
The little son was anointed as Gangapati XIV with Sindhu Putra's
blessing. Everyone recalled how the child was born by a miracle of
Sindhu Putra, some eight years back.

Sindhu Putra also blessed the 'Regent' who was to look after the
land of Ganga and to train Gangapati XIV, until the child came of age.
The Regent was nominated by the Sabha and approved by Gangapatni
ma (mother of Gangapati XIV).

Sindhu Putra caused some confusion by blessing two girls as
prospective brides for Gangapati XIV, without indicating a preference
for either and obviously leaving the final choice to the parents. Of
these two, one was the Regent's five-year-old daughter and the other
was Sindhu Karkarta Sharat's two-year-old granddaughter.

Some felt that Sindhu Putra should have made the selection, blessed
one and not both; but others said that Sindhu Putra always blessed
everyone and everything, sometimes without even knowing who or
what he blessed!

From Ganga, Sindhu Putra reached Sindhu. Muni and Roopa had
died two years earlier, within three days of each other. Some recalled
Roopa's words that Muni and she would always be at the Rocks
together and foolishly a poet said that a pipal tree sprung up on the
edge of the Rocks to hold their spirits. But that pipal tree was simply
an offshoot of a tree Roopa had planted a long time ago, to mark the
birth of Kanta's son who died at the Rocks.

Roopa's father, the once-blind singer, was still alert and active,
despite his advanced age. Some said that God granted him extra years
on earth, for the early years that he was blind.

To the ailing Gatha, Sindhu Putra said, 'You are the only father I
have left.' Gatha died in ecstasy while Sindhu Putra wept.

Sindhu Putra would sometimes sit by the side of his two mothers—
Kanta and Sonama. He would then feel at peace, while Kanta brushed
his hair with her hand and he wondered at their uncomplicated lives
full of faith!

But those moments of peace were few. Everyone in the village and
thousands beyond came to be near him, cheer him and be blessed.
They no longer wanted miracles from him. He was their miracle!

What, then, was the burden in his heart, he wondered. But then,
can a man slice through his multiple personalities to discover the secret

of his guilt and sorrow! A god possibly can; a man cannot; and he knew he was no god.

Yet he accused himself—he remembered that moment of joy and elation, when he reached Ganga, where every chief, from far and near, including Karkarta Sharat, had gathered to witness the anointment of Gangapati XIV. They had all bowed to him in utmost reverence and had even thought it a miracle that he had arrived on the day of the anointment. As it is, Gangapatni ma had prayed in the temple and in her heart that Sindhu Putra may come to bless the ceremony; she even begged the temple-priests to pray likewise. 'This god hears prayers,' they said, when Sindhu Putra appeared.

All the Chiefs at the ceremony had touched his feet and kissed the hem of his garment and he had felt elated. But he forgave himself for that thrill. It was, he rationalized, nothing personal and in their exaggerated respect he simply saw their assurance that they would never revert to their old ways of holding slaves and disrupt freedom and unity. That feeling of elation continued as the repeated cry rang through endless crowds: 'Mahapati!' 'Mahakarta!' 'Periyar!' 'Maharaj!' .... And again, he forgave himself with the realization that the people's love for him was a guarantee that they would never again permit slavery.

It was not so much the ceremonial anointment of Gangapati XIV as a scene of unbridled joy at the reunion with Sindhu Putra. He blessed the new Gangapati and then moved to Sindhu.

Even so, Sindhu Putra felt lonely within himself, as the crowds around him grew. The words that were in his heart, he did not speak. His every mood and movement, every sigh and smile, were noticed. For him there was no privacy.

Sindhu Putra went to Muni's Rocks. That would be his retreat. The less people see me, the easier they will find it to forget me—he thought. He was wrong. Hundreds of boats would line up in the river along the Rocks to view him and seek his blessings.

The once-blind singer lived at the Rocks with the two daughters of Muni and Roopa. He understood something of Sindhu Putra's grief, which arose from the unwilling role imposed on him as a god, and he said, 'There is no lie in him! From his father Bharatjogi, he inherited a dream that was good and godly. Alone he made that dream come true! His self-doubts are human, so long as he is on this earth. But did any god, ever, have a nobler dream or perform a greater miracle?'

The singer quotes also the former Chief of silent tribe: 'A man sees little and grieves much; surely a god who sees all, will grieve all the more.'

But to Sindhu Putra, the singer merely said, 'Remain at the Rocks in peace. They, who line up along the river seek nothing. A simple blessing, a distant nod, a mere raising of the hand, is enough.' The singer was right, he thought. They seek nothing—simply to be blessed. That spiritual solace was enough.

None of the high and mighty came. They had bowed to him at the ceremony of anointment of Gangapati XIV; also, with respect they had bowed when he first arrived in their lands. Often, they sent gifts, big and small. That surely was enough, as his title—Mahakarta, Mahapati, Periyar, Maharaj, or whatever—was simply spiritual and had no power over them.

In public if the high and mighty had to speak of him, their words were laced with honey, but it was all to the good, they felt, that he had shut himself away at the Rocks and did not venture out.

In peace, Sindhu Putra remained at the Rocks. The large Tamala group along with the sons of Tungeri happily left to explore the entire Sindhu region. Only the former Chief of silent tribe and a few others were with him at the Rocks.

Meanwhile, battles continued, far away in scattered, unknown, remote pockets, as commanders, inspired by Sindhu Putra's message, were still at work. Couriers would reach the Rocks to convey to the former chief of silent tribe the glad tidings of this or that victory won, such and such region freed from old tyranny and names of new chiefs appointed, old chiefs expelled or reformed. There would often also be news of how the freed lands had been amalgamated with Ganga or Sapta Sindhu or even set up as a nagara of Dravidham with instructions to Dharmadassa (Tamala Aravalu) to keep an eye on it, so that they function wisely with a proper Council. In several cases though, the land would be on its own, under a new chief, committed to the 'freedom wave' of Sindhu Putra. Here, a poet pounces on the silent Chief to say—

'Words he could never articulate
    With signs, motions to gesticulate;
Truth is what he always told,
    But only a little, much to withhold.'

The poet is clear that the Chief told Sindhu Putra only of the lands freed, and not of the bloodshed and cruelty, nor of the fresh wave of tyranny by the new chiefs. Another poet, however, in a long poem—
The Blindfold of Gods—blames Sindhu Putra and says—

'He knew or should have known;
    The blame is his—his alone.'

The once-blind singer had said that people hungered only for a blessing from Sindhu Putra to gain spiritual solace. He was right but not for long. The high and mighty chiefs needed no spiritual solace;

they were happy with Sindhu Putra cloistered in the Rocks; but there were those who wanted those high and mighty positions for themselves, also those whose authority had been usurped by the new chiefs appointed in their place. And the people? They had their grievances too and hopes and aspirations far beyond spiritual solace. How could you have a god around you and seek only a blessing!

A wit even asked, 'Would not the gods feel ignored and insulted if I seek nothing from them?'

But it was not easy to gain access to Sindhu Putra. The silent Chief would not permit it.

But then what the silent Chief wanted was to spare Sindhu Putra the agony of listening to the woes of so many and opening the flood-gates to a never-ending torrent of visitors. For him, it was enough that Sindhu Putra appeared every dawn and sunset at the commanding balcony of his newly built house at the Rocks to bless all those gathered outside.

But the silent Chief listened long and hard to the old Tamala explorer who came to visit. The explorer spoke of a colony of slaves, freed, but only in name, and working in pitiable conditions, their lot worse than before. He spoke of raids into Jalta lands by armed men from forts at the eastern tip; and though the Jalta lands were united with Sapta Sindhu, Jalta people were halted and harassed if they crossed over to pursue offenders. The three Jalta brothers were away, fighting battles in Sindhu Putra's cause, in distant theatres. Alone, ailing and sightless, their mother watched and grieved over the affairs of her people.

Immediately, the explorer was taken to Sindhu Putra who heard the grim tale. The reference to Jalta's mother affected him—'She is my mother,' he said. For the rest, his faith in Karkarta Sharat was total. 'He is a man of honour. These things have happened without his knowledge and against his wishes.'

When told that the new colony of ex-slaves was too large and the raids on Jalta lands too well-organized for the Karkarta to remain unaware, Sindhu Putra felt hurt at this lack of trust—'I trust Sharatji. Conscience is his best friend.' He turned to the silent Chief, 'Go, place the facts before him and he will instantly set everything right.'

The silent Chief left with the explorer who was to act as his interpreter. Sadly, in Karkarta's town, he learnt of the definite limits to the reach and influence of his master, Sindhu Putra. Spiritual power, by itself, was not enough!

Jagasi who acted as 'door opener' (secretary?) for Karkarta Sharat, insisted on knowing what the message was.

'It is for Karkarta's ears only,' the Chief replied.

'But I am Karkarta's ears! And eyes too!'

'I am sure Karkarta still retains his ears for a message sent personally for him by Sindhu Putra.'

'Sindhu Putra! Of course, to hear him is to obey! I shall soon send for you.'

Two days passed. The former Chief went storming in. Jagasi apologized: 'Karkarta has been so busy, why not catch him any morning, as every dawn he is at Raj Garden, listening to all those who wish to meet him.'

The next dawn, the Chief and explorer were in the garden. It was besieged by throngs of petitioners and it was impossible to catch Karkarta's eye.

They saw Jagasi again who was as cheerful as ever—'All good things come to those who wait. I promise you a meeting in a day or two.'

But the Chief, resolved now on a different approach, said, 'Thank you, but I cannot wait. I have to leave now for Jalta lands.'

'Well, suit yourself. But do see me on your return.'

'Of course, though I wanted to see Sharatji before discussing with Jalta ma the problem of her becoming Karkarta.'

'What!' Jagasi's eyes popped out; but the Chief and the explorer nonchalantly walked out. They did not seem to hear Jagasi calling them back. But messengers ran to halt them.

Karkarta Sharat received them graciously. 'What is this I hear about old Jalta ma aspiring to be Karkarta?'

'It is a high position, high honour,' the Chief replied.

'But at the time of union, she openly declared that she wanted me as Karkarta.'

The Chief nodded sympathetically, 'Maybe she hears that Karkarta is not a lifelong office, but an elected term of seven years.'

'But what chance can she have to win?' Sharat asked. The Chief simply shrugged his shoulders, as if to agree that she had no chance; and Sharat continued, 'What does Sindhu Putra feel about it?'

'How can I speak for my master? Only. . .' he hesitated but Sharat insisted on knowing his unspoken thoughts. The Chief obliged. 'All I know is that Sindhu Putra regarded Jalta ma as his mother. Her three sons fight for his cause. Her people shed their blood for him. She accepted his plea for union with Sindhu. He owes her much! Maybe he can deny her nothing!'

Just as the silent Chief had recently concluded that spiritual power by itself was not enough to command men of influence, Sharatji's mind now ran on similar lines—that earthly power itself has limits; what would happen if Sindhu Putra throws his weight behind Jalta ma at the next election! Blind, old, stupid she may be. But what would happen if Sindhu Putra openly favoured her? She wouldn't win. But the disgrace! He wanted no challenge. He must remain undisputed Karkarta for life and thereafter, his son. Yet his gracious smile did not desert him as he asked, 'But why this sudden, insane ambition? Does she know the problems a Karkarta faces?'

'I don't think she knows. Maybe she is not really interested in all the great things that a great Karkarta must accomplish. She would simply be worried about one or two things, hoping to make a difference. For instance, her worry would be about incursions and raids from Sindhu forts into eastern territory. . . .'

'They shall stop, forthwith,' Sharat thundered. 'I shall see to it. Some of our commanders act as criminals. There will not be a single incursion again. That is my promise.'

'Then she would be worried about much that has already been taken away from her land. . . .'

'That is a small matter. The criminals will be punished.'

'That will give her comfort but she will still wish to regain what they have lost.'

'Of course; there will be restitution. No; more than that. She will get more than they have lost.'

The Chief nodded, obviously impressed with his generosity, 'Yes that will be the best, for sometimes her people exaggerate their losses; and the only other matter in which she can possibly hope to make a difference is in the respect of ex-slave colonies.'

There was determination in Sharat's eyes as the explorer translated the Chief's gestures, 'Since the Jalta lands have no burden of past slavery, she may think it is easy to dismantle the colonies, newly established, to herd ex-slaves into our land, where these unfortunates are forced to work in poor conditions. Maybe she feels that ex-slaves can immediately be helped to rise to the level of our rya.'

With a sweep of his hand, the Chief seemed to suggest that those colonies existed all over, though the explorer had actually mentioned to him only a single colony he had seen.

Slowly Sharat responded, 'Such colonies must be done away with, and surely ex-slaves must have all their rights—equal and indivisible—of the rya. More, in fact, to compensate for their past suffering. I must see to it myself. Too long have I relied on others.'

The Chief was silent. Mentally he noted that Sharat's reply gave away that he knew there were other such colonies. Quietly Sharat asked, 'Is there anything else of concern to Jalta ma?'

'I doubt it. She is not a person with many ideas and she will be happy if these few concerns are fully met. Of course, words may not satisfy her. . . .'

'No,' Sharat interrupted. 'Positive proof is what she shall have.'

'What more can she ask for?' the Chief graciously conceded.

'And her ambition to be Karkarta?' asked Sharat.

'Even I will forcefully persuade her to have no such foolish ambition once she has proof that her real concerns are resolved.'

Sharat liked this turn in the conversation, which had taken long enough to come and was made all the more tedious by the Chief's gestures and their interpretation by the explorer, with too many exchanges between the chief and the explorer so that the Chief's thoughts were correctly expressed.

Sharat had already indulged in the drama of shouting at Jagasi for keeping visitors of such quality away from him for so long. Now, graciously, he invited the Chief and explorer for a meal. All the other visitors were kept at bay; all appointments were cancelled.

Meanwhile, Sharat was thinking, maybe Jalta's mother is furious over the raids in her territory. Yes, they will stop. I will bribe her too, with far more compensation. But why should our ex-slave colonies have bothered her? They are our ex-slaves!... None from Jalta lands! ...In our own land...Far from Jalta territory!...Rarely do Jalta people travel so far inland...Often, they are halted; turned back. So how did this stupid, half-witted, blind woman see or hear about them!

An awesome thought struck him—was it that woman's dream to aspire to be Karkarta? Or was it Sindhu Putra's move to bring her forward as a candidate!... Sharat's mind raced. This man sheltered in the Rock retreat may not, then, be a mere dummy! Then he must probe the minds of the two simpletons before him.

The 'probe' brought him no joy, though the Chief and explorer were both forthcoming in their responses. Sharat expressed his pleasure that Jalta ma came to know about faraway ex-slave colonies and therefore the matter was able to be brought to his attention so that he could rectify it; but he casually asked, 'How did she come to know about the colonies?' The Chief said that it was actually a discovery made by the explorer and the explorer was a talkative person and could keep nothing to himself and therefore a lot of people came to know whatever he discovered, but hereafter he would be told not to blabber to anyone but report only to Sindhu Putra.

It was with great pain and much argument in sign language that the explorer finally translated all this. But the lights flashing in Sharat's mind had a different message. Still he said, 'I thought your friend, the explorer from Dravidham and his team, travelled for pleasure.'

'That too. But they must go from place to place and report everything to Sindhu Putra. After all, he is Mahakarta and he realizes what his duty is as Mahakarta.'

Sharat could have told him that Mahakarta was only a title of honour, with no rights, no powers and no duty. Instead, he said, 'But what would these men from outside know about what happens in our land of Sindhu?'

'Exactly my thought, Karkarta! But just as there are teams from Dravidham and Ganga here, there is a Sindhu team in Dravidham;

and Dravidham teams in Ganga; and Sindhu teams elsewhere. I don't see much merit in that but Mahakarta seems to think it is good to avoid local influences in fact-finding.'

My God, thought Sharat. Sindhu Putra's teams were on the prowl everywhere then! Waiting, watching! Why?

But the former Chief was proving to be a mine of information, despite protests from his explorer friend and translator. 'Actually Karkarta, maybe I am wrong. Mahakarta always tells me that these people from Dravidham are not outsiders. Nor are Ganga people and others. To him, like the people of Sindhu, they belong to Bharat Varsha—Hindus all—though they may be in separate units, under Karkarta in Sindhu or with Gangapati in Ganga. But then, here, there, everywhere, they are one, as he remains the single, common link as Mahakarta, Mahapati, Periyar for all Bharat Varsha.'

Sharat fumed silently—so I serve under this Mahakarta!

But the Chief's next observation assuaged his feelings—'Of course, Mahakarta is not interested at all in the affairs of men. In two years or less, he will retire totally as an ascetic, unconcerned with matters of the earth. Even now he would have, but for his promise that slavery is eradicated all over and that ex-slaves are brought to the level of rya and no part of Bharat Varsha is threatened by another remain.'

So, the imposition is for two years—thought Sharat hopefully. Still he asked, 'You think all this is achievable in two years or less?'

'Why not? He can only pave the way, not resolve everything. Maybe he will increase his teams so that things progress quickly.'

'His teams have no difficulty in gathering information?'

'Who will deny them information? They carry Mahapati seals in Ganga, Periyar seals in Dravidham and Mahakarta seals here.'

'Mahakarta seals? What are those?'

'Oh, simply to indicate that the team is on Mahakarta's business, so that everyone cooperates.'

'May I see the seal?' Sharat requested.

Then began a furious sign-exchange between explorer and Chief. Finally, the Chief said that the seal was with the explorer's team and he had not brought it with him to this meeting, even though he had clear instructions that the seal remain with the leader at all times. However, he would obtain a spare seal from Mahakarta and show it to Karkarta the next time.

Mahakarta! Mahakarta! The Chief kept throwing out the phrase, as though heaven and earth had combined to invest Sindhu Putra with every imaginable power. Sharat no longer had the impulse to shout that Mahakarta was an empty title that meant nothing. Sadly he realized that if the man behind that title decided to put up a dead donkey to fight an election as Karkarta, maybe there would be many who would lend their support.

664 / Return of the Aryan

Outside, at a distance from Karkarta's house, the explorer spoke to the former Chief. 'Our Periyar, Sindhu Putra, told us that conscience is your Karkarta's best friend!'

'Karkarta's dog, too, is his best friend. But did you not notice how roughly Karkarta spoke when the dog barked—and the dog went into a corner and remained quiet, with its tail between its legs.'

'Your own conscience did not impress me, either.'

'Why? You are the one who told all the lies!'

'Under your corrupt manipulations.'

'Yes, I realize, you are not an original thinker.'

'May God save me from such original thinking!'

'Why? Think, old man. Think! The ex-slave colonies will be disbanded! The promise to treat them as rya will be honoured! Raids to Jalta lands will stop! They will even be compensated. Did you ever achieve that much in your lifetime of truth?'

'Yet to attribute false words to Periyar's mouth! And even to that poor lady Jalta ma!'

'That is the fault of your defective translation. Not a single thought did I attribute to Sindhu Putra or Jalta ma.'

'Is that the impression you left with Karkarta Sharatji?'

'The impression given to him was the right one. He will henceforth follow the right path.'

'For how long? A year? Two years?'

'That is all that is needed. Once he raises the slaves to the rya level, how will he turn back? And if raids to Jalta lands stop now, will he resume them when the Jalta brothers return from their battles in full force?'

'And how will you know that all the colonies of ex-slaves are truly dismantled?'

'That is your task, my friend; you told us about one colony; your team will go around to see if any more remain.'

'I am not a spy!'

'No, you are the "eyes" of your Periyar, Sindhu Putra. Did you ever dream of such a high honour when you were languishing as a slave?'

'In your land—while you were its Chief!' the explorer accused.

'That Chief was different, untouched by God. He that stands before you, now, is your friend, your brother.'

'And that friend and brother touched by God, now calls on me to participate in his lies!'

The Chief did not reply. The explorer did not insist. They avoided each other's eyes, perhaps with a single thought—what needs to be done, has to be done. Instead, the explorer asked, 'Could you not at least tell a less outrageous lie? To imply that poor, blind Jalta ma is hoping to be Karkarta! You could have used the name of one of the Jalta brothers!'

'But the outrageous succeeded! The fact though is, I really wasn't thinking. It came on the spur of the moment.'

'I know. Others think first, and act thereafter. With you, it is the opposite. And what was that nonsense about the Mahakarta seal?'

'Merely to anticipate events. You will have your Mahakarta seal before you leave.'

In a town, not far off, a well-known seal-maker was found. 'I work where I work,' he said when the silent Chief's emissary tried to entice him to go to the Rocks.

'You will have the honour of working for Sindhu Putra.'

'Honour! Does it mean I will not be paid?'

'No, it means you will be paid twice—once on earth and again hereafter.'

'I prefer being paid twice on earth.'

'So be it,' the emissary agreed. Terms were settled. The artist left for the Rocks, with mules to carry his equipment.

The Chief demanded ten seals in a hurry—it didn't matter if they were not too artistic. But the artist said, 'Then you should hire a brick-layer or a barber. An artist can only create art.' He agreed to produce one seal every ten days.

The design on the seal? 'Why not a depiction of Bharat Varsha?'— the explorer suggested, explaining the kind of map he had in view.

But the ex-Chief said, 'Frontiers of Bharat Varsha advance every day, everywhere—north, south, east, west—and as Sage Yadodhra said, all who were once together are coming back together.'

'Then why not a circle to show that all those who were apart have come together,' the explorer proposed.

But the artist asked, 'Have all those who were apart come together? Why close the circle. Besides, a circle represents a star or sun and such seals are common.'

The Chief drew a cross to symbolize the growth of Bharat Varsha in all four directions. The artist shook his head, 'It looks like the wooden frame my brother makes for hanging his scarecrow to frighten away birds from his field.'

The Chief drew another figure—a straight line, at which the top branched off in a number of lines in all directions. The artist said, 'With a few lines less at the top, it could look like a pitchfork; with a few more lines at the top, it would look like the broom with which my mother sweeps the floor. Now it simply looks like a plant with needles and no flowers.'

'If you are such a great critic and artist, why don't you come up with a better idea?' asked the explorer.

'No, the Chief's idea is sound. I will work on his lines,' said the artist. He drew an unfamiliar figure. Later, this figure would be known

[1]It was immediately after the distribution of these seals that the figure came to be known as svastika, an auspicious, benedictory, sacred mark, by virtue of its being blessed by Sindhu Putra. Literally, svastika then came to mean a blessing for well-being or good fortune, or simply, a blessing for the fortunate. This meaning is still retained in present-day Sanskrit.

as the auspicious svastika[1] design. It was in the form of a cross with equal arms, each arm having a limb of equal length projecting from its end; and each limb pointed in a different direction.

The chief approved, 'It points in all directions, with a feeling of movement, strength, unity, equality and togetherness in its limbs.'

'Yes,' said the explorer. 'Togetherness, yet with a diversity that does not offend its wholeness.'

Sindhu Putra saw the artist at work. The Chief enlightened him, 'So many seek tokens of your affection; so many need them! These seals will serve that purpose.'

Later, the Chief and explorer brought the svastika design of the seal to Sindhu Putra, who said, 'I like it. It shows flow, movement in all directions, strength, unity, equality, togetherness and diversity.'

They heard him with astonishment; how did he know exactly what they were going to say. But Sindhu Putra laughed, 'Don't be surprised! The artist told me the idea behind it. I would have believed him, if he had said it represented two elephants embracing each other. But as he explained it, I think it is a beautiful symbol that you two gave him.'

'No, the artist came up with the symbol,' the Chief said.

'Well,' said Sindhu Putra. 'The artist said it was your idea which he admired immensely.'

Sometimes, Sindhu Putra watched as the artist worked to cut, saw, round, smooth, and sand steatite (soap-stone) with all kinds of saws, knives and tools. Thereafter, with copper burin (cutting tool), he would carve the svastika design. The seals would then be coated with a smooth, glossy glaze, hardened by fire, with the flame kept away from the seal. Some seals were square or oblong; others cylindrical. A few had svastika with a delicate inlay of beads; others had refined copper containing elements of arsenic and antimony; and some had bronze and tin alloy.

Sindhu Putra tried his hand at cutting steatite, but could not. Nor could he carve. The artist laughed, 'Easy to be a god; but it takes time to be an artist.' Sindhu Putra laughed too. 'I am neither,' he said.

The Chief actually wanted all the seals to be the same but the artist said, 'I do not copy. I will send my cousin to you. He cannot create but he copies beautifully.'

He made fifteen seals, taking only five days per seal, instead of the ten days that he had threatened. 'I would have finished earlier but for your god hindering my work.' When he left, he demanded, and received, wages for two days to reach his town.

Later, his cousin came to work on the seals. He brought a large copper tablet with a pierced hump at the back for suspension—a gift from the artist to Sindhu Putra. The svastika figure was in gold with a slight silver content. The Chief wondered, 'How demanding he was about his wages! And yet he sends a gift of gold that costs far more than his wages!'

The Chief's mind was, however, on more momentous matters. The explorer had left with a seal to rejoin his team. Couriers from the Chief were scurrying all over to assemble four new teams. Their task? To act as Sindhu Putra's 'eyes everywhere and report'. Each team carried Sindhu Putra's seal. The crowds would touch the seal, pray and even weep.

There was no secrecy in the movement of the teams. The seals in their possession simply made them inviolable and encouraged everyone to open their hearts to them. If any injustice was persistent or widespread, the team was to send a report to the Chief for Sindhu Putra. The team could not redress grievance, nor intercede—only report. But often, their mere presence goaded the administrators into remedying matters.

Communications were poor; teams far away; reports, often unable to reach. But no matter. The teams gave hope to the masses.

People put up large metal tablets in their villages with the svastika design, with its message of the oneness of Bharat Varsha emerging clearly in their minds. Even clearer was the message that far above those that ruled them, was their overlord Sindhu Putra, who thought of them, cared for them and would move to redress their grievances. The message to Karkarta, Gangapati's Regent, and the other mighty lords and Chiefs was clear too—Sindhu Putra is watching. His power is not spiritual alone. Deny him not!

Jagasi arrived with boat-loads of gifts for Sindhu Putra. The Chief suppressed the impulse to tell him that he should seek his chance to meet Sindhu Putra on a full-moon day when he mingled with visitors.

Jagasi presented Sharat's gifts to Sindhu Putra and thanked him for the information about the raids on Jalta lands—'Criminals have been punished. This will not happen again. Jalta ma is delighted with the caravans of gifts to compensate her.' He added, 'Ex-slave colonies are no more; every slave is now rya.'

Sindhu Putra was pleased and told the Chief, 'See! I told you the moment Sharatji hears, he will spring into action.'

Jagasi added, 'Karkarta seeks to serve you. He can do far more when family ties are established with Gangapati and a true unity of hearts is achieved between Sindhu and Ganga. Why, Karkarta would even assume the Regent's responsibility so both Ganga and Sindhu move single-mindedly for unity, freedom and justice.'

Again Jagasi sought and was granted a blessing for the marriage of Karkarta's granddaughter with the child-Gangapati. But he was also told that the blessing granted to others must remain as well.

More would have been said but for the timely interruption already arranged by the Chief. Again Sindhu Putra told the Chief, 'Truly, Sharatji is a man of virtue and honour. I trust him fully.'

Silently, the Chief wondered: but he says that of Gangapati's Regent too and of all whom he meets. He loves people not only in the abstract, but each individual, never doubting their word. What is it, then? Indulgence of love—universal and personal? Or is it that the gods are unable to understand duplicity!

The teams increased in number, size and even function. They were fact-finders who were to observe and spread the message of the oneness of Bharat Varsha under Sindhu Putra—but sometimes they would take up issues with local lords, chiefs and headmen; and the excuse that the orders came from Karkarta or Gangapati was not enough. The question was: do they conform to the higher order of Sindhu Putra?

Slowly, spiritual power was transforming itself into earthly power as well. Nandan's eighth great-grandson blamed the Chief of silent tribe and said of Sindhu Putra—

'...Always a pawn, now a pawn...this son of unknown, an orphan from nowhere, with the mind of a goat, was first Bharatjogi's pawn who put a false mask of a god on him. And then came this cold-blooded, silent, tribal chief, with teeth of iron and the mind of a monster, thirsting for the power that rightfully belonged to the lords of the land....'

The explorer laughed when he heard of three more teams going round Sindhu. 'Let us do more than these new-comers,' he told his team.

Gangapati's Regent was livid. 'How dare he send his prowling teams here!' Gangapatni ma was horrified to hear him, 'He is Mahapati. It is his right. His teams do his bidding. That is their privilege.'

With dismay, the Regent saw Sindhu Putra's teams welcomed everywhere, even by the Sabha members. He could have tried to put a stop to it. He could even have ignored Gangapatni ma. She enjoyed respect, but he was the Regent, fully in command, with power over all that happened in the land of Ganga. He was a bold, decisive man, who believed that power shared is power lost; and the Sabha and Gangapatni ma could try to persuade him, but never overrule him.

Yet there was something that the Regent lacked. It was a power which every mother in the land had—to accept or reject marriage-vows offered for her minor child. And the one overpowering ambition of the Regent was that one day his daughter would marry Gangapati XIV and be Gangapatni. He was amazed at Gangapatni ma's hesitation when he offered his daughter's marriage-vows. Sweetly, she mumbled about Sindhu Putra, but he said, 'Sindhu Putra has blessed them.'

'He has also blessed the vows of Sharatji's granddaughter and of six others,' she replied.

'How can he bless so many vows?'

'Why not! It clearly means that whosoever my son marries, the union shall always be blessed.'

'Then why not my daughter,' he pressed. But she said, 'Sindhu Putra must decide He has blessed many; he must choose among the blessed.'

The Regent's courier had left with gifts for Sindhu Putra and returned with blessings again, but not the decision. The Regent himself went, with more gifts, but found Sindhu Putra as indecisive as ever—'How can I choose one over the other? That is a decision for the mother.'

The Regent emphasized the need to choose a girl for Gangapati from the region itself; he urged that uncertainties would lead to ambitions from outsiders and even conspiracies. Sindhu Putra was unmoved.

The Regent's only cheering moment came when Sindhu Putra embraced him in the end and even said, 'It will all be well; wait and you will see.' Even the copper-faced silent Chief sitting with Sindhu Putra had nodded vigorously at the words.

The Chief saw the Regent off. His gestures were explained to the Regent—'Sindhu Putra favours you. . . . Foolish to think otherwise. . . . Did you not hear his last words! Wait. . .It will all be well.' This was no assurance either, but as near to it as it possibly could be.

To his wife, the Regent ranted over Sindhu Putra's inability to decide. But his wife simply said, 'Men decide quickly; gods wait.'

The Regent knew he had to wait for Sindhu Putra's decision. But suppose Sindhu Putra favoured the marriage-vows of someone else! What then?

The Regent's mind was clear—I will surround the child-Gangapati with so much love and affection and so dominate his will and mind that when he grows to a marriageable age, he will listen to me alone, and none else, even when I am no longer Regent. Marriage-vows with another, after all, are not a rope around the neck and surely they can be discarded in adulthood.

Yet the Regent did everything to invite a favourable decision. Regularly, his gifts went to Sindhu Putra. Not because he was Mahapati, for that he regarded simply as a title of respect, but because he had the key to Gangapatni ma's acceptance of marriage-vows.

Gangapatni ma's welcome for Sindhu Putra's teams sobered the Regent. He was amazed with the reaction of the people—bowing, rejoicing, kneeling and praying before Sindhu Putra's seal.

Either to sow seeds of doubt in Gangapatni ma's heart or simply in anger over her enchanted expression as she held the seal, the Regent exclaimed, 'My God! Really, if Sindhu Putra came here, he could take over Gangapati's position and no one would even question him!'

Gangapatni ma was simply amused—seeing nothing of the Regent's anger—and said, 'Of course, but why would Mahapati descend to the lowly position of Gangapati!'

'Mahapati!' 'Mahapati'—the cry rang through the populace as Sindhu Putra's team went along. Later, the team saw the Sabha members, drawing attention to this or that, as though they had an inherent right to demand redress or explanation for what they assumed to be wrong. With politeness, the Regent too heard them, though more to probe their minds; he even invited them to his home, singly and in groups. From the Regent himself, the team demanded nothing. Yet his own people kept reminding him of the different concerns voiced by the team. The message was clear—Mahapati is the overlord Deny him not!

The Regent's heart froze. Swiftly, surely, realization dawned on him—as it had on Karkarta of Sindhu and on many mighty chiefs—that Sindhu Putra was not only a spiritual power but an earthly power as well. Deny him not!

It happened all over again—with people kneeling and praying as Sindhu Putra's team visited Madhya Desa and the lands to the east, north and south of Ganga.

Everywhere people wept, as though Sindhu Putra's hand had reached out to touch them. They felt the thrill of his nearness and the sensation of his strength. No longer would they feel alone—for he, that commanded all the rulers and chiefs of Bharat Varsha was with them too. The chiefs and rulers fumed. They felt diminished. It was a cold, numb emotion—Sindhu Putra is watching. Deny him not!

Jalta the Fourth came to the Rocks to bow to Sindhu Putra. Battles on the eastern front had died down. He and his brothers had won decisive victories and he could now look forward to an era of tranquillity. Jalta embraced the Chief but asked, 'What do you mean by sending your spy-teams?'

'Did they offend you?' the Chief asked.

'Not me. But they annoy the chiefs whom I appointed.'

'And your heart grieves over their annoyance! Why? Are those chiefs very honourable?'

'No, some of them have turned out to be scoundrels. But I thought I should be the one to question and discipline them.'

The Chief took Jalta's hand and put it around his shoulder. 'You and I were slaves together. What does that say to you?' he asked.

'It says that you and I are brothers and we shall never be slaves again.'

'No,' the chief gestured. 'It says no one shall be a slave and we are all brothers.'

Jalta nodded. The Chief continued, 'And there shall be justice for all, as far as we can help it.'

Again Jalta nodded. The Chief continued, 'And the chiefs you appoint are not intended to replace one tyranny by another. They are the ones who must bear the greatest scrutiny. For no one must say that you, my brother, let yourself and your cause down.'

Jalta nodded but the Chief had not finished. 'And those you appoint are not there to serve you but the higher cause of him whom we have sworn to serve.'

Silently Jalta nodded and the Chief asked, 'Tell me, am I wrong?'

'No brother, you are not wrong. But if you were, would I ever say so?'

Smiling, they went to Sindhu Putra together.

The message to the people, far and near, was clear—march to the music of Sindhu Putra; take refuge in him; his mission is timeless; old animosities and dangers are no more; he bears the pain of Bharat Varsha; he holds the promise of Bharat Varsha. Rejoice!

And what of the mighty chiefs and lords! Their power was slipping away. It was as though they retained their position, or could be removed, at the will and pleasure of Sindhu Putra.

What is the future for an oppressor, when the oppressed cease to fear him and when people begin to look to someone else for hope and healing! Fearsome was the power of those chiefs once, but with fear gone, the very foundation of their terror and deception was disappearing. People would hide their faces no more, warmed by the realization that far beyond the insolent might of their chiefs was the greater, more awesome power of him who watched from the Rocks.

But most poets tell us that the chiefs were not frequently removed. Emphatically, in Sindhu Putra's name, the silent Chief ordered:

'Change not the chiefs, change their hearts; give them your love and seek their love in return; go, re-elect them as your own and so shall they be your own; and let every action of theirs be for your good and for the good of Bharat Varsha.'

Much later though, Nandan's poet-great-grandson would say, 'This widely scattered, far flung, never-ending land that they called Bharat Varsha was built on the tears and ruins of rightful chiefs and rulers. . . . And beggars became tyrants and uprooted the lawful masters. . .and everywhere these new, arrogant upstarts wielded the swords of Sindhu Putra that were pitiless, indiscriminate. . . . Ruthless also was his rod of authority held by a single puppet-master, who could speak not, whose face was dark, but not as dark as his black heart and whose eyes glowed with fires as in the deepest pit of hell.'

How far one accepts the judgement of Nandan's eighth great-grandson is open to question. However, he also took pains to describe with sadness, each and every area and region throughout the land, where various chiefs were displaced, disciplined or subordinated by Sindhu Putra's 'legions'. His description only confirms the length and breadth of Bharat Varsha, 'Where many chiefs remained, though vassals, they were fearful of their position and subordinate to the shadow of Sindhu Putra, who alone, unchallenged, commanded this vast land of Hindu.'

And yet the description of Bharat Varsha by this poet, who was always hostile to Sindhu Putra, conforms fully with Sindhu Putra's contemporary poets.

The description which the ancient poets employ in order to outline the frontiers of Bharat Varsha are colourful and varied and sometimes confusing. The names they give to many locations are strange and archaic; and even a poet of those times laments, 'names of regions, mountain peaks, lakes, rivers and seas spring forth, like the hoofs of a thousand horses, all rushing, no one knows where!' Yet, the overall picture of Bharat Varsha that emerges is clear and unmistakable and many ancient poets, concerned with the ithihasa of those times, have taken pains to describe it.

In modern terms, Bharat Varsha, extending from Sindhu and Ganga, was that land mass which included the entire territory of present-day India, Pakistan and Bangladesh.

Also in the north, it went beyond the soaring peaks and plunging valleys of the Himalayas to Tibet to reach lake Manasasarovara (Mansarovar), Mount Kailash, right up to the source of the auspicious Sindhu and mighty Brahmaputra rivers.

Additionally, the land of Newar (Nepal) was included in Bharat Varsha but as the poet adds 'not because the legions inspired by Sindhu Putra imposed it, but because Rishi Newar himself so declared it; but how could he not, when he, a Sanathani from Ganga, knew that all pre-ancient streams of Sanathana, Sanathana Dharma, Sanathani and the sacred Tamala tradition have all come to merge into a single gracious unity—the Hindu!'

The land of Bhuta (Bhutan) was also integrated with Bharat Varsha. Legend has it that it was called the land of Bhuta (ghosts), as several tribal warriors who had found refuge there constantly threatened Rishi Newar and the people of Nepal. They were often described as demons. At the Rishi's urging, legions moved to discipline them.

A massacre ensued in this land of Bhuta in which 'innocents died with the guilty and nights were haunted by ghosts (bhuta)—the naked spirits of those who died such violent deaths and for whom cremation rites were not performed, nor prayers said—though later came Rishi Newar to bless them all and bhutas (ghosts) were bhutas no more and the land was called Bhuta-nah (no ghosts).'

When Rishi Newar saw how gentle and affectionate the locals of Bhuta-nah were, and how terribly the warlords had terrorized them, he demanded an indemnity from the Chief of the silent tribe on behalf of Sindhu Putra. The silent Chief protested, 'Ask for help; why do you call it indemnity?' Rishi Newar argued, 'Help you may refuse; indemnity you cannot. These warlords who terrorized Bhuta-nah fled from the lands under your Sindhu Putra. You should have stopped them, killed them, and seen to it that they created no mischief, anywhere. By what right do you send out criminals to free yourself and terrorize others?' The silent Chief agreed to give the indemnity but said that if help was needed it would be twice as much as the indemnity. The Rishi was a reasonable man and accepted help, instead of indemnity.

Also included within the frontiers of Bharat Varsha was Avagana where everyone called himself Hindu, since the time of Sadhu Gandhara and his son Kush. Moving from Hari Rath, Hindu settlements even intruded into parts of Iran, beyond Lake Namaskar-Namaksar, where several Hindu hermits congregated. (This lake is on the Iran-Afghanistan border—map reference: 34.00n; 60.30e.)

Then there were certain parts of the Land of Brahma (Burma) which were included in Bharat Varsha, though it is difficult to say how far it extended into Burma.

In the south, the land of Vraon (modern Sri Lanka) was always regarded as a part of Bharat Varsha. It was regarded as a sacred place to remind man of his early cruelty against the vraon.

Everyone seems agreed that this vast land mass of Bharat Varsha did not come about as the result of victories by great soldiers and conquerors. Battles there were many, to eradicate slavery, to halt attacks, to discipline raiders, to rescue prisoners, or to protect people. Often, these battles were protracted, with bloodshed and even massacre. But there was no special move to merge or integrate any new territories with Bharat Varsha. Nor was there ever an attempt, even to hint or suggest, that any tribal should become, or call himself, a Hindu, for clearly the 'Song of the Hindu' had restated forcefully the pre-ancient belief that 'He who seeks to convert another to his own faith offends against his own soul, and the will of God, and the law of humanity....'

Yet it was faith that moved millions across the land and fired them with the enthusiasm to regard Bharat Varsha as a cultural reality—Hindus all. Soon, it would emerge as far stronger than a simple cultural entity, when the entire land came, first to be stirred by the diverse cry of Mahakarta, Periyar, Mahapati, soon to be replaced by the one, single, common overriding cry of 'Maharaj,' 'Maharaj.' Literally Maharaj meant 'one who pleases the most (maha—great; raj—pleasing). In common usage, though, it came to mean 'he who commands all lords and chiefs'.

Thus, far beyond a common consciousness and ideology, there arose a triumphant understanding that this land of Bharat Varsha was one, indivisible, from end to end, with Sindhu Putra at the helm, to guide them all—Hindus all.

'Power is elusive unless it is wielded with finesse....The sword is mightier than the spirit; but the sword must remain sheathed until ready to strike....Speech is not intended to reveal a thought but to conceal it....The words we utter are not linked to our feelings nor the action we take....The powerful have no friends, only allies and dependents and they all must be watched lest their loyalties waver....Bonds of friendship and gratitude are good but only so long as they are useful....To regain lost power, one may retrace a step or two, to run forward faster....Yet power must grow lest it stagnate and disappear. . . .'

—('Words of Wisdom' of the Regent of Ganga to Gangapati XIV—5030 BC)

Ganga and Sindhu

5032 BC

Years passed.

'He will outlive us all,' said Karkarta Sharat. He was speaking of Sindhu Putra to his son. Sharat was ailing. His one ray of sunshine was that Sindhu Putra had blessed his son Sauvira's election as Karkarta in the event of his death.

Sharat was seething with anger. He had had to ask Sindhu Putra's blessing for his son. Yet there was no other way out. In his father Nandan's time, the law prohibiting a Karkarta's son succeeding his father was abolished. Even so, when Nandan retired, Sharat himself would not have been elected without Sindhu Putra's blessing.

Since then, Sharat had won the people's love and respect—not only in the traditional land of Sindhu but also in the new lands in the Union.

To the Jalta lands, he was specially generous ever since he heard of Jalta ma's aspiration to be Karkarta. Also, he became considerate to the ex-slaves. His hope lay in the silent Chief's assurance to Jagasi that Sindhu Putra would soon retire, closing his eyes and mind to the affairs of men. But it was not to be. Instead, Sindhu Putra's teams armed with the svastika seal were on the prowl. And he felt forced to welcome them with a smile.

But then the gods have their uses too—Sharat realized. While sickness assailed him, he was consumed by the passion that his son, Sauvira, must succeed him. His own sickness he kept a secret and merely spoke to a few about retiring. But then he heard that some, with ambitions of their own, were muttering that the office of Karkarta should not be degraded to a father-son office. Promptly, he sent his son Sauvira to Sindhu Putra who readily blessed him for Karkarta's office.

'And did you ask Sindhu Putra to bless your daughter's marriage to Gangapati?' questioned Sharat.

'I asked, but he said one thing at a time.' Sauvira replied.

'Did you ask for anything else?'

'No,' Sauvira replied and he saw his father's sadness. Why? Was Sharat, in the sunset of his life, beginning to believe in Sindhu Putra's divinity? Or was it that he expected his son to demonstrate his concern for his father's health by requesting Sindhu Putra to cure him. Quietly,

Sauvira said, 'Father, my intelligence I inherit from Grandfather Nandanji and you. If I suffered from the slightest trace of belief in this... this false god, I would have washed his feet with my tears to seek his blessing for your health.'

Sharat embraced his son, proud that his son understood his unspoken question.

The svastika teams went around announcing that Sindhu Putra had blessed Sauvira to succeed as Karkarta. It was a surprise to everyone. How premature! Elections were two years away! And surely Karkarta Sharat would not retire mid-term and impose a new election! Hardly anyone knew the condition of his health and the few that did, were silent. Jagasi, as always, was wreathed in smiles. Sharat was known to be touring the eastern lands, though he was actually in his ancestral family home, far from Karkarta's town. His son, Sauvira, as senior Council member, was carrying out Karkarta's day-to-day duties, in Karkarta's absence. Surely, if Karkarta was unwell, the son would be near the father! Why this untimely announcement then, that Sauvira must succeed Sharat!

The answer came quickly. With suddenness, they heard the news of Karkarta Sharat's death.

Far more than sadness was the widespread wonder that Sindhu Putra knew!... Knew what was to happen!... That Sharatji was to die!...

And to those who asked, 'If he knew, why did he not prevent it?' the answer had an age-old familiar ring—'Why would he delay Sharatji's moksha!'

Sharat's body, preserved for the journey, raced to Karkarta's town, in horse-drawn carriages, by relays. People grieved. But more than grief was their realization that 'it was to happen when it happened, for had not Sindhu Putra already blessed his son as Karkarta?'

Sauvira fumed but how could he say that it was he who had sought Sindhu Putra's blessing ahead of time! After that meeting with Sindhu Putra, the silent Chief had offered to send out svastika teams to announce Sindhu Putra's blessings for his election. Sauvira demurred— was it not too early? But the Chief smiled. 'Teams move slowly; they take time to reach people; so why not tie and bind all? And tell them that Sindhu Putra has blessed you this day.' Was there a hint in the Chief's smile and words that it was better to commit Sindhu Putra immediately, lest he bless another too, who comes to him later, aspiring for Karkarta's position—for everyone knew that he withheld blessings from none—so why not bind him with an open, public announcement!

Sauvira had agreed instantly, gratefully; and the svastika teams moved briskly to announce it ahead of time. But now, everyone marvelled, in awe and amazement, over the miracle.

Yet Sauvira had to remain silent, his head bent in grief over his father's death, and his heart on fire with a hatred that he dared not express.

Sindhu Putra reached Karkarta's town to pay his respects. This was the first time in years that he had left the Rocks. But he felt he had to. His love for Sharat was immense. And he recalled that Sharat was the one who had first freed the slaves in Sapta Sindhu and united the tribal lands. He was the moving spirit behind what was known as the 'Bharat Programme'. He was the one who called the land of Sindhu and the lands beyond Bharat Varsha to honour Sindhu Putra's father, Bharatjogi. He was the one who had assisted ex-slaves to reach the level of rya. It was he who always sent aid and succour to the tribal lands and magnificent contributions to Jalta ma.

Sindhu Putra was not assailed by the doubts of the silent Chief and the others who saw a motive behind a motive and a secret behind a secret in every word and deed of Sharat. To him, Sharat was a man of goodness, honour and integrity and none dared even hint otherwise in his presence. He who trusted all, disbelieved none, how could he ever doubt Sharat, whose impressive achievements for freedom, unity and justice were far beyond those of any other Karkarta!

There were tears in Sindhu Putra's eyes at Sharat's cremation. Sharat's mother, old and limping, came to him, and through her tears she begged Sindhu Putra, 'Master, bless my son.' And Sindhu Putra replied, 'Mother, I seek his blessing. He is greater than all of us here. He is with God and he is God.' And he folded his hands in 'Namaste,' and began to pray near Sharat's body, ending with 'Bless us all!'

That Sauvira would be elected as Karkarta was a foregone conclusion. He was elected with no opposition. However, a little drama intervened, before the elections. Some said that as Sindhu Putra had blessed Sauvira, the practice of a seven-year term for Karkarta be abolished to make Sauvira a Karkarta for life. To gain support for such a dramatic change, Jagasi and the others approached the silent Chief to persuade Sindhu Putra to lead the campaign. He was after all Mahakarta! Who could deny him!

The Chief seemed sympathetic but later sadly reported that although Sindhu Putra loved and supported Sauvira, he also felt that the people must have the opportunity to demonstrate their renewal of love by voting for him, time and again. It seemed, the Chief disagreed with Sindhu Putra, and even his expression was derogatory; but then as if to rebuke himself for his expression, he said, 'He knows what he is doing; he is the Mahakarta. He decides. He alone!'

Mahakarta Maharaj! The news spread that he had rejected the plea to abolish elections. 'Pity!' admitted the silent Chief. 'It was a confidential request but then so many are so garrulous and babble away without restraint!'

Yet the message was clear. 'Mahakarta decides all. He is supreme.'

Sauvira, twenty-third Karkarta of Sapta Sindhu, again glared at the distant Rocks, with a hatred that he neither named nor described.

Meanwhile, Gangapatni ma had died some four years earlier. The pressure on her had mounted, during her sickness, to decide on the marriage-vows for her son. How wrong, said some, it would be for Gangapati XIV to grow to adulthood, without the mother having fulfilled her basic duty; indeed it was pious to follow Sindhu Putra's advice, but then why did she not request him to decide immediately? But for many, her decision to leave the matter to Sindhu Putra had their profound and reverent acceptance.

One day, when Gangapatni ma had felt particularly weak, and the Regent was by her bedside for some hours, the rumour that she was accepting marriage-vows for his daughter ran rife. Later, when she heard the rumour, she realized that her every nod, sigh and smile would be misconstrued. She exercised her right to attend the next Sabha meeting. Her voice was weak, but the message, clear: Sindhu Putra alone would decide on the marriage-vows of her son. When a voice in the Council requested her to beg Sindhu Putra's decision. She simply said, 'He will decide when he decides. He is Mahapati Maharaj.'

Not too many have commented on why Gangapatni ma chose to leave the decision to Sindhu Putra. Some said, it was an act of faith. Others said, she needed time to know which way the wind was blowing and she was waiting to see if Sharat's son eventually did become Karkarta, and if so, she would prefer her son to marry Karkarta's daughter; but if not, the Regent's daughter was more acceptable.

Yet others whispered that she was against accepting family ties with the Regent; that she disliked him for the contempt he had shown towards her daughter (adopted by her when she was childless; given to her by Sindhu Putra); she loved this daughter as much as she loved her first-born son.

The Regent, on the other hand, treated this girl as someone from a questionable tribal stock, and he denied her free and easy access to her younger brother, though the two children loved each other fondly.

Some even said that it was not merely dislike for the Regent but fear that moved Gangapatni ma. The Regent was a man of power and prestige, which would grow if his daughter were to wed Gangapati and her fear was that he may one day take over the entire domain of Gangapati. If someone argued: surely no one offends against a son-in-law! The counter-argument was: why not, if one has to choose between a son and a son-in-law! Or even between oneself and one's son-in-law! And, in any case, greed for power is an intoxicant that recognizes no bonds of blood or kinship! Why else, they asked, would Gangapatni ma, at every opportunity, speak of Sindhu Putra as Mahapati Maharaj, with sovereign and supreme power over the land of Ganga, and even over Gangapati himself! Would a mother, they asked, ever raise someone to that lofty height, over and above her own son, unless she was frightened that there was another—the Regent himself—with designs of rendering her son powerless! And she knew that Sindhu Putra neither had nor sought earthly ambition and yet his spiritual authority was enough to render her son safe from the Regent's ambition.

But the majority view was dismissive of all such intricate theories. For them, it remained a simple act of faith.

True, Sindhu Putra had said to the Regent's emissaries, that a mother decided on marriage-vows. But Gangapatni ma herself had visited Sindhu Putra and he had blessed her; and there was no doubt in her mind that the time for the acceptance of marriage-vows had not yet come. But even if she did have a doubt, the silent Chief silenced it. 'You come in faith. . . . Can he ever deny you!...Wait, all will be well.'

Yes, she decided; wait she would...even beyond the horizon of her lifetime, if need be. Mahapati Maharaj alone would decide, whenever he willed, and whatever he willed.

Questions were asked—did Mahapati have as much power in Ganga as he did in Sindhu as Mahakarta? The answers differed—depending on who asked and who answered. Earlier, everyone thought that Mahapati or Mahakarta were titles of love, affection, even personal devotion—'He that is above earth, what need has he of power over earth!' But later, people wondered—maybe it was not possible to separate earthly and spiritual power. And now, he had the title of Maharaj that outranked all!

The Regent was on his best behaviour lest Sindhu Putra fling his daughter's suit in his face. But it is not easy to appear perfect when someone keeps watching your every move. When the svastika teams came, they saw much that was wrong. The fault often lay with the teams. In their self-importance, they forgot the clear orders of the silent Chief—'Go, spread Sindhu Putra's message; for the rest, say little; observe more; interfere not; report to local lords but only if crimes are grave.' The teams had asked him—'But if the crimes are grave and the lords listen not, what then?' The Chief's reply was, 'Nothing then! Silent you shall remain; and simply report to me.'

But the teams, intoxicated by the warmth of their welcome, did interfere. The Regent was irritated but steeled himself to tolerate it all, even to redress grievances that the teams had no business to interfere with. Later he even encouraged them and asked for ideas on how to spread Sindhu Putra's name and message further. The delighted teams had thousands of suggestions—possible and impossible—as the Regent kept encouraging their inventiveness; and they saw no need to send reports to the silent Chief. But the Regent, who had already learnt from the teams what exactly their task was, himself sent emissaries—not to complain, but simply to report how fully he had met Sindhu Putra's wishes, conveyed by his teams. The emissaries listed a thousand items completed at the team's demand, though regretfully they also showed how such demands had led to an undue burden on others—

'But the Regent is clear that Sindhu Putra's wishes must be met, whatever the cost.' The emissaries now proceeded to what they said was their main purpose. 'The Regent hopes you will not misunderstand the delay in his evacuation of people from so many areas selected by the team for Sindhu Putra's temple....'

The Chief was ready to explode. At last, he gestured, 'Who wants a temple!'

They chose not to understand him. 'No, please, be not angry. Already hundreds have been evacuated. Most huts and cottages have been demolished. People are being forced out. The team's demands shall be met but so many will be hurt by the removal, the Regent just wants more time, please....'

Furiously, the Chief gestured, 'Stop. The temple is not wanted!'

The emissaries interpreted it as rebuke for the delay. The Regent, they said, worked sleeplessly to meet the team's demand for the temple, whatever the cost or hurt. The temple would be erected in the svastika design and....

The Chief's fists were clenched. He was wishing he had a hundred hands and arms long enough to reach Ganga, so as to strangle the throat of each team member. Somehow he managed to indicate to the emissaries that the temple was not required and all work must cease.

The Chief was met with stony silence. Obviously, they disbelieved that he spoke for Sindhu Putra. What about the team's loud and repeated demand for the temple! Later, he took them to Sindhu Putra. That alone convinced them.

The couriers were already speeding to Ganga with the silent Chief's orders for the team to return forthwith.

The Regent was happy when the team departed because he disliked the fact that someone was overseeing his work and reporting to another.

He was fascinated by the concept of one people and one land of Bharat Varsha—from Ganga to the Himalayas and Tibata in the north; to the isle of Vraon and Dravidham in the south; and from Sindhu in the west to Avagana and the eastern land of Brahma. The idea of unity and togetherness instinctively appealed to him.

The Regent did not even mind that the entire land was called Bharat Varsha. To him, it was just a name and people would soon forget that its inspiration came from Sindhu Putra's father's name—Bharatjogi.

But what the Regent disliked intensely was that Sindhu Putra should be regarded as the supreme leader. That right and title, he felt, must belong to Gangapati.

He recalled the glory of past Gangapatis—and their victorious cry (Har Har Ganga! Har Har Gange!). It was a cry of faith in Ganga and in the legendary force of Gangapati, heard over the centuries from Hari Hara Dwara to Gangasagarsangam and, in many lands, in all directions, far removed from the banks of Ganga.

Was it not galling that the descendant of the illustrious Gangapatis should be viewed as subordinate to this false and fake god!

The Regent was convinced of his objectivity and detachment—he was after all not a Gangapati; he was thinking only of the magnificence of the institution itself. But then he had the ability to mask, sometimes even from himself, his future aspirations; the least he hoped for was that his future grandson should be the next Gangapati, through his daughter's marriage with Gangapati XIV.

The Regent, when he thought of Sindhu Putra's team, realized that this god was not too intelligent. The team, of course, had fallen into the Regent's trap—his subtle hints that suggested the impossible which he even pretended to implement to show that he treated them as Sindhu Putra's commands. He was the one to suggest a huge, magnificent temple for Sindhu Putra, and the team gratefully adopted it as its own. He even pretended to implement this impossible suggestion to show that he treated it as Sindhu Putra's command as conveyed by the team. And he smiled as he recalled reports from his emissaries. How easy it was to outwit them all, so completely! What future could such a dim-witted god and his rabble have! No, Gangapati shall and must remain the supreme reality, for ever.

There were not many to whom the Regent could open his heart. But the one listener that he did have was the child Gangapati. None showered as much love and attention on the boy as the Regent himself. If he had succeeded in distancing the boy from his sister, and even from Gangapatni ma, it was not so much the result of a command as of his affectionate and indulgent approach to the boy. He had carefully selected the people with whom to surround the boy; he always took him on his journeys and saw to it that every whim and wish, every comfort and convenience of the boy was met. After Gangapatni ma's death, they became even closer.

The Regent was Gangapati's real mentor and the training he imparted was gentle and yet persistent. He described the past glory and greatness of the Gangapatis and helped foster a dream for the future.

Also, the Regent employed singers and poets around him; and through stories, tales and anecdotes they would invest the boy's mind with a thirst for a glory that matched the greatness of his invincible ancestors.

Rigours of higher and more intensive training for the boy-Gangapati were yet to come, but even then he was learning that the power of the sword is mightier than the power of the spirit and there is no power greater than that of Gangapati and all must submit to him. It was as though the inscrutable wisdom of providence and the inexorable process of historic destiny had so ordained.

Yet the greater message that the Regent wanted to instil in the young Gangapati was that power could be elusive unless it was wielded with finesse; that the sword must remain sheathed until ready to strike; that speech was not intended to reveal thought but conceal it; that the words we utter were not linked with the action we take; that the powerful have no friends, but only allies and dependents, and that they must all be watched lest their loyalties waver; that to regain lost power, one had to retrace a step or two, to run faster forward; yet power must grow, lest it stagnate and disappear.

The annual spectacle of athletics, sports, song, dance and drama initiated by Gangapati II had continued, becoming more magnificent year by year. With Gangapati as the host, it continued to draw every chief from far and near. Intuitively, instinctively, the boy-Gangapati understood the dislike—sometimes even hatred—of the high and mighty chiefs for Sindhu Putra. Little was said. The hints were subtle and protestations of admiration and reverence for Sindhu Putra were profuse. But the message was clear: there was no connection—none at all—between their words and feelings.

The Regent pointed to the vast territories south of Ganga. Sindhu Putra had passed through those lands to reach Dravidham. Earlier, many of them were barren wastelands with a limited population in scattered pockets. Since then, many displaced ex-slaves and others had settled there; the lands were now green, fertile; but instead of bringing them under Ganga, the silent Chief of Sindhu Putra had conspired to make them separate, independent entities! 'Yes,' the boy softly responded, 'and it is all Gangadesa (Ganga land)'; and the boy paused to whisper, almost inaudibly, 'here and everywhere.'

The Regent felt thrilled. He had no more doubts. The lesson was well-learnt—this boy would always be a man of Ganga and the entire land would be Gangadesa.

Only a few months remained for Gangapati to come of age. Sindhu Putra had not yet moved to select anyone's marriage-vows for him. None expected Sindhu Putra to intervene so late; and obviously the question of marriage-vows in the traditional sense would lapse as soon as Gangapati was an adult. By and large, everyone conformed to parental wishes when choosing a marriage-partner; but Gangapati's parents had exercised no choice; besides how often had the boy said to the Regent, 'You are my teacher, my mentor; you are more than my father and mother to me; always be with me, to guide me.' The Regent had felt his heart warmed at such words of love and gratitude from the boy, who was normally so reserved and reticent with others.

With an effort, the Regent suppressed his impulse to seek a promise from the boy to marry his daughter, but he knew how inauspicious it was—unthinkable—to raise with a minor, the question of choosing his bride. I shall wait—the Regent told himself.

No, the Regent had no doubt of the love and trust always reflected in the boy's actions and on his lips. His anger was actually against his own daughter, who foolishly, rebelliously and repeatedly sought to join Sindhu Putra's ashram—as the Rocks had come to be called.

Many in faith and some with wounds in their hearts had found permanent refuge in the ashram.

At first, when the Regent heard his daughter's plea, he was proud and impressed. Obviously, her move was calculated to secure Sindhu Putra's blessing for her marriage to Gangapati. What else could the brilliant daughter of a brilliant father think! But as he heard more, his mind exploded. She was moved by faith. She insisted. He came as near to hitting her as any father possibly can.

On reflection, however, he felt that it must be her frustration at the delay in acceptance of her marriage-vows that had tempted her to seek an escape; it was simply, he thought, the hurt to a deeply sensitive, young girl, forced into protracted suspense when all her friends have had their marriage-vows accepted years ago. In a rush of feeling, he put his arms around her and his lips to her cheek, and said, 'A great prize, a great dream, a great ambition—takes time for fulfilment.' She saw hope in his words; he saw hope in her smile. But their hopes were different.

The annual spectacle of sports, song, dance and drama was two days away. But it was preceded by momentous celebrations to mark Gangapati's coming of age. That was the day on which Gangapati XIV became the undisputed master of the land of Ganga, in law and fact.

The Regent was Regent no more, but he basked in the glow of a job well done and in the sure hope of greater glories to come.

The lords and chiefs of many lands had gathered. Sauvira, twenty-third Karkarta of Sindhu, saw the glow on the ex-Regent's face and abandoned his idea of pursuing his daughter's suit with Gangapati.

After the ritual ceremony, it was Gangapati XIV who went to Sauvira and untroubled by the presence of many said, 'Karkarta, for you, I have always felt a special friendship. Would you and your daughter object if our friendship became even closer?'

It was an odd, direct, frontal way to propose marriage; but gratefully, Sauvira said, 'For me, Gangapati, it would be an honour which my late father and I always wished for; for my daughter it would be an honour beyond her dreams.'

Simply, Gangapati pointed to the ex-Regent, 'He has always been like a father to me. He will speak to you further about whatever arrangements are necessary.'

The ex-Regent died within himself, but everyone says that he gave the fullest care to the wedding negotiations. He resolved matters of union between Ganga and Sindhu—rights of succession if Karkarta Sauvira had no son; or if Sauvira had a son, but Gangapati had none; action on the frontiers against raids; a common approach to outsiders, joint exploration, discovery, resource-exploitation; so on and so forth.

The ex-Regent died shortly after the wedding. Gangapati ordered a state funeral and mourned him as a son would. Some irrelevant comments apart, everyone agrees that the Regent died of a broken heart as he felt deceived by Gangapati whom he had loved liked a son.

It did not take Karkarta Sauvira and Gangapati XIV too long to understand each other perfectly. If Karkarta was thinking that he would have to brief his son-in-law a great deal, he was mistaken. Young Gangapati had forgotten the Regent, but not the lessons that the Regent had taught. He knew who the real enemy was. It was Sindhu Putra. He was the one who was out to rob Gangapati of his heritage. To him it was clear that the entire ithihasa of the great and glorious Gangapatis was being mocked by the odious charlatan who claimed to call himself Mahapati and Maharaj, to play upon the heartstrings of people. Through his fakery and fraud people had come to regard him as superior to Gangapati, and even accept that his would be the law to prevail over the wish of Gangapati. That this son of a nameless father and an abandoned woman, from nowhere, through the scheming of an ex-Karkarta, should arrogate to himself a position far above thirteen of his illustrious ancestors who had nurtured this land of Ganga with their love, blood, sweat and sacrifice. . . .

There was no need for words. Like Karkarta Sauvira, young Gangapati too looked with eyes of hatred in the direction of the Rocks.

The two men parted with deep understanding and a clear resolve.

Gangapati XIV and Karkarta Sauvira were not the only ones with hate in their hearts. Even more savage was the hatred of the lords and chiefs of many lands—they with wealth, command, influence and vast territories—they who had once held the power of life, death and liberty over their people—were now being subjected to scrutiny from spy-teams sent out by the silent Chief from the Rocks. And some chiefs were even thrown out of their positions! Maybe one day, the man from the Rocks would be asking beggars to mount horses and take up the rod of authority!

Meanwhile, Sindhu Putra gave up much of his isolation and often came out to meet crowds at the Rocks.

The wisdom he sought in silence and loneliness had eluded him. Prayers and meditation gave him no glimpse of the riddle of universal mystery. At the Rocks, many with knowledge and learning congregated. But he could say little except that dharma controls the universe; that it is the law of cause and effect and deed and consequence (karma) that rules individual emancipation and not blind chance or destiny; that human will and human effort help in reshapeing man's environment and future.

How could the wise and learned be impressed by such common-place utterances which they learnt as children in their parent's lap or at the feet of their first guru! And how silent he was about nature and the identity of the Universal spirit and the Ultimate Reality behind the phenomenal world!

But if the wise learnt little from him, he perhaps learnt even less from them; and he once said, 'Why don't we all simply admit that we don't know and perhaps never shall!' Often, he pointed to a snail or a worm in the Rock garden to say, 'that little God's creature possibly knows as much about the Universal Spirit as I do—or maybe he knows more.' He was glad that he said so, for later he found some walking carefully in order to avoid treading on worms in the garden.

All he was sure about was that the universe was alive, the earth was holy and that all life was connected as a part of an eternal and infinite process.

But if the wise and learned were disappointed with him, his devotees were not. They had the calm, smiling assurance that arises from love and faith.

Sometimes, out of reverence for him, his devotees would look grave as he passed by, but he would pinch a little girl and say, 'Give me your smile and make it a part of me,' and she would smile, and so would everyone; and the poet adds, 'thus he passed by, embracing their smile.'

Often now, Sindhu Putra left his Rock-retreat not to attend spectacles, weddings or rituals, but to move on dusty paths and lonely routes, to areas where ex-slaves and others lived in lowly conditions. Thousands followed him. And he would ask that their condition be improved. Sometimes he made demands that were impossible. But slowly, surely, many of his demands were met, as the teams which followed him, kept pestering everyone in power.

To him, poverty was a form of slavery; that the lords of the lands were answerable to those over whom they rule; that they were trustees, and to live better than the least of their fellow-men, was to abuse that trust; that the weakest must have the same opportunity as the strongest; that the Lord above us all cared and Man had a purpose—to seek out God's purpose and will to serve those around him.

The chiefs, far and near, did not need teams from the Rocks to hear these words. Their own men were at the Rocks; and to them Sindhu Putra's purpose was clear—a climate of contempt against them and an aura of sanctity for himself.

*

Annual Ganga spectacles continued to attract chiefs but not only for enticing festivities. There was much to say, more to discuss.

An overwhelming sense of frustration assailed the mighty chiefs and lords. The arrogance of their people astounded them. What shocked them even more was the total ingratitude of Sindhu Putra, who accepted all their magnificent gifts but then did everything he could to spread discontent and sedition.

Like Karkarta Sauvira and his son-in-law, Gangapati XIV, they too looked towards the Rocks with bitter hatred.

The people's love for Sindhu Putra grew.

The chiefs' hatred for Sindhu Putra grew.

One who rose from the 'blackness of black nights, when nights and days were not; and light and dark were not'; and Him who sprang from 'nothingness when nothingness and existence were not,' and He it was who sent this glorious radiance here on earth, 'in the darkest of dark nights that was.'

—(the once-blind singer's cry at the cremation of Sindhu Putra, as he recalls an age-old argument with Bharatjogi, 5015 BC)

'Swifter than sound, faster than light, quicker than
                                                thought
It came—and came with a motion as if it moved not
Yet it moved all that kept far, asunder, apart
And they sang—we all have the same one heart!'

—(The last song sung for Sindhu Putra before he died, 5015 BC)

One who rose from the blackness of black nights, when nights and men were not, and light and dark were not; and I (he) who sprang from 'nothingness when nothingness and existence were not, and He it was who saw this glorious radiance here on earth, in the darkest of dark nights that was.'

—(the once-gifted singer's cry at the cremation of Shadni Putra, as he recalls an age-old argument with Bharatiraji. 501S BC)

'Swifter than sound, faster than light, quicker than thought
It came—and came with a motion as if it moved not
Yet it moved all that kept far, asunder, apart
And they sang—we all have the same one heart.'

—(The last song sung for Shadni Putra before he died. 501S BC)

Death of a God

5015 BC

A scream of anguish rose from the Rocks. Sindhu Putra was dead.

Throughout the land, there was a cry of despair, a prayer for mercy, a sorrowing silence—and each mourned in his own way.

How did that terrible, fateful moment arrive?

It was a day not too different from any other. Sindhu Putra was awake well before dawn and, after a bath, sat for his prayers, as usual. Girls entered, with soft footsteps, bringing large fruit-baskets. He took a little fruit and the baskets went back for distribution among the devotees.

Two girls remained. They chanted, one after another, his favourite hymns. Then one of the them began a song he had not heard before—

'Swifter than sound, faster than light, quicker than thought
It came—and came with a motion as if it moved not
Yet it moved all that kept far, asunder, apart
And they sang—we all have the same one heart!'

The song went on; the second girl joined in, not with words but a soft, delicate tune that seemed to dance around the melody; but she joined in with the words which appeared over and over again as a recurring refrain in the song—'We all have the same one heart!'

Their voices were captivating. Sindhu Putra liked the thought, particularly when the song went on to say that every heart whichever creature it belong to, be they fixed or moving, and of all those that walk, swim, fly or glow, in this multiform creation, in near, remote, open and secret regions—is the same one heart and it is the very heart of the Lord of Creation to whom all pathways lead.

Yet the words of the song were a little laboured and it lacked the flow and imagery of the once-blind singer from whom no doubt she had learnt the song and he asked, 'When did he sing that song?'

She blushed, stammered, 'I...I composed this song....You did not like it?'

He put his arm around her, 'Like it! I loved it. Sing this song for everyone at the prayer session today.'

'Will you be there?' she hopefully asked.

'Nothing shall keep me back from hearing you again.'

Sindhu Putra never had a precise schedule. Sometimes, he would walk into the evening prayer-session in which the Rock-residents and devotees participated. At other times, he would simply stroll in the Rock garden or rest under a pipal tree or move amid throngs of visitors. But there would be days when he would not appear, except to bless them from the balcony. He had no fixed days on which he would fast; nor did he plan ahead when he would visit outside the Rocks—'As the spirit moved him, so did he move.'

How different he was from the silent Chief who was precise and punctual in all things—well, in all except his time to sleep. Sometimes, the Chief would be up all night, 'talking' to returning emissaries, discussing things with teams, writing, planning, thinking.

The explorer would laugh at the Chief and say, 'Perhaps for your dark thoughts you need darkness.' But irrespective of the time he slept, the Chief would wake up at the same time, earlier than Sindhu Putra.

That is why it was surprising that the Chief did not arrive that evening. He always left on time and arrived on time; and he had left the Rocks only for four days for a nearby visit—and had even arranged two meetings at the Rocks for that evening itself.

Sindhu Putra had decided to drag the Chief to the prayer session, to hear the song which the girls sang for him in the morning. He waited, asked the others, but the Chief had not arrived.

Sindhu Putra reached the prayer meeting late. But since everyone knew that he was to join, they waited. He reproached them, 'How can you delay prayers!'

Hymns began; then the song he had heard in the morning. It sounded different, more captivating—but that was not surprising for now it was accompanied by musical instruments and even a chorus of children, who soulfully sang out the oft-repeated refrain—'We all have the same one heart.'

The session over, he walked on the lush grassy path, through the swarming people towards the Rock edge. Everywhere, people lined up saying 'Namaste,' as they let him pass. Some even stood, with children, at the Rock edge where it was slippery. A man in front obligingly took in his arms an infant of someone behind him to bring it closer to receive Sindhu Putra's blessing.

Sindhu Putra passed on. It was, as always, a slow, silent walk; normally, there were only three women behind him with the 108-bead rosary; but this time he had also asked the two singing sisters to join him. From time to time, he responded silently to people's namaste.

Suddenly, when Sindhu Putra was barely three steps away, the man holding another's infant, gently dropped the child in Sindhu Putra's way. The girl behind Sindhu Putra murmured at his carelessness. 'Brother, what have you done!'

Sindhu Putra said nothing but stooped to pick up the baby. The man said, 'Forgive me,' and he too stooped as if to pick up the infant. But his right hand holding a sharp dagger shot out to tear into Sindhu Putra's chest.

Sindhu Putra gasped 'Om!' as he sank to the ground, lifeless, his hands frozen in the gesture of picking up the infant; somehow the hands moved closer to each other. Perhaps he intended his last gesture to be namaste. Instead they pointed to the sky, as though with a question or a complaint to someone above.

The infant, blood-soaked, slept.

No one moved, except the killer. All eyes were riveted on Sindhu Putra. The killer dived from the high rock into the river below. No one halted him. He was seen from the boats lined up on the river. But they knew nothing as yet of what had happened. Some even saw him swim and enter a boat, which had three occupants. They were possibly waiting for him. Fast and furious, the boat rushed to the opposite bank—not to the village but towards the tall grasslands. Just before it reached the bank, it started floundering in all directions, with the current. Later, the boat was found. In it lay the killer's body, but with the face bashed and battered into a pulp so as to make him unrecognizable. Apparently, the three men, having done their deed, abandoned the boat near the opposite bank and swam away to ride away on their horses hidden in the grassland. This conjecture might have been difficult except for the fact that at a distance from the boat, in a narrow pass beyond the grassland lay three bodies of men and three bodies of horses riddled with arrows. But again the faces of the men were battered beyond recognition. Apparently, Sindhu Putra's assassin was killed by three men waiting in the boat and those three were waylaid by others and butchered.

Whoever was behind it all, apparently did not want the killer, nor the three men waiting for him in the river, to be found alive for questioning, or even recognized when dead, lest the trail lead to....

The silent Chief and his four companions were found dead. Among them was the old explorer.

Elsewhere, at spots far and near, many members of the teams sent out by the silent Chief had died. Who killed them and why? And who commanded the killing? No one knew.

Flames from the cremation pyre rose and fell as the fire consumed Sindhu Putra's body.

At the sight of the smoke curling up from the pyre, a mournful cry rose; it subsided as they heard the old, once-blind singer's chant. Was he chanting a prayer? No. His tearful eyes seemed to focus not on the present but far back, into the past. He was thinking of the time when he had hastily been summoned to the Island of Silence where

Bharatjogi kept denying that the three-year-old child was a miracle of God and had said, 'Gods do not come to walk on earth among men.' The singer was smiling now, his thoughts locked in that argument with Bharat—and suddenly, he raised his hand to point beyond the river, to the far horizon, as though he saw Bharat there—and he cried, 'Yes Bharat, yes!'—and then he began his chant:

> *He was the one when rock and tree was one*
> *When air, earth, river, sea was one*
> *When all below, up, above, high was one*
> *When stars, moon, sun, sky was one.*

The chant went on, obscurely, to speak of the one who rose from the 'blackness of black nights, when nights and days were not; and light and dark were not;' and of Him who sprang from 'nothingness when nothingness and existence were not,' and He it was who sent his glorious radiance, here on earth, 'in the darkest of dark nights that was.'

No one understood him; no one realized that at this moment of overwhelming grief, his mind had wandered into an age-old argument with Bharatjogi. But they heard his words and thought that they understood him—that he spoke, not of Bharatjogi but of Bharat Varsha.

Kanta watched as Sindhu Putra's ashes were immersed from the Rocks into Sindhu. She was not grieving over the god that was no more. In her mind was the vision of her little two-day-old son whose ashes were sprinkled from these rocks and whom Muni had blessed as Sindhu Putra. She put her face against the trees which Roopa had planted for her son. She saw the marks of her tears on the tree-trunks. But quickly, the trees absorbed them and the marks vanished. Maybe the trees spoke to her or maybe her heart spoke and she cried out, 'Yes, this is where he began his last journey—this is where it ends— but only to begin anew.' Soulfully, dry-eyed, she spoke, 'He shall come again,' and softly began to hum Muni's song—'He comes, He comes, ever He comes. . . .'

Some joined her song. But many wept and their tears did not stop.

...But then at last, a whisper came in the child's tiny heart, and as he rose with his grandfather's blood on his face, there was a terrible silence inside the core of his being that he did not understand. All he knew was that he was not the rya of those that struck his grandfather down.... Quietly, he said, 'We are not the rya! We are arya.'

—(A child's cry, 5014 BC)

...Clearly, the cry began with an anguished whisper from people's hearts and the desolate realization of their nothingness in a land that disowned them.

...Maybe, it even started as a pitiful lament to pitiless gods!— 'Why have you forsaken us and left us anath (without protection)?'

...Maybe then, a quiet voice spoke, or maybe none spoke, and a voice rose in their hearts, to ask—'How can we be the rya of those that slayed our Sindhu Putra?'

...No longer, then, was it a cry of anguish! No longer a cry to wallow in self-pity! No longer a cry to beat their breasts for the degradation to which others sought to reduce them—'For us, our nath Sindhu Putra slaved and suffered and was slain. We are not them; and they are not us. We are not their rya!'

...'No, we are arya!'

—(From 'Song of the Exile', 5014 BC)

We are the Aryans!

5014 BC

Mahakarta, Mahapati, Periyar, Maharaj was no more. Thousands had followed his footsteps everywhere but, in a sense, he walked alone. He left no successor—no one on whom people could pin their hopes and faith. Adored and cherished, his memory lingered in people's hearts—but there was no one left to guide their footsteps.

The teams which had been sent out by the silent Chief faded away; many disappeared and some were suppressed. Those that remained could do little. Their voice was not the same as the voice people had loved and revered. They were shrill and loud. But the man, who was no more, had been soft and gentle—his voice had been quiet and low, yet audible above the din and shouting of all, thrilling men and moving the lords of the land. To the weak, he had said, 'Shed your fear.' To the strong and powerful he had said, 'This land is yours, theirs and mine. Make it worthy for all of us.'

Now that voice was stilled. The black pall of fear would re-emerge; restraint on the lords would disappear. The hurt he had caused to the powerful was great—the poor do not mind if much remains denied to them—but pain to the mighty lords was greater, not only because of the encroachments on their privilege but more at the shame of being regarded subordinate to his commands, and even to the 'advice' of 'his sub-human, speechless chief who waved his hands, as if he owned the land.'

The high and mighty lords smirked. Said one, 'They are not mourning Sindhu Putra. They are celebrating his second coming—and they sing: He comes, He comes, ever He comes.'

Another asked in mock-fear, 'How long do you think we have before he comes again?'

'Well, his last coming was after a prophecy that raged for a thousand years.'

'Oh, we have time then!'

'Certainly. Enough time to make his Bharat Varsha fit for him.'

'I hear they are also singing that his glorious radiance shall arise when the land is in the blackest of black nights!'

' I am glad. Many oil lamps burn in my house and yours at night.'

'Yes, but I think we should burn lamps in the village-streets also.'

'Good idea! Let us keep thieves and gods away.'

Poets rarely give names—not even their own. So it is not clear who these two speakers were. However, neither Karkarta Sauvira, nor Gangapati XIV nor any of the other mighty chiefs indulged in such open glee. Publicly, they maintained a solemn appearance and joined the mourning over Sindhu Putra's passing away.

So that the masses did not feel dejected that there was no one to listen to their woes and right their wrongs, now that Sindhu Putra was no more, Karkarta Sauvira declared that he felt honour-bound to listen to people in the same way, with the same attention and compassion, as Mahakarta had done. Soon, those around him began to address him by a title that went far beyond mere Karkarta. They would call him Karkarta Mahakarta Maharaj. And others soon learnt that the use of this expanded title encouraged a better hearing from Karkarta.

To prove that people everywhere think alike, poets say that similar changes arose in other lands as well, and in Ganga too, where Gangapati came to be called Gangapati Mahapati Maharaj.

Of course, it meant less to Gangapati than to Karkarta; Gangapati was not subject to the vagaries of elections and succession went from father to son; while Karkarta was elected to serve a seven-year term. But what happens to Karkarta who is also Mahakarta! Surely Mahakarta Maharaj couldn't be subject to elections. To those who still harboured the illusion that Mahakarta was simply a title of respect but not of authority, much was said even by Karkarta Sauvira of the power of Sindhu Putra, that was.

How these new and various titles were to add to the lustre, power and prestige of Karkarta and other lords, would remain to be tested in the future. The present certainty was that armies were on the move everywhere. Poets speak of Karkarta Sauvira's forces moving in two directions; of the thrust of Gangapati's contingents in all the lands around and of the eleven armies of the other mighty chiefs advancing to many lands.

And the lands under attack? These were lands from which petty tyrants were dispossessed by Jalta and other commanders to free them from enslavement. In some of these, new chiefs were appointed, with the silent Chief's approval; but in many, sabhas were set up.

Then there were a vast number of lands, newly cleared, to resettle freed slaves and many others, moving and migrating to a better future. These new lands came under no lord. Monumental efforts had been made to clear these lands, plant fields and farms, irrigate them and even to provide housing and amenities. All these initial efforts came from Sindhu Putra's Rocks, often with the silent Chief's personal supervision.

Later, some tried to follow the trail of massive wealth in Sindhu Putra's hands which allowed him to fund such huge, far-flung projects. Sindhu Putra had, at his disposal, Kanta's wealth, and tremendous revenues that flowed regularly from the temple in Gatha's village. Besides his influence on many devotees had changed the entire texture of their lives and they too donated everything they had. To many other rich devotees, Sindhu Putra would say, 'Help me to improve that new village' and some would respond by 'adopting' that village. He would make the same appeal to artisans, builders, peasants and even singers. For the rest, he had only to extend his hand to Karkarta, Gangapati and the lords everywhere and 'how could those gracious lords ever refuse!'

Nandan's eighth great-grandson strikes a different note and says, 'This horde of wealth came more from the dispossessed chiefs and from Bharatjogi's vast wealth which had been corruptly secreted by him when he was Karkarta and left with his wife Mataji.' Maybe this poet is right about the wealth confiscated by the silent Chief from tyrannical chiefs, but as to secret wealth with Mataji—she had none. What little she left went equally to her two sons and daughter, though they decided that as their parents regarded Sindhu Putra as their son, there should be four shares—one to belong to Sindhu Putra. It is also true that apart from his share, Bharat's younger son 'adopted' one of the new lands and spent all his wealth and time in its welfare.

Additionally, many visiting devotees left their little offerings at the Rocks. Some women took off their small ornaments and even ancient family heirlooms. Little by little, but in an almost unending stream, contributions flowed to the treasury guarded by the silent Chief. Some said, even thieves left a part of their loot in the hope that this pious contribution would wash away their sins.

As if all this was not enough, the silent Chief would sell and even 'auction' little leaves on which Sindhu Putra had written 'Om.'

'How come!' asks a poet, 'that nothing was found after Sindhu Putra departed?' The fact is that Karkarta Sauvira, Gangapati and even other lords had, together, come to the Rocks to collect with reverence, the relics of Sindhu Putra so that 'they be distributed in all the temples of Bharat Varsha, lest it be said that he belonged to the Rocks alone.' The story is that they found very little gold, silver or wealth and whatever was found was immediately given away in charity.

Lands, to which the various armies moved, were not carved out from territories of any lords and chiefs. They were 'abandoned lands, far from the rule and jurisdiction of lords; out of the way, virgin, unclaimed, where rock and weed once abounded, with no sustenance for man, beast or bird; but then men came, inspired by the god from the Rocks, and they made the land lush, green and fertile with their incessant toil and vowed for ever to serve the land with virtue and merit—and though each land bore its separate name, all such lands together came to be known as punya-bhumi (land where virtuous acts are performed—sacred land).'

In these lands, no chiefs were appointed. Sabhas were established on the pattern of Dravidham nagaras but without necessarily giving women a dominant role, as in Dravidham. It was left to the people to elect.

As armies moved to these vast, extensive pockets of punya-bhumi, some asked, 'But why?' The reply was 'To unite. Deep divisions in Bharat Varsha must cease.' Some still argued, 'But to take punya-bhumi! This was not Sindhu Putra's legacy!' The reply: 'His aim was unity... his mission timeless... on our shoulders falls the burden of his greatness... we must pick up the fallen torch... and with faith, forward we must go... unity is our aim... if some fall by the wayside, so be it....'

Some still argued, 'But Sindhu Putra never conquered with force, fire and sword!'

'No!'—was the mocking reply to this simple-minded question. 'What about the heroic battles fought faraway in Sindhu Putra's name by commanders to free slaves and remove repressive chiefs?'

Yes, the sword! Always the sword—to conquer evil as also the spirit!

Relentlessly, the armies moved to punya-bhumi.

Suddenly, then, a cry rose. No one knows how it began or who began it. Some poets say that it was the spirit of Sindhu Putra that cried. But others offer a realistic explanation to say that its inspiration came when an army commander called upon people to leave their land.

'But where do we go?'—people asked. He pointed to the wilderness, far beyond, where their land ended. Again the people cried out, 'There is nothing there!' The commander's reply was, 'That is what you are! Nothing! Leave this land. It belongs to our people.'

'We are the rya,' they shouted.

'Leave! You are not the rya!' the commander thundered.

'This land is ours.'

'You are not of this land.'

'We are rya!' they insisted.

The soldiers' swords gleamed. The villagers stood unmoved. The commander had no wish to order his horsemen to charge and cause bloodshed. He pointed his sword at the throat of the old man who seemed to be their spokesman and said, 'Listen, old man, you have not many years to live but others have. Leave. Go beyond. You can make those rocky barren lands as green as this one. No one shall molest you there, so long as you set no foot here. By midday, if all of you are not gone....'

But here the unpredictable happened. The old man's six-year-old grandson suddenly lunged forward at the commander. Both the old man and the commander moved. Unplanned, unintended, the sword-point went deeper into the throat of the old man. Blood gushed.

The old man was dead.

And all that the six-year-old child was saying to the commander was, 'Let my grandfather go! We are not rya, not rya, not rya!' He only wanted to save his grandfather from the menace and thought that all that the commander wanted was to hear that they were not rya.

The child saw his grandfather fall. He buried his face in his and kept repeating, 'Baba, Baba, you are not rya, not rya.' Somehow he hoped that if his grandfather said that, the commander would restore to him the life that he took away.

But then at last a whisper came in the child's tiny heart and as he rose with his grandfather's blood on his face there was a terrible silence inside the core of his being. Quietly, he said, 'We are not the rya.'

The child no longer said this to gain favour with the commander. There was a silence in his heart that he did not understand. All he knew was that he was not the rya of those that struck his grandfather.

The commander moved away with his men. Outside the heat of battle, he had never killed a man. Perhaps, he would not have grieved if the crowd was rebellious and he had charged, killing many in consequence. He washed his hands in the stream, repeatedly, though he knew the stain was not on his hand but in his heart. He had no wish to menace these people further. There would be other lands—hundreds—from which people had to be moved.

But the villagers hardly noticed the commander moving away with his men. Their eyes were riveted on the little boy, standing next to his grandfather's fallen body, who had said, 'We are not rya'—and as they heard him, it was not the voice of a grieving child; there was no emotion, no tears—neither fear nor despair—neither hate nor anger, but a simple undemonstrative acceptance of a reality—and it came anew to them—'we are not the rya.'

Their thoughts raced back three years, when the boy's father had died, working on the rope-bridge over a ravine, and the child was in shock, without words, without tears. When Sindhu Putra had visited the village, he took the boy in his arms and asked, 'Would you accept me as your father?' Rebelliously the boy replied, 'No, I am my father's son.'

Gently, Sindhu Putra had spoken to him—'I too lost my father and my mother. I was younger than you then....' The child then had tears for someone who had borne greater sorrow. His hand moved to touch Sindhu Putra and with tears he made a concession, 'You shall be my father-friend.'

Father-friend! It was a new relationship, unknown, unheard of. A respected elder, a father-figure, would be called 'uncle'. But Sindhu Putra said, 'Then you will be my son-friend' and thus a new bond was forged. Sindhu Putra invited the boy for a visit to the Rocks. But the boy objected, 'My grandfather will be lonely without me.'

Both the boy and his grandfather had gone to the Rocks for a month. The boy returned with mountains of toys—everyone at the Rocks wanted to give a gift to Sindhu Putra's 'son-friend.'

Ever since his return from the Rocks, the boy had stood apart in the eyes of others. His grandfather was already the head of the village council. His father had toiled for the village with love and lost his life in its service; and his little son had Sindhu Putra as his father-friend.

Now they heard the boy—'We are not the rya.' With an icy chill, the pitiless words echoed in their hearts, and would soon be heard all over—'We are not the rya.'

Yet this was only a tiny village in the vast, unending lands that were called punya-bhumi. Poets tell various stories of how the same cry came to be heard elsewhere. In some villages, commanders pleaded, in others they roared and, in yet others, they charged without warning; at places crowds were mowed down, their huts were burnt and crops destroyed; in others they refused to move and some were slain. At a village, a commander was unhorsed and a reign of terror began, with children roasted on the fire and women thrown into wells.

There were many stories—diverse and different, sad and sentimental—each with its own tale of tears and pathos. Names were different; heroes and villains, diverse; villages far apart. Yet, in essence, where was the difference! Everywhere, all these stories ended with the same cry from the hearts of the people—'We are not the rya!'

Clearly, the cry began with an anguished whisper from people's hearts and their desolate realization of their nothingness in a land that disowned them.

Maybe, the cry started even as a pitiful lament to pitiless gods!— 'Why have you forsaken us and left us anath?'

Maybe then, a quiet voice spoke, or maybe no one spoke and a voice rose in their hearts that asked—'How can we be the rya of those that slayed our nath[1] Sindhu Putra?'

'No, we are arya!'

We are arya!—the cry rose, but it was no longer an agonized cry. It was a cry of conscience—to separate themselves from their oppressors, to cling to their one certainty of Sindhu Putra in the shifting sands around them.

No one knew who had slain Sindhu Putra. The mighty lords and chiefs had publicly mourned his passing away with unrestrained tears. They spoke of their determination to hunt the faceless, nameless killer.

---

[1]Nath meant: protector, master, husband or god. As usual, the addition of 'a' gave it the opposite meaning. Thus anath meant: unprotected, abandoned or orphaned. This practice of attaching 'a' to achieve the opposite meaning continues in Sanskrit and the modern Indian languages, though now under stricter conditions. These strict conditions came later, in the post-Vedic era, when pandits and priestly grammarians intervened to declare the language as fixed and perfected, so that it no longer developed naturally, but strictly within the framework of the rules they prescribed, forgetful of the observation of Muni Manu (not the modern law-giver, but a sage of 5060 BC) that a language that does not grow naturally 'may achieve a great past but never a great future.' The word arya came too, by adding the prefix 'a' to rya; and thus arya came to mean: non-people or exile.

Meanwhile, there were many rumours—that it was a demented lunatic; or a tribal, angry that his land was united with another; or someone whose wife or daughter became a 'bride of Sindhu Putra'; or a drunkard with nothing, whose parents donated their all to Sindhu Putra; or it was the Devil himself; or he who sold his soul to the Devil.

But now a new certainty emerged in the heart of the oppressed—that all those who were terrorizing them were the real killers of Sindhu Putra. But how could that be?—it was only one man who thrust his dagger into the heart of Sindhu Putra! They silenced the question—the Devil comes in ten thousand forms and single or together, he it was that shed the blood of their 'Father'.

The cry of arya was then like a badge of honour—with a deep longing for Sindhu Putra and an intense feeling of trust in his all-conquering love. It was as if the cry gave them a new, distinct identity—with the sensation of being divinely separated from those that shed Sindhu Putra's blood; and they had even the thrill of being 'the chosen ones' who served him with their whole heart and soul. And they were certain that as unrighteousness increased, he would reappear in the dark night for their redemption.

A few poets are misled into believing that the cry of the 'arya' was widespread, extending across the land and skies of all Bharat Varsha, in one single sweep like a giant crusade. Not so. Other poets are realistic and quick to point out that movements, unled and undirected, are never fast-moving.

Meanwhile, the turmoil continued not only in punya-bhumi but throughout the heart of Bharat Varsha. With armies on the move, fresh alliances were forming, new spheres of influence were being established, and recently appointed chiefs were being sacked to make way for new favourites. But those developments distressed only a few at the top.

What affected the vast populace was that even the dispossessed, who had been rehabilitated by Sindhu Putra, were being uprooted anew. Terrified and dazed, they tried to flee and migrate, but they had no place to run to and no place to hide. Every step was a step to nowhere.

Their way to punya bhumi was barred unless they chose to leave for the wastelands beyond. And their cry rose too—'We are arya!'

Yet the cry came not only from the displaced and the uprooted. Some with affluence, secure in their position, and threatened by no one, also joined the cry; they were moved by the pain and tears of others; and as their minds dwelt on Sindhu Putra, the feeling in their hearts was that they too were victims. Many more there were, who, in their soul, reflected the suffering of others, but theirs was a silent despair and they were fearful of the vengeance of the mighty lords of the land. But in their inner ear, came the echo of what Devdatta had once said and Bharatji had repeated—'There is guilt in silence.'

Confusion and chaos spread. Yet the cry of arya rose and surged like a whirlwind. Mighty lords laughed in their contempt and said,

'Yes, you are arya, and so must you be treated—landless, homeless and driven to barren, infertile wastelands beyond our villages and driven again, if by a miracle those lands become luxuriant!'

But to those that banded together to participate in the cry of 'arya' it was like a beam of light that pierced the darkness from their eyes. Suddenly, they found that they were not alone, that thousands joined the cry, that it was a cry of togetherness, of fellow-feeling, of belonging, of comradeship and brotherhood.

Troubled in mind they still were, but no longer did they feel lonely and lost; and the realization dawned on them that they were being tyrannized, not because of their intrinsic inferiority but because those that ruled the land were vile and vicious. With that came a sense of their own dignity and righteousness and even a feeling that they were being hunted because they had chosen to follow the auspicious path of Sindhu Putra.

Thus it was that the cry of arya achieved two different, disparate dimensions and a poet explains it in a two-line dialogue—

'Yes, you are arya,' said the lords, with contempt ineffable.

'Yes, we are arya,' said they, with pride ineffable.

But faith alone! How much could it achieve anything against the mighty lords! And the power of the sword, some said, was mightier than the power of the spirit! Fear thus alternated with faith and sometimes it was all the greater; yet fear arose not so much from the threat of being driven to wastelands of inhospitable terrain as from being herded in separate, isolated areas. Were they being sent there so that it should be easy to pick them up, at will, to be enslaved! Slavery was abolished throughout Bharat Varsha in fact and in law. Yet its memory lingered.

The movement thus began, in fear and faith—fear of the land in which they felt rejected and faith that the spirit of Sindhu Putra would guide their footsteps onto an auspicious path. But there was far more to their faith. They were convinced that the land where they felt disowned had also denied their nath, Sindhu Putra; yet surely Sindhu Putra reigned elsewhere. And hundreds of songs were being sung to radiate this faith.

Such songs, heard everywhere, fired the imagination of receptive listeners, luring them to 'walk the earth where Sindhu Putra walks.'

Yet it is not as if the great migration began overnight. Fear there was that the route to new lands would be difficult and dangerous— but again they thought: can it be more dangerous than remaining here? Another question troubled them: what happens if we find no new lands? But the counter to that was: how is that possible?—did not Sadhu Gandhara go all over—and surely land was there wherever he went! Did not Rishi Newar (of Nepal) find the land he was seeking? Did not. . .? Thus stories of discoverers and explorers were told, of Tirathada who went all over to witness each sanctified spot; and of the brave expeditions which reached the source of Sindhu and Ganga, across the Himalayas and trans-Himalayas, to touch Mount Kailas and Tibata... and to the 108 mouths of the sacred Ganga... and so many faraway lands. Little was said of the intrepid wanderers who died on the way from starvation, exposure or attack and never returned to tell their tale. Yes, danger there would be, they knew, but God would guide them.

Even from themselves, these Aryas tried to suppress the thought that it was fear that tempted them to flee their land—and they would say:

> 'Escapees we are not, nor vagrants, nor aimless wanderers,
> But pilgrims we are, in search of God's land, pure and free.'

Others were even more positive and said: 'We go not for enticement into the unknown, but with the sure knowledge of being near the blaze of unfading glory of our nath (Sindhu Putra).'

Some, to gain courage and take the final, awesome step of leaving their land, wrapped themselves with many comforting self-assurances, and cried out:

> ARYA!
> Noble our aim, noble our thought
> Rya of house of clay we are not!
> ARYA!
> Noble our quest, noble our deed
> Rya, we of distant noble land indeed!
> ARYA!
> Where our Nath, radiant, untouched by evil is He
> There are we rya, noble, pure, free!
> ARYA!
> So ownward in joy!
> No tears, no sighs!
> And if unseeing, our eyes
> Pass that land by,
> We will hear love's cry
> From earth and sky,
> "Come! here am I!"
> And He will bless us then
> And we, Arya no more, Rya again . . . .

Great poetry this was not. But as slogans, they gave comfort and cheer to those that were afraid to move; they exhilarated and intoxicated; and even excited and incited the Arya to move out. But faith and fear?—like light and shadow they cling together and when you embrace one, surely the other waits to embrace you.

But then, if an Arya sought to whisper his fears, another would burst into a song of faith, 'Onward Arya, onward in joy...!' And emotions would then rise to cascade, sweeping past all fears and uncertainties. Thereafter, it was neither a discussion nor a dialogue, nor a debate, but simply a series of songs and declarations, each full of faith in the future.

Later, Nandan's eighth great-grandson asked: 'Where was the scope for fear! Did not the mighty lords and chiefs, Karkarta and Gangapati, and everyone in power, go out of their way to assist the Aryans? Were not the doors of vast treasure-houses opened to equip the Aryans? Were they not given horses, swords, axes, arrows—and even tents and clothing? Like filthy beggars, these Aryans came, swarming before their lords and freely and fondly the benevolent lords gave. Are we then so lost to logic, so bereft of reason, so devoid of sense, as to believe that the Aryans fled from those bounteous patrons who gave them such prodigious help!'

Powerful argument indeed! And powerfully presented! Even persuasive! And, by and large, his facts were right too! Only the conclusion is wrong.

The mighty lords gave liberal help to the Aryans when they moved out because, to them, the Aryans' desire to migrate to faraway lands came like a breath of fresh air. After all, what was their intention in trying to herd these unfortunate Aryans into deserted expanses outside their villages, where nothing grew! Certainly, an immediate advantage was that their lush and green lands could be given to more desirable citizens—for patronage or sale; but beyond that short-term gain was the hope that once again these toiling men, forced to eke out a living in the rocky, toilsome terrain, would renew the land and make it fertile. Then it would again be time to take over those lands and send them out to other uninhabitable areas. As it is, lands from which they were now being displaced were once barren. With unending labour, these men had performed the miracle of making them green. Why could they not keep repeating the miracle!

But now the lure to the lords was even greater. Here they had huge, heroic Aryan groups, fired with the passion to leave Bharat Varsha, to seek out new lands. The lords laughed, though with a new hope springing in their hearts—who knows, some of these miserable Aryans, on this hazardous quest, may even survive to find new lands. Surely then, the lords could move to take over the lands so discovered! True, many of these pathetic Aryans would die in the attempt—but all in a good cause, and their very failure would at least reveal the routes which do not lead to new lands.

The mighty lords were convinced that wealth from the new, faraway lands would be enormous. Why worry then about simply improving the bleak lands outside their villages! And why not encourage this exploration! Obviously, these dull-witted dregs of humanity that moved out as Aryans would know nothing of the rich rewards in these new lands—but surely, they would pave the way. Let us encourage them, resolved the lords.

Were the lords pinning their hopes on something too far-fetched?

Was there a real prospect that the Aryans may find new lands which the lords could take over? The fact is that not all new lands in the past were found by intrepid explorers, with design and intent or even the will to explore. Everyone knew the ancient story—that a drunkard had leapt into Sindhu to retrieve his half-empty liquor-barrel which fell in the river. In the fast flow of the river, somehow the barrel moved faster than he could swim. Before he lost consciousness, he had the sense or good fortune to climb on to a large chunk of driftwood. On that he slept, dead to the world; and apparently all the beasts in the river had kept away from him because he smelt so strongly of liquor. He woke up the next morning. He did not find his liquor-barrel. But he saw there, the confluence of Sindhu river with Sutudhri (Sutlej river in Panchanad—Punjab). He returned sadly without his liquor-barrel but was later delighted when the Sindhu Council of Chiefs presented him with five large, full, liquor-barrels for his amazing discovery of the confluence.

So why was it surprising for the mighty lords to hope that these 'faith-drunk' Aryans might succeed in finding new lands? And if they failed and died in the attempt... so what! Good riddance!

No one should therefore be surprised if the mighty lords encouraged the Aryan migration. From various, scattered pockets, small bands of Aryans were helped with transport, to join together in sizeable groups.

The choice for the Aryans was simple, even virtuous—go empty-handed, unprotected, in the raw, rocky, untamed land in the wild expanse outside the village or heed the call of hope in lands beyond. They chose the lands beyond; and the lords, for once, were generous—ready to offer stores, equipment, food and even draft-animals, horses, swords and arrows. The lords also nominated men to give advice to these Aryans on the different routes to follow—and their intention was to avoid the concentration on one single route; surely much would be revealed, if more routes were taken.

Whenever an Aryan group was overtaken by momentary panic at embarking on a journey into the unknown—the men sent out by the lords were ready not only with words of comfort and cheer, but larger aid in stores and equipment. Singers sent out by the lords would also sing,

> 'Child! be blessed of one mind;
> Go! His glory seek, and find;
> On and on....'

Some Aryan groups paused to wonder that, if the mighty lords supported their move, maybe there was something really wrong with it. But was that reason enough to give it up, when the alternatives were so bleak! Instead, greater wisdom came to them and they spoke of their fear and torments as though they were hesitating—even uncertain—to go so ill-equipped into the lands beyond.

The lords responded with greater generosity. Said one Aryan to another, 'How stupid these clever people are!'

The petty chiefs marvelled at the patience of their lords with the Aryans. They fumed that their lords should demand that so much be given to these miserable creatures. They suggested: let the Aryans be sent to work in barren areas beyond their villages, or be driven out altogether. The lords were magnificently unconcerned, for the burden of their largesse fell on the petty chiefs.

The great migration of the Aryans from Bharat Varsha had begun.

'. . .They did not choose the path they had to tread. It was simply the fantasy of faith that led them on, towards the elusive, unreachable goal of finding a land that was pure and free of evil. . .'

—(Poetess Padma's Song 'The Voice that was Not'—5005 BC)

. . .And then Sage Bharadwaj spoke and said the earth is eternal, and so is man, if he lives in harmony with nature. But also he said that man could not destroy the earth and if he tried that by folly or design, 'then, only mankind shall die but not the eternal ground on which mankind walks, for the decision to destroy the earth rests with all-powerful, limitless God.' But Dharmabila asked, 'If God is that limitess and all-powerful, why is it inconceivable that He created man to be even more powerful than Himself?' Sage Bharadwaj laughed and simply said, 'How many times must I tell you to have your soma wine after our discussions and not before?. . .'

—(From poetess Shaila, 'Much to learn, more to unlearn'— 5005 BC)

'Look for a worm, and a treasure you may find'

(A proverb, current in Sindhu in 5065 BC when earlier Hindu explorers went to the Land of Kosa Karas [literal meaning: Land of Worms; later named, China] to look for silk-worms, but instead found jade.)

God! Bring me not back, as I was
Let me come as a blade of grass
Or a droplet of dew and rain
So this waterless desert blooms again. . .

—(Last Prayer of an Arya who died in Gobi Desert, in Mongolia, 5003 BC)

The Aryans Move

5011 BC

'Poets are descended from cats,' said poet Dharmabila.

He was explaining why there were not many poets among the Aryan bands that left Bharat Varsha. Poets, like cats, he said, were never adventurous; they 'do not like to venture out into uncertain territory; and be it a time of pleasure or pain, the cat will purr and likewise the poet will sing, remaining always at home, clean and well-groomed, with no desire to stray into the dust and debris of the outside world; the cat and the poet carry a tongue to preen themselves, though others can feel its rasplike, coarse quality. Yet both are capable of subtle affection and grace, if you feed them well.'

As a final dig at poets, Dharmabila said that his conclusions were inspired by Sage Bharadwaj. Actually, he was misquoting the Sage. But then he often misquoted the Sage and the Sage did not mind.

Sage Bharadwaj believed that man, though infinitely removed from the perfection of the creator, was close to the perfection of the animal. According to him, trees were the earliest ancestor of man; from trees, man evolved through slow, successive stages—of worms and insects, fowl and fish, birds and beasts, vraon (half-ape, halfman) and vrbila (half-cat, half-man), 'though I cannot say that each of the 108 humans that first evolved, spent the same time in each link of this living chain.' The Sage also added that even the powerful mammoth species that tormented the earth and its creatures in the past became extinct. Thus he emphasized that the earth was eternal and so was man, if he lived in harmony with nature. But otherwise 'only mankind shall die but not the eternal ground on which mankind walks', and thereafter another species will emerge.

Out of fun, poet Dharmabila perverted Sage Bharadwaj's observation on the uncertainty of time that each of the first 108 humans passed in various species towards their final evolution as man. Dharmabila said that the craftiest and trickiest among those 108 passed more time with the fox; the wisest and most reflective with the owl; the fickle, with the butterfly; the strongest, with the lion. And after all these examples, Dharmabila finally declared that the first poet undoubtedly remained longest with the cat.

Incidentally, Dharmabila, though not a poet of fame, was a lover of cats. His observation was 'I love my six cats, more than the wife I don't have'—and from this, one may conclude that he was a bachelor.

Dharmabila's observation, on why poets of renown did not join the Aryan movement out of Bharat Varsha, has very little merit. Largely, these were expeditions of the dispossessed and disinherited. Most of those who joined were from the stock of ex-slaves, fearful of their future in their own land. They wanted to flee from their grim reality and chase a dream.

True, there were several songs about others that joined, moved solely by faith and fellow-feeling. But then songs will often be sung to extol the exceptional or inspirational and not about what is ordinary or expected.

Certainly, the presence of more poets would have added to the knowledge about routes taken by the Aryans and their trials and triumphs on the way. But the fact is that even from groups which had poets, the information was sketchy—related often to what some isolated individuals or teams faced on the way. Also, laments a poet himself, such uncoordinated information when it came, 'was brief and abrupt. . .often rambling and blurred. . .vague and unadorned. . .easy to ignore and easier to forget. . .lacking the inspirational genius of a poet who could weave together in a gracious harmony, the many strange events and isolated incidents.'

And so, though the claim that the poets could have shed more light is valid, some poets actually confused more than they enlightened.

The routes on which the Aryans went were initially no more than twelve. The Aryans converged from hundreds of points to form larger bands, so as to leave on specific routes from their respective regions. There were large and small bands, following each other—some after short, others after long, intervals, often joining together or even parting from each other to go on their own.

Certainly there is much to be said in favour of what Nandan's eighth great-grandson reports on the initial routes selected by the Aryans for their move out of Bharat Varsha.

The first series of routes, which Nandan's great-grandson correctly mentions, began from Avagana. According to him, 'The route to Avagana was traditional and fraught with no danger. . . . For it was here that Sadhu Gandhara first established an ashram; and the city Qandhara was named after him. . . and from there the Sadhu had moved to bring all Avagana up to and beyond Hari Rath under his protection. . .and when he died, the land was left in trust with the headman from Sapta Sindhu, until his son Kush came of age. . . and then began the glorious reign of Lord Kush who married the daughter of Dhrupatta's wife's sister's daughter from Sapta Sindhu, with the blessings of my great-grandfather Karkarta Nandan. . .and always Nandanji, the most illustrious of Karkartas, regularly sent caravans of goods, artisans and assistance to Kush and his land, which always shall be a part of Hindu Varsha... So where was the danger to these wandering Arya bands to go through Avagana, when Kush, magnificent and vigorous himself, despite his venerable age, was there to guide them!... and the request of Karkarta Sauvira to Kush was clear... he had asked that these wanderers be not permitted to remain in Avagana; and must be led out to lands beyond... but should they try to tarry in Avagana, they must be sent back forthwith.... Pity though it is, that Kush misunderstood this request and allowed some Aryans to stay back, choosing those that were valuable to his land, and others too sick and old to travel.... But, honourable as always, Kush sent a message to Karkarta Sauvira, though by mischance, the messenger failed to arrive....'

At Hari Rath in Afghanistan several Aryan bands congregated. Many parted here, too, to branch out on different routes.

Purus who lived by the side of Saraswati river, led his Arya bands towards Lake Namaskar (Namaksar).

'We know not if we shall meet again on this earth,' said Purus while parting from the other Aryan bands. 'But surely we shall reassemble at the feet of the Master in the world beyond.'

'Yes,' said the leader of another band, 'we that saw him live, know that he lives, and so shall we.'

Such a cry of faith came, no doubt, from the heart; and these self-assurances and chants were many, if only to keep their hopes and dreams that somewhere there was a better land, where their lost god awaited them with outstretched arms, alive.

But consistency belongs only to the gods. With human beings, each cry of faith is overtaken often by another cry of despair; and even grief dies only to be replaced by another greater grief.

Six scouts of Aryan bands, which Purus led, were killed outright. They were going ahead of the others and were suddenly overtaken by a group of roving bandits. But as the large columns of Aryan bands, escorted by Kush's men, came into view, the bandits fled. The gruesome sight of these four murdered men and two women brought an overflow of the feeling of dread that lay in the heart of every Aryan who marched.

Purus and his bands reached the area around Lake Namaskar. Already, several Hindu hermits had settled down there—originally from Sapta Sindhu, thereafter from Ganga, and later from Dravidham and elsewhere.

Kush had ordered his men, who were escorting the Aryas, not to let anyone stay back. Karkarta Sauvira's request was clear—to send out all of them to the lands beyond; already Kush had deviated from it by allowing many to remain behind.

A hermit around the lake, however, adopted nine children of those who were killed by bandits on the way. At first, Kush's men insisted that these nine children could not remain. But the hermit glared, ready to shout. The leader of Kush's escort advised his men, 'Look the other way; hermits carry a powerful curse; beware!' They looked the other way; and it seems, some adult Aryas too stayed back with the hermits.

'Purus, the Arya leader, did not object to anyone remaining behind and said, 'Your feelings must be your guide. . . . You must follow the faith that calls loudest to you. . . who knows where the Master needs you!. . . Who knows where we too may retrace our steps!. . .'

Some view this as a lack of faith, as if he feared that after all his wanderings, the object of his quest may elude him. But a poet adds, 'I know of no man of faith, nor a god, who is untouched by anguish and self doubt.'

Of the nine children adopted by the hermit, the eldest—a twelve-year-old—ran to rejoin the Arya bands, a few hours later. At this reunion, it is said that Purus had tears in his eyes.

Yet one aspect is clear. The Arya bands did not go out into new lands with any feeling of triumph or banners flying. The reassuring chants of 'sanctified terrain. . .far. . .somewhere. . .elsewhere. . .' may have been in the depths of their hearts, but their move beyond, to lands unknown, was mournful.

Quietly, they heard the blessing of the hermits at Lake Namaskar and did not even smile when the oldest hermit possibly made a mistake about the name of Purus and said:

'Go then, Purusa, take your Aryas; but as you flee from evil, carry not evil with yourself; and even if you are sacrificed in many parts, let your deeds be noble in the reckoning of God and man; not by one or the other; but in the judgement of both; so that till the end of time, the Arya shall be known as noble.'

Purusa! That is what the hermit had called Purus. Some said—a peculiar mistake indeed, by an enlightened hermit! Others said, it was not a mistake at all!

Purusa had an enticing array of meanings. It meant ideal man; but it also meant 'world spirit' to those sages who conceived the entire universe as an organic whole and various aspects of creation as parts of the macrocosmic unity. There were other sages who synthesized entire human society into one being—the purusa. Often also purusa meant the primeval man, who sacrificed himself to bring justice and freedom to others.

Centuries later, an echo of this would be found in the *Rig Veda* as well, which describes Purusa as possessed of 'Myriad heads, myriad eyes, myriad feet, pervading terrestrial regions. . . and extending beyond the universe by a space of ten fingers.'

Ironically and perversely though, the *Rig Veda* hymns on Purusa would subsequently be distorted and misquoted as sanctioning or condoning different levels of humanity or the caste system which would come to cast its shadow on post-Vedic society long after the return of the Aryans to Bharat Varsha. In point of fact, the pre-ancient songs are clear that primeval man made this sacrifice so that the sacred laws of freedom, justice and equality be honoured and man may protect nature and creation and, if need be, even sacrifice himself in that cause.

The lands beyond Namaskar lake, into which the Arya bands moved, had no special name. The hermits referred to them as the lands of Hari Haran. Long after the Arya bands moved in, it began to be called Hari Haran Aryan or simply the land of Aryan, and from this, later emerged its name—Iran.[1]

It was in the isolation of Hari Haran Aryan (Iran) that the Arya bands rested. Several other bands travelling from Avagana joined them. Purus injured his leg and remained in Iran (Persia) with some Arya groups. Many groups moved on in various directions—in the west to modern Turkey and Iraq; in the south to the Persian Gulf and the Gulf of Oman; and to the north into the erstwhile Soviet Union.

The influx into what was the Soviet Union had begun not only from Iran. Many Aryan bands from Avagana itself moved there, on the routes which Sadhu Gandhara had earlier taken.

Sadly, nine out of every ten that travelled on Sadhu Gandhara's routes, died. Those that went to Iran and beyond did not fare so poorly but, even so, less than half survived.

Purus recovered a little from his leg injury. He himself was impatient to move forward. But during his enforced stay in Iran, he had become the central figure and focal point for protecting Aryan groups and assisting and equipping them to move out in various directions.

And move out they did, all across the west.

It was the sea-route from the mouth of Sindhu river that attracted the Aryas.

From all over in upper Sindhu and elsewhere, the Aryas came to congregate in lower Sindhu. Karkarta Sauvira himself set up comfortable camps for them in lower Sindhu to oversee and encourage their move to lands beyond the sea—to the Persian Gulf and Sumer (modern Iraq).[2]

To avoid hurting the sensitivities of lower Sindhu, Karkarta Sauvira would always refer to these Aryas as 'Arya pilgrims' to emphasize that they were 'of no land, but God's pilgrims to all lands, everywhere, with a purpose that is sacred and intent that is noble.'

---

[1]Later, some said that Iran obtained its other name—Persia—from the Arya leader Purus, who affectionately began to be called 'Purusa' on the basis of the hermit's 'mistake by design'. But resemblance in names could also simply be a coincidence.

[2]The short distance to the Persian Gulf, and thence to Sumer (Mesopotamia—Iraq) and Iran, would not impress anyone today. Even the boat-people of the twentieth century, fleeing from persecution, have crossed far larger distances in their dilapidated, over-crowded, ill-made and ill-equipped boats, while subjected to attacks from pirates. The Aryans of Bharat Varsha went out in more auspicious circumstances; they were fleeing too, but they fled with the active aid and support of those from whom they were fleeing.

The sea voyages of the Aryas began.

As it is, long-distance sea voyages had begun earlier, even in Karkarta Nandan's time. Nandan had given every encouragement so that bigger, faster and safer boats be built and even a ship with 108 oars was developed. The seafarers had then touched the Persian Gulf and thence proceeded to the coast of Sumer between the Euphrates and Tigris rivers. But the men who went in those boats were sailors, mariners and seamen, interested in exploring the sea—and not land. A few stayed back though, to build their huts on the coastline, and even piers and docks for the loading and repair of boats that came infrequently from Sindhu. However, finding no locals nearby, and nothing of real interest to them in the immediate vicinity, their trips inland were few and never too deep.

But the Aryas who crowded into the boats for the Persian Gulf and Sumer were not seafarers. They were frightened, gentle souls, who were stricken with fear—certain that the winds would tear their boats apart and the ocean would open its depths to swallow them. And then even the song, 'Onward, Noble Arya. . .' failed to soothe them.

Shipwrecks did take place since boats were being hastily built in order to meet the large demand.

Suddenly, however, all boat-traffic stopped as the Naudhyaksa (superintendent of ships) of lower Sindhu intervened, demanding that no boat leave, until he and his men had inspected it fully.

Karkarta Sauvira himself rushed to the scene. The 'unfeeling' retort attributed to Naudhyaksa was:

*'I care not how many "faithfuls" drown
But how dare they drag my sea-men down!'*

Nandan's great-grandson also refers to this, not so much to show that Naudhyaksa was unconcerned with the Aryas who drowned and cared only for the safety of his sailors as to show how considerate Karkarta Sauvira was, not only to agree with Naudhyaksa, but to bring in hundreds of men to assist in boat-building.

Most Aryas waiting to be transported to the Persian Gulf and Sumer were also put on the job of repairing and building boats. Many 'unfeeling' lines have again been attributed to Naudhyaksa.

However, Naudhyaksa was not always caustic. He and his men would often sit with the Aryas to explain the finer points of boat-building to them. He also demanded that each Arya—man, woman and child—must learn to be a better swimmer. He concentrated on children, saying, 'Adults have lived long enough, so it does not matter if they drown, though they too should learn to swim if only to save their children, if the need arises, and then they can drown in peace.'

Naudhyaksa also 'persuaded' some Aryas, who became proficient in boat-building, to stay back. He called them 'sailors with land-legs.'

Forcefully, he was warned by Karkarta Sauvira's men that their Karkarta was against keeping back the Aryas. He was not bothered and said, 'Impossible! Don't forget, he is Karkarta Nandan's grandson who helped us to build bigger, better ships. He is the son of Karkarta Sharat whose elder brother was an illustrious naudhyaksa and, at his feet, I learnt my art. He is the one who toiled and died to make a ship of 108 oars a reality. And you tell me that Karkarta Sauvira is so forgetful of his ancestry—and so unenlightened—as to object! Nonsense! You insult your Karkarta! And you insult the memory of his ancestors!'

Karkarta Sauvira heard it all and never objected. But, by and large, it was the 'herd instinct' that prevailed, and the cry came from other Aryas, 'Why do you desert us cruelly at this moment of parting?'— And most of the Arya boat-builders delayed their departure, but eventually, they too left.

Steadily, one after another, the Aryans reached the coast of Sumer.

They moved inland, deeper, coming across many people and settlements. Later, some Arya groups would even mix and mingle with their roving bands which had reached Iran and Afghanistan with Purus.

The existence of quantities of jade excavated in the pre-Aryan Indus valley civilization surprised many. There was no cause for surprise. The clue for the existence of so much jade in the Sindhu civilization is found in the proverb which was current even before Karkarta Sauvira's time—'Look for a worm, and a treasure you may find!'

The background to this proverb needs to be explained:

The source of Sindhu river in Tibata had been discovered by the expedition sent out by Karkarta Bharat. Later, Rishi Skanda Dasa established an ashram there. The ashram attracted a number of locals and one of them presented the Rishi with a treasured possession—a cloth of soft, sleek silk. The Rishi was told that the silk, brought by a traveller from the north, was made from the cocoons of domesticated worms. The traveller had been delighted to exchange his silk cloth with the cotton made in Sapta Sindhu.

The Rishi sent the silk cloth to Karkarta Bharat; and from then on began a series of consultations between the Guild of Weavers and the Guild of Merchants. The weaver's guild was content with the excellent cotton fibre and textiles they were producing, but the merchant's guild went ahead with organizing a team to go north, with the Rishi's help. The team was composed of fifty-four locals from Tibet and six weavers from Sapta Sindhu.

The team of sixty left for the Land of Kosa Karas.[3]

---

[3] Its subsequent name as 'China' or 'Cheena' emerged some 4,000 years later in the eighth century BC, and all the more so, when the Ch'in dynasty began unifying the country in 221 BC, and its king, Shih Huang Ti, claimed the title of sovereign emperor.

After eight years, fifteen members of the team returned. With them, they brought a group of over 450 men, women and children fleeing the anarchy of the Land of Kosa Karas. They had harrowing tales to tell of the brutality, massacres and incessant warfare everywhere in that land. Yet they spoke also of the gentleness and compassion of the many ordinary though powerless people.

The failure of the team was that it did not find areas in China which domesticated silkworms. Its success was that fifteen team members and the group of 450 brought jade. And thus began the proverb 'Look for a worm and a treasure you may find.'

Little is known of the forty-five missing members of the team sent out to the land of Kosa Karas. Fourteen are definitely known to have died during their wandering there. Ten decided to stay back. Of them, one—a weaver from Sindhu—took a wife from Kosa Karas and was immediately unpopular with his wife's family over his failure to appreciate the local custom whereby all childless females—sisters, cousins, aunts—in the family must be regarded as married to the new husband. He had heard about the custom before marriage, but he thought it was to be a spiritual bond, and not a 'body-bond.'

It is not known if he ultimately resisted the temptation or succumbed to it. But one thing is certain. He prayed to his god Skanda—the god of fertility—day and night for a child to be born to his wife, so that she may remain totally outside the amorous advances of any new husband who entered into the familyfold.

God Skanda was apparently impressed with his prayers and on the twenty-fourth night of his marriage, his wife gave birth to twins— a boy and a girl—just two days before another husband entered the family, as a result of the marriage of his wife's elder sister.

This new husband could now command a pool of twenty-nine females from the family, in addition to his own wife, but not the wife of the weaver from Sindhu, or the other women who had borne children.

So much about the weaver from Sindhu is well-known and is substantiated by many. But later, his story came to be wrapped in myths and miracles. He is credited to have sired eighteen children in eight years of marriage. That is not too difficult to believe, as he may have finally adopted the local custom of accepting all childless females in the family as married to him.

But far greater myths arose about him in later centuries—not so much in Bharat Varsha but in the land of Kosa Karas. He came to be known variously as the 'Lord of Grain' or the 'Lord of Millet and Wheat,' or the 'Lord of Soil.' These titles of honour came to him not as a lord of the land, but simply as a cultural hero who taught agriculture to the locals, under the inspiration of his god Skanda. In the Kosa Karas myth, he is said to emerge as a lord who sprang from below (south) to tickle the soil of the earth, to bring forth grains and fruit. His inventions are supposed to have included boats and oars—common in Sindhu but not then in Kosa Karas. He also taught them breeding of domestic fowls. Finally, he retired to Tien Shan (celestial mountains) where his god Skanda used to come for occasional visits.

Several portraits and statues of the Sindhu weaver appear in Kosa Karas, depicting him in a heroic mould.

He was clearly shown as brown-skinned, with eyes and features which distinguished him from the Chinese race and identified him with the kind of statues found in the Indus valley civilization.

Centuries later, for social and political reasons, the Chinese removed and modified portraits and statues of this Bharat Varsha weaver, to show, instead, a legendary figure with Chinese features.

It was in Karkarta Nandan's time that more teams were sent to the Land of Worms. They were better equipped, armed and ably led. They found more jade and some precious stones and metals, but were unable to reach the region of silkworms. Again, the proverb would be heard—'Look for a worm and a treasure you may find.'

Even though a few teams had been sent, it is not as if the route to Kosa Karas or even to Tibet was well-frequented. Only the hardy, intrepid travellers would venture on it.

Yet the Arya bands moved there too, fired by the spark of faith within, that somehow their god would guide them to the 'enchanted land where he himself dwells and reigns.' If a doubt sometimes crept into their minds, they took refuge in their exulting songs—there were always singers and poets whose song-stories were noble to the point of rapture; and they pointed to paths that were without danger for those that tread on them in faith.

Many routes were taken by the Aryas to the north and east. Not all the routes are known with certainty. For the Arya bands often criss-crossed each other, sometimes joining other bands, sometimes separating. At times, bands and even individuals, refused to go on, some staying back, and others returning.

However, the major routes to the east were through the Land of Brahma, which had its autonomous chief, under the sovereignty of Gangapati of Ganga. The treks began through modern East Bengal, Assam and Manipur (Munipur); and thence from upper Burma, the Arya groups moved southwards, some to reach Malaya and Sindpur (later known as Singhpur and, now, Singapore). It was from Malaya and Sindpur, that they would reach Bali and Sumatra by boat.

Gangapati had also organized boats for the sea-journey, just as Karkarta Sauvira had done in Sapta Sindhu. Arya bands worked day and night to build more boats at port Tamralipti (near modern Midnapore district; map reference:. 22.25n; 87.20e) and at ports on the Orissa coast. Boats proceeded along the coasts of Bengal and Burma and after crossing the Bay of Bengal reached Malaya, Sindpur, Hindu Chhaya (Indo-China) and Indonesia.

At Bali, the Aryas would build the first Hindu temple, later at Sindpur, and possibly, at the same time, in Cambodia.

Among the routes to China was also the overland route across Avagana over the Hindu Kush passes to Bactria, thereafter through Central Asia to western China. Another route went through Upper Burma to southwest China. Additionally, there were the sea-routes from the coasts of Indo-China and through the East Indies islands.

Obviously, there were other routes, minor and major and Arya groups, large and small, often deviated to chart a path of their own, in faith, and sometimes even in frustration.

Many routes would thus remain unknown. For instance, a poet relates the story of a group of Aryas in the middle of the Gobi Desert (in Mongolia, with the erstwhile Soviet Union to their north and China to the south; map reference: 43.00n; 106.00e). Of this group of 120, only two survived. The two survivors found shelter near a mountain which they called Hari Haran Mountain (Presently known as Mount Hayrhan, in Mongolia; map reference: 46.50n; 91.40e).

Even this odd incursion, outside any known route, would go unreported, except that the survivor, apparently a poet, wished to recite the prayer of an Arya who died in the Gobi Desert. The prayer was:

> God! Bring me not back, as I was
> Let me come as a blade of grass
> Or a droplet of dew and rain
> So this waterless desert blooms again. . .

The poet goes on for four hundred more lines to speak of the blessing of the dying man so that the waterless 'Gobi Desert may bloom again.'

'...These were not sages, poets, philosophers and thinkers. They were simple men and women, many in fear of persecution, and some fired by the faith that the gods would guide their footsteps to the land of pure. But others there were who listened to the murmur of their own hearts and went out to share the destiny of the abandoned, the lonely and the lost. . . .'

—(From Dharmabila's poem 'They that returned not'— 4990 BC)

'Gods wait; goodness comes first to the land by man's effort; and then only do gods enter. And gods come not to do man's work but to bless him; and they depart in sorrow if man ceases his work.'

—(view expressed by Purus, the Aryan leader in Iran— 5005 BC)

Aryans in Iran

5005 BC

In the distortion of time and memory, some poets have been tempted to go to extraordinary lengths to depict the Aryans as warlike, vigorous, courageous, enterprising souls, overflowing with all the lusty emotions and desires of life, and fired with the passion to explore and discover the world. With superb rhythm, imagery and narrative force, the poets recite not only some of the exploits of the Aryans, but they even speak of a well-coordinated organizational plan—and they ask what seems to them an unanswerable question: how else would they travel from so many points, on different routes, to reach so many destinations?

Aim? There was no aim to discover the world; nor to go out for adventure. The Aryan bands left simply in search of elusive purity. The assassination of Sindhu Putra had left a scar, but not all of them were influenced only by that. The feeling went far beyond and affected even those not emotionally involved with Sindhu Putra.

They saw the decay around themselves and the failure of the land of their birth to protect them. They feared that the evil against them would grow; and somewhere else, they felt, a moral order existed and that was where they must dwell.

A coordinated organizational plan? True, the Aryan bands moved out from many points. But it had to be so. Obviously, it was impossible to cover the vast distances from one end of Bharat Varsha to another in order to congregate at a single departure point. The routes they took were also many—some over land, others over water. It was not really a free choice. The point of departure itself, often, determined the route. So where was the question of a well-coordinated plan! They did not choose the path they had to tread. It was simply the fantasy of faith that led them on towards 'the unreachable goal of finding a land that is pure and free from evil.'

The migration and movement of Aryas from Bharat Varsha continued. They were unaware of shipwrecks, disasters and the sudden deaths that overtook their compatriots in foreign lands.

Many who had reached Sumer and Hari Haran Aryan would stay back, 'their feet weary and their hearts heavy, for their fountain of hope to find the land of the pure had dried up.' But many more, still fired with faith, went on, in different directions, on different routes, finding themselves in faraway lands. Perhaps a hundred volumes are needed to describe the routes they took, the vast numbers of places they went to, and what all they did to protect themselves and their compatriots and, more so, to salvage the lives of the unfortunates living in those areas. At best, here, a synoptic review is all that is possible.

To begin with, much of the land through which Purus and his bands of Aryas passed from Avagana, was unoccupied. Their first contact was with a settlement of people, working under warlords and bandits, with the power of life and death over whoever was around them.

Possibly, bandit-chiefs could easily have wiped out the largely unarmed Arya bands, when they were first seen. But their sheer numbers were frightening; and local bandits could never imagine that such a large 'army' came on a peaceful errand. Maybe, the initial approach by the first Aryan band would have convinced them of the peaceful intent of the new-comers. But the local warlord did not wait for that first approach. He did what he had always done in the past, whenever a large bandit army came into view. The drum-beat sounded, gongs were struck and inhabitants of the village were driven out to the hills, before the Aryas could reach the settlement.

Three young men, three naked women, twelve dogs and cats were left, tied and bound, in the village. This was the usual 'peace-offering' that bandit-lords left, whenever fleeing from a large bandit-army in the hope that they would not be pursued, nor dealt with severely, if caught. It was simply a tribute to a conquering force—an acceptance of temporary sovereignty.

The six tied men and women were intended for the slavery and enjoyment of the new-comers; the dogs and cats, for their eating pleasure.

From a distance, the Aryas saw men, women, and children fleeing. It then occurred to them that their walking-staffs—and the arrows and swords with some—had frightened the locals. They shouted reassuring words and even ran to tell them that they came in friendship, but this frightened the bandit-lord and his men even more; and they cracked their whips to drive their 'human cattle' faster to the hills.

The Aryas freed the twelve cats and dogs and the six men and women. Perhaps the first frightening thought that ran through the minds of these six released persons was: 'why are they letting animals go free—are they amongst those bandits that eat only human flesh?'

Their words were foreign. But a common language was not needed to understand their fright and the suffering of many whom the bandit-lords controlled.

Purus was not from slave-stock. His father was a hermit in the forest of Varanasi. His father had been disappointed in his discussions with

Sindhu Putra who offered no enlightenment on the mystery and identity of the universal spirit.

He was even more disappointed with his son Purus, who did not believe in God, but only in goodness. Later, Purus had taken to wandering, but not like a sadhu or a muni. He enjoyed a dice game and an occasional soma drink. He was proficient in yoga—yet he practised it, not for spiritual release but for physical relaxation.

In his wanderings, Purus had visited the Rocks where Sindhu Putra resided, more out of curiosity than faith. He came away from there as he went in, and despite what many said, he could not believe that Sindhu Putra was a god. To him, Sindhu Putra appeared simply as a lonely individual, surrounded by many in faith, and by some who were scoundrels; but somehow he failed to see in Sindhu Putra the glow of inner peace which a god, or even a man of god, must have in himself. It was as if Sindhu Putra had lost control over events and wondered if what others did in his name was the right course of action.

Purus, then, had taken up residence by the side of the many-splendoured Saraswati river. He acquired barges to transport soma wine for sale. His slogan of 'sacred wine on sacred river' was appealing. Meanwhile, in the midst of his lucrative business, he thought no more of Sindhu Putra.

But the sudden news of Sindhu Putra's assassination struck him like a shattering blow. That night he drank soma and when that did not comfort him, he followed it up with sura.

Since then, Purus identified himself with the cause of the Aryas and led the first Arya band to Iran through Avagana. To many, it would remain a mystery why and how this pleasure-loving man, with no affiliations to Sindhu Putra, joined the cause after his assassination.

Later, a poet said, 'Perhaps it occurred to him anew, that gods are many, and men who proclaim God's name, many more; but men of goodness are few—and the assassination of a man of goodness diminishes us all.'

Maybe, it is the association of men like Purus with the Aryas, that caused some to say that the Aryans went out for conquest and discovery. Certainly, they said, he was not searching for a god, nor the land of pure. As it is, on that arduous journey, he often questioned himself.

The defining moment for Purus came in Iran when he saw the sight of the six unfortunates left as slaves by the bandit-lord. He realized, with even greater force, that it was futile to search here or anywhere, for gods or for the land of pure. 'They are all hidden by heavenly smoke,' he said. 'But it is necessary that as far as man can, he should strive for goodness to make the land pure, fit for the gods to enter.'

Purus advanced his idea, though few understood him and, he said, 'Gods wait; goodness comes first to the land by man's effort and then only do the gods enter. And gods come not to do man's work, but to bless him; and they depart in sorrow if man ceases his work.'

If his thinking was obscure, his orders at least were clear, as he saw the anguish of these six 'slaves.' He said, 'Wherever we go, we shall drive out the bandit-lords and set their slaves free.'

Most of their men could look into their own past and easily relate to this order. But some had questions—'Surely this was not our mission!' Purus was silent; yet others answered for him—'If our goal is to reach a god, and god asks what we did on the way, shall we say that we paused not to do god's work!' Purus had merely nodded and a poet sadly adds, 'The truth is that he was not godly himself.' And this poet goes on to relate the story of how Purus had made his Arya bands carry eight barrels from Bharat Varsha, saying that they contained water from Ganga, Saraswati, Sindhu and five other sacred rivers, and how his men guarded the barrels with their life through steep ascents and treacherous gorges on the route; but the truth was that the barrels contained soma liquor, and when the truth was finally revealed Purus himself cried out, 'It is god's work—to turn water into wine!' The poet adds also, 'I laugh not at those that believe him and I honour them for their faith but the ways of this Purus were truly wayward.'

Wayward, Purus may have been in his belief in the gods, but he was single-minded in his aim to free the slaves. The six 'slaves' left by the bandit-chief now insisted on joining the Aryas.

Guided by the six released 'slaves,' Purus and his bands saw to the release of many, all along the way. Later, Purus realized that the task he had undertaken was not to be treated lightheardly. The bandit-chiefs often fought back or later counter-attacked in force.

Purus had the advantage of numbers with him, but his people lacked the spirit of violence and the skill of warfare. Often then, he engaged in battle-exercises to teach his men to fight and a poet says, 'Aryas made arrows, swords, slingshots and poles with sharp ends; and learnt to wield them all with skill, with the instincts of a killer; and jumped up and down trees, or moved in silence to take the oppressor unawares.'

The Arya bands swelled. More and more were reaching from Avagana. Slaves freed by the Aryas in Iran were joining them, afraid to remain in their old settlements for fear of bandits returning to wreak vengeance.

But it is not as if throughout Iran it was a scene of degradation. Society, though divided largely between a vast number of slaves and a few bandit-chiefs, had men of learning too—mostly ascetics.

The bandit-chiefs were afraid to hurt the ascetics and their disciples. Everyone knew of the curse—that those who harm ascetics will burn in hell and their descendants too will suffer slavery; and as if that was not enough, the curse also fell on those who associated with such persons; with blessings for all who opposed the accursed. Thus, it was a self-fulfilling curse, as anyone harming an ascetic was treated as an outcast by his associates, lest the curse affect them too; and thus isolated, even once-powerful bandit-chiefs were killed or enslaved, as it was the sacred duty of all to oppose them.

Purus began to woo the ascetics. Many were willing. Around these ascetics, villages were formed, with residents declared as disciples, to discourage attacks from bandit-chiefs. Locals were trained to defend themselves and were also called Aryas so that the bandit-chiefs knew that the Arya bands would seek revenge, if they were harmed.

Purus set up Arya camps in coastal regions outside the mountain ring. In these settlements, Hari Haran Aryan witnessed, for the first time, the development of settled village agricultural life. Domestication of animals and plants started, along with a definite shift to tool-making and later to sophisticated farming at a number of places including the sites now known as Asiab, Ali Kosh, Ganj-e-Dareh, Guran, Tepe Sabz, Sialk, Yahya, Godin and Hajji Firuz.

Villages in new settlements followed a simple rectangular pattern devised by the Arya groups. High walls with towers at corners formed the outer face of houses which had flat roofs of mud and straw supported by wood rafters. Cattle and fowl were herded inside the walls.

It was a far cry from the aesthetic villages of Bharat Varsha, but even there, in centuries past, the beginnings were equally modest.

In the centre of the walled village would be the best hut, often unoccupied. That was supposed to house the ascetic, though generally he would be in the forest under a tree or on a rock. Yet an attack on the settlement was regarded as an attack against him, personally.

Purus regularly sent teams to visit all the Arya settlements, so that the bandit-chiefs guilty of violating them were punished. Also, he organized teams along the routes to look after new groups arriving from Avagana and those moving from Iran to Sumer and the Persian Gulf.

Purus married a 'wild girl of the forest.' She was supposed be the daughter of an ascetic. When she was three years old, she was abducted along with her father, mother and several other families, by a team of bandits to a faraway land. Normally bandits have no use for children, but this bandit-chief was merciful and allowed the mother to keep the child, leaving it to the mother's buyer to decide the child's fate. The abducted group was being driven faraway for sale. Days later, another bandit-army attacked the abductors. The mother saw her chance and ran with the girl to a clump of trees. An arrow struck the mother. She still kept running, carrying the child. She fell not too faraway and died. Three days later, a wandering ascetic saw the little girl in the forest. She could tell him little about her people or the town. All that the ascetic could say was that her people came somewhere from the vast plains of 'Oxus and Jaxartes.' The ascetic took the girl along, hoping to leave her with some family on the way. But who wants a three-year-old girl! They went on for days and months. At last, a family took the girl in.

The next morning, the ascetic went on his way, happy to be relieved of his burden. On entering the forest, somehow the darkness around him brought gloom to his heart. Always a wanderer, never before had he faced a feeling of loneliness. Now it came to him like a great stirring from within. He sat under a tree wondering over this strange, despairing emotion. He opened his eyes a long time later, on hearing sounds nearby. This forest, he knew, had no large beasts, only deer, gazelles, foxes, wolves and lynx, and their proximity did not bother him. Nor was he afraid of bandits, who never harmed an ascetic. But actually, what he saw, were people from the settlement searching for the little girl he had left with them. The girl, it seemed, had fled to follow the ascetic into the forest.

The ascetic was now frantic with grief and panic. All his life's indifference to human companionship was washed away in a single tidal wave. Passionately, desperately, he wanted to find the child and keep her with him. For two days, the child could not be found. The people from the settlement went back. The ascetic searched. The agony was not only in his heart. He could even feel the physical pain in his chest.

It was on the third night that he found the sleeping child. And the poet says that the child opened her eyes, unsurprised, as if she was expecting him to come and asked, 'Did you miss me?' Silently, the ascetic gathered her in his arms and went towards the settlement but she pointed in the opposite direction. He understood and promised, 'Never shall I leave you again.' She had fever and he wanted her to rest. Later, after the child was rested and well, they both left through the same forest.

But the ascetic's passion for wandering ended. It was more from habit that he kept moving. At last he settled down in a forest with his 'daughter', in the land that would come to be called Hari Haran Aryan after the Arya bands under Purus entered.

The girl was about fifteen years old when the Arya bands moved in. About her, people said, she 'never walks the earth' and is always swinging from one tree to another, 'afraid of no man or beast.'

It was two years after Purus came to Iran that he saw her or as a poet says, 'She it was who saw him first.' Purus, along with six companions, had been ambushed by a large bandit-group intent on revenge. An arrow had cut deep into his leg. Other arrows struck his horse. In a frenzy of pain the horse bolted, carrying him headlong into the forest, unstoppable until he got caught in a maze of thorny, prickly shrubs which formed the forest ground-cover. Without warning, the horse suddenly stopped, his forelegs high in the air. Purus fell on the ground, striking his head against a tree.

It was the girl who saw him, unconscious. Swinging from tree to tree, she picked up some fruit, to sprinkle fruit-water over Purus. From the broad-leafed evergreens, she selected leaves to press on his bleeding head. With thread-like tree vines, she tied up his leg at various points and carefully took out the arrow. She stopped the blood by finger-pressure and bandaged the wound. Apparently, she had experience, drawn from tending to wounded animals in the forest. Yet she rushed to her father and both came armed with remedies made from trees and plants which they had found useful in treating animals.

They carried Purus to their shelter. Soon they found the horse too. The horse recovered before Purus did.

Later, some Aryas said that the hurt to Purus's head must have been more severe, for he asked the ascetic for the hand of the girl without asking the marriage-customs of her family. They knew that marriage-customs varied wildly, even widely, with sometimes a wife married to more than one husband. For instance, five or six brothers, or even friends, would pool together to get a single wife to serve them all. Nor was there a bar to someone buying a wife or husband.

But Purus asked no questions. He was determined to marry her. All he asked was her name. 'She has no name,' the ascetic said. 'I have always called her "my princess" and she will be your queen for life.'

The wild girl was now shy, fully dressed, her face scrubbed, her hair groomed, no longer wishing to swing from trees.

They were married with the ascetic's simple words, 'You are now husband to my daughter—unborn to me, but my child always—and she is now your wife and queen for ever.'

Even so, the Aryas lit a sacred fire and Purus and his 'queen' went round it, with offerings of grain and flowers. The poet tells us that many animals watched from a distance and would have come nearer but for the sacred fire that was burning too brightly.

The Aryas came to love this once-wild girl. For the older women, she brought, from the forest, wild fruits and flowers which many had not seen—like roses from which she made an enticing perfume. For the young, she made a delicate, subtle perfume from a combination of many flowers, mixed largely with berberis (a prickly-stemmed shrub with yellow flowers). Women, young and old, clustered round her. It did not take her too long to learn the language of Bharat Varsha.

Men were impressed with her ability to ride and throw javelins with perfect aim—but rarely did she show off. Her prowess she reserved for moments of peril. And when those moments passed, she spoke of the bravery of others. For her, it was enough that her husband loved her. She sought no more.

Yet praise her they did and so she said to Purus, 'They love you so much that they praise even your wife!' He laughed, and said, 'I love them too but I don't go about praising their wives.' And with mock-jealousy she retorted, 'Don't you ever dare praise their wives!'

She was even more popular with the Arya Vaids (physicians). From the forest, she found for them almost all the herbal remedies they were seeking and many more they knew nothing about.

She still had no name. They simply called her Purus's queen—or sometimes, even 'Queen,' as Purus himself called her.

Centuries later, this title of 'Queen,' given to her out of love, would lead to a mystery that still remains to be resolved.

Purus died, tragically, twelve years after his marriage.

After his death, she took on many of the duties of Purus to lead the Aryas in Iran and even supervised their movements to other lands.

She remained in Iran, after most Aryans returned to Bharat Varsha. She did not remarry. Her one son and two daughters from Purus also remained with her in Iran, though many locals joined the Aryas to go to Bharat Varsha—tied by bonds of marriage, love or friendship.

Centuries later, someone supposed to be either the forty-eighth or eighty-fourth descendant of this 'Queen' and Purus, is quoted as having said:

'My ancestress was the first Queen of Persia, whose cradle-land was the plain of Oxus and Jaxartes; and a sage who could foretell her great and glorious destiny travelled far, to pick her up from there when she was barely three years old; and the sage brought her to Persia, where he trained her in all the arts; and when the sage was old, and could teach no more, he got her married to a valiant commander of the Aryan armies from the east, who was fated to live for twelve years; later, she herself trained armies of her own, permitting the eastern armies to go back home; but many of them remained to witness the glory of the first and foremost Queen of Persia, whose reign was glorious and great, even though I, a descendant of this illustrious Queen, command no more than thirty-four goats and sheep in this miserable settlement of Rhages from which she ruled the land in righteousness and splendour....And her glory and greatness is ever revealed in the traditional memory of the people and in the Sacred Leaves (books).'

No one knows how reliable this quotation of this real or mythical descendant of the little girl who came from the vast plains of Oxus and Jaxartes is. The mere fact that many cite it is no reason for believing it. Particularly curious is his statement that '. . . her glory and greatness is in. . . . the Sacred Leaves (books).' As it is there is no such record in any sacred book of Bharat Varsha. Nor could the reference be to *Avesta*, the pre-Islamic, Zoroastrian holy book of Iran (and Parsis in India). The fact is that the *Avesta* was composed long centuries after the 'Queen of Persia' is supposed to have come into being, and even this particular descendant may not have been around at the time of its composition. So the eras do not seem to match. In any case, there is no reference in the *Avesta* to this 'Queen of Persia'.

It is of course true that only the fourth part of the original *Avesta* was saved after the Arab conquest of Iran in the seventh century AD, and the rest of it was looted and burnt. But it would be futile to presume that this 'traditional memory' is documented in the lost tracts of the *Avesta* or in its Gathas—the hymns of Zoroaster.

Zoroaster (Zarathushtra or Zartosht) was a poet, prophet, philosopher and reformer who led the wave for establishment of the great religion of Zoroastrianism of Ahura Mazda around 580 BC, a little before the conversion of King Vishtaspa of Chorasmia in 588 BC.[1] Neither in those early Gathas which were written or inspired by Prophet Zoroaster himself, nor in later material, composed long after his time (after 550 BC), is there any clue of the traditional memory of the pre-ancient 'Queen of Persia.' Incidentally, Zoroastrianism now exists only in isolated areas of Iran. The religion however flourishes in India among Parsis whose ancestors found sanctuary in India from the eighth century AD onwards, after the Muslim conquest of Iran. But even in the Parsi hymns inspired in these later centuries, there is no reference to any traditional memory about the 'Queen of Persia' in or around 5000 B.C. The fact however is that Prophet Zoroaster's teachings were concerned with man's lofty pilgrimage to vanquish evil, to accept 'life', to reject 'not life,' in the 'desirable' kingdom yet to come, when evil is destroyed and the 'followers of the lie' are silenced. Thus the *Avesta* and its associated Gathas would hardly be concerned with mere details of prehistory or the 'Queen of Persia,' even assuming that the lost tracts of the *Avesta* are rediscovered. Therefore all that can possibly be said in favour of the quotation of the said descendant of the 'Queen of Persia' is that he was referring to some other 'Sacred Leaves' or books which cannot be found.

Purus had become a man of caution in the years after his marriage. Gone were the days when he willingly courted danger. He concerned himself more and more with protecting Arya bands, rather than rushing headlong into the attack to free slaves from the bandits.

Some said that after marriage, Purus had assumed imperial airs, as he travelled in a chariot or was carried on a chair. But this was because he was unable to run or ride until his leg healed completely; and yet he had to be at more than one place at the same time to inspect and organize.

Rarely did Purus make frontal assaults on the bandit-chiefs and their followers. Often he frightened them into fleeing merely by a show of strength.

With the arrival of more Arya bands and many locals joining Purus, the Arya settlements outside the mountain ring grew.

The largest Arya camp was set up at Bhakti Gaon (town of worship) at Daryachen-je lake. Bhakti Gaon is now named Bakhtegan (map reference: 29.20n; 54.05e). Another large camp was established at Hari

[1]Dates given above, about Poet-Prophet Zoroaster (Zarathushtra), should be regarded as tentative and are based on what most writers have said. My understanding is that these dates are wrong and that Zoroaster lived prior to 1600 BC.

(south of modern Tehran; the area is now called Rey—map reference: 35.35n; 51.25e).

The largest number of camps were however established in Hara (Lord Shiv) region (map reference: 29n; 51e).

The Hara region went through many successive names. After Purus's death it was known as Purus region (or as later Assyrian records show, it was known as Parsumash or Purusmath). Presently it is known as the Parsa or Fars province of Iran. The ruling dynasty of Persians settled here after the overthrow of the Medes in 550 BC.

Purus also insisted on drill, discipline and even showmanship. His Arya bands would move with banners, as though always on the march, fearing no opposition and assured of victory, should anyone attack. He chose four banners for his people:

- For Men of the Mouth—singers, marching ahead with their songs to keep everyone's spirits up; route-finders; scouts moving far in advance to shout in case of danger—a white flag.
- For Men of Arms—fighters and warriors—a green flag.
- For the People of the Breast—women not trained for fighting, children, the old and infirm—a red flag.
- For People of Hands and Feet—artisans, peasants, workers, artists, food-gatherers, untrained for war but expected to protect the Red Flag people if the need arose—a blue flag.

Banners and flags were largely for show, but their movements were also to signal danger and summon help, when the columns were at a distance. Normally though, the white flags would march ahead while the green flags formed an outer ring with the red and blue flags inside the protected ring.

There are those who have tried to see a common link between this four-fold colour (varna) classification of Purus and the caste system which came to distort Hindu society some thousands of years later, in the post-Vedic modern era. There is no connection at all.

Purus's classification of mouth-people, arms-people, breast-people, and feet-people and his identification of them with different flag-colours was simply for the purpose of attack, defence, protection and to ensure that those joining the march, on the way, would know which formation to join and thus avoid a disorderly scramble for a place in the 'army' on the march. Besides, the man leading the 'army' from one settlement to another, or to chart a new area, had to know at a glance how many fighters he had and how many he had to protect—and this determined his movement and route. But there never was a question of who was lower or higher than the other. In any case, as already explained, the caste system never existed in those times and came long after the *Rig Veda*, so much so that Sanskrit has no word for it. But then, as it is, some misguided commentators have even gone to the extent of distorting a later *Rig-Vedic* hymn (X.90) to argue that it sanctions or condones the caste system.

Purus was ambushed by bandit-chiefs. He had foolishly rushed off with three others when a local complained that his wife had been molested by an outsider. He was cut down. His three companions were left dead as they were. But to show the mark of personal vengeance, Purus' body was cut up in several parts—arms, mouth, feet, eyes—and distributed among the attackers to throw on the way, to be eaten by vultures.

There are, then, stories of the vengeance of Purus' wife—how she moved swiftly with armies of locals to hunt the bandits. To the Aryas from Bharat Varsha she said, 'This vengeance is ours.' But some Aryas said, 'Purus was ours before he was yours and for ever now, yours and ours' and they too moved against the bandits under her banner.

Purus' wife caught her husband's murderers but her thrust went beyond. She hunted even those bandits who posed no threat to the Arya settlements. Summarily they were hanged, with followers and families, and their bodies thrown to the vultures.

Her 'ascetic father', old and emaciated, came to accuse her, 'This was not your husband's way! He taught love, mercy and understanding! Vultures devoured his flesh; but you deny him his soul everlasting! And you defile his memory!' She wept and stopped her tempestuous reprisals.

She would shed more tears later when her 'ascetic father' was dying. He had declared his will—'Let my dead body be left, unburied, for vultures and animals to devour, as Purus' body was. Let it be my salute to him to go the same way—and be it also a symbol of my offerings to birds and animals, from whom so much mankind takes!'

When he died, the Aryas built a fire for cremation. The locals dug a grave. But his last 'will' was carried out. The fire remained burning. The grave-pit was left unfilled. Everyone had to leave. But even after a day, his body was untouched. The ascetic's old dog kept the vultures away.

The dog was bleeding, half-blinded by its attacks on vultures. It had to be forcibly taken away. Later, the locals buried the remains of the ascetic's bones.

A poet adds that the dog also died because he refused food. The dog would not be coaxed by the ascetic's daughter whom he loved and kept growling at her. Only in the end, he dragged himself to her, licked her hand and died. Perhaps, at last, the dog understood. Who knows!

Purus' wife declared that, on her death, her body too must be left to the animals and vultures. But it seems that this custom caught on in Iran, on the inspiration of her father, 'and in memory of Purus', even before her death, among the locals.

Purus' wife remained in overall command of the Aryas. Her later history is surrounded by mystery, particularly after most Aryas from Bharat Varsha went to their land.

Although the Aryas from Bharat Varsha did not remain in Iran for very long, the influence they left behind was considerable. This influence is especially noticeable in the Iranian language. Also, the influence still persists, deeply embedded, in Iranian art, culture and their spiritual and religious ethos.

Yet it is true that the Aryas from Bharat Varsha left behind the influence of only one limited aspect of their spiritual philosophy—the philosophy of salvation by following a saviour who is commanded by God to bring revelation. This was combined with the belief that when the earth was defiled by forces of darkness and evil such a saviour would be incarnated in human shape to assist man's soul in its ascension back to its original celestial home. Centuries later, long after the Aryas returned, this view would somehow begin to lead to an attitude of monotheism—of the unwavering belief in an inflexible creed, as though acceptance of a particular metaphysic was necessary for salvation, and its non-acceptance, a sin, meriting punishment in hell. This limited view was a far cry from the kind of polytheism that dominated the landscape of Bharat Varsha. The sages of Ganga, Sindhu and Dravidham clearly held that the scheme of salvation was not limited to those who held a particular view of God's nature and worship; to them such absolutism would be inconsistent with an all-loving, universal God—'There are none that are chosen of God and God is denied to none, for what counts is conduct, not creed.'

How is it then that the Aryas from Bharat Varsha failed to leave the foundation of their belief that God's gracious purpose included all aspirants—whatever their creed—and included even non-aspirants, without a creed! The fact is that these simple Aryas had no sages, philosophers or even poets among them. They had travelled across great distances, some in fear of persecution and many fired by faith in their personal god, to lead them to the land of the pure. What spiritual legacy could they leave behind! Even Purus, who led the Arya bands to Iran, was stirred by a sudden bond of sympathy with the Aryas and not by the belief in any god. A poet tells the following story about Purus:

The Arya groups from Sumer (Iraq) narrated to Purus their sad tales of unfortunate ship-wrecks that killed many on the way. According to them, they prayed 'day and night to god Indra, but the god did not listen, and the cruel sea swallowed them. . .' Someone later asked Purus, 'Is god Indra so unkind?' And Purus replied, 'Gods are capricious; maybe Indra is more capricious than others.'

These light-hearted words became etched in people's memory. Purus had reached such a commanding position that people spoke of him as they speak of legendary heroes, and every word he uttered was remembered, repeated and retold. No wonder then that though the Iranians honoured many gods of Bharat Varsha, Indra was never highly rated.

The *Avesta* of the Zoroastrians, for instance, honours god Mitra, but depicts god Indra as a demon—maybe the result of the lighthearted words of Purus that remained in the traditional Iranian memory for centuries before the *Avesta* was composed.

But then Purus was like that. He believed in no gods—not perhaps even in God, except as a symbol of goodness. Besides, the Aryas did not go out to impose their gods on others, nor to leave behind a legacy of their spiritual belief, since their own tradition itself taught them respect for the beliefs and gods of others.

'God is not a law-giver. He wills a rich harmony; not a colourless uniformity; God does not decree one, single, common creed; He demands no worship in fixed form; He excludes none from His scheme of salvation; He is an all-loving, universal God; For Him every individual is worthy of reverence. . . .'

—(Sumaran, Aryan Leader, in Sumer, Iran—5005 BC)

'. . .And they established their camps and settlements in Sumer (Iraq) at places, still known by the names they gave them— Hindiya, Hari Nath, Ramaji and Sumaran and fourteen others . . .'

—(From the account of a later narrator of events of 5005 BC)

'There is no honour among priests.'

—(Remark by Sumaran who once was a priest—5005 BC)

Aryans Everywhere

5005 BC

Several Arya contingents reached the coastline of the Persian Gulf by boat and thence went to Sumer between the Euphrates and Tigris rivers. But even from Iran, some moved along the Zagros range through the rugged, forbidding ridges and narrow gorges into the plains of Sumer (Mesopotamia).

The Aryas, here, did not have the kind of problems they faced in Hari Haran Aryan. The land had no organized bandit-chiefs or robber-lords. But they had something worse in the shape of the priests who ruled the land and people.

The priest's control was total in each area. People could not leave their area to reside elsewhere, unless priests of both areas agreed and appropriate payments were made.

The priest had no army to enforce his will. He did not need it. His word was law. At his bidding, everyone would move and the offender would be stripped, strangled or hanged—whatever the priest willed.

The priest was prosperous. For the rest, there was widespread poverty, over-reliance on hunting, death often by starvation and animal attacks.

The priest was entitled to a portion of the hunt, produce and goods made by artisans and it was left to him to determine his portion. On the death of a person, all his worldly goods were supposed to belong to the gods and thus went to the priest, who would determine if a part of those goods be given to the survivors of the deceased.

Priesthood was hereditary (unlike Bharat Varsha where a priest was appointed for a term and brahmins as a caste did not exist). On the priest's death, his eldest son succeeded, though occasionally a priest would divide the area so as to favour his other sons as well.

Before the Aryas reached a village in Sumer, they met a few individuals who had fled from their priests' tyranny. These unfortunates were outside the pale of law. Everyone was encouraged to hunt down such renegades; and none could have social contact with them.

From these outcasts, the Aryas understood the power of the priests, though the language-barrier often led to exaggerated gestures and signs.

Yet when the Aryas reached a village, they thought, at first, that their fears had been baseless. The priest welcomed them with delight. The land was endless, but people were few; and the power and prestige of the priest rested on the number of people under him. From a gestured conversation with the Aryas, the priest realized that many of them were hardworking and skilled and he pointed to his vast land to say, 'All this land is yours; make of it what you will.' Some Aryas he sent back, with instructions to guide any more arriving Arya bands to his own area.

The task assigned to the first Arya group was to raise an artificial mountain (Ziggurat—a man-made stepped tower). The Ziggurat was a pile of towers, each a little smaller than the one on which it rested, and the effect from a distance was that of a stepped pyramid. The topmost tower had a small room with a large comfortable bed, perfumed incense and a platform outside the room.

Each priest would want his Ziggurat to be the largest and highest— and some priests, wishing to divide their areas to provide for all their sons, wanted more Ziggurats.[1]

To the Aryas, it appeared like a miniature temple on the inspiration of Mount Meru, which in the Hindu mind was conceived as the mythical seat of the gods.[2] They went about the task of building the Ziggurat with enthusiasm. It was to be their pride and delight.

The gratified priest gave the Aryas every encouragement and saw to it that everyone in the area brought food for them.

The Aryas saw poverty, even starvation, among the people around them. Though at first glance they often found unhappiness, people laughed, joked, and even made merry, certain in their faith that their time for 'great happiness in the great beyond' was to come. They believed it was simply their fate to suffer in their life on earth and on death they would rise to their starlit heaven. Their belief was that they were the fallen angels who for some heinous sin were sent on earth to suffer and so long as they obeyed Gods' commands (conveyed by the priest) on earth, they would, at the end, go back to their heavenly homeland. Meanwhile on earth, God's commands would often be stern, pitiless, demanding and dire, and yet they had to be obeyed without question or qualm, irrespective of personal or family feeling, for such commands were made 'only to test if they should go back as a bright or a dull star, or a star that is shot with deadly lightning that sends

---

[1] A vast pyramidal pile in Babylon, 300 feet square and 300 feet high with top temple in blue glaze, became notorious as the Tower of Babel. However, that is not a Ziggurat of great antiquity, and was built in Nebuchadrezzar II's reign in Babylon, sixth century BC.
[2] Some have suggested that the ancient name for the area as Sumer was derived from Su-Meru (the great Meru of Hindu mythology).

them back not to land, but below, into the bowels of the earth where there is no priest and therefore no way to reach heaven.'

To them the whole of heaven was filled with human beings who had turned into stars, with 6,000 gods above them all, who appeared on earth in the garb of priests.

The multiplicity of the gods never bothered the Aryas. That gods could appear in human shape was also close to their hearts. What they found peculiar was the belief that sorrows and sufferings were also the result of fate—and there was nothing that men could do to alter their destiny. They permitted no room for human will and felt that by total surrender to fate and the commands of the priests, their lives would be freed of impurities.

The Arya belief in karma, on the other hand, was different. The belief simply was that karma in a previous life determined a person's initial social standing, fortune, happiness or misery in this life; but karma certainly excluded fatalism and man had enough free will to rise above his condition to 'raise self by self,' and not be a pawn of fate. By his own effort, it was open to man to transform his weakness into strength and his ignorance into illumination. How could the Arya believe that life simply provided an unfolding of a passive, pre-arranged plan and total slavery to the whims of a priest! Surely, each individual should have the opportunities open to strive until he realized the divine destiny of salvation for which he was intended!

It was after all belief in karma itself that tempted the Aryas to take destiny into their own hands, to go out in search of a better land.

Besides, an Arya, like any other Hindu believed that God was not only a Universal Spirit, but also a personal being, full of love for his creation; and for the Aryas, therefore, it was impossible to imagine that a loving, just God would make the kinds of demands that priests made on their helpless, hapless people. Also, the Aryas found it impossible to accept that God would consign anyone to hell eternal.

The Aryas also believed that to despise another's faith was to despise the people themselves and they had come to love these simple people who shared every thing they had and were cheerful despite their adversity.

It was easy for the Aryas to be tolerant of others' faith, so long as a brutal, merciless assult was not made on them. Yet slowly, some silence, even sullenness, entered into the Aryan soul as they saw the pitiable conditions the people lived in.

Their first sense of horror came when the priest's wife gave birth to a son. It was a day of celebration. Yet a baby born at the same time to another woman was crushed to death, lest its destiny—arising from the stars—rob the priest's son. Messages were also sent to priests of other areas to kill babies born at the same time. All the priests were honour-bound to comply.

What happens if a priest's wife has twins—would not one rob the other of his destiny—asked the Aryas. 'Of course,' was the answer. 'If the twins are a boy and a girl, the girl will be killed. If both are boys, one, weaker or stronger, will be killed. In any case, one of the two has to be killed.'

The second shock to the Aryas came when they learnt that the Ziggurat on which they were working was a different kind of temple. On death, the body of a person was to be taken to the platform of the topmost tower and kept there for two days, so that the gods may view it from the heavens above, to assign the right kind of star.

The priest would also ascend the Ziggurat while the dead body was there. Following him, would be a virgin picked up by the priest from the people. But the 'virgin' could also be the wife of another— and the belief was that selection by the priest 'cleansed her of all prior sex and she came forth chaste, undefiled, shining, like a child of God, and ready for deflowering by a god.' Below, another 'virgin-in-waiting' selected by the priest would be ready, just in case he needed another. After two days, the priest would send the dead body down, as by then its soul was supposed to have ascended to the right star. The body would then be used as a bait to trap animals.

All this the Aryas heard second-hand. It was happening at another Ziggurat far away from the one they were building.

More Arya boat-groups reached them. Many groups from Hari Haran Aryan also joined them. Their pleasure was dampened by the news of Iran—that the land was infested by bandit-lords. And the cheerless thought in their minds was that this land too was corrupted by bandit-priests. What was the difference?—only that a bandit-chief robs with a sword-point at the throat, while a priest robs through terror in the soul! Where was the land of the pure then? Where had all their wandering led them! To what useless, senseless inconsequence!

But the greatest shock was yet to come. News came to the priest that someone had died. He gave instructions for the body to be bathed before being taken to the Ziggurat. There and then, he picked up a woman from his people as the 'virgin' to follow him. She was married and even had two children but his benediction 'cleansed' her of all prior sex. The priest was about to leave when suddenly the desire to taste fresh flesh came over him. He pointed to an Arya girl, thirteen years old. She understood nothing when the priest pointed at her and simply smiled. But an older Arya understood and shouted 'No!'

The old Arya tried to shield the girl. Other Aryas came up. They stood, frozen with fear. Their numbers were large and if they were to put up a fight, there was little the priest could do. Yet, fear of the priest held them back.

The priest regarded himself as a kind, benevolent man, who had always been gracious to these new-comers. He was ready to forgive the foreign fool who had shouted at him. He even regretted his hasty decision to pick up a 'virgin in waiting' from the Aryas. The girl was thin; she hardly had full breasts. But the decision was now unalterable; to change it would mean losing face; and would cast its shadow on future relations with these new-comers who had to be taught unquestioning obedience.

Quietly, the priest asked his people to take the girl; he asked them to leave the foolish Arya, who had shielded her, alone. This was well within their tradition: that a madman not be harmed.

The priest's men started moving to escort the girl. They would have done so, even if such an order was about one of their own children.

Dhrav, one of the Aryas who had come from Iran after a brush with the bandit-chiefs, hastily took out his dagger.

But old Sumaran who had led the first batch of Aryas by the sea-route and was regarded as leader of all the Aryas in this land, put up his hands in a placatory gesture.

Respectfully, Sumaran called out, 'Gracious Lord Priest!—A moment please, for a word in your kind ear, if your lordship permits.'

'What is it?' the priest asked. Everyone stopped. Sumaran walked to the priest and bowed low, 'For your ears alone, gracious Lord Priest.'

The priest glared at his men so that they moved far back, out of earshot. Sumaran spoke quietly, his attitude clearly humble, his face wearing the smile of a slave speaking to a great lord, 'Listen Lord Priest and hear it good. If anyone dares take our girl, I shall personally cut out your testicles with the chisel with which I carve figures on your Ziggurat. And that goes for each member of your family. I swear it on your gods and mine.'

Never, in his wildest nightmares even, had the priest heard anything resembling a threat—neither from the gods nor from man. Fear gripped him. His eyes went to the chisel in Sumaran's hand. Yet how could he recall the order. He stammered, 'But I have already spoken!'

'So be it, Lord Priest,' Sumaran said. 'Let our girl be considered a "virgin-in-waiting". We shall be the ones to bathe and dress her. You may so announce. But if you really send for her, do take the trouble to cut out your own testicles, as my method may not be as painless.'

At last the priest nodded. To his people, he announced, 'They beg to bathe and dress the "virgin-in-waiting" with holy water of their own gods brought by them to do greater honour to our gods. So be it.' If his voice trembled, obviously his men thought that it was in joy that these new-comers should wish to honour the priest's gods.

Sumaran walked back with a low, respectful bow to the priest. Dhrav, Arya veteran from Iran, was now waiting to stab Sumaran, for all he understood was that the girl was to be bathed by them, to be made ready for sex with priest. It is difficult to argue with a hot-headed man brandishing a dagger; deftly, old Sumaran twisted young Dhrav's hand, hit his legs with his own and lifted him on his back.

Dhrav's dagger fell. Dhrav also fell, crashing headlong, on to the ground. Quietly then Sumaran explained.

From a distance, the priest's people watched in dismay. Violence was alien to these gentle people. Even when they killed a man, it would be at the command of the priest, and they would do it swiftly, with mercy and without anger. An animal, ready for the kill, would be treated with gentleness. Only a powerful man was permitted to kill a trapped animal and he was expected to kill it with one blow, so that the animal, unaware, suffered nither fear nor pain. Large, trapped animals would often be fed with herbs mixed with their food, so as to dull their pain from the blow. After the animal's death, the killer and others would bow and pray to the spirit of the departed animal.

Now the locals were shocked as they saw old and respected Sumaran threatened by a dagger and Dhrav with a bleeding head, while the rest of the Aryas shouted. But the priest explained, 'That young lunatic was against treating their own gods lower than our gods by bathing my "virgin-in-waiting" with their holy water.'

The priest's explanation, they saw, was absolutely correct, as Dhrav was kneeling to Sumaran in obvious apology and Sumaran was even embracing him. It even raised Sumaran in their estimation, that he treated a madman like Dhrav with affection. In their own belief too, a mad person was supposed to float in the higher reaches of god's angels.

Also, there was joy in their hearts—that their own gods were rated higher by these Aryans. But initially, there was surprise too; how could one god be lower or higher than another? Someone put a timid question but the priest had no difficulty—'Their gods are false gods. They are devils!' This opened the floodgates of astonishment and against his better judgement, a local asked, 'But, my lord, they are working on our Ziggurat!'

Contemptuously, the priest answered, 'You understand nothing! They are performing penance. It is God's will!' Now their hearts went out to the Aryas—a sinner who repented was surely to be admired; and how much these poor Aryas must have suffered under their false gods!

The priest went up his Ziggurat. The married 'virgin' he had selected followed. The Arya girl, perfumed and decked in flowers, waited below with the Aryas, as if ready for the priest's summons. But she was not summoned. Ignoring a 'virgin-in-waiting' was common, for often the priest needed none else to 'satisfy the gods,' and selection of a 'virgin-in-waiting' was more an honour. But some speculative minds were at work among the locals. Maybe, the Priest did not want a girl who once belonged to false gods until the penance by her people was complete. Their respect for their priest and sympathy for the Aryas, increased.

After the Priest descended from the Ziggurat, Sumaran approached him, 'Gracious lord, we seek permission to leave.' True, the Aryas could leave without permission; their numbers were large and the Priest was powerless to stop them. But they would then be outside the pale of law. No priest anywhere would give them passage. No locals would speak to them. It would be the sacred duty of all to hunt them down. So why go into an uncertain future, in an alien land, and invite an era of bloodshed!

The Priest understood that too. He himself did not want these people any more. Clearly, he foresaw trouble and treason, in the times ahead, from such crude, coarse people who would go to the extent of threatening his sacred, inviolable person. If they raised such a fuss over a plain girl with stunted breasts, how much would they fight if their property was threatened! And they would corrupt the attitude of his own people!

But there was something that the Priest wanted more terribly than his self-esteem; and he said, 'You behave as if you are a law unto yourself. Why don't you, then, go on your own, without my permission?'

'Go we will, with or without permission,' Sumaran said, 'though we prefer to go with your blessing.'

'My blessing has to be earned.'

'Ask what you will.'

'First, none of you shall speak of what we spoke the other day.'

'I promise,' Sumaran said.

'Second, you shall not serve any other priest.' Obviously the priest did not want these useful workers serving another area. Sumaran agreed.

'Third, you will not entice anyone from the area to follow you.'

Sumaran agreed. The priest continued, 'Fourth, while you prepare to leave, you will speak to none of my people here, even if they address you.' Obviously, the priest wanted no corrupting influence on his people.

Sumaran agreed. Now, the priest came to what was nearest to his heart —'Finally, you will leave after the Ziggurat is ready.'

Sumaran hesitated, 'That will take time.'

'I have time,' said the priest, ending the discussion.

The Aryas debated furiously. Dhrav said nothing but the others who came from Iran favoured leaving immediately. 'We did not join the bandit-chiefs there. Why do we need the blessing of a bandit-priest here?'

The difference was explained to them—bandit-chiefs in Iran terrorized people; here the people were behind their priest. But the Iran-veterans argued, 'What can they do to us? They are not fighters!'

And Sumaran asked, 'Are we fighters? Is it to fight that we left our land?' It was then that Dhrav spoke, 'If fight we must, fight we shall. One lives within the conditions that life offers.'

'Really! Then why did we not remain in Bharat Varsha to live within the conditions that life offered there?' Sumaran asked.

'We left to escape the unjust; and here you ask that we associate with the unjust! I say, we go!'

'Go where? From nowhere to nowhere! And leave a trail of blood, everywhere they find us!'

'It won't be our blood!'

'And their blood is cheap?'

Back and forth went the argument. At last no one had anything to say. In silence, they waited for Sumaran to give the decision. They knew he hated to decide when views were divided. Still, that was his task. Suddenly, with a flourish Dhrav took out his dagger and said, 'Brother Sumaran, I may not be a great fighter against you but I challenge you that I am a better builder. Will someone please accept my excellent dagger in exchange for a good hammer to work on the Ziggurat?'

There was laughter but no need for a formal decision. The only question was whether the work on the Ziggurat began right then or the next morning. They began that evening itself.

Fires were lit every night for work to press on. The priest assigned more locals to assist the Aryas. True to Sumaran's promise, the Aryas did not speak to the locals. It shocked the locals. The Priest explained— the Aryas are in their final phase of penance to complete the Ziggurat during which they cannot speak to the people of the true gods.

Again, their hearts went out to the Aryas—how much these poor unfortunates must endure to get away from their false gods!

The locals even prayed to their Priest to ease the Arya penance but he was stern and said, 'The flaming wrath of our righteous gods is roused against their false gods who abominate the earth. Ask for no mercy, no charity for those that once served false gods, lest you too be defiled!'

The Aryas moved out after eleven months of back-breaking labour. The Ziggurat, when complete, was not as tall or ornate as originally hoped. Yet it was one of the tallest pyramidal towers of Sumer.

There was no pride of achievement, no thrill of accomplishment.

Sumaran spoke for them all when he said, 'I wish I could smash this Ziggurat to bits. It is the tower of evil.' To Dhrav he said, 'You were right; one lives in the condition that life offers. We leave behind this monument of evil that will outlast you and me.'

Dhruv understood Sumaran's anguish, 'Evil would have remained, neither more or less, whether we built this monument or not.'

'Yet we left our land to be away from evil and here we participated in it!'

Dhrav did not respond but said, as if speaking to himself, 'Purus said to us in Iran—none can flee evil by fleeing his land.'

They were silent. Each had a question in his heart. Each dreaded the answer.

The priest had given Sumaran information on the layout of the land to reach areas outside the control of any priest. Apparently there were many such areas—wild, barren and uncleared. Nothing prevented a priest from extending his area, so long as it was unoccupied by another priest, but with a limited population and vast area, priests rarely ventured into lands that offered nothing but required great effort.

Some say that the priest gave such information so that the Arya bands did not serve another priest and make him great and strong. Others say, it was to protect other priests from the corrupting Arya influence.

The Aryas moved on. In the areas they crossed, they would be known as 'Aryas of the Clay Tablet', as they carried a tablet of clay from the priest whom they left. It was a kind of an 'exit visa' that repressive governments of the twentieth century would rediscover. The tablet permitted the Aryas to leave the priest's area and go elsewhere; second, it obliged all other priests to permit them to cross their land, unless the Aryas agreed to serve another priest, in which case the original priest decided on the payment he was to receive; third, the Aryas could settle in areas unoccupied by a priest, though a priest could enter that land at any time, in which case the Aryas would either have to leave, or serve the new priest, with a payment being made to the original priest; fourth, none, on death, would be honoured with exposure on a Ziggurat since that would abominate the true gods; but their bodies could serve as bait to trap animals; but here again, those animals would not be sacrificed to the gods; fifth, the Aryas would have to send to the original priest, a share of their hunt, produce, and goods, as decided by the priest; sixth....

The list went on. And so, the idea of this plain clay tablet, with a single graven image, was that sovereignty of the original priest continued, and there was no place to run and hide, for ever.

Dhrav commented, 'Priests here are masterly in making their laws. Do they know as much about their gods?'

'How can you know such laws and gods at the same time?' Sumaran countered. 'Laws were intended to subvert the gods and exploit the exploited.'

'Surely, there are God's laws too!'

'God is not a law-giver. He wills a rich harmony; not a colourless uniformity; God does not decree one, single common creed; He demands no worship in fixed form; He excludes none from His scheme of salvation; He is an all-loving, universal God; for Him, every individual is worthy of reverence....'

'Brother Sumaran, you should have been a priest.'

'I was.'

Dhrav laughed, 'No wonder you could fool the priest here into giving you the "clay tablet." Truly, a priest alone can outwit another priest!' But then seriously, he asked, 'What made you to leave Bharat Varsha?'

'My son and my wife.'

'Where are they?' Dhrav asked.

'My son died years before we left. He had joined Jalta's command to free slaves. He died the next day. My wife died in a shipwreck, on our way to this land.'

Dhrav was silent. Yet there was a question in his eyes. Sumaran answered it. 'No we are not of slave-ancestry. I was a land-owner and wanted to be a hermit, but my wife's brother, who was a Council member, built a temple in my son's memory and I agreed to be its priest. When the cry came from some rya to be arya, my wife knew, and I knew, that our son wanted not a temple, but to protect the exploited. My wife demanded that we leave...I am still following her....'

*

The priest's clay tablet was certainly not invented by the Aryas. It had been in use for centuries in Sumer. That gave the Aryas joyful assurance. Obviously, many locals must be using such clay tablets with the connivance of priests to seek asylum in non-priestly areas.

In their long, tedious journey, they found some such areas, though they were largely deserted, mostly barren; people there, outside priestly control, were a revelation to them. Their day-to-day activity was to hunt and gather food, but with concern for the weak, infirm and the orphaned. They had artists, singers, even hermits.

'Why do you not improve this land?' asked the Aryas.

'Because the priests will then come and take us over!' they countered. 'It is open to a priest to take over any non-priestly land. And what do we do then? Serve the priest? Run elsewhere? No, let the land remain unattractive and untempting to priests.'

'Why do you not unite against the priests?' asked the Aryas

'How do a few trees unite against a million locusts!'

The Aryas viewed the local hermits with respect. Some hermits were immersed in the calculation of time and angles; others, with astronomy, zodiac and its signs. A few were trying to evolve a method of writing through pictographs—an achievement that was just a step below the invention of writing already achieved in Bharat Varsha.

As it is, only a few Aryas, like Sumaran and Dhrav were fully familiar with the art of writing. Many were not.

How artistic these Sumerians were, with their music, painting, sculpture! They made no idols, but figures of animals, birds, men and women with beautiful slender bodies and women suckling children. Local artists saw the seals that the Aryas carried and they made almost exact copies in clay, with every detail of engraving clearly visible.

'Why don't we all go together,' the Aryas asked these locals, 'and settle where the land will hold us all.'

'Send for us when you find such a land,' they replied. 'But if you don't find it, come back and be with us.'

The Aryas went on.

Later, these locals would find asylum in areas where the Aryas settled.

Hindiya is the first known site at which the Aryas established their largest camp. It is now known as Al Hindiya (map reference: 32.33n; 44.13e; south of Baghdad, Iraq).

The second largest Arya camp was at Hari Nath. It is presently known as Hadithah (map reference: 34.07n; 42.23e).

Actually, though, there were many Arya camps spread all over Mesopotamia, between Rama and Ramji on the Euphrates and the bend of Tigris below Sumaran.[3]

In these camps, the Aryas encouraged locals to dyke rivers. In the south—dry, barren and rainless—the Aryas began artificial irrigation, bringing water to large stretches through a widely branching network of canals. The soil was fertile and with irrigation and proper drainage, it would soon become a land of plenty.

Thus began concentration on agriculture rather than hunting, with tree-farming, cattle breeding, weaving, date-palm cultivation, reed utilization, and later even quarrying of limestone and marble.

With local help, the Aryas built a huge granary consisting of six chambers, each holding a different kind of grain and lentil.

They even built a huge Ziggurat, not as a house of evil for misuse by a priest, but as a real temple where people could pray. There was no platform for dead bodies and no priest at all.

In art and aesthetics, in culture and philosophy, the Aryas had as much to teach as learn from the locals who had been uprooted by the priests.

The strange difference was that many of the locals, through earlier persecution, had become atheists, whereas the Aryas who had fled their land after witnessing persecution had achieved greater faith. Yet the locals and Aryas delighted in this difference and it did not divide them. In fact, they all came to call themselves Aryas.

Many stories would be told of how Sumaran—the Arya leader—obtained more and more land for the Aryas from the priests. Some speak of his negotiating skills. Others simply call it crude bribery. But the fact is that promises were given (and fulfilled) for untold wealth to priests, from time to time, if the priests left the Arya areas undisturbed.

If more and more locals joined the Aryas, it hardly bothered the priests. Their compensating revenue rose. That priests pocketed these payments without regard to the established 'law' of compensating the original priest is understandable in terms of Sumaran's explanation—'there is no honour among priests.'

Sumaran should know. He had once been a priest himself.

---

[3]Rama or Ramji (map reference: 33.25n; 43.17e) is now known as Ramadi or ar-Ramadi—113 km west of Baghdad, Iraq. Sumaran (map reference: 34.12n; 43.52e) is now known as Sammarra—110 km north-north-west of Baghdad, Iraq.

'Maybe it is all to the good that you call yourself noble Arya for sometimes men will try to live up to their name and title. But remember! To be called noble is not a personal honour. . . . It demands that we act nobly. It imposes a duty, an obligation. . .it is a title not of arrogance but humility. . .for we ventured out to seek God's glory. . .not our own. . . .'

—(Reminder from Arya leader Sumaran—5004 BC)

'Nothing on earth, nothing in the sky, nothing in the great beyond, nothing now or ever, nothing here and hereafter, can compensate for man's loneliness in life. Go, find a wife for yourself!'

—(Advice from the recluse to Hermit-King Lugal)

'God is a kind soul. He allows the Devil to make laws!'

—(Attributed to King Lugal's mother—date unknown)

New Nobles and the King of Assyria

5005 BC

The Aryas were still in Hari Haran Aryan and Sumer. Many stayed back but many more would leave for other lands.

Yet for every single Arya from Bharat Varsha that moved from there to new lands, there were at least five locals from Sumer and Iran who joined them. Why? Nobody explains fully. Maybe, as a poet says, the locals too came to accept the strange belief of these Aryas, that surely there has to be, somehow, somewhere, a land that is good and pure.

To the locals also it then began to appear inconceivable that every land in this God's earth should be full of fear, hate, turmoil and injustice—'God hides his land of glory. But why?'

Why! So that we accept the challenge of faith to go out in search....

And locals from Hari Haran Aryan and Sumer, who far outnumbered the Aryas from Bharat Varsha, marched to the tune of the same song,

> 'Onward, Noble Arya, onward in joy,
> Onward to the land where waits He;
> Onward to the land, pure and free.'

There were many such songs—and each one proclaimed the noble aim of the Aryas, their noble quest and pursuit, to seek a land that was noble, pure and free. It was not just faith and fervour that these songs voiced. They led to new horizons—an Arya must strive for noble ends and be noble in all his actions and deeds. And in turn, these horizons would lead to a new identity altogether.

Soon, the word 'Arya' lost its original meaning and acquired a new shine. In its origin, no doubt, Arya meant non-people or exiles. But no more. The title Arya itself became a badge of honour, a status of quality, for to be an Arya meant to be noble—for such was their aim and quest. No longer did it indicate the degradation of the uprooted and dispossessed. Instead, it became a mark of nobility for these valiant men, who with 'an upright heart of faith,' were ready to face howling winds and the heat of deserts and the numbing cold and deep snows of the mountains, in their noble quest.

It did not, then, take too long for the word Arya to be considered synonymous with noble. Yet its limitations were also explained by Sumaran at Sumer, when an Arya group was parting from him; and he said, 'Maybe it is all to the good that you call yourself noble Arya, for sometimes, men will try to live up to their name and title. But remember! To be called noble is not a personal honour. . . . It demands that we act nobly. It imposes a duty, an obligation. . .it is a title not of arrogance but of humility. . .for we ventured out to seek God's glory. . .not our own. . . .'

From Iran, some moved along the Zagros range into Armenia. Others from Sumer and Iran would converge in many lands, including those which are now known as Egypt, Syria, Palestine, Israel and parts of Africa.

It was Arya Nilakantha of Bharat Varsha who led the Arya groups consisting largely of locals from Iran and Sumer into Egypt.

Nilakantha had a powerful singing voice and a powerful physique, but he was as gentle as a lamb. Though he was popular, the most respected member in the entire group was the one who was known as Hermit-King Lugal of Assyria.

Lugal was originally from Sumer. He aspired to be a great architect and in his younger days he had built the first Ziggurat in Sumer which was as high as sixty feet. Earlier Ziggurats had been no more than twenty-four feet high—with a single temple-room on a stepped-up flat platform, as his father had often built.

But young Lugal was ambitious and careless. It almost proved to be his undoing. He had made the Ziggurat with mud, mixed with straw and wood-rafters. During a heavy rain-storm, the Ziggurat fell, while the priest and his 'virgin' were there. Two dead bodies were found under the debris—of the priest and of the dead man who was up on the platform for 'viewing by the gods for the selection of his star of after-life.' The 'virgin' was unhurt.

The penalty for causing a priest's death—intentionally or otherwise—was terrible and a culprit had to die 'little by little' and be finally tied up as a live meal for rats, whose numbers were kept small, so that the ordeal lasted longer. It was perhaps the only instance in which cruelty would be added to a punishment.

Lugal fled to a distant forest. As he went deeper, he found he was not the lone human there. A recluse was living under a crumbling mud shelter which no doubt had seen better days.

Lugal kept his distance. He knew that his death penalty would apply equally to anyone who harboured him. Also, if the recluse ever had visitors, his own whereabouts would become known to the priests.

Far away, Lugal built his own shelter, but his desire for human company remained. Often, he followed the recluse, who every morning would go to a treeless, rocky terrain, which rose about the forest. But the recluse did nothing there, except watch the sky and shift the position of stones.

When the rainy season came, the recluse did not emerge for days. Lugal feared that the man was sick and went to his shelter. 'Why did you take so long to come?' the recluse asked and Lugal was surprised that he knew of his proximity.

The recluse was not curious but Lugal told him that he was under a death penalty for killing a priest.

The old man simply said, 'It is not good to kill anyone but if one is fated to kill, it is better to kill a priest than anyone else.'

Kill a priest!—strange words from someone who was the only son of a priest and could have succeeded as a priest!—for that is what this recluse was. Yet, not so strange from a man whose priest-father selected his loving son's wife as the 'virgin' to take up on the Ziggurat.

In disgust, the son had abandoned his home and disappeared before his father and wife descended from the Ziggurat. For some time, the son became a raving lunatic. Later, he found peace in a forest, as a recluse, watching the sun by day and the stars by night.

What the poets call a 'father and son friendship' sprung up between the recluse and Lugal from the moment they met. Lugal wanted the recluse to move to his shelter which kept rain away. The recluse showed him openings, holes, cavities and cuts in his shelter, made so that he could watch the stars at night from various angles as also the play of sunlight during the day. Lugal studied them all. Four months later, he took the recluse again for a visit to his shelter. Lugal had duplicated every opening in his shelter to view the skies and added some more, with shutters to close them fully or partly, and some even in angles, triangles and circles.

From then on the recluse stayed in Lugal's shelter and Lugal too got caught up in the fever of watching the skies, day and night.

With age, the recluse got weaker and half-blind. Lugal acted as his eyes and told him of the observation of the sky. But often the recluse knew without being told and would even correct Lugal's inaccurate observations.

The recluse started sinking into depression. The forty years in the forest were taking their toll. He thought of his father and his wife, no longer with bitterness. He thought of his people and wanted to die in their midst. He loved Lugal like a son. Yet he alone could not fill the recluse's void of loneliness.

But then many refugees, escaping from various priests, found sanctuary in the forest. Lugal assisted them in building shelters and they, in turn, gathered food for the recluse and Lugal. The recluse forgot about the sky, except to tell its stories to the children of the refugees around him. Lugal continued 'sky-watching.'

A priest entered the forest to claim it as his own—with all the residents as his subjects. None of them could have stopped the priest, but the recluse did, with the claim that he, as a priest, had already occupied the forest.

He, a priest! Impossible! More probably a madman! Yet the occupying priest wavered and detailed inquiries began.

Truly, the recluse, being the only son of a priest, was entitled to that office on the day his father died. That entitlement could not be denied. In his absence, it was the son of the recluse who officiated as a priest. But that did not extinguish the right of the recluse to demand that his priesthood be returned.

It was the son of the recluse—the reigning priest—who came. He brought the 'Seal of the Priest' to surrender to his father. They embraced joyfully and in tears. Was the recluse really the father of this priest? The recluse and his 'son' had never seen each other. The son was born eight months after his wife had ascended the Ziggurat with his father; and he would never know if he was his brother or his son.

But it no longer mattered. He was happy to see his 'son', his son's children and grandchildren, and even said a soulful prayer for his wife who, he learnt, had died in childbirth.

His son insisted, but the recluse declined to accept his priesthood. The only request that the recluse made was that his priest-son assume notional jurisdiction over the forest so that no other priest claimed it— and let the 'forest be free under my other son, Lugal.'

The son agreed but begged that the father go back with him immediately.

'Give me a few more days and be with me till then,' the father requested. He died on the third day with a smile, 'I made the gods wait! How beautiful is the end!' Many heard him but none understood. Maybe, he was referring to his wish to die among his people.

The son kept his promise—and more. Lugal was now in command of the forest, with no interference from any priest and with even the right to extend his area, so long as such new lands were unoccupied by a priest.

The son gave many 'indemnities' to several priests to have this 'impossible situation' accepted. From this arose the myth that Lugal of Sumer valiantly vanquished priests of Sumeria to establish his undisputed reign in Assyria.[1] Actually, he was no ruler in the traditional sense; he was simply a Sumerian architect who fled to the forest of Assyria and became a sky-watcher (astronomer); and there he welcomed everyone who was in trouble with priests.

There was quite a few refugees around Lugal. They were under his protection and affectionately called him 'King Lugal'. But he joked, 'I can only be King of Kings here, as all of you here are Kings.'

---

[1]Assyria lay north of Mesopotamia. After the Aryas entered Assyria, its main city came to be called Ashura or Ashur (160 miles north, north-west of modern Baghdad).

Yet Lugal felt terribly lonely without the recluse who was no more.

A messenger came from the priest-son of the recluse—'Brother mine, it was my father's wish that you be married. With care I have chosen three wives for you. Should they not suit you, use them as you will and I will send you more.'

With the messenger came three girls who were sisters.

Lugal remembered the recluse's words in his dying days, 'Nothing on earth, nothing in the sky, nothing in the great beyond, nothing now or ever, nothing here or hereafter, can compensate for man's loneliness in life. Find a wife for yourself, Lugal!'

Lugal had humoured the recluse and said, 'How do I find a wife in this wilderness!'

After deep thought, the recluse had said, 'Then I must ask the gods to find a wife for you.'

Nothing more was said but the recluse certainly spoke to a god—for a priest was no less.

Now came these three women, eager to share Lugal's lonely bed. His first reaction was to protest but the messenger said, 'The Lord Priest has performed the marriage ceremony. But you have freedom.'

Lugal knew what that 'freedom' meant. They were his wives. There was no system of divorce, as such. He could put them to work as his slaves or sell them. If he kept them, they could remarry 666 days after his death. If he sold them, he could buy them back at any time by paying double the price he received. A man could marry any number of wives. A woman could have only a single husband, but she could have sex with others with her husband's permission, provided nobody received direct or indirect payment for such sex. . . Lugal remembered what his mother had once said—'God is a kind soul. He allows the Devil to make laws!'

Lugal saw the silent appeal in the eyes of his three 'brides' and the eldest said, 'Do not deny us.'

Lugal kept the three wives. In the beginning, he made a feeble protest—'Be with me but you are like sisters to me.' Happily, they responded, 'Yes, sisters and wives.'

In a year, Lugal was the proud father of three infants.

Later, the Aryas from Bharat Varsha congregated in his forest to set up a major camp. From there, acting under Lugal's advice, they branched out to other areas in Assyria, unoccupied by priests. In each such area, new settlements arose, attracting the locals.

For himself, Lugal wanted nothing. He had almost given up sky-watching. His three wives and three children were his pride and joy. If he sometimes looked up at the sky, it was as if he expected his own father and mother to be there, smiling at their grandchildren.

How much his mother had wanted him to marry when he was young! Not only she, but his father too had wanted to have grandchildren. But no, his was the single-minded ambition to be the greatest architect in the land—everything else had to wait!

Now, it was the other way round. Three wives and three children later, he was now supervising a vast variety of activities, including the building of houses, cattlesheds, granaries and water-reservoirs. Though some of the ideas came from the Aryas of Bharat Varsha, even they had to acknowledge that he was a superior builder.

Yet Lugal did request a part of the produce from these settlements—but only to 'gift' them to nearby priests. He knew of the growing anger of the priests; and even though the 'new people' were settling in virgin areas, unoccupied by priests, their hostility was on the rise. He placated priests with gifts but wondered—how long can one 'buy' friends! How long will this friendship last!

Lugal prayed for the long life of the recluse's priest-son who was his protection. What about those that would follow him! He was not worried about his own future. But of that of his children and their children! His mind dismissed the wishful hope expressed by some that a day would soon dawn when the priests would be powerless against their settlements. What a foolish hope—he thought—despite their effort to learn all these new ways of self-defence taught by the Aryas.

And Lugal knew that the Aryas themselves were constantly on the move; but even if the Aryas were to remain, the fact was that the priests controlled vast territories and massive numbers of men. Why, even in these settlements, not many would dare oppose a priest's direct order! Old beliefs die slowly and priests, after all, were regarded as gods in human garb.

Maybe—thought Lugal—the Arya hope that somewhere there is land that is pure and free is also foolish.

Lugal had not met Purus, the Arya leader in Iran. But the Aryas spoke of his view—that there was no land that was pure, unless we make it so, by our own will and effort. Purus was right—thought Lugal. But these lands of Sumer and Assyria were far too corrupt; it would require a superhuman effort to release them from the vicious stranglehold of the priests; but surely then, the aim should be to find land that is empty and relatively free from the control of men of evil.

It was then that Lugal felt that for the sake of the future—for the sake of his children—he should join the Arya quest for land elsewhere.

Yet his heart was heavy. The locals in these settlements admired the Aryas; but Lugal was the one to whom they looked up as their leader—emotionally and even materially. He was the one to whom they came with their problems, concerns and hopes.

Lugal remained silent but not for long. He spoke to the locals and was amazed to find them receptive to the idea of his leaving, 'so long as you take us along with you.' Actually, in the end, many had to be persuaded to remain and Lugal said—'If we fail, we return here, if we succeed, you come there. Both ways, we lose nothing.'

Thus left King Lugal, though not a king really, except in the hearts and imaginations of the Assyrian settlers, on his quest of new lands with the Aryas.

For every Arya from Bharat Varsha, there were twenty-four locals—and they too called themselves Arya, the noble.

'Hermit-King Lugal, you be in command!' begged Nilakantha, the Arya leader from Bharat Varsha.

'No,' said Lugal. 'Your faith is greater. You lead.'

Thus left King Lugal, though not a king really, except in the hearts and imaginations of the Assyrian settlers, on his quest of new lands with the Aryas.

For every Arya from Bharat Varsha, there were twenty-four locals—and they too called themselves Arya, the noble.

'Hermit-King Lugal, you be in command!' begged Nilakanta, the Arya leader from Bharat Varsha.

'No,' said Lugal. 'Your faith is greater. You lead.'

'In a better world it is a singer of songs and a dreamer of dreams who must lead mankind.'

'I don't rule heaven. If I did, I would banish the mad god who rules over earth and heaven and permits such cruelties.

—(From the song, 'Hopes of Hutantat'—around 5005 BC)

'He hideth Himself; long the journey,
And crying heart cries "Where is He!"
Arduous the path, much testing on the way
But does glory await the steps of a single day!
No, this is not the end of the end
But the beginning of a beginning, my friend...'

—(From 'Songs of Nila'—around 5005 BC)

Kings of Egypt and the Language of the Gods

5005 BC

After what seemed an eternity, the Aryas under Nilakantha entered Eygpt, along with Hermit-King Lugal. Along the way, as planned, some Arya groups parted to go to other areas—now known as Syria, Palestine, Saudi Arabia, Jordan and Israel. With them went many locals from Iran. But the locals from Sumer and Assyria would not leave King Lugal.

The journey was long and toilsome and before they reached Egypt, many were overcome with melancholy—where are we going and why? They would sing all the louder to keep up their spirits but often the songs did not allay their restless grief. Where was the land in which God ruled in his splendour? Was it all an illusion? But silent they remained, unwilling to share their uneasy forebodings with the others. There were those who understood each other without words and wondered: how powerful and alive we were with faith when we left Bharat Varsha....

Long before they entered Eygpt, they met many on the way, who went their way, groping, as their eyes had been put out. Others had their limbs cut off and tongues torn out because of some minor offence like not completing their allotted work on time, or to set a stern example to other workers on occasion, but also, often, for sport or simply to terrorize.

Such unfortunates lived and died miserably, in poor settlements, even though the land was not fertile. There were also youngsters who were more often than not on the run for fear of being taken to the land beyond—army service for men and slavery or prostitution for women—though prostitution among men was equally common.

The land beyond was called by many names—'Valley of Kings'; 'Land of Sun'; 'Land of Glory'—but the glory belonged to the King and the sun was simply a reflection in the sky of the King's glory.

At first, the Aryas believed that the land had a single king. But as they learnt the language of these people better, they understood that there were thirteen kings. Each king viewed the other with hate and spite and they were all at war with each other. Borders were undefined, raids common and loyalties shifting.

At one settlement, mostly barren, where the Aryas became really friendly with the locals as the result of looking after their sick, a local brought out from hiding two gold cups to offer water to Nilakantha and Lugal.

The truth was soon out. Beyond, in the hills, was a hide-out of robbers, who supported the settlement. In turn, the people there would warn robbers of any strangers around, with designs to catch them. Yet these robbers rarely robbed the living. They were grave-robbers.

In all these kingdoms, each man, on death, would be buried along with all his living wives, in their best clothes and whatever jewellery they had; additionally, there would be items of daily necessity, such as pots and pans, for use on their journey to heaven, through the bowels of the earth. A man of status would, in addition to his wives, have at least one slave buried with him and there would also be a variety of luxury items, including wine and wine-cups to make the journey pleasant. Such a journey was supposed to take twenty-seven days but for those who had a live donkey or horse buried with them, it could take less time, depending on the speed of the donkey or horse.

There was a curse against grave-robbers—that they would never ascend to heaven. This apparently did not deter the grave-robbers. But if caught, they were crucified by fastening on a frame, with wooden nails driven through their arms and legs and their bodies smeared with a honey-like substance to attract flies and ants.

Much of the information on the land beyond came to the Aryas from grave-robbers—how to cross safely, away from the clutches of kings, how to outsmart their little armies and where to hide. They even gave information on the huge catacombs to which the Aryas could run, in case of need—'If soldiers ever enter there, they never come out alive and thieves are too honourable to steal from anyone else hiding there.'

Indeed, the grave-robbers had a high opinion of men of their profession. When they stole from the living, they were convinced that the man must have exploited the poor to amass so much—'for how else is a fortune made except by robbing other's share!' As to grave-robbing, they never approached a grave during the first twenty-seven days that it was supposed to take a person to ascend to heaven and just in case a heavenly traveller turned lame or lost his way, they even waited for fifty-four days, 'For by then, his heavenly ascent is surely accomplished and he needs nothing in the grave any more for the journey. So why burden the earth with what it needs not, but we do!'

Friendly and informative the grave-robbers were, but they knew little of the lands beyond. They felt that the Aryas could at first avoid the river where it was populated and then follow its course to the south where the desert began—'Maybe the river and desert will lead somewhere or maybe nowhere but the north holds no prospect, for the river itself drowns into a huge body of salt-water.'

The river was then called Kemi which means 'black.' This was an allusion to its sediment. Its mud was black enough to earn that name. Later, after the Arya entry into Egypt, the river come to be known as Ar, Ary or Aur. Much later it came to be known as the Nil or Nile from Nila—and some say that it was to honour Nilakantha the Arya leader. Others have a different version, saying that the name Nile could have come from the Greek Neilos which is derived from the Semitic root nahal, meaning a valley or river-valley and hence by extension, a river. This seems too far-fetched.

The Arya 'army' moved on. They were to leave behind their thirty-six men, women and children, too sick and bruised to travel any more. Ajitab, an Arya from Bharat Varsha—though himself well enough to travel—was left behind in charge.

Such farewells had taken place, often before, on the way, but they were always heart-wrenching. The grave-robbers consoled Nilakantha, 'Maybe, we will teach them our arts if they cannot rejoin you.'

Nilakantha laughed, 'No, we have learned much of your language from you. That is enough. Teach us not your arts. But I hope our people will teach you our arts—to sow, plant, to build shelters and live differently and well. Meanwhile protect them.'

They promised, 'With our life and honour!'

Nilakantha believed them. He genuinely felt that one day the Aryas left behind would show these misguided men the way to atone for the past and live well.

Meanwhile, Nilakantha gave them the 'way to die well.' With Lugal guiding him, Nilakantha had searched far beyond the area for a particular wild plant. They found many. Its leaves, sun-dried and pounded, yielded a bitter powder that dulled pain and an overdoze even caused deep sleep. This was his gift to the grave-robbers for use, if ever they were caught and were to be crucified. It would not save their lives but would prevent the torture of a painful, lingering death.

'Be as silent as the graves we rob,' the robbers had warned the Aryas as they moved out. They sang no more and marched with a quieter tread.

Unbidden, dark and gloomy thoughts assailed them and Nilakantha asked Lugal, 'Should we not go back?' But it was too late.

Their mistake lay in assuming that like the grave-robbers they could steal their way into unknown, uninhabited paths. Robbers went in groups of three or four. Here a huge 'army' travelled. The Eygptian rulers had spies everywhere and this large movement could not pass undetected. Also, the Aryas were unsure as they zig-zagged into unknown tracks; and so they went slowly. Superstition had compelled them to decline when a grave-robber had graciously offered to guide them. Their slow, unsure movement gave enough time to the local King to mobilize his men and face what he thought was a challenge. His spies had exaggerated the strength of the oncoming Aryas.

Suddenly, the Aryas stopped. Ahead of them were the local King's men, massed like an ocean. The King's commander shouted from afar, 'Animals! Get down from your animals! Throw down all you carry!' The Aryas complied as Nilakantha repeated the order. He had learnt enough of their language on the way to understand what the commander desired.

The commander was surprised. He expected some resistance or at least the 'enemy' trying to run away. With ten slaves shielding him, he came forward slowly, afraid to be within their immediate arrow-range. But what he saw surprised him. These men and women looked different from his people. Even their clothes! And they had children too!

As a victorious commander, he was entitled to a hundredth part of captured booty in slaves, women and goods. Already, he was eyeing the women, men and their goods, as if relishing his own share.

Yet suddenly, the commander thought of the condition that some blood must flow on his side to be entitled to booty. This condition, perhaps devised originally to reward great warriors, had degenerated into a senseless token formality—and yet it was unavoidable, or else the booty was lost. The commander quickly gave his order. His slaves held the eldest slave and one of them ran a sword through him. Soon his writhing agony stopped. He died.

The Aryas understood nothing of this bloodthirsty rite. But fear gripped them and they thought this was the start of a merciless massacre. Nilakantha moved near the commander with a hand on his dagger. Lugal came forward too. Without an order, the Aryas picked up their weapons and mounted their animals—let us die fighting rather than be slaughtered.

The commander raised his hand and shouted, 'There is naught to fear. None shall he harmed.' But he was afraid too. These newcomers, he knew, could not stand against his superior force. But he feared he would be the first to fall, having come so near. He tried moving back. The Aryas inched forward. He halted and barked, 'Remain where you are! The Sun-god (King) shall soon arrive.' Meanwhile, face to face, he explained to Lugal and Nilakantha that killing the slave was no more than a necessary rite and meant no threat to them. He was simply ensuring that he got a part of the booty due to him. His explanation, instead of reassuring Nilakantha and Lugal, actually terrified them. They looked back at the Aryas as if to translate his words; but said, 'Whatever happens, keep your arms ready to surround the King and the commander.'

At the commander's order, a slave rushed to advise the priest, so that their King was informed of total victory.

Face to face, the two armies stood.

At last, then, the King came. But he was not like his foolish commander, overpowered by greed. He was surrounded by an outer ring of priests and an inner ring of soldiers. He could hardly be seen. Nor did he come near, but halted along the middle of his army. Six priests came to inspect the opposite army and reported back to him.

The King demanded the presence of their commander. Nilakantha insisted on taking Lugal. 'None approaches the Sun-god with a weapon,' the priest said so they went unarmed.

'Kneel, dogs, kneel, before the Sun-god,' the priest barked as they reached the King's group. Nilakantha and Lugal knelt.

The King would have had to shout to speak directly to them. But he spoke through the six priests he had lined up.

'Why do you have two commanders? I asked for one,' was the King's first question. Nilakantha answered, 'Sun-god, I am in command, but we all respect Hermit-King Lugal, so I brought him.'

'The only kings that enter my land are dead kings,' the Sun-god responded.

Nilankantha regretted his foolish response but Lugal spoke, 'Sun-god, I am not a king in the ordinary sense. I am known as king of architects and builders.'

'So what do you come to build here?' asked the Sun-god.

'To build a dream,' said Lugal, but even before conveying the reply to the King, the priest muttered, 'Explain, dog, explain!'

Lugal explained, 'A dream came to me, Sun-god!—that I build a glorious temple in your land to honour you.'

'What need have I of a temple to honour me when, wherever I am, a temple lies unseen beneath my feet!'

'True, Sun-god, but my next dream clarified that doubt. Just as the sun shines in the sky to reflect your glory and is seen by all, there has to be a temple, seen by all on earth, to reflect your glory here.'

'How will a temple reflect my glory? Will you build a sun on earth?'

'Yes, Sun-god, something like the sun—to reflect its glory and yours.'

The man must be mad, the King thought but Lugal had excited his interest. Nilakantha had his mouth open and understood nothing. 'Explain!' the King shouted for the first time.

'Sun-god, like all great architecture, the idea in my dream is profoundly simple. The movement of the sun that revolves around you throws its light differently in various phases. Your temple shall have a number of obelisks in pyramidal and tapering squares. The rising or setting sun would, at different times, gild with a bright gold glow, the tip of each particular obelisk. And in those golden glimpses, each shall observe with awe and reverence, your glory, that is reflected in the sky as it shall be reflected on earth.'

'But surely,' said the King doubtfully, 'sunlight shall fall equally on every obelisk.'

Lugal went on, at length, with his explanation. He was on firm technical ground and had no doubt. But it was all beyond the King's comprehension. 'Bring Hutantat,' he ordered.

Hutantat was the sky-watcher (astronomer) in his land.

Well before Hutantat arrived, Lugal started drawing all kinds of figures on the ground. With the King's permission, Lugal called one of his men—Himatap, an Arya from Bharat Varsha. All along the way, Lugal and Himatap had been engaged in discussing and observing movements of the heavenly bodies including the sun. Himatap was his 'star-pupil'. (It is not clear if by the expression 'star-pupil,' the poet meant that Himatap was the best pupil or a pupil who studied only stars—in any case, the poets did regard the sun as a star too—and the idea was that each god's universe had a star attached to it and the sun was the 'local star to guide the earth'.)

Under Lugal's instruction, Himatap began drawing all kinds of figures on the ground with an arrow-tip—lines, squares, angles, triangles. Even the King came nearer, with his entourage, to watch curiously, while they waited for Hutantat.

Nine soldiers, carrying Hutantat's litter, arrived. Hutantat had no priestly or secular titles. But his claims to fame were many. He often predicted when the river would rise in flood and when it would recede. He knew more about an eclipse than anyone—and predicted it accurately. But more than that, when six kings had joined together to attack the kingdom in the time of the present King's grandfather, he had predicted the defeat of the six kings, even though no more than eighty soldiers were left to fight against them. At his bidding, it was said, 'the river rose, drowning all that came before it and the six kings fled and one even died before reaching his land.'

Since then Hutantat was known as the 'oracle who could alter events.'

Perfunctorily, Hutantat bowed to the King. Anyone else making such a careless bow would have been beheaded on the spot—but he was not anyone else. It was the King who returned the bow. At the King's order, the chief-priest explained the impossible dream of Lugal.

Hutantat left the priest without waiting for him to complete his explanation and walked over to Lugal and Himatap who were still drawing figures on the ground. With impatience, even with anger, Hutantat rubbed off with his feet, one figure drawn by Himatap; he snatched Himatap's arrow and redrew the figure differently and, at a greater distance. Lugal nodded in agreement with the correction.

Then began Hutantat's scrutiny of the figures drawn by Lugal. Hutantat rubbed off no figures but drew and redrew; and Lugal too drew and redrew. It was as if both were discussing, by means of figures, the best way to achieve the objective.

Hutantat ignored two distant interruptions from the impatient King who wanted to know his views immediately.

The King was now being served with choice refreshments. When he sent a priest to call Hutantat, the priest heard Hutantat's insulting shouts to remain away—lest he disturb the figures drawn on the ground.

Lugal and Hutantat were both tired. They stopped and looked at each other in silent appreciation. Lugal felt that Hutantat had the eyes of his mentor—the recluse priest-father—who had taught him all he knew about the sun's movements.

But Hutantat's words were pitiless as he responded to the King's shout—as he said, 'Only a fool would begin such a project.'

The terrible words were spoken. Lugal felt no anger—only sad weariness.

The priests who had known all along that it was an impossible idea, and had said so to the King, were pleased.

The King was already discussing with his commanders how the Aryas be surrounded to avoid undue bloodshed. It pleased him to have so many different looking men and women as slaves.

Lugal hardly heard Hutantat who was speaking to him. 'How can you think of wasting so much time and effort over a useless temple to satisfy the ego of an arrogant king when most people here are hungry, naked and without shelter. Do you know how much it would cost? And the poor here will groan and suffer! Are you without pity?'

'Pity! Yes, I have pity. But for my people too. From what the King's commander said, clearly we are to be enslaved here. It was pity, then, that moved me to offer to build a temple. You think it is wrong to have pity for one's own people!'

'Then it was not a dream that brought you here?'

Ruefully Lugal laughed, 'I have many dreams but this is not one of them. It suddenly occurred to me when we were threatened with slavery or death and I thought it was worth a try.'

'Yet, it is a glorious idea,' Hutantat said almost to himself and fell into a reverie.

Suddenly, Hutantat shouted across to the King's entourage, 'And I must see the site where this temple is to be built.'

'What!' the Chief-priest shouted back. 'I thought the proposal was dead.'

Hotly, Hutantat replied, 'You may be dead yourself. Why don't you ask the King?'

It was the King who spoke, 'But Hutantat, did you not say that only a fool would start such a project!'

'Of course,' Hutantat replied and he pointed his hand at Lugal, 'is he not a fool, who comes from afar, pursuing a dream, not for his glory but yours! And he stands in the sun, his people without food and water, while even your eunuchs are having refreshments with umbrellas over their heads. Certainly he is a fool to start this splendrous project. But only a great King would embark on such a project. Are you a great King?'

The priests winced. Hutantat never called the King by his true title of Sun-god. But to challenge the King's wrath with such impertinence!

The King ignored the question and asked, 'You think the project has merit! You really think so?'

'I don't think so. I know so.'

'It cannot fail?' the King pressed.

'Certainly, it can fail if the sun moves away, elsewhere, for ever; or if the earth under our feet disappears. But otherwise, how can it fail? This dreamer here may be a fool to pursue his dream for your glory, but his dream is solid and splendid, based on the movements of the sky and earth and the manner in which the sun's rays invariably fall. No, it cannot fail.'

There was silence all over. But the King soon ordered four sun-umbrellas to go to Hutantat, Lugal, Nilakantha and Himatap. A refreshment cart was also brought and left for them. Hutantat took a little; Lugal took nothing. He was thinking of all the Aryas—his wives and children among them—sweating in the hot sun, unaware of all that was happening here.

But Hutantat told Lugal, 'Take a little. My insolence they expect and appreciate; yours they may not.' They drank and ate and it occurred to Lugal that Hutantat possibly used his impertinence as a screen.

At last the King spoke, 'Sage Hutantat! Will you help these men to select a temple-site?'

'That I shall,' Hutantat replied. 'But first let a site be found to house them and all their people.'

The Chief-priest spoke, 'Our men will assist too. Surely, not all the people brought by them are needed to work.' The Chief-priest was simply translating the King's desire to have some of these different-looking men and women in his household.

'Are you mad, eunuch!' Hutantat shouted. 'Do you think these people came from so far off to rest here? They too come chasing the dream of this fool for the greater glory of our King. Or is our King's glory of no consequence to you? Do you realize that if a single one of them does not work or is hurt or harmed this project of glory will suffer! So see to it, then, that they are all able to work and he who disturbs or harms them is punished with the highest penalty. You are personally responsible for that.'

Sadly, the Chief-priest looked at the King. They spoke. How could these people all be workers! Some were old and quite a few women had children. The King spoke, 'But Sage Hutantat, some of their women have children...!'

'Exactly, King, exactly!' Hutantat interrupted ecstatically, as though agreeing with him. 'That is what your priest does not understand and never will. They even brought children for the promise of this glory. You are absolutely right, King, and wise too!'

No one understood what he meant. Maybe he did not understand either. Certainly, the King did not understand. But how could he disagree with a sage who not only agreed with him but even called him wise. The King could not recall a single other occasion on which Hutantat had so complimented him.

The King's orders were now clear. All these people were to be well-treated and well-housed and anyone trying to harm them would meet a terrible fate.

Finally, the King said, 'Sage Hutantat, when you select a temple-site, come to me and bring this... this....' He pointed to Lugal; maybe he disliked calling him King Lugal or maybe he forgot his name.

But Hutantat immediately said, 'Certainly, my King, and I shall also bring the King's architect Lugal.'

'King's Architect! Good title! Yes, let that be his,' said the King.

The Chief-priest and the King came forward. The Chief-priest shouted at Lugal, 'Kneel, dog, kneel!' Lugal knelt, bewildered.

The King touched Lugal's head with his whip, gently. The Chief-priest shouted, 'The Sun-god has spoken. And all shall honour you as such. Rise! Honourable King's Architect, rise with honour!'

Obviously, it was a great honour. But the day had been crowded with so many startling events that Lugal did not know whether to laugh or cry.

The King and his entourage left. The commander and his soldiers remained to carry out the King's order to arrange for food and housing for the King's Architect and his people. The commander discussed arrangements with Huntantat and Lugal.

Nilakantha ran to the Aryas. Breathless, laughing, crying, he reached them, unable to utter a word—and they thought he had brought news of the calamity awaiting them. At last he said, 'We are saved! Sing, sing, sing!' And many sang, though others shouted questions at him and at each other, while still others exclaimed, 'Sing! He says we are saved!'

The commander heard the off-key song, with some singing, others stopping midway to ask questions or to hear the answers. To him it sounded like a disorderly lament, 'Why are they bleating like goats and sheep?' he asked. Lugal himself was surprised at the tuneless song.

But Hutantat said, 'They sing in a language that God understands better—the language of goats and sheep.'

'God understands the language of sheep and goats better!' the commander asked. 'How is it then that our King, the Sun-god, does not speak the language of goats and sheep?'

Hutantat wondered if the commander's question was a trap to entice him into saying something indiscreet about the King. He said, 'King knows all he needs to know. It is for you to know better—perhaps the cry of slaughtered slaves, and the lament of those that you call sheep and goats.'

Many heard what Sage Hutantat said—and the story would be told and retold that these outsiders speak the language of the gods!

Language of the gods! Who says so! Why, Hutantat himself! And Hutantat, they knew, was never wrong and never spoke lightly.

The locals, obsessed with the idea of after-life, that awaited them after a brief journey of twenty-seven days from their grave, regarded the coming of the Aryas as auspicious. True, they carried their wives, pots and pans, even slaves and asses to the grave, for their journey to heaven. But to go armed with the language of the gods! Many aspired to crowd around these new-comers to learn their heavenly language.

Some thousands of years later, far into the modern post-Vedic era, possibly around 1200 AD, poetess Satyali of Sind would sing of the echo of Sage Hutantat's words and say, 'The Aryas took our language out to lands distant and near—oh where did they not go and so few came back!—But they left their words on the lips and hearts of many in those strange lands; the strangers were strangers no more and those that returned, rich they came with much they learnt of what was on the lips and in the hearts of them that they left.'

Poetess Satyali also adds something more to the point. She says, 'And then came the venerable priests and they said, "Beware! The language we speak and see is the language that the gods speak and see. Honour therefore its eternal divinity and pure perpetuity and think! Should not God's language always remain perfect and refined!" And who but a senseless poetess like me would argue with a sentiment so noble and lofty! Then the priests pronounced their codes of command to refine the language and make it perfect and fit for the gods. No longer then did it matter *what* a poet said, but *how* he said it. And as my poet-great-grandfather said to the priests, "Beware, for soon it may be that the gods alone shall utter this language of perfection, and humans no more..."

'And I, Satyali, tell you that though fortunately the number of gods has not gone down, unfortunately the number of those that now speak the language of my ancestors is restricted to very few. And I know not how many humans shall speak this language in the time of my great-great-grandson, but I hope, he shall—even if he be the only one so to speak.'

Poetess Satyali mentions no one in particular as a target of her criticism. It may be wrong to assume that her criticism is against Panini—author of *Astadhyayi*, fourth century BC, which contains 3,983 sutras, and an almost equal number of rules affecting Sanskrit; also the criticism may not be against later commentators like Patanjali— author of *Mahabhasya*, second century BC, or Jayadity and Vamana— authors of *Kasika Vritti*, seventh century AD. The fact is that poetess Satyali mentions her poet great-great-grandfather who is identified in her other poems as poet Kundaliya of the sixth century BC—a predecessor of Sage Panini of the fourth century BC. Obviously therefore, poet Kundaliya's criticism, at the least, must be aimed at grammarians before Sage Panini's time. The obscure line of a fourth century BC poet that 'Rishi Panini drank water from the same river as

Kavi (poet) Kundaliya', seems to be irrelevant for this purpose and all it probably means is that both Panini and Kundaliya resided near Sindhu river. As it is, Panini had his ashram at Salatura, situated near an angle formed by the junction of Kabul with Sindhu river, while Kundaliya lived at the mouth of Sindhu near the sea.

The Aryas were now about to leave to follow the commander. Suddenly, a young, shrill voice rose, 'But where is brother Himatap?' They all looked. Far away, alone, was Himatap, where the King and his entourage had been. He was still drawing figures on the ground, untouched by the bewilderment that affected everyone that day.

'What is he doing?' asked Nilakantha.

'He is trying to discover God's law,' Lugal said.

'Yes,' Hutantat rejoined grimly, 'so that the Devil may be served better.'

Nilakantha misunderstood and said, 'Himatap is a good lad.'

Lugal and the others shouted to Himatap to return. Himatap heard and suddenly seemed bewildered at finding himself alone. He had been much too absorbed to notice that the others had left.

The King approved of the temple-site. Hutantat said to Nilakantha, 'Many untruths were spoken to the King. Yet I am bound by the promise that you shall build the temple.'

Nilakantha felt sad that Hutantat doubted the Arya sincerity and said, 'Each of us is honour-bound and I swear by the light of the sun....'

Hutantat smiled, 'Enough! But learn a few rules before you break them. Never swear by the sun. The sun may not object but as all here will tell you, the sun is only a reflection of our Sun-god King, and never annoy him if you hope to die of old age.'

Nilakantha was still hurt, 'But you doubted our sincerity, did you not?'

'Sometimes I doubt the sincerity of God the Creator, too.'

'Sincerity of God!'

'But then, perhaps, God does not exist; so why question his sincerity?'

Nilakantha looked more sad. Hutantat asked playfully, 'Why! Does everyone in your land believe that God exists?'

'Oh no! There are some who disbelive in God.'

'And they are evil men?' asked Hutantat.

'No, not at all. Many are good, though I think they are ... inside them...' he groped for a word.

'Lonely?' Hutantat prompted.

'Yes, there is a loneliness, an emptiness inside them.'

'And you try to bring to them your belief in God?'

'Me! Why? How! Each person reaches his belief himself, within himself.'

'Nothing outside of him influences him?'

'Of course. The winds of influence will be there, from parents, teachers, neighbours, but above all from what his soul tells him.'

'Oh! So you too have a talkative soul!' Hutantat said. 'But tell me, in your land, does a man who disbelieve in God go to heaven?'

Nilakantha too now had the urge to be playful and said, 'No one in our land is expected, ever, to go to heaven.'

'What! You live a life and die. That's all!'

Nilakantha then told him of his belief—that there was no heaven, no hell, but only moksha—reidentification of the human soul with the soul of God, if the individual in his earthly journey lived with righteous karma; or alternatively a chain of rebirths till he achieved righteousness, though no one was ever denied either the opportunity or the hope to achieve salvation.

'And surely this moksha will be denied to those that disbelieve in God?' Hutantat asked.

'Why would it be denied if the man's karma was righteous?'

'Surely God decides!'

'How can God be unjust?'

'You mean that your God is not angered by neglect, nor placated by praise! But then what is the point in believing or disbelieving in God, or loving or hating him, if moksha is unrelated to it?'

'Sometimes, the love for God in a man's heart will overflow. If a man can love his father and wife and even unborn son, grandchild or friend, why is it inconceivable that he loves and believes in God? That love and belief itself will incline an individual to right conduct. But whether he believes in God or not, if his karma is righteous, how can God deny him moksha! How can a just God ever refuse to a man what he has earned!'

Hutantat asked many questions in order to clarify things. But in the end he said, 'Interesting. But I believe none of it.'

Nilakantha smiled, 'That is your privilege, Sage. Many in my land too do not believe it. That is their privilege.'

Hutantat asked with heat, 'You mean there is nobody in your land to tell disbelievers to believe!'

Nilakantha had difficulty in replying. He was wandering how the wise sage could ask such a preposterous question. At last he said, 'But how, by what right...!'

'If you believe, why don't you make others believe?'

'Why? How! If I, a believer, force myself upon another, does the non-believer not have the right to force his non-belief on me?'

'Exactly! And in the end, force will decide whose belief succeeds.'

'But faith achieved through force and assault! What kind of faith would that be? A faith conceived in sin! And he who tries to impose such a faith on another, what kind of a person must he be? Truly, an enemy of God, or one who believes himself above God, for God never demanded what a man should or should not believe....'

Nilakantha stopped with the feeling that he had been lecturing an honoured sage and said, 'Forgive me, Master, I know so little and I have no way with words. But you know we all love and honour you....'

'Even if I don't believe in God?' Hutantat challenged with a smile.

'That, Master, is between God and you. But I simply wanted to respond to your first question, to promise that each of us would work sincerely to see that the temple you have promised the King shall be built.'

Hutantat was serious now. 'Good. The King has released 1,500 slaves for temple-work despite the Chief-priest's protests. They will be freed in my custody when the temple is completed; and the King will give me six villages where they can remain in freedom. Already hundreds of others work in freedom in villages which King gave me three years ago. I care not at all for the temple. But if my promise for the temple fails, no harm may come to me but the axe will surely fall on the slaves.'

Nilakantha was looking at him with a fixed stare. Hutantat thought he had spoken too fast in a language that was still not too familiar to these people. He was about to explain but Nilakantha spoke, 'You saved us! You save slaves! Can God have greater love than that a man should love his creatures so much! I wish I could trade my faith with your karma.'

'Do not give away so much for so little!' Hutantat rejoined.

Even Lugal was thinking, as he saw hundreds of slaves being driven to the temple-site by the whip and the lash, with wounds and sores on their bodies and terror in their eyes, of karma and human free will of which the Aryas had spoken—that the soul was a source of liberty, that a human had the capacity to go beyond his heritage! That no one was denied the hope and opportunity to so advance!

But where was human free will, Lugal wondered. And where did it lead? Nowhere. It was simply an illusion—an escape from one tyranny into another. Did these slaves at the temple-site have free will? Did he have free will? In its land of Sumer, priests were the tyrants and here the King terrorized with priests, commanders and soldiers under him. But what was the difference? Except that here the tyranny was more visible, more naked, more brutal. And now, they were building a temple to the glory and vanity of a King who ruled with indescribable horror! Where had he led his people with this free will? From one horror to another! No, there was no free will; no mysterious, benign presence that governed the universe! Man was simply a pawn of fate, a slave of necessity.

Lugal's gloom actually arose from being rebuffed by the slave-commander who had tersely told him, 'Lord Architect! Tell me what you want these slaves to do and my soldiers shall get it done. Don't tell me how!'

Later, Hutantat told Lugal and Nilakantha, 'The King's Architect cannot interfere with the King's commanders. Only a priest can.'

'Then get Nilakantha appointed a priest,' Lugal urged. 'He sings, he prays, sometimes he even thinks, and his thoughts are always auspicious.'

'Although Nilakantha will gain much by being a priest, he will lose a little too,' Hutantat said.

Hutantat explained: the King appoints ninety-nine priests—no more, no less. He bows to them every morning. He cannot dismiss them. So if he dislikes a priest, or wishes to appoint another, the priest must die. And even those that kill the priest, at the King's command, must die, for it is a sin to strike a priest.

Hutantat continued, 'Maybe, no one sheds tears over a priest's death, as it means one vicious person less; but imagine Nilakantha in that role! After two years, he must lose his manhood and be a eunuch.'

'What!' Lugal and Nilakantha shouted in surprise.

'Yes. For the first 730 days, the priest is permitted the freedom to pick any and every man's wife, sister, daughter, mother and take her to bed. No restrictions, except that he cannot touch the King's wives. All others must submit to his desire. But on the 731st day, the priest undergoes an operation and becomes a eunuch for life.'

'Why this madness?'

'Simple. When the King dies, his queens and his ninety-nine priests are buried with him, alive. Queens are mostly of royal blood, as the King must marry all his sisters, whatever their age. He can marry others too and they too are buried with him. In that cramped grave, where there are so many buried, only eunuch males are allowed lest they corrupt the queens on their celestial journey. But of course, the belief is that when they reach heaven, there is an abundance of everything, including human spare parts; so their manhood is promptly restored and there, too, they can claim any woman that their hearts desire.'

Nilakantha was speechless but Lugal asked, 'Priests and queens— are they the only ones buried alive?'

'No, many slaves. They are castrated too. Why, even horses and asses are castrated before being buried alive with the King, lest his queens begin to suffer from unholy desires during that brief journey to paradise. The only difference is that slaves and animals do not get their spare parts back.'

'Why?'

'Why! Don't ask me! I don't rule heaven,' Hutantat said. 'If I did, the first thing I would do is to banish the God who rules over earth and heaven and permits such revolting cruelties.' He paused to ask, 'Brother Nilakantha, would you like to be a Lord Priest?'

Later, they were told why a priest was castrated during his lifetime. A priest was always with the King. He escorted the queens to the King, served as their teacher and physician. Nobody could see a queen except the priest.

But why not assign such duties to women, they wanted to know. But Hutantat said that women, here, were regarded as fit only for work in the fields or to satisfy man's hunger and produce children.

'But Arya women work! They are even teachers, singers and doctors!'

'Well, maybe they will say Arya men are not manly enough and their women, not feminine enough.'

'Does anyone then wish to be a priest?'

'Why not!' Hutantat explained. 'Two years of riotous living to compensate for castration; then living in the lap of luxury. Sex? But even a eunuch does have some inlets and outlets to satisfy his desires. And remember! He has the absolute certainty of reaching heaven with his manhood restored and bliss everlasting!

'Does anyone believe it?' Nilakantha asked.

'You believe what you believe—they believe what they believe.'

'What do you believe?' Nilakantha pressed.

'I believe everything and nothing,' said Hutantat. 'One day I may know what I should have believed but by then it may not matter!'

Actually, it was Hutantat who secured better treatment for the slaves working for the temple. Most of their heavy work lay outside, like bringing huge stone-blocks and baking bricks, but they were also levelling the huge, hilly terrain of the temple-site.

Nilakantha asked Hutantat, 'The commander is unduly brutal with the slaves. Is there no way that you can get another commander?'

'Another commander will be equally brutal,' Hutantat said, but added after a pause, 'Good idea, Brother Nilakantha! You cannot be a priest, but you could be appointed to serve as a commander.'

'You mean you can appoint me as commander!' Nilakantha asked.

'No, only the King can. But it is a brilliant idea. Yes, you replace the commander and your men replace his soldiers, for they are more brutish than their commander! And certainly, the slaves will respond to your gentleness. They know the King's promise that they will be freed once the temple is complete.'

'I hope the King will remember his promise to free the slaves when the temple is completed.'

'He forgets no promises. He just won't keep them. If I count all his promises to me, I should have had eighty-five villages with thousands of slaves freed. But some promises, sometimes, he keeps. So the problem now is about your ambition to be the King's commander; or are you to remain only the commander of your Aryas?'

'Ambition! But please don't call me a commander of the Aryas,' Nilakantha begged. 'It is Hermit-King Lugal who leads us all. He commands that I march ahead, as I am simply a singer of songs.'

'Yes, Lugal knows too, that in a better world it is a singer of songs and a dreamer of dreams who must lead mankind.'

But Hutantat influenced the commander, not by moral force which only met with indifference but by threatening him. 'You are maltreating and starving the slaves which bothers me not at all, except that it disrupts the King's temple.'

Again said Hutantat to the commander, 'Beware, the King may make you not a priest but priestly (castrated)!'

The commander would have struck down anyone else, but not Sage Hutantat. Often, the King came to the temple-site, demanding Hutantat's presence. Gratefully, the commander would hear Hutantat praising him to the King for his work—and once the King even said to the Chief-priest, 'Remind me to promote the commander when the temple is complete.'

Hutantat also lined up a few Aryas, visibly, to keep watching the treatment of the slaves by the commander and his soldiers. It had its effect and the soldiers no longer interfered with Aryas offering food and water to the slaves, or tending to their wounds and later the soldiers became less harsh with the slaves and sometimes even considerate.

'Work goes slowly,' Hutantat said to Nilakantha, in mock-complaint against the good treatment of the slaves.

'But, auspiciously,' said Nilakantha, happily. 'And I thank you, Master.'

Among the Aryas, Himatap was perhaps the only one unconcerned with the slaves or any other matter. All his dreams and waking thoughts were centred on temple-construction.

The King often came, each time to demand that the temple be made bigger and grander than Lugal's conception. Readily, Hutantat would agree, only to demand more slaves, so that they could be freed at the end, and more villages to house them in.

'Do not promise lightly, my King,' Hutantat said, 'for you know the curse on him that vainly promises in the temple's name, and keeps not his promise.'

The King did not know the curse and asked. But Hutantat only said, 'Too much I honour you, King, to utter such a curse in your presence.'

Thoughtfully, the King promised more slaves, but Hutantat never demanded too much, knowing that each superstition had a limit.

In the centre of the temple, the King demanded a palace, surrounded by tapering obelisks, monolithic shafts with a pyramidal apex, on which the sun's rays gleamed with a golden glow. Yet, he also wanted a place for burial, with his entourage.

'Why not a Ziggurat for the King to ascend to the heavens directly from the sky,' said Lugal, with his Sumerian experience. But he silently realized his mistake—bodies decompose and surely on that open platform, everyone would see the condition of the King's body with horror. Besides, the King's body was not a bait to trap animals, as in Sumeria.

The King's objection was different. 'Grave-robbers steal even from closed pits and an open Ziggurat won't do. Instead, think of how to keep the robbers away from our grave-pits.'

Himatap had a suggestion, 'Let it be a closed pyramid then—closed for ever.'

It was Hutantat, then, who answered the King's doubts—'How will bodies go into an enclosed pyramid?'

'An opening will be there,' explained Hutantat, 'which will be sealed with bricks after the bodies are put in.'

'Is heavenly ascent possible from an enclosed pyramid?' the King asked.

'Yes, the King's spirit is mighty.'

'But what of those that must accompany me?'

'The King's might will guide them too, but holes shall be provided at the top of the pyramid for weaker ones.'

'But so far, heavenly ascents have been made from earth. What if the sky-route is impossible?'

'No problem. The earth will be under your feet.'

Except cost and effort, every problem was considered.

The King's decision: 'Build the pyramid, Hutantat. You will get 900 more slaves, to be freed at the conclusion of construction, with two more villages. No more, but no less. That is a promise.'

Each visit by the King resulted in intense discussion, chiefly among Hutantat, Lugal and Himatap, with all three drawing and redrawing figures, diagrams and lines—sometimes disagreeing, often pondering, and even striking their own foreheads in frustration.

Later Western and Indian historians would write about the theorem of Pythagoras of Samos, a Greek philosopher and mathematician.

Someone could argue that somehow Hutantat, Lugal and Himatap learnt it from Pythagoras—except that Pythagoras lived in the sixth century BC while Hutantat, Lugal and Himatap worked on the first pyramid in Egypt some thousands of years before Pythagoras. But that apart, there are well preserved pyramids and funerary monuments in Egypt, built long centuries before Pythagoras, and it may be worthwhile for Indian historians to take a trip to Egypt to see if this simple theorem was well within the grasp of those simple people.

It is difficult to say who came upon the theorem first—Hutantat the Egyptian, or Lugal the Sumerian and Assyrian, or Himatap the youngster from Bharat Varsha with the Tibetan mother. Chances are that it came from Hutantat the Egyptian, or Lugal the Sumerian, though it is possible that Lugal learnt if from his mentor—the Sumerian recluse, who was the son and father of a priest. In any case, a later poet's claim 'surely this knowledge flowed from my land (India)' has no basis either, except that the Indus Valley finds clearly show that pre-ancient India was well aware of the application of this theorem.

Many poets from Bharat Varsha credit Nilakantha with much that the Aryas did in Egypt. He deserves credit—after all he was the leader, though he distinguished himself largely through self-effacement.

Hutantat was their spokesman with the King and commander. All work was organized by Hutantat and Lugal. Nilakantha was supposed to supervise everyone. But so convinced was he that they were all working excellently, that he hardly supervised, except to appreciate their work. And since he realized that he achieved nothing by supervision, he did what pleased him most—going to the slaves and often serving them food. Sometimes, he detached the Aryas from work to prepare some delicacies for the slaves. But first he would offer them to the commander, and soldiers, then to the slaves. He would talk to the slaves although a lot of them did not understand him, for they had been caught from lands in the African south along the Nile.

Nilakantha would wonder about the darker colour of the slaves' skins. He sometimes sang for them and encouraged them to sing. He understood the sadness in their songs, if not the words. He addressed each slave as 'brother,' in his language.

The commander did not interfere with Nilakantha's contact with the slaves. After all, everyone, even Hutantat, respected Nilakantha as a leader. He was a fool but a delightful fool—thought the commander. The soldiers considered him funny but pleasantly so. Only the slaves regarded him as lovable, without reservation.

Nilakantha was the son of a celebrated singer and the grandson of a poet. Why did he leave with the Aryas? To seek a better life for himself? Maybe to seek a better life for others.

Lugal saw Nilakantha often speaking or singing to the slaves and said what once Hutantat had said, 'Work goes slowly.' And Hutantat too said what Nilakantha had once said, 'But auspiciously, Master.' Both laughed.

Nilakantha saw them from a distance. Somehow he knew they were laughing at him. But even so, he was happy, for so overwrought were these two with work and worry, that it delighted him to see them laugh.

But this is a simplistic view of all that Nilakantha did. He was perhaps the ablest listener. Everyone came to him with their troubles. He listened, rarely saying much. But, often, the mere recitation of woes softens distress.

One wound remained—and that was in every heart. Where was the object of their long quest? Why were they caught in this land? Was it for this that they had left their homeland? Nilakantha had these doubts too and his voice trembled as he sang, 'So onward Arya, onward all...'

What more is wanted from a leader than that he keeps his hurt to himself but cheers his troops and raises their morale and sanity when there is no way of going forward or back!

Poets from Bharat Varsha wrapped many fables and legends around Nilakantha as if he were the inspiration behind all the monuments and mathematics of Egypt.

Even Nilakantha's narration of the story of the Egyptian calendar was misunderstood. Nobody paid attention to the story as a whole. Everyone merely heard the title of the story and assumed that Nilakantha established the Egyptian calendar.

The story simply was that Hutantat who often praised Lugal, once said to Nilakantha, 'Every day, Lugal gives me a lesson in humility, and teaches me something new.' Actually, all that Lugal had done was to prove to Hutantat that a year consisted not of 365 days but 365 1/4 days, 'And I was the foolish one,' said Hutantat, 'to declare to the King's grandfather that the year begins when the brightest star is seen in the morning sky in direct line with the rising sun;[1] and all my observations showed the year to have 365 days—no more, no less.'

Nilakantha knew that in Bharat Varsha, a year was known to have 365 1/4 days; so also in Sumer (Mesopotamia); he did not know how or why. But he was sure that so insignificant an error of a mere 1/4 day hardly mattered and he said so. But Hutantat gravely said, 'It makes a difference of a year in 1,460 years.' Apparently, Hutantat did not view this lightly.

However in the Bharat Varsha calendar, a day was divided into twenty hours, an hour into 100 minutes, and a minute into 100 seconds, and a second into ten subdivisions. In Sumeria, a day had twenty-four hours, each hour sixty minutes, and a minute had sixty seconds, with no subdivisions for seconds. But then, the Sumerians always had six as their sacred number. Everything had to be in multiples of six— whether it be their gods, immortal angels, the number of lashes to punish a culprit, or division of days, minutes and seconds.[2]

Even the man-made cycle of a 'week', as an artificial cluster of seven days, owed its inspiration to the Sumerians. Their proverb was, 'Six days of the priest and one day of sin.' All that this proverb meant was that each person owed his six days, out of seven, to labour for his priest, while the one remaining day was, inauspiciously, for a person's own individual, private pursuits.

People in Bharat Varsha had a ten day week, and the eleventh day was a day of rest and to entertain friends, while the twelveth day was for public festivities; and thereafter the ten day work-week restarted.

It was actually from Sumeria that the system of twenty-four hours for a day, sixty minutes for an hour and sixty seconds for a minute and even the concept of a week as a bouquet of seven days reached the Romans, Christians, and others—and while the origins and routes of borrowings are obscure, it may be that the Sumerian system came to Bharat Varsha not through returning Aryans but later, indirectly, from Europe.

---

[1] The rising of Sirius, the Dog Star, occurs in the morning before sunrise on approximately 19 July (Julian Calendar). Hutantat observed it happening each year at the time when the Nile river rose rapidly. He came to regard that day as the true New Year's Day. His reckoning of a year of 365 days, however, was one quarter of a day too short.

[2] There was then not a great deal of difference between Lugal's calendar of Sumeria (Mesopotamia, Iraq) and Bharat Varsha. Perhaps the main difference was that in Sumeria, the knowledge of the calendar was restricted to a few learned priests and sages, while in Bharat Varsha it was common knowledge, that affected the daily life of everyone.

On the Sumerian's use of multiples of six and Bharat Varsha's preference for multiples of ten, Hutantat asked Himatap, 'Is ten a sacred number in your Bharat Varsha?'

'Not at all,' Himatap said. 'But ten is a convenient number for decimal placement.' But decimals came later. Many say that in its pre-ancient origin, the popularity of number ten arose simply for its convenience—as man had ten fingers and counting up to ten was easy.'

Lugal laughed, 'Maybe, the first Sumerian who began counting had six fingers in his hand; or maybe he had six children and no more and stopped counting after six. Who knows! But the fact is that six has always remained a sacred number with us.'

Nilakantha pleaded so Hutantat took him, along with many others, to bring back Ajitab and the thirty-six sick and injured Aryas they had left behind in his charge at the settlement which was under the protection of grave-robbers.

There was no settlement there, any more; only skeletons of the dead, fleshless bodies, left there to rot. Also, they found no one in the hills where the grave-robbers had their hide-out.

They did not know it but this tragedy was actually related to the temple that the Aryas were building. The King's soldiers had fanned out everywhere to hunt for new slaves to work on the temple. Apparently, everyone too young or too old to serve as a slave was killed and the rest were dragged away as slaves.

Since then, Hutantat sent out his men everywhere to look for any slaves taken from there. None could be located. He tried to console Nilakantha, 'Maybe, your Aryas joined the grave-robbers to escape.'

Nilakantha was in anguish. 'Don't worry,' Lugal said, 'If they are robbing graves, they are working less than we are and living better.' Nilakantha shook his head.

Both Lugal and Hutantat knew what Nilakantha was thinking—would the Aryas who confront the karma of last life, soil their karma for the next life, by commiting the evil of robbing a grave?

They did not want to intrude on Nilakantha's anguish. Yet they were both thinking—each man has his destiny and neither tears nor hope can wipe it away!

There was silence in Nilakantha's heart. Laughter did not come to him as easily as before. Around him, he saw the graveyard of his hopes—his own and of the Aryas who relied on him. How comforting it would be to adopt the philosophy of Hutantat, that our hopes and dreams, our effort and will, matter not; and all is ruled by destiny.

'Let us live like humans even if we must die as beasts.'

—(From 'The King that once commanded the catacomb of cut-throats')

'If God is what I believe Him to be, I am sure He is annoyed with prayers when some duty remains neglected.'

—(Hermit-King Lugal—around 5005 BC)

'Karma is above prayer and piety.'

—(Nilakantha, Arya Leader in Egypt—around 5005 BC)

'It all depends, as before,
On the roll of dice—no more;
Not on the thrower's will or tears
Not our prayers, hopes or fears.
But the unthinking dice unfolds
All that creation's future holds.'

—(From 'Songs of Hutantat', after 5005 BC)

(Let us live, Lesbia, mine, upon it we must die, as boasts

—(From: *The King that once commanded the catacomb of cut-throats*)

If God is what I believe Him to be, I am sure He is annoyed with priests when some duty remains neglected.

—(Hermit-King of Egypt—around 5005 BC)

Karma is slow prayer and piety

—(Nilkantha, Arya Leader in Egypt—around 5005 BC)

It all depends, as before,
On the roll of dice—no more,
Not on the thrower's will or least
Not our prayers, hopes or fears
But the unthinking dice unfolds
All that creation's future holds.

—(From: *Songs of Nilakshi*, after 5005 BC)

Egypt and the Kingdom of Ajitab

5005 BC

Ajitab and his thirty-six Aryas had fled from the hills with the grave-robbers, when the soldiers came to hunt for slaves.

After many adventures, they moved into another Egyptian kingdom. They were caught, enslaved and made to work on stone-excavation. Only four Aryas and sixteen grave-robbers remained to work with Ajitab after two years of dehumanizing brutality. The rest died, collapsing where they worked.

Ajitab organized a mass escape. Twelve guards and eighty slaves died, but Ajitab escaped with four Aryas, thirteen grave-robbers and 460 other slaves. On the way, they attacked numerous places where many slaves worked. Minor skirmishes were many and their initial success, spectacular. Their ranks swelled but their days seemed numbered as soldiers throughout the kingdom were collecting for an all out assault on them.

There was a near-revolt of slaves against Ajitab. He wanted to press on, to be ahead of the soldiers hunting them. But many slaves felt invulnerable with their numbers and wanted to stay back to loot, steal and fight.

Ajitab allowed defections, while he pressed on. Perhaps that saved him and his group, as battles raged against the slaves who stayed back. He reached the hills from where they had originally fled. But the hills were no longer safe.

By devious paths, in the pitch dark of night, he reached the catacombs with 110 slaves including four Aryas and eleven grave-robbers.

The catacombs were safe but only for thieves, robbers and cut-throats. There were many hiding places, trenches and tunnels. For soldiers, it was a deadly place, not only because of the cut-throats there but also because they had a greater horror of contagion, as many lepers lived there.

Early on, Ajitab became involved in a deadly tussle with Dahzur, the chief of the catacombs. Dahzur had strangled the previous chief. He had then turned his ferocity against the lepers and had them burnt alive; thereafter, he cleansed the catacombs of many old robbers who in their youth had stolen much from outside but were now dependent on charity; finally, he began a reign of terror against many whose personal loyalty he suspected. At the end, Dahzur's command was absolute. He demanded a share of loot from everyone in the catacombs and enforced the demand ruthlessly. Those who objected, somehow disappeared mysteriously. He never ventured out but gave close attention to the teams which left the catacombs to loot. His planning was faultless but some teams were caught. He shed no tears, as there were many who brought in a great deal.

Dahzur had welcomed Ajitab's group. He recognized the grave-robbers with Ajitab and was pleased at the addition to his strength.

Soon after, a team was to be sent out to loot. One team-member was sick. Dahzur asked an Arya to go instead. The Arya declined. Dahzur insisted, but in good humour, ready to be gracious to a new-comer who was unaware of his power. But Ajitab intervened, 'Enough! Did you not hear him say that he shall not go!'

Dahzur exploded within. He saw it as a challenge and decided that this was as good a time as any to set an example; he motioned to three henchmen. They moved to Ajitab, one with a dagger unsheathed.

With the instinct of a hunted slave, sharpened by years of danger and adversity, Ajitab did not wait for the three to reach him. He lunged at Dahzur's throat. The more powerful Dahzur fell at this unexpected, ferocious attack and Ajitab fell over him with a vicious grip on his throat. The man with the dagger misjudged his blow and stabbed Ajitab in a fleshy part; but the searing pain only tightened Ajitab's grip over Dahzur's throat. He heard a gurgle. Suddenly, with a jerk, he got up, and the three who were trying to pull him away, fell off-balance. He started hitting out, unseeing and madly.

In a flash, many from his own group rose to join the fight. But no one attacked Ajitab. Someone said quietly, 'Dahzur is dead.'

Ajitab nodded as though he knew. He walked away slowly, bleeding but unsupported. In his shelter, four Aryas washed and bandaged his wound. Then he half-fainted.

Later, the three who sought to attack him were brought, ready to be killed. But Ajitab said, 'Let them go. They were under orders.'

From that day, though in slow stages, they began treating Ajitab as the chief. He demanded that the lepers who entered should not be killed. Separate areas were reserved for them. Nor were the old and infirm to be eliminated. Ajitab did not demand a share; but a share was still payable, in trust for lepers, the old and infirm. The trash, dirt and garbage in the catacombs was burnt; medicine and herbal remedies were stocked. He asked them to locate and smuggle into the catacombs a slave who knew the use of these remedies.

He wanted more trenches and tunnels to hide and fight from, if ever there was an attack; a reservoir to store water; more shelters, amenities: 'Let us live like humans even if we must die as beasts.'

Ajitab even put the oldest to light work. He used them also to go well-dressed, trailing after raiding parties, so that if the raiders were arrested, he would know where they had been taken.

Twice, he arranged their rescue, due to this ploy.

His men had located two slaves with physicians' knowledge in a group of forty-eight. Ajitab himself led the attack and, as a result, the entire slave-group was freed and smuggled into the catacombs.

But Ajitab was astounded that these freed men were being treated as slaves in the catacombs. He tried to put a stop to it. He failed. Quickly, he learnt a bitter lesson which Dahzur knew but he did not— that the way to reach the hearts of these ruthless cut-throats in catacombs was not always through gentleness.

With the ferocity of a convert and with a savagery that Dahzur would have envied, he enforced his will and after the blood-bath, declared, 'Anyone who enslaves another shall be chained and left outside the catacombs as a soldier's reward.'

No one thereafter challenged Ajitab. He was the King of the Catacombs and his wish was law in this kingdom of cut-throats, murderers and thieves.

There was much that remained unsaid between Ajitab and the four Aryas with him. But each knew the anguish of the other! They thought of those innocent times, as if it were centuries ago, when they left home, singing—'Noble Arya onward, on...'—and now they lived to loot, kill and crush, while every savage dagger, unseen, remained aimed at their hearts! God! where have you guided our footsteps? And why? Is it your karma or ours?

Suddenly, astounding news filtered to the catacombs—that about a 100 miles away, the Aryas were building a temple!

A hundred miles! What could 100 miles matter to men who had traversed thousands? Yet they paused. That would be a route with danger at every twist and turn. But an old robber volunteered to carry Ajitab's message to the temple-site—and all ex-slaves were ready too. It was decided that the old man would go with six ex-slaves carrying a coffin, as if it were being carried for burial. Nobody would attack a coffin, nor a grave, for the first twenty-seven days. Even so, the ex-slaves would go visibly armed, so that no one was tempted to attack.

At the last moment, one of the four Aryas insisted on going with them.

'Only four of us are left,' Ajitab pleaded. But the Arya rejoined, 'Would it matter if none were left!'

Ajitab understood the anguish, but insisted, 'I don't know what our Aryas are doing there. Maybe they are captives. If they are, we must organize an attack from the catacombs to free them. Please!'

'No, let me die; let me be a slave; but I cannot live here... in this..., this kingdom of yours....' Suddenly tears came to his eyes, 'Forgive me, brother Ajitab, but let me go.... Last night I swore I would not remain here, neither to kill, nor hurt anyone.... If I must remain here, you will grieve over my dead body sooner....'

'Go with God,' Ajitab said.

More than the anguish in Ajitab's heart was the revolt in his soul— 'God, there is evil in me but I know not who needs more forgiveness —you or me!'

Ajitab embraced the Arya with tears as he left. The Arya went as the father of the child in the coffin carried by the six slaves. The old robber accompanied the group as the grandfather.

No one felt tempted to attack them all along the route; but as they neared the temple-site, a soldier suspected them. He had seen such a ploy by thieves before. He called other soldiers and demanded they put the coffin down for inspection.

The Arya knew his moment had come; he was sorry that the others too would die with him. He claimed sole responsibility, as none of the others knew anything. A soldier shoved him aside but the officer looked hard and wondered—he looks different, speaks with an accent, certainly not a local! 'Are you Arya?' the officer asked and he replied, 'Yes, yes, I am Arya!' Still suspicious, the officer ordered, 'Sing the Arya song!' Startled, he sang—'Noble Arya...onward...on.'

'Enough, stop! Now give me some Arya names,' the officer commanded.

He recited the names—'Nilakantha, Lugal, Himatap....'

'What about Hutantat?' the officer asked. The Arya said nothing, not sure if it was a trap or not, for he knew no Hutantat. But the officer was already convinced that he had an Arya before him. Still, he demanded to know what was in the coffin. The old man simply pointed to the Arya, then to the sky and the temple-site. He pretended to be dumb so that he told no lies. The officer understood nothing but he remembered the King's warning of the highest penalty for those that harmed the Aryas of the temple-site. He asked the Arya's name and at his order, a soldier rushed to the temple-site.

Four hours they waited, guarded but unharmed. And then Nilakantha, Lugal and many others arrived.

None of the Aryas at the temple-site slept that night.

At dawn Hutantat, Nilakantha and some others left with the reunited Arya and the old robber. On the way, not only the Arya but the old man thanked the officer and soldiers so volubly that they wondered how it was that the old man who was totally dumb the day before, could now speak. But the old man simply pointed to Hutantat for the miracle. Everyone knew Hutantat's power of prophecy. But now some would regard him as man of miracles, too.

They all waited at a distance from the catacombs and through devious paths, the old robber went in and brought out Ajitab and the three Aryas.

Joyously, they travelled together to the temple-site. Nilakantha had no words, no songs—his heart too full with the wonder of Ajitab and four others restored to them. Tears, he often had, for the many that they had lost, but this was not the moment for those tears.

Yet Nilakantha's joy was short-lived. Ajitab had passed only two nights at the temple-site when he flared up in a violent temper. 'You make slaves work for you here!'

Nilakantha explained. It only led to Ajitab's contempt. Nilakantha did not even retort that Ajitab stole, lied, even killed to save himself.

In his heart, Nilakantha realized that to hold an innocent in captivity was a sin, more heinous than any of Ajitab's sins in self-defence. He knew also that not all Ajitab's offences were to protect himself. But it did not occur to Nilakantha—then or ever—to list Ajitab's sins and exonerate himself—'each is answerable for his sin, and not in relation to the sins of another.'

Instead, Nilakantha pleaded and Ajitab asked, 'Is this why you led us here?'

Nilakantha pleaded, to no avail. Ajitab was clear. 'So long as I am here, I shall try to free these slaves.'

'We are under oath to Sage Hutantat to complete the temple,' Nilakantha said.

'I am under no such oath,' Ajitab said.

'The oath binds us all.'

'Not me.'

Nilakantha was silent. He knew a little of Ajitab's story. Ajitab's father and mother had been held as slaves in Bharat Varsha, although slavery had been declared unlawful. Some time after his father's death, when Ajitab was six years old, his mother was molested by the slave-owner. His mother shrieked. Ajitab was stricken with fear. His three-year-old sister ran to her mother. The slave-owner picked up the girl and threw her forcefully against a rock, smashing her head. In panic, the child Ajitab ran, and while running, he saw stones, and the thought even flashed through his mind that he should hurl them at his sister's killer and mother's ravisher. But he was much too frightened and kept running. Meanwhile, the slave-owner had calmed his passion on the unconscious mother. When she gained consciousness, she saw her daughter's dead body; her son was missing; and in her daze, she imagined that he too was dead. She jumped into the well. Ajitab came back and saw his sister and mother being cremated. He ran away again.

Since then Ajitab had died a hundred deaths. In every nightmare, he saw stones that lay unpicked and unhurled at the slave-owner and sometimes he saw fragments of his sister's smashed head, though more often, he would see flames from the cremation of his sister and mother—flames that leapt and laughed to mock him.

A sadhu sheltered him. From the sadhu, he learnt yoga, but after a while he lost interest in it. He wanted to learn to fight, aim an arrow, throw a dagger, wield a sword. 'Why?' asked the sadhu.

'Because I am a coward,' Ajitab said. The sadhu knew he was not a coward but simply a child and did not want him to grow up thinking he was a coward. So the sadhu taught him as much as he could and then left him in charge of an old pupil who trained athletes, wrestlers and fighters.

At sixteen, Ajitab went to his old village to kill the slave-owner. But the slave-owner was dead, having been stung by a deadly scorpion.

He returned to the sadhu who asked him, 'You did not wish to kill the slave-owner's children?'

'No,' he said. 'Only cowards kill children.' The sadhu embraced him.

Since then, Ajitab's life had been purposeless. He went back as assistant to his teacher to train others to fight. When the Aryas left the land, he joined them, hoping for a better land, elsewhere.

But even while Ajitab was being brutalized as a slave in Egypt's adjoining kingdom, he decided what he would devote his life to. A vague whisper of that role stirred in his heart when the forty-eight slaves were smuggled into the catacombs and his men tried to use them as slaves. He was merciless with those who did not listen to him to leave the slaves alone. Soon, however, his mind shifted to concerns of self-survival and protecting his mates in the catacombs.

But now, as he saw the masses of slaves at the temple-site, he knew what his purpose in life was to be—to free slaves, anywhere and everywhere.

Nilakantha and Ajitab sat facing each other, without speaking. In those silent moments, each understood more of the solitary anguish of the other. Both knew that their faith in finding the land of pure had dwindled and this long journey had been in vain.

Yet, both thought of how selfish they had been in their desire to seek the land of spirit for themselves, where they could live untrammelled by sorrows, tears and bloodshed, unmindful of the brutal tyranny that others faced.

Nilakantha took Ajitab's hand and pleaded, 'Our hearts are the same, our goals no different: freedom of these slaves and safety of our people. That is why we have to complete the temple.'

Ajitab's fury was spent, 'Don't worry, I shall not interfere.'

But Nilakantha's glow of ecstasy died, as Ajitab continued, 'By your will, I shall leave as an Arya.' It sounded cruel because of the play on the word 'Arya' which had always meant exile and was now beginning to acquire a different connotation and mean a person who acts with nobility.

Clearly, he implied, that it was Nilakantha's tolerance of slavery at the temple that was forcing him to go out as an exile.

'I would rather run a sword through myself than dream of exiling you,' Nilakantha said.

Ajitab apologized. He realized it was his inner frustration that had made him blame the gracious Nilakantha. He added, 'No, I leave by my will. You have to look after your temple and slaves here. I shall look for slaves elsewhere.'

Perhaps only Hutantat understood Ajitab's resolve and said, 'Each man comes to his decision, himself. Yet a man who lives in the desert must know the source of water; a man in the high mountains must learn to protect himself against falling rocks; a man in the river must know how to avoid crocodiles.'

Nobody understood. But he explained, 'Your heart tells you to free slaves. So be it. But your head must come to terms with that decision. What will you do when the slaves are free? Leave them to be hunted again! Where will they run and hide? In your catacombs! Today, the soldiers ignore the catacombs. But when you shelter numerous slaves there, will the King stay his hand? Each there will die in unspeakable horror. You will die happy, perhaps in the vain belief that you died to fulfil a mission—but you are the one to doom your own mission from the very start.'

Ajitab glared, while Hutantat continued, 'And what karma will you teach the slaves while they hide in the catacombs—to steal, loot, kill! Apart from arts of violence, is there any art that you yourself know? So, you will simply raise legions of robbers and murderers out of slaves, so that they rob others of life and liberty, before they too vanish into nothingness! Is that why you left your land, Arya?'

Pitilessly, Hutantat continued, 'I suppose you will also unfurl the Arya flag over your thieving, murdering slaves, so that the Arya name and mission is always dipped in dishonour in the ithihasa of this country, if not in yours and everywhere else!'

Ajitab shook his head but Hutantat added, 'And finally, your achievement will be that the Aryas here too shall be wiped out for the dishonour of associating with you—you! who must be known as a great freedom fighter, ready to lay down his life for his cause, regardless of the doom of slaves and eternal dishonour to Aryas!'

'You know that is not my purpose,' Ajitab said.

'No, it is only the inevitable consequence of what is in your immature mind.'

'And you think I should happily live here like Nilakantha?'

'No, each man must heed the call in his heart. It is beyond you, even to understand the extent of Nilakantha's silent, living sacrifice. One day when you and Aryas like you understand, you will turn to him with tenderness and gratitude.'

'I am ready to touch Nilakantha's feet now,' Ajitab joked.

'It will be an empty gesture, like the glorious death you foresee for yourself. But remember, dying is easy. It is life that presents difficult choices and sometimes a man must condemn himself to live, when there are promises to keep and when duty inescapable beckons. What kind of a dream is it, that not only the dreamer must die, but along with him the dream itself be cursed and dishonoured by all!'

'Sage, I understand not a word of what you say.'

'I feared as much. Nilakantha understands; Lugal understands; many will. But certainly, it is beyond you. To understand it, you need courage in your heart and not hotheaded rashness.'

Nilakantha feared that Ajitab would explode. He did not. He was humble and contrite and said, 'You are right, Sage. All I hear is the voice in my heart that tells me what I should go after. That voice re-echoes within me and I know I do not hear it in vain. I shall not shut it out. But for the rest you are right. I do not know how I should respond to its call. Perhaps, your words alone shall show me the way.'

Later, quietly, Hutantat clarified to Ajitab, 'First, you will have to leave here as a renegade Arya, unloved and despised by the Aryas here. Nor must you ever call yourself an Arya. Second, the catacombs must not shelter slaves as that will invite massive attacks by the King's forces. Third, there are larger areas, barren and deserted, where only lizards live, which are reachable through the mountains, paths difficult for soldiers to cross; and slaves may live there while you teach them the only art you know. Fourth, as a thief never robs from one house only, it will be folly to restrict your activity to this kingdom alone, unless you want undivided attention from the King here. You have to diversify.'

'But other kingdoms are faraway!' Ajitab said.

'For a man who has travelled this far, you are really very modest! And where do you think your hide-outs will be—next to the catacombs? No, you will have to go much further.'

'But Sage, how are slaves to live in those barren areas?'

'I am glad you asked. Perhaps a glimmer of understanding is coming into your mind—that it is easy to die but difficult to live. Yes, slaves must learn to make those areas fertile. You too must learn, in order to teach!'

'But that will take time!' Ajitab replied.

'What else does life have except time! From birth to death, there is only time. A fool fritters it away, the wise guard it.'

For days Ajitab remained at the temple-site. Hutantat took him to his own villages that had once been barren but now were lush and green, with freed slaves working under his protection.

'I have a few freed slaves who have the same dream as you,' Hutantat said. 'If they are ungrateful and run away from here to join you, there is nothing I can do.'

Hutantat and Ajitab then spoke of faraway barren areas, the way to reach them, the method to tap water, the route to neighbouring kingdoms and the location of possible hide-outs everywhere.

Finally, Hutantat advised, 'See my hut there! It has a great deal a thief can want. When you are ready, ransack the hut and take everything away.'

'Steal from you?' Ajitab asked, shocked.

'Why not! What else will a renegade do! You will "steal" also from the Aryas at the temple-site! They must distance themselves from you.'

'So I appear as a dishonourable thief and a common scoundrel, condemned and scorned by all those I love!'

'It is your choice, remember? The only question is: do you fight for yourself and your name alone or for your dream?'

Irrelevantly, Ajitab said, 'My little sister died with her head smashed; my mother threw herself in a well.'

'I know,' Hutantat said, for Nilakantha had told him.

'They died in vain and I shall die in dishonour.'

'Your sister and your mother did not die in vain. Their death inspires you and your cause. You shall not die in dishonour. You shall die for a cause that is larger than your life, far above the empty pretence of honour and virtue; and you shall die only in your body; for the spirit remains alive, inspiring others to reach out for the day that is to come.'

'Am I doing the right thing, Sage?'

'That judgement must be yours. All I know is that whether you live or die, I shall pray for you, day and night, far more than I pray for myself and my soul.'

Hutantat and Ajitab were together often after that. Escorted by soldiers and Hutantat's freed slaves, they travelled to far off lands. Ostensibly, the purpose was to look for materials for the king's temple. But the real purpose was that Ajitab may see areas, routes, hide-outs and possible sanctuaries. Surreptitiously, a few freed slaves left Hutantat's lands; and Hutantat ostensibly made anxious inquiries everywhere but shrugged his shoulders—'They had a right to leave. But to depart without a word of farewell!' Many sympathized, 'What ingratitude!' But some said, 'This is the result of giving freedom to the undeserving!'

For some time, Ajitab's plans were known only to Hutantat, Lugal, Nilakantha and the Aryas who were with him in the catacombs. Later, of course, Larali came to know too.

Larali was the one who had once been nominated 'virgin-in-waiting' by a priest in Sumeria but was rescued. Since then, she had moved with the Aryas to Hermit-King Lugal's domain in Assyria and thence to Egypt.

It was when the Aryas rested at the grave-robber's settlement, on the outskirts of Egypt, that Ajitab and Larali spoke words of love to each other. Both felt in their hearts that at their next meeting they would speak of an abiding relationship.

Larali and Ajitab were to be in the first batch to move out from the grave-robber's settlement. At the last minute, Nilakantha asked Ajitab to wait. Meanwhile, Larali moved with the first batch. They were certain that soon Nilakantha and Ajitab would race to join them. Nilakantha always led the very first batch—and in any case, the second, third and even the last batch were to follow closely.

But Nilakantha had bigger concerns on his mind. The Arya expected to remain with thirty-five sick and injured had been showing off, jumping from hill to hill; unfortunately, he lost his footing and could not walk or ride for a month. Nilakantha could not leave an injured man to look after the sick. He told Ajitab, 'This high jumper was to look after thirty-five. Now you look after thirty-six.'

Larali's batch went ahead. Instead of Nilakantha, someone was singing, 'Onward, Arya, onward on....' But Larali was looking not onward but backward to catch a glimpse of Ajitab following her.

Even when they were entering Egypt, Larali had not lost her anchor of faith. Despite stories told by the grave-robbers of the terror in this kingdom, a hope sprang up among most Aryas that the auspicious land of their quest was not too far. It was actually one Arya's faith that spread to many. From the grave-robbers he had learnt that here, the river (later, named as Nile) flowed from south to north and finally drowned in the great water. This learned Arya knew that in Bharat Varsha all rivers flowed from north to south into the sea. If a river here flowed backwards, surely this was the land of hope—he thought. Nobody knew why this man cried out that the land of glory was soon to come but his cry of faith touched them. After all, it was faith that had made them leave their homeland and their hurt over their loss of faith was very deep. Many took up his cry.

How could Larali then fear that Ajitab was lost! Even at the temple-site, her hope remained alive. But later, the chilling news that only skeletons were found at the settlement and that there was no trace of Ajitab and the thirty-six others came; and Larali who was once a 'virgin-in-waiting' said to herself, 'Always, it is my destiny to "wait." '

After which many asked for her hand in marriage but she declined and to herself said, 'I wait.'

Months multiplied, and then suddenly, unexpectedly, came a lone Arya from the catacombs, bringing the joyous tidings that Ajitab and three others were alive and safe. Yet, she feared to ask him the question that wrenched her heart. Instead, she asked, 'How is your leg?' for he was the one whose leg was injured in the bravado of leaping from hill to hill, forcing Ajitab to stay back at the settlement, to look after the sick. 'My leg is fine, so also is he who looked after me and my leg—and he loves you, always, every moment, waking, dreaming, sleeping!'

What a strange way to speak of God, thought some, for none knew of the bond between her and Ajitab and yet this Arya—for long a co-slave with Ajitab—certainly knew. They smiled and Larali said to herself—'At last, my waiting is done.'

Not so. When Ajitab came, he looked into Larali's eyes, held her hand, but the question he was to ask, to bind them forever, remained unasked. Later, Ajitab even avoided her. Is it possible for a man to contemplate marriage while he charts such a perilous path for himself! Is there hope of his survival as he tilts against kingdoms to free their slaves? He was ready to die, certain that his death would not be in vain; that someone, somewhere, would pick up the fallen torch to continue the struggle. But marriage! Out of the question.

Once only did Ajitab pour his heart out to her, to speak not of love but of what lay ahead of him and she was silent.

Thereafter, he would be away for weeks with Hutantat. When he came, he would be surrounded by people; but she saw only him, and in a voice that did not falter, said, 'There was one question I forgot to ask you that day. Do you or do you not love me?' Quietly, he too, unmindful of the others, said 'Yes. Always.'

Her voice rose, 'Brother Nilakantha, I shall marry Ajitab. Please perform the ceremony.' They had no regular priest. The task to perform marriage and other rites fell on Nilakantha.

But Nilakantha was taken aback and said, 'But Ajitab has not spoken.' The husband-to-be always had to be the first to declare his desire to marry and, at the same time, take the five-fold marriage-vow promising his wife, 'piety, permanence, pleasure, property and progeny.'

But Larali replied to Nilakantha, 'My husband-to-be is simply too tongue-tied, too timid, too afraid to speak.'

Timid and afraid! Ajitab! Impossible. But Ajitab spoke now, 'Yes, Brother Nilakantha, please, I wish to marry Larali now....'

Nilakantha pleaded, 'Wait....' But he chose the wrong word; and Larali stormed, 'Wait! I have waited enough! And all because of you!'

Poor Nilakantha! He knew nothing of Larali's longings when he had asked Ajitab stay back at the settlement but then, everyone always blamed him—and he did not know why, and everyone also loved him—and again he did not know why.

But now he was on sure ground and said firmly, 'I never perform a marriage without taking a bath first.' Even Larali laughed, 'That much I shall wait.' And Ajitab said, 'Then hurry, Brother!'

Hutantat put his arm around Larali and drew her aside to ask, 'Daughter, do you know what Ajitab is to do and why and where?' And she answered, 'I know what and why. But as to where, surely, I shall soon know as I shall always be with him.'

Gravely, Hutantat said, 'Yet it may be a place of no return.'

In her heart she had no fear of the future. She was only afraid of the Sage who may possibly influence Ajitab, even now, not to marry, for the sake of the task he was to undertake.

But she spoke the right words when she said, 'I have no mother, no father. Bless me Sage and give me away as the bride.'

He held her to his bosom, 'So be it, child, if that is your destiny. My blessing you have. May your union be fruitful. But then accept, in good grace, destiny's wounds and triumphs.'

Her reply, she formed in her heart, but did not voice, 'I make my own destiny to meet my destiny.'

They were married

Ajitab and Larali shared only a few nights of love. For days and weeks, he would be away with Hutantat or sometimes on his own. Many said, 'He was a secret lover; and now a secret husband.' Some felt sorry for Larali. What had she done to deserve such neglect from her husband?

Many even saw a more terrible aspect of Ajitab—for anxiously, he was trying to prepare himself for the role of the renegade who deserts the Arya. He openly quarrelled with Hutantat, Lugal and Nilakantha and was never respectful. Some, including the commander, soldiers and slaves, wondered: 'Why do they tolerate him?' But then Ajitab was held out as a master in locating and selecting the right building-materials for the temple 'and Hutantat and the Aryas will go to any lengths, in the King's cause, to build the best temple.'

Meanwhile Ajitab quietly visited the catacombs. Of the forty-eight freed slaves there, many left for a distant area to work on the land. Freed slaves from Hutantat's land were already there with the necessary implements.

Four months after his marriage, Ajitab's arrangements to move were nearly complete. 'A few days more and we leave,' he told Larali.

'You must go alone,' she replied. 'I can wait. Your child cannot.' He was delighted that he was to be a father. But he teased her too, 'You said you would be careful.'

She laughed, 'Destiny! After all, Sage Hutantat blessed our union, wishing it to be fruitful.'

Anxiously, he asked, 'Do you want me to delay my departure?'

'No,' she insisted. 'Your task remains. Let no one accuse my unborn child of delaying your purpose.'

'Our unborn child,' he corrected her pleasantly.

'Yet I must speak for him, if you will not.'

Suddenly, some five months after his marriage, Ajitab disappeared. Ajitab was to leave with the three Aryas who were with him in the catacombs. It never occurred to him that the fourth Arya who left the catacombs at the last minute would wish to join. Yet the night before Ajitab was to leave, he went to the fourth Arya, simply to say farewell.

They had left Bharat Varsha together; they were the best of friends and they had slaved side by side and suffered together in the adjoining kingdom and seen many comrades die.

'Perhaps we shall meet again, perhaps not; but think well of me,' Ajitab said.

'I shall think well of you, whatever happens; whatever you do!' Arya said. 'But you are right to desert me; I deserted you once before.'

'You did not desert me. I deserted myself then.'

'And now, you don't want me with you! I deserve it.'

He went with them.

Every Arya at the temple-site felt desolate at Ajitab's desertion. They had seen him in moments of joy, interrupted by quarrels with

Hutantat, Lugal and Nilakantha. But how could they know that he was acting the part of one who was to desert! Their shock came when they learnt that he had even robbed a hut containing Hutantat's valuables.

The King, who heard it from his gleeful Chief-priest, sympathized with Hutantat and learnt that the fugitive Arya had robbed his Arya brethren too. 'I thought all these Aryas were honourable,' said the King.

'The best fruit-tree can be attacked by worms,' Hutantat said.

'True. If out of my nine sister-wives two are rotten, surely these many Aryas are entitled to have a few scoundrels.'

'Well said King. You are truly profound,' Hutantat responded.

Pleased, the King added, 'But I shall ask everyone to hunt for the renegade so that he meet his fate.'

'No, King. Your words of wisdom were spoken when you said that anyone harming an Arya will receive the highest penalty. So let him alone. If by chance he is seen, he should be allowed to go his way.'

'But he may steal elsewhere!' the King objected.

'Yes, but if he is caught he must be brought to the Aryas unharmed. He has hurt them terribly. They must be the ones to punish him. How grateful they will be and how mightily they will work for you!'

'You speak wisely, Sage Hutantat,' said the King.

'When I am in the presence of my King who is the fount of wisdom, what else can flow from my lips!'

The King was delighted.

No one saw it as cause and effect—for the events were separated by time and distance, but four months after Ajitab left the temple-site, attacks started on various posts to free large numbers of slaves.

Meanwhile, work continued on the temple-complex. The entire surface of the hill and even its sides were flattened and smoothed, as though it was all a man-made monument. Bricks to cover the top of the hill were being baked and glazed. The sides were not to be covered with bricks, as it was intended to hide their view by steps running all along the four sides, so that the hill itself appeared a 'stepped square'. Meanwhile there were make-shift ladders to go up the 'squared' hilltop. Surrounding the hill, below, was to be an ornamental garden; and already areas had been cleared, a stream diverted and trees planted, with spaces earmarked for housing soldiers and slaves in artificial valleys and wide trenches, dug up for that purpose; and the aim was that from a distance, not even the hut-roofs should be seen, and the entire area should present an aesthetic appearance.

On the hill, the outer structure of the palace was ready and two out of the twenty-five obelisks had been erected.

Lugal was viewed as the creator of the temple-complex because he had originally conceived of the idea. But it was Himatap who was everywhere, supervising the digging, erecting, clearing and experimenting. Often, Himatap would run to Lugal for ideas, advice, calculations and even help and inspiration. But then he would improve on those ideas and try to erect something far more ambitious than that which Lugal had conceived. Sometimes he would have a construction demolished, only to rebuild it differently, because a better idea had come to him.

Lugal would try to stop him—'Brother Himatap, we build all this not for the glory of God but to satisfy the vanity of a tyrant who cannot distinguish between what is perfect and what is flawed. Build well but do not seek perfection. The sooner we finish, the sooner we may be free.'

Himatap would agree for the moment, but in the joy of building would forget all else. Everything was erased from his mind except the perfection of what he built. Nothing else mattered.

At last, Lugal intervened, 'We will be judged not by your grand conception but simply by what we promised the King. Concentrate on that and for the rest, let others worry.'

Lugal insisted that the obelisks should be erected at the end. He was the one who had boasted to the King of his ability to erect obelisks whose tips would attract the golden glow of the rising and setting sun at different times. The conception was clearly in his mind, as though he could touch the tip of an unbuilt obelisk and see the sun's glow on his fingers. But a theoretical conception and actual construction were not the same; and Lugal remembered the first Ziggurat he had erected in Sumer—thoughtfully conceived and elegantly built—and yet it fell in the first rainstorm.

It was with this fear that Lugal had urged that the obelisks be erected last, and hopefully, the King on seeing the grandeur of the other structures, would forget about the obelisks. But Hutantat told him, 'The King never forgets a pledge made to him.'

Himatap was delighted to be unleashed on erecting the obelisks. The idea that Lugal's conception might not work did not even occur to him. His mind-set simply was to work on it and if it failed, he would re-calculate and begin anew. Time and effort meant nothing to him.

But fortune smiled on them. Lugal's calculations, over which Hutantat and Himatap had also worked tirelessly, were flawless. When the first obelisk was ready, the sun's glow shone on its top pyramidal tip, every day at the same time. They did not have to look at the obelisk. Looking simply at the sky, with the obelisk behind, Himatap would raise his hand to signal when the sun's glow would hit the obelisk—and it was indeed so!

A miracle—many said; Lugal and Hutantat agreed that Himatap was the miracle-maker. They said—the human mind can conceive anything but to bring that conception alive requires genius.

Many poets have said much about Himatap's ancestry and his life and times in Eygpt. To summarize: Himatap's grandfather was one of the 140 explorers who, in Karkarta Bharat's time, went across the trans-Himalayas to find the source of Sindhu river. He was one of the few who survived, but he lost his eyesight from the sun's reflection 'leaping back from ice in the mountains.' The grandfather never returned to Sapta Sindhu but remained in Tibet and married a local Tibetan girl. His only daughter also married a local Tibetan. Their son was named Himatap in loving memory of his grandfather (Himatap meant the heat of snow; hima — snow; tap or tapas — heat).

Later, even after most of the Aryas left Egypt to return to Bharat Varsha, Himatap remained in Egypt. He married a girl from Egypt. A hundred girls from Egypt wanted to marry him, as he had announced that his wife did not have to die and be buried on his death for as he declared, who would then pray for him, when he was no more!

To a Tibetan it was unthinkable that he should die with none to pray for him. And the belief was that it was not just a person's karma and prayers that counted but also the prayers of others on his behalf.

To the men from Egypt who argued against his stand, he even joked that his wife could not be buried with him, as he, like all Hindus, would be cremated. But still they asked, 'Why then can the wife not be cremated with the husband?'

Himatap was revolted for he could not conceive of a more heinous sin and asked, 'Would not such a sin damage my soul and the souls of all my children and grandchildren?' And here the poet intervenes to add, 'A Hindu he was, yet he also had the Tibetan belief that our sins jeopardize the souls of our children—but then the echo of that ancient thought lies in many Hindu hearts too.'

In disgust, the Egyptian men asked Himatap, 'You will then leave your wife to be claimed by any man?' But he said, 'God will claim her in His own time.'

But then Himatap also rejected the marriage proposals of hundreds of Egyptian girls. As a Hindu, he said he would be married only to one wife, lifelong, and he had already selected his loving bride.

The fact is that Himatap's wife could neither be buried nor cremated with him. She died after sixteen years of marriage after having given birth to four children and he outlived her by years. He did not remarry.

It has been said that Himatap was the direct ancestor of Imhotep who in the reign of the Egyptian King Djoser (Zoser), around 2500 BC, was a great thinker, physician and philosopher, as also the greatest of all the architects of Egypt. Imhotep built for King Djoser the first great limestone step-pyramid and exquisite monuments around it—and a poet says 'so noble was the conception and so wonderful its execution, that it would always bear testimony to the greatness of King Djoser and his master-builder, Imhotep, of an honoured ancestry that began with the blind who found or discovered the auspicious, far off river-source in the land of Bharat and whose grandson built the first great sun-obelisk in this land.'

But others point out that apart from many such clues, there is no clear, direct link to tie up Imhotep's ancestry with Himatap. Reference to the 'blind' may not be to the blind grandfather of Himatap but could be to another blind man who located another river-source. Again, the 'auspicious' river-source cannot be said to refer to Sindhu exclusively, as all rivers were considered auspicious. Nor would 'far off river-source' necessarily mean Sindhu, as the fact is that every river-source is far off; and even the river Nile stretches 4,000 miles from its remote head-stream before merging with the Mediterranean. Similarly, it is just possible that the reference to 'sun-obelisk' may not be to the one built by Himatap, but by someone else later.

Thus the question of a link-up between Himatap and Imhotep must lie in the lap of future researchers.

The King was delighted with the obelisk that captured the sun's glow. So visibly impressed was he that Hutantat promptly asked for more villages and more slaves to be freed.

'Villages, I shall give,' the King said, 'but for slaves, wait until all the obelisks are ready. I have difficulties at the moment.'

'How can you, King of all, have difficulties!' Hutantat asked.

But the King spoke of mysterious attacks on slave-posts. 'But soon they will be found, and then you will have what you seek.'

Attacks on the slave-posts continued. They all seemed so senseless. There was no effort to steal anything at those posts—only to free the slaves. And how long could a run-away slave hide—and where? Detection was unavoidable, as each slave was branded on the left and right upper-arms. A slave would have to cut off both his arms in order to plead that he never was a slave. Punishment for escape was horrible and continuing. No wonder, the slave-guards were so careless and lax.

But attacks came on the slave-posts in a series and then suddenly stopped; but only to start and stop in the next kingdom; then to begin and end in another; and thus the round continued and restarted.

To begin with, it mattered little to the kings. The loss of slaves simply meant that they had to pick up others to fill their place. With the exception of those who held priestly or official titles from the King, everyone was regarded as a slave—irrespective of whether or not they were branded on their upper-arms. The only difference was that the branded slave was kept for certain work at a particular place under the direct supervision of soldiers, with no freedom of movement; while all others—peasants and artisans—had limited freedom, though most of what they produced was for the King. It was certainly the unquestioned privilege of the King to have any of those peasants and artisans taken to be branded as slaves; and sometimes this was done—though not too often as the King realized that the kingdom loses by sending out artisans and peasants as branded slaves. Yet, now, with the frequent attacks to free branded slaves, peasants and artisans were being branded.

No wonder, when the King was dazzled by the second obelisk too, Hutantat asked not for slaves, but a title for all the Aryas so that they were immune from slavery, by any whim of the King's priests and others.

As it is, the King had given the title of 'King's Architect' to Lugal at their very first meeting. He now asked, 'What title do you seek for them?' Hutantat suggested, 'Soldiers of the King's Architect.' But firmly, the Chief-priest intervened, 'Only the King has soldiers.'

Hutantat did not care what title was given; any King's title would prevent all future designs to brand the Aryas as slaves. He knew that some had even been given titles of 'King's Donkey', 'King's Fool' and 'Carrier of King's Shit-Pot', and they too were immune from slavery.

Pleasantly, Hutantat said, 'Very well, give them the title of Arya.'

But the King asked 'Arya! what does that mean?' The King thought that Arya simply indicated the lands from which these strangers came.

Hutantat said, 'Arya means noblemen who work for a noble cause.'

But again, the Chief-priest said, 'Noble! Only priests, commanders and King's Architects are noble!'

Hutantat shouted back, 'So I suppose your King is not noble; nor the men who work on his noble temple. Do you want me to tell these people that they work for a King who is not noble? And you, eunuch, are you the enemy of the King yourself?'

The Chief-priest wilted. Anyone else would be cut down by the sword for saying that much—but not Hutantat.

Pleasantly, the King said, 'Yes, I shall give them all the title of Arya, except one.' And while Hutantat worried, the King pointed to Himatap to say, 'He shall be given the title of Master Builder.'

With feeling, Hutantat said, 'Oh King! To be in your shadow is to learn wisdom! And how I wish it could flow to your priests, as well!' But he added, 'Yet, it may demean and degrade your Master Builder in the eyes of all, if his commander Nilakantha is not honoured.'

Quickly, the King asked, 'And what prevents me from giving a commanders's title to this Nila...?'

'Nothing my King! Nothing is beyond you and your power and your Majesty!' said Hutantat—and before the Chief-priest could interfere, Hutantat shouted to Nilakantha, 'Kneel, dog, kneel!'

Nilakantha was bewildered, but that was the ritual for receiving a title; and Lugal too had received his title of King's Architect with the same ritual. Nilakanatha knelt and the King's whip touched him.

With sadness, the Chief-priest intoned to the kneeling Nilakantha, 'The Sun-god has spoken. And all shall honour you as such. Rise, Honourable King's Commander, rise with honour.'

Himatap too knelt like a 'dog' but rose honoured as the King's Master Builder. Then came the turn of the other Aryas. But they were too many, and the King's hand was tiring. The Chief-priest said, 'Enough for the day....'

Hutantat interrupted, 'Yes, enough, my King; you make the ritual and you unmake it. Enough, if you flick the whip in the air, while they all kneel, and I shall leave their names with the King's clerk'— and he shouted to all the Aryas, 'Kneel dogs kneel. All of you!'

Gratefully, the King flicked his whip in the air and the Chief-priest again intoned, 'Rise, Honourable King's Aryas, rise with honour.'

There is a poet who says that the next day Hutantat met the King's clerk with the names of all the Aryas at the temple-site who were deemed to be honoured with the King's title and he 'even added five more names—of the elusive and absconding Ajitab and his four Arya companions—to the list.' Would Hutantat be so dishonest! The poet himself says:

'Would this man cheat and lie?
Oh! he could be low and high
Sometimes sweet and syrupy servile
But then to appear vicious and vile
Oh! this man of pure heart
Could play each and every part!'

The Aryas were completely unaware of all that came to them with the King's titles, apart from the red bands they wore. Hutantat said, 'All it means is that no one can ever enslave you; but then the guarantee of liberty—is it not superior even to the guarantee of life?' No one disagreed and he added, 'But to Himatap, King's Master Builder, there are many rights; and even more are the rights of the King's Commander, Nilakantha.'

Among Nilakantha's privileges, that Hutantat mentioned, was the authority to free slaves and make them soldiers under his command.

Nilakantha pleaded, 'Oh brother, brother, let us free every slave here and make him a soldier!'

Hutantat smiled, 'No, that much authority you do not have. You can free only unbranded slaves.'

'But practically all of them are branded,' Nilakantha wailed.

'Thirty-six are unbranded,' Hutantat said. He knew the exact number of unbranded slaves. Those thirty-six had come later, to be branded on arrival! But Hutantat had pleaded with the commander, 'If you brand them now, for days they will be unable to work with the pain and blisters from hot branding. Why delay the King's work! Wait for a lull in the work.'

The commander agreed to wait—and a lull there never was. They remained unbranded. Now it was open to Nilakantha to demand that they be freed.

'But the commander may object,' Nilakantha feared.

'Don't worry,' Hutantat said. 'You have rights as the King's Commander. But even so, tell him you need fifty soldiers. Surely, as King's Commander, you can demand that pitiful number. He will hate to lose a single soldier—and then tell him that you will accept unbranded slaves, instead. He will be delighted; he may even kiss you on your cheeks.'

The commander did not kiss Nilakantha but agreed that the unbranded slaves be made soldiers. He wanted to lose not a single soldier of his.

Nilakantha was the proud commander of thirty-six soldiers who had once been slaves.

Hutantat smiled, 'Brother Nilakantha, these are your thirty-six noble deeds to count towards your karma!'

'No, Master, this is your karma!' Nilakantha said.

'What will I do with karma, friend, when the Goddess that rules me is unconcerned with deeds, unmoved by intention and untouched by pleas!'

'What kind of a Goddess is that?' Nilakantha asked.

'That one and only Goddess—the Goddess of destiny.'

'But surely, she too follows the law?' Nilakantha said.

'Oh yes, hers is the inexorable, relentless law—law of dice—and by a throw of dice, she determines the future of us all.'

'But that is no law,' Nilakantha objected.

Hutantat shook his head and softly chanted:

'Why not!
It all depends, as before
On the roll of dice—no more;
Not on the thrower's will or tears
Not our prayers, hopes or fears.
But the unthinking dice unfolds
All that Creation's future holds.'

'You mean, the Goddess herself is not in control!' Nilakantha asked.

'Who can control a roll of dice!' Hutantat said.

'Brother, is life then nothing but a meaningless play of chance forces? That we rise from nothing to end in nothing!'

'I don't know what we rise from. But I am content, if it all ends in nothingness... yes, eternal forgetfulness.'

Nilakantha was silent. It was not in him to quarrel with another's faith. But suddenly he spoke in a voice broken with emotion, 'Brother Hutantat, you are far greater than all of us Aryas.'

'And how did you reach this profound conclusion?' Hutantat mocked.

'We seek salvation through good karma. You seek nothing—neither salvation nor bliss. And yet, seeking no reward or return, your karma is pure. Your soul reflects the sufferings of others. Pain of another brings tears to your eyes....'

Hutantat interrupted, 'I suppose you will soon say that the sun rises and sets over my head! But Brother Nilakantha, think! If man had control over his thoughts and deeds, why would he ever contemplate evil? Why would he build on the shaky foundation of the anguish, despair and terror of others? If the road to salvation is as clear and unambiguous as you say, would not people perform great deeds of mercy and charity?'

'But you do!' Nilakantha interrupted.

'The evil I do, the good I do; the evil and good we all do; every step we take, every word we utter—they are all destiny's roles assigned to each one,' Hutantat said.

'And God, the creator, is without a role!'

'You who will build this temple and depart—what influence will you have over the lives of those that come to occupy it? None. Perhaps God built the world and departed.'

That night Nilakantha prayed—'God, I pray for a soul nobler than us all—I know not what to ask—but I simply pray.'

Ajitab's attacks continued. One action followed another in swift succession. Each attack brought its harvest of freed slaves.

But Ajitab learnt bitter lessons too. He had hoped to convert the slaves into a cohesive force to free others and initially, they cooperated. Later, they failed in discipline. Defying orders, they would pursue and attack fleeing guards even after their objective to free slaves was achieved; they would even loot and burn slave-posts; and while returning, they would attack innocent targets on the way.

The worst was that all semblance of discipline broke down when they remained too long in their areas. Then there were violent fights, for no reason at all, except to show superiority against weaker slaves.

Ajitab's terrible tongue-lashings had an effect, but it did not last long. His entire plan went awry. What he had hoped was to create a disciplined force of freed slaves who would not only free others, but also learn the art of peace, to till the land and be self-sufficient. But instead, these freed slaves, dehumanized and brutalized by the terror of the past, learnt not sympathy for others but a strange desire to hurt those who had never harmed them before.

Sometimes, Ajitab even saw their smoldering rage against himself when he tried to curb their violence. But he had learnt much in the catacombs and could be as brutal. Once, he ordered that four of them be hanged for beating an old man to death. Again, for a woman's rape, he had two hanged and sixteen flogged for not intervening and stopping it.

Ajitab felt unclean and soiled but he saw no way out, except a reign of terror against any crime by his men. He felt that no one would understand what he was doing. But Hutantat would have—destiny.

Where he failed even more, was to make the freed slaves tend to land or cattle. To them, freedom was freedom—have we exchanged the King's slavery for this new slavery! And their restlessness turned into senseless violence against each other, the longer they stayed back in their hide-outs.

Quickly, Ajitab learnt that he had to keep his men on the move and attack more often, if any kind of discipline was to be maintained.

His attacks on the slave-posts became more frequent than he had originally intended. But the attacks were no longer only on the slave-posts. He had to attack even the King's granaries, as their own land was hardly productive.

Lessons of discipline during those attacks were learnt by the freed slaves, gradually and forcefully. They found that those who tarried behind to loot on their own were often caught by the King's soldiers; and it was easy to imagine how mercilessly they would be tortured.

It did not then take long for them to turn into a real fighting force, when disobedience led to capture; and death itself was certainly preferable to being caught alive. Many lost their lives; but even so, they had far more men than Ajitab had planned.

Attacks on the King's granaries and food-stores multiplied.

The King's men went round in all directions to probe. On the way, some commanders even suspected the location of their hide-outs. But why go into inhospitable, possibly fortified, terrain! Yet having come all the way, the commanders went extra miles to have easy pickings. And they vandalized the lands of adjoining kingdoms.

These kingdoms had already suffered from Ajitab's attacks. Now with these attacks by commanders, their suspicion that frequent attacks to free slaves were also inspired by the same source—the vile King who was planning to have a magnificent temple built in his honour—grew into a certainty.

The fact is that the King was boasting about the temple. When he saw the first obelisk, with the sun's golden glow at the predetermined time, his enthusiasm knew no bounds and he said 'from one end of the earth to another, there will be no such magnificent temple anywhere.'

True, his idea about the size of earth was limited, and did not go beyond the few kingdoms around him. Certainly, for him and for his people the world ended where the 'river [Nile] was drowned in the great waters [Mediterranean]'.

In the Egyptian mind, the land of Egypt, with its thirteen kingdoms, was then regarded as a planet on its own, unrelated to any other land, cut off as it was by a cruel sea in the north and vast, barren deserts in all other directions. The sea itself was regarded as a monstrous killer. To them, the rhythm of the river was the rhythm of life. If the sea could drown their auspicious river, what would it not do to humans! No boat would ply in the sea. Even to look at it may bring evil.

Spies and informers of other kingdoms had many tales to tell their own masters; they spoke of the visions of glory that this temple-building King suffered from. And to their kings they reported all this.

The adjoining kings gritted their teeth and made their arrangements to attack.

Ajitab's 'slave army' moved into an elaborate ambush in the adjoining kingdom. Ajitab barely saved himself. One Arya with him died and thirty of his men were killed outright. Many were wounded, and had to be left behind. That the bulk of Ajitab's men escaped was due not only to their fighting skill, but the enemy's failure to pursue. The carnage on the enemy's side was frightening too, despite their superior forces.

Now, there was no doubt in the mind of the 'victors' that it was the 'temple-builder' King who was behind all such attacks. The dead Arya was clearly recognizable. So the King had imported men beyond the deserts to mount his nefarious attacks! The dead and wounded slaves, as they saw, were all branded and this to them was a clear clue too. So this shameless King stole their slaves to fight against them! And he keeps his soldiers in reserve to strike a crushing blow at us!

Ajitab counted his losses. They were far too many. He did not know that a large number of his men had fled in the opposite direction, deeper into the land of the adjoining kingdom. But even if he had known, there was no way he could go to their rescue.

A scream of anguish rose in the adjoining kingdom. Most of Ajitab's men, who had fled in the opposite direction, regrouped. They could not go back to rejoin Ajitab but they had a clear, danger-free route ahead, with almost the entire army massed far behind, celebrating their victory, torturing captives and burying their dead.

And these leaderless men, each branded with the mark of a slave, with terror in their hearts, went on to strike terror all round. When they came across a soldier with four slaves, they killed not only the soldier, but also the slaves who refused to join them. For no reason at all, they killed bystanders. They ransacked huts for food but then waited also to burn them. No one knows why.

News of their violence and viciousness would reach the commanders and the King of that land but only much later; and then the number of these fugitives was so exaggerated that the commanders paused to muster larger forces before pursuing them. Some commanders even rushed in the wrong direction to give an impression of pursuit with no intention of jeopardizing their own safety.

At last, sense dawned on these leaderless fugitives—maybe there was hope since they hadn't been caught for so long! They fled faster, without wasting time in senseless murder and mayhem and would only stop to snatch essential food and attack slave-posts to increase their numbers.

They also decided that he who killed the first guard at a slave-post would be their leader, though when the attack was over, they could not agree which of the three contenders had killed first. In sheer disgust, the choice fell on the fourth.

The first order that the new leader gave was to change their route. He feared that they would be caught easily if they kept going in the same direction. Away from the river, he avoided habitations and led them through deserted areas and forests. Their numbers had swollen with the newly-freed slaves, though they did not have weapons to go around.

Beyond the forest, they came upon two unsuspecting soldiers. They killed the soldiers. The slave-leader and another then put on the solider's clothes along with their armbands; thereafter, it appeared as though two soldiers were leading slaves on some official errand; and they went on unmolested.

Some five days later, two dead, half-naked soldiers were found with their armbands missing. Suspicion immediately fell on the slave-army. The spot where the dead soldiers were found lay on the direct route to a different kingdom, though a detour could lead to yet another.

Messages were rushed to both kingdoms, to watch out for villainous attacks from the murderous forces of the temple-builder King.

The slave-fugitives moved into a formidable trap. The slave-leader was wounded but killed himself. He did not want to be taken alive and had promised himself he would die laughing for the few months of liberty that destiny had granted him.

Meanwhile, Ajitab returned to his headquarters only to find some outsiders watching from a distance. He did not know whose spies they were but quickly decided to evacuate to another area, with his entire 'slave-army'. He had three such areas, each at a distance from the other. Through criss-cross routes he reached another area, but now the informers of other kingdoms were vigilant and news of slave-armies, moving and marching, reached the various Kings.

To what purpose were these slave-armies on the move—wondered the Kings. And they were led by the same kind of people who were building the temple for that vicious King! What else but a prelude to an all-out attack against them.

Ajitab would have been shocked to know that his slave-armies were viewed by the other Kings as tools of the temple-builder King. That King would have called on the sun itself to bear witness that he had nothing to do with that renegade Ajitab and his men. But the King hardly had a chance to explain.

The four Kings from adjoining kingdoms conferred and conspired and their armies moved from different directions. Their objectives:

- To kill the temple-building King;
- To destroy his temple;
- To kill the aliens recruited by the King from the deserts beyond, to build his nefarious temple;

● To divide his kingdom among the four attacking Kings and any other kings who would join the attack.

Two more Kings joined the four Kings in their attack. It is said that this was the first time that Kings attacked the land of another without warning. But the attacking Kings were convinced that the 'first attacks' came not from them but from the temple-building King, with no warning, notice, parleys or provocation.

The first objective of the attacking armies was soon achieved. The King was at a resort, with two of his sister-queens and all his priests. A commander was there with many soldiers but hardly enough to halt a sudden, unexpected attack.

The dazed King was instantly beheaded. His eyes were taken out, so that whatever chance he had of seeing his way to heaven, was lost. His head was mounted on a tall spear to be immersed with his body into the monstrous sea from which none could ever ascend to heaven.

He would never be buried. The question of burying his wives, priests, or slaves, alive long with him, never arose.

The sister-wives and priests were spared, for no one would dishonour women from a royal household or dare harm a priest.

No one knows what happened to the various priests of the beheaded King, but the Chief-priest killed himself by running his sword through his body, and declaring with his dying breath that he be thrown into the sea along with his dead royal master. And the poet adds, '....he knew that his soul in the sea would wander in hell, never achieving paradise, and never would he meet his royal master there, for each one is alone in hell and meets no one except grinning demons who poke burning stakes in every opening of your body. But then he said—let me suffer the same fate... and perhaps a lonely cry will reach out to let my master know that he wanders not alone....'

After their first flush of victory, so easily achieved, the victorious Kings foresaw no future obstacles to achieving all their objectives. Their armies moved leisurely so that the lifeless head of the dead King be seen by all, for total submission to the conquerors.

Then they moved in two directions with no secrecy in their movements or objectives—one army moved to seize the King's sons so that no pretenders be left to dispute their mastery; and the second army moved to the temple, to demolish it and wipe out the alien builders there.

But the conquering Kings then decided not to destroy the temple since it would now belong to them, but only to wipe out the aliens working on it.

'To the temple; to the temple; and kill the aliens there!'—was their shout to the army.

The armies often halted on the way. The Kings accepted the homage of the dead King's commanders. 'None shall be hurt or harmed,' the Kings said. 'Inform the populace of our rightful victory; and of the defeat, death and dishonour of him whose head is stuck on the top of the spear.'

While the Kings marched in triumph, slowly, majestically, the news of the King's death reached Hutantat. He grieved—'He had the brain of a flea but he was a good man, far better than the scouldrels who come now.'

Even of the Chief-priest, Hutantat said, 'I called him a eunuch but he was not a eunuch at heart. He was a man.'

But grief could wait. What worried Hutantat was the openly announced onslaught to destroy the temple and kill the Aryas who were building it. Why, he wondered. He had no reason to suspect that Ajitab was seen as the dead King's puppet and that all the Aryas were seen as his partners in crime.

It was time to act, not think! Hutantat went to the commander, who too had heard all, and had either to submit to the new masters or die.

Hutantat asked, 'Of what use is your submission to them when their anger is against the temple and those that built it? Why will they spare you when you too have assisted at the temple?'

'But I had my orders,' the commander replied.

'So had these Aryas. Yet they are unprotected.'

Hutantat suggested to him to flee with his soldiers—'Hide and resurface when things are quiet.'

'But what will I do with the slaves here?'

'Leave them here. Nilakantha is also the King's Commander.'

The commander laughed, despite his worries. Yet, it was a way out. He said, 'Sage, you are good to me.'

'I will do even better; if the conquering Kings listen to me, I shall say that you hated the temple and all the Aryas so that no one seeks to harm you.'

The commander hoped that every King would listen to the Sage who was honoured and respected everywhere. 'I am grateful,' he said.

But Hutantat said, 'I too need something. You and your soldiers must leave most of your weapons behind.'

The commander understood the purpose of the request. 'Sage! Gladly I shall do so. But these Aryas have no chance. Weapons would avail nothing against those formidable armies. They will all be slaughtered.'

'I fear so too. But to some people what matters is not whether they live or die but *how* they live and die.'

The commander nodded. He did more than leave weapons behind. He went to the arsenal, three miles away, with Hutantat. The guards there were already in a panic as terrible rumours were afloat everywhere. He dismissed the guards saying that he and his soldiers would take charge of the arsenal and granary next door, lest there be looting in these disordered, uncertain times. The guards were delighted to be relieved of a duty that would probably bring disaster to them and quickly left.

'It is all yours,' the commander said to Hutantat.

'Thank you, you are really good to me,' Hutantat said gratefully.

The commander and his soldiers left. All work on the temple stopped. Every Arya was now engaged on removing weapons and food from the arsenal and granary to store at the temple-site.

Hutantat turned to the slaves—'The soldiers have left. You are free to leave.'

'Where do we go, Master? All of us would be hunted as slaves everywhere. Let us remain as slaves here.'

'You know the Arya way! There will be no slaves here! They will set you free but free to do what! To die with them here!'

But really he was going too fast for them. To them it was unthinkable that a branded slave could be freed. It was as if the brand on their upper-arms was a heavenly decree that no earthly power could erase. Why! Even after death they would be recognized in the sky as branded slaves and set apart in a horrible hell. It was not only in the eyes of others that they felt degraded but in their own too.

Hutantat explained, '. . .The freedom to depart is yours. Outside, you may have a chance. If you remain here, your freedom is illusory, momentary—for die you surely shall, with these Aryas.'

'But we are branded slaves!'

'The brand is not in your soul nor in your heart. It is not even a birthmark. Destiny willed that someone degrade you and you felt degraded. Now destiny turns and you can escape or die here!'

'We will die here, free, Master!'

Grimly, Hutantat explained, 'You have time to decide and each must take his own decision. But when the armies move here, the moment of decision will be gone. Then you shall be treated as soldiers here, waiting for the moment of crucifixion. The Aryas will fight to the last, but what chance do they have against the mighty armies of the conquering Kings! Be under no illusion, then. Death here is inescapable.'

'But we will die free, Master!' repeated a slave.

'You can also escape free,' Hutantat said and went to Nilakantha.

It was Nilakantha who now addressed the slaves:

'I, Nilakantha, King's Commander, in the absence of the departed King, hereby assume control of this temple-site, and declare you all free; I hereby order that you are free to leave any moment until the armies can be seen by the sharpest eye from this distance; further, I grant to those that remain with us the title of Noble Arya; and I grant to those that leave us, the title of Arya's Friend, so that none shall ever dare enslave them, anywhere, anytime.'

A slave asked, 'Sage! Does he have this authority?'

Hutantat glared, 'He thinks he has the authority. You think you are a slave. I think all here are doomed. We all think. But does thinking make it so! How easy then to think, rethink, to make, unmake and re-make. Go, think for yourself!'

Nilakantha did not hold even the branch of a tree, in the absence of the King's whip, while conferring titles on the slaves. All he had said to the slaves was at the prompting of Hutantat. But his eyes were now closed and a vision passed through his mind of a day long past, in his childhood, when his eight-year-old sister held him in her arms, as Sindhu Putra was about to leave with the men of Jalta and the Silent Tribe, who had just been released from slavery; the child Nila was then only two years old, but he remembered that he was the first to hear and be blessed by Sindhu Putra with the chant of 'Tat tvam asi'.

Nilakantha's lips were now moving, as though in silent communion with someone unseen. Then slowly, he spoke with a tremor in his voice and said, 'I spoke to you in the name of the King. No, that was wrong. I speak to you in God's name. You are free, my brother and sisters, always. You are free; Tat Tvam Asi.'

Hutantat was standing by, ready to shout the words of the King's ritual—'Kneel, dogs, kneel', so that the ceremony of the title-award to the slaves be properly completed. He remained silent. Strange, he thought; every slave had disbelief on his face when he spoke in the King's name. But now... they seemed to believe his every word... and yet they knew that only the King could speak in God's name, not even the Chief-priest.

Lugal said to Hutantat, 'When Nila thinks, he thinks powerfully.'

'His faith is powerful,' Hutantat replied.

Farewells, laughter, tears.

Of the thirty-six slaves who were made soldiers after Nilakantha became the King's Commander, twenty-five left. They were unbranded, with the best chance of being able to merge with the population, unrecognized as former slaves. But four returned the next day, even though no danger threatened them outside.

Of the branded slaves, the poet says, 'One out of every eight left, with food and arms for the journey; but one of every ten that left, returned the next day and two out of every thirty-three that left returned after two days ....' Was the poet setting an arithmetical problem or simply wanting to confuse? But maybe his poem does not survive fully.

Many freed slaves too moved from Hutantat's villages to the temple-site.

The palace structure in the temple was now the granary and the arsenal. Hurriedly, a wall was improvised, with small openings from which defenders may watch, aim arrows, or hurl stones. Except Himatap, whose mind was still on the temple, everyone had the task of collecting stones to keep them at the site.

Lugal said, 'Don't let Himatap go out. He will drop everything he picks up and will even lose his way.' He was not joking. He knew how Himatap almost 'sleep-walked' whenever absorbed with the problem of temple construction whirling in his mind. But later Himatap had a job too—to break each brick inside the temple to give it a jagged edge.

All around, everyone else deserted the area. The rumour that the Kings had come to destroy the temple and its builders was now known. Nobody wished to remain where soon arrows were to fly.

To the Aryas, it was all extremely mysterious. They had never wanted the temple! They had to work on it or be slaves. All they were now seeking was to leave this land but they were not being allowed to go.

Grimly Hutantat said, 'They will not let you go alive.'

'But why?'—and he replied, 'There is no reason in unreason!'

'But we want no fight,' Nilakantha said.

'Not a question of what you want. It is what you get; an alternative to self-defence is death by torture or the brand of a slave.'

Lugal and many others collected thorny bushes; the hill-sides, which were supposed to have had steps all round, were now filled with those sharp needles, to obstruct climbing. Day and night they worked and Lugal said, 'Maybe we will be asleep when the enemy comes charging in.'

Lugal then organized what saddened many. The plants and trees, on the approach to the temple-site, were cut down. Lugal said, 'Let them have no cover to hide, to aim their arrows.' Instead, he not only had the thorny bushes spread all over but had many planted with roots.

Nilakantha said, 'Brother, they will take months to grow!' Lugal said, 'Maybe years,' and Hutantat nodded.

And an anguished voice again rose, silently, in Nilakantha's heart— 'Was it for this that we left our land!'

Their most tedious, back-breaking job was to store water. The diverted stream reached below the hill but it would be unreachable if the temple was surrounded. Every hut around was scoured for pots and pans, as many had deserted the area. From Hutantat's villages too came every vessel there was to hold water. His man went around, buying, begging, stealing water-jars. They were kept, filled to the brim. Ditches were dug in the palace floor and lined with bricks to hold water.

Lugal commented, 'We are destroying this place, before the Kings reach to destroy it. But why not!'

When Himatap wondered what a man with rope-scaffolding was doing on the top of an obelisk, Lugal said, 'See! He is bald, and he thinks the sun will glow more brightly on his head than on the obelisk!'

But the man was simply there to watch out for the army's approach.

Everything, Hutantat wanted was completed in time. The Kings were slow in coming. Homage on the way meant much to them.

At last, the man from the top of the obelisk cried out that the army was on its way. Perhaps a few hours more and they would be at the site.

Everyone collected around Hutantat and he said: 'There are tears in my heart, but I shall not bring them to my eyes, for I must see you all clearly, and it may be the last time we are together. So let us part smiling.'

But there were tears all round. Everyone had hoped that Hutantat would remain. But Lugal had shouted, 'Who then will speak for you outside, while we remain holed up like rats in here!'

Hutantat embraced Lugal and whispered much in his ear. His last words were to Nilakantha, 'I have little hope from these six jackals who call themselves Kings. But they cannot harm you if you remain firm here. Beware of treachery. Refuse to leave without arms. Refuse to leave at their timing. Refuse, unless they withdraw. They cannot be here for ever. I may not come but someone will come to tell you if they withdraw, back to their lands, or if any ambush awaits you.'

They embraced.

Hutantat paused to kiss Ajitab and Larali's baby-daughter—perhaps his gesture to the youngest Arya there. Then slowly he went down the heavy makeshift steps. He was the last to use those steps. Soon many descended from the temple by rope-ladders to break them, section by section.

Hutantat knew two Kings. The other Kings knew him by reputation. A King kindly said, 'You seek mercy for these Aryas in vain. My own kingdom was ravaged by their attacks. They even stole our slaves to raise "slave-armies" to attack us.'

It took time but Hutantat at last understood. 'But that was done by a renegade Arya, Ajitab, who deserted them to battle on his own. The Aryas are not guilty; and the King whom you killed knew nothing.'

'Be not so foolish as to make a liar out of me,' the King commanded. 'I demanded an attack on the kingdom for the vileness of its King and the complicity of these alien temple-builders. Did I lie?'

'But...,' Hutantat began but the King warned him, 'Take no risks with your life and liberty. Leave before I change my mind.'

The King shouted to those around him. 'If this Sage ever approaches me or any other King, cut out his tongue and throw him out.'

Even the other Kings were surprised at such treatment of a known Sage.

But there was much on the minds of the Kings. Four sons of the dead King were caught and beheaded. The fifth and last son of the King—a six-month-old infant—was missing. A maid had smuggled him out and could not be found. Her husband was blinded and her father killed—still no clue!

The temple-defenders still had two days to enjoy the stillness beyond. With rope-ladders they could go down, bathe in the stream, replenish water, bushes and firewood. They continued to keep watch.

The Kings were in a bad mood, quarreling over division of territory and their failure to locate the missing infant-son of the dead King.

The Kings retired to a pavilion prepared for them on the river bank and more troops were sent out to hunt for the dead King's infant.

A small battalion left for the temple to arrest everyone there. The decision on the fate of the temple, they decided, could wait.

Meanwhile, an old man and a woman with a bundle approached the temple. The man spoke the code word to prove that he came from Hutantat. A rope-ladder was sent down. He climbed up with the woman and the infant. The message from Hutantat was terse:

'Guard this infant as you would guard my one and only son. The Kings have rejected my plea. Expect no mercy from them.'

The old man left. The woman and infant remained. Obviously, she was the mother, as she was breast-feeding the baby. A sympathetic question about the baby's father frightened her. Maybe an unwed mother they thought and asked no more

Perched on a high hill, the temple stood like a fort. There was no way that the small force sent against it could succeed. But it marched with supreme confidence, expecting to instantly seize everyone inside for slaughter.

'Brother Nila,' Lugal said, 'let yours be the first arrow.'

Nilakantha's arrow sped. The attackers were faraway but the arrow was aimed to warn them of the limit of their advance. Only one arrow—the attackers laughed. Their arrows came one after the other but the temple was beyond their range and the arrows fell faraway from the hill. Yet the barrage continued—it gave them a feeling of power. And they advanced beyond the spot where Nilakantha's arrow fell.

Lugal shouted. The invaders did not hear. The defenders did. Arrows sped from the temple. The invaders halted. Four of them were hit. Their leader shouted commands and now their arrows flew without pause.

A few advanced and most ran to form a semicircle. More were hit. Another angry command from their leader; and they halted and watched their men in the front being hit with arrows and stones.

Quickly, they retreated behind Nilakantha's first arrow. The wounded were trying to return. Nilakantha ordered his people to stop. Many stopped, but the newly-freed slaves kept aiming at the wounded.

By shouts and force, Nilakantha stopped them. Some of the injured outside were obviously dead with many arrows stuck in them. Then came the lull. Nilakantha complained bitterly against aiming at the injured.

Lugal said, 'As commander, feel free to behead those who disobeyed you. But be happy that the point is well made. Expect no mercy from the attackers and show no mercy so that they fear to advance.'

Not a single enemy arrow had fallen near the temple. An Arya said, 'God was on our side.' Lugal was angry, 'God is on everyone's side, theirs, ours, the killers and the killed!' Actually, Lugal was annoyed, not with those that had aimed at the wounded, but with the six Aryas who were last at their posts since their prayers had not been completed. He continued, 'If God is what I believe Him to be, I am sure He gets annoyed with prayers when some duty remains neglected.'

'Brother, you put it differently,' said Nila. 'But what you say is near to our heart too—that karma is above prayer and piety.'

'Yet there were those who forgot that and came late!'

Nilakantha nodded and looked sadly at the culprits.

Shouts came from the watchers at the wall and obelisk. Everyone rushed to their posts. The attackers were moving up, behind arrow-range, away from each other, obviously to avoid being easy targets for opposing arrows; they soon ran forward, some straight, others circuitously, hoping to reach spots from where their arrows would be effective. They failed.

And they rushed back even faster. Those among the wounded who could, were limping back painfully. Others just lay there, unable to move.

The sky was filled with vultures circling overhead. The Aryas shuddered.

The attackers now waited beyond arrow-range. Again, the watchers shouted and they all rushed to their posts.

The commander and two men approached from the enemy lines, their arms raised high. Lugal shouted, 'Let them come, unharmed.' They simply picked up the wounded, unmoving men and went back slowly.

The attackers now passively waited at a distance—possibly postponing reporting their failure. At last they left, well before sunset.

A grateful cry rang out in the temple. But Lugal said warningly, 'They will be back, stronger, larger, better armed and ably led.'

Even though they were not expected to attack at night, watch was kept.

Nilakantha saw enemy arrows stuck in thorny bushes—obviously undamaged. He ordered the six Aryas who were last at their posts to go and collect them, 'with feet, hands and legs bandaged, lest the thorns prick us.' They had ample arrow-stocks and Lugal wondered if he was merely punishing the six. But then Nilakantha punished himself too, for he went with them. After recovering the arrows, the six were given the task of filling buckets from the stream, to be pulled up by a rope from the temple by others, to replenish the water used during the day.

Exhausted, they returned by rope-ladders. Lugal was still up and Nilakantha said, 'We are back from our prayers.' Lugal laughed, 'If such are our prayers, the enemy has no chance, Brother.'

They had five days of respite. The Kings were livid. The entire kingdom was grovelling at their feet. How was it possible that these miserable aliens dared to stand up to them! But since the defeated commander spoke of terrible losses, the Kings waited for their large armies to regroup.

On the sixth day, at sunrise, a formidable army marched, led by cavalry. Its commander was certain of an easy path to the hilltop. How else were so many up there! His horsemen led and the foot-soldiers followed. But then he made the same mistake as the first commander. The horses presented easier targets; they got caught in thorny bushes, while arrows rained on them. The horsemen and foot-soldiers got trampled as arrows, stones and jagged bricks rained on them.

The commander then had a drum-beat sounded for his soldiers to return. The defenders thought it signalled another wave of attack. Their arrows flew, unable to distinguish between retreating, wounded and arriving soldiers. Even the boy-drummer went forward to beat the drum, as not too many soldiers were returning. He too was hit and lay dead, his drum by his side.

The commander viewed the situation grimly. He sent for burning torches. They came. Himself, alone, he rode, within arrow range, holding two torches. He threw the torches at the dry, thorny bushes. Every arrow missed him. One torch hit the dry bushes. Many horsemen then repeated the exercise. Two horsemen were hit but the bushes begun burning.

'There is water in my head but no brain,' Lugal said. 'Why did I not drench the bushes with water to avoid fire?'

Nilakantha promised, 'Let this day pass; tonight we will spread more bushes and drown them with water.'

But it was not to be. Sunset came. The enemy remained. They erected tents for the commander and his officers. The soldiers remained in the open. Obviously, it was to be a siege—and then assault.

The commander kept sending out his men who would rush back as soon as a volley of arrows appeared from the temple. He was neither teasing nor courting danger but simply testing the temple's arrow-range. He sent many men to the sides and back who tried the same ploy.

Lugal ordered, 'Aim your arrows short.' Only the soldiers at the back were foolishly near. The rest, prudently, remained far. But far or near, the stream below remained surrounded, no more within reach.

All night, the enemy kept up a battle of nerves. Many slept, but some galloped close, inviting arrows—maybe to see whether the defenders were on guard. They were, but in the moonlight the arrows found their mark only if they were lucky. And what would a few casualties matter to such a huge army!

Morning clarified the enemy's planning. Long ladders were openly being built. Soldiers with spears and swords covered with animal skins were practising with shields.

'An assualt with ladders and shields to avoid our arrows,' Lugal said, 'and we must fight not behind our walls but from the top.' His fear, he kept to himself, and his ordered architect's mind went into the steps to be taken.

The next morning, they saw the dead body of an old man, strung up on a ladder. It was the same old man who had earlier brought the woman and the infant to the temple. Apparently, he had been trying to sneak into the temple with Hutantat's message and was caught.

But in the afternoon, they saw something more horrible. It was Hutantat's body and the bodies of twelve others, mounted on ladders. Something died within them all.

Later, Lugal spoke to them with a calmness which came of extreme shock. 'We weep together, we pray together, but more remains to be done.' They understood and Nilakantha said, 'Yes, they killed the best and noblest Arya amongst us all. But he lives—always—in our hearts.'

The defenders saw a cavalcade that stirred the enemy lines, with decorated umbrellas and canopies. Obviously, the six conquering Kings.

Soon the enemy-commander walked up to the temple, his arms raised. He gestured for permission to ascend. A rope-ladder was thrown out to him.

The commander greeted Nilakantha coldly. Lugal sent everyone away. He did not want anyone to be recognized if they were ever to escape and sat nearby, head down, as if he were praying.

The commander said, 'I have been asked by the Kings to forgive you all if the infant is given to us.'

'What infant?' Nilakantha asked.

'The infant which Hutantat brought here.'

'Sage Hutantat brought no infant here.' Nilakantha said. He was truthful. It was Hutantat's messenger who had brought the infant.

'Then give me all the infants here,' the commander said.

Nilakantha shook his head. The commander said, 'Your life, your freedom depends on it.'

'Of what use is life or freedom without honour!'

'You come from the deserts beyond. Of what use is this infant to you?' the commander asked.

'Which infant?' Nilakantha asked.

The commander looked at him with respect and said, 'You will all die but truly shall I regret it.'

The commander left. They all rushed to Nilakantha, 'What did he say?'

Nilakantha replied shortly, 'He demanded the impossible.'

Lugal nodded and silenced their questions—'Ask no more!' They silently wondered what terrible demands had been made that Nilakantha and Lugal would not even speak.

Left alone, Nilakantha and Lugal wondered too. Why were the Kings seeking the infant that Hutantat sent with a request to guard him like 'my one and only son.' Was he really Hutantat's son from the woman who brought him to the temple? True, she shed tears when she saw Hutantat's dead body. But didn't they all? And why should the Kings want the dead Hutantat's infant son! It made no sense. They gave up.

For the next two nights, the enemies continued their shrieking and galloping—forward and back—unmindful of casualties, maybe to frighten the defenders or keep them sleepless, tired and nervous. On the third night, well before dawn, Lugal took his little revenge and arrows rained on those at the back who had imprudently slept within range. Their casualties were many, but the commotion, far more. Even the enemy-commander rushed out of his tent, thinking that the defenders had come out to attack.

The next morning Nilakantha again saw the distant cavalcade of the Kings. He sadly thought of the enemy dead below the temple. 'Those soldiers were innocent. These Kings are responsible,' he said.

Lugal nodded, 'Criminals are always on top. They go free. Only innocents remain as soldiers and servants to shed blood for criminals, in the vain belief that they serve a worthy cause.'

Hurriedly, the bodies of Hutantat and the twelve others were being removed by the soldiers.

Lugal concluded, 'The assault shall soon begin. Maybe the Kings are pressing the commander to attack.'

Lugal was right. The commander wanted ten more days. The Kings gave him till the next morning.

At sunrise, the attack began. Enemy waves, protected by shields, rushed up with tall ladders. The cavalry galloped ahead of them to take the brunt of the arrows, as if the casualties did not matter, so long as the foot-soldiers reached the temple hill with their ladders.

But they had only 100 ladders. The defenders were ready. Led by Lugal, more than 200 waited on the top of the wall to pounce on the ladders as they rested against the hill.

From each alternate wall-cavity in the temple, burning torches were being thrown. The other wall-cavity continued showering arrows. The enemy attack was ill-conceived and hasty, with too many men trying to do too little, and only sixty ladders stood against the temple wall, to be toppled by the defenders. And the enemy cavalry itself blocked its own men from running back to safety from the burning torches.

Even so, the Arya lost twelve men, due to their own foolish enthusiasm to rush too quickly at the ladders and go down with them; and even more foolishly, to stand on the edge of the hill and strike the enemy soldiers on the ladders, while the other Aryas tried to topple them.

But down below, in the enemy ranks, chaos and confusion and cries of the dying and the wounded sounded.

From a safe distance, the Kings saw the carnage in their ranks with all the ladders toppled and their men trapped.

The Kings left. Only then did the commander dare to sound the retreat-drum.

Much is said by the poets on the glowing victory of the Aryas over a commander who was one of the best in the land. Actually, it was due to the temple's commanding position on the hill-top but far more, because of the folly of the Kings, who ignored their commander's plea to give him time to prepare fully for a difficult assualt.

The Kings were stern and unforgiving to the commander. He had failed to get the infant, believed to be the King's son, hidden by Hutantat in the temple. He had failed in his attack. They replaced the commander.

But the Kings paused before ordering the new assault. They had the confession, under torture, from two captured slaves who had left the temple earlier. Clearly, the temple had an Arya commander, appointed by the earlier King; but he had no soldiers and only untrained slaves under him; the rest were his own Aryas, who were simply builders, singers and worshippers, but not fighters.

But then the Kings wondered—if they had no real fighters, how did they cause such havoc among their troops! Obviously, it was their commander who alone planned it all and his must be the skill and inspiration, to 'place his puppets properly to frighten our spiritless cowards who ran away.' If they enticed away their commander would not their entire resistance collapse?

A King's Chief-priest walked towards the temple, arms raised. 'Refuse him entry,' some said. Their hearts were anguished over the twelve Aryas whose bodies were scattered below.

But Nilakantha said, 'There are others to save. Maybe he offers a way out.' Lugal nodded. A rope-ladder was thrown for the Chief-priest.

The priest graciously bowed, 'It is by command of the six Kings that I request you to meet them.'

'Why? What do they want?' Nilakantha asked.

'What can Kings want! Nothing. They desire that you leave the temple to them and be in peace, free to remain to work for them or free to leave with honour, as you wish.'

'But that is all we want—to leave.'

'So be it. The Kings will even pay handsomely for the work you did on the temple.'

'There is no demand for an infant?'

The Priest laughed, 'That was a foolish mistake. No, all your people—infants, men, women—go with you.'

'Good. What guarantees of our safety have we?'

'The six Kings will themselves give you their oath.'

'Then why did so many have to die, before?'

The Priest smiled, 'Now the Kings fully believe what they suspected before—that this temple holds the power of the Sun-god and its builders are blessed. If they needed proof positive, it was your victory of so few against so many. Never will the Kings dream of attacking you in the temple or anywhere, for they believe that any harm to you diminishes them all.'

'Yet your troops are massed there!' Nilakantha said.

'Any moment, orders will reach them to depart.'

Lugal spoke, 'Why must our commander go to the King? You can tell us the arrangements for our safety to depart.'

The Priest was annoyed. 'Who is he?' he asked, unable to see even Lugal's face, who sat as if absorbed in prayers.

'He is King Lugal...' Nilakantha began but Lugal interrupted, 'I am a priest here.'

The Chief-priest wondered—they even have a king here who calls himself a priest; but truly that is how it should be and only priests should be Kings! Respectfully he said, 'In that case, Lord priest, you too may join your commander to see the Kings. But who am I to take an oath for your security on behalf of the Kings! How can I command armies to protect you to go where you wish! Surely, these oaths and orders must come from the Kings.'

Impulsively Nilakanatha said, 'I am ready....'

But Lugal cut in, 'Yes, the commander is ready to give you his answer in two days. He has to consult all.'

The Chief-priest smiled, 'It is for the commander to speak.'

Lugal glared at Nilakantha who said, 'Yes, I must consult... two days.'

'So be it,' the Chief-priest said. 'I shall come again.'

But Lugal asked, 'Meanwhile, your troops will move back, twenty or thirty miles away?'

The Chief-priest nodded, 'Of course; instantly.'

And Lugal added, 'We will keep your ladders, tents, everything in the temple for safety.'

'Yes, please do that. And should you need any food or anything else, I shall have it sent to you.'

'No, we have everything,' Lugal replied.

The rope-ladder was dropped. But before leaving, the Chief-priest spoke to Lugal, 'Lord Priest, I honour and respect a priest like you who questions and checks everything. Do join your commander to see the Kings. And you will realize that they will be generous beyond your dreams for the great temple you leave behind.'

Still, Lugal asked, 'Why can I not go instead of the commander?'

But the Chief-priest said, 'Why make the Kings feel small when they ask for your commander? But certainly, you and even many others may join him. It is always nice and proper for a commander to go well-attended.'

Nilakantha later apologized to Lugal, 'Forgive me for wishing to rush to the Kings without waiting to consult you.'

'We have been brothers too long to apologize to each other,' Lugal said. 'But I fear the Kings are up to no good. There is treachery in their hearts.'

They all discussed it but were unsure of what this new development meant. Suddenly, from the obelisk the cry came—'Army moves!'

The Chief-priest was right. The army was leaving.

Discussion was halted. The bodies of the twelve Aryas had first to be brought up for the last rites. The three who were from Bharat Varsha were cremated and the nine locals were buried in a grove at a distance from the temple.

Lugal said, 'They will have died in vain, if we sit back to mourn.'

Groups were sent out to replenish water from the stream; bring stores and ladders, left by the enemy; drag the enemy dead away from the temple approaches; collect thorny bushes for spreading later; flood the approaches with water, so that the bushes remained wet.

'No sleep, no rest, only work and more work for two days,' Lugal said to them. He did not even supervise. He was speaking to Nilakantha, who asked, 'What is your suspicion?'

'That they will kill you.'

'How will my death serve them?'

'You command the Aryas here.'

'Brother Lugal, you are in command! I serve only to voice your orders.'

'And what will happen to the Aryas if you die?'

'The torch is safe in your hands.'

'And what of their hearts, their morale!'

'It will hurt them, yes,' Nilakantha replied. 'As it hurt us terribly when we saw Sage Hutantat's body. But that only increased our resolve to fight.'

'Yes, Hutantat's death had that effect. But another blow will shatter them. I know it will shatter me.'

Nilakantha put his arm around Lugal's shoulder. 'Brother, do we have a choice? The Kings promise safety. But suppose we spurn their offer! We sit back and fight here—for what!—and how long! Can time and events wait? Can we win! Never! So one day we will try to escape and they will simply cut us down. Why not, instead, get their oath to leave us alone to go our way!'

'Only, I have a ghastly, nightmarish feeling that they mean treachery.'

'Treachery to what end! Only to kill me! One single life! What can it avail them! All right, even so, what are the two sides of this dice? I stake my life to gain freedom for us all. And if I don't stake it, we all die in any case—it is only a matter of time. So if they kill me, I will simply have died a little earlier.'

Lugal was silent but Nilakantha again asked, 'What can they hope to gain by killing me? Do they expect that you will then kiss their hands and be ready for slaughter!'

Though all the others were busy at the temple they knew of Nilakantha's hopes and Lugal's fears. Nobody wanted Nilakantha to go but there was no alternative.

They saw Lugal—this man of reason—rent with perplexity, but then even he could not understand what the Kings hoped to gain by enticing Nilakantha. Were the Kings really sincere? They that killed Hutantat. But maybe the Kings wanted to avoid more bloodshed! Maybe they wanted to rush back to their kingdoms and wished to resolve all this peacefully!

Yet they saw Lugal's grief. But then they knew his compassion and tenderness and they also knew that he loved Nilakantha like a brother.

'All will be well. I slept only for an hour but I had a beautiful dream,' Nilakantha said.

'Your beautiful dreams always come true?' Lugal asked.

'This one will. I dreamt that we were all back in Bharat Varsha and you were with us too.'

'Then your endless journeying is over?'

'Yes, Purus was right. Our land is beautiful. It is we who fail if we do not keep it pure.'

Many gathered. Nilakantha spoke. 'I am telling Hermit-King Lugal of my dream of going back to our land.'

They nodded. Once their dream, too, had been to find a pure land elsewhere. Not any more.

The Chief-priest arrived. They were all there, refusing to remain away, while Nilakantha was to leave.

Graciously, the Chief-priest smiled at them all, 'I see you have watered the approaches to your temple.'

Lugal replied, 'Yes, too much blood, carnage and death was there! We had to wash it.'

The Priest nodded appreciatively, 'Very auspicious.'

Nilakantha was going around. He kissed Larali's child. The Chief-priest came forward to look, 'Beautiful child. Your son?'

Larali replied, 'My daughter.'

Lovingly, the Priest picked up the child, fondling it. He checked what he wanted to check and looked around. He saw no other infant, as it was well-hidden in the granary with his mother.

But the smile did not leave the Chief-priest's face. He turned to Nilakantha and asked, 'Ready?'

Nilakantha nodded. Casually, the Priest said, 'It would be nice if you came attended. Commanders always have attendants.'

A freed slave pleaded, 'Master, let me come!' Nilakantha saw Lugal nod.

Nilakantha and the slave went with the Chief-priest.

'Kneel, dog, kneel.' Nilakantha was ordered as he approached the Kings. But it did not worry him. This was the ritual in the King's presence. And here were six Kings in this river-side pavilion.

'Welcome, Commander,' a King said pleasantly. 'Now, go with our men to the temple. Ask all your men to come out with their hands up in the air and bring out the infant.'

Nilakantha stared. Was it a joke?

But the King said, 'We are not joking. You had better obey.'

Hoarsely, Nilakantha said, 'I would rather die.'

'Honourable choice,' said the King. 'Foolish, but honourable. Oblige him.' The King looked at his men.

They held Nilakantha. An axe was poised to strike, when the King said, 'No blood here! There!' They dragged him to the river.

Nilakantha's neck was severed from his body. His head fell into the river. They threw his body in.

The Kings looked and then turned their attention to the food before them.

Nilakantha's soldier was held tight by the captors. The Chief-priest hit his face with a stick. 'Listen, dog, go to the temple. Tell them to throw the infant down instantly. We will then be merciful to all. Understood!' The soldier nodded. They escorted him near the temple.

Meanwhile, Lugal and the others waited. Weary, tired, dazed, after two days of ceaseless work and worry, they still could not sleep. Their most gruesome experience was removing the twelve Arya bodies from below and then dragging the countless enemy bodies away. Each felt sick with grief and revulsion. And now, the uncertainty over Nilakantha's fate!

Suddenly there was a movement! It was their own soldier returning with many others. The others remained behind. The soldier moved forward. Surely, Nilakantha was following! A rope-ladder was lowered. Their soldier came up.

He was besieged—'Where is Nilakantha?' They saw his tears. There was silence. At last he spoke, 'River Kemi (black river)[1] is red now with Master Nila's blood... red, re river... Master Nila... Nila...river....' He was sobbing.

The King's men who had escorted the soldier waited beyond arrow-range. 'What do they want?' Lugal asked.

The soldier said 'They wait for the infant,' and he repeated the message of the Chief-priest.

Hurriedly, Lugal collected a bundle and went to the wall, as if holding a baby. He gestured. A man detached himself from the group below and came forward, motioning to Lugal to throw down the infant.

---

[1] There are some who say that Egypt's river which was till then known as Kemi (black) then came to be called Nila.

Lugal simply pointed to the rope-ladder. The man went back to consult but returned to ascend. 'Give me the infant,' he demanded.

Lugal grovelled, 'Master, we will give the child. But will you then be merciful to us?'

'Yes, Kings are merciful.'

'But Master, we beg. Promise us mercy.'

'Yes, I shall speak to the commander.'

'Master, where is the commander?' Impatiently, the man pointed beyond the wall and Lugal wailed, 'But Master, that is not the commander. We know the commander. He was here before.'

'You fool, it is the new commander! The old commander is no more!'

'Master, we mean no offence, but then let the Chief-priest come; we know him. We know none else. He is gracious.'

The man stormed. Cravenly, Lugal heard him, head bowed. The man left in anger.

A debate was on in the pavilion of the six Kings. The report was clear: dispirited men in the temple, frightened women, crying children; and their spokesman grovelling like a dog, with his tail between his legs, begging for a personal promise of mercy from the Chief-priest.

'Send the commander,' the Chief-priest advised. He had no wish to risk his precious life. But the commander argued, 'They say they don't know me and will only deal with someone they know.'

'Then let the old commander go,' the Chief-priest said.

'But they were told he was no more.'

'Why did we give that information?'

One of the Kings spoke to the Chief-priest, 'That question can wait. What is important is that you go and bring the infant.'

The Chief-priest looked at his own King. 'I know their spokesman. He is a sly fox. It is a trap.'

'Trap for what? To kill you! No one kills a Chief-priest.'

'They are aliens, bound by no scruples,' said the Chief-priest.

'And they will sacrifice all hope only to kill you?'

'They have no hope,' the Chief-priest said miserably.

'He who lives, hopes. He dies hoping,' the King said. But the Chief-priest was without hope.

The King continued, 'And you worry over your life when we must have the infant!'

The Chief-priest made one last appeal, 'Sun-god, consider the insult to your Majesty if they lay hands on your Chief-priest!'

'It is a sorrow I shall bear,' the King replied brutally. 'What I cannot bear is your cowardice.'

The Chief-Priest went to the temple. He felt like a lamb going to slaughter. But he sadly thought—God blessed lambs with no such fore-knowledge—only man knows where he goes. He forgot to raise his arms, but a rope-ladder waited for him.

If the Chief-priest had any hope, it left him as soon as he saw Lugal's cold expression.

'Speak the truth for once in your life, before you die. Who is the infant?' Lugal asked.

'Surely you know!' the Priest answered. 'He is the King. The last son of the last King.'

'But they have overtaken the kingdom. Why kill him?'

'They cannot be Kings while he lives. The law!'

Lugal was thinking—Everyone has a law and all laws are mad!

He asked, 'But the child's mother—she does not look like a queen!'

'She is no mother,' replied the Priest. 'She is the wet-nurse who breast-feeds the baby. She smuggled the child out.'

'But why this mad rush to kill the infant?' Lugal asked.

'The Kings always fear being absent from their kingdom for too long. They have to go back.'

Both were silent. Sombrely, Lugal asked, 'You know why we sent for you'

The Priest nodded. Lugal continued, 'You may pray before you die.'

'I prayed before I came,' the Priest said.

They looked at each other. Each fell into thought. They looked inside, within themselves.

The Priest saw the rope in Lugal's hand. Quietly, he asked, 'If possible, could you kill me by the sword? You can hang me, thereafter.'

Lugal nodded. Courteously, the Priest said, 'Thank you.'

Lugal picked up the sword. Its point caught the Priest's unprotected throat. Blood gushed forth.

The Chief-priest was dead.

Lugal spoke to everyone, 'I killed not in anger, nor for revenge. I killed to let them know that they can expect no mercy from us. But more! So that you expect no mercy from them, ever. Remember that as we die, whether together or one by one! But we must try to live— for Hutantat had a dream to save this infant; and Nilakantha had a dream that we all go to his land. Anyone who dies needlessly hurts that dream. The Kings must rush back to their kingdom. They have no time. We have.'

The limp body of the Chief-priest was hanging from the temple wall. His men, who waited at a distance, watched horrified. Two came forward to see closely, their arms raised. They came nearer. Arrows were aimed from the temple, for Lugal had warned, 'They that come to speak to us mean more harm than those who shoot arrows at us.' The temple arrows hit one. He lay there. The other, wounded, rushed back.

'To hang a Chief-priest!' The commander reported to the Kings. 'To aim at our men with arms raised! They are inhuman!'

'Be inhuman with them, yourself!' the Kings commanded.

Strangely, the enemy army did not appear for the next five days. But when they came, Lugal knew why there had been a delay. Hundreds of slaves came carrying huge wooden ramps; heavy ladders with steps; long poles with fire-torches at the end. Long lines of the enemy army followed.

What had the defenders done meanwhile? Nothing, except to dig ditches to store more water, spread thorny bushes outside and wet them.

And those huge ramps! They were being assembled right there to make them even huger. Hundreds were carrying them, sheltered below from arrows, and keeping them against the temple walls; and then the men, perhaps even horses, would rush on to those ramps, while innumerable heavy ladders were raised everywhere.

Multitudes of slaves were driven to the area, hour by hour, to work on the ramps, ladders and siege-works. The enemy was planning war with even itself. Fences were being erected so that the enemy soldiers could not retreat or rush back—they had to go forward and kill or die.

If there was a hope in the temple, it was voiced by Lugal, 'Join me to pray that we die like warriors. That is what we all are—Arya warriors—each one of us, no matter where this journey began.'

He spoke also of the fate of those that were caught alive—'It shall be far more terrible than death,' he said.

It was the first time Lugal had called for prayers. It was always Nilakantha's task. They prayed with tears. Prayers concluded, they embraced each other. Later there might not be time to say farewell. Egyptian freed slaves, branded slaves, Hutantat's soldiers, men from Bharat Varsha, Iranians, Sumerians, Assyrians—Aryas all.

The mother-nurse of the infant-King came forward. She asked Lugal, 'Bless me Father as Arya and this infant-King who shall be Arya.'

Lugal replied, 'You are Arya and so is the infant-King.'

They all embraced her and kissed the infant.

Somehow, they did not seem dejected any more. Only Larali. Hers was a difficult task.

'You must live,' Lugal had said to Larali. 'While they massacre everyone, maybe a moment of confusion will arise. Lead the infant-King, his nurse, your infant, and the other children to safety if you can.'

Lugal had pointed to the spots from which the rope-ladder would run and the bundles in which the children would be wrapped and thrown down safely. 'Even if one child is saved, it will not be in vain,' he said.

Lugal tried to comfort Larali. He said, 'Dying is a necessity but we can turn it into an art and when the time comes for us to die, it must be time for you to live.'

And then Lugal said something unexpected, 'I choose you, not because you have your own infant, not because you must meet your husband Ajitab, but because of my faith.'

'What faith?' she asked.

'My faith tells me that everything repeats itself in time, out of time, in life, out of life. And I know, my dear virgin-in-waiting, whenever someone forces you to wait, something good always happens.'

She smiled through her sorrow, 'You really believe it?'

'Yes, mine is the faith that you will meet your husband, that he will kiss his infant daughter, that your life will be complete, fulfilled.'

Her eyes filled up with tears, 'My life will not be complete, Father Lugal, if you are not with us.' He took her in his arms and she wept.

There was still time for the onslaught to begin, so long as the multitudes of slaves remained in the enemy area.

Regularly now, for the last two days, slaves were being driven out in droves, many unable to walk, having worked under the whip and lash day and night. Now only a few hundred slaves remained. Apparently, they were to carry the ramps and ladders for the soldiers to scale the temple wall.

Ladders and ramps were being brought nearer to the temple. Everywhere out in the enemy area was activity, excitement. So the attack begins in the morning—thought Lugal.

He gazed at the moon—'Farewell, moon of tonight! Look for us elsewhere tomorrow night!'

He turned back to speak to them all, 'Let us sleep early, sleep well and rise early. The attack comes at sunrise, I am sure.'

Lugal himself did not sleep. He went round the temple. It pleased him that his watchers were alert and the rest were sleeping peacefully. We have all come to terms with destiny, he thought.

He lay down to sleep. Three hours before sunrise, something woke him up. He peered out into the dim light. No movement. He called out to those on watch. 'Nothing,' they replied. Sheer nervousness, he thought.

But then it came, like a distant thunderstorm. The watch called out. The noise increased in volume. Lugal stood on the top of the wall. He saw nothing. The obelisk-watchers saw some burning torches in the far distance. 'Why do they need more army units?'—Lugal wondered aloud. Everyone was up by now.

'Our moment arives,' Lugal said. Still, he was sure that the attack would not begin before sunrise. He saw the usual torches burning in front of the ramps and ladders. They remained unmoved. Obviously, the slaves would need an hour to bring the ramps against the temple wall and now, judging by the distant noise, the enemy was waiting for even more troops to arrive.

He cried, 'Larali! Live to tell how many they needed to fight against us!'

Suddenly, the distant noise was no more. Nor could the obelisk-watchers see the faraway torches. Maybe, some large movement of soldiers, elsewhere—thought Lugal—and not new enemy units coming in.

Nobody in the temple slept any more. Their task was simple. To fight with arrows and swords but mostly to throw burning torches on the ramp carriers and, inside the temple, on those that tried to surround Larali and the children.

Fortunately, they did not lack torches to burn. Their own arsenal was full; and when the enemy had evacuated after the Chief-priest's first visit, they had left behind an endless supply. They also intended to leave burning torches on the temple floor to obstruct enemy movement.

An hour before sunrise, drums sounded in the enemy camp. The slaves were rushing up with ramps and ladders. Lugal looked around. Everyone nodded—a prayer in each heart. And then they began to light torches.

Hundreds of slaves carried many ramps all round the temple. Arrows would be ineffective against the slaves sheltered below the ramps.

The ramp-carriers stopped at the thorny bushes. But in the frontline, sheltered under the ramps, were also those who had long pointed poles. With those they swept aside the bushes to make way for the slaves to go through.

Burning torches thrown by the Aryas on the ramps were ineffective. Torches hurled on the ground slowed them down but those too were swept away with the long poles.

Slowly, inexorably, the ramps moved forward.

Lugal looked around at the Aryas, as if to see them for the last time. All his arrangements had failed so far and he thought—these good people deserve a better organizer than I. He considered going down by the rope-ladder to throw burning torches directly at the ramp-carriers. But there were soldiers under the ramps too. They would cut down his group to pieces, before it could reach. Better to die here.

Enemy soldiers were forming lines with shields and spears. Horsemen were ahead.

And then came a deafening roar, as if a thousand demons were shrieking. It rose in volume. Lugal saw little in the dim light. The ramps were still faraway. What then was this pandemonium?

There was confusion everywhere. The enemy lines became disorderly. The ramps however, continued to move. Suddenly, even the ramps stopped. Then a few ramps fell, maybe crushing many who carried them. Everyone was running, here, there and everywhere. The slaves and soldiers who extricated themselves from under the ramps were running too, within the temple's arrow-range.

Who was chasing whom? In his bafflement, all that Lugal did was to order everyone to stop aiming arrows and hurling torches.

The tumult increased but no one attacked. Everyone watched from the temple. But they were witnesses to a drama that they did not comprehend. There was no tranquillity in their minds. Their hearts were pounding with each roar from outside. Suddenly, an Arya cried out, 'I always knew God would come to save us!'

It was Ajitab. He came with his legions of slaves and cut-throats from the catacombs.

Long before Hutantat was killed, he sent six messengers to Ajitab. Two had reached Ajitab. Since then Ajitab had been marching, stopping only to attack slave-posts and increase his numbers. His last stop was at the catacombs. His adventures on that long march were many but with most of the soldiers diverted to attack the temple, his perils were few.

At the last moment, before nearing the temple, his numbers grew even more with all the slaves who until recently had worked for the enemy army under the lash.

There was slaughter all around the the temple. Yet it took six hours for Ajitab to reach the temple hill. Deliriously they shouted. Lugal asked Larali to throw down the ladder.

Larali was in Ajitab's embrace. He kissed his infant. Someone said, 'Ajitab you are our saviour!'

But Ajitab's own cry was more astonished as he looked at his infant, 'I am a father! A father!'

He asked where Nilakantha was. They told him.

'That river shall flow with blood,' he shouted.

But Lugal said, 'Let them die who deserve to die. But let their blood not pollute Nila's River!'

Everyone was talking to Ajitab, all at once. Outside, confusion still reigned. But the most repetitive cry—resonant and booming—was, 'King Ajitab, Ajitab, King Ajitab.'

Some asked, 'They call you King!'

Ajitab dismissed it, 'I was called the King of Catacombs when I led thieves and robbers for a time. The title still seems to unite freed slaves around me and adds to their spirit and morale.'

'Who but a King could save us!' an Arya said.

'I am no King,' Ajitab retorted. 'Lugal is the one whom we call King.' And he picked up the infant-King, 'And we have a real King too.'

'And outside, six Kings wait to kill him,' Lugal said.

'They will die,' Ajitab said evenly.

Ajitab was in the temple less than three hours. Then he left. 'Why?' everyone cried. But he said his army of ex-slaves would go wild with bestiality and brutality unless he was out there to control them. 'My men will guard the temple outside. Let them not come up. They are not a well-ordered lot.'

Ajitab returned after nine days. All six Kings had been caught. They were stabbed in the heart and left to rot by the side of the river. 'Let them keep watching the river where Nila's blood flowed,' Ajitab said.

But the next day, the bodies of five out of the six Kings were missing from the riverbank. A poet explained, 'The Chief-priests of the five Kings took away their bodies to bury them. Only the body of the King whose Chief-priest was killed at the temple remained rotting by the riverbank. Why would the Chief-priests of other Kings help a King who sends his own Chief-priest to premature death! And for him came the vultures.'

From then on, Ajitab's visits to the temple were brief.

In the temple, every heart had a single question—How long shall we be here in this land?—and each asked, 'How long!'

And Himatap said, 'Long, very long,' but he was thinking of the damage to the temple, with the water ditches and battered walls, broken bricks and burning torches—and he felt that all that must now be repaired.

Peace came slowly to the six kingdoms and then in all the thirteen kingdoms. It was a peace imposed by Ajitab's contingents. Soon all the kingdoms would have a single name—Kingdom of Ajitab. Its name as Kingdom of Egypt would come later and, as said some, as an adaptation of Kingdom of Ajitab.

But then Ajitab was no longer called the King. Nor was Lugal so called. Ajitab had a title though—King's Commander-in-Chief. And Lugal had a title too—King's Keeper (Regent).

The title of King belonged solely and exclusively to the infant, the last son of the King who was killed by the six attacking Kings.

The infant's real mother had been spared initially, but was later killed as the six Kings suspected her of conspiring to smuggle him out. The wet-nurse who had protected the infant-King had the title of 'King's Mother.'

Many months later, the Aryas left the kingdom. Their quest was over and now they were homeward bound, with no desire to go elsewhere. They were escorted by a large contingent of Ajitab's well-trained, disciplined troops. Everyone who was at the temple left with them, except Himatap—King's Builder, Lugal—King's Keeper, Ajitab—King's Commander, Larali, King's Mother and two infants—Larali's daughter and the infant-King.

'Come with us,' the Aryas pleaded with Lugal. For, as they said, 'The best of Aryas must not remain behind.' But Lugal had promises to keep. He thought of Hutantat's message about the infant-King—'Guard the infant as you would guard my one and only son.' He would keep faith.

And he thought, when the infant was safe, secure and grown, he would go to Assyria and Sumeria. There was a dream in Lugal's mind about his homeland—a dream that was vague and formless but sometimes it was also persistent like the lament of a bird that had lost its mate.

Lugal would leave the kingdom sixteen years later, when the King was grown and fully in command. The King called himself Arya, bound by his oath to govern righteously by the noble Arya code of conduct.

Meanwhile, Lugal had abolished slavery in the kingdom. Anyone who disobeyed and kept a slave would have his upper-arms branded, apart from his wealth being confiscated. There were no eunuch Chief-priests or priests in the kingdom any more. Marrying one's sister was considered incestuous.

Ajitab, Larali and their two sons—fourteen and twelve years old—left with Lugal. Their daughter, who was born in the temple, was left behind. She had married the King. Poets say that she and the King fell in love when they were infants together in the temple.

For three years, Lugal and Ajitab would be in the thick of fighting in Assyria and Sumeria. They had brought troops from the kingdom of Ajitab. But their larger support came from the Aryas there and the locals who joined the Aryas.

Lugal would soon be the undisputed ruler of Assyria and Sumeria. He had no imperial ambition. But King, he had to be, if exploitation by the priests was to be suppressed and the noble Arya Code, introduced.

Ajitab remained as Lugal's commander for another two years. Then he left with Larali and four sons.

Lugal kept back Ajitab's nineteen-year-old son. He told Larali, 'You have too many sons; I have none.'

Lugal promised to leave Sumeria after three years for a visit to Bharat Varsha. He did. He nominated his son (Ajitab and Larali's son, adopted by him), as his Regent and successor.

The Aryas who had returned to Bharat Varsha long ago, thronged to meet this Sumerian Lugal of whom it was said that he was the highest and noblest of all Aryas.

Lugal never went back to his homeland and passed his last days on the banks of the Ganga—and when someone asked him if he had understood the mystery of the universe, he said he had not even grasped the mystery of the Aryas of Bharat Varsha who left their land of promise, purity and glory for an elusive quest into the unknown.

Thus it is, that this Arya Sakaru from Ganga, whose mother came from Saketa (Ayodhya), and father from Sindhu, was chosen as leader of hundreds of settlements that merged to form a single tribe under him, in the area beyond the northern boundary of the Russian Caucasus between two rivers, Kuma (draining into the Caspian sea) and Kuban (flowing into the Black Sea)....

Sakaru wanted to call it the 'Tribe of the Horse', for he had taught them to domesticate, love and respect the horse as 'man's friend' and not for wanton, cruel sacrifice....But the tribe came to call itself 'Sakaru's Tribe'....

—(Adaptations from 'Stories of Pamira—Granddaughter of Sakaru')

'...But many Aryas who came were prisoners of their own dream. To them, the whisper of that dream spoke louder than any warnings. That there was grim brutality and bestiality in these new lands actually strengthened them—it had to be total darkness that leads to total light. They scoffed at those that warned—"All they have is the triumph of being alive; but what is life, if the dream dies!" No, we shall not stop in our quest for the land of the pure; the dream shall not die...'

—(From the 'Dream that Died'—after 5005 BC)

'Their goal? Back to Hari Haran Aryan and then to Bharat Varsha....What of the Land of the Pure then? If we cannot reach it, maybe God will bring it to us....Maybe, it is only up in high heaven....'

—(The cry of an Arya stranded along the Caspian Sea—after 5005 BC)

Aryas in Europe

5005 BC

To the Aryas in Iran, Sumeria and Assyria, the realization came quickly that those lands were not the sacred destinations of their seeking. Their minds were assaulted by images of the cruelty all around.

Purus, who led the Aryas in Iran, had already recovered from his initial shock and his mind was crystal clear—that there was no land of purity anywhere, except when man made it so by his own effort.

Many Aryas would come to agree with Purus and they would stay back—their wandering days over—and their only dream to return to Bharat Varsha. But often it was only a dream. They feared that the journey back would be as perilous as their journey out.

But not everyone heard the voice of Purus. To some it did not reach at all. True, the Aryas from Iran, Sumeria and Assyria met and mingled—but not as much or as often as would be expected in the day and age of fast, unlimited communications. Different events as they occurred in one area rarely came to be known in another.

Besides, Purus did not lay down the law. He himself was no longer torn by doubt or perplexity. His mind was set on remaining in Iran or returning to Bharat Varsha when the opportunity arose. But that was a personal decision. To the pilgrim Aryas who wished to go forward in faith, he said, 'I hope I am wrong, though for myself, my journey is over; yet I honour your footsteps that go out to seek the land of pure. . . .'

Thus it was that even those who were of Purus's view assisted huge contingents that left for the land that would come to be known as the Kingdom of Ajitab and later, as Egypt.

One request was always made to those that left—'Somehow send us word of where, how and what you reach.' But it was an impossible request. Certainly, no news came from Egypt while the entire Arya contingent was forced to labour on the King's temple there. But absence of information did not deter the faith of many; and in wishful hope they said—surely all is well as none rush back here to seek help.

Meanwhile more Arya teams arrived in Sumeria from Sindhu; and the stream of Arya pilgrims from Bharat Varsha through Avagana to Iran continued. Right until his death, Purus and his men saw to it that, as far as possible, these Arya bands were assisted to reach areas of safety, throughout Iran, Sumeria and Assyria. After his death, this task was taken over, even more zealously, by his wife. Her own view was similar to her husband's though differently expressed—'Be proud, Noble Aryas! With God's help and yours Hari Haran Aryan is the land that we shall make the Land of Pure! Be with us; though honoured be your footsteps, wherever they lead.'

But many who came were prisoners of their own dream. What Purus and his wife said, meant little. To them, the whisper of their dream spoke louder than any warnings. That there was grim brutality and bestiality in Iran and Sumeria, compared to Bharat Varsha, actually strengthened them—it has to be total darkness to lead to total light, they said. No, we shall not stop in our quest for the Land of the Pure; the dream shall not die.

Some even had contempt for those that held Purus' view—'All they have is the triumph of being alive; but what is life, if the dream dies!'

Yet those that wished to leave were not without apprehension over what dangers lay ahead. Their dream was large but otherwise they felt small, afraid and ignorant. The land-routes, they knew, were littered with savages who robbed, murdered and enslaved. Besides, Nilakantha had already led a large caravan by land; so why duplicate the effort; hopefully later, there would be continuous mutual enrichment, as each group was able to send information out to the other.

Thus it was that several groups decided to leave from Iran by sea. Among those who encouraged this decision were seamen of Sapta Sindhu, who had reached Sumer, the Persian Gulf and Iran by sea.

Blessed as these seamen were with a familiarity with the long, navigable rivers and deep harbours opening to the Sindhu sea, the sea-route did not hold much terror for them. Shipwrecks there had been, but those were due to faulty planning and haste. This time they would plan and build better; even slower; and all the boats would leave together so that any boat in trouble had instant help.

A river entrance to the Caspian sea in Iran became the centre of boat-building. Locals watched the Arya flotilla of boats in wonder. It was not the number of boats, but the size of each boat that they viewed with awe. Hundreds of Aryas, with no intention of going themselves, had assisted the sea-going Aryas in building those boats. Their massive size only increased the fear that they would sink rather than sail.

But sail they did, beautifully and majestically, at the initial trials. And many more Aryas then—including locals in Iran—conquered their fear and began to join the flotilla.

Each boat had its own commander. The entire flotilla, however, was under the joint command of two brothers, Atul and Atal, who were the grandsons of Dhrupatta, the twentieth Karkarta of the Sindhu clan. Actually they were not his natural grandsons but were among the eighteen children adopted by Dhrupatta's son who had immersed himself in the task of the welfare of the tribe which was responsible for Dhrupatta's death in tragic circumstances.

Thus they sailed into the Caspian sea where none had gone before. Perhaps the first mistake arose from the command-ship itself. Dhrupatta's grandsons, in their enthusiasm, wanted it to go faster; the broad, open sea fascinated them and they were not content to hug the coastline as originally planned. Other boats tried to keep pace; but soon, because of the vagaries of the wind and waywardness of the command-ship, the flotilla split into groups.

A boat, looking in vain for those that went ahead, ran aground on the coastline. A few boats slowed down in order to assist.

Ahead, the flotilla went on through fog, thunder and lightning. The winds were more in command than the crew. They were committed to the unknown—and even if they wished to return, they could not.

But the fact is that their faith that God would grant it to them to reach their goal remained as unshakeable.

Meanwhile, the floundering ship needed help. Four ships rallied to its assistance. And in horror witnessed one of those ships scattered by a sudden gust of storm; it then hit some rocks and sank. And although it was near the coastline, more than half the persons on the ship were cast into the abyss of the sea, never to be recovered.

Nor was there any hope of saving the ship which had floundered earlier. Unseen rocks had damaged its bottom. Everyone had to swim to the coastline, with many later trips to bring out the food and supplies. Thereafter, all energies were diverted to towing the three undamaged ships to the shoreline.

Far in the distance, two more ships were coming towards them. There was no way to warn them of the treacherous coastline. One of them hit the hidden rocks and capsized. However, no one was hurt and they all swam ashore.

The second ship saw the danger and veered away from the coastline. It slowed down. Its commander, Sakaru, jumped into the sea and swam to assess the assistance needed by the stranded Aryas. But with dismay he saw that his own ship could not wait for him to return. Strong winds sent it forward. 'My own son exiles me,' he said, ruefully.

His son Rohrila was his next-in-command on the ship and was an excellent seaman. Only that morning Sakaru had complimented his son, 'You are a better seaman than I am,' and the son had cheekily replied, 'But I always knew that!'

Sakaru was certain that his son would bring the ship back to pick him up as soon as possible. But even so, there was no possibility that with two ships already lost, all the stranded Aryas could be taken on the remaining ships. Each ship had sailed with a full load.

They all waited at the mountainous coastline for days on end. No ship passed by. Even Sakaru's hope for his son's return dimmed. Food and essentials they had, from their ships. For fresh water, there was rain and mountain-depressions serving as reservoirs. Weeks went by.

They tied and secured their ships. Carrying all their supplies, they first moved northward, to avoid difficult mountains, and then circuitously to the west. Somewhere, they hoped, the mountainous region would end and perhaps then there would be trees from which they could build boats.

At last, on a day that was bright with sun, the high cliffs were behind them and they moved to the grasslands.

They got their first shock when they heard a thunderous roar like that of a fast approaching hurricane. But it was simply a herd of thousands of wild horses stampeding. The Aryas, now, had no doubt—if there were horses here, people could not be faraway! They went on—a little carefully though—for, their experience in Iran had taught them that people could be hostile too.

The area they had reached was below what is now known as Stavropol, beyond the northern boundary of the Russian Caucasus, between two rivers, Kuma and Kuban, though those rivers have changed their course, somewhat, since then.

They had their first casualty there. Arya Dharmavir died from no apparent cause, though they spoke of his age, exhaustion and the 'hurt to his heart as his daughter died in the capsized ship.' The area in which Arya Dharmavir died is now known in Russia as Armavir (map reference: 45.00n; 41.08e).

After trudging along, the Aryas reached a settlement which was friendly and curious. Its entire population lived under one roof, that went on and on, in undivided sections, made up of dry grass, supported by poles. The locals had hardly any utensils or articles of day to day use, apart from the horse-skins they wore and the patches of dry grass on the mud floor on which they slept. It looked more like a camp than a settlement, but that is how they lived.

The locals generously made place for their Arya visitors. Many rushed to add extensions to the grass-roof; but that was for themselves, as they gave up their own places on the mud floor with the dry grass for their visitors' comfort.

Sakaru had a quarrel with the local chief, all of it in gestures, as the Chief wanted to give up his own place to Sakaru. The Chief was the only one to have a canopy over his head, made up of horse-skins and supported on poles.

The language barrier prevented the Aryas from learning much. They wondered why the locals were all cramped together when there was so much land around. Wild animals, the locals explained, did not attack when they were all together; and if they did, it was easier to resist. They pointed to the mounds of stones around their sleeping areas. Those were the only weapons for attack and defence.

But the Aryas, as they rested there recovering from their bruises and exhaustion, found that it was not a village as such—simply a huge, extended 'family' that kept growing. Their customs, as the Aryas slowly began to understand, were vastly different from those of the Aryas.

There were no marriages at all. Each person was free to have sex with the other and there were no bars on a man sleeping even with his daughters—as no one knew who was whose daughter. There was however a customary prohibition against sleeping with the mother, though there was nothing against having sex with a sister. A person could co-habit with the same woman for any length of time, but it was open to any woman to seek sex from any man or vice versa.[1]

Sex was a ritualized affair—a bath before and a bath after; a perfumed paste of flowers to be applied to the body; and except on full-moon day, the booking of partners had to be made a day in advance and the act itself could begin only after the couple slept side by side 'in love for an eighth part of the night'. Nobody was really counting, but all these guidelines meant that one did not simply give in to sudden, momentary urges.

Thus exclusiveness in sex was frowned upon and even group sex was favoured, in order to give the entire village a large family feeling of togetherness. To them, the idea of a man and wife, solely for each other, and having children identifiable as their very own, was too ridiculous even to think about—apart from the fear that it could lead to the formation of separate families, hostile to each other.

They had a complicated calendar whereby nobody could have sex on certain days and it was connected with the size of the moon, except that when it rained and the moon was covered by clouds, the prohibition was off. Practically, it meant that sex was available for about eight days out of every twenty-eight.

Everyone in the settlement loved children; they never raised their voices and were rarely angry. They had no art other than making crude toys for children. They loved round stones which would be covered by layers of horse skin. Young and old played games with this 'ball'. Every victory with the ball would be punctuated by dances—vigorous rather than artistic.

Their season of youth was short. They were not a healthy lot. To the Aryas it seemed that it was due to their sole reliance on horse-meat.

There were wild horses all over. But they were not partners or friends of humans. Nor was the horse domesticated. The villagers would hurl stones at selected horses. When the horse was disabled, more stones would be pelted at the horse until it was helpless and unmoving and finally a rock would be used to smash it to death.

To the locals a horse provided flesh to eat, skin for clothing and manure for fuel. But horses were killed not for this purpose alone.

---

[1]It is not as if a man or woman was obliged to have sex with another on such a demand being made. Everyone was free to refuse but this 'tap' clearly meant that they could not continue sex with their earlier partners; and that they must have sex with others as well and, at least, as often as with their previous partners.

Over the pit in which a dead person was buried, the head of a pure white horse would be kept, to be replaced from time to time. If a child died, there would be five horse-heads and, if the Chief died, ten horse-heads, and all these were to be replaced regularly. The flesh of these horses would not be eaten nor their skins used.

The customs of the locals shocked the Aryas although they realized sex, marriage and family were personal or social affairs and there was no one true way of dealing with them.

But the brutality to the horses revolted the Aryas. When the locals next met to stone a horse, Sakaru, with a heavy heart, aimed arrows at the horse, killing it. Better to kill it outright than have it stoned—he thought.

The locals were fascinated with the Arya bows and arrows and surprised that only two arrows were sufficient to kill a horse. Yet they left that dead horse alone and started on another because they thought it was unsporting to kill a horse with a distant arrow. What chance did the horse have against an unseen, distant arrow! What chance did he have against stones? Why, he could bolt, leaving the other horses as victims— 'and sometimes, we even come away, without killing a single horse, as they all flee faster than our stones.'

Sakaru remained with the sorrow of having needlessly killed a noble animal.

The locals domesticated no cattle. They drank no milk, except for breast-feeding during their infancy. They killed no animals other than the horse, for food. If wild animals ever came, they were stoned but never eaten.

As it is, wild animals kept away from man. For them too, there were enough horses to go around and horseflesh was certainly tastier than human flesh. Besides, men made the task of wild animals much easier; horses, wounded and fleeing from stones hurled by men, were easy prey for wild animals. In fact it so came to pass that whenever men began throwing stones at horses, wild animals collected expectantly. At times, little jackals and foxes would be eating a horse, injured by stones, unable to move, yet not dead.

Why did they kill and eat only horses? They had a myth to support it—'When the Goddess gave birth to human children, all the animals gathered to admire them. The largest among the female animals quickly ate two human children. The Goddess cursed the animal and the animal crashed to earth from heaven; but it takes forty million sunsets for a crashing body to reach earth from heaven; and meanwhile, as the animal was pregnant, it gave birth to two animal-children on the way and they too fell, but the mother fell before and the animal-children landed on her soft belly though later that soft belly hardened to become the mountains behind. Meanwhile, the animal-children, unable to feed on the long way to earth, had become smaller and smaller and they are the present-day horses. So when human beings came to earth, they had permission to eat horses, who were descended from the dreaded female-animal who ate the first two human children.'

There was no hatred for the horses. They were not at fault for the original sin of their First Mother. But that original sin was enough to justify man's killing and eating horses. What did man eat before he ate horses, the Aryas asked. Funny question! Humans, they said, came after all animals and certainly after the horse.

Wistfully, Sakaru said to his Aryas, 'I would give up my quest, if only I could show them the way to understand and love a horse.'

They agreed, though their most pressing concern was to locate areas where trees for boat-building could be found. They had very little food saved from the ship. But the vegetation around had roots, even wild fruits and mushrooms to offer. Why did the locals not eat them? 'That food is for horses. We eat as man should,' they said. The Aryas had no idea of the lifespan of these people but it was obviously not more than thirty-five years though their boast was that they lived longer than any animal and certainly longer than horses.

The Aryas left behind much of their gear to look for the right trees. They came across another settlement. Customs, rituals and even man's relationship with the horses were the same there too. They found suitable trees, not too far away. They would be right for the small boats, but that is all they had hoped for.

The Aryas returned with the wood for their boats, to the first settlement. Their shock was great. The locals had killed innumerable horses to provide skins for the roof under which the Aryas slept and a skin-canopy, specially for the Arya leader Sakaru.

The locals gave up everything to assist the Aryas in carrying wood and building boats. They had never seen a boat before but were helpful in many ways.

Sakaru gave up everything to capture horses. He wanted to show the locals that the horse was a wonderful friend who could carry man above others, give man power and speed, haul goods, and was also good for sport.

Sakaru even created a myth of his own—that 'the horse, sad at his First Mother's original sin of eating human children, is keen to do penance and support man in every way.' But old myths die hard.

Sakaru had difficulties in capturing and training horses. For many centuries, the horses had had no enemy greater than man. If the horses had a conception of evil, man obviously ranked as the most malignant of all devils. Yet with patience and gentleness, Sakaru trained the horses which he captured and earned their respect and even affection. He would need them to haul boats to the coastline but meanwhile he was more keen on developing an understanding between horse and man, among the locals.

The Aryas were gathering and planting food too. They could not offer it as food to the locals. But they did serve it as medicine for those who were in bad health—and many were. To the children, mare's milk was being served not as food but medicine. Often, the locals found the 'medicine' to be tastier than the monotony of everyday horse-flesh. But what was more dramatic was the improvement in their health.

It took the Aryas over two years to return to the Caspian coastline. Patiently they had worked on the boats. Now with these boats and the ships they had left, tied and secured at the coast line, they could go on.

Sakaru had mixed feelings about leaving; somehow he felt needed here. But he was the best seaman among the Aryas. He had led them on from the coastline, kept up their morale and taught them boat-building. He saw the appeal in their eyes. He would leave too—he decided. The Aryas were his first responsibility.

Their goal? Back to Hari Haran Aryan—and then, God willing, back to Bharat Varsha. What of the land of the pure then! Maybe Purus was right. Maybe it was only high up in heaven!

A cry of despair rose in the Arya hearts as they inspected their ships which they had left on the coastline. The wind and weather had not harmed them as much as the worms had. They had almost eaten the timbers. The boats were no longer seaworthy and were beyond repair.

They went back to the settlement.

Meanwhile Sakaru's son, Rohrila, took over command after his father jumped out to assist the stranded Aryas. But the wind was merciless. His ship lurched forward, unstoppable, buffeted by storms. All he hoped was to steer clear of the coastline and avoid rocks, seen and unseen. Then came the time when he could neither go forward nor back but had to circle around.

When the winds cleared, there was a roar of joy, as Rohrila and his companions saw another ship ahead, and the feeling of loneliness, in the vast expanse, was gone. But tragically, the ship ahead was breaking up on the coastline, bit by bit. Rohrila would not stop to assist it and was later called hard-hearted. He was. His first responsibility was to his own ship.

Later, when the winds calmed and he returned, the ship was nowhere to be seen. Everyone was keen that he go where Sakaru had left the ship. He did that, circling the sea. He even saw the abandoned ships lined up on the coastline but no sign of life. He dared not take his ship to the rocky coastline. He dared not leave his ship to less experienced men. For days he remained moving up and down but had no luck.

Now, everyone on Rohrila's ship wanted to go back to Hari Haran Aryan and thence back to their own homeland.

What of the Land of the Pure, then? If they could not reach it, maybe God would bring it to them. Was it any different from what Purus had said—that man makes his own land pure?

They had chosen to travel by sea to avoid robbers and thieves. But nature was no less cruel. They had seen ships broken up on the way, with their men drowning and their commander even unable to rescue his own father!

Rohrila safely guided his ship back to Hari Haran Aryan.

But then he was single-minded in his purpose. He had to take the ships, he insisted, with the Arya warriors, to the land where his father was stranded. He pleaded—not his father alone but so many Aryas were there and no one knew in what condition!

But the ships were already being built, not for the Caspian sea, but for the journey back to Bharat Varsha. Why, he asked. By all means, give up your quest for the Land of Pure, but surely you do not go with the impurity of deserting your own Aryas in distress! Are you Noble Aryas then?

When someone slyly remarked that Rohrila was not thinking of saving stranded Aryas but rescuing his father, he simply said, 'Very well, I shall not bring my father back even when I find him.'

Rohrila's words proved prophetic. He led a flotilla of seven ships to find Sakaru and the others. They were found. A touching reunion between father and son took place. All the Aryas left except for Sakaru and sixteen others.

How could Sakaru leave! He was in the thick of his programme of domesticating horses, cattle, fowl and even wild dogs. How strange, he thought, in his own land it was the dog, then cattle, fowl and later the horse that were domesticated. Here, the horse came first.

Once he had said that to the local Chief who had laughed, 'No Sakaru. You were the first to be domesticated by us and thereafter, you domesticated us all. Everything good then follows.'

At first, Sakaru had not understood and attributed it to his insufficient understanding of the Chief's language. Later, he knew that the Chief spoke carefully.

The Chief was nearly forty years old and he had suddenly called everyone to declare his last will. He said, after him, Sakaru would be the Chief.

Sakaru had laughed and in bravado had said that if they agreed to eat what he prescribed and never stone horses, and have no horse-heads over their graves, he would accept. And the Chief said, 'I knew you would so ask. I come ready to say yes.' They all stared at the Chief—how could he give up horse-heads on his burial!

The Chief had died three days before Rohrila arrived to pick up his father. Sakaru was now the new Chief.

Does a Chief desert his people?

Sakaru remained.

In Sakaru's time itself, many nearby settlements merged to form a tribe. Horse and man became the best of friends. The horse ploughed fields, brought in harvest and tracked cattle. Above all, it proudly carried them above those who trudged on foot. Men and women of this tribe became accomplished archers, shooting arrows from horses for sport.

Later they would become talented artists too, but that was after Rohrila came six years later, bringing his wife Rausini and daughter Pamira and a group of twenty-two artists to settle down there.

Sakaru's introduction of a system of 'marriage' had limited success even though he created the myth that the children they all loved would live longer and healthier with such a system.

After him, Rohrila tried but far more success was achieved during the time of Pamira—Sakaru's granddaughter.

Thus it was that a new tribe composed of hundreds of settlements was formed under Sakaru—this man whose mother came originally from Saketa (next to modern-day Ayodhya) and father from Sukkur or Sakkar (presently in Sind, Pakistan).

Sakaru wanted to call it the 'Tribe of the Horse'. But the tribe came to call itself Sakaru's tribe or Saka tribe. In later centuries, archaeologists would call them Scythians or Seythians. However in Bharat Varsha their name would always be what they called themselves—Sakaru or Saka.

'Do not impose this arrogance on us! No man has the right to call himself a messenger of God.'

—(Aryas' plea to Priest Ugera of Finland who called them God's Messengers)

'These Aryas will not question what gods you believe in. They honour them all. But do not call yourself Arya until you learn their belief in goodness.'

—(Declaration of Priest Ugera of Finland to his people after 5005 BC)

'A plant will grow whether a saint or a sinner plants the seed.'

—(Arya Leader Atal—after 5005 BC)

On To Finland, Sweden, Norway

5005 BC

Meanwhile, the flotilla led by Dhrupatta's grandsons, Atul and Atal, sailed through the Caspian Sea to reach Europe's largest river, presently known as the Volga.

The Aryans called this the Ra Ra river.[1]

Sailing up the Volga, the Arya flotilla reached its confluence with river Kama.

Two more Arya boats capsized at the confluence of the Ra (Volga) and the river they called Omtar (now known as Oka). A coherent account of where they stopped and what mishaps and adventures they met with on the way in the Russian lands would take months to relate. But it was near the source of the Ra that they finally left their boats and went trudging on foot, until they reached the southern part of the country now known as Finland.

The initial enthusiasm of the Aryas had disappeared. Their experience at each stopping place had given them the frightful feeling that the Land of Pure, for which they set out, was nowhere within their reach.

They had seen their ships scatter and their men drown. The song of 'Noble Arya, onward on. . .', which always inspired them before, was still on their lips but was now an empty, ritual murmur that no longer came from the heart.

It had taken them four years to reach Finland and there were only 1,220 left out of the 6,080 that had left Iran. Their hope was that the many left behind them in the Caspian sea were unharmed and had found a safe haven somewhere.

---

[1]Atal gave this river the name Ra Ra. He was simply making an imitative, repetitive sound of the thundering roar of the river as it fell into the Caspian sea. A later poet says that the name given by Atul to the Volga was not Ra Ra but Hara (title of Shiva); another says that it was Hari Hara (Vishnu and Shiva) and was shortened to Ra. But this is doubtful, an Arya boat broke apart at the river's mouth, and another capsized soon after. The possibility therefore is that river was given not an auspicious name, but this frightening name of Ra Ra. Later the Aryas would shorten the name and call it the Ra river.

The Aryas set up their camp in Finland. Harsh reality had taught them on the way that their first imperative was to defend themselves. They built protective fences around the land they farmed and tried to live in seclusion from the others.

But the locals came, one after another, and then in batches. They were all old men and women, often hungry, starving, ill, distressed and dying.

There was a language barrier and so the Aryas could only wonder whether these old people were hermits uprooted by sudden storms or animal attacks. Or whether they were simply exiles.

The system, they later found out, was simple. Every old person, unable to work, had to leave his group and fend for himself. But how can you have such a heartless system, asked the Aryas. 'It is not heartless,' they were told. 'We did it to our fathers; and they, to theirs; how can the tribe flourish or even survive, unless it casts off its useless burden of old people? The old can neither march nor hunt but will only tie down the younger, productive members. Indeed, there were tribes in the remote past which carried young and old alike, but those tribes withered away.'

'And the helpless ones must leave?' the Aryas asked.

'Children are the really helpless ones,' they said. 'They are loved, cherished, protected, for they are the future promise. What promise does old age hold? Don't you people retire?'

'We do,' the Aryas replied. 'Then we become hermits and pray and meditate.'

'We can do that too, if we want.'

But the Aryas explained that it was everyone's duty to help, if a hermit was unable to fend for himself.

'Even if he is not of your tribe?' they asked.

'A hermit belongs to all the tribes,' the Aryas replied.

'Do animals, fish and birds rush over to you to be eaten?'

'No, our land gives us what we eat.'

'Your land, then, must be rich?' the old people said.

'Land is always rich. Everywhere.'

Clearly, these refugees saw that it was so, at least in the sprawling Arya camp. There were neat rows of plants; even cattle there was not for slaughter but for milk and breeding and fowl for eggs.

The refugees wanted to move after their immediate distress was over; they were a proud people and sought no extended hospitality or charity from the Aryas. As it is they had left their tribes on their own, when they realized that their useful days were over. Nobody had to tell them to leave.

But the Aryas insisted that these refugees remain. 'You can help us,' they said, 'to learn your language, farm more land, milk cattle, domesticate fowl.'

These were tasks the old could do as well as the youth and so the refugees stayed. The youngsters in their tribes may have been proficient in stone-throwing to kill animals or marching endlessly to hunt, but in this job involving the tender, patient care of land, cattle and fowl, perhaps old age was an advantage. They discovered new vitality while doing a useful job. The Aryas also had the same feeling as Sakaru did about his Saka tribe (Scythians), that it was the all-meat diet of these people which made them prematurely old and unhealthy.

Word went round that the old were welcome at the camp of these strange Aryas. They came in droves. But they were a proud people. They wanted work and not a hand-out; each one worked to the best of his or her ability. Often food would be in short supply when too many came. But they would never steal, nor take anything that did not belong to them. If they found eggs, they would bring them to the camp; if they caught a fowl, that too would be brought to the camp. This was now their very own tribe. They belonged.

The Aryas did not know it but these old people were their best protection. Word had travelled that these strangers offered refuge to their old and infirm. Sometimes, a group brought their old to leave them at the Arya camp. The system itself may have decreed the abandonment of the old as useless, but it is not as if every bond of affection was snapped at parting. Every time an old man left, there was silent sorrow, even though much remained unsaid. And when the tribes learnt that there was a group that gave shelter, food, comfort and even good health to their old fathers, mothers and grandfathers, their hearts went out to the Aryas.

Initially, the locals suspected the motives of the Aryas and came to check on them. But they found around their old people, not the curtain of isolation, but of respect and dignity.

Who could then attack the Aryas! Word even went forth that an attack against the Aryas would be treated as an attack against themselves. The old sheltering with the Aryas said they would die rather than allow an Arya to be harmed.

Tribal warfare was common in the land. But never would their sense of honour permit the locals to steal from another. They had to kill or enslave the other tribe before they took their goods—by right of conquest. Thus the Arya's tools and implements which the locals envied, and even their surplus food lying all over the extensive Arya lands, remained untouched.

But something more dramatic happened. Slowly, the locals realized what the Aryas were doing. They too began to progress from their existence as hunters and fishermen to a more settled life as agriculturists.

Some old refugees, sheltered by the Aryas, felt refreshed and renewed and even wanted to visit their tribes to show them how to make implements and tools, and how to make their land productive. Atul said to them, 'But come back! We shall be lonely without you.' And the hearts of these old men warmed with the sense of belonging.

When these old refugees reached their tribes, their own people wondered—'They left us old but they return young!' For, there was a new tone of authority in them. What will self-respect not do!

And the old came back to the Aryas, bringing their youngsters to learn how to set up fields and farms.

An old man once brought his entire tribe along with the tribal Priest Ugera to the Aryas to learn farming.

Atul told Priest Ugera of many of their adventures and delays on the way from Bharat Varsha and Iran.

Priest Ugera said, 'Our people should have learnt these arts of farming much earlier, but the Devil kept your people away from us.'

Atul, who was an artist, stood on the pedestal of the statue on which he was working, and looking at his reflection in the water said, 'The Devil exists as much as my reflection in water.'

This observation of Atul remains firmly in the traditional memory of Finland even today, but with a different meaning. Priest Ugera himself inspired the myth that God stood on top of a statue and 'ordered his reflection in the water to rise and this became the Devil!'

But Ugera was not at fault since that was how he had understood Atul's observation. From the other Aryas he had learnt of dualism—of good against evil. Was it any different from God against Devil. And when the Aryas spoke of God giving man the ability to scatter seeds and make the earth fruitful and smiling, was it not a defeat of the Devil and the unmasking of his deceit! But why did God bring up the Devil? Was it because growth was not possible without challenge?

To begin with, it confused Priest Ugera that every Arya he talked to, gave him a different conception of God. But then that was the Hindu way. Each was entitled to his own view of the Ultimate Reality without disrespect to the views of others. But later Ugera understood that all these stories were the many stories of God and it was folly to attach oneself to a single view or dogma.

Priest Ugera was even more fascinated by the stories about Shiva Lingum (phallic symbol), and for his people he evolved a conception of god of the sky (Skaj, 'the creator and birth-giver', and also Niskepas, 'the great inseminating god who is all knowing and all seeing and can grant great and gracious boons, but approach him not lightly for what is trivial').

The Priest had a long mud pillar made, representing it as a symbol of Shiva Lingum and the world order. The Aryas smiled, for in their own land they had not seen such a tall representation of the Shiva Lingum. But later, when the top mud portion fell off and Priest Ugera was sad, they all pitched in to make baked bricks and Ugera's joy knew no bounds as the tall pillar once again rose to a commanding height.

Priest Ugera's affection for the Aryas grew, but not because of their success in tapping wealth from the earth. He was fascinated by their myths and moral values; and he even wondered if this success arose as a result of the Arya's spiritual outlook. But Atal laughed, 'A plant will grow whether it be a saint like you or a sinner like my brother Atul, who plants the seed.' Atal always lovingly called his brother Atul, a sinner, as he devoted all his time not to caring for the land, but to his painting and sculpting.

Ugera wanted his people to learn from the spiritual values of the Aryas. But initially the impact on his people was more social than spiritual. When the tribes which settled in the vicinity of the Arya lands wanted to call themselves Aryas, Ugera emphatically said, 'No. You have not earned that privilege.' They protested, 'The Aryas honour our gods and they do not ask that we must honour their gods.'

But Ugera replied, 'They care not what gods we believe in. But goodness they believe in. And do not call yourself Arya until you learn to treat your old and infirm the Arya way.'

Priest Ugera's words began to be heeded, even in the lands beyond, now known as Scandinavia. He was their most renowned priest and poet. For him, as a priest, there was no threat of exile in old age; yet he spoke with fire and sang with passion. His words went to the heart of his people and he said—'God gave some of our people long life but you condemn your old to isolation and slow death. Are we to learn nothing from these noble Arya "messengers" whom God sent over mountains, seas and rivers to speak to us of their traditions of honour?'

Even the Aryas protested. 'Do not impose this arrogance on us. No man has the right to call himself a messenger of God.'

But Ugera said, 'God sends a message, though the messenger himself may be unaware that he carries God's message. Did you not tell me that the song of the jatayu birds guided the Hindu Tribes to your Sindhu river? I am sure God sent the jatayu birds; but did the jatayu know why he was sent?'

Opinion may have remained divided about the extent of the jatayu's knowledge of the message; but among Priest Ugera's people, slowly and surely, the system moved to respect old age and it became a point of honour with the tribes to keep their old and infirm until their dying day with respect and dignity.

Priest Ugera's words, inspired by the Aryas, still remain in the traditional memory of Scandinavia in their attention to the aged and the retired.

Priest Ugera called the Aryas and the locals who clustered round them the 'Moksa' (moksha) people. He explained the Arya belief in moksha to say that they all would be gods, as their right karma would free them from the bonds of birth and rebirth and their souls would merge with the soul of God, as 'One without the Second.' Till today, this pre-ancient Arya belief of 'Moksha people' continues to influence the tradition of the Finno-Ugric people who inhabit the regions of Scandinavia, Siberia, the Baltic areas and Central Europe.

New religions, with monolithic superstructures and inflexible dogmas have entered these places but cannot displace the traditional belief in the moksha people which still holds sway in these regions.

The emptiness at the core of the Aryan hearts remained. The realization grew that the whisper of their dream, to seek out the Land of the Pure, was based on fantasy. There was slavery, injustice, misery and tears all around; and if they were able to reach out and touch a few hearts, it was simply a drop in the vast ocean.

Many Aryas, led by Priest Ugera, spent two years in neighbouring countries, now known as Sweden and Norway. The situation there was no different.

Their desolation was all the greater as there was no possibility of going back the same way. Their boats, in a terrible state, were abandoned near the source of Ra. Nor did time erase their memory of the terror of the Caspian sea.

Yet they had no intention of remaining in the Land of Ugera (Finland). A new dream had formed in their mind—to search no more, but go back to their homeland: Bharat Varsha.

'It does not matter how many shed tears over a man's death. Be concerned with life, not with death! One cannot eat or drink tears, nor buy horses or houses with them.'

—(Advice to Bala, Arya leader, from his prospective father-in-law)

Their wealth, power and eminence were based on the poverty, misery and hunger of the people inland. That barrier must never break. The poor must remain poor or else who knows, the unthinkable may come to pass, and even the rich may suffer!

—(The situation of the eighty-nine ruling families of Lithuania—around 5005 BC)

'The dream, that promised so much was over. They woke up to the reality that the Land of Pure existed nowhere.

—(From the 'Arya Cry' in Lithuania—around 5005 BC)

Aryans in Lithuania, Baltic States and Elsewhere

5005 BC

The Aryas from the Land of Ugera made small boats to cross over the narrow strip of water now known as the Gulf of Finland. Thereafter they hoped to travel by land to find the route that led to Bharat Varsha. What if they couldn't find it? It was a chilling thought that they wanted to shut out. Priest Ugera put it in words—'Be back here, if God wills it; this is my home and yours.'

Only Atul, the artist, and twenty-six Aryas stayed behind. Priest Ugera's son and 280 locals went with the returning Aryas. Many more went but only for a short while, to bring back the boats. These boats were the Arya's parting gifts to the people of Ugera who had earlier seen only basket boats—dangerous and unable to hold more than one person.

As soon as the Aryas crossed over to the other side of the Gulf, they received hostile and baleful glares from many groups of locals there.

But as they trudged wearily inland, they were astounded to see people greeting them. Some even stopped, smiled and called them Arya.

It dawned on them, then, that some Aryas had already reached this land. Breathlessly, they asked by words, gestures and signs. The locals pointed southwards.

They now went on with joy—deep ecstatic joy.

What had actually happened was that the several boats that had followed the command-ship into the Caspian sea and then the Ra river had got left behind because they were slower. But then, while Atul and Atal's contingent had gone to the Land of Ugera, these Aryas found themselves on a different route and reached what is now known as Lithuania.

The locals in Lithuania kept collecting around these Aryas who now came from Ugera. Some would escort them to the next village; from then on, others would take over. There were greetings and good cheer all round. They even greeted them with Namaste and Om. There was now no doubt in the minds of the new-comers that other groups of Aryas had already arrived in that land, in large numbers.

There was also terrible poverty all round. Yet when the Aryas offered them the food they had brought, the locals took the tiniest portion, out of courtesy.

The locals ran in relays, day and night, from one village to the next, to inform the Aryas in Lithuania about their comrades arriving from Ugera.

Suddenly, unexpectedly, after long weary marches, the two groups of Aryas—from Ugera and Lithuania—met face to face. There was a roar of delight and then silence as each ran to embrace the other.

Each felt like a parent whose lost sons had been restored.

The Aryas from Lithuania had brought wine. 'To old dreams, to new dreams,' said the Arya leader, Bala, as he raised his wine cup.

Everyone drank. It was a long time since the Aryas from Ugera had tasted wine! It tasted like nectar.

Bala—who commanded the Aryas in Lithuania—had a dream that was different from those that arrived from Ugera. He too had moved out of Bharat Varsha fired by the dream to reach the Land of Pure. That dream was no more. And yet he had no wish to return to Bharat Varsha—'Let me remain where I am needed'. Although, many of his affectionate memories were centred around his homeland.

Bala had been a farmer when he left Bharat Varsha. His mother and later his father, died in peace. The parents of the girl he was expected to marry had climbed the social ladder and acquired greater ambition for their daughter. He was delighted to release her from the marriage-vow. For himself, he desired nothing, coveted nothing. But somehow he heard and re-heard the Arya cry to seek out the Land of Pure. Almost on an impulse, he joined them.

Bala saw abject misery and poverty in the land of Lithuania. His affection for his own homeland grew but along with it grew his determination to remain among these unfortunate people.

The entire coastline of the Baltic sea and river was controlled by eighty-nine families; each had over 100 members. They alone had the right to fish. Anyone else seeking to fish there had to comply with the condition of sharing the major part of their catch with these families and performing services for them.

These families developed as a race apart with contact only among themselves, never with the locals inland, except as servants and serfs. Occasionally, a man or a woman would be taken from among the locals for pleasure and sent back, rewarded with supplies of fish.

The families had viewed the arrival of 800 Aryas under Bala with indifference. Nobody had questioned their authority before and nobody—they were sure—would, in the future.

The landscape was bleak. Nothing edible for man seemed to grow there; but there was enough for migratory birds and small animals.

Bigger animals were highly prized, and when caught or killed, fetched a handsome reward in fish from the families that ruled the sea and rivers. But large animals were difficult to catch or kill, in the absence of all hunting implements, other than sticks and stones. Everything that moved or flew was eaten, including ants, frogs, insects, reptiles, mongoose, bats, cats, dogs, roaches and rats.

No attempt had been made towards agriculture or the domestication of livestock. If many starved or suffered from malnutrition, they had no complaints; it was all fate and arose from the supreme order determined by Laima, the Goddess of Destiny.

Bala, who led the Aryas, had a simple mind. He acknowledged destiny's role; but as a farmer he knew that the earth responds to effort. The soil in Lithuania was mostly sandy and at places, marshy; but Bala put his Aryas to work, not only to plough the land but to raise livestock. Initially, he was afraid of the locals, but without cause, for they neither stole nor battled to possess anyone's goods.

The Aryas were fortunate to capture four horses and when they were domesticated, it was not difficult to go far, to capture cattle for breeding milk and wild fowl to domesticate them for eggs.

To Bala belongs the credit for introducing butter and egg-nog (a mixture of eggs and milk) in the Baltic States. That is what his mother used to serve him, sometimes, as a child. Bala's masterstroke was however different. He had seen his father making wine from fruits. There were no such fruits here in Lithuania, but he tried to make wine from mushrooms and vegetables. He failed.

But, far away, on one of their horse-rides the Aryas saw a few plants with edible berries. Bala succeeded in making wine from them, though it was more bitter than sweet. He then had these berry plants transplanted to the Arya lands. But their growth was slow and he relied on collecting berries from marshy lands, until his plants and fruit trees came up.

Bala had encouraged the locals to work on the Arya lands. The locals expected it to be no different from working for the eighty-nine families, where they received a tiny part of their produce. Instead, here, they got it all.

He never gave wine to the locals. Instead, he sent it as a gift to the families. They wanted to buy it. It took days to negotiate the price.

He was permitted by the families to send 100 persons for two days to fish as much as they wished. Bala was ready. Three Aryas had already prepared nets, and practised with the locals. They went, with ninty-seven locals and their catch was phenomenal.

To Bala, then, belongs the dubious, unsporting honour of starting net-fishing in these waters and all that can be said in his favour is that he was a vegetarian and never ate meat or fish; and the idea of net-fishing was given to him by the fishermen in the Arya group. And the catch was so stupendous that hundreds of villagers were invited to feast on it.

These momentary thrills apart, there was growing melancholy in the Arya camp in Lithuania. The dream, with which they had left their homeland, had promised so much. But the dream was over. They had woken up to the reality that the Land of Pure did not exist. Yet this truth did not liberate their hearts. Their affection for their homeland grew; but with it came a silent, profound grief and tormenting questions—what folly tempted us to leave our homes?—how do we return to our gracious rivers and sacred soil?—are we to die in this wilderness like tired, old animals unloved, alone and empty?

Bala remained untouched by the storm in the hearts of the Aryas around him. He remembered his father who was not very prosperous but always gave much to his neighbours. 'Their need is greater,' he would say. When his father died, there were tears in the eyes of every villager. But the man whose daughter Bala was to marry lectured to him, 'It does not matter how many shed tears over a man's death. Be concerned with life, not death! One cannot eat or drink tears, nor buy horses and houses with them.' Later, the lectures stopped, when Bala complied with the request to release the man's daughter from her marriage-vow.

As he viewed this wilderness, Bala thought of his father's words— 'Their need is greater'—and he decided he would stay back, even if there was the prospect of return.

Bala worked like a slave but was also a slave-driver, except that he did not command with a whip and lash but begged and pleaded.

The Aryas had enough for themselves and even for the locals who worked with them. But Bala encouraged the locals to bring in more people to till more land and until those lands were productive, the locals were given food and other necessities as an 'advance'.

A few Aryas feared that the locals would run off with this 'advance' and even with the tools given to them to work on the land. But this fear was foolish. It never even occurred to the locals to flee when a debt was unpaid. Once a woman came to work for the Aryas and declined her 'advance' as she was the wife of a local who had fallen sick after receiving his 'advance'.

Later, The Aryas knew that many were working with the eighty-nine families to clear debts that their fathers and grandfathers had incurred.

Bala received a setback. The families found out that the exquisite wine he sold came from the berry plant. He had never kept that a secret. Hundreds of serfs and servants went out to collect the plants. The families failed to make wine out of it, unaware of the process. But so many plants were uprooted that it was difficult for Bala's men to locate more.

But this upset helped Bala in the long run. He experimented more with the few berry plants his men found, by mixing them with wild herbs and flowers. The concoction he produced was no longer light; it was bitter, intoxicating, but somehow its taste lingered, with a continuing desire to have a little more.

Bala's price of this 'wine' went up ten times but the families did not care. The waters were boundless with inexhaustible fishstocks; so how did it matter if these aliens came to fish for a few days, in return for this cherished wine?

Yet the principle itself bothered the 'wise' among the families. Their wealth, power and eminence were based on the poverty, misery and hunger of the people inland. That barrier must never break. The poor must remain poor or else who knows, the unthinkable may come to pass, and even the rich may suffer!

And so the families reached an instant decision—this Arya chief, who makes such great wine, must remain away from the locals.

Ceremoniously, a procession of 890 servants and serfs left the living quarters of the families. Each carried a tray made of bones on which every kind of fish and seafood was decoratively placed. The Aryas understood nothing but every local did. It was a marriage proposal from the families for Bala, the Arya leader.

This was the first time that the families had sought a husband or wife from outside. All their marriages otherwise were among themselves.

But horror of horrors! Bala refused. Instead of gratitude at this extraordinary honour, his mind went to the family of the girl in Bharat Varsha who was to marry him—'They wanted me not to be me but them.' He had released that girl from marrying him and wished her well; his wishes had come true; she became the wife of a rich and powerful man. But he still remembered that ineffable feeling of freedom when the marriage-vow was no more.

But maybe there was a stronger reason for Bala to shut this golden door of opportunity. A year earlier in Lithuania, a local girl had come to work in place of her father who died. The father had received an 'advance' and she felt responsible for the unpaid debt. Bala never subscribed to this heartless system of 'unpaid' debt from father to children and discouraged her—and when she insisted said, 'But how are you responsible! He is dead....' He saw her tears but did not realize that he had said something heartless. He had. His poor knowledge of their language was at fault. In their language, animals died, humans did not. What human destiny ruled was that each human had four lives—the first in hell, the second on earth and the third among the eighty-nine families who controlled fishing rights and the fourth in paradise.

Bala attributed the tears to her father's death and all he understood was that she insisted on working. He looked at her slender, delicate figure and instead of hard labour on land, asked her to milk cattle. But she had no experience of milking and cattle can sense the nervousness and fear of those that seek to milk them. She was hit on her head.

Later, Bala was sad at the hurt to her heart when he called her father 'dead,' and again, the hurt to her head by sending her to milk cattle, without showing her how.

But was that a foundation for love? Bala himself did not know what it was. As far as he knew, love came after marriage and not before—that was the system of the times he lived in, when marriage-vows were exchanged in childhood and people married early.

All he knew dimly was that he liked this girl near him; and he kept her to work on the flowers and herbs that he used for making wines.

Earlier, Bala had been much too preoccupied to think of marriage. Now, the marriage proposal turned his thoughts in that direction.

And in his mind came the vision of this local girl who mixed herbs and flowers for his wine-making. There was a yearning in his heart that he did not understand.

He spoke to Mathuran, the oldest Arya, who said, 'Brother, marry her; you will be very happy.'

Bala married the girl

The eighty-nine families may in time have forgiven the insult of having their marriage proposal rejected. But to marry a local girl immediately thereafter and have a public display with free flowing wine among the Aryas and locals alike!

A cold war between the families and the Aryas began. Its first salvos were tame. The families refused to buy wine from the Aryas. Fishing requests by locals were totally denied. Immediate payment of all debts owed by the locals were demanded.

None of this hurt the Aryas. Yet there was concern. Would this cold war lead to something worse?

But then came the joyous, fantastic news that a huge contingent of Aryas was coming from the north towards them. All else was forgotten. It was Mathuran who said, 'Brother Bala, I told you, your marriage with her will bring bliss. Truly, she is what they call Laima, the Lady of Luck and Happiness!'

Actually, in the Lithuanian conception, Laima was the Goddess of Destiny; but the word Laima, from its root-word, also meant 'luck' or 'happiness.' Mathuran heard the locals when they cried out with joy at her wedding that she was 'lucky' and 'happy' to marry the Arya chief. Thereafter, Mathuran and most of the Aryas referred to Bala's wife as Laima. The locals were intrigued initially but later they too began calling her 'Laima' and, a few centuries later, a myth emerged that it was Bala's wife who was the first Laima, the Goddess of Destiny. She was credited to have enticed, with her magical powers, men from another planet so that they would bring joy and prosperity to her 'chosen people' and then she married the handsomest of them all, and took him to her celestial home, from which she still watches her 'chosen land'.

A sketch by a local artist, of Bala's wife at her wedding, has survived, and the work of this artist would inspire in the Baltic States, portraits of Laima, the fair-skinned Goddess with her husband of dark skin, black hair and brown eyes.

But the fact is that belief in Laima, the Goddess of Destiny, of unlimited power, existed firmly in the Baltic area, long before Bala's marriage. In fact, the Arya effort had been to make the locals believe that human will could alter the course of human destiny.

The Aryas from Ugera were now with them. After a joyous reunion and a thousand questions, their minds turned to their most heartfelt wish—to return to Bharat Varsha!

Atal, the Arya-leader from Ugera, simply said, 'We came by sea and river but we will go back by land in the same general direction if we find it. The rest, we must leave to the gods.'

Bala remained silent but many Aryas from Lithuania agreed, 'Danger is there, as before. But now there will be no ships to lead us astray and away from each other.'

Others spoke of the dangers of remaining in Lithuania, now that the families were angry. The locals had reported that the families were sharpening their weapons.

Actually whatever the eighty-nine families were planning was now on hold. They wanted to teach a sharp lesson to the Aryas; but they had seen an Arya contingent crossing over from the sea and had wondered—are the Aryas summoning others to assist them?—how did they know what we planned?—how did they send word over the sea?—how did their men come so quickly?—do they have more contingents hiding elsewhere?

Meanwhile, as many Aryas spoke of their fervent wish to return, Mathuran interrupted, 'I want to go back to my homeland and I want to remain here too. My heart belongs to both places.'

Someone rejoined, 'There is a myth that Dhumarta was loved so much by two maidens that they cut him in two and each took a piece away, saying that half Dhumarta was better than none; and both maidens lived unhappily ever after. Shall we cut you in two pieces, Mathuran!'

No one laughed. The echo of what Mathuran had said was in many hearts. Atal turned to Bala, 'You have been silent!'

'For me, there is no going back,' Bala said.

Many gasped, 'Why?' Bala remained silent. He did not want to say that this land needed him. His father was ridiculed when he treated another's need as important; and yet his father's example influenced many. But Bala had no wish either to be laughed at or to influence.

Someone said, 'Bala is staying on because his wife is from here.'

But Atal said, 'Nothing prevents his wife from coming with him!' And quietly added, 'My brother Atul stayed in Ugera. I knew the reason. Yet he himself spoke of it only when we were parting from him.'

'What reason?' asked some.

'Who am I to speak the heart of another?' Atal said. 'Bala will no doubt tell you when we part from him.'

But the irrepressible Mathuran shouted, 'I know, I know why Bala will not leave! They need him here! This land needs him. I will remain too. I won't go!'

Later, a few came to Bala with the inevitable question—'Should we stay back?'

Bala replied, 'Your feelings must guide you.'

When they insisted, he said, 'Since you ask this question, obviously there are two voices in your heart. You must not stay here with your mind clouded and convictions unsettled. For you will not be able to leave later.'

About sixty Aryas including twenty women decided to stay back. But Atal was in no hurry to leave. He was concerned about the sixty remaining behind.

With Mathuran and Laima as interpreters, Atal questioned the locals. The families were angry. They had 9,000 adult members and many more serfs who would also fight alongside them.

The families had sticks with large sharp fish bones that hurt terribly. Their short sticks with pointed fish bones could hurt even more. They hurled those over long distances at the local children who entered their area without permission. They had 8,000 horses. Maybe more. They rode well; took exercise; played athletic games. Had they ever battled before? No, not in living memory.

Atal's last question—do they have bows and arrows?—the locals did not understand. Atal showed them bow and arrows. The families obviously had no arrows. This was the only bit of information that pleased Atal.

The next day, Atal demanded that around the Arya camp, ditches be dug so deep and wide that horses would not be able to jump across them. The ostensible purpose was to grow special plants for wine. All 2,000 Aryas worked on the ditches, except the sixty remaining behind. These sixty went to a scheduled spot with Atal.

'You are unfit to stay back,' Atal thundered when he found that only fourteen of them had good aim. As it is, in Lithuania, the Aryas had never practised with bow and arrows, lest the locals learn and start hunting animals, instead of planting crops.

Atal assigned his best marksmen to teach them. He gave his ultimatum—'Either you all learn to shoot or I cannot leave you behind.'

Atal then wanted walls built around the Arya camp. Bala objected, 'the families will see it as a provocation.'

Atal said, 'That is less harmful than your being vulnerable to them.' But he advised—'Let the locals know that the walls have been built for climbing creepers and vines to make liquor.'

Bala often diverted the people building these defensive walls to work on land.

Atal warned him, 'You left Iran under my command. My command does not cease because we separated.'

'Do we neglect land! Food is necessary to live.' Bala protested.

'Life is necessary to live,' Atal rejoined.

'Do you think sixty of us can defeat thousands?'

'That we must determine later,' Atal said. 'If I fear you cannot survive against them, I will not leave you behind.'

'No, I must stay back,' Bala pleaded.

'Of course you must. I shall not interfere with your decision to remain. But that will determine whether we leave or remain here to protect you.'

'You mean you will give up leaving for my sake,' Bala asked.

'Your sake! My sake! Bala, how did these differences emerge in your mind?'

Now Bala was frantic to help with the defensive works. He did not want it on his conscience that all the Aryas had stayed back on his account.

Their daily exercise with archery continued. Bala swore that he could shoot a target with his eyes closed. Atal remained dissatisfied with their progress. Practice continued. Bala said, 'The families mean no mischief. They have never battled before.'

Atal replied, 'Good, but if they do, you may have to teach them never to battle again.'

Bala was certain that he was delaying Atal's departure and now was frantic to do everything, possible and impossible, to improve the defences so that they met with Atal's satisfaction.

But Atal had many plans. He wanted to capture horses.

A hundred Aryas, with many locals, went searching high and low for wild horses. Strangely, information came from a serf of the families, of a faraway valley where herds of wild horses roamed.

The families, it seemed, went to that valley, sometimes to hurl short sticks with sharp fish bones at the horses and to kill them for horse-meat. They never captured horses to domesticate them since they had their own pet horses for generations. The offspring of those horses were enough for riding and sport. They never killed their pet horses for meat. Their old and infirm horses, like their old and sick serfs, were treated kindly, well-cared for, well-fed, until their death, and then they were buried ceremoniously.

Atal set up a camp in the valley with hundreds of other Aryas. For seven months they remained there, uprooting trees, making fences, enclosures and corrals to capture the wild horses. Their success, slow at first, was phenomenal later. They captured 1,100 horses. But he wanted over 2,000—to leave 100 with Bala and the rest for his men for their journey back.

The families watched in anger. They were unconcerned about the ditches and walls in the Arya camps; they thought those were for plants to make liquor. But there was much more that troubled them.

A poet points out that the families never intended serious bloodshed or battle. All they had in mind was a demonstration of superiority, as their fabled ancestors had done—to ride out, strike some with sharp sticks, burn a few huts, take a few women as prisoners, men too and release them after a while. Surely, the lesson then would be clear.

In their own lifetime, the families had never had to teach such a lesson but their ancestral memory was alive with many such examples.

There was also the earlier ancestral memory of how their First family rose to command the sea and waters in the land and with what valour, glory and bloodshed, it subjugated everyone. Out of that first family grew these eighty-nine families, the proud successors of that illustrious line; and though at times, in the dim and distant past, the locals had misbehaved, for the last three generations they had been so docile that the question of teaching them a sharp lesson never arose.

But now with the coming of the Aryas, something had gone wrong with the locals too. It was as though their aura of reverence for the families was not the same.

The families halted their plan for teaching the Aryas a sharp lesson when the large Arya contingent arrived from Ugera. From their servants they learnt that all the Aryas were soon to leave. Good riddance—they thought.

But months passed and the Aryas stayed on.

Atal kept horses only for the Aryas. But while looking for horses, Atal's men captured cattle too. He freely gave cattle to the locals in return for their help in capturing horses.

The families now watched with growing anger. They saw the locals with cattle. They saw hundreds of horses in the Arya camp. No doubt, the Aryas would soon be asking local beggars to mount horses and ride like lords.

Serfs of the families reported to their masters about the indifference with which the locals spoke to them. No longer did hordes of locals collect to offer services in return for permission to fish. None of this affected the families' lifestyle, but they saw the change in the locals' attitude and fumed.

Strangely, Atal was far more popular with the locals than Bala was. Atal made them laugh. Bala was more intent on work. Atal put them through the high adventure of capturing horses. He even gave them cattle, without demanding a promise that they would not kill it. Bala was quiet, serious-minded and would insist that cattle was for breeding and milking, never to be killed to eat.

According to a poet, Atal suspected that after he left, Bala and the sixty Aryas would be wiped out by the families. Therefore, the poet says, Atal was keen for the war with the families to begin while he was there with his full contingent. This poet then goes into a rambling account of how the war with the families started.

Under Atal's order, every Arya practised horse-riding. One day, Mathuran and Isran were enjoying their horse-ride. They stopped to chat with the locals, as usual. Among the locals was Isran's favourite ten-year-old boy. Isran often put the boy on his horse and they would both ride out together. This time the boy was foolish. While Mathuran and Isran chatted with the locals, the boy got on to the horse and started goading and prodding it. The horse, sensing the young rider's uncertainty, bolted, while the frightened boy hung on to the horse for dear life. Mathuran leapt on his horse to overtake the errant boy and horse.

The fleeing horse entered a colony which had shacks belonging to the families. These were not family homes. Such shacks were all over, for the families to rest on the way, when travelling. Here the horse suddenly stopped, finding no exit. A serf, angry at this invasion of the family shacks, kicked the fallen boy and hit the horse with a sharp fishbone stick. The horse bolted back to the Arya camp.

But then Mathuran came charging in, on his horse; and whether out of viciousness or fear, the serf threw the stick at Mathuran. It hit Mathuran in the face. Bleeding profusely, Mathuran picked up the fallen boy, put him on his horse and left. The boy was unconscious. Mathuran fainted as soon as he reached the boy's home.

That evening, it was clear that Mathuran had lost his eye. He did not know who had hit him in the family shacks. It was certainly not a family member so it had to have been a servant or a serf.

Atal sent the Aryas to the shacks to demand that the families surrender, within a day, whosoever was guilty. The serfs threatened the Aryas with sticks. The Aryas quickly left after announcing their message.

It may be that the serfs did not inform the families of this impertinent message. It may be that none knew who the guilty serf was.

But the next day, Atal went with many Aryas to the living quarters of the families. In the presence of many others, he grabbed and abducted a family member, announcing, as he left, that the man would be released only when the guilty person was delivered.

Atal's action sent shock-waves though the local population and consternation was rife even in the Arya camp. To abduct and imprison a member of the families! Did he not know that their person was inviolate? That they were above the law? That none may even approach them except at their command?

Even Bala begged, 'Brother Atal, there are better ways to. . . .' But Atal interrupted, 'I shall think of those ways, later, Brother.'

The Arya camp remained on the alert.

All the locals left the Arya camp lest the guilt fall on their heads too. In their view, what Atal had done was terrible and something far more terrible was bound to follow. Accusingly they looked at Atal, the man they had admired so much, for now he was about to shatter their peaceful way of life.

Atal seemed unabashed and simply cried, 'Laima! Laima!.'

In a few hours, serfs from the families came. They threw a man bound and gagged on the ground.

Atal released the family member. He had been well-treated but there was blazing anger in his eyes as he left.

The serf delivered by the families was still where they had left him. Bala was frantic and asked Atal, 'What will you do with him? Blind his eye! Will it bring back Mathuran's eye?' And when Atal did not respond, Bala shouted, 'What makes you think it is the man who hurt Mathuran?'

There was no certainty. It was an old serf, deaf and dumb. Mathuran could not identify him with his blinded vision. The ten-year-old boy would never agree to identify him.

Quietly, Atal said, 'I never intended to hurt the serf. Our quarrel is with the families.'

There was silence in the Arya camp. The locals remained away. All work stopped. They expected an attack that day itself. Nothing happened.

That night the Aryas said to Kataria who often led their prayers, 'Brother Kataria, pray that God may protect us.'

Atul said, 'No, brother, let us pray to each other that we protect ourselves. That is our duty, not God's. Let us not ask God to take sides, nor ask Him to do what we must do ourselves.'

Perhaps for the first time, Bala, rebelliously, raised his voice, 'Do you, Brother Atal, assume for yourself the right to tell us how we pray and what we seek from God!'

Humbly, Atal replied, 'No, Brother; I spoke for myself, of my own grief, and of the anguish of many—that we did not fight for what was our right in Bharat Varsha itself; that in our folly of reliance on God, we abandoned our homeland; that we devoted our energies not to protecting righteousness in our land, but fled to knock at other doors to find ourselves.' He paused and softly added, 'The dream was there within our reach and grasp but we left to chase it elsewhere. That was not God's doing. And what we do now, shall not be God's doing but ours.'

The attack came on the third day. But strangely, not on the Aryas.

Hundreds of serfs went, many on horses, to attack the locals. Clearly they knew which locals had been working for the Aryas. Those were the first to be taught a lesson.

Their intention was not to kill; only to burn a few huts and leave the mark of fish-bone sticks on a few faces.

But violence sometimes assumes a life of its own. Six locals died, possibly when they sought to save others. Two were however singled out for death—the ten-year-old boy who had foolishly found himself in the family shacks on his runaway horse and his father. His mother was let off with tell-tale marks of fish-bone on her face.

Yet the locals did not try to run to the Arya camp for refuge. Only a few came, fearing that the serfs were hunting them specially. From them, the Aryas learnt that the heads of the ten-year-old boy and his father had been paraded on tall sticks to strike terror in all hearts.

The attack on the Aryas came two days later. Grim-faced, determined to teach an unforgettable lesson, 5,000 horsemen left the family quarters. They halted at a distance from the Arya camp. Their serfs, mostly on foot, lit up torches that each family member held, to burn the camp. Sharp sticks lay in their saddle-bags.

The horsemen charged. But did they have a chance? Arrows rained on them suddenly, from 2,000 marksmen in the Arya camp. Horses and riders fell on each other. Cries of the wounded and dying rent the air as their bodies crashed into the mud. Some lay burning with their own torches. And yet those that rushed headlong could not stop—unable even to understand what was happening. Many reached the ditch, only to fall to the deadly arrows.

Dazed and demoralized, many of them fled while others staggered off. And even when they escaped beyond the range of arrows, they rode or ran wildly.

Somewhere along the way they stopped and did what men crazed with rage and humiliation do. Instead of returning home to lick their wounds or to renew their attacks on the Aryas, they went into the village, hitting, hacking, crushing every man, woman and child they came across.

It was an unplanned, cowardly assault and later even they did not understand what brought it on; but at that moment, their impotent fury over their debacle against the Aryas had to find an outlet.

Some family members retreated, not to attack the locals but to rally the huge throng of serfs. They realized that the Aryas had these mysterious flying arrows, against which they were powerless and their own horses provided an easy target.

Serfs were now dispatched with burning torches and sticks to bring their wounded back and to hurt the enemy.

The serfs marched; but scattered even faster than their masters. They too rushed to the village for easy pickings.

A lull ensued. The villagers were now rushing to the Arya camp to seek sanctuary. It was difficult to distinguish a friend from a foe. But later, many were allowed in and they told their tale of horror.

'They are without pity,' the villagers wept.

'So shall we be,' Atal promised.

The sun was about to set, but a bright flame-coloured light was still there. Atal rode with 850 Aryas, far into the family compound. They were not expected. A scream arose.

Atal perhaps simply intended to warn the families that there was no safety from the Aryas if their hostility continued. The Aryas, however, were amateurs at this deadly game and, like all amateurs, they caused more harm than necessary; their own fear made them hit harder and later a poet would say, 'No man is as violent as a man of peace when suddenly he must wield a sword.'

At the point of his spear, Atal made the family serfs release the horses in their stables. There were only 450 horses in that compound.

But Atal saw the carnage by his men and had no desire to raid the other compounds. In good order, he retreated with his men.

The dead and dying were everywhere. A returning Arya with Atal tried to assist a few wounded family members. They seemed grateful, but one of them rained blows on him with his fish-bone stick. His head split. He died that night. He was the only Arya casualty on that day on which so many others died.

That night, the family Patriarch came, on a litter, with serfs carrying torches. Atal readily gave permission for the bodies of the dead and wounded to be carried away by the serfs.

The next day, the Patriarch came again and Atal responded to his question to say, 'Peace is all we want.'

'But peace there was, until you came!' the Patriarch replied.

'Peace there was, only for the families,' Atal said.

'But there have to be masters and servants.'

'Then let the families assume the role of servants, having been masters for so long.'

Peace was reached.

The property and person of the families shall not be violated. None shall interfere with their serfs. Everything taken from the family compounds (including the horses) shall be restored. In turn, the families shall attack neither the Aryas nor the locals. There shall be no reprisal or vengeance for lives already lost. The locals shall not be taught to use, nor given, arrows. The Aryas also shall not use them against anyone or in the presence of any locals, lest the locals learn the art. The Aryas shall show the families the method of making wine and liquor.

The sticking point was the right to fish. Atal's demand: seas and waters belong to all. The Patriarch's view: they have always belonged to the families. Atal's counterpoint: then it is high time that the roles be reversed. Final decision: wherever on the waterfront there is a house, shack, structure or compound already built by the families, no local shall fish there or within 10,000 footsteps on either side. The families may build more structures on the waterfront and the restriction of 4,000 steps shall apply to the new structures. The families can fish anywhere even if the locals have structures on that waterfront.

Later, some criticized Atal. They said he should have demanded freedom for the serfs and refused privileges to the families. They argued that he had the upper-hand and could have wiped out the families—did the ten-year-old boy, hundreds of locals, and our one Arya die in vain?

Others contend that Atal knew the situation. His force was small; a single victory does not guarantee all victories; many Aryas would have died; their return to their homeland would have been delayed. And were these first steps not enough to lead the locals to eventual equality?

Atal was now ready to return. He had remained there for eighteen months. Even the family Patriarch, who became friendly with him, asked, 'Was it to war with us that you waited this long?'

Atal confessed that it was his need of horses. As it is, he had only 1,400 horses for his contingent of nearly 2,200.

'Then, why did you agree to return our horses?' the Patriarch asked.

'You asked for them,' Atal replied.

'Let me then loan you 800 horses,' the Patriarch offered.

'Loan? How can I return the loan?'

'Your men know how to capture horses. Let their first 800 horses be mine.'

'But if they cannot catch 800 horses?' Atal asked.

'Let it be a gift then.' Atal accepted the horses.

Some warned Atal, 'The patriarch wants you to leave so that the Aryas here are unprotected and hence this gift to hasten your departure.'

They were wrong. As it is, the families had lost their aura of invincibility after their defeat by the Aryas. Respect for the families among the locals vanished with their senseless raids; who could erase the memory of the parade with the head of a ten-year-old boy held aloft. Many mourned their dead and carried marks of the families' brutality on their bodies. No longer could the families be regarded as benevolent nobility.

And if fear and respect disappear, can an exploiter exploit any more?

Atal was certain that if ever a conflict erupted, it would be the families that would need protection from the locals. He was told that the locals did not fight. 'Now they will; they have their fishing rights to protect,' he said. 'Make a man rich and he will fight for his land.'

Meanwhile, the Arya camp was turned into a hospital to look after the wounded and to console the locals who had lost their near and dear ones. The Aryas looked at them with compassion, tended to their wounds and treated them with tenderness. Bala and his men also went round to assist the locals in rebuilding their destroyed huts. Of the locals, a poet says, the red glare went out of their eyes, their hearts were touched, their panic disappeared, replaced by calm strength; and perhaps some spoke and others not but in their hearts was the same thought, 'that they would rather die than ever allow an Arya to be harmed.'

Yes, Atal was convinced that Bala's group would be able to protect itself.

In a secluded area, Atal's men were working on making a boat. Thirty men carried it, as a gift from Atal, to the family Patriarch. It was his way of thanking the Patriarch for his 'loan' or 'gift' of 800 horses and was perhaps an insurance for the future.

Yet work on the boat had begun long before that gift of horses or even the conflict with the families began. Atal had intended it for Bala's group, in case they ever had to flee. Clearly, he had told them of the land of Ugera and how to cross over there from the Gulf. But now the boat was gifted to the Patriarch while Bala's group learnt enough to make boats on their own.

The Patriarch was fascinated with the boat. The families were delighted. The locals were awed. How different was this magnificent boat from their basket-boats! But the message was also clear. There is no limit to the wonders of these Aryas: their exquisite wines; boats bigger than huts; milk and butter; clothes out of thread made from tree-offerings; clothes from cattle-hair; musical-strings from horse-hair; nets for fish and fowl; corrals for horses; and arrows that fly . . . .

Yes; clearly, the unspoken message was—it was better to have these Aryas as friends and partners and not as strangers and enemies.

Many locals begged Atal that they be allowed to go with him. 'No,' said Atal, 'he who abandons his home belongs nowhere.' Later, he relented; sixty-six locals who had captured their own horses would go with him.

The time came for Atal to depart. Affectionately, Bala's wife said, 'You waited all this time for my husband's sake, is it not?'

'No, I waited here for my sake,' Atal replied. Laima smiled as if disbelieving him and he added, 'Maybe I thought of my father, grandfather, maybe Bala, our children, yours, all.'

'My children shall go to Bharat Varsha,' Laima said.

'Yes, they must,' Atal earnestly replied.

Atal begged Bala, 'Please don't touch my feet.'

'Why not? You are elder. . . and . . . and your footsteps shall reach Bharat Varsha earlier than mine.'

The moment of parting came for Atal and his contingent. There were tears in many eyes.

Atal embraced Bala. He embraced Laima, but through her tears she asked that he should embrace her not once but twice, 'One for me and one for the Arya I carry inside me.'

Joyfully, Atal shouted out the happy news to all. Smiling, with their eyes still moist with tears, they left.

*

This ends Atal's story in the Baltic States. His contingent left, hugging the Baltic coast, towards the land that is now known as Poland.

Peacefully, Bala and his group continued to live in Lithuania.

Six months later, the entire area erupted in joy as Laima gave birth to a son. It should have passed off as an ordinary event, but 'No,' said the locals, 'there is reason to celebrate; it is the first Arya born here!' He was their first, their very own Arya! Was he not born to their Laima, their own local girl! How could they not celebrate!

Bala and Laima's son was named Atalvia (so named to honour Atal).

Later, Bala tried to return the 800 recently captured horses to the family Patriarch but he declined saying that he had gifted, not loaned, his horses.

Slowly, but surely, distinctions between the families and locals started disappearing. Much of that arose due to the rising affluence of the locals from fishing privileges, boat-building, housing, agriculture and cattle-breeding. No doubt, it would take a century or two until the last remnants of any notion of nobility of the families was laid to rest.

Fourteen years later, Atalvia, eldest son of Bala and Laima, left Lithuania with Mathuran and 218 locals who called themselves Aryas. It took them five years to reach Bharat Varsha. Mathuran died soon after reaching home.

Atalvia met Atal in Bharat Varsha. Atal said, 'I adopted you as my own son in my heart when your mother said you were inside her. But I renounce that adoption if you will be my son-in-law.' Actually, Atal was a bachelor but had adopted his twin brother Atul's daughter who had arrived from Ugera, accompanied by hundreds. Atul had married the daughter of Priest Ugera. Atalvia and Atul's daughter were married. They remained in Bharat Varsha.

Thirty years later, Laima arrived in Bharat Varsha with many others bringing Bala's ashes for immersion at Varanasi. She stayed back with her son Atalvia, his wife and four children.

*

The close links between the languages of Lithuania and the Baltic states with pre-ancient Sanskrit are there for everyone to see. Almost half their words are adapted from Sanskrit. The relationship between pre-ancient Sanskrit and the Baltic languages was even closer at one time. But that was before learned grammarians in Bharat Varsha intervened, with their rules and codes, to transform Sanskrit into an unnaturally rigid language resulting in the death of this most elegant and expressive of all languages.

But quite apart from the affinity of languages is the evidence of closeness in the extensive folklore of the Baltic States and Bharat Varsha. Baltic folk songs and folk tales—perhaps the most extensive of all the European peoples—show a definite influence of the folklore of Bharat Varsha. That Bharat Varsha's contact continued with the Baltic states long after Bala is also clear from the similarity between the material structure of dainas (the four-line folk songs of the Baltics) and the short verses of the Rig Veda. Baltic dainas reveal a high level of artistic expression and their subject matter often followed the Rig Veda in its conception of the totality of human life, strong individualism, high ethical standards and love of nature.

The religion of the Baltics also came to be centred around gods called Deva and Devas (Dievas)—friendly and benevolent gods— assisted by a number of lesser gods patterned largely on the conception of the Aryas from Bharat Varsha. Their god Saule (sun) follows so closely, in specific functions and attributes, the Hindu god Surya that none can doubt close and continuing contact between the two peoples.

The same goes for the treatment of practically all those who occupy a central place in the pantheon of the Baltic gods. The old Baltic conception of Laima, the Goddess of Destiny, did undergo a change under the Arya influence, and this Goddess was no longer regarded as inexorable and inflexible. Although she was still believed to control human destiny at birth, an individual had the opportunity to lead his life well or badly; she also determined the moment of a person's death, arguing sometimes about it with the friendly, benevolent god, Deva (Dievas).

New religions that have entered into the Baltic region have had their inescapable influence. These new religions try to curb the tendency to intellectualize the Ultimate Reality; any philosophy, fancy or romance or even the spirit of tolerance, if it deviates from their rigid dogma, is frowned upon.

Even so, till today, in the Baltic mind, the pre-ancient Hindu folklore and the traditional memory of the Aryas, remains.

There are several other areas in Europe where the Aryas from Bharat Varsha went. Certainly, they went to Germany, about which, fortunately, considerable information is available.

But there were other regions too, to which the Aryas travelled. Unfortunately, the routes and the accounts of their travels are lost in the mists of time.

One source speaks of the Aryas of Bharat Varsha in Italy. But the account lacks a beginning and an end; and only a little of the rest survives. But then a later source points out that the ancient Italian culture is largely unconcerned with pre-Roman Italy and everything else is stamped out.

From the little that survives one can say that the Aryas established camps in Italy in the area that came to be known as Hindurya or Indurya.

Later, after centuries, this Italian area of Hindurya or Indurya would come to be known as Eturia, which in present-day terms corresponds to parts of Latium, Tuscany (Toscana), Umbria and possibly Campania.

The Aryas of Bharat Varsha in Italy came to be called Aryasenna (army of Aryans) or Ryasenna (people's army). Ryasenna was the people's army organized by the Aryas but composed largely of the locals, to stop human sacrifice and prevent abduction of people for slavery. According to Herodotus, Rasenna (Ryasenna of Aryas) came from the East through Lydia or in general from the Aegean and probably through the Island of Lemnos.

But even with this information it is difficult to pinpoint their route or adventures and accomplishments.

Only a few fragments remain of the influence of the Aryas in Italy. They were the first to introduce the funeral rites of cremation. A theory was advanced by the Arya leader there that worms enter into the body the moment a person dies (contrary to the common belief that worms attack a body only after decomposition). Neither the name of this arya leader nor the scientific evidence for this theory has been given. Instead, Dhanawantri's name has been mentioned.

Certainly, the Aryas introduced agriculture and the domestication of animals and fowls in Italy. Additionally, they are associated with Mandalas (intricate geometrical patterns).

The Arya leader's son—Gaipal—is known to have introduced the flute in Italy. The later predilection of the Italians for the flute was due to Gaipal's obsession; and the flute would accompany Italian banquets and even the flogging of slaves and love-making, though the Aryas of Bharat Varsha did not use the flute for such purposes. For the rest, little is known of how far the Aryas influenced their moral, social, aesthetic and intellectual values.

*

Apart from Italy, clues are littered everywhere, of Arya bands visiting many other areas.

One source, which survives only in part says, 'Eagerly, they went there and for long they could not leave but the imprint they left on that area, which centuries and centuries later would blossom forth as the fountain-head of European civilization, culture, literature and philosophy. . . and yet there was so much that they then found repulsive in that land where men remained married to men and women were regarded only as producers of offspring, but entitled neither to love nor tenderness nor comfort, and that land had neither real rivers nor forests nor tall trees.'

'Children, today I shall sing of the ancient gods of Germany.'
'Banaji, were they honoured as gods only in Germany?'
'Oh no, many lands in Europe honoured them. For instance, in England:
—Wednesday was named after the German god Odin (Woden).
—Thursday was named after the German god Thor.
—Friday was named after the German goddess Frigga.'
'But Banaji, were they also gods of the Aryas of Bharat Varsha?'
'No, children, they were heroic humans and friends of our Aryas. Together, they vanquished all their enemies to reunite the German tribes.'
'Then Banaji, how did they become gods?'
'Nothing is impossible for story-tellers and myth-makers.'
'Are they still regarded as gods in Europe?'
'No, children. New religions disallow gods of others.'
'So Banaji, the old gods vanish!'
'No children. Memory remains.'

—(From 'Songs of Bana Bhagat, Wandering Minstrel')

Aryans in Germany

5005 BC

Through the Black sea and river Danube, a large Arya contingent eventually reached the land presently known as Germany. The contingent was led by the three sons of Manu of Tungeri.

The influence that these three sons of Manu left in Germany is both profound and lasting. Even 4,000 years later (in AD 98), Cornelius Tacitus in his historical work, the *Germanica* (*De Origine et situ Germanorum*), relates that according to their ancient songs, the Germans were descended from the three sons of Manu and that the people of that area came to be known as Tungeri.

Tacitus was, of course, a renowned historian of the first century AD; he was a great public orator and high official in the Roman Empire. Some of his information about Germany also came from his father-in-law, Gnaeus Julius Agricola, Roman Consul, and later Roman Governor of Britain.

Actually though, Tacitus was wrong in suggesting that the German people were descended from the sons of Manu of Tungeri. The fact is that the Germans existed long before the three sons of Manu of Tungeri led the Arya contingent to Germany around 5000 BC.

For the rest, Tacitus is right—certainly there were innumerable songs about the three sons of Manu, throughout the German lands and the name Tungeri came to be adopted by the people there.

As it is, in Germany and even in the Bharat Varsha of today, there is a great deal of mystery about the origins of Manu of Tungeri, whose three sons crossed the Sindhu sea to reach Iran and thence from Turkey travelled first through the Black Sea and thereafter by river Danube to reach Germany.

Some say that Manu of Tungeri's father was a dacoit who may have come to Avagana either from the north (Russia?) or from the west (Iran?). He joined a gang of robbers and raiders camped at Sindhan in Avagana. It was the same camp which Sadhu Gandhara attacked to free the region from the brutality of raiders.

Everyone at Sindhan were overpowered and captured by Sadhu Gandhara but Manu's father was treated kindly. The reason was simple. He had a one-year-old child in his arms and it was assumed that he was a victim of the robbers and was not a culprit, himself.

When they asked him about his wife and the mother of the child, he had tears in his eyes. Obviously, the raiders must have killed or sold his wife as a slave—they thought—and everyone was sympathetic.

Soon, the Sindhan camp was converted into an ashram. The child, the youngest there, was loved and his 'father' was treated kindly.

But some refugees who came to the ashram recognized the child's 'father' as a robber. Sadhu treated this as a case of mistaken identity as the refugees often made mistakes in their eagerness to catch criminals.

The next day, the child's 'father' fled, stealing a horse, a sword and a few belongings of the others. The child was left behind.

Sadhu saw everyone's love for the child turn into contempt and was surprised that people should attach a father's guilt to a one-year-old. He promptly announced that this was not the child of that dacoit, but simply an infant who was cruelly snatched by dacoits from the loving embrace of his murdered parents. When the Sadhu was asked about the identity of the child's parents, he had no difficulty. He said it was the child of Manu—a learned sage.[1]

The child now sprang back into everyone's affection with the Sadhu's announcement. Some may have had lingering doubts, for after all, Manu's title is earned at an advanced age and it was odd that a Manu should have a one-year-old child. But they realized that for a child to be born, a man's age does not matter; only a woman has to be young, as nature, in its infinite wisdom, ordains that in each child's life there should be many years of mother's love and care—though a father was at best an asset.

Yet again, their doubts came to the forefront when, six years later, the dacoit who was briefly known as the child's father was mortally wounded in an encounter. He asked about the child at the ashram. Quickly, the child came but the dacoit had died by then.

The child wept. They told the child, 'He was not your father. He is nothing to you.' But the child replied, 'He called me his son!'

The elders did not understand the orphan's world. He wanted to belong—to love, not to judge, his father.

A later poet gives a clearer account. The poet, first, based his version on the last words of the dacoit before he died. The decoit was asked if he was really the child's father and he replied, 'I saved him once, he saved me once; and the bond lives, he will save me after I die.' Many regarded the dacoit's words as the ramblings of a dying man. But this poet had no difficulty in explaining them. According to him, when the

---

[1]Manu is a title that recurs in Bharat Varsha through the ages. Normally, it was accorded to a person who sought to discover God's laws—physical and spiritual—to convey his knowledge to others. Manu, then, was regarded as distinct from a hermit, muni, yogi, sadhu or rishi, who were concerned chiefly with the matters of the spirit, meditation, yoga or worship, though it was also common for a hermit, for instance, to be known as Manu, if engaged in the discovery of God's law. Thus a hermit, who studied astronomy, mathematics, or devised rules for 'seen' (written) language, could be called Manu.

real parents of the child were killed by raiders, the child had wrapped his tiny arms around the leg of the dacoit who felt sorry for the child and decided to save him.

Later when Sadhu Gandhara attacked, it was the child in his lap that saved the dacoit. Maybe, the dacoit even hoped that the child would pray of him, to bend God's will to grant him paradise. . . .

The seven-year-old child now was disenchanted with the Sadhu's ashram at Sindhan. He had begged that they dig a grave for the dacoit whom he regarded as his dead father. No, they said, the bosom of the earth was too sacred for robbers.

The child left the ashram; after years—and none knows how and when—he reached the heartland of Bharat Varsha. There too he was a wanderer; finally, at the age of twenty-two he settled on the banks of the Tungabhadra river (map reference 15.57n; 78.15e). He had no name as such, except that Sadhu Gandhara had called him Manu's son at Sindhan, to fit in with his story that he was the son of a Manu, murdered by dacoits.

At Tungeri (Tungabhadra river), he experimented with herbs and became renowned for his healing powers, both with humans and animals. He taught his healing art to many. No longer was he known as Manu's son but as a Manu himself—Manu of Tungeri.

No one knows for certain if he was the son of a Manu or a dacoit, or a poet. But he was a Manu in his own right.

Yet a greater mystery remained about his three sons.

When Sindhu Putra went to the Land of Tamala (Dravidham), Sage Yadodhra went to meet Manu of Tungeri. But Manu died, just before Yadodhra reached, leaving behind three children, no more than five years old, who were known to be his sons. Manu of Tungeri was known to be very old when he died, with no women nearby; and it was difficult to believe that these three dark-skinned children were the sons of Manu of Tungeri who was so fair.

The three went with Yadodhra to Sindhu Putra who adopted them as his sons; but they would always be known as the sons of Manu of Tungeri.

For the three sons of Manu of Tungeri, who commanded an Arya flotilla from Bharat Varsha, it was an enchanted voyage over the Sindhu sea up to Hari Haran Aryan. They suffered no shipwrecks or mishaps.

But there was much in Iran that they found distasteful. Purus, the Arya leader in Iran, had no cheering information. He spoke of Arya disappointment everywhere in Iran and in nearby Sumeria and Assyria.

Why not give up this journeying, Purus asked. But those who were with the sons of Manu of Tungeri asked—why not try elsewhere!

Many Aryas, disenchanted with Iran, Sumeria and Assyria, joined them and their numbers grew. They knew that two huge contingents had left—one by land (which eventually went on to find its way to

Egypt) and the other by the Caspian sea (which reached three different destinations—Russian Scythia, Scandinavia and the Baltic States).

Tungeri's group moved towards the land presently known as Turkey. Their experience was gruesome. Their numbers were large, their weapons many, but they had to remain on guard against sneak attacks and robbery. This certainly was not the land of their seeking.

When the sons of Manu of Tungeri tried to be friendly, even to give away gifts, the locals saw it as a sign of weakness and their demands and attacks grew.

The difficulties multiplied as they went deeper inland. The thought of returning to Iran and thence to Bharat Varsha began to seem more and more attractive.

But then as they saw the inviting spectacle of the vast body of water (the Black sea), their minds went to their smooth passage on the Sindhu Sea; and their imagination drew bold strokes, leaving a hope in their hearts that beyond those waters lay the land of their quest.

They camped near the Black sea for over a year and built boats.

Their voyage for the most part through the Black sea was smooth. They saw in the calm sea, a portent of things to come—a fulfilment of their dreams at their journey's end.

But a long way off, sudden storms whipped up the waters. A boat separated and was lost, never to be seen again. Two boats capsized, though except for a woman, everyone was rescued.

Ahead and around, more terrible storms were forming. The sky was overcast and the sea assumed a savage aspect; its currents gave up their sense of direction, as if intent on forming whirlpools to suck in the Arya boats. Was this not the very image of the funeral of all their hopes and dreams and of life itself?

And then the Aryas did what they knew best—they prayed. And the poet is certain that it was this prayer that dispersed the threatening clouds, dissipated the storm and brought calm to the turbulent waters; and lest we doubt the poet's words, he says, 'Remember! Among those that prayed were also the sons of Manu of Tungeri—they that Sindhu Putra graciously adopted!'

The poet continues, his heart full of gratitude, not only at the sudden calming of the sea but at the far greater wonder which the Aryas saw. To their left was a river, calm and tranquil. They called it the river Dana—for surely this was the 'bounteous gift from the gods'.

Thus the name of river Danube in every country bears the closest relationship to its original name Dana, which the Aryas gave to it. However, some may regard this similarity as simply a coincidence.[2]

---

[2]Dana river is commonly known as the Danube. It is the second largest river of Europe, after Ra (Volga). Along its course of 1,770 miles, it passes through many countries. But each country has a different name for it: in the Soviet Union, it is known as Dunay; in Bulgaria and Yugoslavia, they call it Dunav; in Romania, it is known as Dunarea; in Czechoslovakia, its name is Dunaj; in Hungary, it is called Duna; in Germany and Austria, it is known as Donau.

Slowly, the Aryas proceeded up the river. They often stopped, but only when the banks were deserted. Somehow, for reasons they never understood, they faced hostility from the people on the banks. People threw stones at their boats and ran when the Aryas tried to come close to the bank.

Did the locals fear that these strangers were some sea-monsters with innumerable heads and arms, intent on mischief against them?

Fortunately, there were many deserted banks to serve their needs to repair the boats and rest. But they always had to remain on guard.

Months passed. The voyage continued. At times, they forced their way to the banks, even with people around; and the locals would then flee while the Aryas remained for months waiting for the weather to turn merciful.

Doubts, even despair, would assail them on this endless voyage. The shadows on the river, even when it was calm and serene, began to appear like spirits of demons. The land around the banks was inhospitable. The dream that once inspired them lay dormant and the agonized question in their minds now was—where are we going and why?

It had taken them more than two years to complete their 1,770 mile journey on the river Dana. Now there was nowhere for them to go, for they had reached the end of the river, where it rose to the mountains of West Germany.

The locals saw the Aryas disembark. They did not run away but kept their distance. The Aryas were in a quandary. Should they remain or return? But their boats were no longer seaworthy and needed extensive repairs. Their own need for rest on land was urgent. The locals, however, did not respond to their friendly gestures and appeared to be more hostile than curious.

The next day, the local crowd grew larger. It grew excited as an old man reached them. Apparently, he was highly respected by the locals. Indeed, he was. Odin—their most renowned priest.

Slowly, Priest Odin approached the Aryas. He was shivering, as he asked his question, which the sons of Manu of Tungeri did not understand. At last, he raised his finger up to the sky, and then to the earth, as if to ask where they came from. One of Manu of Tungeri's sons pointed to the earth, to deny that they came from heaven.

It was the wrong answer. The gesture terrified the old man. Actually, his question was whether the Aryas came from the sky, where heaven was located or from below the earth—the nether world—where hell was located. The idea that these Aryas belonged to the mortal world of earth itself did not readily come to Odin's superstitious mind; nor had it occurred to the vast crowd watching the Aryas.

There was perhaps a good reason for it. The locals had never seen boats as large as theirs; they had never seen such strange bows and arrows; their dress was different; the speed with which they put up their tents was something remarkable.

But none of this mattered so much. What astounded them most was the dark skins, black hair and brown eyes of these people and they were certain that these strangers came, not from the earth but from a different realm altogether. Their own world, they knew, was peopled by men with blond hair, blue eyes and fair skins, and however enticing the different colours of these visitors, the locals could not conceive that there existed a part of the earth where people could be so different.

In their own local festivals, the actors appearing as devils or angels would colour their skins and hair, black. But in their real world, these colours did not exist on the faces and figures of men and women.

Even so, the visit from the higher or nether world would not have been so frightening except for the age old prophecy that either angels would arrive to transport mankind to the moon or devils would come to take them to the lower world, where wolf-headed women, serpents and malignant spirits would be laughing at them while they burnt in slow fires every day, and were thrown in a deep, dark well to be stung by scorpions and wasps each night.

The tragedy about this prophecy was that it was restricted not just to individuals, but affected the entire tribe. The fault of any of its individuals would result in the tribe being damned. And amongst the greater sins was also the failure to maintain the purity of the tribe, for instance, marriage with the member of another tribe or allowing a deformed child to live.

Even old Odin, who now appeared before the Aryas, was responsible for allowing his own child, born with a birth defect, to live. Thus he himself had contributed to the impurity of his race.

The deeply-rooted local belief simply was that each member of the tribe had to be pure and blameless, but if even a single member strayed from the path of purity, the entire tribe must suffer the nether world. There was no individual salvation. All rose or fell together.

The Tungeri sons were unaware of the devastating effect their reply had on the old man. They were busy ordering a cask of wine to be opened in order to serve the guest.

They had brought these wine-casks from Sapta Sindhu. They remained untouched for nobody was permitted to drink during the voyage. Even now, they wanted the drink not for themselves but for their guest, to earn his friendship and goodwill.

But Odin shivered all the more. He was deep in the throes of his superstition. He was sure he was being offered the last draught of the Devil and then this life would be no more, his eyes would close, and he would move to his eternity in hell. He pleaded, begged, to be given five days to put his affairs in order.

The Tungeri sons did not understand; they saw the old man's emphasis on his five fingers, and thought that the old man was simply pleading that he had given up drinking five years earlier. But what a kind, courteous man he was—they thought—to have tears in his eyes for refusing a drink from his hosts! With gestures they assured him that they understood. The Tungeri sons themselves never touched wine. They told him so. Odin understood; they were not insisting that he drink; he looked so relieved and grateful that one of the Tungeri sons was touched by his courtesy. He brought out a svastika seal and gave it to the old man as a gift.

With words and gestures he explained that it was the svastika seal of Sindhu Putra, his adoptive father, who was now in heaven and his finger was raised to the sky to indicate heaven.

A thrill went through Odin. He thought he understood now. Reverently he placed the svastika seal against his breast.

In the old man's heart, suddenly, rose joy ineffable; in his eyes, tears unstoppable. Now he knew—surely these celestial beings were not the emissaries of the Devil but of God in heaven; if they now came from the nether world, it was no doubt God who had sent them there for inspiration, a visit, or whatever; but they held a seal from God in heaven! And they were in effect leaving it to him to take the last draught of the Devil, or instead, this seal of God! Humbly, he bowed to the Tungeri sons and was about to place his hands near their feet; but one of them quickly raised him and instantly they were locked in an embrace.

Limply, Odin lay in Tungeri's embrace, unable to move, even to think. He knew, as everyone in his race did, that to be in the embrace of a Devil's emissary is to die instantly and go to the nether world; and to be locked in an angel's bosom also means the end of life, to be instantly transported to heaven.

The old man's whole life flashed before his eyes; he did not want to die, even to go to the highest heaven; there was something terribly urgent he wanted to do, for his unfortunate son before he died. Heaven and hell could wait. But that, as even a child would tell him, was impossible. Everyone knew that even the founder of their illustrious race had begged but was denied a moment after his embrace with the angel. No, there was no escape from that eternal, inexorable law. Oh, my son! My son!

Odin came out of the embrace, numb and dazed, his eyes closed, for he wanted to shut out the sight of whatever awaited him in the land of the dead. But nothing seemed to have changed. The earth was firm under his feet. The familiar sounds of the living were all around. Am I not dead then! Have I died without knowing I am dead? Is there no difference, then, between the dead and the living?

Then like the passing shadow of a fast-flying bird, his own superstition, formed by his ancestors of centuries past, vanished into nothingness. Still, he lacked the strength to speak. Everything was drained from him. Silently, he pointed to the wine-cask. Gladly, they poured soma wine for him.

Odin felt ecstatic joy as he sipped his wine. His mind clearing now. He looked at them all closely—from the dark skinned Tungeri sons to others of lighter complexions. He saw the colour differences in the hair and eyes of many. Yet they were together as a single tribe!

He had many questions but did not know how to ask them. The Tungeri sons sketched lines to show how they had come from beyond the river. But that was impossible, he gestured. Surely the river went into the forbidden realm of the gods? No, he was told, it merges into bigger waters (the Black sea) which leads to many lands, thence to another sea (Sindhu sea) and, finally, to the land of Bharat Varsha.

Even in the midst of his wine, old Odin had a sobering thought—there was a vast world beyond their river; and many tribes lived in the land of these strangers. Yet they did not kill each other, even though the complexion and physiognomy of some was different from others.

Yet he had a terrible doubt—why did this tribe of dark people come here? With all their gestures, the Tungeri sons could not explain that they had set out with the impossible dream to seek the Land of Pure. All that Odin understood was that they were wandering everywhere.

But why wander around, far from home, without lust, hunger, hatred or greed—Odin wondered. Clearly their gestures implied that they left, not for want of food, floods or the ill-will of gods. Why then? Were they going to enslave people and select sacrificial victims for the altar of their gods?

But if that was their intention why would they not say so? Odin's own tribe never fought deceitfully. Openly and boldly, they informed the other tribes of their intention to attack. Other tribes too never marched stealthily. Their tradition of honour and gallantry would never allow such treachery.

Only robber-bands or thieves attacked without warning. No, battles must be pre-announced. And if some unforeseen tragedy overtook the enemy tribe—like floods or a priest's death—the onslaught was postponed.

Odin was a priest—one of the twelve—of his tribe. He had to ask the awesome question about their intention, even though it was undignified.

Amongst them always, the arriving tribe stated its intention, openly and frankly. To ask, was to be suspicious, even insulting. Yet, he felt, he had no choice. He pointed to the swords and daggers, arrows which they had shown in response to his curiosity; and he asked, with gestures that were eloquent and expressive whether all these weapons were intended to cut the throats and pierce the breasts of his own tribe.

The question saddened the Aryas; but then they knew of the bloodshed in Iran, Turkey, Sumeria and Assyria. These people obviously had good reason to ask.

With every possible gesture, they reassured the old man that they came in peace, that the locals here they considered their brothers; that they sought nothing, wanted nothing, coveted nothing but harmony. The Aryas even started embracing each other and then pointed at the locals standing at a distance to show the affection they felt for them.

Odin looked into their friendly eyes, into their open, honest countenance. They were people of honour, he was certain, and the path they would take would never be one of treachery.

His parting from the Aryas was friendly. He gestured that he welcomed their stay in the forest. The Aryas wondered, though—was he suggesting that they not venture too far out of the forest? But then the forest was so vast. It had everything. They had no intention of moving out.

Till today, the forest occupied by the Aryas is known as the Black Forest (Schwarzwald: schwarz—black, wald—wood or forest).

Tungeri's hut was later erected at a place now known in Germany as Karlsruhe (map reference: 49.03n; 8.24e). When the Aryas set up camp there, it was called Kararuhe (which meant 'appearance of black people' or 'place of rest or leisure of black people'). Subsequently, it was named Karlsruhe, after King Karl established his lodge there.

Presently, the colour of the Indian skin can, by and large, be described as brown—be it light or dark. But it was not always so.

Anthropological and physiognomical studies are many and, without going into tiresome detail, it may be mentioned that the skin colour of the Bharat Varsha races was far darker before 5000 BC, than it is today.

A slight lightening of the skin colour came in with the integration of the northern tribes during the time of Bharat, nineteenth Karkarta of the Sindhu clan and also with the integration of Ladakh, Kashmir and other mountainous regions, after the success of the trans-Himalayan expedition organized by Karkarta Bharat, which saw the source of the Sindhu river in Tibet.

Closer links led to intermarriage and this had its effect on the skin colour.

The second phase came with the integration of Avagana with Sindhu in Karkarta Dhrupatta's time.

Of equal importance in the integration of the mountain tribes were the expeditions by the Gangapatis from Haridwar to the source of the Ganga river in Gaimukh in the Himalayas. The extension of the Ganga civilization right up to Gangasagarsangam, led to further integration.

Thereafter came Sindhu Putra's influence (as Mahakarta, Mahapati, Maharaj and Periyar). The frontiers of Bharat Varsha came to include all the present lands of India, Pakistan, Bangladesh, Afghanistan, Nepal, Tibet, Śri Lanka, Bhutan and east Burma.

Again, this assimilation had its effect on the skin colour.

Even so, the skin colour of the Aryas who left Bharat Varsha around 5000 BC was still dark, not so much brown but nearer black.

Thereafter, it really needs no study to demonstrate how the present transformation of skin colour from darker to lighter brown has taken place. The Aryas left India in large numbers. Many married there. They brought back their wives and children on their return. But more so, many locals came with them, inspired by the faith and values of the Aryas of Bharat Varsha. These locals came in large numbers from Iran, Assyria, Sumeria, Egypt, Germany, Finland, Sweden, Lithuania, Estonia, Latvia, Scythia, Poland, and even from Turkey, Italy, Spain and Greece.

Assimilation of these overseas tribes who joined the Aryas returning to their homeland of Bharat Varsha has undoubtedly had its gradual effect on the eventual skin colour of the people of this land.

But certainly, in 5000 BC, the skin colour, in particular of the Tungeri sons, who were even darker than the rest, justified the name 'Black Forest'. Equally appropriate was the name Kararuhe for the place where the Tungeri hut was erected.

To the fair-skinned locals who had never seen such dark-complexioned people before, it was a spectacular sight; and it should surprise no one that when the locals began to respect the Arya values, ideals and ethics, they commemorated these places (Black Forest and Kararuhe) with names to honour the advent of the Aryas.

*

Names such as Black Forest were given by the locals at an early stage, before they learnt to mix and mingle with the Aryas. But the practice continued; and such names were given to everything associated with the Aryas. For instance, their boats were called 'boats of the black people'. Again, their language was called 'black speech' and even their arrows, 'black arrows'.

But far more spectacular was the naming of the sea as the 'Black sea', as the name itself came to have some dramatic and profound consequences on European mythology, folklore, and even their exploration. This too needs to be explained:

For reasons explained above, the Black sea itself was so named after Bharat Varsha. The Aryas crossed it to reach Germany. These Aryas were naturally the first to use this sea from Turkey to join river Dana and finally reach the source of the river in the Black Forest mountains. Strangely, the Germans named it the Black sea before even setting their eyes on it, after the Aryas explained to them, at length, the route they had taken to reach their land. At that stage, it was still a mythical sea in the German mind, as their earlier conception of it was that there was nothing bigger than the waters and rivers around them, which went on endlessly, until they finally led to the home of the gods.

Later when many Germans joined the Aryas, on their return to Bharat Varsha, and saw for themselves this vast sea, it ceased to be mythical; and its name, the Black sea, became all the more common.

Not only the Germans but, much later, people living in the land now known as Turkey also came to call it Kara Dengiz (literal meaning: Black sea).

The question, how is it that the forest, camp and the sea were all called black, but not the river by which the Aryas came to Germany has been asked. The answer is simple. The Aryas had already given the name to that river as Dana (God's bounty which saved them from the storm-tossed Black sea) and no one felt it proper to change its name.

Names, by themselves, hardly matter. Yet the name Black sea itself led, later, to a celebrated Greek legend, which even today is regarded in the European mind and literature as quasi-historical in the sense that events in that legend are accepted as having really occurred and its heroes and heroines are believed to have actually lived.

Simply stated, the Greek legend speaks of the heroic voyage of Jason and the Argonauts who set out across the Black sea in search of the golden fleece to be found in a kingdom of black people there.

This thrilling saga has been embellished by folk tales and fiction over the centuries, but is believed to have a definite substratum of history. What is undoubtedly accepted as true is that the voyage of Jason and the Argonauts did take place but despite their heroism it was doomed to fail.[3]

The fact is that there never was a kingdom of black people in the Black sea. Nor was there a golden fleece, anywhere there. But what then was the inspiration for the fable?

One can hardly blame the poet who inspired it. It is not as if he simply heard of the Black sea and his versatile mind jumped to the conclusion that a black kingdom flourished there; no, his imagination was reinforced also by the known fact that the black people (from Bharat Varsha) were settled for a long time in Turkey on the Black sea coastline, and then crossed over the sea, to Germany.

Equally strong was the basis for the belief in the existence of the golden fleece. In its origin, the belief possibly arose from a German song. Translated, the song says:

> Thus led by gold under the skin of a sheep
> Came the black, from black deep
> And the Black Forest, to which the white river led
> With homage, bowed the golden head.

---

[3]It is possible to argue that the heroic voyage of Jason and the Argonauts over the Black Sea (to find the Golden Fleece with the Kingdom of Black People), never took place and that too is a fable in itself. Maybe. But the story of the Golden Fleece is deeply rooted in the European mind and literature as quasi-historical and there is no doubt that its inspiration arises from the voyages of the early Aryans.

This poem was translated by an Arya poet but was long ignored due to the obscurities of the line—'Thus led by gold under the skin of a sheep'. Later, the poem became clearer. Each of its lines was explained as follows:

- The command-boat of the Aryas had, at its helm, the large golden svastika, under an umbrella (canopy), brought by the sons of Manu of Tungeri from Bharat Varsha. The poet assumed that the canopy cloth was made of wool from sheepskin (statues placed outdoors were often under umbrellas or canopies, as a mark of respect or for protection from the sun and rain).
  It was this auspicious svastika which they hoped would lead them in safety to the place of their seeking (actually, it was golden; not gold).
- The black people sailed over the Black sea.
- The white river Dana then led them to the Black Forest.
- Germans (of blonde and gold hair) bowed to the Aryas in homage.

How this or similar poems reached Greece and inspired the Greek fable of the Golden Fleece is a matter for conjecture.

*

Odin, the old priest, who had met the Aryas, was certain that his colleagues would agree to a peaceful attitude towards this new wandering tribe of black people. He was the first to reach the Aryas, as his home was nearby, though other priests had also been hastily summoned.

All twelve priests and the Chief-Priest gathered two days later and their meeting was stormy. It need not have been. The spoken wrath of the priests was against this new tribe which, in their superstition, they regarded as a symbol of evil, because it was so monstrously different.

But their unspoken wrath was also against Odin. He had not before realized how unpopular he was with his colleagues, and the more he supported the Aryas, the greater was their venom.

The reasons for his unpopularity need to be explained. A priest enjoyed a position of wealth, prestige and honour. Wealth came to the priests from offerings made to them on days of sacrifice, which were thirteen in a year of 339 days. Before each sacrifice, the priests had to publicly immerse themselves in ritual prayers for thirteen days. Gifts to priests participating in sacrificial prayers were so lavish that even in dire sickness, a priest would have himself carried there.

If the chief of the tribe died, his successor was appointed from among the priests. Normally, the position went to the Chief-Priest, but not always. That decision rested with the Council of thirty-nine.

In fact, every recommendation by the priests had to be approved by the Council. (Maybe this was their way of achieving checks and balances.)

Thus, the priests spent the 169 days of public prayers on thirteen annual sacrifices. The number increased when a battle against another tribe was won and enemy prisoners were taken for human sacrifice.

The formal meetings of priests took only a few days. For the remaining days, the fiction remained that the priests were engaged in private prayers—though everyone saw that such free time was devoted to entertainment.

Yet, two years earlier, Odin annoyed his priestly colleagues. He stopped attending sacrificial prayers. Initially it was understandable, as his son was just born. But his absence continued, and later he said he would pass all his time in private prayers.

Odin left his priestly cottage and went to live with his wife and new-born son and a nurse in a hut far into the forest. Out of curiosity, the priests visited him at his hut. He discouraged their visits and would not speak, remaining engrossed in prayers when the visitors came.

The institution of hermits was unknown in that land then. No one was reputed to have retired to silence and solitude and certainly not a priest, who led a charmed life with choice liquor, music, entertainment and rights of intimacy with virgins selected for sacrifice.

But it may be that the hermit's appeal is timeless. The priests laughed at Odin but not others. As news of his seclusion spread, people came in large numbers. Odin begged for silence lest his communion with the gods be disturbed. People even built fences for him so that visitors to seek his blessings remained at a distance. But there was no way to prevent throngs of people collecting beyond those barriers.

Something strange will always occur whenever crowds collect for blessings. Some are healed by miracles of their own faith and credit the healing to the blessing. Others spread the word of those miracles, if only to prove that they knew something that many did not. Whatever the reason, faith in Odin's blessings grew. The crowds grew too. Many left gifts—a clear proof that their wishes had come true. Odin sometimes mingled with the crowds to distribute the gifts left by so many. That only sent Odin's popularity soaring.

The priests were furious with Odin as his popularity rose.

The Chief of the tribe was old and not likely to live much longer and the priests feared that the Council of thirty-nine might select the odious Odin, by-passing all the other priests, including the Chief-Priest. Already there were rumours that some Council members were enchanted with Odin.

As for Odin himself, he was leading the life of a lie for the last two years. Earlier, he had been popular with the priests. He had hunted, drunk, and sung with them and even delighted them with his poetry and painting. If he had a sorrow, it was that he married late and his nine years of marriage had not given him a child.

At last a son was born. He was ecstatic. He saw tears in the eyes of his wife and the nurse. They were not tears of joy. The child was born with a twisted foot.

The law was clear and inexorable. Anyone with a birth defect must die. How else can the purity and strength of the race be ensured!

The law respected no one. Once, even a child of the Chief of tribe had to die as he was born deformed. The Chief had tears in his eyes but came forward himself to announce the birth defect, and with it, the death of the child.

For Odin, there was no way out. He knew it. His wife knew it. The nurse knew it. But Odin shut out that knowledge. Iron entered his soul. I shall keep my son—he said.

Swearing his wife and nurse to secrecy, he covered the child's body in blankets and carried it out to accept everyone's congratulations, as if all was well.

Odin had no clear idea of what he wanted—maybe to keep the child for a few days but then what? He had already broken the law brazenly. The law of 'race-cleansing' was clear. A deformed child cannot be allowed to live even for a day. Perhaps there was some sense in this senselessness—to prevent bonds of affection from growing, to make a later parting even more difficult, leading to the temptation to break the law.

Later, Odin thought, that if he could keep his child invisible for two or three years, he could then fake an accident to show that the foot-injury was not a birth-deformity but arose from an accident. Many had tried this trick before but too soon after birth, leading to suspicion and arrest. He would wait.

But a priest and his family were highly visible and it would not be easy to sustain the charade!

Finally, he reached his decision. He would remain in isolation on the pretext of devoting his time to personal prayers to commune with the gods. With his wife, nurse and baby, he went with his 360 thralls (slaves) to a remote area, next to a stream. His thralls erected a hut, then sheds, to store his supplies. Thereafter, they hauled rocks, felled trees and dug ditches to make the approaches to his hut difficult. He then freed his thralls and no one knew or suspected his baby's defect.

Since then, Odin did not join public prayers and attended only a few meetings with the priests. But the wave of admiration for Odin came soon after and with it, waves of people.

Certainly, Odin was not at prayer in his hut. He had simply hoped to be left alone, so that no one discovered his secret and, meanwhile, he would paint and even compose poems while enjoying the proximity of his wife and the baby.

The nurse had 'bought' a healthy baby from a mother willing to part with her son for a large sum. There were now two children in Odin's hut—one that was hidden and the other that was displayed.

Distant watchers saw the baby playing and frolicking; at times, Odin took the child to the crowds. The baby—they all saw—was healthy and whole.

The day came for the real child to have a 'safe' fall from a tree and fake a foot-injury.

But messengers came rushing to Odin to announce the sudden arrival of a strange new tribe. Other priests were sent for but Odin was the nearest. As a priest, it was his duty to check on behalf of everyone if there was any danger. He went.

His meeting with the Aryas convinced Priest Odin that they had no hostile intent and would soon return after they repaired their boats and even built larger ones. Actually, Odin hoped that his own people would learn boat-building from the Aryas.

Now as Odin sat formally with the priests, his every view was dismissed with contempt. The conclusion—this Arya tribe was evil and had to be wiped out.

Odin felt the heat of their personal anger against him. But he remained unperturbed. Priests rarely recommended war with the tribes. A defeated tribe had to surrender six priests to the victors for human sacrifice. No wonder then that the priests never chose war and only the Council of thirty-nine or the Tribe-Chief took such decisions.

Odin shrugged his shoulders as if, to say, 'Very well; consult the Council and Tribe-Chief and if war it is to be, tell the new tribe.'

'War!' thundered the Chief-Priest, 'Who spoke of war? They are not a tribe. They are thieves, robbers. We don't war on robbers!'

Odin protested, 'Lord Priest, they are not robbers. But have it your own way. They can be told to leave.'

'Are you mad? So they leave, taking their boats and all they have! I hear they even have gold.'

'I saw no gold with them,' Odin said.

'How could you! You were too busy drinking their liquor and embracing them!'

Odin realized that the bystanders had obviously been questioned. Simply, he said, 'That was necessary to assess their intention.'

'Really! And they gave you a gift of gold?'

Odin showed his svastika seal. The Chief-Priest laughed, 'Is that all they gave you! These robbers are not generous. We should make them part with all they have.'

'I wonder,' asked Odin, 'who is the robber? They that came with gold, or they that wish to take it away from them!'

The Chief-Priest controlled his anger. 'Try to study this seal, Odin! See the rods pointing in all directions. They rob everywhere. What is our duty, then?'

'At least to tell them to leave, as I promised them they could stay in the forest,' said Odin.

'That right you did not have.'

'Certainly, I had the right. A priest speaks for everyone in their absence. All I must now do is to tell them to leave.'

'You will do nothing of the sort,' the Chief-Priest ordered. 'You will have no contact with them. I don't want them warned. Do you understand?'

'I do. They are to be killed while they sleep. But Lord Priest, is this your decision or everyone's?' He continued, as all the priests nodded, 'I see, it is the decision of all. Who am I then to question or disobey?'

The Chief-Priest asked, 'I want a priestly promise from all that none will speak to anyone of today's discussions lest it reach the ears of the new people.' Each gave the priestly promise. Odin gave the promise readily; the Chief-Priest asked, 'Your word to the Aryas to stay troubles you no more?'

'If it does not trouble you, why should it trouble me?' Odin replied, 'That word I gave on behalf of all the priests. And now my solemn priestly promise overrides all.'

The meeting ended. The Chief-Priest smiled at Odin, 'Do not grieve. Too long have you secluded yourself to understand realities. Go enjoy your two huts, two women and two children.'

Odin nodded miserably but his heart raced. Two children? Did he know something? Quietly, he left. But his mind remained confused. Two women, yes—his wife and nurse. Two huts, yes—one in which to live and the other in which to store goods. No problem. But the two children! How did he know? Had the nurse been indiscreet? Did the thralls who escorted the nurse when she went to buy the baby suspect something? Did someone see his child's defect before he moved out? How? Who? Above all, the awesome question: did he know of the birth-deformity of his son? But if he knew, why had he not unmasked Odin? Why should he? Would he not wait for the most dramatic moment? Maybe when the Tribe-Chief died, he would make the denouncement, so that he would be nominated Tribe-Chief. But he was already Chief-Priest and bound to be Tribe-Chief!

Day by day, Odin's mind got more clouded. Was it simply a slip of the tongue—two women, two huts, two children? Maybe. But then why that silky smile? He was too crafty to speak carelessly. Why did he speak at all, except to frighten Odin with the sword he held over him forever!

From fear, his mind moved to certainty, in the next few days—for how long will he spare me? He is bound to unmask me; my child, wife, nurse, the other baby will be killed. My own person, as a priest, is inviolable and they will leave it to me to kill myself. Should I have obeyed the law and killed my child? No, he shouted defiantly, hurling his fist against the floor.

Closely, he questioned the nurse. Could anyone have detected the birth-defect of the child? She was positive that no one could have. The child was always well-covered.

But the nurse also gave him some terribly disquieting information. The village-woman, from whom she had brought the other child, had been among the crowd outside the hut, twice. The nurse had never given that woman her identity when buying the child from her and ignored her, pretending not to recognize her even when she came to speak to her, outside the hut; and when the woman asked how her child was doing, the nurse told her that she must be mistaking her for someone else. The woman went back, disappointed. The only information that the woman gave the nurse was that she had moved from her original village as she was now married to the man who looked after the upkeep of the house of the Chief-Priest. The next time, when the woman came, she did not speak to the nurse but she had come with a number of people and, among them, the nurse recognized two servants of the Chief-Priest. But the nurse did not consider that strange as many came to collect outside the hut to seek Odin's blessings. In fact, the nurse was satisfied that the woman had believed her story of mistaken identity as she did not speak to her on this second occasion.

Odin was clear in his mind now. Loki, the Chief-Priest, knew. That smirk on Loki's face was not innocent, nor was his reference to 'two children' a slip of the tongue.

Odin's decision was made. In the dead of night, with his wife, nurse, and two bundled children, he left for the Arya camp. Surprisingly, the route was active, with so many locals having pitched camps nearby. He was challenged six times by his own people, but who would question Odin—'He goes wherever god's voice guides his footsteps.' It was Odin who asked why so many sentries were in these deserted areas. They knew nothing except that they were so ordered. Amazing!—thought Odin—how quickly had the Tribe-Chief's approval been obtained for attack!

He reached long after midnight, to find the Aryas asleep, unaware of the impending danger. Leave—Odin warned them—leave tonight, when nobody is watching. His gestures were clear. There was danger, terrible danger. The message sank in. But at night, where could they go? By land, they would be chased and hounded. By river, yes, though that was fearful too on a moonless night, but their boats were in poor condition; the journey had taken its toll; their repairs would take days and months.

After the last visit of Odin, in their assumed safety, they had taken apart the rafters from their boats to repair and refashion them. No, there was no question of some Aryas running away and others remaining behind. They all must live or die together.

Odin was in a daze. He wanted no battle. In his confused mind, he had thought that, once warned, the Aryas would flee and he was ready to flee with them. But he had no idea of the distances involved, nor of the danger and hostility that the Aryas had met everywhere en route.

For Odin, there was no going back. He had been seen on the way and his people would know where he was. But how could he remain with these people who were to fight his own people!

Oh, for one crime how many crimes have I to commit! All he could think of was that he would neither go back nor join the Aryas in their fight against his people.

Odin knew the philosophy of his times in the tribe—that men are frail and fallible creatures who require strong leadership and firm discipline to behave properly and function effectively. Only the Tribe-Chief and priests are strong. It was for the priests to establish a lofty moral order that each one in the tribe would adhere to—'or else, the impurity of a single individual will contaminate many and the entire tribe shall then decay and crumble....'

He recalled how Thor, the illustrious founder of their race, had ordered an intense search of that decay; and how hundreds were caught and wiped out in a single day, not in hatred or anger, but with compassion, only to ensure that the tribe was not corroded with those who were born retarded, handicapped, ill-formed or limbless. 'The weeds must be pulled out,' Thor had said, 'or else they will crowd out the flowers.'

It was then a single tribe. As its people moved to different areas, new tribes were formed, with new interests, new pursuits, new ideas and even new animosities. Yet they all honoured Thor, that single, illustrious founder and each tribe regarded him as their own. Each tribe also honoured its own priests as the strongest of all individuals.

But now, Odin did not feel strong and powerful. He felt like a futile waste in time and space.

Odin decided to leave his wife, nurse and two children with the Aryas. He himself would go out to die.

He would hang himself by his own hand. That is what the gods would demand for the crime of threatening the purity of his race. Yet, in his mind, he bargained with the gods—'See gods! I do not harm the purity of my race. I leave my child to these Aryas. His impurity shall be theirs and shall not soil my tribe. And for my crime of sheltering him for two years and violating my priestly vows by warning the Aryas, I shall give up my life. Is that not enough! Surely a priest's life is worth a thousand! In return, protect my child, my wife, nurse and the other child. They are blameless—I am the one who forced my crime on them.'

Odin looked around in the Arya hut. The Tungeri sons had left the hut to warn their men and to prepare to defend themselves. The nurse was asleep, unconcerned—what can go wrong when the priest is with you? The two children were also asleep. Frigga, his wife, had tears in her eyes.

Had he spoken aloud or had she understood what was passing through his mind! Frigga said, 'I want to come with you.'

Miserably, Odin looked at the sleeping child. She understood, but said, 'Your gods are wrong....'

He pressed his hand to her mouth to stop her blasphemy. This was no moment to annoy the gods. He had just struck a bargain with them—his own life, to protect his family's. By this surrender to the gods he felt free in his deepest being and purified of all sins. Yes, he had heard the voice that never let anyone down—the voice of Thor, the illustrious founder of his race. My son will bring no impurity to my race and I too shall pay the supreme penalty of surrendering my life for this momentary disobedience.

He looked at his wife's anxious face, 'Frigga, dearest, do not try to shake my resolve. There is no way out, except that I die.'

'What will your death avail?' she asked. 'You think Loki will spare your child after... after....'

Soberly Odin replied, 'No, Frigga, fear not; Loki hates me. But what has he against you? With my death, his hatred shall be no more.... And you will be sheltered by these Aryas....'

'For how long?' Frigga cried. 'This forest is soon to be attacked. And this refuge will be our tomb. And these Aryas?—Those that do not die instantly will be sacrificed to the gods. Only...only my son...' Frigga wept. She knew that her son could not be sacrificed to the gods but could certainly be strangled to death.

'Frigga, try and understand, Loki is your cousin. Ties of blood will prevent him....'

She laughed bitterly, 'Ties of blood did not prevent Loki from plotting against my father.'

'But that was only so that Loki himself could become the Chief-Priest,' Odin replied. 'And after your father's death, how gracious he was to your brothers, sisters and to you. He even helped your brother to....'

'Yet he always hated you!'

'Yes, but with my death that hatred shall cease. By pursuing you what can he hope to gain?'

'Gain? He will show the tribe that for their sake he is ready to persecute his own. Your illustrious founder, Thor, did that.'

Odin knew the story. Thor's brother-in-law was a cripple from birth. Thor had him killed.

'You grieve unduly,' Odin said. 'Loki may hate me. There are those who love me. They will protect you. If these Aryas can flee, go with them. If they cannot flee, rejoin your people and claim that you were prevented by the Aryas to come out. As for our son, do what we decided. A fall from the tree, an accident, a hurt to his leg....'

*

Odin was about to embrace Frigga again as he said, 'There is no other way; let me part....'

'I cannot part from you, my husband. I part from a priest. Bless me as a priest when you leave.'

She knew she had hurt him with those words. She wept. And quietly, he said, 'So long as I live, I am unforgiven by man. I need their forgiveness not in life but in death. Only from you, I need....'

She embraced him; and words tumbled out of her, like a lament that could neither flow nor stop, '...What can I deny you!... But you are wrong...your gods are wrong...gods that do not love have no right to live...they are the ones that are retarded...they are the ones who must be sacrificed...and not a little, innocent baby...no, gods must learn to forgive...to love.... All you did for your son was out of love.... You are a better god than those unfeeling, unseeing, sightless gods.... You are better, nobler...gods are not...you are merciful....'

There was a cold chill in Odin's superstitious heart. What was she saying! He knew that the gods never forgave an insult. He prayed, 'Gods, forgive her! It is a momentary madness. It will pass...forgive her.'

He kissed his wife. He kissed the sleeping nurse on her forehead. He kissed the other child and turned to his own. With a rush of feeling, he kissed the child on his lips, eyes, forehead. Surprisingly, the child was smiling in his sleep, maybe, in the midst of a pleasant dream. Softly, Odin said, 'My son! Nothing more can I give you. Only my love and that will remain till the end.' He kissed the child again. But suddenly the child opened his eyes, looked around and went into his father's embrace.

'Why is Mother crying?' the child asked. Odin did not reply.

'Why is nurse sleeping?' asked the child. That Odin could answer and said, 'Because she is tired.'

'But she never sleeps when I am awake.'

Odin smiled and said, 'Goodbye, I must go.'

'Where?' asked the child.

'To meet God.'

The sleepy child closed his eyes. Odin waited a moment, held his wife's hands and left the tent. He paused outside the tent to look at the starry sky and moved. But suddenly, he heard the child's shrill cry. He went back in.

Excitedly, the child was saying, 'Don't go, Father! God is here. You will not find him outside. He is here! Here! With me! Here!'

Odin was staring at the child. Frigga said, 'Listen to your child! He speaks with the voice of God!'

Odin's gaze was glued to his child's eyes, awake, bright, with no sleep in them. They were the eyes of a god, he thought. The child said, 'Yes, father! God is here.' and went back to sleep.

Now here, we are left at the mercy of the poets. They sing variously, and at length, their songs overflowing with rapture. But their message is the same—'that the child had seen a vision of the God that exists within us all....' Yet, there are also poets who are direct and forthright and one of them says, 'The child saw nothing of the sort. And let me now parade all the circumstances for you in a simple manner so that your simple minds can grasp this simple fact. Hear me then:

'The child's father, Odin, had given the svastika seal presented to him by the Tungeri brothers to his son. When the child had asked what it was, Odin had said that it was the seal that belonged to the God of the people that came from a land from away. And when the child heard that his father was going out to look for a god, he wondered why since the god was there with him. The child opened his eyes.

'Yes, the svastika seal was still there. "Why is my father leaving then? Does he think I lost it? How can I lose god's seal?" The child clutched the seal and cried out, "Don't go! Don't go! God is here, with me, with me!"

'Hear ye then my friend! That is simply how the unseen god of all gods sprang before Odin's mind's eye and his wife's—minds that were steeped in superstition, self-doubt and despair. But then that is how most gods are born and made.'

*

The fact then emerges that the child's simple, innocent remark, 'God is here! God is here!' was treated by both Odin and Frigga as the words of an oracle.

Their aching hearts wanted to believe what the child said and perhaps that is why they believed him.

Quietly, Odin said, 'I shall not go.'

Frigga said, 'Yes. You must not go.'

'If God wills me to die, so be it; but He is the one who will send for me,' Odin said.

'God wants you to live,' said Frigga

'But I broke my priestly promise.'

'You broke the promise to Devil Loki. God will be pleased,' Frigga said.

'I broke the commandment of Thor.'

'Thor wanted to commit incest with his sister and to have his brother-in-law killed. His was not the commandment of God,' said Frigga.

'Then what is God's commandment?' Odin asked.

'To love.'

'But I love my people too. Do I desert them and stay here among their enemies with whom my people will fight?'

'Who made them enemies?' asked Frigga. 'Did you not say they were simple wanderers on God's earth?'

'That they are.'

'Then Loki made them enemies. Loki is the devil. You will side with the devil?'

'No, but I will not fight against my people,' Odin said.

'No, that you shall not. God wills us to love, not to battle.'

Odin nodded but the instinct of the mother came uppermost in her, and she said, 'Yet if someone seeks to harm my child, he must burn here, as he will burn later in hell.'

The Tungeri brothers returned to their hut. They knew nothing of the upheaval in the superstitious hearts of Odin and his wife—where one superstition had replaced another.

As it is, when Odin had suddenly arrived in their camp, they had thought that they understood something of his anguish. Obviously, out of the goodness of his heart, he had come to warn them to flee, as he feared that his tribe would attack them if they remained. But there was no way they could rush out, until their boats were ready and that, he understood, would take time. They also realized that Odin obviously wanted to flee with them because his tribe would be angry with him for revealing their plan to the Aryas. And yet he seemed to be anguished, not about himself, but only about the son with the twisted foot. It seemed that he was pleading that the Aryas should look after him. The language barrier made it impossible for the Aryas to understand Odin's terror about the child or the customs of his land.

One of them had simply petted the child and lifted his finger to the sky to indicate that God above would look after the child.

Odin himself had seen nothing extraordinary in that gesture—a mere assurance of God's mercy and grace. But now Odin saw that gesture differently. He was certain that the Aryas were saying that his son had communion with the Gods.

Now as the Tungeri brothers returned to the hut, Odin's heart was bursting to tell them that he too had understood at last. With rapture he pointed to his son and high up to the sky. Seriously and repeatedly. The Tungeris nodded, happy that Odin was reassured of God's protection for his son. They had no way of knowing what was passing through the minds of Odin and his wife and what brought on that look of faith, wonder and repture. They simply nodded.

Odin's gestures made it clear to the Aryas that he would remain aloof from their fight with his people. They understood and respected that.

The attack began.

Initially, arrows flew. But in the thickly wooded forest, they were ineffective. A tree would halt an arrow before it hit the intended target. It would have to be a hand-to-hand fight.

The attackers had, as their chief weapons, burning torches and long lances with one pointed end hardened by fire. Many also carried wooden shields strengthened with animal skins. Their plan was simply to surround the Aryas and then launch a sharp attack on them from all directions, using the woods as cover.

Fearlessly, the attackers came. There was naught to fear—they were told. They would be facing a gang of robbers and thieves and not a fighting tribe. And even the rules of warfare were not to apply—the injured enemy must be slaughtered there itself; and only the 'whole' must be taken as prisoners for a sacrifice to the gods.

On an impulse, Odin left his hut where he was to remain sheltered with his family. He went towards the attackers. The Aryas wanted to stop him but they saw his resolute expression. Odin went on.

From a distance, the attackers did not recognize Odin. They laughed. Obviously, the robbers were sending someone to plead for mercy. Well, they would cut off his legs. But their leader said, 'No, let him come and have his say. Then we will cut his tongue out and send him back.'

But then they saw that it was Odin. They gasped and then bowed. 'Go back,' said Odin. 'They are good people. Do not seek to harm them.'

'But they are robbers, Lord Priest!' The commander said.

'No, they are God's people,' Odin replied. 'We are the ones who seek to rob them.'

'Our orders come from the Tribe-Chief and Chief-Priest,' the commander pleaded.

'My orders come from Him that is higher than them.'

'From Thor?' asked the startled commander.

'No, higher than Thor.'

The commander wilted, 'But what shall I say to honoured Loki.'

'Say to him that if he hears not the higher voice, he shall be smitten. And for his crime, all of us will be smitten. The hour of peril is nigh. The tribe shall crumble and be humbled into the pit of the nether world.'

'I. . .I dare not say that to him, Master,' the commander pleaded.

'Good! Better it is not to consort with evil.'

Evil! He had just called the Chief-Priest evil!

The poet here tells us that Chief-Priest Loki may or may not have been evil, but he certainly was foolish to have sent out forces against the Aryas which were in the area nearest to the Black Forest, for that was the very area in which Priest Odin resided. And Odin's renown in that area was unsurpassable. But then, how was Loki to know of Odin's desertion and it was probably easier to muster up forces closest to the area in which the Aryas were.

The commander still continued his weak protest, 'My Lord Priest, you still wear the Chief-Priest's sacred ring!'

'You are right, son,' Odin said, looking at the offending finger that wore the priestly ring blessed by the Chief-Priest. 'Marks of evil do not leave us easily.' He took out the ring, threw it on the ground, took a burning torch from a soldier, put its flame on the ring and said, 'Bring your torches nearer, let this evil burn, so that your hearts are cleansed; and then you may hear God's voice and not the voice of evil Loki.'

Hesitantly, as though against their will, some brought torches to burn the evil ring; and the thought came to them that they were scorching evil from their hearts.

Here, again, the poet intervenes to tell us that this was no play-acting on Odin's part—it was simply the case of one superstition taking the place of another. Somehow, says the poet, Odin's superstition now found its echo in the hearts of others too—for it was their most respected priest—a hermit, a healer, a miracle-worker—who spoke to them. And he said that a superstition could not disappear into nothingness. It had to be replaced by a higher superstition. For instance, if you believed that a monster had ten heads, no one could make you believe that it had only one head; but if someone respected came along to tell you that the monster had not ten but a hundred heads, you would be ready to accept it. Superstition grows; it cannot subside.

The commander and his men remained bewildered. They knew they would not attack. But what were they to do? How would they go back? With what face? What were they to say? Never before had a soldier ignored the call of his tribe. They had always been ready to lay down their lives, even when defeat and death were certain. The honour of the individual and the honour of the tribe called for such supreme sacrifice. But now this desertion! Was it not cowardice?

'What are we to do, Lord Priest?' they asked Odin in agony.

'Do?' Odin asked. 'Do what your honour demands that you do. You must protect these Aryas.'

'And forsake our own tribe!'

'Only to save it. To help it to keep its covenant with God.'

'But our covenant with our tribe? Our tribe will forsake us.'

'Then there is a higher destiny for you. You shall belong to the tribe of the Arya, the people of God.'

Thus failed this first attack, before it really started. Many stood wavering. Many more left, not knowing what to believe. But some remained, determined to prevent onslaughts on the Aryas, as their respected Priest Odin advised. With Odin, they moved into the forest to meet the Aryas.

The commander left with a few of them, uncertain in mind. But as he moved away, the effect of Odin's words withered. 'I am a fool to have allowed him to speak,' he said to himself. But he realized that it was impossible now to rally his men for an all-out attack—they were too much under the spell of Odin's words.

Dejected, the commander thought on—how will I explain to my superiors? But what is there to explain? It was Priest Odin who stopped us! And how am I expected to fly in the face of a direct command from a priest? But surely, you knew the priest was a deserter? No, I did not, until he spoke—and then it was too late. Really! Did he not say, the Chief-Priest was evil! Did he not arrogate to himself the right to speak on behalf of the gods above Thor? Did he not burn his priestly ring? Even then, you did not suspect that he was a deserter? Why you even bent your own fire-torch to burn the priestly ring blessed by the Chief-Priest! What would you have done to anyone else if he did that in the field of battle to prevent our men from attacking? Why, I would have cut anyone else down, but not a priest. Priests are inviolable. Yes, priests are inviolable, but not the Aryas. Why did you call off the attack? I did not call it off. My men deserted me. But not all; some were still with you!

These were the tortuous thoughts and self-doubts whirling in the commander's mind. All he knew now was that somehow he had to save his face against the Aryas. But the men with him were very few. So many groups had formed, each with its own thoughts and fears. Some had gone with Odin. Others remained on the edge of the forest, lost in their own doubts; some had gone their own way, wondering, wavering.

The commander feared that it was all his fault. He had failed in his resolve at the decisive moment, charmed by Odin's words. Now, he regretted it deeply.

He led the men with him inside the forest simply to make a show of force—enough to satisfy his superiors that he did all this despite the desertions enticed by a renegade priest.

Through a gap in the trees, the commander saw the Arya huts. Enough if we throw fire torches and burn them, he thought.

The commander deployed his men along the line and gave orders, 'As soon as I shout my command, aim fire-torches at the huts and then we all run to the village.'

His next-in-command pleaded, 'Don't do that. Order the men off.'

The commander flared up, 'Why didn't you go with that priest then?'

'No, my duty is to follow you. But there was goodness in his words and wisdom.'

'And there is treachery in your words,' the commander shot back. 'Now light your torch and throw.'

'That I shall not,' the next-in-command said.

All the frustration of the past hours in the commander's soul exploded. He waved the burning torch in his deputy's face as if to hit him with it. They grappled for it. Somehow, the torch struck the commander's face. The commander roared in pain. That, thought his men—far along the line—was the command to hurl their torches. They threw them and ran.

At the village, the soldiers halted. 'Where is the commander?' they asked. And the next-in-command also asked, 'Where is he?'

Meanwhile, the few local soldiers who had joined Odin reached the Aryas. Gratefully, the Tungeri brothers and other Aryas welcomed them. Frigga too came out of her hut.

But suddenly then, fire-torches began to rain on their huts. Fire struck the hut which was reserved for Odin. The nurse, who was sleeping, woke up and carried out both children, shielding them with her body. She was on fire herself. Outside, she collapsed, falling over the children. The Aryas rushed to roll her on the ground to smother the flames.

The nurse was dead.

Frigga's voice rose, 'Let him who ordered this burning burn on earth as he will burn in hell.'

She was cursing Loki. But it was the commander who was found later, burnt to a cinder. Nobody knew that it was his next-in-command that had hit him with the torch and run away and the burning dry gass had done the rest.

All that everyone realized was that Frigga had a powerful curse.

If Odin and Frigga's child had a birth defect, nobody would know about it, ever. It was the blazing fire in the hut that charred his foot. Part of his leg was also seared and singed by the fire. The child was in agony; and some feared for its life. The other child, who was known as the son of the nurse, was unhurt. In the presence of all the locals and Aryas he was adopted by Odin and Frigga as their own son.

After that one of the Tungeri brothers was always by the bedside of Odin's child, sometimes praying, but often applying herbal extracts and compresses to the child's blistered foot and leg. This was the least, thought the Aryas, that was due to the child of Odin who had come to warn and protect them. And Odin had even brought locals to assist them.

To Odin and Frigga's anxious inquiries if their son would live, the Tungeri brothers simply pointed heavenwards—'God's will shall be done.'

But suddenly, after days of vigil, in the midst of his prayers, one of the Tungeri brothers saw a half smile forming on the lips of the child. In joy, he cried out, 'Bal Deva, Bal Deva' (power of god; will of god).

He did not even complete his prayers. Odin and Frigga had heard his shout in terror and thought their child was no more. But now they watched fascinated. The child opened its eyes and smiled.

The Aryas collected and echoed the cry, 'Bal Deva! Bal Deva!'

Every day of the child's agony had built up the anguish in the hearts of the Aryas. They had felt the child's wound personally, for they felt that his family had come to protect them and the child had suffered! Now that fearful tension was no more. The child would live. They were ecstatic and each of them felt as though their own child had been spared.

Odin, Frigga and the locals would repeat 'Bal Deva' without comprehending it. Later, they would find out that it meant the power and will of the gods. But again, they would not fully understand it— what they thought was 'not that the child was saved by the will and power of god but that the child had, within himself, god's will and power.'

Thenceforth, the child would be called Bal Deva and later epics, myths, stories and fables would be woven around this child who came to be known in the mythology of Germany and Europe as 'God Bal Deva (Balder, Baldr) son of God Odin and Goddess Frigga, at whose feet bowed all, for with one foot he put all the dwarfs to flight and took on the sorrows of the Aryas whom his father and mother had vowed to protect.'

Many locals left the Aryas, a few never to return; but others left to bring back their belongings and even their families. They came back, not only with their own families but with others too. Odin's words of brotherhood with the Aryas—people of God—were being repeated all over.

Already, Odin had left his mark on many during his two years as a hermit. And they came, in hope, in faith and to be healed.

Chief-Priest Loki was irritated beyond endurance. There was little that he understood. Nobody could give him a coherent account. All he understood was that Odin had broken the priestly vow and was sheltered in the Arya camp. A priest turning traitor was unheard of and unimaginable!

And soldiers deserting! Never before had this happened! And it was all due to that odious Odin. And the commander dead and burnt mysteriously! And what did the Aryas suffer? A few burnt huts. Not a single Arya had died!

Yet Loki was glad that Odin and Frigga had not died. Let Odin live in ignominy, he thought, when he finally unmasked him.

Loki was sorry to hear that the nurse had died. He would have loved to hear her confess, under torture of the rack, how Odin and Frigga had conspired criminally with her to hide the birth defect of the child.

Loki had under his thumb the woman who had sold the child to the nurse. But it would have been nice, he thought, to make the nurse confess too, to this continuing crime! But maybe some thralls freed by Odin would know. Yes and then Odin could be unmasked by his own men to add that final blow to his humiliation.

Loki issued orders, 'Let all those who were Odin's thralls be arrested and brought here.'

As to the Aryas' survival, Loki was not worried. It was only one insignificant contingent that had gone against them. Now, he would send a formidable force and make sure that none of them were from Odin's area.

There was only one cloud on Loki's horizon. Neither he nor the Tribe-Chief could order the death of Odin. Nobody could. A priest could not be harmed. But Odin had thrown his priestly ring and burnt it in the fire! Even so, the other priests were firmly of the view that once anointed, a priest's person was sacred. How could other priests lose for themselves this privilege that separated them from all the rest! Well, let Odin live! In shame and humiliation, unmasked and scorned!

Frigga must die, decided Loki. Her son must die. Odin will hold no ring so he cannot participate in public prayers or sacrifice. Yes, let him live!—A living death it will be.

Loki was not the only one shocked by Odin's conduct. There was consternation among all the priests, the Council of thirty-nine, and the Tribe-Chief. The Aryas had to be wiped out. They were the emissaries of the devil to so tempt a priest.

Loki demanded a large army, under his direct orders. So be it, said everyone.

But something happened to bring everything to a standstill. The Tribe-Chief died. Many agreed that he was old, ailing, overdue for death. But there were some who said it was Frigga's curse that did it.

The Council of thirty-nine met. This was no time to make waves—with one priest, a traitor; an alien Arya gang of robbers at their doorstep; and desertions in their midst. Quickly, in keeping with tradition, the decision was taken to approve Chief-Priest Loki as the Tribe-Chief.

Ceremonies intervened. Those were more important to Loki than any attack against the Aryas. Retribution against Odin could wait. Strictly, it wasn't even necessary, any more, as Loki had kept the unmasking of Odin in reserve, to use it only if anyone opposed him as Tribe-Chief. But even though this high honour and position was now his, he still had the burning desire to make Odin suffer.

Even the rounding up of the ex-thralls of Odin went slowly, as so many ceremonies intervened. And with this delay, the news among the thralls spread. Some were caught but others fled to the Arya camp. Those that were caught would not admit, even under 'harsh' questioning, that they had seen Odin's child with a birth defect.

The thralls were paraded before the 'mother' from whom the nurse had bought the baby. Loki hoped that she would recognize the two men who were with the nurse when she came to buy the baby. She could not.

The thirty-nine days of ceremonies of the anointment of the Tribe-Chief were over. A formidable army was being assembled to attack the Aryas.

But from Odin's area too, locals were trickling to the Arya camp to be with their mentor. Loki was not bothered. Good; let all the traitors congregate at a single place to be annihilated with one stroke.

But before a victory of arms, Loki wanted a moral victory—to raise the righteous indignation of his tribe against the criminal conduct of Priest Odin. Frigga was his cousin; therefore Odin, a sort of brother-in-law; but he wanted to let the tribe know that he was of the mould of Thor who had denounced his own brother-in-law for the good of the tribe.

To the shocked audience of Priests, Council and others, he announced the charge against Odin, of criminally hiding the birth defect of his son. He could not say that he knew this all along, for to hide another's crime was as bad as being a criminal yourself. No, he had obtained the evidence only now.

The tribe-criers, with a drum-beat, went around everywhere to repeat Loki's speech throughout the tribe; and every charge against Odin was catalogued. It was not surprising, that in Odin's area, two of the tribe-criers were beaten with their drums tied to their backs, 'So that you with always know that your god is in front of you and your backside behind you.'

After his masterly speech, Tribe-chief Loki ceremoniously ordered Odin's effigy to be hanged. He was doing what the illustrious founder of the race had done. The priest was inviolable; but not his effigy. It was supposed to warn the priest of public scorn and suggest to him to do to himself what was done to his effigy.

But it all backfired, terribly. The illustrious founder of the race may have done that. But Loki was not the founder of the race. Nor was he regarded as illustrious, yet. The priests were hurt. True, many were angry with Odin, but they had all pleaded that he should not be harmed. Yet Loki was doing it by the backdoor—by hanging his effigy to suggest to Odin that he kill himself.

The Council of thirty-nine was annoyed. None of them really liked Loki. They knew he was power-hungry. They knew his intrigue against his own pious uncle (Frigga's father) to jockey himself into the position of Chief-Priest. Prior to that even, there was much that was not honest in his conduct as a priest. If only Odin had not taken the awesome step of deserting to an alien gang, he would have been considered for the position of Tribe-Chief. If only the exceptional disorder of many desertions had not occurred, they could have considered another priest. And now, Loki was making wild accusations and even hanging Odin's effigy! Not that what Odin did was right, but they were upset about the division of the tribe! And besides what proof did Loki have?

But proof Loki had. Or did he? The nurse was no more. Odin's former thralls were uncooperative. But he still had the 'mother' whose baby was taken by the nurse.

But he found that he no longer had the 'mother' of the baby, either.

The ex-thralls of Odin, paraded before the 'mother' of the baby, did not know what it was all about. Nor did they even know that they were being questioned so brutally under the orders of the Tribe-Chief himself. They simply saw a minor official brutalizing them and then parading them before a woman who was the wife of the Chief-Priest's servant. So that meant that she was the one responsible, thought the thralls.

One ex-thrall escaped harsh questioning by blurting out that the nurse never went about her business with the thralls, but was always with her foster-brothers, cousins and uncles who resided in a distant settlement. The 'mother' and her husband went quickly with the thrall to that settlement, to see if she could identify anyone. But the husband and wife never returned. Nobody knows what happened to them. A poet says, 'Maybe an accident, for pious was this ex-thrall and would never take a human life to benefit himself.' But another poet says, 'True, true, never would he take a human life, but they that followed Loki were reptiles. This "mother" and her husband hungered not for their child but simply wanted to serve Loki. What kind of a mother was she! And who spoke of a thrall's benefit to himself, when he had a god (Odin) to serve!'

There were six in the Council of thirty-nine who felt personally affected. They distanced themselves from Odin's association with the alien Aryas but they were perturbed by the Tribe-Chief's announcement, that 'I shall not violate a priest's person, but those that consorted with Odin, at any time, shall meet a cruel fate.' Actually, Loki meant Frigga, her child, and the locals who were now in the Arya camp. But his statement was far too sweeping. There were six who were known to have supported Odin as Tribe-Chief, prior to his desertion. Then there were two others, whose daughters were cursed by Odin's blessing while he was a hermit. 'Are we the targets too?'—they asked themselves. The fact is that the inviolability of priests did not apply to the Council of thirty-nine.

But there were objective voices too in the Council. And openly, they demanded of Loki, 'What proof do you have?'

'Proof!' Loki sneered. He asked that the mother of the child, from whom the nurse bought the child, be brought before the Council.

But the mother could not be found. He was told that she went to a distant village a few days ago 'under your orders' and had not returned. 'No problem,' he said. 'She will be back soon. And then you will know all.'

Thus Loki raised their expectations.

Meanwhile, he regaled them with the story of how Odin's child was born with a birth defect. How Odin had hidden that fact and had pretended to be a hermit; meanwhile, his nurse had bought a baby, whose mother would come to tell the story; that the baby was shown to everyone while the defective baby was hidden; and finally, that Odin, finding that he was to be unmasked, had rushed off to hide with the gang of robbers and thieves who called themselves the Aryas. 'Yes, you will have the proof. The mother of the baby bought by the nurse shall come to tell you the truth.'

They waited—agog with excitement.

The news reached almost everyone in the tribe. People came in droves to hear the testimony of the 'mother.' But days passed. The witness was nowhere to be found. Some said that she was dead; others said that she was in the Arya camp. But many laughed—'She never existed, except in the brain of great Loki. Or if she existed, she spoke the truth. So Loki made her disappear.'

There were serious poems though that severely criticized Loki and one spoke crudely to say that Loki's story originated from 'maggots in the inside flesh of Loki's brain.' This was the first time that a Tribe-

Chief was so dishonoured by a poet. The previous practice had been either to sing the praise of the Tribe-Chief or say nothing at all.

Loki's emergence, therefore, did bring about a new art in German poetry—ridicule and criticism of the master of the tribe—unknown and unheard of before.

There was much that angered people. Loki's reliance on 'dead' witnesses like the nurse, the 'missing witnesses' like the mother and her husband, may have been forgiven. But no one could forgive his crude and obviously false charge against a poor child, whose foot was burnt in a blazing fire and who was even now hovering between life and death. How dare he call this present injury a birth defect! One may as well castigate a soldier who loses a leg in battle. And then the malicious charge that Odin went into self-imposed exile to hide the child's defect angered them. Here was a saintly, godly man who loved and blessed all.

And Frigga! How could Loki accuse Frigga! She, who shed tears whenever anyone was troubled, hurt or dead! She that came with grieving heart, weeping for others! She that brought gifts and aid to the needy! Did ever any other priest's wife do that! No, the priests took; they never gave. And Frigga's father! What a saintly soul he had been!

The blow to Loki's prestige also came from people's suspicions. If Loki could fabricate such crude and wild charges against Odin, Frigga and the child, could it be, that somehow, Loki had also conspired to force Odin to join the alien tribe of the Aryas! What could he have done to achieve that? Were there limits to Loki's duplicity and subterfuge?

Or was it. . .was it that these new people. . .were really and truly a tribe of God! Maybe that was why Odin was drawn to them.

But more was yet to come! Suddenly, the news spread like wild fire that Odin's child lived. . .and had the power and will of God— Bal Deva. Who says so, they asked. Has the oracle of Thor spoken? No, it is the voice of gods above Thor! How do you stop superstition from galloping forward?

The trickle to the Arya camp grew.

Then there were those whose babies were strangled because of birth defects. Tears came to them, anew, in memory of those they had lost. Whether they believed or disbelieved the story that Odin's child was born with a birth defect no longer mattered. The fact was that Loki had charged him with that accusation. Odin's effigy was hanged. Frigga, his wife, and Bal Deva, his child, were threatened with a sentence of death. Their hearts went out to Odin. And they cried, 'He who fights against Odin aims his dagger at us!'

Odin's ex-thralls had fled to the Arya camp for sanctuary. They were being hunted to give evidence against Odin's child. They sought safety and were ready to be Odin's thralls again. But by now Odin had learnt enough of the Aryas to understand that one could not be an Arya and yet hold a slave. And he asked his ex-thralls, 'If you were ready to live with me as my thralls, will you not live with me as my brothers?' And again, the news spread that the thralls lived there as the brothers of Priest Odin and all Aryas! Equality with a priest! With the Aryas! And they called these good people robbers and thieves! Who could then blame the thralls if they escaped to hide with the Aryas!

Even those that lost their thralls wondered—what kind of a new Tribe-Chief have we. All these disturbances and even the thralls vanishing. It had never happened before. What ill-wind had this Tribe-Chief brought?

But it was the emergence of the new god, Bal Deva that stirred the poets.

And the poets sang of Priest Odin—the godly; of Frigga—the weeping goddess; and Bal Deva—who had the power of the gods that soar above Thor. The poets were certain that the people would accept their every word.

True, the people accepted much of what poets the said, but they were bewildered too. One could hardly blame them. They did not live in the television age where the attention span over any news item lasted a few hours, if not minutes. For them, anything new had to be discussed, debated, rediscussed and redebated, with everyone having expressed and reiterated his or her view. But when the news and songs came with such startling rapidity there was a breathless wonder.

Certainly, the people were bewildered. Loki was not. He had sense enough to realize that somehow his arrows against Odin had missed their mark. And nothing is so galling to a Tribe-Chief who meets with ridicule and criticism from the poets. He deeply regretted the loss of age-old values. Thor would promptly have roasted such criminal poets alive. Even those that followed Thor!

Could anyone even imagine such blasphemous utterances against the Tribe-Chief! The law was clear. He who offends against the destiny of the Tribe-Chief offends the entire tribe and it was the duty of everyone to report such criminals.

The time for reckoning would come—Loki was certain. Meanwhile, the Arya camp had to be attacked. Once the Aryas were wiped out, the tribe, he thought, would kiss his hands. Their boats, their gold, even their women would belong to him. And he would keep nothing. He would give it all to the tribe. They would then wallow in the memory of their ingratitude and repent.

Loki's mind was made up. He gave his orders. A formidable force was ready to march against the Aryas.

The poets were wrong. In their overweening vanity they had thought that Loki would not be able to raise a great force. But, obviously, the poets had misunderstood the temperament of their own soldiers.

To the German soldier, orders were orders—and if the lawful authority gave those orders, all questions ceased.

In Loki's words to the soldiers and commanders, there was a touch of piety. He said, 'See that no harm comes to Priest Odin or his family. In my view, he is simply misguided and I long to hold him in my embrace. Show no mercy to the men of the Aryas but spare their women and their property. If any of our men are with the Aryas, deal with them gently; be assured, they are the prisoners of the Aryas. These Arya robbers must be wiped out. For the rest, mercy is our mission.'

The army moved. The poets were aghast; the people, surprised; many were shocked. And some in the tribe accosted the commander and soldiers, 'There are our people too with the Aryas. You move against them!'

But the commander was clear, 'No, we shall not harm our people. We go to destroy the robbers and thieves—the Aryas.'

'But they are men of God!' said many.

The commander laughed. Nervously, many soldiers joined in the laughter. Sometimes though, the commander said, 'Everyone is a man of god—even thieves and robbers. We will kill them only to send them quickly to their god. Their god itself we will leave to Thor to destroy.'

'But their God is higher than Thor!'

'Really! Who is he?' asked the commander.

'Bal Deva!'

'Well he may be higher than Thor, but then here I stand; and my arrow can pierce a bird that flies higher.'

'You do not understand, Lord-commander. He is Bal Deva, the son of Lord-Priest Odin!'

'Oh Odin's son! Two years old!' the commander. 'And you expect Thor to fear a two-year-old! Thor! He that destroyed the devils of the nether world with one wave of his hand! He that conquered giants, dwarfs and the demons of chaos and brought order, so that all the gods came to touch his feet in humility, wonder, awe and reverence!'

But often the commander said not a word. His booming laughter or his contemptuous sneer said it all.

Yet, the soldiers felt there was something missing, something lost. Whenever in the past they had marched to do battle, there had been applause, waving, laughter, with men cheering, children waving and women blowing kisses.

Why this sullenness now, wondered the soldiers, but in their hearts they too knew the answer.

Their most cheerless time came when they passed through the area near which Odin had resided as a hermit and in a mournful tune, a poet sang 'Our bravest go out to kill the best;

> Gods to kill, Gods to waste;
> Oh make haste. . .make haste!

The commander stopped. He hit the poet. The people with the poet helped him up; but his eight-year-old daughter ran and asked a soldier on the march, 'Why did you hit my father?'

The soldier stopped and the march of the soldiers behind him halted. 'No, little one, I did not hit him. The commander hit him.'

But the girl asked, 'Why did you allow him to hit my father?'

The soldier smiled. 'We don't allow the commander. He is the one who orders us.'

The commander tuned back, unhappy that the soldiers at the back had stopped. 'You are a beast, a beast,' the girl shouted at him.

The commander was angry and raised his hand, as if to hit the girl. The soldier shielded the girl. 'No commander, no,' said the soldier. 'She is a child.'

The commander glared. 'I was not going to hit her. I was just trying to frighten her.'

'It is not good to frighten children,' the soldier replied.

The commander glared at the soldier. The soldier did not lower his eyes. Perhaps, he had an eight-year-old girl himself. Or perhaps he understood the anguish of the girl. Or perhaps, he was no longer proud to be a part of the mission. Yet the commander knew that this was a soldier who loved discipline and respected authority.

'Start marching!' the commander barked.

He waited for the soldiers to reform their lines. The girl cried out to the passers-by, 'The commander hit my father.'

'Why?' asked some.

'Because this commander is a beast, a beast,' the girl shouted, unafraid. Silently, the commander went to take his position in front.

They would hear the curse again, 'Beast! Beast!' as they passed.

The commander shrugged his shoulders, unconcerned—let the dogs bark. But there was hurt in the hearts of the soldiers. Were they being driven to a heartless mission?

Never before had the soldiers seen any difference or distance between themselves and the people. Their hearts were always in unison. Why then this gulf, now? They marched, but no longer with pride.

The soldiers' destination was the Black Forest which was not too far off. Rest, the commander decided, they would take near the forest. It was best to remain away from the inhospitable, cheerless 'Odin' area, where the villagers had neither grace, nor sense, nor manners.

In front of the Black Forest, Loki's army rested. It was a mistake to give such a clear notice of their arrival to the Aryas. But the Aryas themselves were not keeping watch. They were far behind, deep in the forest. The frontline defence was taken over by the locals.

In fact Odin was surprised at first to see what the Aryas were doing. All boat-building activity had stopped. Every moment of their time was devoted to defensive works—digging trenches, building walls, felling trees. This, thought Odin, was not the way to fight.

In Odin's tribes, the opposing armies faced each other openly with lances, daggers, swords and shields—charge, counter-charge, regroup, charge. True, many hid behind the cover of trees to aim their arrows, but there never was as much effort to conceal themselves as the Aryas were engaged in. It was only after a defeat that the soldiers made an effort to hide themselves in pits, under boulders and elsewhere, to avoid being caught for human sacrifice; but that came later and no one started with the idea of hiding and running.

But then, thought Odin, his own tribe was not fighting along its traditional lines. These Aryas were being treated as robbers. They were very few, while the resources of his tribe were inexhaustible. No wonder, then, that the Aryas were preparing their places of hiding. But could they really hide, he wondered.

Odin knew that his tribe would attack suddenly, without notice or warning. His scouts were already in position. But then the commander's decision to march right up to the approaches of the Black Forest and rest his tired troops there made Odin's task easier.

Odin's army of locals was hidden behind the shelter of trees at the outer fringe of the forest. Their bows and arrows were ready. Their hearts were not—should they fight their own tribe?

Loki's army moved towards the forest.

Odin ordered his men to come out of cover; they massed behind him. The two armies gazed at each other across the distance—away from the range of arrows and lances.

Odin ordered his men to stop where they were, out in the open—neither to move, nor to strike. What was in his mind! That Loki's army be the first to strike?

Odin went forward alone, with slow steps, towards the opposing army. What did he hope for? Did he expect a 'repeat' of his last performance when the miserable little contingent simply evaporated, and even its commander died mysteriously! These were not the troops from his own area—these were disciplined soldiers, picked up from remote parts where Priest Odin's name was heard, even respected, but not worshipped.

Odin was well within their arrow-range. He moved on. He was now even within the range of a lance-throw.

'Stop!' shouted the commander. 'Or else you will die like the dog that you are.' The commander had no intention of letting Odin come too near. He knew what had happened on the last occasion that Odin had cast a seditious spell on the troops to make them desert their commander, who now lay burnt and dead.

Odin stopped.

The commander shouted, 'Tell the men of your tribe to throw down their arms and surrender. They will not be harmed. We are only after the Arya robbers.'

'They are not robbers,' Odin replied. 'Your men will have to kill us all—your own people, your very own, we, who are your flesh and blood before you reach the Aryas. I beg you. . . .'

Odin did not finish. This was precisely the kind of talk that the commander wanted to avoid.

The commander threw his lance, straight and direct, at Odin. He was the most accomplished lance-thrower within the tribe and he aimed at Odin's mouth, from which the words of sedition were flowing Odin fell.

The soldiers were shocked. To kill a priest! That too during parleys! When he was unarmed! Some could even recall Loki's words at the last salute when the army departed—'No harm must come to Odin; he is simply misguided and I long to hold him in my embrace. . . .' And yet their commander killed a priest—a priest, inviolable, innocent, unarmed, unthreatening! But the soldiers did not know what the commander had been quietly told by the Tribe-Chief.

A cry of anguish rose from the defenders of the forest. No one ordered them. Yet it seems that with one will they rushed—not at the opposing army but to the fallen Odin.

The commander's arrows sped at them. Some fell. But still they rushed. Then came the arrows from the soldiers in a quick volley—as the soldiers thought that it was a rush at them. But it was not. The soldiers had seen men running towards them wildly and their instinct of self-preservation had taken over.

But the locals from the forest were all only rushing to reach Odin's fallen body. No one thought of hitting the enemy or protecting the Aryas or themselves. All that was erased from their minds. They had but one thought—to reach Odin.

All of them had thrown away their shields, their bows and arrows. Most of them had only their weapons strapped to their bodies, like daggers and short swords. But they came, now, not to fight but to mourn Odin. And many fell on the way—victims to the unthinking arrows of the soldiers.

They ignored the soldiers, ignored the arrows and simply stood around Odin, while a few of them lifted Odin's body.

The soldiers stopped their arrows. Now they knew—some even with a terrible pang in their hearts—that their commander had killed an innocent, unarmed priest; and they had killed those that came only to mourn their priest and pick up his fallen body.

They were German soldiers—proud of their honour, gallantry and courage. And a later poet would even sing melodramatically, that in the dead bodies of the innocent that their arrows killed, they saw not the corpses of men, but the corpses of their own honour and gallantry.

Odin's body was picked up by his men. Silently, mournfully, they started to move back towards the forest. None of them even looked at the soldiers.

But it was the commander who demanded attention. He had no intention of letting all these men go into the forest. He gestured to the four who carried Odin's body to proceed to the forest. Yes, he thought, let Odin's dead body be in the depths of the forest, lest it lead to a furore here. The rest, he ordered, must remain here. He wanted no fighters against himself—and now that these fools had rushed there, he wanted them to go nowhere else.

The four carrying Odin's body proceeded to the forest. A few more followed them. The rest stood, uncertain, listless, as though all will had left them.

The commander shot his arrows at those who were following the four, carrying Odin. One fell. Then another. But the commander gave up. There were not more than ten in any case—why worry!

He turned to the many standing around like lost children, looking towards the few who were proceeding to the forest. He raised his hand and shouted, 'If any of you tries to leave, he will die like a dog.'

It was an ex-thrall of Odin. He saw the commander's raised hand. Maybe he did not even hear what the commander said. He mumbled something—a prayer!—a vow! a curse—a cry from the heart!

'What did you say,' asked the commander, ready to strike if the man had said something unpleasant and ready to reward, if he had sworn loyalty.

Again, the poet says, the thrall did not hear the words. His eyes were riveted on the commander's hand that held another lance. All else had disappeared from his view. Yes, this was the hand that threw the lance at his master Odin. The thrall jumped at the commander. The lance went through the thrall's shoulder; but the thrall's dagger went pounding again and again into the commander:

The thrall, with a lance cutting right through his shoulder, still had the will to keep striking the commander. Both of them died—'the thrall gallantly, the commander foolishly, for he came too near, believing he was facing men whose blood had run cold and who knew not where to turn after their Odin had fallen.'

With his dying breath, the commander's last words were, 'Kill them, kill them. . . kill all. . .kill. . . .'

His soldiers did not hear those dying words. Only Odin's men did. There would later even be a controversy as to whether it was the thrall who uttered those words or the commander. Most of Odin's men ran towards the forest, fearing that the soldiers would shoot their arrows at them. But the soldiers did not. Some would criticize the soldiers later—'What cowards these, that intervened not, to save their commander.' But the fact is they could not have saved the commander, whose supreme self-confidence in his invulnerability had made him go too near men he thought had lost their will and spirit. In any case, the tussle between the thrall and the commander took a split second, though poems about them would take hours, if not days to recite.

Yet later, some of the soldiers refuted the charge of cowardice and, quoting the poets, said that they had been led by a coward. And went on detailing the horrendous crimes of the commander, who had hit a poet, was ready to hit his eight-year old-daughter, and finally killed a priest 'unarmed, godly, residing with men of god.'

The fantasies and contradictions of poets aside it was clear that most of Odin's men rushed back to the forest. Still many stood by, fascinated by the struggle between the thrall and the commander. When that ended in the death of both, they still stood by, dazed.

The German army is never without a commander. Instantly, on his death, the commander's deputy took over command. At his order, the soldiers now moved ominously towards the many men of Odin, standing by listlessly. Others, ceremoniously, picked up the fallen commander's body.

But why did these men of Odin not run! Were they afraid that arrows and lances would fly after them if they ran? But others had run and they were unharmed. Nobody is able to explain.

The soldiers came face to face with the immobile force. They were wary, for they realized what had happened to the commander when he thought that these supine creatures had no will to fight.

'Throw down your weapons,' the new commander ordered. But most of them had no arms. A few had daggers in their belts. They threw them on the ground.

'Kill us, Brother,' said Hansa, an old man amongst them.

'Why would I kill you?' asked the new commander.

'You killed our Odin, the best, the bravest, the noblest among us,' Hansa lamented.

'I did not kill him but perhaps he had to die.'

The old man's eyes met the commander's and he said, as though pronouncing a judgement, 'You killed him,' and then he looked at the soldiers, and said, 'You all killed him, each one of you.'

'You would not speak so much if this lance went through your stupid mouth,' said the commander.

'I would not then speak; but you will know, all the same, always, that you killed him, you all killed him.' He straightened himself, 'Come, let your lance strike!'

But the new commander had no wish to strike the unarmed old man. Kindly he said, 'Brother, we come not to kill our brothers. I am sorry about Priest Odin.'

The old man was pitiless, 'Yet you killed him. All of you.'

Even the soldiers' eyes were downcast. They had a feeling now that they were all a party to the crime of their commander.

The new commander spoke, 'Please understand; we have nothing against you. You are our people. We are after the robber Aryas there.'

'We are all Aryas. There are no robbers here. It is Loki, the robber, who sends you to rob.'

The commander's hand gripped his lance. But he controlled himself. 'Move over,' he ordered, 'all of you. And remain here. Do not try to go to the forest.'

'Where will you go, Brother?' the old man asked.

'We will go to the forest and bring those Aryas out.'

'Then you must kill us before you go. We shall not let you go.'

The man was mad, the commander was convinced. 'Move, old man, move,' he said gently.

But the old man stood there. With the back of his hand, the commander hit the old man in an attempt to move him away. The old man fell. None of Odin's men helped the old man to rise. But they all stood, resolutely, to block the commander.

'Do you all really, truly want to die?' the commander asked. He himself put out his hand to help the old man to rise. But the old man cried, 'Do not, do not give me your hand, Brother. It is red with my master's blood!'

The commander turned away, purple with rage. He looked at his soldiers. 'Move them and hit any that oppose.'

His soldiers stood. Passive. None of them moved. None of them attempted to move.

Again the poet intervenes to tell us—they were the flowers of the tribe's soldiery; they had never disobeyed the order of their commanders. They would leap to their death and destruction, kill and be killed, but would never question the command of a superior. Yet there they stood—their mind solely on a single question—had they killed Odin?

The soldiers' gaze went to the forest. Bodies were lying everywhere. Those were the men that they had hit when Odin fell. Cautiously, men were coming from out of the forest to pick up their bodies. Yes, thought the soldiers, we were responsible for their deaths.

Without orders, the soldiers moved sideways. Some moved back. They could, easily and effortlessly, have broken through Odin's men, unarmed and non-violent as they were.

The new commander was in a quandary—where did he go from here. The target, he knew, was the forest. There lay the enemy who was to be wiped out.

But he looked at his men, perhaps he looked into his own heart and he realized his army had lost its spirit. That spirit, he knew, as an intangible, mysterious force—the morale that moved men to give their last breath to achieve something without counting the cost to themselves—something which made men feel that they were doing something bigger and nobler than themselves. But now he felt drained and he knew that his men were drained.

He pointed to a spot at the back and quietly ordered, 'We camp here.'

Many said later that it was a mistake. He should have rushed into the forest. As it is, all the locals in the forest who had joined the Arya cause were demoralized and in dire distress over Odin's condition. The commander would have had a walk-over. The Aryas themselves were shaken.

The Tungeris clustered around Odin's prostrate body, tending to him. Fortunately, the commander's lance had not smashed his face. Odin had turned his face when the lance crashed into him. It had cut deep into the side of his face. He had lost one eye irretrievably. But would he lose his life? It seemed so.

There was a wound in every Arya's heart. The first attack had burnt Odin's son. His nurse had died. Now Odin lay at death's door. By all counts, over sixty of them had been killed by soldiers outside the forest—all of them locals, all those who had followed Odin.

Yet the commander remained camped outside, when he could have walked in and crushed all resistance. They said he was his own enemy.

Spectators watched from a distant village. They could not tell that it was Odin who fell. When they saw the army camped, cautiously, curiously, they came. They went back with the heart-broken lament that Odin had fallen.

Four hours later, men, women and children came from the village —all heading towards the forest. But that was only the beginning. Hour by hour, others followed. They were all going there to pay their respects to Odin and be with those whom Odin sought to protect.

The commander and his soldiers saw these endless processions. They could have prevented them. They could have demanded that everyone turn back, there and then, peacefully, to their villages. But could they really have done that? Perhaps not, when they could not even stand the resoluteness of one, single, unarmed, old, frail man.

Dusk was falling. More and more villagers were still going into the forest, making a long detour, to avoid a collision with the army.

But the commander did not have the heart to stop the flow. It was his own deputy that came to his help, 'How many of our own people will we have to kill when we move into the forest? What glory will there be in that victory?'

'Glory! There never will be glory, never any honour.... We lost that when Priest Odin was struck. Why we did that—I will never understand.'

'But that is what the Tribe-Chief ordered,' the deputy said.

'Nonsense! I heard the Tribe-Chief myself. He asked for utmost consideration to Odin.'

'I heard him when he spoke to the commander. He said that Odin should be left neither here, nor in the forest, not in fact anywhere on earth.'

'Why was I not told?'

'It was not for me to report to you what I heard the Tribe-Chief say to the commander. It was for the commander to tell you.'

'Why is it that you were with the commander and not I when the Tribe-Chief spoke to him?'

'But you were not expected to join this contingent! You interrupted your leave of absence and suddenly arrived from nowhere.'

Yes, from nowhere to nowhere, the new commander thought. Still he asked, 'But who else was with you when the Tribe-Chief spoke?'

'None, except the Tribe-Chief's brother. But in my presence, the commander spoke to his orderly, to convey these instructions to the next in command, if something happened to him on the way.'

'I have taken over command. But the orderly has said nothing about it to me,' the new commander said.

'Why should he? The deed has been done. But don't worry, he is bound to speak to you. He will even tell you how our own people who have joined these Arya robbers are to be taught a lesson.'

The new commander went to the orderly.

It was an hour later that the commander spoke to his troops.

'I have to leave. Do not ask why. . . My reasons are compelling. . . personal. . . You will be led by. . . an able commander. . . who knows where he goes. . . Good bye.'

A commander does not desert in the middle of a campaign! Certainly not when his own senior has just died and when all honour of victory shall be his.

Yet the drummer-boy, who was not much of a soldier, asked, 'Lord-commander, bad news from home?'

Kindly, the commander looked at the boy, 'Yes, son. News from somewhere we all come from.'

We all—he had said. Must be a catastrophe affecting his entire family—thought some. Others thought differently. They asked no more.

That he left alone, in the night itself, desiring not even the attendance of his orderly, only proved that the news he had received had been heart-rending, though they had seen no messenger arrive or leave.

The new commander spoke to them, 'Sleep early and well. At dawn, we must begin the attack.' He outlined for them the formation and method of attack and finally asked, 'Any questions?'

Only one question came, 'Why did the commander leave?'

'I am your commander and I have not left,' he shortly replied.

'No, we mean the last commander. Why—where did he go?'

'It was not the purpose of this meeting to discuss the reasons or the whereabouts of the last commander. As a commander, he exists no more. As a friend, he remains; and it would be unfriendly to pursue a question that he requested must remain unasked.'

They were silent, each with his own thoughts, or perhaps with the same thought. Why did he go? Where? No one takes the awesome step of deserting when battle is a few hours away. Certainly not a commander! Certainly not an officer of his calibre! Why even a miserable soldier would not do that! There was dishonour in defection. A nightmarish feeling stole over some.

The next morning, sixty-two soldiers were missing.

The commander, who left did not join the Aryas. He went home and 'then to homelessness'— though it is not clear what exactly the poet here means by 'homelessness'. Nor is it correct that the sixty-two soldiers who left went to the Black Forest. From all accounts, only six were with the Aryas.

The new commander saw with dismay the absence of sixty-two soldiers. In no way did it really diminish the strength of his formidable force. But why then did he pause? Why did he not attack? No one answers the question. All right, if you don't attack, why do you allow people to enter the forest? Why not a siege, a show of force, a threat? Again, no answers. Yet the new commander was known as a brave man, not a patient man, a man of action, not reflection.

He simply decided to send a message to the Tribe-chief while he waited. The message spoke of the fall of Odin, the death of the first commander, the departure of the second, and the desertion by sixty-two soldiers, as well as the entry of many—too many—locals going into the forest, and the possibility of bloodshed, not only among the Aryas but the people of the tribe who were congregated in the forest. And yet the message said not a word about what the commander proposed to do, nor did he ask for instructions. The last two words of his message were mysterious too, 'I wait.'

Loki was far away. It took time for the messengers to reach him. He exploded, 'Wait for what? Wait to attack? Wait for my reply? Wait to be dismissed? For what?'

The messengers could not enlighten him.

Loki asked, 'Is he attacking or is he not? Is he a fool?'

'He is the commander, Lord Tribe-Chief,' replied the chief messenger with unmistakable reproach in his voice.

Loki glared but the messengers asked, 'Is there a reply? Or do we go back without a reply?'

'There is no reply,' said Loki grimly. 'And you do not go back. Consider yourself out of the army.'

It annoyed Loki that the messengers were profuse in their thanks.

Loki sent his own brother. He was to congratulate and honour the commander if he had attacked and won; or to dismiss him if he had failed to attack. The brother was then to take over command. Two priests and two members of the Council of thirty-nine were sent with the brother, so as to leave no doubt about the transfer of command and to keep up the morale of the attacking troops, just in case the inept commander had demanded it, somehow. The brother was not as senior as the man he was to replace—and was even junior to his deputies. But in times of crisis, seniority does not matter! And to be of the family of the Tribe-Chief surely conferred something far more precious than mere seniority!

The Priests and Council members had many faults. But their virtue was that they travelled leisurely, taking time to learn and grasp much on the way. It was not their fault if they could not keep up with the brother of the Tribe-Chief; they even failed to appreciate his impatience over their slow pace. 'We are not going too slowly, Brother; it is you who try to go too fast; better to reach refreshed.' The fact also is that the two priests were unhappy. Odin's reported death hurt them personally and deeply. They may have disliked Odin. But like them, he was a priest. And the Tribe-Chief had reacted as if it was a pariah dog that died. And now this Tribe-Chief's brother was telling them to rush—this man with such a junior rank in the army! Were the priests then at the mercy of every lackey who chose to command. Oh Thor! How had the priests fallen so low!

Even the two Council members were angry with the brother.

They said to the priests, 'You go too fast and by this folly you will miss seeing the tribe's problems on the way.'

'True, very true,' said the priests.

Meanwhile strange events were occurring outside the Black Forest where the army was camped. And many remarked on how strange it was that the commander allowed men from the forest to come and speak to him and his soldiers! Could there, they asked, be a better (or worse) way of spreading sedition? And Hansa, the old man who had stood resolutely, unarmed, ready to die, in front of the last commander, even brought food for the soldiers from the Arya kitchen. But then there was very little available in the village beyond. Ordinarily, the village which worshipped Odin, would have refused to serve the army. But Hansa said, 'They are our brothers.'

The villagers argued, 'They came to kill our god.'

Hansa's reply was, 'Does a brother cease to be a brother, then! And who can kill a god! Odin lives! He lives!'

This was the first time that they heard the news that Odin was not dead. At first, they disbelieved it—perhaps Hansa meant it in the spiritual sense—that gods do not die. And even the soldiers said, 'Never did our late commander's lance fail to kill.'

'It was not the failure of your commander. It was the success of your god,' said Hansa.

But then, everyone came to know that Odin lived. He had lost an eye, though. 'How can a god lose his eye?'—they asked.

'Gods make sacrifices too. Did not Odin's son Bal Deva lose his foot to save the Aryas?'

But the greatest surprise was not that Odin lived. The greater surprise was that the soldiers rejoiced that Odin lived. A cloud lifted from their hearts, for their hands—they had felt—were red with Odin's blood, even though the lance had been thrown by another.

Even the old man Hansa had said so. But later Hansa had apologized to all the soldiers, 'Brothers, forgive me, I spoke from want of faith. No, your hands are pure, blameless, auspicious. How can I even hate the commander! He restored our faith in our god.'

Mad, this Hansa was. Mad, he is—they thought. But may God give us this ineffable madness of infinite love! They loved him. They laughed at him. Yet they envied him. They listened to him.

But some soldiers asked, 'One day, we will have to attack. Will you love us then?'

But his answer perplexed them, 'If you will love me after I die, why will I not love you before I die! I know not how love starts; but I know now that it does not cease. Man dies. Love does not.'

But then this Hansa had intrigued not just his own people. The Aryas were charmed by him, too. Later poets of Bharat Varsha said that Hansa was influenced by the Aryas. They were wrong. Hansa was what he was, before he even understood the language of the Aryas.

When Hansa could converse with the Aryas, the Tungeri brothers asked, 'Why are you called Hansa?'

'Why not! My father gave me the name,' said Hansa.

But then he explained what Hansa meant. It meant a person who joins many to form a league to do violence to the violent.

The Tungeri brothers laughed. They saw the connection between Hansa and their own word himsa. One of them said, 'Hansa, no. You should be called Ahansa.'

'What would that mean?' Hansa asked.

'It would mean that you are in league with many to do non-violence to the violent.'

'Oh, merely, by adding 'a', you give my name the opposite meaning?'

'Exactly.'

But Hansa said, 'No, I cannot change the name that my father gave. But you can call me Hansa that does Ahansa.'

*

At last, the brother of the Tribe-Chief and his party reached the army, outside the Black Forest. With contempt, he viewed the commander and his troops. The two priests and two Council members were respectful but the brother was brusque. He did not even wait for the Council members to announce respectfully that the Tribe-Chief wanted him to be the new commander. Such messages were to be conveyed with finesse and not in the presence of the troops and eavesdroppers. They were always accompanied by a plea to the commander who was being removed, to guide the new commander. It had to be ensured that he went neither in anger nor felt insulted. There also has to be a hint of a higher command waiting for him. The transition had to be smooth so that the soldiers knew nothing of the heartburn of those that lead them.

The Priests and Council members had rehearsed in their minds, and even discussed, the delicacy with which they would handle this transition. But the Tribe-Chief's brother ruined it all with his impatient bluntness.

'It gives me great pleasure to renounce this command,' said the commander and then he pointed to the priest and Council members and included them in his insult. 'Will they be your chief officers and advisers?'

'I told you, they are Council members and priests,' said the brother of the Tribe-Chief. 'Can you not see their rings?'

'Forgive me,' the dismissed commander said to the priests and Council members. 'In the glare of the dazzling glory of the Tribe-Chief's brother, all else was blinded. And you are so tongue-tied in his presence! How could I believe you to be respected priests and Council members? Recently though I saw a priest of honour who wore no priestly ring!'

Contemptuously, he turned from them to speak to his soldiers, 'Men, I have just been relieved of command. I bid you goodbye. Your command now is in the hands of this. . .this. . .brother of the Tribe-Chief. And he brings the Council members and priests to see that you obey.'

It was an unfair insult to the priests and Council members. But the commander felt unfairly insulted too—not by the dismissal but by the manner of dismissal—and the more so, because he was replaced by a blustering, bullying junior. He had expected his own deputy to replace him. As it is, the German army always marched with an hierarchy of officers, so that if one fell another was ready to take over. The dismissed commander himself was the third such officer. He had nine more in line and at least five of them were senior to the Tribe-Chief's brother in military service.

After this terse address to his men, the dismissed commander moved towards his tent to remove his belongings.

'Commander!' shouted someone and the new commander—the Tribe-Chief's brother—responded, 'Yes!'

It was the commander's deputy who had stepped out. Brutally, he told the new commander, 'I speak not to you; I speak to my commander.'

The deputy now addressed the dismissed commander, 'I do not wish to serve in the unit.'

The dismissed commander would possibly have said that he was no longer in command, but the new commander was angry and said, 'Consider yourself dismissed.'

'What I consider or do not consider is my business,' replied the deputy. 'As to my dismissal, that right is not yours unless your brother is dead and you are a priest and have been nominated by the Council of thirty-nine to be Tribe-Chief.'

Carefully now, the new commander spoke, 'I did not mean dismissal in the sense you choose to understand. I meant that your request to leave is acceptable. Report wherever you must for your new assignment.'

Without a word of thanks, the deputy left.

Four officers came out. Wearily, the new commander asked, 'You too wish to move away?'

They nodded. Nothing was said.

The commander nodded. Nothing was said. The four officers left.

The priests wanted to speak to the soldiers. A priest began addressing them. The soldiers moved away in disrespect. If they had been ordered to listen, they would have. But in the absence of an order, they felt that they did not have to listen to those that came as puppets and witnesses to insult their command. And the new commander thought—if they lack respect for me, how can they honour the priests and Council members!

> *All values disappear;*
> *Nothing remains of yester-year;*
> *Neither respect nor fear;*
> *Since Black aliens came near.'*

The poet's lament related to the astounding events taking place. Commanders deserting the army; officers openly insulting lawfully-appointed commanders; and the horrendous disrespect being displayed to priests and Council members. But more was yet to come.

The dismissed commander left. The four officers, who chose transfer, left. But Hansa came, as usual, with food from the Arya kitchen.

'Why are we having food from the Aryas?' the new commander asked.

'There is no other place to get food for so many of us.'

'Good. Soon their kitchen will be ours,' the commander said and then he asked, pointing to Hansa and his companions, 'who are they?'

'They are Odin's men,' they said.

A priest intervened to say, 'But Odin is dead!'

The priest was taken aback as a chorus replied, 'Odin lives! Odin lives! Odin Lives!' Many more joined in—as if it was a chant.

'He lives!' the commander asked, astounded.

'He lives! He lives,' was the reply.

'Then he must die! We were told a falsehood!' The brutal words sped out of his lips. He just did not have the finesses of his brother, the Tribe-Chief.

'What falsehood?' an officer asked.

'The falsehood that Odin was dead!'

'That was no falsehood! He died. He now lives. He sacrificed his eye to save the Aryas,' the officer replied. Others nodded.

The commander stood aghast. I have an army of deserters and demented lunatics—he thought. Still he asked, 'But the Tribe-Chief was not informed that Odin lives.'

'He came to life after the message was sent.'

Yes, they were mad. He was convinced. 'Well, he will have to die again,' he said.

'Who will kill him?' some asked.

'You will. I will. We will. He must die.'

The answer was clear. The mist disappeared. They knew now that the commander did not throw a lance at Odin out of a temper-tantrum. The mission, obviously, right from the beginning, was to kill Odin. Still an officer asked, 'Lord-Commander, why is it necessary to kill Odin?'

'Because he violated Thor's law. He hid his son who was born with a birth defect and took shelter with the Aryas.'

'That is a lie,' a Council-member shouted.

'I speak the words of the Tribe-Chief,' the commander frostily said.

'A lie, be it spoken by anyone, still remains a lie,' the Council member said. 'I do not say that the Tribe-Chief invented the lie. But he believed the lie of others.'

'You do not know all the facts,' the commander said.

'It is my business to know facts—and lies,' the Council member replied.

'I would like to go and see Odin,' the priest said.

'We will move into the forest tomorrow. You will see him, dead or alive,' said the commander.

Immediately, the commander went with the officers for a tour of the area. Having arrived only that morning, he was tired physically and emotionally. Yet he had to demonstrate that he took his duties seriously.

The priests asked the drummer-boy, 'What can you do with that drum?'

'Everything, Lord-Priest. I can call on soldiers to attack, to retreat, to. . . .'

'Can you call all the soldiers to assemble here?'

'Of course, if the commander orders,' the boy said.

'But, of course, I ask you in the commander's name.'

The boy beat the drum—an emergency call. Everyone turned up.

The priest spoke to them all, 'You did not wish to hear me earlier. But give me only a moment. I speak to you of Priest Odin.'

He had their attention. He continued, 'It is not for me to judge. I do not know who threw the lance in Odin's face and who wanted him to die—and why. But this I know. He is a priest—honour him or not. But a priest he is—and he among you who seeks to harm him commits a sin against God and a crime against man.'

The commander was away with the officers, inspecting the area. He heard the drum. He rushed back and was told what the priest had said. 'What idiots my brother has sent with me!'—he said to himself, but he did not quarrel with the priest and later only said, to make the priest feel small, 'You did not tell the truth to the drummer-boy!'

'There are truths and there are higher truths,' the priest said. The other priest nodded and so did the Council members.

The commander had no wish to argue, any more. Let none kill Odin, he said to himself. Odin shall die by my hand. Tomorrow at dawn, I attack!

At dawn, the army had evaporated!

The officers remained. There were, however, no more than 600 soldiers left, out of the formidable army that had proudly marched to the Black Forest.

None of the twelve sentries had deserted. And the sentry-chief said, 'The task given to us was to watch for attack; no one asked that we guard against our men leaving; or hold them prisoners.'

'They were not our men,' the commander exploded. 'They were deserters!'

The sentry-chief seemed unimpressed and said, 'Lord-Commander, none of our sentries left. They knew it was their duty to guard.'

The words were soft yet ominous—did he mean that the sentries would have deserted too, if the duty to guard had not been imposed on them?

There was rage and hate in the commander's heart. He felt like strangling the two priests. He was convinced that they, with their words of sedition, had caused this mass-desertion. But he quietly asked, 'Which way did the deserters go? To the forest?'

But the sentry-chief replied, 'No, Lord-Commander, it was in the opposite direction that our soldiers went.'

Our soldiers! The commander looked murderously at the sentry-chief. At this moment, the commander had room in his heart to hate everyone. But he looked at the drummer-boy and quietly said, 'Summon everyone.'

The remaining soldiers lined up before him. They knew why so many had left. Fear of God! Curse of god! Blessing of Odin! Love of Hansa! Villainy of Tribe-Chief! Cry of child Bal Deva! Tears of mother Frigga!. . .oh a hundred reasons! 'Soldiers we are, killers not!'

But the 600 soldiers also knew why they had remained. It was the soldier's code of honour—and that code overrode all fear, tears, curses and cries. It maybe that some remained too, hoping that with the desertion of so many, the commander himself would desert the field of battle; and there would be no need then to violate their code of honour as soldiers. But those were very few and they were wrong. The commander had no intention of deserting the battlefield. He had enough rage in his heart to war with all the gods in the firmament. Yet his words were quiet as he addressed his soldiers.

'Many have deserted us,' he said. 'Perhaps that is good. Those with the evil of desertion in their hearts, those that violate the soldier's sacred code of honour, those that seek to put this gallant tribe to shame, what could they have achieved for us, except to weaken our resolve and halt our advance! We now move and let the Aryas learn what it is to face the soldiers of this great tribe. I know they shall not remember it for long, for they shall be dead and gone. Move!'

Brave words! And the commander died bravely too. With him, died his 160 soldiers and the drummer-boy. Over 400 locals died.

Among the locals that died in the forest was Hansa. He too had demanded a sword to face the army as it came marching in. Someone had said to him, 'But you are not a man of violence!' His reply was, 'That I am not. Nor am I a coward, I hope.'

Hansa went with his sword. No one knows if he knew how to wield a sword. No one knows if he hurt anyone. No one knows whose lance struck him in his chest. All they knew was that he died and they wept.

The locals in the Black Forest with the Aryas lost over 400 lives. The Aryas of Bharat Varsha? Only two died. The Arya defence line was deep inside the forest. The two who died were the ones carrying the news of how the battle was progressing.

Everyone had a strange question. Bal Deva, son of Odin, lost his foot in the first battle. Odin lost his eye in the second. Would the Gods demand another sacrifice from Odin's family in this third battle?

The Gods had. Frigga wept, 'Two brothers I lost! One of blood, one of heart!'

They knew who the brother of heart was. Hansa. But the brother of blood? It was the commander, the brother of the Tribe-Chief, her cousin.

'You weep for him?' asked some, in surprise. She wept and wept more and asked, 'Who will then weep for him, if none of you will?'

Frigga's heart was full. She remembered this cousin who was the playmate of her childhood days. She was afraid of his elder brother. But so was he and they had laughed at him behind his back, even when he became Chief-Priest. They did not know he would become Tribe-Chief but even if they had known, they would have laughed.

She remembered her little cousin now—not the commander that died. How they laughed, played, frolicked and grew up together!

Yes, Frigga and her little cousin were grown up, when she was to marry Odin. The cousin had kissed her on the mouth, passionately, when he heard the news of her marriage. She blushed and stammered, 'That was not the kiss of a brother!'

'It was not meant to be a brotherly kiss,' he had said. And asked 'Why do you marry an old man?'

'He is a man of honour,' she hotly replied.

'Honour! What has honour to do with loving, kissing, caressing. . . .'

'My father says I must marry him,' Frigga interrupted.

'Does your father know that I am in love with you?'

'Maybe; that is why he wants me to marry him.'

He laughed, 'I thought you loved me, too.'

'I shall always love you. You always were and shall be my brother.' And she had kissed him on the cheek.

Now, they told her, it was the commander who came to kill them that died. No, she knew, it was her cousin, her brother, the playmate of her childhood days, who had died. And she wept.

Hansa was right. Love does not die. Not hers, anyway.

Since then, they called Frigga the mother for she wept for every child on earth.

Months later, in a jovial moment, an Arya child asked, 'Mother Frigga, you shed tears often and you laugh so little!'

It was Odin who intervened, 'Please, no. When she laughs, she sheds more tears and they never stop.'

It was true for Frigga laughed at Odin's reply and with that laughter came the never-ending stream of her tears.

But those tears?—they were of joy. Her son had recovered. Her husband had recovered. And God, she felt, was right in her heart.

The Aryas felt that the hour of peril had passed. It was time, they thought, to build boats to return. They were wrong.

Along the river, Loki's men waited, ready for the kill.

Attacks on the forest came—more to frighten, harass and keep up the pressure, lest the tribe assume that the war was lost. No one from the villages could go to the forest. The area where Odin had once resided and that had come to be known as Odin's, became a cluster of ghost villages. Some say that Loki's man sacked it. Others say that most of the villagers left to join the Aryas. Perhaps the truth lies somewhere inbetween.

Loki's men who now attacked the forest on a 'hit and run' basis, were of a different kind. They came not to fight as soldiers, but as brutal prowlers, to maim and kill. Villagers, thralls, others seeking to go to the forest were, for them, the easiest prey. Sometimes though they attacked in force from various points in the forest.

In the months that went by, fourteen Aryas from Bharat Varsha died from those attacks. Of the locals, a great many were killed. But figures vary wildly.

Those were difficult times in the forest. It had turned into a teeming city. Fighters were few and those that needed protection, far too many.

The villagers came stealthily, crawling at night, from various routes. Those that were caught by Loki's men met with savagery.

Suddenly, however, all restrictions, it seemed, had been lifted. Everyone was free to enter the forest, unrestricted.

More villagers, more thralls escaping from all over, came in. Problems arose with so many men, women and children in the forest. But there was a sigh of relief too. No longer were Loki's men guarding the access.

It was then that the Aryas received more disquieting news. A thrall from another tribe stole into the forest. He told them that word had gone to every tribe from Loki, to participate in the attack on the bands of robbers and thieves congregated in the forest.

Each tribe which so participated in the attack was promised a share of the loot to be grabbed from the Aryas. Their share? It would depend on the number of fighters each tribe sent. For each person from another tribe who lost a limb, his share would be triple. For each that died, the tribe would receive six times the amount.

Food, lodging and other amenities would be provided by Loki's tribe to other tribes, without affecting their share of the loot.

All the Aryas would be enslaved for distribution to the other tribes in the same proportion as other loot. The locals, too, in the forest, irrespective of what tribe they belonged to, would be subject to slavery in the same way as the alien Aryas, for distribution to other tribes.

The thrall had even more information. Other tribes wondered why they were being pursued so much, with such generous offers. Their suspicions rose, as Loki kept pressing them. They wanted to know what would happen if the Aryas did not have as much as Loki said they did. No problem, they were told. If less than that was found with the Aryas, his tribe would make up the difference. But would it be Loki's decision if a dispute arose over the distribution of loot and slaves? Not at all, said Loki. All the tribes should elect a single team of judges whose decision would bind them all. There was another question. Would Loki try to move away the locals hiding in the forest, to reduce their share of the slaves? No, said Loki; as of now, no one would be allowed to leave the forest; whosoever tried would be thrust back forcibly. More, much more, Loki promised—those that tried to enter the forest, would be free to go in, to swell the number of eventual slaves.

A later poet tells us that in that land, in those times, falsehood did not play a part in diplomacy. Negotiations were difficult. But in the end, if a word was given by the Tribe-Chief, it was like a bond, irrevocable and irreversible.

No one doubted Loki's word. Nor did Loki contemplate breaking it.

The tribes moved. Not only their armies but also their thralls, their ruffians and their cut-throats. The share of each tribe depended on the number of men it brought into the field.

Their weapons varied but each 'soldier' carried a rope with which to tie the slaves. The slogan was—'Kill to cause terror, but kill less, catch more.'

The Aryas boats were getting ready. Odin said to the Tungeri brothers, 'You could make a dash for it when hostilities break out. We will keep them busy. No one will be watching for you in the excitement of battle.'

'Will you come with us?' they asked.

'There was a time when I would have given my life to come with you. But now...' said Odin, and his hand went to the vast numbers of locals milling around. 'How can I leave them behind?'

'Exactly,' smiled one of the Tungeris. 'And the same question overpowers us too—how can we leave you and them behind?'

'You owe us nothing,' said Odin. 'You do not belong to this land. You must leave when the battle begins or it will be too late.'

The Tungeri brothers laughed and one of them said, 'You are right. We owe you nothing, except our life, that you saved. We don't belong to this land. But you belong in our hearts. And strangely, my two brothers and all the Aryas believe these are good enough reasons for us to stay together and, if need be, die together.'

'It is a mistake for you to remain, a grave error. . .' Odin pleaded.

'Our error began when we left our homeland,' Tungeri smiled.

'Then why were you all rushing these last few days and nights to complete your boats?'

'Boats! But they have a purpose to serve.'

'What purpose? To make a gift of them to Loki?' Odin asked.

'Frigga has to take the children away,' Tungeri said.

'What?' Both Odin and Frigga shouted.

Tungeri explained. True, they had given up everything, even the thought of defence and used every ounce of strength to complete the work on the boats. The locals had helped too. But the boats were not for their escape. He continued, 'As soon as the attack begins, all the children—Arya and local—must rush into the boats. The only adults to go with the children will be the Arya boatsmen who must row the boats. But there will be one more—the mother of all these children—Frigga. From now on, all children will be camped near the boats. So will the boatmen. So will Mother Frigga. At a signal from us, the boats will leave. Our Aryas will run along the river and divert anyone watching with evil design. Hopefully, we will ensure that the boats get beyond harm's reach. And the children, then, will be in the charge of God and Mother Frigga. Can we ask for a more powerful, more benevolent combination? Maybe they will all reach Bharat Varsha. If not, some other place of safety, God willing.'

Frigga said, 'You think I will leave my husband behind!'

Tungeri said, 'No. You will be with your son Bal Deva. Wherever you are, wherever Bal Deva is, your husband is.'

Strangely, Frigga had no tears. Her eyes were hard. Firmly, she repeated, 'I shall not leave my husband.'

Calmly, Tungeri responded, 'That is your decision. It was not easy for us to persuade the boatmen to leave. They wanted to stay back to die alongside us. But we insisted that they had a higher duty. I shall not try to persuade you. I just did not want all these children to go motherless. If you can persuade Odin to go with you, along with the children, I shall welcome it. . . .'

Frigga looked at Tungeri's eyes, filled with sadness and resolution. She wept. 'I shall go; I shall go. My husband's place is here. . . . Mine, I know. . .with the children.'

The sense of panic in the forest disappeared and was replaced by a calm strength. They knew they were fated to die. Who could withstand the combined onslaught of all the tribes! But it seemed to matter less and less. Ever since the news had come that there was to be such a concerted attack, the Aryas had desperately been trying to complete building the boats. Clearly, the Aryas were intending to flee—and why not, thought the locals. They had no hope of survival and this was not their land; so why should they not flee? Yet, somehow, the locals had felt forsaken, lonely, lost.

But now they knew! The Aryas were staying back to die with them, if need be.

The Aryas too understood what it was—'We are all brothers,' they said. And with a smile, mingled with sadness, remembered Hansa. Earlier when Hansa's grasp of the Aryan language had not been very good, he had said, 'All brothers are men,' and it had taken the Aryas some time to realize that what he had meant was 'all men are brothers.'

Loki was able to satisfy some of his own people that this was the beginning of a cooperation among the tribes which would eventually lead to unity. They had been a single tribe once, under Thor; should they not be united again? Perhaps some hoped that if indeed that elusive unity was achieved, Loki would be displaced. But then everyone knew that unity was simply a dream.

Some even remembered Kvasir, grandson of Thor, in whose time, from a single tribe, they broke into two and then into three tribes, and finally, in succeeding generations, there were twelve tribes.

Old Kvasir had been tricked. He had sent his trusted advisers, with full powers, to the negotiations to sort out the differences, in order to avoid a partition of land and tribes; but his own men, greedy for personal power, had contrived to outwit him and whipped up such a frenzy of disunity that a split was unavoidable. Old Kvasir retired in anguish from his position of chief of a tribe that had split into two. His sense of honour prevented him from blaming anyone but himself. Yet his dream remained that the tribes would one day reunite. Even in his retirement, he was loved. But he was assassinated, as some thought that he was trying to be too considerate to the other tribe that had split and did not understand that he was a dreamer who was pursuing a dream. He has, ever since, been held in fond esteem.

But that was a long time ago. The dream of unity was no more. It was like an empty murmur in a troubled sleep; and everyone realized that disunity, like all other evils, would only grow; and that it was impossible to undo the divisions and partitions among tribes to bring about the age-old dream of unity, of that lone man who died for it. At the core of their hearts, people may want unity, but how do people matter, when the personal ambitions of those that lead them lie in keeping them divided?

Even so, some were touched by Loki's words of unity. They were among the trusting few who judged mostly by their leader's words and not actions and did not realize that the honoured name of the old man who died chasing the dream of unity was often on the lips of the most dishonourable men in the land, who had achieved positions of eminence, prestige and power.

Everyone in the forest waited for the blow to fall as the tribes gathered. Loki's negotiations had taken a long time. Some tribes were yet to arrive and clearly the decision reached was that all the tribes should strike together.

The Aryas and locals in the Black Forest had one certainty— whatever happened, they would sell their lives dearly. There would be no bravado; no feats of heroism. They would not fight in the open, not even behind the cover of trees, but from pits, ditches, shelters and some of them would even be covered with domes. Only the tallest trees with thick foliage would be utilized, where a single fighter may wait at the tree-top, with a canopy and scaffolding to shelter him and his stones and arrows. Nor would many congregate at a single point, waiting for slaughter. Each fighter would be an 'army' unto himself. To reach him, the enemy would have to cross the obstacle of fallen trees, avoid the cross-aiming of arrows and stones, and navigate the sheltering walls.

What then? Extinction? The only silver lining lay in their hope that the children would be safe. Mother Frigga would be with them.

Yes, through our children, our tribe shall live—Odin's tribe!

Odin's tribe! Yes, that is what many locals in the forest called themselves, initially. Odin shook his head in disapproval. Then some women said—we shall live through our children and Frigga is the one who leads them to safety. Should we not call ourselves Frigga's tribe? It was Frigga who then said, 'No, the Tungeri brothers lead us. They send our children to safety. Maybe we shall be in their Bharat Varsha before. . .they reach. Should we not call ourselves the Tungeri tribe?'

But the Tungeri brothers shook their heads. 'We are all God's tribe.'

Strange, says a poet, that people waiting to die should concern themselves with matters as trivial as hunting for a name for their tribe!

Even more strange, that Odin should continue to compose poetry and say that he is able to look within himself better, now that he has only one eye! Strange also, that Frigga weeps no more but only laughs, though tears come to her eyes whether she laughs or weeps!

Strange, too, that the locals still continue to learn the language of the Aryas!—do they to converse in it after they die?

Strange, moreover, that the Tungeri brothers should continue their sessions with the locals asking questions about life, afterlife, karma, moksha, dharma, bhakti and, even more, about the reality, personality and duality of the universal spirit, creation of the universe, evolution of man, conception of time and space and so many other abstract and philosophical concepts of the Hindu! And so many questions about the roots of Hinduism in Sanathana Dharma and Sanathana!

And the poet asked himself—why this senseless urge for more knowledge when it would matter no more and life itself would end! Why seek wisdom when wisdom matters no more! Or is it our intention to confuse God with our superior knowledge when life has ended!

Still more strange, says the poet, is the fact that they spoke, smiled, chatted, joked, laughed and sang as though the certainty of death did not matter any more. They were not like wild women and doomed men under a sentence of death. The women dressed well, cared for their appearance and even took time to part their hair properly, as usual, and apply the red dot on their foreheads, as the locals had learnt from the Aryas.

And the men! They never forgot to admire the women.

Thus the poet goes on and finally says—'perhaps when we come to terms with the fact that we are soon to die, our perceptions deepen and suddenly we are what we were as children—truly human.'

Another poet criticizes this poet as 'full of airy nothings on everything but short on facts.' He says that this poet failed to mention that every bachelor Arya married a local girl in 'those that they regarded to be their last days.' How many marriages? But here this poet too faces us with an 'airy nothing.'

All he tells us is that thus there were many moments of music and dance, frolic and festivity, laughter and mirth, love and longing in the forest. And the couples said that they would be true to each other all their lives—and never did they even ask themselves how short that life was to be!

But they knew that each day was a boon.

*

Strange, says a poet. These Aryas and locals in the Black Forest did not even pray that their lives be spared. They prayed only for the safety of the children who were to be rushed out by boat. For themselves, they asked for nothing.

Why? Is it because they thought that it was impossible that they be saved! Did they then lack faith? Did they believe that there were limits to God's miracle! Did they believe that God could not perform the impossible!

Yet the impossible became possible. Was it an act of God? No, it was an act of man.

Thus it was that the Aryas were saved! Suddenly, unexpectedly, came Atal and his 2,000 horsemen from Lithuania!

What would 2,000 men matter against the combined army of 12 tribes? Very little. But 2,000 horses! An animal they had never seen before!

Oh gods! Gods! They ride on wolves! These black devils!

All coherent accounts are lost for the poets are incoherent when they speak of this miracle.

The terror of the twelve tribes outside the forest was unimaginable. Their armies vanished but their hatred was intense and single-minded.

So Loki knew! they said to themselves. He knew then, that we were to face not human beings but monster-men riding on wolves!

Wolves with four legs below and two legs above! Wolves with a wolf-face below and a human face above!

No wonder Loki was offering us so much, they said. Oh fools we! To believe that Loki was giving away so much for a mere attack on robbers! And he pits us against monsters!

The armies of the twelve tribes collapsed, not with a war-cry but with a shriek of terror.

They fled, rushing back not to their homelands, but deep inside Loki's lands, for deadly vengeance.

Loki's body was ripped apart—his head sightless—his legs and arms scattered—maybe these monster-wolves from the Black Forest would halt to eat Loki's flesh and forget to pursue them!

But mob-terror stops nowhere. On their way to their homelands, soldiers of various tribes vandalized every tribe, everywhere. Promises to them had been violated—they felt—so they violated and crushed everyone and everything in sight.

*

Was it really a miracle that suddenly, out of the blue, Atal arrived to the rescue? The explanation was simple.

Atal had followed the Baltic coastline from Lithuania. Somewhere, he changed direction.

On the way, Atal's men were learning the shifting, ever-changing language of the people they met. Sometimes, the language varied slightly and at others, considerably, but always with shades and patterns that were faintly common and recognizable. There came a time when their horses frightened the people they met. But their friendly approach reassured the strangers.

Somewhere along the route, they were advised by a friendly person to watch out, for men and women like them were being hunted for 'butchery and slavery', by all the tribes of the land, in a forest far-away, that was now called the 'Black Forest.'

'Where?' asked Atal and then he and his men rode on 'wings of thunder.'

How can you then call this rescue a miracle! 'Ah,' say the poets, 'He that guideth the miracle hideth Himself!'

Maybe!

This should end the story of the Aryas in Germany. But not really.

Atal was among the first to leave along with some men from his contingent. They went by the boats which were intended for the children and Frigga. But then many more boats were also built. Frigga and the children did not need to go now that there was no danger. Even so, a few Arya and local children left with Atal. All the locals who had come from Finland and Lithuania also went with Atal.

Joining him were also the Aryas from Bharat Varsha who had married local girls.

The horses were left behind under the Tungeri brothers' command.

Many of Atal's men remained. They would leave later with the Tungeri brothers and the rest of the Aryas.

Much remained to be done. There was a desperate cry of agony from all the tribes as the soldiers from the twelve armies went on their mindless rampage. These tribes had seen danger before but never as acutely as this. They were quivering under the heel of ruthless men who were senselessly killing, burning and looting. Villages all over were witnessing a bloodbath and the merciless tearing apart of families. Many were orphaned. Some lost a son, a few all their loved ones. They came swarming out of their shattered villages. But there was no place to run and hide. A cry of pain was wrung from their souls by the measureless torment through which they passed. There was a broken prayer for mercy everywhere.

The looters laughed.

Frigga wept.

Odin moved with Atal and the Tungeri brothers' forces.

Did Odin move to bind the wounds only in his tribe? No. Every tribe was God's tribe, he said, as the Tungeri sons had said earlier; and Frigga wept for them all.

Months passed. But, at last, in Germany (or the Land of Tungeri, as it was called), there was only one tribe, as all the tribes had shed their separate identities and merged under Odin's leadership as a single tribe. And then it was as old Kvasir had dreamt and died for—one great tribe. They said it was the 'sword' that united them. But others said it was the sword that had divided them but it was Odin's mercy and the Aryas' love and Bharat Varsha's svastika that united them.

What should they call this united tribe now? Again some said—'The tribe of Tungeris?'

The Tungeris objected, 'Call it Odin's tribe, if a name has to be given—for it is Odin, who united you.'

'No,' said Odin. 'Let it be called the "Tribe of Aryans".' Odin had the last word and so it was named the 'Tribe of Aryans'. Somehow though, Frigga called it the Aryan tribe of svastika. She could not forget that her son had clutched the svastika seal in his tiny hand to prevent his father from going out to hang himself.

That indeed ends the story of the Aryas of Bharat Varsha in Germany. The horses were left with Odin since his men were now accomplished horsemen.

Led by the Tungeri brothers the Aryas left by river Dana and then on to the Black sea, to Turkey, and thence to Hari Hara Aryan and finally to Bharat Varsha. With them went many locals from Germany; and many more would follow, year after year.

Of their mishaps, triumphs and adventures, volumes can (and should) be written. But it is enough to say that a Tungeri brother was killed in Turkey in tragic circumstances. The second Tungeri died in a shipwreck, not too far from the Sindhu coast. The third son reached Bharat Varsha.

This Tungeri recited the names of all those that died and prayed for them all—but he did not mention his two brothers. They asked him why; he said, 'So long as I live, they live; so long as they die, I die.' Some understood him; some did not.

The story of the Aryas of Bharat Varsha in Germany ends. But not the story of the locals in Germany who called themselves the Aryas.

In later centuries, Odin would come to be honoured as a god in the mythology of Germany, Norway, Sweden, Iceland, Denmark and other European nations, particularly England.

But the honour of godhood in Germany went equally to his weeping wife Frigga and his son Bal Deva.

As a God, Odin is described variously in the later literature of Germany and Europe.

He is known as the god of poetry—but also much more. He is known as the god of occult wisdom which he acquired as the result of his hanging. His hanging is presented as a symbolic act of 'sacrifice to himself'; and a poet quotes him, 'A moment came when I desired my death, but Mother (Frigga) spoke to me—Oh foolish me, I heard her not! And then my son spoke and I was hearing him not! But then my father (God eternal) thundered in my heart to say, "Deny them not, for both mother and son speak with My voice"—and clearly I heard them, then; and could I deny them any more? But Guardian Spirits had heard my vow that by hanging I must go. And Loki came to my rescue, as they whispered in his ear and promptly he hanged a likeness of me in straw and wood. And the Guardian Spirits smiled to say, "Your sacrifice by hanging is performed." Oh God! multiply such Guardian Spirits in my land, and in every land.'

But many more fables surrounded Odin, the god. His effigy was said to be hanging for 'nine endless nights' on the World Tree. Later, the effigy was pierced with a lance to show how the commander stabbed Odin. But then what did the World Tree do? It turned into a horse, and the tree came to be known as Yggdrassil, i.e., Odin's horse (this of course commemorates the sudden appearance of horses on the German scene which enabled Odin to straddle Germany and pacify and unite the Germans into a single tribe known as the 'Tribe of Aryans' or the 'Aryan Tribe of Svastika').

Thus, Odin, through his symbolic death by the hanging of his effigy, acquired 'the wisdom that belongs only to the dead.'

As such, Odin was regarded as the god of the hanged. But then another kind of reputation also got attached to him later. He came to be credited with the art of communicating with the dead and it was said that he could make hanged men talk. But this fabled reputation was unjustly earned. The fact is that Odin ordered the hanging of many, from among the 'soldiers' of the twelve tribes who continued on their murdering and looting spree. Around their necks, ropes were strung with a threat to hang them, if they did not reveal where they had hidden the loot or the people they had captured as slaves. Fortunately, these 'hanged' men talked, faced between life and death, and thus was Odin's reputation for necromancy earned. The fact is that Odin was never too gentle with those that kept vandalizing and certainly not with those who still held unfortunates as slaves.

Odin is always shown in German fables as fighting against a monstrous wolf. But that again was a reference to the horse that suddenly appeared in Germany, to the terror of many, for they saw it as an incarnation of the wolf. But the fable simply was that Odin destroyed the monstrous self of the wolf but preserved the gentler self. 'For nothing is wholly evil, not even the monstrous wolf, for in him too lurks the gentleness of Him, the Creator.' Thus it was .hat Odin, having destroyed the monstrousness of the wolf, brought forth the gentler self of the wolf—the horse—and it was this gentle, lovable horse that helped to heal the wounds of the twelve tribes and united them into a single tribe.

Odin is also shown as chaining carrion beasts, ravens and wolves as images of those that treacherously betrayed Kvasir to disunite the tribe. When poets praise Odin for his dream of unity, he is obscurely quoted as saying, '. . .that dream was the soul-blood of Kvasir. Render then to Kvasir the praise that is his; and let none speak of Odin's theft of that dream. . . .'

But the fables also speak of Odin praising Loki for speaking of the need to unite tribes. Obviously, Odin wanted to avoid divisions in the land. Similarly Odin praised Thor too, as in his time, the tribe remained one and had not splintered into twelve fragments.

Odin had lost his eye when the commander's lance had ripped through his face. But German fables are clear that this god Odin sacrificed his eye in order to gain inner knowledge. In later centuries, a few Germans would go about with a patch on one of their eyes to gain inner vision and wisdom. By such disuse and atrophy, it is said, some actually lost the vision in their patched eye. It is not known, however, if they gained inner vision and wisdom.

But over the centuries, as the fables multiplied, Odin would also have many questionable worshippers. Lawless men regarded him as their god. His cult spread to renegades and Vikings; and he was regarded as a god who broke the most sacred of oaths, even the oaths on the holy ring, but never his personal word. This was a throw-back to Odin having violated the priestly vow (that he would not divulge Loki's plans to attack the Aryas). Pirates and lawless men swore by Odin, if they meant to keep their word, but broke every other oath.

But all these fables and fantasies came later. Clearly, Odin led his united tribe with compassion; and he felt for the sorrows of all, trying to move heaven and earth to bring comfort and unity to his people.

He abolished the law of 'tribe-cleansing' and a baby could not be harmed for a birth defect. He also abolished human and animal sacrifices.

*

And Frigga? German fables remember her not only as the wife of Odin and mother of Bal Deva, but as a Goddess in her own right. She was the mother of all and one who wept for all God's children; and 'her tears cleansed all spirits and washed away all sorrows,' and with 'her tears, the earth rose refreshed.' She is known also as Terra Mater (earth mother) and when she is with us, 'there is gladness, rejoicing and peace and weapons disappear.' She is named as Friia in the second Merseburg Charm. Often, German and European fables equate her with Venus and her name survives in 'Friday' (Old English Frigedaeg) from *Dies Veneris*, Venus' Day.

Bal Deva was known as the one with the will and power of God even before the German fables conferred godhood on Odin and Frigga.

Bal Deva is always referred to in the German fables as the 'Spotless' god. Every fable thus bends backwards to emphasize that he was not born with a birth defect and that it was simply a canard that arose in Loki's diseased mind.

In German fables, Bal Deva is also shown as the innocent, suffering god. He is supposed to have had dream-forebodings, at the age of two, about his father Odin's resolve to kill himself, but quickly rose from his sleep to dissolve his father's resolve. Bal Deva, the fables say, had dream-forebodings about his own death too, but his mother Frigga took an oath of protection from all creatures—living and dead; from all elements like fire and water; all things like stones and tress; and from all witches that brought diseases and illnesses. Somehow, Frigga missed taking a vow from the small, insignificant mistletoe. Loki took the mistletoe and gave it to the blind god Hod who hurled it as a shaft through Bal Deva's body. All creatures sent messengers to Hel, the goddess of Death. She agreed to spare Bal Deva if all things, creatures, elements and witches would weep for him. They all did, except a giantess who was none other than Loki in disguise. But with the will and power of god that Bal Deva had, Frigga rose high up to the heaven, and there she wept and her tears rained and rained; and Hel, goddess of Death, clearly saw that all were weeping. And while it rained, Bal Deva extended his tiny hand to protect the goddess of fire who shivers with cold whenever it rains; and, in gratitude, the goddess of fire came to cover the birth defect of Bal Deva.

*

Fables and fiction apart, at the age of about sixteen, Bal Deva suddenly disappeared from the Land of Tungeri and at the age of twenty-six, he reached Bharat Varsha. There, some called him the grandson of Manu of Tungeri, as he was supposed to have been adopted by the last, surviving Tungeri son. But that is not correct. He actually married Nanna, the daughter of the Tungeri son. From her, he had four sons and four daughters. For most of his life, he lived near the confluence of Sindhu river with the Sindhu sea. In his last years, however, he was at Hari Hara Dwara. He was cremated on the banks of the Ganga at Varnash.

*

These Aryan gods—Odin, Frigga, Bal Deva—were honoured in Germany. But in Bharat Varsha nobody knew them as gods. They were simply friends of the Aryas of Bharat Varsha. They had fought against a common enemy and had for many years, lived, loved, laughed and wept together and ultimately triumphed.

Certainly the Aryas from Bharat Varsha did not go to England.

The English were a mongrel race, outside the periphery of any civilized knowledge or culture at the time the Aryas travelled to Europe.

Even for long centuries thereafter, a vast shadow of darkness and ignorance remained over Britain.

Much later, slowly, successive continental cultures came to exercise their civilizing influence, even though the fact is that for a long time, England was mired in superstition, filth, poverty, slavery, incest, homosexual activity, child-abuse, brigandage, human sacrifice, cannibalism and the killing of old parents.

Later, it was the German civilizing influence that left its mark in Britain.

The German Aryan gods came to be honoured in England—in particular Odin, Frigga and Bal Deva. Also Thor, honoured by Odin, came to be respected.

In the beginning though, even the Germans ridiculed the English and said that Britain honoured only Loki—a god who was a 'changer of shape, from a vulture to a rat to a reptile to a seal.' This was intended to highlight the then well-known English trait of refusing to honour any word or vow, using all the deviousness and deception in their power to break it, for they lacked courage and relied largely on creating dissension among others.

Loki was also known as a deceiver who cheated the gods and gave birth to many evils; and the Germans were therefore convinced that Loki, and the people of England, were ideally suited to each other.

But as the civilizing influence of the German Aryas grew in England, Odin, Frigga and Bal Deva began to shine in the eyes and minds of the English.

Odin named as Woden in England would have Wednesday named for him.

Frigga, Odin's wife, would have Friday named for her.

Bal Deva, supposed to have the will power of god, had no day named for him, due to a superstition that it might render all other days inauspicious. His influence was thus regarded as all pervasive.

Even Thor, though not of Odin's family, but honoured by Odin, had Thor's day (Thursday) named for him.

But then the German Aryan gods, though unknown in India as gods, were honoured everywhere else in Europe, particularly in Scandinavia, Iceland and Britain.

While the ancient gods of Germany came to be honoured in many parts of Europe, the fact remains that it is now purely a matter of history.

These gods could not stand the onslaught of Christianity with its pressure of a positive, monotheistic, forceful creed which demanded that all other gods be renounced.

But somehow in Germany, the traditional memory of these gods still remains.

Epilogue

The Aryas had left from many parts of Bharat Varsha but not from Dravidham.

Many groups of Aryas came from the lands of Sindhu, Ganga and Saraswati to Dravidham, hoping to find routes which would lead them to distant destinations.

Dharmalila,[1] the headman of Dravidham, was astounded.

'But why brothers, why?' asked Dharmalila. To him the idea of people leaving for the unknown in search of a new home seemed ridiculous. He said so.

The groups of refugees told their story. It was a familiar tale of deceit, greed and plunder by the lords of the land.

'Help us,' they pleaded with Dharmalila. 'We must join the other Aryas. Many have already left.'

'Help you, I shall,' promised Dharmalila. 'But be with us in this land that is yours and mine.'

'No master, others have departed long ago to find the land that is safe, blessed and pure.'

'Here walked one who was purer than us all. Make this again then, with your effort, the land of pure,' said Dharmalila. He did not know it, but his words echoed the thought of Purus, the Arya leader in Iran.

Much more was said by the stragglers. Dharmalila silenced their doubts, 'Yes, be with us for six months—a year. If you don't like us, I will help you to leave. I promise.'

They stayed.

Many groups came thereafter, all intent on leaving. Again, Dharmalila cried, 'Brothers, sisters, what madness is this! Here you have lands waiting to be made fertile, long valleys, coastal ranges, spectacular sea-shores. But they matter not so much. Here you will enjoy the fruits of your labour and you will live with us as our own.'

They too stayed in Dravidham.

A series of strange messages also reached Dharmalila then. They came from Karkarta of Sindhu, Gangapati of Ganga and many other

---

[1]Dharmalila was the son of Dharmadassa, the Tamala Aravalu (speechless Tamala), who was left in charge of Dravidham by Sindhu Putra as Periyar. Dharmadassa retired as a hermit; and by the decision of the Dravidham Nagara Councils, the office went to Dharmalila.

mighty lords and chiefs. None of them was aware that Dharmalila was dissuading groups from leaving. These messages simply requested Dharmalila to help various groups, that might reach Dravidham, to depart. The messages spoke of everlasting gratitude for such help and even promised to share with Dharmalila the information on the wealth and lands eventually found by these stragglers.

Dharmalila's response to these messages was polite, even enthusiastic. From this some concluded that he would assist the Aryas to depart from his land. But this was not so. He simply welcomed groups that came and encouraged them to stay back.

But there was little that Dharmalila could do to discourage the flow of Aryas from other parts of Bharat Varsha. He sent a few of his men out, to Ganga, Sindhu and elsewhere. His men came back to report that the Arya movement and migration was widespread. 'Like a tidal wave,' said some; but they were exaggerating as messengers and envoys often do.

'But why,' asked Dharmalila, 'why were so many Aryas leaving?' The reasons, he was told, were many and varied and his people did not even understand most of them. But mostly, it was a cry in their souls.

'Nonsense,' retorted Dharmalila. But then some said—how could Dharmalila understand such a reason! His was the deep-seated joy of wrestling with the soil rather than the soul.

But Dharmalila did understand. He sent messages to many, including Rishi Newar (Nepal), Manu Sachal (who now led Yadodhara's ashram), Ekantra, Baldana (Sage Bharadwaj's spiritual successor), Sage Kundan and poetess Chitra. He wanted them all to stop the Arya migration.

Dharmalila was a young man and his messages had the anger of a warm-hearted youth. What was his plea to these learned men? Declare that he who leaves for lands elsewhere betrays his land; and the waters he crosses to reach there are not auspicious....'

Some laughed. But many understood Dharmalila's anger and anguish. Yet what could these philosophers, sages, rishis and poets do? Their congregations and disciples heard them, but they had never intended to leave with the Aryas, in any case.

It was Rishi Newar who travelled to meet Dharmalila.

He complained to Dharmalila, 'How can you speak of betrayal by those that flee! You are calling the victims the culprits. The crime is committed by the mighty lords of the land; and corruption lies in the uncontrolled urges of our rulers.'

Dharmalila heard all this silently; and Newar challenged, 'You, who are virtually the Periyar of this land, will naturally find it difficult to accept that rulers are corrupt.'

'No,' Dharmalila said. 'These lords are a hundredfold more evil than they appear to be.'

'Why do you then blame the people?'

'Because the fault is with the people. The rulers do what they have to do. But the failure is not theirs, nor does it lie in the land but in ourselves. The fight should have begun here. You do not forsake your land for the evil of a few!...'

'Few?' Rishi Newar interrupted.

'All right, many. You yourself did not abandon Newar and they say only twelve of you were left, but your spirit kept them on, fighting, until the evil was rooted out.'

'You exaggerate my role, son. It was the spirit of my men that kept them fighting.'

'Exactly. What else am I seeking in Bharat Varsha except the spirit of a man who would fight!'

It is said that Rishi Newar, always thoughtful, was even more thoughtful when he left Dravidham.

But it was too late. Most of the Aryas had already left from various parts of Bharat Varsha. Those that were still leaving were far beyond the reach of Dharmalila's words. Only the stragglers who found their way to Dravidham could be persuaded to remain.

In a complex, mysterious way, and even totally out of context, Dharmalila's words would ring through the ages—'Declare that he who leaves for lands elsewhere, betrays his land; and the waters he crosses to reach there are not auspicious.'

Many spiritual personalities then repeated Dharmalila's words, so much so that later, in the post-Vedic era, long after the *Rig Veda*, there were those who said that the religion of the Hindu prevented him from travelling abroad and crossing the seas—and some spoke of smrti-rules against crossing the ocean, foreign travel and contact with foreigners, abroad.

Thus it was that many centuries later, long after the Aryas had departed and returned, Dharmalila's words would echo mindlessly, irrelevantly and unconnectedly with the purpose he then had in mind.

Priests of the post-Vedic era embraced these words with delight and fervour and in effect, said, 'Truly, it is inauspicious to travel over waters and oceans; but fear not; with special prayers performed by us (for a suitable fee), all such sins are washed away.'

Historians—amazingly, even some Indian historians, writers, thinkers, opinion-makers trained in the best schools and universities of England—pointed to this 'age-old' 'religious' prohibition against foreign travel, and said—'Surely, then the Aryas could not originate from Bharat Varsha. How could they violate the age-old, religious law!'

The fact, however, is that this taboo was neither 'age-old', nor 'religious' nor a 'law'. In the *Rig Veda* there are references to marine navigation, including many references to 'the treasures of the oceans,' 'gains of sea-trade,' 'ships with hundred oars,' and 'shipwrecks'. Clearly, these and many such references in the *Rig Veda* and elsewhere prove that the ancients of Bharat Varsha knew the oceans and sailed in ships to distant lands.

In any case, the doubts of the historians should have vanished with the finds in the Indus Valley. These excavations indicate ports, naval dockyards and harbour works which presuppose a sound knowledge of hydrography and marine engineering in pre-Vedic times, long before the emergence of the Aryans. Also, there is evidence from numerous seals, artifacts, implements and even anchor stones, that show the familiarity that the pre-Vedic ancients had with ocean-going ships which they used for long voyages for settlement abroad and trade.

It is true that the historians were taken unawares by the finds of the Indus valley, as they had already pronounced their hasty judgments, well before those excavations, that the Aryans came from 'anywhere, everywhere, elsewhere, but not from here.' With the evidence of the Indus valley finds facing them, the historians said little, except that some of them simply added that the Indus valley was pre-Aryan. Thus they simply restated what was obvious, but after recovering from their initial surprise, their imagination soared and they added that the Aryans sprang neither from Sindhu, nor Ganga, nor Saraswati, nor the Dravidham civilizations nor from anywhere in Bharat Varsha but came from somewhere else. They did not say from where. They kept pointing successively and alternatively to various regions of the world from which the Aryans 'might' have come. By the last count, twenty-two such regions have been mentioned by the historians, any one of which, they say, could possibly be the homeground of the Aryans. They admit, though, that none of those regions had the level of civilization that the finds of the Indus valley reveal; even more clear is their admission that at that time, none of those regions had the high level of literature, music and aesthetics of the Aryans of Bharat Varsha. The only evidence that the historians offered was that the language of those regions had many words common to Bharat Varsha. Obviously, it had to be so. The Aryas that went out from Bharat Varsha to all those regions, naturally influenced those languages and were influenced in turn.

The final argument left with the Indian writers was that 'all the western historians have concluded that the Aryans did not emerge from India.' And they named those eminent historians, one after another, in an impressive list. And the argument of the western historians was that 'Indian historians, writers, thinkers and high-level opinion-makers of India, also agree with our assessment.' This spirit of international accord is no doubt touching, but it neither recreates history nor reveals the life and times of the Aryans.

*

Poets of Dravidham may be correct in saying that Dharmalila even sent emissaries to Lord Kush of Avagana and Rishi Bongla of Gangasagarsangam. He requested both of them to dissuade the Aryas from departing for the 'pathless wild', and even to advise those that had already left, to return.

But the poets exaggerate the effect of these messages. Long before Dharmalila's messengers reached, the Aryas had left.

Long thereafter, the Aryas would return.

Yet the Aryas returned not because they heard Dharmalila's cry. No, it was the cry that rose in their own hearts—in Germany, Finland, Norway, Denmark, Sweden, Scythia, Turkey, Spain, Assyria, Sumer, Egypt, Lithuania, Italy, Iran—everywhere. The dream had vanished.

Thousands of these gentle, frightened souls had forced themselves, in joy, and pain, to yield to the obscure urge to search for the land of pure. Now they knew; there was no land of the pure, anywhere, except where they themselves made it so. They wanted to go back to the healing power of their home, heritage and roots.

From all over Europe, the Aryas of Bharat Varsha travelled back. Most of them gathered in Iran. Many locals too joined them. And they all built boats, though some of them returned by land too, from Avagana.

In Iran, Purus's wife—who later would be known to some, as the Queen of Persia—was the guiding spirit.

The ships of the Aryans sailed home.

*

'Did you bring the world with yourself?' asked Sage Durgan with heavy irony.

'No, Sage, we brought ourselves back,' said Kamalpati, the Arya leader in Spain.

'But I am told you and your Aryas claim that you discovered many lands and people!'

'No Sage, it would be ludicrous for us, and insulting to them, to claim that we discovered them. They were there for thousands of years before we showed up.'

'Yet I am told they honoured you, respected you and bathed you in all their love and devotion.'

'No, Sage, we slaved and suffered, at least in the beginning. Later, they realized we meant no harm and that we were their friends, out to help them. That is how we parted; and a few of them have even come with us.'

'But then you could have had all the power, wealth, and attention from those people there. Who will bother about you here? Why return then?'

The Sage's wife, Sitavati, herself a Sage in her own right, interrupted, 'You can acquire all you want and still feel empty if you are uprooted from your home and land. That ache remains!'

'Why do you interrupt a conversation, Sitavati?' asked the Sage.

'I learnt that from you.' she said with a smile and turned to Kamalpati, 'But then why did you leave your home in the first place?'

As Sage Durgan often says, we all have to lose ourselves sometimes, to find ourselves.'

The Sage asked, 'Did I say that? I must guard against such foolish utterances that are misconstrued and misapplied by the ignorant.'

'What will you and the other Aryas do now?' Sitavati asked.

'Each of us has a dream,' Kamalpati said.

'Each of you?' Sitavati said. 'What each of you dreams remains a dream. Only when you all dream together does reality begin.'

Sage Durgan said, 'Forget about your dreams. Learn all you can; learn first to read the seen (written) language.'

'But Sage, I learnt that in your ashram before I left.'

'Yes I remember now; you were not one of my gifted pupils. Still, go out, learn to write about our land, people, their music, poetry, culture, aesthetics, philosophy, hopes, aspirations—and even their courage to stay back, to fight evil, rather than flee at the first whiff of smoke, as you did. Yes, write about their capacity to suffer and meet it with courage, instead of escaping.'

Kamalpati smiled at the Sage's caustic words and asked, 'Am I the right person to write about the courage of these people?'

'Why not? It takes courage to live their life. Does it not take courage to write about them? A brave man lives. Any coward can write. And, there is much to write. Bharat Varsha has progressed much in your absence—maybe because of the absence of people like....'

Kamalpati's smile deepened. Nothing that the Sage said, nothing that anyone said, would rob him of the happiness within. He was back home, back at last!

Sindhu flowed on.

Ganga flowed on.

Saraswati flowed on.

Kauveri flowed on.

Kamalpati gazed at the peaceful countryside and felt a glow of happiness and peace within. He was home—in Hindu Varsha, Bharat Varsha! Arya Varsha!

If there was a dark age to follow, Kamalapati did not know about it.

But then even today, who in this land—sieged within and without—knows of the dark age ahead!

Here ends the novel *Return of the Aryans*, but not the saga of the Aryans.

READ MORE IN PENGUIN

In every corner of the world, on every subject under the sun. Penguin represents quality and variety—the very best in publishing today.

For complete information about books available from Penguin—including Puffin, Penguin Classics and Arkana—and how to order them, write to us at the appropriate address below. Please note that for copyright reasons the selection of books varies from country to country.

In India: Please write to *Penguin Books India Pvt. Ltd. 11, Community Centre, Panchsheel Park, New Delhi, 110017*

In the United Kingdom: Please write to *Dept JC, Penguin Books Ltd. Bath Road, Harmondsworth, West Drayton, Middlesex, UB7 ODA, UK*

In the United States: Please write to *Penguin Putnam Inc., 375 Hudson Street, New York, NY 10014*

In Canada: Please write to *Penguin Books Canada Ltd. 10 Alcorn Avenue, Suite 300, Toronto, Ontario M4V 3B2*

In Australia: Please write to *Penguin Books Australia Ltd. 487, Maroondah Highway, Ring Wood, Victoria 3134*

In New Zealand: Please write to *Penguin Books (NZ) Ltd. Private Bag, Takapuna, Auckland 9*

In the Netherlands: Please write to *Penguin Books Netherlands B.V., Keizersgracht 231 NL-1016 DV Amsterdam*

In Germany: Please write to *Penguin Books Deutschland GmbH, Metzlerstrasse 26, 60595 Frankfurt am Main, Germany*

In Spain: Please write to *Penguin Books S.A., Bravo Murillo, 19-I'B, E-28015 Madrid Spain*

In Italy: Please write to *Penguin Italia s.r.l., Via Felice Casati 20, I-20104 Milano*

In France: Please write to *Penguin France S.A., 17 rue Lejeune, F-31000 Toulouse*

In Japan: Please write to *Penguin Books Japan, Ishikiribashi Building, 2-5-4 Suido, Tokyo 112*

In Greece: Please write to Penguin Hellas Ltd, dimocritou 3, GR-106 71 Athens

In South Africa: Please write to *Longman Penguin Books Southern Africa (Pty) Ltd, Private Bag X08, Bertsham 2013*